THE
WRITER'S
HANDBOOK
2001

Barry Turner has worked on both sides of publishing, as an editor and marketing director and as an author. He started his career as a journalist with *The Observer* before moving on to television and radio. He has written over twenty books including *A Place in the Country*, which inspired a television series, and a best-selling biography of the actor, Richard Burton.

His recent work includes a radio play, travel articles, serialising books for *The Times*, editing the magazine *Country* and writing a one-man show based on the life of the legendary theatre critic, James Agate. This is his fourteenth year as editor of *The Writer's Handbook* and his third as editor of *The Statesman's Yearbook*.

THE
WRITER'S HANDBOOK
2001

EDITOR

BARRY TURNER

First published 1988
This edition published 2000 by
Macmillan
an imprint of Macmillan Publishers Ltd,
25 Eccleston Place, London SW1W 9NF
Basingstoke and Oxford
Associated companies throughout the world
www.macmillan.co.uk

9 8 7 6 5 4 3

A CIP catalogue record for this book is available from the British Library

ISBN 0 333 78181 3

Credits

Publisher *Morven Knowles*
Editor *Barry Turner*
Editorial Assistant *Jill Fenner*
Poetry Editor *Peter Finch*
Contributors *Lynda La Plante*
            Donald Trelford
            David Whitaker
Tax and Finance Advisor *Ian Spring*
Production *Dominic Saraceno*

Typeset by Heronwood Press, Medstead, Hants
Printed and bound in Great Britain by Mackays of Chatham plc, Kent

Contents

Beware the Writer-friendly Computer

Barry Turner

In the beginning was the word; not, as some would like us to think, a screen and a keyboard. I have nothing against technology. Anything that simplifies the routine of daily living has to be welcomed. But I object to the view, more often assumed than openly expressed, that the human input, creativity if you like, is secondary to the machine.

An early warning of the shape of things to come flashed up at me over thirty years ago when I was at the University of Oregon. America was then suffering a collective nervous breakdown brought on by the fear that the Russians were winning the space race. If they could be first out there what might they not be achieving down here? The response was to pour millions of dollars into education in the hope that the system would turn out higher-grade scientists and engineers. Pedagogic skills were reassessed and refined. As a lecturer in education, I was a ringside witness to the introduction of the latest teaching aids. Television entered the classroom and there was something called programmed learning which had the student fielding questions on a simple computer. All very impressive. Trouble was, with so much effort going on how to teach, no one seemed to be much interested in what was being taught. It was a victory of style over substance.

The classroom revolution soon carried over to Britain where the same cockeyed reasoning prevailed. With attention focused on teaching methodology, the curriculum suffered by neglect. The priorities shifted so dramatically that in the end what was being taught was determined more by favoured modes of instruction than by the needs of the student.

And so it goes. Today, all the talk is of achieving computer literacy. The fact that a large number of young people can barely string together a few words to make a logical sentence is apparently of secondary concern. In the same way that in some people's eyes the advent of the pocket calculator removed the need to learn mathematics, the grammar and spelling checks in computer programs take away the incentive for acquiring basic English.

What nonsense. The capacity for expressing thoughts clearly and succinctly, not to say interestingly, is reserved to the human brain and no computer is going to change that. Yet even experienced writers can be made to believe that technology is able to assist and even take over the basic functions of the creative process.

Some years ago, when Ludovic Kennedy was Chairman of the NCR Award, he observed that most books are 20,000 words too long. He blamed the computer. All those beautiful words, so neatly tabulated on the screen; how hard it is to strike out the superfluous adjective, the repetitive sentence. In the absence of hard print, it is almost impossible to judge a work as a whole. The screen can accommodate at most 200 words and keying back and forth to check what has gone before and after is no substitute for revising the printed text where inconsistencies can more easily be spotted. Susan Hill is among the select few authors who stand firm against what she calls the mechanisation of literature. 'There is nothing like having to write every word down for making you think about the value of what you have to say. Machines seem to have a mind of their own.'

Sadly, too many of Susan Hill's peers have become mesmerised by technology. For them, Parkinson's law needs to be revised; work expands not to fill the time available but to keep machines operating at full capacity.

Over-dependence on the computer has all but put an end to conventional copy-editing. If the grammar and spelling checks fail to detect an error it can hardly be worth worrying about. It is a neat argument but one that is frequently proved unjustified. Recently, I received a computer-printed direct debit form which invited me to 'sign hear'. The sender could hardly blame the spell check, though he had a good try. It had never occurred to him that his computer might not recognise the distinction between 'here' and 'hear'.

A small matter. But careless editing of letters, not to mention e-mails which are often an incomprehensible jumble of disconnected thoughts, has carried over to the editing of all printed material, including books. So accustomed are we to grammatical errors and structural defects, many publishers no longer find it economically viable to employ copy-editors. Even when mistakes stand out a mile, readers seldom complain. As a *Sunday Telegraph* critic observes, 'tautologies, malapropisms, migraine-inducing syntax, sentences without apparent subjects or verbs and metaphors so mixed they'd do credit to Moulinex' pass without comment. It is almost as if the virtues of high tech (cheaper printing, faster turnaround, sharper presentation) are assumed to compensate for poor writing.

Computer buffs, with their contempt for knowledge outside their own narrow sphere, promote this view. Not long ago, a self-appointed expert on adapting technical wizardry to the needs of authors came up with a new computer programme specifically designed for aspiring writers. It incorporated a work pacer which flashed up a signal whenever the user showed signs of failing to meet his target of so many words an hour. A more depressing misunderstanding of the essence of creativity it is hard to visualise. The example is not isolated. A contempt for language is characteristic of every computer manual.

But if the machine-minded are predictably inclined to push their own interests, what is less obvious is why opinion leaders, politicians in particular, put computer literacy ahead of any other cultural attainment. Is it just the economic potential of ever-expanding service industries that appeals or is there a more sinister motive? Reflecting that the 'lack of linkage to and dependence upon the machine is being increasingly understood as an affront to the body politic', David Mamet takes to his old-fashioned typewriter to consider Newt Gingrich's sugges-

tion that the plight of the underprivileged world be a
computer on to every ghetto schoolroom desk.

    This was the occasion of mirth on the part of his detractors.
an inept, untutored and disingenuous attempt to suggest soci
ment. But perhaps his suggestion reveals a deeper, an unconsciou
standing of the role of the machine.
    What did he want from the poor, and what possible good could their
use of the computer do for him? It could get the poor to shut up.
    *Jafsie and John Henry – Essays on Hollywood, Bad Boys and Six Hours of
Perfect Poker,* David Mamet (Faber & Faber)

    Could it be that the same Orwellian vision has entered the imagination of
New Labour?

UK Publishers

AA Publishing
The Automobile Association, Fanum House, Basingstoke, Hampshire RG21 4EA
☎0990 448866   Fax 01256 491974
Managing Director *John Howard*
Editorial Director *Michael Buttler*

Publishes maps, atlases and guidebooks, motoring, travel and leisure. About 100 titles a year.

Abacus
See **Little, Brown & Co (UK)**

ABC-Clio Ltd
Old Clarendon Ironworks, 35a Great Clarendon Street, Oxford OX2 6AT
☎01865 311350   Fax 01865 311358
Email oxford@abc-clio.ltd.uk
Website www.abc-clio.com
Managing Director *Tony Sloggett*
Editorial Director *Dr Robert G. Neville*

Formerly Clio Press Ltd. *Publishes* academic and general reference works, social sciences and humanities. Markets, outside North America, the Web, CD-ROM publications and reference books of the American parent company. Art Bibliographies *S. Charles*. SERIES *World Bibliographical*; *Clio Montessori*.
Royalties paid twice-yearly.

Abington Publishing
See **Woodhead Publishing Ltd**

Absolute Classics
See **Oberon Books**

Absolute Press
Scarborough House, 29 James Street West, Bath BA1 2BT
☎01225 316013   Fax 01225 445836
Email sales@absolutepress.demon.co.uk
Managing/Editorial Director *Jon Croft*
FOUNDED 1979. *Publishes* food and wine-related subjects as well as travel guides and the *Streetwise Maps* series of city maps. About 10 titles a year. Lead title for 1999: *Icons – 50 Twentieth Century Gay Icons*. *Outlines*, launched in summer 1997, is a new series of monographs on gay and lesbian

creative artists. No unsolicited mss. Synopses and ideas for books welcome.
Royalties paid twice-yearly.

Abson Books London
5 Sidney Square, London E1 2EY
☎020 7790 4737   Fax 020 7790 7346
Email absonbooks@aol.com
Chairman *M. J. Ellison*
FOUNDED 1971 in Bristol. *Publishes* language glossaries and curiosities. No unsolicited mss; synopses and ideas for books welcome.
Royalties paid twice-yearly.

Academic Press
See **Harcourt Brace and Company Ltd**

Academy Group Ltd
John Wiley & Sons, 4th Floor, International House, 7 High Street, Ealing Broadway, London W5 5DB
☎020 8326 3800   Fax 020 8326 3801
Chairman *John Jarvis*
Commissioning Editor *Maggie Toy*
Approx. Annual Turnover £2 million
FOUNDED 1969. Became part of John Wiley & Sons, Inc. group in 1997. *Publishes* architecture and design. Welcomes unsolicited mss, synopses and ideas.
Royalties paid annually.

Acair Ltd
Unit 7, 7 James Street, Stornoway, Isle of Lewis, Scotland HS1 2QN
☎01851 703020   Fax 01851 703294
Email acair@sol.co.uk
Specialising in matters pertaining to the Gaidhealtachd, Acair publishes books in Gaelic and English on Scottish history, culture and the Gaelic language. 75% of their children's books are targeted at primary school usage and are published exclusively in Gaelic.
Royalties paid twice-yearly.

Actinic Press
See **Cressrelles Publishing Co. Ltd**

Addison Wesley Longman
See **Pearson Education**

Adelphi
See **David Campbell Publishers Ltd**

Adlard Coles Nautical
See **A & C Black (Publishers) Ltd**

African Books Collective
The Jam Factory, 27 Park End Street, Oxford OX1 1HU
☎01865 726686   Fax 01865 793298
Email abc@dial.pipex.com
Website www.africanbookscollective.com

FOUNDED 1990. Collectively owned by its 17 founder member publishers. Exclusive distribution in N. America, UK, Europe and Commonwealth countries outside Africa for 44 African member publishers. Concentration is on scholarly/academic, literature and children's books. Mainly concerned with the promotion and dissemination of African-published material outside Africa. Supplies African-published books to African libraries and organisations.

Age Concern Books
1268 London Road, London SW16 4ER
☎020 8765 7200   Fax 020 8765 7211
Approx. Annual Turnover £500,000
Publishing arm of Age Concern England. *Publishes* related non-fiction only. No fiction. About 18 titles a year. Unsolicited mss, synopses and ideas welcome.

Airlife Publishing Ltd
101 Longden Road, Shrewsbury, Shropshire SY3 9EB
☎01743 235651   Fax 01743 232944
Email airlife@airlifebooks.com
Website www.airlifebooks.com
Editorial Head *Peter Coles*
Approx. Annual Turnover £3 million
IMPRINTS
Airlife Specialist aviation titles for pilots, historians and enthusiasts. Also naval and military history. About 60 titles a year. TITLES *Air War Korea; Airlife's Airliner Series; Special Operations Aviation; Combat Carriers.*
Swan Hill Press Country pursuits, horse riding, mountaineering, fishing, natural history and decorative art. About 35 titles a year. TITLES *Salmon, Trout and Charr of the World; Encyclopedia of Falconry; The Healthy Horse.*
Unsolicited mss, synopses and ideas for books welcome.
Royalties paid annually; twice-yearly by arrangement.

Ian Allan Publishing Ltd
Riverdene Business Park, Molesey Road, Hersham, Surrey KT12 4RG
☎01932 266600   Fax 01932 266601
Email info@ianallanpub.co.uk
Website www.ianallanpub.co.uk
Chairman *David Allan*
Managing Director *Tony Saunders*
Specialist transport publisher – atlases, maps, railway, aviation, road transport, military, maritime, reference. About 80 titles a year. Send sample chapter and synopsis (with s.a.e.). Manages distribution and sales for third party publishers.
IMPRINTS **Dial House** sporting titles; **Midland Publishing** (see entry); **OPC** railway titles.

J. A. Allen & Co.
An imprint of Robert Hale Ltd, Clerkenwell House, 45–47 Clerkenwell Green, London EC1R 0HT
☎020 7251 2661   Fax 021 7490 4958
Email allenhorsebooks@lineone.net
Publisher *Caroline Burt*
Approx. Annual Turnover £750,000
FOUNDED 1926 as part of J. A. Allen & Co. (The Horseman's Bookshop) Ltd. Bought by **Robert Hale Ltd** in 1999. *Publishes* equine and equestrian non-fiction. About 20 titles a year. Mostly commissioned, but willing to consider unsolicited mss of technical/instructional material related to all aspects of horses and horsemanship.
Royalties paid twice-yearly.

Allen Lane
See **Penguin UK**

Allison & Busby
114 New Cavendish Street, London W1M 7FD
☎020 7636 2942   Fax 020 7323 2023
Publishing Director *David Shelley*
FOUNDED 1967. *Publishes* contemporary fiction, writers' guides and crime fiction. IMPRINT **London House** Biography, history, topical issues, mind, body and spirit, the paranormal and health. About 80 titles a year. Send synopses with two sample chapters, not full mss. No replies without s.a.e.

Amber Lane Press Ltd
Cheorl House, Church Street, Charlbury, Oxfordshire OX7 3PR
☎01608 810024   Fax 01608 810024
Chairman *Brian Clark*

Managing Director/Editorial Head
Judith Scott

FOUNDED 1979 to publish modern play texts. *Publishes* plays and books on the theatre. About 4 titles a year. TITLES *Strange Fruit* Caryl Phillips; *The Best of Friends* Hugh Whitemore (play texts); *Coriolanus in Deutschland* Steven Berkoff; *Prokofiev* David Gutman. 'Expressly *not* interested in poetry.' No unsolicited mss. Synopses and ideas welcome.
Royalties paid twice-yearly.

AMCD (Publishers) Ltd
PO Box 182, Altrincham, Cheshire WA15 9UA
☎0161 434 5105   Fax 0161 434 5105
Email j.s.adams@talk21.com
Website www.amcd.co.uk
Managing Director *John Stewart Adams*

FOUNDED 1988. *Publishes* financial directories, books on China, local history, business books and foreign language dictionaries. Took over the Jensen Business Books imprint in 1993 and is well placed in electronic reference after developing its own software. In conjunction with JHC (Technology) Ltd, AMCD offers publishers access to the electronic book market with their reference, dictionary and directory Pop-Up© software packages which can handle most languages. About 5 titles a year. TITLES *Deregulation of the Gold Market in China (2000); Financial Dictionaries – Chinese, Japanese, Russian, Spanish, French; Around Haunted Croydon; Handguide to the Placenames of Alderley Edge.* Ideas for business books and books on European history, China or the Far East welcome in synopsis form (no mss). No poetry, fiction or historical romance. Final mss must be on disk.
Royalties paid twice yearly.

Amsco
See **Omnibus Press**

Anchor
See **Transworld Publishers**

Andersen Press Ltd
20 Vauxhall Bridge Road, London SW1V 2SA
☎020 7840 8701/8700   Fax 020 7233 6263
Website www.andersenpress.co.uk
Managing Director/Publisher *Klaus Flugge*
Editorial Director *Janice Thomson*
Editor, Fiction *Audrey Adams*

FOUNDED 1976 by Klaus Flugge and named after Hans Christian Andersen. *Publishes* children's high-quality picture books and hardback fiction.

Seventy per cent of their books are sold as co-productions abroad. TITLES *Elmer* David McKee; *Greyfriars Bobby* Ruth Brown; *I Want My Potty* Tony Ross; *Badger's Parting Gifts* Susan Varley; *Teddy, Where Are You?* Ralph Steadman; *Jack's Fantastic Voyage* Michael Foreman; *Suddenly!* Colin McNaughton; *Junk* Melvin Burgess. Unsolicited mss welcome for picture books; synopsis in the first instance for books for young readers up to age 12. No poetry or short stories.
Royalties paid twice-yearly.

The Angel's Share
See **Neil Wilson Publishing Ltd**

Anness Publishing Ltd
Hermes House, 88–89 Blackfriars Road, London SE1 8HA
☎020 7401 2077   Fax 020 7633 9499
Chairman/Managing Director *Paul Anness*
Publisher/Partner *Joanna Lorenz*

FOUNDED 1989. *Publishes* highly illustrated co-edition titles: general non-fiction – cookery, crafts, interior design, gardening, photography, decorating, lifestyle and children's. About 400 titles a year. IMPRINTS **Lorenz Books**; **Aquamarine**; **Hermes House**; **Peony Press**; **Southwater**.

Antique Collectors' Club
5 Church Street, Woodbridge, Suffolk IP12 1DS
☎01394 385501   Fax 01394 384434
Email sales@antique-acc.com
Website www.antique-acc.com
Managing Director *Diana Steel*
Director *Brian Cotton*

FOUNDED 1966. Has a five-figure membership spread over the United Kingdom and the world. The Club's magazine *Antique Collecting* is sold on a subscription basis (currently £25 p.a.) and is published 10 times a year. It is sent free to members who may also buy the Club's books at special pre-publication prices. *Publishes* specialist books on antiques and collecting. The price guide series was introduced in 1968 with the first edition of *The Price Guide to Antique Furniture.* Subject areas include furniture, silver/jewellery, metalwork, glass, textiles, art reference, ceramics, horology. Also books on architecture and gardening. RECENT TITLES *Dictionary of Bird Artists of the World* Christine Jackson; *Antique Glass* John Sandon; *19th Century Lustreware* Michael Gibson; *My Kind of Garden* David Hicks. Unsolicited synopses and ideas for books welcome. No mss.
Royalties paid quarterly as a rule, but can vary.

Anvil Press Poetry Ltd

Neptune House, 70 Royal Hill, London
SE10 8RF
☎020 8469 3033   Fax 020 8469 3363
Email anvil@anvilpresspoetry.com
Website www.anvilpresspoetry.com

Editorial Director *Peter Jay*

FOUNDED 1968 to promote English-language
and foreign poetry, both classic and contemporary, in translation. English list includes
Peter Levi, Dick Davis, Dennis O'Driscoll and
Carol Ann Duffy. Translated books include Bei
Dao, Celan, Dante, Lalić, Baudelaire, Lorca
and Neruda. Preliminary enquiry required for
translations. Unsolicited book-length collections of poems are welcome from writers
whose work has appeared in poetry magazines.
Please enclose adequate return postage.

Authors' Rating With a little help from the
Arts Council, Anvil has become one of the
foremost publishers of living poets.

Apollos

See **Inter-Varsity Press**

Apple

See **Quarto Publishing** under **UK Packagers**

Appletree Press Ltd

The Old Potato Station, 14 Howard Street
South, Belfast BT7 1AP
☎028 9024 3074   Fax 028 9024 6756
Email reception@appletree.ie
Website www.appletree.ie

Managing Director *John Murphy*
Creative Manager *Rob Blackwell*

FOUNDED 1974. *Publishes* cookery and other
small-format gift books, plus general non-
fiction of Irish and Scottish interest. TITLES
Little Cookbook series (about 40 titles); *Ireland:
The Complete Guide.* No unsolicited mss; send
initial letter or synopsis.
   Royalties paid twice-yearly in the first year,
annually thereafter. For the *Little Cookbook* series,
a standard fee is paid.

Aquamarine

See **Anness Publishing Ltd**

Arc Publications

Nanholme Mill, Shaw Wood Road,
Todmorden, Lancashire OL14 6DA
☎01706 812338   Fax 01706 818948
Website www.arcpublications.co.uk

Publishers *Rosemary Jones, Angela Jarman*

General Editor *Tony Ward*
Associate Editors *John Kinsella* (International),
   David Morley (UK), *Jean Boase-Beier*
   *(*Translations)

FOUNDED in 1969 to specialise in the publication
of contemporary poetry from new and estab-
lished writers both in the UK and abroad.
AUTHORS John Goodby, Miklos Ragnoti
(Hungary), C. K. Stead, Andrew Johnson (New
Zealand), Tariq Latif, Donald Atkinson, Tomas
Saluman (Slovenia), James Sutherland Smith,
Gail Dendy (South Africa). 10 titles a year.
Authors submitting material should ensure that it
is compatible with the current list and should
enclose s.a.e. if they wish mss to be returned.

Argentum

See **Aurum Press Ltd**

Aris & Phillips Ltd

Teddington House, Warminster, Wiltshire
BA12 8PQ
☎01985 213409   Fax 01985 212910
Email Aris.Phillips@btinternet.com
Website www.arisandphillips.com

Managing/Editorial Director *Adrian Phillips*
Editor, Hispanic Classics *Lucinda Phillips*

FOUNDED 1972 to publish books on Egyptology.
A family firm which has remained independent.
Publishes academic, classical, oriental and his-
panic. About 20 titles a year. TITLES *Campo Libre*
(series); *Mammals of Ancient Egypt* Osborn; *The
Reign of Ramesses IV* A. J. Peden; *The Third
Intermediate Period in Egypt (1100–650BC)* K. A.
Kitchen. With such a highly specialised list,
unsolicited mss and synopses are not particularly
welcome, but synopses will be considered.
   Royalties paid twice-yearly.

Arkana

See **Penguin UK**

Arms & Armour Press

See **Cassell**

Arnold

See **Hodder Headline Plc**

Arrow

See **Random House Group Ltd**

Artech House

46 Gillingham Street, London SW1V 1AH
☎020 7596 8750   Fax 020 7630 0166
Email jlancashire@artechhouse.co.uk
Website www.artechhouse.com

Managing Director (USA) *William M. Bazzy*
Senior Commissioning Editor *Dr Julie Lancashire*

FOUNDED 1969. European office of Artech House Inc., Boston. *Publishes* electronic engineering, especially telecommunications, computer communications, computing, optoelectronics, signal processing, digital audio and video, intelligent transportation systems and technology management (books, software and videos). 60–70 titles a year. Unsolicited mss and synopses considered.

Royalties paid twice-yearly.

Ashgate Publishing Ltd

Gower House, Croft Road, Aldershot, Hampshire GU11 3HR
☎01252 331551   Fax 01252 317446
(Ashgate)/344405 (Gower)
Email info@ashgatepub.co.uk
Website www.ashgate.com *and*
   www.gowerpub.com

Chairman *Nigel Farrow*

FOUNDED 1967. *Publishes* business and professional titles under the **Gower** imprint and humanities, social sciences, law and legal studies under the **Ashgate** imprint. Acquired **Lund Humphries**, art books publisher, in December 1999 (see entry).

DIVISIONS **Ashgate** *Sarah Markham* Social sciences; *John Smedley* History/Variorum collected studies; *Rachel Lynch* Music and history; *Pamela Edwardes* Art history; *John Hindley* Aviation studies. **Gower** *Jo Gooderham* Business and management; *Jonathan Norman* Training resources; *John Irwin* Law and legal studies. Access the websites for information on submission of material.

Ashmolean Museum Publications

Ashmolean Museum, Beaumont Street, Oxford OX1 2PH
☎01865 278009   Fax 01865 278018
Website www.ashmol.ox.ac.uk

Publisher/Editorial Head *Ian Charlton*

The Ashmolean Museum, which is wholly owned by Oxford University, was FOUNDED in 1683. The first publication appeared in 1890 but publishing did not really start in earnest until the 1960s. *Publishes* European and Oriental fine and applied arts, European archaeology and ancient history, Egyptology and numismatics, for both adult and children's markets. About 8 titles a year. No fiction, American/African art, ethnography, modern art or post-medieval history. Most publications are based on and illustrated from the Museum's collections.

IMPRINTS **Ashmoleum Museum Publications**; **Griffith Institute** (Egyptology imprint). Recent TITLES *Techniques of Drawing; Glass; Turner Watercolours; English Delft; Catalogue of Islamic Coins; Turner and Oxford.* No unsolicited mss.

Royalties paid annually.

Aspire Publishing

See **Greenzone Publishing**

Associated University Presses (AUP)

See **Golden Cockerel Press Ltd**

The Athlone Press

1 Park Drive, London NW11 7SG
☎020 8458 0888   Fax 020 8201 8115
Email athlonepress@btinternet.com

Managing Director *Doris Southam*
Editorial Head *Tristan Palmer*

FOUNDED 1949 as the publishing house of the University of London. Now wholly independent, but preserves links with the University via an academic advisory board. *Publishes* archaeology, architecture, art, economics, film studies, performance studies, history, history-of-ideas, history-of-science, law, eating disorders, psychiatry, literary criticism, psychic, medical, Asia, philosophy, politics, religion, science, sociology, women's/feminist issues. Anticipated developments in the near future: more emphasis on cultural studies, history of ideas, women's/feminist studies and environmental issues, including medicine. About 45 titles a year. Unsolicited mss, synopses and ideas for academic books welcome.

Royalties paid annually. *Overseas associates* The Athlone Press, c/o Transaction Publishers, 390 Campus Drive, Somerset, NJ 08873, USA.

Atlantic Europe Publishing Co. Ltd

Greys Court Farm, Greys Court, Nr Henley on Thames, Oxfordshire RG9 4PG
☎01491 628188   Fax 01491 628189
Email info@AtlanticEurope.com
Websites:www.AtlanticEurope.com *and*
   www.curriculumVisions.com

Directors *Dr B. J. Knapp, D. L. R. McCrae*

Closely associated, since 1990, with Earthscape Editions packaging operation. *Publishes* full-colour, highly illustrated children's non-fiction in hardback for international co-editions. Not interested in any other material. Main focus is on National Curriculum titles, especially in the fields of mathematics, science, technology, social history and geography. About 25 titles a year. Unsolicited synopses and ideas for non-fiction curriculum-based books welcome but s.a.e. essential for return of submissions.

Royalties or fees paid depending on circumstance.

AUP (Associated University Presses)

See **Golden Cockerel Press Ltd**

Aurum Press Ltd

25 Bedford Avenue, London WC1B 3AT
☎020 7637 3225   Fax 020 7580 2469
Email aurum@attglobal.net
Managing Director *Bill McCreadie*
Editorial Director *Piers Burnett*
Approx. Annual Turnover £1.89 million

FOUNDED 1977. Formerly owned by Andrew Lloyd Webber's Really Useful Group, now owned jointly by Piers Burnett, Bill McCreadie and Sheila Murphy, all of whom worked together in the '70s for André Deutsch. Committed to producing high-quality, illustrated/non-illustrated adult non-fiction in the areas of general human interest, art and craft, lifestyle, sport and travel. About 60 titles a year. IMPRINTS **Argentum** Practical photography books; **Jacqui Small** high-quality lifestyle books.

Royalties paid twice-yearly.

Autumn Publishing Ltd

North Barn, Appledram Barns, Birdham Road, Near Chichester, West Sussex PO20 7EQ
☎01243 531660   Fax 01243 774433
Managing Director *Campbell Goldsmid*
Editorial Director *Ingrid Goldsmid*

FOUNDED 1976. Publisher of highly illustrated children's books. About 50 titles a year. Unsolicited synopses and ideas for books welcome if they come within relevant subject areas.

Payment varies according to contract; generally a flat fee.

Award Publications Limited

1st Floor, 27 Longford Street, London NW1 3DZ
☎020 7388 7800   Fax 020 7388 7887
Email info@award.co.uk

FOUNDED 1958. *Publishes* children's books, both fiction and reference. 40 titles in 1999. IMPRINT **Horus Editions**. No unsolicited mss, synopses or ideas.

Azure

See **Society for Promoting Christian Knowledge**

B & W Publishing Ltd

29 Inverleith Row, Edinburgh EH3 5QH
☎0131 552 5555   Fax 0131 552 5566
Directors *Campbell Brown, Steven Wiggins*

FOUNDED 1990. *Publishes* general fiction and non-fiction, including memoirs, sport, cookery and guidebooks. Ideas for books welcome. Send synopsis and sample chapter with s.a.e. or return postage.

Royalties paid twice-yearly.

Baillière Tindall

See **Harcourt Brace and Company Ltd**

Duncan Baird Publishers

Castle House, 75–76 Wells Street, London W1P 3RE
☎020 7323 2229   Fax 020 7580 5692
Email james@dbairdpub.co.uk
Managing Director *Duncan Baird*
Editorial Director *Bob Saxton*
Approx. Annual Turnover £5 million

FOUNDED in 1992 to publish and package co-editions overseas and went on to launch its own publishing operation in 1998. *Publishes* illustrated cultural reference, world religions, health, mind, body and spirit, lifestyle, graphic design. 20 titles in 1999. No unsolicited mss. Synopses and ideas welcome; approach in writing in the first instance with s.a.e. No fiction or UK-only subjects.

Royalties paid twice-yearly.

Bantam/Bantam Press

See **Transworld Publishers**

Barefoot Books Ltd

Editorial & Rights: PO Box 95, Kingswood, Bristol BS15 5BH
☎0117 9328885   Fax 0117 9328881
Email edit@barefoot-books.com
Website www.barefoot-books.com
Sales, Marketing & Management:
18 Highbury Terrace, London N5 1UP
☎020 7704 6492 Fax 020 7359 5798
Managing Director *Nancy Traversy*
Publisher *Tessa Strickland (at Bristol office)*
Approx. Annual Turnover £1 million

FOUNDED in 1993. *Publishes* high-quality children's picture books, particularly new and traditional stories from a wide range of cultures. 40 titles in 1999. TITLES *The Gigantic Turnip* Alexei Tolstoy; *Stories from the Opera* Shahrukh

Husain; *Tales of Wisdom and Wonder* Hugh Lupton. No unsolicited mss.
Royalties paid twice-yearly.

Authors' Rating Writers of children's books would do well to keep track of Barefoot which, from small beginnings, is building a quality list that must be the envy of bigger publishers.

Barny Books
The Cottage, Hough on the Hill, Near Grantham, Lincolnshire NG32 2BB
☎01400 250246   Fax 01400 250246
Managing Director/Editorial Head
Molly Burkett
Business Manager *Tom Cann*
Approx. Annual Turnover £10,000

FOUNDED with the aim of encouraging new writers and illustrators. *Publishes* mainly children's books but moving into adult fiction and non-fiction. TITLES *Adventures of Builder Bob* Robert Street; *The Rutland Osprey* Molly Burkett; *Once Upon a Wartime* (series); *Eric's War* Cathy Ryan. Too small a concern to have the staff/ resources to deal with unsolicited mss. Writers with strong ideas should approach Molly Burkett by letter in the first instance. Also runs a readership and advisory service for new writers (£10 fee for short stories or illustrations; £20 fee full-length stories).
Royalties Division of profits 50/50.

Authors' Rating A gutsy small publisher with a sense of fun which appeals to youngsters.

Barrie & Jenkins
See **Random House Group Ltd**

B. T. Batsford Ltd
9 Blenheim Court, Brewery Road, London N7 9NT
☎020 7700 7611   Fax 020 7700 4552
Email info@batsford.com
Website www.batsford.com
Chairman *John Needleman*
Publisher *Roger Huggins*
Approx. Annual Turnover £2 million

FOUNDED in 1843 as a bookseller, and began publishing in 1874. Acquired by the Chrysalis Group plc in 1999. A world leader in books on chess, arts and craft. *Publishes* non-fiction: archaeology, bridge and chess, cinema, crafts and hobbies, fashion and costume, graphic design and gardening. About 100 titles a year.
Royalties paid twice in first year, annually thereafter.

Authors' Rating After a troubled three years, when authors' complaints of poor treatment

became standard, Batsford finally went into receivership from which it was rescued by Chrysalis Books, owners of **Salamander Books** and **Robson Books**.

BBC Worldwide Ltd
80 Wood Lane, London W12 0TT
☎020 8433 2000   Fax 020 8433 3707
Website www.bbcworldwide.com
Editorial Manager *Richard Larkham*
Approx. Annual Turnover £450 million

Publishes TV tie-in and stand-alone titles including books which, though linked with BBC television or radio, may not simply be the 'book of the series'. Also TV tie-in titles for children. About 90 titles a year. TITLES *Delia Smith's How to Cook*; *Walking With Dinosaurs*; *Ground Force Practical Garden Projects*. Unsolicited mss (which come in at the rate of about 20 weekly) are rarely accepted. However, strong ideas well expressed will always be considered, and promising letters stand a chance of further scrutiny.
Royalties paid twice-yearly.

Authors' Rating Publishing scare story of the year was the announcement from BBC Worldwide that publishing plans included an imprint specifically tied to broadcasting output. Rivals saw this as an attempt by the BBC to muscle in on their territory with all the advantages of television promotion. On the other hand, BBC Worldwide is surely justified in trying to hold on to its big name authors who tend to wander off to other publishers when their books are not TV related. First indications of serious intent came with the announcement of a whole raft of celebrity biographies with Terry Wogan, Esther Rantzen and Stuart Hall heading the list. Meanwhile, Delia Smith, Michael Palin *et al* chalk up new sales records with their TV inspired books. BBC Worldwide is investing heavily in US book and video publishing.

Bedford Square Press
See **NCVO Publications**

Belair
See **Folens Limited**

Belitha Press
See **Collins & Brown**

Bellew Publishing Co. Ltd
Nightingale Centre, 8 Balham Hill, London SW12 9EA
☎020 8673 5611   Fax 020 8675 2142
Email bellewsubs@hotmail.com

Chairman *Ian McCorquodale*
Managing Director *Ib Bellew*
Approx. Annual Turnover £600,000

FOUNDED 1983. Publisher and packager. *Publishes* craft, art and design, fiction, illustrated non-fiction, general interest, religion and politics. About 10 titles a year. TITLES *We Believe* Alfred Gilbey; *Chronicle* Alan Wall; *The Danube Testament* Ingrid Mann; *On Depiction: Critical Essays on Art* Avigdor Arikha. No unsolicited mss. 'We do not record any unsolicited submissions, unless sent registered.' Synopses with specimen chapters welcome.
Royalties paid annually.

Ben Gunn
See **SB Publications**

David Bennett Books
See entry under **UK Packagers**

Berg Publishers
150 Cowley Road, Oxford OX4 1JJ
☎01865 245104   Fax 01865 791165
Email enquiry@berg.demon.co.uk
Website www.berg.demon.co.uk

Editorial & Managing Director *Kathryn Earle*
Production Director *Sara Everett*

Also **Oswald Wolff Books** imprint. *Publishes* scholarly books in the fields of history, fashion, cultural studies, social sciences and humanities. About 45 titles a year plus one journal, *Fashion Theory*. TITLES *The Untouchables of India* Robert Deliege; *Social Change in the 20th Century* Thomas C. Patterson; *The Maximum Surveillance Society* Clive Norris and Gary Armstrong; *The Culture of Sewing* Barbara Burman; *Fashion Spreads* Paul Jobling. No unsolicited mss. Synopses and ideas for books welcome.
Royalties paid annually.

Berkswell Publishing Co. Ltd
PO Box 420, Warminster, Wiltshire BA12 9XB
☎01985 840189   Fax 01985 840189

Managing Director *John Stidolph*

FOUNDED 1974. *Publishes* illustrated books, royalty, heritage, country sports, biography, books about Wessex and *The Churchwarden's Yearbook*. No fiction. About 4 titles a year. Unsolicited mss, synopses and ideas for books welcome.
Royalties paid according to contract.

Berlitz Publishing Co. Ltd
4th Floor, 9–13 Grosvenor Street, London W1X 9FB
☎020 7518 8300   Fax 020 7518 8310

Email publishing@berlitz.co.uk
Website www.berlitz.com
Chairman *H. Yokoi*
Managing Director *R. Kirkpatrick*

FOUNDED 1970. Part of Berlitz International, which also comprises language instruction and translation divisions. *Publishes* travel and language-learning products only: travel guides, phrasebooks and language courses. SERIES *Pocket Guides; Berlitz Complete Guide to Cruising and Cruise Ships; Phrase Books; Pocket Dictionaries; Business Phrase Books; Self-teach: Rush Hour Commuter Cassettes; Think & Talk; Berlitz Kids*. No unsolicited mss.

BFI Publishing
British Film Institute, 21 Stephen Street, London W1P 2LN
☎020 7255 1444   Fax 020 7436 7950
Website www.bfi.org.uk

Head of Publishing *Andrew Lockett*
Approx. Annual Turnover £500,000

FOUNDED 1982. Part of the **British Film Institute**. *Publishes* academic and general film/television-related books. About 30 titles a year. TITLES *Film Classics* (series); *Modern Classics* (series); *The Cinema Book, revised edition* eds. Pam Cook and Mieke Bernink; *BFI Film & Television Handbook* (annual) Eddie Dyja. Unsolicited synopses and ideas preferred to complete mss.
Royalties paid annually.

BFP Books
Focus House, 497 Green Lanes, London N13 4BP
☎020 8882 3315   Fax 020 8886 5174
Chief Executive *John Tracy*
Commissioning Editor *Stewart Gibson*

FOUNDED 1982. The publishing arm of the Bureau of Freelance Photographers. *Publishes* illustrated books on photography, mainly aspects of freelancing and marketing pictures. No unsolicited mss but ideas welcome.

Big Fish
See **Collins & Brown**

Clive Bingley Books
See **Library Association Publishing Ltd**

Birlinn Ltd
Unit 8 Canongate Venture, 5 New Street, Edinburgh EH8 5BH
☎0131 556 6660   Fax 0131 557 6250
Email info@birlinn.co.uk
Website www.birlinn.co.uk

Managing Editor *Hugh Andrew*
FOUNDED 1992. Acquired **John Donald Publishers** in 1999 (see entry). *Publishes* Gaelic, Scottish interest and history. 80 titles in 1999. No unsolicited mss; synopses and ideas welcome. *Royalties* paid.

A. & C. Black (Publishers) Ltd
35 Bedford Row, London WC1R 4JH
☎020 7242 0946   Fax 020 7831 8478
Email enquiries@acblack.co.uk
Chairman *Charles Black*
Deputy Chairman *David Gadsby*
Managing Directors *Charles Black, Jill Coleman*
Approx. Annual Turnover £7.75 million
(Group turnover)

Publishes children's and educational books, including music, for 3–15-year-olds, arts and crafts, ceramics, fishing, ornithology, nautical, reference, sport, theatre and travel. About 125 titles a year. Acquisitions brought the Herbert Press' art, design and general books, Adlard Coles' sailing list and Christopher Helm's natural history and ornithology lists into A. & C. Black's stable. Bought by **Bloomsbury Publishing** in May 2000.
   IMPRINTS **Adlard Coles Nautical; The Herbert Press; Christopher Helm**. TITLES *New Mermaid* drama series; *Who's Who; Writers' & Artists' Yearbook; Blue Guides* travel series; *Rockets* and *Graffix* children's series. Initial enquiry before submission of mss appreciated.
   Royalties Payment varies according to contract.
Authors' Rating Publisher of the venerable rival to *Writer's Handbook*; also *Who's Who* which has enhanced its reputation with an entry for the editor of *Writer's Handbook*.

Black Ace Books
PO Box 6557, Forfar DD8 2YS
☎01307 465096   Fax 01307 465494
Website www.blackacebooks.com
Managing Directors *Hunter Steele, Boo Wood*
FOUNDED 1991. *Publishes* new fiction, Scottish and general; some non-fiction including biography, history, philosophy and psychology. 36 titles in print. IMPRINTS **Black Ace Books, Black Ace Paperbacks** TITLES *Succeeding at Sex and Scotland, Or the Case of Louis Morel* Hunter Steele; *Spitfire Girls* Carol Gould; *The Evolution of Hypnotism* Derek Forrest. Completed books only. No unsolicited mss. 'Send only: one-page covering letter, one-page synopsis, one full page of text and large s.a.e. If possible, include one-page recommendation from suitable referee such

as published author, book reviewer or university teacher of literature. No poetry, children's, cookery, DIY, religion.'
   Royalties paid twice-yearly.

Black Butterfly Children's Books
See **Writers and Readers Ltd**

Black Dagger Crime
See **Chivers Press Ltd**

Black Lace
See **Virgin Publishing Ltd**

Black Spring Press Ltd
2nd Floor, 126 Cornwall Road, London SE1 8TQ
☎020 7401 2044   Fax 020 7401 2055
Email bsp@blackspring.demon.co.uk
Directors *Simon Pettifar, Maja Prausnitz*
FOUNDED 1986. *Publishes* fiction, literary criticism, biography. About 5 titles a year. TITLES *King Ink 2* Nick Cave; *The Mortdecai Trilogy* Kyril Bonfiglioli; *The Tenant* Roland Topor; *Beautiful Losers* Leonard Cohen; *The Terrible News* collection of Russian short stories by Zamyatin, Babel, Kharms, *et al.* No unsolicited mss.
   Royalties paid twice-yearly.

Black Swan
See **Transworld Publishers**

Blackie & Co. Publishers
107–111 Fleet Street, London EC4A 2AB
☎020 7936 9021   Fax 020 7936 9100
Email editors@blackie.org
Website www.blackie.org
Editorial Head *John Bree*
Editor *Jill Redgrave*

A new company which *publishes* scientific/ environmental books: popular and academic, humour, literature, crime, fiction, non-fiction, pets (for adults and children), heritage, educational, computers/the Internet. Plans to publish 20/30 titles a year. TITLES *Time to Kill* B. Moorhouse; *A Quest for the Comic Meaning in Literature* Carol Joyce and Margaret Dunn; *Where Seagulls Dare* Gary Hogg. No unsolicited mss.
   Royalties paid annually.

Blackstaff Press Ltd
Blackstaff House, Wildflower Way, Apollo Road, Belfast BT12 6TA
☎028 9066 8074   Fax 028 9066 8207
Email books@blkstaff.dnet.co.uk
Director/Editorial Head *Anne Tannahill*

FOUNDED 1971. *Publishes* mainly, but not exclusively, Irish interest books, fiction, poetry, history, politics, illustrated editions, natural history and humour. About 25 titles a year. Unsolicited mss considered, but preliminary submission of synopsis plus short sample of writing preferred. Return postage *must* be enclosed.

Royalties paid twice-yearly.

Authors' Rating This Belfast publisher is noted for a strong backlist, 'wonderfully well-presented catalogues and promotional material'.

Blackwell Publishers Ltd

108 Cowley Road, Oxford OX4 1JF
☎01865 791100   Fax 01865 791347
Website www.blackwellpublishers.co.uk

Chairman *Nigel Blackwell*
Managing Director *René Olivieri*
Approx. Annual Turnover £23.7 million

FOUNDED 1922. A rapidly expanding Anglo-American company. The focus is on international research journals and undergraduate textbooks in social sciences, business and humanities; computer-aided instruction on PC applications. About 300 titles a year (joint venture with **Polity Press**) and over 250 journals.

DIVISIONS **Books** *Philip Carpenter* **Journals** *Sue Corbett, Claire Andrews, Philippa Scoones*. Unsolicited synopses with specimen chapter and table of contents welcome.

Royalties paid annually. *Overseas associates* Blackwell Publishers Inc., Maldon, MA; Info-Source Inc., Orlando, FL

Authors' Rating Continuing expansion is thanks largely to successful exploitation of the US academic market where Blackwell scores more than half its total sales.

Blackwell Science Ltd

Osney Mead, Oxford OX2 0EL
☎01865 206206   Fax 01865 721205
Website www.blackwell-science.com

Chairman *Nigel Blackwell*
Group Managing Director *Robert Campbell*
Managing Director (UK) *Jon Conibear*
Publishing Directors *Dr Andrew Robinson* (Medicine); *Simon Rallison* (Science); *Dr Jon Walmsley* (Professional)
Approx. Annual Turnover £105 million (Group turnover)

FOUNDED 1939. Rapid growth since the 1970s along with expansion into Europe in the late 1980s. Also owner of Danish academic publisher Munksgaard. *Publishes* medical, professional (including Fishing News Books) and science.

About 400 titles a year, plus 350 journals, now available on-line. TITLES *Diseases of the Liver and Biliary System* Sherlock; *Essential Immunology* Roitt; *Textbook of Dermatology* Champion. Unsolicited mss and synopses welcome.

Royalties paid annually. *Overseas subsidiaries* in USA, Australia, Japan, Hong Kong, Paris, Berlin and Vienna; editorial offices in London and Edinburgh.

Authors' Rating Blackwell Science's main business is in scientific journals, mostly produced in partnership with learned societies, and medical publishing. Much of the growth is in mainland Europe where Blackwell Science has offshoots in Berlin, Paris and Vienna.

Blake Publishing

3 Bramber Court, 2 Bramber Road, London W14 9PB
☎020 7381 0666   Fax 020 7381 6868

Managing Director *John Blake*
Deputy Managing Director *Rosie Ries*

FOUNDED 1991 and rapidly expanding. Bought the assets of Smith Gryphon Ltd in 1997 when that publishing house went into receivership. *Publishes* mass-market non-fiction. No fiction, children's, specialist or non-commercial. About 50 titles a year. No unsolicited mss; synopses and ideas welcome. Please enclose s.a.e.

Royalties paid twice-yearly.

Authors' Rating Unashamedly mass-market with its celebrity titles, tailor-made for press serialisation.

Blandford Press

See **Cassell**

Bloodaxe Books Ltd

PO Box 1SN, Newcastle upon Tyne NE99 1SN
☎01434 240500   Fax 01434 240505
Email editor@bloodaxebooks.demon.co.uk
Website www.bloodaxebooks.demon.co.uk

Chairman *Simon Thirsk*
Managing/Editorial Director *Neil Astley*

Publishes poetry, literature and criticism, and related titles by British, Irish, European, Commonwealth and American writers. 95 per cent of the list is poetry. About 50 titles a year. TITLES include two major anthologies, *The New Poetry* Hulse, Kennedy and Morley (eds.); *Sixty Women Poets* Linda France (ed.); *No Truth With the Furies* R. S. Thomas (**Nobel Prize** nominee); *Selected Poems* Jenny Joseph; *Poems* J. H. Prynne; *Poems 1960–2000* Fleur Adcock;

recent collections by Selima Hill, Helen Dunmore and Peter Reading. Unsolicited poetry mss welcome; send a sample of no more than 10 poems with s.a.e., 'but if you don't read contemporary poetry, don't bother'. Authors of other material should write in the first instance.

Royalties paid annually.

Authors' Rating Assisted by regional Arts Council funding, Bloodaxe is one of the liveliest and most innovative of poetry publishers with a list that takes in some of the best of the younger poets.

Bloomsbury Publishing Plc

38 Soho Square, London W1V 5DF
☎020 7494 2111   Fax 020 7434 0151
Website www.bloomsbury.com
Chairman/Chief Executive *Nigel Newton*
Publishing Directors *Alexandra Pringle, Liz Calder, Kathy Rooney, Matthew Hamilton, Sarah Odedina, Jonathan Glasspool*
Approx. Annual Turnover £16 million

FOUNDED 1986 by Nigel Newton, David Reynolds, Alan Wherry and Liz Calder. Over the following years Bloomsbury titles were to appear regularly on *The Sunday Times* bestseller list and many of its authors have gone on to win prestigious literary prizes. In 1991 Nadine Gordimer won the **Nobel Prize for Literature**; Michael Ondaatje's *The English Patient* won the 1992 **Booker Prize**; Tobias Wolff's *In Pharaoh's Army* won the Esquire/Volvo/Waterstone's Non-Fiction Award in 1994; in 1997 Anne Michaels' *Fugitive Pieces* won both the **Orange Prize for Fiction** and the Guardian Fiction Prize, Joanna Traynor's *Sister Josephine* won the SAGA Prize and Jane Urquhart's *The Underpainter* won the Governor General's Prize in Canada. J. K. Rowling's *Harry Potter and the Philosopher's Stone, Harry Potter and the Chamber of Secrets* and *Harry Potter and the Prisoner of Azkaban* won the **Nestlé Smarties Book Prize** in 1997, 1998 and 1999 respectively. Published *The Encarta World English Dictionary* in 1999. Acquired **A. & C. Black (Publishers) Ltd** in May 2000.

Publishes literary fiction and non-fiction, including general reference. AUTHORS Margaret Atwood, T. C. Boyle, Daniel Goleman, David Guterson, John Irving, Jay McInerney, Will Self, Hunter S. Thompson, Rupert Thomson, Joanna Trollope. Unsolicited mss and synopses welcome; no poetry.

Royalties paid twice-yearly.

Authors' Rating What a year for Bloomsbury.

Having scaled the heights of the bestseller lists with Harry Potter, brought to fruition a deal with Bill Gates to co-produce the *Encarta World English Dictionary* (Microsoft produces the CD-ROM version), and announced a move into Hollywood with a plan to sell books direct to the studios, it was hardly surprising that Bloomsbury should be declared Publisher of the Year at the British Book Awards.

Boatswain Press
See **Kenneth Mason Publications Ltd**

Bobcat
See **Omnibus Press**

Bodley Head
See **Random House Group Ltd**

The Book Guild Ltd

Temple House, 25 High Street, Lewes, East Sussex BN7 2LU
☎01273 472534   Fax 01273 476472
Email info@bookguild.co.uk
Website www.bookguild.co.uk
Chairman *George M. Nissen CBE*
Managing Director *Carol Biss*

FOUNDED 1982. *Publishes* fiction, human interest, media, children's fiction, academic, natural history, naval and military, biography, art. Approx. 80 titles a year. Expanding mainstream list plus developing the human interest/media genre.

DIVISIONS/TITLES
Media *Lifting the Lid* Betty Box. **Fiction** *Six Feet Under* Howard Hodgson. **Children's** *Underneath the Underground I & 2* Anthea and Wendy Turner. **Photography** *The Edwardian Eye of Andrew Pitcairn Knowles* Richard Pitcairn Knowles. **Travel** *Foothold on Antarctica* Charles Swithinbank. **History** *British Chimney Sweeps* Benita Cullingford. **Motoring** *The Car Import Guide* Richard Bowman.

IMPRINT **Temple House Books** Nonfiction: *The Fitzroy* Sally Fiber; *Colditz, Last Stop* Jack Pringle. Unsolicited mss, ideas and synopses welcome.

Royalties paid twice-yearly.

Authors' Rating Regularly advertises for authors who may be asked to cover their own production costs. But in promoting its services, The Book Guild is more up-front with its clients than the typical vanity publisher who promises the earth and delivers next to nothing.

Borderlines Biographies
See **Seren**

Boulevard Books & The Babel Guides
8 Aldbourne Road, London W12 0LN
☎020 8743 5278   Fax 020 8743 5278
Email raybabel@dircon.co.uk
Website www.raybabel.dircon.co.uk
Managing Director *Ray Keenoy*

Specialises in contemporary world fiction by young writers in English translation. Existing or forthcoming series of fiction from Brazil, Italy, Latin America, Low Countries, Greece, and elsewhere. The Babel Guides series of popular guides to fiction in translation started in 1995.

DIVISONS
Latin American *Ray Keenoy* TITLE *Hotel Atlantico* J. G. Noll. **Italian** *Fiorenza Conte* TITLE *The Toy Catalogue* Sandra Petrignani. **Brazil** *Dr David Treece* TITLE *From the Heart of Brazil* (anthology). **Low Countries** *Prof. Theo Hermans.* **Greece** *Marina Coriolano-Likourezos.* **Babel Guides to Fiction in Translation** *Ray Keenoy* Series Editor TITLES *Babel Guide to Italian Fiction in Translation; Babel Guide to the Fiction of Portugal, Brazil & Africa in Translation; Babel Guide to French Fiction in English Translation; Babel Guide to Jewish Fiction.*
Suggestions and proposals for translations of contemporary fiction welcome. Also seeking contributors to forthcoming Babel Guides (all literatures).
Royalties paid annually.

Bounty
See **Octopus Publishing Group**

Bowker–Saur
Windsor Court, East Grinstead House, East Grinstead, West Sussex RH19 1XA
☎01342 326972   Fax 01342 336192
Website www.bowker-saur.com
Group Publishing Director
Gerard Dummett
Managing Director *Charles Halpin*
Publisher *Geraldine Turpie*

Owned by Reed Elsevier, Bowker-Saur is part of Reed Business Information in the UK. *Publishes* library reference, library science, bibliography, biography, African studies, business and professional directories. Unsolicited mss will not be read. Approach with ideas only. *Royalties* paid annually.

Boxtree
See **Macmillan Publishers Ltd**

Marion Boyars Publishers Ltd
24 Lacy Road, London SW15 1NL
☎020 8788 9522   Fax 020 8789 8122
Email marion.boyars@talk21.com
Website www.marionboyars.co.uk
Editor *Karen McCrossan*
Editor, Non-fiction *Ken Hollings*

FOUNDED 1975, formerly Calder and Boyars. *Publishes* biography and autobiography, economics, fiction, literature and criticism, music, philosophy, poetry, politics and world affairs, psychology, sociology and anthropology, theatre and drama, film and cinema, women's studies. About 30 titles a year. AUTHORS include Georges Bataille, Ingmar Bergman, Heinrich Böll, Hortense Calisher, Jean Cocteau, Clive Collins, Warwick Collins, Carlo Gébler, Julian Green, Ivan Illich, Pauline Kael, Ken Kesey, Kenzaburo Oe, Hubert Selby, Igor Stravinsky, Frederic Tuten, Eudora Welty, Judith Williamson, Tom Wiseman. Unsolicited mss not welcome for fiction or poetry; submissions from agents preferred. Unsolicited synopses and ideas welcome for non-fiction.
Royalties paid annually. *Overseas associates* Marion Boyars Publishers Inc., 237 East 39th Street, New York, NY 10016, USA.

Boydell & Brewer Ltd
PO Box 9, Woodbridge, Suffolk IP12 3DF
☎01394 411320

Publishes non-fiction only, principally medieval studies. All books commissioned. No unsolicited material.

BPS Books
St Andrews House, 48 Princess Road East, Leicester LE1 7DR
☎0116 2549568   Fax 0116 2470787
Website www.bps.org.uk
Publications Manager *Joyce Collins*
Editor *Jon Reed*

Book publishing division of The British Psychological Society. *Publishes* a wide range of academic and applied psychology, including specialist monographs, textbooks for teachers, managers, doctors, nurses, social workers, and schools material; plus general psychology and some electronic publishing. 10–15 titles a year. Proposals considered.

Bradt Travel Guides
19 High Street, Chalfont St Peter,
Buckinghamshire SL9 9QE
☎01753 893444   Fax 01753 892333
Email info@bradt-travelguides.com
Website www.bradt-travelguides.com
Managing Director *Hilary Bradt*
Editorial Head *Tricia Hayne*
Approx. Annual Turnover £400,000
FOUNDED in 1974 by Hilary Bradt. *Specialises* in
travel guides to off-beat places. 10 titles in 1999.
TITLES *Guide to Ethiopia; Madagascar; Mali;
Zanzibar; Cuba,* etc.; *Wildlife Guide to Madagascar;
Galapagos; Antarctica; Rail Guides to USA; Greece;
India; By Road Guides.* No unsolicited mss; syn-
opses and ideas for travel guidebooks welcome.
Royalties paid twice-yearly.

Brassey's
9 Blenheim Court, Brewery Road, London
N7 9NT
☎020 7700 7611   Fax 020 7700 4552
Website www.brasseys.com
Chairman *John Needleman*
Began life as *Brassey's Naval Annual* in 1886 to
become the most important publisher of serious
defence-related material in the world. Acquired
by the Chrysalis Group plc in 1999. *Publishes*
books and journals on defence, international
relations, military history, maritime and aeronautical subjects and defence terminology.
IMPRINTS **Brassey's**; **Conway Maritime
Press** Naval history and ship modelling;
Putnam Aeronautical Books Technical and
reference.
Royalties paid annually.

Nicholas Brealey Publishing Ltd
36 John Street, London WC1N 2AT
☎020 7430 0224   Fax 020 7404 8311
Website www.nbrealey-books.com
Managing Director *Nicholas Brealey*
FOUNDED 1992. Innovative books for business
that address the most critical and interesting
issues of the new century – from business to consumer behaviour, from cross-cultural titles to
those promoting understanding of global change
within the new economy. 20 titles a year. TITLES
*The Electronic B@zaar; The Soul of the New
Consumer; The Power Laws; The 80/20 Principle;
High Tech/Low Touch; Breaking Through the
Culture Shock; The Dance of Change.* No fiction,
poetry or leisure titles. No unsolicited mss; synopses and ideas welcome.
Royalties paid twice-yearly.

Authors' Rating Looks to be succeeding in
breaking away from the usual computer-speak
business manuals to publish information and
literate texts. Lead titles have a distinct trans-
Atlantic feel.

The Breedon Books Publishing Co. Ltd
Breedon House, 3 Parker Centre, Derby
DE21 4SZ
☎01332 384235   Fax 01332 292755
Email breedonbooks@netmatters.co.uk
Chairman/Managing Director
A. C. Rippon
Approx. Annual Turnover £1 million
FOUNDED 1983. *Publishes* autobiography, biog-
raphy, local history, old photographs, heritage
and sport. 40 titles in 1999. Unsolicited mss,
synopses and ideas welcome if accompanied by
s.a.e. No poetry or fiction.
Royalties paid annually.

Breese Books Ltd
164 Kensington Park Road, London W11 2ER
☎020 7727 9426   Fax 020 7229 3395
Email MBreese999@aol.com
Chairman/Managing Director *Martin
Ranicar-Breese*
FOUNDED 1975 to produce specialist conjuring
books and then went on to establish a more
general list. Breese Books has now closed its
general publishing division and is concentrating
on Sherlock Holmes pastiches. There is little
point in submitting material on any subjects
other than the above.

Authors' Rating Having cut back on his publishing programme Martin Breese is offering a
Critical Eye Service to advise authors on how to
make their work saleable. There are no guaran-
tees of publication and there is a charge but for
some, straight practical advice may be useful.

Brimax
See **Octopus Publishing Group**

Bristol Classical Press
See **Gerald Duckworth & Co. Ltd**

British Academic Press
See **I. B. Tauris & Co. Ltd**

The British Academy
10 Carlton House Terrace, London
SW1Y 5AH
☎020 7969 5200   Fax 020 7969 5300
Email secretary@britac.ac.uk

Website www.britac.ac.uk

Publications Officer *J. M. H. Rivington*
Publications Assistant *J. English*

FOUNDED 1901. The primary body for promoting scholarship in the humanities, the Academy publishes many series stemming from its own long-standing research projects, or series of lectures and conference proceedings. Main subjects include history, philosophy and archaeology. About 15 titles a year. SERIES *Auctores Britannici Medii Aevi; Early English Church Music; Fontes Historiae Africanae; Records of Social and Economic History.* Proposals for these series are welcome and are forwarded to the relevant project committees. The British Academy is a registered charity and does not publish for profit.
Royalties paid only when titles have covered their costs.

The British Library
96 Euston Road, London NW1 2DB
☎020 7412 7704   Fax 020 7412 7768

Publishing Manager *David Way*
Approx. Annual Turnover £950,000

FOUNDED 1979 as the publishing arm of The British Library's London Collections to publish works based on the historic collections and related subjects. *Publishes* bibliographical reference, manuscript studies, illustrated books based on the Library's collections, and book arts. TITLES *Historical Source Book for Scribes; English Maps – A History; The British Library Writers' Lives Series; Landmarks in Western Science.* About 35 titles a year. Unsolicited mss, synopses and ideas welcome if related to the history of the book, book arts or bibliography. No fiction or general non-fiction.
Royalties paid annually.

British Museum Press
46 Bloomsbury Street, London WC1B 3QQ
☎020 7323 1234   Fax 020 7436 7315
Website www.britishmuseum.co.uk

Managing Director *Patrick Wright*
Head of Publishing *Emma Way*

The book publishing division of The British Museum Company Ltd. FOUNDED 1973 as British Museum Publications Ltd; relaunched 1991 as British Museum Press. *Publishes* ancient history, archaeology, ethnography, art history, exhibition catalogues, guides, children's books, and all official publications of the British Museum. Around 50 titles a year. TITLES *Egypt; Indigo; Sutton Hoo: Burial Ground of Kings?; The Atlantic Celts: Ancient People or Modern Invention?; The Classical Cookbook; How to Read Egyptian*

Hieroglyphs. Synopses and ideas for books welcome.
Royalties paid twice-yearly.

Brockhampton Press
See **Caxton Publishing Group**

Andrew Brodie Publications
PO Box 23, Wellington, Somerset TA21 8YX
☎01823 665345   Fax 01823 665345
Email andrew@abp-ltd.demon.co.uk
Website www.abp-ltd.demon.co.uk

Chairman *Andrew Brodie*
Approx. Annual Turnover £200,000

FOUNDED 1992. *Publishes* children's books. 19 titles in 1999. TITLES *Times Tables Today; Spelling Today; Maths Today; Pink Pig Turns Brown.* Unsolicited mss, synopses and ideas for books welcome; send a letter in the first instance.
Royalties paid annually.

John Brown Publishing Ltd
The New Boathouse, 136–142 Bramley Road, London W10 6SR
☎020 7565 3000   Fax 020 7565 3055

Chairman/Managing Director *John Brown*

FOUNDED 1986. *Publishes* adult comic annuals; *Viz* magazine; strange phenomena. 5 titles in 2000.
DIVISION **Fortean Times Books** *Mike Dash* Does not welcome unsolicited mss.
Royalties paid twice-yearly.

Brown, Son & Ferguson, Ltd
4–10 Darnley Street, Glasgow G41 2SD
☎0141 429 1234   Fax 0141 420 1694
Email info@skipper.co.uk
Website www.skipper.co.uk

Chairman/Joint Managing Director
T. Nigel Brown

FOUNDED 1850. *Specialises* in nautical textbooks, both technical and non-technical. Also Boy Scout/Girl Guide books, and Scottish one-act/ three-act plays. Unsolicited mss, synopses and ideas for books welcome.
Royalties paid annually.

Bryntirion Press (formerly Evangelical Press of Wales)
Bryntirion House, Bridgend, Mid-Glamorgan CF31 4DX
☎01656 655886   Fax 01656 656095
Email press@draco.co.uk

Chief Executive *Gerallt Wyn Davies*
Press Manager *Huw Kinsey*

Approx. Annual Turnover £100,000

Owned by the Evangelical Movement of Wales. *Publishes* Christian books in English and Welsh. 1999 TITLES *Draw Near to God; Putting Asunder; Beginning at the Beginning; Let Everybody Praise the Lord.* No unsolicited mss; synopses and ideas welcome.

Royalties paid annually.

Bucknell University Press
See **Golden Cockerel Press Ltd**

Burns & Oates
See **Search Press**

Business Books
See **Random House Group Ltd**

Business Education Publishers Ltd
The Teleport, Doxford International, Sunderland, Tyne & Wear SR3 3XD
☎0191 525 2400   Fax 0191 520 1815
Managing Director *P. M. Callaghan*
Approx. Annual Turnover £400,000

FOUNDED 1981. *Publishes* business education, economics and law for BTEC and GNVQ reading. Currently expanding into further and higher education, computing, community health services, travel and tourism, occasional papers for institutions and local government administration. Unsolicited mss and synopses welcome.

Royalties paid annually.

Business Press
See **Thomson Learning**

Butterworth-Heinemann International
See **Reed Educational & Professional Publishing**

Butterworths Tolley
Tolley House, 2 Addiscombe Road, Croydon, Surrey CR9 5AF
☎020 8686 9141   Fax 020 8686 3155
Managing Director *Stephen Stout*

Part of Reed Elsevier Legal Division.

DIVISIONS **Tolley Publishing; Charles Knight Publishing; Payroll Alliance; Butterworths Tax Publications**. Unsolicited mss, synopses and ideas welcome.

C&B Publishing Plc
See **Collins & Brown**

Cadogan Guides
West End House, 11 Hills Place, London W1R 1AG
☎020 7287 6555   Fax 020 7734 1733
Email guides@morrispub.co.uk
Editorial Director *Vicki Ingle*
FOUNDED 1982. *Publishes* travel guides.

Calder Publications Ltd
126 Cornwall Road, London SE1 8TQ
☎020 7633 0599   Fax 020 7633 0599
Email enquiries@calderpub.demon.co.uk
Website www.paris-anglo.com/calder
Chairman/Managing Director/ Editorial Head *John Calder*

Formerly John Calder (Publishers) Ltd. A publishing company which has grown around the tastes and contacts of John Calder, the iconoclast of the literary establishment. The list has a reputation for controversial and opinion-forming publications; Samuel Beckett is perhaps the most prestigious name. The list includes all of Beckett's prose and poetry. *Publishes* autobiography, biography, drama, literary fiction, literary criticism, music, opera, poetry, politics, sociology. AUTHORS include Antonin Artaud, Marguerite Duras, Martin Esslin, Erich Fried, P. J. Kavanagh, Robert Menasse, Robert Pinget, Luigi Pirandello, Alain Robbe-Grillet, Nathalie Sarraute, L. F. Celine, Eva Figes, Claude Simon, Howard Barker (plays), ENO opera guides. *No new material accepted.*

Royalties paid annually.

Authors' Rating Known for his patronage of eccentric talents, John Calder is one of the few publishers to carry the flag for the English language '... which is in great danger of disappearing under the American vernacular'.

California University Press
See **University Presses of California, Columbia & Princeton Ltd**

Cambridge University Press
The Edinburgh Building, Shaftesbury Road, Cambridge CB2 2RU
☎01223 312393   Fax 01223 315052
Website www.cup.cam.ac.uk
Chief Executive *R. J. Mynott*

The oldest printer and publisher in the world with long-established branches in the USA and Australia and more recently established branches in Spain, Africa, South America and

East Asia. Winner of The Queen's Award for Export Achievement in 1998. Over the last ten years, Cambridge has opened many new offices around the world. Its books are sold in more than 200 countries. Publications include the Cambridge Histories and Companions, encyclopedias and dictionaries; the **Canto** series; popular science and scientific and medical reference; major ELT courses; coursebooks for the National Curriculum; Cambridge Reading; and Cambridge Low Price Editions for the developing world. *Publishes* academic/educational and reference books for English-language markets worldwide, at all levels from primary school to postgraduate, together with a list of Spanish titles. Also ELT, Bibles and over 140 academic journals. Over 23,000 authors in 106 different countries and about 1800 new titles a year.

PUBLISHING GROUPS
Bibles *C. J. Wright* **ELT** *C. J. F. Hayes* **Science Publishing** *A. E. Crowden* **Humanities and Social Sciences** *A. M. C. Brown* **Professional Publishing** *R. W. A. Barling* **Education** *A. C. Gilfillan* **Journals** *C. Guettler*. Synopses and ideas for educational, ELT and academic books are welcomed (and preferable to the submission of unsolicited mss). No fiction or poetry.
Royalties paid twice-yearly.

Authors' Rating The difficulties facing a prestigious academic press in the age of high technology were revealed recently in the *Bookseller* where Michael Holdsworth, business development director of CUP, reported that over 8000 titles on the CUP list sold less than 100 copies in a year. Printing on demand or going on-line would seem to be the answer but authors will need to be reassured that their interests are taken into account.

Camden Press Ltd

46 Colebrooke Row, London N1 8AF
☎020 7226 2061   Fax 020 7226 2418
Chairman *Bob Borzello*
FOUNDED 1985. *Publishes* social issues; all books are launched in connection with major national conferences. DIVISION **Publishing for Change** *Bob Borzello* TITLE *Living with the Legacy of Abuse.* IMPRINT **Mindfield** TITLES *Hate Thy Neighbour: The Race Issue; Therapy on the Couch.* No unsolicited material. Approach by telephone in the first instance.
Royalties paid annually.

Camden Softcover Large Print
See **Chivers Press Ltd**

David Campbell Publishers Ltd

Gloucester Mansions, 140a Shaftesbury Avenue, London WC2H 8HD
☎020 7539 7600   Fax 020 7379 4060
Website www.everyman.uk.com
Managing Director *David Campbell*
Approx. Annual Turnover £3.5 million
FOUNDED 1990 with acquisition of Everyman's Library (established 1906) bought from J. M. Dent. *Publishes* classics of world literature, pocket poetry anthologies, music companion guides and travel guides. AUTHORS include Bulgakov, Bellow, Borges, Forster, Grass, Mann, Nabokov, Orwell, Rushdie, Updike and Waugh. No unsolicited mss. IMPRINT **Adelphi** Illustrated books.
Royalties paid annually.

Campbell Books
See **Macmillan Publishers Ltd**

Candle Books
See **Angus Hudson** under **UK Packagers**

Canongate Books Ltd

14 High Street, Edinburgh EH1 1TE
☎0131 557 5111   Fax 0131 557 5211
Email info@canongate.co.uk
Website www.canongate.net
Publisher *Jamie Byng*
Approx. Annual Turnover £1.75 million
FOUNDED 1973. Independent publisher, following a management buyout in October 1994. *Publishes* a wide range of fiction and non-fiction. Strong Scottish slant to part of the house.

IMPRINTS
Canongate Classics Adult paperback series dedicated solely to important works of Scottish literature; **Canongate Crime** Paperback series featuring writers from all around the world, includes **Canongate Crime Classics** dedicated to reprinting lost classics of the genre; **Canongate International** New imprint for fiction in translation; **Kelpie** Children's paperback fiction series; **Payback Press** Afro-American, Black orientated fiction and non-fiction; music, history, politics, biography and poetry; **Rebel Inc.** Promotion of new writing – fiction, poetry and non-fiction – as well as underground and neglected classics. About 100 titles a year. Synopses preferred to complete mss.
Royalties paid twice-yearly.

Authors' Rating Started as a purely Scottish publisher but now extends to a wide range of new writing and contemporary issues.

Canterbury Press Norwich
See **Hymns Ancient & Modern Ltd**

Canto
See **Cambridge University Press**

Capall Bann Publishing
Freshfields, Chieveley, Berkshire RG20 8TF
☎01635 247050/248711/247050   Fax 01635 247050/248711/247050
Chairman *Julia Day*
Editorial Head *Jon Day*

FOUNDED 1993 with three titles and now have over 180 in print. Family-owned and -run company which *publishes* British traditions, folklore, computing, boating, animals, alternative healing, environmental, Celtic lore, mind, body and spirit. 40 titles in 1998. TITLES *Practical Spirituality; Celtic Lore; Handbook of Fairies; Talking to the Earth; Bruce Roberts' Boatbuilding*. Synopses and ideas for books welcome. No fiction or poetry.
Royalties paid quarterly.

Jonathan Cape Ltd
See **Random House Group Ltd**

Carcanet Press Ltd
Conavon Court, 12–16 Blackfriars Street, Manchester M3 5BQ
☎0161 834 8730   Fax 0161 832 0084
Email pnr@carcanet.u-net.com
Website www.carcanet.co.uk
Chairman *Kate Gavron*
Managing Director/Editorial Director
Michael Schmidt

Since 1969 Carcanet has grown from an undergraduate hobby into a substantial venture. Robert Gavron bought the company in 1983 and it has established strong Anglo-European and Anglo-Commonwealth links. Winner of the **Sunday Times Small Publisher of the Year** award in 2000. *Publishes* poetry, academic, literary biography, fiction in translation and translations. About 50 titles a year, including the *P. N. Review* (six issues yearly). AUTHORS John Ashbery, Edwin Morgan, Elizabeth Jennings, Iain Crichton Smith, Natalia Ginzburg, Eavan Boland, Stuart Hood, Leonardo Sciascia, Christine Brooke-Rose, Pier Paolo Pasolini, C. H. Sisson, Donald Davie.
Royalties paid annually.

Authors' Rating Ever in the forefront of imaginative publishing, Carcanet has taken a step closer to the source of its literary creativity by setting up a postgraduate Writing School at Manchester Metropolitan University. (See entry under **Writers' Courses, Circles and Workshops.**)

Cardiff Academic Press
St Fagans Road, Fairwater, Cardiff CF5 3AE
☎029 2056 0333   Fax 029 2055 4909
Managing Director *R. G. Drake*
Academic publishers.

Carfax Publishing
See **Taylor & Francis Group plc**

Carlton Books Limited
20 Mortimer Street, London W1N 7RD
☎020 7612 0400   Fax 020 7612 0401
Email enquiries@carltonbooks.co.uk
Website www.carlton.com
Managing Director *Jonathan Goodman*
Publishing Director *Piers Murray Hill*
Approx. Annual Turnover £11 million

FOUNDED 1992. Owned by Carlton Communications, Carlton's books are aimed at the mass market for subjects such as TV tie-ins, lifestyle, computer games, sport, health, new age, puzzles, popular science and rock'n'roll. *Publishes* illustrated leisure and entertainment. Prime UK customers include the Book Club and WHSmith. No unsolicited mss; synopses and ideas welcome. No novels, science fiction, poetry or children's books.
Royalties paid twice-yearly.

Authors' Rating Linked to the largest programme producer in the ITV network, Carlton Books has built a reputation on co-editions for the international market and television tie-ins. Noted for speed of taking a book from first idea to publication. Carlton Books recently launched a US publishing operation.

Carroll & Brown Publishers Limited
20 Lonsdale Road, London NW6 6RD
☎020 7372 0900   Fax 020 7372 0460
Email carbro.gen@virgin.net
Managing Director *Amy Carroll*
Approx. Annual Turnover £3.5 million

FOUNDED in 1989 as a packaging operation; commenced publishing in 2000. *Publishes* practical cookery, health, gardening, lifestyle, mind, body and spirit. TITLES *Three Bowl Cookbook; Get Fit, Feel Fantastic; Meditations for Pregnancy; The Natural History of the Unnatural World*. Synopses/ideas for illustrated books welcome; approach in writing in the first instance. No fiction.
Fees paid instead of royalties.

Frank Cass & Co Ltd

Newbury House, 890–900 Eastern Avenue,
Newbury Park, Ilford, Essex IG2 7HH
☎020 8599 8866   Fax 020 8599 0984
Email info@frankcass.com
Website www.frankcass.com
Chairman *Frank Cass*
Managing Director *Stewart Cass*
Managing Editor *Andrew Humphrys* (Books
  Editor)
Publishes books and journals in the fields of politics, international relations, military and security studies, history, Middle East and African studies, economics, development studies. TITLES *Central Asia Meets the Middle East* ed. David Henashin; *In Pursuit of Military Excellence* Shimon Naveh; *Knowing Your Friends* Martin S. Alexander; *Nothing Sacred* David Alvarez and Robert A. Graham; *The Liberian Civil War* Mark Huband.

DIVISIONS
Woburn Press Educational list TITLES *Her Majesty's Inspectorate of Schools Since 1944* John E. Dunford; *Going Comprehensive in England and Wales* Alan C. Kercknoff. **Vallentine Mitchell/ Jewish Chronicle Publications** Books of Jewish interest TITLES *The Library of Holocaust Testimonies* series; *The Jewish Yearbook 1998* ed. Stephen Massil; *The Jewish Travel Guide; Soldier of Jerusalem* Uzi Narkiss. Unsolicited mss considered but synopsis with covering letter preferred.
  Royalties paid annually.

Cassell

Wellington House, 125 Strand, London
WC2R 0BB
☎020 7420 5555   Fax 020 7240 7261
Website www.cassell.co.uk
Managing Director *John Mitchinson*
FOUNDED 1848 by John Cassell. Bought by Collier Macmillan in 1974, then by CBS Publishing Europe in 1982. Returned to independence in 1986 as Cassell plc and a string of acquisitions. Acquired by the **Orion Publishing Group** in December 1998. *Publishes* general non-fiction, poetry, reference and illustrated.

IMPRINTS
Cassell General Books TITLES *Poems on the Underground; Cordon Bleu Complete Cookery Techniques; Cacti: The Illustrated Dictionary; Shaker.*
  Arms & Armour Press *Angus MacKinnon* TITLES *First World War Sourcebook; Napoleonic Weapons & Warfare; Great Battles of the Royal Navy.*
  Blandford Press *Stuart Booth* TITLES *Make*

Your Own Electric Guitar; Celebration of Maritime Art; Spiders of the World; Celtic Art Sourcebook.
  Ward Lock *Margaret Little* TITLES *Home & Garden Style; Mrs Beeton's Book of Cookery and Household Management; Ward Lock Gardening Encyclopedia.*
  Victor Gollancz Orion House, 5 Upper St Martin's Lane, London WC2H 9EA ☎0171 240 3444 *Mike Petty* TITLES *Lost Gardens of Heligan; About a Boy* Nick Hornby; *Beat Route* Jools Holland.

Authors' Rating New ownership has brought a welcome infusion of energy to Cassell where there is enthusiasm for product that will help build an ambitious publishing programme. Seven Dials, a new paperback illustrated imprint, begins publishing from August 2000 with titles ranging from cookery and gardening to travel and heritage.

Castle Publications

See **Nottingham University Press**

Kyle Cathie Ltd

122 Arlington Road, London NW1 7HP
☎020 7692 7215   Fax 020 7692 7260
Email kcathie@aol.com
FOUNDED 1990 to publish and promote 'books we have personal enthusiasm for'. *Publishes* non-fiction: cookery, food and drink, health and beauty, style/design, reference and occasional books of classic poetry. TITLES *Feel Fabulous Forever* Josephine Fairley and Sarah Stacey; *Patricia Wells at Home in Provence; Rejuvenating a Garden* Stephen Anderton. About 25 titles a year. No unsolicited mss. 'Synopses and ideas are considered in the fields in which we publish.'
  Royalties paid twice-yearly.

Catholic Truth Society (CTS)

40–46 Harleyford Road, London SE11 5AY
☎020 7640 0042   Fax 020 7640 0046
Email ctsfergal@mcmail.com
Chairman *Rt. Rev. Peter Smith*
General Secretary *Fergal Martin*
Approx. Annual Turnover £500,000
FOUNDED originally in 1868 and re-founded in 1884. *Publishes* religious books – Roman Catholic; a variety of doctrinal, moral, biographical, devotional and liturgical publications; including a large body of Vatican documents and sources. Unsolicited mss, synopses and ideas welcome if appropriate to their list.
  Royalties paid annually.

Caucasus World
See **Curzon Press Ltd**

Causeway Press Ltd
PO Box 13, 129 New Court Way, Ormskirk, Lancashire L39 5HP
☎01695 576048   Fax 01695 570714
Chairman/Managing Director
M. Haralambos
Approx. Annual Turnover £2 million
FOUNDED in 1982. *Publishes* educational textbooks only. 10 titles in 1999. TITLES *Mathematics for SEG; Geography in Focus; Psychology in Focus; Sociology in Focus; Business Studies; British History in Focus.* Unsolicited mss, synopses and ideas welcome.
Royalties paid annually.

Caxton Publishing Group
20 Bloomsbury Street, London WC1B 3QA
☎020 7636 7171   Fax 020 7636 1922
Email office@caxtonpublishing.com
Website www.caxtonpublishing.com
Chairman *Stephen Hill*
Managing Director *John Maxwell*
Approx. Annual Turnover £4 million
FOUNDED 1999. *Specialises* in reprinting out-of-print works for the 'value' market worldwide and commissioning new general non-fiction publications in reference, cookery, gardening and children's. 150 titles a year.
DIVISIONS/ IMPRINTS
Brockhampton Press Ltd Children's fiction and non-fiction. **Caxton Editions Ltd** General non-fiction, reference and military. **Knight Paperbacks Ltd** Fiction. No unsolicited mss; synopses and ideas welcome; send letter in the first instance.
Royalties paid twice-yearly.

CBA Publishing
Bowes Morrell House, 111 Walmgate, York YO1 9WA
☎01904 671417   Fax 01904 671384
Website www.britarch.ac.uk
Publications Officer *Kathryn Sleight*
Approx. Annual Turnover £80,000
Publishing arm of the **Council for British Archaeology**. *Publishes* academic archaeology reports, practical handbooks, yearbook, *British Archaeology* (bi-monthly magazine), *Young Archaeologist* (club's magazine), monographs, archaeology and education. TITLES *St Oswald's Priory; Archaeology and Conservation in Ironbridge; Conservation and Change in Historic Towns; Recording and Analysing Graveyards.*
Royalties not paid.

CBD Research Ltd
Chancery House, 15 Wickham Road, Beckenham, Kent BR3 5JS
☎020 8650 7745   Fax 020 8650 0768
Email cbdresearch@compuserver.com
Website www.glen.co.uk/cbd/
Chairman *G. P. Henderson*
Managing Director *S. P. A. Henderson*
Approx. Annual Turnover £500,000
FOUNDED 1961. *Publishes* directories and other reference guides to sources of information. About 6 titles a year. No fiction.
IMPRINT **Chancery House Press** Non-fiction of an esoteric/specialist nature for 'serious researchers and the dedicated hobbyist'. Unsolicited mss, synopses and ideas welcome.
Royalties paid quarterly.

Centaur Press
See **Open Gate Press**

Century
See **Random House Group Ltd**

Chadwyck-Healey Ltd
The Quorum, Barnwell Road, Cambridge CB5 8SW
☎01223 215512   Fax 01223 215513
Website www.chadwyck.co.uk
General Manager *Steven Hall*
Approx. Annual Turnover £9.5 million
Part of Bell & Howell. *Publishes* humanities and literary databases on the Web, CD-ROM and microform. Key TITLES include *KnowUK; Literature Online; The English Poetry Database; Periodical Contents Index; KnowEurope.* No unsolicited mss. Synopses and ideas welcome for reference works only.
Royalties paid annually.

Chambers Harrap Publishers Ltd
7 Hopetoun Crescent, Edinburgh EH7 4AY
☎0131 556 5929   Fax 0131 556 5313
Website www.chambersharrap.com
Managing Director *Maurice Shepherd*
Administrator *Catherine Johnson*
Publishes dictionaries, reference, and local interest. The imprint was founded in the early 1800s to publish self-education books, but soon diversified into dictionaries and other reference works. The acquisition of Harrap

Publishing Group's core business strengthened its position in the dictionary market, adding bilingual titles, covering almost all the major European languages, to its English-language dictionaries. About 24 titles a year. Send synopsis with accompanying letter rather than completed mss.

Chameleon
See **André Deutsch Ltd**

Chancery House Press
See **CBD Research Ltd**

Channel 4 Books
See **Macmillan Publishers Ltd**

Geoffrey Chapman
See **Continuum International Publishing Group Ltd**

Paul Chapman Publishing Ltd
See **Sage Publications Ltd**

Chapman Publishing
4 Broughton Place, Edinburgh EH1 3RX
☎0131 557 2207   Fax 0131 556 9565
Email editor@chapman-pub.co.uk
Website www.chapman-pub.co.uk

Managing Editor *Joy Hendry*

A venture devoted to publishing works by the best of the Scottish writers, both up-and-coming and established, published in *Chapman* magazine, Scotland's leading literary quarterly. Has expanded publishing activities considerably over the last two years and is now publishing a wider range of works though the broad policy stands. *Publishes* poetry, drama, short stories, books of contemporary importance in 20th-century Scotland. About 4 titles a year. TITLES *Carlucco & the Queen of Hearts; The Blasphemer* George Rosie; *Gold of Kildonan; Songs of the Grey Coast; Whins* George Gunn; *The Collected Shorter Poems* Tom Scott; *Alien Crop* Janet Paisley; *Good Girls Don't Cry* Margaret Fulton Cook. No unsolicited mss; synopses and ideas for books welcome.

Royalties paid annually.

Chapmans Publishers
See **The Orion Publishing Group Ltd**

Charnwood
See **F. A. Thorpe (Publishing) Ltd**

Chatham Publishing
See **Gerald Duckworth & Co Ltd**

Chatto & Windus Ltd
See **Random House Group Ltd**

Cherrytree Books
See **Evans Brothers**

Child's Play (International) Ltd
Ashworth Road, Bridgemead, Swindon, Wiltshire SN5 7YD
☎01793 616286   Fax 01793 512795
Email allday@childs-play.com
Website www.childs-play.com

Chief Executive *Neil Burden*

FOUNDED in 1972, Child's Play is an independent publisher specialising in learning through play, whole child development, life-skills and values. *Publishes* books, games and A-V materials. TITLES Books: *Big Hungry Bear; There Was an Old Lady; Puzzle Island; Children of the Sun; Ten Beads Tall; Pocket Pals; Sliders; Big Books and Storysacks*; Games: *Dizzy Bizzy; Safe Places; Arithmetic Lotto*. Unsolicited mss welcome. Send s.a.e. for return or response. Expect to wait two months for a reply.

Royalties Outright or royalty payments are subject to negotiation.

Chimera Book Publishers
Sheraton House, Castle Park, Cambridge CB3 0AX
☎01223 370012   Fax 01223 370040

Senior Editor *D. W. Stern*
Editor *R. Sabir*

Publishes fiction and non-fiction, general interest, biography, autobiography, children's, history, humour, science fiction, erotica and crime. TITLES *Tern* Sarah Jenkins; *When a Man Carries the Lamp* Mike Bolger; *Fields of Amaranth* Ross Merren. Unsolicited mss, synopses and ideas considered if accompanied by return postage.

Royalties paid twice-yearly.

Chivers Press Ltd
Windsor Bridge Road, Bath BA2 3AX
☎01225 335336   Fax 01225 310771
Email sales@chivers.co.uk
Website www.chivers.co.uk

Managing Director *Julian R. Batson*
Approx. Annual Turnover £9 million

Publishes reprints for libraries mainly, in large-print editions, including biography and autobiography, children's, crime, fiction and spoken word cassettes. No unsolicited material.

IMPRINTS **Chivers Large Print; Gunsmoke Westerns; Galaxy Children's Large Print;**

Camden Softcover Large Print; Paragon Softcover Large Print; Windsor Large Print; Black Dagger Crime. Chivers Audio Books (see entry under **Audio Books**).
Royalties paid twice-yearly.

Christian Focus Publications
Geanies House, Fearn, Tain, Ross-shire
IV20 1TW
☎01862 871011   Fax 01862 871699
Email efp@geanies.org.uk
Website www.christianfocus.com
Chairman *R. W. M. Mackenzie*
Managing Director *William Mackenzie*
Editorial Head *Malcolm Maclean*
Children's Editor *Catherine Mackenzie*
Approx. Annual Turnover £900,000
FOUNDED 1979 to produce children's books for the co-edition market. Now a major producer of Christian books. *Publishes* adult and children's books, including some fiction for children but not adults. No poetry. About 70 titles a year. Unsolicited mss, synopses and ideas welcome from Christian writers. Publishes for all English-speaking markets, as well as the UK. Books produced for Australia, USA, Canada, South Africa.
IMPRINTS **Christian Focus** General books; **Mentor** Specialist books; **Christian Heritage** Classic reprints.
Royalties paid twice-yearly.

Chrysalis Books Limited
10 Blenheim Court, Brewery Road, London
N7 9NT
☎020 7700 7444
Website www.chrysalisbooks.co.uk

The holding company for the book publishing division of the media group, Chrysalis Group Plc, encompassing **Brassey's** (incorporating **Conway Maritime Press** and **Putnam Aeronautical Books**), **B. T. Batsford**, Greenwich Editions (promotional books and reprints), Ramboro Books (remainder books), **Robson Books** and **Salamander Books**.

Churchill Livingstone
See **Harcourt Brace and Company Limited**

Cicerone Press
2 Police Square, Milnthorpe, Cumbria LA7 7PY
☎015395 62069   Fax 015395 63417
Email info@cicerone.demon.co.uk
Website www.cicerone.demon.co.uk
Managing/Editorial Director
Jonathan Williams

FOUNDED 1969. Guidebook publisher for outdoor enthusiasts. About 30 titles a year. No fiction or poetry. TITLES *Walking in the Alps*; *Jordan: Walks, Treks, Caves and Climbs*; *County* and *Long Distance Walking* series of guides. No unsolicited mss; synopses and ideas considered.
Royalties paid twice-yearly.

CIMA Books
32 Great Sutton Street, London EC1V 0NB
☎020 7253 7960   Fax 020 7253 7967
Email mail@cimabooks.co.uk
Website www.cimabooks.co.uk
Managing Director *Mark Collins*
Publisher *Cindy Richards*
FOUNDED in 1999 by Mark Collins and Cindy Richards (both formerly with Collins & Brown) 'to offer flexibility by being small, selling co-edition rights to overseas publishers'. *Publishes* lifestyle and interiors, mind, body and spirit. About 12 titles a year. No unsolicited mss, synopses or ideas.
Royalties paid twice-yearly.

Citron Press
Suite 155, Business Design Centre, 52 Upper Street, London N1 0QH
☎020 7288 6024   Fax 020 7288 6196
Email citronpress@citronpress.co.uk
Website www.citronpress.co.uk
Managing Director *Nikki Connors*
Operations Director *Steve Connors*
Editorial Director *Fiona Stewart*
ESTABLISHED in 1998 to publish and promote new fiction the Citron Press New Authors' Co-operative has now published over 130 titles. *Publishes* contemporary new fiction as paperback originals. No poetry or children's fiction. No unsolicited mss or agents. Citron Press' advocates include Martin Amis and Sebastian Faulks. TITLES *Toilet Elephant* Nick Johnston-Jones; *Fragile State* David Turner; *Cold Snap* Kelvin Mason; *Sensible Shoes* Julie Alpine. For details of submission procedure contact Citron Press free on 0800 013 6533 or e-mail or visit the website.

Authors' Rating Set up as an authors cooperative, Citron has moved closer to traditional publishing with the scrapping of its £400 membership fee. But supplicants are still liable for a £50 reading fee. If a ms is accepted Citron acquires worldwide rights to the title for 20 years. A deal with Hilton Hotels allows for a Citron Book for Bedtime to be charged to guests' bills – a civilised alternative to the Hollywood movie.

Claridge Press

Horsell's Farmhouse, Sunday Hill,
Brinkworth, Wiltshire SN5 5AF
☎01666 510272   Fax 01666 510013
Managing Editor *Andrea Downing*

FOUNDED 1987. Developed from the quarterly
Salisbury Review. Publishes current affairs – political, philosophical and sociological – from a right-
wing viewpoint. SERIES *Thinkers of our Time*.
TITLES *Falsification of the Good; Understanding
Youth; Some Turn to Mecca to Pray: Islamic Values
in the Modern World; KGB Lawsuits*. Unsolicited
mss welcome within given subject areas.
Royalties paid according to contract.

Clarion

See **Elliot Right Way Books**

T. & T. Clark

59 George Street, Edinburgh EH2 2LQ
☎0131 225 4703   Fax 0131 220 4260
Email ggreen@tandtclark.co.uk
Website www.tandtclark.co.uk
Managing Director/Editorial Head
Geoffrey Green

FOUNDED 1821. *Publishes* religion, theology,
philosophy and law, for academic and professional markets. About 35 titles a year, including
journals. TITLES *Church Dogmatics* Karl Barth;
*Scottish Law Directory; The Law of Contracts and
Related Obligations in Scotland* David M. Walker.
Unsolicited mss, synopses and ideas for books
welcome.
Royalties paid annually.

James Clarke & Co.

PO Box 60, Cambridge CB1 2NT
☎01223 350865   Fax 01223 366951
Email publishing@jamesclarke.co.uk
Website www.jamesclarke.co.uk
Managing Director *Adrian Brink*

Parent company of **The Lutterworth Press**
(see entry). *Publishes* scholarly and academic
works, mainly theological, directory and reference titles. TITLES *Encyclopedia of the Middle Ages*
(book and CD-ROM versions); *New Testament
in its Literary Environment; Mystical Theology of the
Eastern Church; Libraries and Society*. Approach in
writing with ideas in the first instance.

Richard Cohen Books

An Imprint of Metro Publishing Ltd,
19 Gerrard Street, London W1V 7LA
☎020 7734 1411   Fax 020 7734 1811
Consulting Publisher *Peter Day*

Publishes biography, current affairs, travel, his-
tory, politics and the arts. First titles published in
1995. The company went out of business in
October 1998 and was reconstituted under
Metro as an independent publishing division. No
erotica, DIY, children's, reference or fiction.
TITLES *Siegfried Sassoon* John Stuart Roberts;
C. B. Fry Iain Wilton; *Rupert Brooke* Nigel Jones.
No unsolicited mss.
Royalties paid twice-yearly.

Authors' Rating The living proof of the pre-
carious nature of small-scale, quality publishing
Richard Cohen has been rescued yet again, this
time by Metro Books. He is now a wholly-
owned subsidiary of Metro. Long may his editorial talents thrive.

Peter Collin Publishing Ltd

1 Cambridge Road, Teddington, Middlesex
TW11 8DT
☎020 8943 3386   Fax 020 8943 1673
Email info@pcp.co.uk
Website www.pcp.co.uk
Chairman *P. H. Collin*

FOUNDED 1985. *Publishes* dictionaries only,
including specialised dictionaries in English for
students and specialised bilingual dictionaries for
translators (French, German, Swedish, Spanish,
Greek, Chinese, Hungarian). About 10 titles a
year. Synopses and ideas welcome. No unsolicited mss; copy must be supplied on disk.
Royalties paid twice-yearly.

Collins

See **HarperCollins Publishers Ltd**

Collins & Brown
(C&B Publishing plc)

London House, Great Eastern Wharf, Parkgate
Road, London SW11 4NQ
☎020 7924 2575   Fax 020 7924 7725
Email info@cb-publishing.co.uk
Website www.cb-publishing.co.uk
Approx. Annual Turnover £25 million

FOUNDED 1989. Independent publisher. Acquired Pavilion Books Ltd in 1997 and David
Bennett Books in 1998. *Publishes* illustrated non-
fiction: practical photography, crafts, gardening,
decorating, lifestyle and cookery. No fiction,
poetry or local interest. About 400 titles a year.
DIVISION **C&B Children's Books**. GROUP
IMPRINTS Adult Non-fiction: **Collins & Brown**
Publisher *Colin Ziegler*, **Pavilion Books** (see
entry); Children's Non-fiction: **Belitha Press**
Publisher *Colin Webb* **David Bennett Books**

(see entry under **UK Packagers**); **Big Fish**
Publisher *Chester Fisher*. No unsolicited mss; outlines with s.a.e. only.
Royalties paid twice-yearly.

Colonsay Books
See **House of Lochar**

Columbia University Press
See **University Presses of California, Columbia & Princeton Ltd**

Compendium Publishing Ltd
1st Floor, 43 Frith Street, London W1V 5TE
☎020 7287 4570   Fax 020 7494 0583
Email compendium@compuserve.com
Managing Director *Alan Greene*
Editorial Director *Simon Forty*

FOUNDED 1996. *Publishes* and packages for international publishing companies – general non-fiction: history, reference, hobbies, children's, transport and militaria. 25 titles in 1999. IMPRINT **Windrow & Greene** Military books. No unsolicited mss; synopses and ideas preferred.
Royalties paid twice-yearly.

Condé Nast Books
See **Random House Group Ltd**

Condor
See **Souvenir Press Ltd**

Conran Octopus
See **Octopus Publishing Group**

Constable & Robinson
3 The Lanchesters, 162 Fulham Palace Road, London W6 9ER
☎020 8741 3663   Fax 020 8748 7562
Email enquiries@constablerobinson.com
Website www.constablerobinson.com
Non-Executive Chairman *Benjamin Glazebrook*
Managing Director *Nick Robinson*
Directors *Jan Chamier, Nova Jayne Heath, Adrian Andrews*
Approx. Annual Turnover £5 million

Constable & Co FOUNDED in 1890 by Archibald Constable, a grandson of Walter Scott's publisher. Robinson Publishing Ltd FOUNDED in 1983 by Nick Robinson. In December 1999 Constable and Robinson combined their individual shareholdings into a single company, Constable & Robinson Ltd.
IMPRINTS **Constable** (Hardbacks) *Carol O'Brien*, Editorial Director *Publishes* biography

and autobiography, crime fiction, general and military history, psychology, travel, climbing, landscape photography and outdoor pursuits guidebooks. **Robinson** (Paperbacks) *Krystyna Green* Senior Commissioning Editor *Publishes* crime, science fiction, *Daily Telegraph* health books, the Mammoth series, psychology, true crime, military history and *Smarties* children's books. Unsolicited sample chapters, synopses and ideas for books welcome. No mss; no e-mail submissions. Enclose return postage.

Authors' Rating The merging of two small but highly regarded independent publishers promises well for authors who enjoy close attention from their editors. The broad scope of the fiction and non-fiction lists suggests a flexible response to book proposals.

Consultants Bureau
See **Kluwer Academic/Plenum Publishers**

Consumers' Association
See **Which? Books/ Consumers' Association**

The Continuum International Publishing Group Ltd
Wellington House, 125 Strand, London WC2R 0BB
☎020 7420 5555   Fax 020 7420 7261
Website www.continuum-books.com
Chairman & Managing Director
   Philip Sturrock
Approx. Annual Turnover £9 million

FOUNDED in 1999 by a buy-out of the academic and religious publishing of **Cassell** and the acquisition of Continuum New York. *Publishes* academic and religious books. 250 titles in 1999. DIVISIONS **Academic** *Janet Joyce* IMPRINTS **Pinter**; **Leicester University Press**; **Mansell** TITLES *Theory and Practice of Counselling; Reflective Teaching in the Primary School.* **Religious** *Robin Baird-Smith* IMPRINTS **Geoffrey Chapman**; **Mowbray** TITLES *Pilgrims in Rome; Jerome Biblical Commentary.* **General Books** *Robin Baird-Smith.* Unsolicited synopses and ideas within the subject areas listed above welcome; approach in writing in the first instance. *Overseas associate* The Continuum International Publishing Group Inc., New York.
Royalties paid twice-yearly.

Conway Maritime Press
See **Brassey's**

Thomas Cook Publishing

PO Box 227, Peterborough PE3 6PU
☎01733 503571   Fax 01733 503596
Head of Publishing *Kevin Fitzgerald*
Approx. Annual Turnover £1.7 million

Part of the Thomas Cook Group Ltd, publishing commenced in 1873 with the first issue of Cook's Continental Timetable. *Publishes* guidebooks, maps and timetables. About 20 titles a year. No unsolicited mss; synopses and ideas welcome as long as they are travel-related.
Royalties paid annually.

Leo Cooper

See **Pen & Sword Books Ltd**

Corgi

See **Transworld Publishers**

Cornwall Books

See **Golden Cockerel Press Ltd**

Coronet

See **Hodder Headline Plc**

Countryside Books

2 Highfield Avenue, Newbury, Berkshire
RG14 5DS
☎01635 43816   Fax 01635 551004
Email info@countrysidebooks.co.uk
Publisher *Nicholas Battle*

FOUNDED 1976. *Publishes* local interest paperbacks on regional subjects, generally by English county. Local history, genealogy, walking and photographic, some transport. Over 250 titles available. Unsolicited mss and synopses welcome but no fiction, poetry, natural history or personal memories.
Royalties paid twice-yearly.

Cressrelles Publishing Co. Ltd

10 Station Road Industrial Estate, Colwall,
Malvern, Worcestershire WR13 6RN
☎01684 540154   Fax 01684 540154
Managing Director *Leslie Smith*

Publishes a range of general books, drama and chiropody titles. IMPRINTS **Actinic Press** Specialises in chiropody; **J. Garnet Miller Ltd** Plays and theatre texts; **Kenyon-Deane** Plays and drama textbooks.

Cromwell Publishers

Eagle Court, Concord Business Park,
Manchester M22 0RR
☎0161 932 6402   Fax 0161 932 6001
Email editorial@cromwellpublishers.co.uk
Website www.cromwellpublishers.co.uk

FOUNDED 1995. *Publishes* fiction and non-fiction in paperback format: memoirs, biography, autobiography, religion/inspirational, popular sciences, young children, health. 'May consider some poetry.' No cookery, academic, manuals or erotica. 60 titles to date. No unsolicited mss; send synopsis and one sample chapter with return postage to New Submissions. IMPRINTS **Cromwell Children**; **Cromwell Publishing**.
Royalties paid annually.

Authors' Rating Liable to ask authors to contribute towards costs of publication.

Croom Helm

See **Routledge**

Crossway

See **Inter-Varsity Press**

The Crowood Press Ltd

The Stable Block, Crowood Lane, Ramsbury,
Marlborough, Wiltshire SN8 2HR
☎01672 520320   Fax 01672 520280
Email crowood@crowood.demon.co.uk
Website www.crowood.demon.co.uk
Chairman *John Dennis*
Managing Director *Ken Hathaway*

Publishes sport and leisure titles, including animal and land husbandry, climbing and walking, maritime, country sports, equestrian, fishing and shooting; also chess and bridge, crafts, dogs, gardening, natural history, aviation, military history and motoring. About 70 titles a year. Preliminary letter preferred in all cases.
Royalties paid annually.

James Currey Publishers

73 Botley Road, Oxford OX2 0BS
☎01865 244111   Fax 01865 246454
Chairman *James Currey*
Managing Director/Editorial Director
Douglas H. Johnson

FOUNDED 1985. A specialist publisher. *Publishes* academic paperback books on Africa, the Caribbean and Third World: history, anthropology, economics, sociology, politics and literary criticism. Approach in writing by post with synopsis if material is 'relevant to our needs'.
Royalties paid annually.

Curzon Press Ltd

15 The Quadrant, Richmond, Surrey
TW9 1BP
☎020 8948 4660   Fax 020 8332 6735

Managing Director *Malcolm G. Campbell*

Specialised scholarly publishing house. *Publishes* academic/scholarly books on history and archaeology, languages and linguistics, philosophy, religion and theology, sociology and anthropology, cultural studies and reference, mainly in the context of Asia but also Africa. IMPRINTS **Caucasus World**; **Japan Library**.

Cygnus Arts

See **Golden Cockerel Press Ltd**

Dalesman Publishing Co. Ltd

Stable Courtyard, Broughton Hall, Skipton, North Yorkshire BD23 3AE

☎01756 701381   Fax 01756 701326

Email editorial@dalesman.co.uk

Website www.dalesman.co.uk

Editor *Terry Fletcher*

Publishers of *Dalesman, Cumbria and Lake District* and *Peak District* magazines, and regional books covering Yorkshire, the Lake District and the Peak District. Subjects include crafts and hobbies, geography and geology, guidebooks, history and antiquarian, humour, travel and topography. Unsolicited mss considered on all subjects. About 20 titles a year.

Royalties paid annually.

Terence Dalton Ltd

Water Street, Lavenham, Sudbury, Suffolk CO10 9RN

☎01787 249291   Fax 01787 248267

Website www.lavenhamgroup.co.uk

Director/Editorial Head *Elisabeth Whitehair*

FOUNDED 1967. Part of the Lavenham Group Plc, a family company. *Publishes* non-fiction and currently contract-publishes water and environment books for Chartered UK Institution. No unsolicited mss; send synopsis with two or three sample chapters. Ideas welcome.

Royalties paid annually.

The C. W. Daniel Co. Ltd

1 Church Path, Saffron Walden, Essex CB10 1JP

☎01799 521909   Fax 01799 513462

Email daniel_publishing@dial.pipex.com

Website www.cwdaniel.com

Managing Director *Ian Miller*

Approx. Annual Turnover £1 million

FOUNDED in 1902 by a man who knew and was a follower of Tolstoy, the company was taken over by its present directors in 1973. Output has increased following the acquisition in 1980 of health and healing titles from the Health Science Press, the purchase of Neville Spearman Publishers' metaphysical list in 1985 and the list of L. N. Fowler in 1998. *Publishes* New Age: alternative healing and metaphysical. About 15 titles a year. No fiction, diet or cookery. Unsolicited synopses and ideas welcome; no unsolicited mss.

Royalties paid annually.

Darf Publishers Ltd

277 West End Lane, London NW6 1QS

☎020 7431 7009   Fax 020 7431 7655

Website www.darfpublishers.co.uk

Chairman/Managing Director *M. B. Fergiani*

Editorial Head *A. Bentaleb*

Approx. Annual Turnover £500,000

FOUNDED 1982 to publish books and reprints on the Middle East, history, theology and travel. *Publishes* geography, history, language, literature, oriental, politics, theology and travel. About 10 titles a year. TITLES *Moslems in Spain; Travels of Ibn Battuta; Elementary Arabic; Travels in Syria and the Holy Land* Burckhardt.

Royalties paid annually. *Overseas associates* Dar Al-Fergiani, Cairo, Tripoli and Tunis.

Darton, Longman & Todd Ltd

1 Spencer Court, 140–142 Wandsworth High Street, London SW18 4JJ

☎020 8875 0155   Fax 020 8875 0133

Email mail@darton-longman-todd.co.uk

Editorial Director *Brendan Walsh*

Approx. Annual Turnover £1 million

FOUNDED in 1959. In July 1990 DLT became a common ownership company, owned and run by staff members. The company is a leading ecumenical, predominantly Christian, publisher, with a strong emphasis on spirituality, theology and the ministry and mission of the Church. About 50 titles a year. TITLES include *Jerusalem Bible; New Jerusalem Bible; God of Surprises; Audacity to Believe*. Sample material for books on theological or spiritual subjects considered.

Royalties paid twice-yearly.

David & Charles Children's Books

Winchester House, 259–269 Old Marylebone Road, London NW1 5XJ

☎020 7616 7200   Fax 020 7616 7201

Editorial Director *Mandy Suhr*

FOUNDED 1994. Formerly Levinson Children's Books; acquired by **David & Charles Publishers** in 1997. *Publishes* board books,

novelty books, picture books and gift collections for children of 0–12 years. Unsolicited mss, synopses and ideas welcome.
Royalties paid twice-yearly.

David & Charles Publishers
Brunel House, Forde Road, Newton Abbot, Devon TQ12 4PU
☎01626 323200   Fax 01626 323317
Email mail@davidandcharles.co.uk
Website www.davidandcharles.co.uk
Managing Director *Neil Page*
Approx. Annual Turnover £16.8 million
FOUNDED 1960 as a specialist company. Bought back from **Reader's Digest** in 1997. Acquired Godsfield Press in June 1998. *Publishes* illustrated non-fiction for international markets, specialising in crafts, art techniques, interiors, gardening, equestrian and countryside, mind, body and spirit and children's. No fiction, poetry or memoirs. About 60 titles a year. TITLES *Jazz Up Your Junk; Garden Transformations; Crafts Made Easy Series; Badminton Horse Trials; The Organic Café Cookbook; Egg Day; Illustrated Encyclopedia of Well Being.* Unsolicited mss will be considered if return postage is included; synopses and ideas welcome.
Royalties paid twice-yearly.

Christopher Davies Publishers Ltd
PO Box 403, Swansea, West Glamorgan SA1 4YF
☎01792 648825   Fax 01792 648825
Managing Director/Editorial Head
Christopher T. Davies
Approx. Annual Turnover £100,000
FOUNDED 1949 to promote and expand Welsh-language publications. By the 1970s the company was publishing over 50 titles a year but a subsequent drop in Welsh sales led to the establishment of a small English list which has continued. *Publishes* biography, cookery, history, sport and literature of Welsh interest. About 4 titles a year. TITLES *English/Welsh Dictionaries; Ivor Allchurch M.B.E., Biography; Historic Gower; Who's Who in Welsh History.* No unsolicited mss. Synopses and ideas for books welcome.
Royalties paid twice-yearly.

Authors' Rating A favourite for Celtic readers and writers.

Giles de la Mare Publishers Ltd
PO Box 25351, London NW5 1ZT
☎020 7485 2533   Fax 020 7485 2534
Email gilesdelamare@dial.pipex.com

Chairman/Managing Director
Giles de la Mare
Approx. Annual Turnover £45,000
FOUNDED 1995 and commenced publishing in April 1996. *Publishes* mainly non-fiction, especially art and architecture, biography, history, music. TITLES *Married to the Amadeus* Muriel Nissel; *Venice: An Anthology Guide* Milton Grundy; *History at War* Noble Frankland; *Duchess of Cork Street* Lillian Browse; *The Weather of Britain* Robin Stirling; *Vermeer* Lawrence Gowing; *Erasmus Darwin* Desmond King-Hall; *Shakespeare and the Prince of Love* Anthony Arlidge. Unsolicited mss, synopses and ideas welcome after initial telephone call.
Royalties paid twice-yearly.

Dean
See **Egmont Children's Books**

Debrett's Peerage Ltd
Brunel House, 55a North Wharf Road, Paddington, London W2 1XR
☎020 7915 9660   Fax 020 7724 2089
Email people@debretts.co.uk
Website www.debretts.co.uk
Chairman *Christopher Haines*
Managing Director *Simone Kesseler*
FOUNDED 1769. The company's main activity (in conjunction with **Macmillan**) is the quinquennial *Debrett's Peerage and Baronetage* (published in 2000) and annual *Debrett's People of Today* (also available on CD-ROM). Debrett's general books are published under licence through **Headline**.
Royalties paid twice-yearly.

Dedalus Ltd
Langford Lodge, St Judith's Lane, Sawtry, Cambridgeshire PE17 5XE
☎01487 832382   Fax 01487 832382
Email DedalusLimited@compuserve.com
Chairman *Juri Gabriel*
Managing Director *Eric Lane*
Approx. Annual Turnover £175,000
FOUNDED 1983. *Publishes* contemporary European fiction and classics and original literary fiction in the fields of magic realism, surrealism, the grotesque and bizarre. 13 titles in 1999. TITLES *The Decadent Traveller; The Arabian Nightmare* Robert Irwin; *Theodore* Christopher Harris; *When the Whistle Blows* Jack Allen; *Music in a Foreign Language* Andrew Crumey (winner of the **Saltire Best First Book Award** in 1994). Welcomes submissions for original fiction and books suitable for its list but says: 'most people

sending work in have no idea what kind of books Dedalus publishes and merely waste their efforts'. Particularly interested in intellectually clever and unusual fiction. A letter about the author should always accompany any submission. No replies without s.a.e.

DIVISIONS/IMPRINTS **Original Fiction in Paperback**; **Contemporary European Fiction 1992–2000**; **Dedalus European Classics**; **Empire of the Senses**; **Bizarre Literary Concept Books**.

Royalties paid annually.

Authors' Rating A small, quality publisher which actually recognises that good books can come from foreign language writers.

University of Delaware
See **Golden Cockerel Press Ltd**

JM Dent
See **The Orion Publishing Group Ltd**

André Deutsch Ltd
76 Dean Street, London W1V 5HA
☎020 7316 4450   Fax 020 7316 4499
Website www.vci.co.uk

Managing Director *A. Ogilvie*
Editorial Director *Louise Dixon*
Approx. Annual Turnover £5.3 million

FOUNDED in 1950 by André Deutsch, who eventually ended his long association with the company in 1991 (died April 2000). In 1995 the company was acquired by video and audio publisher and distributor VCI plc, who were in 1998 acquired by the Kingfisher Group. In the past three years six distinct and successful imprints have been developed, two for children: **Madcap**, offering innovative, fun and accessible titles and **André Deutsch Classics**, a range of hardback classic books at paperback prices. For adults there is **Chameleon**, the commercial imprint that covers comedy, humour, sport, TV tie-ins, music and film, the **André Deutsch** label which covers biography, sport, cookery, entertainment and current affairs, the **Manchester United** imprint under which the company looks after all the publishing interests of the football club, and the **Granada Media** imprint, under which the television company's high profile books are published.

Authors' Rating Who would have thought of Deutsch, one-time darling of the literary greats, as the publisher of Glen Hoddle, Cliff Richard and the Spice Girls. But that is what comes from

association with the highly successful video and audio publisher Video Collection International, in turn owned by Kingfisher. Many Deutsch titles are linked to VCI products but there is also a thriving children's list.

Dial House
See **Ian Allan Publishing Ltd**

Diva Books
Worldwide House, 116/134 Bayham Street, London NW1 0BA
☎020 7482 2576   Fax 020 7284 0329
Website www.prowler.co.uk

Contact *Gillian Rodgerson*

Part of the Millivres – Prowler Group. New lesbian imprint. *Publishes* literary and popular fiction, non-fiction. TITLES *Needlepoint* Jenny Roberts; *The Comedienne* V. G. Lee; *Emerald Budgies* Lee Maxwell. 'Rights by negotiation.'

Dolphin Book Co. Ltd
Tredwr, Llangrannog, Llandysul SA44 6BA
☎01239 654404   Fax 01239 654002

Managing Director *Martin L. Gili*
Approx. Annual Turnover £5000

FOUNDED 1957. Small publishing house specialising in Catalan, Spanish and South American books for the academic market. TITLES *Elegies de Bierville/Bierville Elegies* Carles Riba, Catalan text with English translation by J. L. Gili; *The Late Poetry of Pablo Neruda* Christopher Perriam; *Hispanic Linguistic Studies in Honour of F. W. Hodcroft; Salvatge cor/Savage Heart* Carles Riba; Catalan text with English translations by J. L. Gili. Unsolicited material not welcome.

Royalties paid annually.

John Donald Publishers Ltd
Unit 8 Canongate Venture, 5 New Street, Edinburgh EH8 5BH
☎0131 556 6660   Fax 0131 557 6250

Managing Director *Hugh Andrew*

Bought by **Birlinn Ltd** in 1999. *Publishes* academic and scholarly, agriculture, archaeology, architecture, economics, textbooks, guidebooks, local, military and social history, religious, sociology and anthropology. About 20 titles a year.

Royalties paid annually.

Donhead Publishing Ltd
Lower Coombe, Donhead St Mary, Shaftesbury, Dorset SP7 9LY
☎01747 828422   Fax 01747 828522

Email jillpearce@donhead.com
Website www.donhead.u-net.com
Contact *Jill Pearce*

FOUNDED 1990 to specialise in publishing how-to books for building practitioners; particularly interested in architectural conservation material. *Publishes* building, architecture and heritage only. 6 titles a year. TITLES *Encyclopaedia of Architectural Terms; A Good Housekeeping Guide to Churches and their Contents; Cleaning Historic Buildings; Brickwork; Practical Stone Masonry; Conservation of Timber Buildings; Surveying Historic Buildings; English Heritage Directory of Building Limes; Heritage, Sands and Aggregates; Creative Re-use of Buildings; Journal of Architectural Conservation* (3 issues yearly). Unsolicited mss, synopses and ideas welcome.

Dorling Kindersley Ltd

9 Henrietta Street, London WC2E 8PS
☎020 7836 5411   Fax 020 7836 7570
Website www.dk.com
Chief Executive *Anthony Forbes Wilson*
Publisher *Christopher Davis*
Approx. Annual Turnover
  UK £29.1 million; US £36.5 million

FOUNDED 1974. Packager and publisher of illustrated non-fiction: cookery, crafts, gardening, health, travel guides, atlases, natural history and children's information and fiction. Launched a US imprint in 1991 and an Australian imprint in 1997. Acquired Henderson Publishing in 1995 and was purchased by Pearson plc for £311 million in 2000. About 175–200 titles a year.

  DIVISIONS **Adult**; **Children's**; **Interactive Learning**; **Vision** (video). TITLES *Eyewitness Guides; Eyewitness Travel Guides; BMA Complete Family Health Encyclopedia; RHS A–Z Encyclopedia of Garden Plants; Children's Illustrated Encyclopedia; The Way Things Work.* Unsolicited synopses/ideas for books welcome.

Authors' Rating A victim of its own energy and originality, DK is now part of Pearson which has the resources to develop the list and to put a large part of it on-line. There were mistakes along the way, notably the hugely expensive overproduction of *Star Wars* books but nothing can detract from DK's achievement in education and self-learning, both sectors having benefited from DK's highly structured, colourful guides and manuals. Authors who are experiencing DK for the first time should be aware that in this area of publishing personalities are secondary to the team effort.

Doubleday
See **Transworld Publishers**

Ashley Drake Publishing Ltd

PO Box 733, Cardiff CF4 6WE
☎029 2052 2229   Fax 029 2052 2229
Email post@ashleydrake.com
Website www.ashleydrake.com
Chairman *Ashley Drake*
Approx. Annual Turnover £70,000

FOUNDED 1995. *Publishes* academic, trade and Welsh-language books. 20 titles in 1999. No unsolicited mss; synopses and ideas for the Welsh Academic Press and Ashley Drake Publishing imprints welcome. No scientific or computing books.

IMPRINTS
Ashley Drake Publishing Sport, music, cookery and general trade. TITLES *When Pele Broke Our Hearts – Wales and the 1958 World Cup; Welsh Names for Children – The Complete Guide.* **Welsh Academic Press** English language academic, scholarly humanities and social sciences. TITLES *The American West; The Electoral Handbook of Wales 1900–1999; Celtic Radicals* and *Celtic Poetry Library* series. **Gwasg Addysgol Cymru** Welsh-language educational titles. TITLES *Dyddiadur Anne Frank (Diary of Anne Frank).* **Y Ddraig Fach** Welsh-language titles for children. Welsh editions of Ladybird/Disney minihardbacks: *Crwca Notre Dame (Hunchback of Notre Dame); Pocahontas.*
  Royalties paid annually.

Drake Educational Associates

St Fagans Road, Fairwater, Cardiff CF5 3AE
☎029 2056 0333   Fax 029 2055 4909
Managing Director *R. G. Drake*
Educational publisher.

Dref Wen

28 Church Road, Whitchurch, Cardiff CF14 2EA
☎029 2061 7860   Fax 029 2061 0507
Chairman *R. Boore*
Managing Director *G. Boore*

FOUNDED 1970. *Publishes* Welsh language and bilingual children's books, Welsh and English educational books for Welsh learners. Over 50 titles in 1999. No unsolicited material.
  Royalties paid annually.

Dryden Press
See **Harcourt Brace and Company Limited**

Duck Editions
See **Gerald Duckworth & Co. Ltd**

Gerald Duckworth & Co. Ltd
61 Frith Street, London W1V 5TA
☎020 7434 4242   Fax 020 7434 4420
Email info@duckworth-publishers.co.uk
Website www.duckw.com
Publisher/CEO *Thomas H. Hedley*
Editorial Director *Sarah Such*
Approx. Annual Turnover £2 million

FOUNDED 1898 by Gerald Duckworth. Original publisher of Virginia Woolf. Other early authors include Hilaire Belloc, John Galsworthy, D. H. Lawrence and George Orwell. Duckworth is a general trade publisher with eminent authors such as Beryl Bainbridge and John Bayley in addition to a strong academic division.

IMPRINTS/DIVISIONS
Bristol Classical Press Classical texts and modern languages; **Chatham Publishing** Maritime history; **Duck Editions** FOUNDED 1998. Contemporary literary fiction and non-fiction; **Duckworth Academic**; **Duckworth General**. No unsolicited mss; synopses and sample chapters only. Enclose s.a.e. or return postage for response/return.

Royalties paid twice-yearly at first, annually thereafter.

Authors' Rating Once noted for erudition and books by Beryl Bainbridge, Duckworth has re-invented itself as a publisher for the youth market. A new imprint, Duck Editions, offering an intriguing collection of quirkish titles, will attract submissions from way-out authors who find that their work does not fit easily into conventional publishing. Another sign of aggressive expansion is the creation of Drake Films to commission screenplays which may be taken on to production or sold as part of a production package.

Duncan Petersen Publishing Limited
31 Ceylon Road, London W14 0PY
☎020 7371 2356   Fax 020 7371 2507
Directors *Andrew Duncan, Mel Petersen*

FOUNDED 1986. Publisher and packager of childcare, business, antiques, birds, nature, atlases, walking and travel books. IMPRINT **Duncan Petersen** SERIES *Charming Small Hotel Guides; Independent Traveller's Guides; Backroads Driving Guides; On Foot* (city walking guides). Unsolicited synopses and ideas for books welcome.
Fees paid.

Martin Dunitz Ltd
The Livery House, 7–9 Pratt Street, London NW1 0AE
☎020 7482 2202   Fax 020 7267 0159
Website www.dunitz.co.uk
Managing Director *Martin Dunitz*
Production Director *Rosemary Allen*
Journals Manager *Ian Mellor*

Acquired by the **Taylor & Francis Group plc** in 1999. *Publishes* specialist medical and dentistry atlases, texts, pocketbooks, slide atlases and CD-ROMs aimed at an international market. Particular areas of focus are psychiatry, neurology, cardiology, orthopaedics, dematology, oncology and bone metabolism. The company won the Queen's Award for Export Achievement in 1991. 90–100 titles a year. Unsolicited synopses and ideas welcome but no mss. TITLES *International Journal of Cardiovascular Interventions, International Journal of Psychiatry in Clinical Practice, Journal of Cutaneous Laser Therapy; Amyotrophic Lateral Sclerosis and Other Motor Neuron Disorders.*
Royalties paid twice-yearly.

Eagle
See **Inter Publishing Ltd**

Earthlight
See **Simon & Schuster**

Earthscan Publications
See **Kogan Page Ltd**

Ebury Press
See **Random House Group Ltd**

Economist Books
See **Profile Books**

Edinburgh University Press
22 George Square, Edinburgh EH8 9LF
☎0131 650 4218   Fax 0131 662 0053
Website www.eup.ed.ac.uk
Chairman *David Martin*
Managing Director *Timothy Wright*
Editorial Director *Jackie Jones*

Publishes academic and scholarly books (and journals): gender studies, geography, history – ancient, classical, medieval and modern, Islamic studies, linguistics, literary criticism, media and cultural studies; philosophy, politics, Scottish studies, theology and religious studies. About 100 titles a year.

IMPRINTS **Polygon** *Publishes* fiction and poetry, general trade books, Scottish literary, cultural and oral history; **Polygon@Edinburgh** Scottish politics and culture.

No unsolicited mss for EUP titles; mss welcome for Polygon and Polygon@Edinburgh but must be accompanied by s.a.e. for reply/return; letter/synopsis preferred in the first instance. *Royalties* paid annually.

Éditions Aubrey Walter
BCM 6159, London WC1N 3XX
Email aubrey@gmppubs.co.uk
Director *Aubrey Walter*

Publishes visual work by gay artists and photographers, usually in the form of a monograph showcasing one artist's work. TITLES *Life and Work of Henry Scott Tuke* Emmanuel Cooper; *The Bear Cult* Chris Nelson; *Paintings* Sadao Hasegawa; *The Erotic Art of Duncan Grant*; *Nubile Nostalgia* photos by Stephen Garkii. Work may be submitted on disk, transparency, photocopy or photograph.
Payment One-off fee negotiable.

Egmont Children's Books
239 Kensington High Street, London W8 6SA
☎020 7761 3500   Fax 020 7761 3510
Email <firstname>.<lastname>@ecb.egmont.com
Managing Director *Susannah McFarlane*

Part of the Egmont Group (Copenhagen), Egmont Children's Books comprises the original imprints of Heinemann Young Books and Methuen Children's Books (both over 100 years old), and Hamlyn Children's Books. *Publishes* children's picture books, fiction and non-fiction; licensed characters for children. About 350 titles a year.
IMPRINTS **Mammoth** TITLES *The Ghost of Thomas Kempe; The Little Prince; Tintin.* **Heinemann**; **Methuen** TITLES *Thomas the Tank Engine; Winnie-the-Pooh;* **Dean**. No unsolicited mss. Synopses and ideas welcome; approach in writing with s.a.e.
Royalties paid twice-yearly.

Authors' Rating Building on a list of indestructible classics ranging from Pooh to Thomas the Tank Engine, Egmont has made the bold move into children's books in translation, a marvellous opportunity for youngsters to find out what appeals to their continental cousins.

Egmont World Limited
Deanway Technology Centre, Wilmslow Road, Handforth, Cheshire SK9 3FB
☎01625 650011   Fax 01625 650040
Managing Director *Ian Findlay*

Publishing Director *David Riley*
Publishing Manager *Nina Filipek*

Sister company of **Egmont Children's Books**. Part of the Egmont Group, Denmark. *Specialises* in children's books for home and international markets: activity, sticker, baby, early learning, novelty/character books and annuals. SERIES *Mr Men; I Can Learn; Learning Rewards.* 'Unsolicited material rarely used.' Egmont World does not accept responsibility for the return of unsolicited submissions.

Element Books Ltd
The Old School House, The Courtyard, Bell Street, Shaftesbury, Dorset SP7 8BP
☎01747 851448   Fax 01747 855721
Chairman/Publisher *Michael Mann*
Publisher *Julia McCutchen*
Approx. Annual Turnover £17 million

FOUNDED 1978. Winners of The Queen's Award for Export Achievement 1999. An independent general publisher whose aim is 'to make available knowledge and information to aid humanity in a time of major transition'. *Publishes* general non-fiction in hardback and paperback, including full-colour, illustrated gift books and children's books. 'We publish in the areas of holistic lifestyle, health and complementary therapies; self-help and personal development; psychology; world religions and spiritual traditions; divination and related areas.' TITLES *Cracking the Apocalypse Code; The Keys to Avalon; Illustrated Bloodline of the Holy Grail*. No unsolicited mss or synopses without an introductory letter and s.a.e.
Royalties paid twice-yearly.

Authors' Rating Confusion reigned early in the year when a refinancing programme was accompanied by complaints from authors and freelancers of late payments.

11:9
See **Neil Wilson Publishing Ltd**

Edward Elgar Publishing Ltd
Glensanda House, Montpellier Parade, Cheltenham, Gloucestershire GL50 1UA
☎01242 226934   Fax 01242 262111
Email info@e-elgar.co.uk
Website www.e-elgar.co.uk
Chairman *Alex Ryan*
Managing Director *Edward Elgar*

FOUNDED 1986. International publisher in economics, the environment, public policy and social sciences. 234 titles in 1999. TITLES *The International Handbook of Environmental Sociology;*

Institutional Economics; The Legacy of Milton Friedman as Teacher. No unsolicited mss; synopses and ideas in the subject areas listed above welcome. Approach by letter or e-mail; no telephone inquiries.
Royalties paid annually.

Elliot Right Way Books
Kingswood Buildings, Lower Kingswood, Tadworth, Surrey KT20 6TD
☎01737 832202   Fax 01737 830311
Email info@right-way.co.uk
Website www.right-way.co.uk
Managing Directors *Clive Elliot, Malcolm G. Elliot*

FOUNDED 1946 by Andrew G. Elliot. *Publishes* how-to titles and instruction books on a multifarious list of subjects including cookery, DIY, family financial and legal matters, family health, fishing, looking after pets, motoring, popular education, puzzles, jokes and quizzes. All the early books were entitled *The Right Way to . . .* but this format became too restrictive. No fiction, poetry or biography. IMPRINTS **Right Way** Instructional paperbacks in B format; **Clarion** Promotional/ bargain series of 'how-to' books. Unsolicited mss, synopses and ideas for books welcome.
Royalties paid annually.

Ellipsis London Ltd
2 Rufus Street, London N1 6PE
☎020 7739 3157   Fax 020 7739 3175
Email <name>@ellipsis.co.uk
Website www.ellipsis.com
Contact *Tom Neville*

FOUNDED 1992. Formerly a subsidiary of Zurich-based Artemis Verlags AG but now an independent publishing house. *Publishes* architecture, unpopular culture and music; contemporary art on CD-ROM. About 30 titles a year. No unsolicited mss, synopses or ideas.
Royalties paid annually.

Aidan Ellis Publishing
Whinfield, Herbert Road, Salcombe, South Devon TQ8 8HN
☎01548 842755   Fax 01548 844356
Email aidan@aepub.demon.co.uk
Website www.demon.co.uk/aepub
Partners/Editorial Heads *Aidan Ellis, Lucinda Ellis*

FOUNDED in 1971. *Specialises* in general trade books and non-fiction. TITLES *Eternity Regained* – final part of Marguerite Yourcenar's autobio-

graphical trilogy; *Presumed Dead* Eunice Chapman; *Reunited! Loved Ones Traced by the Red Cross* Michael Johnstone; *The Royal Gardens in Windsor Great Park* Charles Lyte; *Trees For Your Garden* Roy Lancaster. Ideas and synopses welcome (return postage please).
Royalties paid twice-yearly.

Elm Publications/Training
Seaton House, Kings Ripton, Huntingdon, Cambridgeshire PE17 2NJ
☎01487 773254   Fax 01487 773359
Managing Director *Sheila Ritchie*

FOUNDED 1977. *Publishes* textbooks, teaching aids, educational resources, educational software and languages, in the fields of business and management for adult learners. Books and teaching/training resources are generally commissioned to meet specific business, management and other syllabuses. 'We are actively seeking good training materials for business/ management, especially tested and proven.' About 30 titles a year. Ideas are welcome; first approach in writing with outline or by a brief telephone call.
Royalties paid annually.

Elsevier Science Ltd
The Boulevard, Langford Lane, Kidlington, Oxford OX5 1GB
☎01865 843000   Fax 01865 843010
Website www.elsevier.nl
Managing Director *Gavin Howe*

Parent company **Reed Elsevier**, Amsterdam. Now incorporates Pergamon Press. *Publishes* academic and professional reference books, scientific, technical and medical books, journals, CD-ROMs and magazines.
DIVISION **Elsevier and Pergamon** *Barbara Barrett, Peter Desmond, Chris Lloyd, Paul Evans.* Unsolicited mss, synopses and ideas for books welcome.
Royalties paid annually.

Emissary Publishing
PO Box 33, Bicester, Oxfordshire OX6 7PP
☎01869 323447   Fax 01869 324096
Editorial Director *Val Miller*

FOUNDED 1992. *Publishes* mainly humorous paperback books; no poetry or children's. Runs a biennial Humorous Novel Competition in memory of the late Peter Pook and publishes the winning novel (s.a.e. for details). No unsolicited mss or synopses.
Royalties paid twice-yearly.

Empiricus Books
See **Janus Publishing Company Ltd**

Enitharmon Press
36 St George's Avenue, London N7 0HD
☎020 7607 7194   Fax 020 7607 8694
Email books@enitharmon.demon.co.uk
Director *Stephen Stuart-Smith*

FOUNDED 1967. An independent company with
an enterprising editorial policy, Enitharmon has
established itself as one of Britain's leading
poetry presses. Patron of 'the new and the
neglected', Enitharmon prides itself on the success of its collaborations between writers and
artists. *Publishes* poetry, literary criticism, fiction,
art and photography. TITLES include *April* and *A
Short Survey of Surrealism* both by David
Gascoyne; *Feminine Endings* and *Views and
Distances* both by Vernon Scannell; *A Different
Country* Anthony Thwaite. No unsolicited mss.
Royalties paid according to contract.

Epworth Press
c/o Methodist Publishing House, 20 Ivatt
Way, Peterborough, Cambridgeshire PE3 7PG
☎01733 332202   Fax 01733 331201
Chairman *Dr John A. Newton, CBE*
Editor *Gerald M. Burt*

Publishes Christian books only: philosophy, biblical studies, theology, pastoralia and social concern. No fiction, poetry or children's. A series
based on the text of the *Revised Common
Lectionary*, entitled *Companion to the RCL*, was
launched in 1998 and the two new series
Exploring Methodism and *Thinking Things Through*
continue. About 10 titles a year. TITLES *Methodist
Spirituality* Gordon S. Wakefield; *Book of Jeremiah*
Henry McKeating; *Grain in Winter* Donald
Eadie. Unsolicited mss considered but write to
enquire in the first instance. Authors wishing to
have mss returned must send sufficient postage.
Royalties paid annually.

Essentials
See **How To Books Ltd**

Euromonitor
60–61 Britton Street, London EC1M 5NA
☎020 7251 8024   Fax 020 7608 3149
Website www.euromonitor.com
Chairman *R. N. Senior*
Managing Director *T. J. Fenwick*
Approx. Annual Turnover £9 million

FOUNDED 1972. International business infor-
mation publisher specialising in library and
professional reference books, market reports,
electronic databases, journals and CD-ROMs.
Publishes business reference, market analysis and
information directories only. About 200 titles a
year.
DIVISIONS **Market Direction & Reports**
S. Holmes; **Reference Books & Directories**
S. Hunter. TITLES *Credit & Charge Cards: The
International Market*; *Europe in the Year 2000*;
European Marketing Handbook; *European
Directory of Trade and Business Associations*; *World
Retail Directory and Sourcebook*.
Payment is generally by flat fee.

Europa Publications Ltd
18 Bedford Square, London WC1B 3JN
☎020 7580 8236   Fax 020 7636 1664
Email sales@europapublications.co.uk
Website www.europapublications.co.uk
Managing Director *P. A. McGinley*
Approx. Annual Turnover £5 million

Owned by the **Taylor & Francis Group plc**.
FOUNDED 1926 with the publication of the first
edition of *The Europa Year Book*. *Publishes*
annual reference books on political, economic
and commercial matters. About 3 titles a year.
No fiction, biography or poetry. Enquiries in
writing only.
Royalties paid annually.

Evangelical Press of Wales
See **Bryntirion Press**

Evans Brothers Ltd
2A Portman Mansions, Chiltern Street,
London W1M 1LE
☎020 7935 7160   Fax 020 7487 5034
Email sales@evansbrothers.co.uk
Managing Director *Stephen Pawley*
International Publishing Director *Brian Jones*
UK Publisher *Su Swallow*
Approx. Annual Turnover £3.5 million

FOUNDED 1908 by Robert and Edward Evans.
Originally published educational journals, books
for primary schools and teacher education. After
rapid expansion into popular fiction and drama,
both were sacrificed to a major programme of
educational books for schools in East and West
Africa. A new UK programme was launched in
1986 followed by the acquisition of Hamish
Hamilton's non-fiction list for children in 1990.
Acquired interests in Cherrytree Books and
Zero to Ten in 1999. *Publishes* UK children's
and educational books, and educational books
for Africa, the Caribbean and Latin America.
About 90 titles a year.

IMPRINTS **Cherrytree Books** Publisher
Angela Sheehan; **Zero to Ten** 327 High Street,
Slough, Berkshire SL1 1TX Publisher *Anna
McQuinn*. Unsolicited mss, synopses and ideas
for books welcome.
Royalties paid annually. *Overseas associates* in
Kenya, Cameroon, Sierra Leone; Evans Bros
(Nigeria Publishers) Ltd.

Everyman
See **The Orion Publishing Group Ltd**

Everyman's Library
See **David Campbell Publishers Ltd**

University of Exeter Press
Reed Hall, Streatham Drive, Exeter, Devon
EX4 4QR
☎01392 263066   Fax 01392 263064
Email uep@exeter.ac.uk
Website www.ex.ac.uk/uep/
Publisher *Simon Baker*

FOUNDED 1956. *Publishes* academic books:
archaeology, classical studies, history, maritime
studies, English literature (especially medieval),
linguistics, European studies, modern languages
and literature, film history, Arabic studies and
books on Exeter and the South West. About 40
titles a year. Proposals welcomed in the above
subject areas.
Royalties paid annually.

Exley Publications Ltd
16 Chalk Hill, Watford, Hertfordshire
WD1 4BN
☎01923 248328   Fax 01923 818733
Email editorial@exleypublications.co.uk
Managing/Editorial Director *Helen Exley*

FOUNDED 1976. Independent family company.
Publishes giftbooks, quotation anthologies,
social stationery and humour. All in series only
– no individual titles. About 65 titles a year.
DIVISIONS **Gift Series** TITLES *To a Very
Special Friend, Daughter, Mother, ...; Golf, Book
Lovers, Dog, Friendship Quotations*. **Cartoon
Series** TITLES *The Fanatics Guide to Golf, Cats,
Dads*, etc. **Words on Series** TITLES *Courage,
Joy, Hope, Serenity, Wisdom*, etc. No unsolicited
mss. 'Writers needed who can create personal
thank you and loving messages. Emotion that's
never sugary or sentimental.'

Faber & Faber Ltd
3 Queen Square, London WC1N 3AU
☎020 7465 0045   Fax 020 7465 0034
Website www.faber.co.uk

Chairman *Matthew Evans*
Managing Director *Toby Faber*
Approx. Annual Turnover £10 million

Geoffrey Faber founded the company in the
1920s, with T. S. Eliot as an early recruit to the
board. The original list was based on contemporary poetry and plays (the distinguished
backlist includes Eliot, Auden and MacNeice).
Publishes poetry and drama, children's, fiction,
film, music, politics, biography, wine.

DIVISIONS
Children's *Suzy Jenvey* AUTHORS Terry Deary,
Gaye Hicyilmaz, Russell Stannard; **Wine** *Toby
Faber* TITLES *Burgundy; Bordeaux*; **Fiction** *Jon
Riley* AUTHORS P. D. James, Peter Carey, Giles
Foden, Michael Frayn, Kazuo Ishiguro, Milan
Kundera, Hanif Kureishi, John Lanchester, John
McGahern, Andrew O'Hagan; **Plays** *Peggy
Butcher*, **Film** *Walter Donohue* AUTHORS Samuel
Beckett, Alan Bennett, David Hare, Brian Friel,
Harold Pinter, Tom Stoppard, John Boorman,
Joel and Ethan Coen, John Hodge, Woody
Allen, Martin Scorsese, Quentin Tarantino;
Music *Belinda Matthews* AUTHORS Humphrey
Burton, Alexander Goehr, Donald Mitchell,
Mark Steyn, Elizabeth Wilson; **Poetry** *Paul
Keegan* AUTHORS Seamus Heaney, Ted Hughes,
Douglas Dunn, Tom Paulin, Simon Armitage;
Non-fiction *Julian Loose* AUTHORS John Carey,
Adam Phillips, Darian Leader, Jan Morris, Jenny
Uglow.
Royalties paid twice-yearly.

Authors' Rating A strong back list is probably
the main reason why Faber used to convey an
air of complacency. But all this has changed
with an organisational shakeup and greater
concentration on innovative marketing. Faber
is particularly strong on poetry and the performance arts. A pointer to the future is the
poetry database set up as a joint venture with
Chadwyck-Healey.

Fairleigh Dickinson University Press
See **Golden Cockerel Press**

Falmer Press
11 New Fetter Lane, London EC4P 4EE
☎020 7583 9855   Fax 020 7842 2303
Senior Commissioning Editor *Anna Clarkson*

Part of **Taylor & Francis Group plc**.
Publishes educational books/materials for all
levels. Largely commissioned. Unsolicited mss
considered.
Royalties paid annually.

Farming Press

Miller Freeman, Miller Freeman House, Sovereign Way, Tonbridge, Kent TN9 1RW
☎01732 364422

Contact *Editorial Dept.*

Owned by United News & Media Plc. *Publishes* specialist books and videos on farming, agriculture and rural life. About 15 books and videos a year. Synopses and ideas on the subject areas listed above considered; no unsolicited mss.

Royalties paid twice-yearly.

Fernhurst Books

Duke's Path, High Street, Arundel, West Sussex BN18 9AJ
☎01903 882277   Fax 01903 882715
Email sales@fernhurstbooks.co.uk
Website www.fernhurstbooks.co.uk

Chairman/Managing Director *Tim Davison*

FOUNDED 1979. For people who love watersports. *Publishes* practical, highly-illustrated handbooks on sailing and watersports. No unsolicited mss; synopses and ideas welcome.

Royalties paid twice-yearly.

Financial Times Management

See **Pearson Education**

Findhorn Press Ltd

The Park, Findhorn, Moray IV36 3TY
☎01309 690582   Fax 01309 690036
Email books@findhorn.org
Website www.findhornpress.com

Directors *Karin Bogliolo, Thierry Bogliolo*
Approx. Annual Turnover £320,000

FOUNDED 1971. *Publishes* mind, body, spirit, new age and healing. 9 titles in 1999. Unsolicited synopses and ideas welcome if they come within their subject areas. No children's books, fiction or poetry.

Royalties paid twice-yearly.

Firefly Publishing

See **Helter Skelter Publishing**

First & Best in Education Ltd

Unit K, Earlstrees Court, Earlstrees Road, Corby, Northamptonshire NN17 4AX
☎01536 399004   Fax 01536 399012
Email firstbest9@aol.com
Website www.schools.co.uk

Publisher *Tony Attwood*
Senior Editor *Katy Charge*

Publishers of over 1000 educational books of all types for all ages of children and for parents and teachers. No fiction. All books are published as being suitable for photocopying and/or as electronic books. Currently launching 10 new titles a month and 'keenly looking for new authors all the time'. TITLES *Raising Grades Through Study Skills; Parents Survival Guide Series; Business Sponsorship of Secondary Schools; Revision, Study and Exam Techniques Guide.* IMPRINTS **Multi-Sensory Learning** (see entry) and **School Improvement Reports**. In the first instance send s.a.e. for details of requirements and current projects to *Julia Perkins*, Editorial Dept. at the address above.

Royalties paid twice-yearly.

Fitzgerald Publishing

PO Box 804, London SE13 5JF
☎020 8690 0597

Managing Editor *Tim Fitzgerald*
General Editor *Andrew Smith*

FOUNDED 1974. *Specialises* in scientific studies of insects and spiders. 1–2 titles a year. TITLES *Tarantulas of the USA; Scorpions of Medical Importance* and *Earth Tigers – Tarantulas of Borneo* (TV/video documentary). Unsolicited mss, synopses and ideas for books welcome. Also considers video scripts for video documentaries. New video documentary: *Desert Tarantulas.*

Fitzjames Press

See **Motor Racing Publications**

Fitzroy Dearborn Publishers

310 Regent Street, London W1R 5AJ
☎020 7636 6627   Fax 020 7636 6982
Email postroom@fitzroydearborn.demon.co.uk
Website www.fitzroydearborn.com

Managing Director *Daniel Kirkpatrick*
Publishers *Lesley Henderson, Roda Morrison*
Commissioning Editors *Mark Hawkins-Dady, Anne-Lucie Norton, Gillian Lindsey, Jonathan Dore*

Publishes reference books: the arts, history, literature, business, science and the social sciences. About 50 titles a year. TITLES *Encyclopedia of the Novel* ed. Paul Schellinger; *International Encyclopedia of the Stock Market* ed. Michael Sheimo; *Encyclopedia of Historians & Historical Writing* ed. Kelly Boyd; *International Dictionary of Black Composers* ed. Samuel A. Floyd. IMPRINT **Glenlake Business Books**. Unsolicited mss, synopses and ideas welcome for reference books.

Royalties paid twice-yearly. *US associate* Fitzroy Dearborn Publishers, 919 North Michigan Ave., Suite 760, Chicago, IL 60611.

Fitzwarren Publishing

PO Box 6887, London N19 3SG
☎01296 632627   Fax 01296 630028
Contact *Julie Stretton*

Publishes two or three books a year, mainly layman's handbooks on legal matters. All books published so far have followed a rigid 128-page format. Written approaches and synopses from prospective authors welcome. Authors, although not necessarily legally qualified, are expected to know their subject as well as a lawyer would.
Royalties paid twice-yearly.

Five Star

See **Serpent's Tail**

Flame

See **Hodder Headline Plc**

Flamingo

See **HarperCollins Publishers Ltd**

Flicks Books

29 Bradford Road, Trowbridge, Wiltshire BA14 9AN
☎01225 767728   Fax 01225 760418
Email flicks.books@dial.pipex.com
Publishing Director *Matthew Stevens*

FOUNDED 1986. Devoted solely to publishing books on the cinema and related media. TITLES *Queen of the 'B's: Ida Lupino Behind the Camera* ed. Annette Kuhn; *By Angels Driven: The Films of Derek Jarman* ed. Chris Lippard. Unsolicited mss, synopses and ideas within the subject area are welcome.
Royalties paid annually or twice yearly.

Flint River Press Ltd

See **Philip Wilson Publishers Ltd**

Floris Books

15 Harrison Gardens, Edinburgh EH11 1SH
☎0131 337 2372   Fax 0131 346 7516
Email floris@floris.demon.co.uk
Managing Director *Christian Maclean*
Editors *Christopher Moore, Gale Winskill*
Approx. Annual Turnover £350,000

FOUNDED 1977. *Publishes* books related to the Steiner movement, including The Christian Community, as well as arts & crafts, children's, history, religious, science, social questions and Celtic studies. No unsolicited mss. Synopses and ideas for books welcome.
Royalties paid annually.

Fodor's

See **Random House Group Ltd**

Folens Limited

Albert House, Apex Business Centre, Boscombe Road, Dunstable, Bedfordshire LU5 4RL
☎01582 472788   Fax 01582 472575
Email folens@folens.com
Website www.folens.com
Chairman *Dirk Folens*
Managing Director *Malcolm Watson*

FOUNDED 1987. Leading educational publisher. About 150 titles a year. IMPRINTS **Folens**; **Belair**. Unsolicited mss, synopses and ideas for educational books welcome.
Royalties paid annually.

For Beginners™

See **Writers and Readers Ltd**

Fortean Times Books

See **John Brown Publishing Ltd**

W. Foulsham & Co.

The Publishing House, Bennetts Close, Slough, Berkshire SL1 5AP
☎01753 526769   Fax 01753 535003
Chairman *R. S. Belasco*
Managing Director *B. A. R. Belasco*
Approx. Annual Turnover £2.2 million

FOUNDED 1819 and now one of the few remaining independent family companies to survive takeover. *Publishes* non-fiction on most subjects including lifestyle, travel guides, family reference, cookery, diet, health, DIY, business, self improvement, self development, astrology, dreams, MBS. No fiction. IMPRINT **Quantum** Mind, Body and Spirit titles. Unsolicited mss, synopses and ideas welcome. Around 60 titles a year.
Royalties paid twice-yearly.

Foundery Press

See **Methodist Publishing House**

Fount

See **HarperCollins Publishers Ltd**

Fountain Press Ltd

2 Gladstone Road, Kingston-upon-Thames, Surrey KT1 3HD
☎020 8541 4050   Fax 020 8547 3022
Email fountprs@dircon.co.uk
Managing Director *H. M. Ricketts*
Approx. Annual Turnover £750,000

FOUNDED 1923 when it was part of the Rowntree Trust Social Service. Owned by the

British Electric Traction Group until 1982 when it was bought out by the present managing director. *Publishes* mainly photography and natural history. About 25 titles a year. TITLES *Photography Yearbook*; *Wildlife Photographer of the Year*; *Antique and Collectable Cameras*; *Camera Manual* (series). Unsolicited mss and synopses welcome.
Royalties paid twice-yearly.

Authors' Rating Highly regarded for production values, Fountain has the reputation for involving authors in every stage of the publishing process.

Fourth Estate Ltd
6 Salem Road, London W2 4BU
☎020 7727 8993   Fax 020 7792 3176
Email general@4thestate.co.uk
Website www.4thestate.co.uk
Chairman/Managing Director *Victoria Barnsley*
Publishing Director *Christopher Potter*
Approx. Annual Turnover £17 million
FOUNDED 1984. Independent publisher with strong reputation for literary fiction and up-to-the-minute non-fiction. *Publishes* fiction, popular science, current affairs, biography, humour, self-help, travel, reference. About 100 titles a year.
DIVISIONS **Literary Fiction/Non-fiction**; **General Fiction/Non-Fiction** TITLES *Fermat's Last Theorem* Simon Singh; *Nigel Slater's Real Food* Nigel Slater; *The Giant, O'Brien* Hilary Mantel; *Laura Blundy* Julie Myerson; *Man of the Hour* Peter Blauner; *The Perfect Storm* Sebastian Junger; *The Diving Bell and the Butterfly* Jean-Dominique Bauby; *Karl Marx* Francis Wheen; *Longitude* Dava Sobel; *Close Range* Annie Proulx; *If Only It Were True* Marc Levy. No unsolicited mss; synopses welcome.
IMPRINT **Guardian Books** in association with *The Guardian*.
Royalties paid twice-yearly.

Authors' Rating An energetic and imaginative publisher with a talent for picking unlikely bestsellers.

Free Association Books Ltd
57 Warren Street, London W1P 5PA
☎020 7388 3182   Fax 020 7388 3187
Email fab@fa-b.com
Website www.fa-b.com
Managing Director/Publisher *T. E. Brown*
Publishes psychoanalysis and psychotherapy, psychology, cultural studies, sexuality and gender, women's studies, applied social sciences. TITLES *The Rumour*; *The Scientification of Love*;

Self-Esteem; *Stress and Emotion*; *History of the Circle*; *Fetish*. Always send a letter in the first instance accompanied by a book outline.
Royalties paid twice-yearly. Overseas associates ISBS, USA; Astam, Australia.

W. H. Freeman
Macmillan Press, Houndsmill, Basingstoke, Hampshire RG21 6XS
☎01256 329242   Fax 01256 330688
President *Elizabeth Widdicombe* (New York)
Sales & Marketing Director *Margaret Hewinson*
Part of W. H. Freeman & Co., USA. *Publishes* academic, agriculture, animal care and breeding, archaeology, artificial intelligence, biochemistry, biology and zoology, chemistry, computer science, economics, educational and textbooks, engineering, geography and geology, mathematics and statistics, medical, natural history, neuroscience, palaeontology, physics, politics and world affairs, psychology, sociology and anthropology, and veterinary. Freeman's editorial office is in New York (Basingstoke is a sales and marketing office only) but unsolicited mss can go through Basingstoke. Those which are obviously unsuitable will be sifted out; the rest will be forwarded to New York.
Royalties paid annually.

Samuel French Ltd
52 Fitzroy Street, London W1P 6JR
☎020 7387 9373   Fax 020 7387 2161
Email theatre@samuelfrench-london.co.uk
Website www.samuelfrench-london.co.uk
Chairman *Charles R. Van Nostrand*
Managing Director *Vivien Goodwin*
FOUNDED 1830 with the object of acquiring acting rights and publishing plays. *Publishes* plays only. About 50 titles a year. Unsolicited mss considered only after initial submission of synopsis and specimen scene. Such material should be addressed to the Performing Rights Department.
Royalties paid twice-yearly for books; performing royalties paid monthly, subject to a minimum amount.

Authors' Rating Thrives on the amateur dramatic societies who are forever in need of play texts. Editorial advisers give serious attention to new material but a high proportion of the list is staged before it goes into print. Non-established writers are advised to try one-act plays, much in demand by the amateur dramatic societies but rarely turned out by well-known playwrights.

David Fulton (Publishers) Ltd

Ormond House, 26/27 Boswell Street,
London WC1N 3JD
☎020 7405 5606   Fax 020 7831 4840
Email mail@fultonbooks.co.uk
Website www.fultonbooks.co.uk

Chairman/Publisher *David Fulton*
Managing Director *David Hill*
Editorial Director *John Owens*
Approx. Annual Turnover £1.5 million

FOUNDED 1987. *Publishes* non-fiction: books
for teachers and teacher training at B.Ed and
PGCE levels for early years, primary, secondary and virtually all aspects of special education; geography for undergraduates. In 1995,
David Fulton set up a Fulton Fellowship in
Special Education (see entry under **Bursaries,
Fellowships and Grants**). About 65 titles a
year. No unsolicited mss; synopses and ideas
for books welcome.

Royalties paid twice-yearly.

Authors' Rating David Fulton has shown
how niche publishing can succeed even in a
difficult market. Known chiefly for books on
learning difficulties, he gets most of his ideas
and authors by going to education conferences.

Gaia Books Ltd

66 Charlotte Street, London W1P 1LR
☎020 7323 4010   Fax 020 7323 0435
Website www.gaiabooks.co.uk

Also at: 20 High Street, Stroud,
Gloucestershire GL5 1AZ
☎01453 752985 Fax 01453 752987

Managing Director *Joss Pearson*

FOUNDED 1983. *Publishes* ecology, health, natural living and mind, body & spirit, mainly in
practical self-help illustrated reference form for
Britain and the international market. About 12
titles a year. TITLES *Healing Drinks; The Feng
Shui Kitchen; The Healing Energies of Earth; The
Edible Container Garden; Pilates; The Fertility
Plan.* Most projects are conceived in-house but
outlines and mss with s.a.e. considered. 'From
submission of an idea to project go ahead may
take up to a year. Authors become involved
with the Gaia team in the editorial, design and
promotion work needed to create and market a
book.'

Gairm Publications

29 Waterloo Street, Glasgow G2 6BZ
☎0141 221 1971   Fax 0141 221 1971

Chairman *Prof. Derick S. Thomson*

FOUNDED 1952 to publish the quarterly Gaelic
periodical *Gairm* and soon moved into publishing other Gaelic material. Acquired an old
Glasgow Gaelic publishing firm, Alexander
MacLaren & Son, in 1970. *Publishes* a wide
range of Gaelic and Gaelic-related books: dictionaries, grammars, handbooks, children's,
fiction, poetry, biography, music and song.
TITLES *The Companion to Gaelic Scotland; Derick
Thomson's collection of poems, Meall Garbh/The
Rugged Mountain.* Catalogue available.

Galaxy Children's Large Print
See **Chivers Press Ltd**

J. Garnet Miller Ltd
See **Cressrelles Publishing Co. Ltd**

Garnet Publishing Ltd

8 Southern Court, South Street, Reading,
Berkshire RG1 4QS
☎0118 9597847   Fax 0118 9597356
Email enquiries@garnet-ithaca.demon.co.uk
Website www.garnet-ithaca.co.uk

Managing Director *Ken Banerji*

FOUNDED 1992 and purchased Ithaca Press in
the same year. *Publishes* art, architecture, photography, archive photography, cookery, travel
classics, travel, comparative religion, Islamic
culture and history, foreign fiction in translation. Core subjects are Middle Eastern but list
is rapidly expanding to be more general. About
30 titles in 1999.

IMPRINTS

Ithaca Press *Adel Kamal* Specialises in postgraduate academic works on the Middle East,
political science and international relations.
About 20 titles in 1999. TITLES *The Making of
the Modern Gulf States; The Palestinian Exodus;
French Imperialism in Syria; Philby of Arabia.*
Garnet Publishing *Emma Hawker* TITLES *The
Story of Islamic Architecture; Traditional Greek
Cooking; Jerusalem: Caught in Time; World Fiction*
series. Unsolicited mss not welcome – write
with outline and ideas first plus current c.v.

Royalties paid twice-yearly. *Sister companies:*
All Prints, Beirut; Garnet France, Paris.

Gay Men's Press

PO Box 3220, Brighton, East Sussex
BN2 5AU
☎01273 672823   Fax 01273 672159
Website www.prowler.co.uk

Contact *Peter Burton*

Part of the Millivres – Prowler Group. *Publishes*
books on gay-related issues: non-fiction and a
wide range of fiction from literary to popular.

TITLES *Lemon Gulch* Donovan O'Malley; *Fatal Shadows* Josh Lanyon; *Air From Other Planets* Andrew Clements; *Mirrors of Narcissus* Guy Willard. Work should be submitted on disk. Send synopsis with sample chapters rather than complete mss.

Royalties negotiable.

Gay Times Books

Worldwide House, 116/134 Bayham Street, London NW1 0BA
☎020 7482 2576   Fax 020 7284 0329
Website www.prowler.co.uk

Contact *Simon Topham*

Part of the Millivres – Prowler Group. New imprint linked with *Gay Times*, the gay news magazine. TITLES *Gay Planet* Eric Chaline (encyclopedia for gay men); *The Gay Times Book of Short Stories; New Century, New Writing.* 'Rights by negotiation.'

Gazelle Books

See **Angus Hudson** under **UK Packagers**

Geddes & Grosset

David Dale House, New Lanark ML11 9DJ
☎01555 665000   Fax 01555 665694

Publisher *R. Michael Miller*
Approx. Annual Turnover £2.2 million

FOUNDED 1989. Publisher of children's and reference books. Unsolicited mss, synopses and ideas welcome. No adult fiction.

Stanley Gibbons Publications

5 Parkside, Christchurch Road, Ringwood, Hampshire BH24 3SH
☎01425 472363   Fax 01425 470247

Chief Executive *P. Fraser*
Editorial Head *D. Aggersberg*
Approx. Annual Turnover £3 million

Long-established force in the philatelic world with over a hundred years in the business. *Publishes* philatelic reference catalogues and handbooks. Approx. 15 titles a year. Reference works relating to other areas of collecting may be considered. TITLES *How to Arrange and Write Up a Stamp Collection; Stanley Gibbons British Commonwealth Stamp Catalogue; Stamps of the World.* Foreign catalogues include Japan and Korea, Portugal and Spain, Germany, Middle East, Balkans, China. Monthly publication *Gibbons Stamp Monthly* (see entry under **Magazines**). Unsolicited mss, synopses and ideas welcome.

Royalties by negotiation.

Robert Gibson & Sons Glasgow Limited

17 Fitzroy Place, Glasgow G3 7SF
☎0141 248 5674   Fax 0141 221 8219
Email Robert.GibsonSons@btinternet.com

Chairman/Managing Director
R. G. C. Gibson

FOUNDED 1850 and went public in 1886. *Publishes* educational books only, and has been agent for the Scottish Certificate of Education Examination Board since 1902 which, in 1997, became the Scottish Qualification Authority. About 40 titles a year. Unsolicited mss preferred to synopses/ideas.

Royalties paid annually.

Ginn & Co

See **Reed Educational & Professional Publishing**

Mary Glasgow Publications

See **Stanley Thornes (Publishers) Ltd**

Glenlake Business Books

See **Fitzroy Dearborn Publishers**

Godsfield Press Ltd

See **David & Charles Publishers**

Golden Cockerel Press Ltd

16 Barter Street, London WC1A 2AH
☎020 7405 7979   Fax 020 7404 3598
Email lindesay@btinternet.com

Directors *Tamar Lindesay, Andrew Lindesay*

FOUNDED 1980 to distribute titles for US-based Associated University Presses Inc., New Jersey. *Publishes* academic titles mostly: art, film, history, literary criticism, music, philosophy, sociology and special interest. About 120 titles a year.

IMPRINTS **AUP: Bucknell University Press; University of Delaware; Fairleigh Dickinson University Press; Lehigh University Press; Susquehanna University Press**. Also: **Cygnus Arts** Non-academic books on the arts; **Cornwall Books** Trade hardbacks.

Authors' Rating Very much attuned to American interests with trans-Atlantic spelling and punctuation predominating. Some writers may find the process wearisome but those who persevere win through to a wider market.

Victor Gollancz

See **Cassell**

Gomer Press

Wind Street, Llandysul, Ceredigion SA44 4QL
☎01559 362371   Fax 01559 363758
Email gwasg@gomer.co.uk
Website www.gomer.co.uk
Chairman/Managing Director *J. H. Lewis*
FOUNDED 1892. *Publishes* adult fiction and non-fiction, children's fiction and educational material in English and Welsh. About 100 titles a year (65 Welsh; 35 English).
IMPRINTS **Gomer Press** *Bethan Matthews*. **Pont Books** *Mairwen Prys Jones*. No unsolicited mss, synopses or ideas.
Royalties paid twice-yearly.

Gower

See **Ashgate Publishing Ltd**

GPC Books

See **University of Wales Press**

Graham & Trotman

See **Kluwer Law International**

Graham & Whiteside Ltd

Tuition House, 5–6 Francis Grove, London SW19 4DT
☎020 8947 1011   Fax 020 8947 1163
Website www.graham-whiteside.com
Managing Director *Alastair M. W. Graham*
FOUNDED 1995. Part of the Gale Group. *Publishes* annual directories for the business and professional market with titles dating back to 1975 originally published by Graham & Trotman. 22 annual directories, including: *Major Companies of Europe; Major Companies of the Arab World; Major Companies of the Far East and Australasia.* Proposals for new projects welcome.
Royalties paid annually.

Graham-Cameron Publishing

The Studio, 23 Holt Road, Sheringham, Norfolk NR26 8NB
☎01263 821333   Fax 01263 821334
Editorial Director *Mike Graham-Cameron*
Art Director *Helen Graham-Cameron*
FOUNDED 1984 as a packaging operation. *Publishes* illustrated factual books for children, institutions and business; also biography, education and social history. TITLES *Up From the Country; In All Directions; The Holywell Story; Let's Look at Dairying.* No unsolicited mss.
Royalties paid annually. *Subsidiary company*: Graham-Cameron Illustration (agency).

Granada Media

See **André Deutsch Ltd**

Granta Books

2–3 Hanover Yard, Noel Road, London N1 8BE
☎020 7704 9776   Fax 020 7354 3469
Website www.granta.com
Associate Publisher *Gail Lynch*
Publishing Director *Neil Belton*
FOUNDED 1979. *Publishes* literary fiction and general non-fiction. About 25 titles a year. No unsolicited mss; synopses and sample chapters welcome.
Royalties paid twice-yearly.
Authors' Rating After a brave try at breaking into general publishing with quality fiction, Granta has pulled back, cutting its title output by half and aligning its programme more closely with the editorial policies of *Granta* magazine.

W. Green (Scotland)

See **Sweet & Maxwell Ltd**

Green Books

Foxhole, Dartington, Totnes, Devon TQ9 6EB
☎01803 863260   Fax 01803 863843
Email greenbooks@gn.apc.org
Website www.greenbooks.co.uk
Chairman *Satish Kumar*
Managing Editor *John Elford*
Approx. Annual Turnover £200,000
FOUNDED in 1987 with the support of a number of Green organisations. Closely associated with *Resurgence* magazine. *Publishes* high-quality books on a wide range of Green issues, including economics, politics and the practical application of Green thinking. No fiction or books for children. TITLES *Forest Gardening* Robert A. de J. Hart; *Eco-Renovation* Edward Harland; *The Growth Illusion* Richard Douthwaite; *The Green Lanes of England* Valerie Belsey; *The Organic Directory* ed. Clive Litchfield. No unsolicited mss. Synopses and ideas welcome.
Royalties paid twice-yearly.

Greenhill Books/ Lionel Leventhal Ltd

Park House, 1 Russell Gardens, London NW11 9NN
☎020 8458 6314   Fax 020 8905 5245
Email LionelLeventhal@compuserve.com
Website www.greenhillbooks.com
Managing Director *Lionel Leventhal*
FOUNDED 1984 by Lionel Leventhal (ex-**Arms**

& Armour Press). *Publishes* aviation, military and naval books, and its Napoleonic Library series. Synopses and ideas for books welcome. No unsolicited mss.
Royalties paid twice-yearly.

Greenzone Publishing
(incorporating **Aspire Publishing**)
24 Higher Kings Avenue, Exeter, Devon EX4 6JP
☎01392 662246   Fax 01392 252517
Email aspire@xcentrex.force9.co.uk
Managing Editor *Patricia Hawkes*
FOUNDED 1994. *Publishes* popular fiction and non-fiction including autobiography, biography and political. 1999 TITLES included *Who Really Killed Rachel?* Colin Stagg and David Kessler. No unsolicited material; no e-mail submissions. Send s.a.e. for guidelines.

Gresham Books Ltd
46 Victoria Road, Summertown, Oxfordshire OX2 7QD
☎01865 513582   Fax 01865 513582
Managing Director *Paul A. Lewis*
Approx. Annual Turnover £300,000
A small specialist publishing house. *Publishes* hymn and service books for schools and churches, school histories, also craftbound choir and orchestral folders and Records of Achievement. TITLES include music and melody editions of *Hymns for Church and School*; *The School Hymnal; Praise and Thanksgiving*. No unsolicited material but ideas welcome.

Griffith Institute
See **Ashmolean Museum Publications Ltd**

Grisewood & Dempsey
See **Kingfisher Publications plc**

Grub Street
The Basement, 10 Chivalry Road, London SW11 1HT
☎020 7924 3966/7938 1008
Fax 020 7738 1009
Email post@grubstreet.co.uk
Website www.grubstreet.co.uk
Managing Director *John Davies*
FOUNDED 1982. *Publishes* cookery, food and wine, health, military and aviation history books. About 20 titles a year. Unsolicited mss and synopses welcome in the above categories.
Royalties paid twice-yearly.

Guardian Books
See **Fourth Estate Ltd**

Guild of Master Craftsman Publications Ltd
166 High Street, Lewes, East Sussex BN7 1XU
☎01273 477374   Fax 01273 478606
Chairman *A.E. Phillips*
Approx. Annual Turnover £2 million
FOUNDED 1974. Part of G.M.C. Services Ltd. *Publishes* woodworking, craft and gardening books, magazines and videos. 40 titles in 1999. Unsolicited mss, synopses and ideas for books welcome. No fiction.
Royalties paid twice-yearly.

Guinness World Records Ltd
338 Euston Road, London NW1 3BD
☎020 7891 4567   Fax 020 7891 4501
Email info@guinnessrecords.com
Website www.guinnessrecords.com
Chairman *Ray Joy*
Managing Director *Christopher Irwin*
Publishing Director *Ian Castello-Cortes*
Television Director *Michael Feldman*
Approx. Annual Turnover £7 million
FOUNDED 1954 to publish *The Guinness Book of Records*, now the highest-selling copyright book in the world, published in 35 languages. The list now includes international four-colour popular reference, music and film titles. Ideas and synopses welcome as is contact from projective researchers, editors and designers.

Gunsmoke Westerns
See **Chivers Press Ltd**

Gwasg Addysgol Cymru
See **Ashley Drake Publishing Ltd**

Gwasg Carreg Gwalch
12 Iard Yr Orsaf, Llanrwst, Conwy LL26 0EH
☎01492 642031   Fax 01492 641502
Email books@carreg-gwalch.co.uk
Website www.carreg-gwalch.co.uk
Managing Editor *Myrddin ap Dafydd*
FOUNDED in 1990. *Publishes* Welsh language; English books of Welsh interest – history, folklore, guides and walks. 90 titles in 1999. Unsolicited mss, synopses and ideas welcome.
Royalties paid.

Gwasg Prifysgol Cymru
See **University of Wales Press**

Peter Halban Publishers

22 Golden Square, London W1R 3PA
☎020 7437 9300   Fax 020 7437 9512
Email books@halbanpublishers.com
Directors *Peter Halban, Martine Halban*
FOUNDED 1986. Independent publisher. *Publishes* biography, autobiography and memoirs, history, philosophy, theology, politics, literature and criticism, Judaica and world affairs. 6–8 titles a year. No unsolicited material. Approach by letter in first instance.
Royalties paid twice-yearly for first two years, thereafter annually in December.

Robert Hale Ltd

Clerkenwell House, 45–47 Clerkenwell Green, London EC1R 0HT
☎020 7251 2661   Fax 020 7490 4958
Chairman/Managing Director *John Hale*
FOUNDED 1936. Family-owned company. *Publishes* adult fiction (but not interested in category crime, romance or science fiction) and non-fiction. No specialist material (education, law, medical or scientific). Acquired **NAG Press Ltd** in 1993 with its list of horological, gemmological, jewellery and metalwork titles and **J. A. Allen & Co. Ltd** in 1999 with its extensive list of horse and dog books. Over 250 titles a year. TITLES *Ballet: A Complete Guide* Robert Greskovic; *Orangutans, Wizards of the Rainforest* Anne E. Russon; *How to Control Your Anger Before It Controls You* Albert Ellis Ph.D; *Depraved English* Peter Novobatzky and Ammon Shea; *Sean Connery – A Celebration* Robert Sellars; *Judge Me Not* John D. MacDonald; *Redemption* Howard Fast. Unsolicited mss, synopses and ideas for books welcome.
Royalties paid twice-yearly.

Authors' Rating Smiled upon in a recent Society of Authors survey on author relations, Robert Hale has carved out a profitable niche for popular non-fiction.

Halsgrove

Halsgrove House, Lower Moor Way, Tiverton, Devon EX16 6SS
☎01884 243242   Fax 01884 243325
Email sales@halsgrove.com
Website www.halsgrove.com
Joint Managing Directors *Simon Butler, Steven Pugsley*
Approx. Annual Turnover £1.5 million
FOUNDED in 1990 from defunct Maxwell-owned publishing group, it has grown into the region's largest publishing and distribution group, specialising in books, video and audio tapes. *Publishes* local history, cookery, biography. 130 titles in 1999. Also established a series of local interest magazines in southern England. No fiction or poetry. Unsolicited mss, synopses and ideas for books of regional interest welcome.
Royalties paid annually.

The Hambledon Press

102 Gloucester Avenue, London NW1 8HX
☎020 7586 0817   Fax 020 7586 9970
Email office@hambledon.co.uk
Chairman/Managing Director/ Editorial Head *Martin Sheppard*
FOUNDED 1980. *Publishes* British and European history from post-classical to modern. Currently expanding its list to include history titles with a wider appeal including more biographies. 25–30 titles a year. TITLES *The White Death: A History of Tuberculosis* Thomas Dormandy; *Victorian Girls: Lord Lyttelton's Daughters* Sheila Fletcher; *A Muse of Fire: Literature, Art and War* A. D. Harvey. No unsolicited mss; send preliminary letter. Synopses and ideas welcome.
Royalties paid annually. *Overseas associates* The Hambledon Press (USA), Ohio.

Hamilton & Co (Publishers) Ltd

10 Stratton Street, Mayfair, London W1X 5FD
☎020 7546 8646   Fax 020 7546 8570
Email editorial@hamilton-and-co.demon.co.uk
Website www.hamilton-and.co.uk
Managing Editor *Mal Sykes*
Editor *Margo Whiteley*
FOUNDED 1997. *Publishes* fiction and non-fiction: memoirs, autobiography, biography, war, children's and historical. Around 25 titles a year. TITLES *Cut to the Chase* Steve Emecz; *Unholy Terror* Duncan Measor; *John McEnroe's Golden Years* James Harbridge. No unsolicited mss; synopses and sample chapters with return postage only.
Royalties paid annually.

Authors' Rating Liable to ask authors to contribute towards costs of publication.

Hamish Hamilton/Hamish Hamilton Children's
See **Penguin UK**

Hamlyn Children's Books
See **Egmont Children's Books**

Hamlyn Octopus
See **Octopus Publishing Group**

Harcourt Brace and Company Limited

32 Jamestown Road, London NW1 7BY
☎020 7424 4200
Fax 020 7482 2293/7485 4752
Website www.harcourt-international.com

Owned by US parent company. *Publishes* scientific, technical and medical books, college textbooks, educational & occupational test. No unsolicited mss. IMPRINTS **Academic Press**; **Baillière Tindall**; **Dryden Press**; **Churchill Livingstone**; **Holt Rinehart and Winston**; **Mosby International**; **T. & A. D. Poyser**; **W. B. Saunders & Co. Ltd.**; **Saunders Scientific Publications**.

Harlem River Press

See **Writers and Readers Ltd**

Harlequin Mills & Boon Ltd

Eton House, 18–24 Paradise Road, Richmond, Surrey TW9 1SR
☎020 8288 2800   Fax 020 8288 2899
Website www.eharlequin.com
Managing Director *F. Gejrot*
Editorial Director *Karin Stoecker*
Approx. Annual Turnover £25 million
FOUNDED 1908. Owned by the Canadian-based Torstar Group. *Publishes* romantic fiction and historical romance. Over 600 titles a year.

IMPRINTS

Mills & Boon Presents /**Mills & Boon Enchanted** (50–55,000 words) Contemporary romances with international settings, focusing on hero and heroine. **Mills & Boon Medical Romance** *Sheila Hodgson* (50–55,000 words) Modern medical practice provides a unique background to love stories. **Mills & Boon Historical Romance** *Linda Fildew* (75–80,000 words) Historical romances. **MIRA** *Linda Fildew* (minimum 100,000 words) Individual women's fiction.
Mills & Boon Temptation titles are acquired through the Canadian office. **Silhouette Desire**, **Special Edition**, **Sensation** and **Intrigue** imprints are handled by US-based **Silhouette Books** (see **US Publishers**). Please send query letter in the first instance. Tip sheets and guidelines for the Mills & Boon series available from the website or Harlequin Mills & Boon Editorial Dept. (please send s.a.e.).
Royalties paid twice-yearly.

Authors' Rating In the wake of the Bridget Jones phenomenon, Mills & Boon has appealed for more younger authors to write 'real life'

romances. A competition has been launched to encourage 18- to 30-year-olds to send in manuscripts. But while Mills & Boon invariably scores high sales for its titles, royalty payments are generally below the trade average. Those who want to know how this niche publisher came to prominence will enjoy *Passion's Fortune, The Story of Mills & Boon* (OUP, £25) described by one reviewer as a 'good book about bad books'.

Harley Books

Martins, Great Horkesley, Colchester, Essex CO6 4AH
☎01206 271216   Fax 01206 271182
Email harley@keme.co.uk
Managing Director *Basil Harley*
FOUNDED 1983. Natural history publishers specialising in entomological and botanical books. Mostly definitive, high-quality illustrated reference works. TITLES *The Moths and Butterflies of Great Britain and Ireland; Dragonflies of Europe; The Flora of Hampshire; The Liverwort Flora of the British Isles; The Spiders of Great Britain and Ireland.*
Royalties paid twice-yearly in the first year, annually thereafter.

HarperCollins Publishers Ltd

77–85 Fulham Palace Road, London W6 8JB
☎020 8741 7070   Fax 020 8307 4440
Website www.harpercollins.co.uk
Also at: Freepost PO Box, Glasgow G4 0NB
☎0141 772 3200 Fax 0141 306 3119
Chief Executive *Jane Friedman*
Executive Chairman/Publisher *To be appointed*
Approx. Annual Turnover £200 million
Publisher of high-profile authors such as Jeffrey Archer, J. G. Ballard, Fay Weldon, John Major and Frank McCourt. Owned by News Corporation. Since 1991 there has been a period of consolidated focus on key management issues which has led to various imprints being phased out in favour of others, among them Grafton and Fontana which have been merged under the HarperCollins paperback imprint. **Booker Prize** and **Pulitzer Prize** winners in 1997.

DIVISIONS
Trade Divisional Managing Director *Adrian Bourne*. Publishing Directors *Nick Sayers* (Fiction); *Michael Fishwick* (Non-fiction); *Susan Watt*. IMPRINTS **Collins Crime**; **Collins Willow** (sport) Publishing Director *Michael Doggart*; **Flamingo** (literary fiction, both hardback and paperback) Publishing Director *Philip Gwyn Jones*; **HarperCollins Audiobooks** (see

entry under **Audio Books**); **HarperCollins Entertainment** Publishing Director *Val Hudson*; **HarperCollins Paperbacks**; **Tolkien**; **Voyager** (science fiction/fantasy) Publishing Director *Jane Johnson*. Over 650 titles a year, hardback and paperback. No longer accepts unsolicited submissions.

Thorsons Divisional Managing Director *Stephen Bray*. Health, nutrition, business, parenting, popular psychology, positive thinking, self-help, divination, therapy, recovery, feminism, women's issues, mythology, religion, yoga, tarot, personal development, sexual politics, biography, history, popular culture. About 250 titles a year.

Children's Divisional Managing Director *Kate Harris*. IMPRINTS **Picture Lions**; **HarperCollins Audio** (see entry under **Audio Books**); **Jets** Quality picture books and book and tape sets for under 7s; all categories of fiction for the 6–14 age group; dictionaries for pre-school and primary. About 250 titles a year. No longer accepts unsolicited mss.

Reference Divisional Managing Director *Stephen Bray*. IMPRINTS **HarperCollins**; **Collins New Naturalist Library**; **Collins Gems**; **HC Illustrated**; **Janes** (military); **Times Books**; **Times Atlases** Encyclopedias, guides and handbooks, phrase books and manuals on popular reference, art instruction, illustrated, cookery and wine, crafts, DIY, gardening, military, natural history, pet care, Scottish, pastimes. About 120 titles a year.

Educational Divisional Managing Director *Kate Harris*. Textbook publishing for schools and FE colleges (5–18-year-olds): all subjects for primary education including the **Letterland** imprint and the **Collins Study and Revision Guides**. Strong presence in all major secondary and curriculum areas; sociology, business studies and economics in FE. (Former Holmes McDougall, Unwin Hyman, Mary Glasgow Primary Publications, and part of Harcourt, Brace & Co. educational imprints have been incorporated under Collins Educational.) About 90 titles a year.

Dictionaries Divisional Managing Director *Kate Harris*. IMPRINTS **Collins**; **Collins Cobuild**; **Collins Gem** Includes the *Collins English Dictionary* range with dictionaries and thesauruses, *Collins Bilingual Dictionary* range (French, German, Spanish, Italian, etc.), and the *Cobuild* series of English dictionaries, grammars and EFL books. About 50 titles a year.

Religious Divisional Managing Director *Adrian Bourne*. A broad-based religious publisher across all denominations. IMPRINTS **Harper-Collins**; **Fount**; **Marshall Pickering** Extensive range covering both popular and academic spirituality, music and reference. Marshall Pickering: bibles, missals, prayer books, and hymn books. About 150 titles a year.

HarperCollins Cartographic Divisional Managing Director *Stephen Bray*. The cartographic division and Times Books now joined as one division. IMPRINTS **Collins**; **Collins Longman**; **Nicholson/Ordnance Survey**; Maps, atlases and guides (Collins; Collins Longman); leisure maps, educational titles (Collins Longman); London titles (Nicholson); waterway guides (Nicholson/Ordnance Survey); reference and non-fiction. About 30 titles a year.

Authors' Rating It was an exciting year for HarperCollins. After Britain's largest consumer book publisher achieved an impressive recovery from flat results to a thumping 11 per cent increase in turnover, bucking the market trend, Eddie Bell unexpectedly resigned as executive chairman. So far, there is no hint of a replacement but some observers anticipate a successor from across the Atlantic. Meanwhile, more resources have been allocated to authors' advances and there is a new imprint, HarperCollins Entertainment, which publishes spin-offs from News International's television and other entertainment output.

Harrap

See **Chambers Harrap Publishers**

Harvard University Press

Fitzroy House, 11 Chenies Street, London WC1E 7ET
☎020 7306 0603   Fax 020 7306 0604
Email info@HUP-MITpress.co.uk
Website www.hup.harvard.edu

Director *William Sisler*
General Manager *Ann Sexsmith*

European office of **Harvard University Press**, USA. *Publishes* academic and scholarly works in history, politics, philosophy, economics, literary criticism, psychology, sociology, anthropology, women's studies, biological sciences, classics, history of science, art, music, film, reference. All mss go to the American office: 79 Garden Street, Cambridge, MA 02138. (See entry under **US Publishers**.)

The Harvill Press Ltd

2 Aztec Row, Berners Road, Islington, London N1 0PW
☎020 7704 8766   Fax 020 7704 8805
Website www.harvill.com

Publisher *Christopher MacLehose*
Editorial Director *Guido Waldman*

FOUNDED in 1946, the Harvill list was bought by Collins in 1959, of which it remained an imprint until returning to its original independent status in early 1995. *Publishes* literature in translation (especially Russian, Italian and French), English literature, quality thrillers, illustrated books and Africana, plus the occasional literature anthology. 90–100 titles in 1999. AUTHORS Mikhail Bulgakov, Raymond Carver, Richard Ford, Peter Høeg, Robert Hughes, Giuseppe T. di Lampedusa, Peter Matthiessen, Haruki Murakami, Boris Pasternak, José Saramago, W. G. Sebald, Aleksandr Solzhenitsyn. Synopses and ideas welcome. No educational or technical books.
Royalties paid twice-yearly.

Authors' Rating Strong on translated fiction, the two-way traffic means that Harvill's English language writers tend to do well in Europe. Relations with authors are said to be close and friendly.

Haynes Publishing

Sparkford, Near Yeovil, Somerset BA22 7JJ
☎01963 440635 Fax 01963 440825
Email info@haynes-manuals.co.uk
Website www.haynes.co.uk
Chairman *John H. Haynes, OBE*
Approx. Annual Turnover £28.7 million

FOUNDED in 1960 by John H. Haynes. Family-run business. The mainstay of its programme has been the *Owners' Workshop Manual*, first published in the mid 1960s and still running off the presses today. Indeed the company maintains a strong bias towards motoring and transport titles. Acquired **Sutton Publishing Ltd** in March 2000 (see entry). *Publishes* DIY service and repair manuals for cars, motorbikes and general leisure plus other related topics.
IMPRINT **Haynes** *Matthew Minter* Service and repair manuals; *Mark Hughes* Motoring, motor sport, cars, motorcycles, home, DIY and leisure titles. Unsolicited submissions welcome if they come within the subject areas covered.
Royalties paid twice-annually. *Overseas subsidiaries* Haynes Manuals Inc., California, USA, Editions Haynes S.A., France, Haynes Publishing Nordiska AB, Sweden.

Authors' Rating Up to a few months ago, Haynes was one of the most specialist of specialist publishers. If you wanted to write a car manual OK; otherwise forget it. But all this changed when Haynes bought Sutton Publishing, noted

for its social and regional history books. It could be that the continuing success of Haynes with its core titles will lead to further acquisitions. But novelists shouldn't hold their breath.

Hazar Publishing Ltd

147 Chiswick High Road, London W4 2DT
☎020 8742 8578 Fax 020 8994 1407
Managing Director *Gregory Hill*
Editorial Head *Marie Clayton*
Approx. Annual Turnover £700,000

FOUNDED 1993, An independent publisher of high-quality illustrated books. *Publishes* children's picture books and pop-up books and adult non-fiction on design and architecture. About 15 titles a year.
Royalties paid twice-yearly.

Hazleton Publishing

3 Richmond Hill, Richmond, Surrey TW10 6RE
☎020 8948 5151 Fax 020 8948 4111
Publisher/Managing Director *R. F. Poulter*

Publisher of the leading Grand Prix annual *Autocourse*, now in its 49th edition. *Publishes* high-quality motor sport titles including annuals. TITLES *Motocourse; Rallycourse*. About 13 titles a year. No unsolicited mss; synopses and ideas welcome. Interested in all motor sport titles.
Royalties payment varies.

Headline
See **Hodder Headline Plc**

William Heinemann
See **Random House Group Ltd**

Heinemann Educational
See **Reed Educational & Professional Publishing**

Heinemann Young Books
See **Egmont Children's Books**

Helicon Publishing Ltd

42 Hythe Bridge Street, Oxford OX1 2EP
☎01865 204204 Fax 01865 204205
Email admin@helicon.co.uk
Website www.helicon.co.uk
Managing Director *David Attwooll*
Editorial Director *Hilary McGlynn*
Approx. Annual Turnover £3.5 million

FOUNDED 1992 from the management buy-out of former Random Century's reference division. Led by David Attwooll, the buy-out included the Hutchinson encyclopedia titles and databases, along with other reference titles. Helicon is now a 100% subsidiary of WHSmith. The Helicon list, which is represented by Hodder & Stoughton Educational, is increasing its range of reference titles, particularly in history, science and current affairs and is maintaining its lead in electronic publishing, especially in the area of on-line licensing, where it has relationships with several key UK and US blue-chip service providers. TITLES *The Hutchinson Encyclopedia.* Electronic: *The Penguin Hutchinson Reference Suite; The Hutchinson Educational Encyclopedia 2000; The Hutchinson Science Suite; The Hutchinson History Suite.*

Christopher Helm Publishers Ltd
See **A. & C. Black (Publishers) Ltd**

Helter Skelter Publishing
4 Denmark Street, London WC2H 8LL
☎020 7836 1151   Fax 020 7240 9880
Email helter@skelter.demon.co.uk
Website www.skelter.demon.co.uk
Contact *Sean Body*
FOUNDED 1995. *Publishes* books on music and film. About 8–10 titles a year. IMPRINTS **Helter Skelter Publishing**; **Firefly Publishing**. Unsolicited mss, synopses and ideas welcome.

Henderson Publishing
See **Dorling Kindersley Ltd**

Ian Henry Publications Ltd
20 Park Drive, Romford, Essex RM1 4LH
☎01708 749119   Fax 01708 749119
Managing Director *Ian Wilkes*
FOUNDED 1976. *Publishes* local history, transport history and Sherlockian pastiches. 8–10 titles a year. TITLES *Chelmsford at War; Sherlock Holmes and The Midnight Bell; Lost Parish Churches of Essex.* No unsolicited mss. Synopses and ideas for books welcome.
Royalties paid twice-yearly.

The Herbert Press
See **A. & C. Black (Publishers) Ltd**

Hermes House
See **Anness Publishing Ltd**

Nick Hern Books
The Glasshouse, 49a Goldhawk Road, London W12 8QP
☎020 8749 4953   Fax 020 8746 8746
Email info@nickhernbooks.demon.co.uk

Chairman/Managing Director *Nick Hern*
Approx. Annual Turnover £400,000
FOUNDED 1988. Fully independent since 1992. *Publishes* books on theatre and film: from how-to and biography to plays and screenplays. About 30 titles a year. No unsolicited play-scripts. Synopses, ideas and proposals for other theatre material welcome. Not interested in material unrelated to the theatre or cinema.

Hippo
See **Scholastic Ltd**

Historic Military Press
See **SB Publications**

HMSO
See **The Stationery Office Publishing**

Hobsons Publishing
159–173 St John Street, London EC1V 4DR
☎020 7336 6633   Fax 020 7490 2422
Website www.hobsons.com
Chairman *Martin Morgan*
Group Managing Director *Christopher Letcher*
Approx. Annual Turnover £17.7 million
FOUNDED 1973. A division of Harmsworth Publishing Ltd, part of the Daily Mail & General Trust. *Publishes* course and career guides, under exclusive licence and royalty agreements for CRAC (Careers Research and Advisory Bureau); computer software; directories and specialist titles for employers, government departments and professional associations. TITLES *Graduate Employment and Training; Degree Course Guides; The Which Degree Series; Which University* (CD-ROM); *The POST-GRAD Series: The Directory of Graduate Studies; The Directory of Further Education.*

Hodder & Stoughton
See **Hodder Headline Plc**

Hodder Headline Plc
338 Euston Road, London NW1 3BH
☎020 7873 6000   Fax 020 7873 6024
Group Chief Executive *Tim Hely Hutchinson*
Approx. Annual Turnover £93.2 million
Formed in June 1993 through the merger of Headline Book Publishing and Hodder & Stoughton. Headline was formed in 1986 and had grown dramatically, whereas Hodder & Stoughton was 125 years old with a diverse range of publishing. About 2000 titles a year. The company was acquired by the WHSmith Group plc in 1999.

DIVISIONS
Headline Book Publishing Managing Director *Amanda Ridout*. **Non-fiction** Publishing Director *Heather Holden-Brown*; **Fiction** Publishing Director *Jane Morpeth*; **Headline** *Anne Williams*; **Headline Feature** *Bill Massey*; **Review** *Geraldine Cooke*. *Publishes* commercial and literary fiction (hardback and paperback) and popular non-fiction including biography, cinema, countryside, food and wine, popular science, TV tie-ins and sports yearbooks. IMPRINTS **Headline**; **Headline Feature**; **Review**. AUTHORS Catherine Alliott, Ronan Bennett, Raymond Blanc, Martina Cole, Josephine Cox, Lucy Ellmann, John Francome, Ken Hom, Jennifer Johnston, Cathy Kelly, Dean Koontz, James Patterson, Anthony Worrall Thompson.

Hodder & Stoughton General Managing Director *Martin Neild*, Deputy Managing Director *Sue Fletcher*. **Non-fiction** *Roland Philipps*; **Sceptre** *Carole Welch*; **Fiction** *Carolyn Mays*; **Audio** (See entry under **Audio Books**). *Publishes* commercial and literary fiction; biography, autobiography, history, self-help, humour, travel and other general interest non-fiction; audio. IMPRINTS **Hodder & Stoughton**; **Lir**; **Coronet**; **Flame**; **New English Library**; **Sceptre**. AUTHORS Dickie Bird, Melvyn Bragg, John le Carré, Justin Cartwright, Charles Frazier, Elizabeth George, Thomas Keneally, Stephen King, Ed McBain, Malcolm Gluck, Rosamunde Pilcher, Mary Stewart.

Hodder & Stoughton Educational Managing Director *Philip Walters*. **Humanities, Tests, Science & Scotland** *Lis Tribe*; **Languages, Business, Psychology, English and Mathematics** *Tim Gregson-Williams*; **Teach Yourself**; **Trade Education** *Jo Osborne*. Textbooks for the primary, secondary, tertiary and further education sectors and for self-improvement. IMPRINT **Hodder & Stoughton Educational**.

Hodder Children's Books Managing Director *Mary Tapissier*. IMPRINTS **Hodder Children's Books**; **Signature**; **Wayland**. AUTHORS Enid Blyton, John Cunliffe, Lucy Daniels, Mick Inkpen, Hilary McKay, Joan Lingard, Jenny Oldfield, Christopher Pike.

Hodder & Stoughton Religious Managing Director *Charles Nettleton*. **Bibles & Liturgical** *Emma Sealey*; **Christian paperbacks** *Judith Longman*. Bibles, commentaries, liturgical works (both printed and software), and a wide range of Christian paperbacks. IMPRINTS **New International Version of the Bible**; **Hodder Christian Books**.

Arnold Managing Director *Richard Stileman*. **Humanities** *Chris Wheeler*; **STM** *Nick Dunton*; **Health Sciences** *Georgina Bentliff*; **Journals** *Mary Attree*. Academic and professional books and journals.

Royalties paid twice-yearly

Authors' Rating Why should WHSmith buy a leading publisher such as Hodder Headline? Moreover, why should WHSmith pay such a thumping good price – £185 million – for a leading publisher? Retail analysts point to the need for the big chains to control their supply lines though both Hodder and WHSmith made strenuous efforts to reassure authors and other publishers that Hodder would retain its independence. A long-awaited move into the US market can now be expected. Also, the resources are in place for further investment in new talent.

Holt Rinehart & Winston
See **Harcourt Brace and Company Limited**

Honeyglen Publishing Ltd
56 Durrels House, Warwick Gardens, London W14 8QB
☎020 7602 2876   Fax 020 7602 2876
Directors *N. S. Poderegin, J. Poderegin*

FOUNDED 1983. A small publishing house whose output is 'extremely limited'. *Publishes* history, philosophy of history, biography and selective fiction. No children's or science fiction. TITLES *The Soul of India; A Child of the Century* Amaury de Riencourt; *With Duncan Grant in South Turkey* Paul Roche; *Vladimir, The Russian Viking* Vladimir Volkoff; *The Dawning* Milka Bajic-Poderegin; *Quicksand* Louise Hide. Unsolicited mss welcome.

Horus Editions
See **Award Publications Limited**

House of Lochar
Isle of Colonsay, Argyll PA61 7YR
☎01951 200232   Fax 01951 200232
Email Lochar@colonsay.org.uk
Chairman *Kevin Byrne*
Managing Director *Georgina Hobhouse*
Approx. Annual Turnover £95,000

FOUNDED 1995 on a tiny island, taking advantage of new technology and mains electricity and taking over some 20 titles from Thomas and Lochar. About 10 titles a year. *Publishes* mostly Scottish – history, topography, transport and fiction. IMPRINTS **House of Lochar** TITLES *The Crofter and the Laird; The Clyde in Pictures;*

Alexander III. AUTHORS (fiction) Neill Gunn, Naomi Mitchison, Marion Campbell. **Colonsay Books** TITLES *Summer in the Hebrides.* **West Highland Series** Mini walking guides. No poetry or books unrelated to Scotland or Celtic theme. Unsolicited mss, synopses and ideas welcome if relevant to subjects covered.
Royalties paid annually.

How To Books Ltd
3 Newtec Place, Magdalen Road, Oxford OX4 1RE
☎01865 793806   Fax 01865 248780
Email info@howtobooks.co.uk
Website www.howtobooks.co.uk
Publisher/Managing Director Giles Lewis
A fast-growing independent reference publisher which *publishes* three popular SERIES: **How To** Practical, accessible and encouraging books to help people improve their lives and develop their skills; *Pathways* Inspiring, informative books for thoughtful readers wanting to develop themselves and realise their potential; **Essentials** Handy, crisp and approachable books teaching specific skills to busy people. Over 50 titles a year. Subjects covered include business and management, living and working abroad, personal finance, self-employment and small business, computers and the net, career development, career choices, personal development, student guides and study skills, home and family, creative writing. New book proposals are 'very welcome. Authors are given assistance and guidance in the development of their books.'
Royalties paid annually.

Human Horizons
See **Souvenir Press Ltd**

Human Science Press
See **Kluwer Academic/Plenum Publishers**

Hunt & Thorpe
See **John Hunt Publishing Ltd**

John Hunt Publishing Ltd
46a West Street, New Alresford, Hampshire SO24 9AU
☎01962 736880   Fax 01962 736881
Email john@johnhuntpub.demon.co.uk
Approx. Annual Turnover £1.5 million
Publishes children's and religious titles only – about 25 a year. IMPRINTS **Hunt & Thorpe**; **John Hunt Publishing**; **Arthur James**. Unsolicited material welcome.

C. Hurst & Co.
38 King Street, London WC2E 8JZ
☎020 7240 2666   Fax 020 7240 2667
Email hurst@atlas.co.uk
Website www.hurstpub.co.uk
Chairman/Managing Director
   Christopher Hurst
Editorial Heads *Christopher Hurst,*
   Michael Dwyer
FOUNDED 1967. An independent company, cultivating a concern for literacy, detail and the visual aspects of the product. *Publishes* contemporary history, politics and social science. About 20 titles a year. TITLES *The Origins of Japanese Trade Supremacy; The Rwanda Crisis – History of a Genocide; Listening People, Speaking Earth: Contemporary Paganism; Yugoslavia's Bloody Collapse; Following Ho Chi Minh – Memoirs of a North Vietnamese Colonel.* No unsolicited mss. Synopses and ideas welcome.
Royalties paid twice in first year, annually thereafter.

Hutchinson
See **Random House Group Ltd**

Hymns Ancient & Modern Ltd
St Mary's Works, St Mary's Plain, Norwich, Norfolk NR3 3BH
☎01603 612914   Fax 01603 624483
Chairman *Very Rev. Dr Henry Chadwick KBE*
Chief Executive *G. A. Knights*
Publisher, Canterbury Press Norwich
   Christine Smith
Publisher, RMEP *Mary Mears*
Approx. Annual Turnover £4 million
Publishes hymn books for churches, schools and other institutions. All types of liturgical and general religious books and material for religious and social education. Owns SCM-Canterbury Press Ltd of which **SCM Press Ltd** is a division (see entry). IMPRINTS **Canterbury Press Norwich** Liturgical and general religious books TITLES *Exciting Holiness; Gospel of the Lord; Women of the Passion; Rhythm of Life* series; *Re-pitching the Tent.* **Religious and Moral Education Press (RMEP)** Religious, social and moral books for primary and secondary schools, assembly material and books for teachers and administrators. **G. J. Palmer & Sons Ltd** TITLES *Church Times* (see entry under **Magazines**); *The Sign* and *Home Words* – two monthly nationwide parish magazine inserts. Ideas welcome; no unsolicited mss.
Royalties paid annually.

Icon Books Ltd

Grange Road, Duxford, Cambridge CB2 4QF
☎01763 208008   Fax 01763 208080
Email icon@mistral.co.uk
Website www.iconbooks.co.uk
Managing Director *Peter Pugh*
Editorial Head *Richard Appignanesi*
Publishing Director *Jeremy Cox*

FOUNDED 1992. SERIES **Introducing** Cartoon introductions to the key figures and issues in the history of science, psychology, philosophy, religion and the arts TITLES *Introducing Psychology; Introducing Philosophy*. **Readers' Guides** Student guides to critical writings TITLES *James Joyce's Ulysses; The Fiction of Martin Amis*. **Postmodern Encounters** Provocative mini-essays exploring a key theme in the work of a major thinker in the areas of psychology, philosophy and science.
Royalties paid twice yearly. *Overseas associates* Totem Books, USA. Distributed by the Penguin Group.

Idol

See **Virgin Publishing Ltd**

The In Pinn

See **Neil Wilson Publishing Ltd**

Independent Voices

See **Souvenir Press Ltd**

The Industrial Society

Robert Hyde House, 48 Bryanston Square, London W1H 7LN
☎020 7479 2000   Fax 020 7723 7375
Website www.indsoc.co.uk
Head of Publishing *Carl Upsall*
Approx. Annual Turnover (Publishing Division) £1.6 million

Industrial Society Publications, which is part of The Industrial Society (a registered charity committed to making work fulfilling), has been publishing books for over 20 years. *Specialises* in business, management, self-development, training, staff development, human resources – both books and special reports. TITLES *Communication Skills – A Practical Handbook; Fifty Ways to Personal Development; Body Talk – Skills of Positive Image; Navigating Complexity; Career Guides: Travel and Tourism, Sport, Retailing*. Unsolicited mss, synopses and ideas welcome. No fiction or illustrated non-fiction.
Royalties paid twice-yearly.

Institute of Personnel and Development

IPD House, Camp Road, London SW19 4UX
☎020 8263 3387   Fax 020 8263 3850
Email publish@ipd.co.uk
Website www.ipd.co.uk

Part of IPD Enterprises Limited. *Publishes* people management and training titles. A list of 200 titles. Unsolicited mss, synopses and ideas welcome.
Royalties paid annually.

Inter Publishing Ltd

6–7 Leapale Road, Guildford, Surrey GU1 4JX
☎01483 306309   Fax 01483 579196
Email eagle_indeprint@compuserve.com
Managing Director *David Wavre*
Approx. Annual Turnover £500,000

FOUNDED 1990. *Publishes* religious plus some gift and art books. About 24 titles a year. IMPRINT **Eagle**. Unsolicited mss, synopses and ideas for books welcome.
Royalties paid twice-yearly.

Inter-Varsity Press

38 De Montfort Street, Leicester LE1 7GP
☎0116 2551754   Fax 0116 2542044
Email ivp@uccf.org.uk
Website www.ivpbooks.com
Chairman *Ralph Evershed*
Chief Executive *Frank Entwistle*

FOUNDED mid-'30s as the publishing arm of Universities and Colleges Christian Fellowship, it has expanded to wider Christian markets worldwide. *Publishes* Christian belief and lifestyle, reference and bible commentaries. About 50 titles a year. No secular material or anything which fails to empathise with ortho-dox Protestant Christianity.
IMPRINTS **IVP**; **Apollos**; **Crossway** TITLES *The Bible Speaks Today; Science, Life and Christian Belief* Berry and Jeeves. No unsolicited mss; synopses and ideas welcome.
Royalties paid twice-yearly.

International Thomson Publishing

See **Thomson Learning**

Internet Handbooks

Unit 5 Dolphin Building, Queen Anne's Battery, Plymouth, Devon PL4 0LP
☎01752 262626   Fax 01752 262641
Email editor@internet-handbooks.co.uk
Website www.internet-handbooks.co.uk
Owner *International Briefings Ltd*

Managing Director *Roger Ferneyhough*

FOUNDED in 1998 by Roger Ferneyhough following his sale of **How To Books** in 1996. *Publishes* practical step-by-step guides to help the reader get the most out of the Internet with the series set to grow to around 30 titles. 11 titles in 1999. TITLES *The Internet for Writers; Find It On the Internet; Marketing Your Business on the Internet; Personal Finance on the Internet.* The Internet Handbooks website offers substantial and free online help on a broad range of topics for all Internet users. Welcomes material for books about the Internet; a telephone call is advised in the first instance.

Royalties paid annually.

Intrigue
See **Harlequin Mills & Boon Ltd**

Isis Publishing Limited
7 Centremead, Osney Mead, Oxford OX2 0ES
☎01865 250333   Fax 01865 790358
Managing Director *John Durrant*

Publishes large-print books – fiction and non-fiction; audio books (see entry under **Audio Books**). TITLES *The Colour of Magic* Terry Pratchett; *Return to Sunset House* Lady Fortescue; *Christine* Stephen King. No unsolicited mss as Isis undertakes no original publishing.

Royalties paid twice-yearly.

Ithaca Press
See **Garnet Publishing Ltd**

IVP
See **Inter-Varsity Press**

Jacqui Small
See **Aurum Press Ltd**

Arthur James
See **John Hunt Publishing Ltd**

Jane's Information Group
163 Brighton Road, Coulsdon, Surrey CR5 2HY
☎020 8700 3700   Fax 020 8763 1006
Website www.janes.com
Managing Director *Alfred Rolington*

FOUNDED 1898 by Fred T. Jane with the publication of *All The World's Fighting Ships.* Now part of The Thomson Corporation. In recent years management has been focusing on growth opportunities in its core business and in enhancing the performance of initiatives like Jane's information available online and on CD-ROM. *Publishes* magazines and yearbooks on defence, aerospace and transport topics, with details of equipment and systems; plus directories and strategic studies. Also *Jane's Defence Weekly* (see entry under **Magazines**).

DIVISIONS
Magazines *Dominic Vaughan* TITLES *Jane's Defence Weekly; Jane's International Defense Review; Jane's Airport Review; Jane's Defence Upgrades; Jane's Navy International.* **Publishing** *Karen Heffer, Fabiana Angelini* TITLES *Defence, Aerospace Yearbooks.* **Geopolitical** *Peter Felstead* TITLES *Jane's Intelligence Review; Foreign Report; Jane's Sentinel* (regional security assessment). **Transport** *Alan Condron* TITLES *Transportation Yearbooks;* CD-ROM and electronic development and publication. Unsolicited mss, synopses and ideas for reference/yearbooks welcome.

Royalties paid twice-yearly. *Overseas associates* Jane's Information Group Inc., USA.

Janus Publishing Company Ltd
76 Great Titchfield Street, London W1P 7AF
☎020 7580 7664   Fax 020 7636 5756
Email publisher@januspublishing.co.uk
Managing Director *Sandy Leung*

Publishes fiction, human interest, memoirs, philosophy, mind, body and spirit, religion and theology, social questions, popular science, history, spiritualism and the paranormal, poetry and young adults. About 400 titles in print. IMPRINTS **Janus Books** Subsidy publishing; **Empiricus Books** Non-subsidy publishing. TITLES *The Anarchists in the Spanish Civil War; Nature of the Self; Healing Connections; Politics and Human Nature; Tales of French Corsairs and Revolutions; Child of the Thirties; Napoleon 1813.* Unsolicited mss welcome.

Royalties paid twice-yearly. Agents in the USA, Australia, South Africa and Asia.

Authors' Rating Authors may be asked to cover their own productions costs but Janus seems to be moving into legitimate publishing with its Empiricus imprint.

Japan Library
See **Curzon Press Ltd**

Jarrold Publishing
Whitefriars, Norwich, Norfolk NR3 1TR
☎01603 763300   Fax 01603 662748
Managing Director *Caroline Jarrold*

Part of Jarrold & Sons Ltd, the printing and publishing company FOUNDED in 1770. *Publishes* UK tourism and travel, sports and leisure, history, gift books and calendars. Material tends to be of a high pictorial content. About 30 titles a year. Unsolicited mss, synopses and ideas welcome but before submitting anything, approach in writing to the Managing Director.

Royalties paid twice-yearly.

Jensen Business Books
See **AMCD (Publishers) Ltd**

Jets
See **HarperCollins Publishers Ltd**

Jewish Chronicle Publications
See **Frank Cass & Co Ltd**

John Jones Publishing Ltd
Unit 12, Clwydfro Business Centre, Lon Parcwr, Ruthin LL15 1NJ
☎01824 705272/704856   Fax 01824 705272
Email mail@johnjonespublishing.ltd.uk
Website www.johnjonespublishing.ltd.uk
Managing Director *John Idris Jones*

FOUNDED 1989. *Publishes* paperback non-fiction about Wales, its culture, topography and history (including autobiography), the history of the Celts and the Tudor period. Titles are specially commissioned or re-publications of important older books which have gone out of print. TITLES *Wild Wales; I Bought a Mountain; Hovel in the Hills; The Pagan Celts; Speak Welsh.* Approach in writing with s.a.e.

Michael Joseph
See **Penguin UK**

Kahn & Averill
9 Harrington Road, London SW7 3ES
☎020 8743 3278   Fax 020 8743 3278
Email kahn@averill23.freeserve.co.uk
Managing Director *Mr M. Kahn*

FOUNDED 1967 to publish children's titles but now specialises in music titles. A small independent publishing house. *Publishes* music and general non-fiction. No unsolicited mss; synopses and ideas for books considered.

Royalties paid twice-yearly.

Karnak House
300 Westbourne Park Road, London W11 1EH
☎020 7243 3620   Fax 020 7243 3620
Managing Director *Amon Saba Saakana*
FOUNDED 1979. *Specialises* in African and Carib-

bean studies. *Publishes* anthropology, education, Egyptology, history, language and linguistics, literary criticism, music, parapsychology, prehistory. No poetry, humour or sport. About 12 titles a year. No unsolicited mss; send introduction or synopsis with one sample chapter. Synopses and ideas welcome.

Royalties paid twice-yearly. *Overseas subsidiaries* The Intef Institute, and Karnak House, Illinois, USA.

Kelpie
See **Canongate Books Ltd**

Kenilworth Press Ltd
Addington, Buckingham, Buckinghamshire MK18 2JR
☎01296 715101   Fax 01296 715148
Email editorial@kenilworthpress.co.uk
Chairman/Managing Director *David Blunt*
Approx. Annual Turnover £500,000

FOUNDED in 1989 with the acquisition of Threshhold Books. The UK's principal instructional equestrian publisher, producing the official books of the British Horse Society, the famous *Threshold Picture Guides*, and a range of authoritative titles sold around the world. About 10 titles a year.

IMPRINT **Kenilworth Press** TITLES *British Horse Society Manuals; Dressage with Kyra; A Modern Horse Herbal; For the Good of the Rider; No Foot, No Horse; Threshold Picture Guides 1–44.* Unsolicited mss, synopses and ideas welcome but only for titles concerned with the care or riding of horses or ponies.

Royalties paid twice-yearly.

Kenyon-Deane
See **Cressrelles Publishing Co. Ltd**

Laurence King
71 Great Russell Street, London WC1B 3BN
☎020 7831 6351   Fax 020 7404 9273
Email enquiries@laurence-king.co.uk
Website www.laurence-king.co.uk
Chairman *Robin Hyman*
Managing Director *Laurence King*

FOUNDED 1991. Publishing imprint of UK packager **Calmann & King Ltd** (see entry under **UK Packagers**). *Publishes* full-colour illustrated books on art history, the decorative arts, carpets and textiles, graphic design, architecture and interior design. Unsolicited material welcome.

Royalties paid twice-yearly.

Kingfisher Publications Plc

New Penderel House, 283–288 High Holborn, London WC1V 7HZ
☎020 7903 9999   Fax 020 7242 4979
Email sales@kingfisherpub.co.uk
Chairman *Bertil Hessel*

Formerly Larousse plc until 1997 when the company name changed to Kingfisher Publications Plc. FOUNDED 1994 when owners, Groupe de la Cité (also publishers of the Larousse dictionaries in France), merged their UK operations of Grisewood & Dempsey and **Chambers Harrap Publishers Ltd** (see entry).
DIVISION **Kingfisher** *Ann-Janine Murtagh*, Publishing Director, Fiction, *Gill Denton* Non-fiction. Founded in 1973 by Grisewood & Dempsey Ltd. *Publishes* children's fiction and non-fiction in hardback and paperback: story books, rhymes and picture books, fiction and poetry anthologies, young non-fiction, activity books, general series and reference. No unsolicited mss accepted.
Royalties paid bi-annually where applicable.

Jessica Kingsley Publishers Ltd

116 Pentonville Road, London N1 9JB
☎020 7833 2307   Fax 020 7837 2917
Email post@jkp.com
Website www.jkp.com
Managing Director *Jessica Kingsley*
Senior Editor *Helen Parry*
Editor *Amy Lancaster-Owen*

FOUNDED 1987. Independent publisher of books for professionals and academics on social and behavioural sciences, including special needs, arts therapies, child psychology, psychotherapy (including forensic psychotherapy), psychoanalysis and social work. Over 100 titles a year. TITLE *Asperger Syndrome – A Guide for Parents and Professionals* Tony Attwood. 'We are actively publishing and commissioning in autism and Asperger Syndrome. We welcome suggestions for books and proposals from prospective authors. Proposals should consist of an outline of the book, a contents list, assessment of the market, and author's c.v. and should be addressed to Jessica Kingsley. Complete manuscript should not be sent.' No fiction or poetry.
Royalties paid twice-yearly.

Kingsway Publications

Lottbridge Drove, Eastbourne, East Sussex BN23 6NT
☎01323 437700   Fax 01323 411970
Email books@kingsway.co.uk
Chairman *Peter Fenwick*

Managing Director *John Paculabo*
Editorial Contact *Mrs C. Owen*
Approx. Annual Turnover £1.5 million

Part of Kingsway Communications Ltd, a charitable trust with Christian objectives. *Publishes* Christian books: Bibles, Christian testimonies, renewal issues. No poetry, fiction or unsolicited submissions accepted. About 40 titles a year.
IMPRINT **Kingsway** TITLES *No Flowers, Just Lots of Joy* Fiona Castle; *Questions of Life* Nicky Gumbel; *The Life Application Bible*.
Royalties paid twice-yearly.

Kluwer Academic/ Plenum Publishers

New Loom House, 101 Back Church Lane, London E1 1LU
☎020 7264 1910   Fax 020 7264 1919
Email mail@plenum.co.uk
Website www.plenum.co.uk
Managing Director *Dr Ken Derham*
Editor *Joanna Lawrence*

FOUNDED 1966. A division of **Kluwer Academic/Plenum Publishing**, New York. The London office is the editorial base for the company's UK and European operations. *Publishes* postgraduate, professional and research-level scientific, technical and medical textbooks, monographs, conference proceedings and reference books. About 300 titles (worldwide) a year.
IMPRINTS **Consultants Bureau**; **Kluwer Academic/Plenum Publishers**; **Plenum Press**; **Human Science Press**. Proposals for new publications will be considered, and should be sent to the editor.
Royalties paid annually.

Kluwer Law International

Sterling House, 66 Wilton Road, London SW1V 1DE
☎020 7821 1123   Fax 020 7630 5229
Director of Operations *Marcel Nieuwenhuis*

FOUNDED 1995. Parent company: Wolters Kluwer Group. Kluwer Law International consists of three components: the law list of Graham & Trotman, Kluwer Law and Taxation and Martinus Nyhoff. *Publishes* international law. 200 titles a year. Unsolicited synopses and ideas for books on law at an international level welcome.
Royalties paid annually.

Charles Knight Publishing
See **Butterworths Tolley**

Knight Paperbacks Ltd
See **Caxton Publishing Group**

Kogan Page Ltd

120 Pentonville Road, London N1 9JN
☎020 7278 0433   Fax 020 7837 3768/6348
Email kpinfo@kogan-page.co.uk
Website www.kogan-page.co.uk *or*
www.earthscan.co.uk

Managing Director *Philip Kogan*
Approx. Annual Turnover £8 million

FOUNDED 1967 by Philip Kogan to publish *The Industrial Training Yearbook*. In 1992 acquired Earthscan Publications. *Publishes* business and management reference books and monographs, education and careers, marketing, personal finance, personnel, small business, training and industrial relations, transport, plus journals. Further expansion is planned, particularly in the finance and high-tech, EC publications areas, yearbooks and directories, and international business reference. About 280 titles a year.

DIVISIONS

Kogan Page *Pauline Goodwin, Philip Mudd, Peter Chadwick.* **Earthscan Publications** *Jonathan Sinclair Wilson* Has close associations with the International Institute for Environment and Development and with the Worldwide Fund for Nature. *Publishes* Third World issues and their global implications, and general environmental titles, both popular and academic. About 50 titles a year. Unsolicited mss, synopses and ideas for books welcome.

Royalties paid twice-yearly.

Authors' Rating Long established as the businessman's friend this firmly independent publisher has strong views on what sells and is usually right.

Ladybird Books

See **Penguin UK**

Landmark Publishing Ltd

Waterloo House, 12 Compton, Ashbourne, Derbyshire DE6 1DA
☎01335 347349   Fax 01335 347303
Email landmark@clara.net

Chairman *Mr R. Cork*
Managing Director *Mr C. L. M. Porter*
Approx. Annual Turnover £350,000

FOUNDED in 1996 following the demise of Moorland Publishing. *Publishes* itinerary-based travel guides and industrial history. 36 titles in 2000. No unsolicited mss; telephone in the first instance.

Royalties twice-yearly.

Larousse plc

See **Kingfisher Publications plc**

Lawrence & Wishart Ltd

99A Wallis Road, London E9 5LN
☎020 8533 2506   Fax 020 8533 7369
Email lw@l-w-bks.demon.co.uk
Website www.l-w-bks.co.uk

Managing Director/Editor *Sally Davison*

FOUNDED 1936. An independent publisher with a substantial backlist. *Publishes* current affairs, cultural politics, economics, history, politics and education. 15–20 titles a year. TITLES *A New Modernity; Liberty or Death; The Struggle for Democracy in Britain 1780–1830; Rosa Luxemburg: An Intimate Portrait.*

Royalties paid annually, unless by arrangement.

The Learning Institute

Honeycombe House, Bagley, Wedmore, Somerset BS28 4TD
☎01934 713563   Fax 01934 713492
Email courses@inst.org
Website ds.dial.pipex.com/institute

Managing Director *Kit Sadgrove*

FOUNDED 1994 to publish home-study courses in vocational subjects such as garden design, writing and computing. *Publishes* subjects that show the reader how to work from home, gain a new skill or enter a new career. Interests include self-improvement, interior design, hobbies, parenting, health, careers, music and investment. TITLES *Become a Freelance Photographer; Master the Art of Painting.* Authors guidelines sent on receipt of s.a.e. No unsolicited mss; send synopses and ideas only.

Royalties paid quarterly.

Lehigh University Press

See **Golden Cockerel Press Ltd**

Leicester University Press

See **Continuum International Publishing Group Ltd**

Lennard Associates Ltd

Windmill Cottage, Mackerye End, Harpenden, Hertfordshire AL5 5DR
☎01582 715866   Fax 01582 715121
Email mailbox@lenqap.demon.co.uk

Chairman/Managing Director *Adrian Stephenson*

FOUNDED 1979. Publisher of sporting yearbooks, personality books, and television associated titles. YEARBOOKS *The Cricketers' Who's Who; RFU Club Directory; Official PFA Footballers' Factfile; British Boxing Yearbook; European Tour Yearbook.* No unsolicited mss.

IMPRINTS **Lennard Publishing**; **Queen Anne Press**. Acquired the latter and most of its assets in 1992.
Payment Both fees and royalties by arrangement.

Letterland
See **HarperCollins Publishers Ltd**

Charles Letts
See **New Holland Publishers (UK) Ltd**

Lionel Leventhal Ltd
See **Greenhill Books**

Levinson Children's Books
See **David & Charles Children's Books**

Dewi Lewis Publishing
8 Broomfield Road, Heaton Moor, Stockport SK4 4ND
☎0161 442 9450   Fax 0161 442 9450
Email mail@dewilewispublishing.com
Website www.dewilewispublishing.com
Contacts *Dewi Lewis, Caroline Warhurst*
Approx. Annual Turnover £240,000

FOUNDED 1994. *Publishes* fiction, photography and visual arts. 16 titles in 1999. TITLES *Industry of Souls* Martin Booth (shortlisted for the 1998 **Booker Prize**); *Common Sense* Martin Parr; *New York 1954–5* William Klein. Mss in the above categories are welcome, provided return postage is enclosed; no synopses or ideas, please.
Royalties paid twice-yearly.

Lexis-Nexis
See **Reed Elsevier plc**

John Libbey & Co. Ltd
PO Box 276, Eastleigh SO50 5YS
☎023 8065 0208   Fax 023 8065 0259
Email johnlibbey@aol.com
Website www.johnlibbey.com
Chairman/Managing Director *John Libbey*

FOUNDED 1979. *Publishes* medical books and cinema/animation books and journals. *Specialises* in epilepsy, neurology, nuclear medicine, nutrition and obesity. Synopses and ideas welcome. *Overseas subsidiaries* John Libbey Eurotext Ltd, France; John Libbey & Co. Pty. Ltd, Australia.

Librapharm Ltd
Gemini House, 162 Craven Road, Newbury, Berkshire RG14 5NR
☎01635 522651   Fax 01635 36294
Chairman *Mr M. W. Frost*

Managing Director *Dr P. L. Clarke*
Approx. Annual Turnover £500,000

FOUNDED 1995 as a partial buyout from Kluwer Academic Publishers (UK) academic list. *Publishes* medical and scientific books and periodicals. IMPRINT **Petroc Press**. TITLES *Neighbour: The Inner Consultation*; *Moulds: Emergencies in General Practice*; *Primary Care Psychiatry* (journal); *Current Medical Research and Opinion* (journal). Unsolicited mss, synopses and ideas for medical books welcome.
Royalties paid twice-yearly.

Library Association Publishing
7 Ridgmount Street, London WC1E 7AE
☎020 7255 0590/020 7255 0505 (text phone)
Fax 020 7255 0591
Email lapublishing@la-hq.org.uk
Website www.la-hq.org.uk/lapublishing
Managing Director *Janet Liebster*

Publishing arm of **The Library Association**. *Publishes* library and information science, monographs, reference, IT training materials and bibliography aimed at library and information professionals. About 35 titles a year.

IMPRINTS
Library Association Publishing; **Clive Bingley Books** Over 200 titles in print, including *Walford's Guide to Reference Material* and *AACR2*. Unsolicited mss, synopses and ideas welcome provided material falls firmly within the company's specialist subject areas.
Royalties paid annually.

Frances Lincoln Ltd
4 Torriano Mews, Torriano Avenue, London, NW5 2RZ
☎020 7284 4009   Fax 020 7267 5249
Managing Director *Frances Lincoln*
E-mail: francesl@frances-lincoln.com *or* janettao@ *or* annef@ etc.

FOUNDED 1977. *Publishes* highly illustrated non-fiction: gardening, art and interiors, spirituality and healing, health, crafts, children's picture and information books; and stationery. About 60 titles a year.

DIVISIONS
Adult Non-fiction *Kate Cave* TITLES *Chatsworth* Duchess of Devonshire; *The Gravel Garden* Beth Chatto; *Beatrix Potter: At Home in the Lake District* Susan Denyer; **Children's General Fiction and Non-fiction** *Janetta Otter-Barry* TITLES *The Wanderings of Odysseus* Rosemary Sutcliffe, illus. Alan Lee; *Amazing Grace, Grace*

& Family Mary Hoffman, illus. Caroline Binch; **Stationery** *Anne Fraser* TITLES *RHS Diary and Address Book*; *National Gallery Diary and Address Book.* Synopses and ideas for books considered. *Royalties* paid twice-yearly.

Authors' Rating To gardening and interior design has been added a trail-blazing children's list. Expansion is promised.

Linden Press
See **Open Gate Press**

Linford Romance/
Linford Mystery/Linford Western
See **F. A. Thorpe (Publishing) Ltd**

Lion Publishing
Peter's Way, Sandy Lane West, Oxford OX4 5HG
☎01865 747550   Fax 01865 747568
Email custserv@lion-publishing.co.uk
Website www.lion-publishing.co.uk
Managing Director *Paul Clifford*
Approx. Annual Turnover £6.77 million
FOUNDED 1971. A Christian book publisher, strong on illustrated books for a popular international readership, with rights sold in over 100 languages worldwide. *Publishes* a diverse list with Christian viewpoint the common denominator. All ages, from board books for children to multi-contributor adult reference, educational, paperbacks and colour co-editions and gift books.
DIVISIONS **Adult** *Celia Walden*; **Children's and Giftlines** *Charlotte Stewart.* Unsolicited mss welcome provided they have a positive Christian viewpoint intended for a wide general and international readership. Synopses, proposals and ideas also welcome.
Royalties paid twice-yearly.

Lir
See **Hodder Headline Plc**

Little, Brown & Co. (UK)
Brettenham House, Lancaster Place, London WC2E 7EN
☎020 7911 8000   Fax 020 7911 8100
Chief Executive *David Young*
Publisher *Ursula Mackenzie*
Approx. Annual Turnover £36.8 million
FOUNDED 1988. Part of Time-Warner Inc. Began by importing its US parent company's titles and in 1990 launched its own illustrated non-fiction list. Two years later the company took over former Macdonald & Co. *Publishes* hardback and paperback fiction, literary fiction, crime, science fiction and fantasy; and general non-fiction, including illustrated: architecture and design, fine art, photography, biography and autobiography, cinema, gardening, history, humour, travel, crafts and hobbies, reference, cookery, wines and spirits, DIY, guidebooks, natural history and nautical.
IMPRINTS
Abacus *Richard Beswick* Literary fiction and non-fiction paperbacks; **Orbit** *Tim Holman* Science fiction and fantasy; **Little Brown/Warner** *Alan Samson, Barbara Boote, Hilary Hale* Mass-market fiction and non-fiction; **X Libris** *Sarah Shrubb* Women's erotica; **Illustrated** *Julia Charles* Hardbacks; **Virago** (see entry). Approach in writing in the first instance. No unsolicited mss.
Royalties paid twice-yearly.

Authors' Rating A quality publisher that manages to cover an impressive range of new writing. A big push for Orbit, the science fiction and fantasy imprint, suggests that SF is back in fashion. If so, it is typical that Little, Brown should be taking a lead in a subject that other publishers find difficulty in selling.

Liverpool University Press
4 Cambridge Street, Liverpool L69 7ZU
☎0151 794 2233   Fax 0151 794 2235
Website www.liverpool-unipress.co.uk
Managing Director/Editorial Head
Robin Bloxsidge
LUP's primary activity is the publication of academic and scholarly books and journals but it also has a limited number of trade titles. Although its principal focus is on the arts and social sciences, in which it is active in a wide variety of disciplines, the LUP list includes some STM books. 30–40 titles a year. TITLES *The Ionian Islands in the Bronze Age and Early Iron Age; Temple Festival Calendars of Ancient Egypt; Gainsborough's Vision; The Irish Border History, Politics, Culture; Environmental Pollution Studies; Millions Like Us: British Culture in the Second World War; Gresford: The Anatomy of a Disaster; Joseph Brodsky and the Baroque; A Study of Ted Hughes.*
Royalties paid annually.

Livewire Books for Teenagers
See **The Women's Press**

London House
See **Allison & Busby**

Lonely Planet Publications

10A Spring Place, London NW5 3BH
☎020 7428 4800   Fax 020 7428 4828
Email go@lonelyplanet.co.uk
Website www.lonelyplanet.com
Owner *Lonely Planet (Australia)*
General Manager *Charlotte Hindle*
Editorial Head *Katharine Leck*
Approx. Annual Turnover £30 million

FOUNDED in 1973 by Tony and Maureen Wheeler to document a journey from London across Asia to Australia. Since then, Lonely Planet has grown into a global operation with headquarters in Melbourne and offices in Paris, California and London. *Publishes* travel guidebooks, phrasebooks, travel literature, pictorial books, city maps, regional atlases, diving and snorkelling, walking, cycling, wildlife, healthy, restaurant, pre-departure guidebooks. In 2000 Lonely Planet set up a commercial travel slide library called **Lonely Planet Images** (lpi@lonelyplanet.com.au). No unsolicited mss; synopses and ideas welcome.
   Royalties negotiable.

Lorenz Books

See **Anness Publishing Ltd**

Peter Lowe (Eurobook Ltd)

PO Box 52, Wallingford, Oxfordshire OX10 0XU
☎01865 858333   Fax 01865 858263
Email eurobook@compuserve.com
Managing Director *Peter Lowe*

FOUNDED 1968. *Publishes* popular science and illustrated adult non-fiction. No unsolicited mss; synopses and ideas (with s.a.e.) welcome. No adult fiction.

Lund Humphries

Gower House, Croft Road, Aldershot, Hampshire GU11 3HR
☎01252 3315514   Fax 01252 3685954
Email info@ashgatepub.co.uk
Website www.ashgate.com
Chairman *Nigel Farrow*
Publishing Director *Lucy Myers*

Publisher of fine art books. First title appeared in 1895. Part of **Ashgate Publishing** since December 1999. *Publishes* art, architecture, photography, design and graphics. Publishers of exhibition catalogues in association with museums and galleries, and of the annual *Guide to Art Exhibitions*. About 20 titles a year. Unsolicited mss welcome but initial introductory letter preferred. Synopses and ideas for books considered.
   Royalties paid twice-yearly.

Authors' Rating Sold to Ashgate Publishing at the end of last year, the Lund Humphries list fits well into Ashgate's art history and contemporary art lists, which has to be good news for authors.

The Lutterworth Press

PO Box 60, Cambridge CB1 2NT
☎01223 350865   Fax 01223 366951
Email publishing@lutterworth.com
Website www.lutterworth.com
Managing Director *Adrian Brink*

The Lutterworth Press dates back to the 18th century when it was founded by the Religious Tract Society. In the 19th century it was best known for its children's books and magazines, both religious and secular, including *The Boys' Own Paper*. Since 1984 it has been an imprint of **James Clarke & Co** (see entry). *Publishes* religious books for adults and children, adult non-fiction, children's fiction and non-fiction. TITLES *Lutterworth Dictionary of the Bible; Doctor of Souls; Cosmic Puberty; The Millennium and the Book of Revelation; Meetings That Work.* Approach in writing with ideas in the first instance.
   Royalties paid annually.

Macdonald & Co.

See **Little, Brown & Co. (UK)**

McGraw-Hill Publishing Company

McGraw-Hill House, Shoppenhangers Road, Maidenhead, Berkshire SL6 2QL
☎01628 502500   Fax 01628 770224
Email alfred_waller@mcgraw-hill.com
Website www.mcgraw-hill.co.uk
Publishing Director, Europe *Alfred Waller*

FOUNDED 1899. Owned by US parent company. Began publishing in Maidenhead in 1965, having had an office in the UK since 1899. *Publishes* business and economics, accountancy, finance, computer science and business computing for the academic, student and professional markets. Around 50 titles a year. Unsolicited mss, synopses and ideas welcome.
   Royalties paid twice-yearly.

Macmillan Publishers Ltd

25 Eccleston Place, London SW1W 9NF
☎020 7881 8000   Fax 020 7881 8001
Website www.macmillan.com
Chief Executive *Richard Charkin*
Approx. Annual Turnover £220 million
(Book Publishing Group)

FOUNDED 1843. Macmillan is one of the largest publishing houses in Britain, publishing approximately 1400 titles a year. In 1995, Verlagsgruppe Georg von Holtzbrinck, a major German publisher, acquired a majority stake in the Macmillan Group. In 1996, Macmillan bought Boxtree, the successful media tie-in publisher and, in 1997, purchased the Heinemann English language teaching list from Reed Elsevier. Unsolicited proposals, synopses and mss are welcome in all divisions of the company (with the exception of Macmillan Children's Books). Authors who wish to send material to Macmillan General Books should note that there is a central submissions procedure in operation. Send a synopsis and the first 3–4 chapters with a covering letter and return postage to the Submissions Editor, 25 Eccleston Place, London SW1W 9NF.

DIVISIONS

Macmillan Press Ltd
Brunel Road, Houndmills, Basingstoke, Hampshire RG21 6XS
☎01256 329242 Fax 01256 3479476

Managing Director *Dominic Knight*. **Academic** *Josie Dixon*; **College: Humanities & Social Sciences Division** *Frances Arnold*; **Business, Computer Science & Engineering** *Chris Glennie*; **Professional Business & Management Division** *Stephen Rutt*; **Journals** *David Bull*. *Publishes* textbooks, monographs and journals in academic and professional subjects. Publications in both hard copy and electronic format.

Macmillan Heinemann
English Language Teaching
Macmillan Oxford, 4 Between Towns Road, Oxford OX4 3PP
☎01865 405700 Fax 01865 405701
Email elt@mhelt. com
Website www.mhelt.com

Managing Directors *Mike Esplen, Chris Harrison*; Publishing Directors *Sue Bale, Alison Hubert*. *Publishes* a wide range of ELT titles and educational books for the international education market.

Pan Macmillan
(Eccleston Place address, as above). Chairman *Adrian Soar*. *Publishes* under **Macmillan, Pan, Picador, Papermac, Sidgwick & Jackson, Boxtree, Channel 4 Books, Macmillan Children's Books, Campbell Books** imprints.

Macmillan (FOUNDED 1843) Publisher *Jeremy Trevathan*, Editorial Directors (fiction) *Beverley Cousins, Peter Lavery*. *Publishes* novels, detective fiction, sci-fi, fantasy and horror. Editorial Director (non-fiction) *Georgina Morley*. *Publishes* autobiography, biography, business and industry, economics, gift books, health and beauty, history, humour, natural history, travel, philosophy, politics and world affairs, psychology, film and theatre, gardening and cookery, encyclopedias, popular science. Editorial Director (reference) *Morven Knowles*. *Publishes* trade reference titles.

Pan (FOUNDED 1947) Publisher *Clare Harington*. *Publishes* fiction: novels, detective fiction, sci-fi, fantasy and horror. Non-fiction: general non-fiction, sports and games, film and theatre, travel, gardening and cookery.

Papermac (FOUNDED 1965) Publisher *Clare Harington*. Serious non-fiction: history, biography, science, political economy, cultural criticism and art history.

Picador (FOUNDED 1972) Publisher *Peter Straus*, Senior Editorial Director *Ursula Doyle*, Deputy Publishing Director *Maria Rejt*. *Publishes* literary international fiction and non-fiction.

Sidgwick & Jackson (FOUNDED 1908) Editorial Director *Gordon Wise*. *Publishes* popular non-fiction with strong personality or marketable identity, from celebrity and showbusiness to ancient mystery, music and true-life adventure to illustrated lifestyle and branded books. Also military history list.

Macmillan Children's Books (Eccleston Place address) Managing Director *Kate Wilson*; **Black & White** *Sarah Davies*; **Full Colour** *Alison Green*. IMPRINTS **Macmillan, Pan, Campbell Books**. *Publishes* novels, board books, picture books, non-fiction (illustrated and non-illustrated), poetry and novelty books in paperback and hardback. No unsolicited material.

Boxtree Publisher *Clare Hulton*. *Publishes* books linked to and about television and film. About 100 titles a year. TITLES *Dilbert; Father Ted; The Motley Fool; Who Wants to be a Millionaire?; James Bond; Randall and Hopkirk*. **Channel 4 Books** Publisher *Ms Charlie Carman*. *Publishes* TV tie-in titles – books that stand on their own merits and not just the 'book of the series'. About 50 titles a year. TITLES *Friends; Water Colour Challenge; Time Team; Dawson's Creek; Frasier; South Park*.

Holtzbrinck Online Publishing
(Eccleston Place address) Managing Director *Ian Jacobs* Editorial Director *Jane Turner*. *Publishes* works of reference in academic, professional and vocational subjects; online resources. TITLES *The New Grove Dictionary of Music and Musicians* ed. Stanley Sadie; *The Dictionary of Art* ed. Jane Turner.
Royalties paid annually or twice-yearly depending on contract.

Authors' Rating Macmillan is no longer Macmillan except in name. After 156 years, the family has sold its stake to Holtzbrinck, the majority shareholder, which has now acquired the rest of the company to couple it with newspaper, television, radio and other book publishing interests centred on Stuttgart. As to the future, there is much talk of Internet publishing. A lot depends on the reception to changes in the reference division, the new edition of *Grove's Dictionary of Music*, the Nature Publishing Group and, in particular, to Holtzbrinck Online Publishing, a company in the making, all of which represents an investment in reference so large that even the splendid *Writer's Handbook* and *Statesman's Yearbook* pale into the minor league. Back in the world of hard print, Pan has built an enviable list of popular authors who command a large share of the consumer market.

Madcap
See **André Deutsch Ltd**

Magi Publications
1 The Coda Centre, 189 Munster Road, London SW6 6AW
☎020 7385 6333   Fax 020 7385 7333
Publisher *Monty Bhatia*
Editor *Linda Jennings*
Approx. Annual Turnover £2.5 million
Publishes children's picture and novelty books for ages 0–9. No texts over 1200 words. About 24 titles a year. Unsolicited mss, synopses and new ideas welcome, but please telephone first.
Royalties paid annually.

Mainstream Publishing Co. (Edinburgh) Ltd
7 Albany Street, Edinburgh EH1 3UG
☎0131 557 2959   Fax 0131 556 8720
Directors *Bill Campbell, Peter MacKenzie*
Approx. Annual Turnover £2.75 million
Publishes art, autobiography/biography, current affairs, health, sport, history, illustrated and fine editions, photography, politics and world affairs, popular paperbacks. Over 80 titles a year. Ideas for books considered, but they should be preceded by a letter, synopsis and s.a.e. or return postage.
Royalties paid twice-yearly.

Authors' Rating A Scottish company aiming for a British profile. Keen on finding authors who 'can develop with us'.

Mammoth
See **Egmont Children's Books**

Management Books 2000 Ltd
Cowcombe House, Cowcombe Hill, Chalford, Gloucestershire GL6 8HP
☎01285 760722   Fax 01285 760708
Email m.b.2000@virgin.net
Website www.mb2000.com
Managing Director *Nicholas Dale-Harris*
Marketing *Nicholas Murphy*
Approx. Annual Turnover £500,000
FOUNDED 1993 to develop a range of books for executives and managers working in the modern world of business, supplemented with information through other media like seminars, audio and video. *Publishes* business and management and sponsored titles. About 30 titles a year. Unsolicited mss, synopses and ideas for books welcome.

Manchester United Books
See **André Deutsch Ltd**

Manchester University Press
Oxford Road, Manchester M13 9NR
☎0161 273 5539   Fax 0161 274 3346
Email mup@man.ac.uk
Website www.man.ac.uk/mup
Publisher/Chief Executive *David Rodgers*
Approx. Annual Turnover £2 million
FOUNDED 1903. MUP is Britain's third largest university press, with a list marketed and sold worldwide. Remit consists of occasional trade publications but mainly A-level and undergraduate textbooks and research monographs. *Publishes* in six main areas: literature and cultural studies, history and history of art, politics, economics, design, film and media. About 120 titles a year, plus journals. DIVISIONS **Humanities** *Matthew Frost*; **History/Art History/Religion** *Vanessa Graham*; **Politics and Economics** *Tony Mason*. Unsolicited mss welcome.
Royalties paid annually.

George Mann Books

PO Box 22, Maidstone, Kent ME14 1AH
☎01622 759591   Fax 01622 209193
Chairman/Managing Director *George Mann*

FOUNDED 1972, originally as library reprint publishers, but has moved on to other things with the collapse of the library market. *Publishes* original non-fiction and selected reprints. Not considering new fiction for publication. 'Will only consider and respond to authors who, in the present publishing climate, are prepared to support some of the costs of publication. Unsolicited material not accompanied by return postage will neither be read nor returned.'
Royalties paid annually.

Mansell

See **Continuum International Publishing Group Ltd**

Manson Publishing Ltd

73 Corringham Road, London NW11 7DL
☎020 8905 5150   Fax 020 8201 9233
Email manson@man-pub.demon.co.uk
Chairman/Managing Director *Michael Manson*
Approx. Annual Turnover £700,000

FOUNDED 1992. *Publishes* scientific, technical, medical and veterinary. 15 titles in 1999. No unsolicited mss; synopses and ideas will be considered.
Royalties paid twice-yearly.

Marc

See **Monarch Books**

Marshall Pickering

See **HarperCollins Publishers Ltd**

Marshall Publishing

See **Marshall Editions Ltd** under **UK Packagers**

Marston House

Marston House, Marston Magna, Yeovil, Somerset BA22 8DH
☎01935 851331   Fax 01935 851372
Managing Director/Editorial Head *Anthony Birks-Hay*

FOUNDED 1989. Publishing imprint of book packager Alphabet & Image Ltd. *Publishes* fine art, architecture, ceramics. 4 titles a year.
Royalties paid twice-yearly, or flat fee in lieu of royalties.

Kenneth Mason Publications Ltd

Dudley House, 12 North Street, Emsworth, Hampshire PO10 7DQ
☎01243 377977   Fax 01243 379136
Chairman *Kenneth Mason*
Managing Director *Piers Mason*
Approx. Annual Turnover £500,000

FOUNDED 1958. *Publishes* diet, health, fitness, nutrition and nautical. No fiction. About 15 titles a year. Initial approach by letter with synopsis only. IMPRINT **Boatswain Press**.
Royalties paid twice-yearly (Jun/Dec) in first year, annually (Dec) thereafter.

Kevin Mayhew Publishers

Buxhall, Stowmarket, Suffolk IP14 3BW
☎01449 737978   Fax 01449 737834
Email info@kevinmayhewltd.com
Chairman *Kevin Mayhew*
Managing Director *Gordon Carter*
Commissioning Editors *Jonathan Bugden, Helen Elliott*
Approx. Annual Turnover £4 million

FOUNDED in 1976. One of the leading sacred music and Christian book publishers in the UK. *Publishes* religious titles – liturgy, sacramental, devotional, also children's books and school resources. 300 titles in 1999. TITLES *Hymns Old & New (Anglican Edition); More Things to do in Children's Worship.* Unsolicited synopses and mss welcome; telephone prior to sending material, please.
IMPRINT **Palm Tree Press** *Kevin Mayhew* Bible stories, colouring/activity and puzzle books for children.
Royalties paid annually.

Melrose Press Ltd

St Thomas Place, Ely, Cambridgeshire CB7 4GG
☎01353 646600   Fax 01353 646601
Chairman *Richard A. Kay*
Managing Director *Nicholas S. Law*
Approx. Annual Turnover £2 million

FOUNDED 1960. Took on its present name in 1969. *Publishes* biographical who's who reference only (not including *Who's Who*, which is published by **A. & C. Black**).
DIVISION **International Biographical Centre** *Jon Gifford.* TITLES *International Authors and Writers Who's Who; International Who's Who in Music; Who's Who in Asia and the Pacific Nations.*

Mentor

See **Christian Focus Publications**

Mercat Press

53 South Bridge, Edinburgh EH1 1YS
☎0131 556 6743   Fax 0131 557 8149
Email enquiries@jthin.co.uk
Website www.jthin.co.uk/merchome.htm

Chairman/Managing Director
D. Ainslie Thin
Editorial Heads *Tom Johnstone, Seán Costello, Camilla James*

FOUNDED 1971 as an adjunct to the large Scottish-based bookselling chain of James Thin. Began by publishing reprints of classic Scottish literature but now produces a wide range of new non-fiction titles. In 1992 the company acquired the bulk of the stock of Aberdeen University Press and the backlist expanded greatly as a result. In 1999 it took over some 60 titles from the Stationery Office's Scottish heritage list. New titles are added regularly. *Publishes* Scottish classics reprints and non-fiction of Scottish interest. This includes walking guides and historical and literary books. TITLES *West Highland Way, Official Guide* Bob Aitken and Roger Smith; *25 Walks* series; *Golden City, Scottish Children's Street Games and Songs* James Ritchie; *The Scots Kitchen* F. Marian McNeill. Unsolicited synopses of non-fiction Scottish interest books, preferably with sample chapters, are welcome. No new fiction or poetry.
Royalties paid annually.

Merehurst

Ferry House, 51–57 Lacy Road, London
SW15 1PR
☎020 8355 1480   Fax 020 8355 1499

Group CEO/Publisher *Anne Wilson*
Chief Operating Officer *Sharon Miller*
Approx. Annual Turnover £3 million

Owned by Australian media group Murdoch Magazines Pty Ltd. *Publishes* full-colour non-fiction: homes and interiors, gardening, cookery, craft, cake decorating and DIY. About 46 titles a year. Synopses and ideas for books welcome; no unsolicited mss.
Royalties paid twice-yearly.

The Merlin Press Ltd

PO Box 30705, London WC2E 8QD
☎020 7836 3020   Fax 020 7497 0309
Email info@merlinpress.co.uk

Managing Director *Anthony W. Zurbrugg*

FOUNDED 1956. *Publishes* economics, history, philosophy, left-wing politics. TITLES *Necessary and Unnecessary Utopias: Socialist Register 2000;*

The Romantics: England in a Revolutionary Age E. P. Thompson. About 10 titles a year. No fiction.
Royalties paid twice-yearly.

Methodist Publishing House

20 Ivatt Way, Peterborough, Cambridgeshire
PE3 7PG
☎01733 332202   Fax 01733 331201
Website www.mph.org.uk

Chair *Dudley Coates*
Chief Executive *Brian Thornton*
Approx. Annual Turnover £2 million

FOUNDED 1800. Owned by the Methodist Church. *Publishes* a wide range of books, magazines and resources which are sold to Christians in the UK and overseas. 20 titles in 1999. Launching a new bi-monthly magazine *Flame* with a target readership of 35,000. IMPRINTS **Epworth Press** (see entry); **Foundery Press** *Brian Thornton*. Unsolicited mss, synopses and ideas welcome; send sample chapter and contents with covering letter.
Royalties paid twice-yearly.

Methuen Children's Books

See **Egmont Children's Books**

Methuen Publishing Ltd

215 Vauxhall Bridge Road, London
SW1V 1EJ
☎020 7828 2838   Fax 020 7233 9827
Email <name>@methuen.co.uk

Managing Director *Peter Tummons*
Publishing Director *Michael Earley*
Publisher, General Books *Max Eilenberg*

FOUNDED 1889. Methuen was owned by Reed International until it was bought by Random House in 1997. Purchased by a management buy-out team in 1998, it is now independent. *Publishes* fiction and non-fiction; drama, film, performing arts, humour. 60 titles in 1999. DIVISIONS **General** *Max Eilenberg*; **Drama, Film, Theatre** *Michael Earley*. No unsolicited mss; synopses and ideas welcome. Prefers to be approached via agents or a letter of inquiry. No first novels, cookery books, personal memoirs.
Royalties paid twice-yearly.

Authors' Rating Having escaped the conglomerate embrace, the once proud drama publisher is back in business with a revitalised programme including a repackaging of leading backlist titles. On the general side, there are plans for 35 to 40 new titles a year.

Metro Books

Metro Publishing Ltd, 19 Gerrard Street, London W1V 7LA
☎020 7734 1411   Fax 020 7734 1811
Email metro@metro-books.com
Managing Director *Susanne McDadd*
Publishing Director *Alan Brooke*

FOUNDED 1995. *Publishes* general non-fiction – biography, current affairs, popular psychology, health and cookery. 26 titles in 2000. TITLES *Real Fast Vegetarian Food* Ursula Ferrigno; *Can Reindeer Fly?* Roger Highfield; *The Paras* John Parker; *Class Act* Linda Lee-Potter. IMPRINT of Metro Publishing Ltd: **RCB (Richard Cohen Books** – see entry) Biographies of Rupert Brooke, Siegfried Sasson and C. B. Fry. No unsolicited mss. Send outline, sample chapter, c.v., sales and marketing ideas plus s.a.e. in the first instance.
Royalties paid twice-yearly.

Authors' Rating Author friendly publisher credited with good communications and readiness to involve writers in production decisions.

Michelin Tyre plc

The Edward Hyde Building, 38 Clarendon Road, Watford, Hertfordshire WD1 1SX
☎01923 415000   Fax 01923 415052
Website www.michelin-travel.com

FOUNDED 1900 as a travel publisher. *Publishes* travel guides, maps and atlases, children's I-Spy books. Travel-related synopses and ideas welcome; no mss.

Midland Publishing – An imprint of Ian Allan Publishing Ltd

24 The Hollow, Earl Shilton, Leicester LE9 7NA
☎01455 847256   Fax 01455 841805
Publisher *N. P. Lewis*

Publishes aviation, military and railways. No wartime memoirs. No unsolicited mss; synopses and ideas welcome.
Royalties paid quarterly.

Harvey Miller Publishers

2 Byron Mews, Hampstead, London NW3 2NQ
☎020 7284 4359   Fax 020 7267 8764
Editorial Director *Mrs Elly Miller*

FOUNDED 1974. *Publishes* serious studies in the history of art only. Approx. 6 titles a year. No unsolicited mss; synopses and ideas welcome.
Royalties paid annually.

Miller's
See **Octopus Publishing Group**

Mills & Boon
See **Harlequin Mills & Boon Ltd**

Mindfield
See **Camden Press Ltd**

Minerva Press Ltd

6th Floor, Canberra House, 315–317 Regent Street, London W1R 7YB
☎020 7580 4114   Fax 020 7580 9256
Email mail@minerva-press.co.uk
Website www.minerva-press.co.uk
Managing Director *Angelina Anton*

FOUNDED in 1992, but the imprint can be traced back to 1792. *Publishes* fiction and non-fiction; memoirs/biography, poetry, religion, philosophy, history and children's. 300 titles in 1999. TITLES *Hope – thirteen very personal accounts of surviving breast cancer* Clare Shvili; *The Taming of the Gorillas* Bob Campbell; *Beyond Hope Street* Glen Williams. Specialises in new authors. Unsolicited mss, synopses and ideas for books welcome.
Royalties paid twice-yearly. Offices in Miami, New Delhi and Rio de Janeiro, with representation in Australia.

Authors' Rating Liable to ask authors to contribute towards costs of publication.

MIRA
See **Harlequin Mills & Boon Ltd**

The MIT Press Ltd

Fitzroy House, 11 Chenies Street, London WC1E 7ET
☎020 7306 0603   Fax 020 7306 0604
Email info@HUP-MITpress.co.uk
Director *F. Urbanowski*
General Manager *A. Sexsmith*

Part of **The MIT Press**, USA. *Publishes* academic, architecture and design, art history and theory, bibliography, biography, business and industry, cinema and media studies, computer science, cultural studies and critical theory, economics, educational and textbooks, engineering, environment, linguistics, medical, music, natural history, philosophy, photography, physics, politics and world affairs, psychology, reference, scientific and technical, neurobiology and neuroscience. All mss go to the American office: 5 Cambridge Centre, Cambridge, MA 02142. (See entry under **US Publishers**.)

Mitchell Beazley
See **Octopus Publishing Group**

Monarch Books
Concorde House, Grenville Place, London
NW7 3SA
☎020 8959 3668   Fax 020 8959 3678
Email tonyc@angushudson.com
Directors *Tony Collins, Jane Collins*

Now an imprint of **Angus Hudson Ltd** (see
entry under **UK Packagers**). *Publishes* an
independent list of Christian books across a
wide range of concerns. About 30 titles a year.

IMPRINTS **Monarch** Upmarket, social concern issues list covering a wide range of areas
from psychology to future studies, politics, etc.,
all with a strong Christian dimension; **Marc**
Leadership, mission and church growth titles.
Unsolicited mss, synopses and ideas welcome.
'Regretfully, no poetry or fiction.'

Monitor Press Ltd
Suffolk House, Church Field Road, Sudbury,
Suffolk CO10 2YA
☎01787 378607   Fax 01787 880201
Website www.monitorpress.co.uk
Publisher *Zöe Turner*

Part of LLP Professional Publishing, a trading
division of Informa Publishing Group Ltd.
Publishes a range of legal, tax and business to business newsletters, special reports and books aimed
at senior management and professional practices.
25 newsletter titles a year. Unsolicited synopses
and ideas welcome. Initial approach in writing.

Mosby International
See **Harcourt Brace and Company Limited**

Motor Racing Publications
Unit 6, The Pilton Estate, 46 Pitlake,
Croydon, Surrey CR0 3RY
☎020 8681 3363   Fax 020 8760 5117
Website www.oberon.co.uk/mrp
Chairman/Editorial Head *John Blunsden*
Approx. Annual Turnover £500,000

FOUNDED soon after the end of World War II
to concentrate on motor-racing titles. Fairly
dormant in the mid '60s but was reactivated in
1968 by a new shareholding structure. John
Blunsden later acquired a majority share and
major expansion followed in the '70s. About
10–12 titles a year. *Publishes* motor-sport history, classic car collection and restoration, road
transport, motorcycles, off-road driving and
related subjects.

IMPRINTS **Fitzjames Press**; **Motor Racing
Publications** TITLES *Grand Prix Cars 1945–65*
M. Lawrence; *Jeep CJ to Grand Cherokee*
J. Taylor; *MG From A–Z* J. Wood; *Land Rover
Discovery* J. Taylor. Unsolicited mss, synopses
and ideas in specified subject areas welcome.
Royalties paid twice-yearly.

Mowbray
See **Continuum International Publishing
Group Ltd**

Multi-Sensory Learning Ltd
Earlstrees Court, Earlstrees Road, Corby,
Northants NN17 4HH
☎01536 399003   Fax 01536 399012
Email pipattwood@aol.com
Senior Editor *Philippa Attwood*

Publishes materials and books related to dyslexia;
the multi-sensory learning course for dyslexic
pupils needing literacy skills development, plus
numerous other items on assessment, reading,
maths, music, etc. for dyslexics. Keen to locate
authors able to write materials for dyslexic people
and for teachers of dyslexics.

John Murray (Publishers) Ltd
50 Albemarle Street, London W1X 4BD
☎020 7493 4361   Fax 020 7499 1792
Chairman *John R. Murray*
Managing Director *Nicholas Perren*

FOUNDED 1768. Independent publisher. *Publishes* general trade books, educational (secondary
school and college textbooks) and Success
Studybooks.

DIVISIONS **General Books** *Grant McIntyre*;
Educational Books *Nicholas Perren*. Unsolici-
ted material discouraged.
Royalties paid twice yearly.

Authors' Rating Noted for scholarly books
that appeal to the wider readership.

NAG Press Ltd
See **Robert Hale Ltd**

National Trust Publications
36 Queen Anne's Gate, London SW1H 9AS
☎020 7222 9251   Fax 020 7222 5097
Website bookshelf.nationaltrust.org.uk
Chairman *Charles Nunneley*
Director-General *Martin Drury*
Publisher *Margaret Willes*

Publishing arm of The National Trust, FOUNDED
in 1895 by Robert Hunter, Octavia Hill and
Hardwicke Rawnsley to protect and conserve

places of historic interest and beauty. *Publishes* gardening, cookery, handbooks, social history, architecture, general interest and children's books. About 15 titles in 1999. TITLES *Literary Trails; The Art of Dress; Flora Domestica; Children of the Great Country Houses; Hadrian's Wall: An Historic Landscape.* No unsolicited material.
Royalties paid twice-yearly.

Nautical Data Ltd
12 North Street, Emsworth, Hampshire PO10 7DQ
☎01243 377977   Fax 01243 379136
Email info@nauticaldata.com
Website www.nauticaldata.com
Managing Director *Piers Mason*
Approx. Annual Turnover £750,000
FOUNDED 1999. Part of **Macmillan Publishers Ltd**. *Publishes* nautical almanacs and pilots. 6 titles in 1999. No unsolicited mss; synopses and ideas welcome. No fiction or non-nautical themes.
Royalties paid twice-yearly.

NCVO Publications
Regent's Wharf, 8 All Saints Street, London N1 9RL
☎020 7713 6161   Fax 020 7713 6300
Website www.ncvo-voc.org.uk
Publications Manager *Maria Kane*
Approx. Annual Turnover £140,000
FOUNDED 1928. Publishing imprint of the National Council for Voluntary Organisations, embracing former Bedford Square Press titles and NCVO's many other publications. The list reflects NCVO's role as the representative body for the voluntary sector. *Publishes* directories, management and trustee development, legal, finance and fundraising titles of primary interest to the voluntary sector. TITLES *The Voluntary Agencies Directory; Grants from Europe; The Good Trustee Guide; The Good Campaigns Guide; The Good Financial Management Guide.* No unsolicited mss as all projects are commissioned in-house.
Royalties paid twice-yearly.

Nelson – A division of Stanley Thornes (Publishers) Ltd
Nelson House, Mayfield Road, Walton on Thames, Surrey KT12 5PL
☎01932 252211   Fax 01932 246109
Website www.nelson.co.uk
CEO/Managing Director *Dominic Richardson*
FOUNDED 1798. Part of the Wolters Kluwer Group of companies. Major educational publisher of printed and electronic product, from pre-school to Higher Education, with emphasis on requirements of National Curriculum, GCSE, A Level, GNVQ and NVQ. Publisher of a range of material for the Caribbean market. TITLES *GAIA: Geography, An Integrated Approach; The Wider World; Nelson English; Nelson Maths; Wellington Square; Route Nationale; Encore Tricolore; Zickzack Neu; World of Sport Examined; New Balanced Science; Bath Science.*
Royalties paid twice-yearly.

Authors' Rating The problems of the education sector were underlined early in the year when Nelson was sold to Stanley Thornes, a subsidiary of Wolters Kluwer. With combined sales of over £40 million, the new structure will help distribution, particularly in the primary schools where Nelson's books do best.

Thomas Nelson & Sons Ltd
See **Nelson**

New Beacon Books Ltd
76 Stroud Green Road, London N4 3EN
☎020 7272 4889   Fax 020 7281 4662
Chairman *John La Rose*
Managing Director *Sarah White*
Approx. Annual Turnover £120,000
FOUNDED 1966. *Publishes* fiction, history, politics, poetry and language, all concerning black people. 1 title in 1999. No unsolicited material.
Royalties paid annually.

New English Library
See **Hodder Headline Plc**

New Holland Publishers (UK) Ltd
24 Nutford Place, London W1H 6DQ
☎020 7724 7773   Fax 020 7724 6184
Email postmaster@nhpub.co.uk
Managing Director *John Beaufoy*
Editorial Head *Yvonne McFarlane*
Approx. Annual Turnover £5 million
FOUNDED 1956. Relaunched 1987 with new name and editorial identity. New directions and rapid expansion transformed the small specialist imprint into a publisher of illustrated books for the international market. In 1993, they diversified further with the acquisition of the Charles Letts Publishing Division list. In 1997, their parent company (New Holland Struik Group, S. Africa) acquired Southern Book Publishers, and their sister company (New Holland Australia) acquired the natural history and lifestyle divisions of Reed Australia. *Publishes*

non-fiction, specialising in natural history, travel, cookery, cake decorating, crafts, gardening, DIY and outdoor sports. TITLES *Dive Sites Series; Top Dive Sites of the World; Climber's Handbook; Globetrotter Travel Guides and Maps; Bill Oddie's Birds of Britain and Ireland; Seabirds of the World; Design and Decorate Series; No-Time Party Cakes; Design Source Books.* No unsolicited mss; synopses and ideas welcome.
Royalties paid twice-yearly.

Nexus
See **Virgin Publishing Ltd**

Nexus Special Interests
Nexus House, Azalea Drive, Swanley, Kent BR8 8HY
☎01322 660070   Fax 01322 667633
Website www.nexusmedialtd.co.uk
Contact *Jackie Hollingsworth*

Publishes aviation, engineering, leisure and hobbies, modelling, electronics, health, craft, wine and beer making, woodwork. Send synopses rather than completed mss.
Royalties paid twice-yearly.

NFER-Nelson Publishing Co. Ltd
Darville House, 2 Oxford Road East, Windsor, Berkshire SL4 1DF
☎01753 858961   Fax 01753 856830
Website www.nfer-nelson.co.uk
Managing Director *Michael Jackson*

FOUNDED 1981. Jointly owned by the Thomson Corporation and the National Foundation for Educational Research. *Publishes* educational and psychological tests and training materials. Main interest is in educational, clinical and occupational assessment and training material. Unsolicited material welcome.
Royalties vary according to each contract.

Nia
See **The X Press**

Nicholson
See **HarperCollins Publishers Ltd**

James Nisbet & Co. Ltd
78 Tilehouse Street, Hitchin, Hertfordshire SG5 2DY
☎01462 438331   Fax 01462 431528
Chairman *E. M. Mackenzie-Wood*

FOUNDED 1810 as a religious publisher and expanded into more general areas from around 1850 onwards. The first educational list appeared in 1926 and the company now specialises in educational material and business studies. About 5 titles a year. No fiction, leisure or religion. No unsolicited mss; synopses and ideas welcome.
Royalties paid twice-yearly.

NMS Publishing Limited
Royal Museum, Chambers Street, Edinburgh EH1 1JF
☎0131 247 4026   Fax 0131 247 4012
Email ltaylor@nms.ac.uk
Website www.nms.ac.uk
Chairman *Mark Jones*
Director *Lesley A. Taylor*
Approx. Annual Turnover £250,000

FOUNDED 1987 to *publish* non-fiction related to the National Museums of Scotland collections: academic and general; children's; archaeology, history, decorative arts worldwide, history of science, technology, natural history and geology, poetry. 14 titles in 1999. TITLES *Scotland's Past in Action* series; *The Scottish Home; Domestic Culture in the Middle East; Agates; Harmony and Contrast: A Journey Through East Asian Art; Thistle at War; Souvenirs: Hieland Foodie; Plastics: Collecting and Conserving; Precious Cargo; Scots' Lives; Jewellery Moves; Scottish Coins; Chinese Lacquer; Spirit of Flight.* No unsolicited mss; only interested in synopses and ideas for books which are genuinely related to NMS collections and to Scotland in general.
Royalties paid twice-yearly.

No Exit Press
See **Oldcastle Books Ltd**

Nonesuch Press
See **Reinhardt Books Ltd**

Northcote House Publishers Ltd
Horndon House, Horndon, Tavistock, Devon PL19 9NQ
☎01822 810066   Fax 01822 810034
Managing Director *Brian Hulme*

FOUNDED 1985. Recently launched a new series of literary critical studies, in association with the British Council, called *Writers and their Work. Publishes* education management, literary criticism, educational dance and drama. A new series of study aids for A-level students and undergraduates in the humanities is in preparation. 20 titles in 1999. 'Well-thought-out proposals, including contents and sample chapter(s), with strong marketing arguments welcome.'
Royalties paid annually.

Nottingham University Press

Manor Farm, Main Street, Thrumpton,
Nottingham NG11 0AX
☎0115 9831011   Fax 0115 9831003
Email editor@nup.com
Website www.nup.com
Managing Editor *Dr D. J. A. Cole*
Approx. Annual Turnover £250,000

Initially concentrated on agricultural and food
sciences titles but has now branched into new
areas including engineering, lifesciences, medicine, law and sport. Sports books published
under subsidiary, Castle Publications. TITLES
*Global 2050; Lung Function Tests; Diet,
Lipoproteins and Coronary Heart Disease; Chinese
Herbs in Animal Nutrition; Progress in Pig Science.*
Castle Publications TITLES *The Mental Game
of Golf; The Natural Sportsman; Rinks to Arenas,
10 Years of British Ice Hockey.*
Royalties paid twice-yearly.

Oak

See **Omnibus Press**

Oberon Books

521 Caledonian Road, London N7 9RH
☎020 7607 3637   Fax 020 7607 3629
Email oberon.books@btinternet.com
Publishing Director *James Hogan*
Managing Director *Charles D. Glanville*

Publishes play texts (usually in conjunction with
a production) and theatre books. *Specialises* in
contemporary plays and translations of
European classics. IMPRINTS **Oberon Books**;
Absolute Classics. AUTHORS/TRANSLATORS
Rodney Ackland, Michel Azama, Simon Bent,
Steven Berkoff, Ranjit Bolt, Ken Campbell,
Barry Day, Marguerite Duras, Dario Fo,
Jonathan Gems, Pam Gems, Trevor Griffiths,
Sir Peter Hall, Giles Havergal, Rolf Hochhuth,
Michael Kilgarriff, Robert David MacDonald,
Kenneth McLeish, Adrian Mitchell, Sheridan
Morley, Gregory Motton, Stephen Mulrine,
Jimmy Murphy, Meredith Oakes, Stewart
Parker, David Pownall, Roland Rees, Colin
Teevan, Colin Winslow, Charles Wood.

Octagon Press Ltd

PO Box 227, London N6 4EW
☎020 8348 9392   Fax 020 8341 5971
Website www.octagonpress.com
Managing Director *George R. Schrager*
Approx. Annual Turnover £100,000

FOUNDED 1972. *Publishes* philosophy, psychology, travel, Eastern religion, translations of

Eastern classics and research monographs in
series. 4–5 titles a year. Unsolicited material
not welcome. Enquiries in writing only.
Royalties paid annually.

Octopus Publishing Group

2–4 Heron Quays, London E14 4JP
☎020 7531 8400   Fax 020 7531 8650
Website www.octopus-publishing.co.uk
Chief Executive *Derek Freeman*
Approx. Annual Turnover £45 million
(Group)

A new company formed following a management buyout of Reed Consumer Books from
Reed Elsevier plc in August 1998.

Conran Octopus
Fax 020 7531 8627
Email info-co@conran-octopus.co.uk
Website www.conran-octopus.co.uk

Managing Director *Caroline Proud* Quality
illustrated lifestyle books, particularly interiors,
design, cookery, gardening and crafts TITLES
The Essential House Book Terence Conran; *Fork
to Fork* Monty Don; *Passion for Seafood* Gordon
Ramsey; *New Retail* Rasshied Din.

Hamlyn Octopus
Email info-ho@hamlyn.co.uk
Website www.hamlyn.co.uk

Managing Director *Alison Goff* Popular non-
fiction, particularly cookery, gardening, craft,
sport, health, film and music TITLES *Larousse
Gastronomique; Hamlyn Book of Gardening;
Hamlyn Book of DIY & Decorating.*

Mitchell Beazley/Miller's
Fax 020 7537 0773
E-mail info-mb@mitchell-beazley.co.uk
Website www.mitchell-beazley.co.uk

Publisher/Managing Director *Jane Aspden*
Quality illustrated reference books, particularly
food and wine, gardening, interior design and
architecture, antiques, general reference TITLES
*Hugh Johnson's Pocket Wine Book; The New Joy of
Sex; Miller's Antiques and Collectibles Price Guides.*

Philip's
Fax 020 7531 8460
Email george.philip@philips-maps.co.uk
Website www.philips-maps.co.uk

Managing Director *John Gaisford* World atlases,
globes, astronomy, road atlases, encyclopaedias,
thematic reference TITLES *Philip's Atlas of the
World; Philip's Modern School Atlas; Philip's Guide
to the Stars and Planets; Ordnance Survey Street
Atlas; Philip's Millennium Encyclopaedia.*

Brimax
Fax 020 7531 8607
Email brimax@brimax.octopus.co.uk

Managing Director *Laura Bamford* Mass-market board and picture books for children, age groups 1–10.

Bounty
Fax 020 7531 8607
Email bountybooksinfo-bp@bountybooks.co.uk

Managing Director *Laura Bamford* Bargain and promotional books. New, repackaged and reissued titles.

Royalties paid twice-yearly/annually, according to contract in all divisions.

Oldcastle Books Ltd
18 Coleswood Road, Harpenden, Hertfordshire AL5 1EQ
☎01582 761264   Fax 01582 712244
Email info@noexit.co.uk
Website www.noexit.co.uk
Managing Director *Ion S. Mills*

FOUNDED 1985. *Publishes* crime fiction and gambling non-fiction. 20 titles in 1999. *No unsolicited mss*; synopses and ideas for books within the two areas of interest welcome.
   IMPRINTS **No Exit Press** TITLES *Burglar In the Rye* Lawrence Block; *Mr Blue* Eddie Bunker; **Oldcastle Books** TITLES *Little Book of Poker* David Spanier.
   Royalties paid twice-yearly.

Oldie Publications
45/46 Poland Street, London W1V 4AU
☎020 7734 2225   Fax 020 7734 2226
Website www.theoldie.co.uk
Chairman *Richard Ingrams*

FOUNDED in 1992. Book publishing arm of *The Oldie* magazine. *Publishes* compilations from the magazine, including cartoon books. TITLES *I Once Met; Dictionary For Our Time; The Fourth Oldie Annual; Jennifer's Diary: By One Fat Lady* Jennifer Paterson. No unsolicited mss; synopses and ideas (with return postage) welcome.

OM Publishing
See **Paternoster Publishing**

Michael O'Mara Books Ltd
9 Lion Yard, Tremadoc Road, London SW4 7NQ
☎020 7720 8643   Fax 020 7627 8953
Email <firstname.lastname>@
   michaelomarabooks.com

Chairman *Michael O'Mara*
Managing Director *Lesley O'Mara*
Approx. Annual Turnover £5 million

FOUNDED 1985. Independent publisher. *Publishes* general non-fiction, royalty, history, humour, anthologies and reference. TITLES *Diana: Her True Story* Andrew Morton; *The Seven Wonders of the World* John Romer; *I Don't Believe It!* Richard Wilson. Unsolicited mss, synopses and ideas for books welcome.
   Royalties paid twice-yearly.

Authors' Rating From Diana to Monica via Morton. The route to riches may look simple enough but plenty of other publishers have lost their way. The list is building with fun titles ideal for the gift market.

Omnibus Press
Book Sales/Music Sales Ltd, 8–9 Frith Street, London W1V 5TZ
☎020 7434 0066   Fax 020 7734 2246
Email chris.charlesworth@musicsales.co.uk
Editorial Head *Chris Charlesworth*

FOUNDED 1971. Independent publisher of music books, rock and pop biographies, song sheets, educational tutors, cassettes, videos and software. IMPRINTS **Amsco**; **Bobcat**; **Oak**; **Omnibus**; **Wise Publications**. Unsolicited mss, synopses and ideas for books welcome.
   Royalties paid twice-yearly.

Oneworld Publications
185 Banbury Road, Oxford OX2 7AR
☎01865 310597   Fax 01865 310598
Email oneworld@cix.co.uk
Website www.oneworld-publications.com
Editorial Director *Juliet Mabey*

FOUNDED 1986. Distributed worldwide by **Penguin Books**. *Publishes* adult non-fiction across a range of subjects from world religions and social issues to psychology and philosophy. 30 titles in 1999. A series on world religions was launched in 1994 with authors such as Geoffrey Parrinder, Keith Ward, Klaus Klostermaier and John Hicks. A series of concise encyclopedias has been launched on world religions, a new series of short histories of countries is planned for 2000 and a new series on philosophy is planned for 2001. Lead TITLE for 1999: *The Fifth Dimension* John Hicks. No unsolicited mss; synopses and ideas welcome, but should be accompanied by s.a.e. for return of material and/or notification of receipt. No autobiographies, fiction, poetry or children's.
   Royalties paid annually.

Onlywomen Press Ltd

40 St Lawrence Terrace, London W10 5ST
☎020 8354 0796   Fax 020 8960 2817
Email onlywomen_press@compuserve.com
Website www.onlywomenpress.com
Editorial Director *Lilian Mohin*
FOUNDED 1974. *Publishes* feminist and lesbian
books only: literary fiction, genre fiction
(crime, sci-fi, romance), non-fiction (feminist
theory, literary criticism) and poetry. Up to 6
titles a year. Unsolicited mss, synopses and
ideas welcome. Submissions should be accompanied by s.a.e. for response and/or return of
material as well as a covering letter 'identifying
the author and suggesting reasons to consider
publishing her work'.

OPC

See **Ian Allan Publishing Ltd**

Open Gate Press (incorporating Centaur Press 1954)

51 Achilles Road, London NW6 1DZ
☎020 7431 4391   Fax 020 7431 5129
Email books@opengatepress.co.uk
Managing Directors *Jeannie Cohen, Elisabeth
Petersdorff*
FOUNDED in 1989 to provide a forum for psychoanalytic social and cultural studies. *Publishes*
psychoanalysis, philosophy, social sciences,
politics, literature, religion, animal rights, environment. SERIES *Psychoanalysis and Society.*
Also publishes a journal of psychoanalytic social
studies, *New Analysis.* IMPRINTS **Open Gate
Press**; **Centaur Press**; **Linden Press**. Since
the acquisition of Centaur Press, Open Gate
Press is continuing its work, in particular the
Kinship Library – a series on the philosophy,
politics and application of humane education,
with special focus on the subject of animal
rights and its relevance to the human condition. Synopses and ideas for books and articles
welcome.
Royalties paid twice-yearly.

Open University Press

Celtic Court, 22 Ballmoor, Buckingham,
Buckinghamshire MK18 1XW
☎01280 823388   Fax 01280 823233
Email enquiries@openup.co.uk
Website www.openup.co.uk
Managing Director *John Skelton*
Approx. Annual Turnover £3 million
FOUNDED 1977 as an imprint independent of the
Open University's course materials. *Publishes*
academic and professional books in the fields
of education, management, sociology, health
studies, politics, psychology, women's studies.
No economics or anthropology. Not interested
in anything outside the social sciences. About
100 titles a year. No unsolicited mss; enquiries/
proposals only.
Royalties paid annually.

Orbit

See **Little, Brown & Co. (UK)**

Orchard Books

See **The Watts Publishing Group Ltd**

The Orion Publishing Group Limited

Orion House, 5 Upper St Martin's Lane,
London WC2H 9EA
☎020 7240 3444   Fax 020 7240 4822
Chairman *Jean-Louis Lisimachio*
Chief Executive *Anthony Cheetham*
Managing Director *Peter Roche*
Approx. Annual Turnover £60 million
FOUNDED 1992 by Anthony Cheetham,
Rosemary Cheetham and Peter Roche.
Incorporates Weidenfeld & Nicolson, JM Dent
and Chapmans Publishers. Acquired **Cassell** in
1998 (see entry).

DIVISIONS
Orion Managing Director *Malcolm Edwards*
IMPRINTS **Orion** General Publishing Director
Jane Wood Hardcover fiction/non-fiction;
Orion Business *Martin Liu* Business books;
Orion Media Publishing Director *Trevor
Dolby* Film and TV; **Orion Children's**
Managing Director *Judith Elliott* Children's
fiction/non-fiction.
   Weidenfeld & Nicolson Managing Direc-
tor *Ion Trewin* IMPRINTS **Weidenfeld General**
Publishing Director *Rebecca Wilson* General
non-fiction, biography and autobiography;
Phoenix House Publishing Director *Maggie
McKernan* Literary fiction; **Weidenfeld
Illustrated** Publisher *Michael Dover* Illustrated
non-fiction.
   Mass Market IMPRINTS **Orion**; **Phoenix**;
Phoenix Illustrated; **Everyman**.

Authors' Rating The Phoenix imprint is
expanding its history list with expectations of
300 new titles over two years. Having made
several acquisitions, Cassell being the latest, the
foundations are there for further growth across
the whole of Orion.

Osprey Publishing Ltd

Elms Court, Chapel Way, Botley, Oxford
OX2 9LP
☎01865 727022   Fax 01865 727017/727019
Email osprey@ospreypublishing.com
Website www.ospreypublishing.com
Managing Director *Jonathan Parker*
Editor, Military *Lee Johnson*
Editor, History *Jane Penrose*
Editor, Aviation *Tony Holmes*

Publishes Illustrated history, military history and aviation from around the world. FOUNDED 1969, Osprey became independent from **Reed Elsevier** in February 1998. 98 titles in 1999.
MILITARY SERIES *Order of Battle; Men-at-Arms; Elite Campaign; New Vanguard; Warrior.* HISTORY SERIES *Landmarks in History.* AVIATION SERIES *Aircraft of the Aces; Combat Aircraft; Aviation Pioneers; Aviation Elites.* No unsolicited mss; synopses and ideas welcome.
Royalties paid twice-yearly.

Peter Owen Ltd

73 Kenway Road, London SW5 0RE
☎020 7373 5628/7370 6093
Fax 020 7373 6760
Email admin@peterowen.u-net.com
Chairman *Peter Owen*
Editorial Director *Antonia Owen*

FOUNDED 1951. *Publishes* biography, general non-fiction, English-language literary fiction and translations, sociology. 'No genre or children's fiction; the company only rarely takes on first novels.' AUTHORS Jane Bowles, Paul Bowles, Shusaku Endo, Anna Kavan, Jean Giono, Anaïs Nin, Jeremy Reed, Peter Vansittart. 35–40 titles a year. Unsolicited synopses welcome for non-fiction material; mss should be preceded by a descriptive letter and synopsis with s.a.e.
Royalties paid twice-yearly. *Overseas associates* worldwide.

Authors' Rating Peter Owen has been described as 'a publisher of the old and idiosyncratic school'. He has seven Nobel prize-winners on his list.

Oxford University Press

Great Clarendon Street, Oxford OX2 6DP
☎01865 556767   Fax 01865 556646
Email enquiry@oup.co.uk
Website www.oup.co.uk
Chief Executive *Henry Reece*
Approx. Annual Turnover £300 million

A department of the university, OUP grew from the university's printing works and devel-

oped into a major publishing business in the 19th century. *Publishes* academic books in all categories: student texts, scholarly journals, schoolbooks, ELT material, dictionaries, reference, music, bibles, electronic publishing, as well as paperbacks, general non-fiction and children's books. Around 3000 titles a year.

DIVISIONS
Academic *I. S. Asquith* Academic and college titles in all disciplines; dictionaries and non-lexical reference, trade books, journals and electronic publishing. TITLES *Concise Oxford Dictionary*; *Birds of the Western Palearctic*; **Educational** *F. E. Clarke* National Curriculum courses and children's literature; **ELT** *P. R. Mothersole* ELT courses and dictionaries. OUP welcomes first-class academic material in the form of proposals or accepted theses.
Royalties paid twice-yearly. *Overseas subsidiaries* Sister company in USA; also branches in Australia, Canada, East Africa, Hong Kong, India, Japan, New Zealand, Pakistan, Singapore, South Africa. Offices in Argentina, Brazil, France, Germany, Greece, Italy, Mexico, Spain, Taiwan, Thailand, Turkey, Uruguay. Joint companies in Malaysia, Nigeria and Germany.

Authors' Rating Subject to the vagaries of overseas markets, OUP has undertaken a 'rigorous management of costs' which includes the closure of Oxford Interactive Learning (a distance learning unit) and a decision to stop publishing contemporary poetry, a list which has gone to Carcanet. Academic and education publishing continues to thrive but the advance of the Net suggests more changes are on the way.

Palm Tree Press
See **Kevin Mayhew Publishers**

G. J. Palmer & Sons Ltd
See **Hymns Ancient & Modern Ltd**

Pan
See **Macmillan Publishers Ltd**

Papermac
See **Macmillan Publishers Ltd**

Paragon Press

1A Tower Square, Leeds, West Yorkshire
LS1 4HZ
☎0113 2095771   Fax 0113 2095600
Email info@ParagonPress.org.uk
Website www.ParagonPress.org.uk
Managing Editor *Reggie Sharp*

FOUNDED 1998. *Publishes* fiction and non-fiction

and books for children. DIVISIONS **Paragon Children** *The Wizard's Spell* series of books for little children. All written in-house but suggestions for other titles welcome. **Paragon Education** Ideas always welcome. TITLES *Teach Your Child Maths; Planning for Effective Teaching.* Initial approach by e-mail or in writing. **Paragon** Popular football/mystery novels of Steve Bruce: *Strike! Sweeper! Defender!* AUTHORS Alex Crawford, Hope Dubé, James Lansbury. SERIES **Paragon Summaries** Short factual series for higher and further education. TITLES *Auguste Comte; Scott Fitzgerald; Sigmund Freud*; **Paragon Lists** Books of lists and information both general and academic. All written in-house. No unsolicited mss; check Website or write with large s.a.e. for submission guidelines.

Authors' Rating Liable to ask authors to contribute towards cost of publication.

Paragon Softcover Large Print
See **Chivers Press Ltd**

Partridge Press
See **Transworld Publishers**

Paternoster Publishing
PO Box 300, Kingstown Broadway, Carlisle, Cumbria CA3 0QS
☎01228 512512   Fax 01228 593388
Publishing Director *Mark Finnie*
Editorial Coordinator *Nancy Lush*
Approx. Annual Turnover £2 million
A division of STL Ltd. IMPRINTS: **The Paternoster Press** FOUNDED 1936. *Publishes* religion and learned/church/life-related journals. Over 60 titles a year. TITLES *Complete Short Works of J. I. Packer, All's Well* R. T. Kendall.

OM Publishing FOUNDED 1966. *Publishes* Christian books on evangelism, discipleship and mission. About 30 titles a year. TITLES *Operation World* Patrick Johnstone; *You Can Change the World* Jill Johnstone; and many titles by Elisabeth Elliot and A. W. Tozer. Unsolicited mss, synopses and ideas for books welcome.
Royalties paid twice-yearly.

Pathways
See **How To Books Ltd**

Pavilion Books Ltd
London House, Great Eastern Wharf, Parkgate Road, London SW11 4NQ
☎020 7350 1230   Fax 020 7350 1261
Email <firstname.surname>@pavilionbooks.co.uk

Website www.pavilionbooks.co.uk
Publisher/Managing Director *Colin Webb*
Publishing Director, Children's Books *Pamela Webb*
Publishing Director, Adult Books *Vivien James*
Acquired by **C&B Publishing plc** in 1997. *Publishes* illustrated books in children's, biography, cookery, gardening, humour, art sport and travel. Unsolicited mss not welcome. Ideas and synopses for non-fiction titles and children's fiction considered.
Royalties paid twice-yearly

Payback Press
See **Canongate Books Ltd**

Pearson Education
Edinburgh gate, Harlow, Essex CM20 2JE
☎01279 623623   Fax 01279 431059
Website www.pearsoned-ema.com
Contracts & Copyrights Department Manager *Brenda Gvozdanovic*
FOUNDED in 1998 following the merger of Addison Wesley Longman, Financial Times Management and **Simon & Schuster**'s educational list. *Publishes* a range of curriculum subjects, including English language teaching for students at primary and secondary school level, college and university, as well as for professionals. Address all unsolicited mss to the Manager, Contracts and Copyrights Department.
Royalties paid twice-yearly. *Overseas associates* worldwide.

Authors' Rating Consolidating its position as the world's leading educational publisher, Pearson has come to a deal with America OnLine, making it AOL's preferred supplier of educational content. It had to happen, of course, but increasing attention to the Net has not, as yet, dampened Pearson enthusiasm for hard print publishing.

Pen & Sword Books Ltd
47 Church Street, Barnsley, South Yorkshire S70 2AS
☎01226 734734   Fax 01226 734438
Website www.pen-and-sword.co.uk
Chairman *Sir Nicholas Hewitt*
Chief Executive *Charles Hewitt*
One of the leading military history publishers in the UK. *Publishes* non-fiction only, specialising in naval and aviation history, WW1, WW2, Napoleonic, autobiography and biography. Also publishes *Battleground* series for battlefield

tourists. About 100 titles a year. IMPRINTS **Leo Cooper**; **Wharncliffe Publishing** (see entry). Unsolicited synopses and ideas welcome; no unsolicited mss.

Royalties paid twice-yearly. *Associated company* **Wharncliffe Publishing**.

Penguin UK

27 Wrights Lane, London W8 5TZ
☎020 7416 3000   Fax 020 7416 3099
Website www.penguin.co.uk

President *David Wan*
CEO (UK) *Anthony Forbes Watson*
Approx. Annual Turnover £99.1 million

Owned by Pearson plc. The world's best-known book brand and for more than 60 years a leading publisher whose adult and children's lists include fiction, non-fiction, poetry, drama, classics, reference and special interest areas. Reprints and new work.

DIVISIONS

Penguin General Books Managing Director *Helen Fraser* Adult fiction and non-fiction is published in hardback under Michael Joseph, Viking and Hamish Hamilton imprints. Paperbacks come under the Penguin imprint. IMPRINTS **Viking/Penguin** Publisher *Juliet Annan* Publishing Director *Tony Lacey*; **Hamish Hamilton** Publisher *Simon Prosser*; **Michael Joseph/Penguin** Publishing Director *Tom Weldon* Unsolicited mss discouraged.
   Penguin Press Managing Director *Andrew Rosenheim* Publishing Director *Stuart Proffitt* Academic adult non-fiction, reference, specialist and classics. IMPRINTS **Allen Lane**; **Arkana** Mind, body and spirit; **Buildings of England**; **Classics**; **Penguin Books** Approach in writing only.
   Frederick Warne Publisher *Sally Floyer* Classic children's publishing and merchandising including *Beatrix Potter™*; *Flower Fairies*; *Orlando*. **Ventura** Publisher *Sally Floyer* Producer and packager of *Spot* titles by Eric Hill.
   Ladybird Books Managing Director *Michael Herridge* FOUNDED in the 1860s. Children's home learning consumer books for the mass market internationally, with an emphasis on books for babies, toddlers, pre-school and under-8s. About 200 titles a year. IMPRINT **Ladybird Disney**. Also Ladybird audio cassette/book series (see entry under **Audio Books**).
   Penguin Children's Books Managing Director *Philippa Milnes-Smith* Hardback IMPRINTS **Hamish Hamilton Children's**; **Viking Children's**; Paperback IMPRINT **Puffin** Publishers *Penny Morris* (fiction, poetry and picture

books), *Richard Scrivener* (media and popular non-fiction). Leading children's paperback list, publishing in virtually all fields, including fiction, non-fiction, poetry, picture books, media-related titles. No unsolicited mss; synopses and ideas welcome.
   Penguin Audiobooks (see entry under **Audio Books**).
Royalties paid twice-yearly. *Overseas associates* worldwide.

Authors' Rating Newcomers are sometimes frustrated by Penguin giving so much attention to its backlist. But the promising authors who do get lucky benefit by association with the many great names on the list and a world recognised media brand. In any event, the backlist has been given another boost with a redesign and relaunch of Classic Biography and History titles. Overall, Penguin intends concentrating on 'books we believe have a real shot at becoming successful'. Whether this means more or less risk taking remains to be seen. Reading on-line is much favoured. Penguin UK is one of four European publishers that have teamed up with Microsoft to publish a range of books in electronic format.

Peony Press

See **Anness Publishing Ltd**

Pergamon Press

See **Elsevier Science Ltd**

Persephone Books

28 Great Sutton Street, London EC1V 0DS
☎020 7253 5454   Fax 020 7253 5656
Email sales@persephonebooks.co.uk
Website www.persephonebooks.co.uk

Managing Director *Nicola Beauman*

FOUNDED 1999. *Publishes* reprint fiction and non-fiction, mostly 'by women, for women and about women'. 12 titles a year. TITLES *William – An Englishman* Cicely Hamilton; *Fidelity* Susan Glaspell; *Good Evening, Mrs Craven* Mollie Downes; *Consequences* E. M. Delafield. No unsolicited material.
   Royalties paid twice-yearly

Petroc Press

See **Librapharm Ltd**

Phaidon Press Limited

Regent's Wharf, All Saints Street, London N1 9PA
☎020 7843 1000   Fax 020 7843 1010
Email <name>@phaidon.com

Chairman/Publisher *Richard Schlagman*
Managing Director *Andrew Price*
Deputy Publisher *Amanda Renshaw*
Editorial Heads *Karen Stein* (Architecture and Design), *Pat Barylski* (Art and Ideas Series), *Gilda Williams* (Contemporary Art), *Chris Boot* (Photography)
Approx. Annual Turnover £16 million

Publishes quality books on the visual arts, including fine art, art history, architecture, design, photography, decorative arts, music and performing arts. Recently started producing videos. About 100 titles a year. Unsolicited mss welcome but 'only a small amount of unsolicited material gets published'.
Royalties paid twice-yearly.

Authors' Rating Secure in the knowledge that Gombrich's classic megaseller *The Story of Art* has still a long way to run (so far it has sold over six million copies in 23 languages), Phaidon continues on expansionist course. But there were a couple of jolts last year. The company settled out of court with the Matisse estate who claimed copyright infringement and, on a separate issue, with one of its authors who had criticised in print certain aspects of his book's publication.

Philip's
See **Octopus Publishing Group**

Phillimore & Co. Ltd
Shopwyke Manor Barn, Chichester, West Sussex PO20 6BG
☎01243 787636   Fax 01243 787639
Email bookshop@phillimore.co.uk
Website www.phillimore.co.uk
Chairman *Philip Harris*
Managing Director *Noel Osborne*
Approx. Annual Turnover £1 million

FOUNDED in 1897 by W. P. W. Phillimore, Victorian campaigner for local archive conservation in Chancery Lane, London. Became the country's leading publisher of historical source material and local histories. Somewhat dormant in the 1960s, it was revived by Philip Harris in 1968. *Publishes* British local and family history, including histories of institutions, buildings, villages, towns and counties, plus guides to research and writing in these fields. About 70 titles a year. No unsolicited mss; synopses/ideas welcome for local or family histories.
IMPRINT **Phillimore** *Noel Osborne* TITLES *Domesday Book; A History of Essex; Carlisle; The Haberdashers' Company; Channel Island Churches; Bolton Past; Warwickshire Country Houses.*
Royalties paid annually.

Phoenix/Phoenix House/ Phoenix Illustrated
See **The Orion Publishing Group Ltd**

Piatkus Books
5 Windmill Street, London W1P 1HF
☎020 7631 0710   Fax 020 7436 7137
Email info@piatkus.co.uk
Website www.piatkus.co.uk
Managing Director *Judy Piatkus*
Approx. Annual Turnover £5.5 million

FOUNDED 1979 by Judy Piatkus. The company is customer-led and is committed to publishing fiction, both commercial and literary, and non-fiction. *Specialises* in publishing books and authors 'who we like to build for long-term success as well as short-term!' *Publishes* fiction, biography and autobiography, health, Mind, Body and Spirit, popular psychology, self-help, history, science, business and management, cookery 'and other books that tempt us'. In 1996 launched a list of mass-market non-fiction and fiction titles. About 175 titles a year (70 of which are fiction). DIVISIONS **Non-fiction** *Gill Bailey* TITLES *Optimum Nutrition Bible* Patrick Holford; *Clear Your Clutter with Feng Shui* Karen Kingston. **Fiction** *Judy Piatkus* TITLES *Hot Property* Zoë Barnes; *Big Trouble* Dave Barry; *River's End* Nora Roberts; *Three Women* Marge Piercy. Piatkus are expanding their range of books and welcome synopses and first three chapters.
Royalties paid twice-yearly.

Authors' Rating Achieving a strong position in the paperback market is the latest sign that Piatkus is heading for the big time. Authors enjoy the excitement of belonging to a publishing team with a real sense of purpose.

Picador
See **Macmillan Publishers Ltd**

Piccadilly Press
5 Castle Road, London NW1 8PR
☎020 7267 4492   Fax 020 7267 4493
Email books@piccadillypress.co.uk
Publisher/Managing Director *Brenda Gardner*
Approx. Annual Turnover £800,000

FOUNDED 1983. Independent publisher of children's and parental books. 30 titles in 1999. Welcomes approaches from authors 'but we would like them to know the sort of books we do. We will send a catalogue (please enclose s.a.e.)'. No adult or cartoon-type material.
Royalties paid twice-yearly.

Pictorial Presentations
See **Souvenir Press Ltd**

Picture Lions
See **HarperCollins Publishers Ltd**

Pimlico
See **Random House Group Ltd**

Pinter
See **Continuum International Publishing Group Ltd**

Pitkin Unichrome
Healey House, Dene Road, Andover, Hampshire SP10 2AA
☎01264 409200   Fax 01264 334110
Email guides@pitkin-unichrome.com
Website www.britguides.com
Managing Director *Heather Hook*

Pitkin Guides, FOUNDED in 1947, was part of Reed Books from 1988 to March 1998 when it merged with Unichrome. *Publishes* illustrated souvenir guides.

Plenum Publishers/Plenum Press
See **Kluwer Academic/Plenum Publishers**

Pluto Press Ltd
345 Archway Road, London N6 5AA
☎020 8348 2724   Fax 020 8348 9133
Managing Director *Roger Van Zwanenberg*
Publishing Director *Anne Beech*

FOUNDED 1970. Has developed a reputation for innovatory publishing in the field of non-fiction. *Publishes* academic and scholarly books across a range of subjects including cultural studies, politics and world affairs, social sciences and socialist, feminist and Marxist books. About 50–60 titles a year. Synopses and ideas welcome if accompanied by return postage.

Point
See **Scholastic Ltd**

The Policy Press
University of Bristol, 34 Tyndall's Park Road, Bristol BS8 1PY
☎0117 9546800   Fax 0117 9737308
Managing Director *Alison Shaw*
Approx. Annual Turnover £250,000

The Policy Press is a specialist publisher of policy studies. Material published, in the form of books, reports, practice guides and journals, is taken from research findings and provides critical discussion of policy initiatives and their impact, and also recommendations for policy change. 45–50 titles per year. No unsolicited mss; brief synopses and ideas welcome.

Politico's Publishing
8 Artillery Row, London SW1P 1RZ
☎020 7931 0090   Fax 020 7828 8111
Email publishing@politicos.co.uk
Website www.politicos.co.uk
Chairman *John Simmons*
Managing Director *Iain Dale*
Approx. Annual Turnover £250,000

FOUNDED 1998. Sister company to Politico's Bookstore in Westminster. *Publishes* political books. 25 titles in 1999. TITLES *In My Own Time* Jeremy Thorpe; *Farewell My Lords* Austin Mitchell; *Politico's Guide to Parliament* Susan Child. Unsolicited mss, synopses and ideas welcome; telephone in the first instance.
Royalties paid annually.

Polity Press
65 Bridge Street, Cambridge CB2 1UR
☎01223 324315   Fax 01223 461385

FOUNDED 1984. All books are published in association with **Blackwell Publishers**. *Publishes* archaeology and anthropology, criminology, economics, feminism, general interest, history, human geography, literature, media and cultural studies, medicine and society, philosophy, politics, psychology, religion and theology, social and political theory, sociology. Unsolicited synopses and ideas for books welcome.
Royalties paid annually.

Polygon/Polygon@Edinburgh
See **Edinburgh University Press**

Pont Books
See **Gomer Press**

Pop Universal
See **Souvenir Press Ltd**

Portland Press Ltd
59 Portland Place, London W1N 3AJ
☎020 7580 5530   Fax 020 7323 1136
Email editorial@portlandpress.com
Website www.portlandpress.com
Chairman *Professor A. J. Turner*
Managing Director *G. D. Jones*
Editorial Director *Rhonda Oliver*
Approx. Annual Turnover £2.5 million

FOUNDED 1990 to expand the publishing activities of the Biochemical Society (1911). *Publishes* biochemisty and medicine for graduate, postgraduate and research students. Expanding the list to include schools and general readership. 5 titles in 1999. TITLES *A Leaf in Time; Mitochondria and Cell Death; Lifelong Learning Policy and Research.* Unsolicited mss, synopses and ideas welcome. No fiction.

Royalties paid twice-yearly.

T. & A. D. Poyser
See **Harcourt Brace and Company Limited**

Princeton University Press
See **University Presses of California, Columbia & Princeton Ltd**

Prion Books Ltd
Imperial Works, Perren Street, London NW5 3ED
☎020 7482 4248   Fax 020 7482 4203
Managing Director *Barry Winkleman*
Editor *Andrew Goodfellow*

Formerly a packaging operation but began publishing under the Prion imprint in 1987. *Publishes* non-fiction: humour, popular culture, historical and literary reprints, beauty, food and drink, sex, psychology and health. About 40 titles a year. Unsolicited mss, synopses and ideas welcome only with s.a.e.

Royalties paid twice-yearly.

Profile Books
58A Hatton Gardens, London EC1N 8LX
☎020 7404 3001   Fax 020 7404 3003
Email info@profilebooks.co.uk
Website www.profilebooks.co.uk
Managing Director *Andrew Franklin*
Approx. Annual Turnover £1.5 million
FOUNDED 1996. *Publishes* serious non-fiction including current affairs, history, politics, psychology, cultural criticism, business and management. Winner of the **Sunday Times Small Publisher of the Year Award** 1999/2000.
IMPRINTS **Profile Books** *Andrew Franklin*; **Economist Books** *Stephen Brough.* No unsolicited mss.

Royalties paid twice-yearly.

Authors' Rating Living up to its credit as *Sunday Times* Small Publisher of the Year, Profile has achieved impressive growth while maintaining author-friendly relations.

Prowler Books/Zipper Books
3 Broadbent Close, 20 Highgate High Street, London N6 5GG
☎020 8340 7711   Fax 020 8347 7667
Website www.prowler.co.uk

Contact *Nick Hilton*
Part of the Millivres – Prowler Group. *Publishes* gay male erotica. TITLES *Overload* ed. David Laurents; *The Initiation* David Keane; *Gladiator School* Ben Elliott. Looking for mss of 60–80,000 words. Rights bought for single printing, non-royalty deals.

Publishing House
Trinity Place, Barnstaple, Devon EX32 9HJ
☎01271 328892   Fax 01271 328768
Email publishinghouse@vernoncoleman.com
Website www.vernoncoleman.com
Managing Director *Vernon Coleman*
Editorial Head *Sue Ward*
Approx. Annual Turnover £500,000
FOUNDED 1989. Self-publisher of fiction, health, humour, animals, politics. TITLES *Bodypower; Village Cricket Tour; How to Publish Your Own Book* all by Vernon Coleman. No submissions.

Puffin
See **Penguin UK**

Pulp Books
PO Box 12171, London N19 3HB
☎020 7561 1387
Website www.pulpfact.demon.co.uk

Specialises in new contemporary British fiction. Currently producing 20–25 titles a year and expanding. TITLES *Go* Simon Lewis; *Serious Time* Joe Ambrose; *Do What You Want* Chris Savage King; *Random Factor* and *Technopagan* (both short fiction collections) under the **Pulp Faction** imprint. Only previously unpublished work considered.

Royalties paid annually.

Pushkin Press Ltd
22 Park Walk, London SW10 0AQ
☎020 7349 9367   Fax 020 7352 0098
Email pushkinpressltd@compuserve.com
Chairman *Melissa Ulfane*
Editorial Head *Oliver Berggruen*
Approx. Annual Turnover £500,000
Publishes novels, essays and poetry drawn from the best of classic and contemporary European literature. Welcomes unsolicited mss, synopses and ideas for books which come within these areas. No popular/commercial fiction/non-fiction.

Royalties paid twice-yearly.

Putnam Aeronautical Books
See **Brassey's**

Quadrille Publishing Ltd

Alhambra House, 27–31 Charing Cross Road, London WC2H 0LS
☎020 7839 7117   Fax 020 7839 7118

Chairman *Sue Thomson*
Managing Director *Alison Cathie*
Publishing Director *Anne Furniss*

FOUNDED in 1994 by four ex-directors of Conran Octopus, with a view to producing a small list of top-quality illustrated books. *Publishes* non-fiction, including craft, cookery, gardening, interior design and decoration, health. 17 titles in 2000. TITLES *A Chef for All Seasons* Gordon Ramsay; *RHS New Classic Gardens*; *Space Within: Reshape Your Home for Contemporary Living* Jane Withers. No unsolicited mss; synopses and ideas welcome. No fiction or children's books.
Royalties paid twice-yearly.

Quantum

See **W. Foulsham & Co.**

Quartet Books

27 Goodge Street, London W1P 2LD
☎020 7636 3992   Fax 020 7637 1866

Chairman *Naim Attallah*
Managing Director *Jeremy Beale*
Publishing Director *Stella Kane*
Approx. Annual Turnover £1 million

FOUNDED 1972. Independent publisher. *Publishes* contemporary literary fiction including translations, popular culture, biography, music, history, politics and some photographic books. Unsolicited mss with return postage welcome; no poetry, romance or science fiction.
Royalties paid twice-yearly.

Queen Anne Press

See **Lennard Associates Ltd**

Quiller Press

46 Lillie Road, London SW6 1TN
☎020 7499 6529   Fax 020 7381 8941

Managing/Editorial Director
Jeremy Greenwood

Specialises in sponsored books and publications sold through non-book trade channels as well as bookshops. *Publishes* architecture, biography, business and industry, children's, collecting, cookery, DIY, gardening, guidebooks, humour, reference, sports, travel, wine and spirits. About 10 titles a year. TITLES *Willis Faber Book of Tennis and Rackets* Lord Aberdare; *Mews Style* Sebastian Deckker; *In Vanity Fair* Roy Matthews and Peter Mellini. Most ideas originate in-house. Unsolici-

ted mss not welcome unless the author sees some potential for sponsorship or guaranteed sales.
Royalties paid twice-yearly.

Radcliffe Medical Press Ltd

18 Marcham Road, Abingdon, Oxfordshire OX14 1AA
☎01235 528820   Fax 01235 528830
Email contact.us@radcliffemed.com
Website www.radcliffe-oxford.com

Managing Director *Andrew Bax*
Editorial Director *Gillian Nineham*
Commissioning Editor *Liz Walker*
Approx. Annual Turnover £1.5 million

FOUNDED 1987. Medical publisher which began by specialising in books for general practice and health service management. *Publishes* health policy books, clinical, management, training materials and CD-ROMs. 80 titles in 1999. Unsolicited mss, synopses and ideas welcome. No non-medical or medical books aimed at lay audience.
Royalties paid twice-yearly.

The Ramsay Head Press

9 Glenisla Gardens, Edinburgh EH9 2HR
☎0131 662 1915   Fax 0131 662 1915
Email conrad.wilson@genie.co.uk

Managing Directors *Conrad Wilson,*
Mrs Christine Wilson

FOUNDED 1968 by Norman Wilson OBE. A small independent family publisher. *Publishes* biography, cookery, Scottish fiction and non-fiction, plus the bi-annual literary magazine *InScotland*. About 3–4 titles a year. TITLES *When It Works It Feels Like Play* Tessa Ransford; *The Happy Land* Howard Denton and Jim C. Wilson. Synopses and ideas for books of Scottish interest welcome.
Royalties paid twice-yearly.

The Random House Group Ltd

Random House, 20 Vauxhall Bridge Road, London SW1V 2SA
☎020 7840 8400   Fax 020 7233 6058
Email enquiries@randomhouse.co.uk
Website www.randomhouse.co.uk

Chief Executive/Chairman *Gail Rebuck*
Deputy Chairman *Simon Master*
Managing Director *Ian Hudson*

Random's increasing focus on trade publishing, both here and in the US, has been well rewarded, with sales continuing to grow over the last year. Random House Group Ltd is the parent company of three separate publishing divisions and of **Transworld** (see entry). The three divisions are: General Books, the Group's largest publishing division; Children's Books, and Ebury Press Special Books. General Books is divided into two operating groups, allowing hardcover editors to see their books through to publication in paperback. The literary imprints Jonathan Cape, Secker & Warburg, Yellow Jersey Press and Chatto & Windus work side by side with paperback imprints Vintage and Pimlico to form one group; trade imprints Century, William Heinemann and Hutchinson go hand-in-hand with Arrow to form the other group.

IMPRINTS
Jonathan Cape Ltd ☎020 7840 8576 Fax 020 7233 6117 Publishing Director *Dan Franklin* Biography and memoirs, current affairs, fiction, history, photography, poetry, politics and travel. IMPRINT **Yellow Jersey**.

Secker & Warburg ☎020 7840 8649 Fax 020 7233 6117 Editorial Director *Geoff Mulligan* Principally literary fiction with some non-fiction.

Chatto & Windus Ltd ☎020 7840 8522 Fax 020 7233 6117 Publishing Director *Alison Samuel* Art, belles-lettres, biography and memoirs, current affairs, essays, poetry, fiction, history, politics, philosophy, translations and travel.

Century (including **Business Books**) ☎020 7840 8555 Fax 020 7233 6127 Publisher *Kate Parkin*, Publishing Director Non-fiction *Mark Booth* General fiction and non-fiction, plus business management, advertising, communication, marketing, selling, investment and financial titles.

William Heinemann ☎020 7840 8400 Fax 020 7233 6127 Publishing Director Fiction *Lynne Drew*, Publishing Director Non-fiction *Ravi Mirchandani* General non-fiction and fiction, especially history, biography, science, crime, thrillers and women's fiction.

Hutchinson ☎020 7840 8564 Fax 020 7233 7870 Publishing Director *Sue Freestone* General fiction and non-fiction including notably belles-lettres, current affairs, politics, travel and history.

Arrow ☎020 7840 8516 Fax 020 7233 6127 Publishing Director *Andy McKillop* Mass-market paperback fiction and non-fiction.

Pimlico ☎020 7840 8630 Fax 020 7233 6117 Publishing Director *Will Sulkin* Large-format quality paperbacks in the fields of history, biography, popular culture and literature.

Vintage ☎020 7840 8531 Fax 020 7233 6127 Publisher *Caroline Michel* Quality paperback fiction and non-fiction. Vintage was founded in 1990 and has been described as one of the 'greatest literary success stories in recent British publishing'.

Children's Books ☎020 7840 8400 Fax 020 7233 6058 Managing Director *Gill Evans* IMPRINTS **Hutchinson** Publishing Director *Caroline Roberts*; **Jonathan Cape** Publishing Director *Tom Maschler*; **Bodley Head** Publishing Director *Anne McNeil*; **Red Fox** and **Tellastory** Publishing Director *Pilar Jenkins*.

Ebury Press Special Books ☎020 7840 8400 Fax 020 7840 8406 Managing Director *Amelia Thorpe*, Publisher *Fiona MacIntyre*, Associate Publisher *Julian Shuckburgh* IMPRINTS **Ebury Press**; **Vermilion**; **Rider**; **Barrie & Jenkins**; **Condé Nast Books**; **Fodor's**. Art, antiques, biography, Buddhism, cookery, gardening, health and beauty, homes and interiors, personal development, spirituality, travel and guides, sport, TV tie-ins. About 150 titles a year. Unsolicited mss, synopses and ideas for books welcome.

Royalties paid twice-yearly for the most part.

Authors' Rating With Random House and Transworld in its portfolio, not to mention Book Club Associates, Germany-based Bertelsmann is a leading force in British and American publishing. Random is seldom out of the bestseller list. On the other hand, proper attention is given to new writers who occupy nearly a third of the fiction frontlist. Newcomers who do not contact a specific editor have their synopses and manuscripts passed on to freelance readers.

Ransom Publishing Ltd

Ransom House, Unit 1, Brook Street, Watlington, Oxfordshire OX9 5PP
☎01491 613711   Fax 01491 613733
Email ransom@ransompublishing.co.uk
Website www.ransom.co.uk

Managing Director *Jenny Ertle*

FOUNDED 1995 by ex-McGraw-Hill publisher. Partnerships formed with, among others, Channel 4 and the ICL. *Publishes* educational and consumer multimedia and study packs. Over 30 CD-ROMs, most with educational support packs. TITLES include *The Little Monsters* series; *Whale of a Tale* series including maths, science, language and geography; *Tom Paint; The Castle Under Siege; The History of the Universe; The History of Life; Rivers* plus natural history CD-ROMs.

Ravette Publishing Limited

Unit 3 Tristar Centre, Star Road, Partridge Green, West Sussex RH13 8RA
☎01403 711443   Fax 01403 711554
Email ravettepub@aol.com

Chairman/Managing Director
Margaret Lamb
Approx. Annual Turnover £350,000
FOUNDED 1995. A small independent publisher producing a range of best-selling series for both adults and children, including Garfield and Disney. A new range of Peanuts titles is about to added to the list. *Publishes* children's, fiction and humour. 20 titles in 1999. Unsolicited mss, synopses and ideas welcome; approach by post.
Royalties paid twice-yearly.

Reader's Digest Association Ltd
11 Westferry Circus, Canary Wharf, London E14 4HE
☎020 7715 8000   Fax 020 7715 8181
Email gbeditorial@readersdigest.co.uk
Website www.readersdigest.co.uk
Managing Director *Andrew Lynam-Smith*
Editorial Head *Cortina Butler*

Publishes gardening, natural history, cookery, history, DIY, travel and word books. About 20 titles a year. TITLES *Family Encyclopedia of World History; Know Your Rights; Yesterday's Britain; Foods That Harm, Foods That Heal; Country Walks and Scenic Drives.*

Reaktion Books
79 Farringdon Road, London EC1M 3JU
☎020 7404 9930   Fax 020 7404 9931
Email info@reaktionbooks.co.uk
Managing Director *Michael R. Leaman*

FOUNDED in Edinburgh in 1985 and moved to its London location in 1988. *Publishes* art history, architecture, Asian studies, cultural studies, design, film, history, photography and travel. About 20 titles a year. TITLES *Written on the Body: The Tattoo in European and American History* ed. Jane Caplan; *Animal Rights: Political and Social Change in Britain since 1800* Hilda Kean; *Cool Rules* Dick Pountain and David Robins; *Vermeer's Wager: Speculations on Art History, Theory and Museums* Ivan Gaskell. No unsolicited mss; synopses and ideas welcome.
Royalties paid twice-yearly.

Reardon Publishing
56 Upper Norwood Street, Leckhampton, Cheltenham, Gloucestershire GL53 0DU
☎01242 231800
Website www.reardon.co.uk
Managing Editor *Nicholas Reardon*

FOUNDED in the mid 1970s. Family-run publishing house specialising in local interest and tourism in the Cotswold area. Member of the

Outdoor Writers Guild. *Publishes* walking and driving guides, and family history for societies. 10 titles a year. TITLES *The Cotswold Way* (video); *The Cotswold Way Map; Cotswold Walkabout; Cotswold Driveabout; The Donnington Way; The Haunted Cotswolds.* Unsolicited mss, synopses and ideas welcome with return postage only. See also **WALKfree Productions Ltd** under **Audio Books**.
Royalties paid twice-yearly.

Rebel Inc.
See **Canongate Books Ltd**

Red Fox
See **Random House Group Ltd**

William Reed Directories
Broadfield Park, Crawley, West Sussex RH11 9RT
☎01293 613400   Fax 01293 610322
Email directories@william-reed.co.uk
Website www.foodanddrink.co.uk
Editorial Manager *Ian Tandy*

William Reed Directories, a division of William Reed Publishing, was ESTABLISHED in 1990. Its portfolio includes 13 titles covering the food, drink, non-food, catering, retail and export industries. The titles are produced as directories, market research reports, exhibition catalogues and electronic publishing.

Reed Educational & Professional Publishing
Halley Court, Jordan Hill, Oxford OX2 8EJ
☎01865 311366   Fax 01865 314641
Website www.repp.co.uk
Chief Executive *John Philbin*

A member of the **Reed Elsevier plc** group, REPP incorporates Heinemann Educational, Ginn and Butterworth-Heinemann in the UK; Greenwood Heinemann and Rigby in the USA; Rigby Heinemann in Australia.
    Heinemann Educational Fax 01865 314140 Managing Director *Bob Osborne*, Primary *Paul Shuter*, Secondary *Kay Symons*. Textbooks/literature/other educational resources for primary and secondary school and further education. Mss, synopses and ideas welcome.
    Ginn & Co Fax 01865 314189 Managing Director *Paul Shuter*, Editorial Director *Jill Duffy*. Textbook/other educational resources for primary and secondary schools.
    Butterworth-Heinemann International Linacre House, Jordan Hill, Oxford OX2 8EJ
☎01865 310366 Fax 01865 310898 Managing

Director *Philip Shaw*, Engineering & Technology *Neil Warnock-Smith*, Business *Kathryn Grant*, Medical *Geoff Smaldon*. Books and electronic products across business, technical, medical and open-learning fields for students and professionals.

Royalties paid twice-yearly/annually, according to contract in all divisions.

Reed Elsevier plc

25 Victoria Street, London SW1H 0EX
☎020 7222 8420   Fax 020 7227 5799
Website www.r-e.com

2 Park Avenue, 7th Floor, New York, NY 10016, USA
☎001 212 448 2300 Fax 001 212 448 2196

Van de Sande Bakhuyzenstraat 4, 1061 AG Amsterdam, The Netherlands
☎00 31 20 515 9341 Fax 00 31 20 683 2617

Chief Executive Officer UK *Crispin Davis*

Reed Elsevier plc group is one of the world's leading publishers of scientific, legal, taxation, reference, educational, professional and business materials.

DIVISIONS **Reed Educational & Professional Publishing** (see entry); **Reed Elsevier Legal Division**; **Elsevier Science** (see entry); **Butterworths** Halsbury House, 35 Chancery Lane, London WC2A 1EL ☎020 7400 2500 Fax 020 7400 2842 *Publishes* legal and accountancy textbooks, journals, law reports, CD-ROMs and online services; **Butterworths Tolleys** (see entry); **Lexis-Nexis**.

Authors' Rating After an accident-prone five years during which Reed Elsevier revealed a distressing tendency to lose chief executives, this Anglo-Dutch company has at last got its act together. Ninety per cent of investment for the next three years is earmarked for the Internet, a sure indicator, as if it was needed, of the way legal, scientific and professional publishing is moving.

Regency House Publishing Limited

3 Mill Lane, Broxbourne, Hertfordshire EN10 7AZ
☎01992 479988   Fax 01992 479966

Chairman *Brian Trodd*
Managing Director *Nicolette Trodd*
Approx. Annual Turnover £1.3 million

FOUNDED 1991. Publisher and packager of mass-market non-fiction. 20 titles in 1999. No unsolicited mss; synopses and ideas for books welcome. No fiction.

Royalties paid twice-yearly.

Reinhardt Books Ltd

Flat 2, 43 Onslow Square, London SW7 3LR
☎020 7589 3751

Chairman/Managing Director
Max Reinhardt
Director *Joan Reinhardt*

FOUNDED in 1887 as H. F. L. (Publishers), it was acquired by Max Reinhardt in 1947, changing its name to the present one in 1987. First publication under the new name was Graham Greene's *The Captain and the Enemy*. Also publishes under the **Nonesuch Press** imprint. AUTHORS include Mitsumasa Anno, Alistair Cooke and Maurice Sendak. New books are no longer considered.

Royalties paid according to contract.

Religious & Moral Educational Press (RMEP)

See **Hymns Ancient & Modern Ltd**

Review

See **Hodder Headline plc**

Richmond House Publishing Company Ltd

Douglas House, 3 Richmond Buildings, London W1V 5AE
☎020 7437 9556   Fax 020 7287 3463
Email sales@rhpco.demon.co.uk

Managing Directors *Gloria Gordon, Spencer Block*

Publishes directories for the theatre and entertainment industries. TITLES *British Theatre Directory 2000; Artistes and Agents 2000; London Seating Plan Guide.* Synopses and ideas welcome.

Rider

See **Random House Group Ltd**

Robinson Publishing Ltd

See **Constable & Robinson Ltd**

Robson Books

10 Blenheim Court, Brewery Rod, London N7 9NT
☎020 7700 7444   Fax 020 7700 4552

Publisher *Jeremy Robson*
Editorial Head *Lorna Russell*

FOUNDED 1973. Part of the Chrysalis Group plc. *Publishes* general non-fiction, including biography, cookery, gardening, guidebooks, health and beauty, humour, travel, sports and games. About 70 titles a year. Unsolicited synopses and ideas for books welcome (s.a.e. essential for reply).

Royalties paid twice-yearly.

Naomi Roth Publishing

154 Tachbrook Street, London SW1V 2NE
☎020 7834 6351   Fax 020 7233 5848

Managing Director *Naomi Roth*

FOUNDED in 2000 by Naomi Roth, formerly of **B. T. Batsford**, to publish quality non-fiction: business/management, lifestyle, style and photography. TITLE *Workaholism: Getting a Life in the Killing Fields of Work*.

Rotovision

Sheridan House, 112/116A Western Road, Hove, East Sussex BN3 1DD
☎01273 727268   Fax 01273 727269
Website www.RotoVision.com

Managing Director *Brian Morris*
Commissioning Editor *Natalia Price-Cabrera*

FOUNDED 1996. Rapidly-expanding visual arts publishers with a strong emphasis on education and inspiration. *Publishes* graphic design, photography, web design, advertising, film, architecture. 21 titles in 1999. TITLES *Art Director Confesses ....* Mike Salisbury; *Organic Architecture* Javier Senosiain; *100 Designs/100 Years* Mel Byars. No unsolicited mss; written synopses and ideas welcome; no phone calls, please. No academic or fiction.

Flat fee paid.

Round Hall

See **Sweet & Maxwell Ltd**

Roundhouse Publishing Group

Millstone, Limers Lane, Northam, North Devon EX39 2RG
☎01237 474474   Fax 01237 474774
Email roundhse@compuserve.com

Editorial Head *Alan Goodworth*

ESTABLISHED 1991. *Publishes* cinema and media-related titles. TITLES *Cinema of Oliver Stone; Cinema of Stanley Kubrick; Cinema of Martin Scorsese; Italian Cinema; Toms, Coons, Mulattoes, Mammies and Bucks*. Represents and distributes a broad range of non-fiction publishing houses throughout the UK and Europe. No unsolicited mss.

Royalties paid twice-yearly.

Routledge

11 New Fetter Lane, London EC4P 4EE
☎020 7583 9855   Fax 020 7842 2298
Website www.routledge.com

Managing Director *Roger Horton*
Publishing Directors *Claire L'Enfant, Alan Jarvis, Mary MacInnes*
Approx. Annual Turnover £35.5 million (Group)

Routledge was formed in 1987 through an amalgamation of Routledge & Kegan Paul, Methuen & Co., Tavistock Publications, and Croom Helm. Subsequent acquisitions include the Unwin Hyman academic list from **HarperCollins** (1991), *Who's Who* and historical atlases from **Dent/Orion** (1994), archaeology and ancient history titles from **Batsford** (1996), and the E & FN Spon imprint from ITP Science (1997). In 1998, Routledge became a subsidiary of **Taylor & Francis Group plc** (see entry). *Publishes* academic and professional books and journals in the social sciences, humanities, health sciences and the built environment for the international market. Subjects: addiction, anthropology, archaeology, architecture, Asian studies, biblical studies, the built environment, business and management, civil engineering, classics, heritage, construction, counselling, criminology, development and environment, dictionaries, economics, education, environmental engineering, geography, health, history, Japanese studies, journals, language, leisure studies and leisure management, linguistics, literary criticism, media and culture, Middle East, nursing, philosophy, politics, political economy, psychiatry, psychology, reference, social administration, social studies and sociology, therapy, theatre and performance studies, women's studies. No poetry, fiction, travel or astrology. About 900 titles a year. Send synopses with sample chapter and c.v. rather than complete mss.

Royalties paid annually and twice-yearly, according to contract.

Ryland Peters and Small Limited

Cavendish House, 51–55 Mortimer Street, London W1N 7TD
☎020 7436 9090   Fax 020 7436 9790
Email info@rps.co.uk

Managing Director *David Peters*
Publishing Director *Alison Starling*
Art Director *Gabriella Le Grazie*

FOUNDED 1996. *Publishes* highly illustrated lifestyle books aimed at an international market, covering gardening, cookery, interior design. No fiction. No unsolicited mss; synopses and ideas welcome.

Royalties paid twice-yearly.

S.C.P. Publishers Ltd (trading as Scottish Cultural Press)

Unit 13d, Newbattle Abbey Business Annexe, Newbattle Road, Dalkeith EH22 3LJ
☎0131 660 6366   Fax 0131 660 6414
Email scp@sol.co.uk

Directors *Avril Gray, Brian Pugh*

FOUNDED 1992. *Publishes* Scottish interest titles, including cultural literature, poetry, archaeology, local history. DIVISION **S.C.P. Children's Ltd (trading as Scotish Children's Press)** Children's fiction and non-fiction. Unsolicited mss, synopses and ideas welcome provided return postage is included.
Royalties paid.

Sage Publications

6 Bonhill Street, London EC2A 4PU
☎020 7374 0645   Fax 020 7374 8741
Website www.sagepub.co.uk

Managing Director *Stephen Barr*
Editorial Director *Ziyad Marar*

FOUNDED 1971. *Publishes* academic books and journals in humanities and the social sciences. Bought academic and professional books publisher Paul Chapman Publishing Ltd in April 1998.
Royalties paid twice-yearly.

Saint Andrew Press

Board of Communication, Church of Scotland, 121 George Street, Edinburgh EH2 4YN
☎0131 225 5722   Fax 0131 220 3113
Email cofs.standrew@dial.pipex.com
Website www.churchnet.org.uk

Publishing Manager *Lesley Ann Taylor*
Approx. Annual Turnover £225,000

FOUNDED in 1954 to publish and promote the 17-volume series *The Daily Study Bible New Testament* by Professor William Barclay. Owned by the Church of Scotland Board of Communication. *Publishes* religious, Scottish local interest and some children's books. No fiction. 16 titles in 1999. No unsolicited mss; synopses and ideas preferred.
Royalties paid annually.

St Pauls Publishers

187 Battersea Bridge Road, London SW11 3AS
☎020 7978 4300   Fax 020 7978 4370
Email editions@stpauls.org.uk

Managing Director *Karamvelil Sebastian*

Publishing division of the Society of St Paul.

Began publishing in 1914 but activities were fairly limited until around 1948. *Publishes* religious material only: theology, catechetics, scripture, prayer books, children's material and biography. Unsolicited mss, synopses and ideas welcome. About 50 titles a year.

Salamander Books Ltd

8 Blenheim Court, Brewery Road, London N7 9NT
☎020 7700 7799   Fax 020 7700 3572

Managing Director *David Spence*
Editorial Director *Charlotte Davies*

FOUNDED 1973. Part of the Chrysalis Group plc. *Publishes* colour illustrated books, mainly on collecting, cookery, interiors, gardening, music, crafts, military, aviation, pet care, sport and transport. About 30 titles a year. No unsolicited mss but synopses and ideas for the above subjects welcome.
Royalties Outright fee paid instead of royalties.

Sangam Books Ltd

57 London Fruit Exchange, Brushfield Street, London E1 6EP
☎020 7377 6399   Fax 020 7375 1230
Email sangambks@aol.com

Executive Director *Anthony de Souza*

Traditionally an educational publisher of school and college level textbooks. Also *publishes* art, India, medicine, science, technology, social sciences, religion, plus some fiction in paperback.

Sapphire

See **Virgin Publishing Ltd**

W. B. Saunders & Co. Ltd/ Saunders Scientific Publications

See **Harcourt Brace and Company Ltd**

SB Publications

c/o 19 Grove Road, Seaford, East Sussex BN25 1TP
☎01323 893498   Fax 01323 893860
Email sales@sbpublications.swinternet.co.uk
Website www.sbpublications.swinternet.co.uk

Managing Director *Steve Benz*

FOUNDED 1987. *Specialises* in local history, including themes illustrated by old picture postcards and photographs; also travel, guides (town, walking), maritime history and railways. 25 titles a year.
IMPRINTS **Historic Military Press; Benn Gunn** TITLES *Lewes Then and Now; Curiosities of*

East Sussex; A Dorset Quiz Book. Also provides marketing and distribution services for local authors.
Royalties paid annually.

Sceptre
See **Hodder Headline Plc**

Scholastic Ltd
Villiers House, Clarendon Avenue, Leamington Spa, Warwickshire CV32 5PR
☎01926 887799   Fax 01926 883331
Website www.scholastic.co.uk
Chairman *M. R. Robinson*
Managing Director *David Kewley*
Approx. Annual Turnover £50 million
FOUNDED 1964. Owned by US parent company. *Publishes* children's fiction and non-fiction and education for primary schools.

DIVISIONS
Scholastic Children's Books *Richard Scrivener* Commonwealth House, 1–19 New Oxford Street, London WC1A 1NU ☎020 7421 9000 Fax 020 7421 9001 IMPRINTS **Scholastic Press** (hardbacks); **Hippo** (paperbacks); **Point** (paperbacks) TITLES *Postman Pat; Rosie & Jim; Tots TV; Horrible Histories; Goosebumps; Point Horror.*

Educational Publishing *Anne Peel* (Villiers House address) Professional books and classroom materials for primary teachers, plus magazines such as *Child Education, Junior Education, Art & Craft, Junior Focus, Infant Projects, Nursery Projects; Literacy Time.*

Red House Book Clubs *David Teale, Victoria Birkett* Cotswold Business Park, Witney, Oxford OX8 5YT ☎01993 893456 Fax 01993 776813 The Book Club group sells to families at home through The Red House Book Club, the Red House School Book Clubs (four different clubs catering for children from 4–15), and the Red House International Schools Club.

School Book Fairs *Will Oldham* The Book Fair Division sells directly to children, parents and teachers in schools through 27,000 weeklong book events held in schools throughout the UK.
Royalties paid twice-yearly.

Authors' Rating Came out top in a recent Society of Authors survey of author-friendly publishers.

SCM Press
9–17 St Albans Place, London N1 0NX
☎020 7359 8033   Fax 020 7359 0049
Email scmpress@btinternet.com

Editor *Alex Wright*
Approx. Annual Turnover £1 million
Publishes religion and theology from an open and inter-faith perspective, with some ethics and philosophy. About 40 titles a year. Relevant unsolicited mss and synopses considered if sent with s.a.e.
Royalties paid annually.

Authors' Rating Leading publisher of religious ideas with well-deserved reputation for fresh thinking. At SCM, 'questioning theology is the norm'.

Scottish Cultural Press/Scottish Children's Press
See **S.C.P. Publishers Ltd**

Scribner
See **Simon & Schuster**

Seafarer Books
102 Redwald Road, Rendlesham, Woodbridge, Suffolk IP12 2TE
☎01394 420789   Fax 01394 461314
Email info@seafarerbooks.com
Website www.seafarerbooks.com
Sole Proprietor *Patricia M. Eve*
FOUNDED 1968. *Publishes* sailing titles, with an emphasis on the traditional. AUTHORS Jack London, Erskine Childers, Frank Mulville, Bjorn Larsson. No unsolicited mss; preliminary letter essential before making any type of submission.
Royalties paid twice-yearly.

Search Press Ltd/Burns & Oates
Wellwood, North Farm Road, Tunbridge Wells, Kent TN2 3DR
☎01892 510850   Fax 01892 515903
Email searchpress@searchpress.com
Website www.searchpress.com
Managing Director *Martin de la Bédoyère*
FOUNDED 1847. *Publishes* (Search Press) full-colour art, craft, needlecrafts; (Burns & Oates) theology, history, spirituality, reference.
DIVISIONS **Academic** *Paul Burns* TITLES include *Butler's Lives of the Saints*, new full edition, 12 volumes. **Craft** *Rosalind Dace* Books on papermaking and papercrafts, painting on silk, art techniques and embroidery.
Royalties paid annually.

Secker & Warburg
See **Random House Group Ltd**

Sensation
See **Harlequin Mills & Boon Ltd**

Seren
First Floor, 2 Wyndham Street, Bridgend
CF31 1EF
☎01656 663018   Fax 01656 649226
Email seren@seren.force9.co.uk
Website www.seren-books.com
Chairman *Cary Archard*
Managing Director *Mick Feltin*
Approx. Annual Turnover £100,000

FOUNDED 1981 as a specialist poetry publisher
but has now moved into general literary pub-
lishing with an emphasis on Wales. *Publishes*
poetry, fiction, literary criticism, drama, biog-
raphy, art, history and translations of fiction. 25
titles in 1999.
    DIVISIONS **Poetry** *Amy Wack* AUTHORS
Owen Sheers, Tony Curtis, Sheenagh Pugh,
Duncan Bush, Deryn Rees-Jones. **Drama** *Amy
Wack* AUTHORS Edward Thomas, Charles Way,
Lucinda Coxon. **Fiction**, **Art**, **Literary
Criticism**, **History**, **Translations** *Mick Felton*
AUTHORS Christopher Meredith, Leslie Norris,
Gwyn Thomas.
    IMPRINT **Border Lines Biographies** TITLES
*Bruce Chatwin; Dennis Potter; Mary Webb; Wilfred
Owen; Raymond Williams.* Unsolicited mss, syn-
opses and ideas for books welcome.
    Royalties paid twice yearly.

Serpent's Tail
4 Blackstock Mews, London N4 2BT
☎020 7354 1949   Fax 020 7704 6467
Email info@serpentstail.com
Website www.serpentstail.com
Contact *Laurence O'Toole*
Approx. Annual Turnover £650,000

FOUNDED 1986. Won the *Sunday Times* **Small
Publisher of the Year Award** (1989) and the
Ralph Lewis Award for new fiction (1992).
Serpent's Tail has introduced to British audiences a number of major internationally known
writers. Noted for its strong emphasis on design
and an eye for the unusual. *Publishes* contemporary fiction, contemporary gay fiction and non-
fiction, including works in translation, crime,
popular culture and biography. No poetry,
romance or fantasy. About 40 titles a year.

IMPRINTS
Serpent's Tail TITLES *Hero of the Underworld*
Jimmy Boyle; *Whatever* Michel Houellebecq;
Altered State Matthew Collin; *Pornocopia*

Laurence O'Toole. **Five Star** TITLES *Acid
Casuals* Nicholas Blincoe; *Always Outnumbered,
Always Outgunned* Walter Mosley; *Bombay
Talkie* Ameena Meer. Send preliminary letter
outlining proposal with a sample chapter. No
unsolicited mss. Prospective authors unfamiliar
with Serpent's Tail are advised to study the list
before submitting anything.
    Royalties normally paid annually.

Authors' Rating A publisher noted for originality which means doing what the conglomerates are unwilling or unable to do. An exciting
fiction list much praised by its own and other
publishers' authors.

Severn House Publishers
9–15 High Street, Sutton, Surrey SM1 1DF
☎020 8770 3930   Fax 020 8770 3850
Email info@severnhouse.com
Website www.severnhouse.com
Chairman *Edwin Buckhalter*
Editorial *Marisa McGreevy*

FOUNDED 1974. A leader in library fiction
publishing. *Publishes* hardback fiction: romance
science fiction, horror, fantasy, crime. About
140 titles a year. No unsolicited material.
Synopses/proposals preferred through *bona fide*
literary agents only.
    Royalties paid twice-yearly. *Overseas associates*
Severn House Publishers Inc., New York.

Sheffield Academic Press
Mansion House, 19 Kingfield Road, Sheffield
S11 9AS
☎0114 2554433   Fax 0114 2554626
Email admin@sheffac.demon.co.uk
Website www.shef-ac-press.co.uk
Managing Director *Mrs Jean R.K. Allen*
Approx. Annual Turnover £1.5 million

FOUNDED in 1976. Originally known as JSOT
Press. Now the leading academic publisher of
biblical titles. Recently expanded its list to
include archaeology, literary studies, history
and culture, languages, contemporary European studies, scientific, professional, reference.
112 titles in 1999. Unsolicited mss, synopses
and ideas welcome. No fiction.
    IMPRINTS **Sheffield Academic Press** *Jean
Allen*; **Subis**.
    Royalties paid annually

Sheldon Press
See **Society for Promoting Christian
Knowledge**

Shepheard-Walwyn (Publishers) Ltd

Suite 34, 26 Charing Cross Road, London
WC2H 0DH
☎020 7240 5992   Fax 020 7379 5770
Email books@shepheard-walwyn.co.uk
Website www.craft-fair.co.uk/
    shepheardwalwyn/

Managing Director *Anthony Werner*
Approx. Annual Turnover £150,000

FOUNDED 1972. 'We regard books as food for
the mind and want to offer a wholesome diet
of original ideas and fresh approaches to old
subjects.' *Publishes* general non-fiction in three
main areas: Scottish interest; gift books in calligraphy and/or illustrated; history, political
economy, philosophy. About 5 titles a year.
Synopses and ideas for books welcome.
    Royalties paid twice-yearly.

The Shetland Times Ltd

Prince Alfred Street, Lerwick, Shetland
ZE1 0EP
☎01595 693622   Fax 01595 694637
Email publishing@shetland-times.co.uk
Website www.shetland-books.co.uk

Managing Director *Robert Wishart*
Publications Manager *Charlotte Black*

FOUNDED 1872 as publishers of the local newspaper. Book publishing followed thereafter plus
publication of monthly magazine, *Shetland Life*.
Publishes anything with Shetland connections –
local and natural history, music, crafts, maritime.
Prefers material with a Shetland theme/connec-
tion.
    Royalties paid annually.

Shire Publications Ltd

Cromwell House, Church Street, Princes
Risborough, Buckinghamshire HP27 9AA
☎01844 344301   Fax 01844 347080
Website www.shirebooks.co.uk

Managing Director *John Rotheroe*

FOUNDED 1967. *Publishes* original non-fiction
paperbacks. About 25 titles a year. No unsolicited material; send introductory letter with
detailed outline of idea.
    Royalties paid annually.

Authors' Rating You don't have to live in the
country to write books for Shire but it helps.
With titles like *Church Fonts, Haunted Inns* and
Discovering Preserved Railways there is a distinct
rural feel to the list. Another way of putting it, to
quote John Rotheroe, Shire specialises in 'small
books on all manner of obscure subjects'.

Sidgwick & Jackson

See **Macmillan Publishers Ltd**

Sigma Press

1 South Oak Lane, Wilmslow, Cheshire
SK9 6AR
☎01625 531035   Fax 01625 536800
Email info@sigma.press
Website www.sigmapress.co.uk

Chairman/Managing Director *Graham Beech*

FOUNDED in 1980 as a publisher of technical
books. Sigma Press now publishes mainly in the
leisure area. *Publishes* outdoor, local heritage,
myths and legends, sports, dance and exercise.
Approx. 45 titles in 1999. No unsolicited mss;
synopses and ideas welcome. DIVISION **Sigma
Leisure** TITLES *The Coniston Tigers* (biography);
*Salsa & Merengue Step-by-Step; How to Run a
Marathon; Laugh Away the Fat.*
    Royalties paid twice-yearly.

Signature

See **Hodder Headline Plc**

Silhouette Desire

See **Harlequin Mills & Boon Ltd**

Simon & Schuster

Africa House, 64–78 Kingsway, London
WC2B 6AH
☎020 7316 1900   Fax 020 7316 0331

Managing Director *Ian Chapman*
Editorial Directors *Clare Ledingham, Martin
    Fletcher, Helen Gummer*

FOUNDED 1986. Offshoot of the leading
American publisher. *Publishes* general fiction,
including science fiction under its **Earthlight**
imprint (Editor *John Jarrold*) and non-fiction in
hardback and paperback. Literary fiction and
non-fiction is published in trade paperback
under the **Scribner** imprint. No academic or
technical material.
    Royalties paid twice-yearly.

Authors' Rating Having disposed of its US
education divisions to Pearson, S&S is building
its list of consumer books. After the successful
Pocket Books paperback list came the launch
of a children's list, a science fiction and fantasy
list, and a new upmarket paperback imprint.

Skoob Books Ltd

11A–15 Sicilian Avenue, Southampton Row,
London WC1A 2QH
☎020 7404 3063   Fax 020 7404 4398
Email books@skoob.com
Website www.skoob.com

Editorial office: 76A Oldfield Road, London
N16 0RS ☎/Fax 020 7275 9811
Managing Director *I. K. Ong*
Editorial *M. Lovell*

Publishes literary guides, cultural studies, esoterica/occult, poetry, new writing from the Orient. No unsolicited mss, synopses or ideas. TITLES *Where We Are* Lucien Stryk; *Skoob Directory of Secondhand Bookshops*; *The Necronomicon* George Hay; *Haunting the Tiger* K. S. Maniam.

Smith Gryphon Ltd
See **Blake Publishing**

Colin Smythe Ltd
PO Box 6, Gerrards Cross, Buckinghamshire
SL9 8XA
☎01753 886000   Fax 01753 886469
Managing Director *Colin Smythe*
Approx. Annual Turnover £1.8 million
FOUNDED 1966. *Publishes* Anglo-Irish literature, drama; criticism and history. About 15 titles a year. No unsolicited mss. Also acts as literary agent for a small list of authors including Terry Pratchett.
Royalties paid annually/twice-yearly.

Society for Promoting Christian Knowledge (SPCK)
Holy Trinity Church, Marylebone Road,
London NW1 4DU
☎020 7387 5282   Fax 020 7388 2352
Website www.spck.or.uk
Director of Publishing *Simon Kingston*
FOUNDED 1698, SPCK is the third oldest publisher in the country. IMPRINTS **SPCK** Editorial Director *Joanna Moriary* Theology, academic, liturgy, prayer, spirituality, Biblical studies, educational resources, mission, pastoral care, gospel and culture, worldwide. **Sheldon Press** Editorial Director *Liz Marsh* Popular medicine, health, self-help, psychology. **Triangle** Editor *Alison Barr* Popular Christian paperbacks. **Azure** Senior Editor *Alison Barr* General spirituality.
Royalties paid annually.

Authors' Rating Religion with a strong social edge.

Southwater
See **Anness Publishing Ltd**

Souvenir Press Ltd
43 Great Russell Street, London WC1B 3PA
☎020 7580 9307/8 & 7637 5711/2/3
Fax 020 7580 5064

Chairman/Managing Director *Ernest Hecht*
Independent publishing house. FOUNDED 1951. *Publishes* academic and scholarly, animal care and breeding, antiques and collecting, archaeology, autobiography and biography, business and industry, children's, cookery, crafts and hobbies, crime, educational, fiction, gardening, health and beauty, history and antiquarian, humour, illustrated and fine editions, magic and the occult, medical, military, music, natural history, philosophy, poetry, psychology, religious, sociology, sports, theatre and women's studies. About 55 titles a year. Souvenir's Human Horizons series for the disabled and their carers is one of the most pre-eminent in its field and recently celebrated 20 years of publishing for the disabled.
IMPRINTS/SERIES **Condor; Independent Voices; Human Horizons; Pictorial Presentations; Pop Universal; The Story-Tellers**. TITLES *Chocolate Therapy* Murray Langham; *Ancient Siege Warfare* Paul Bentley Kern; *Solutions for Writers* Sol Stein; *The Hand-Reared Boy* Brian W. Aldiss; *The Complete Book of Spells, Curses and Magical Recipes* Leonard R. N. Ashley; *Dyspraxia: The Hidden Handicap* Amanda Kirby; *The Magician of Karakosk* Peter S. Beagle. Unsolicited mss considered but initial letter of enquiry preferred.
Royalties paid twice-yearly.

Authors' Rating Souvenir is entering its fiftieth year with its founder Ernest Hecht, one of publishing's great eccentrics, still very much in control. The extraordinary range of books that appear in the Souvenir catalogue suggests a sharp business brain combined with an idiosyncratic sense of humour. What more could authors want of their publisher?

SPCK
See **Society for Promoting Christian Knowledge**

Neville Spearman
See **The C. W. Daniel Co. Ltd**

Special Edition
See **Harlequin Mills & Boon Ltd**

Spectrum
See **F. A. Thorpe (Publishing) Ltd**

Spellmount Ltd
The Old Rectory, Staplehurst, Kent TN12 0AZ
☎01580 893730   Fax 01580 893731
Email enquiries@spellmount.com
Website www.spellmount.com

Managing Director *Jamie Wilson*
Approx. Annual Turnover £450,000
FOUNDED 1983. *Publishes* history and military history. About 30 titles a year. Synopses/ideas for books in these specialist fields welcome, enclosing return postage.
Royalties paid biannually for two years, then annually.

E & FN Spon
See **Routledge**

Springer-Verlag London Limited
Sweetapple House, Catteshall Road,
Godalming, Surrey GU7 3DJ
☎01483 418800   Fax 01483 415144
Email postmaster@svl.co.uk
Website www.springer.co.uk
Managing Director *John Watson*
Editorial Director *Beverley Ford*
Approx. Annual Turnover £5 million
The UK subsidiary of Bertelsmann Springer of Germany. *Publishes* science, technical and medical books and journals. About 150 titles a year, plus journals. Specialises in computing, engineering, medicine, mathematics, astronomy and food science. All UK published books are sold through Springer's German and US companies as well as in the UK. Not interested in social sciences, fiction or school books but academic and professional science and amateur astronomy mss or synopses welcome.
Royalties paid annually.

Stainer & Bell Ltd
PO Box 110, 23 Gruneisen Road, London
N3 1DZ
☎020 8343 3303   Fax 020 8343 3024
Email post@stainer.co.uk
Website www.stainer.co.uk
Managing Directors *Carol Y. Wakefield,*
Keith M. Wakefield
Publishing Director *Nicholas Williams*
Approx. Annual Turnover £750,000
FOUNDED 1907 to publish sheet music. *Publishes* music and religious subjects related to hymnody. Unsolicited synopses/ideas for books welcome. Send letter enclosing brief précis.
Royalties paid annually.

Harold Starke Publishers Ltd
Pixey Green, Stradbroke, Near Eye, Suffolk
IP21 5NG
☎01379 388334   Fax 01379 388335
Directors *Harold K. Starke, Naomi Galinski*

Publishes adult non-fiction, medical and reference. No unsolicited mss.
Royalties paid annually.

The Stationery Office Ltd
St Crispins, Duke Street, Norwich, Norfolk
NR3 1PD
☎01603 622211   Fax 01603 694313
(Editorial)
Website www.itsofficial.co.uk
Chief Executive *Fred J. Perkins*
Approx. Annual Turnover £250 million
Formerly HMSO, which was FOUNDED 1786. Became part of the private sector in October 1996. 11,000 new titles each year with 50,000 titles in print. Publisher of material sponsored by Parliament, government departments and other official bodies. Also commercial publishing in the following broad categories: business and professional, environment, transport, education, law and heritage. Unsolicited material may be considered if suitable; s.a.e. with synopsis/samples should be sent in the first instance to *Doug Fox*, Head of Venture Publishing at The Stationery Office, Publications Centre, 51 Nine Elms Lane, London SW8 5DR.

Stevens
See **Sweet & Maxwell Ltd**

STM
See **Hodder Headline Plc**

The Story-Tellers
See **Souvenir Press Ltd**

Straightline Publishing Ltd
29 Main Street, Bothwell, Glasgow G71 8RD
☎01698 853000   Fax 01698 854208
Chairman *Frank Docherty*
Editors *B. Taylor, P. Bellew*
FOUNDED 1989. *Publishes* magazines and directories – trade and technical – books of local interest. 11 titles in 1999. TITLES *Cabletalk; Information Builder.* No unsolicited material.
Royalties paid annually.

Subis
See **Sheffield Academic Press**

Summersdale Publishers
46 West Street, Chichester, West Sussex
PO19 1RP
☎01243 771107   Fax 01243 786300
Email enquiries@summersdale.com
Website www.summersdale.com

Directors *Stewart Ferris, Alastair Williams*
Editor *Elizabeth Kershaw*
Approx. Annual Turnover £1 million
FOUNDED 1990. *Publishes* non-fiction: humour, travel literature, self-help, biography, sport, gift books, cookery. TITLES *Snowball Oranges; The Gringo Trail; Running a Hotel on the Roof of the World; The Trail to Titicaca; Drinking Games; The Bumper Book of Chat-up Lines.* 50 titles in 2000. No unsolicited mss; synopses and ideas welcome. *Royalties* paid.

Susquehanna University Press
See **Golden Cockerel Press**

Sutton Publishing Ltd
Phoenix Mill, Thrupp, Stroud, Gloucestershire GL5 2BU
☎01453 731114   Fax 01453 731117
Managing Director *David Hogg*
Publishing Director *Peter Clifford*
Approx. Annual Turnover £5.5 million
FOUNDED 1978. Acquired by **Haynes Publishing** in March 2000. *Publishes* academic, archaeology, biography, countryside, history, military, regional interest, local history, pocket classics (lesser known novels by classic authors), transport. About 240 titles a year. Send synopses rather than complete mss.
Royalties paid twice-yearly.

Authors' Rating Now part of Haynes Publishing, this imaginative history publisher will almost certainly benefit from stronger marketing and distribution.

Swan Hill Press
See **Airlife Publishing Ltd**

Sweet & Maxwell Ltd
100 Avenue Road, London NW3 3PF
☎020 7393 7000   Fax 020 7393 7010
Email <name>@sweetandmaxwell.co.uk
Website www.sweetandmaxwell.co.uk
Managing Director *Wendy Beechar*
FOUNDED 1799. Part of The Thomson Corporation. *Publishes* legal and professional materials in all media, looseleaf works, journals, law reports and on CD-ROM. About 150 book titles a year, with live backlist of over 700 titles, 75 looseleaf services and more than 80 legal periodicals. Not interested in material which is non-legal. The legal and professional list is varied and contains many academic titles, as well as treatises and reference works in the legal and related professional fields.

IMPRINTS **Sweet & Maxwell**; **Sweet & Maxwell Asia**; **Stevens**; **W. Green (Scotland)** General Manager *Martin Redfern*; **Round Hall/Sweet & Maxwell (Ireland)** General Manager *Elanor McGarry.* Ideas welcome. Writers with legal/professional projects in mind are advised to contact the company at the earliest possible stage in order to lay the groundwork for best design, production and marketing of a project.
Royalties and fees paid according to contract.

Take That Ltd
PO Box 200, Harrogate, North Yorkshire HG1 2YR
☎01423 507545   Fax 01423 526035
Website www.takethat.co.uk
Chairman/Managing Director *C. Brown*
FOUNDED 1986. Independent publisher of computing, finance and gambling titles (books and magazines). TITLES *Understand Financial Risk in a Day; Complete Beginner's Guide to the Internet; Successful Spread Betting.* About 10 titles a year. Unsolicited synopses for books welcome; 'no s.a.e., no reply'.
Royalties paid twice-yearly.

Tango Books
See **Sadie Fields Productions Ltd** under **UK Packagers**

I. B. Tauris & Co. Ltd
Victoria House, Bloomsbury Square, London WC1B 4DZ
☎020 7831 9060   Fax 020 7831 9061
Website www.ibtauris.com
Chairman/Publisher *Iradj Bagherzade*
Managing Director *Jonathan McDonnell*
FOUNDED 1984. Independent publisher. *Publishes* general non-fiction and academic in the fields of international relations, current affairs, history, politics, cultural, media and film studies, Middle East studies. Joint projects with Cambridge University Centre for Middle Eastern Studies, Institute for Latin American Studies and Institute of Ismaili Studies. *Distributes* The New Press (New York) outside North America. *Represents* **The Curzon Press** in the UK. IMPRINTS **Tauris Parke Books** Illustrated books on architecture, travel, design and culture. **Tauris Parke Paperbacks** Trade titles, including art and art history. **British Academic Press** Academic monographs. Unsolicited synopses and book proposals welcome.
Royalties paid twice-yearly.

Tavistock Publications
See **Routledge**

Taylor & Francis Group plc
11 New Fetter Lane, London EC4P 4EE
☎020 7583 9855   Fax 020 7842 2298
Website www.tandf.co.uk
Chairman *Robert Kiernan*
Chief Executive *Anthony Selvey*
Approx. Annual Turnover £40.2 million
FOUNDED 1798 with the launch of *Philosophical Magazine* which has been in publication ever since (now a solid state physics journal). The company is privately owned with strong academic connections among the major shareholders. **Falmer Press** (see entry) joined the group in 1979 and it doubled its size in the late '80s with the acquisition of Crane Russak in 1986 and Hemisphere Publishing Co in 1988. In 1995, acquired Lawrence Erlbaum Associates Ltd and Brunner/Mazel in 1997, adding to the growing list of psychology publications. In 1996, UCL Press Ltd was purchased, adding further to its portfolio of publications in science and humanities. In 1997, Garland Publishing Inc., New York, and in 1998 Routledge Publishing Holdings Ltd, including Carfax Publishing and E & FN Spon were acquired. The most recent additions to the Taylor & Francis Group are Europa Publications Ltd, the reference book publisher covering international affairs, politics and economics, and **Martin Dunitz Ltd** (see entry) in 1999. *Publishes* scientific, technical, education titles at university, research and professional levels. About 1600 titles a year. Unsolicited mss, synopses and ideas welcome.
   Royalties paid yearly. *Overseas office* Taylor & Francis Inc., Philadelphia, PA and New York, Hemisphere Publication Services, Singapore, Taylor & Francis AS, Norway and Sweden.

Teach Yourself
See **Hodder Headline Plc**

Telegraph Books
1 Canada Square, Canary Wharf, London E14 5DT
☎020 7538 6826   Fax 020 7538 6064
Website www.booksonline.co.uk
Owner *Telegraph Group Ltd*
Publisher *Susannah Charlton*
Approx. Annual Turnover £2.3 million
Concentrates on Telegraph branded books in association/collaboration with other publishers. Also runs Telegraph Books Direct, a direct mail, phone-line bookselling service and off-the-page sales for other publishers' books. *Publishes* general non-fiction: journalism, business and law, cookery, education, gardening, wine, guides, sport, puzzles and games. About 50 titles a year. Only interested in books if a Telegraph link exists. No unsolicited material.
   Royalties paid twice-yearly.

Tellastory
See **Random House Group Ltd**

Temple House Books
See **The Book Guild Ltd**

Thames and Hudson Ltd
181A High Holborn, London WC1V 7QX
☎020 7845 5000   Fax 020 7845 5050
Email mail@thameshudson.co.uk
Website www.thameshudson.co.uk
Managing Director *Thomas Neurath*
Editorial Head *Jamie Camplin*
Approx. Annual Turnover £20 million
Publishes art, archaeology, architecture and design, biography, fashion, garden and landscape design, graphics, history, illustrated and fine editions, mythology, music, photography, popular culture, style, travel and topography. 200 titles a year. SERIES *World of Art; New Horizons; Celtic Design; Chic Simple; Cutting Edge; Fashion Memoir; Hip Hotels; Most Beautiful Villages; Prospects for Tomorrow.* TITLES *20th Century Fashion; The Book of Kells; David Bailey Archive; Henri Cartier-Bresson; Derek Jarman's Garden; Love & Desire; Sensation; The Earth from the Air; The Seventy Wonders of the Ancient World; The Shock of the New; Vision: Fifty Years of British Creativity; Website Graphics NOW.* Send preliminary letter and outline before mss.
   Royalties paid twice-yearly.

Authors' Rating Fifty years in the business, Thames and Hudson has a fine record of publishing quality illustrated books on art and design. The World of Art series, a huge range of modestly priced, scholarly books, is probably the best of its kind anywhere in the world. Financial success rests on producing the sort of books that easily carry over to other languages.

Thomson Learning
Berkshire House, 168–173 High Holborn, London WC1V 7AA
☎020 7497 1422   Fax 020 7497 1426
Email info@itpuk.co.uk
CEO (Worldwide) *Bob Christie*

Editorial Head *Julian Thomas*
Websites: www.thomsonlearning.co.uk *or* www.businesspress.co.uk

FOUNDED 1993. Formerly International Thomson Publishing, part of the Thomson Corporation and as such has offices worldwide with the UK office being reported to by Copenhagen (for Europe), Turkey (Middle East) and South Africa. *Publishes* education. IMPRINT **Business Press** TITLES *Management and Cost Accounting* Drury; *Strategy – Process, Content, Contact* DeWitt and Meyer. Unsolicited material aimed at students is welcome but telephone in the first instance to check out the idea.
Royalties vary according to contract.

Stanley Thornes (Publishers) Ltd

Ellenborough House, Wellington Street, Cheltenham, Gloucestershire GL50 1YW
☎01242 228888   Fax 01242 221914
Managing Director *Oliver Gadsby*
Approx. Annual Turnover £20 million
FOUNDED 1972. Part of the Wolters-Kluwer Group. *Publishes* secondary school and college curriculum textbooks and primary school resources. About 200 titles a year. Unsolicited mss, synopses and ideas for books welcome if appropriate to specialised list.
IMPRINT **Mary Glasgow Publications** Foreign-language teaching materials and teacher support.
Royalties paid annually.

F. A. Thorpe (Publishing) Ltd

The Green, Bradgate Road, Anstey, Leicester LE7 7FU
☎0116 2364325   Fax 0116 2340205
Chairman *David Thorpe*
Group Chief Executive *Robert Thirbly*
Approx. Annual Turnover £500,000
Part of the Ulverscroft Group. *Publishes* fiction and non-fiction large print books. No educational, gardening or books that would not be suitable for large print. 444 titles in 1999. DIVISIONS **Charnwood; Ulverscroft.** IMPRINTS **Linford Romance; Linford Mystery; Linford Western; Spectrum.** No unsolicited material.

Thorsons

See **HarperCollins Publishers Ltd**

Times Books

See **HarperCollins Publishers Ltd**

Titan Books

144 Southwark Street, London SE1 0UP
☎020 7620 0200   Fax 020 7620 0032
Email editorial@titanmail.com
Managing Director *Nick Landau*
Editorial Director *Katy Wild*
FOUNDED 1981. Now a leader in the publication of graphic novels and film and television tie-ins. *Publishes* comic books/graphic novels, film and television titles. About 70–80 titles a year.
IMPRINTS **Titan Books** TITLES *Batman; Superman; Alien; Star Trek; Star Wars; The Simpsons; The X Files; The Avengers.* No unsolicited fiction or children's books please. Ideas for film and TV titles considered; send synopsis/outline with sample chapter. No e-mail submissions. Author guidelines available.
Royalties paid twice-yearly.

The Toby Press

146 New Cavendish Street, London W1M 7FG
☎020 7580 5440   Fax 020 7580 5442
Email toby@tobypress.com
Website www.tobypress.com
Chairman *M. Miller*
FOUNDED 1999. *Publishes* fiction only and markets the books directly to readers through its website and the *Toby Press Review*, a quarterly magazine. About 20 titles a year. TITLES *Failing Paris* Samantha Dunn; *Absence* Raymond Tallis; *Cardiofitness* Alessandra Montrucchio. Send first chapters only; 'unsolicited mss will *not* be returned'.
Royalties paid quarterly. *Overseas subsidiary* in the USA.

Tolkien

See **HarperCollins Publishers Ltd**

Tolley Publishing

See **Butterworths Tolley**

Transworld Publishers, A division of the Random House Group Ltd

61–63 Uxbridge Road, London W5 5SA
☎020 8579 2652   Fax 020 8579 5479
Email info@transworld-publishers.co.uk
Managing Director/CEO *Mark Barty-King*
Approx. Annual Turnover £65 million
FOUNDED 1950. A subsidiary of **Random House, Inc.**, New York, which in turn is a wholly-owned subsidiary of Bertelsmann AG, Germany. *Publishes* general fiction and non-fiction, children's books, sports and leisure.

DIVISIONS
Adult Trade *Patrick Janson-Smith, Larry Finlay*
IMPRINTS **Anchor** *John Saddler;* **Bantam**
Francesca Liversidge; **Bantam Press** *Sally Gaminara;* **Corgi; Black Swan** *Bill Scott-Kerr;*
Doubleday *Marianne Velmans;* **Partridge Press** *Alison Barrow.* AUTHORS Kate Atkinson,
Bill Bryson, Catherine Cookson, Jilly Cooper,
Nicholas Evans, Frederick Forsyth, Robert
Goddard, Germaine Greer, Stephen Hawking,
Anne McCaffrey, Andy McNab, Terry
Pratchett, James Redfield, Gerald Seymour,
Danielle Steel, Joanna Trollope, Mary Wesley.
Children's & Young Adult Books *Philippa
Dickinson* IMPRINTS **Doubleday** (hardcover);
**Picture Corgi; Corgi Pups; Young Corgi;
Corgi Yearling; Corgi; Corgi Freeway;
Bantam** (pbk). AUTHORS Ian Beck, Malorie
Blackman, Anthony Browne, Helen Cooper,
Peter Dickinson, Dick King-Smith, Francine
Pascal, K. M. Peyton, Terry Pratchett, Philip
Pullman, Robert Swindells, Jacqueline Wilson.
Royalties paid twice-yearly. *Overseas associates*
Random House Australia Pty Ltd; Random
House New Zealand; Random House (Pty)
Ltd (South Africa).

Authors' Rating What with the strong pound
and troublesome overseas markets, Transworld
would have been hard put to keep up its run of
increased sales. But a flat year still leaves this
publisher unchallenged as one of the best in the
business, an object lesson in making quality
pay. For frontlist paperbacks, according to the
Bookseller, 'no one can touch Transworld'.

Trentham Books Ltd

Westview House, 734 London Road, Stoke
on Trent, Staffordshire ST4 5NP
☎01782 745567   Fax 01782 745553
Chairman/Managing Director
Dr John Eggleston
Editorial Head *Dr Gillian Klein*
Approx. Annual Turnover £1 million

Publishes education (nursery, school and higher),
social sciences, intercultural studies and law for
professional readers *not* for children and parents.
Also academic and professional journals. No fiction, biography or poetry. About 25–30 titles a
year. Unsolicited mss, synopses and ideas welcome if relevant to their interests. Material only
returned if adequate s.a.e. sent.
Royalties paid annually.

Triangle

See **Society for Promoting Christian
Knowledge**

Trident Press Ltd

Empire House, 175 Piccadilly, London
W1V 9DB
☎020 7491 8770   Fax 020 7491 8664
Email admin@tridentpress.ie
Website www.tridentpress.com
Managing Director *Peter Vine*
Approx. Annual Turnover £550,000

FOUNDED 1997. *Publishes* TV tie-ins, natural
history, travel, geography, underwater/marine
life, history, archaeology, culture and fiction. 8
titles in 1999. DIVISIONS **Fiction/General
Publishing** *Paula Vine;* **Natural History** *Peter
Vine.* TITLES *Red Sea Sharks; The Elysium
Testament; BBC Wildlife Specials; UAE in Focus.*
No unsolicited mss; synopses and ideas welcome, particularly TV tie-ins. Approach in
writing or *brief* communications by e-mail, fax
or telephone.
Royalties paid annually.

Trotman & Co. Ltd

2 The Green, Richmond, Surrey TW9 1PL
☎020 8486 1150   Fax 020 8486 1161
Website www.trotmanpublishing.co.uk
Chairman *Andrew Fiennes Trotman*
Publishing Director *Morfydd Jones*
Approx. Annual Turnover £3 million

Publishes general careers books, higher education guides, teaching support material, employment and training resources. About 50 titles a
year. TITLES *Degree Course Offers; Getting into
Oxford or Cambridge; Students' Money Matters.*
Unsolicited material welcome. Also active in
the educational resources market, producing
recruitment brochures.
Royalties paid twice-yearly.

20/20

See **The X Press**

UCL Press Ltd

See **Taylor & Francis Group**

Ulverscroft

See **F. A. Thorpe (Publishing) Ltd**

University Presses of California, Columbia & Princeton Ltd

1 Oldlands Way, Bognor Regis, West Sussex
PO22 9SA
☎01243 842165   Fax 01243 842167
Email lois@upccp.demon.co.uk

Publishes academic titles only. US-based editorial offices. Over 200 titles a year. Enquiries only.

Usborne Publishing Ltd
83–85 Saffron Hill, London EC1N 8RT
☎020 7430 2800 Fax 020 7430 1562
Email mail@usborne.co.uk
Website www.usborne.com

Managing Director *Peter Usborne*
Editorial Director *Jenny Tyler*
Approx. Annual Turnover £13.6 million

FOUNDED 1973. *Publishes* non-fiction, fiction, computer books, puzzle books and music for children and young adults. Some titles for parents. Up to 100 titles a year. Non-fiction books are written in-house to a specific format and therefore unsolicited mss are not normally welcome. Ideas which may be developed in-house are sometimes considered. Fiction for children may be considered. Keen to hear from new illustrators and designers.
Royalties paid twice-yearly.

Authors' Rating Having sorted out its distribution problems, Usborne is concentrating efforts on developing a children's list distinguished by the precept that learning can be fun.

Vallentine Mitchell
See **Frank Cass & Co Ltd**

Ventura
See **Penguin UK**

Vermilion
See **Random House Group Ltd**

Verso
6 Meard Street, London W1V 3HR
☎020 7437 3546 Fax 020 7734 0059
Website www.versobooks.com

Chairman *George Galfalvi*
Managing Director *Colin Robinson*
Approx. Annual Turnover £2 million

Formerly New Left Books which grew out of the *New Left Review*. *Publishes* politics, history, sociology, economics, philosophy, cultural studies, feminism. TITLES *No One Left to Lie To* Christopher Hitchens; *Redemption Song* Mike Marqusee; *The Challenge of Carl Schmitt* Chantal Mouffe; *Limits to Capital* David Harvey; *Adventures in Marxism* Marshall Berman; *Machiavelli and Us* Louis Althusser; *High Art Lite* Julian Stallabrass; *The Judge and the Historian* Carlo Ginzburg. No unsolicited mss; synopses and ideas for books welcome.
Royalties paid annually. *Overseas office* in New York.

Authors' Rating Dubbed by the *Bookseller* as 'one of the most successful small independent publishers'.

Viking/Viking Children's
See **Penguin UK**

Vintage
See **Random House Group Ltd**

Virago Press
Little, Brown & Co. (UK), Brettenham House, Lancaster Place, London WC2E 7EN
☎020 7911 8000 Fax 020 7911 8100

Publisher *Lennie Goodings*
Senior Editor/Publisher, Vs *Sally Abbey*
Editor, Virago Modern Classics
Imogen Taylor
Approx. Annual Turnover £2.5 million

FOUNDED in 1973 by Carmen Callil, Virago has just passed its quarter century of publishing fiction and non-fiction books of quality by women. *Publishes* approximately 50 new books a year in the areas of autobiography, biography, fiction, history, politics, psychology and women's issues. IMPRINTS **Virago Modern Classics** 20th century reprints; **Virago Vs** AUTHORS Margaret Atwood, Maya Angelou, Gail Anderson-Dargatz, Nina Bawden, Jennifer Belle, Sarah Dunant, Marilyn French, Gaby Hauptman, Michele Roberts, Natasha Walter, Sarah Waters. Send synopsis and sample chapter and return postage with all unsolicited material.
Royalties paid twice-yearly.

Virgin Publishing Ltd
Thames Wharf Studios, Rainville Road, London W6 9HT
☎020 7386 3300 Fax 020 7386 3360
Website www.virgin-books.com

Chairman *Robert Devereux*
Managing Director *Rob Shreeve*
Approx. Annual Turnover £15 million

The Virgin Group's book publishing company. *Publishes* non-fiction, reference and large-format illustrated books on entertainment and popular culture, particularly music, TV tie-ins and books about film, showbiz, sport, biography, autobiography and humour. Launched a series of travel guides in 1999. No poetry, short stories, individual novels, children's books.

DIVISIONS/IMPRINTS
Non-fiction: **Virgin** Editorial Director *Humphrey Price*; Senior Editor, Humour, TV tie-ins and Entertainment *Rod Green*; Senior

Editor, Reference *David Gould*; Senior Editor, Music *Ian Gittins*; Music Scout *Stuart Slater*; Senior Editor, Sport *Jonathan Taylor*.

Illustrated books: Editorial Director *Carolyn Thorne*; Editor *James Bennett*.

Fiction: **Virgin**; **Black Lace** Senior Editor *Kerri Sharp*; **Idol** and **Sapphire** Editor *Kathleen Bryson*; **Nexus** Editor *James Marriott*.

Royalties paid twice-yearly.

The Vital Spark
See **Neil Wilson Publishing Ltd**

Volcano Press Ltd
PO Box 139, Leicester LE2 2YH
☎0116 2706714   Fax 0116 2706714
Email asaf@volcano.u-net.com
Chairman *F. Hussain*
Managing Director *A. Hussain*

FOUNDED 1992. *Publishes* academic non-fiction in the following areas: Islam, women's studies, human rights, Middle East, strategic studies and cultural studies. About 15 titles a year. TITLES *Beyond Islamic Fundamentalism*; *Islam in Britain*; *Islamic Fundamentalism in Britain*; *Islam in Everyday Life: An Introduction*; *Women in the Islamic Struggle*. No unsolicited mss; synopses and ideas welcome. No fiction, poetry or plays.

Royalties paid twice-yearly.

Voyager
See **HarperCollins Publishers Ltd**

University of Wales Press
6 Gwennyth Street, Cathays, Cardiff CF24 4YD
☎029 2023 1919   Fax 029 2023 0908
Email press@press.wales.ac.uk
Website www.wales.ac.uk/press
Director *Susan Jenkins*
Deputy Director *Richard Houdmont*
Approx. Annual Turnover £425,000

FOUNDED 1922. *Publishes* academic and scholarly books in English and Welsh in four core areas: history, Welsh and Celtic Studies, European Studies, religion and philosophy. 60 titles in 1999.

IMPRINTS **GPC Books**; **Gwasg Prifysgol Cymru**; **University of Wales Press** TITLES *The Visual Culture of Wales: Industrial Society* Peter Lord; *The Contemporary Challenge of Modernist Theology* Paul Badham; *Editing Women* ed. Anne M. Hutchinson. Unsolicited mss considered.

Royalties paid annually.

Walker Books Ltd
87 Vauxhall Walk, London SE11 5HJ
☎020 7793 0909   Fax 020 7587 1123
Editors *Vanessa Clarke, Caroline Royds, Sally Christie*
Approx. Annual Turnover £31.7 million

FOUNDED 1979. *Publishes* illustrated children's books, children's fiction and non-fiction. About 300 titles a year. TITLES *Where's Wally?* Martin Handford; *Five Minutes' Peace* Jill Murphy; *Can't You Sleep, Little Bear?* Martin Waddell & Barbara Firth; *Guess How Much I Love You* Sam McBratney & Anita Jeram; *MapHead* Lesley Howarth. Unsolicited mss welcome.

Royalties paid twice-yearly.

Authors' Rating Some of the best loved titles in contemporary children's fiction but non-fiction has not done so well. On the lookout for the next bestseller.

Wallflower Press
16 Chalk Farm Road, Camden Lock, London NW1 8AG
☎020 7485 0110   Fax 020 7485 0101
Email info@wallflowerpress.co.uk
Website www.wallflowerpress.co.uk
Managing Director *Yoram Allon*
Chief Editor *Del Cullen*
Approx. Annual Turnover £100,000

FOUNDED 1999. *Publishes* academic and popular film studies and related media and cultural studies. 9 titles in 2000. Unsolicited mss, synopses and ideas welcome. No fiction or academic material not related to the arts, humanities and social sciences.

Royalties paid twice-yearly.

Ward Lock
See **Cassell**

Ward Lock Educational Co. Ltd
1 Christopher Road, East Grinstead, West Sussex RH19 3BT
☎01342 318980   Fax 01342 410980
Owner *Ling Kee (UK) Ltd*

FOUNDED 1952. *Publishes* educational books (primary, middle, secondary, teaching manuals) for all subjects, specialising in maths, science, geography, reading and English and currently focusing on Key Stages 1 and 2.

Frederick Warne
See **Penguin UK**

Warner
See **Little, Brown & Co. (UK)**

Warner Chappell Plays Ltd
See entry under **UK Agents**

Franklin Watts
See **The Watts Publishing Group Ltd**

The Watts Publishing Group Ltd
96 Leonard Street, London EC2A 4XD
☎020 7739 2929   Fax 020 7739 6487
Email <gm>@wattspub.co.uk
Managing Director *Marlene Johnson*

Part of Groupe Lagardere. *Publishes* children's
non-fiction, reference, information, gift, fiction,
picture and novelty. About 300 titles a year.
IMPRINTS **Franklin Watts** *Philippa Stewart*
Non-fiction and information; **Orchard Books**
Francesca Dow Fiction, picture and novelty books.
Unsolicited mss, synopses and ideas for books
welcome.
Royalties paid twice-yearly. *Overseas associates*
in Australia and New Zealand, US and Canada.

Wayland Publishers Ltd
See **Hodder Headline Plc**

Weidenfeld & Nicolson Ltd
See **The Orion Publishing Group Ltd**

Welsh Academic Press
See **Ashley Drake Publishing Ltd**

West One (Trade) Publishing Ltd
Kestrel House, Duke's Place, Marlow,
Buckinghamshire SL7 2QH
☎01628 487722   Fax 01628 487724
Email sales@west-one.com
Website www.westoneweb.com
Chief Executive *Martin Coleman*
Approx. Annual Turnover £2 million

Publishes travel guides and cartography, inclu-
ding RAC publications. TITLES include *RAC
Inspected Hotels Guide to UK and Ireland; France for
the Independent Traveller; Europe for the Independent
Traveller; Road Atlas Great Britain and Ireland.*
Unsolicited synopses and ideas welcome.

Westzone Publishing Ltd
27 Adam and Eve Mews, London W8 6UG
☎020 7376 1415   Fax 020 7376 1416
Email westzone@westzonepublishing.com
Website www.westzonepublishing.com
Chairman *Gavin Aldred*
Managing Director *Nicholas Kenney*

Editorial Head *Gigi Giannuzzi*
Approx. Annual Turnover £2 million

Launching in September 2000 with a projected
output of 30 titles a year. Cutting-edge photo-
reportage books. 'Takes photography, culture
and contemporary art in a new direction.'
Unsolicited mss, synopses and ideas welcome;
approach by letter in the first instance. No
children's or educational books.
Royalties paid quarterly.

Wharncliffe Publishing
47 Church Street, Barnsley, South Yorkshire
S70 2AS
☎01226 734222   Fax 01226 734438
Chairman *Sir Nicholas Hewitt*
Chief Executive *C. Hewitt*
Imprint Manager *Mike Parsons*

An imprint of **Pen & Sword Books Ltd**.
Wharncliffe is the book and magazine publishing arm of an old-established, independently
owned newspaper publishing and printing
house. *Publishes* local history throughout the
UK, focusing on nostalgia and old photographs. SERIES **Aspects**. Unsolicited mss,
synopses and ideas welcome but return postage
must be included with all submissions.
Royalties paid twice-yearly.

Which? Books/ Consumers' Association
2 Marylebone Road, London NW1 4DF
☎020 7830 6000   Fax 020 7830 7660
Website www.which.net
Director *Sheila McKechnie*
Head of Publishing *Gill Rowley*

FOUNDED 1957. Publishing arm of the
Consumers' Association, a registered charity.
Publishes non-fiction: information, reference
and how-to books on travel, gardening, health,
personal finance, consumer law, food, careers,
crafts, DIY. Titles must offer direct value or
utility to the UK consumer. 25–30 titles a year.
IMPRINT **Which? Books** *Gill Rowley* TITLES
*Good Food Guide; Good Skiing and Snowboarding
Guide; The Which? Hotel Guide; The Which?
Wine Guide.* No unsolicited mss; send synopses
and ideas only.
Royalties, if applicable, paid twice-yearly.

J. Whitaker & Sons Ltd
12 Dyott Street, London WC1A 1DF
☎020 7420 6000   Fax 020 7836 2909
Website www.whitaker.co.uk
Managing Director *Martin Whitaker*

FOUNDED in 1858 by bookseller Joseph Whitaker and remained independent until acquired by BPI, American subsidiary of the Dutch group VNU, in 1999. Published *Whitaker's Almanac* from 1868 until the title was sold to the Stationery Office in 1997. Provides a range of services for the book trade including the **ISBN Agency**, BookBank, SourceData and Book Track. *Publishes* bibliographic reference products. TITLES *Whitaker's Books in Print*; *Information Age*; *Directory of Publishers (The Red Book)*; and the journal of the book trade, *The Bookseller*.

Whittet Books Ltd

Hill Farm, Stonham Road, Cotton, Stowmarket, Suffolk IP14 4RQ
☎01449 781877   Fax 01449 781898
Email annabel@whittet.dircon.co.uk
Managing Director *Annabel Whittet*

Publishes natural history, pets, poultry, horses, rural interest. Unsolicited mss, synopses and ideas for books welcome.
Royalties paid twice-yearly.

Whurr Publishers Ltd

19B Compton Terrace, London N1 2UN
☎020 7359 5979   Fax 020 7226 5290
Email info@whurr.co.uk
Chairman/Managing Director *Colin Whurr*
Approx. Annual Turnover £1 million

FOUNDED in 1987. *Publishes* speech and language therapy, nursing, psychology, psychotherapy, business and management, dyslexia, audiology. No fiction and general trade books. 40 titles in 1999. Unsolicited mss, synopses and ideas welcome within their specialist fields only. 'Whurr Publishers believes authors can be best served by a small, specialised company' combining old-fashioned service with the latest publishing technology.
Royalties paid twice-yearly.

Wild Goose Publications

Iona Community, Unit 16, Six Harmony Row, Glasgow G51 3BA
☎0141 440 0985   Fax 0141 440 2338
Email alex@wgp.iona.org.uk
Website www.iona.org.uk
Editorial Head *Sandra Kramer*
Approx. Annual Turnover £200,000

The publications division of the Iona Community was ESTABLISHED in 1985 to publish topical books covering the teachings and ideals of the Community founded in 1938 by Lord Macleod. *Publishes* mind, body and spirit books,

religious songbooks, meditations and music. 9 titles in 1999. TITLES *A Wee Worship Book; Protest for Peace; Dandelions and Thistles*. Unsolicited mss, synopses and ideas welcome; approach in writing in the first instance. No fiction.
Royalties paid twice-yearly.

Wiley Europe Ltd

Baffins Lane, Chichester, West Sussex PO19 1UD
☎01243 779777   Fax 01243 775878
Website www.wiley.co.uk
Managing Director *Dr John Jarvis*
Publishing Directors *Steven Mair, Mike Davis, Ernest Kirkwood*
Approx. Annual Turnover £56 million

FOUNDED 1807. *US parent company*. *Publishes* professional, reference trade and text books, scientific, technical and biomedical.

DIVISIONS **Earth Sciences & Architecture** *Sarah Stevens*; **Life/Medical, Technology & Stats** *Mike Davis*; **College Division** *Simon Plumtree*; **Physical Sciences & Engineering** *Ernest Kirkwood*; **Business & Finance, Psychology** *David Wilson*. Unsolicited mss welcome, as are synopses and ideas for books.
Royalties paid annually.

Authors' Rating A favourite with academics. Authors seem to like the way their books are presented. The American connection helps.

Neil Wilson Publishing Ltd

Suite 303a, The Pentagon Centre, 36 Washington Street, Glasgow G3 8AZ
☎0141 221 1117   Fax 0141 221 5363
Email enquiries@nwp.sol.co.uk
Website www.nwp.co.uk
Chairman *Gordon Campbell*
Managing Director/Editorial Director *Neil Wilson*
Approx. Annual Turnover £300,000

FOUNDED 1992. *Publishes* Scottish interest and history, biography, humour and hillwalking, whisky and beer; also cookery and Irish interest. About 10 titles a year. NWP manages the **11:9** fiction imprint for new Scottish writing, launched in 2000, which is financed under the New Directions Lottery fund, distributed by the Scottish Arts Council. In addition, three non-fiction IMPRINTS were launched in 2000: **The In Pinn** Outdoor pursuits; **The Angel's Share** Whisky, drink and food-related subjects; **The Vital Spark** Humour. Unsolicited mss, synopses and ideas welcome. No politics, academic or technical.
Royalties paid twice-yearly.

Philip Wilson Publishers Ltd

143–149 Great Portland Street, London
W1N 5FB
☎020 7436 4490   Fax 020 7436 4403
Email pwp4364485@aol.com
Chairman *Philip Wilson*

FOUNDED 1976. *Publishes* art, art history,
antiques and collectables. 11 titles in 1999.
DIVISIONS **Philip Wilson Publishers Ltd**;
Flint River Press Ltd *Philip Wilson*.

Windhorse Publications

11 Park Road, Moseley, Birmingham
B13 8AB
☎0121 449 9191   Fax 0121 449 9191
Email windhorse@compuserve.com
Chairman *Dharmashura*
Editorial Head *Sara Hagel*
Approx. Annual Turnover £250,000

FOUNDED 1977. *Publishes* meditation and
Buddhism and biographies of Buddhists. Associated with the FWBO, a world-wide Buddhist
movement. 6 titles in 1999. TITLES *A Survey of
Buddhism; Introducing Buddhism; Meditation; Who
is Buddha?*. Unsolicited mss, synopses and ideas
welcome; approach by letter or e-mail in the first
instance.
Royalties paid quarterly.

Windrow & Greene

See **Compendium Publishing Ltd**

The Windrush Press

Little Window, High Street, Moreton in
Marsh, Gloucestershire GL56 0LL
☎01608 652012/652025   Fax 01608 652125
Email windrush@windrushpress.com
Website www.windrushpress.com
Managing Director *Geoffrey Smith*
Editorial Head *Victoria Huxley*

FOUNDED 1987. Independent company.
Publishes biography, history, military history,
humour. About 10 titles a year. TITLES *Waterloo:
A Near Run Thing; A Traveller's History of
Australia; Key to the Sacred Pattern; Endeavour: The
Story of Captain Cook's First Great Voyage*. Send
synopsis and letter with s.a.e.
Royalties paid twice-yearly.

Windsor Large Print

See **Chivers Press Ltd**

Wise Publications

See **Omnibus Press**

WIT Press

Ashurst Lodge, Ashurst, Southampton,
Hampshire SO40 7AA
☎023 8029 3223   Fax 023 8029 2853
Email marketing@witpress.com
Website www.witpress.com
Owner *Computational Mechanics International Ltd,
Southampton*
Chairman *Professor C. A. Brebbia*
Managing Director/ Editorial Head *Lance
Sucharov*

FOUNDED in 1980 as Computational Mechanics
Publications to publish engineering analysis titles.
Changed to WIT Press to reflect the increased
range of publications. *Publishes* scientific and
technical, mainly at postgraduate level and
above, including architecture, environmental
engineering, bioengineering. 50 titles in 1999.
TITLES *The Revival of Dresden; Applied Virtual
Instrumentation; Seismic Isolation; The Sustainable
City: Urban Regeneration and Sustainability*. Unsolicited mss, synopses and ideas welcome;
approach by post or e-mail. No non-scientific or
technical material or lower level (school- and
college-level texts).
Royalties paid annually. *Overseas subsidiary*
Computational Mechanics, Inc., Billerica, USA.

Woburn Press

See **Frank Cass & Co Ltd**

Oswald Wolff Books

See **Berg Publishers**

The Women's Press

34 Great Sutton Street, London EC1V 0LQ
☎020 7251 3007   Fax 020 7608 1938
Website www.the-womens-press.com
Managing Director *Elsbeth Lindner*
Approx. Annual Turnover £1 million

Part of the Namara Group. First title published
in 1978. *Publishes* women only: quality fiction
and non-fiction. Fiction usually has a female
protagonist and a woman-centred theme.
International writers and subject matter
encouraged. Non-fiction: books for and about
women generally; gender politics, race politics,
disability, feminist theory, health and psychology, literary criticism. About 50 titles a year.
IMPRINTS
Women's Press Crime; **Women's Press
Handbooks Series**; **Livewire Books for
Teenagers** Fiction and non-fiction series for
young adults. Synopses and ideas for books

welcome. No mss without previous letter, synopsis and sample material.
Royalties paid twice-yearly.

Authors' Rating The year has been marked by jazzier presentation and sharper marketing. A prime aim is to move up the ranks of fiction publishers with at least one lead title each season.

Woodhead Publishing Ltd

Abington Hall, Abington, Cambridge
CB1 6AH
☎01223 891358   Fax 01223 893694
Email wp@woodhead-publishing.com
Website www.woodhead-publishing.com

Chairman *Alan Jessup*
Managing Director *Martin Woodhead*
Approx. Annual Turnover £1.3 million

FOUNDED 1989. *Publishes* engineering, materials technology, finance and investment, food technology, environmental science. TITLES *Welding International* (journal); *Reinforced Plastics Durability; Meat Science 6e; Base Metals Handbook; Foreign Exchange Options.* About 40 titles a year.
DIVISIONS **Woodhead Publishing** *Martin Woodhead;* **Abington Publishing** (in association with the Welding Institute) *Patricia Morrison.* Unsolicited material welcome.
Royalties paid annually.

Wordsworth Editions Ltd

Cumberland House, Crib Street, Ware, Hertfordshire SG12 9ET
☎01920 465167   Fax 01920 462267
Email enquiries@wordsworth-editions.com
Editorial Office: 6 London Street, London W2 1HL ☎020 7706 8822 Fax 020 7706 8833
Email laelia.hartnoll@wordsworth-editions.com

Directors *M. C. W. Trayler, E. G. Trayler*
Chief Editor *L. K. Hartnoll*
Approx. Annual Turnover £4 million

FOUNDED 1987. *Publishes* classics of English and world literature, reference books, poetry, children's classics, military history. About 75 titles a year. No unsolicited mss.

Writers and Readers Ltd

PO Box 29522, London N1 8FB
☎020 7226 2522   Fax 020 7359 1406
Email begin@writersandreaders.com
Website www.writersandreaders.com

Publisher *Glenn Thompson*

FOUNDED 1974. *Publishes* children's books, black history, documentary and comic books. 10 titles in 1999.

DIVISIONS **For Beginners**™ *Vastiana Belfon* TITLES *Philosophy for Beginners; Brecht for Beginners;* **Black Butterfly Children's Books** *Deborah Dyson* TITLE *Big Friend, Little Friend;* **Harlem River Press** *Deborah Dyson* TITLES *Revolutionary Suicide; Silent Terror.* No unsolicited mss; synopses and ideas welcome; approach by letter in the first instance. No poetry.
Royalties paid annually. *Overseas office* in New York.

X Libris

See **Little Brown & Co. (UK)**

The X Press

6 Hoxton Square, London N1 6NU
☎020 7729 1199   Fax 020 7729 1771
Email vibes@xpress.co.uk

Chairman *Dotun Adebayo*
Managing Director *Steve Pope*

LAUNCHED in 1992 with the cult bestseller *Yardie*, The X Press is the leading publisher of Black-interest fiction in the UK. Also *publishes* general fiction and children's fiction. 28 titles in 1999. IMPRINTS **The X Press** TITLES *Yardie; Baby Father;* **Nia** TITLE *In Search of Satisfaction;* **20/20** TITLE *Curvy Lovebox.* Send mss rather than synopses or ideas (enclose s.a.e.). No poetry.
Royalties paid annually.

Y Ddraig Fach

See **Ashley Drake Publishing Ltd**

Y Lolfa Cyf

Talybont, Ceredigion SY24 5AP
☎01970 832304   Fax 01970 832782
Email ylolfa@ylolfa.com
Website www.ylolfa.com/

Managing Director *Robat Gruffudd*
Editor *Lefi Gruffudd*
Approx. Annual Turnover £650,000

FOUNDED 1967. Small company which publishes mainly in Welsh. It handles all its own typesetting and printing too. *Publishes* Welsh language publications; Celtic language tutors; English language books about Wales for the visitor; nationalism and sociology (English language). 30 titles in 1999. Expanding slowly. TITLES *My Kingdom of Books* Richard Booth; *The Welsh Learner's Dictionary* Heini Gruffudd; *Burning Down the Dosbarth* David Greenslade. Not interested in any English language books except political and Celtic. Write first with synopses or ideas.
Royalties paid twice-yearly.

Yale University Press (London)

23 Pond Street, London NW3 2PN
☎020 7431 4422   Fax 020 7431 3755
Managing Director/Editorial Director
John Nicoll
FOUNDED 1961. Owned by US parent company. *Publishes* academic and humanities. About 200 titles (worldwide) a year. Unsolicited mss and synopses welcome if within specialised subject areas.
Royalties paid annually.

Authors' Rating A publisher with a marvellous talent for turning out scholarly books which also appeal to the general reader. Academic writers who want to reach a wider audience should take note.

Roy Yates Books

Smallfields Cottage, Cox Green, Rudgwick, Horsham, West Sussex RH12 3DE
☎01403 822299   Fax 01403 823012
Chairman/Managing Director *Roy Yates*
Approx. Annual Turnover £120,000
FOUNDED 1990. *Publishes* children's books only. No unsolicited material as books are adaptations of existing popular classics suitable for translation into dual-language format.
Royalties paid quarterly.

Yellow Jersey

See **Random House Group Ltd**

Zastrugi Books

PO Box 2963, Brighton, East Sussex BN1 6AW
☎01273 566369   Fax 01273 566369/562720
Chairman *Ken Singleton*
FOUNDED 1997. *Publishes* English-language teaching books only. No unsolicited mss; synopses and ideas for books welcome.
Royalties paid twice-yearly.

Zed Books Ltd

7 Cynthia Street, London N1 9JF
☎020 7837 4014   Fax 020 7833 3960
Email hosie@zedbooks.demon.co.uk
Website www.zedbooks.demon.co.uk
Approx. Annual Turnover £1 million
FOUNDED 1976. *Publishes* international and Third World affairs, development studies, women's studies, environmental studies, cultural studies and specific area studies. No fiction, children's or poetry. About 40 titles a year.

DIVISIONS **Development & Environment** *Robert Molteno*; **Women's Studies**, **Cultural Studies** *Louise Murray*. TITLES *The Development Dictionary* ed. Wolfgang Sachs; *Staying Alive* Vandana Shiva; *The Autobiography of Nawal* Nawal El Saadawi. No unsolicited mss; synopses and ideas welcome though.
Royalties paid annually.

Zero to Ten

See **Evans Brothers Ltd**

Electronic and Internet Publishers

AuthorsOnline

Adams Yard, Maidenhead Street, Hertford, Hertfordshire SG14 1DR
☎01992 503151   Fax 020 7681 2847
Email theeditor@authorsonline.co.uk
Website www.authorsonline.co.uk
Owner AuthorsOnLine Ltd.
Chairman/Managing Director *Richard Fitt*
Approx. Annual Turnover
£250,000–500,000
FOUNDED 1997. Internet publisher whose aim is 'to help authors secure hard-copy contracts and for established authors to re-publish books that are no longer reprinted and on which publishing rights have reverted'. £25 is charged to publish the manuscript on the AuthorsOnline website plus annual hosting fee of £10 per week while it remains on-line. Interested in all types of books; submit mss by post or e-mail. For more information, access the website.

Context Limited

Grand Union House, 20 Kentish Town Road, London NW1 9NR
☎020 7267 8989   Fax 020 7267 1133
Email postmaster@context.co.uk
Website www.context.co.uk
FOUNDED 1986. Electronic publisher of UK and European legal and offical information on CD-ROM, on-line and the Internet. TITLE *JUSTIS Cartoons* CD-ROM, developed jointly with the **Centre for the Study of Cartoons and Caricature** at the University of Kent (see entry under **Library Services**), contains over 18,000 political cartoons published in British newspapers from 1912 to 1990. No unsolicited mailshots; enquiries only.

DNA Books

PO Box 166, Stevenage SG1 5UF
Email editor@dnabooks.co.uk
Website www.dnabooks.co.uk
Editor *Dr Stephen Nottingham*
FOUNDED 2000. *Publishes* electronic books (e-books) in the areas of popular science, science and popular culture and guides to the Internet. Unsolicited synopses and ideas welcome.
Royalties of 50% paid annually.

ePublish Scotland

236 Magdala Terrace, Galashiels, Selkirkshire
TD1 2HT
☎01896 752109
Email info@epublish-scotland.com
Website www.epublish-scotland.com
Managing Director *John Brewer*
FOUNDED 1999. *Publishes* in electronic format with an emphasis on educational material. 'We wish to expand our range of products and encourage other authors to consider distributing their work through us.' Welcomes synopses and ideas; approach by e-mail in the first instance.

Notting Hill Electronic Publishers

Vicarage House, 58–60 Kensington Church Street, London W8 4DB
☎020 7937 6003   Fax 020 7937 0003
Email info@nottinghill.com
Website www.nottinghill.com *or*
   www.dancerdna.com
Chairman *Andreas Whittam Smith*
Managing Director *Ben Whittam Smith*
FOUNDED 1994. Award-winning electronic publisher created by Andreas Whittam Smith, founder of *The Independent*. *Publishes* art and popular science on CD-ROMs and websites, and creates 'sound to light' software. TITLES *International Athletics; The Art of Singing; The Evolution of Life; Dancer DNA.*

Online Originals

Priory Cottage, Wordsworth Place, London
NW5 4HG
☎020 7267 4244
Email editor@onlineoriginals.com
Website www.onlineoriginals.com
Managing Editor *David Gettman*
Commissioning Editor *Dr Christopher Macann*
Publishes book-length works on the Internet only. Acquires global electronic rights (including print-on-demand and digital reading) in literary fiction, intellectual non-fiction, drama, fiction for young readers (ages 8–16). No poetry, fantasy, how-to, self-help, picture books, cookery, hobbies, crafts or local interest. 60 titles in 1999. TITLES *Sister Blister* Sam Smith; *Hangdog Hall* James Leigh; *The Glass Palace Chronicle* Patricia le Roy. Unsolicited mss, synopses and ideas for books welcome. *All* communications are by e-mail and authors must have Internet access. Submissions or enquiries on paper or diskette will be discarded. Guidelines available from the e-mail address above.
Royalties paid annually (50% royalties on standard price of £4 or $7).

Reardon and Rawes

56 Upper Norwood Street, Leckhampton, Cheltenham, Gloucestershire GL53 0DU
☎01242 231800
Editor *Julian Rawes*
FOUNDED 1996. *Publishes* re-issues of out-of-print titles in electronic/multimedia format. Non-fiction historical titles only. TITLES *Picture of Bristol – A Guide* Rev. John Evans; *Proverbs and Family Mottoes* J. A. Mair; *Wessex to Essex* Rosemary Barham. Unsolicited mss welcome.
Royalties not paid.

Virtual Volumes

Ashanti, 61 Lower Road, Chorleywood, Hertfordshire WD3 5LA
☎01923 443326   Fax 01923 282750
Email kaq56@dial.pipex.com
Editors *Diana Flower, Andrew Macgregor*
Websites: www.virtualvolumes.com
   www.booksinspace.com
   www.treelessbooks.com
Publishes general fiction and non-fiction, children's and environmental issues. Electronic publishing only. Particularly interested in out-of-print titles and will look at any niche market. 'We aim to bring a wide range of writing to the world's readers.' Welcomes unsolicited mss but prefers synopsis, first 2 chapters of completed works only. 'Please e-mail in the first instance for guidelines or send an enquiry letter only with s.a.e. Submissions on paper will be returned or discarded.'
Royalties of 50% paid monthly.

The Cheque is in the Post – Authors and Their Earnings

There are no rules, only guiding principles for authors' earnings. The Society of Authors has negotiated minimum terms with most of the top publishers but the only figures mentioned in these agreements are percentages such as the royalties an author can expect on hardback and softcover sales at home and abroad. But even these guidelines are open to interpretation.

Old hands remember the days when it was standard for a publisher to offer 10 per cent on hardback and 7½ per cent on paperback with built-in increases tied to volume of sales. No longer. High-pressure marketing now requires a more flexible approach. Concessions to powerful booksellers by way of increased discounts have to be paid for and it can well be that the writer is asked to take a lower royalty so that his book may be sold more aggressively. Fair or unfair? Who is to say until the cheque arrives in the post and the author jumps for joy or rings the Samaritans.

Electronic rights complicate matters still further. The Society of Authors supports an 80:20 division of the proceeds in the writer's favour. Publishers are inclined to switch the advantage or compromise on a 50:50 split. Exports are another contentious area. Contracts usually provide for royalties to be based not on the UK published price but on the price or net receipts received by the publishers. It is not at all unusual for an author to hear good news – that a container-load of his books has joined the export drive – followed by the bad news – the deal was done at such a cheap rate that earnings will be derisory.

When it comes to the advance on royalties, the money that kick-starts a book, an author (or his agent) needs to have a realistic view of his value in the marketplace. Big names get big advances. The six- or seven-figure deal is a regular item of literary news. Last year, Salman Rushdie's agent Andrew Wylie was after £20 million for a five-book deal, though he subsequently lowered his sights to a modest £1.5 million. Heaven knows what J. K. Rowling makes from her stories about the schoolboy wizard, Harry Potter, but it's certain she will never starve.

The big names may be great writers. But then again, they may not. For every Rushdie or Rowling there is a name famous for anything but writing – a royal, a Hollywood star, a maverick businessman – famous, perhaps, for just being famous, who will be inspired by a publisher waving a large cheque. You can understand the reasoning. A personality who is regularly in the headlines is more likely to attract the bookshop passing trade than an unknown – however talented the latter and however bovine the former.

There are exceptions that prove the rule. Barely a week passes without a trumpeted discovery of a bestseller in the making, plucked from obscurity by a sharp-eyed publisher or agent. But million-dollar deals can prove as ephemeral as the newspapers which give them prominence. Publishers quote astronomical sums to beat up public interest; they neglect to mention that the six-figure advance is often conditional on the sale of rights, be they paperback, foreign, film or television. If the deals do not come through, neither does the money. One young innocent given the star treatment reappeared in the news a year later. She was spotted on the dole queue.

Needless to say, flash-Harry publishing does not extend to authors judged to be respectable but not mega-sellers. The best they can hope for is a sum equivalent to 60 per cent of projected royalties on a first edition, split three ways, on signature of contract, on delivery of manuscript and on publication. Marketing people, who tend towards a low view of public taste, are squeezing the sales estimates of books that might be described as 'literary' with the inevitable result that advances too are tighter. They don't always get it right. For *Birdsong*, Sebastian Faulkes was paid a measly £25,000 advance. The book turned into one of the most popular novels of the decade with more than 500,000 copies sold. Insiders suggested re-titling the book *Going For a Song*.

There are other examples of quality authors selling in large numbers – Roddy Doyle, Helen Fielding, Bill Bryson, Minette Walters, Robert Harris, to take names at random – but the fact remains that publishers are ever more reluctant to chance their arm. Advances are down (a promising novelist starting out on a career is lucky to get more than £2,000 up front) and fewer titles are being published. The upside is that more books are being bought than ever before and that radio, television and the movie industry rely increasingly on book publishers for their new material. There are fortunes to be made but by whom and for what remains a tantalizing mystery.

Irish Publishers

An Gúm

Cúirt Fhreidric, Sr. Fhreidric Thuaidh, Baile Átha Cliath 1, Republic of Ireland
☎00 353 1 8892229   Fax 00 353 1 8731140
Email gum@educ.irlgov.ie
Senior Editor *Seosamh Ó Murchú*
Editors *Antain Mag Shamhráin, Máire Nic Mhaoláin*

FOUNDED 1926. Formerly the Irish language publications branch of the Department of Education and Science. Has now become part of the North/South Language Body established under the Good Friday Agreement to provide general reading, textbooks and dictionaries in the Irish language. *Publishes* educational, children's, music, lexicography and general. Little fiction or poetry. About 50 titles a year. Unsolicited mss, synopses and ideas for books welcome. Also welcomes reading copies of first and second level school textbooks with a view to translating them into the Irish language.
Royalties paid annually.

Anvil Books

45 Palmerston Road, Dublin 6, Republic of Ireland
☎00 353 1 4973628   Fax 00 353 1 4968263
Managing Director *Rena Dardis*

FOUNDED 1964 with the emphasis on Irish history and biography. Expansion of the list followed to include more general interest Irish material and in 1982 The Children's Press was established. *Publishes* Irish history, biography (particularly 1916–22), folklore and children's fiction (for ages 9–14). No adult fiction, poetry, fantasy, short stories or illustrated books for children under 9. About 7 titles a year. Only books of Irish interest considered. Send synopsis only with International Reply Coupons; unsolicited mss will not be returned.

DIVISIONS **General** TITLES *On Another Man's Wound*; *The Workhouses of Ireland*; *The Norman Invasion of Ireland*. **The Children's Press** TITLES *Kids Can Cook*; *Drawing Made Easy*; *Riverside Soccer Books*; *Riders by the Grey Lake*.
Royalties paid annually.

Ashfield Press

See **Blackhall Publishing**

Attic Press Ltd

c/o Cork University Press, Crawford Business Park, Crosses Green, Cork, Co. Cork, Republic of Ireland
☎00 353 21 321715   Fax 00 353 21 315329
Publisher *Sara Wilbourne*

FOUNDED 1988. Began life in 1984 as a forum for information on the Irish feminist movement. *Publishes* teenage fiction, and non-fiction (history, women's studies, politics, biography). About 10 titles a year. Does not accept unsolicited proposals in adult fiction.
Royalties paid twice-yearly.

Blackhall Publishing

26 Eustace Street, Dublin 2, Republic of Ireland
☎00 353 1 6773242   Fax 00 353 1 6773243
Email blackhall@eircom.net
Managing Director *Gerard O'Connor*
Commissioning Editor *Tony Mason*

Publishes business and law books. Main subject areas include accounting, finance, management, marketing and law books aimed at both students and professionals in the industry. TITLES *The Caring Economy*; *Brandwatching*; *Individuals and Enterprise*; *Attracting Lifetime Customers*. IMPRINTS **Ashfield Press** Irish-interest books, both fiction and non-fiction. TITLES *Music for Middlebrows*; *The Brothers Behan*. **Inns Quay**. Unsolicited mss and synopses welcome.
Royalties paid annually.

Blackwater Press

c/o Folens Publishers, Hibernian Industrial Estate, Greenhills Road, Tallaght, Dublin 24, Republic of Ireland
☎00 353 1 4137200   Fax 00 353 1 4137280
Email john.o'connor@folens.ie
Chief Executive *Dirk Folens*
Managing Director *John O'Connor*

Part of Folens Publishers. *Publishes* political, sports, fiction (*Anna O'Donovan*) and children's (*Deidre Whelan*). 84 titles in 1999.

Bradshaw Books

Tigh Filí, Thompson House, MacCurtain Street, Cork, Republic of Ireland
☎00 353 21 509274   Fax 00 353 21 551617

Email admin@cwpc.ie
Website indigo.ie/~cwpc1
Managing Director *Maire Bradshaw*
Literature Office *Liz Willows*
FOUNDED 1985. *Publishes* poetry, short stories, women's issues, spiritual, children's books. 6 titles in 1999. SERIES *Cork Literary Review; Eurochild; Millennium Poets.* Submit letter, synopsis, sample chapters and s.a.e.
Royalties not generally paid.

Brandon Book Publishers Ltd
See **Mount Eagle Publications Ltd**

Edmund Burke Publisher
Cloonagashel, 27 Priory Drive, Blackrock, Co. Dublin, Republic of Ireland
☎00 353 1 2882159   Fax 00 353 1 2834080
Email deburca@indigo.ie
Website indigo.ie/~deburca/deburca.ie
Chairman *Eamonn De Búrca*
Approx. Annual Turnover £150,000
Small family-run business publishing historical and topographical and fine limited-edition books relating to Ireland. TITLES *Annals of the Four Masters; The Irish Fiants of the Tudor Sovereigns; Irish Stuart Silver; Irish Names of Places* Joyce; *Burke People and Places* E. Bourke; *Trias Thaumathurga* J. Colgan; *History of the Kingdom of Kerry* Cusack; *Scots Mercenary Forces in Ireland* G. A. Hayes-McCoy; *The Dean's Friend* Alan Harrison; *Manners and Customs of the Ancient Irish* Eugene O'Curry; *The Annals of Ulster, A Connacht Man's Ramble* Costello; *The Three Candles, a Bibliographical Catalogue* de Búrca. Unsolicited mss welcome. No synopses or ideas.
Royalties paid annually.

Butterworth Ireland Limited
26 Upper Ormond Quay, Dublin 7, Republic of Ireland
☎00 353 1 8731555   Fax 00 353 1 8731378
Chairman *P. Woods (UK)*
Tax Editor – Managing *Susan Keegan*
Legal Editor – Managing *Louise Leavy*
Subsidiary of Butterworth & Co. Publishers, London, (**Reed Elsevier** is the holding company). Leading publisher of Irish law and tax titles. *Publishes* solely law and tax books. 18 titles in 1999. Unsolicited mss, synopses and ideas welcome for titles within the broadest parameters of tax and law.
Royalties paid twice-yearly.

The Children's Press
See **Anvil Books**

The Chronicle of Ireland
PO Box 3847, Foxrock, Dublin 18, Republic of Ireland
☎00 353 1 2352657   Fax 00 353 1 2850157
Managing Editor *Harry Walsh*
Publishes the Chronicle of Ireland series, a two-volume annual review of the coverage by the main national media of the political, commercial and social developments in Ireland, North and South. IMPRINT **"G" Gulliver Book**.

Cló Iar-Chonnachta
Indreabhán, Connemara, Galway, Republic of Ireland
☎00 353 91 593307   Fax 00 353 91 593362
Website www.cic.ie
Chairman/Director *Micheál Ó Conghaile*
Editor *Róisin Ní Mhianáin*
Approx. Annual Turnover 250,000
FOUNDED 1985. *Publishes* fiction, poetry, plays and children's, mostly in Irish, including translations. Also publishes cassettes of writers reading from their own works. 15 titles in 1999. TITLES *Aran Song* John Canter; *Facing South* Patrick Gallager; *The Village Sings* Gabriel Fitzmaurice; *Out in the Open* Cathal ó Searcaigh.
Royalties paid annually.

The Columba Press
55A Spruce Avenue, Stillorgan Industrial Park, Blackrock, Co. Dublin, Republic of Ireland
☎00 353 1 2942556   Fax 00 353 1 2942564
Website www.columba.ie
Chairman *Neil Kluepfel*
Managing Director *Seán O'Boyle*
Email: sean@columba.ie (editorial) *or* info@columba.ie (general)
Approx. Annual Turnover £800,000
FOUNDED 1985. Small company committed to growth. *Publishes* religious and counselling titles. 30 titles in 1999. (Backlist of 225 titles.) TITLES *Theology and Modern Irish Art* Gesa Thiesseu; *A Sacramental People* Gunn and Drumm. Unsolicited ideas and synopses rather than full mss preferred.
Royalties paid twice-yearly.

Cork University Press
Crawford Business Park, Crosses Green, Cork, Co. Cork, Republic of Ireland
☎00 353 21 902980   Fax 00 353 21 315329
Email corkunip@ucc.ie
Website www.ucc.ie/corkunip
Publisher *Sara Wilbourne*
Editor *Eileen O'Carroll*

FOUNDED 1925. Relaunched in 1992, the Press *publishes* academic and some trade titles. 26 titles in 2000. Two journals, *Irish Review* (bi-annual), an interdisciplinary cultural review, and *The Irish Journal of Feminist Studies* (bi-annual), are now part of the list. Unsolicited synopses and ideas welcome for textbooks, academic monographs, belles lettres, illustrated histories and journals.
Royalties paid twice-yearly.

Drumlin Publications

Nure, Manorhamilton, Co. Leitrim, Republic of Ireland
☎00 353 72 55237   Fax 00 353 72 56063
Editor *Proinnsíos Ó Duigneáin*
Director, Marketing & Production
Betty Duignan

Publishes local, social and family history, any county and biography. Well researched and referenced work only. Ideas welcome; submit specimen chapter or complete ms.

C. J. Fallon Limited

Lucan Road, Palmerstown, Dublin 20, Republic of Ireland
☎00 353 1 6166400   Fax 00 353 1 6166499
Email cjfallon@iol.ie
Website www.cjfallon.ie
Owner *Adare Printing Group plc*
Managing Director *Henry McNicholas*
Editorial Head *Niall White*

FOUNDED 1927. Educational publishers for first and second level schools in Ireland. 25 titles in 1999. Unsolicited mss, synopses and ideas welcome; approach in writing in the first instance. No non-educational material considered.
Royalties paid annually.

Flyleaf Press

4 Spencer Villas, Glenageary, Co. Dublin, Republic of Ireland
☎00 353 1 2806228   Fax 00 353 1 8370176
Email Flyleaf@indigo.ie
Website www.flyleaf.ie
Managing Director *Dr James Ryan*

FOUNDED 1981 to publish natural history titles. Now concentrating on family history and Irish history as a background to family history. No fiction. TITLES *Irish Records; Longford and its People; Tracing Your Kerry Ancestors; Tracing Your Dublin Ancestors.* Unsolicited mss, synopses and ideas for books welcome.
Royalties paid twice-yearly.

Four Courts Press Ltd

Fumbally Lane, Dublin 8, Republic of Ireland
☎00 353 1 4534668   Fax 00 353 1 4534672
Email info@four-courts-press.ie
Website www.four-courts-press.ie
Chairman/Managing Director *Michael Adams*
Director *Martin Healy*
Approx. Annual Turnover £500,000

FOUNDED 1972. *Publishes* mainly scholarly books in the humanities. About 60 titles a year. Synopses and ideas for books welcome.
Royalties paid annually.

Gateway

See **Gill & Macmillan**

Gill & Macmillan

10 Hume Avenue, Park West, Dublin 12, Republic of Ireland
☎00 353 1 5009500   Fax 00 353 1 5009599
Website www.gillmacmillan.ie
Managing Director *M. H. Gill*
Approx. Annual Turnover £6.5 million

FOUNDED 1968 when M. H. Gill & Son Ltd and Macmillan Ltd formed a jointly owned publishing company. *Publishes* biography/autobiography, history, current affairs, literary criticism (all mainly of Irish interest), guidebooks, cookery. Also educational textbooks for secondary and tertiary levels. About 100 titles a year. Contacts: *Hubert Mahony* (educational); *Fergal Tobin* (general); *Ailbhe O'Reilly* (tertiary textbooks). IMPRINTS **Newleaf** *Eveleen Coyle* Popular health, psychology, mind, body and spirit; **Gateway** Spirituality, cosmic issues, environment, alternative science. Unsolicited synopses and ideas welcome. Not interested in fiction or poetry.
Royalties paid subject to contract.

Goldcrest

See **Poolbeg Press Ltd**

Inns Quay

See **Blackhall Publishing**

Institute of Public Administration

57–61 Lansdowne Road, Dublin 4, Republic of Ireland
☎00 353 1 2697011   Fax 00 353 1 2698644
Email Sales@ipa.ie
Website www.ipa.ie
Chairman *Michael Quinn*
Director-General *John Gallagher*
Publisher *Tony McNamara*
Approx. Annual Turnover £600,000

FOUNDED 1957 by a group of public servants, the Institute of Public Administration is the Irish public sector management development agency. The publishing arm of the organisation is one of its major activities. *Publishes* academic and professional books and periodicals: history, law, politics, economics and Irish public administration for students and practitioners. 9 titles and 6 reprints in 1999. TITLES *Administration Yearbook & Diary; Sources of Economic Information; A New Partnership in Education; A Vital National Interest: Ireland in Europe 1973–98.* No unsolicited mss; synopses and ideas welcome. No fiction or children's publishing.
Royalties paid annually.

Irish Academic Press Ltd
44 Northumberland Road, Ballsbridge, Dublin 4, Republic of Ireland
☎00 353 1 6688244   Fax 00 353 1 6601610
Email info@iap.ie
Website www.iap.ie
Chairman *Frank Cass (London)*
Managing Editor *Linda Longmore*
Approx. Annual Turnover £250,000
FOUNDED 1974. *Publishes* academic monographs and humanities. 17 titles in 1999. Unsolicited mss, synopses and ideas welcome.
Royalties paid annually.

Irish Management Institute
Sandyford Road, Dublin 16, Republic of Ireland
☎00 353 1 2078400   Fax 00 353 1 2955150
Email hannawac@imi.ie
Website www.imi.ie
Chief Executive *Barry Kenny*
Approx. Annual Turnover £10 million
FOUNDED 1952. The Institute, owned by its members, both corporate and individual, works to improve the practice of management. Offers managers a wide range of management development services. *Publishes* a newsletter, *Management Focus* on a bi-monthly basis, distributed to members. Other publications include periodic economic reports and management research and texts. Mss, synopses and ideas relevant to Irish management practice welcome.
Royalties paid annually.

The Lilliput Press
62–63 Sitric Road, Arbour Hill, Dublin 7, Republic of Ireland
☎00 353 1 6711647   Fax 00 353 1 6711233
Email info@lilliputpress.ie
Website www.lilliputpress.ie

Chairman *Brendan Barrington*
Managing Director *Antony Farrell*
Approx. Annual Turnover £200,000
FOUNDED 1984. *Publishes* non-fiction: literature, history, autobiography and biography, ecology, essays; criticism; fiction and poetry. About 20 titles a year. TITLES *Ulysses: The Dublin Edition; The Growth Illusion* (ecology); *Gander at the Gate* (autobiography); *Nature in Ireland; Visiting Rwanda; Life of Theobald Wolfe Tone; The Marriage at Antibes* (fiction); *The Aran Islands* (photography). Unsolicited mss, synopses and ideas welcome. No children's or sport titles.
Royalties paid annually.

Marino Books
See **Mercier Press Ltd**

Mercier Press Ltd
PO Box No 5, 5 French Church Street, Cork, Co. Cork, Republic of Ireland
☎00 353 21 275040   Fax 00 353 21 274969
Website www.indigo.ie/mercier
Also at: 16 Hume Street, Dublin 2
☎00 353 1 661 5299 Fax 00 353 1 661 8583
Chairman *George Eaton*
Managing Director *John F. Spillane*
E-mail: (Cork office): books@mercier.ie
(Dublin office): books@marino.ie
FOUNDED 1944. One of Ireland's largest publishers with a list of approx 250 Irish interest titles. IMPRINTS **Mercier Press** *Mary Feehan* Children's, politics, history, mind, body, spirit. **Marino Books** *Jo O'Donoghue* Fiction, current affairs, women's interest. TITLES *The Course of Irish History*; all of John B. Keane's works; *Mortally Wounded; Real Cool; The Celtic Tiger: The Inside Story of Ireland's Boom Economy.* Unsolicited mss, synopses and ideas welcome.
Royalties paid annually.

Mount Eagle Publications Ltd
Dingle, Co. Kerry, Republic of Ireland
☎00 353 66 9151463   Fax 00 353 66 9151234
Publisher *Steve MacDonogh*
Approx. Annual Turnover £350,000
FOUNDED in 1997, Mount Eagle took over Brandon Book Publishers in December of that year. Strong Irish fiction and some non-fiction. About 15 titles a year. Not seeking unsolicited mss.

Newleaf
See **Gill & Macmillan**

The O'Brien Press Ltd
20 Victoria Road, Rathgar, Dublin 6,
Republic of Ireland
☎00 353 1 4923333   Fax 00 353 1 4922777
Email books@obrien.ie
Website www.obrien.ie
Chairman/Managing Director
Michael O'Brien
Editorial Director *Íde Ní Laoghaire*
FOUNDED 1974 to publish biography and books
on the environment. Also *publishes* business,
adult fiction, crime, popular biography, music
and travel. In recent years the company has
become a substantial force in children's publish-
ing, concentrating mainly on juvenile novels.
No poetry or academic. About 40 titles a year.
Unsolicited mss (with return postage enclosed),
synopses and ideas for books welcome.
Royalties paid annually.

Oak Tree Press
Merrion Building, Lower Merrion Street,
Dublin 2, Republic of Ireland
☎00 353 1 6761600   Fax 00 353 1 6761644
Email oaktreep@iol.ie
Website www.oaktreepress.com
Managing Director *Brian O'Kane*
FOUNDED 1992. Specialist publisher of business
and professional books: accounting, finance,
management and law, aimed at students and
practitioners in Ireland, the UK and USA.
About 30 titles a year. TITLES *The Accountant's
Guide to Excel; Winning Business Proposals;
Success Skills for Managers; Once a Customer,
Always a Customer; The Small Business Guide to
the Internet.* Unsolicited mss and synopses wel-
come; send to *David Givens*, General Manager,
at the address above.
Royalties paid twice-yearly.

On Stream Publications Ltd
Cloghroe, Blarney, Co. Cork, Republic of
Ireland
☎00 353 21 385798   Fax 00 353 21 385798
Email info@onstream.ie
Website www.onstream.ie
Chairman/Managing Director *Roz Crowley*
Approx. Annual Turnover £200,000
FOUNDED 1992. Formerly Forum Publications.
Publishes academic, fiction, cookery, wine,
general health and fitness, local history, rail-
ways, photography and practical guides. About
6 titles a year. TITLES *Dealing With Chronic
Pain; A Pinch of This – Tastes of Home-Cooking;
The Ultimate Guide to Meeting the Opposite Sex.*

Synopses and ideas welcome. No children's
books.
Royalties paid annually.

Poolbeg Press Ltd
123 Baldoyle Industrial Estate, Baldoyle,
Dublin 13, Republic of Ireland
☎00 353 1 8321477   Fax 00 353 1 8321430
Email poolbeg@iol.ie
Website www.poolbeg.com
Contact *Kieran Devlin*
FOUNDED 1976 to publish the Irish short story
and has since diversified to include all areas of
fiction (literary and popular), children's fiction
and non-fiction, and adult non-fiction: history,
biography and topics of public interest. About
70 titles a year. Unsolicited mss, synopses and
ideas welcome (mss preferred). No drama.
IMPRINTS **Poolbeg** (paperback and hardback); **Children's Poolbeg**; **Goldcrest**; **Wren**.
Royalties paid twice-yearly.

Real Ireland Design Ltd
27 Beechwood Close, Boghall Road, Bray,
Co. Wicklow Republic of Ireland
☎00 353 1 2860799   Fax 00 353 1 2829962
Managing Director *Desmond Leonard*
Producers of calendars, diaries, posters, greetings cards and books, servicing the Irish tourist
industry. *Publishes* photography and tourism.
About 2 titles a year. No fiction. Unsolicited
mss, synopses and ideas welcome.
Royalties paid twice-yearly.

Relay Publications
Tyone, Nenagh, Co. Tipperary, Republic of
Ireland
☎00 353 67 31734   Fax 00 353 67 31734
Email relaybooks@eircom.net
Managing Director *Donal A. Murphy*
FOUNDED 1980. *Publishes* regional history.
4 titles in 1999. Not interested in fiction.
Royalties paid twice-yearly.

Royal Dublin Society
Science Section, Ballsbridge, Dublin 4,
Republic of Ireland
☎00 353 1 6680866   Fax 00 353 1 6604014
Email carol.power@rds.ie
Website www.rds.ie
President *Col. W. A. Ringrose*
FOUNDED 1731 for the promotion of agriculture,
science and the arts, and throughout its history
has published books and journals towards this
end. Publishers hired on contract basis. *Publishes*

conference proceedings, biology and the history of Irish science. TITLES *Agricultural Development for the 21st Century*; *The Right Trees in the Right Places*; *Agriculture & the Environment*; *Water of Life*; *Science, Technology & Realism*; *Science Centres for Ireland*; *Blueprint for a National Irish Science Centre*; occasional papers in *Irish Science & Technology* series.
Royalties not generally paid.

Royal Irish Academy

19 Dawson Street, Dublin 2, Republic of Ireland
☎00 353 1 6762570   Fax 00 353 1 6762346
Executive Secretary *Patrick Buckley*
Editor of Publications *Rachel McNicholls*
Approx. Annual Turnover (publication sales) £100,000
FOUNDED in 1785, the Academy has been publishing since 1787. Core publications are journals but more books published in last 13 years. *Publishes* academic, Irish interest and Irish language. About 7 titles a year. Welcomes mss, synopses and ideas of an academic standard.
Royalties paid annually, where applicable.

Salmon Publishing Ltd

Knockeven, Cliffs of Moher, Co. Clare, Republic of Ireland
☎00 353 65 7081941   Fax 00 353 65 7081621
Email salpub@iol.ie
Website www.salmonpoetry.com
Managing Director *Jessie Lendennie*
Approx. Annual Turnover £100,000
FOUNDED 1982. *Publishes* contemporary Irish and international poetry. 20 titles in 1999. TITLES *The White Page/An Bhileog Bhán: Twentieth Century Irish Women Poets* ed. Joan McBreen; *The Portable Creative Writing Workshop* Pat Boran; *Story Hunger* Jerah Chadwick; *A Curb in Eden* Joseph Enweiler; *Split the Lark: Selected Poems* R. T. Smith.
Royalties paid twice-yearly.

Tír Eolas

Newtownlynch, Doorus, Kinvara, Co. Galway, Republic of Ireland
☎00 353 91 637452   Fax 00 353 91 637452
Publisher/Managing Director *Anne Korff*
Approx. Annual Turnover £50,000
FOUNDED 1987. *Publishes* books and guides on ecology, archaeology, folklore and culture. TITLES *The Book of the Burren; The Shannon Floodlands; Not a Word of a Lie; The Book of Aran; Women of Ireland, A Biographic Dictionary; Kinvara,*

A Seaport Town on Galway Bay. Unsolicited mss, synopses and ideas for books welcome. No specialist scientific and technical, fiction, plays, school textbooks or philosophy.
Royalties paid annually.

Town House and Country House

Trinity House, Charleston Road, Ranelagh, Dublin 6, Republic of Ireland
☎00 353 1 4972399   Fax 00 353 1 4970927
Email books@townhouse.ie
Managing Director *Treasa Coady*
FOUNDED 1980. *Publishes* commercial fiction, art and archaeology, biography and environment. About 20 titles a year. TITLES *Love Like Hate Adore* Deirdre Purcell; *Mary, Mary* Julie Parsons; *Now is the Time* Sr. Stanislaus Kennedy; *Wild Wicklow* Richard Nairn and Miriam Crowley. Unsolicited mss, synopses and ideas welcome. No children's books.
Royalties paid twice-yearly.

Veritas Publications

7–8 Lower Abbey Street, Dublin 1, Republic of Ireland
☎00 353 1 8788177   Fax 00 353 1 8786507
Email publications@veritas.ie
Chairman *Diarmuid Murray*
Director *Fr Sean Melody*
FOUNDED 1969 to supply religious textbooks to schools and later introduced a more general religious list. Part of the Catholic Communications Institute. *Publishes* religious books only. About 30 titles a year. Unsolicited mss, synopses and ideas for books welcome.
Royalties paid annually.

Wolfhound Press

68 Mountjoy Square, Dublin 1, Republic of Ireland
☎00 353 1 8740354   Fax 00 353 1 8720207
Website www.wolfhound.ie
Managing Director *Seamus Cashman*
FOUNDED 1974. Member of **Clé** – the Irish Book Publishers Association. *Publishes* art, biography, children's, fiction, general non-fiction, history, photography, literature, literary studies, audio and gift books. About 30 titles a year. TITLES *Famine; Leading Hollywood; Eye Witness Bloody Sunday; Father Brown's Titanic Album*. Unsolicited mss (with synopses and s.a.e.) and ideas welcome.
Royalties paid twice-yearly.

Wren

See **Poolbeg Press Ltd**

Irish Literary Agents

The Book Bureau Literary Agency/ Script to Screen Ltd

1st Floor, 4 Great Strand Street, Dublin 1
Republic of Ireland
☎00 353 1 6670528/8735023
Fax 00 353 1 8735078
Email lez@script2screen.net
Website www.script2screen.net

Contacts *Geraldine Nichol (Book Bureau),*
Lez Barstow (Script to Screen)

FOUNDED 1998. *Handles* all fiction (popular and literary) – thrillers, women's and Irish novels. No horror, science fiction, childrens, poetry. Script to Screen *handles* writers for film, television, radio and theatre. No reading fee. CLIENTS Padraig Kelly, Grace McKenna, Bill Murphy, Paddy Reid. Send preliminary letter, synopsis and first five chapters; return postage/s.a.e. essential. *Commission* Home 10%; US 15%; TV, Film & Translation 20%.

The Lisa Richards Agency

15 Lower Pembroke Street, Dublin 2
Republic of Ireland
☎00 353 1 6624880   Fax 00 353 1 6624884
Email fogrady@eircom.net

Contact *Faith O'Grady*

FOUNDED 1998. *Handles* commercial and literary fiction, thrillers, non-fiction, children's books; TV, film, radio and theatre scripts. No

science fiction. Approach with 3–4 chapters and a synopsis of the rest. No reading fee. CLIENTS Colm Keena, Pauline McLynn, David O'Doherty, S. O'Donovan, Martin Malone. *Commission* Home 10%; UK 15%; US & Translation 20%. *Overseas associate* **The Marsh Agency** for translation rights.

Script to Screen Ltd

See **The Book Bureau Literary Agency/ Script to Screen Ltd**

Jonathan Williams Literary Agency

Ferrybank House, 6 Park Road, Dun Laoghaire, Co. Dublin Republic of Ireland
☎00 353 1 2803482   Fax 00 353 1 2803482

Contact *Jonathan Williams*

FOUNDED 1980. *Handles* general trade books: fiction, auto/biography, travel, politics, history, gardening, cookery, sport and leisure, humour, reference, social questions, photography. Some poetry, business and children's, but less of a speciality. No plays, science fiction, mind, body and spirit, computer books, theology, multimedia, motoring, aviation. No reading fee unless 'the author wants a very fast opinion'. Initial approach by phone or letter. *Commission* Home 10%; US 10–15%; Translation 15%. *Overseas associates* Borderline Literary Agency, Italy; Lora Fountain Agency, France.

Audio Books

Abbey Home Entertainment Group Ltd
13 Blenheim Terrace, St John's Wood, London NW8 0EH
☎020 7625 3600   Fax 020 7625 3100
Managing Director *Anne Miles*

Abbey were the instigators (previously as MSD Holdings) in the development of the spoken word. With over 20 years' experience in recording, marketing and distribution of audio, book and cassette, their catalogue includes major children's story characters such as *Thomas the Tank Engine, Postman Pat, Goosebumps* and *Winnie the Pooh*. *Specialises* in children's audio cassettes. 50 titles in 1999. Ideas from authors and agents welcome.

BBC Radio Collection
Woodlands, 80 Wood Lane, London W12 0TT
☎020 8433 2230   Fax 020 8433 3851
Email radio.collection@bbc.co.uk
Owner *BBC Worldwide Ltd*
Publisher *Jan Paterson*
Editorial Director *Mary Kalemkerian*

ESTABLISHED in 1988 as The BBC Radio Collection, BBC Audio releases material associated with BBC Radio and Television. *Publishes* fiction and drama, non-fiction, poetry, children's and sound effects. TITLES *BBC Radio Shakespeare; Alan Bennett; This Sceptred Isle; Hancock; Steptoe; Round The Horne; Agatha Christie; Sherlock Holmes*. Almost all releases sourced from BBC Radio and Television. Unsolicited work not accepted.

Canongate Audio
See **Canongate Books** under **UK Publishers**

Cavalcade Story Cassettes
See **Chivers Audio Books**

Chivers Audio Books
Windsor Bridge Road, Bath BA2 3AX
☎01225 335336   Fax 01225 310771
Website www.chivers.co.uk
Managing Director *Julian Batson*
Part of **Chivers Press Ltd**. *Publishes* a wide range of titles, mainly for library consumption and direct mail. Fiction, autobiography, children's and crime. 290 titles in 1999. TITLES *The Soldier's Return* Melvyn Bragg; *The Remorseful Day* Colin Dexter; *The Real James Herriot* Jim Wight; *Stonehenge* Bernard Cornwell; *The Double Act* Jacqueline Wilson.
IMPRINTS **Chivers Audio Books, Chivers Children's Audio Books, Cavalcade Story Cassettes**.

Corgi Audio
Transworld Publishers Ltd, A division of the Random House Group Ltd, 61–63 Uxbridge Road, London W5 5SA
☎020 8579 2652   Fax 020 8231 6666
Managing Director *Mark Barty-King*

Publishes fiction, autobiography, children's and humour. TITLES *Discworld Series* Terry Pratchett; *Notes From a Small Island* Bill Bryson and other travel writing; *A Kentish Lad* Frank Muir; *The Horse Whisperer* Nicholas Evans.

Cover To Cover Cassettes Ltd
PO Box 112, Marlborough, Wiltshire SN8 3UG
☎01672 562255   Fax 01672 564634
Email email@covertocover.co.uk
Website www.covertocover.co.uk
Managing Director *Helen Nicoll*

Publishes complete and unabridged audio books of classic 19th and 20th century fiction – Jane Austen, Charles Dickens, Anthony Trollope, plus children's titles – *Worst Witch* Jill Murphy; *Sheep-Pig* Dick King-Smith; *Story of Tracy Beaker* Jacqueline Wilson; *In Your Garden* Vita Sackville-West (book/cassette). 26 titles in 1999.

CSA Telltapes Ltd
101 Chamberlayne Road, London NW10 3ND
☎020 8960 8466   Fax 020 8968 0804
Email michelle@csatelltapes.demon.co.uk
Managing Director *Clive Stanhope*

FOUNDED 1989. *Publishes* fiction, children's, short stories, poetry, travel, biographies. Over 100 titles to-date. Tends to favour quality/classic/nostalgic/timeless literature for the 30+ age group. TITLES *Carry on Jeeves* P. G. Wodehouse;

Alfie Bill Naughton; *The Third Man* Graham Greene; *Hideous Kinky* Esther Freud; *Room at the Top* John Braine; *Midwich Cuckoos* John Wyndham; *How Proust Can Change Your Life* Alain de Botton. Ideas for cassettes welcome.

CYP Limited

The Fairway, Bush Fair, Harlow, Essex CM18 6LY
☎01279 444707   Fax 01279 445570
Email enquiries@cypmusic.co.uk
Website www.kidsmusic.co.uk

Joint Managing Directors *Mike Kitson, John Bassett*

FOUNDED 1978. *Publishes* children's material for those under 10 years of age; educational, entertainment, licensed characters (i.e. *Mr Men; Little Miss*). Ideas for cassettes welcome.

Faber.Penguin Audiobooks

27 Wrights Lane, London W8 5TZ
☎020 7416 3000   Fax 020 7416 3289
Email audio@penguin.co.uk
Website www.penguin.co.uk

3 Queen Square, London WC1N 3AU
☎020 7465 0045 Fax 020 7465 0108

Publishing Manager *Anna Hopkins*
    (at Wrights Lane address)
Publishing Director *Joanna Mackle*
    (at Queen Square address)

A joint venture between **Penguin Books** and **Faber & Faber**. *Publishes* 25–30 titles per year, drawing on the strength of Faber's authors. AUTHORS Ted Hughes, Philip Larkin, Garrison Keillor, Sylvia Plath, T. S. Eliot, Wendy Cope, William Golding, Seamus Heaney and Paul Muldoon.

Halsgrove

See entry under **UK Publishers**

HarperCollins AudioBooks

77–85 Fulham Palace Road, London W6 8JB
☎020 8741 7070   Fax 020 8307 4517 (adult)/
8307 4291 (children's)

The Collins audio and video company was acquired in the mid-eighties but the video section was later sold.

ADULT

Managing Director *Adrian Bourne* **Publisher** *Rosalie George Publishes* a wide range including popular and classic fiction, non-fiction, Shakespeare and poetry. 60 titles in 1999. TITLES *'Tis* Frank McCourt; *Iris: A Memoir* John Bayley; *Black Notice* Patricia Cornwell; *Inconceivable* Ben

Elton; *John Major: The Autobiography*; *Losing My Virginity* Richard Branson.

CHILDREN'S DIVISION
Publishing Director *Gail Penston* **Senior Editors** *Stella Paskins, Gillie Russell* (fiction) *Publishes* picture books/cassettes and story books/cassettes as well as single and double tapes for children aged 2–13 years. Fiction, songs, early learning, poetry etc. 60 titles in 1999. AUTHORS C. S. Lewis, Roald Dahl, Enid Blyton, Robin Jarvis, Colin and Jacqui Hawkins, Ian Whybrow, Lynne Reid Banks, Robert Westall, Jean Ure, Nick Butterworth, Judith Kerr.

Hodder Headline Audio Books

338 Euston Road, London NW1 3BH
☎020 7873 6000   Fax 020 7873 6024
Website www.hodder.co.uk

Publisher *Rupert Lancaster*
Editor *Helen Garnons-Williams*

LAUNCHED in 1994 with 50 titles. A strong list, especially for theatre, vintage radio, film tie-ins, poetry plus fiction and non-fiction. Approx 200 titles in 1999. AUTHORS Louis de Bernières, Dickie Bird, John LeCarré, Alex Ferguson, Stephen King, Ellis Peters, Rosamunde Pilcher, Terry Waite, Mary Wesley.

Isis Audio Books

7 Centremead, Osney Mead, Oxford OX2 0ES
☎01865 250333   Fax 01865 790358

Managing Director *John Durrant*
Editorial Head *Veronica Babington Smith*

Part of **Isis Publishing Ltd**. *Publishes* fiction and a few non-fiction titles. AUTHORS include Virginia Andrews, Barbara Taylor Bradford, Edwina Currie, Leslie Thomas, Douglas Adams, Terry Pratchett.

Ladybird Books Ltd

Ground Floor, 39 Stoney Street, Nottingham NG1 1LX
☎0115 9486900   Fax 0115 9486901

Managing Director *Michael Herridge*

Part of the **Penguin Group**. Only *publishes* recordings of titles which appear on the Ladybird book list. TITLES *The Railway Children; Gulliver's Travels; Little Red Riding Hood; Puss in Boots; Farmyard Stories for Under Fives*.

Laughing Stock Productions

81 Charlotte Street, London W1P 1LB
☎020 7637 7943   Fax 020 7436 1646

Managing Director *Colin Collino*

FOUNDED 1991. Issues a wide range of comedy

cassettes from family humour to alternative comedy. 12–16 titles per year. TITLES *Red Dwarf; Shirley Valentine* (read by Willy Russell); *Rory Bremner; Peter Cook Anthology; Sean Hughes; John Bird and John Fortune; Eddie Izzard.*

Macmillan Audio Books

25 Eccleston Place, London SW1W 9NF
☎020 7881 8000   Fax 020 7881 8001
Email a.muirden@macmillan.co.uk
Website www.macmillan.co.uk
Owner *Macmillan Publishers Ltd*
Manager *Alison Muirden*

FOUNDED 1995. *Publishes* adult fiction, non-fiction and autobiography, focusing mainly on lead book titles and releasing audio simultaneously with hard or paperback publication. About 25–40 titles a year. AUTHORS Wilbur Smith, Ken Follett, Colin Dexter, Clare Francis, Minette Walters, Michael Ondaatje, Helen Fielding, Elizabeth Jane Howard, Martin Cruz Smith, Colin Forbes, James Herbert, Jackie Collins, Kathy Lette, Janet Evanovich, Brett Easton-Ellis, Joy Adamson, Niall Williams, Lynda La Plante.

Mr Punch Productions

139 Kensington High Street, London W8 6SU
☎020 7368 0088   Fax 020 7368 0051
Email editor@mrpunch.com
Managing Director *Stewart Richards*

FOUNDED 1995. Independent producer of audio books – drama and non-fiction. Over 70 titles with SERIES including *Classic Journals; Hollywood Playhouse*, Oscar-winning films specially adapted for the radio and performed by many of the original stars; *Variety Bandbox*, archive variety radio; *Classic Radio Drama; Great British Trials*, dramatised versions of original trial transcripts. TITLES *Wisdens; The Letters & Journals of Lord Nelson; Wonderful Life; Rebecca; Scott of the Antarctic; Tales From the Old Testament.* 'Always interested in non-fiction ideas that are suitable for performing in the first person (single- or multi-voice production).'

Naxos AudioBooks

18 High Street, Welwyn, Hertfordshire
AL6 9EQ
☎01438 717808   Fax 01438 717809
Email Naxos_Audiobooks@compuserve.com
Website www.naxosaudio-books.com
Owner *HNH International, Hong Kong*
Managing Director *Nicolas Soames*

FOUNDED 1994. Part of Naxos, the classical budget CD company. *Publishes* classic and modern fiction, non-fiction, children's and junior classics, drama and poetry. TITLES *Paradise Lost* Milton; *Ulysses* Joyce; *Kim* Kipling; *Decline and Fall of the Roman Empire* Gibbon.

Penguin Audiobooks

27 Wrights Lane, London W8 5TZ
☎020 7416 3000   Fax 020 7416 3289
Email audio@penguin.co.uk
Website www.penguin.co.uk
Owner *Penguin Books Ltd*
Head of Audio Publishing *Anna Hopkins*

Launched in November 1993 and has rapidly expanded since then to reflect the diversity of Penguin Books' list. *Publishes* mostly fiction, both classical and contemporary, non-fiction, autobiography and an increasing range of children's titles under the **Puffin Audiobooks** imprint. Approx. 70 titles a year. Contemporary AUTHORS include: Dick Francis, Barbara Vine, Anne Fine, Gillian Cross, John Mortimer, Roald Dahl, Tom Clancy, Sue Townsend, Philip Ridley.

Puffin Audiobooks

See **Penguin Audiobooks**

Random House Audiobooks

20 Vauxhall Bridge Road, London SW1V 2SA
☎020 7840 8400   Fax 020 7233 6127
Owner *Random House Group Ltd.*
Managing Director *Kate Parkin*
Manager *Victoria Williams*

The audiobooks division of Random House started early in 1991. Acquired the Reed Audio list in 1997. *Publishes* fiction, non-fiction and self help. 27 titles in 1999. AUTHORS include John Grisham, Stephen Fry, Charles Handy, Patricia Cornwell, Michael Crichton and Ruth Rendell.

CHILDREN'S DIVISION IMPRINT **Tellastory** AUTHORS include Jane Hissey, Shirley Hughes, David McKee and Michael Palin.

Rickshaw Productions

64 Fields Court, Warwick CV34 5HP
☎0780 3553214   Fax 01926 402490
Email rickprod@aol.com
Website www.rickshawtalkingbooks.co.uk
Executive Producer *Ms L. J. Fairgrieve*

FOUNDED 1998. *Publishes* adult fiction, specialising in Eastern and Far Eastern literature, both classic and modern. Also looking for unpublished new writers of any genre apart from poetry and children's. TITLES *Chinese Classic Stories* read by Martin Jarvis; *Chinese Women's*

Stories read by Miriam Margolyes. Ideas for cassettes welcome.

Simon & Schuster Audio

Africa House, 64–78 Kingsway, London
WC2B 6AH
☎020 7316 1900   Fax 020 7316 0332
Email darren.nash@simonandschuster.co.uk
Audio Manager *Darren Nash*

Simon & Schuster Audio began by distributing their American parent company's audio products. Moved on to repackaging products specifically for the UK market and in 1994 became more firmly established in this market with a huge rise in turnover. *Publishes* adult fiction, self help, business, Star Trek and Alien Voices titles. TITLES *Mr MacGregor* Alan Titchmarsh; *The Time Machine* H. G. Wells; *Popcorn* Ben Elton; *The 7 Habits of Highly Successful People* Stephen R. Covey; *Deja Dead* Kathy Reichs; *Star Trek IX: Insurrection* J. M. Dillard; *Ramses* Christian Jacq.

Smith/Doorstop Cassettes

The Poetry Business, The Studio, Byram Arcade, Huddersfield, West Yorkshire
HD1 1ND
☎01484 434840   Fax 01484 426566
Email edit@poetrybusiness.co.uk
Website www.poetrybusiness.co.uk
Co-directors *Peter Sansom, Janet Fisher*

Publishes poetry, read and introduced by the writer. AUTHORS Carol Ann Duffy, Simon Armitage, Les Murray, Ian McMillan, Sujata Bhatt.

Soundings

Kings Drive, Whitley Bay, Tyne & Wear
NE26 2JT
☎0191 253 4155   Fax 0191 251 0662
Managing Director *John Durrant*

FOUNDED in 1982. *Publishes* fiction and non-fiction; crime, romance. About 190 titles a year. AUTHORS include Angus McVicar, Barbara Cartland, Catherine Cookson, Olivia Manning, Derek Tangye, Lyn Andrews, Susan Sallis, Mary Jane Staples, Alexander Fullerton, Patrick O'Brian, Pamela Oldfield.

Tellastory

See **Random House Audiobooks**

WALKfree Productions Ltd

Reardon Publishing, 56 Upper Norwood Street, Leckhampton, Cheltenham, Gloucestershire GL53 0DU
☎01242 231800
Website www.reardon.co.uk
Publishing/Sales Director *Nicholas Reardon*

FOUNDED 1996, produces, in association with the Ordnance Survey, *WALKfree AudioGuides* which 'cultivate a new form of country walking experience in the countryside'. The audio tape is accompanied by a 16-page guide book containing an Ordnance Survey Travelmaster map extract plus outline route maps. Each guide also offers advice on convenient places for refreshment and local contacts. TITLES *The Cotswolds; Peak District; Hadrian's Wall.*

Poetry as Ordinary Life

Peter Finch

'Poetry is now part of ordinary life – more read, more written, more discussed, more valued than it ever was,' remarked the Poet Laureate on World Book Day recently. The subject of one of his biographies, the late Philip Larkin did not agree. 'I think we got much better poetry when it was all regarded as sinful or subversive, and you had to hide it under the cushion when somebody came in,' he once remarked. But the world is now a completely different shape. Even TV newsreaders and football players are not unknown to quote the odd bit of verse. Poetry has ceased totally to be an arcane art. It is now central on the everyday curriculum. It is hard to remember those days in the 70s when Craig Raine's *Martians* were as new as it got and most of the population regarded verse as a sort of sissy irrelevancy. Poetry was invisible, operating largely out of pamphlets and in dark pub rooms in the dead of night. But now, new Millennium, new values, and we can't get enough of the stuff.

Centrepiece of poetry's new position in society in recent times has been the Poetry Society's imaginative (and well-Lottery-funded) *Poetry Places* scheme. Here poetry has been given the chance to reach the parts that other arts do not. Poets have worked in communities distant from the literary centre, reading, popularising, demonstrating and getting people who have hardly ever put pen to paper to try their own hands at creating verse. There have been poets working in the Surrey hills with the Countryside Commission, with taxi drivers and their clients in London, with farmers in Cornwall, with locals etching verse onto bus shelters in Blackpool, commemorating the mining tradition in Cleveland, with off-shore workers on the Arco gas platform in the North Sea, with visitors to the Botanic Gardens Glasgow, in the City of London, running online Internet residencies, working with the Red Cross, on the railways in West Yorkshire and, famously, at the Millennium Dome. Simon Armitage, an accessible popular and genuine poet if their ever was one, is poetry's contribution to our national celebration.

'Poetry is the only thing that makes anything happen' – Paul Durcan.

Oxford University Press may have abandoned its poetry list to others but this did not stop the industry from putting out more than two and a half thousand new poetry books last year. Picador, the mass market paperbacker, is trying its hand at poetry CDs. Bloomsbury has published *Versability*, a poetry game for adults while most gift shops now offer *Magnetic Poetry* – sets of magnets with which you compose your own lyrics on the front of the fridge. The Poetry Society has produced a CD-ROM *Poetry Forager* which delivers poetry appropriate to its users' moods. Michael Lee in Richmond is managing PIWR – Poems In the Waiting Room – which should solve a few of the vacant looks

among visitors to the doctors. Where else can the stuff go? Already Tony Blair
has read alongside the Poet Laureate to the TUC and National Poetry Day has
attracted a bunch of promotions the like of which Screaming Lord Sutch would
have approved. There have been poetry contests among 1700 London dial-
a-cab drivers and their clients. Lines have been projected onto buildings and
tattooed onto skin in Salisbury. In St Peter's Square, Manchester the public have
been invited to scratch poetry onto a giant plaster limb. The poetry doctor has
been permanently in this year.

But let us not get carried too far with the tide. Much of the apparent accept-
ability of verse is only skin deep. Check what books people are reading on the
Underground or in airport lounges. Not much sign of the bards there. Nor will
you find verse on the magazine racks at WH Smiths. Once you get inside it
much poetry turns out actually to demand something from its readers most of
them don't want to give. In your face performances at a Poetry Slam may win
the poets instant crowd adulation but for long term viability they need to make
things just that little bit harder. 'Poetry, for all its obligation to be social, must
not be excessively crowd-pleasing if it wants to be worthy of the name. It must
not be afraid of difficulty' – Andrew Motion. There are quite a number of poets
out there on the circuit who could do well to heed that advice.

If your poems are flowing out at a rate of knots then maybe now is the time
to spend a little more time tinkering with them. The best poem is probably not
the one you declare to be complete just as it came. Certainly, it is possible to
produce masterpieces swiftly and for re-writes to beat the excitement out of a
piece but generally things are improved by consideration, deletion, amendment,
comprehensive revision and in many cases by chucking the things in the bin. As
a breed poets tend to overproduce. We have far too much verse kicking around
the system. We are flooded by data anyway, the poetry we encounter needs to
be of the absolute best.

And the best way to get yourself in a position to produce such work? You can
read the rest of this *Handbook* poetry section for firm and relevant advice on the
shape of the scene, where to send you material and how things click. But to get
on the single best activity in which to engage is reading. Worry about writing
later, first discover what poetry actually is.

What should you read?

Taking this advice to heart means putting some time in at the bookshop and at the
library. Be as open and catholic as you can in your selection. Ensure you check out
the whole scene – the past, the present, mainstream English literature along with
work in translation, the obvious poets you find you like as well as those you find
difficult. Appreciation will not come without effort. Stay the course.

Ask at your booksellers for their recommendations. Check Waterstone's or
Blackwells, who both do a good job. A few years back Waterstone's brought out

their own *Waterstone's Guide to Poetry Books* edited by Nick Rennison which provided a decent map. Most shops these days carry a basic stock, but if you need a specialist then get hold of the Poetry Library's current list of shops with a specific interest in poetry. Enquire at your local library. Start with a recent anthology of contemporary verse. You'll be spoilt for choice here, the Millennium's end has rushed a whole crop of century definers into print. To get a broad view of what's going on, not only should you read Simon Armitage and Robert Crawford's Penguin *British and Irish Poetry Since The War*; Sean O'Brien's *The Firebox* (Picador); Michael Schmidt's *The Harvill Book of Twentieth-Century Poetry In English* (Harvill); Hulse, Kennedy and Morley's Bloodaxe *The New Poetry*; Peter Forbes' *Scanning The Century* (Viking); and Ian Sinclair's *Conductors of Chaos* (Picador); but Richard Caddel and Peter Quartermain's *Other: British and Irish Poetry since 1970* (Wesleyan); Sarah-Jane Lovett's *Oral* (Sceptre); Lemn Sissay's *The Fire People – A Collection of Contemporary Black British Poets* (Payback Press); Jeni Couzyn's *The Bloodaxe Book of Contemporary Women Poets*; Linda France's *Sixty Women Poets* (Bloodaxe); Tony Frazer's *A State Of Independence* (Stride); *Poems For The Millennium Volume Two: From Postwar to Millennium* edited by Jerome Rothenberg and Pierre Joris (California) and *Postmodern American Poetry,* a really splendid selection edited by Paul Hoover (Norton). This last title might be harder to find but will be worth the effort. Fill in with a standard overview of poetry in English since Chaucer. Ted Hughes and Seamus Heaney's two Faber anthologies *The Rattle Bag* and *The School Bag* are good scatter guns. For a more balanced historical view try Christopher Rick's *The Oxford Book of English Verse,* Helen Gardner's *New Oxford Book of English Verse,* John Hayward's *Penguin Book of English Verse*, the great *Norton Anthology of Poetry* or long-term standby *Palgrave's Golden Treasury* (OUP).

Progress to the literary magazine. Write off to a number of the magazine addresses which follow this article and ask the price of sample copies. Enquire about subscriptions. Expect to pay a little but inevitably it will not be a lot. It is important that poets read not only to familiarise themselves with what is currently fashionable and to increase their own facility for self-criticism, but to help support the activity in which they wish to participate. Buy – this is vital for little mags, it is the only way in which they are going to survive.

First steps to getting published

Are you personally convinced that your work is ready? If you are uncertain, then most likely that will be the view of everyone else. Check your text for glips and blips. Rework it. Root out any clichés or archaic poetry expressions such as O, doeth, bewild'd and the like. Drop any of what Peter Sansom calls 'spirit of the age' poetry words. Do without shards, lozenges, lambent patina, and stippled seagulls. If you work with rhyme attempt to avoid the obvious. Check that any metre you may be using actually works. Try not to clank. If by this time your writing still sounds okay, then go ahead.

Internet

Poetry's appearance on the Internet has turned from a trickle to a flood. No longer a mere extension of conventional print, it is now a substitute which you ignore at your peril. Growth over the past year has been phenomenal. With the advent of free access and complimentary Web space an increasing number of poetry enthusiasts, publishers and activists have set up sites. Some have abandoned conventional print to operate solely online; others have launched without ever having known ink and paper. Cyberspace – the place where it all happens – is a mirror of the conventional world. The electronic replicates the real. Here are online books, magazines, historical and contemporary archives, reference works, creative tools, discussion forums and news round-ups. Many dedicate themselves entirely to poetry.

Journals

Online magazines range from those which mirror their print-based cousins (and in some cases are simply direct copies) to completely innovative, interactive compilations which mix sound and action with the text. The Net is no static place. It can provide movement, video, sound and user-defined typeface along with actual text. Some mags (e-zines, online journals) offer playable recordings of their poets performing, others give space for readers to add criticism. More and more are opening chat rooms where readers can exchange views. All use the hyper-link, a method of moving instantly from one section of the site to another or off the site altogether. The difference between online and print-based magazines becomes more apparent when you discover that what you get when you call them up is not simply the current issue but access to the entire back catalogue. All searchable, storable (put them on your hard drive) and, best of all, free.

Geography dissolves on-line. America is no further and no more costly to access than Britain. One of the great mags, John Tranter's *Jacket,* is based in Australia. It's just as easy to read as one of the UK's most engaging, George Simmers' *Snakeskin* or Rick Lupert's Los Angeles *Poetry Super Highway.* In fact, half the time, the user has no idea precisely where the site being accessed is physically based. Place ceases to matter, language takes over. Online journals can range from the terrible to the terrific. For my money the aforementioned *Jacket,* *Perihelion* and Jennifer Ley's *Riding The Meridian* are three of the world's best. Not all is in English, either. For information about the Welsh strict metres have a look at *Cartref Cynghanedd ar y We* (The Home of Cynghanedd on the Web).

How do you contribute? As with all poetry ventures, read first. Will you fit in? If you think so then send your poems by e-mail, no s.a.e. needed. A few brave journals will accept work by snail mail from the not yet connected (*New Hope International* insists on this method) although most prefer to deal electronically. Online mag editors hate re-keying, it goes against the grain. And you'll more than likely get an instant answer. Little waiting around for six weeks before your poems return, rejected, through your letter-box. Online is quick.

Cyberspace is huge. Some of the sites which list online journals, such as *Peter Howard's Poetry Contacts*, seem to go on for days. Starting your own mag is easy – frictionless, Microsoft's Bill Gates calls it – and size presents few difficulties. Standards are therefore pretty variable. Not only are the UK's computer literate newbies up there but America, Canada and Australia's too.

Competitions

Naturally there is an online variant to the more traditional send five pounds and your best work contests. A number actively canvass entries from the un-connected and offer Net publication as the prize. For some poets this will no doubt be sufficient reward. Others accept online entries and chose their winners by asking readers to vote – again online. With some you pay by sending a cheque or keying in your credit card details. Others offer free entry. BT insisted that entrants for their Roger McGough-judged Millennium blockbuster signed up for their talk21 e-mail service (also free) before submitting. No hassle, you got complimentary entry and a portable Web e-mail address. BT got your details and a direct route onto your home PC. The selling point for all these competitions is judged to be the enormous audience supposedly sitting around out there in front of their screens. The potential certainly is large - forty or fifty million users already connected and with more joining every day. Yet how many actually bother to access poetry remains debatable. The Web counters which publicly log visitors to sites are notoriously untrustworthy but even if most of them only tell half truths they are still recording a pretty large number of readers.

Books

If you tire of contributing to the websites of others then start your own. A whole collection of verse online will present relatively little difficulty. Most Internet Service Providers, both the ones you pay for as well as the free services, offer an amount of free Web space to users. This means that with the aid of some Web authoring software you can put your work online. Hosting your own *Home Page* is certainly not beyond anyone capable of using conventional computer word processing packages. (See the article So You Want Your Own Web Site on page 174). If you'd like to see the kind of thing that's possible have a look at poet John Kinsella's Home Page, or for that matter my own, *The Peter Finch Archive*. If you are reticent get a fan to set up a site devoted to your works. This has happened to David Gascoyne, to J. H. Prynne, Maya Angelou, Ivor Cutler, Benjamin Zephaniah and others. Otherwise go to it on your own. If you have a recording of yourself doing your stuff then get one jump ahead. Put that up on the site too.

Groups

To reduce the poet's traditional feeling of isolation the Net presents a number of opportunities. World-wide poets, once they've got over the stunning breadth of

Net facilities, are usually hard to shut up. E-mail provides one vehicle. Here bands of poets circulate their work, their criticisms and their views of world literature. Join a group (no cost, just ask) and you'll find a daily delivery of e-mails in your in-box. Some groups are moderated which means that contributions are filtered by a controlling individual although most are free-for-alls. Discussion can range from the moronic to the stimulating. *The British and Irish Poets Group* established by Ric Caddel and *Cyber Poets* set-up by Peter Howard are two worth looking at.

A variant on e-mail discussion groups are Usernet Newsgroups. Newsgroups run through their own dedicated software (provided by your ISP as part of your subscription) and are open to contributions from anyone anywhere. Articles are delivered to your browser for consumption. If you want to contribute then type it up and it's done. The principle poetry newsgroups, *rec.arts.poems* and *alt.arts.poetry.comments*, offer pretty varied fare. By their world-wide nature they tend to be American dominated and standards of contribution are not always that high. But they are places where you can get an instant reaction to your latest poem. There are also a few masterclasses out there with established poets offering online advice. At Lion Chadwyck-Healey have used Matthew Sweeney and Evan Boland. John Burnside was cyberpoet for the Poetry Society. *The Opening Line*, a major collaboration between The Word Hoard and Yorkshire Arts Circus, offers tutor-led workshops for those who want to experiment.

Tools and resources

The Net offers a multitude of these. There are online spell-checkers (in many languages), thesauri, an anagram creator, Shakespeare and Bible concordances, a rhyming dictionary. The archives of universities (particularly in America) offer the great poetry of the past in comprehensive quantity. Download facsimile editions of *The Germ* (the first ever poetry magazine from 1850) or hear Seamus Heaney recite. Read the complete works of Blake, find out what powered the Beat generation, discover how Hardy worked, check the roots of modern verse. Not only can you find the texts themselves but entire critical apparatuses, historical contexts, biographies, bibliographies, portraits, names of lovers, and shoe sizes for most of the great poets of the world. You can access information on poetry readings or check at the British Council for data on literature festivals. Students seems to revel in posting their dissertations. Archives want their knowledge made available to everyone. Interested in a particular style? Haiku? Visual poetry? Traditional forms? They've all got their sites.

E-commerce

E-commerce – shopping on the Net using a credit card – has certainly arrived as far as books are concerned. The big Internet bookshops – bol.com and Amazon – both offer searchable lists for that difficult-to-obtain poetry title. Buying online is generally safe and swift although as with all mail order never 100% perfect. The UK *Poetry Book Society* which acts as a poetry book club (see **Organisations of Interest to Poets**) is also taking advantage of Internet sales.

How to find them

Use the search engine. The big ones – *Yahoo, InfoSeek, Web Crawler, Excite, AltaVista* – can return enormous lists in response to keying in the word *poetry*. I got 149,529 results out of *AltaVista*. Much easier is to log onto one of a number of poetry resource sites which run clickable lists of relevant pages. The UK Poetry Society, The Poetry Library and the *Poetry Review*'s 'Web watcher' Peter Howard's home page are worth consulting. The *Poetry Web Ring* links poetry pages (and parts of pages) world-wide. Follow it and you'll be up for days stuffing your head with verse. Ted Slade's *Poetry Kit* provides poetry, competitions, resource lists plus a whole raft of self-help articles. And for a good world-wide look try *Pif Magazine*.

Where next?

New forms and ideas arrive all the time. trAce, a major online writing project set up at Nottingham-Trent University with support from the Arts Council, is signposting many of the ways Net writing can go. Hypertext poetry – a form of verse which relies entirely on the Net's ability to jump from link to link is becoming a significant artistic force. Check Rob Kendall's *Wordcircuits* for leads. The opportunities for poets are as huge as the Net itself. Get involved now.

Some Web addresses for poets:

Annedd y Cynganeddwyr	www.geocities.com/Athens/Acropolis/1998/
British Poets e-mail list	www.mailbase.ac.uk/lists/british-poets/
Chadwyck-Healey (poetrydatabase)	lion.chadwyck.co.uk
Electronic Poetry Centre	wings.buffalo.edu/epc
Jacket (magazine)	www.jacket.zip.com.au
John Kinsella	www.geocities.com/SoHo/Square/8574/
New Hope International (magazine)	www.nhi.clara.net/nhihome.htm
The Opening Line (workshops)	www.openingline.co.uk
Perihelion (magazine)	webdelsol.com/Perihelion
Peter Finch Archive	dialspace.dial.pipex.com/peter.finch/
Peter Howard's Poetry Page	www.hphoward.demon.co.uk/poetry
Pif Magazine	www.pifmagazine.com
Poetry Book Society	www.poetrybooks.co.uk
Poetry Kit (magazine)	www.poetrykit.org/
The Poetry Library	www.rfh.org.uk/poetry/index.htm
The Poetry Society (UK)	www.poetrysoc.com/index.htm
Riding The Meridian	www.heelstone.com/meridian/
Rob Kendall's Home Page	wordcircuits.com/kendall/
Snakeskin (magazine)	homepages.nildram.co.uk/~simmers/
Trace	trace.ntu.ac.uk/

Commercial publishers

Despite the obvious possibilities of making something from poetry in the traditional hard copy commercial market place the number of those conglomerate publishers involved is actually pretty limited. Where once there were a multitude of mainstream poetry imprints there are now only three or four. Poetry is increasingly seen today as the quality line which enhances a publisher's list. It is rarely there to make profit but more often to impart class and fashion to the list. Despite a decade of poetry booms the stuff is still a commercial risk. Compared to other lines slim volumes are, with a few exceptions, slow sellers. Their editors are almost always part-time or have other jobs within the company and are never allowed to publish what they would really like.

The obvious exception to this approach is long-term market leader and envy of the whole business **Faber & Faber**. Here editor Paul Kegan, who handles adult work, along with Jane Feaver, in charge of work for children, preside over a list which continues to be as important to the firm as when T. S. Eliot inaugurated it more than seventy years ago. The best poetry does transcend the limits of the traditional market, they believe. This is the imprint most poets would like to join. The greats of the twentieth century are here – Pound, Eliot, Plath, Hughes, Larkin. Seamus Heaney made half-a-million in sales when he won the Nobel prize. Wendy Cope regularly sells into five figures. The imprint is built on distinctively designed class and on the roster of contemporary poets are some of the best we have – Simon Armitage, Derek Walcott, Don Paterson, Glyn Maxwell, Andrew Motion, Jo Shapcott, Hugo Williams, Paul Muldoon, Douglas Dunn. Kegan will read all manuscripts submitted. Send a brief covering letter and a sample of your writing (10–20 poems) not forgetting s.a.e. if you think this is where you'll fit in. The Faber Web site is at www.faber.co.uk.

Until recently Faber's leading place was followed closely by the **Oxford University Press** contemporary list of Sean O'Brien, D. J. Enright, Tobias Hill, Penelope Shuttle, Moniza Alvi, Peter Porter, Fleur Adcock and others. But the bottom line talks. The list has gone. 'Ninety per cent sell under 200 copies,' reported director Andrew Potter. Those few poets who didn't jump to either Faber or Bloodaxe now appear on an Oxford Poets list put out by Carcanet Press. At Oxford what remains is backlist and historical erudition. Poetry is the past.

The commercial editor most admired for his taste is still **Cape**'s Robin Robertson. His list is by no means all things to all people. Peter Redgrove, Matthew Sweeney, John Burnside, Sharon Olds and Michael Longley are typical. Roberston, himself a fine poet, produces five to six titles annually – all books, no anthologies and with a number sourced from the other side of the Atlantic. The care taken in their production is obvious. Check them out, these books look worth the money. Worth trying? Yes but potential contributors should never waste anyone's time by not looking at the list first. Poetry at fellow Random House press, **Chatto & Windus**, is now in the hands of Rebecca Carter. Some of the imprint's old vigour is now seeping back with an output of two or three titles a year including Alan Jenkins, Fred D'Aguiar and Kate Clanchy. But unless supported by a strong recommendation from an established fellow practitioner Carter does not want to see unsolicited manuscripts. Both Chatto and Cape preview examples from their lists in the poem for the day section of the Random House website at www.randomhouse.co.uk.

The **Harvill Press** runs one of the smaller commercial poetry lists, publishing one or two new titles annually. Central are the works of Paul Durcan and the late Raymond Carver. It also publishes Michael Schmidt's neatly controversial anthology *The Harvill Book of Twentieth Century Poetry In English*. It will look at new manuscripts but chances are slim. New writers would be better off starting elsewhere.

Among the other commercial houses activity appears to be limited to nominal titles, anthologies or back-list obligations. Liz Calder at **Bloomsbury** reprints poetry classics and work for children (including Benjamin Zephaniah and Adrian Henri) along with the occasional adult titles from the likes of Anne Michaels. **Cassell** anthologises the poems from the London Underground (which sell so well you'd think they'd be encouraged to try something else). **Element** puts out spiritual highs (such as the work of Jay Ramsay). **Souvenir** anthologises cats and dogs. **Dent** recycles Rimbaud and Irish humanism. **Granta** does Blake Morrison. **HarperCollins** ties in humour and first aid with Channel 4. **Methuen** sticks with John Hegley. **Orion** has R. S. Thomas, Ben Okri and the Illustrated Poetry Please. **Boxtree** has Purple Ronnie. Some specialist interests are dealt with at **Lion** (Christian verse) and **Oscars** (gay) – but it isn't a lot.

The smaller operators

Not all commercial publishing is vast and conglomerate. A few independents still exist and on their lists poetry occasionally occurs. **Payback Press**, an imprint of **Cannongate Books**, has been testing the water. Northern Ireland general publisher, **Blackstaff Press**, brings out one or two poetry titles annually. Sioban Campbell, Carol Rumens and John Hewitt are typical. Welsh family firm **Gwasg Gomer** produces tidy editions of Brian Morris (Lord Morris of Castle Morris), Nigel Jenkins and Tony Conran. Formerly *Sunday Times* Small Publisher of the Year, **Polygon** (which is an imprint of **Edinburgh University Press**) continues to mix Gaelic with English as part of its 'poetry for the new generation' policy. Jackie Jones and Robert Crawford are editors. The press has at least half-a-dozen poets on the list including Donny O'Rourke, Rody Gorman, Liz Lochhead and W.N. Herbert. Check their *The Dream State: The New Scottish* Poets. Send in if you are part of the Scottish renaissance.

Universities

With the collapse of OUP's contemporary interest activity among UK presses is sparse. Reprints and literary studies at Cambridge, the same at Manchester. At the

University of Wales Press, which publishes a splendid series of collected works from Welsh poets, you need to be dead. American university presses such as Nebraska, **Harvard**, **Chicago**, Michigan, Ohio, **Yale**, Duke, Northeastern, **Iowa**, **Syracuse** and **California** along with W.W. Norton do an increasing amount of verse but exclusively by Americans. No chances there. In Austria, however, the University of Salzburg Press, now renamed Poetry Salzburg, has embarked on a steady programme of substantial poetry volumes from the less commercial. Run by Wolfgang Görtschacher with financial help from its founder, James Hogg, the press output is around half-a-dozen volumes annually. Workmanlike if not brilliantly designed, these books fill a niche unoccupied by anyone else. Salzburg rescues the neglected and spotlights the new. Typical authors include James Kirkup, Peter Russell, Eric Mottram, Alexis Lykiard, Alison Bielski and William Oxley. Hogg and Görtschacher along with Fred Beake also run *The Poet's Voice* magazine and have published a number of anthologies drawn from the little mags including a best of *Ore*, *Stride* and *Outposts*. Görtschacher's studies of the British Little Mag scene are also Salzburg highlights. Despite its Austrian location the majority of the poetry is British in origin.

Women

There were days when **Virago** was out front here but no longer. Becoming part of **Little, Brown** clearly means becoming less partisan. In poetry terms the company does little more now than bring out the obvious (Margaret Atwood, Jean Binta Breeze, Merle Collins, Maya Angelou) along with the occasional anthology. At **The Women's Press**, Virago's traditional competitor, the situation is much the same. Original good intentions have gone, to be replaced by keeping Alice Walker in print. **The Onlywomen Press**, however, have kept their interest. Lilian Mohin tries to publish two poetry titles annually. Marilyn Hacker, Elana Dykewomon and Kate Foley are typical. Their anthology *Not For The Academy: Lesbian Poets* fills a niche. Generally, however, women poets are better served by the poetry specialists. More of them anon.

The mass-market paperback

The popular end is where many poets imagine the best starting place to be. Paperback houses were founded to publish inexpensive reprints of hard-covered originals and, despite years of innovation and market posturing, to a large extent still fulfil this role. Being neither cheap nor (in sales terms) that popular poetry does not really fit in. Check the empires of **Arrow**, **Vista**, **Corgi**, **Headline** and **Mills & Boon**. If you discount the inspirational, you won't find a book of verse between them. **Vintage**, to their credit, publishes the occasional anthology and runs reprints of Iain Sinclair but he is also a successful novelist. Elsewhere nothing, although there are two exceptions. At **Penguin**, where things are always different, poetry has a significant role. With a commercial ear ever to the ground the company has correctly assessed the market for contemporary and traditional verse and systematically and successfully filled it. Reprinting important volumes pioneered by poetry presses such as **Anvil, Carcanet** and **Bloodaxe**, originating historic and thematic anthologies, reviving classic authors and producing a multitude of translations en route, Penguin continues to provide an almost unrivalled introduction to the world of verse. But appearances aside, this is most certainly no place for the beginner. 'As a large trade publisher, we publish only anthologies plus a handful of famous poets,' publishing director Tony Lacey told me. 'We leave the discovering of poets to the specialists. The smaller presses can take risks: we cannot.' The company acts as main publishers for a select group of sure sellers which includes James Fenton, Geoffrey Hill, Craig Raine, and Roger McGough. The main thrust remains the re-packaging of proven bards such as Simon Armitage, Carol Ann Duffy, U.A. Fanthorpe and Dannie Abse, a good range of modern poets in translation along with larger sets from the likes of William Empson, Allen Ginsberg and John Ashbery. The *Penguin Modern Poets* second series of loosely connected trios has thirteen volumes and represents an excellent cross-section of British and Irish contemporary verse. The company's poetry overview anthology, the Simon Armitage and Robert Crawford edited *British and Irish Poetry Since The War*, is a must. Despite these obvious winners Lacey sees the whole market for verse as small, despite the hype. Penguin on-line is at www.penguin.com.

Penguin's nearest rival, **Picador**, the literary imprint from **Pan Macmillan**, is now exhibiting considerable vigour. Under the commanding eye of successful and non-metropolitan poet Don Patterson it has moved into high gear putting out a stream of successful anthologies including Iain Sinclair's *Conductors of Chaos*, Sean O'Brien's *The Firebox* and an anthology of 'new poetry for the new century', *Last Words*. These have been backed by a CD sampler of readings by Picador poets and a steadily increasing range of individual collections. Patterson will bring out at least six new titles annually. The list includes Robin Robertson, Paul Farley, Kate Clanchy, Kathleen Jamie, Carol Ann Duffy, Billy Collins, Michael Donaghy and others. Worth trying here? 'Certainly: 10 poems better than a full length ms, but establish some track record in the reputable journals first,' advises Patterson.

The specialists

Poetry is available, despite commercial disparagement. But where? With the specialist independents, the small army of semi-commercial operations which are scattered across the country. They are run by genuine poetry enthusiasts whose prime concern is not so much money as the furtherance of their art. Begun as classic small presses which soon outgrew the restraints of back-bedroom offices and under-the-stairs warehousing they are now a real force on the poetry scene.

You can find them in Waterstones, you can see them in Blackwells and at Ottakars. Most (but not all) receive grant aid, without which their publishing programmes would be sunk. They are models of what poetry publishing should be – active, involving, alert and exciting. They promote their lists through readings, tours, websites and broadcasts and they involve their authors in the production and sales of their books. Never before have new poets been faced with so many publishing opportunities. And if there is any criticism then this is it. Too many books jamming the market. Just how does the reader see through the flood? By reputation I guess. Two have emerged well ahead of the pack – **Carcanet** and **Bloodaxe**. Along with Faber these two now dominate British poetry publishing.

Taking them alphabetically the first of these is Neil Astley's acclaimed **Bloodaxe Books**. Publishing forty titles annually the press brings out more poetry books than any other British imprint. Picking up poets dropped by the commercial operators, discovering new ones and selling on to the world's anthologists, this is certainly one of poetry's best proving grounds. Based in Newcastle upon Tyne and begun in the late 70s, the press is unhindered by a past catalogue of classical wonders or an overly regional concern. It relentlessly pursues the new. Astley presents the complete service from thematic anthologies, world greats and selected works to slim volumes by total newcomers. The press has its own range of excellent handbooks to the scene including Paul Hyland's *Getting Into Poetry* and Peter Sansom's *Writing Poems* along with an increasing range of critical volumes. Best poetry sellers are their anthologies: Linda France's *Sixty Women Poets*, Jenni Couzyn's *Contemporary Women Poets*, their decade-framing anthology *The New Poetry*. With commendable concern to stay ahead Bloodaxe is pushing *New Blood,* an anthology of poets whose first books were published during the past decade, Edna Longley's great *Bloodaxe Book of Twentieth Century Poetry* and Herbert and Hollis' *Strong Words*, an important collection of manifestos and poetics. Bloodaxe relishes the chance to publish work from outside the standard English mainstream – Ireland, Scotland and Wales are all well represented, as our more traditional UK outsiders such as J. H. Prynne. There is a multi-media thrust – a series of poets on CD and cassette (including a revival of the British Council's recordings of contemporary poets), and a Bloodaxe website (www.bloodaxebooks.demon.co.uk). Bloodaxe will not go rusty with age. Newcomers are advised to send a sample rather than a full collection. 'If you don't read contemporary poetry we are unlikely to be interested in your work,' comments Astley. Apart from the company's catalogue (which is a sampler in itself) a simple way to taste the imprint's range is to try their anthology *Poetry With An Edge.*

The second, **Carcanet Press**, has been the consistent recipient of critical accolades from the great and the good. Publishing four Nobel Prize-winning authors and four Pulitzers helps. And recently, with the fall of OUP, Carcanet has taken over what remains of their list. Although it is no longer exclusively a publisher of verse, putting out fiction, criticism, lives and letters, the press still gives poetry pre-eminence. It has over 600 titles in print and reps in forty-two countries. Managing director Michael Schmidt agrees with Auden's observation that most people who read verse read it for some reason other than the poetry. He fights the tide with his own mainstream journal *PN Review*. Carcanet has a policy of serious quality. 'I am strongly aware of the anti-modernist slant in a lot of poetry publishing, and publish to balance this,' he comments. 'Most submissions we receive come from people ignorant of the list to which they are submitting. Nothing is more disheartening than to receive a telephone call asking whether Carcanet publishes poetry.' The press has a four-part editorial programme: to publish new writing, to dust down substantial but neglected figures of this and earlier centuries, to encourage the translation of poetry, and to publish poets' prose and work relating to modern poetry. Typical of their list are Ian Macmillan, John Ashbery, Gillian Clarke, Allen Curnow, Edwin Morgan, Les Murray, Sophie Hannah, Miles Champion, Eavan Boland and bestseller Elizabeth Jennings. Carcanet has an air of purpose about it. 'We avoid the technicolour and pyrotechnic media razzmatazz,' says Schmidt. Have a look at their Web site (www.carcanet.co.uk) which is complete with a secure online bookselling facility. New poets are welcome to submit, but check both your own past performance as well as Carcanet's style before you go ahead. Schmidt's *New Poetries* anthologies give an idea where his taste is going next.

Production standards among other specialists can be equally as good as Carcanet and Bloodaxe, although annual output (and as a consequence opportunity for the new poet) is substantially less.

Anvil Press Poetry, under founder Peter Jay, has now done thirty years of independent, alternative publishing and a recent activity shows the press to be as vigorous as ever. Founded as a small press in 1968 Anvil was an early alternative to the Fabers of the poetry scene. Jay still runs his original group of poets – Harry Guest, Peter Levi, Anthony Howell and Heather Buck – although he is adamant that he avoids cliques. If they are right for the imprint new poets will be taken on. Jay has continued his abiding interest in poetry in translation publishing titles from Li Po, Lorca, Bei Dao, Trakl, Gumilyov and others. Anvil is justly proud of its claim of keeping British poetry open to new work from all over the world. Editions have a subdued style with as much attention paid to presentation inside the book as out. Their runaway best-seller is Carol Ann Duffy, with Matthew Sweeney and Ken Smith's anthology, *Beyond Bedlam*, 'poems written out of mental distress', not far behind. The kind of thing Anvil uses can be best sampled in Jay's anthology *The Spaces of Hope*, 'the most memorable work encountered in thirty years of independent publishing'.

Enitharmon Press represents quality, cares about presentation and operates 'at the unfashionable end' of the poetry publishing spectrum. Its books, often concerned with the process of bringing together word and image, are produced to the highest of standards. Enitharmon has little interest in fashion. The press is, as Anne Stevenson put it, 'dedicated to a poetry of the human spirit in an age of rampant commercialism'. Owner Stephen Stuart-Smith continues a policy of publishing between eight and ten volumes annually by new, established and unjustly neglected poets. Typical of the list are Pascale Petit, Myra Schneider, Vernon Scannell, Edwin Brock and Anthony Thwaite. The press has seen a recent surge in interest in the anthology, bringing out volumes covering the Thames, The Exeter Riddles, and a first from The Poetry School. 'It seems unlikely that many new names will be added to the list, as Enitharmon is the only major poetry publisher in Britain which receives no regular subsidy' – which is a pity. We need more from publishers like Stuart-Smith.

Seren Books is a Welsh-based literary house publishing novels, short fiction, biographies and critical texts. Started by Cary Archard as an offshoot of the magazine *Poetry Wales*, the imprint still maintains a solid interest in verse, publishing at least eight new single author volumes annually. In receipt of Arts Council of Wales sponsorship, the bias towards work from Wales and the border regions is both admirable and inevitable. Poetry editor Amy Wack reads *everything* submitted but admits that she has only ever accepted one unsolicited manuscript in her entire tenure. Poets should read more, she told me. Editions are quality productions with plenty of attention paid to design inside and out. Typical recent poets include Forward winner Sheenagh Pugh, Deryn Rees-Jones, Paul Henry, Robert Minhinnick and Tony Curtis. Their major best-seller is Dannie Abse's *Twentieth Century Anglo-Welsh Poetry*. A good example of their work is the anthology *Burning The Bracken*. They have also published their own guide to the scene, *The Poetry Business*.

Tony Ward's **Arc Publications**, based in Lancashire, publishes a dozen poetry titles annually. 'We publish work that we believe important, innovative, and of outstanding quality,' Ward told me. The imprint has David Morley and John Kinsella on the board and maintains a backlist of approaching 100 titles. Ivor Cutler, John Kinsella and John Hartley-Williams are top sellers. The press has recently launched a series aimed at bringing significant foreign poets to the attention of English audiences. The press Web site is at www.arcpublications.co.uk. Prospective poets should not expect a quick response and most certainly should familiarize themselves with the Arc list before sending. 'There are simply too many family/angst/therapy writers believing, without any hint of editing or rewriting, they are God's gift' is the official line. You have been warned.

Rupert Loydell's **Stride** has gathered a good reputation for catholic taste and running risks. Based in the south-west recent cut-backs in grant aid have sadly reduced output from fifteen to six books annually. The back list runs to more than 200 titles ranging from the totally unknown to the famous. Stride almost perfectly fills the gap between the avant-garde and the user-friendly. No one else operates in this niche. 'We are interested in linguistically innovative work,' says Loydell, 'as well as work in more traditional genres that reinvent the way we see the world.' The press runs individual collections, criticism and interviews, along with a range of excellent alternative anthologies. Stride responds to submissions swiftly; invariably within three weeks and often within three days. Recent successes include Colin Falck, Peter Redgrove, Robert Sheppard and their series of interviews on poetics, *Binary Myths*. Check Stride's anthology *Ladder To The Next Floor* for a sampler of how the press got where it is or look at their Web site (www.madbear.demon.co.uk/stride/).

Peterloo Poets, based in Cornwall, represents poetry without frills, without fuss and most definitely without the avant-garde. Run by Harry Chambers, the press aims to publish quality work by new and neglected poets, some of them late starters (although if you have been flogging your stuff around the circuit for years and got nowhere then Chambers is unlikely to be your saviour); to co-publish with reputable presses abroad (Goose Lane in Canada, Storyline Press and the University of Pittsburgh in the States, and **Cló Iar Chonnacta** in Ireland); and to establish a Peterloo list of succeeding volumes by a core of poets of proven worth. Chambers avoids anthologies and has finished with magazines and newsletters. The press sticks to books, running an active backlist of nearly 200 titles. Bestsellers include U. A. Fanthorpe, John Mole with his collections for children, John Whitworth's *From The Sonnet History*, John Latham and Dana Gioia. Recent additions include Anna Crowe and Alison Pryde. The Peterloo Centre has now opened in a converted chapel at Calstock, a venture not without its funding difficulties. Now in its twenty-third year, it runs its own poetry competition (£2000 first prize – see entry under **Prizes**) and insists that prospective contributors to the press have had at least six poems in reputable magazines. Send a full manuscript accompanied by a stamped envelope large enough to carry it back to you. Chambers currently takes a couple of months to reply and is full to 2002.

There are other presses with less prodigious outputs but whose editions are still up there with the best of them. In Northumberland Margaret and Peter Lewis's **Flambard Press** has maintained its stature. Begun in 1991, it now publishes around four titles annually in the Bloodaxe style. With aid from Northern Arts, the press is particularly interested in new and neglected poets especially from the North and the Borders. William Scammell and Amanda White are typical poets. They also publish H. R. F. Keating's crime fiction in verse. Gladys Mary Coles has developed her **Headland Publications** into a regular Peterloo clone. Her interest centres on north-west England and north Wales: Brian Wake, Herbert Williams and Joseph Clancy top the list. Ken Edwards' **Reality Street Editions** specializes in 'linguistically innovative writing by women and men on both sides of the Atlantic'. Publishing a small number of single-author volumes, translations and ground-breaking anthologies along with a series of four-poet showcases, the press takes the new poetry seriously although it offers little scope for the newcomer. Typical authors include Barbara Guest, Cris Cheek and Denise Riley. The press has also published book/CD packages and runs an excellent Web site (freespace.virgin.net/reality.street/). Nicholas Moore's **Etruscan Books** carries the flame for avant-garde poetry and performance with an excellent series of readers, chapbooks and multi-contributor volumes backed up by extensive poetry tours and festival appearances. Poets include Alice Notley, Maggie O'Sullivan, Bill Griffiths and Tom Pickard.

At the self-styled poetry capital of Britain, no other place than Huddersfield,

Janet Fisher and Peter Sansom run **Smith/Doorstop,** the poetry imprint of their enterprising **Poetry Business** (see **Organisations of Interest to Poets**). The press produces a mixture of pamphlets, full-length collections and stylish cassettes. Cliff Yates, Martin Stannard, Jo Haslam, Carcanet Press MD Michael Schmidt, and Michael Laskey are typical authors. Simon Armitage, Carol Ann Duffy and Ian McMillan feature in the cassette series.

Jessie Lendennie runs **Salmon Publishing** from the Cliffs of Moher, Co. Clare with connections at Spruce Island, Alaska, where they are planning a North American poetry centre and writers' retreat. The press publishes some of the best-designed titles in the West. An Irish connection is pretty useful when trying here although Salmon do look at material from further afield. Typical poets include Adrian Rich, Rita Ann Higgins, Theo Dorgan, Ann Zell, James Simmons and Mary O'Donnell. Their anthology of contemporary Irish women poets, *The White Page*, is a terrific achievement. Salmon has an excellent Web site (www.salmonpoetry.com). And if the poetry is not flowing you can book in to a Salmon residential Creative Writing Workshop – £100 for the weekend.

Peepal Tree is the largest independent publisher of Caribbean, South Asian and black British poetry. Founded in 1986 it now produces around eight poetry titles annually. Typical poets include Kwame Dawes, Marcia Douglas, Cyril Dabydeen and Stewart Brown. Editors Jeremy Poynting and Hannah Banister read over 1000 submissions annually and are not known for their speedy responses. Send five or six examples of your work along with a biographical note and wait. You can get a Peepal Tree catalogue and news updates by e-mail (hannah@peepal.demon.co.uk).

Elsewhere, Roland John's **Hippopotamus Press** slowly fills the middle ground with Edward Lowbury, and Lotte Kramer and Lewis Davie's prose outfit, **Parthian Books** has appointed a poetry editor and is putting out fine editions of Richard Gwyn and Ifor Thomas.

As technology continues to make life easier for publishers, it becomes harder to draw the line between the poetry specialists and the classic small presses. Maybe by now such a division does not exist at all.

The traditional outlets

Poetry has a place in our national press but traditionally a small one. *The Independent* runs a daily poem, so does the *Express*. The *Guardian* features verse from time to time as do all the serious Sunday heavies. The *Times Literary Supplement* gives over considerable space on a regular basis but it does have its favourites. The *London Review of Books* shows a similar interest although neither appear very keen to use unsolicited work from the mailbox. The *London Magazine* has the reputation for being the fastest responder in the business (you walk to the post box, mail your poems, then return home to find them rejected and waiting for you on the mat). Auberon Waugh relishes stuffy tradition at The

Literary Review. Among other weeklies and monthlies the situation is fluid. Poetry gets in when someone on the staff shows an interest. Check your targets along the shelves at WHSmith's. Local newspapers and freesheets occasionally devote pages to contributions from readers, mostly dire doggerel and largely unpaid, although it is publication. If your paper hasn't joined in yet try sending your work in. Much of this might sound quite reassuring for the poet but the truth is that were poetry to cease to exist overnight, then these publications would continue to operate without a flicker. Who, other than the poets, would notice?

The regional anthologies

Running in parallel with the high ground literary approach of much of the poetry world are empires largely unknown to the taste-makers and ignored by the critics. The biggest, Ian and Tracy Walton's **Forward Press** in Peterborough, now turns over £1.5 million annually, has almost 5000 titles in print, and reckons to account for around ten percent of all verse published in the UK. Depressed with 'twenty years of not being able to enjoy poetry' because it was inevitably obscure, the couple have moved from back kitchen to factory unit in the service of 480,000 active British verse scribblers. 'A high proportion of the thousands of letters we receive tell us that many people find poetry over-complex and difficult to understand' runs one of their brochures. For more than a decade since it was founded, Forward Press has enthusiastically promoted an 'accessible, sincere poetry which everyone can relate to'. The higher realms are not for them. Publishing under a number of imprints including **Poetry Now**, **Anchor Books** and **Triumph House**, the operation receives thousands of contributions annually. Poets are sourced through free editorial copy in regional newspapers. The contributors flow in their hundreds. 'It is a bit like amateur dramatics,' Ian told me, 'anyone can take part.'

Forward's outstanding success is built on its approachability. The Waltons and their team of exclusively young editors include as many as 160 poems in each anthology. Submissions under thirty lines are preferred. Costs are kept down by using in-house printing equipment coupled to serviceable bindings. If you want to see your work in print, and for most contributors this is the whole *raison d'être* for writing, then you have to buy a copy. For many poets this will be their first appearance in book form and chances are they will purchase more than a single copy. This is not a traditional vanity operation. No one is actually being ripped off nor are the publishers raking in exorbitant profits. Page for page their titles are not much more expensive than those of Cape or Faber and are cheaper than the output of some little presses. However, distribution is patchy – not many Forward titles make the shelves of our national chains. As for many of the small presses, interested parties are encouraged to buy direct. Forward's critics claim that quality is being neglected in exchange for quantity. Dumb down your criteria for inclusion, cram the poems in, sell more copies. Undoubtedly the genuine literary achievement of appearing in one of Forward's books is questionable. But in mitigation it must be said that for some writers this will be their much-needed beginning and for others the only success they are ever going to get.

Forward's much criticized royalty payment scheme has been replaced with the *Forward Press Top 100 Awards* which annually offer a total of £10,000 to the best of the poets published in their many anthologies.

In addition to their schools and regional collections, Forward runs two magazines, *Poetry Now* and *Triumph Herald* (which specializes in Christian verse), a print and design service for self-publishers, and **Poetry Now Introducing** – a series of books from single authors. Their **Writers' Bookshop** imprint publishes a most useful series of guides to the publishing scenes in Britain, America and Australia including subject and genre guides, directories and handbooks. Forward offers the complete poetry life. If *Season's Delight, Poetic Bond, Happy Days, Cleansing Thoughts*, and *Portraits of Life* sound like your scene send for the group's newsletters (Remus House, Coltsfoot Drive, Woodston, Peterborough PE2 9JX), ring them (01733 890099), check their Web site (www.forwardpress.co.uk) or e-mail your request (suzy@forwardpress.co.uk). You'll find no dubious accommodation address dealing here but, on the other hand, few literary giants either.

Envious of Forward's success at catching the hearts and minds of most of the UK's poetry hobbyists, a good number of rival empire-builders have risen in their wake. Regional poetry anthologies, 'Best of Britain collections' and compendiums of English, Scottish, Irish and Welsh verse abound. Contributions are sourced through notices on library walls, local freesheets, local radio and through direct mail. These operations vary from the glossy to a number of pathetically produced and, one hopes, short-lived incarnations based in the non-metropolitan sticks. No actual rip-off occurs and contributors get in whether they purchase or not. But if you want to see your work then you must buy and the books can cost upwards of £20. Before agreeing to contribute check the press's output. Do not submit blindly, research their back list. It is what Faber would demand of you. The rule applies to the whole poetry scene.

The small press and the little magazine

Hobbyist publishing ventures have been with us for quite a long time. And today it seems easier than ever to get your own small mag into the market place or to bring out your own book. Technologically literate poets are everywhere. Publishing has been stripped of its mystery. Access to decent printers and the computers that drive them are commonplace. Desktop publishing and word processing software make it so easy to do. Disposable income has gone up. Poets in growing numbers are able and willing to establish competent one-person publishing operations, turning out neat, professional-looking titles on a considerable scale.

These are the small presses and little magazines. They sell to new and often non-traditional markets rarely finding space on bookshop shelves, where they are regarded as unshiftable nuisances. Professional distribution is still the age-old problem, using as it does conventional routes. But as publication shifts into cyberspace the Internet is becoming the great leveller. For now small mags mostly go hand-to-hand among friends – at slams, readings, concerts, creative writing classes, literary functions and via subscriptions – and are liberally exchanged among all concerned. The network is large. The question remains: is anyone out there not directly concerned with the business of poetry actually reading it? But that is another story.

Statistically, the small presses and the little magazines are the largest publishers of new poetry in terms of range and circulation. They operate in a bewildering blur of shapes and sizes everywhere from Brighton to Birmingham and Aberystwyth to Aberdeen. Have a look at Derrick Woolf's fine *Poetry Quarterly Review* (Coleridge Cottage, Nether Stowey, Somerset TA5 1NQ), or Andy Cox's broad ranging *Zene* (5 Martins Lane, Witcham, Ely, Cambs CB6 2LB; www.tta-press.freewire.co.uk). There are also two excellent browsable small magazine information Web sites: Daniel Trent's Little Magazines (www.little-magazines.co.uk), which exhibits flair and information in equal measure, and Gerald England's New Hope International (www.nhi.clara.net/mg.htm).

This country's best poetry magazines all began as classic littles. Between them *PN Review*, *Ambit*, *The Devil*, *Outposts*, *Orbits*, *Poetry Review*, *Rialto*, *Acumen*, *Staple*, *The North*, *Smiths Knoll*, *Envoi* and *Stand* do not come up to even half the circulation of journals like *Shooting Times* and *Practical Fishkeeping* – which says a lot about the way our society values its poetry. Nonetheless, taken as a group, they will get to almost everyone who matters. They represent poetry as a whole. Read these and you will get some idea of where the cutting edge is. In the second division in terms of kudos lie the regional or genre specialists such as *HU* (Irish poetry), *Poetry Scotland*, *The New Welsh Review*, *Poetry Wales*, *Poetry Ireland*, *Psycopoetica* (psychologically based poetry), *Krax* (humorous verse), *Writing Women*, *Christian Poetry Review*, *Snapshots Haiku Magazine* and *Time Haiku*. All these magazines are well produced, sometimes with the help of grants, and all represent a specific point of view. In Wales there is *Barddas* for poets using the strict meters and in Scotland *Lallans* for poets working in Lowland Scots. The vast majority of small magazines, however, owe no allegiance and range from fat irregulars like *The Reater* (powered by a Lottery grant), quality general round-ups like *Billy Liar*, *Tears In The Fence*, *Obsessed With Pipework* and *Seam* (small enough to slide up your sleeve), to pamphlets like *The Yellow Crane* (interesting new poems), *The Red Wheelbarrow* (so much depends), *The Interpreter's House* (the best prose and verse that the editor can get), *Iota* (recent poetry), *Poetry Monthly* (run by poets for poets), *The Poetry Church* (a magazine of Christian poetry), *Slipstream* (risk-takers welcome) and *Swagmag* (the magazine of Swansea's writers and artists). Some, like *The Penniless Press,* are for the poor of pocket and the rich of mind, *Sub Voicive* doesn't like you smoking, while *The News That Stays News* is a private affair. If you can't find a magazine that suits you and your style then you can't be writing poetry. On the other hand, if you are really sure you are then start your own.

Among the small presses there is a similar range. **Maquette** dips its toe in the new wave; **Rockingham Press** stays safe, solid and conventional; **Odyssey**, the side-line of *Poetry Quarterly Review*, based at the aptly named Coleridge Cottage in Somerset, mixes the mainstream with the wobbling edge; **Dangaroo** has Third World and ethnic concerns. **The Collective** works the Welsh marches; **Staple First Editions** insists on the new and unsafe. **Poetical Histories** works with the innovative, as do **Words Worth** and **Alfred David Editions**. **Redbeck** follows David Tipton's reliable ear with at least a dozen pamphlets each year and an increasing number of quality full scale books which put this press among those on the rise. **Y Lolfa** publishes unofficial bards. These kinds of presses are the obvious place for the new writer to try first. Indeed it is where many have. Who put out T. S. Eliot's first? A small publisher. Dannie Abse, Peter Redgrove, James Fenton and Dylan Thomas, the same. R. S. Thomas, Ezra Pound and Edgar Allen Poe didn't even go that far – they published themselves.

Poetry for children

The thing to remember here is that children rarely buy poetry for themselves nor are there poetry magazines aimed at them. On the other hand there are a great number of children's poets out there – Duffy, McGough, Henri and Patten would be much lesser authors if they'd ignored the under-eighteens. The schools system regularly pays poets to read to their classes and teach their children. Macmillan, Faber, Penguin, Walker and a few other publishers run specialist children's poetry lists. The market switches between the traditional and the hilarious – *Whizz, Bang, Orang-Utan* compiled by John Foster is a typical title. If you have appropriate work send in a few samples marked for the attention of the children's poetry editor. But do not imagine this market to be easy nor a place where you can unload your adult failures. Kids do not suffer fools gladly. For more information check with the Poetry Society, which publishes a number of poetry in schools checklists along with a handbook.

Cash

A lot of writers new to the business are surprised to learn that their poetry will not make them much money. For most, being a poet is not really much of an occupation. You get better wages delivering papers. There will be the odd £10 from the better heeled magazine, perhaps even as much as £60 or so from those periodicals lucky enough to be in receipt of a grant, but generally it will be free copies of the issues concerned, thank you letters and little more. Those with collections published by a subsidized, specialist publisher can expect a couple of hundred as an advance on royalties. Those using the small presses can look forward to a handful of complimentary copies. On the Internet, published poets get nothing at all. The truth is that poetry itself is undervalued. You can earn money writing about it, reviewing it, lecturing on it, teaching it or, certainly, by giving public performances (£100 standard here, £900 or more if you are Roger McGough, several thousand if you are Seamus Heaney). In fact, most things in the poetry business will earn better money than the verse itself. This isn't capitalism, this is art.

Readings

Since the great Beat Generation Albert Hall reading of 1964, there has been an ever-expanding phenomenon of poets on platforms, reading or reciting their stuff to an audience that can be anywhere between raptly attentive and fast asleep. Jaci Stephen, writing in the *Daily Mirror*, reckoned readings to be like jazz. 'Both involve a small group of people making a lot of noise, and then, just when you think it's all over, it carries on.' But I believe there can be a magic in the spoken poem: when it's good it can be sublime. Yet for some writers the whole thing has devolved so far as to become a branch of the entertainment industry or, in the case of poetry slams (see Competitions, below), an opportunity to show off in front of friends. Whichever way you view it, it is certainly an integral part of the business and one in which the beginner is going to need to engage sooner or later. Begin by attending and see how others manage. Watch out for local events advertised at your local library or ring your local arts board. Poets with heavy reputations can often turn out to be lousy performers while many an amateur can really shake it down. Don't expect to catch every image as you listen. Readings are not places for total comprehension but more for glancing blows. Treat it as fun and it will be. If you are trying things yourself for the first time, make sure you've brought your books along to sell, stand upright, drop the shoulders, gaze at a spot at the back of the hall and blow.

Music

Poetry has also made a number of inroads into the music business. There was a time when this meant Spike Milligan standing up and spouting in front of a jazz band or middle-of-the-road brass run behind John Betjeman reciting his best but no longer. There are quite a number of poets now working with musicians, starting bands or using pre-recorded backing tracks. The advent of rap, hip-hop and the ready use of the speech sample as a component part of dancefloor beats has turned the public ear. Dub poets – such as Linton Kwesi Johnson – have long used reggae as a backdrop for their words and the likes of Americans Sonja Sohn, Saul Williams and Dana Bryant have been softening up the cool crowd with their funk-backed hooks. This is certainly a non-traditional approach well away from poetry's conventional involvement with literature and with books.

Scorsese has found space for Sohn in *Bringing Out The Dead*. Check the clubs to hear more and expect what you find to be nothing like what you expected.

Competitions

Poetry competitions have been the vogue for decades now with the most unlikely organizations sponsoring them. The notion here is that anonymity ensures fairness. Entries are made under pseudonyms so that if your name does happen to be Andrew Motion, then this won't help you much. Results seem to bear this out too. The big competitions run biennially by the **Arvon Foundation** with the help of commercial sponsors, the **Academi's** Cardiff International and the **Poetry Society's** National, attract an enormous entry and usually throw up quite a number of complete unknowns among the winners. And why do people bother? Cash prizes can be large – thousands of pounds – but it costs at least a pound a poem to enter, and often much more than that. If it is cash you want, then the Lottery scratch-cards are a better bet. And there has been a trend for winners to come from places like Cape Girardeau, Missouri and Tibooburra, Australia. The odds are getting longer. Who won the last Arvon? I don't remember. But if you do fancy a try then it is a pretty innocent activity. You tie up a poem for a few months and you spend a few pounds. Winners' tips include reading the work of the judges to see how they do it, submitting non-controversial middle-of-the-road smiling things, and doing this just before the closing date so you won't have to wait too long. Try two or three of your best. Huge wodges are costly and will only convince the judges of your insecurity. Have a look at *The Ring of Words* (Sutton Publishing), an excellent anthology of Arvon winners and runners-up. For contests to enter watch the small mags, write to your regional arts board, check out *The New Writer* (one of the best listings around), *Poetry London*, *Writer's News* or the listings in *Orbis* magazine, look on the notice board at your local library, or write for the regularly updated list from the **Poetry Library** in London (see **Organisations of Interest to Poets**).

Combining both competition and reading is the **Poetry Slam**. Here allcomers are given the opportunity to strut their stuff for around three closely-timed minutes before a usually not all that literary crowd. Points are awarded much in the styles as those for ice skating. You get them for a combination of performance and audience reaction. Scatology and street-wise crowd pleasing are more likely to get you through the rounds than closely-honed work. The events, which involve much shouting, can be a lot of fun.

Radio and TV

The BBC centre, most of its efforts on National Poetry Day and its poll to find the Nation's Favourite. This is useful programming focus for the Beeb enabling it to put verse in the mouths of presenters, newscasters and personalities throughout its networks and to actually get an immediate reaction. The public vote by letter, fax and e-mail or through the BBC's Web site. Beyond the star-studded half an hour where the results get revealed there is also a useful spin-off in the form of the BBC-published *The Nation's Favourite Poem* anthology, which inevitably hits the best-sellers. Generally, however, coverage is slight. The regular slots are all on radio, naturally enough. It is so hard to make verse visually appealing. Some producers have tried, notably Peter Symes at BBC2. Symes' approach is to avoid the poem illustrated and to concentrate instead on documentary-style collaborations between commissioned poet and film-maker. Film-maker Brian Hill produced a splendid collaboration with Simon Armitage for Channel Four despite Armitage's remark that by 'far and away the worst flicks are the ones that dabble in poetry'. Digital TV, however, with its almost insatiable appetite for material is an emerging market. BBC Knowledge has already tried televized poetry slams. Poetry can also occasionally be found ladled between the music on MTV but inevitably by the media promoted bards. On Radio Four Susan Roberts produces *Fine Lines* from Manchester, which features pairs of poets in discussion, and is keen to work with poets on drama productions. Mary Sharp looks after the Four's regular Sunday 4.30 strand with *Poetry Please* (a listeners' request show which uses only published material). There are also occasional features. On Radio Three, Tim Dee has commissioned poets to write pieces with radio in mind. His *Radio Poems* has included George Szirtes, Michael Hofmann, Mark Beeson, Ken Smith, Peter Reading and others. Fiona McLean produces *Best Words*, an occasional poetry magazine programme fronted by Michael Rosen. It is also worth listening out for the Sunday feature programme on Three which includes poetry in its range. Radio One puts poetry into some of its evening slots, showcasing poets who have high street-cred. The World Service has Michael Rosen's *Poems By Post*, which features listeners' requests. Independent radio, especially *Classic FM*, is trying verse as fillers. It's an enlarging but difficult market although the BBC is pretty definite about having no remit to use 'unpublished or amateur verse'. If you are determined to put your verse on air then local radio offers better possibilities. Try sending in self-produced readings on cassette (if you are any good at it) or topical poetry which regional magazine programmes could readily use. Don't expect to be paid much.

Starting up

Probably the best place will be locally. Find out through the library or the nearest arts board which writers' groups gather in your area and attend. There you will meet others of a like mind, encounter whatever locally produced magazines there might be and get a little direct feedback on your work. 'How am I doing?' is a big question for the emerging poet and although criticism is not all that hard to come by, do not expect it from all sources. Magazine editors, for example, will rarely have the time to offer advice. It is also reasonable to be suspicious of that offered by friends and relations – they will no doubt be only trying to please. Writers' groups present the best chance for poets to engage in honest mutual criticism. But if you'd prefer a more detached, written analysis of your efforts and are willing to pay a small sum, then you could apply to *Prescription*, the service operated nationally by the Poetry Society (22 Betterton Street, London WC2H 9BU), to the service run by the Arts Council of Wales (see **Arts Councils and Regional Arts Boards**) or to those run on an area basis by your local arts board. There are also a number of non-subsidized critical services which you will find advertised in writers' magazines.

Read; if it's all a mystery to you, try Tony Curtis' *How to Study Modern Poetry* (Macmillan); Matthew Sweeney and John Hartley Williams' *Teach Yourself Writing Poetry* or Peter Sansom's excellent *Writing Poems* (Bloodaxe); or my own *The Poetry Business* (Seren). How real poets actually work can be discovered by reading C. B. McCully's the *Poet's Voice and Craft* (Carcanet) or *How Poets Work* (Seren). After all this, if you still think it's appropriate, try sending it in.

How to do it

Increase your chances of acceptance by following simple, standard procedure:

- Type or print on a single side of the paper, A4 size, single-spacing with double between stanzas, exactly as you'd wish your poem to appear when printed.
- Give the poem a title, clip multi-page works together, include your name and address at the foot of the final sheet. Avoid files, plastic covers, stiffeners and fancy clips of any sort.
- Keep a copy, make a record of what you send where and when, leave a space to note reaction.
- Send in small batches – six is a good number – with a brief covering letter saying who you are. Leave justification, apology and explanation for your writers' group.
- Include a self-addressed, stamped envelope of sufficient size for reply and/or return of your work.
- Be prepared to wait some weeks for a response. Don't pester. Be patient. Most magazines will reply in the end.
- Never send the same poem to two places at the same time.
- Send your best. Work which fails to fully satisfy even the author is unlikely to impress anyone else.

Where?

Try the list which follows. This is by no means the whole UK small-press scene but only those where potential contributors might stand a chance. Even here do not expect unrelenting positive responses: magazines get overstocked, editors change, addresses shift, policy alters, operators run out of steam. Be prepared to hunt around and for a lot of your work to come back. You can help improve things by buying copies. Send in an s.a.e. asking how much. The total market is vast and if you want to go further than the *Writer's Handbook* listings then you could consult the following: the *Small Press Guide* (which only covers journals – Writers' Bookshop, Remus House, Coltsfoot Drive, Woodston, Peterborough PE2 9JX), *Light's List of Literary Magazines*, which contains both UK and US addresses (John Light, The Lighthouse, 37 The Meadows, Berwick upon Tweed, Northumberland TD15 1NY), Dee Rimbaud's bargain *AA Small Press Listings* (£2.00 only to Acid Angel, 35 Falkland St., GFL, Glasgow G12 9QZ), the Internet directories New Hope International and Little Magazines (see The Small Press and Little Magazine, above) and Chantelle Bentley's Po*et's Market* (F&W Publications, Inc.) or Len Fulton's *Directory of Poetry Publishers* (Dustbooks), the two main American directories.

Scams and cons

With poetry overpopulated by participants it is not surprising that the con artist should make an appearance. There are plenty of people out there taking money off beginner writers and offering very little in return. The traditional vanity anthology, once the staple of the trickster, is fortunately in retreat. They have been hounded to silence largely by the **National Poetry Foundation**'s Johnathon Clifford (you can read about his campaigns in his self-published *Vanity Press & The Proper Poetry Publishers*). Nonetheless variations and embellishments on the old approach surface steadily. These include offers to put your poetry to music setting you off on the road to stardom, readings of your verse by actors with deep voices to help you break into the local radio market (there isn't one) and further requests for cash to have entries on you appear in leather-bound directories of world poets. Everyone appears, including your uncle. There are bogus competitions where entry fees bear no relation to final prize money (or such prize money turns out never to be forthcoming) and the advertised 'publication of winners in anthology form' often means shelling out more for what will turn out to be a badly printed abomination crammed full of weak work. Poets should look very carefully at any-thing which offers framed certificates, scrolls or engraved wall hangings. They should also be wary of suggestions that they have come high in the State of Florida's Laureateship Contest (or some such like) and have been awarded a calligraphed testimonial. Presentation usually occurs at a three-day festival held in one of the state's most expensive hotels. To get your bit of paper you need to stay for all three days and it is you who has to settle the bill. If you try your luck at a no-entry-fee, advertised in the Sunday papers international competition, don't be too surprised to find you've made it through round one – that happens to every-one. The scam starts with round two when they ask you for money.

How do you spot the tricksters? They change their names and addresses at will. They bill themselves as Foundations, Societies, Libraries, National Associations,

Guilds. They sound so plausible. If you have the slightest suspicion then check with the Poetry Society (see **Organisations of Interest to Poets**). In the poetry world genuine advertisements for contributions are rare. And if anyone asks you for money then forget it. It is not the way things should be done.

The next step

Once you have placed a few poems you may like to consider publishing a book-let. There are as many small presses around as there are magazines. Start with the upmarket professionals by all means – Jonathan Cape, Faber & Faber – but be prepared for compromise. The specialists and the small presses are swifter and more open to new work.

If all else fails you could do it yourself. Blake did, so did Walt Whitman. Modern technology puts the process within the reach of us all and if you can put up a shelf, there is a fair chance you will be able to produce a book to go on it. Read my *How to Publish Yourself* (Allison & Busby), or Peter Domanski's *A Practical Guide To Publishing Books Using Your PC* (Domanski-Irvine Books). Remember that publishing the book may be as hard as writing it but marketing and selling it is quite something else. Check Alison Baverstock's *How To Market Books* (Kogan Page) if you really want to get ahead.

The listings

None of the lists of addresses which follow is exhaustive. Publishers come and go with amazing frequency. There will always be the brand-new press on the look-out for talent and the projected magazine desperate for contributions. For up to the minute information check with some of the **Organisations of Interest to Poets** (see page 150). Poetry has a huge market. It pays to keep your ear to the ground. The magazines and presses listed here have all been active during the past eighteen months and most (although be warned, *not all*) have indicated a willingness to look at new work. Those with a positive un-interest in receiving unsolicited work have been excluded. In all cases check before sending. Ask to see a catalogue or a sample copy. Good luck.

Poetry presses

Anchor Books *(Poetry – an imprint of the Forward Press group)* Steve Twelvetree, Remus House, Coltsfoot Drive, Woodston, Peterborough PE2 9JX
☎01733 898102 Fax 01733 313524
Email suzy@forwardpress.co.uk
Website www.forwardpress.co.uk

Anvil Press Poetry *(Contemporary British Poetry)* See entry under **UK Publishers** *Peter Jay*, Neptune House, 70 Royal Hill, London SE10 8RT
☎020 8469 3033
Fax 020 8469 3363
Email anvil@anvilpresspoetry.com

Arc Publications *(Contemporary poetry from new and established writers both in the UK and abroad)* See entry under **UK Publishers**. Incorporating **Littlewood Arc** *Tony Ward,* Nanholme Mill, Shaw Wood Road, Todmorden, Lancs OL14 6DA
☎01706 812338 Fax 01706 818948
Email arc.publications@virgin.net

Arktos *(Underground writers) Maxine* – PO Box 471, Bromley, Kent

Aural Images *(Poetry, youth arts workshops) Susan & Alan White,* 5 Hamilton Street, Astley Bridge, Bolton, Lancs BL1 6RT

The Bad Press PO Box 76, Manchester M21 8HJ Website www.thebadpress.co.uk

BB Books *(Post-Beat poetics and counterculture theoretic. Iconoclastic rants and anarchic psycho-cultural tracts)* See also **Global Tapestry Journal** *Dave Cunliffe,* Spring Bank, Longsight Road, Copster Green, Blackburn, Lancs BB1 9EU
☎01254 249128

Big Little Poem Books *(Contemporary approaches to the lyric and epigram)* See also **Door to Everywhere** magazine *Robert Richardson,* 3 Park Avenue, Melton Mowbray, Leics LE13 0JB
☎01664 850228 Fax 01664 850228

Blackwater Press *(Contemporary poetry from new and established writers)* PO Box 5115, Leicester LE2 8ZD ☎0116 2238703

Blade Press *Jane Holland,* Maynrys, Glen Chass, Port St Mary, Isle of Man IM9 5PN

Blaxland Tan *(Publishers of the annual poetry groups register and The Poets Reference Book) John Jarrett,* 12 Matthews Road, Taunton, Somerset TA1 4NH ☎01823 324423 Fax 01823 324423

Bloodaxe Books *(Britain's leading publisher of new poetry)* See entry under **UK Publishers** *Neil Astley,* PO Box 1SN, Newcastle upon Tyne NE99 1SN ☎01434 240500 Fax 01434 240505
Email editor@bloodaxebooks.demon.co.uk
Website www.bloodaxebooks.demon.co.uk

Bogle-L'Ouverture Press Ltd *(Promoting an independent voice of the experiences of black people) Eric L. Huntley,* PO Box 2186, London W13 9ZO
☎020 8579 4920 Fax 020 8579 4920

Bootlet Editions 44 Knightsbridge Street, Glasgow G13 2YN

The Celtic Cross Press *(Private press publishing signed and numbered limited editions) Rosemary & Nigel Roberts,* Ovins Well House, Low Street, Lastingham, York YO6 6TJ
☎01751 417298 Fax 01751 417739

Email books@ccpress.ndirect.co.uk Website www.praxis.co.uk/ppuk/celtic.htm#top

Chrysalis Poetry Pamphlets *(Chrysalis – the poet in you – correspondence course) Jay Ramsay,* PO Box 17, Yelverton, Devon PL20 6YF

The Collective Press *(Non-profit promoter and publishers of contemporary poetry) John Jones,* Penlanlas Farm, Llantilio Pertholey, Y-fenni, Gwent NP7 7HN ☎01873 856350
Email john.jones@which.net

Community of Poets Press *(Increasing focus on printing and publishing original artwork with poetry/text) Philip Bennetta,* Hatfield Cottage, Chilham, Kent CT4 8DP
☎01227 730787 Fax 01227 732134
Email bennetta.artco@virginnet.co.uk

Conybeare Publishing *(Poetry, drama and art/architecture in Wales) Jonathan A. Jones,* 27 Conybeare Road, Victoria Park, Cardiff CF5 1GB ☎029 2038 4682
Fax 029 2040 5411 Email conybeare. publishing@breathemail.net

Corbie Press *(Scottish and European literature, art, philosophy, some poetry)* See also **Epoch** magazine *Neil Mathers,* 57 Murray Street, Montrose, Angus DD10 8JZ
☎01674 672625

Dangerous Cardigans 4 Devon Place, Bridgetown, Totnes, Devon TQ5 5AE

Deco Partnership *(Illustrated gift poetry) Barbara Dordi,* 114 Broadway, Herne Bay, Kent CT6 8HA

Diehard Publishers *(Poetry and drama, mainly Scottish)* See also **Poetry Scotland** magazine *Ian King,* 3 Spittal Street, Edinburgh EH3 9DY ☎0131 229 7252

Dionysia Press Ltd *(Poems, short stories, plays, reviews, articles)* See also **Understanding** magazine *Denise Smith,* 20a Montgomery Street, Edinburgh EH7 5JS
☎0131 478 0927 Fax 0131 478 2572

Enitharmon Press *(Poetry and criticism) Stephen Stuart-Smith,* 36 St George St, London N7 0HD ☎020 7607 7194 Fax 020 7607 8694
Email books@enitharmon.demon.co.uk

Erran Publishing *(Non-profit supporter of third world charities)* See also **Poetic Hours** magazine *Nick Clark,* 43 Willow Road, Carlton, Notts NG4 3BH
Email erran@arrowgroup.freeserve.co.uk

Etruscan Books *(Modernist, sound, visual poetry, US/UK poets) Nicholas Johnson,* 24a Fore Street, Buckfastleigh, South Devon TQ11 0AA

Ex Libris Press *(Local history, poetry, walking) Roger Jones,* 1 The Shambles, Bradford on

Avon, Wiltshire BA15 1JS
☎01225 863595 Fax 01225 863595
Flambard *(Concentrates on poetry but also publishes fiction, especially crime and mystery)* Peter Elfed Lewis, Stable Cottage, East Fourstones, Hexham, Northumberland NE47 5DY ☎01434 674360 Fax 01434 674178 Email admin@signature-books.co.uk

Flarestack Publishing *(Considers first collections for A5 stapled pamphlet publication)* See also **Obsessed With Pipework** magazine Charles Johnson, Redditch Library, 15 Market Place, Redditch B98 8AE ☎01527 63291 Fax 01527 68571 Email flare.stack@virgin.net

Forward Press *(General poetry and short fiction anthologies)* See also **Poetry Now**, **Triumph House** and **Poetry UK** Ian Walton, Remus House, Coltsfoot Drive, Woodston, Peterborough PE2 9JX ☎01733 890099 Fax 01733 313524 Email forward_press@compuserve.com Website www.forwardpress.co.uk

Gomer Press/Gwasg Gomer *(Welsh interest)* See entry under **UK Publishers** Sue Davies, Llandysul, Dyfed SA44 4BQ ☎01559 362371 Fax 01559 363758

Headland Publications *(Fine editions of poetry; anthologies)* Gladys Mary Coles, Ty Coch, Galltegfa, Ruthin, Denbighshire LL15 2AR ☎0151 625 9128 Fax 0152 625 9128

Hippopotamus Press *(First collections of verse from those with a track record in the magazine)* See also **Outposts Poetry Quarterly** Roland John, 22 Whitewell Road, Frome, Somerset BA11 4EL ☎01373 466653 Fax 01373 466653

Honno *(The Welsh women's press)* Gwenllian Dafydd, Alisa Craig, Heol Y Cawl, Dinas Powys, Bro Morgannwg CF64 4AH ☎01970 623150 Fax 01970 626765 Email gol.honno@virgin.net

Hub Editions *(Poetry, experimental writing, high-class hand-made products)* Colin Blundell, Longholm, East Bank, Wingland, Sutton Bridge, Spalding, Lincolnshire PE12 9YS

I*D Books *(Poetry, fiction, local history)* Clive Hopwood, Connah's Quay Library, High Street, Connah's Quay, Deside, Clwyd ☎0161 226 3419

Ihsan Communication *(Poetry, short stories, social commentaries with emphasis on race, culture and youth)* PO Box 550, Bradford, W. Yorks BD10 0YF Website www.ihsan.org.uk

In Books *(Coffee table visions of Wales)* Gwenda Williams, PO Box 105, Cardiff CF14 5YB

Intimacy Books *(Innovative writers/artists)* See also **Intimacy** magazine Adam Mckeown, 11c Elizabeth House, Alexandra Street, Maidstone, Kent ME14 2BX ☎01622 670419 Email adam.mckeown@kent.gov.uk

K. T. Publications (Kite Books) *(Kite modern poetry series includes two poets per book)* See also **The Third Half** magazine Kevin Troop, 16 Fane Close, Stamford, Lincolnshire PE9 1HG ☎01780 754193

Katabasis *(English poetry and bilingual editions of Latin American poetry. For humanity against neoliberalism)* Dinah Livingstone, 10 St Martin's Close, London NW1 0HR .☎020 7485 3830 Fax 020 7485 3830 Email katabasispress@netscapeonline.co.uk

Kronos Books/Bayeux Arts Inc Spantech House, Lagham Road, South Godstone, Surrey

Lapwing Publications *(Small first collections in pamphlet form)* Dennis & Rene Greig, 1 Ballysillan Drive, Belfast BT14 8HQ ☎028 9039 1240 Fax 028 9039 1240

Little Big Words Poetry Press Paul D Nicklin, 62 Willowhale Green, Bognor Regis, West Sussex PO21 4LW ☎07930 269061

Y Lolfa *(Welsh language press)* Talybont, Ceredigion SY24 5AP ☎01970 832304 Fax 01970 832782 Email ylolfa@ylolfa.com Website www.ylolfa.com

Mariscat Press *(Currently publishing poetry pamphlets only)* Hamish Whyte & Others, 3 Mariscat Road, Glasgow G41 4ND ☎0141 423 7291 Email davidmemenemy@compuserve.com

Mo-Saic Imprints PO Box 177, Nottingham NG3 5SU

Morning Star Publications *(Visual folios and pocketbooks)* Alex Finlay, PO Box 23143, Edinburgh EH11 1BG

Mudfog Press *(The best new writers from Teesside)* Andy Croft & Others, 11 Limes Road, Linthorpe, Middlesbrough TS5 7QR ☎012642 864428 Fax 012642 264955 Email cleveland.arts@onyxnet.co.uk

Mynah Poets 13 Belvedere, Balby, Doncaster DN4 9DU

New Hope International *(Poetry booklet publisher)* See also **Aabye** and **NHI Review** Gerald England, 20 Werneth Avenue, Gee Cross, Hyde, Cheshire SK14 5NL ☎0161 351 1878 Email newhope@iname.com Website www.nhi.clara.net/ONLINE.HTM

Oasis Books *(Pamphlets and books of poetry and prose)* See also **Oasis** magazine *Ian Robinson*, 12 Stevenage Road, Fulham, London SW6 6ES ☎020 7736 5059

Odyssey Poets *(Poetry/prose; first collections; interim booklets; full collections)* See also **PQR** magazine *Derrick Woolf*, Coleridge Cottage, Nether Stowey, Somerset TA5 1NQ ☎01278 732662 Email pqrrev@aol.com

The Old Style Press *(Fine hand-printed books with text and images)* *Frances & Nicholas McDowel*, Catchmays Court, Llandogo, Nr Monmouth, Gwent NP45 4TN ☎01291 689226

The One Time Press *(Poetry of the forties in limited letterpress editions. Illustrated)* *Peter Wells*, Model Farm, Linstead Magna, Halesworth, Suffolk IP19 0DT ☎01986 785422

Original Plus *(Requires something extra – another language or markedly original)* See also **The Journal** *Sam Smith*, 11 Heatherton Park, Bradford on Tone, Taunton, Somerset TA4 1EV ☎01823 461725 Email smithsssj@aol.com

The Other Press *(Experimental poetry by women)* *Frances Presley* 19 Marriott Road, London N4 3QN ☎020 7272 9023 Email fpresley@compuserve.com

Othername Press *(Poetry and surrealism)* 14 Rosebank, Rawtenstall, Rossendale BB4 7RD

Peepal Tree Press *(Best in Caribbean and South Asian writing from around the world)* *Jeremy Poynting*, 18 King's Avenue, Leeds, W. Yorks LS6 1QS ☎0113 2451703 Fax 0113 2468368 Email hannah@peepal.demon.co.uk

Peterloo Poets *(Contemporary English poets)* *Harry Chambers*, The Old Chapel, Sand Lane, Calstock, Cornwall PL18 9QX ☎01822 833473

Pikestaff Press *(Poetry – mainly pamphlets – in traditional English verse forms)* *Robert Roberts*, Ellon House, Harpford, Sidmouth, Devon EX10 0NH ☎01395 568941

Poems in the Waiting Room *(Pamphlets for the medical waiting rooms)* *Michael Lee*, PO Box 488, Richmond TW9 4SW Email leelda@globalnet.co.uk

The Poetry Business *Peter Sansom & Others*, The Studio, Byram Arcade, Westgate, Huddersfield, W. Yorks HD1 1ND ☎01484 434840 Fax 01484 426566 Email edit@poetrybusiness.co.uk Website www.poetrybusiness.co.uk

Poetry Monthly Press See also **Poetry Monthly** magazine *Martin Holroyd*, 39 Cavendish Road, Long Eaton, Nottingham NG10 4HY ☎0115 9461267 Email martinholroyd@compuserve.com Website ourworld.compuserve.com/home page/martinholroyd

Poetry Now *Remus House, Coltsfoot Drive, Woodston, Peterborough PE2 9JX ☎01733 890099 Fax 01733 323524 Email forward_press@compuserve.com Website www.forwardpress.co.uk

Poetry Now Young Writers *(Publishers of children's poetry)* See also **Scribbler!** Magazine. *Andrew Head*, Remus House, Coltsfoot Drive, Woodston, Peterborough PE2 9JX ☎01733 890066 Fax 01733 323524 Email forward_press@compuserve.com Website www.forwardpress.co.uk

Poetry Salzburg *Wolfgang Görtschacher*, Universität Salzburg, Institut für Anglistik, A-5020 Salzburg, Austria

Poetry Today *(Part of the Forward Press group)* Remus House, Coltsfoot Drive, Woodston, Peterborough PE2 9JX ☎01733 890099 Fax 01733 323524 Email forward_press@compuserve.com Website www.forwardpress.co.uk

Polygon Books *(Prize-winning independent literary publisher specialising in new fiction and poetry)* See entry under **UK Publishers** *Alison Bowden*, **Edinburgh University Press**, 22 George Square, Edinburgh EH8 9LF ☎0131 650 4213 Fax 0131 662 0053 Email polygon@eup.ed.ac.uk Website www.eup.ed.ac.uk/polygon

Psychopoetica Publications *(Psychologically-based poetry)* *Geoff Lowe*, Dept of Psychology, University of Hull, Hull HU6 7RX Fax 01482 465599 Website www.fernhse.demon.co.uk/ eastword/psycho

Puddle Press *Geoff Sawers*, 2b Hamilton Court, Taunton, Somerset TA1 2PA

QQ Press *(Poetry)* See also **Quantum Leap** magazine *Alan Carter*, York House, 15 Argyle Terrace, Rothesay, Isle of Bute

Raunchland Publications *(Limited edition poetry/graphics booklets)* *John Mingay*, 18 Canon Lynch Court, Dunfermline, Fife KY12 8AU Email raunchland@hotmail.com

Reality Street Editions *(New poetry from Britain, Europe and America)* *Ken Edwards*, 4 Howard Court, Peckham Rye, London SE15 3PH Email reality.street@virgin.net

Red Candle Press *('Traditionalist poetry is our great interest.')* See also **Candelabrum Poetry Magazine** *Michael Leonard McCarthy*, 9 Milner Road, Wisbech, Cambridgeshire PE13 2LR ☎01945 581067

Rialto Publications See also **The Rialto** magazine *Michael Mackmin*, PO Box 309, Aylsham, Norwich, Norfolk NR11 6LN

Rive Gauche Publishing *(Poetry by women writing and performing in Bristol)* P.V.T. West, 69 Lower Redland Road, Bristol BS6 6SP ☎0117 9745106

Robooth Publications *(Voice and verse – runs the Big Poetry Catalogue)* See also **Voice & Verse** magazine *Ruth Booth*, 7 Pincott Place, London SE4 2ER ☎020 7277 8831 Fax 020 7277 8831 Email robooth@gofornet.co.uk

Seshat *(Cross-cultural perspectives in poetry and philosophy)* See also **Seshat** magazine *Terence Duquesne & Others*, PO Box 9313, London E17 8XL

Shearsman Books *(Radical poetry)* See also **Shearsman** magazine *Tony Frazer*, Lark Rise, Fore Street, Kentisbeare, Cullompton, Devon EX15 2AD ☎01884 266174 Fax 01884 266174 Email shearsman@appleonline.net

Shoestring Press *(Poetry and fiction) John Lucas*, 19 Devonshire Avenue, Beeston, Nottingham NG9 1BS ☎0115 9251827

Signature Sunhouse, 2–4 Little Peter Street, Manchester M15 4PS ☎0161 834 8767 Fax 0161 834 8656 Email admin@signature-books.co.uk

SMH Books *(Real-life books, including poetry and memoirs) Sandra M.H. Saer*, Pear Tree Cottage, Watersfield, Pulborough, West Sussex RH20 1NG ☎01798 831260 Fax 01798 831906 Email smhbooks@freeserve.co.uk

Sol Publications *(Poetry)* See also **Sol Poetry Magazine** *Malcolm E. Wright*, 24 Fowler Close, Southchurch, Southend on Sea, Essex SS1 2RD Email maelstrom@solpubs.freeserve.co.uk Website www.solpubs.freeserve.co.uk

Sound & Language *(Poetry)* See also **Language Alive** magazine *Crisaz Cheek*, 85 London Road South, Lowestoft, Suffolk NR33 0AS Email cris@slang.demon.co.uk

Staple First Editions *(Currently resting)* See **Staple** magazine *Don Measham*, Tor Cottage, 81 Cavendish Road, Matlock, Derbyshire DE4 3HD

Stonebridge Publications Ballard, Kilnaboy, Co Clare, Republic of Ireland ☎00 353 87 234 7892

Stop Press *Malcolm Wiseman*, 263 Nether Street, Finchley, London N3 1PD

Stride Publications See entry under **Small Presses** *(Innovative poetry, anthologies, essays and interviews) Rupert Loydell*, 11 Sylvan Road, Exeter, Devon EX4 6EW Email rml@madbear.demon.co.uk Website www.madbear.demon.co.uk/stride/

Summer Palace Press *(Poetry and prose) Kate and Joan Newmann*, Cladnageeragh, Rilbeg, Kilcar, Co Donegal, Republic of Ireland ☎00 353 73 38448 Fax 00 353 73 38448

Survivors' Poetry Scotland *(For survivors of the mental health system)* See also **Nomad** magazine 30 Cranworth Street, Hillhead, Glasgow G12 8AG ☎0141 357 6838 Email sps@spscot.co.uk Website www.spscot.co.uk

Tabla *(Publisher of the annual Tabla Book of New Verse) Dr Stephen James*, 13a Shirlock Road, London NW3 2HR Fax 0117 9288860 Email stephen.james@bristol.ac.uk

Tarantula Publications *(Collections of poetry)* See also **Brando's Hat** magazine *Sean Body*, 14 Vine Street, Salford, Manchester M7 3PG ☎0161 792 4593 Fax 0161 792 4593 Email tarantula_pubs@lineone.net

Terrible Workpress *(New innovative and non-mainstream poetry)* See also **Terrible Work** magazine *Tim Allen*, 21 Overton Gardens, Mannamead, Plymouth, Devon PL3 5BX

Totem *(Publishers of contemporary literature and art) Fiifi Annobil*, 60 Swinley House, Redhill Street, Regent's Park, London NW1 4BB ☎020 7387 7216

Triumph House *(A Christian imprint publishing several anthologies annually)* See also **Triumph Herald** magazine *Steve Twelvetree*, Remus House, Coltsfoot Drive, Woodston, Peterborough PE2 9JX ☎01733 890099 Fax 01733 313524 Email suzy@forwardpress.co.uk Website www.forwardpress.co.uk

United Press Ltd *(Publishes poetry and prose including national poetry anthology) Peter Quinn*, 1 Yorke Street, Burnley, Lancs BB11 1HD ☎01282 459533 Fax 01282 412679 Email mail@upltd.co.uk Website www.upltd.co.uk

Ventus Books *(Publisher of plays, scores and poems by Tony Breeze)* See also

Playwrights Publishing Co *Tony Breeze*, 70 Nottingham Road, Burton Joyce, Notts NG14 5AL ☎0115 9313356

Windhorse Publications *(Body, mind and spirit)* 11 Park Road, Moseley, Birmingham B13 8AB ☎0121 449 9191 Fax 0121 449 9191 Email windhorse@compuserve.com

The Windows Project See also **Smoke** magazine *David Ward*, First Floor, Liver House, 96 Bold Street, Liverpool L1 4HY ☎0151 709 3688

Words Worth Books *(Innovative literary, visual & performance work; formerly Zimmer Press)* Alaric Sumner, BM Box 4515, London WC1N 3XX Email a.sumner@dartington.ac.uk

Writers Forum *(Innovative language and visual poetries)* See also **And** magazine *Bob Cobbing*, 89a Petherton Road, London N5 2QT ☎020 7226 2657

Writers' Own Publications *Mrs E. M. Pickering*, 121 Highbury Grove, Clapham, Bedford MK41 6DU ☎01234 365982

Yorkshire Art Circus Ltd *(Community publisher)* See entry under **Small Presses** and see also **The Opening Line** magazine, School Lane, Glass Houghton, Castleford, W. Yorks WF10 4QH ☎01977 550401

Zum Zum Books *(Wild, brilliant, deep, sensuous, philosophical poetry)* Neil Oram, Goshem, Bunlight, Drumnadrochit, Inverness-shire IV3 6AH ☎01456 450402

Poetry magazines

Many poetry magazines have links with or are produced by companies listed in **Poetry Presses**

A Bard Hair Day *(Quarterly magazine for poetry, short stories and articles – part of Writing Partners)* See also **The Word** magazine *Ian Deal*, 289 Elmwood Avenue, Feltham, Middlesex TW13 7QB ☎020 8751 8652 Website www.partnersinpoetry.freeserve.co.uk

AABye *(Contemporary international poetry journal open to all genres)* Gerald England, 20 Werneth Avenue, Gee Cross, Hyde, Cheshire SK14 5NL ☎0161 351 1878 Email newhope@iname.com Website www.nhi.clara.net/nhihome.htm

Acid Angel *(If you hate the lit scene then this is your sort of mag!)* See also **Fire in the Blood** *Dee Rimbaud*, 35 Falkland Street (gfl), Glasgow G12 9QZ ☎0141 221 1223 Email acidangel@acidity.globalnet.co.uk Website www.writhe.net/rimbaud

Acorn *(Magazine of the Dublin writers workshop)* Kevin Higgins, 35 Glenard Crescent, Salthill, Galway, Republic of Ireland Email kpiggins@hotmail.com

Acumen *(Good poetry, intelligent articles and wide-ranging reviews)* See also **Long Poem Group Newsletter** *Patricia Oxley*, 6 The Mount, Higher Furzeham, Brixham, Devon TQ5 8QY ☎01803 851098 Fax 01803 851098

The Affectionate Punch *(Quality writing,well presented poetry up to 40 lines, fiction to 1500)*

Andrew Tutty, 35 Brundage Road, Manchester M22 0BY

Agenda *(Quarterly poetry magazine, founded 1959)* William Cookson, 5 Cranbourne Court, Albert Bridge Road, London SW11 4PE ☎020 7228 0700 Fax 020 7228 0700

Ambit *(Poetry, fiction, graphics, arts, reviews)* Martin Bax, 17 Priory Gardens, London N6 5QY Website www.ambit.co.uk

And *(Visual and linguistically innovative poetries)* See also **Writers Forum** press *Bob Cobbing & Adrian Clarke*, 89a Petherton Road, London N5 2QT ☎020 7226 2657

Animal Crackers *(Short stories, poems, anecdotes and jokes about pets and their owners)* Derek George James, 31 Somerset Road, Barry, Vale of Glamorgan CF62 8BL Email d.g.james@net.ntl.com

Areopagus *(A Christian-based arena for creative writers)* Julian Barritt, 107 Coopers Green, Bicester, Oxon OX6 9US Email jbarritt@areopagus.freeserve.co.uk Website www.churchnet.org.uk/ areopagus/index.html

Awen *(Poetry and vignette-length fiction of any style/genre)* David John Tyrer, 38 Pierrot Steps, 71 Kursaal Way, Southend on Sea, Essex SS1 2UY

Backdrop *(New poets)* Steve Jones, Flat 61, Elm Grove, Hayling Island PO11 9EA

Bad-Breakfast All Day *(Fiction, poetry and graphics from Britain and North America)* Philip Boxall, 43 Kingsdown House, Amhurst Road, London E8 2AS ☎0033 (0)235 403326 Fax 0033 (0)235 403326 Email boxall@badpress.com Website www.badpress.com

The Big Spoon *(New writing, culture, photography and the visual arts)* Martin Crawford, 32 Salisbury Court, Belfast BT7 1DD ☎028 90 232353 Fax 028 90 232650 Email martin_crawford@lineone.net

Blade *(On the cutting edge of poetry)* See also **Blade Press** *Jane Holland*, Maynrys, Glen Chass, Port St Mary, Isle of Man IM9 5PN

Blue Print *(Artwork, poetry and prose)* Bejamin Beaumont, 2 Norwood Grove, Leeds, W. Yorks LS6 1DT

Blueprint *(Creative journal)* Jess Poole, LUU Creative Journal Society, Leeds University Union, University of Leeds, W. Yorks

Borderlines *(Journal of the Anglo-Welsh Poetry Society)* Dave Bingham & Kevin Bamford, Nant Y Brithyll, Llangynyw, Welshpool, Powys SY21 0JS ☎01938 810263

Brando's Hat *(Poems, longer poems, poetry sequences)* See also **Tarantula Publications** Sean Body, 14 Vine Street, Salford, Manchester M7 3PG ☎0161 792 4593 Fax 0161 792 4593

Braquemard *(Forty pages of excellent poetry, prose and artwork)* David Allenby, 20 Terry Street, Hull HU3 1UD

The Brobdignagian Times *(Poetry, very short fiction, cover art)* Giovanni Malito, 96 Albert Road, Cork, Republic of Ireland

Bukowski Zine *(Works of Charles Bukowski)* Ricki Hollywood, Little Lagoon, PO Box 11271, Wood Green, London N22 8BE

The Burning Bush *(Bi-annual literary mag – poetry and prose, urban contemporary)* Michael Begnal & Others, 35 Glenard Crescent, Salthill, Galway, Republic of Ireland ☎00 353 91 525020 Email kphiggins@hotmail.com

Candelabrum Poetry Magazine *(Twice-yearly poetry, mostly traditional)* See also **Red Candle Press** Michael Leonard McCarthy, 9 Milner Road, Wisbech, Cambs PE13 2LR

Chapman *(The best in Scottish and international writing; well-established writers and the up-and-coming)* See also **Chapman Publishing** under **UK Publishers**. Joy M. Hendry, 4 Broughton Place, Edinburgh EH1 3RX

☎0131 557 2207 Fax 0131 556 9565 Email chapman_pub@netdirect.co.uk

The Coffee House *(Poetry, short prose and visual art, featuring new and familiar local and international voices)* Deborah Tyler-Bennett, Charnwood Arts, Fearon Hall, Rectory Road, Loughborough, Leics LE11 1PL ☎01509 269416 Fax 01509 238010 Email charnwood_arts@ndirect.co.uk Website www.charnwood-arts.co.uk

Colonies SF Magazine *(Gloss sf magazine)* See also **Voyage** magazine John Dunne, 14 Honour Avenue, Goldthorne Park, Wolverhampton WV4 5HH ☎01902 652999 Fax 01902 652999 Email john@voyage99.freeserve.co.uk Website www.zyworld.com/voyagemag/colonies.htm

Community of Poets *(Community and organisational life and learning)* See also **Community of Poets Press** Philip Bennetta, Hatfield Cottage, Chilham, Kent CT4 8DP Email bennetta@cpoetspress.freeserve.co.uk Website www.cpoetspress.freeserve.co.uk

Connections *(The literary scene in the South East)* Narissa Knights, 13 Wave Crest, Whitstable, Kent CT5 1EH

Corpses and Clarinets *(Poetry)* Simon Jennor, 51 Waterloo Street, Hove, East Sussex BN3 1AH

CPR Internations *(Aims to provide a platform for new and established poets who also happen to be Christian)* Frances T Lewis, Grendon House, 8 Laxay, Lochs, Isle of Lewis H52 9PJ ☎01851 830418 Fax 01851 830412 Email grendon.house@virginnet.co.uk Website planet-scotland.com

Critical Quarterly Blackwell Publishers, 108 Cowley Road, Oxford OX4 1JF

Current Accounts *(Poetry, short fiction, articles – magazine of the Bank Street Writers' Group)* 16–18 Mill Lane, Horwich, Bolton, Lancs BL6 6AT

Cyphers *(Irish literary magazine: poetry, prose, reviews)* Eilean Ní Chuilleanain, 3 Selskar Terrace, Ranelagh, Dublin 6, Republic of Ireland Fax 00 353 1497 8866

The David Jones Journal *(Articles, information, reviews and inspired works)* Anne Price-Owen, The David Jones Society, 48 Sylvan Way, Sketty, Swansea SA2 9JB ☎01792 206144 Fax 01792 205305 Email anne.price-owen@sihe.ac.uk

The Devil *(Prose, poetry, fiction, reviews, major interviews)* Formerly **The Printer's Devil** 247 Gray's Inn Road, London WC1X 8JR ☎020 8994 7767

Dial 174 *(Poetry, short stories, articles, travelogues, artwork, etc.) Joseph Hemmings*, 21 Mill Road, Watlington, King's Lynn, Norfolk PE33 0HH ☎01553 811949

Door-To-Everywhere *(Poem card series)* See also **Big Little Poem Books** press *Robert Richardson*, 3 Park Avenue, Melton Mowbray, Leics LE13 0JB

Dream CatcherLiterary Arts *(Poetry, prose, b/w photographs, from national and international contributors) Paul Sutherland*, 4 St John Street, York YO3 7QT ☎01904 628138 Fax 01904 628138 Website www.openingline.co.uk/magazines/dreamcatcher

Eastern Rainbow *(Focuses on 20th century culture via poetry, prose and art)* See also **Peace and Freedom** magazine *Paul Rance*, 17 Farrow Road, Whaplode Drove, Spalding, Lincs PE12 0TS

Eclipse *(Bi-monthly poetry mag – all types and styles welcome) Elizabeth Boyd*, 53 West Vale, Neston, Cheshire CH64 9SE

The Engine *Paul Murphy*, 3 Ardgreenan Drive, Belfast BT4 3FQ Email quinqureme@hotmail.com

Envoi *(Poetry, sequences, features, reviews, competitions) Roger Elkin*, 44 Rudyard Road, Biddulph Moor, Stoke-on-Trent, Staffs ST8 7JN

Epoch Magazine *(Scottish and European literature, art, philosophy, some poetry)* See also **Corbie Press** *Neil Mathers*, 57 Murray Street, Montrose, Angus DD10 8JZ ☎01674 672625

Federation *(Magazine of the Federation of Workers Writers & Community Publishers) Tim Diggles*, 67 The Boulevard, Tunstall, Stoke-on-Trent ST6 6BD ☎01792 8222327 Fax 01792 8222327 Email fwwcp@cwcom.net Website www.fwwcp.mcmail.com

Fire *(Poetry: alternative, unfashionable, experimental, spiritual, demotic; occasional experimental prose) Jeremy Hilton*, 3 Holywell Mews, Holywell Road, Malvern WR14 4LF

Fire in the Blood *(Anthology of prose, poetry celebrating the drug culture)* See **Acid Angel** magazine *Dee Rimbaud*, 35 Falkland Street (gfl), Glasgow G12 9QZ ☎0141 221 1223 Email acidangel@acidity.globalnet.co.uk Website www.writhe.net/rimbaud

First Time *(New poets) Josephine Austin*, The Snoring Cat, 136 Harold Road, Hastings, East Sussex TN35 5NN

Flaming Arrows *(Stories, poetry, contemplative, metaphysical, spiritual themes grounded in senses) Leo Regan*, County Sligo V.E.C., Riverside, Sligo, Republic of Ireland ☎00 353 71 45844 Email leoregan@tinet.ie Website www.artspark.com/home/sligovec

For Poets *(Poetry and advice) Carole Baldock*, PO Box 1009, Storrington, Pulborough, West Sussex RH20 3YT ☎01903 747224 Fax 01903 746238

Gairm *(All-Gaelic literary quarterly) Derek Thomson*, 29 Waterloo Street, Glasgow G2 6BZ ☎0141 221 1971

Gargoyle See also **Black Spring Press Ltd** 152 Harringay Road, London N15 3HL ☎020 8292 7350 Fax 020 7401 2055 Email bsp@blackspring.demon.co.uk

Gentle Reader *(Quarterly fiction and poetry. Welcomes new poets) Lynne E. Jones*, 8 Heal Pen Y Bryn, Penyrheol, Caerphilly CF83 2JX ☎029 2088 6369 Email lynne_jones@hotmail.com

Glasshouse Electric *(Experimental poetry and word art) J. Rogerson*, West Lodge, Highlane, Liverpool L9 7AB

Global Tapestry Journal *(Global Bohemia, post-Beat and counterculture orientation)* See also **BB Books** *Dave Cunliffe*, Spring Bank, Longsight Road, Copster Green, Blackburn, Lancs BB1 9EU ☎01254 249128

Helicon *(Non-genre poetry mag which pays contributors) Shelagh Nugent*, Cherrybite Publications, Linden Cottage, 45 Burton Road, Little Neston, South Wirral L64 4AE ☎0151 353 0967 Email helicon@globalnet.co.uk

How Do I Love Thee? *(The magazine for love poetry)* See also **Poetry Life** magazine *Adrian Bishop*, 1 Blue Ball Corner, Water Lane, Winchester, Hants SO23 0ER Email adrian.bishop@virgin.net Website www.freespace.virgin.net/poetry.life/

HU – The Honest Ulsterman *(Ireland's premier journal for new poems, prose, articles) Tom Clyde*, 49 Main Street, Greyabbey, Co Down BT22 2NP

Interchange *(Poetry, reviews and articles from Wales and the rest of the world) Stuart Kime*, Dept. of English, U.C.W. Aberystwyth, Aberystwyth, Ceredigion SY23 3DY Fax 01970 622530 Email smk6@aber.ac.uk Website www.aber.ac.uk/~engwww/

The Interpreter's House *(Poems and stories up to 2500 words, new and established writers) Merryn Williams*, 10 Farrell Road, Wootton, Bedfordshire MK43 9DU

Intimacy *(Communication experienced as nakedness – innovative arts and literature)* See also **Intimacy Books** *Adam McKeown*,

11c, Elizabeth House, Alexandra Street, Maidstone, Kent ME14 2BX ☎01622 670419 Email adam.mckeown@kent.gov.uk

Iota *(Poetry and reviews. Iota, having no particular hobby-horses, poets are free to ride their own)* David Holliday, 67 Hady Crescent, Chesterfield, Derbyshire S41 0EB ☎01246 276532

Island *(New poetry inspired by nature and human relationships with the earth)* Robert Ford, 3 Kinsway, Balderton, Newark, Notts NG24 3DJ

The Journal *(Poems in translation alongside poetry written in English)* Sam Smith, 11 Heatherton Park, Bradford on Tone, Taunton, Somerset TA4 1EV ☎01823 461725 Email smithssj@aol.com

The Journal *(Post-modernist poetry and prose)* Billy Mills & Catherine Walsh, 37 Grosvenor Court, Templeville Road, Templeogue, Dublin 6 W, Republic of Ireland

Juju *(Quarterly poetry magazine with an unusual – possibly disturbing – view of the everyday world)* P. Sanders, 39 Walnut Street, Belfast BT7 1EN

Konfluence *(Good quality crafted poetry – West Country bias but no regional/generic exclusivity)* Mark Floyer, Bath House, Bath Road, Nailsworth, Glos GL6 0JB ☎01453 835896 Fax 01453 8355587

Krax *Light-hearted, contemporary poetry, short fiction and graphics)* Andy Robson, 63 Dixon Lane, Wortley, Leeds, W. Yorks LS12 4RR

Lallans *(The literary magazine for writing in Scots)* Scots Language Society, A.K. Bell Library, York Place, Perth PH2 8AP ☎01738 440199

Lateral Moves *(Poems, stories, articles, humour, listings, letters, interviews, how-tos, quotes, artwork, reviews, jokes)* Nick Britton & Alan White, 5 Hamilton Street, Astley Bridge, Bolton, Lancs BL1 6RJ

The Layabout *(Short stories, cartoons, poetry)* Henry Ramsager, 45 St Bedes Crescent, Cambridge CB1 3TZ

Lexicon See entry under **Magazines** Francis Anderson, PO Box 754, Stoke on Trent ST1 4BU

Links *(Poetry magazine committed to quality writing and reviews)* Bill Headdon, Bude Haven, 18 Frankfield Rise, Tunbridge Wells, Kent TN2 5LF

Little Girl *(Gay/lesbian short stories, poetry)* Michael Coleman, 18 Sunningdale Avenue, Sale Cheshire M33 2PH

London Magazine See entry under **Magazines** *Alan Ross, 30 Thurloe Place,* London SW7 2HQ

The Long Poem Group Newsletter *(Newsletter of the Long Poem Group)* William Oxley, 6 The Mount, Higher Furzeham, Brixham, S. Devon TQ5 8QY ☎01803 851098 Fax 01803 851098

Magma *(New poetry plus poetry reviews and interviews)* David Boll, The Stukely Press, 43 Keslake Road, London NW6 6DH Email magmapoems@aol.com Website www.dcs.qmw.ac.uk/~timk/magma

Manifold Magazine of New Poetry *(Original and translated poetry, poetry gossip, etc.)* Vera Rich, 99 Vera Avenue, Grange Park, London N21 1PR ☎020 8360 3202 Fax 020 8360 3202 Email verarich@clara.co.uk Website www.members.xoom.com/mainfoldpoet

Merseyside Arts Magazine *(Data on local activity)* Bernard F. Spencer, PO Box 21, Liverpool L19 3RX Email merseyside. arts.monthly@cablenet.co.uk

Metre *(A magazine of international poetry and critical prose)* David Wheatley, Dept of English, Trinity College, Dublin 2, Republic of Ireland

Monomyth *(Poetry, prose and articles; all genres, styles and lengths considered. New writers welcome)* See also **Awen** magazine Richard T. Burman & Others, 99 Sandringham Road, Southend on Sea, Essex SS1 2UG

Moonstone *(Pagan/Pantheistic poetry)* Talitha Clare, SOS, The Old Station Yard, Settle N. Yorks BD24 9RP Email talclare.moonstone@virgin.net

MPT – Modern Poetry in Translation Daniel Weissbort, MPT, School of Humanities, King's College London, Strand, London WC2R 2LS ☎020 7848 2360 Fax 020 784 2145 Website www.kcl.ac.uk/mpt

Nasty Piece of Work *(Quarterly mag of morbid, sick and macabre horror fiction and poetry)* David A. Green, 20 Drum Mead, Petersfield, Hants GU22 3AQ

Never Bury Poetry *(Quarterly, founded 1989. International reputation; each issue has a different theme)* Jean Tarry, Bracken Clock, Troutbeck Close, Hawkshaw, Bury, Lancs BL8 4LJ ☎01204 884080 Email j.tarry@zen.co.uk

New Horizon *(Poems, short stories, art work from new and experienced writers; quarterly)* Soumyen

Maitra, 64 Acacia Avenue, Huyton, Liverpool L36 5TP ☎0151 489 5179 Email souyen@maitras.freeserve.co.uk

Nomad *(Poetry and creative writing by survivors of the mental health system, of abuse or addictions) Gerry Loose*, Survivors Press, 30 Cranworth Street, Glasgow G12 8AG ☎0141 357 6838 Fax 0141 357 6939 Email sps@spscot.co.uk Website www.spscot.co.uk

The North *(Contemporary poetry, some fiction and graphics, extensive reviews)* See also **Smith/Doorstop Books** *Peter Sansom & Janet Fisher*, The Studio, Byram Arcade, Westgate, Huddersfield, W. Yorks HD1 1ND ☎01484 434840 Fax 01484 426566 Email edit@poetrybusiness.co.uk Website www.poetrybusiness.co.uk

Northwords *(Poetry, short fiction and reviews, focusing on the North) Angus Dunn*, The Stable, Long Road, Avoch, Ross-shire IV9 8QR ☎01381 621561 Email stable@cali.co.uk

Oasis *(Poetry, short fiction, essays, reviews, etc.)* See also **Oasis Books** *Ian Robinson*, 12 Stevenage Road, Fulham, London SW6 6ES ☎020 7736 5059

Obsessed With Pipework *(Open quarterly 'poetry to surprise and delight with a high-wire aspect')* See also **Flarestack Publishing** *Charles Johnson*, Redditch Library, 15 Market Place, Redditch B98 8AR ☎01527 63291 Fax 01527 68571 Email flare.stack@virgin.net

The Opening Line *(For readers and writers – magazine of Yorkshire Arts Circus and the Word Hoard)* Cultural Industries Centre, School Lane, Glasshoughton, Castleford, W. Yorks WF10 4QH ☎01977 603028 Email office@openingline.co.uk Website www.openingline.co.uk

Orbis *(An independent international quarterly of poetry and prose with many reader-friendly features) Mike Shields*, 27 Valley View, Primrose, Jarrow, Tyne & Wear NE32 5QT ☎0191 489 7055 Fax 0191 430 1297

Outposts *(Longest surviving independent poetry magazine in the UK)* See also **Hippopotamus Press** *Roland John*, 22 Whitewell Road, Frome, Somerset BA11 4EL ☎01373 466653 Fax 01373 466653

Panda *(Poetry and prose) Esmond Jones*, 46 First Avenue, Clase, Swansea SA6 7LL Email esmond.jones@cableol.co.uk

Passport *(Short fiction, poetry and articles) Gordon Rockett*, The Writer's Co-operative, 6 Chaplin Grove, Crownhill, Milton Keynes MK8 0DG Website www.writerscooperative.currantbun.com

Peace and Freedom *(Humanitarian/ecologically-minded arts mag)* See also **Eastern Rainbow** *Paul Rance*, 17 Farrow Road, Whaplode Drove, Spalding, Lincs PE12 0TS Email peaceandfreedom@lineone.net Website lineone.net/~peaceandfreedom

Peer Poetry *(80-page poetry bi-annual; publisher's winners' collections; sae for details) Paul Amphlett*, 26 Arlington House, Bath Street, Bath BA1 1QN ☎01225 445298

The Penniless Press *(Quarterly for the poor pocket and the rich mind. Poetry, fiction, essays) Alan Dent*, 100 Waterloo Road, Ashton, Preston, Lancs PR2 1EP ☎01772 736421

Pennine Ink *(Poetry and prose) John Carley*, Mid Pennine Gallery, Yorke Street, Burnley, Lancs BB11 1HD

Piffle *(Articles, poetry, cartoons and stories)* 98 Nightingale Lane, Hornsey, London N8 7QY

Planet *(The Welsh Internationalist – current affairs, arts, environment) John Barnie*, PO Box 44, Aberystwyth SY23 3ZZ ☎01970 611255 Fax 01970 611197 Email planet.enquiries@planetmagazine. org.uk

Planet Prozac *(Short fiction, poetry and humour; scifi, fantasy, gothic horror and the bizarre) Stephen E. Bennion*, 31a Waldron Avenue, Brierley Hill, Dudley DY5 3RU Fax 01384 835819

PN Review See also **Carcanet Press** under **UK Publishers** *Michael Schmidt*, 4th Floor, Conavon Court, 12-16 Blackfriars Street, Manchester M3 5BQ

Poetic Hours *(Non-profit supporter of third world charities)* See also **Erran Publishing** *Nick Clark*, 43 Willow Road, Carlton, Notts NG4 3BH Email erran@arrowgroup.freeserve.co.uk

Poetic Licence *(New poetry, rotating editorial team, fresh perspectives) Peter L. Evans*, 70 Aveling Close, Purley, Surrey CR8 4DW ☎020 8645 9956

Poetry Can Bulletin *(News of poetry in the Bristol area)* Unit 11, Kuumba Project, Hepburn Road, Bristol BS2 8UD ☎0117 9426976 Fax 0117 9441478 Email angela@poetrycan.demon.co.uk

The Poetry Church *(Free sample)* See also **Feather Books** under **Small Presses** *Rev J. Waddington Feather*, Fair View, Old Coppice, Lyth Bank, Shrewsbury, Shropshire SY3 0BW ☎01743 872177 Fax 01743 872177

Email john@waddysweb.free.uk
Website www.waddysweb.com

Poetry File *(Poems for children – 5 to 16 – two editions per year) Neil Rathmell,* Arts Advisor, Arts & Media, 5 Belmont Street, Shrewsbury SY1 1TE ☎01743 243755 Fax 01743 344773

Poetry Ireland Review/Eigse Eireann *(Quarterly journal of poetry and reviews) Niann Morris,* Bermingham Tower, Upper Yard, Dublin Castle, Dublin 2, Republic of Ireland ☎00 353 1 671 4632 Fax 00 353 1 671 4634 Email poetry@iol.ie Website www.poetryireland.ie

Poetry Life *(Devoted to the business of poetry – articles and interviews)* See also **How Do I Love Thee?** *Adrian Bishop,* 1 Blue Ball Corner, Water Lane, Winchester, Hants SO23 0ER Email adrian.bishop@virgin.net Website freespace.virgin.net/poetry.life/

Poetry London *(Poetry, listings, information)* Formerly **Poetry London Newsletter** *Anna Robinson,* 1a Jewel Road, London E17 4QU Email editors@plondon.demon.co.uk Website www.poetrylondon.co.uk

Poetry Monthly *(Well-crafted, dynamic, fresh and individual poems) Martin Holroyd,* 39 Cavendish Road, Long Eaton, Nottingham NG10 4HY ☎0115 9461267 Email martinholroyd@compuserve.com

Poetry Nottingham International *(Poetry, articles, letters, features, reviews, 48–56 pages, quarterly) Cathy Grindrod & Others,* 71 Saxton Avenue, Heanor, Derbyshire DE75 7PZ

Poetry Review *(Quarterly forum on the state of poetry) Peter Forbes,* Poetry Society, 22 Betterton Street, London WC2H 9BU ☎020 7420 9883 Fax 020 7240 4818 Email poetrysoc@dial.pipex.com Website www.poetrysoc.com

Poetry Scotland *(All-poetry broadsheet with Scottish emphasis)* See also **Diehard Publishers** *Sally Evans,* 3 Spittal Street, Edinburgh EH3 9DY ☎0131 229 7252

Poetry UK Newsletter *(For people who write poetry) Kelly Deacon,* PO Box 304, Peterborough, Cambs PE2 9NX ☎01733 898102 Fax 01733 898108 Email poetry_uk@lineone.net

Poetry Wales *(Focuses on new and established poets from Wales plus translations, articles and reviews)* See also **Seren Books** under **UK Publishers** *Robert Minhinnick,* First Floor,

2 Wyndham Street, Bridgend CF31 1EF ☎01656 663018 Fax 01656 639226 Email pw@seren.force9.co.uk Website www.seren-books.com

PQR – Poetry Quarterly Review *(In-depth reviews of mainstream/small press poetry)* See also **Odyssey Poets** press *Derrick Woolf,* Coleridge Cottage, Nether Stowey, Somerset TA5 1NQ ☎01278 732662 Email pqrrev@aol.com

Presence *(Haiku, senryu, tanka, renku and related poetry in English) Martin Lucas,* 12 Grovehall Avenue, Leeds, W. Yorks LS11 7EX Email: smartin.lucas@talk21.com Website members.netscapeonline.co.uk/ haikupresence

Prop *(Poetry, short fiction plus related essays, reviews and interviews) Stephen Blythe & Chris Hart,* 31 Central Avenue, Farnworth, Bolton, Lancs BL4 0AU Email chris.hart@dial.pipex.com

Psychopoetica *(A magazine of psychologically-based poetry)* See also **Psychopoetica Publications** *Geoff Lowe,* Dept of Psychology, University of Hull, Hull HU6 7RX Fax 01482 465599 Website www. fernhse.demon.co.uk/eastword/psycho

Pulsar *(Hard hitting/inspirational poetry – quarterly) David Pike,* 34 Lineacre, Grangepark, Swindon, Wilts SN5 6DA ☎01793 875941 Fax 01793 875941 Email david. pike@virgin.net Website www.i-way. co.uk/~swindonlink/poetry.html

Purple Patch *(Poetry mag founded 1976 – includes reviews and gossip column) Geoff Stevens,* 25 Griffiths Road, West Bromwich B71 2EH

Quantum Leap *(User-friendly magazine – encourages new writers – all types of poetry)* See also **QQ Press** *Alan Carter,* York House, 15 Argyle Terrace, Rothesay, Isle of Bute

The Quarterly Muse *(Inspiring, friendly publication with quarterly theme) Jane Reid,* 5 Grosvenor Close, Great Sankey, Warrington, Cheshire WA5 1XQ ☎01925 574476 Email jane@gjsreid.free-online.co.uk

The Reater *(No flowers, just blunt chiselled poetry) Shane Rhodes,* Wrecking Ball Press, 18 Church Street, Northcave, Brough, E. Yorks HU15 2LW ☎01430 424346

The Rialto *('Simply the best' – Carol Ann Duffy)* See also **Rialto Publications** *Michael Mackmin,* PO Box 309, Aylsham, Norwich, Norfolk NR11 6LN

Rising *(Hard-boiled poetry brewed in a bathtub) Tim Wells,* 80 Cazenove Road, Stoke

Newinton, London N16 6AA
Email timmywells@hotmail.com
Website www.geocities.com/soho/bistro/
6754/rising.html

Roundyhouse *(The poetry scene in Wales and beyond) Sally Roberts Jones & Others* PO Box 433, Swansea SA1 6WX
Email herbert@williams63.fsbusiness.co.uk

Saltburn Scene *(Science, rock music, poetry, folk and fairy lore, history − local and otherwise) Mark Beevers*, Glenside Cottage, Glenside Terrace, Saltburn, Cleveland TR12 1SS

Scribbler! *(Publishers of children's poetry)* See also **Poetry Now Young Writers** press *Andrew Head* , Remus House, Coltsfoot Drive, Woodston, Peterborough, Cambs PE2 9JX ☎01733 890066
Fax 01733 313524
Email forward_press@compuserve.com
Website www.forwardpress.co.uk

Seam *(New poetry by established and new poets) Maggie Freeman & Others*, PO Box 3684, Danbury, Chelmsford, Essex CM3 4GP

Second Light *Dilys Wood*, 67 Dulwich Village, London SE21 7BJ

Seshat *(Cross-cultural perspectives in poetry and philosophy) Terence Duquesne & Others*, PO Box 9313, London E17 8XL

Shearsman *(Quarterly journal of contemporary British and American poetry, some translations)* See also **Shearsman Books** *Tony Frazer*, Lark Rise, Fore Street, Kentisbeare, Cullompton, Devon EX15 2AD ☎01884 266174 Fax 01884 266174
Email shearsman@appleonline.net

The Shop!: A Magazine of Poetry *(International but with emphasis on Irish poetry) John Wakeman*, The Rectory, Toormore, Goleen, Co Cork, Republic of Ireland Email wakeman@iol.ie

Slacker *(Literary mag − emphasis on new writers) David Brewster*, Flat 1/L, 3 MacIntyre Place, Paisley PA2 6EE
Email slackerpublications@yahoo.co.uk

Slipstream *(Poetry, fiction, writing) Cathy Cullis*, 4 Crossways, Crookham Village, Fleet, Hampshire GU13 0TA
Email cathy@cullis.demon.co.uk

Smiths Knoll *(Clear, honest, well-crafted poems) Roy Blackman & Michael Laskey* 49 Church Road, Little Glemham, Woodbridge, Suffolk IP13 0BJ

Smoke *(Poetry, graphics, short prose − 24pp − bi-annual)* See also **The Windows Project** *Dave Ward*, The Windows Project, 1st Floor, Liver House, 96 Bold Street, Liverpool L1 4HY ☎0151 709 3688

South (incorporating **Doors**) *(Poetry for the Southern Counties) Michael Fealty*, Word and Action, 61 West Borough, Wimborne, Dorset BH21 1LX ☎01202 889669
Fax 01202 881061
Website wanda@wanda.demon.co.uk

Southfields *(Poetry, essays, reviews. A Scottish little mag with wide-ranging concerns) Richard Price & David Kinloch*, 8 Richmond Road, Staines TW18 2AB

The Spice Box *(Contemporary poetry by new and established writers)* Formerly **Wire**. *Malcolm Napier*, 1 Alanbrooke Close, Knaphill, Surrey GU21 2RU

Stand *(Quarterly magazine of poetry, fiction, reviews and cultural criticism) John Kinsella*, School of English, University of Leeds, Leeds, W. Yorks LS2 9JT
☎0113 2334794 Fax 0113 2334791
Email stand@english.novel.leeds.ac.uk
Website saturn.vcu.edu/~dlatane/stand.html

Staple New Writing *(Mainstream poetry and fiction magazine, established 1982; not a closed shop)* See also **Staple First Editions** *Bob Windsor & Don Mesham*, Tor Cottage, 81 Cavendish Road, Matlock, Derbyshire DE4 3HD

The Stinging Fly PO Box 6016, Dublin 8, Republic of Ireland

Subtext *(Your free guide to new writing in the North of England) Clare Malcolm*. New Writing North, 7-8 Trinity Chare, Quayside, Newcastle upon Tyne NE1 3DF
☎0181 232 9991 Fax 0191 230 1883
Email subtext.nwn@virgin.net

Superfluity *Peter Larkin*, Scribbled Publications, PO Box 6234, Nottingham NG2 5EX

Tandem *(Poetry, some prose, reviews. Encourages young writers. Annual poetry competition) Michael J. Woods*, 13 Stephenson Road, Barbourne, Worcester WR1 3EB
☎01905 28002
Email mjw@tandem-poetry. demon.co.uk
Website www.tandem-poetry.demon.co.uk

Tears In The Fence *(Magazine looking for the unusual, perceptive, risk-taking, lived and visionary literature) David Caddy*, 38 Hod View, Stourpaine, Nr Blandford Forum, Dorset DT11 8TN ☎01258 456803
Fax 01258 454026
Email westrow@clara.net

10th Muse *(A5, stapled, nonist, poems and reviews, neither matter no spirit but sexy) Andrew Jordan*, 33 Hartington Road, Southampton SO14 0EW

Terrible Work *(New innovative and non-main-stream poetry plus reviews and art)* See also **Terrible Workpress** *Tim Allen,* 21 Overton Gardens, Mannamead, Plymouth, Devon PL3 5BX

The Text *(Loose-leaf magazine for fiction, experimental writing and long poems) Keith Jafrate,* The Word Hoard, Kirklees Media Centre, 7 Northumberland Street, Huddersfield HD1 1RL ☎01484 452070 Fax 01484 455049 Email hoard@zoo.co.uk

The Third Half *(Looking for a good script – do you have one?)* See also **K. T. Publications** *Kevin Troop,* 16 Fane Close, Stamford, Lincs PE9 1HG ☎01780 754193

Thumbscrew *(International journal of poetry and poetry-related criticism) Tim Kendall* PO Box 657, Oxford OX2 6PH Email tim.kendall@bristol.ac.uk Website www.bristol.ac.uk/thumbscrew

Triumph Herald *(Christian writers' magazine with poetry, stories and articles written by subscribers)* See also **Triumph House** press *Steve Twelvetree,* Remus House, Coltsfoot Drive, Woodston, Peterborough, Cambs PE2 9JX ☎01733 890099 Fax 01733 323524 Email suzy@forwardpress.co.uk Website www.forwardpress.co.uk

Under Surveillance *Eddie Harriman,* 107 Southover Street, Brighton, East Sussex BN2 2UA

Upstart! *(Literary magazine) Carol Barac,* 19 Cawarden, Stantonbury, Milton Keynes MK14 6AH ☎01908 317535

Urthona *(The arts from a spiritual perspective)Ratnagarbha Shantigarbha,* 3 Coral Park, Henley Road, Cambridge CB1 3EA ☎01223 566567 Fax 01223 566568 Email urthona@windhorse.freeserve.com

Various Artists *(Poetry and graphics) Tony Lewis Jones,* 34 Northleaze, Long Ashton, Bristol BS41 9HT

Voice & Verse *(Quarterly with a wide range of poetry, articles, news, reviews, etc.)* See also **Robooth Publications** *Ruth Booth,* 7 Pincott Place, London SE4 2ER ☎020 7277 8831 Fax 020 7277 8831 Email robooth@gofornet.co.uk

Voyage Short Story & Poetry Magazine *(A5 colour, glossy multi-genre stories and poems by new, developing and established writers)* See also **Colonies SF Magazine** *John Dunne,* 14 Honour Avenue, Goldthorne Park, Wolverhampton WV4 5HH ☎01902 652999 Fax 01902 652999 Email john@voyage99.freeserve.co.uk Website www.zyworld.com/voyagemag/ voyage_magazine.htm

Wasafiri *(Literary journal of African, Asian, Caribbean and black British writing) Susheila Nasta,* Dept. of English, Queen Mary and Westfield College, Mile End Road, London E1 4SN ☎020 7775 3120 Fax 020 8980 6200 Email wasafiri@qmw.ac.uk

The Word Hoard *(News of the arts development cooperative including some poetry)* See also **The Opening Line** magazine Kirklees Media Centre, 7 Northumberland Street, Huddersfield, W Yorks HD1 1RL ☎01484 452070 Fax 01484 455049 Email hoard@zoo.co.uk Website www. wordhoard.co.uk/homepage.htm

The Word *(Quarterly journal that deals with mysteries of the spirit – part of Writing Partners)* See also **A Bard Hair Day** magazine *Ian Deal,* 289 Elmwood Avenue, Feltham, Middlesex TW13 7QB ☎020 87518652

Write Here! Right Now! *(Monthly magazine for amateur writers in Yorkshir & Lincolnshire) Rachel J Webb,* 11 Commonside, Crowle, North Lincs DN17 4EX Email writehererightnow@hotmail.com

Writers' Cauldron *(Short stories and featured poets)* PO Box 241, Oakegates, Shropshire TF2 9XZ

The Yellow Crane *(Interesting new poems from South Wales and beyond) Jonathan Brookes,* 20 Princes Court, The Walk, Roath, Cardiff CF2 3AU

Zine-on-a-Tape *(The small press magazine recorded on an audio cassette)* Formerly **Super-Trouper.** *Andrew Savage* 33 Kearsley Road, Sheffield S2 4TE Email andy@andysav. free-online.co.uk Website www.andysav. free-online.co.uk/zine.htm

Organisations of interest to poets

A survey of some of the societies, groups and other bodies which may be of interest to practising poets. Organisations not listed should send details to the Editor for inclusion in future editions.

Academi – The Welsh National Literature Promotion Agency
3rd Floor, Mount Stuart House, Mount Stuart Square, Cardiff Bay, Cardiff CF10 5FQ
☎029 2047 2266 Fax 029 2049 2930
Email post@academi.org
Website www.academi.org

North Wales Office: Ty Newydd, Llanystumdwy, Cricith, Gwynedd LL52 0LW

West Wales Office: Dylan Thomas Centre, Somerset Place, Swansea SA1 1RR

Chief Executive *Peter Finch*

The writers' organisation of Wales with special responsibility for literary activity, writers' residencies, writers on tour, festivals, writers' groups, readings, tours, exchanges and other development work. **Yr Academi Gymreig/The Welsh Academy** won the 1998 Arts Council of Wales franchise for Wales-wide literature development. It has offices in Cardiff and fieldworkers based in North and West Wales. *Publishes* the Lottery-funded *Encyclopedia of Wales*, the Welsh-medium literary magazine *Taliesin*, the *Academi English– Welsh Dictionary*, co-publisher of *The New Welsh Review* along with a number of other projects. The Academi sponsors a range of annual contests including the prestigious **Cardiff International Poetry Competition**. Publishes *A470* a bi-monthly literary information magazine.

Apples & Snakes
Battersea Arts Centre, Lavender Hill, London SW11 5TN
☎020 7924 3410 Fax 020 7924 3763
Email apples@snakes.demon.co.uk

Contacts *Geraldine Collinge, Roger Robinson, Malika Booker*

A unique, independent promotional organisation for poetry and poets – furthering poetry as an innovative and popular medium and cross-cultural activity. A&S organises an annual programme of over 150 events (including their London season which actively pushes new voices), tours, residencies and festivals as well as operating a Poets-in-Education Scheme and a non-profit booking agency for relevant poets.

Arts Councils and Regional Arts Boards
For a full list of addresses see **Arts Councils and Regional Arts Boards**

The Arvon Foundation
See entry under **Professional Associations**

Association of Small Press Poets
7 Pincott Place, London SE4 2ER
☎020 7277 8831 Fax 020 7277 8831
Email robooth@gofornet.co.uk

Coordinator *Ruth Booth*

Fledgling association of poets wishing to increase the sales of their work. Publishes *The Big Poetry Catalogue* as a sales tool, the newsletter *Appraisal*, and offers various competitions, appraisal services and discounts on *Robooth Publications*, the ASPP coordinator's own press. Membership charges are on a sliding scale starting from £18. There will be a Web site soon.

The British Haiku Society
35 Downs Park West, Westbury Park, Bristol BS6 7QH
☎0797 965 6775
Website dspace.dial.pipex.com/town/place/xst19/index.htm

Secretary *Alan J Summers*

Formed in 1990. Promotes the appreciation and writing within the British Isles of haiku, senyru, tanka, haibun and renga by way of tutorials, workshops, exchange of poems, critical comment and information. The Society runs a haiku library and administers the annual James W. Hackett Award. *Publishes The Haiku Kit* teaching pack and the quarterly journal, *Blithe Spirit*.

The Eight Hand Gang
5 Cross Farm, Station Road, Padgate, Warrington WA2 0QG

Secretary *John F. Haines*

An association of SF poets. *Publishes Handshake*, a single-sheet newsletter of SF poetry and information available free in exchange for an s.a.e.

The Little Magazine Collection, Poetry Store and Alternative Press Collections

University College London, Gower Street, London WC1E 6BT
☎020 7380 7796   Fax 020 7380 7727
Contact *John Allen*

Housed at University College London Library, these are the fruits of Geoffrey Soar and David Miller's interest in UK and US alternative publishing, with a strong emphasis on poetry. The Little Magazines Collection runs to over 3600 titles mainly in the more experimental and avant-garde areas. The Poetry Store consists of over 12,200 small press items, mainly from the '60s onwards, again with some stress on experimental work. In addition, there are reprints of classic earlier little magazines, from Symbolism through to the present. Anyone who is interested can consult the collections, and it helps if you have some idea of what you want to see. Bring evidence of identity for a smooth ride. The collections can be accessed by visiting the Manuscripts and Rare Books Room at University College at the above address between 10.00am and 5.00pm on weekdays. Most items are available on inter-library loans.

The Northern Poetry Library

Central Library, The Willows, Morpeth, Northumberland NE61 1TA
☎01670 534524/534514   Fax 01670 534513
Email amenities@northumberland.gov.uk

Membership available to everyone in Cleveland, Cumbria, Durham, Northumberland and Tyne and Wear. Associate membership available for all outside the region. Over 15,000 books and magazines for loan including virtually all poetry published in the UK since 1968. Access to English Poetry, the full text database of all English Poetry from 600 - 1900. Postal lending available too. In association with MidNag publishes *Red Herring*, a poetry magazine.

The Poet's House/Teach na hÉigse

Clonbarra, Falcarragh, Co Donegal, Republic of Ireland
☎00 353 65470 Fax 00 353 74 65471
Email phouse@iol.ie
Director *Janice Fitzpatrick Simmons*

Set in the heart of Donegal Gaeltacht, the centre offers a year-long residential MA along with three ten-day summer courses (to apply send three poems). During each session there are three resident and six visiting poets. Recent poets have included Peter Sir, Paul Durcan, James Simmons, Frank Ormsby and Medbh McGuckian.

The Poetry Book Society

Book House, 45 East Hill, London SW18 2QZ
☎020 8870 8403 Fax 020 8877 1615
Website poetrybooks.co.uk
Director *Clare Brown*

For readers, writers, students and teachers of poetry. Founded in 1953 by T. S. Eliot and funded by the Arts Council, the PBS is a unique membership organisation providing up-to-date and comprehensive information about poetry from publishers in the UK and Ireland. Members receive the quarterly *PBS Bulletin* packed with articles by poets, poems, news, listings and access to discounts of at least 25% off featured titles. These range from modern classics to contemporary works. There are three membership packages – two of which include a number of new books specially selected by the Society's panel of experts, along with a special package for teachers. Subscriptions start at £10. The PBS also runs the annual **T. S. Eliot Prize** for the best collection of new poetry.

The Poetry Business

The Studio, Byram Arcade, Westgate, Huddersfield, West Yorkshire HD1 1ND
☎01484 434840   Fax 01484 426566
Email edit@poetrybusiness.co.uk
Website www.poetrybusiness.co.uk
Administrators *Peter Sansom, Janet Fisher*

Founded in 1986, the Business publishes *The North* magazine and books, pamphlets and cassettes under the **Smith/Doorstop** imprint. It runs an annual competition and organises monthly writing Saturdays. Send an s.a.e. for full details.

The Poetry Can

Unit 11, Kuumba Project, 20–22 Hepburn Road, Bristol BS2 8UD
☎0117 942 6976   Fax 0117 944 1478
Email hester@poetrycan.demon.co.uk
Website www.poetrycan.demon.co.uk
Coordinator *Hester Cockcroft*

Founded in 1995, tthe Poetry Can is a poetry development agency working across the Bristol and Bath area. It runs poetry readings, supports the creative and professional development of poets and publishes a bi-monthly bulletin of poetry news and activity.

Poetry Ireland/Eigse Eireann

Bermingham Tower, Upper Yard, Dublin Castle, Dublin, Republic of Ireland
☎00 353 1 6714632   Fax 00 353 1 6714634
Writers in Schools Scheme ☎00 353 674 9860
Email poetry@iol.ie
Website www.poetryireland.ie

Director *Theo Dorgan*
General Manager *Niamh Morris*

The national poetry organisation for Ireland, supported by Arts Councils both sides of the border. Publishes a quarterly magazine *Poetry Ireland Review* and a bi-monthly newsletter of upcoming events and competitions as well as organising tours and readings by Irish and foreign poets and the National Poetry Competition, open to poets working in both Irish and English. Administers the Austin Clarke Library, a collection of over 6000 volumes, runs the Writers in Schools Scheme in the Republic and is a partner in the European Poetry Translation Network.

The Poetry Library

Royal Festival Hall, Level 5, London SE1 8XX
☎020 7921 0943/0664
Fax 020 7921 0939
Email poetrylibrary@rfh.org.uk
Website: www.poetrylibrary.org.uk

Librarian *Mary Enright*

Founded by the Arts Council in 1953. A collection of 45,000 titles of modern poetry since 1912, from Georgian to Rap, representing all English-speaking countries and including translations into English by contemporary poets. Holds two copies of each title: one for loan, one for reference; a wide range of poetry magazines and ephemera from all over the world plus cassettes, records and videos, many available on loan. There is also a children's poetry section with a teacher's resource collection.

An information service compiles lists of poetry magazines, competitions, publishers, groups and workshops, available from the Library on receipt of a large s.a.e. or from the Web site. It also has a noticeboard for lost quotations, through which it tries to identify lines or fragments of poetry which have been sent in by other readers.

General enquiry service available. Membership is free but proof of identity and address are essential to join. Open 11.00am to 8.00pm, Tuesday to Sunday. The Library's Web site is one of the best poetry resources on the Net.

Beside the Library is *The Voice Box*, a performance space especially for literature. For details of current programme ring 020 7921 0906.

Poetry London Newsletter

1a Jewel Road, London E17 4QU
Email editors@plondon.demon.co.uk

Contacts *Anna Robinson* (listings), *Pascale Petit* (poetry editor), *Scott Verner* (reviews).

Published three times a year, *Poetry London* includes poetry by new and established writers, reviews of recent collections and anthologies, features on issues relating to poetry, and an encyclopaedic listing of virtually everything to do with poetry in the capital and the South East, with a limited coverage of events elsewhere.

The Poetry School

1a Jewel Road, London E17 4QU
☎020 8985 0090/8223 0401

Coordinator *Mimi Khalvati*

Funded by the London Arts Board the School offers a core programme of tuition in reading and writing poetry through a series of workshops, courses, masterclasses and seminars. Tutors include Matthew Sweeney, Michael Donaghy, Jane Duran and Alison Fell. The School also provides a forum for practitioners to share experiences, develop skills and extend appreciation of the traditional and innovative aspects of their art.

The Poetry Society

22 Betterton Street, London WC2H 9BU
☎020 7240 4810 Fax 020 7240 4818
Email: poetrysoc@dial.pipex.com
Website: www.poetrysoc.com

Chair *Judith Palmer*
Director *To be appointed*

Founded in 1909, which ought to make it venerable, the Society exists to help poets and poetry thrive in Britain. In the past decade it has undergone a renaissance, reaching out from its Covent Garden base to promote the national health of poetry in a range of imaginative ways. Membership costs £32 for individuals. *Poetry News* membership is £15. Current activities include:

- Quarterly magazine of new verse, views and criticism, *Poetry Review*, editor Peter Forbes.
- Quarterly newsletter, *Poetry News*.
- Promotions, events and cooperation with Britain's many literature festivals, poetry venues and poetry publishers.
- Competitions and awards, including the annual **National Poetry Competition** in association with BT (£5000 first prize).
- A manuscript-diagnosis service, *The Poetry Prescription*, which gives detailed reports on submissions. Reduced rates for members.

- Seminars, fact sheets, training courses, ideas packs.
- Provides information and advice, publishes books, posters and resources for schools and libraries. Education membership costs £45/ £25 and includes *The Young Poetry Pack*, *Poetry Book* for primary schools and *Jumpstart Poetry* for secondary schools, colourful poetry posters for Keystages 1 to 4. Many of Britain's most popular poets, including Michael Rosen, Roger McGough and Jackie Kay, contribute, offering advice and inspiration.
- The Poetry Café serving snacks & drink to members, friends and guests, part of *The Poetry Place*, a venue for many poetry activities – readings, poetry clinic, workshops and poetry launches. This space is available for bookings.

Recent projects include *Poetry Places*, a national programme of residencies and placements.

Point

Halsesteenweg 31-22, B-9402 Ninove, Belgium
☎00 32 54 32 4748   Fax 00 32 54 32 4660
Email elpoeta@point-editions.com
Website www.point-editions.com

Director *Germain Droogenbroodt*

Founded as Poetry International in 1984, Point is based in Belgium. A multilingual publisher of contemporary verse from *established* poets, the organisation has brought out more than 60 titles in at least eight languages, including English. Editions run the original work alongside a verse translation into Dutch made in co-operation with the poet. The organisation's Website is highly developed and features much English language verse. Point also co-organises an annual international poetry festival.

Regional Arts Boards

See **Arts Councils and Regional Arts Boards**

Scottish Poetry Library

5 Crichton's Close, Canongate, Edinburgh EH8 8DT
☎0131 557 2876
Email inquiries@spl.org.uk
Website spl.org.uk

Librarian *Penny Duce*

A comprehensive reference and lending collection of work by Scottish poets in Gaelic, Scots and English, plus the work of British and international poets. Stock includes books, tapes, videos, news cuttings and magazines. Borrowing is free to all. Services include: a postal lending scheme, for which there is a small fee, a mobile library which can visit schools and other centres by arrangement, exhibitions, bibliographies, publications, information and promotion in the field of poetry. There is an online catalogue and computer index to poetry and poetry periodicals. The membership scheme costs £15 annually. Members receive a newsletter and support the library.

Survivors' Poetry

Diorama Arts Centre, 34 Osnaburgh Street, London NW1 3ND
☎020 7916 5317 Fax 020 7916 0830
Email survivors@survivorspoetry.org.uk

Director *Clare Douglas*
Administration *Demet Dayamch*

A unique national literature organisation which promotes poetry by survivors of mental distress through workshops, readings and performances to audiences all over the UK. It was founded in 1991 by four poets with first-hand experience of the mental heaalth system. Survivors' community outreach work provides training and performance workshops and publishing projects. A survivor is defined as: someone with a current or past experience of psychiatric hospitals; a recipient of ECT, tranquillisers or other medication; a user of counselling and therapy services; a survivor of sexual abuse or child abuse; anyone who has empathy with the experience of survivors.

Survivors' Poetry Scotland

30 Cranworth Street, Glasgow G12 8AG
☎00141 357 6838 Fax 0141 357 6939
Email sps@spscot.co.uk
Website www.spscot.co.uk

Project Manager *Chris Balance*
Administrator *Wallace MacBain*
Managing Editor *Gerry Loose*

Promotes poetry by survivors of mental distress through a poetry magazine, *Nomad*, published three times a year; writing workshops (four a week in Glasgow); and monthly performance evenings. SPS is setting up local groups across Scotland.

Tŷ Newydd

Llanystumdwy, Criccieth, Gwynedd LL52 0LW
☎01766 522811 Fax 01766 523095
Email tynewydd@dial.pipex.com
Website academi.org/tynewyd

Director *Sally Baker*

An independent Arvon-style residential writers

centre run by the Talisin Trust from the one-time home of Lloyd George in North Wales. The programme (in both Welsh and English) has a regular poetry content. (See also **Writers' Courses, Circles and Workshops**.) Among the many tutors to-date have been: Gillian Clarke, Wendy Cope, Roger McGough, Carol Ann Duffy, Liz Lochhead, Peter Finch and Paul Henry. Send for the centre's descriptive leaflets and a copy of its newsletter.

Small Presses

Aard Press
c/o Aardverx, 31 Mountearl Gardens, London SW16 2NL
Managing Editor *D. Jarvis, Dawn Redwood*
FOUNDED 1971. *Publishes* artists' bookworks, experimental/visual poetry, 'zines, eonist literature, topographics, ephemera and international mail-art documentation. Very small editions. No unsolicited material or proposals.
Royalties not paid. No sale-or-return deals.

Abbey Press
Abbey Grammar School, Courtenay Hill, Newry, Co. Down BT34 2ED
☎028 3026 3142   Fax 028 3026 2514
Also at: 24 Martello Park, Old Seahill, Craigavad, Co. Down BT18 0DG
☎028 9042 2209 Fax 028 9042 2209
Editor *Adrian Rice*
Administrator *Mel McMahon*
FOUNDED in 1997, Abbey Press is a fast growing literary publisher with a strong poetry list. Also *publishes* biography, memoirs, fiction, history, politics, Irish language and academic. Send synopsis, sample of work, biographical note and s.a.e.

ABCD
See **Allardyce, Barnett, Publishers**

Agneau 2
See **Allardyce, Barnett, Publishers**

AK Press/AKA Books
PO Box 12766, Edinburgh EH8 9YE
☎0131 555 5165   Fax 0131 555 5215
Email ak@akedin.demon.co.uk
Website www.akuk.com
Managing Editor *Alexis McKay*
AK Press grew out of the activities of AK Distribution which distributes a wide range of radical (anarchist, feminist, etc.) literature (books, pamphlets, periodicals, magazines), both fiction and non-fiction. *Publishes* politics, history, situationist theory, occasional fiction in both book and pamphlet form. About 12 titles a year. Proposals and synopses welcome if they fall within AK's specific areas of interest.
Royalties paid.

Akros Publications
33 Lady Nairn Avenue, Kirkcaldy, Fife KY1 2AW
☎01592 651522
Publisher *Duncan Glen*
FOUNDED 1965. *Publishes* poetry collections, pamphlets and anthologies; literary essays and studies; travel books with a literary slant; local histories and memoirs. About 10 titles a year. Ideas for books welcome; no unsolicited mss.
Royalties paid twice-yearly.

The Alembic Press
Hyde Farm House, Marcham, Abingdon, Oxon OX13 6NX
☎01865 391391   Fax 01865 391322
Email AlembicPrs@aol.com
Owner *Claire Bolton*
FOUNDED 1976. Publisher of hand-produced books by traditional letterpress methods. Short print-runs. *Publishes* bibliography, book arts and printing, miniatures and occasional poetry. Book design and production service to like-minded authors wishing to publish in this manner. No unsolicited mss.

Allardyce, Barnett, Publishers
14 Mount Street, Lewes, East Sussex BN7 1HL
☎01273 479393   Fax 01273 479393
Publisher *Fiona Allardyce*
Managing Editor *Anthony Barnett*
FOUNDED 1981. *Publishes* art, literature and music. About 3 titles a year. IMPRINTS **Agneau 2**, **ABCD**, **Allardyce Book**. Unsolicited mss and synopses cannot be considered.

Anglo-Saxon Books
Frithgarth, Thetford Forest Park, Hockwold cum Wilton, Norfolk IP26 4NQ
☎01842 828430   Fax 01842 828332
Email asbooks@englisc.demon.co.uk
Website www.englisc.demon.co.uk
Managing Editor *Tony Linsell*
FOUNDED 1990 to promote a greater awareness of and interest in early English history and culture. Originally concentrated on Old English texts but now also publishes less academic, more popular titles. Seeking titles for all periods of English history. *Publishes* English history, cul-

ture, language and society. About 5–10 titles a year. Unsolicited synopses welcome but return postage necessary.

Royalties – standard rate.

Athelney

1 Providence Street, King's Lynn, Norfolk PE30 5ET   Fax 01842 828332

Managing Editor *John Cooper*

FOUNDED 2000. *Publishes* nationalism in general; English nationalism in particular. Unsolicited outlines/contents, page/first chapter welcome. Please enclose return postage.

Royalties – standard rate.

AVERT

AIDS Education and Research Trust, 4 Brighton Road, Horsham, West Sussex RH13 5BA

☎01403 210202   Fax 01403 211001

Email avert@dial.pipex.com

Website www.avert.org

Managing Editor *Annabel Kanabus*

Publishing arm of the AIDS Education and Research Trust, a national registered charity established 1986. *Publishes* books and leaflets about HIV infection and AIDS. About 3 titles a year. Unsolicited mss, synopses and ideas welcome.

Royalties paid accordingly.

M. & M. Baldwin

24 High Street, Cleobury Mortimer, Kidderminster DY14 8BY

☎01299 270110   Fax 01299 270110

Email mb@mbaldwin.free-online.co.uk

Managing Editor *Dr Mark Baldwin*

FOUNDED 1978. *Publishes* local interest/history, WW2 codebreaking and inland waterways books. Up to 5 titles a year. Unsolicited mss, synopses and ideas for books welcome (not general fiction).

Royalties paid.

Bardon Enterprises

6 Winter Road, Southsea, Hampshire PO4 9BT

☎023 9287 4900   Fax 023 9287 4900

Email info@bardonia.softnet.co.uk

Website www.soft.net.uk/bardonia

Managing Director *W. B. Henshaw*

FOUNDED 1996. *Publishes* music, art, biographies, poetry, academic books and sheet music. 6 titles in 1999 plus 35 pieces of music. Unsolicited mss, synopses and ideas welcome. No pictorial books.

BB Books

See under **Poetry Presses**

The Better Book Company

Warblington Lodge, The Gardens, Warblington, Near Havant, Hampshire PO9 2XH

☎01428 682937   Fax 01428 681736

Website www.betterbook.com

Managing Editor *James Jude Garvey*

FOUNDED 1996. *Publishes* fiction, histories, poetry, religious, scientific, company histories. 12 titles in 1999. Offers a complete editorial, design, printing and marketing service to self-publishing authors in all genre. No unsolicited mss but will consider synopses and ideas; telephone in the first instance.

Royalties paid.

Between the Lines

9 Woodstock Road, London N4 3ET

☎020 7272 8719   Fax 020 8374 5736

Email betweenthelines@lineone.net

Website www.pbk.co.uk/btl/

Editorial Board *Peter Dale, Ian Hamilton, Philip Hoy, J. D. McClatchy*

FOUNDED 1998. *Publishes* extended interviews with leading contemporary poets. By mid-2001, it is planned to have eleven volumes in print, featuring W. D. Snodgrass, Michael Hamburger, Anthony Thwaite, Anthony Hecht, Donald Hall, Thom Gunn, Richard Wilbur, Seamus Heaney, Paul Muldoon, Donald Justice and Hans Magnus Enzensberger. Each volume features a career sketch, comprehensive bibliography and a representative selection of quotations from the poets' critics and reviewers.

Black Cat Books

See **Neil Miller Publications**

The Bonaventura Press

Bagpath, Tetbury, Gloucestershire GL8 8YG

☎01453 860827   Fax 01453 860487

Email famosa@iname.com

Website www.bonaventura.co.uk

Managing Editor *Janet Sloss*

FOUNDED 1995. Self-publishing venture.

The Book Castle

12 Church Street, Dunstable, Bedfordshire LU5 4RU

☎01582 605670   Fax 01582 662431

Email bc@book-castle.co.uk

Website www.book-castle.busclub.net

Managing Editor *Paul Bowes*

FOUNDED 1986. *Publishes* non-fiction of local interest (Bedfordshire, Hertfordshire, Buckinghamshire, Oxfordshire, Northamptonshire, the Chilterns). 6+ titles a year. About 70 titles in print. Unsolicited mss, synopses and ideas for books welcome.

Royalties paid.

Book-in-Hand Ltd

20 Shepherds Hill, London N6 5AH
☎020 8341 7650 Fax 020 8341 7650
Email books@book-in-hand.demon.co.uk

Contact *Ann Kritzinger*

Print production service for self-publishers. Includes design and editing advice to give customers a greater chance of selling in the open market.

Bookmarque Publishing

26 Cotswold Close, Minster Lovell,
Oxfordshire OX8 5SX
☎01993 775179

Managing Editor *John Rose*

FOUNDED 1987. Publishing business with aim of filling gaps in motoring history of which it is said 'there are many'. *Publishes* motoring history, motor sport and 'general' titles. About 8 titles a year (increasing). All design and typesetting of books done in-house. Unsolicited mss, synopses and ideas welcome on transport titles. S.a.e. required for reply or return of material or for advice on publishing your work.

Royalties paid.

Bozo

BM Bozo, London WC1N 3XX
Managing Editors *John & Cecilia Nicholson*

FOUNDED 1981. Began by producing tiny pamphlets (*Patriotic English Tracts*) and has gained a reputation as 'one of England's foremost pamphleteers'. *Publishes* historical analyses, apocalyptic rants, wry/savage humour and political 'filth'. Considerable expansion of titles is underway. No unsolicited mss, synopses or ideas.

Royalties not paid.

Brantwood Books

PO Box 144, Orpington, Kent BR6 6LZ
☎01689 833117 Fax 01689 833117
Email brantwood@planxty.com
Website www.planxty.com/brantwood

Publisher *Philip Turner*

Publishes highly illustrated, limited edition print runs of specialist cinema titles, ranging from Russian cinema architecture to 32-page illus-

trated guides to British and North American cinema circuit histories.

DIVISIONS **Brantwood Books** and **Outline Publications** UK/US cinema circuit and film studio histories; **Brantwood Biographical** Biographies of movie moguls, producers and directors; **Brantwood Miniature Life** Series of outline biographies of popular movie stars; **Brantwood Technical** Screen, film and camera/projector topics. Ideas which can be adapted to a 32-page format are welcome.

Brilliant Publications

The Old School Yard, Leighton Road,
Northall, Dunstable, Bedfordshire LU6 2HA
☎01525 222844 Fax 01525 221250
Email brilliantpublications.compuserve.com
Website www.brilliantpublications.co.uk

Publisher *Priscilla Hannaford*

FOUNDED 1993. *Publishes* books for teachers, parents and others working with 0–13-year-olds. About 10–15 titles a year. SERIES *How to Dazzle at ...* (9–13-year-olds with special needs); *How to be Brilliant at ...* (7–11-year-olds); *How to Sparkle at ...* (5–7-year-olds); *Activities* (3–5-year-olds). Submit synopsis and sample pages in the first instance: authors are advised study the format of existing books before submitting synopses.

Royalties paid twice-yearly.

Business Innovations Research

Tregeraint House, Zennor, St Ives, Cornwall
TR26 3DB
☎01736 797061 Fax 01736 797061
Email great-ideas@ukgateway.net
Website www.great-ideas.com

Managing Director *John T. Wilson*

Publishes business books and newsletters, home study courses, and guidebooks. Production service available to self-publishers.

Businesslike Publishing

'Bluepool', Strathoykel, Ardgay, Inverness-shire
IV24 3DP
☎01549 441211 Fax 01549 441366
Website www.dorian.blue@btinternet.com

Managing Editor *Iain R. McIntyre*

FOUNDED 1989. Provides a printing and publishing service for members of the **Society of Civil Service Authors**. *Publishes* magazines, collections of poetry, short stories (not individual poems or short stories) and Scottish history. About 2 titles a year. Ideas/synopses accepted. No unsolicited mss.

Royalties generally not paid but negotiable in some circumstances.

C K Publishing

151 Brookfield Road, Cheadle, Cheshire
SK8 1EY
☎0161 491 6074
Email editor@writersmuse.co.uk *or*
calum@cheadle.u-net.com
Website www.writersmuse.co.uk
Managing Editor *Calum Kerr*

Publishes novels and poetry collections; also
Writer's Muse, a bi-monthly creative writing
magazine featuring short stories, poetry, reviews,
articles, biography, etc. Unsolicited mss welcome; no synopses or ideas. S.a.e. essential.
Royalties paid for book collections. No payment for *Writer's Muse* magazine – free copies.

Cartmel Press Associates

Old Orchard, Barber Green, Grange-over-
Sands, Cumbria LA11 6HU
☎015395 36390
Email dguthrie@ndirect.co.uk
Managing Editor *D. M. Guthrie*

FOUNDED in 1983 to publish art monographs
and now publishing full-length biographies of
established artists. No unsolicited mss; synopses
and ideas welcome.
Royalties paid.

Chameleon HH Publishing

The Quarry House, East End, Witney,
Oxfordshire OX8 6QA
☎01993 880223   Fax 01993 880236
Email marion@chameleonhh.co.uk *&*
david@chameleonhh
Website www.chameleonhh.co.uk
Directors *David Hall, Marion Hazzledine*

FOUNDED 1997. CD-ROM and Web publishers
on behalf of commercial publishers, institutes,
associations and government bodies. Also, **E-
and I-Commerce** – welcomes unsolicited mss
for electronic publishing from self-publishers.
Consulting and advice on CD-ROM and Web
publishing.

Charlewood Press

7 Weavers Place, Chandlers Ford, Eastleigh,
Hampshire SO53 1TU
☎023 8026 1192
Email gponting@clara.net
Website www.home.clara.net/gponting/
index-page11.html
Managing Editors *Gerald Ponting, Anthony
Light*

FOUNDED 1987. Publishes local history books on
the Fordingbridge area, researched and written
by the two partners and leaflets on local walks.
No unsolicited mss.
Royalties not paid.

The Cheverell Press

Great Cheverell Mill, Devizes, Wiltshire
SN10 5UP
☎01380 816877   Fax 01380 816878
Managing Editor *Sarah de Larrinaga*

Publishes careers, media and performing arts. No
fiction. IMPRINTS **The Cheverell Press**; **First
Hand Books**. Currently using researchers/
writers on a fee basis, rather than royalties. No
unsolicited mss. Started as a self–publisher and
has produced a self–publishers information pack.
Write for details.

Chrysalis Press

7 Lower Ladyes Hills, Kenilworth,
Warwickshire CV8 2GN
☎01926 855223   Fax 01926 856611
Managing Editor *Brian Boyd*

FOUNDED 1994. *Publishes* fiction, literary criticism and biography. No unsolicited mss.
Royalties paid.

Clinamen Press Ltd

Enterprise House, Whitworth Street West,
Manchester M1 5WG
☎0161 237 3355   Fax 0161 237 3727
Email bstebbing@clinamen.net
Website www.clinamen.net

FOUNDED 1998. *Publishes* philosophy, literary
criticism and art theory. 6 titles in 1999. No
unsolicited mss; two sample chapters with
covering letter welcome.

CNP Publications

The Roseland Institute, Gorran, St Austell,
Cornwall
☎01726 843501   Fax 01726 843501
Managing Editor *Dr James Whetter*

FOUNDED 1975. *Publishes* quarterly journal *The
Cornish Banner/An Baner Kernuak*; also poetry
booklets of Celtic design, political essays,
Cornish history. 1–2 titles a year. Cornish history published under the **Lyfrow Trelyspen**
imprint. Unsolicited mss, synopses and ideas
welcome.
Royalties not paid.

Codex Books

PO Box 148, Hove, East Sussex BN3 3DQ
☎01273 728000   Fax 01273 205502
Email codex@codexbooks.co.uk

Website www.codexbooks.co.uk
Managing Editor *Hayley Ann*
FOUNDED 1994. *Publishes* 'cutting edge fiction', journalism and non-fiction. Includes cyber punk, pulp, experimental fiction, gay fiction and music-related titles. AUTHORS include Billy Childish, Stewart Home, Tania Glyde and Jeff Noon. Has also released spoken word CDs featuring Kathy Acker, Alan Moore and Iain Banks. Prefers to receive sample (approx. 50pp) with brief synopsis and author info, following introductory phone call.
Royalties paid.

Copperfield Books
Hillbrook House, Lyncombe Vale Road, Bath BA2 4LS
☎01225 442835   Fax 01225 319755
Email sales@www.darcybook.com
Website www.darcybook.com
Managing Director *John Brushfield*
Publishes paperback fiction and general non-fiction. No unsolicited mss; 'we only commission books to our own specification'.

Corvus Books
See **ignotus press**

The Cosmic Elk
68 Elsham Crescent, Lincoln LN6 3YS
☎01522 820922
Email heather@hobden.fsbusiness.co.uk
Contact *Heather Hobden*
FOUNDED in 1988 to publish *John Harrison and the Problem of Longitude* (now in its 7th edition). Continues to produce booklets in science and history, and associated products such as the John Harrison tea towel, exhibition posters, etc. 'New work always welcome on science or history topics (not fiction or children's). Please e-mail or telephone first to discuss.'

Crescent Moon Publishing and Joe's Press
PO Box 393, Maidstone, Kent ME14 5XU
Email orders@crescentmoon.org.uk
Website www.crescentmoon.org.uk
Managing Editor *Jeremy Robinson*
FOUNDED 1988 to publish critical studies of figures such as D. H. Lawrence, Thomas Hardy, André Gide, Walt Disney, Rilke, Leonardo da Vinci, Mark Rothko, C. P. Cavafy and Hélène Cixous. *Publishes* literature, criticism, media, art, feminism, painting, poetry, travel, guidebooks,

cinema and some fiction. Literary magazine, *Passion*, launched February 1994. Quarterly. Twice-yearly anthology of American poetry, *Pagan America*. About 15–20 titles per year. Unsolicited mss, synopses and ideas welcome but approach in writing first and send an s.a.e.
Royalties negotiable.

Crown House Publishing
Crown Buildings, Bancyfelin, Carmarthen SA33 5ND
☎01267 211345   Fax 01267 211882
Website www.crownhouse.co.uk
Editorial Director *David Bowman*
Publishing Director *Bridget Shine*
FOUNDED 1998. *Publishes* titles in the areas of psychology, Neuro-Linguistic Programming (NLP), personal growth, stress management, business, health and hypnosis. The aim of our list is to both demystify the latest psychological advances, particularly in the fields of NLP and hypnosis, and provide professional therapists, consultants and trainers with books detailing the latest cutting-edge developments in their field. Approx. 20 titles a year.
Royalties paid twice-yearly.

Daniels Medica
Zetland House, Cley Next The Sea, Norfolk NR25 7RS
☎01263 740230   Fax 01263 740343
Email daniels@breathe.co.uk
Publisher *Dr Victor G. Daniels*
Educational materials and training packs for the pharmaceutical industry.

Dionysia Press Ltd
See under **Poetry Presses**

Dog House Publications
18 Marlow Avenue, Eastbourne, East Sussex BN22 8SJ
☎01323 729214
Email doghouse@rapport.softnet.co.uk
Website www.soft.net.uk/rapport/
Managing Editor *Silvia Kent*
FOUNDED 1990. Publishes books and booklets on dog training and behaviour. 'We no longer accept unsolicited mss. Following a major restructuring in 1997, we have reduced the range of our titles to concentrate on new editions of our best sellers.' Free training and dog care booklets available to charities on request.
Royalties paid.

The Dragonby Press
15 High Street, Dragonby, Scunthorpe, North Lincolnshire DN15 0BE
☎01724 840645
Email rah.williams@virgin.net
Website freespace.virgin.net/rah.williams/
Managing Editor *Richard Williams*

FOUNDED 1987 to publish affordable bibliography for reader, collector and dealer. About 3 titles a year. Unsolicited mss, synopses and ideas welcome for bibliographical projects only.
Royalties paid.

Dramatic Lines
PO Box 201, Twickenham TW2 5RQ
☎020 8296 9502   Fax 020 8296 9503
Email mail@dramaticlinespublishers.co.uk
Website www.dramaticlinespublishers.co.uk
Managing Editor *John Nicholas*

FOUNDED to promote drama for young people. Publications with a wide variety of theatrical applications including classroom use and school assemblies, drama examinations, auditions, festivals and theatre group performance. Unsolicited drama related mss, proposals and synopses welcome.
Royalties paid.

Education Now Publishing Cooperative Ltd
113 Arundel Drive, Bramcote Hills, Nottingham NG9 3FQ
☎0115 9257261   Fax 0115 9257261
Website www.gn.apc.org/edheretics
Managing Editors *Dr Roland Meighan, Philip Toogood*

A non-profit research and writing group set up in reaction to 'the totalitarian tendencies of the 1988 Education Act'. Its aim is to widen the terms of the debate about education and its choices. *Publishes* reports on positive educational initiatives such as flexi-schooling, mini-schooling, small schooling, home-based education and democratic schooling. 4–5 titles a year. No unsolicited mss or ideas. Enquiries only.
Royalties generally not paid.

Educational Heretics Press
113 Arundel Drive, Bramcote Hills, Nottingham NG9 3FQ
☎0115 9257261   Fax 0115 9257261
Website www.gn.apc.org/edheretics
Directors *Janet & Roland Meighan*

Non-profit venture which aims to question the dogmas of schooling in particular and education

in general, and establish the logistics of the next learning system. No unsolicited material. Enquiries only.
Royalties not paid but under review.

EKO Fund
Wedgwood Memorial College, Barlaston, Staffs ST12 9DG
☎01782 372105   Fax 01782 372393
Managing Editor *Brian W. Burnett*

FOUNDED January 1996 to publish modern, lively books and magazines in and about Esperanto. Unsolicited mss, synopses and ideas welcome.
Royalties paid.

Enable Enterprises
PO Box 1974, Coventry CV3 1YG
☎0800 3588484   Fax 0870 1332447
Email writers@enableenterprises.com
Website www.enableenterprises.co.uk
Contact *Simon Stevens*

Enable Enterprises provides a wide range of accessibilty and disability services including publications on relevant issues. It welcomes unsolicited material related to accessibility and disability issues.

Feasac Press
See **ignotus press**

Feather Books
Fair View, Old Coppice, Lyth Bank, Shrewsbury, Shropshire SY3 0BW
☎01743 872177   Fax 01743 872177
Email john@waddysweb.freeuk.com
Website www.waddysweb.com
Managing Director *Rev. John Waddington-Feather*
Directors *David Grundy, Tony Reavill*

FOUNDED 1980 to publish writers' group work. All material has a strong Christian ethos. *Publishes* poetry (mainly, but not exclusively, religious); Christian mystery novels (the Revd. D. I. Blake Hartley series); Christian children's novels; seasonal poetry collections and *The Poetry Church* magazine. 20 titles a year. Produces poetry, drama and music CD/cassettes. No unsolicited mss, synopses or ideas. All correspondence to include s.a.e. please.

Fern House
19 High Street, Haddenham, Ely, Cambridgeshire CB6 3XA
☎01353 740222   Fax 01353 741987
Email info@fernhouse.com
Website www.fernhouse.com

Managing Editor *Rodney Dale*

FOUNDED 1995. *Publishes* non-fiction with a bias towards biography, reference and technology. 4 titles in 1999. Unsolicited synopses and ideas welcome. Preliminary approach by letter, telephone or the website preferred.
Royalties paid.

First Hand Books
See **The Cheverell Press**

Five Leaves Publications
PO Box 81, Nottingham NG5 4ER
☎0115 9693597
Email fiveleaf01@surfaid.org
Contact *Ross Bradshaw*

FOUNDED 1995 (taking over the publishing programme of Mushroom Bookshop), producing 6–8 titles a year. *Publishes* fiction, poetry, politics and Jewish Interest. Publisher of several books by Michael Rosen. Titles normally commissioned.
Royalties and fees paid.

Forth Naturalist & Historian
University of Stirling, Stirling FK9 4LA
☎01259 215091   Fax 01786 464994
Email Lindsay.Corbett@stir.ac.uk
Website www.stir.ac.uk/theuni/forthnat/
Also at: 30 Dunmar Drive, Alloa, Clackmannanshire FK10 2EH
Honorary Editors *Lindsay Corbett, Neville Dix*

FOUNDED 1975 by the collaboration of Stirling University members and the Central Regional Council to promote interests and publications on central Scotland. Aims to provide a 'valuable local studies educational resource for mid-Scotland schools, libraries and people'. Runs an annual symposium: Man and the Landscape. *Publishes* naturalist, historical and environmental studies and maps, including 1890s maps 25" to the mile – 24 of Central Scotland areas/places with historical notes. Over 20 selected papers from the annual *The Forth Naturalist & Historian* are published in pamphlet form. Welcomes papers, mss and ideas relevant to central Scotland.
Royalties not paid.

Frontier Publishing
Windetts, Kirstead, Norfolk NR15 1BR
☎01508 558174   Fax 01508 550194
Managing Editor *John Black*

FOUNDED 1983. *Publishes* travel, photography and literature. 2–3 titles a year. No unsolicited mss; synopses and ideas welcome.
Royalties paid.

Galactic Central Publications
Imladris, 25A Copgrove Road, Leeds, West Yorkshire LS8 2SP
Email philsp@compuserve.com
Managing Editor *Phil Stephensen-Payne*

FOUNDED 1982 in the US. *Publishes* science fiction bibliographies. About 4 titles a year. All new publications originate in the UK. Unsolicited mss, synopses and ideas welcome.

The Gargoyle's Head
Chatham House, Gosshill Road, Chislehurst, Kent BR7 5NS
☎020 8467 8475   Fax 020 8295 1967
Managing Editor *Jennie Gray*

FOUNDED 1990. *Publishes* a six-monthly magazine and newsletter plus books and supplements on Gothic and macabre subjects. History, literary criticism, reprints of forgotten texts, biography, architecture, art, etc., usually with a gloomy and black-hued flavour. About 4 titles a year. Synopses and ideas welcome.
Flat fee paid.

Geological Society Publishing House
Unit 7, Brassmill Enterprise Centre, Brassmill Lane, Bath BA1 3JN
☎01225 445046   Fax 01225 442836
Website bookshop.geolsoc.org.uk
Managing Editor *Mike Collins*

Publishing arm of the Geological Society which was founded in 1807. *Publishes* undergraduate and postgraduate texts in the earth sciences. 25 titles a year. Unsolicited mss, synopses and ideas welcome.
Royalties not paid.

Glosa
PO Box 18, Richmond, Surrey TW9 1WD
☎020 8274 9094
Managing Editors *Wendy Ashby, Ronald Clark*

FOUNDED 1981. *Publishes* textbooks, dictionaries and translations for the teaching, speaking and promotion of Glosa (an international, auxiliary language); also a newsletter and journal. Rapid growth in the last couple of years. In 1994 launched *Sko-Glosa*, a publication for and by younger students of Glosa to be distributed to schools in different countries. Also in 1994 published several fairy stories and activity pages for school children who are learning Glosa in school. Unsolicited mss and ideas for Glosa books welcome.

Gothic Press

PO Box 542, Highgate, London N6 6BG
Managing Editor *Robin Crisp*

Specialist publisher of Gothic titles in quality, case editions. Mostly non-fiction at present (*Carmel: Authentic Sequel to Bram Stoker's Dracula* is a notable exception). *Publishes* mysticism, supernatural, history, biography, Gothic novels. No unsolicited mss; synopses and ideas might be welcome.

Flat fee paid.

Grace Publishing

11 Hargood Road, London SE3 8HR
☎020 8856 8877   Fax 020 8856 8877
Email pgrace@lineone.net
Managing Editors *Joe Wilson, Sola Akande*

FOUNDED 1987. *Publishes* non-fiction; religious (Christianity), economic/regional, Third World development and issues. 'Intelligent controversy and concrete issues.' 1 title in 1999. Unsolicited mss, synopses and ideas welcome; approach by post or e-mail with copy of manuscript in the first instance.

Royalties paid.

Grant Books

The Coach House, New Road, Cutnall Green, Droitwich, Worcestershire WR9 0PQ
☎01299 851588   Fax 01299 851446
Email golf@grantbooks.co.uk
Website www.grantbooks.co.uk
Managing Editor *H. R. J. Grant*

FOUNDED 1978. *Publishes* golf-related titles only: course architecture, history, biography, etc., but no instructional material. New titles and old, plus limited editions. About 6 titles a year. Unsolicited mss, synopses and ideas welcome.

Royalties paid.

Great Northern Publishing

PO Box 202, Scarborough, North Yorkshire YO11 3GE
☎01723 581329   Fax 01723 581329
Email books@greatnorthernpublishing.co.uk
Website www.greatnorthernpublishing.co.uk
Senior Editor *Diane Crowther*

FOUNDED in 1999, originally as a journal/newsletter and general publisher and also as a self-publishing venture. Offers full publishing service, including advice on marketing and sales to first-time authors as well as museums, charities, groups and businesses. *Publishes* fiction and non-fiction in most genres; no romantic, religious, political or feminist books.

2 titles in 1999. No unsolicited mss; send letter in the first instance.

Royalties paid twice-yearly.

Grevatt & Grevatt

9 Rectory Drive, Newcastle upon Tyne NE3 1XT
Chairman/Editorial Head
   Dr S. Y. Killingley

FOUNDED 1981. Alternative publisher of works not normally commercially viable. Three books have appeared with financial backing from professional bodies. *Publishes* academic titles and conference reports, particularly language, linguistics and religious studies. Some poetry also. No unsolicited mss. Synopses and ideas should be accompanied by s.a.e. Offers typesetting, editing and other services; s.a.e. with enquiries.

Royalties paid annually (after first 500 copies).

GRM Publications

PO Box 213, Leeds LS6 4YQ
☎0113 2752456   Fax 0113 2752456
Managing Editors *Graham Wade,*
   Elizabeth Wade

FOUNDED 1996. Publishes monographs on classical music and musicians.

GSSE

11 Malford Grove, Gilwern, Abergavenny, Monmouthshire NP7 0RN
☎01873 830872
Email GSSE@zoo.co.uk
Owner/Manager *David P. Bosworth*

Publishes newsletters (main publication, *OLS News*) and booklets describing classroom practice (at all levels of education and training). Ideas welcome – particularly from practising teachers, lecturers and trainers describing how they use technology in their teaching.

Royalties paid by arrangement.

The Guerrilla Press

B.M. Betelguise, London WC1N 3XX
Website
www.geocities.com/CapitolHill/6743
Managing Editor *Tim Telsa*

FOUNDED in 1997 'to challge the authority of psychiatric care'. *Publishes* political – mainly work of an anarchist nature – 'that would be ignored by most publishers'. About 10 titles a year. Unsolicited mss, synopses and ideas welcome; send letter with description of proposed mss plus return postage.

Royalties not paid.

Happy House

3b Castledown Avenue, Hastings, East Sussex
TN34 3RJ
☎01424 434778

FOUNDED 1992 as a self-publishing venture for a Dave Arnold/Martin Honeysett collaboration of poetry and cartoons.

Haunted Library

Flat 1, 36 Hamilton Street, Hoole, Chester,
Cheshire CH2 3JQ
☎01244 313685   Fax 01244 313685
Email pardos@globalnet.co.uk
Website www.users.globalnet.co.uk/~pardos/
   GS.html
Managing Editor *Rosemary Pardoe*

FOUNDED 1979. *Publishes* a twice-yearly ghost story magazine in the antiquarian tradition of M. R. James. The magazine publishes stories, news and articles. No unsolicited mss.
   Royalties not paid.

Heart of Albion Press

2 Cross Hill Close, Wymeswold,
Loughborough, Leicestershire LE12 6UJ
☎01509 880725
Email albion@indigogroup.co.uk
Website www.indigogroup.co.uk/albion/
Managing Editor *R. N. Trubshaw*

FOUNDED 1990 to publish books and booklets on the East Midlands area. *Publishes* mostly local history. Future publications on CD-ROM only. No unsolicited mss.
   Royalties negotiable.

Hermitage Press

77 Old Tiverton Road, Exeter, Devon
EX4 6NG
☎01392 213843   Fax 01392 213843
Managing Editor *John Evans*

FOUNDED 2000. *Publishes* books about books, nature conservation, spiritual path; also *The Dial*, a literary quarterly (see entry under **Magazines**). No unsolicited mss; send synopses and ideas by post or fax.
   Royalties paid.

Hilmarton Manor Press

Calne, Wiltshire SN11 8SB
☎01249 760208   Fax 01249 760379
Email hilmartonpress@lineone.net
Chairman/Managing Director *Charles Baile de Laperriere*

Publishes fine art reference only. *Royalties* paid.

Horseshoe Publications

PO Box 37, Kingsley, Frodsham, Cheshire
WA6 8DR
☎01928 787477 (Afternoons and evenings)
Managing Editor *John C. Hibbert*

FOUNDED in 1994, initially to publish work of Cheshire writers. Poetry, short stories and own writing. 9 titles in 1999. Shared cost publishing considered in certain circumstances. Reading fee on full mss £25. Unsolicited mss, synopses and ideas in the realm of commercial fiction welcome. S.a.e. for return.

ignotus press

BCM-Writer, 27 Old Gloucester Street,
London WC1N 3XX
☎01530 831916   Fax 01530 831916
Email ignotus@hotmail.com
Publisher *Suzanne Ruthven*

Specialises in full length esoteric non-fiction and fiction of all traditions although writers are advised to send s.a.e. for authors' guidelines before submitting material for consideration. All mss are checked for accuracy and knowledge of subject by specialists who will reject New Age idealism, fantasy, 'mind, body & spirit'. Also *publishes* *Comhairle*, the official journal of the Comhairle Cairde. The articles and features published in the quarterly magazine illustrate the range of material sought by any of the ignotus press imprints. Sample copies available priced £3 from the publisher.
   IMPRINTS **Corvus Press** *Christine Sempers* A5 booklets and spiral-bound workbooks on a world-wide range of esoteric and mysteries techniques. **Feasac Press** *Frances Denton* The cultural aspects of esoteria, i.e. history, anthopology, psychology and sociology of the different traditions, including art and craft, short fiction, poetry, music and performance art.
   Royalties paid.

Inner Sanctum Publications

75 Greenleaf Gardens, Polegate, East Sussex
BN26 6Q
☎01323 484058
Email books@ethericrealms.com
Website www.ethericrealms.com
Managing Editor *Mary Hession*

FOUNDED in 1999 to *publish* spiritual books. 3 titles in 1999. Unsolicited mss, synopses and ideas welcome; approach in writing in the first instance.
   Royalties not paid.

Intellect Books
E.F.A.E., Earl Richards Road North, Exeter,
Devon EX2 6AS
☎01392 475110   Fax 01392 475110
Email books@intellect-net.com
Website www.intellectbooks.com
Publisher *Masoud Yazdani*
Assistant Publisher *Robin Beecroft*

A multidisciplinary publisher for both individual
and institutional readers. Tracks newest developments in digital creative media – art, film, television, design, etc. - and examines distinct theories in education, language, gender study and
international culture through scholarly articles.
Also publishes in AI, computer science and
human-computer interaction in books, journals
and website.
Royalties paid.

Iolo
38 Chaucer Road, Bedford MK40 2AJ
☎01234 270175   Fax 01234 270175
Managing Director *Dedwydd Jones*

Publishes Welsh theatre-related material and campaigns for a Welsh National Theatre. Ideas on
Welsh themes welcome; approach in writing.

Ivy Publications
72 Hyperion House, Somers Road, London
SW2 1HZ
☎020 8671 6872
Proprietor *Ian Bruton-Simmonds*

FOUNDED 1989. *Publishes* educational, science,
fiction, philosophy, children's, travel, literary
criticism, history, film scripts. No unsolicited
mss; send two pages, one from the beginning
and one from the body of the book, together
with synopsis (one paragraph) and s.a.e. No
cookery, gardening or science fiction.
Royalties paid annually.

JAC Publications
28 Bellomonte Crescent, Drayton, Norwich,
Norfolk NR8 6EJ
☎01603 861339
Managing Editor *John James Vasco*

Publishes World War II Luftwaffe history only.
Unsolicited mss welcome. No synopses or ideas.
Royalties paid.

The Jupiter Press
Oracle House, 1–3 Gospel End Road,
Sedgley, Dudley, West Midlands DY3 3LT
☎01902 665477   Fax 01902 678655
Managing Editor *Gordon Drury*

FOUNDED 1995. Looking for niche market and
information publications, particularly sport-
orientated (golf and soccer), also quiz, puzzles
and games content. Also interested in clairvoy-
ance, esoteric subjects. Synopses and ideas for
books welcome.
Royalties paid.

Katabasis
See under **Poetry Presses**

Richard Kay Publications
80 Sleaford Road, Boston, Lincolnshire
PE21 8EU
☎01205 353231
Email rebecca@richardkay.freeserve.co.uk
Managing Editor *Richard Kay*

FOUNDED 1970. Non-profit motivated publisher
of local interest (Lincolnshire) material: dialect,
history, autobiography and biography, philosophy, medico-political and contemporary dissent
on current affairs. About 6 titles a year. No unsolicited mss; synopses and ideas welcome.
Royalties paid if appropriate.

Kittiwake
3 Glantwymyn Village Workshops, Nr.
Machynlleth, Montgomeryshire SY20 8LY
☎01650 511314   Fax 01650 511602
Email david@perrocarto.co.uk
Website www.perrocarto.co.uk
Managing Editor *David Perrott*

FOUNDED 1986. *Publishes* guidebooks only,
with an emphasis on careful design/produc-
tion. Unsolicited mss, synopses and ideas for
guidebooks welcome. Specialist research, writing, cartographic and electronic publishing
services available.
Royalties paid.

The Lindsey Press
Unitarian Headquarters, 1–6 Essex Street,
Strand, London WC2R 3HY
☎020 7240 2384   Fax 020 7240 3089
Email ga@unitarian.org.uk
Convenor *Kate Taylor*

ESTABLISHED at the end of the 18th century as a
vehicle for disseminating liberal religion. Took
the name of The Lindsey Press at the beginning
of the 20th century (after Theophilus Lindsey,
the great Unitarian Theologian). *Publishes* books
reflecting liberal religious thought or Unitarian
denominational history. Also worship material
– hymn books, collections of prayers, etc. No
unsolicited mss; synopses and ideas welcome.
Royalties not paid.

Logaston Press

Logaston, Woonton, Almeley, Herefordshire
HR3 6QH
☎01544 327344

Managing Editors *Andy Johnson, Ron Shoesmith*

FOUNDED 1985. *Publishes* guides, archaeology, social history, rural issues and local history for Wales, the Welsh Border and West Midlands. 8–10 titles a year. Unsolicited mss, synopses and ideas welcome. Return postage appreciated.
Royalties paid.

Luath Press Ltd

543/2 Castlehill, The Royal Mile, Edinburgh
EH1 2ND
☎0131 225 4326   Fax 0131 225 4324
Email gavin.macdougall@luath.co.uk
Website www.luath.co.uk

Managing Editor *G. H. MacDougall*

FOUNDED 1981. *Publishes* mainly books with a Scottish connection. About 20–30 titles a year. Unsolicited mss, synopses and ideas welcome; 'committed to publishing well-written books worth reading'.
Royalties paid.

Lyfrow Trelyspen

See **CNP Publications**

Madison Publishing Ltd

Fairway House, 27 Comyn Road, London
SW11 1QB
☎0370 873399   Fax 020 7585 0079

Managing Director *Nathan Andrew Iyer*

FOUNDED 1995. *Publishes* British fiction. No unsolicited mss. Synopses (no more than 2pp) and ideas welcome.

Marine Day Publishers

64 Cotterill Road, Surbiton, Surrey KT6 7UN
☎020 8399 7625

Managing Editor *Anthony G. Durrant*

FOUNDED 1990. Part of The Marine Press Ltd. *Publishes* local history.
Royalties not paid.

Matching Press

1 Watermans End, Matching Green, Harlow, Essex CM17 0RQ
☎01279 731308

Publisher *Patrick Streeter*

FOUNDED 1993. *Publishes* biography, autobiography, social history and fiction. Enquiries welcome.
Royalties paid.

Maypole Editions

22 Mayfair Avenue, Ilford, Essex IG1 3DQ
☎020 8252 3937

Contact *Barry Taylor*

Publisher of plays and poetry in the main. 2–3 titles a year. Unsolicited mss welcome provided return postage is included. Poetry always welcome for collected anthologies. Poems should be approximately 30 lines long, broadly covering social concerns, ethnic minorities, feminist issues, romance, travel, lyric rhyming verse. No politics. The annual collected anthology is designed as a small press platform for first-time poets who might not otherwise get into print, and a permanent showcase for those already published who want to break into the mainstream. Catalogue £1, plus s.a.e. 'Please be patient when sending work because of the huge volume of submissions.' Exempt Charity Status.

Meadow Books

22 Church Meadow, Milton under Wychwood, Chipping Norton, Oxfordshire OX7 6JG
☎01993 831338

Managing Director *C. O'Neill*

FOUNDED 1990. Published *A Picture of Health* and *More Pictures of Health*.

Mercia Cinema Society

19 Pinder's Grove, Wakefield, West Yorkshire WF1 4AH
☎01924 372748
Email mervyn.gould@virgin.net

Managing Editor *Brian Hornsey*

FOUNDED 1980 to foster research into the history of picture houses. *Publishes* books and booklets on the subject, including cinema circuits and chains. Books are often tied in with specific geographical areas. Unsolicited mss, synopses and ideas.
Royalties not paid.

Meridian Books

40 Hadzor Road, Oldbury, West Midlands B68 9LA
☎0121 429 4397

Managing Editor *Peter Groves*

FOUNDED 1985 as a small home-based enterprise following the acquisition of titles from Tetradon Publications Ltd. *Publishes* walking and regional guides. 4–5 titles a year. Unsolicited mss, synopses and ideas welcome if relevant. Send s.a.e. if mss is to be returned.
Royalties paid.

Mermaid Turbulence

Annaghmaconway, Cloone, Leitrim Republic
of Ireland
☎00 353 78 36134   Fax 00 353 78 36134
Managing Director *Mari-Aymone Djeribi*
Approx. Annual Turnover £10,000

FOUNDED in 1993 with the first issue of
Element, an international annual literary journal. *Publishes* essays, fiction, poetry, history and
artists' books. 7 titles in 1999. Unsolicited mss,
synopses and ideas welcome. No pulp fiction.
Approach in writing, enclosing s.a.e.
   Royalties paid annually.

Merton Priory Press Ltd

67 Merthyr Road, Whitchurch, Cardiff
CF14 1DD
☎029 2052 1956   Fax 029 2062 3599
Email merton@dircon.co.uk
Managing Director *Philip Riden*

FOUNDED 1993. *Publishes* academic and mid-
market history, especially local, industrial and
transport history; also distributes for small publishers working in the same field. About 6 titles
a year. Full catalogue available.
   Royalties paid twice-yearly.

Neil Miller Publications

Mount Cottage, Grange Road, Saint
Michael's, Tenterden, Kent TN30 6EE
Managing Editor *Neil Miller*

FOUNDED 1994. *Publishes* short tales with a twist,
comedy, suspense, mystery, fantasy, science fiction, horror and the bizarre under the **Black Cat
Books** imprint. Also *publishes* paperbacks: classics, rare tales, tales of the unexpected. New
authors always welcome. Evaluation and critique
service available for large mss. 'We seek short
story writers, in any genre. No unsolicited/un-
requested mss, please. In the first instance, send
£7.75 and large 45-pence s.a.e. for author's
package, which includes free book listing hundreds of possible publication outlets for new
authors. We have published 170 new authors
since 1994. We will help and advise on anything
well written and researched. Now accepting
novels and short poems.'

Millers Dale Publications

7 Weavers Place, Chandlers Ford, Eastleigh,
Hampshire SO53 1TU
☎023 8026 1192
Email gponting@clara.net
Website www.home.clara.net/gponting/
   index-page10.html

Managing Editor *Gerald Ponting*

FOUNDED 1990. *Publishes* books on local history
related to central Hampshire. Also books related
to slide presentations by Gerald Ponting. Ideas
for local history books on Hampshire considered.

Minority Rights Group

379 Brixton Road, London SW9 7DE
☎020 7978 9498   Fax 020 7738 6265
Email minority.rights@mrgmail.org
Website www.minorityrights.org
Deputy Head of Communications *Angela
   Warren*

FOUNDED in the late 1960s, MRG works to
raise awareness of minority issues worldwide.
Publishes books, reports, educational material
on minority rights. 8–10 titles a year.

Mohr Books

345 Old Birmingham Road, Bromsgrove B60
1NX
☎0121 447 7897   Fax 0121 445 1063
Email Mohr_Books@compuserve.com
Website www.welcome.to/Mohr_Books
Managing Director *Eileen Mohr*
Approx. Annual Turnover £13,000

FOUNDED 1995. *Publishes* Christian books for
adults and children. 1–2 titles a year. No unsolicited mss; telephone in the first instance. No
New Age or books not biblically Christian.
   Royalties paid twice-yearly.

Morton Publishing

PO Box 23, Gosport, Hampshire PO12 2XD
Managing Editor *Nik Morton*

FOUNDED 1994. *Publishes* fiction – genre novellas
(eg crime, science fiction, fantasy, horror, western), max. 20,000 words; short story anthologies
– max. 4000 words per story. Unsolicited synopses and ideas for books welcome; enclose s.a.e.
Also offers literary agent service of guidance and
advice (fees on application)
   Royalties paid annually.

Need2Know

Remus House, Coltsfoot Drive, Woodston,
Peterborough PE2 9JX
☎01733 898103   Fax 01733 313524

Managing Editor *Kerrie Pateman*

FOUNDED 1995 'to fill a gap in the market for
self-help books'. Need2Know is an imprint of
Forward Press (see under **Poetry Presses**).
Publishes contemporary health and lifestyle
issues. Mss, synopses and ideas for books welcome with return postage. It is important to

ensure the project fits in with the series and that the subject is not already covered. For further information and an author brief, call *Kerrie Pateman.*

Payment Advance plus 15% royalties.

Nimbus Press

18 Guilford Road, Leicester LE2 2RB
☎0116 2706318   Fax 0116 2706318
Email clifford.sharp@nimbuspress.demon.co.uk
Managing Editor *Clifford Sharp*
Assistant Editor *Justin Moulder*

FOUNDED in 1991 to encourage churches to use drama in worship. *Publishes* Christian drama, humour, Christian apologetics, etc. Plays of no more than 30 minutes' length and suitable for church drama groups welcome. 5 titles in 1999.
Royalties paid.

Norvik Press Ltd

School of Languages, Linguistics & Translation Studies, University of East Anglia, Norwich, Norfolk NR4 7TJ
☎01603 593356   Fax 01603 250599
Email norvik.press@uea.ac.uk
Website www.uea.ac.uk/llt/norvik_press
Managing Editors *Janet Garton,*
Michael Robinson

Small academic press. *Publishes* the journal *Scandinavica* and books related to Scandinavian literature. About 4 titles a year. Interested in synopses and ideas for books within its *Literary History and Criticism* series. No unsolicited mss.
Royalties paid.

Nyala Publishing

4 Christian Fields, London SW16 3JZ
☎020 8764 6292
Fax 020 8764 6292/0115 9819418
Email nyala.publish@geo-group.demon.co.uk
Editorial Head *J. F. J. Douglas*

FOUNDED 1996. Publishing arm of Geo Group. *Publishes* biography, travel and general non-fiction. No unsolicited mss; synopses and ideas considered. Also offers a wide range of publishing and publishing services.
Royalties paid twice-yearly.

Orpheus Publishing House

4 Dunsborough Park, Ripley Green, Ripley, Guildford, Surrey GU23 6AL
☎01483 225777   Fax 01483 225776
Email orpheuspubl.ho@btinternet.com
Managing Editor *J. S. Gordon*

FOUNDED 1996. *Publishes* 'well-researched and properly argued' books in the fields of occult science, esotericism and comparative philosophy/religion. 'Keen to encourage good (but sensible) new authors.' In the first instance, send maximum 3-page synopsis with s.a.e.
Royalties by agreement.

Outline Publications

See **Brantwood Books**

Palladour Books

Hirwaun House, Aberporth, Nr. Cardigan, Ceredigion SA43 2EU
☎01239 811658   Fax 01239 811658
Managing Editors *Jeremy Powell/Anne Powell*

FOUNDED 1986. Started with a twice-yearly issue of catalogues on the literature and poetry of World War I. Occasional catalogues on World War II poetry have also been issued. No unsolicited mss. *Royalties* not paid.

Parapress Ltd

5 Bentham Hill House, Stockland Green Road, Tunbridge Wells, Kent TN3 0TJ
☎01892 512118   Fax 01892 512118
Email e.imlay.parapress@virgin.net
Managing Editor *Elizabeth Imlay*
Production and Promotion *Alison Dalby*

FOUNDED 1993. *Publishes* animals, autobiography, biography, history, literary criticism, military and naval, music, self-help, sports. Some self-publishing. About 12 titles a year.

Parthian

53 Colum Road, Cardiff CF10 3EF
☎029 2034 1314   Fax 029 2034 1314
Email rlparthian@yahoo.co.uk
Website www.parthianbooks.co.uk
Chairman *Gillian Griffiths*
Publisher *Richard Davies*

FOUNDED in 1993. *Publishes* contemporary Welsh fiction, drama and poetry in English, also translations of Welsh language fiction. No unsolicited mss; synopses with sample chapters and ideas welcome.
Royalties paid annually.

Partizan Press

816–818 London Road, Leigh on Sea, Essex SS9 3NH
☎01702 473986   Fax 01702 473986
Website www.caliverbooks.demon.co.uk
Managing Editor *David Ryan*

Caters for the growing re-enactment and wargaming market. *Publishes* military history, with

particular regard to the 17th and 18th centuries. Six military magazines published.
Royalties paid.

Partnership Publishing Ltd
56 Market Street, Wellington, Telford,
Shropshire TF1 1DT
☎01952 415334   Fax 01952 406762
Email partnership.publishing@pipexdial.com
Managing Director *Steve Rooney*
Publisher of *Bus and Coach Professional; AVRO Recovery Operator; ETA Going Green; Wellington News.* Offers full magazine publication services, including design and production, editorial and advertising sales service.

Past and Present Publishing
See **Silver Link Publishing Ltd**

Paupers' Press
27 Melbourne Road, West Bridgford,
Nottingham NG2 5DJ
☎0115 9815063   Fax 0115 9815063
Email stan2727uk@aol.com
Website members.aol.com/stan2727uk/
   pauper.htm
Managing Editor *Colin Stanley*
FOUNDED 1983. *Publishes* extended essays in booklet form (about 15,000 words) on literary criticism and philosophy. About 6 titles a year. Limited hardback editions of bestselling titles. No unsolicited mss but synopsis and ideas for books welcome.
Royalties paid.

Peepal Tree Press Ltd
17 King's Avenue, Leeds, West Yorkshire
LS6 1QS
☎0113 2451703   Fax 0113 2459616
Email hannah@peepal.demon.co.uk
Managing Editor *Jeremy Poynting*
FOUNDED 1985. *Publishes* fiction, poetry, drama and academic studies. *Specialises* in Caribbean, Black British and South Asian writing. About 18 titles a year. In-house printing/finishing facilities. AUTHORS include **Forward Poetry Prize** winner Kwame Dawes. 'Please send an A5 s.a.e. with a 38p stamp for a copy of our submission guidelines.' Write or 'phone for a free catalogue.
Royalties paid.

The Penniless Press
100 Waterloo Road, Ashton, Preston,
Lancashire PR2 1EP

Managing Editor *Alan Dent*
Publishes quarterly magazine with literary, philosophical, artistic and political content, including reviews of poetry, fiction, non-fiction and drama. Prose of up to 3000 words welcome. No mss returned without s.a.e.
Payment Free copy of magazine.

Pentaxion Ltd
180 Newbridge Street, Newcastle upon Tyne
NE1 2TE
☎0191 232 6189   Fax 0191 232 6190
Email pentaxion@pentaxion.force9.co.uk
Publishing Manager *Alison Ross*
Publishes academic, educational, medical, arts and professional studies. CD-ROMs and Web-based multimedia development. No unsolicited mss; synopsis and ideas welcome. 'Under certain circumstances we will enter into joint ventures with authors.'
Royalties paid.

Pexa Publications
5 Grove Road, Whetstone, Leicestershire
LE8 6LN
☎0116 2750472/3   Fax 0116 2750472
Email pexapub.freeserve.co.uk
Managing Editor *Ian Dench*
FOUNDED 1997. *Publishes* workbooks for children aged 6–12. No fiction. No unsolicited mss; synopsis and ideas for books welcome. Approach by fax in the first instance.
Royalties paid twice-yearly.

Pipers' Ash Ltd
'Pipers' Ash', Church Road, Christian
Malford, Chippenham, Wiltshire
SN15 4BW
☎01249 720563   Fax 0870 0568916
Email pipersash@supamasu.demon.co.uk
Website www.supamasu.demon.co.uk
Managing Editor *Mr A. Tyson*
FOUNDED 1976 to publish technical manuals for computer-controlled systems. Later broadened the company's publishing activities to include individual collections of contemporary short stories, science fiction short stories, poetry, short novels, local histories, children's fiction, philosophy, biographies, translations and general non-fiction. 18 titles a year. Synopsis and ideas welcome; 'new authors with potential will be actively encouraged'. Offices in New Zealand and Australia.
Royalties paid annually.

Planet

PO Box 44, Aberystwyth, Ceredigion
SY23 5ZZ
☎01970 611255   Fax 01970 611197
Email planet.enquiries@planetmagazine.org.uk
Website www.planetmagazine.org.uk

Managing Editor *John Barnie*

FOUNDED 1985 as publishers of the arts and
current affairs magazine *Planet: The Welsh
Internationalist* and branched out into book
publishing in 1995. All books so far have been
commissioned. Unsolicited synopses and ideas
welcome.
Royalties paid.

Playwrights Publishing Co.

70 Nottingham Road, Burton Joyce,
Nottinghamshire NG14 5AL
☎0115 8449896

Managing Editors *Liz Breeze, Tony Breeze*

FOUNDED 1990. *Publishes* one-act and full-length
plays. Unsolicited scripts welcome. No synopses
or ideas. Reading fees: £15 one act; £30 full
length.
Royalties paid.

Pomegranate Press

3 Dolphin House, St Nicholas Lane, Lewes,
Sussex BN7 2JZ
Email sussexbooks@compuserve.com
Website ourworld.compuserve.com/
homepages/sussexbooks

Managing Editor *David Arscott*

FOUNDED in 1992 by writer/broadcaster David
Arscott, who also administers the **Sussex
Book Club**. *Specialises* in books about Sussex.
IMPRINT **Pomegranate Practicals** how-to
books. No unsolicited mss; synopses and ideas
for books welcome.
Royalties paid twice-yearly.

David Porteous Editions

PO Box 5, Chudleigh, Newton Abbot,
Devon TQ13 0YZ
☎01626 853310   Fax 01626 853663

Publisher *David Porteous*

FOUNDED 1992 to produce high quality colour
illustrated books on hobbies and leisure for the
UK and international markets. *Publishes* crafts,
hobbies, art techniques and needlecrafts. No
poetry or fiction. 3–4 titles a year. Unsolicited
mss, synopses and ideas welcome if return
postage included.
Royalties paid twice-yearly.

Power Publications

1 Clayford Avenue, Ferndown, Dorset
BH22 9PQ
☎01202 875223   Fax 01202 875223
Email powerpublications@freeserve.co.uk

Contact *Mike Power*

FOUNDED 1989. *Publishes* local interest, pub
walk guides and mountain bike guides. 2–3
titles a year. Unsolicited mss/synopses/ideas
welcome.
Royalties paid.

Praxis Books

Sheridan, Broomers Hill Lane, Pulborough,
West Sussex RH20 2DU
☎01798 873504
Email 100543.3270@compuserve.com
Website www.beckysmith.demon.co.uk

Proprietor *Rebecca Smith*

FOUNDED 1992. *Publishes* reissues of Victorian
fiction, memoirs, diaries and general interest.
15 titles to date. Unsolicited mss accepted with
s.a.e. No fiction, children's or humour. Editing
service available. Flexible funding negotiable. 'I
am most likely to accept work with a clearly
identifiable market.'

Primrose Hill Press Ltd

58 Carey Street, London WC2A 2JB
☎020 7405 7484   Fax 020 7405 7459
Email info@primrosehillpress.co.uk

Managing Director *Brian H. W. Hill*

FOUNDED in 1997, having taken over the stock
and projects in progress of Silent Books Ltd.
Publishes general art titles, wood engraving,
poetry and books for the gift market, 'all high
quality productions'. No fiction. About 12
titles a year. Unsolicited mss, synopses and
ideas welcome.

QED of York

1 Straylands Grove, York YO31 1EB
☎01904 424242   Fax 01904 424381
Email qed@enterprise.net

Managing Editor *John Bibby*

Publishes and distributes resource guides and
learning aids, including laminated posters, for
mathematics and science. Synopses (3pp) and
ideas for books welcome. QED arranges publicity for other small presses and has many contacts overseas. Also provides publishing services
for other publishers and arranges exhibitions at
Frankfurt, LIBF, educational conferences, etc.
Royalties by agreement.

QueenSpark Books
49 Grand Parade, Brighton, East Sussex
BN2 2QA
☎01273 571710   Fax 01273 571710

A community writing and publishing group
run mainly by volunteers who work together
to write and produce books. Since the early
1970s they have published 60 titles: local autobiographies, humour, poetry, history and politics. Free writing workshops and groups held
on a regular basis. New members welcome.

Redstone Press
7A St Lawrence Terrace, London W10 5SU
☎020 7352 1594   Fax 020 7352 8749
Email redstone.press@virgin.net
Website jrothenstein@redstonepress.co.uk
Managing Editor *Julian Rothenstein*

FOUNDED 1987. *Publishes* art and literature.
About 5 titles a year. No unsolicited mss; syn-
opses and ideas welcome but familiarity with
Redstone's list advised in the first instance.
Royalties paid.

The Robinswood Press
30 South Avenue, Stourbridge, West
Midlands DY8 3XY
☎01384 397475   Fax 01384 440443
Email robinswoodpress@cwcom.net
Website www.robinswood.co.uk
Managing Editor *Christopher J. Marshall*

FOUNDED 1985. *Publishes* education, particularly
teacher resources, SEN and Waldorf. About 3–5
titles a year. Unsolicited mss, synopses and ideas
welcome. *Royalties* paid.

Rogue Gene Publications
107 High Street, Pershore, Worcestershire
WR10 1EQ
Managing Editor *Rob Kirbyson*

FOUNDED in 1999 to publish *Rage Before Croquet*
as a forum for more maverick cartoons and
humour. Content 70% cartoons, 30% text. Unsolicited material welcome; approach in writing.
Royalties not paid.

Route
See **Yorkshire Art Circus Ltd**

Scottish Cultural Press
Unit 13d, Newbattle Abbey Business Annexe,
Newbattle Road, Dalkeith EH22 3LJ
☎0131 660 6366   Fax 0131 660 6414
Email scp@sol.co.uk
Chair/Managing Editor *Jill Dick*

Children's Press Administrator *Avril Gray*

FOUNDED 1992. Began publishing in 1993.
Publishes Scottish interest titles, including
cultural, literature, poetry, archaeology, local
history, children's fiction and non-fiction.
IMPRINTS **Scottish Cultural Press**, **Scottish
Children's Press**. Unsolicited mss, synopses
and ideas welcome provided return postage is
included. *Royalties* paid.

Serif
47 Strahan Road, London E3 5DA
☎020 8981 3990   Fax 020 8981 3990
Managing Editor *Stephen Hayward*

FOUNDED 1994. *Publishes* cookery, Irish and
African studies and modern history; no fiction.
Ideas and synopses welcome; no unsolicited mss.
Royalties paid.

Sherlock Publications
6 Bramham Moor, Hill Head, Fareham,
Hampshire PO14 3RU
☎01329 667325
Email sherlock.publications@btinternet.com
Managing Editor *Philip Weller*

FOUNDED to supply publishing support to a
number of Sherlock Holmes societes. *Publishes*
Sherlock Holmes and other Conan Doyle
studies only. About 14 titles a year. No unsolicited mss; synopses and ideas welcome.
Royalties not paid.

Silver Link Publishing Ltd
The Trundle, Ringstead Road, Great
Addington, Kettering, Northamptonshire
NN14 4BW
☎01536 330588   Fax 01536 330588
Website www.slinkp-p.demon.co.uk
Managing Editor *Peter Townsend*

FOUNDED 1985 in Lancashire, changed hands
in 1990 and now based in Northamptonshire.
Small independent company specialising in
nostalgia titles including illustrated books on
railways, trams, ships and other transport subjects. *Publishes* post-war nostalgia on all aspects
of social history under the **Past and Present
Publishing** imprint.
Fees paid.

Spacelink Books
115 Hollybush Lane, Hampton, Middlesex
TW12 2QY
☎020 8979 3148
Managing Director *Lionel Beer*

FOUNDED 1986. Named after a UFO magazine

published in the 1960/70s. *Publishes* non-fiction titles connected with UFOs, Fortean phenomena and paranormal events. No unsolicited mss; send synopses and ideas. Publishers of *TEMS News* for the Travel and Earth Mysteries Society. Distributors of wide range of related titles and magazines.

Royalties and fees paid according to contract.

Stenlake Publishing

Ochiltree Sawmill, The Lade, Ochiltree, Ayrshire KA18 2NX
☎01290 423114   Fax 01290 423114

Publishes local history, railways, shipping, aviation and industrial. 36 titles in 1999. Unsolicited mss, synopses and ideas welcome if accompanied by s.a.e. Freelance writers with experience in above fields also sought for specific commissions.

Royalties or fixed fee paid.

Stone Flower Limited

9 The Drive, Ilford, Essex IG1 3EY
Managing Editor *L. G. Norman*

FOUNDED 1989. *Publishes* biography, law, humour and general fiction. Currently developing a new-style series of legal and general textbooks. Will consider mss, synopses and ideas only if sent with s.a.e. or IRC. Approach in writing in the first instance.

Stride

11 Sylvan Road, Exeter, Devon EX4 6EW
Email RML@madbear.demon.co.uk
Website www.madbear.demon.co.uk/stride/
Managing Editor *Rupert Loydell*

FOUNDED in 1982 as a magazine and booklet series. Since the mid-1980s, the press has published paperback editions of imaginative new writing. *Publishes* poetry, experimental fiction, criticism, reviews, interviews, arts (particularly experimental music). 18 titles in 1999. Unsolicited mss preferred to synopses. Ideas for future books welcome. Approach in writing only (with s.a.e.).

Royalties sometimes paid; free copies usually.

T.C.L. Publications

8 Hywel Way, Pembroke SA71 4EF
☎01646 685637
Managing Editor *Duncan Haws*

FOUNDED 1966 as Travel Creatours Limited (TCL). *Publishes* nautical books only – the *Merchant Fleet* series (38 vols.). 3 titles in 1999.

Unsolicited mss welcome, 'provided they are in our standard format and subject matters'.

Royalties paid.

Tamarind Ltd

PO Box 52, Northwood, Middlesex HA6 1UN
☎020 8866 8808   Fax 020 8866 5627
Email TamrindLTD@aol.com
Managing Editor *Verna Wilkins*

FOUNDED 1987 to publish picture books which give Black children a high, unselfconscious, positive profile. Won Gold Award for Best Product, Nursery & Creche Exhibition, 1994; featured BBC TV Words and Pictures: *Time to Get Up, Dave and the Tooth Fairy*; Book of the Month, Junior Education: *Profile of Benjamin Zephaniah* 1999. All titles sold into both trade and educational markets. Age range: 2–12.

Tarquin Publications

Stradbroke, Diss, Norfolk IP21 5JP
☎01379 384218   Fax 01379 384289
Email enquiries@tarquin-books.demon.co.uk
Website www.tarquin-books.demon.co.uk
Managing Editor *Gerald Jenkins*

FOUNDED 1970 as a hobby which gradually grew and now *publishes* mathematical, cut-out models, teaching and pop-up books. Other topics covered if they involve some kind of paper cutting or pop-up scenes. 7 titles in 2000. No unsolicited mss; letter with 1–2 page synopses welcome.

Royalties paid.

Tartarus Press

5 Birch Terrace, Hangingbirch Lane, Horam, East Sussex TN21 0PA
☎01435 813224
Email tartarus@pavilion.co.uk
Website freepages.pavilion.net/users/tartarus
Proprietor *Raymond Russell*
Editor *Rosalie Parker*

FOUNDED 1987. *Publishes* fiction, short stories, essays and local history. Also books by and about Arthur Machen. About 12 titles a year. 'Please do not send submissions. We cater to a small, collectable market; we solicit the fiction we publish.'

Thames Publishing

14 Barlby Road, London W10 6AR
☎020 8969 3579
Publishing Manager *John Bishop*

FOUNDED 1970. *Publishes* music, and books about English music and musicians, particularly of this century but not pop. About 4 titles a year. No unsolicited mss; send synopses and ideas in first instance.

Trafford Publishing
Suite 6E, 2333 Government Street, Victoria, British Columbia Canada V8T 4P4
☎001 250 383 6864   Fax 001 250 383 6804
Email editorial@trafford.com
Website www.trafford.com

Managing Editor *Bruce Batchelor*

FOUNDED 1995. A self-publishing venture offering 'on-demand publishing ... serving authors from 12 countries'. Books are usually published and publicised within 6 to 8 weeks. Package price is US$950. All genres welcome. Preferred approach by e-mail.
Royalties paid.

Tuckwell Press Ltd
The Mill House, Phantassie, East Linton, East Lothian EH40 3DG
☎01620 860164   Fax 01620 860164
Email tuckwellpress@sol.co.uk
Website www.tuckwellpress.co.uk

Managing Director *John Tuckwell*

FOUNDED 1995. *Publishes* history, archaeology, literature, ethnology, biography, architecture, gardening history, genealogy, palaeography, with a bias towards Scottish and academic texts, also north of England. 120 titles in print. No unsolicited mss but synopses and ideas welcome if relevant to subjects covered.
Royalties paid annually.

UNKN
Highfields, Brynymor Road, Aberystwyth, Ceredigion SY23 2HX
☎01970 627337   Fax 01970 627337

Managing Editor *Niall Quinn*
Publisher *Siobhán O'Rourke*

FOUNDED 1995 originally to promote the work of poets engaged in the production of experimental and marginal text.

Veritam
Pilgrims, Redway, Porlock, Minehead, Somerset TA24 8QF
☎01643 862637
Email neil.trickett@virgin.net

Managing Editor *Neil Trickett*

FOUNDED 1998. *Publishes* fiction with a strong philosophical/literary thrust. Also non-fiction with 'uncompromising efforts to find reality'. 2 titles in 1999. No unsolicited mss; synopses and ideas considered. Approach in writing in the first instance.
Royalties paid 'where appropriate'.

Wakefield Historical Publications
19 Pinder's Grove, Wakefield, West Yorkshire WF1 4AH
☎01924 372748
Email kate@airtime.co.uk

Managing Editor *Kate Taylor*

FOUNDED 1977 by the Wakefield Historical Society to publish well-researched, scholarly works of regional (namely West Riding) historical significance. 1–2 titles a year. Unsolicited mss, synopses and ideas for books welcome.
Royalties not paid.

Paul Watkins Publishing
18 Adelaide Street, Stamford, Lincolnshire PE9 2EN
☎01780 756793   Fax 01780 756793

Proprietor *Shaun Tyas*

Publishes non-fiction – medieval, academic, biography, nautical, local history. No fiction. Distributor for the English Place-Name Society and the Richard III and Yorkist History Trust. 20 titles in 2000. Unsolicited mss, synopses and ideas for books welcome.
Royalties vary according to contract.

Whittles Publishing
Roseleigh House, Latheronwheel, Caithness KW5 6DW
☎01593 741240   Fax 01593 741360
Email whittl@globalnet.co.uk
Website www.users.globalnet.co.uk/~whittl

Managing Editor *Dr Keith Whittles*

FOUNDED 1986 to offer freelance commissioning and consulting. Started publishing a few years ago in the field of civil engineering and surveying. Also general books with a marine/Scottish theme. 7 titles in 1999. Unsolicited mss, synopses and ideas welcome on appropriate themes.
Royalties paid annually.

Witan Books & Publishing Services
Cherry Tree House, 8 Nelson Crescent, Cotes Heath, via Stafford ST21 6ST
☎01782 791673

Managing Editor *Jeff Kent*

FOUNDED in 1980 for self-publishing and commenced publishing other writers in 1991. *Publishes* general books, including biography, education, environment, geography, history, politics, popular music and sport. 1 title in 2000.

Witan Publishing Services, which began as an offshoot to help writers get their work into print, offers guidance, editing, proofreading etc. Unsolicited mss, synopses and ideas welcome (include s.a.e.).

Royalties paid.

Woodstock Books

The School House, South Newington,
Banbury, Oxfordshire OX15 4JJ
☎01295 720598   Fax 01295 720717

Chairman/Managing Director *James Price*
Approx. Annual Turnover £50,000

FOUNDED1989. *Publishes* literary reprints only. Main series: *Revolution and Romanticism, 1789–1834; Hibernia: Literature and Nation in Victorian Ireland.* No unsolicited mss.

The Worple Press

12 Havelock Road, Tonbridge, Kent TN9 1JE
☎01732 367466   Fax 01732 352057
Email theworpleco.@aol.com

Managing Editors *Peter Carpenter,
Amanda Knight*

FOUNDED 1997. Independent publisher specialising in poetry, art and alternative titles. 4 titles in 2000. No unsolicited mss. Write or phone for catalogue and flyers.

Royalties paid.

Writers' Bookshop

Remus House, Coltsfoot Drive, Woodston,
Peterborough PE2 9JX
☎01733 898103   Fax 01733 313524

Managing Editor *Kerrie Pateman*

Writers' Bookshop is an imprint of Forward Press (see under **Poetry Presses**). *Publishes* writers' aids in the form of directories and how-to guides. Best-known annual title is the *Small Press Guide.* For further information and an author brief, call *Kerrie Pateman.*

Payment Advance plus 15% royalties.

Xavier Music Ltd

PO Box 17, Abergavenny NP8 1XA
☎01874 730897   Fax 01874 730897
Email xavier@so-strong.com
Website www.so-strong.com

Managing Editor *Peter Lloyd*

Opened the books division in 1993 to publish poetry and works by Labi Siffre. *Publishes* poetry and one-act plays. No unsolicited material.

Royalties not paid.

Yorkshire Art Circus Ltd

School Lane, Glasshoughton, Castleford, West Yorkshire WF10 4QH
☎01977 550401   Fax 01977 512819
Email admin@artcircus.org.uk
Website www.artcircus.org.uk

Books Coordinator *Ian Daley*

FOUNDED 1986. *Publishes* contemporary fiction (novels and short stories) and local interest (Yorkshire and Humberside) under their **Route** imprint. No local history, children's, poetry, reference or nostalgia. Unsolicited mss discouraged; authors should send for fact sheet first. Write or ring for free catalogue.

Royalties paid.

So, You Want Your Own Web Site

Peter Finch

'Big changes used to take generations or centuries. This one won't take that long ...' **Bill Gates**, *The Road Ahead*

What is the Internet? It's another place. It's a 24–hour, geographically bound-aryless, data-filled, electronic version of the world we actually live in. It has all we need intellectually, artistically, and culturally and provides this mostly for free. What other future is there? Things are definitely going this way. It's hard to be a writer and not be touched by the Internet. It's a resource tool, a worldwide shop, an information exchange, a cultural depository, a proving ground, a con-tact point, a chat show, a rubbish tip, a data dump. How can we do without it? I know there are those of you out there still successfully using stand–up Remingtons and quarto paper. The practise has served you well for decades. Why should you change? But this is the new millennium and the planet has moved on.

Why writers should have their own home pages

On the Web users can establish what are known as home pages. This takes only the smallest amount of application. Home Pages – personal Web sites – are places users maintain which others worldwide can visit and read. Costs are usually minimal and the amount of data that can be put up there almost limitless. As a writer do you really need one of these? If you are an author with a future or even simply a writer with a past then you do. A Web site of your own has a thousand uses: it's a calling card, a personal exhibition, an updateable bibliography, a biographic display, a sales point, a creative outlet, a personal news bulletin, a depository for critical comment, a discussion forum, an advertising hoarding, a photo album, and a place where the work itself can be published – in full or in compact form.

For many it is this last item that provides the main attraction. You can put your poems online or your novel, your short stories, your history of the Yorkshire coal-fields, your political treatise or your memoirs. Size doesn't matter. Alexander Thynn, Lord Bath, already has two volumes of his autobiography, *Strictly Private*, up there and he's only reached 1956 (www.lordbath.co.uk). Others simply list who and where they are and what they do.

With your own Web sites there will no longer be any need to scrabble about for those kind words others may have said about us in order to convince festival organisers to book us or editors to give us that commission. The sending of expensive parcels containing copies of our works to support claims for our literary brilliance will be over. Students enquiring as to our credentials can simply be pointed to the site. Our works can be sampled, read in full, sold on in hard copy form, submitted to publishers, made to sing and dance and be read live (if we are up to it) any time of day or night, all on-line. All we do is point the world to www.you.com (or something similar) and let the Web do the rest.

Web sites impart status. Not everyone has one yet. They can also save money, enhance reputation and provide a magnificent outlet for creativity. Mine is called The Peter Finch Archive (dspace.dial.pipex.com/peter.finch) which, although rather grandly named, does make the point. I do a lot of things. I maintain it myself but visitors do not discover that until they browse through to the end of it. It is my shopfront on the world.

Before you engage in launching yours have a look around the Web at what others have done. One of the earliest, that of the author and journalist Jane Dorner, provides a host of links (dspace.dial.pipex.com/jane.dorner/). Jane is also author of the indispensable *The Internet: A Writer's Guide* (A&C Black).

What can you put up there?

At its simplest the Web is text-based which means that anything you've written can be turned into a Web page without too much difficulty. If you are working on a word processor and save your work as a text file then you are half way there. If you don't then you might have to engage in an amount of re-keying or scanning in the pages but it is still not a complex task. If you are a poet you could start your site with a selection of your best work. A novelist might want to put up Chapter One as a taster and then include instructions as to where visitors might go in order to read the rest. Local historians include whole essays, playwrights Web-publish a sample script, journalists post a range from their output. Once author site-builders have the bit between their teeth they move on to publishing complete works. And while it is text-only size matters little. Some publishers are experimenting with putting everything online. Sales will still come, they reason, because Web surfers will not be willing to suffer the fag of hour-long graphic downloads and the still with us difficulty encountered when trying to read the results in bed.

But after a time text-only can become rather dull. The Web handles graphics well and writers with sites are becoming dab hands at graphic enhancement, the introduction of illustration (which can be animated, if you wish), and those terrific photo shots of the author in action. Some have gone further and posted sound files of themselves reading (or being interviewed). Such embellishments are not difficult to manage but do use up Web space. Authors with a penchant for these things and an ability to use the technology are also including video files, although as of yet the quality of moving pictures on the Internet remains poor. There are two further common site enhancements that appear to appeal to writers with home pages the world over: the links page, where authors nominate other writers, organisations and sources of information that they think their visitors might like to see; and the guest book or discussion forum. This latter piece of interactive magic is relatively simple to manage and establishes a place among the home pages where visitors can leave their comments on what they've read or can initiate discussion with others who may come along. In my experience much of the comment left turns out to be of the 'Hi, this is Dave from the pub' variety although seriousness does occasionally break through.

Setting up – the basics

What do you need? Well, without really wanting to state the obvious, a computer and a connection to the Internet, although there are an increasing number of people who run their sites using either a cybercafé or the machine of a friend. But if you are a writer then you should already own a machine capable of word processing. Connect up your modem and go online. You can manage this with a creaky 286 and legacy Windows if you have to but it's a lot easier if you have a decent, recent computer. Expect this to cost at least £600.

The data which makes up your Web site will reside on a big computer (a server) somewhere which has a permanent connection to the Internet. Usually this will be that of your ISP (Internet Service Provider). Most ISPs allocate an amount of free Web space to all their clients. If you don't run with an ISP then you can use some of the freespace available at places like GeoCities (geocities.yahoo.com/home/)and Freeservers (freeservers.com). Upside – no cost. Downside – your site will carry their advertising.

Web pages are composed using html, a computer language which, lucky for us, is almost as simple as pre-Windows word processing. Html uses tags which tell visitors' Web browsers how the text should be displayed. bold, for example, will give us **bold**. Simple enough. You can avoid the code completely if you want by using one of the many WYSIWYG (What You See Is What You Get) editors available which will set up your pages for you. Microsoft Woed has a rudimentary version built-in. Basic Web building software often comes bundled on your ISP's set-up disks. Better are dedicated site maintenance packages such as FrontPage and Dreamweaver. But for my money you can't beat getting your hands just that little bit dirty with the code itself. Learn it from Mac Bride's *Teach Yourself HTML* or one of the many other handbooks which litter the shelves at Waterstones.

Setting up your first page could not be simpler:

```
<html>
<head>
<title>
```

```
My Home Page
</title>
</head>
<body>
<center>
here it is then
</center>
</body>
</html>
```

Save that as a text file, change the file extension from txt to htm, and view it through a browser (Internet Explorer (IE) and Netscape Navigator are the most common) and you'll get the words 'here it is then' in the centre of a clear grey screen. No more complicated than that.

If you've a computer within reach then why not try it out? How does it look? Fine and basic, certainly, but be assured that it won't look quite the same on the machines of others. Much will depend on what model of computer they are, their operating systems, their screen sizes and resolutions and, even more significantly, which browsers their users run. Most Web authors try to put both IE and Netscape on their computers in order to test things out. Both those bits of software happen to be free, so why not.

Colour can be added by inserting a few extra lines of code. <BODY BGCOLOR =FFFF00> will get you a bright yellow background. <FONT COLOR=000080> will get you dark blue text. Putting in </FONT COLOR> turns the color (note the American spelling here) off again.

Images, photographs and drawings, need to be scanned in as GIFs or JPEGs and run in the appropriate place on the page. Put in the code, <IMG SRC= 'pictureofme.jpg'>, where you want them on the page and the visitor's Web browser will assemble image and text into a viewable whole.

The various pages that will comprise your Web site are linked together with hyperlinks, a set of clickable codes which enables Web browsers to move back and forth through the information you chose to put on the web.

HTML has many parallels with word processing. Once you've learned the basics and can compose a simple letter you move on to more complex arrangements such as bulleted lists, indented paragraphs, tables, boxes and headline display type. Beyond that lie the wonders of image mapping, Java, ActiveX and a multitude of further bells and whistles. The Web is a dynamic place.

If you are stuck them simply take a look at how others have managed. At any given web page tell your browser to 'View Source' and there, magically before you, will be the complete HTML code that's been used. Lift the bits you want and adapt them to your own circumstances. No one will mind.

Once you've written your pages and tested them locally on your home computer, uploading them to the server is usually a matter of a few clicks. ISPs inevitably offer free file transfer software.

Getting visitors

The big Internet myth is that the millions of users out there are all waiting just for you. Put your site up and they'll flock to visit in their thousands. Despite extravagant claims you'll hear from other home page owning netheads believe me, they won't. Competition is fierce. Authors will need to work hard at drumming up traffic. Make sure you offer something worth visiting. Spend time registering your site with the main search engines. Go in for link exchanges with fellow practitioners and the main writers' organisations. Put your Web address on all your outgoing correspondence. And keep things up to date. Nothing is worse than the site which says, boldly, 'Last updated December 1997'. Visitors want to know how things are today.

Where to get help

There are copious quantities of help around. The Internet is fast becoming a national obsession. Read your Sunday papers, check the monthly glossies – .Net is particularly good for those starting out. Of the many Web handbooks available there are two which have helped me more than most: Mac Bride's *Teach Yourself HTML Publishing On The World Wide Web* (Hodder & Stoughton), and Angus J. Kennedy, *The Internet – The Rough Guide* (Rough Guides/Penguin). And for writers I recommend: Jane Dorner, *The Internet – A Writer's Guide* (A. & C. Black), and Trevor Lockwood and Karen Scott, *A Writer's Guide to the Internet* (Allison & Busby).

Useful Web Sites at a Glance

Many of these and other useful websites for writers can be found in
The Internet for Writers by Nick Daws (ISBN 1-84025-308-8), one of a series
of books published by Internet Handbooks.

Academi (Welsh Academy/Yr Academi Gymreig)
www.academi.org
News of events, publications and funding for Welsh-based literary events. (See entry under **Professional Associations and Societies**.)

Alliance of Literary Societies
www.sndc.demon.co.uk/als.htm
Details of societies and events. (See entry under **Professional Associations and Societies**.)

Amazon Bookshop
www.amazon.co.uk
Access to more than 1.5 million UK published titles. Simple search facility, shopping services online with significant discounts on some titles.

Ancestry
www.ancestry.com/
Family history information – databases, articles and other sources of genealogical data.

The Arts Council of England
www.artscouncil.org.uk
Includes information on applying for funding, publications and the National Lottery. (See entry under **Arts Councils and Regional Arts Boards**.)

Arvon Foundation
www.arvonfoundation.org
Information on the three Arvon centres in the UK. (See entry under **Professional Associations and Societies**.)

Association for Scottish Literary Studies
www.arts.gla.ac.uk/ScotLit/ASLS
The educational charity promoting the languages and literature of Scotland. (See entry under **Professional Associations and Societies**.)

Association of Authors' Representatives (AAR)
www.aar-online.org
US agents' organisation including list of current members. (See entry under **Professional Associations and Societies**.)

Authors' Licensing and Copyright Society (ALCS)
www.alcs.co.uk
Details of membership, news, publications, legal issues and rights, plus links to related sites. (See entry under **Professional Associations and Societies**.)

BBC
www.bbc.co.uk
Access to all BBC departments and services.

BOL
www.bol.com
Books and music online; a database of over 1.5 million titles with a simple search engine and many discounts.

British Association of Picture Libraries and Agencies (BAPLA)
www.bapla.org.uk
Free telephone referrals available from the BAPLA database through this Web site. (See entry under **Professional Associations and Societies**.)

British Centre for Literary Translation
www.literarytranslation.com
A joint Web site with the British Council containing workshops by leading translators, contacts and networks, and listings of translation conferences, seminars and events. (See entry under **Professional Associations and Societies**.)

British Council
www.briishtcouncil.org
Information on the Council's English Language services, education programmes, science and health links, and information exchange. (See entry under **Professional Associations and Societies**.)

British Film Institute (bfi)
www.bfi.org.uk
Information on the services offered by the Institute. (See entry under **Professional Associations and Societies**.)

British Library
www.bl.uk
Reader service enquiries, information on collections, links to the various Reading Rooms and exhibitions. OPAC 97 is a free service enabling users to trace material held in the major reference and document supply collections. (See related entries under **Libraries**.)

Children's Writing Resource Center
www.write4kids.com
US Web site – the 'official web gathering place for children's writers', whether published or beginners. Includes special reports, advice, chat links, news on the latest best-sellers and links to related sites.

Complete Works of William Shakespeare
the-tech.mit.edu/Shakespeare/works.html
Access to the text of the complete works with search facility, quotations and discussion pages.

Copyright Licensing Agency Ltd (CLA)
www.cla.co.uk
Copyright information, customer support and information on CLA services. (See entry under **Professional Associations and Societies**.)

Creators' Copyright Coalition
www.gn.apc.org/media/cccindex.html
Formed in 1995 in response to several UK publishers' assault on freelances' rights in their work. Links to affiliated organisations, updates on the Coalition's campaign and a guide to the basics of copyright.

Crime Writers' Association (CWA)
www.twbooks.co.uk/cwa/cwa.html
Web site of the professional crime writers' association. (See entry under **Professional Associations and Societies**.)

The Eclectic Writer
www.eclectics.com/writing/writing.html
US Web site offering a selection of articles on advice for writers on topics such as 'Proper Manuscript Format', 'Electronic Publishing', 'How to Write a Synopsis' and 'Motivation'. Also a Character Chart for fiction writers and an online discussion board.

Electronic Telegraph
www.telegraph.co.uk
The Daily Telegraph online – one of the first UK national newspapers to establish itself on the web.

Encyclopaedia Britannica
www.eb.com
A subscription gives access to the entire *Encyclopaedia Britannica* database as well as Merriam-Webster's *Collegiate Dictionary and the Britannica Book of the Year*. (A 30-day free trial is available.) EB online also gives links to more than 130,000 sites selected, rated and reviewed by Britannica editors.

The English Association
www.le.ac.uk/engassoc
News, publications, conference and membership information. (See entry under **Professional Associations and Societies**.)

Federation of Worker Writers and Community Publishers (FWWCP)
www.fwwcp.mcmail.com
Links to members of the FWWCP, the Federation magazine, information on membership. (See entry under **Professional Associations and Societies**.)

Film Angels
www.filmangel.co.uk
A unique Web site established in March 2000 by Hammerwood Film Productions in conjunction with Pan European Films and Mirabilis Films to create a shop window for writers and would-be film angels alike. Writers submit a short synopsis which can be displayed for a pre-determined period, for a fee, while would-be angels are invited to finance a production of their choice.

Financial Times
www.ft.com
Financial Times online.

Guide to Grammar and Style
www.andromeda.rutgers.edu/~jlynch/Writing/
A guide to grammar and style which is organised alphabetically, plus articles and links to other grammatical reference sites.

Great Books Online
www.bartleby.com
An ever-expanding list of great books – 'currently thousands of works by hundreds of authors' – published online for reference, free of charge.

The Guardian
www.guardian.co.uk
Web site of *The Guardian* and *The Observer* newspapers online.

Guide to Grammar and Writing

webster.comment.edu/HP/pages/darling/
grammar.htm

Produced by Charles Darling, Professor of
English and Humanities at the Capital Community Technical College in Connecticut. In
addition to invaluable information on grammar
and punctuation, the Web site offers interactive
quizzes and a free 'Ask Grammar' service.

Hansard

www.parliament.the-stationery-
office.co.uk/pa/cm/cmhansrd.htm

The official record of debates and written
answers in the House of Commons. The tran-
script of each day's business appears at noon on
the following weekday.

House of Commons Research Library

www.parliament.uk/commons/lib/research/
rpintro.htm

Gives access to the text of research reports prepared for MPs on a wide range of current issues.

HTML Writers Guild

www.hwg.org

US organisation offering resources, support,
representation and education for web authors.
(See entry under **Professional Associations
and Societies**.)

The Independent

www.independent.co.uk

The *Independent* newspaper online.

Ingenta

www.ingenta.com

Established in 1998, Ingenta is the largest online
academic research service in the UK. Formed
through a public/private partnership with the
University of Bath, the site offers 'free searching
of millions of academic and professional articles
from thousands of journals online'.

Inkspot – The Writer's Resource

www.inkspot.com

Canadian website offering over 2000 pages of
information about the craft and business of
writing, discussion forums and networking
opportunities.

Institute of Linguists

www.iol.org.uk

Discussion forum, news on regional societies,
job opportunities, 'Find a Linguist' service,
and *The Linguist* magazine. (See entry under
Professional Associations and Societies.)

Institute of Translation and Interpreting (ITI)

www.iti.org.uk

Web site of the professional association of translators and interpreters, with the ITI Directory,
publications, training and membership information. (See entry under **Professional
Associations and Societies**.)

Internet Bookshop

www.bookshop.co.uk

'Europe's largest online bookshop.'

Internet Classics Archive

classics.mit.edu/titles.d.html

Includes 441 works of classical literature by 59
different authors. Mostly Greek and Roman
works with some Chinese and Persian. All are
in English translation

Journalism UK

www.octopod.demon.co.uk/journ_uk.htm

A Web site for UK-based journalists who write
for text-based publications. Includes links to
newspapers, magazines, e-zines, news sources
plus information on jobs, training and organisations.

The Library Association

www.la-hq.org.uk

The professional body for librarians and
information managers. (See entry under
Professional Associations and Societies.)

The Mirror

www.mirror.co.uk

The Mirror newspaper online.

National Union of Journalists (NUJ)

www.gn.apc.org/media/nuj.html

Represents those journalists who work in all
sectors of publishing, print and broadcasting.
(See entry under **Professional Associations
and Societies**.)

Novel Advice Newsletter

www.noveladvice.com

A free US journal aimed at the fiction writer;
full text of current and past issues online.

PEN

www.pen.org.uk

Web site of the English Centre of International
PEN. News of events, membership details.
(See entry under **Professional Associations
and Societies**.)

Poets and Writers Online
www.pw.org
A US site containing publishing advice, a directory of writers, online bookstore, literary links, news, articles on aspects of writing, grants and awards.

Producers Alliance for Cinema and Television (PACT)
www.pact.co.uk
Publications, jobs in the industry, production companies, membership details. (See entry under **Professional Associations and Societies**.)

Publishers Association
www.publishers.org.uk
Information about the Association and careers in publishing, also 'Getting Published' pages. (See entry under **Professional Associations and Societies**.)

Pure Fiction
www.purefiction.com
Described as 'the Web site for anybody who loves to read – or aspires to write – bestselling fiction'. Contains book reviews, writing advice, a writers showcase and an online bookshop.

Royal Society of Literature
www.rslit.org
Information on lectures, discussions and readings; membership details and prizes. (See entry under **Professional Associations and Societies**.)

Science Fiction Foundation Collection
www.liv.ac.uk/~asawyer/sffchome.html
The research library of the Science Fiction Foundation, based at the University of Liverpool. Includes links to the Foundation, the John Wyndham archive, the Foundation's journal and other SF collections and associations. (See entry under **Professional Associations and Societies**.)

Scottish Arts Council
www.sac.org.uk
Information on funding and events; 'Image of the Month' and 'Poem of the Month'. (See entry under **Arts Councils and Regional Arts Boards**.)

Scottish Book Trust
www.scottishbooktrust.com
Information on the Trust's activities and a link to its Book Information Service. (See entry under **Professional Associations and Societies**.)

Scottish Library Association
www.slainte.ac.uk
Links to various services and major Scottish websites and information on people, organisations, libraries, events and resources of Scottish interest. (See entry under **Professional Associations and Societies**.)

Scottish Publishers Association
www.scottishbooks.org
Links to members' websites; information on activities and publications. (See entry under **Professional Associations and Societies**.)

Screenwriters and Playwrights Home Page
www.teleport.com/~cdeemer/scrwriter.html
A website designed to 'meet the special needs of screenwriters and playwrights', maintained by US screenwriter Charles Deemer. Links to a discussion forum and 'Screenwright', an electronic screenwriting course.

Screenwriters Online
screenwriter.com/insider/news.html
Described as the 'only professional screenwriter's site run by major screenwriters who get their scripts and screenplays made into movies'. Contains screenplay analysis, expert articles and *The Insider Report*.

Self Publishing
www.SelfPublishing.co.uk
Set up to allow writers to advertise their books on the Internet. Mostly of appeal to self-published authors but open to everyone by publishing a 'taster' of one chapter of a novel or equivalent for other books. Applications must be made via the Web site or directly to Ethan Lee, 13 St Brigid Road, Heath, Cardiff CF14 4LB.

Society of Authors
www.writers.org.uk/society/
Includes FAQs for new writers, diary of events, membership details, links to publishers' and other societies' Web sites. (See entry under **Professional Associations and Societies**.)

Society of Freelance Editors and Proofreaders (SFEP)
www.sfep.org.uk
Basic information about the Society. (See under **Professional Associations and Societies**.)

Society of Indexers
www.socind.demon.co.uk
Indexing information for publishers and

authors, 'Electronic Indexers Available' pages. Membership information. (See entry under **Professional Associations and Societies**.)

South Bank Centre, London
www.sbc.org.uk
Links to the Royal Festival Hall, the Hayward Gallery and Poetry Library; news of literature events.

The *Sun*
www.the-sun.co.uk
Website of the *Sun* newspaper.

The Times
www.the-times.co.uk
Website of *The Times* newspaper.

trAce Online Writing Community
www.trace.ntu.ac.uk
Based at Nottingham Trent University, trAce is a '24-hour online community' for writers and readers worldwide to share and critique their work, discuss favourite books and talk. Also holds occasional (live) conferences and workshops. Links to a wide range of useful sites for writers.

The Arts Council of Wales
www.ccc-acw.org.uk
Information on publications, council meetings, the arts in Wales. Links to other arts websites. (See entry under **Arts Councils and Regional Arts Boards**.)

The Web Writer
www.geocities.com/Athens/Parthenon/
8390/TOC.htm
A site for writers who want to write for publication on the web. A wide range of information and advice includes getting online, choosing a computer, saving money on your PC, dealing with Windows, software information, research-

ing online, how to build a Web site, being a writer, Web site issues.

Welsh Academy – see **Academi**

Welsh Books Council (Cyngor Llyfrau Cymru)
www.cllc.org.uk and www.gwales.com
Information about books from Wales, editorial and design services, 'Wales Book Day'. (See entry under **Professional Associations and Societies**.)

Writers Guild of Great Britain
www.writers.org.uk/guild/
A wide range of information including rates of pay, articles on topics such as copyright, news, writers' resources and industry regulations. (See entry under **Professional Associations and Societies**.)

Writers and their Copyright (W.A.T.C.H.)
www.lib.utexas.edu/hrc/watch.html
Database of copyright holders in the UK and North America. (See entry under **Professional Associations and Societies**.)

WritersNet
www.writers.net
A free service, the site contains *The Internet Directory of Published Writers* and *The Internet Directory of Literary Agents* and aims to be a 'comprehensive matchmaking resource for writers, editors, publishers and literary agents on the net'.

WWWebster Dictionary/WWWebster Thesaurus
www.m-w.com/home.htm
Merriam-Webster Online. Includes a search facility for words in the *Webster Dictionary* or *Webster Thesaurus*; word games, 'Word of the Day' and Language Info Zone.

UK Packagers

Aladdin Books Ltd

28 Derry Street, London W1P 0LD
☎020 7323 3319   Fax 020 7323 4829
Email aladdin2@dircon.co.uk
Managing Director *Charles Nicholas*
Approx. Annual Turnover £3.5 million

FOUNDED in 1979 as a packaging company but with joint publishing ventures in the UK and USA. *Commissions* children's fully illustrated, non-fiction reference books. 40 titles in 1999. IMPRINTS **Aladdin Books** *Bibby Whittaker* Children's reference; **Nicholas Enterprises** *Charles Nicholas* Adult non-fiction; **The Learning Factory** *Charles Nicholas* Early learning concepts 0–4 years. Will consider synopses and ideas for children's non-fiction with international sales potential only. No fiction.
Fees usually paid instead of royalties.

The Albion Press Ltd

Spring Hill, Idbury, Oxfordshire OX7 6RU
☎01993 831094   Fax 01993 831982
Chairman/Managing Director
Emma Bradford

FOUNDED 1984. *Commissions* illustrated trade titles, particularly children's. About 4 titles a year. TITLES *From a Distance* Jane Ray and Julie Gold; *The Little Mermaid and other Fairy Stories* Isabelle Brent. Unsolicited synopses and ideas for books not welcome.
Royalties paid; fees paid for introductions and partial contributions.

Alphabet & Image Ltd

See **Marston House** under **UK Publishers**

Archival Facsimiles Limited

The Old Bakery, 52 Crown Street, Banham, Norwich, Norfolk NR16 2HW
☎01953 887277   Fax 01953 888361
Email erskpres@aol.com
Chief Executive *Crispin de Boos*

FOUNDED 1986. Specialist private publishers for individuals and organisations. Produces scholarly reprints and limited editions for academic/business organisations in Europe and the USA, ranging from leather-bound folios of period print reproductions to small illustrated booklets.

Under the **Erskine Press** imprint publishes books on Antarctic exploration, general interest autobiographies and medical related 'Patient's Guides' (*Hip & Knee Replacement*; *Chronic Fatigue Syndrome*). No unsolicited mss. Ideas welcome.
Royalties paid twice-yearly.

AS Publishing

73 Montpelier Rise, London NW11 9DU
☎020 8458 3552   Fax 020 8458 0618
Managing Director *Angela Sheehan*

FOUNDED 1987. *Commissions* children's illustrated non-fiction. No unsolicited synopses or ideas for books, but approaches welcome from experienced authors, editors and illustrators in this field.
Fees paid.

BCS Publishing Ltd

2nd Floor, Temple Court, 109 Oxford Road, Cowley, Oxford OX4 2ER
☎01865 770099   Fax 01865 770050
Managing Director *Steve McCurdy*
Approx. Annual Turnover £350,000

Commissions general interest non-fiction for the international co-edition market.

Belitha Press Ltd

London House, Great Eastern Wharf, Parkgate Road, London SW11 4NQ
☎020 7978 6330   Fax 020 7223 4936
Publishing Director *Chester Fisher*
Editorial Director *Mary-Jane Wilkins*

FOUNDED 1980. *Commissions* children's non-fiction in all curriculum areas. About 125 titles a year. All titles are expected to sell in at least four co-editions. TITLES *World Cities; The Other Half of History; Life in Victorian Times; Our Earth; Future Tech; Speedy Machines; Building Works; Looking at Animals*. IMPRINT **Big Fish** *Chester Fisher* Children's interactive non-fiction. TITLES *Quiz Master; Internet Action*. No unsolicited mss. Synopses and ideas for books welcome from experienced children's writers.

Bellew Publishing Co. Ltd

See entry under **UK Publishers**

Bender Richardson White

PO Box 266, Uxbridge, Middlesex UB9 5BD
☎01895 832444   Fax 01895 835213
Email brw@brw.co.uk

Partners *Lionel Bender, Kim Richardson,*
  Ben White

FOUNDED 1990 to produce illustrated non-fiction for children aged 7–14 for publishers in the UK and abroad. 40 titles in 1999. Unsolicited material not welcome.

Fees paid.

David Bennett Books Ltd

Kiln House, 210 New Kings Road, London
SW6 4NZ
☎020 7731 6444   Fax 020 7731 6554

Managing Editor *Helen Mortimer*
Art Director *Andrew Crowson*

FOUNDED 1989. Part of **C&B Publishing plc**. Producer of children's books: picture and novelty books, interactive and board books, baby gifts and non-fiction for babies and toddlers. Synopses and ideas for books welcome. Unsolicited mss may not be returned. No fiction or poetry.

Payment Both fees and royalties.

Big Fish

See **Belitha Press Ltd**

Book Packaging and Marketing

3 Murswell Lane, Silverstone, Towcester,
Northamptonshire NN12 8UT
☎01327 858380   Fax 01327 858380
Email martin@marixevans.freeserve.co.uk

Contact *Martin F. Marix Evans*

FOUNDED 1989. Essentially a project management service, handling books demanding close designer/editor teamwork or complicated multi-contributor administration, for publishers, business 'or anyone who needs one'. Mainly illustrated adult non-fiction including military, travel, historical, home reference and coffee-table books. No fiction or poetry. 5–8 titles a year. Proposals considered but rarely come to fruition; most books are bespoke by publishers. Additional writers are sometimes required for projects in development. TITLES *Canals of England; Contemporary Photographers*, 3rd ed.; *Michelin's Paris in Your Pocket; The Battles of the Somme 1916–18; The Boer War.*

Payment Authors contract direct with client publishers; fees paid on first print usually and royalties on reprint but this depends on the publisher.

Breslich & Foss Ltd

20 Wells Mews, London W1P 3FJ
☎020 7580 8774   Fax 020 7580 8784
Email sales@breslichfoss.com

Directors *Paula Breslich, K. B. Dunning*
Approx. Annual Turnover £1.5 million

Packagers of non-fiction titles only, including art, children's, crafts, gardening and health. Unsolicited mss welcome but synopses preferred. Include s.a.e. with all submissions.

Royalties paid twice-yearly.

Brown Wells and Jacobs Ltd

Forresters Hall, 25–27 Westow Street, London
SE19 3RY
☎020 8771 5115   Fax 020 8771 9994
Email postmaster@popking.demon.co.uk
Website www.bwj.org

Managing Director *Graham Brown*

FOUNDED 1979. *Commissions* non-fiction, novelty, pre-school and first readers, natural history and science. About 40 titles a year. Unsolicited synopses and ideas for books welcome.

Fees paid.

Calmann & King Ltd

71 Great Russell Street, London WC1B 3BN
☎020 7831 6351   Fax 020 7404 9273
Email enquiries@calmann-king.co.uk
Website www.calmann-king.com

Chairman *Robin Hyman*
Managing Director *Laurence King*

FOUNDED 1976. *Commissions* books on art, the decorative arts, design, architecture, graphic design, carpets and textiles. About 40 titles a year. Unsolicited synopses and ideas for books welcome.

Royalties paid twice-yearly.

Cameron Books (Production) Ltd

PO Box 1, Moffat, Dumfriesshire DG10 9SU
☎01683 220808   Fax 01683 220012
Email info@cameronbooks.co.uk
Website www.cameronbooks.co.uk

Directors *Ian A. Cameron, Jill Hollis*
Approx. Annual Turnover £350,000

Commissions contemporary art, including environmental art, film, design, collectors' reference, educational reference, conservation, natural history, social history, decorative arts, esoteric gardening and cookery. About 6 titles a year. Unsolicited synopses and ideas for books welcome.

Payment varies with each contract.

Carroll & Brown Publishers Limited
See entry under **UK Publishers**

Chancerel International Publishers Ltd
120 Long Acre, London WC2E 9PA
☎020 7240 2811   Fax 020 7836 4186
Email chancerel@chancerel.com
Managing Director *W. D. B. Prowse*

FOUNDED 1976. *Commissions* educational books, and *publishes* language-teaching materials in most languages. Language teachers/writers often required as authors/consultants, especially native speakers other than English.
Payment generally by flat fee but royalties sometimes.

Roger Coote Publishing
Gissing's Farm, Fressingfield, Eye, Suffolk IP21 5SH
☎01379 588044   Fax 01379 588055
Email rgc@ndirect.co.uk
Director *Roger Goddard-Coote*

FOUNDED 1993. Packager of children's and adult non-fiction for trade, school and library markets. About 40 titles a year. No fiction. Include s.a.e. for return.
Fees paid; no royalties.

Diagram Visual Information Ltd
195 Kentish Town Road, London NW5 2JU
☎020 7482 3633   Fax 020 7482 4932
Managing Director *Bruce Robertson*

FOUNDED 1967. Producer of library, school, academic and trade reference books. About 10 titles a year. Unsolicited synopses and ideas for books welcome.
Fees paid; no payment for sample material/ submissions for consideration.

Direct Image Publishing
PO Box 17, Kendal, Cumbria LA8 8BE
☎015395 68936   Fax 015395 68932
Email enquiries@directimageprod.demon.co.uk
Website www.directimageprod.co.uk
Co-directors *Chris Ware, Elaine Ware*

A sub-division of **Direct Image Productions Ltd**. FOUNDED in 1992 to support video training programmes. *Publishes* outdoor pursuits, outdoor education titles and teachers' resource material, usually as part of a video and book package. Developing an outdoor leisure series and launching an outdoor magazine, *Challenge*, with the Association for Outdoor Learning. No unsolicited mss; approach with letter and outline of idea in the first instance.
Payment One-off fee paid.

Dorling Kindersley Ltd
See entry under **UK Publishers**

Duncan Petersen Publishing Limited
See entry under **UK Publishers**

Eddison Sadd Editions
St Chad's House, 148 King's Cross Road, London WC1X 9DH
☎020 7837 1968   Fax 020 7837 2025
Email postmaster@edd-sadd.demon.co.uk
Managing Director *Nick Eddison*
Editorial Director *Ian Jackson*
Approx. Annual Turnover £3.5 million

FOUNDED 1982. Produces a wide range of popular illustrated non-fiction, with books published in 25 countries. Ideas and synopses are welcome but titles must have international appeal.
Royalties paid twice yearly; flat fees paid when appropriate.

Erskine Press
See **Archival Facsimiles Limited**

Expert Publications Ltd
Sloe House, Halstead, Essex CO9 1PA
☎01787 474744   Fax 01787 474700
Email expert@lineone.net
Chairman *Dr. D. G. Hessayon*

FOUNDED 1993. Produces the Expert series of books by Dr. D. G. Hessayon. Currently 18 titles in the series, including *The NEW Flower Expert; The Evergreen Expert; The NEW Vegetable & Herb Expert; The Flowering Shrub Expert; The Container Expert*. No unsolicited material.

Haldane Mason Ltd
59 Chepstow Road, London W2 5BP
☎020 7792 2123   Fax 020 7221 3965
Email haldane.mason@dial.pipex.com

FOUNDED 1994. *Commissions* adult and children's illustrated non-fiction and young children's fiction. 30 titles in 1999. Unsolicited synopses and ideas welcome; approach in writing in the first instance. No adult fiction.
Fees paid.

Angus Hudson Ltd

Concorde House, Grenville Place, Mill Hill, London NW7 3SA

☎020 8959 3668   Fax 020 8959 3678

Email coed@angushudson.com

Managing Director *Nicholas Jones*
Approx. Annual Turnover £3.5 million

FOUNDED 1977. Management buyout from Maxwell Communications in 1989. Leading packager of religious co-editions. *Commissions* Christian books for all ages and co-editioning throughout the world. About 150 titles a year. Publishes under **Candle Books**; **Gazelle Books** and **Monarch Books** (see entry under **UK Publishers**) imprints. Prototype dummies complete with illustrations welcome for consideration. Synopses for text books welcome; no unsolicited mss, please.

Royalties paid.

The Learning Factory

See **Aladdin Books Ltd**

Lexus Ltd

13 Newton Terrace, Glasgow G3 7PJ

☎0141 221 5266   Fax 0141 226 3139

Email pt@lexus.win-uk.net

Managing/Editorial Director
P. M. Terrell

FOUNDED 1980. Compiles bilingual reference, language and phrase books. About 10 titles a year. TITLES *Rough Guide Phrasebooks; Collins Italian Concise Dictionary; Harrap Study Aids; Hugo's Phrase Books; Harrap Shorter French Dictionary* (revised); *Impact Specialist Bilingual Glossaries; Oxford Student's Japanese Learner.* No unsolicited material. Books are mostly commissioned. Freelance contributors employed for a wide range of languages.

Payment generally flat fee.

Lionheart Books

10 Chelmsford Square, London NW10 3AR

☎020 8459 0453   Fax 020 8451 3681

Senior Partner *Lionel Bender*
Partner *Madeleine Samuel*
Designer *Ben White*
Approx. Annual Turnover £250,000

A design/editorial packaging team. Titles are primarily commissioned from publishers. Highly illustrated non-fiction for children aged 8–14, mostly natural history, history and general science. About 20 titles a year.

Payment generally flat fee.

Market House Books Ltd

2 Market House, Market Square, Aylesbury, Buckinghamshire HP20 1TN

☎01296 484911   Fax 01296 437073

Email mhb_aylesbury@compuserve.com

Directors *Dr Alan Isaacs, Dr John Daintith, Peter Sapsed*

FOUNDED 1970. Formerly Laurence Urdang Associates. *Commissions* dictionaries, encyclopedias and reference. About 15 titles a year. TITLES *Concise Medical Dictionary; Brewer's 20th Century Phrase and Fable; Oxford Dictionary for Science Writers and Editors; Oxford Dictionary of Accounting; Bloomsbury Thesaurus; Larousse Thematica* (6 volume encyclopedia); *Collins English Dictionary; The Macmillan Encyclopedia; Grolier Bibliographical Encyclopedia of Scientists* (10 vols); *Oxford Paperback Encyclopedia; Oxford International Business Dictionary; Penguin Biographical Dictionary of Women; Penguin Shakespeare Dictionary; Penguin Dictionary of Plant Sciences; Oxford Dictionary of Medicines.* Unsolicited material not welcome as most books are compiled in-house.

Fees paid.

Marshall Editions Ltd

The Orangery, 161 New Bond Street, London W1Y 9PA

☎020 7291 8222   Fax 020 7291 8233

Website www.marshalleditions.com

Publisher *Barbara Anderson Marshall*
Editorial Director (adult titles) *Ellen Dupont*
Editorial Director (children's) *Linda Cole*

FOUNDED 1977. *Commissions* non-fiction, including health, gardening, lifestyle, self-improvement, leisure, popular science and visual information for children. Also Marshall Publishing which *publishes* business training, education and consumer reference titles.

Monkey Puzzle Media Ltd

Gissing's Farm, Fressingfield, Eye, Suffolk IP21 5SH

☎01379 588044   Fax 01379 588055

Email rgc@ndirect.co.uk

Chairman/Managing Director
Roger Goddard-Coote
Editorial Director *Alex Edmonds*

FOUNDED 1998. Packager of adult and children's non-fiction for trade, school, library and mass markets. About 40 titles a year. No fiction or textbooks. Synopses and ideas welcome. Include s.a.e. for return.

Fees paid; no royalties.

Mike Moran Productions Ltd

33 Warner Road, Ware, Hertfordshire
SG12 9JL
☎01920 466003   Fax 01920 466003
Chairman/Managing Director *Mike Moran*

Packager and publisher. TITLES *MM Publisher
Database; MM Printer Database* (available in UK,
European and international editions).

Nicholas Enterprises
See **Aladdin Books Ltd**

Orpheus Books LImited

2 Church Green, Witney, Oxfordshire
OX8 6AW
☎01993 774979   Fax 01993 700330
Email post@orpheusbooks.demon.co.uk
Chairman *Nicholas Harris*
Production Director *Joanna Turner*
Approx. Annual Turnover £5 million

FOUNDED 1993. *Commissions* children's non-
fiction. 12 titles in 1999. No unsolicited material.
Fees paid.

Oyster Books Ltd

Unit 4, Kirklea Farm, Badgworth, Axbridge,
Somerset BS26 2QH
☎01934 732251   Fax 01934 732514
Managing Director *Tim Wood*

FOUNDED 1985. Packagers of books and book/
toy/gift items for children of pre-school age to
ten years. About 20 titles a year. Most material
is created in-house.
Payment Usually fees paid.

Parke Sutton Ltd

Orchard House, Grange Farm, Ashwellthorpe,
Norfolk NR16 1ET
☎01508 489212   Fax 01508 489212
Director *Ian S. McIntyre*

FOUNDED 1982. Packages books for publishers.
Unsolicited synopses and ideas for books welcome. S.a.e. essential. Also publishing consultant.
Royalties paid twice yearly; fees sometimes
paid rather than royalties.

Playne Books Limited

Chapel House, Trefin, Haverfordwest,
Pembrokeshire SA62 5AU
☎01348 837073   Fax 01348 837063
Director *Gill Davies*
Design & Production *David Playne*

FOUNDED 1987. *Commissions* early learning titles
for young children – fun ideas with an educational slant and novelty books. Also highly illus-

trated and practical books on any subject.
Unsolicited synopses and ideas for books wel-
come, but by post only.
Royalties paid 'on payment from publishers'.
Fees sometimes paid instead of royalties.

Mathew Price Ltd

The Old Glove Factory, Bristol Road,
Sherborne, Dorset DT9 4HP
☎01935 816010   Fax 01935 816310
Email mathewp@mathewprice.com
Chairman/Managing Director *Mathew Price*
Approx. Annual Turnover £1 million

Commissions full-colour novelty picture books
and fiction for young children plus children's
non-fiction for all ages.
Fees sometimes paid instead of royalties.

Quarto Publishing

The Old Brewery, 6 Blundell Street, London
N7 9BH
☎020 7700 6700/7333 0000
Fax 020 7700 4191/7700 0077
Website www.quarto.com
Chairman *Laurence Orbach*

FOUNDED 1976. Britain's largest book packager. *Commissions* illustrated non-fiction, including painting, graphic design, visual arts, history, cookery, gardening, crafts. *Publishes* under
the Apple imprint. Unsolicited synopses/ideas
for books welcome.
Payment Flat fees paid.

Reader's Digest Children's Publishing Ltd

King's Court, Parsonage Lane, Bath BA1 1ER
☎01225 463401   Fax 01225 460942
Email brian.cearnes@readersdigest.co.uk
Website www.childrens-books.com
Managing Director *Brian Cearnes*
Approx. Annual Turnover £9 million

Part of the Reader's Digest Group. *Commissions*
children's projects in novelty or interactive formats – acetate, pop-up, toy add-ons. Also religious list. About 100 titles a year.
Royalties or flat fee according to contract.

Regency House Publishing Limited
See entry under **UK Publishers**

Sadie Fields Productions Ltd

4C/D West Point, 36–37 Warple Way,
London W3 0RG
☎020 8746 1171   Fax 020 8746 1170
Email sheri@tangobooks.co.uk

Directors *David Fielder, Sheri Safran*

FOUNDED 1981. Children's books with international co-edition potential: pop-ups, three-dimensional, novelty, picture and board books, 1500 words maximum. About 30 titles a year. Approach with preliminary letter and sample material in the first instance. *Publishes* in the UK under the **Tango Books** imprint.

Royalties based on a per-copy-sold rate and paid in stages.

Salariya Book Company Ltd

25 Marlborough Place, Brighton, East Sussex BN1 1UB
☎01273 603306   Fax 01273 693857
Email salariya@fastnet.co.uk

Managing Director *David Salariya*

FOUNDED 1989. Children's information books – fiction, history, art, music, science, architecture, education and picture books.

Payment by arrangement.

Savitri Books Ltd

115J Cleveland Street, London W1P 5PN
☎020 7436 9932   Fax 020 7580 6330

Managing Director *Mrinalini S. Srivastava*
Approx. Annual Turnover £200,000

FOUNDED 1983 and since 1998, Savitri Books has also become a publisher in its own right (textile crafts). Keen to work 'very closely with authors/illustrators and try to establish long-term relationships with them, doing more books with the same team of people'. *Commissions* illustrated non-fiction, crafts, New Age and nature. About 7 titles a year. Unsolicited synopses and ideas for books 'very welcome'.

Royalties 10–15% of the total price paid by the publisher.

Sheldrake Press

188 Cavendish Road, London SW12 0DA
☎020 8675 1767   Fax 020 8675 7736
Email mail@sheldrakepress.demon.co.uk
Website www.sheldrakepress.demon.co.uk

Publisher *Simon Rigge*
Approx. Annual Turnover £250,000

Commissions illustrated non-fiction: history, style, travel, cookery and stationery. TITLES *The Shorter Mrs Beeton; The Victorian House Book; The Power of Steam; The Railway Heritage of Britain; Wild Britain; Wild France; Wild Spain; Wild Italy;* and *Wild Ireland; Amsterdam: Portrait of a City* and Kate Greenaway stationery books. Synopses and ideas for books welcome, but not interested in fiction.

Fees or royalties paid.

Stonecastle Graphics Ltd/ Touchstone

Old Chapel Studio, Plain Road, Marden, Tonbridge, Kent TN12 9LS
☎01622 832590   Fax 01622 832592
Email touchstone@touchstone.ndirect.co.uk
Website www.touchstonedesign.co.uk

Partners *Paul Turner, Sue Pressley*
Editorial Head *Sue Pressley*
Approx. Annual Turnover £300,000

FOUNDED 1976. Formed additional design/packaging partnership, Touchstone, in 1983. *Commissions* illustrated non-fiction general books – motoring, health, sport, leisure, home interest and popular culture. 20 titles in 1999. TITLES *Pregnancy – A Week-by-Week Guide; Tracing Your Ancestors; Entertaining in Style; Popular Freshwater Tropical Fish; The History of British Bikes.* Unsolicited synopses and ideas for books welcome.

Fees paid.

Templar Publishing

Pippbrook Mill, London Road, Dorking, Surrey RH4 1JE
☎01306 876361   Fax 01306 889097
Email editorial@templarco.co.uk
Website www.templarco.co.uk

Managing Director/Editorial Head
  Amanda Wood
Approx. Annual Turnover £6 million

FOUNDED 1981. A division of The Templar Company plc. *Commissions* novelty and gift books, picture books and children's illustrated non-fiction. 100 titles a year. Synopses and ideas for books welcome.

Royalties by arrangement.

Toucan Books Ltd

Fourth Floor, 32–38 Saffron Hill, London EC1N 8FH
☎020 7404 8181   Fax 020 7404 8282

Managing Director *Robert Sackville-West*
Approx. Annual Turnover £1,600,000

FOUNDED 1985. *Specialises* in international co-editions and fee-based editorial, design and production services to film. *Commissions* illustrated non-fiction only. About 20 titles a year. TITLES *The Eventful Century; The Earth, Its Wonders, Its Secrets; Leith's Cookery Bible; Charles II; The Complete Photography Course; Journeys into the Past* series; *People and Places.* Unsolicited synopses and ideas for books welcome. No fiction or non-illustrated titles.

Royalties paid twice-yearly; fees paid in addition to or instead of royalties.

Touchstone
See **Stonecastle Graphics Ltd**

Webb & Bower (Publishers) Ltd
9 Duke Street, Dartmouth, Devon TQ6 9PY
☎01803 835525   Fax 01803 835552
Managing Director *Richard Webb*

FOUNDED 1975. Specialises in licensing illustrated non-fiction books from its portfolio of 350 titles.
Royalties paid twice-yearly.

Windrow & Greene
See **Compendium Publishing Ltd** under **UK Publishers**

Wordwright Publishing
8 St Johns Road, Saxmundham, Suffolk IP17 1BE
☎01728 604204   Fax 01728 604029
Email wordwright@clara.co.uk

Contact *Charles Perkins*

FOUNDED by ex-editorial people 'so good writing always has a chance with us'. *Commissions* illustrated non-fiction: social history and comment, military history, women's issues, sport. *Specialises* in military and social history, natural history, science, art, cookery, and gardening. About 6–8 titles a year. Unsolicited synopses/ideas (a paragraph or so) welcome for illustrated non-fiction.
Payment usually fees but royalties (twice-yearly) paid for sales above a specified number of copies.

Working Partners Ltd
1 Albion Place, London W6 0QT
☎020 8748 7477   Fax 020 8748 7450
Email enquiries@workingpartnersltd.co.uk

Contact *Ben Baglio, Rod Ritchie*

Specialises in children's mass-market series fiction books. Creators of *Animal Ark; Puppy Patrol; Puppy Tales; Heartland; Sheltie; Survive!.* No unsolicited mss.
Payment Both fees and royalties by arrangement.

Zöe Books Ltd
15 Worthy Lane, Winchester, Hampshire SO23 7AB
☎01962 851318   Fax 01962 843015
Managing Director *Imogen Dawson*
Director *Bob Davidson*

FOUNDED 1990. *Specialises* in full-colour information and reference books for schools and libraries worldwide. *Publishes* about 30 titles a year. Does *not* publish picture books or fiction. No freelance work available.
Fees paid.

Book Clubs

David Arscott's Sussex Book Club

3 Dolphin House, St Nicholas Lane, Lewes, Sussex BN7 2JZ

☎01273 470100   Fax 01273 470100

Email sussexbooks@compuserve.com

Website www.ourworld.compuserve.com/ sussexbooks

FOUNDED January 1998. *Specialises* in books about the county of Sussex. Represents all the major publishers of Sussex books and offers a wide range of titles.

Artists' Choice

PO Box 3, Huntingdon, Cambridgeshire PE18 0QX

☎01832 710201   Fax 01832 710488

Specialises in books for the amateur artist at all levels of ability.

BCA (Book Club Associates)

Greater London House, Hampstead Road, London NW1 7TZ

☎020 7760 6500   Fax 020 7760 6901

With two million members, BCA is Britain's largest book club organisation. Consists of 22 book clubs, catering for general and specific interests: Ancient & Medieval History Book Club, The Arts Guild, The Book Club of Ireland, The Christian Book Club, Discovery, The Book Club for Children, The English Book Club, Ergo, Escape, The Travel Book Club, Fantasy and Science Fiction, History Guild, Home Software World, The Literary Guild, Military and Aviation Book Society, Mind, Body & Spirit, Mystery and Thriller Club, Quality Paperbacks Direct, Railway Book Club, World Books, Mango, Taste, Escape, The Fiction Club and Computer Books Direct.

Books for Children (Time-Life Entertainment Group Ltd)

Brettenham House, Lancaster Place, London WC2E 7RL

☎0171 322 1400   Fax 020 7322 1488

Editor *Sian Hardy*

Editorial Director *Jill Morse*

Hardcover and paperback books for children from newly-born to teenage. Also occasional adult fiction and non-fiction – cookery, family interest, parenting guides.

Cygnus Books

PO Box 15, Llandeilo, Carmarthenshire SA19 6YX

☎01550 777701   Fax 01550 777569

Email enquiries@cygnus-books.co.uk

Website www.cygnus-books.co.uk

'Books for your next step in spirituality and complementary health care.' See website for over 1000 hand-picked titles. Also publishes *The Cygnus Review* magazine which features 50–60 reviews on new mind, body, spirit titles each month.

The Folio Society

44 Eagle Street, London WC1R 4FS

☎020 7400 4222   Fax 020 7400 4242

Fine editions of classic fiction, history and memoirs; also some children's classics.

Letterbox Library

Children's Book Cooperative, Unit 2D/ 2nd Floor, Leroy House, 436 Essex Road, London N1 3QP

☎020 7226 1633   Fax 020 7226 1768

Hard and softcover, non-sexist and multi-cultural books for children from one to teenage.

Poetry Book Society

See entry under **Organisations of Interest to Poets**

Readers Union Ltd

Brunel House, Newton Abbot, Devon TQ12 2DW

☎01626 323200   Fax 01626 323318

Has ten book clubs, all dealing with specific interests: Country Review, The Craft Club, Craftsman Society, Equestrian Society, The Gardeners Society, Life Matters, Needlecrafts with Cross Stitch, Focal Point, Ramblers & Climbers Society, Today's Family.

Red House Book Clubs

See **Scholastic Ltd** under **UK Publishers**

The Softback Preview (Time-Life UK)

Brettenham House, Lancaster Place, London WC2E 7TL

☎020 7322 1422   Fax 020 7322 1488

Senior Editor *Sarah Willis*
Editorial Director *Jill Morse*

Mainly serious non-fiction.

The Women's Press Book Club

The Women's Press, 34 Great Sutton Street,
London EC1V 0DX
☎0171 251 3007   Fax 020 7608 1938
Website www.the-womens-press.com

'Best women writers from more than 70 pub-lishers.' Fiction, biography and autobiography; popular mind, body and spirit; health and self-help; also a collection of women's studies, social issues and current affairs.

Writers Book Society

PO Box 6058, Nairn IV12 4WB
☎01667 453351   Fax 01667 452365

Specialises in books for writers.

UK Agents

Abbey Literary Agency and Associates

QAF Queen Adelaide, Queen Adelaide, Ely, Cambridgeshire CB7 4TZ
☎01353 69992
Email abbey@callnetuk.com

Contact *John Bree, Belinda Crawford*

FOUNDED 1999. *Handles* general fiction, TV and film, computing, humour, cookery, non-fiction, science fiction, suspense, historical, military, children's, biography, short stories, magazine articles and erotica. 'We welcome submissions from all minority groups whom we are promoting.' Nominal reading fee may be charged for unpublished authors (terms on application). CLIENTS Gavin Miller (US), Elizabeth Baker, Shirley Topton, Melissa Myers, Brian Shah. Unsolicited mss considered but synopsis and sample chapters preferred in the first instance. Please include return postage. *Commission* Home 10%; USA & Translation 20%.

Sheila Ableman Literary Agency

122 Arlington Road, London NW1 7HP
☎020 7485 3409 Fax 020 7485 3409
Email sheila@ableman.freeserve.co.uk

Contact *Sheila Ableman*

FOUNDED 1999. *Handles* commercial and literary fiction and non-fiction including history, science, travel, biography and autobiography. *Specialises* in TV tie-ins. No poetry, children's, cookery, gardening or sport. Unsolicited mss welcome. Approach in writing with publishing history, c.v., synopsis, three chapters and s.a.e. for return. No reading fee. *Commission* Home 15%; US & Translation 20%.

The Agency (London) Ltd★

24 Pottery Lane, Holland Park, London W11 4LZ
☎020 7727 1346 Fax 020 7727 9037
Email info@theagency.co.uk

Contacts *Stephen Durbridge, Leah Schmidt, Sebastian Born, Julia Kreitman, Bethan Evans, Hilary Delamere, Katie Haines, Wendy Gresser*

FOUNDED 1995. *Handles* children's fiction, TV, film, theatre, radio scripts. No adult fiction or non-fiction. Send letter with s.a.e. No reading fee. CLIENTS William Boyd, Andrew Davies, Jimmy McGovern, Lucy Gannon. *Commission* Home 10%; US various.

Gillon Aitken Associates Ltd★

29 Fernshaw Road, London SW10 0TG
☎020 7351 7561 Fax 020 7376 3594

Contacts *Gillon Aitken, Clare Alexander, Antony Harwood*

FOUNDED 1977. *Handles* fiction and non-fiction. No plays or scripts unless by existing clients. Send preliminary letter, with synopsis and return postage, in the first instance. No reading fee. CLIENTS Pat Barker, Sebastian Faulks, Helen Fielding, Germaine Greer, Alan Hollinghurst, Susan Howatch, A. L. Kennedy, Douglas Kennedy, Pauline Melville, V. S. Naipul, Tim Parks, Caryl Phillips, Piers Paul Read. *Commission* Home 10%; US 15%; Translation 20%.

Michael Alcock Management

7 Kensington Church Court, London W8 4SP
☎020 7938 4332 Fax 020 7938 4677
Email michaelalcock@compuserve.com

Contact *Michael Alcock*

FOUNDED 1997. *Handles* general non-fiction including current affairs, biography and memoirs, history, lifestyle, health and personal development; some literary and commercial mainstream fiction. No unsolicited mss; approach by letter giving details of writing and other media experience, plus synopsis and s.a.e. (for fiction send first two chapters as well). No reading fee. CLIENTS Michael Brunson, James Burke, Tom Dixon, Philip Dunn, Kevin Gould, Mark Griffiths, Kathryn Marsden, Lynne Robinson, Barnaby Rogerson, Ruby & Millie. *Commission* Home 15%; US and Translation 20%.

Jacintha Alexander Associates

See **Lucas Alexander Whitley**

Darley Anderson Literary, TV & Film Agency★

Estelle House, 11 Eustace Road, London SW6 1JB
☎020 7385 6652 Fax 020 7386 5571
Email darley.anderson@virgin.net

Contacts *Darley Anderson, Kerith Biggs* (Crime/ Foreign Rights), *Elizabeth Wright* (Women's Fiction/Love Stories/'Tear jerkers'), *Petra Sluka* (Non-Fiction), *Carrie Goodman* (Children's books/TV)

Run by an ex-publisher with a sympathetic touch and a knack for spotting and encouraging talent, known to have negotiated an advance of over £1 million and a Hollywood film deal for one first-time novelist and a £350,000 advance in the UK for another. *Handles* commercial fiction and non-fiction; children's fiction; also scripts for film and TV. No academic books or poetry. *Special interests* Fiction: all types of thrillers and women's and young male fiction, including contemporary romantic sagas, women in jeopardy; also crime (American/hard-boiled/cosy/ historical), horror, comedy, all types of American and Irish novels. Non-fiction: celebrity autobiographies, biographies, 'true life' women in jeopardy, relevatory history and science, popular psychology, self-improvement, diet, health, beauty, fashion, humour/cartoons, gardening, cookery, inspirational and religious. Send letter and outline with first three chapters; return postage/s.a.e. essential. CLIENTS Anne Baker, Gyles Brandreth, Paul Carson, Lee Child, Martina Cole, John Connolly, Joseph Corvo, Joan Jonker, Frank Lean, Carole Matthews, Lesley Pearse, Allan Pease, Adrian Plass, Ben Richards, Mary Ryan, Fred Secombe, Rebecca Shaw, Peter Sheridan, Linda Taylor. *Commission* Home 15%; US 20%; Translation 22½%; TV/Film/Radio 20%. *Overseas associates* APA Talent and Literary Agency (LA/ Hollywood); and leading foreign agents throughout the world.

Anubis Literary Agency
79 Charles Gardner Road, Leamington Spa, Warwickshire CV31 3BG
☎01926 832644 Fax 01926 311607
Contact *Steve Calcutt, Maggie Heavey*

FOUNDED 1994. *Handles* mainstream adult fiction, especially historical, horror, crime and women's. Also literary fiction. Scripts for film and TV. No children's books, poetry, short stories, journalism, academic or non-fiction. No unsolicited mss; send a covering letter and brief (one-page) synopsis (s.a.e. essential). No telephone calls. No reading fee. *Commission* Home 15%; US & Translation 20%.

Author Literary Agents
53 Talbot Road, Highgate, London N6 4QX
☎020 8341 0442/07989 318245 (mobile)
Fax 020 8341 0442

Email agile@authors.co.uk
Website www:authors.co.uk
Contact *John Havergal*

'New writers and creatives welcome. Most fiction and non-fiction genres and media considered, especially content which targets million-plus well researched and clearly defined readerships and audiences.' Email or s.a.e. for guidelines key to submission.

Azure Literary Agency
5 Laxey Road, Edgbaston, Birmingham B16 0JQ
☎0121 420 4493/07760 477987
Fax 0121 420 4493
Email azureagency@hotmail.com
Website hometown.aol.com/azureagents/ myhomepage/index.html
Contact *John Lewis*

FOUNDED 1999. *Handles* general and adult fiction, including some science fiction and fantasy; also non-fiction – mainly historical. *Specialises* in screenplays for film and TV, including comedy. No poetry or romance. No unsolicited mss; send synopsis with 2/3 chapters. For film and TV screenplays, send synopsis. Full manuscript will be requested if interested. S.a.e. essential. Synopses may be e-mailed. No reading fee. *Commission* Home 10%; USA & Translation 20%.

Yvonne Baker Associates
8 Temple Fortune Lane, London NW11 7UD
☎020 8455 8687 Fax 020 8458 3143
Contact *Yvonne Baker*

FOUNDED 1987. *Handles* scripts for TV, theatre, film and radio. Books extremely rarely. No poetry. Approach by letter giving as much detail as possible, including s.a.e. No reading fee. *Commission* Home 10%; US & Translation 20%.

Black C.A.T. Literary Agents
Queen Adelaide Farm, Queen Adelaide, Ely, Cambridgeshire CB7 4TZ
☎01353 663013 Fax 01353 663013
Email bcat@cellnetuk.com
Contacts *Vanessa Carter-James, John Charles, Roland Frederick*

FOUNDED 1999. *Handles* women's issues, music, media, theatre, plays/scripts, current affairs, health, education, adventure, European matters, fiction and non-fiction. No erotica. Reading fee of £65. 'Helps the unknown author to achieve publication. Advice on possible quality self-publishing.' CLIENTS D. Barrie, B. Croft, J. H. Miller.

Send synopsis with three specimen chapters and return postage. *Commission* Home 10%; US 20%.

Blake Friedmann
Literary Agency Ltd★
122 Arlington Road, London NW1 7HP
☎020 7284 0408 Fax 020 7284 0442
Email <firstname>@blakefriedmann.co.uk

Contacts *Carole Blake* (books), *Julian Friedmann* (film/TV), *Conrad Williams* (original scripts/radio), *Isobel Dixon* (books)

FOUNDED 1977. *Handles* all kinds of fiction from genre to literary; a varied range of specialised and general non-fiction, plus scripts for TV, radio and film. No poetry, juvenile, science fiction or short stories (unless from existing clients). *Special interests* commercial women's fiction, literary fiction, upmarket non-fiction. Unsolicited mss welcome but initial letter with synopsis and first two chapters preferred. Letters should contain as much information as possible on previous writing experience, aims for the future, etc. No reading fee. CLIENTS Ted Allbeury, Jane Asher, Joanna Briscoe, Elizabeth Chadwick, Teresa Crane, Barbara Erskine, Maeve Haran, John Harvey, Ken Hom, Glenn Meade, Lawrence Norfolk, Joseph O'Connor, Michael Ridpath, Tim Sebastian. *Commission* Books: Home 15%; US & Translation 20%. Radio/TV/Film: 15%. *Overseas associates* throughout Europe, Asia and the US.

David Bolt Associates
12 Heath Drive, Send, Surrey GU23 7EP
☎01483 721118 Fax 01483 721118

Contact *David Bolt*

FOUNDED 1983. *Handles* fiction and general non-fiction. No books for small children or verse (except in special circumstances). No scripts. *Special interests* fiction, African writers, biography, history, military, theology. Preliminary letter with s.a.e. essential. Reading fee for unpublished writers. Terms on application. CLIENTS include Chinua Achebe, David Bret, Joseph Rhymer, Colin Wilson. *Commission* Home 10%; US & Translation 19%.

Book Affairs Ltd
See entry under **Miscellany**

BookBlast Ltd
21 Chesterton Road, London W10 5LY
☎020 8968 3089 Fax 020 8932 4087

Contact *Address material to the company*

HANDLES traditional and underground literature. No poetry, plays, light romance, science fiction, horror, travel, fantasy, children's, cookery, gardening, health. No unsolicited mss. No submissions on disk, by fax or e-mail. Preliminary letter, synopsis, biographical information and s.a.e. essential, also names of agents and publishers previously contacted. *Commission* Home 10%; US & Translation 20%; TV & Radio 15%; Film 20%.

Alan Brodie Representation Ltd
(incorporating **Michael Imison**
Playwrights Ltd)
211 Piccadilly, London W1V 9LD
☎020 7917 2871 Fax 020 7917 2872
Email info@alanbrodie.com

Contacts *Alan Brodie, Sarah McNair*

FOUNDED 1989. *Handles* theatre, film and TV scripts. No books. Preliminary letter plus professional recommendation and c.v. essential. No reading fee but s.a.e. required. *Commission* Home 10%; Overseas 15%.

Rosemary Bromley
Literary Agency
Avington, Near Winchester, Hampshire
SO21 1DB
☎01962 779656 Fax 01962 779656

Contact *Rosemary Bromley*

FOUNDED 1981. *Handles* non-fiction. Also scripts for TV and radio. No poetry or short stories. *Special interests* natural history, leisure, biography and cookery. No unsolicited mss. No fax enquiries. Send preliminary letter with full details. Enquiries unaccompanied by return postage will not be answered. CLIENTS Elisabeth Beresford, Linda Birch, Gwen Cherrell, Teresa Collard, Estate of Fanny Cradock, Glenn Hamilton, Cathy Hopkins, Keith West, Ron Wilson, John Wingate. *Commission* Home 10%; US 15%; Translation 20%.

Felicity Bryan★
2A North Parade, Banbury Road, Oxford
OX2 6LX
☎01865 513816 Fax 01865 310055

Contact *Felicity Bryan*

FOUNDED 1988. *Handles* fiction of various types and non-fiction with emphasis on history, biography, science and current affairs. No scripts for TV, radio or theatre. No crafts, how-to, science fiction or light romance. No unsolicited mss. Best approach by letter. No reading fee. CLIENTS Karen Armstrong, Humphrey Carpenter, John Charmley, Liza Cody, Artemis Cooper, Angela

Huth, Diarmaid MacCulloch, James Naughtie, John Julius Norwich, Iain Pears, Rosamunde Pilcher, Matt Ridley, Miriam Stoppard, Roy Strong. *Commission* Home 10%; US & Translation 20%. *Overseas associates* Andrew Nurnberg, Europe; several agencies in US.

Peter Bryant (Writers)
94 Adelaide Avenue, London SE4 1YR
☎020 8691 9085 Fax 020 8692 9107
Contact *Peter Bryant*

FOUNDED 1980. *Special interests* animation, children's fiction and TV sitcoms. Also *handles* drama scripts for theatre, radio, film and TV. No reading fee for these categories but return postage essential for all submissions. CLIENTS include Isabelle Amycs, Joe Boyle, Andrew Brenner, Jimmy Hibbert, Penny Lloyd, Allan Plenderleith, Ruth Silvestre, Peter Symonds, George Tarry. *Commission* 10%. *Overseas associate* Hartmann & Stauffacher, Germany.

Juliet Burton Literary Agency
2 Clifton Avenue, London W12 9DR
☎020 8762 0148 Fax 020 8743 8765
Contact *Juliet Burton*

FOUNDED 1999. *Handles* fiction and non-fiction. *Special interests* crime and women's fiction. No plays, film scripts, articles, poetry or academic material. No reading fee. Approach in writing in the first instance; send synopsis and two sample chapters with s.a.e. No unsolicited mss. *Commission* Home 10%; US & Translation 20%.

Campbell Thomson & McLaughlin Ltd★
1 King's Mews, London WC1N 2JA
☎020 7242 0958 Fax 020 7242 2408
Contacts *John McLaughlin, Charlotte Bruton*

FOUNDED 1931. *Handles* fiction and general non-fiction, excluding children's. No plays, film/TV scripts, articles, short stories or poetry. No unsolicited mss or synopses. Preliminary letter with s.a.e. essential. No reading fee. *Overseas associates* Fox Chase Agency, Pennsylvania; Raines & Raines, New York.

Capel & Land
See **Simpson Fox**

Casarotto Ramsay and Associates Ltd
National House, 60–66 Wardour Street, London W1V 3HP
☎020 7287 4450 Fax 020 7287 9128

Email agents@casarotto.uk.com
Film/TV/Radio *Jenne Casarotto, Tracey Smith, Rachel Swann, Charlotte Kelly*
Stage *Tom Erhardt, Mel Kenyon*
(**Books** handled by **Lutyens and Rubinstein**)

Took over the agency responsibilities of Margaret Ramsay Ltd in 1992, incorporating a strong client list, with names like Alan Ayckbourn, Caryl Churchill, Willy Russell and Muriel Spark. *Handles* scripts for TV, theatre, film and radio. No unsolicited material without preliminary letter. CLIENTS include J. G. Ballard, Edward Bond, Simon Callow, David Hare, Terry Jones, Neil Jordan, Willy Russell, David Yallop. *Commission* Home 10%; US & Translation 20%. *Overseas associates* worldwide.

Celia Catchpole
56 Gilpin Avenue, London SW14 8QY
☎020 8255 7200 Fax 020 8288 0653
Contact *Celia Catchpole*

FOUNDED 1996. *Handles* children's books – artists and writers. No TV, film, radio or theatre scripts. No unsolicited mss. *Commission* Home 10% (writers) 15% (artists); US & Translation 20%. Works with associate agents abroad.

Chapman & Vincent
The Mount, Sun Hill, Royston, Hertfordshire SG8 9AT
☎01763 245005 Fax 01763 243033
Contacts *Jennifer Chapman, Gilly Vincent*

A small agency whose clients come mainly from personal recommendation. The agency aims to look after only a small number of predominantly non-fiction writers and is not actively seeking clients but happy to consider really original work. Does not handle poetry, children's books or genre fiction. Please do not telephone or submit by fax. Write with two sample chapters and enclose s.a.e. CLIENTS include George Carter, Leslie Geddes-Brown, Sara George, Rowley Leigh, John Miller, Dorit Peleg. *Commission* Home 15%; US & Europe 20%.

Mic Cheetham Literary Agency
11–12 Dover Street, London W1X 3PH
☎020 7495 2002 Fax 020 7495 5777
Contact *Mic Cheetham*

ESTABLISHED 1994. *Handles* general and literary fiction, crime and science fiction, and non-fiction. No film/TV scripts apart from existing clients. No children's, illustrated books or poetry. No unsolicited mss. Approach in writing with publishing history, first two chapters and return postage. No reading fee. CLIENTS include Iain Banks, Carol Birch, Anita Burgh, Laurie Graham, Toby Litt, Ken MacLeod, China Miéville, Antony Sher. *Commission* Home 10%; US & Translation 20%. Works with **The Marsh Agency** for all translation rights.

Judith Chilcote Agency★

8 Wentworth Mansions, Keats Grove, London NW3 2RL
☎020 7794 3717 Fax 020 7794 7431
Contact *Judith Chilcote*

FOUNDED 1990. *Handles* commercial fiction, TV tie-ins, health and nutrition, sport, cinema, self-help, popular psychology, biography and autobiography, cookery and current affairs. No academic, science fiction, children's, short stories, film scripts or poetry. No approaches by e-mail. Send letter with c.v., synopsis, three chapters and s.a.e. for return. No reading fee. *Commission* Home 15%; Overseas 20–25%.

Teresa Chris Literary Agency

43 Musard Road, London W6 8NR
☎020 7386 0633
Contact *Teresa Chris*

FOUNDED 1989. *Handles* crime, general, women's, commercial and literary fiction, and non-fiction: health, travel, cookery, lifestyle, sport and fitness, gardening, etc. *Specialises* in crime fiction and commercial women's fiction. No scripts. Film and TV rights handled by co-agent. No poetry, short stories, fantasy, science fiction or horror. Unsolicited mss welcome. Send query letter with first two chapters plus two-page synopsis (*s.a.e. essential*) in first instance. No reading fee. CLIENTS include Susan Clark, Tamara McKinley, J. Wallis Martin, Marguerite Patten. *Commission* Home 10%; US 15%; Translation 20%. *Overseas associates* Thompson & Chris Literary Agency, USA; representatives in most other countries.

Mary Clemmey Literary Agency★

6 Dunollie Road, London NW5 2XP
☎020 7267 1290 Fax 020 7267 1290
Contact *Mary Clemmey*

FOUNDED 1992. *Handles* fiction and non-fiction – high-quality work with an international market. No science fiction, fantasy or children's books. TV, film, radio and theatre scripts from existing clients only. No unsolicited mss. Approach by letter only giving a description of the work in the first instance. S.a.e. essential. No reading fee. CLIENTS include Paul Gilroy, Sheila

Kitzinger, Ray Shell, Elaine Showalter, Prof. David Wiggins; US & Canadian clients: The Bukowski Agency, **Frederick Hill Associates**, Lynn C. Franklin Associates Ltd, The Miller Agency, Roslyn Targ Literary Agency Inc. *Commission* Home 10%; US & Translation 20%. *Overseas Associate* Elaine Markson Literary Agency, New York.

Jonathan Clowes Ltd★

10 Iron Bridge House, Bridge Approach, London NW1 8BD
☎020 7722 7674 Fax 020 7722 7677
Contacts *Ann Evans, Isobel Creed, Lisa Whadcock*

FOUNDED 1960. Pronounced 'clewes'. Now one of the biggest fish in the pond, and not really for the untried unless they are true high-flyers. Fiction and non-fiction, plus scripts. No textbooks or children's. *Special interests* situation comedy, film and television rights. No unsolicited mss; authors come by recommendation or by successful follow-ups to preliminary letters. CLIENTS David Bellamy, Len Deighton, Elizabeth Jane Howard, Doris Lessing, David Nobbs, Gillian White and the estate of Kingsley Amis. *Commission* Home & US 15%; Translation 19%. *Overseas associates* **Andrew Nurnberg Associates**; Sane Töregard Agency.

Elspeth Cochrane Personal Management

11–13 Orlando Road, London SW4 0LE
☎020 7622 0314 Fax 020 7622 5815
Contact *Elspeth Cochrane*

FOUNDED 1960. *Handles* fiction, non-fiction, biographies, screenplays. Subjects have included Richard Burton, Marlon Brando, Sean Connery, Clint Eastwood, Lord Olivier. Also scripts for all media, with special interest in drama. No unsolicited mss. Preliminary letter, synopsis and s.a.e. is essential in the first instance. CLIENTS include Royce Ryton, Robert Tanitch. *Commission* 12½% ('but this can change; the percentage is negotiable, as is the sum paid to the writer').

Rosica Colin Ltd

1 Clareville Grove Mews, London SW7 5AH
☎020 7370 1080 Fax 020 7244 6441
Contact *Joanna Marston*

FOUNDED 1949. *Handles* all full-length mss, plus theatre, film, television and sound broadcasting. Preliminary letter with return postage essential; writers should outline their writing credits and whether their mss have previously been submitted elsewhere. May take 3–4 months to consider full mss; synopsis preferred in the first instance. No reading fee. *Commission* Home 10%; US 15%; Translation 20%.

Conville & Walsh Limited
311 New Kings Road, London SW6 4RF
☎020 7731 8407/7720 7618
Email Patrick.Walsh@ukgateway.net

Directors *Clare Conville, Patrick Walsh*

ESTABLISHED 2000 by Clare Conville (ex-**A. P. Watt**) and Patrick Walsh (ex-**Christopher Little Literary Agency**). *Handles* literary and commercial fiction plus serious, narrative non-fiction. Particularly interested in first novelists. CLIENTS Mike Cordy, Steve Erikson, Colin and Jacqui Hawkins, Hector Macdonald, Harland Miller, Rebecca Ray, Patrick Redmond, Simon Singh, Isabel Wolff and the estate of Francis Bacon. *Commission* Home 15%; US & Translation 20%.

Jane Conway-Gordon★
1 Old Compton Street, London W1V 5PH
☎020 7494 0148 Fax 020 7287 9264

Contact *Jane Conway-Gordon*

FOUNDED 1982. Works in association with **Andrew Mann Ltd**. *Handles* fiction and general non-fiction, plus occasional scripts for TV/radio/theatre. No poetry or science fiction. Unsolicited mss welcome; preliminary letter and return postage essential. No reading fee. *Commission* Home 10%; US & Translation 20%. *Overseas associates* **McIntosh & Otis, Inc.**, New York; plus agencies throughout Europe and Japan.

Rupert Crew Ltd★
1A King's Mews, London WC1N 2JA
☎020 7242 8586 Fax 020 7831 7914
Email (correspondence only)
rupertcrew@compuserve.com

Contacts *Doreen Montgomery,*
Caroline Montgomery

FOUNDED 1927. International representation, handling volume and subsidiary rights in fiction and non-fiction properties. No plays or poetry, journalism or short stories. Preliminary letter and return postage essential. No reading fee. *Commission* Home 15%; Elsewhere 20%.

Curtis Brown Group Ltd★
Haymarket House, 28/29 Haymarket, London SW1Y 4SP
☎020 7396 6600 Fax 020 7396 0110
Email cb@curtisbrown.co.uk

Also at: 37 Queensferry Street, Edinburgh EH2 4QS
☎0131 225 1286/1288 Fax 0131 225 1290

Chairman *Paul Scherer*
Group Managing Director *Jonathan Lloyd*
Directors *Mark Collingbourne* (Finance), *Tim Curnow* (Joint MD, Australia), *Fiona Inglis* (Joint MD, Australia)
Books, London *Jonathan Lloyd, Anna Davis, Jonny Geller, Hannah Griffiths, Ali Gunn, Camilla Hornby, Anthea Morton-Saner, Peter Robinson, Vivienne Schuster, Mike Shaw, Elizabeth Stevens*
Books, Edinburgh *Giles Gordon, Jane Bradish-Ellames*
Foreign Rights *Diana Mackay, Carol Jackson, Kate Cooper*
Film/TV/Theatre *Nick Marston* (MD, Talent Division), *Ben Hall, Peter Murphy, Philip Patterson*

Long-established literary agency, whose first sales were made in 1899. Merged with John Farquharson, forming the Curtis Brown Group Ltd in 1989. Also represents directors, designers, presenters and actors. *Handles* a wide range of subjects including fiction, general non-fiction, children's books and associated rights (including multimedia) as well as film, theatre, TV and radio scripts. Outline for non-fiction and short synopsis for fiction with two or three sample chapters and autobiographical note. No reading fee. Return postage essential. Also represents directors, designers, presenters and actors. *Commission* Home 10%; US & Translation 20%. *Overseas associates* in Australia, Canada and the US.

Judy Daish Associates Ltd
2 St Charles Place, London W10 6EG
☎020 8964 8811 Fax 020 8964 8966

Contacts *Judy Daish, Sara Stroud,*
Deborah Harwood

FOUNDED 1978. Theatrical literary agent. *Handles* scripts for film, TV, theatre and radio. No books. Preliminary letter essential. No unsolicited mss.

Caroline Davidson Literary Agency
5 Queen Anne's Gardens, London W4 1TU
☎020 8995 5768 Fax 020 8994 2770

Contact *Caroline Davidson*

FOUNDED 1988. *Handles* fiction and non-fiction, including archaeology, architecture, art, astronomy, biography, cookery, crafts, design, fitness, gardening, health, history, medicine, music, natural history, reference, science, self-help and how-to, TV tie-ins. Many highly illustrated books. Finished, polished first novels positively welcomed. No occult, short stories, children's, plays or poetry. Writers should send an initial letter giving details of the project, including the first 50 pages of their novel if a fiction writer, together with c.v. and return postage. Submissions without the latter are not considered or returned. CLIENTS include Susan Aldridge, Robert Baldock, Nigel Barlow, John Brackenbury, Elizabeth Bradley, Lisa Chaney, Stuart Clark, Andrew Dalby, Emma Donoghue, Robert Feather, Anissa Helou, Paul Hillyard, Tom Jaine, Adrian Lyttelton, Huon Mallalieu, Simon Nolan, Diane Purkiss. *Commission* US, Home, Commonwealth, Translation ·12½%; occasionally more (20%) if sub-agents are involved.

Merric Davidson Literary Agency

12 Priors Heath, Goudhurst, Cranbrook, Kent TN17 2RE
☎01580 212041 Fax 01580 212041
Email mdla@msn.com

Contacts *Merric Davidson, Wendy Suffield*

FOUNDED 1990. *Handles* fiction, general non-fiction and children's books. No scripts. No academic, short stories or articles. Particularly keen on contemporary fiction. No unsolicited mss. Send preliminary letter with synopsis and biographical details. S.a.e. essential for response. No reading fee. CLIENTS include Valerie Blumenthal, Alys Clare, Francesca Clementis, Murray Davies, Harold Elletson, Alison Habens, Frankie Park, Mark Pepper, Luke Sutherland. *Commission* Home 10%; US 15%; Translation 20%.

Felix de Wolfe

Garden Offices, 51 Maida Vale, London W9 1SD
☎020 7289 5770 Fax 020 7289 5731

Contact *Felix de Wolfe*

FOUNDED 1938. *Handles* quality fiction only, and scripts. No non-fiction or children's. No unsolicited mss. No reading fee. CLIENTS include Jan Butlin, Robert Cogo-Fawcett, Brian Glover, Sheila Goff, John Kershaw, Bill MacIlwraith, Angus Mackay, Gerard McLarnon, Braham Murray, Julian Slade, Malcolm Taylor, David Thompson, Paul Todd, Dolores Walshe. *Commission* Home 12½%; US 20%.

Dorian Literary Agency (DLA)

Upper Thornehill, 27 Church Road, St Marychurch, Torquay, Devon TQ1 4QY
☎01803 312095 Fax 01803 312095

Contact *Dorothy Lumley*

FOUNDED 1986. *Handles* mainstream and commercial full-length adult fiction; specialities are women's (including contemporary and sagas), crime and thrillers; horror, science fiction and fantasy. Also, limited non-fiction: primarily self-help and media-related subjects; plus scripts for TV and radio. No poetry, children's, theatrical scripts, short stories, academic or technical. Introductory letter with synopsis/outline and first chapter (with return postage) only please. Equiries or submissions by fax or e-mail will not be acceptable. No reading fee. CLIENTS include Gillian Bradshaw, Stephen Jones, Brian Lumley, Amy Myers, Dee Williams. *Commission* Home 10%; US 15%; Translation 20–25%. Works with agents in most countries for translation.

Anne Drexl

8 Roland Gardens, London SW7 3PH
☎020 7244 9645

Contact *Anne Drexl*

FOUNDED 1988. *Handles* commercially orientated women's fiction. Ideas welcome for business-related books. Strong interest in juvenile fiction. Writers should approach with preliminary letter and synopsis (including s.a.e.). No reading fee. *Commission* Home 12½%; US & Translation 20% (but varies depending on agent used).

Toby Eady Associates Ltd

9 Orme Court, London W2 4RL
☎020 7792 0092 Fax 020 7792 0879
Email toby@tobyeady.demon.co.uk *or*
  jessica@tobyeady.demon.co.uk

Contacts *Toby Eady, Jessica Woollard*

Handles fiction, and non-fiction. No film/TV scripts or poetry. *Special interests* China, Middle East, Africa, India. Approach by personal recommendation, letter. CLIENTS Jung Chang, Fadia Faqir, Ma Jian, David Landau, Kenan Makiya, Nuha Al Radi, Lin Ping, Amir Taheri, Xinran Xue, Bernard Cornwell, Mark Burnell, Julia Blackburn, Fiammetta Rocco, Francesca Marciano, Kuki Gallmann, John Carey, Shyama Perera, Ann Wroe. *Commission* Home 10–15%; Elsewhere 20%. *Overseas associates* USA – Ed Breslin; France – La Nouvelle Agence; Germany – Mohrbooks; Holland –

Jan Michael; Scandinavia, Italy, Spain – Rosie Buckman; China – Joanne Wang.

Eddison Pearson Ltd
3rd Floor, 22 Upper Grosvenor Street, London W1X 9PB
☎020 7629 2414 Fax 020 7629 7181
Email box1@eddisonpearson.com
Contact *Clare Pearson*

FOUNDED 1995. *Handles* literary fiction and non-fiction, contemporary fiction, children's books, poetry for the literary market. Please enquire in writing, enclosing s.a.e. E-mail enquiries also welcome. No unsolicited mss. No reading fee. *Commission* Home 10%; US & Translation 15%.

Edwards Fuglewicz★
49 Great Ormond Street, London WC1N 3HZ
☎020 7405 6725 Fax 020 7405 6726
Contacts *Ros Edwards, Helenka Fuglewicz*

FOUNDED 1996. *Handles* fiction (literary and commercial); non-fiction: biography, current affairs, business books, music and film. No scripts. Unsolicited mss welcome; approach in writing in the first instance with covering letter giving brief c.v., up to three chapters and a synopsis (enclose s.a.e. for return of mss); disks and e-mail submissions not acceptable. No reading fee. *Commission* Home 10%; US & Translation 20%.

Faith Evans Associates★
27 Park Avenue North, London N8 7RU
☎020 8340 9920 Fax 020 8340 9910
Contact *Faith Evans*

FOUNDED 1987. Small agency. *Handles* fiction and non-fiction. New clients by personal recommendation only; no unsolicited mss or phone calls, please. CLIENTS include Melissa Benn, Madeleine Bourdouxhe, Eleanor Bron, Caroline Conran, Helen Falconer, Midge Gillies, Ed Glinert, Saeed Jaffrey, Helena Kennedy, Cleo Laine, Seumas Milne, Tom Paulin, Christine Purkis, Sheila Rowbotham, Lorna Sage, Hwee Hwee Tan, Marion Urch, Harriet Walter, Elizabeth Wilson, Andrea Weiss. *Commission* Home 15%; US & Translation 20%. *Overseas associates* worldwide.

Lisa Eveleigh Literary Agency★
26a Rochester Square, London NW1 9SA
☎020 7267 5245 Fax 020 7485 6960
Email eveleigh@dial.pipex.com
Contact *Lisa Eveleigh*

FOUNDED 1996. *Handles* literary and commercial fiction and non-fiction. No scripts, science fiction or historical fiction. *Specialises* in rock biography, health and astrology. Unsolicited mss welcome; preliminary letter with synopsis (plus three chapters for fiction) and return postage required. No reading fee. CLIENTS include Christina Balit, Philip Casey, Mary Flanagan, Paul Heiney, Lisa Kopper, Irma Kurtz, Margaret Leroy, Libby Purves, Grace Wynne-Jones. *Commission* Home 10%; US & Translation 20%. *Associates* Translation: **Gillon Aitken Associates Ltd**; US: Anderson Grinberg Literary Management.

John Farquharson★
See **Curtis Brown Group Ltd**

Film Rights Ltd
See **Laurence Fitch Ltd**

Laurence Fitch Ltd
483 Southbank House, Black Prince Road, Albert Embankment, London SE1 7SJ
☎020 7735 8171 Fax 020 7582 6046
Contact *Brendan Davis*

FOUNDED 1952, incorporating the London Play Company (1922) and in association with Film Rights Ltd (1932). *Handles* scripts for theatre, film, TV and radio only. No unsolicited mss. Send synopsis with sample scene(s) in the first instance. No reading fee. CLIENTS include Carlo Ardito, Hindi Brooks, John Chapman & Ray Cooney, John Graham, Glyn Robbins, Gene Stone, the estate of Dodie Smith, Edward Taylor. *Commission* UK 10%; Overseas 15%. *Overseas associates* worldwide.

Jill Foster Ltd
9 Barb Mews, Brook Green, London W6 7PA
☎020 7602 1263 Fax 020 7602 9336
Email agents@jfl.uninet.co.uk
Contacts *Jill Foster, Alison Finch, Ann Foster, Simone Bassi, Ali Howarth, Simon Williamson*

FOUNDED 1976. *Handles* scripts for TV, drama and comedy. No fiction, short stories or poetry. No unsolicited mss; approach by letter in the first instance. No reading fee. CLIENTS include Colin Bostock-Smith, Jan Etherington and Gavin Petrie, Phil Ford, Rob Gittins, Julia Jones, Peter Tilbury, Peter Tinniswood, Susan Wilkins. *Commission* Home 12½%; US & Translation 15%.

Fox & Howard Literary Agency

4 Bramerton Street, London SW3 5JX
☎020 7352 8691 Fax 020 7352 8691
Contacts *Chelsey Fox, Charlotte Howard*
FOUNDED 1992. A small agency, specialising in non-fiction, that prides itself on 'working closely with its authors'. *Handles* biography, history and popular culture, reference, business, gardening, mind, body and spirit, self-help, health. No scripts. No poetry, plays, short stories, children's, science fiction, fantasy and horror. No unsolicited mss; send letter, synopsis and sample chapter with s.a.e. for response. No reading fee. CLIENTS Sarah Bartlett, Simon Collin, Professor Bruce King, Tony Clayton Lea, Marion Shoard, Mary Stewart, Jane Struthers. *Commission* Home 10–15%; US & Translation 20%.

French's

9 Elgin Mews South, London W9 1JZ
☎020 7266 3321 Fax 020 7286 6716
Contact *Mark Taylor*
FOUNDED 1973. *Handles* fiction and non-fiction; and scripts for all media. No religious or medical books. No unsolicited mss. 'For unpublished authors we offer a reading service at £60 per ms, exclusive of postage.' Interested authors should write in the first instance. *Commission* Home 10%.

Futerman, Rose & Associates★

17 Deanhill Road, London SW14 7DQ
☎020 8286 4860 Fax 020 8286 4861
Email GRose17@aol.com
Website www.caso.clara.net
Academic/Politics/Current Affairs
  Vernon Futerman
Music/Art *Alexandra Groom*
Fiction/Show Business/TV & Film
  Scripts *Guy Rose*
Theatre Scripts *Christopher Oxford*
FOUNDED 1984. Formerly Vernon Futerman Associates. *Handles* fiction and non-fiction, including biography, show business, music, art, politics; also scripts for TV, film and theatre. No unsolicited mss; send preliminary letter with a brief resumé, detailed synopsis and s.a.e. CLIENTS include Lorraine Chase, Valerie Grosvenor Myer, Susan George, Diana Douglas Darrid, Alexander Connor, Nigel St John Groom, Sir Martin Ewans, Hon. Kingsley Fielding, Angus Graham-Campbell, Angela Meredith, Sue Lenier, Joseph Miller, Aubrey Dillon-Malone, Russell Warren Howe, Judy Upton, Simon Woodham, Peter King, Professor Wu Ningkun,

Sally Becker. *Commission* Literature: Home 12½%; Overseas: 17½%. Drama/Screenplays: Home 15%; Overseas 20%. *Overseas associates* USA, Canada, Australia, South Africa, France, Germany, Austria, Switzerland.

Jüri Gabriel

35 Camberwell Grove, London SE5 8JA
☎020 7703 6186 Fax 020 7703 6186
Contact *Jüri Gabriel*
Handles quality fiction, non-fiction and (almost exclusively for existing clients) film, TV and radio rights/scripts. Jüri Gabriel worked in television, wrote books for 20 years and is chairman of **Dedalus** publishers. No short stories, articles, verse or books for children. Unsolicited mss ('two-page synopsis and three sample chapters in first instance, please') welcome if accompanied by return postage and letter giving sufficient information about author's writing experience, aims, etc. CLIENTS include Nigel Cawthorne, Diana Constance, Stephen Dunn, Miriam Dunne, Pat Gray, Duncan Green, James Hawes, Robert Irwin, Mike Jay, Mark Lloyd, David Madsen, David Miller, Prof. Cedric Mims, John Outram, Dr Stefan Szymanski, Dr Terence White, John Wyatt, Dr Robert Youngson. *Commission* Home 10%; US & Translation 20%.

Eric Glass Ltd

28 Berkeley Square, London W1X 6HD
☎020 7629 7162 Fax 020 7499 6780
Contact *Janet Glass*
FOUNDED 1934. *Handles* fiction, non-fiction and scripts for publication or production in all media. No poetry, short stories or children's works. No unsolicited mss. No reading fee. CLIENTS include Marc Camoletti, Charles Dyer and the estates of Rodney Ackland, Jean Cocteau, Philip King, Wolf Mankowitz, Robin Maugham, Beverley Nichols, Jack Popplewell, Jean-Paul Sartre, Arthur Schnitzler. *Commission* Home 10%; US & Translation 20% (to include sub-agent's fee). *Overseas associates* in the US, Australia, France, Germany, Greece, Holland, Italy, Japan, Poland, Scandinavia, South Africa, Spain.

Global Writers' & Authors' Guild

157 Gloucester Road South, Kensington, London SW7 4TH
Email globalwriters_authorsguild@hotmail.com
password: globalwriters
Director *Lady Bilek von Sternberg*
Chief Executive *Andrew Dempsey*
FOUNDED in 1997 in the Czech Republic.

Worldwide theatrical film and literary agency with offices in Prague, Vienna, Budapest and Munich. *Handles* film, TV, stage scripts, non-fiction and general fiction, especially crime, suspense, drama, murder, mysteries, adventure, thrillers. 'GWAG is always interested in hearing from new and previously unpublished authors.' Approach in writing only. Reading/assessment fee £75. *Commission* Home 10–15%; US 20%.

David Godwin Associates

55 Monmouth Street, London WC2H 9DG
☎020 7395 6110 Fax 020 7240 9992

Contacts *David Godwin, Penny Jones*

FOUNDED 1996. *Handles* literary and general fiction, non-fiction, biography. No scripts, science fiction or children's. No reading fee. Send covering letter with first three chapters. *Commission* Home 10%; Overseas 20%.

Annette Green Authors' Agent

6 Montem Street, London N4 3BE
☎020 7281 0009 Fax 020 7686 5884
Email agreen@literaryagency.freeserve.co.uk

Contact *Material should be addressed to the Company*

FOUNDED 1998. *Handles* literary and general fiction and non-fiction, upmarket popular culture, biography and memoirs. No dramatic scripts, poetry, or children's. Preliminary letter and s.a.e. essential. No reading fee. CLIENTS include Nick Barlay, Bill Broady, Max Kinnings, Maria McCann, Ian Marchant. *Commission* Home 15%; US & Translation 20%.

Christine Green Authors' Agent★

40 Doughty Street, London WC1N 2LF
☎020 7831 4956 Fax 020 7405 3935

Contact *Christine Green*

FOUNDED 1984. *Handles* fiction (general and literary) and general non-fiction. No scripts, poetry or children's. No unsolicited mss; initial letter and synopsis preferred. No reading fee but return postage essential. *Commission* Home 10%; US & Translation 20%.

Louise Greenberg★

The End House, Church Crescent, London N3 1BG
☎020 8349 1179 Fax 020 8343 4559
Email louisegreenberg@msn.com

Contact *Louise Greenberg*

FOUNDED 1997. *Handles* fiction and non-fiction; TV and film scripts. No poetry, health

or sport. No reading fee. Unsolicited mss welcome but send letter in first instance; s.a.e. essential. *Commission* Home 10%; US 15%; Translation 20%. *Dramatic associate* **Micheline Steinberg Playwrights' Agent**.

Greene & Heaton Ltd★

37 Goldhawk Road, London W12 8QQ
☎020 8749 0315 Fax 020 8749 0318

Contacts *Carol Heaton, Judith Murray, Antony Topping*

A small agency with a varied list of clients. *Handles* fiction (no science fiction, fantasy or children's books) and general non-fiction. No original scripts for theatre, film or TV. No reply to unsolicited submissions without s.a.e. and/or return postage. CLIENTS Mark Barrowcliffe, Geraldine Bedell, Bill Bryson, Kate Charles, Jan Dalley, Colin Forbes, Michael Frayn, P. D. James, Mary Morrissy, John Ramster, William Shawcross, Sarah Waters. *Commission* Home 10%; US & Translation 20%.

Gregory & Radice Authors' Agents★

3 Barb Mews, London W6 7PA
☎020 7610 4676 Fax 020 7610 4686
Email info@gregoryradice.co.uk

Contact *Jane Gregory*
Editorial *Lisanne Radice, Suzanne Amphlet*
Rights *Jane Barlow*

FOUNDED 1987. *Handles* full-length fiction and non-fiction. *Special interest* crime, suspense, thrillers, literary and commercial fiction, politics. 'We are particularly successful in selling foreign rights.' No original plays, film or TV scripts (only published books are sold to film and TV). No science fiction, fantasy, poetry, academic or children's books. No reading fee. Editorial advice given to own authors. No unsolicited mss; send a preliminary letter with synopsis and first three chapters (plus return postage). Short submissions by fax or e-mail. *Commission* Home 15%; Newspapers 20%; US & Translation 20%; Radio/TV/Film 15%. Is well represented throughout Europe, Asia and USA.

David Grossman Literary Agency Ltd

118b Holland Park Avenue, London W11 4UA
☎020 7221 2770 Fax 020 7221 1445

Contact *Address material to the Company*

FOUNDED 1976. *Handles* full-length fiction and general non-fiction – good writing of all kinds and anything healthily controversial. No verse or technical books for students. No original screenplays or teleplays (only works existing in volume form are sold for performance rights). Generally works with published writers of fiction only but 'truly original, well-written novels from beginners' will be considered. Best approach by preliminary letter giving full description of the work. All material must be accompanied by return postage. No approaches or submissions by fax or e-mail. No unsolicited mss. No reading fee. *Commission* Rates vary for different markets. *Overseas associates* throughout Europe, Asia, Brazil and the US.

Margaret Hanbury Literary Agency★

27 Walcot Square, London SE11 4UB
☎020 7735 7680 Fax 020 7793 0316
Email mhanbury@mhanbury.demon.co.uk

Contact *Margaret Hanbury*

Personally-run agency representing quality fiction and non-fiction. No plays, scripts, poetry, children's books, fantasy, horror. No unsolicited approaches at present. *Commission* Home 15%; Overseas 20%.

Roger Hancock Ltd

4 Water Lane, London NW1 8NZ
☎020 7267 4418 Fax 020 7267 0705
Email hancockltd@aol.com

Contact *Address material to the Company*

FOUNDED 1961. *Special interests* drama and light entertainment. Scripts only. No books. Unsolicited mss not welcome. Initial phone call required. No reading fee. *Commission* 10%.

A. M. Heath & Co. Ltd★

79 St Martin's Lane, London WC2N 4AA
☎020 7836 4271 Fax 020 7497 2561

Contacts *Bill Hamilton, Sara Fisher, Sarah Molloy, Victoria Hobbs*

FOUNDED 1919. *Handles* fiction, general non-fiction and children's. No dramatic scripts, poetry or short stories. Preliminary letter and synopsis essential. No reading fee. CLIENTS include Joan Aiken, Christopher Andrew, Bella Bathurst, Anita Brookner, Helen Cresswell, Patricia Duncker, Geoff Dyer, Katie Fforde, Lesley Glaister, Graham Hancock, Hilary Mantel, Hilary Norman, Susan Price, John Sutherland, Adam Thorpe, Barbara Trapido. *Commission* Home 10–15%; US & Translation 20%; Film & TV 15%. *Overseas associates* in the US, Europe, South America, Japan and the Far East.

Rupert Heath

Lindengasse 40, Nuremberg 90419 Germany
☎00 49 39 31067 Fax 00 49 39 31069
Email rupheath@hotmail.com

Contact *Rupert Heath*

FOUNDED 2000. In association with the **Andrew Lownie Literary Agency**. Rupert Heath works between Germany and London, with London-based administration/accounts office. *Handles* general fiction and non-fiction, mainly history, biography and autobiography, current affairs, popular science, the arts and some popular culture. No scripts, short stories, poetry or children's. Approach with e-mail or letter (synopsis, sample champter and s.a.e.). No reading fee. *Commission* Worldwide 15%.

Hermes *the Literary Agency*

5 Thames House, Manor House Lane, Datchet, Berkshire SL3 9EB
☎01753 620781

Contact *Susan Wells*

FOUNDED 1993. *Handles* full-length fiction only, *specialising* in the high-concept/techno-thriller genre – manuscripts and screenplays. Unsolicited, fully revised mss accepted with s.a.e. (also for acknowledgement), c.v., one-page synopsis, telephone numbers and copies of all rejections. No sample chapters or outlines. No reading fee. No telephone calls. CLIENTS include Sam Christopher. *Commission* Home 15%; US & Translation 20%; Motion Picture 20%.

David Higham Associates Ltd★

5–8 Lower John Street, Golden Square, London W1R 4HA
☎020 7437 7888 Fax 020 7437 1072

Scripts *Elizabeth Cree, Nicky Lund, Georgina Ruffhead, Gemma Hirst*
Books *Anthony Goff, Bruce Hunter, Jacqueline Korn, Caroline Walsh, Daniela Bernardelle*

FOUNDED 1935. *Handles* fiction and general non-fiction: biography, history, current affairs, etc. Also scripts. Preliminary letter with synopsis essential in first instance. No reading fee. CLIENTS include John le Carré, Stephen Fry, Jane Green, James Herbert, Jeremy Paxman. *Commission* Home 10%; US & Translation 20%.

Vanessa Holt Ltd★

59 Crescent Road, Leigh-on-Sea, Essex SS9 2PF
☎01702 473787 Fax 01702 471890
Email vanessa@holtlimited.freeserve.co.uk

Contact *Vanessa Holt*

FOUNDED 1989. *Handles* general fiction, non-fiction and non-illustrated children's books. No scripts, poetry, academic or technical. *Specialises* in crime fiction, commercial and literary fiction, and particularly interested in books with potential for sales abroad and/or to TV. No unsolicited mss. Approach by letter in first instance; s.a.e. essential. No reading fee. *Commission* Home 15%; US & Translation 20%; Radio/TV/Film 15%. Represented in all foreign markets.

Kate Hordern Literary Agency
18 Mortimer Road, Clifton, Bristol BS8 4EY
☎0117 9239368 Fax 0117 9731941

Contact *Kate Hordern*

FOUNDED 1999. *Handles* quality literary and commercial fiction including women's, suspense and genre fiction; also general non-fiction including history, cultural history, popular science. No children's books. Approach in writing in the first instance with details of project. Synopsis required for fiction; proposal/chapter breakdown for non-fiction. Sample chapters on request only. S.a.e. essential. No reading fee. CLIENTS Richard Bassett, Frances Chapman, Jeff Dawson, Paul Grieve. *Commission* Home 15%; US & Translation 20%. *Overseas associates* Carmen Balcells Agency, Spain; Synopsis Agency, Russia and various agencies in Asia.

Valerie Hoskins
20 Charlotte Street, London W1P 1HJ
☎020 7637 4490 Fax 020 7637 4493
Email ValerieHoskinsAss@compuserve.com

Contacts *Valerie Hoskins, Rebecca Watson*

FOUNDED 1983. *Handles* scripts for film, TV and radio. *Special interests* feature films, animation and TV. No unsolicited scripts; preliminary letter of introduction essential. No reading fee. *Commission* Home 12½%; US 20% (maximum).

Tanja Howarth Literary Agency★
19 New Row, London WC2N 4LA
☎020 7240 5553/7836 4142
Fax 020 7379 0969
Email tanja.howarth@virgin.net

Contact *Tanja Howarth*

FOUNDED 1970. Interested in taking on both fiction and non-fiction from British writers. No children's books, plays or poetry, but all other subjects considered providing the treatment is intelligent. *No unsolicited mss.* Preliminary letter preferred. No reading fee. Also an established agent for foreign literature, particularly from the German language. *Commission* Home 15%; Translation 20%.

ICM
Oxford House, 76 Oxford Street, London W1N 0AX
☎020 7636 6565 Fax 020 7323 0101

Contacts *Greg Hunt, Cathy King, Hugo Young, Michael McCoy, Alan Radcliffe, Sue Rodgers, Jessica Sykes*

FOUNDED 1973. *Handles* film, TV and theatre scripts. No books. No unsolicited mss. Preliminary letter essential. No reading fee. *Commission* 10%. *Overseas associates* ICM, New York/Los Angeles.

IMG Literary UK
The Pier House, Strand on the Green, Chiswick, London W4 3NN
☎020 8233 5000 Fax 020 8233 5001
IMG Literary US, 825 Seventh Avenue, Ninth Floor, New York, NY 10009
☎001 212 489 5400 Fax 001 212 246 1118

Chairman *Mark H. McCormack*

Agents *Sarah Wooldridge (UK), Mark Reiter, David McCormick, Carolyn Krupp (US), Fumiko Matsuki (Japan)*

Handles celebrity books, sports-related books, commercial fiction, non-fiction and how-to business books. No theatre, children's, poetry or academic books. *Commission* Home & US 20%; Elsewhere 25%.

Michael Imison Playwrights Ltd
See **Alan Brodie Representation Ltd**

Intercontinental Literary Agency
33 Bedford Street, London WC2E 9ED
☎020 7379 6611 Fax 020 7379 6790
Email ila@ila-agency.co.uk

Contacts *Anthony Guest Gornall, Nicki Kennedy, Jessica Buckman*

FOUNDED 1965. *Handles* translation rights only for, among others, the authors of **Peters Fraser & Dunlop**, London; **Lucas Alexander Whitley**, London; Harold Matson Co. Inc., New York.

International Copyright Bureau Ltd
22A Aubrey House, Maida Avenue, London W2 1TQ
☎020 7724 8034 Fax 020 7724 7662

Contact *Joy Westendarp*

FOUNDED 1905. Now mainly representing authors' estates and not taking on new clients. *Commission* Home 10%; US & Translation 19%. *Overseas agents* in New York and most foreign countries.

International Scripts

1 Norland Square, London W11 4PX
☎020 7229 0736 Fax 020 7792 3287

Contacts *Bob Tanner, Pat Hornsey, Jill Lawson*

FOUNDED 1979 by Bob Tanner. *Handles* most types of books (non-fiction and fiction) and scripts for most media. No poetry, articles or short stories. Preliminary letter plus s.a.e. required. CLIENTS include Zita Adamson, Simon Clark, Paul Devereux, Ed Gorman, Peter Haining, Julie Harris, Robert A. Heinlein, Anna Jacobs, Richard Laymon, Nick Oldham, Mary Ryan, John and Anne Spencer, Jerry Sykes, **Barrons** (USA), Masquerade Books (USA). *Commission* Home 15%; US & Translation 20%. *Overseas associates* include Ralph Vicinanza, USA; Thomas Schlück, Germany; Yanez, Spain; Eliane Benisti, France.

John Johnson (Authors' Agent) Limited★

Clerkenwell House, 45/47 Clerkenwell Green, London EC1R 0HT
☎020 7251 0125 Fax 020 7251 2172

Contacts *Andrew Hewson, Margaret Hewson, Elizabeth Fairbairn*

FOUNDED 1956. *Handles* general fiction and non-fiction. No science fiction, technical or academic material. Scripts from existing clients only. No unsolicited mss; send a preliminary letter and s.a.e. in the first instance. No reading fee. *Commission* Home 10%; US 15–20%; Translation 20%.

Jane Judd Literary Agency★

18 Belitha Villas, London N1 1PD
☎020 7607 0273 Fax 020 7607 0623

Contact *Jane Judd*

FOUNDED 1986. *Handles* general fiction and non-fiction: women's fiction, crime, thrillers, literary fiction, humour, biography, investigative journalism, health, women's interests and travel. 'Looking for good contemporary women's fiction but not Mills & Boon-type.' No scripts, academic, gardening or DIY. Approach with letter, including synopsis, first chapter and return postage. Initial telephone call helpful in the case of non-fiction. CLIENTS include Patrick Anthony, the John Brunner estate, Jillie Collings, Andy Dougan, Jill Mansell, Jonathon Porritt, Rosie Rushton, Manda Scott. *Commission* Home 10%; US & Translation 20%.

Juvenilia

Avington, Near Winchester, Hampshire SO21 1DB
☎01962 779656 Fax 01962 779656

Contact *Rosemary Bromley*

FOUNDED 1973. *Handles* young/teen fiction and picture books; non-fiction and scripts for TV and radio. No poetry or short stories unless part of a collection or picture book material. No unsolicited mss. Send preliminary letter with full details of work and biographical outline in first instance. Preliminary letters unaccompanied by return postage will not be answered. No enquiries by phone or fax. CLIENTS include Paul Aston, Elisabeth Beresford, Linda Birch, Denis Bond, Terry Deary, Steve Donald, Ann Evans, Gaye Hicyilmaz, Tom Holt, Tony Maddox, Phil McMylor, Elizabeth Pewsey, Saviour Pirotta, Eira Reeves, Kelvin Reynolds, James Riordan, Peter Riley, Malcolm Rose, Cathy Simpson, Margaret Stuart Barry, Keith West. *Commission* Home 10%; US 15%; Translation 20%.

Michelle Kass Associates★

36–38 Glasshouse Street, London W1R 5RH
☎020 7439 1624 Fax 020 7734 3394

Contacts *Michelle Kass, Tishna Molla, Emily Rosser*

FOUNDED 1991. *Handles* literary fiction and film primarily. Also TV, radio and theatre scripts. Approach with telephone call/explanatory letter in the first instance. No reading fee. *Commission* Home 10%; US & Translation 15–20%.

Frances Kelly★

111 Clifton Road, Kingston upon Thames, Surrey KT2 6PL
☎020 8549 7830 Fax 020 8547 0051

Contact *Frances Kelly*

FOUNDED 1978. *Handles* non-fiction, including illustrated: biography, history, art, self-help, food & wine, complementary medicine and therapies, New Age; and academic non-fiction in all disciplines. No scripts except for existing clients. No unsolicited mss. Approach by letter with brief description of work or synopsis, together with c.v. and return postage. *Commission* Home 10%; US & Translation 20%.

Paul Kiernan

PO Box 120, London SW3 4LU
☎020 7352 5562 Fax 020 7351 5986

Contact *Paul Kiernan*

FOUNDED 1990. *Handles* fiction and non-fiction, including autobiography and biography, plus specialist writers like cookery or gardening. Also scripts for TV, film, radio and theatre (TV and film scripts from book-writing clients only). No unsolicited mss. Preferred approach is by letter or personal introduction. Letters should include synopsis and brief biography. No reading fee. CLIENTS include K. Banta, Lord Chalfont, Ambassador Walter J. P. Curley, Sir Paul Fox. *Commission* Home 15%; US 20%.

Knight Features

20 Crescent Grove, London SW4 7AH
☎020 7622 1467 Fax 020 7622 1522

Contacts *Peter Knight, Gaby Martin, Ann King-Hall, Andrew Knight*

FOUNDED 1985. *Handles* motor sports, cartoon books, puzzles, business, history, factual and biographical material. No poetry, science fiction or cookery. No unsolicited mss. Send letter accompanied by c.v. and s.a.e. with synopsis of proposed work. CLIENTS include Frank Dickens, Christopher Hilton, Gray Jolliffe, Angus McGill, Barbara Minto, Frederic Mullally. *Commission* dependent upon authors and territories. *Overseas associates* United Media, US; Auspac Media, Australia.

Labour and Management Limited (tricia sumner – literary agency)

Milton House, Milton Street, Waltham Abbey, Essex EN9 1EZ
☎01992 711511/614527
Fax 01992 711511.614527
Email TriciaSumner@email.msn.com

Contact *Tricia Sumner*

FOUNDED 1995. *Specialises* in literary fiction, biography, general non-fiction, theatre, TV, radio and film. *Special interests* in multi-cultural, gay, feminist and anti-establishment writing. No unsolicited mss. Covering letter and brief synopsis and sample chapters essential, together with s.a.e. No reading fee. CLIENTS include Marion Baraitser, Richard Doyle, John R. Gordon, Barry Grossman, Sophia Kingshill, Roland Moore, Catherine Muschamp, Adrian Sellars. *Commission* Home 12½%; Overseas 20%.

Cat Ledger Literary Agency★

33 Percy Street, London W1P 9FG
☎020 7436 5030 Fax 020 7631 4273

Contact *Cat Ledger*

FOUNDED 1996. *Handles* non-fiction: popular culture – film, music, sport, travel, humour,

biography, politics; investigative journalism; fiction (non-genre). No scripts. No children's, poetry, fantasy, science fiction, romance. No unsolicited mss; approach with preliminary letter, synopsis and s.a.e. No reading fee. *Commission* Home 10%; US & Translation 20%.

Barbara Levy Literary Agency★

64 Greenhill, Hampstead High Street, London NW3 5TZ
☎020 7435 9046 Fax 020 7431 2063

Contacts *Barbara Levy, John Selby*

FOUNDED 1986. *Handles* general fiction, non-fiction and film and TV rights. No unsolicited mss. Send detailed preliminary letter in the first instance. No reading fee. *Commission* Home 10%; US 20%; Translation by arrangement, in conjunction with **The Marsh Agency**. *US associate* Arcadia Ltd, New York.

Limelight Management★

33 Newman Street, London W1P 3PD
☎020 7637 2529 Fax 020 7637 2538
Email limelight.management@virgin.net

Contacts *Fiona Lindsay, Linda Shanks*

FOUNDED 1991. *Handles* general non-fiction and fiction books; cookery, gardening, antiques, interior design, wine, art and crafts and health. No TV, film, radio or theatre. Not interested in science fiction, short stories, plays, children's. *Specialises* in illustrated books. Unsolicited mss welcome; send preliminary letter (s.a.e. essential). No reading fee. *Commission* Home 15%; US & Translation 20%.

Litopia® Corporation Ltd

186 Bickenhall Mansions, Bickenhall Street, London W1H 3DE
☎020 7224 1748 Fax 020 7224 1802
Email enquiries@litopia.com
Website www.litopia.com

Managing Director *Peter Cox*

FOUNDED in 1993 by author Peter Cox to manage a restricted number of clients. 'We are prepared to consider any author, known or unknown, with major international potential.' Sells directly to key overseas markets with particular emphasis on the USA. 'Litopia personnel visit New York once a month.' No radio or theatre scripts. No unsolicited mss; prospective clients must follow the submissions procedure as explained on Litopia's Website. No reading fee. CLIENTS Stephen Twigg, Michelle Paver, Peggy Brusseau, Senator Orrin Hatch, Commodore Scott Jones, USN, Professor Jane Plant, CBE. *Commission* by negotiation.

The Christopher Little Literary Agency (1979)★

10 Eel Brook Studios, 125 Moore Park Road, London SW6 4PS

☎020 7736 4455 Fax 020 7736 4490

Email christopher@christopherlittle.net

Fiction/Non-fiction *Christopher Little*
Office Manager *Emma Schlesinger*

FOUNDED 1979. *Handles* commercial and literary full-length fiction, non-fiction. *Special interests* crime, thrillers, popular science and narrative, and investigative non-fiction. No poetry, plays, science fiction, fantasy, textbooks, illustrated children's books or short stories. No reading fee. Send detailed letter ('giving a summary of present and future intentions together with track record, if any'), synopsis and/or first two chapters and s.a.e. in first instance. CLIENTS include Marcus Berkmann, Harriet Castor, Mike Dash, John Gordon Davis, Ginny Elliot, John Emsley, Penny Faith, Caron Freeborn, Janet Gleeson, Brian Hall, Jamie Holland, Tom Holland, Vivien Kelly, Kristin Kenway, Alastair MacNeill, Robert Mawson, Darren O'Shaughnessy, Marcus Palliser, Ruriko Pilgrim, A. J. Quinnell, Candace Robb, Peter Rosenberg, J. K. Rowling, Laura Roychowdhuri, Alan Smith, Frank Tallis, Laura Thompson, John Watson, James Whitaker, John Wilson. *Commission* Home 15%; US, Canada, Translation, Motion Picture 20%.

London Independent Books

26 Chalcot Crescent, London NW1 8YD

☎020 7706 0486 Fax 020 7724 3122

Proprietor *Carolyn Whitaker*

FOUNDED 1971. A self-styled 'small and idiosyncratic' agency. *Handles* fiction and non-fiction reflecting the tastes of the proprietors. All subjects considered (except computer books and young children's), providing the treatment is strong and saleable. Scripts handled only if by existing clients. *Special interests* boats, travel, travelogues, commercial fiction. No unsolicited mss; letter, synopsis and first two chapters with return postage the best approach. No reading fee. *Commission* Home 15%; US & Translation 20%.

The Andrew Lownie Literary Agency★

17 Sutherland Street, London SW1V 4JU

☎020 7828 1274 Fax 020 7828 7608

Email lownie@globalnet.co.uk

Website www.andrewlownie.co.uk

Contact *Andrew Lownie*

FOUNDED 1988. *Specialises* in non-fiction, especially history, biography, current affairs, military history, UFOs, reference and packaging celebrities and journalists for the book market. Formerly a journalist, publisher and himself the author of 12 non-fiction books, Andrew Lownie's CLIENTS include Norma Major, Gloria Hunniford, Patrick MacNee, the Marquess of Bath, Ken Bates, Jeremy Thorpe, Sir John Mills, Juliet Barker, Timothy Good, Nick Pope, RIchard Rudgley, Alan Whicker, the Joyce Cary estate, Lawrence James, editors of the *Oxford Classical Dictionary* and *Cambridge Guide to Literature in English*, Guy Bellamy. Approach with letter, synopsis, sample chapter and s.a.e. Translation rights handled by **The Marsh Agency**. *Commission* Worldwide 15%.

Lucas Alexander Whitley★ (incorporating **Jacintha Alexander Associates**)

14 Vernon Street, London W14 0RJ

☎020 7471 7900 Fax 020 7471 7910

Email law@lawagency.co.uk

Contacts *Mark Lucas, Julian Alexander,*
Araminta Whitley, Roger Houghton,
Sally Hughes, Celia Hayley, Lucinda Cook,
Peta Nightingale

FOUNDED 1996. *Handles* full-length general and literary fiction and non-fiction. No plays, poetry, textbooks, children's books or fantasy. Film and TV scripts handled for established clients only. S.a.e. essential. No e-mailed submissions. *Commission* Home 15%; US & Translation 20%. *Overseas associates* worldwide.

Lutyens and Rubinstein★

231 Westbourne Park Road, London W11 1EB

☎020 7792 4855 Fax 020 7792 4833

Partners *Sarah Lutyens, Felicity Rubinstein*
Submissions *Susannah Godman*

FOUNDED 1993. *Handles* adult fiction and non-fiction books. No TV, film, radio or theatre scripts. Unsolicited mss accepted; send introductory letter, c.v., two chapters and return postage for all material submitted. No reading fee. *Commission* Home 10%; US & Translation 20%.

Duncan McAra

28 Beresford Gardens, Edinburgh EH5 3ES

☎0131 552 1558 Fax 0131 552 1558

Contact *Duncan McAra*

FOUNDED 1988. *Handles* fiction (literary fiction) and non-fiction, including art, architecture, archaeology, biography, military, travel and books of Scottish interest. Preliminary letter, synopsis and sample chapter (including return postage) essential. No reading fee. *Commission* Home 10%; Overseas by arrangement.

Bill McLean Personal Management
23B Deodar Road, London SW15 2NP
☎020 8789 8191
Contact *Bill McLean*
FOUNDED 1972. *Handles* scripts for all media. No books. No unsolicited mss. Phone call or introductory letter essential. No reading fee. CLIENTS include Dwynwen Berry, Graham Carlisle, Jeff Dodds, Jane Galletly, Patrick Jones, Lynn Robertson Hay, Tony Jordan, Bill Lyons, John Maynard, Michael McStay, Les Miller, Ian Rowlands, Jeffrey Segal, Ronnie Smith, Barry Thomas, Frank Vickery, Mark Wheatley. *Commission* Home 10%.

McLean and Slora Agency
20A Eildon Street, Edinburgh EH3 5JU
☎0131 556 3368 Fax 0131 624 4029
Contact *Barbara McLean*
FOUNDED 1996. *Handles* literary fiction; some non-fiction including biography. *Specialises* in books of Scottish interest. No science fiction, children's books, poetry or scripts. No unsolicited mss. Send preliminary letter, synopsis, sample chapter(s); s.a.e. essential. No initial reading fee. CLIENTS Tom Bryan, John Herdman, Ruari McLean. *Commission* Home 15%; US & Translation 20%.

Eunice McMullen
Children's Literary Agent Ltd
38 Clewer Hill Road, Windsor, Berkshire SL4 4BW
☎01753 830348 Fax 01753 833459
Contact *Eunice McMullen*
FOUNDED 1992. *Handles* all types of children's material from picture books to teenage fiction. Particularly interested in younger children's fiction and illustrated texts. Has 'an excellent' list of picture book illustrators. In need of strong picture book texts to pair with existing illustrators who don't write themselves. Authors with track record in this area only. *No unsolicited scripts.* CLIENTS include Wayne Anderson, Reg Cartwright, Richard Fowler, Charles Fuge, Adrian Henri, Simon James, Susie Jenkin-Pearce, Angela McAllister, Graham Oakley, Sue Porter, Susan Winter, David Wood. *Commission* Home 10%; US 15%; Translation 20%.

Andrew Mann Ltd★
1 Old Compton Street, London W1V 5PH
☎020 7734 4751 Fax 020 7287 9264
Email manscript@compuserve.com
Contacts *Anne Dewe, Tina Betts*
FOUNDED 1975. *Handles* fiction, general non-fiction and film, TV, theatre, radio scripts. No unsolicited mss. Preliminary letter, synopsis and s.a.e. essential. No reading fee. *Commission* Home 15%; US & Translation 20%. *Overseas associates* various.

Manuscript ReSearch
PO Box 33, Bicester, Oxfordshire OX6 7PP
☎01869 323447 Fax 01869 324096
Contact *Graham Jenkins*
FOUNDED 1988. Principally *handles* scripts suitable for film/TV outlets. Will only consider book submissions from established clients. Preferred first approach from new contacts is by letter with brief outline and s.a.e. *Commission* Home 10%; Overseas 20%.

Marjacq Scripts Ltd
34 Devonshire Place, London W1N 1PE
☎020 7935 9499 Fax 020 7935 9115
Email enquiries@marjacq.com
Website www.marjacq.com
Contact *Mark Hayward*
HANDLES general fiction and non-fiction, and screenplays. Special interest in crime, sagas and science fiction. No poetry, children's books or plays. Send synopsis and three chapters; will suggest revision for promising mss. No reading fee. *Commission* Home 10%; Overseas 20%.

The Marsh Agency★
11/12 Dover Street, London W1X 3PH
☎020 7399 2800 Fax 020 7399 2801
Email enquiries@marsh-agency.co.uk
Website www.marsh-agency.co.uk
Contacts *Paul Marsh, Susanna Nicklin*
FOUNDED 1994. International rights specialists. No TV, film, radio or theatre. No unsolicited mss. CLIENTS include several British and American agencies and publishers. *Commission* 10%.

Martinez Literary Agency
60 Oakwood Avenue, Southgate, London N14 6QL
☎020 8886 5829
Contacts *Mary Martinez, Francoise Budd*
FOUNDED 1988. *Handles* high-quality fiction, children's books, arts and crafts, interior design,

alternative health/complementary medicine, autobiography, biography, popular music, sport and memorabilia books. Not accepting any new writers. *Commission* Home 15%; US, Overseas & Translation 20%; Performance Rights 20%.

MBA Literary Agents Ltd★
62 Grafton Way, London W1P 5LD
☎020 7387 2076 Fax 020 7387 2042
Email agent@mbalit.co.uk

Contacts *Diana Tyler, John Richard Parker, Meg Davis, Laura Longrigg*

FOUNDED 1971. *Handles* fiction and non-fiction, TV, film, radio and theatre scripts. No poetry. Works in conjunction with agents in most countries. Also UK representative for **Writers House**, the Donald Maass Agency and the **Susan Schulman Agency**. No unsolicited mss. CLIENTS include Campbell Armstrong, A. L. Barker, estate of Harry Bowling, Jeffrey Caine, Glenn Chandler, Andrew Cowan, Patricia Finney, Maggie Furey, Sue Gee, the estate of B. S. Johnson, Paul J. McAuley, Anne McCaffrey, Sir Roger Penrose, Susan Oudot, Anne Perry, Gervaise Phinn, Iain Sinclair, Mark Wallington, Douglas Watkinson, Paul Wilson, Valerie Windsor. *Commission* Home 15%; Overseas 20%; Theatre/TV/Radio 10%; Film 10–20%.

Midland Exposure
4 Victoria Court, Oadby, Leicestershire LE2 4AF
☎0116 271 8332 Fax 0116 281 2188
Email partners@midlandexposure.co.uk
Website www.midlandexposure.co.uk

Partners *Cari Crook, Lesley Gleeson*

FOUNDED 1996. *Handles* short fiction for magazines only. *Specialises* in women's, teenage and children's magazine fiction. No books. 'Keen to encourage new writers.' Unsolicited mss welcome. Please ring for current reading fee. *Commission* Home 15–25%; US 20%.

Jay Morris & Co., Authors' Agents
Suite 112, 91 Western Road, Brighton, East Sussex BN1 2NW

Directors *Jay Morris (Managing), Professor Phillida Kanta (Children's Dept)*
Assistant Directors *Toby Tillyard-Burrows, Zoë Wasson*

FOUNDED 1994. *Handles* full-length mainstream commercial adult fiction: racy sagas, gay erotica, horror, children's fantasy, women in power (not women's issues), thrillers and crime. List full. Approaches come through personal recommendation. Unsolicited material not welcome. Reading fee charged. CLIENTS include Lord Douglas, Piers de Villias, Elika Rise, Dolores Denning. *Commission* Home 15%; Overseas 20%.

William Morris Agency (UK) Ltd★
1 Stratton Street, London W1X 6HB
☎020 7355 8500 Fax 020 7355 8600

Film/TV *Tanya Cohen*
Stage *Sophie Simpson*
Books *Stephanie Cabot*

FOUNDED 1965. Worldwide theatrical and literary agency with offices in New York, Beverly Hills and Nashville and associates in Sydney. *Handles* film, TV, stage scripts; fiction and general non-fiction. No unsolicited film, TV or stage material *at all*. Mss for books with preliminary letter. No reading fee. *Commission* Film/TV/Theatre/UK Books 10%; US Books & Translation 20%.

Michael Motley Ltd
42 Craven Hill Gardens, London W2 3EA
☎020 7723 2973 Fax 020 7262 4566

Contact *Michael Motley*

FOUNDED 1973. *Handles* all subjects, except science fiction, horror, short mss (e.g. journalism), poetry and original dramatic material. No unsolicited mss. No reading fee. CLIENTS include Simon Brett, Richard Denny, K. M. Peyton, Annette Roome, Barry Turner. *Commission* Home 10%; US 15%; Translation 20%. *Overseas associates* in all publishing centres.

The Narrow Road Company
182 Brighton Road, Coulsdon, Surrey CR5 2NF
☎020 8763 9895 Fax 020 8763 9329
Email narrowroad@freeuk.com

Contacts *Richard Ireson, Karen Pierce-Goulding, Amanda Colclough*

FOUNDED 1986. Part of the Narrow Road Group. Theatrical literary agency. *Handles* scripts for TV, theatre, film and radio. No novels or poetry. No unsolicited mss; approach by letter with c.v. and one-page synopsis. Interested in writers with some experience and original ideas. CLIENTS include David Halliwell, Sheila Kelley, Deepak Verma, Alex Lowe.

William Neill-Hall Ltd
Loganholm, Tiscott Hill, Stibb, Nr Bude, Cornwall EX23 9HL
☎01288 355335 Fax 01288 355335
Email wneill-hall@msn.com

Contact *William Neill-Hall*

FOUNDED 1995. *Handles* general non-fiction, religion. No TV, film, theatre or radio scripts; no fiction or poetry. *Specialises* in religion, sport, history and current affairs. No unsolicited mss. Approach by phone or letter. Enclose return postage. No reading fee. CLIENTS Mary Batchelor, Archbishop of Canterbury (George Carey), Richard Foster, Juliet Janvrin, Jennifer Rees Larcombe, Peter Owen-Jones, Heather Pinchen, David Pytches, Mary Pytches. *Commission* Home 10%; US 15%; Translation 20%.

New Authors Showcase
See entry under **Miscellany**

The Maggie Noach Literary Agency★
22 Dorville Crescent, London W6 0HJ
☎020 8748 2926 Fax 020 8748 8057
Email m-noach@dircon.co.uk
Contact *Maggie Noach*

FOUNDED 1982. Pronounced 'no-ack'. *Handles* a wide range of well-written books including general non-fiction, especially biography, commercial fiction and non-illustrated children's books for ages 7–12. No scientific, academic or specialist non-fiction. No poetry, plays, short stories or books for the very young. Recommended for promising young writers but *very* few new clients taken on as it is considered vital to give individual attention to each author's work. Unsolicited mss not welcome. Approach by letter (*not by telephone or e-mail*), giving a brief description of the book and enclosing a few sample pages. Return postage essential. No reading fee. *Commission* Home 15%; US & Translation 20%.

Andrew Nurnberg Associates Ltd★
Clerkenwell House, 45–47 Clerkenwell Green, London EC1R 0HT
☎020 7417 8800 Fax 020 7417 8812
Email all@nurnberg.co.uk
Directors *Andrew Nurnberg, Klaasje Mul, Sarah Nundy*

FOUNDED in the mid-1970s. *Specialises* in foreign rights, representing leading authors and agents. Branches in Moscow, Bucharest, Budapest, Prague, Sofia, Warsaw and Riga. *Commission* Home 15%; US & Translation 20%.

Alexandra Nye
44 Braemar Avenue, Dunblane, Perthshire FK15 9EB
☎01786 825114
Contact *Alexandra Nye*

FOUNDED 1991. *Handles* fiction and topical non-fiction. *Special interests* literary fiction, historicals and some children's (novels for 7–12 age range). Unsolicited mss welcome (s.a.e. essential for return). Preliminary approach by letter, with synopsis, preferred. Reading fee for supply of detailed report. CLIENTS Dr Tom Gallagher, Harry Mehta, Robin Jenkins. *Commission* Home 10%; US 20%; Translation 15%.

David O'Leary Literary Agents
10 Lansdowne Court, Lansdowne Rise, London W11 2NR
☎020 7229 1623 Fax 020 7727 9624
Email d.o'leary@virgin.net
Contact *David O'Leary*

FOUNDED 1988. *Handles* fiction, both popular and literary, and non-fiction. Areas of interest include thrillers, history, popular science, Russia and Ireland (history and fiction). No poetry or science fiction. No unsolicited mss but happy to discuss a proposal. Ring or write in the first instance. No reading fee. CLIENTS include James Barwick, David Crackanthorpe, James Kennedy, Jim Lusby, Gretta Mulrooney. *Commission* Home 10%; US 10%. *Overseas associates* Lennart Sane, Scandinavia/Spain/South America; Tuttle Mori, Japan.

Deborah Owen Ltd★
78 Narrow Street, Limehouse, London E14 8BP
☎020 7987 5119/5441 Fax 020 7538 4004
Contacts *Deborah Owen, Dawn Fozard*

FOUNDED 1971. Small agency specialising in representing authors direct around the world. *Handles* international fiction and non-fiction (books which can be translated into a number of languages). No scripts, poetry, science fiction, children's or short stories. No unsolicited mss. No new authors at present. CLIENTS include Penelope Farmer, Amos Oz, Ellis Peters, Charlie Ross, Delia Smith. *Commission* Home 10%; US & Translation 15%.

Owen Robinson Literary Agents
20 Tolbury Mill, Bruton, Somerset BA10 0DY
☎01749 812008 Fax 01749 812008
Email jpr@owenrobinson.netlineuk.net
Contact *Justin Robinson*

FOUNDED 1998. *Handles* fiction and non-fiction. No plays, film scripts, poetry or short stories. No reading fee (ms appraisal, copy editing and wordprocessing available on request). No unsolicited mss. Approach in writing with s.a.e. in the first instance; send synopsis and three sample chapters subsequently. CLIENTS include Michael Holt, Valerie Kershaw, Roger Nichols. *Commission* Home 10%; US & Translation 15–20%.

Mark Paterson & Associates★

10 Brook Street, Wivenhoe, Colchester, Essex CO7 9DS
☎01206 825433 Fax 01206 822990
Email info@mark.paterson.co.uk
Contacts *Mark Paterson, Mary Swinney, Penny Tyndale-Hardy*

FOUNDED 1961. World rights representatives of authors and publishers handling many subjects, with specialisation in psychoanalysis and psychotherapy. CLIENTS range from Balint, Bion, Casement and Ferenczi, through to Freud and Winnicott; plus Hugh Brogan, Peter Moss and the estates of Sir Arthur Evans, Hugh Schonfield and Dorothy Richardson. No fiction, scripts, poetry, children's, articles, short stories or 'unsaleable mediocrity'. No unsolicited mss, but preliminary letter and synopsis with s.a.e. welcome. *Commission* 20% (including sub-agent's commission).

John Pawsey

60 High Street, Tarring, Worthing, West Sussex BN14 7NR
☎01903 205167 Fax 01903 205167
Contact *John Pawsey*

FOUNDED 1981. Experience in the publishing business has helped to attract some top names here, but the door remains open for bright, new talent. *Handles* non-fiction: biography, politics, current affairs, show business, gardening, travel, sport, business and music; and fiction. Will consider any well-written novel except science fiction, fantasy and horror. *Special interests* sport, current affairs and popular fiction. No drama scripts, poetry, short stories, journalism or academic. Preliminary letter with s.a.e. essential. No reading fee. CLIENTS include Jonathan Agnew, Dr David Lewis, David Rayvern Allen, Patricia Hall, Elwyn Hartley Edwards, Peter Hobday, Jon Silverman. *Commission* Home 10–15%; US & Translation 19%. *Overseas associates* in the US, Japan, South America and throughout Europe.

Maggie Pearlstine Associates Ltd★

31 Ashley Gardens, Ambrosden Avenue, London SW1P 1QE
☎020 7828 4212 Fax 020 7834 5546
Email post@pearlstine.co.uk
Contact *Maggie Pearlstine*
FOUNDED 1989. Small, selective agency. *Handles*

general non-fiction and fiction. Special interest: history, current affairs, biography and health. No children's, poetry, horror, science fiction, short stories or scripts. Seldom takes on new authors. Prospective clients should write an explanatory letter and enclose s.a.e. and the first chapter only. No submissions accepted by fax, e-mail or from abroad. No reading fee. CLIENTS Debbie Beckerman, John Biffen, Matthew Baylis, Kate Bingham, Menzies Campbell, Kim Fletcher, Dr Frank Furedi, Uri Geller, Roy Hattersley, Rachel Holmes, Prof Lisa Jardine, Charles Kennedy, Mark Leonard, Prof Nicholas Lowe, Alex Parsons, Claire Macdonald, Dr Raj Persaud, Prof Lesley Regan, Hugo Rifkind, Jackie Rowley, Henrietta Spencer-Churchill, Alan Stewart, Jack Straw, Prof Robert Winston, Shaun Woodward. Translation rights handled by **Gillon Aitken Associates Ltd**. *Commission* Home 12½% (fiction), 10% (non-fiction); US & Translation 20%; TV, Film & Journalism 20%.

Pelican Literary Agency

3 Kirkwood Green, Lindley, Huddersfield, West Yorkshire HD3 3WN
Contact *Ray Lodge*

FOUNDED 1998. *Handles* fiction and general non-fiction – memoirs, autobiography, biography, erotica, travel and children's stories. No poetry, scripts, academic, manuals, cookery and crafts. No unsolicited mss. Send synopsis with one sample chapter with return postage. No reading fee. *Commission* Home 10%; US & Translation 15%.

Peters Fraser & Dunlop Group Ltd
See **PFD**

PFD★

Drury House, 34–43 Russell Street, London WC2B 5HA
☎020 7344 1000
Fax 020 7836 9539/7836 9541
Email postmaster@pfd.co.uk
Website www.pfd.co.uk

Joint Chairmen *Anthony Jones, Tim Corrie*
Managing Director *Anthony Baring*
Books *Caroline Dawnay, Michael Sissons, Pat Kavanagh, Charles Walker, Rosemary Canter, Robert Kirby, Simon Trewin, Annabel Hardman, James Gill*
  Serial *Pat Kavanagh, Carol MacArthur*
Film/TV *Anthony Jones, Tim Corrie, Norman North, Charles Walker, Vanessa Jones, St. John Donald, Rosemary Scoular, Natasha Galloway, Jago Irwin, Louisa Thompson*

Actors *Maureen Vincent, Ginette Chalmers, Dallas Smith, Lindy King, Ruth Young, Lucy Brazier, Chris Harris*
Theatre *Kenneth Ewing, St John Donald, Nicki Stoddart, Rosie Cobbe*
Children's *Rosemary Canter*
Multimedia *Rosemary Scoular*

FOUNDED 1988 as a result of the merger of A. D. Peters & Co. Ltd and Fraser & Dunlop, and was later joined by the June Hall Literary Agency. *Handles* all sorts of books including fiction and children's, plus scripts for film, theatre, radio and TV material. Prospective clients should write 'a full letter, with an account of what he/she has done and wants to do and enclose, when possible, a detailed outline and sample chapters'. Enclose s.a.e. No reading fee. CLIENTS include Julian Barnes, Alan Bennett, Alain de Botton, A. S. Byatt, estate of C. S. Forester, Nicci Gerard, Robert Harris, Nick Hornby, Clive James, Andrew Miller, Nancy Mitford, John Mortimer, Andrew Motion, Douglas Reeman, Ruth Rendell, Anthony Sampson, Gerald Seymour, Tom Stoppard, Emma Thompson, Joanna Trollope, estate of Evelyn Waugh. *Commission* Home 10%; US & Translation 20%.

Charles Pick Consultancy Ltd★
3/3 Bryanston Place, London W1H 7FN
☎020 7402 8043 Fax 020 7724 5990
Email 100551.3554@compuserve.com
Contacts *Martin Pick, Sandra Sljivic*

FOUNDED 1985. *Handles* Fiction and non-fiction general books. Deals only with scripts by existing clients. No unsolicited mss. Pefers an approach to be made on the recommendation of someone qualified in their field. Send preliminary letter with a short description/synopsis. CLIENTS Wilbur Smith, Peter O'Toole, Deirdre Purcell, Julie Parsons. *Commission* Home 15%; US & Translation 20%; Film 20%.

Laurence Pollinger Limited★
18 Maddox Street, London W1R 0EU
☎020 7629 9761 Fax 020 7629 9765
Email LaurencePollinger@compuserve.com
Contact *Gerald J. Pollinger*
Adult List *Lorella Belli*
Children's List *Lesley Hadcroft*
Permissions/Foreign Rights *Heather Chalcroft*

FOUNDED 1958. A successor of Pearn, Pollinger & Higham. *Handles* all types of general trade adult and children's fiction and non-fiction books; some screenwriting, electronic media and illustrators. CLIENTS include Michael Coleman, Michael Cox, Vera Chapman, Allan Frewin

Jones, Jonathan Gabay, Philip Gross, Gene Kemp, Adrienne Kennaway, Alan MacDonald, Gary Paulsen, Nicholas Rhea and Sue Welford. Also the estates of H. E. Bates, Erskine Caldwell, D. H. Lawrence, W. Heath Robinson, William Saroyan and other notables. Unsolicited material welcome if preceded by letter. *Commission* Home & US 15%; Translation 20%.

Shelley Power Literary Agency Ltd★
Le Montaud, 24220 Berbiguières, France
☎00 33 55329 6252 Fax 00 33 55329 6254
Email puissant@easynet.fr
Contact *Shelley Power*

FOUNDED 1976. Shelley Power works between London and France. This is an English agency with London-based administration/accounts office and the editorial office in France. *Handles* general commercial fiction, quality fiction, business books, self-help, true crime, investigative exposés, film and entertainment. No scripts, short stories, children's or poetry. Preliminary letter with brief outline of project (plus return postage as from UK or France) essential. 'We do not consider submissions by e-mail.' No reading fee. *Commission* Home 10%; US & Translation 19%.

PVA Management Limited
Hallow Park, Worcester WR2 6PG
☎01905 640663 Fax 01905 641842
Email pvamanltd@aol.com
Managing Director *Paul Vaughan*

FOUNDED 1978. *Handles* non-fiction only. Please send synopsis and sample chapters together with return postage. *Commission* 15%.

Radala & Associates
17 Avenue Mansions, Finchley Road, London NW3 7AX
☎020 7794 4495 Fax 020 7431 7636
Contacts *Richard Gollner, Neil Hornick, Anna Swan, Andy Marino*

FOUNDED 1970. *Handles* quality fiction, non-fiction, drama, performing and popular arts, psychotherapy. Also provides editorial services, initiates in-house projects and can recommend independent professional readers if unable to read or comment on submissions. No poetry or screenplays. Prospective clients should send a short letter plus synopsis (maximum 2pp), first two chapters (double-spaced, numbered pages) and s.a.e. for return. *Commission* Home 10%; US 15–20%; Translation 20%. *Overseas associates* **Writers House, Inc.** (Al Zuckerman), New York; plus agents throughout Europe.

Rogers, Coleridge & White Ltd★

20 Powis Mews, London W11 1JN
☎020 7221 3717 Fax 020 7229 9084

Contacts *Deborah Rogers, Gill Coleridge, Patricia White, David Miller*
Foreign Rights *Ann Warnford-Davis, Laurence Laluyaux*

FOUNDED 1967. *Handles* fiction, non-fiction and children's books. No poetry, plays or technical books. No unsolicited mss, please and no submissions by fax or e-mail. Rights representative in UK and translation for several New York agents. *Commission* Home 10%; US 15%; Translation 20%. *Overseas associates* ICM, New York.

Frederick Rosschild Security

55 Lark Way, Bradwell, Norfolk NR31 8SB
☎01493 443243

Contact *Frederick Rosschild*

FOUNDED 1994. *Handles* fiction and non-fiction. *Specialises* in political books. No scripts, religion or short stories. Unsolicited mss welcome; approach in writing – no telephone calls. *Commission* Home 12%; US 24%.

Hilary Rubinstein Books

32 Ladbroke Grove, London W11 3BQ
☎020 7792 4282 Fax 020 7221 5291

Contact *Hilary Rubinstein*

FOUNDED 1992. *Handles* fiction and non-fiction. No poetry or drama. Approach in writing in the first instance. No reading fee but return postage, please. CLIENTS Lucy Irvine, Eric Lomax, Donna Williams. *Commission* Home 10%; US & Translation 20%. *Overseas associates* **Ellen Levine Literary Agency** New York; **Andrew Nurnberg Associates** (European rights).

Uli Rushby-Smith Literary Agency

72 Plimsoll Road, London N4 2EE
☎020 7354 2718 Fax 020 7354 2718

Contacts *Uli Rushby-Smith*

FOUNDED 1993. *Handles* fiction and non-fiction, commercial and literary, both adult and children's. Film and TV rights handled in conjunction with a sub-agent. No plays or poetry. Approach with an outline, two or three sample chapters and explanatory letter in the first instance (s.a.e. essential). No reading fee. *Commission* Home 10%; US & Translation 20%. Represents UK rights for **Curtis Brown**, New York (children's) and 2.13.61 in the USA, Penguin (Canada), the Alice Toledo Agency (NL) and Columbia University Press.

Rosemary Sandberg Ltd

6 Bayley Street, London WC1B 3HB
☎020 7304 4110 Fax 020 7304 4109
Email rosemary@sandberg.demon.co.uk

Contact *Rosemary Sandberg*

FOUNDED 1991. In association with **Ed Victor Ltd**. *Handles* children's picture books and novels. *Specialises* in children's writers and illustrators. No unsolicited mss as client list is currently full. *Commission* 10%.

Tessa Sayle Agency★

11 Jubilee Place, London SW3 3TE
☎020 7823 3883 Fax 020 7823 3363

Books *Rachel Calder*
Film/TV *Jane Villiers, Matthew Bates*

Handles fiction: literary novels rather than category fiction; non-fiction: current affairs, social issues, travel, biographies, historical; TV and film scripts. No plays, poetry, children's, textbooks, science fiction, fantasy, horror or musicals. No unsolicited mss. Preliminary letter essential, including a brief biographical note and (for books) a synopsis and two or three sample chapters; (for scripts) an outline and sample pages. No reading fee. CLIENTS Books: Stephen Amidon, Peter Benson, Pete Davies, Margaret Forster, Georgina Hammick, Paul Hogarth, Andy Kershaw, Phillip Knightley, Rory MacLean, Denise Mina, Ann Oakley, Kate Pullinger, Ronald Searle, Gitta Sereny, William Styron, Chris Wallace, Mary Wesley. Drama: William Corlett, Shelagh Delaney, Marc Evans, John Forte, Stuart Hepburn, David Hilton, Chris Monger, Sue Townsend. *Commission* Home 10%; US & Translation 20%. *Overseas associates* Elaine Markson Literary Agency and Darhansoff & Verrill, USA; translation rights handled by **The Marsh Agency**.

Seifert Dench Associates

24 D'Arblay Street, London W1V 3FH
☎020 7437 4551 Fax 020 7439 1355
Website www.seifert-dench.co.uk

Contacts *Linda Seifert, Elizabeth Dench, Michelle Arnold*

FOUNDED 1972. *Handles* scripts for TV and film. Unsolicited mss will be read, but a letter with sample of work and c.v. (plus s.a.e.) is preferred. CLIENTS include Peter Chelsom, Tony Grisoni, Stephen Volk. *Commission* Home 10–15%. *Overseas associates* include: William Morris/Sanford Gross and C.A.A., Los Angeles.

The Sharland Organisation Ltd

The Manor House, Manor Street, Raunds,
Northamptonshire NN9 6JW
☎01933 626600 Fax 01933 624860
Email tsoshar@aol.com

Contacts *Mike Sharland, Alice Sharland*

FOUNDED 1988. *Specialises* in national and
international film and TV negotiations. Also
negotiates multimedia, interactive TV deals
and computer game contracts. *Handles* scripts
for film, TV, radio and theatre; also non-
fiction. Markets books for film and handles
stage, radio, film and TV rights for authors. No
scientific, technical or poetry. No unsolicited
mss. Preliminary enquiry by letter or phone
essential. *Commission* Home 15%; US &
Translation 20%. *Overseas associates* various.

Vincent Shaw Associates Ltd

20 Jay Mews, Kensington Gore, London
SW7 2EP
☎020 7581 8215 Fax 020 7225 1079
Email vincentshaw@clara.net

Contact *Vincent Shaw*

FOUNDED 1954. *Handles* TV, radio, film and
theatre scripts. Unsolicited mss welcome.
Approach in writing enclosing s.a.e. No phone
calls. *Commission* Home 10%; US & Translation by negotiation. *Overseas associate* Herman
Chessid, New York.

Sheil Land Associates Ltd★

43 Doughty Street, London WC1N 2LF
☎020 7405 9351 Fax 020 7831 2127
Email info@sheilland.co.uk

Agents, UK & US *Sonia Land, Luigi Bonomi,
Sam Boyce, Vivien Green, John Rush
(film/drama/TV)*
Foreign & US *Amelia Cummins, Paul Rainbow*

FOUNDED 1962. (Incorporates Richard Scott
Simon Ltd 1971 and Christy & Moore 1912.)
Handles full-length general, commercial and literary fiction and non-fiction, including: social
politics, military history, gardening, thrillers,
crime, romance, fantasy, drama, biography,
travel, cookery and humour, UK and foreign
estates. Also theatre, film, radio and TV scripts.
One of the UK's more dynamic agencies, Sheil
Land represents over 300 established clients and
welcomes approaches from new clients looking
either to start or to develop their careers. Known
to negotiate sophisticated contracts with publishers. Preliminary letter with s.a.e. essential. No
reading fee. CLIENTS Peter Ackroyd, John
Blashford-Snell, Simon van der Borgh, Melvyn

Bragg, Stephanie Calman, Catherine Cookson
Estate, Lynda Chater, Seamus Deane, Alan
Drury, John Fowles, Alan Garner, Susan Hill,
HRH The Prince of Wales, Richard Holmes,
John Humphries, Bernard Kops, Charlotte
Lamb, Richard Mabey, Colin McDowell, Van
Morrison, Patrick O'Brian Estate, Esther
Rantzen, Pam Rhodes, Martin Riley, Colin
Shindler, Tom Sharpe, Brian Sibley, Alan
Titchmarsh, Rose Tremain, Sally Ward, John
Wilsher, Paul Wilson. *Commission* Home
10–15%; US & Translation 20%. *Overseas associ-
ates* **Georges Borchardt, Inc.** (Richard Scott
Simon). UK representatives for **Farrar, Straus
& Giroux, Inc**. US Film and TV representa-
tion: CAA, H.N. Swanson, and others.

Caroline Sheldon
Literary Agency★

71 Hillgate Place, London W8 7SS
☎020 7727 9102

Contact *Caroline Sheldon*

FOUNDED 1985. *Handles* adult fiction, in particular women's, both commercial and literary
novels. Also full-length children's fiction. No
TV/film scripts unless by book-writing clients.
Send letter with all relevant details of ambitions
and four chapters of proposed book (enclose
large s.a.e.). No reading fee. *Commission* Home
10%; US & Translation 20%.

Silent Partners Ltd

c/o D.J. Harper International, 18 Redwood
Road, Yew Tree Estate, Walsall, West
Midlands
☎0411 320949

Contact *Jonathan Stuart-Brown*

Handles full-length screenplays with particular
interest in pieces about the lives of Catholic
Saints. No unsolicited mss; send a letter in the
first instance. 'Completely unsolicited material
goes into the bin unread or even the shredder
but everyone who phones gets a call back and a
chance to state their case.'

Jeffrey Simmons

10 Lowndes Square, London SW1X 9HA
☎020 7235 8852 Fax 020 7235 9733

Contact *Jeffrey Simmons*

FOUNDED 1978. *Handles* biography and autobiography, cinema and theatre, fiction (both
quality and commercial), history, law and
crime, politics and world affairs, parapsychology
and sport (but not exclusively). No science fic-
tion/fantasy, children's books, cookery, crafts,

hobbies or gardening. Film scripts handled only if by book-writing clients. *Special interests* personality books of all sorts and fiction from young writers (i.e. under 40) with a future. Writers become clients by personal introduction or by letter, enclosing a synopsis if possible, a brief biography, a note of any previously published books, plus a list of any publishers and agents who have already seen the mss. *Commission* Home 10–15%; US 15%; Translation 20%.

Simpson Fox Associates★

52 Shaftesbury Avenue, London W1V 7DE
☎020 7434 9167 Fax 020 7494 2887
Email georgina@simpson-fox.demon.co.uk

ESTABLISHED 1973. As we went to press it was announced that Georgina Capel (formerly Fox) has left Simpson Fox to form a new agency with Anita Land called Capel & Land. Simpson Fox no longer represents authors.

Capel & Land are based at 29 Wardour Street, London W1V 3HB. ☎020 7734 2414 Fax ☎020 7734 8101. CLIENTS Julie Burchill, Mo Mowlem, Christina Odone, Andrew Roberts, Henry Porter, Petronella Wyatt.

Robert Smith Literary Agency★

12 Bridge Wharf, 156 Caledonian Road, London N1 9UU
☎020 7278 2444 Fax 020 7833 5680

Contact *Robert Smith*

FOUNDED 1997. *Handles* non-fiction; biography, health and nutrition, cookery, lifestyle, showbusiness and true crime. No scripts, fiction, poetry, academic or children's books. No unsolicited mss. Send a letter and synopsis in the first instance. No reading fee. CLIENTS include Neil and Christine Hamilton, James Haspiel, Christine Keeler, Norman Reid, Mike Reid, Christopher Warwick. *Commission* Home 15%; US & Translation 20%. *Overseas associates* Frédérique Poretta Literary Agency (France); Thomas Schlück Literary Agency (Germany).

Elaine Steel

110 Gloucester Avenue, London NW1 8HX
☎020 8348 0918 Fax 020 8341 9807
Email ecmsteel@aol.com

Contact *Elaine Steel*

FOUNDED 1986. *Handles* scripts and screenplays. No technical or academic. Initial phone call preferred. CLIENTS include Les Blair, Anna Campion, Michael Eaton, Brian Keenan, Troy Kennedy Martin, Rob Ritchie, Ben Steiner. *Commission* Home 10%; US & Translation 20%.

Abner Stein★

10 Roland Gardens, London SW7 3PH
☎020 7373 0456 Fax 020 7370 6316

Contact *Abner Stein*

FOUNDED 1971. Mainly represents US agents and authors but *handles* some full-length fiction and general non-fiction. No scientific, technical, etc. No scripts. Send letter and outline in the first instance rather than unsolicited mss. *Commission* Home 10%; US & Translation 20%.

Micheline Steinberg Playwrights' Agent

409 Triumph House, 187–191 Regent Street, London W1R 7WF
☎020 7287 4383 Fax 020 7287 4384

Contact *Micheline Steinberg*

FOUNDED 1988. *Specialises* in plays for stage, TV, radio and film. Best approach by preliminary letter (with s.a.e.). Dramatic associate for **Laurence Pollinger Limited**. *Commission* Home 10%; Elsewhere 15%.

tricia sumner – literary agency

See **Labour and Management Limited**

The Susijn Agency

820 Harrow Road, London NW10 5JU
☎020 8968 7435 Fax 020 8354 0415
Email LSusijn@aol.com

Contact *Laura Susijn*

FOUNDED April 1998. *Specialises* in selling rights worldwide in literary fiction and non-fiction. Preliminary letter, synopsis and first two chapters preferred. No reading fee. Also represents non-English language authors and publishers for UK, US and translation rights worldwide. *Commission* Home 15%; US & Translation 15–20%.

J. M. Thurley Management

30 Cambridge Road, Teddington, Middlesex TW11 8DR
☎020 8977 3176 Fax 020 8943 2678
Email JMThurley@aol.com

Contact *Jon Thurley*

FOUNDED 1976. *Handles* full-length fiction, non-fiction, TV and films. Particularly interested in strong commercial and literary fiction. Will provide creative and editorial assistance to promising writers. No unsolicited mss; approach by letter in the first instance with synopsis and first three chapters plus return postage. No reading fee. *Commission* Home 15%; US & Translation 15%.

Lavinia Trevor Agency*

7 The Glasshouse, 49A Goldhawk Road, London W12 8QP
☏020 8749 8481 Fax 020 8749 7377

Contact *Lavinia Trevor*

FOUNDED 1993. *Handles* general fiction and non-fiction, including popular science. No poetry, academic or technical work. No TV, film, radio, theatre scripts. Approach with a preliminary letter, a brief autobiography and first 50–100 typewritten pages. S.a.e. essential. No reading fee. *Commission* rate by agreement with author.

Jane Turnbull*

13 Wendell Road, London W12 9RS
☏020 8743 9580 Fax 020 8749 6079
Email agents@cwcom.net

Contact *Jane Turnbull*

FOUNDED 1986. *Handles* fiction and non-fiction. No science fiction, sagas or romantic fiction. *Specialises* in biography, history, current affairs, health and diet. No unsolicited mss. Approach with letter in the first instance. No reading fee. Translation rights handled by **Gillon Aitken Associates Ltd**. *Commission* Home 10%; US 15%; Translation 20%.

Utopia Media Associates

22c Belfort Road, London SE15 2JD
☏020 7639 7981 Fax 020 7252 9309
Email christopher.norris@utopiamedia.co.uk
Website www.utopiamedia.co.uk

Contact *Christopher Norris*

FOUNDED 1998. *Handles* adult fiction and non-fiction (trade), children's books, TV, film, radio and theatre scripts. No poetry. *Specialises* in subjects with potential for sale in many different media; 'Utopia Media is "story-led", not "medium-led".' Interactive Website. No unsolicited mss. Authors by referral. No reading fee. *Commission* Home & US 15%; Translation 20%.

Ed Victor Ltd*

6 Bayley Street, Bedford Square, London WC1B 3HB
☏020 7304 4100 Fax 020 7304 4111

Contacts *Ed Victor, Graham Greene, Maggie Phillips, Sophie Hicks*

FOUNDED 1976. *Handles* a broad range of material but leans towards the more commercial ends of the fiction and non-fiction spectrums. No scripts, no academic. Takes on very few new writers. After trying his hand at book publishing and literary magazines, Ed Victor, an ebullient American, found his true vocation. Strong opinions, very pushy and works hard for those whose intelligence he respects. Loves nothing more than a good title auction. Please telephone in the first instance. No unsolicited mss. CLIENTS include Douglas Adams, Frederick Forsyth, Josephine Hart, Jack Higgins, Erica Jong, Kathy Lette, Erich Segal, Lisa St Aubin de Terán and the estates of Raymond Chandler, Dame Iris Murdoch, Sir Stephen Spender and Irving Wallace. *Commission* Home 15%; US 15%; Translation 20%.

Walker Associates

31 Algar Grove, London NW1 9UG
☏020 7813 9352 Fax 020 7813 9352

Contacts *Michael Walker, John Hastings, Alison Butler*

FOUNDED 1999. *Handles* fiction, both popular and literary, TV drama. *Specialises* in psychological thrillers/horror and humour. No poetry, short stories or children's fiction. No reading fee. Unsolicited mss welcome. Prospective clients should send preliminary letter including brief c.v., synopsis and first three chapters; s.a.e. essential for return. *Commission* Home 10%; US & Translation 20%.

Cecily Ware Literary Agents

19C John Spencer Square, London N1 2LZ
☏020 7359 3787 Fax 020 7226 9828

Contacts *Cecily Ware, Gilly Schuster, Warren Sherman*

FOUNDED 1972. Primarily a film and TV script agency representing work in all areas: drama, children's, series/serials, adaptations, comedies, etc. No unsolicited mss or phone calls. Approach in writing only. No reading fee. *Commission* Home 10%; US 10–20% by arrangement.

Warner Chappell Plays Ltd

Griffin House, 161 Hammersmith Road, London W6 8BS
☏020 8563 5888 Fax 020 8563 5801

Contact *Michael Callahan*

Formerly the English Theatre Guild, Warner Chappell are now both agents and publishers of scripts for the theatre. No unsolicited mss; introductory letter essential. No reading fee. CLIENTS include Ray Cooney, John Godber, Peter Gordon, Debbie Isitt, Arthur Miller, Sam Shepard, John Steinbeck. *Overseas representatives* in the US, Canada, Australia, New Zealand, India, South Africa and Zimbabwe.

Watson, Little Ltd★
Capo Di Monte, Windmill Hill, London
NW3 6RJ
☎020 7431 0770 Fax 020 7431 7225
Email sz@watlit.demon.co.uk
Contacts *Sheila Watson, Mandy Little,*
Sugra Zaman

Handles fiction and non-fiction. *Special interests*
history, popular science, psychology, self-help
and business books. No scripts. Not interested
in authors who wish to be purely academic
writers. Send preliminary ('intelligent') letter
with synopsis. *Commission* Home 15%; US
24%; Translation 19%. *Overseas associates*
worldwide.

A. P. Watt Ltd★ *www.apwatt.co.uk*
20 John Street, London WC1N 2DR
☎020 7405 6774 Fax 020 7831 2154
Email hpw@hpwatt.co.uk
Directors *Caradoc King, Linda Shaughnessy,*
Derek Johns, Joanna Frank, Sam North

FOUNDED 1875. The oldest-established literary
agency in the world. *Handles* full-length type-
scripts, including children's books, screenplays
for film and TV, and plays. No poetry, aca-
demic or specialist works. No unsolicited mss
accepted. CLIENTS include Quentin Blake,
Marika Cobbold, Helen Dunmore, Nicholas
Evans, Giles Foden, Janice Galloway, Martin
Gilbert, Nadine Gordimer, Linda Grant, Colin
and Jacqui Hawkins, Michael Holroyd,
Michael Ignatieff, Mick Jackson, Philip Kerr,
John Lanchester, Alison Lurie, Jan Morris,
Andrew O'Hagan, Graham Swift, Colm
Toibin and the estates of Wodehouse, Graves
and Maugham. *Commission* Home 10%; US &
Translation 20%.

John Welch, Literary Consultant & Agent
Milton House, Milton, Cambridge CB4 6AD
☎01223 860641 Fax 01223 440575
Contact *John Welch*

FOUNDED 1992. *Handles* military history, aviation, history, biography and sport. No poetry,
children's books or scripts for radio, TV, film
or theatre. Already has a full hand of authors so
no new authors being considered at present.
CLIENTS include Alexander Baron, Michael
Calvert, Paul Clifford, Timothy Jenkins,
Norman Scarfe, Peter Trew, Jason Woolgar,
David Wragg. *Commission* Home 10%.

Dinah Wiener Ltd★
12 Cornwall Grove, Chiswick, London
W4 2LB
☎020 8994 6011 Fax 020 8994 6044
Email dinahwiener@enterprise.net
Contact *Dinah Wiener*

FOUNDED 1985. *Handles* fiction and general
non-fiction: auto/biography, popular science,
cookery. No scripts, children's or poetry.
Approach with preliminary letter in first
instance, giving full but brief c.v. of past work
and future plans. Mss submitted must include
s.a.e. and be typed in double-spacing. CLIENTS
include Catherine Alliott, T. J. Armstrong, Joy
Berthoud, Malcolm Billings, Alison Brodie,
Hugh Brune, Guy Burt, Victoria Corby, David
Deutsch, Robin Gardiner, Jenny Hobbs, Mark
Jeffery, Tania Kindersley, Mary Long, Daniel
Snowman, Peta Tayler, Marcia Willett.
Commission Home 15%; US & Translation
20%.

Michael Woodward Creations Ltd
Parlington Hall, Aberford, West Yorkshire
LS25 3EG
☎0113 2813913 Fax 0113 2813911
Email art@mwc.uk.com
Contact *Michael Woodward, Janet Woodward*

FOUNDED 1979. International licensing company with own in-house studio. Worldwide
representation for artists and illustrators.
Current properties include *Rambling Ted,*
Teddy Tum Tum, Railway Children, Kit 'n' Kin,
Bad Taste Bears, Robots in Big Boots. New artists
should forward full-concept synopses with
sample illustrations. Scripts or stories not
accepted without illustration/design or concept mock-ups. No standard commission rate;
varies according to contract.

National Newspapers

Departmental e-mail addresses are too numerous to include in this listing. They can be obtained from the newspaper's main switchboard or the department in question

Daily Mail

Northcliffe House, 2 Derry Street, Kensington, London W8 5TT
☎020 7938 6000 Fax 020 7937 4463
Owner *Associated Newspapers/Lord Rothermere*
Editor *Paul Dacre*
Circulation 2.4 million

In-house feature writers and regular columnists provide much of the material. Photo-stories and crusading features often appear; it's essential to hit the right note to be a successful *Mail* writer. Close scrutiny of the paper is strongly advised. Not a good bet for the unseasoned. Accepts news on savings, building societies, insurance, unit trusts, legal rights and tax.
   News Editor *Tony Gallagher*
   City Editor *Michael Walters*
   'Money Mail' Editor *Tony Hazell*
   Political Editor *David Hughes*
   Education Editor *Tony Halpin*
   Diary Editor *Nigel Dempster*
   Features Editor *Veronica Wadley*
   Literary Editor *Jane Mays*
   Sports Editor *Bryan Cooney*
   Femail Lisa Collins

Weekend: Saturday supplement **Editor** *Heather McGlone*

Daily Record

Anderston Quay, Glasgow G3 8DA
☎0141 248 7000 Fax 0141 242 3340
Website www.record-mail.co.uk
Owner *Mirror Group Newspapers*
Editor-in-Chief *Martin Clarke*
Circulation 685,536

Mass-market Scottish tabloid. Freelance material is generally welcome.
   News Editor *Gordon Hay*
   Features Editor *Aileen Easton*
   Business Editor *Colin Calder*
   Education *Carlos Alba*
   Political Editor *Dave King*
   Sports Editor *James Traynor*
   Women's Page *Roz Paterson*
   Magazine Editor *Jan Patience*

Daily Sport

19 Great Ancoats Street, Manchester M60 4BT
☎0161 236 4466 Fax 0161 236 4535
Website www.dailysport.co.uk
Owner *Sport Newspapers Ltd*
Editor *Jeff McGowan*
Circulation 235,000

Tabloid catering for young male readership. Unsolicited material welcome; send to News Editor.
   News Editor *Pam McVitie*
   Sports Editor *Marc Smith*

Daily Star

Ludgate House, 245 Blackfriars Road, London SE1 9UX
☎020 7928 8000 Fax 020 7922 7960
Website www.megastar.co.uk
Owner *United News & Media*
Editor *Peter Hill*
Circulation 614,738

In competition with *The Sun* for off-the-wall news and features. Freelance opportunities available.
   Executive Editor *Henry Macrory*
   Deputy Editor *Hugh Whittow*
   Features Editor *Dawn Neesom*
   Sports Editor *Jim Mansell*

The Daily Telegraph

1 Canada Square, Canary Wharf, London E14 5DT
☎020 7538 5000 Fax 020 7513 2506
Website www.telegraph.co.uk
Owner *Conrad Black*
Editor *Charles Moore*
Circulation 1.03 million

Unsolicited mss not generally welcome – 'all are carefully read and considered, but only about one in a thousand is accepted for publication'. As they receive about 20 weekly, this means about one a year. Contenders should approach the paper in writing, making clear their authority for writing on that subject. No fiction.

News Editor *Richard Spencer* Tip-offs or news reports from *bona fide* journalists. Must phone the news desk in first instance. Maximum 200 words. *Payment* minimum £40 (tip).

Arts Editor *Sarah Crompton*
Business Editor *To be appointed*
Political Editor *George Jones*
Diary Editor *Sam Leith* Always interested in diary pieces; contact *Peterborough* (Diary column).
Education *John Clare*
Environment *Charles Clover*
Features Editor *Richard Preston* Most material supplied by commission from established contributors. New writers are tried out by arrangement with the features editor. Approach in writing. Maximum 1500 words.
Literary Editor *Kate Summerscale*
Sports Editor *David Welch* Occasional opportunities for specialised items.
Style/Wellbeing Editor *Jane Taylor*
Payment by arrangement.

Daily Telegraph Weekend: Saturday colour supplement. **Editor** *Rachel Simhon*. *T2*: Saturday tabloid for under-16s. **Editor** *Kitty Melrose*. Website: www.t2online.com

The Express/
The Express on Sunday
Ludgate House, 245 Blackfriars Road, London SE1 9UX
☎020 7928 8000 Fax 020 7620 1654
Website www.expressnewspapers.co.uk
Owner *United News and Media*
Editor *Rosie Boycott*
Circulation 1.09 million(*Express*)/
1 million (*Express on Sunday*)

Now being run as a seven-day publication with *The Express* published Monday to Friday, *The Express on Saturday* and *The Express on Sunday*, with all editors working for each publication. The general rule of thumb is to approach in writing with an idea; all departments are prepared to look at an outline without commitment. Ideas welcome but already receives many which are 'too numerous to count'.

News Editor, Express *Sean Rayment*
News Editor, Sunday Express *Simon Young*
Diary Editor *John McEntee (William Hickey)*
Features Editor *John Price*
Business Editor *Steven Day*
Political Editor *Tony Bevins*
Financial Editor *Robert Miller*
Education Editor *Dorothy Lepkowska*
Literary Editor *Maggie Pringle*
Sports Editor *Mike Allen*
Planning Editor (News Desk) should be circulated with copies of official reports, press releases, etc., to ensure news desk cover at all times.

Saturday magazine **Editor** *Sally Ferrari*

Express on Sunday Magazine: colour supplement. **Editor** *To be appointed*. No unsolicited mss. All contributions are commissioned. Ideas in writing only.
Payment negotiable.

Financial Times
1 Southwark Bridge, London SE1 9HL
☎020 7873 3000 Fax 020 7873 3076
Email <firstname>.<lastname>@ft.com
Website www.ft.com
Owner *Pearson*
Editor *Richard Lambert*
Circulation 449,151

FOUNDED 1888. UK and international coverage of business, finance, politics, technology, management, marketing and the arts. All feature ideas must be discussed with the department's editor in advance. Not snowed under with unsolicited contributions – they get less than any other national newspaper. Approach in writing with ideas in the first instance.

News Editor *Lionel Barber*
Features Editor *John Gapper*
Arts Editor *Peter Aspden*
Financial Editor *Robert Peston*
Literary Editor *Jan Dalley*
Diary Editor *Michael Cassell*
Education *Jim Kelly*
Environment *Vanessa Houlder*
Political Editor *Brian Groom*
Small Businesses *Katherine Campbell*
Sports Editor *Patrick Harverson*

Weekend FT and *the business*. **Editor** *Julia Cuthbertson*
Monthly magazine. **Editor** *Gillian de Bono*

The Guardian
119 Farringdon Road, London EC1R 3ER
☎020 7278 2332 Fax 020 7837 2114
Website www.guardian.co.uk
Owner *The Scott Trust*
Editor *Alan Rusbridger*
Circulation 387,442

Of all the nationals *The Guardian* probably offers the greatest opportunities for freelance writers, if only because it has the greatest number of specialised pages which use freelance work. But mss must be directed at a specific slot.

News Editor *Clare Margetson* No opportunities except in those regions where there is presently no local contact for news stories.

Arts/Literary Editor *Claire Armitstead*
Executive Financial Editor *Paul Murphy*
Managing Editor, City *Steve Bosfield*
On Line *Vic Keegan* Science, computing and technology. A major part of Thursday's paper, almost all written by freelancers. Expertise essential – but not a trade page; written for 'the interested man in the street' and from the user's point of view. Computing/communications (Internet) articles should be addressed to *Jack Schofield*; science articles to *Tim Radford*. Mss on disk or by e-mail (neil.mcintosh@guardian.co.uk).

Diary Editor *Matthew Norman*
Education Editor *Will Woodward* Expert pieces on modern education welcome.
Environment *John Vidal*
Features Editor *Ian Katz* Receives up to 50 unsolicited mss a day; these are passed on to relevant page editors.
Guardian Society *David Brindle* Focuses on social change in the new Millennium – the forces affecting us, from environment to government policies. Top journalists and outside commentators.
Media Editor *Janine Gibson* Nine pages a week, plus 'New Media'. Outside contributions are considered. All aspects of modern media, advertising and PR. Background insight important. Best approach is by e-mail (janine.gibson @guardian.co.uk)
Political Editor *Mike White*
Sports Editor *Ben Clissitt*
Women's Page *Libby Brooks* Runs three days a week. Unsolicited ideas used if they show an appreciation of the page in question. Maximum 800–1000 words. Write, e-mail (libby.brooks@guardian.co.uk) or fax on 020 7239 9935.

The Guardian Weekend Saturday issue. **Editor** *To be appointed.* **The Guide** *Tim Lusher.*

The Herald (Glasgow)

195 Albion Street, Glasgow G1 1QP
☎0141 552 6255 Fax 0141 553 3335
Website www.theherald.co.uk
Owner *Scottish Media Group*
Editor *Harry Reid*
Circulation 101,079

The oldest national newspaper in the English-speaking world, The Herald, which dropped its 'Glasgow' prefix in February 1992, was bought by Scottish Television in 1996. Lively, quality, national Scottish daily broadsheet. Approach

with ideas in writing or by phone in first instance.

News Editor *Bill McDowall*
Arts Editor *Keith Bruce*
Business Editor *Robert Powell*
Diary *Tom Shields*
Education/Environment *Liz Buie*
Sports Editor *Iain Scott*
Herald Magazine *Cate Devine*

The Independent

1 Canada Square, Canary Wharf, London E14 5DL
☎020 7293 2000 Fax 020 7293 2435
Website www.independent.co.uk
Owner *Independent Newspapers*
Editor *Simon Kelner*
Circulation 224,534

FOUNDED October 1986. *The Independent* and *The Independent on Sunday* were acquired by Irish tycoon Tony O'Reilly's Independent Newspapers from Mirror Group Newspapers in March 1998. Particularly strong on its arts/media coverage, with a high proportion of feature material. Theoretically, opportunities for freelancers are good. However, unsolicited mss are not welcome; most pieces originate in-house or from known and trusted outsiders. Ideas should be submitted in writing.

News Editor *Jason Burt*
Features *Laurence Earle*
Arts Editor *Ian Irvine*
Business Editor *Jeremy Warner*
Education *Judith Judd*
Environment *Michael McCarthy*
Literary Editor *Boyd Tonkin*
Political Editor *Andrew Grice*
Sports Editor *Paul Newman*
Travel Editor *Jeremy Atiyah*

The Independent Magazine: Saturday supplement. **Editor** *Andrew Tuck.* **The Information Editor** *Nick Coleman.*

Independent on Sunday

1 Canada Square, Canary Wharf, London E14 5DL
☎020 7293 2000 Fax 020 7293 2043
Website www.independent.co.uk/sindy/sindy.html
Owner *Independent Newspapers*
Editor *Janet Street-Porter*
Circulation 252,304

FOUNDED 1986. Regular columnists contribute most material but feature opportunites exist. Approach with ideas in first instance.

News Editor *Barry Hugill*
Focus Editor *Catherine Pepinster*
Arts Editor *Jenny Turner*
Culture Editor *Simon O'Hagan*
Comment Editor *Charlie Courtauld*
Business Editor *Jason Nissé*
Education Editor *Judith Judd*
Literary Editor *Suzi Feay*
Environment *Geoffrey Lean*
Political Editor *Jonathan Carr-Brown*
Sports Editor *Neil Morton*
Associate Editor, Arts *Marcus Field*
Travel Editor *Jeremy Atiyah*

Review supplement. **Editor** *Richard Askwith.*

International Herald Tribune

181 avenue Charles de Gaulle, 92200 Neuilly-sur-Seine, France
☎0033 1 4143 9300 Fax 0033 1 4143 9338
Website www.iht.com

Editor *Michael Getler*
Circulation 225,000

Published in France, Monday to Saturday, and circulated in Europe, the Middle East, North Africa, the Far East and the USA. General news, business and financial, arts and leisure. Uses regular freelance contributors. Query letter to Features Editor in first instance.
  Features Editor *Katherine Knorr*
  Managing Editor *Walter Wells*

The Mail on Sunday

Northcliffe House, 2 Derry Street, Kensington, London W8 5TS
☎020 7938 6000 Fax 020 7937 3829

Owner *Associated Newspapers/Lord Rothermere*
Editor *Peter Wright*
Circulation 2.24 million

Sunday paper with a high proportion of newsy features and articles. Experience and judgement required to break into its band of regular feature writers.
  News Editor *(Miss) Ray Clancy*
  Financial Editor *Alex Brummer*
  Business Editor *Ruth Sunderland*
  Diary Editor *Nigel Dempster*
  Features Editor/Women's Page *Sian James*
  Literary Editor *Marilyn Warnick*
  Education Editor *Rosie Waterhouse*
  Industrial/Environment Editor *Christopher Leake*
  Political Editor *Simon Walters*
  Sports Editor *Daniel Evans*

Night & Day: review supplement. **Editor** *Christena Appleyard*

You – The Mail on Sunday Magazine: colour supplement. Many feature articles, supplied entirely by freelance writers. **Editor** *Dee Nolan*
  Features Editor *Victoria Hinton*

The Mirror

1 Canada Square, Canary Wharf, London E14 5AP
☎020 7293 3000 Fax 020 7293 3409
Website www.mirror.co.uk

Owner *Mirror Group Newspapers*
Editor *Piers Morgan*
Circulation 2.26 million

No freelance opportunities for the inexperienced, but strong writers who understand what the tabloid market demands are always needed.
  News Editor *David Leigh*
  Features Editor *Mark Thomas*
  Political Editor *Peter MacMahon*
  Business Editor *Clinton Manning*
  Education Editor *Richard Garner*
  Showbusiness Diary Editor *Richard Wallace*
  Sports Editor *Des Kelly*

Morning Star

1st Floor, Cape House, 787 Commercial Road, London E14 7HG
☎020 7538 5181 Fax 020 7438 5125
Email morsta@geo2.poptel.org.uk

Owner *Peoples Press Printing Society*
Editor *John Haylett*
Circulation 9,000

Not to be confused with the *Daily Star*, the *Morning Star* is the farthest left national daily. Those with a penchant for a Marxist reading of events and ideas can try their luck, though feature space is as competitive here as in the other nationals.
  News Editor *Chris Kasrils*
  Features & Arts Editor *Mike Parker*
  Political Editor *Mike Ambrose*
  Foreign Editor *Brian Denny*
  Sports Editor *Amanda Kendal*

News of the World

1 Virginia Street, London E1 9XR
☎020 7782 1000 Fax 020 7583 9504
Website www.newsoftheworld.co.uk

Owner *News International plc/Rupert Murdoch*
Editor *Rebekah Wade*
Circulation 4 million

Highest circulation Sunday paper. Freelance contributions welcome. News and features editors welcome tips and ideas.
  Assistant Editor (News) *Phil Taylor*
  Assistant Editor (Features) *Gary Thompson*

Business/City Editor *Peter Prendergast*
Political/Environment Editor *Ian Kirby*
Sports Editor *Mike Dunn*

Sunday Magazine: colour supplement. **Editor** *Judy McGuire*. Showbiz interviews and strong human-interest features make up most of the content, but there are no strict rules about what is 'interesting'. Unsolicited mss and ideas welcome.

The Observer

119 Farringdon Road, London EC1R 3ER
☎020 7278 2332 Fax 020 7713 4250
Email editor@observer.co.uk
Website www.observer.co.uk
Owner *Guardian Newspapers Ltd*
Editor *Roger Alton*
Circulation 409,295

FOUNDED 1791. Acquired by Guardian Newspapers from Lonrho in May 1993. Occupies the middle ground of Sunday newspaper politics. Unsolicited material is not generally welcome, 'except from distinguished, established writers'. Receives far too many unsolicited offerings already. No news, fiction or special page opportunities. The newspaper runs annual competitions which change from year to year. Details are advertised in the newspaper.

Executive Editor, News *Andy Malone*
Features Editor *Gaby Wood*
Arts Editor *Jane Ferguson*
Review Editor *Lisa O'Kelly*
Comment Editor *Mike Holland*
Business News Editor *Andy Beven*
City Editor *Paul Farrelly*
Education Correspondent *Martin Bright*
Environment Editor *Anthony Browne*
Literary Editor *Robert McCrum*
Sports Editor *Brian Oliver*

Life: arts and lifestyle supplement. **Editor** *Sheryl Garratt*.

Scotland on Sunday

108 Holyrood Road, Edinburgh EH8 8AS
☎0131 620 8620 Fax 0131 620 8491
Website www.scotsman.com
Owner *Scotsman Publications Ltd*
Editor *John McGurk*
Circulation 84,265

Scotland's top-selling quality broadsheet. Welcomes ideas rather than finished articles.

News Editor *Ian Stewart*
Political Editor *Iain Martin*

Scotland on Sunday Magazine: colour supplement. **Editor** *Margot Wilson*. Features on personalities, etc.

The Scotsman

108 Holyrood Road, Edinburgh EH8 8AS
☎0131 620 8620 Fax 0131 620 8616 (Editorial)
Website www.scotsman.com
Owner *Scotsman Publications Ltd*
Editor *Rebecca Hardy*
Circulation 78,973

Scotland's national newspaper. Many unsolicited mss come in, and stand a good chance of being read, although a small army of regulars supply much of the feature material not written in-house.

News Editor *Magnus Llewellin*
Business Editor *Ken Symonds*
Education *Seonag MacKinnon*
Environment *Christopher Cairn*
Features Editor *Stewart Kirkpatrick*
Book Reviews *Catherine Lockerbie*

I-Mag **Editor** *Nicola McCormack*

The Sun

1 Virginia Street, London E1 9BD
☎020 7782 4000 Fax 020 7782 4108
Email <firstname>.<lastname>@the-sun.co.uk
Website www.the-sun.co.uk
Owner *News International plc/Rupert Murdoch*
Editor *David Yelland*
Circulation 3.56 million

Highest circulation daily with a populist outlook; very keen on gossip, pop stars, TV soap, scandals and exposés of all kinds. No room for non-professional feature writers; 'investigative journalism' of a certain hue is always in demand, however.

Head of News *Graham Dudman*
News Editor *Sue Thompson*
Head of Features *Peter Picton*
Features Editor *Sam Carlisle*
Head of Sport *Paul Ridley*
Sports Editor *Ted Chadwick*
Woman's Editor *Vicki Grimshaw*
Fashion Editor *Catherine Westwood*

Sunday Business

193 Marsh Wall, London E14
☎020 7418 9601 Fax 020 7418 9605
Owner *Press Holdings*
Editor *Jeff Randall*
Circulation 68,119

LAUNCHED April 1996 and 'relaunched' February 1998. National newspaper dedicated to business, finance and politics.

Deputy Editor *Richard Northedge*
News Editor *Frank Kane*
Features Editor *Vivien Goldsmith*
City Editor *Richard Wachman*

Sunday Herald

195 Albion Street, Glasgow G1 1QP
☎0141 302 7800 Fax 0141 302 7809
Email editor@sundayherald.com
Website www.sundayherald.com
Owner *Scottish Media Group*
Editor *Andrew Jaspan*
Circulation 54,316

Also at: 10 George Street, Edinburgh EH2 2DU
☎0131 200 8100 Fax 0131 200 8088

LAUNCHED February 1999. New Scottish seven-section broadsheet aimed at the 20–45 age group.
Deputy Editor *Richard Walker*
News Editor *David Milne*
Features Editor *Barry Didcock*
Political Editor *Douglas Fraser*
Sports Editor *Donald Cowey*
Magazine Editor *Charlotte Ross*

Sunday Mail

Anderston Quay, Glasgow G3 8DA
☎0141 248 7000 Fax 0141 242 3587
Website www.record-mail.co.uk
Owner *Trinity Mirror plc*
Editor *Peter Cox*
Circulation 847,776

Popular Scottish Sunday tabloid.
News Editor *Iain Ferguson*
Features Editor *Susie Cormack*
Women's Page *Melanie Reid*

Seven Days: weekly supplement. **Editor** *Liz Steele.*

Sunday Mirror

1 Canada Square, Canary Wharf, London
E14 5AP
☎020 7293 3000 Fax 020 7293 3939
Website www.sundaymirror.co.uk
Owner *Trinity Mirror plc*
Editor *Colin Myler*
Circulation 1.89 million

Receives anything up to 100 unsolicited mss weekly. In general terms, these are welcome, though the paper patiently points out it has more time for contributors who have taken the trouble to study the market. Initial contact in writing preferred, except for live news situations. No fiction.
News Editor *Paul Field* The news desk is

very much in the market for tip-offs and inside information. Contributors would be expected to work with staff writers on news stories.
Personal Finance *Niki Chesworth*
City Reporter *Joia Shillingford*
Features Editor *Jane Johnson* 'Anyone who has obviously studied the market will be dealt with constructively and courteously.' Cherishes its record as a breeding ground for new talent.
Sports Editor *Steve McKenlay*

Personal: colour supplement. **Editor** *Kate Bravery.*

Sunday People

1 Canada Square, Canary Wharf, London
E14 5AP
☎020 7293 3000 Fax 020 7293 3517
Website www.people.co.uk
Owner *Trinity Mirror plc*
Editor *Neil Wallis*
Circulation 1.51 million

Slightly up-market version of *The News of the World*. Keen on exposés and big-name gossip. Interested in ideas for investigative articles. Phone in first instance.
News Editor *David Wooding*
Features Editor *Alison Phillips*
Political Editor *Nigel Nelson*
Sports Editor *Lee Clayton*
Travel Editor *Richard Allen*

The People Magazine. **Editor** *Amanda Cable.* Approach by phone with ideas in first instance.

Sunday Post

2 Albert Square, Dundee DD1 9QJ
☎01382 223131 Fax 01382 201064
Email post@dcthomson.co.uk
Website www.sundaypost.com
Owner *D. C. Thomson & Co. Ltd*
Editor *Russell Reid*
Circulation 700,000

Contributions should be addressed to the editor.

Sunday Post Magazine: monthly colour supplement. **Editor** *Maggie Dun.*

Sunday Sport

19 Great Ancoats Street, Manchester M60 4BT
☎0161 236 4466 Fax 0161 236 4535
Website www.sundaysport.co.uk
Owner *David Sullivan*
Editor *Mark Harris*
Circulation 217,668

FOUNDED 1986. Sunday tabloid catering for a particular sector of the male 15–35 readership.

As concerned with 'glamour' (for which, read: 'page 3') as with human interest, news, features and sport. Unsolicited mss are welcome; receives about 90 a week. Approach should be made by phone in the case of news and sports items, by letter for features. All material should be addressed to the news editor.

Assistant Editor, News Simon Dean Offbeat news, human interest, preferably with photographs.

Features Editor Sarah Stephens Regular items: glamour, showbiz and television, as well as general interest.

Sports Editor Marc Smith Hard-hitting sports stories on major soccer clubs and their personalities, plus leading clubs/people in other sports. Strong quotations to back up the news angle essential.

Payment negotiable and on publication.

Sunday Telegraph

1 Canada Square, Canary Wharf, London E14 5DT
☎020 7538 5000 Fax 020 7538 6242
Website www.telegraph.co.uk

Owner Conrad Black
Editor Dominic Lawson
Circulation 805,069

Right-of-centre quality Sunday paper which, although traditionally formal, has pepped up its image to attract a younger readership. Unsolicited material from untried writers is rarely ever used. Contact with idea and details of track record.

News Editor Chris Boffey
Features Editor Sandy Mitchell
City Editor Neil Bennett
Political Editor Joe Murphy
Education Editor Martin Bentham
Arts Editor Anna Murphy
Environment Editor David Harrison
Literary Editor Miriam Gross
Diary Editor Adam Helliker
Sports Editor Jon Ryan

Sunday Telegraph Magazine Editor Lucy Tuck

The Sunday Times

1 Pennington Street, London E1 9XW
☎020 7782 5000 Fax 020 7782 5658
Website www.sunday-times.co.uk

Owner News International plc/Rupert Murdoch
Editor John Witherow
Circulation 1.39 million

FOUNDED 1820. Tendency to be anti-establishment, with a strong crusading investigative tradition. Approach the relevant editor with an idea in writing. Close scrutiny of the style of each section of the paper is strongly advised before sending mss. No fiction. All fees by negotiation.

News Editor Tim Kelsey Opportunities are very rare.

News Review Editor Sarah Baxter Submissions are always welcome, but the paper commissions its own, uses staff writers or works with literary agents, by and large. The features sections where most opportunities exist are Style and The Culture.

  Culture Editor Helen Hawkins
  Business Editor Andrew Lorenz
  City Editor Kirstie Hamilton
  Education Editor Judith O'Reilly
  Science/Environment Jonathan Leake
  Literary Editor Caroline Gascoigne
  Sports Editor Alex Butler

Style Editor Jeremy Langmead

Sunday Times Magazine: colour supplement. **Editor** Robin Morgan. No unsolicited material. Write with ideas in first instance.

The Times

1 Pennington Street, London E1 9XN
☎020 7782 5000 Fax 020 7488 3242
Website www.the-times.co.uk

Owner News International plc/Rupert Murdoch
Editor Peter Stothard
Circulation 711,457

Generally right (though features can range in tone from diehard to libertarian). The Times receives a great many unsolicited offerings. Writers with feature ideas should approach by letter in the first instance. No fiction.

  Deputy Editor Ben Preston
  News Editor John Wellman
  Features Editor Lorraine Butler
  Associate Editor Brian MacArthur
  City/Financial Editor Patience Wheatcroft
  Diary Editor Mark Inglefield
  Arts Editor Sarah Vine
  Education John O'Leary
  Environment Nick Nuttall
  Literary Editor Erica Wagner
  Political Editor Phil Webster
  Sports Editor David Chappell

Weekend Times Editor Jane Wheatley

The Times Magazine: Saturday supplement. **Editor** Nicholas Wapshott
  Times 3 Editor Sandra Parsons

Freelance Rates – Newspapers

Freelance rates vary enormously. The following minimum rates, set by the National Union of Journalists, should be treated as guidelines. The NUJ has no power to enforce minimum rates on newspapers that do not recognise the Union. It is up to freelancers to negotiate the best deal they can.

National Newspapers

(Including *The Herald, Sunday Herald, Daily Record, Sunday Mail, The Scotsman, Scotland on Sunday, Evening Standard*)

Features (including reviews, obituaries, etc)
Broadsheet rates start at under £200 per 1000 words and as low as £100 in Scotland, but sums of over £500 are common. Payment of less than £210 for London-based nationals is not acceptable. Tabloids often pay considerably more than broadsheets though items are usually shorter.

News
News may be paid for per 1000 words or by the day. When payment is by the word, the minimum should be £210 per 1000 words or pro rata. (Applies to all areas of news reporting, including sport.)

Day Rates
A low minimum of £115, but preferably £125 or more. Accept day rates only if required to be in the office for the day.

Exclusives
These can command very high fees, depending on how much the newspaper wants the story. A prominent position for the piece should command £500 or more. A guaranteed minimum of at least £260 should be negotiated in case it appears further down the page in a shorter form.

Colour Supplements
Seek payment of double all the rates given above.

Cartoons
Cartoon size: 1 column b&w £100, thereafter subject to individual negotiation. For a colour cartoon charge at least double the above rate. (All rates quoted are for one British use.)

Crosswords
15 × 15 squares and under: at least £110; 15 × 15 squares and over: at least £140.

Regional & Provincial Newspapers (England & Wales)

Features
Minimum Rate (for features submitted on spec) Weekly newspapers: £1.85 for up to and including 10 lines; 19p per line thereafter. Daily, evening and Sunday newspapers: £3.24 for up to and including 10 lines; 32p per line thereafter.

News
Minimum Lineage (usually 4 words) Rate Weekly newspapers: £1.80 for up to and including 10 lines; 18p per line thereafter. Daily, evening and Sunday newspapers: £3.10 for up to and including 10 lines; 31p per line thereafter.

Cartoons
Single Frame: at least £55
Feature Strip: £102

Crosswords
At least £64.

Freelancing – A Survivor's Kit

Donald Trelford

The first cheque I ever received from a newspaper for a freelance contribution was for three guineas (which shows how long ago it was) and the accompanying slip from the accounts department of the *Sunday Mercury* in Birmingham bore the cryptic words: 'To drowning three children'. When I showed it to my father, his only comment was: 'Funny sort of job you've got yourself into'.

At the time I was doing a holiday shift on my local paper in Coventry while on vacation from Cambridge University. One Saturday I was covering the tragic story of the three children, who had drowned after falling into a claypit, when a fellow reporter said it was worth filing a few paragraphs about it to the news desks of the national Sundays and offered me the *Sunday Mercury* as a friendly gift to a newcomer while he saved the big-paying tabloids for himself.

Having caught on to this method of augmenting a meagre provincial pay-packet, I daringly wrote to the Sports Editor of the *Observer*, then Christopher Brasher, the former Olympic gold medallist. I pointed out that Coventry, then a major force in English rugby, were badly served by the *Observer*, which hardly ever covered their matches. I added that they had an important fixture against Cardiff the following weekend and obligingly offered to report the match myself if they had no-one else available. Much to my astonishment, they took me up on the offer and invited me to file 300 words by 5pm on Saturday. Over forty years later I still recall opening their telegram, then the standard way of ordering copy, with open-mouthed joy. In fact, I still have it somewhere. They only paid two guineas, but it was the launch of my sports-writing career.

Writing to editors out of the blue in this way is not, however, a course I would generally recommend to aspiring freelance writers. I was lucky, I later discovered, in that my offer arrived just as the newspaper was looking for a Midlands rugby correspondent, and they decided to try me out. The lesson, I suppose, is that timing is everything for a freelance. Unless you are already close to a newspaper, you are unlikely to know when they are on the look-out for a new writer. On the other hand, if you don't tell them about yourself, they will never know that you're available. It's the freelancer's Catch 22.

Here are three guiding principles for freelance wannabes: know your market, find your niche, and never give up. Read newspapers and magazines thoroughly, including specialist publications. Nothing annoys an editor more than receiving a letter that clearly betrays the fact that the writer hasn't read his publication, such as proposing an article on a subject they have recently published or one that lies outside their range. In this respect it is also important to ensure that the individual to whom you address your article or letter is actually still there.

Don't be shy of ringing up the office in advance and double-checking with the switchboard or a secretary.

Try to offer material that is unlikely to be supplied by the publication's own staff writers. Study their house style and get a feeling for the kind of features they like to commission from outside. There are trends in feature coverage, some of them seasonal – this month the articles may be all be about fitness and riding bicycles, the next computers, then personal relationships or bringing up children. The subjects tend to come round and round again. If you can anticipate these trends, or spot them early, you may find a more receptive audience for your ideas. Once you get to know the market, you should feel instinctively which is the appropriate outlet for a particular idea.

I stress the word 'idea', for it is nearly always better to submit a story proposal rather than a finished article, certainly to national newspapers and major magazines. Uncommissioned articles occasionally find their way into print if they are outstandingly well written or cover a subject that is entirely new, but not often in my experience, and hardly ever from a writer unknown to the publication. It can be a disheartening business to know that your article is rapidly going out of date as it yellows in a feature editor's in-tray. There is also the risk – dare I say it? – that a staff writer may borrow or steal an idea from an uncommissioned feature that lands in the office and do a similar piece himself. I have known cases where this has happened, and the freelance has little or no comeback. If you challenge the publication, they can give you the time-honoured (and legally correct) reply that there is no copyright in ideas.

Obviously, your ideas for articles are more likely to be commissioned if they know you already. So you have to get a foot in the door. Easier said than done, of course, when you are dealing with busy people. The best approach is always through a personal recommendation. An editor or features editor will naturally be more inclined to see a writer recommended by someone whose judgement he or she respects. A carefully prepared and presented portfolio of cuttings – not too many or they can look forbidding – may be enough to earn an interview, but more often than not they will be returned unread with a note from a secretary saying they have all the writers they need. Nevertheless, it is vital for a freelance to keep cuttings methodically in case of sudden need. This is a case of 'do as I say, rather than do as I do', as I have to admit that I tend to leave my own cuttings in a pile, unsorted and unfiled, and therefore impossible to lay my hands on in a hurry.

Contacts are precious to a freelance. Look after them and keep an up-to-date contacts book. Obviously, an editor who has once accepted your copy is someone to be nurtured, and if he or she can be tempted to an occasional drink, so much the better. But a careful line has to be drawn between being so pushy you become a bore and so retiring that you miss the chance of further commissions. In this sense a telephone call or a letter is less pushy than an e-mail, which may clutter up a busy editor's in-box.

When you make an approach, especially when it results in a meeting, it is important to go prepared with some written ideas and not waste an editor's time with idle chat in the hope that they will produce the ideas. They may well do so, once they know and like your writing, but you should never count on it. Be ready with an answer for the direct question: 'What would you like to write for us?' Another personal tip for freelances: try to restrain your temper if a paper treats you badly, as they sometimes will (by accepting a piece, for example, then dropping it at the last minute because something more urgent has come up, or paying you late, as they nearly all do). You are a supplicant, at least initially until your worth is known, and you cannot afford to make enemies. Besides, the editor you bawl out may well reappear in another guise on another publication next month, or even become very important indeed.

Find out as much as you can about your target publications. This is best done by reading them thoroughly, as I said before, but it is a good idea to keep in touch as well with trade publications which might tell you about a coming change in a publication's editorial style or personnel. They will also give you advance notice about new publications to whom you might apply. Get around to press conferences and try to get yourself invited to drinks parties or awards ceremonies where you can mingle with other journalists and pick up new contacts and hear about possible openings. When you meet someone who works for a publication you are interested in writing for, pump them for all they are worth about what kind of material they are looking for and gaps in their coverage. It can also be useful to probe gently about office politics, who's in and who's out, and above all to discover who are the coming young executives for you to target with ideas.

The other key principle is finding a niche. This may not be a subject you eventually want to write about. The point is that it should be a subject that is likely to get you into print and into a newspaper office, and from there you can work your way up to a position where they will trust you enough to let you write what you want. You may, for example, want to be a foreign correspondent, but there is no point asking for such a big job if you have no experience and the paper doesn't know who you are and what you are capable of. As an editor, I had to reject many such naïve approaches.

I recall similarly naïve, and sometimes arrogant, applications from people who assumed that their academic qualifications – with PhDs in political science or medicine – would automatically make them great journalists and that it would be my newspaper's clear duty and great good fortune to employ them. I had to explain to them gently that acquiring the arts of communication and the skills of investigation were at least as important as academic degrees. For every Dr Tom Stuttaford, who writes so gracefully in *The Times*, there are a hundred doctors with a prose style as impenetrable as their medical notes.

John Sweeney, now an award-winning foreign correspondent, first came to my notice on the *Observer* as a persistent freelance with a line in stories about the nuclear plant at Sellafield. Because these stories ran legal risks, he had to come into the office to defend them to the news desk and lawyers, and before long he seemed to be part of the furniture. He gradually infiltrated his way onto the staff, with beneficial results all round. Not all freelances want a staff job, of course, but it still helps to get contracts and commissions if your face is familiar around the office.

Another way of getting inside an office is to volunteer for holiday or summer shifts. For this purpose it helps to have as many skills as possible, especially I.T. Even if your ambition is to be a film critic rather than a sub-editor, it will do no harm to learn copy-handling skills. Editing other people's copy may improve your own. It will also give you easier access to an office and earn you more professional respect.

Taking a hot breaking story to a news editor is a surefire way to catch his attention, but these opportunities are naturally few and far between. But a freelance with time on his hands, or based in a region where there is a major running story, can make himself invaluable to a news desk by becoming an expert on it and remaining available to monitor any new developments. Nearly all national newspapers have given up on full-time regional correspondents, so a provincial freelance's address and telephone number can be useful to them.

Jonathan Foster, who mainly writes for the *Independent* from Sheffield, is one of the first freelances called by any news desk when there is a new development to be explained in the Jamie Bulger child murder story. The Hillsborough tragedy in Sheffield was another rolling story where regional freelances built up an expertise on which news desks came to rely. Likewise with the child abuse scandal in a children's home in North Wales. In cases like this, a freelance may obtain an advance for a book and can provide newspapers with continuing stories that come to light in the course of his or her research.

For obvious reasons, travel writing is a popular source of income and pleasure for freelances. The 'pleasure' element has to be stressed, because the actual fee for the resulting travel report may be barely enough to justify the time spent on the trip, which prevents you writing about anything else and may cut you off from other possible commissions while you are away. The key to getting these invitations is to make yourself known to the public relations companies who act for national tourist boards or resort developers. They will, of course, expect you to have a firm commission from a newspaper or magazine. But this can work both ways: if you tell an editor you are going to a particular place and would like to offer a piece when you get back, few of them would refuse. They have big supplements to fill at the turn of every year.

One of my outlets is the British Airways magazine, *High Life*. A couple of years ago the editor rang me out of the blue to say that he was too busy to accept a trip to Barbados, travelling by Concorde, and could I possibly take his place? But blue-chip offers like that only tend to arrive when a magazine knows you well. As it happens, that excursion led to a welcome return trip last year and to a friendly relationship with the resort developer involved.

In the 1980s, during the massive upheavals in Eastern Europe and the former Soviet Union, capital cities which had previously been out of bounds to resident journalists, such as Bucarest and Riga, suddenly became important news centres. Few newspapers could afford to fund a permanent bureau, so a new market for freelances suddenly opened up. Some young Britons took a gamble and went to live in these places to set up as freelances, having made contact with various news desks before leaving London. They calculated that they could live there almost as cheaply as in Britain and were sitting on a story that interested the media all over the world. It was both an adventurous and a commercially sound idea. Even if they didn't stay for ever, at least they would make close contacts with British papers which might offer them jobs on their return.

Something like this had happened to me two decades before. I was sent out to Africa by the Thomson Organisation at the age of twenty-four to edit a paper they owned in Nyasaland, which renamed itself Malawi on becoming independent. That was a saga in itself, struggling to report both sides of a civil war at a time when the new African ruler had declared a state of emergency and made it a criminal offence, punishable by five years in jail, to publish anything 'likely to undermine public confidence in the government'. Even Margaret Thatcher never went that far! My predecessor as editor and, as it turned out, my successor, were both expelled from the country, while I managed to hang on by my fingertips.

One reason I was glad to do so was the amount of freelance work available in Africa at that time. British and French colonies were becoming independent with varying degrees of violence. Southern Rhodesia, now Zimbabwe, declared itself independent of Britain under the rebel leadership of Ian Smith. Nigeria and the former Congo were ablaze with civil wars. Few British papers had more than one resident correspondent in the whole of the continent and their foreign desks had no real sense of the distances involved. I would suddenly receive a message from a paper like the *Daily Mail* asking me for 700 words on the situation in Lagos or Kinshasa within a couple of hours, when it would take at least a couple of days to get there. But I managed, by one means or another, usually with the help of British High Commission staff, including MI6 agents sheltering under their wing, to cobble something together.

I established regular arrangements with *The Times*, the *Observer* and the BBC and wrote occasional pieces for nearly everyone, including newspapers and radio stations in South Africa and the United States. My freelance business was so successful that I was able to use the accrued funds to buy a four-bedroom house in Kew when I returned to London. Even more important than that, the reason I returned to London was to take up a job as Deputy News Editor of the *Observer* – a job for which I could never have aspired if they hadn't got used to me through my freelance reports from Africa.

At the *Observer* I kept an eye out for freelances like myself trying to make a name and a living for themselves in Africa. One, in particular, stood out, reporting from the Biafran war. His name was Frederick Forsyth, who went on to fame and fortune as a thriller writer. The early reporting and investigative skills he acquired as a freelance war reporter were certainly a help to his future career, as I'm sure he would acknowledge. I shudder now with embarrassment at the way I used to hack his copy on the news desk because I thought it was sometimes over-emotional.

In those days we filed by telex and occasionally by expensive and unreliable telephone lines. When reporting from territories in former British colonial Africa, the messages were relayed through London; from French Africa they went via Paris. It was long before fax or e-mail, which have made it almost irrelevant these days where you happen to be filing from. I can send my *Daily Telegraph* column from a holiday home in Majorca without anyone even knowing where I am. For freelances, this communications revolution has brought obvious benefits, allowing writers to work from home among their books and family, with easy access to the Internet for research. For many writers it is no longer vital to be in London, which might have been unthinkable for them a few years ago. The continuing and sometimes bewildering developments in digital technology, especially the growth of on-line media, are creating new jobs for journalists all the time, as websites need constant updating with fresh material which can be supplied from anywhere. The radical changes in employment practices over the past decade or so have blurred the distinction between staff and contract workers. More and more publishing functions are being devolved to so-called 'outworkers', as in the textile trade. It is only a slight exaggeration to say that we are all becoming freelances now. Rupert Murdoch has described the role of journalists in the digital age as that of 'bit providers' serving computer technology. This may sound undignified, even demeaning, for the pride of creative people, but it also opens the door to new job opportunities that could never have been imagined when I started my career. These are exciting times for journalists who are prepared to move with them.

Donald Trelford was Editor of the Observer *from 1975–93 and is now Professor of Journalism Studies at Sheffield University and President of the Media Society.*

Regional Newspapers

Regional newspapers are listed in alphabetical order under town. Thus the *Evening Standard* appears under 'L' for London; the *Lancashire Evening Post* under 'P' for Preston.

Aberdeen

Evening Express (Aberdeen)

PO Box 43, Lang Stracht, Mastrick, Aberdeen
AB15 6DF
☎01224 690222 Fax 01224 699575
Owner *Northcliffe Newspapers Group Ltd*
Editor *Donald Martin*
Circulation 68,191

Circulates in Aberdeen and the Grampian region. Local, national and international news and pictures, sport. Family platforms include *What's On*, *Counter* (consumer news), *Eating Out Guide*, *Family Days Out*. Unsolicited mss welcome 'if on a controlled basis'.

    News Editor *Sally McDonald* Freelance news contributors welcome.

    Payment £30–60.

The Press and Journal

PO Box 43, Lang Stracht, Mastrick, Aberdeen
AB15 6DF
☎01224 690222 Fax 01224 663575
Owner *Northcliffe Newspapers Group Ltd*
Editor *Derek Tucker*
Circulation 104,548

Circulates in Aberdeen, Grampians, Highlands, Tayside, Orkney, Shetland and the Western Isles. A well-established regional daily which is said to receive more unsolicited mss a week than the *Sunday Mirror*. Unsolicited mss are nevertheless welcome; approach in writing with ideas. No fiction.

    News Editor *David Knight* Wide variety of hard or off-beat news and features relating especially, but not exclusively, to the North of Scotland.

    Sports Editor *Jim Dolan*
    Women's Page *Susan Mansfield*
    Payment by arrangement.

Barrow-in-Furness

North West Evening Mail

Abbey Road, Barrow in Furness, Cumbria
LA14 5QS
☎01229 821835 Fax 01229 840164
Email news@nwemail.co.uk
Website www.nwemail.co.uk
Owner *CN Group Ltd*
Editor *Sara Hadwin*
Circulation 20,815

All editorial material should be addressed to the editor.

    Assistant Editor (Production) *Bill Myers*
    Sports Editor *Leo Clarke*

Basildon

Evening Echo

Newspaper House, Chester Hall Lane,
Basildon, Essex SS14 3BL
☎01268 522792 Fax 01268 282884
Owner *Newsquest Media Group (a Gannett company)*
Editor *Martin McNeill*
Circulation 47,000

Relies almost entirely on staff and regular outside contributors, but will very occasionally consider material sent on spec. Approach the editor in writing with ideas. Although the paper is Basildon-based, its largest circulation is in the Southend area.

Bath

The Bath Chronicle

Windsor House, Windsor Bridge Road, Bath
BA2 3AU
☎01225 322322 Fax 01225 322291
Owner *BUP Plc*
Editor *David Gledhill*
Circulation 17,501

Local news and features especially welcomed.
    Deputy Editor *John McCready*
    News Editor *Paul Wiltshire*
    Features Editor *Matt Mills*
    Sports Editor *Neville Smith*

Belfast

Belfast Telegraph

Royal Avenue, Belfast BT1 1EB
☎028 9026 4000 Fax 028 9055 4506/4540
Owner *Trinity International Holdings Plc*

Editor *Edmund Curran*
Circulation 124,530

Weekly business supplement.
   Deputy Editor *Jim Flanagan*
   News Editor *Paul Connolly*
   Features Editor *John Caruth*
   Sports Editor *John Laverty*
   Business Editor *Francess McDonnell*

The Irish News
113/117 Donegall Street, Belfast BT1 2GE
☎028 9032 2226 Fax 028 9033 7505

Owner *Irish News Ltd*
Editor *Noel Doran*
Circulation 50,334

All material to appropriate editor (phone to check), or to the news desk.
   Head of Content *Fiona McGarry*
   Arts Editor *Tim Brannigan*
   Sports Editor *John Haughey*
   Women's Page *Ann Molloy*

Sunday Life
124–144 Royal Avenue, Belfast BT1 1EB
☎028 8026 4300 Fax 028 9055 4507

Owner *Trinity International Holdings plc*
Editor/General Manager *Martin Lindsay*
Circulation 96,612
   Deputy Editor *Dave Culbert*
   Features Editor *Sue Corbett*
   Sports Editor *Jim Gracey*

Ulster News Letter
46–56 Boucher Crescent, Belfast BT12 6QY
☎028 9068 0000 Fax 028 9066 4412

Owner *Century Newspapers Ltd*
Editor *Geoff Martin*
Circulation 33,853

Supplements: *Farming Life* (weekly); *Belfast Newsletter*; *Bangor News*.
   Deputy Editor *Mike Chapman*
   News Editors *Ric Clark/Steven Moore*
   Features Editor *Geoff Hill*
   Sports Editor *Brian Millar*
   Fashion & Lifestyle/Property Editor
   Sandra Chapman
   Business Editor *Adrienne McGill*
   Agricultural Editor *David McCoy*

Birmingham
Birmingham Evening Mail
28 Colmore Circus, Queensway, Birmingham
B4 6AX
☎0121 236 3366 Fax 0121 233 0271

Owner *Trinity Mirror Plc*
Editor *Ian Dowell*
Circulation 138,828

Freelance contributions are welcome, particularly topics of interest to the West Midlands and Women's Page pieces offering original and lively comment.
   News Editor *Steve Dyson*
   Features Editor *Paul Cole*
   Women's Page *Diane Parkes*

Birmingham Post
28 Colmore Circus, Queensway, Birmingham
B4 6AX
☎0121 236 3366 Fax 0121 625 1105

Owner *Trinity Mirror Plc*
Publisher *Dan Mason*
Circulation 21,833

One of the country's leading regional newspapers. Freelance contributions are welcome. Topics of interest to the West Midlands and pieces offering lively, original comment are particularly welcome.
   News Editor *Chris Russon*
   Features Editor *Chris Burton*
   Women's Page *Ros Dodd*

Sunday Mercury (Birmingham)
28 Colmore Circus, Queensway, Birmingham
B4 6AZ
☎0121 236 3366 Fax 0121 234 5877

Owner *Trinity Mirror Plc*
Editor *Fiona Alexander*
Circulation 110,501
   Assistant Editor (News & Features) *Bernard Cole*
   Assistant Editor (Sport) *Lee Gibson*

Blackburn
Lancashire Evening Telegraph
Newspaper House, High Street, Blackburn,
Lancashire BB1 1HT
☎01254 678678 Fax 01254 680429
Website www.thisislancashire.co.uk

Owner *Newsquest Media Group Ltd (a Gannett company)*
Editor *Peter Butterfield*
Circulation 43,919

News stories and feature material with an East Lancashire flavour (a local angle, or written by local people) welcome. Approach in writing with an idea in the first instance. No fiction.
   News/Features/Women's Page Editor
   NickNunn

Blackpool
The Gazette (Blackpool)
PO Box 20, Avroe House, Avroe Crescent,
Blackpool, Lancashire FY4 2DP
☎01253 400888 Fax 01253 361870

Owner *RIM*
Managing Director *Philip Welsh*
Editor *To be appointed*
Circulation 40,002

Unsolicited mss welcome in theory. Approach in
writing with an idea. Supplements: *The Result*
(sport, Monday); *Eve* (women, Tuesday); *Wheels*
(motoring, Wednesday); *Property* (Thursday); *Big
Weekend* (entertainment, Friday); *Sevendays*
(entertainment & leisure, Saturday).
   Sports Editor *Jonathan Lee*

Bolton
Bolton Evening News
Newspaper House, Churchgate, Bolton,
Lancashire BL1 1DE
☎01204 522345 Fax 01204 365068
Email ben_editorial@newsquest.co.uk
Website www.thisislancashire.co.uk

Owner *Newsquest Media Group Ltd (a Gannett
company)*
Editor *Mark Rossiter*
Circulation 42,035

Business, children's page, travel, local services,
motoring, fashion and cookery.
   News Editor *Lyn Ashwell*
   Features Editor/Women's Page
      Angela Kelly

Bournemouth
Daily Echo
Richmond Hill, Bournemouth, Dorset BH2
6HH
☎01202 554601 Fax 01202 292115

Owner *Newscom Plc*
Managing Editor *Ian Murray*
Editor *Neal Butterworth*
Circulation 45,090

FOUNDED 1900. Has a strong features content
and invites specialist articles, particularly on
unusual and contemporary subjects but only
with a local angle. Supplements: business, education, homes and gardens, motoring, what's
on, *Weekender*. Regular features on weddings,
property, books, local history, green issues, the
Channel coast. All editorial material should be
addressed to the **News Editor** *Andy Martin*.
   Payment on publication.

Bradford
Telegraph & Argus (Bradford)
Hall Ings, Bradford, West Yorkshire BD1 1JR
☎01274 729511 Fax 01274 723634
Website www.thisislancashire.co.uk

Owner *Newsquest Media Group Ltd (a Gannett
company)*
Editor *Perry Austin-Clarke*
Circulation 51,838

No unsolicited mss – approach in writing with
samples of work. No fiction.
   News Editor *Damian Bates* Local features
and general interest. Showbiz pieces. 600–1000
words (maximum 1500).
   Sports Editor *Alan Birkinshaw*
   Features Editor *Jan Brierley*

Brighton
Evening Argus
Argus House, Crowhurst Road, Hollingbury,
Brighton, East Sussex BN1 8AR
☎01273 544544 Fax 01273 505703
Email simonb@argus-btn.co.uk
Website www.thisisbrighton.co.uk

Owner *Newsquest (Sussex) Ltd*
Editor-in-Chief *Simon Bradshaw*
Circulation 50,285
   News Editor *Ian Carter*
   Sports Editor *Chris Giles*

Bristol
Evening Post
Temple Way, Bristol BS99 7HD
☎0117 9343000 Fax 0117 9343575
Email mail@epost.co.uk
Website www.epost.co.uk

Owner *Bristol United Press plc*
Editor *Mike Lowe*
Circulation 79,346
   News Editor *Kevan Blackadder*
   Features Editor *Matthew Shelley*
   Sports Editor *Chris Bartlett*

Western Daily Press
Temple Way, Bristol BS99 7HD
☎0117 9343000 Fax 0117 9343574

Owner *Bristol Evening Post & Press Ltd*
Editor *Ian Beales*
Circulation 56,679
   Sports Editor *Bill Beckett*
   Women's Page *Lynda Cleasby*

Burton upon Trent

Burton Mail
65–68 High Street, Burton upon Trent,
Staffordshire DE14 1LE
☎01283 512345 Fax 01283 515351

Owner *Burton Daily Mail Ltd*
Editor *Brian Vertigen*
Circulation 18,456

Fashion, health, wildlife, environment, nostalgia,
financial/money (Monday); consumer, motoring
(Tuesday); women's world, rock (Wednesday);
property (Thursday); motoring, farming, what's
on (Friday); what's on, leisure (Saturday).
  News/Features Editor *Andrew Parker*
  Sports Editor *Rex Page*
  Women's Page *Bill Pritchard*

Cambridge

Cambridge Evening News
Winship Road, Milton, Cambridge CB4 6PP
☎01223 434434 Fax 01223 434415

Owner *Cambridge Newspapers Ltd*
Editor *Colin Grant*
Circulation 42,503
News Editor *Helen Montgomery*
  Business Editor *Jenny Chapman*
  Sports Editor *Cyrus Pundole*
  Women's Page *Angela Singer*

Cardiff

South Wales Echo
Thomson House, Havelock Street, Cardiff
CF10 1XR
☎029 2022 3333 Fax 029 2058 3624
Website www.totalwales.com

Owner *Trinity Mirror Plc*
Editor *Robin Fletcher*
Circulation 75,959

Circulates in South and Mid Glamorgan and
Gwent.
  Head of News & Design *Mark Waldron*
  Head of Features & Development
    Tom Edwards
  Head of Sport *Carl Difford*

Wales on Sunday
Thomson House, Havelock Street, Cardiff
CF10 1XR
☎029 2022 3333 Fax 029 2025 8725

Owner *Trinity International Holdings plc*
Editor *Alan Edmunds*
Circulation 62,286

LAUNCHED 1989. Tabloid with sports supple-

ment. Does not welcome unsolicited mss.
  News Editor *Ceri Gould*
  Features/Women's Page *Mike Smith*
  Sports Editor *Paul Abbandonato*

The Western Mail
Thomson House, Havelock Street, Cardiff
CF10 1XR
☎029 2022 3333 Fax 029 2058 3652
Email nfowler@wme.co.uk
Website www.totalwales.com

Owner *Trinity Mirror Plc*
Editor *Neil Fowler*
Circulation 64,172

Circulates in Cardiff, Merthyr Tydfil, Newport,
Swansea and towns and villages throughout
Wales. Mss welcome if of a topical nature, and
preferably of Welsh interest. No short stories or
travel. Approach in writing to the editor. 'Usual
subjects already well covered, e.g. motoring,
travel, books, gardening. We look for the
unusual.' Maximum 1000 words. Opportunities
also on women's page. Supplements: Saturday
Magazine; Welsh Homes; Country and Farming;
Business; Sport, Motoring.
  Deputy Editor *Simon Farrington*
  Assistant Editor *Alastair Milburn*
  Head of Content *Lee Wenham*
  Sports Editor *Mark Tattersall*

Carlisle

News & Star
Newspaper House, Dalston Road, Carlisle,
Cumbria CA2 5UA
☎01228 612600 Fax 01228 612601

Owner *Cumbrian Newspaper Group Ltd*
Editor *Keith Sutton*
Circulation 25,375
Assistant Editor *Nick Turner*
  Deputy Editor *Steve Johnston*
  Sports Editor *Mike Gardner*
  Women's Page *Jane Loughran*

Chatham

Kent Today
395 High Street, Chatham, Kent ME4 4PQ
☎01634 830600 Fax 01634 829484

Owner *Kent Messenger Group*
Editor *Ron Green*
Circulation 21,567
  Assistant Editor (Production) *Neil Webber*
  Business Editor *Trevor Sturgess*
  Community Editor *David Jones*
  Sports Editor *Mike Rees*

Cheltenham

Gloucestershire Echo

1 Clarence Parade, Cheltenham,
Gloucestershire GL50 3NY
☎01242 271900 Fax 01242 271848
Owner *Northcliffe Newspapers Group Ltd*
Editor *Anita Syvret*
Circulation 25,426

All material, other than news, should be addressed to the editor.
   News Editor *Owen Jones*

Chester

Chronicle Newspapers (Chester & North Wales)

Chronicle House, Commonhall Street,
Chester CH1 2BJ
☎01244 340151 Fax 01244 340165
Email B.Adams@chron8.demon.co.uk
Website www.cheshirenews.co.uk
Owner *Trinity Mirror Plc*
Editor-in-Chief *Eric Langton*

All unsolicited feature material will be considered.

Colchester

Evening Gazette (Colchester)

Oriel House, 43–44 North Hill, Colchester,
Essex CO1 1TZ
☎01206 506000 Fax 01206 508274
Email irene_kettle@essex-news.co.uk
Website www.thisisessex.co.uk
Owner *Newsquest (Essex)*
Editor *Irene Kettle*
Circulation 28,206

Monday–Friday daily newspaper servicing north and mid-Essex including Colchester, Harwich, Clacton, Braintree, Witham, Maldon and Chelmsford. Unsolicited mss not generally used. Relies heavily on regular contributors.
   Features Editor *Iris Clapp*

Coventry

Coventry Evening Telegraph

Corporation Street, Coventry CV1 1FP
☎024 7663 3633 Fax 024 7655 0869
Email editorial@go2coventry.co.uk
Owner *Trinity Mirror Plc*
Editor *Alan Kirby*
Circulation 82,417

Unsolicited mss are read, but few are published. Approach in writing with an idea. No fiction. All unsolicited material should be addressed to the editor. Maximum 600 words for features.
   News Editor *John West*
   Features Editor *Paul Simoniti*
   Sports Editor *Roger Draper*
   Women's Page *Barbara Argument*
   Payment negotiable.

Darlington

The Northern Echo

Priestgate, Darlington, Co. Durham DL1 1NF
☎01325 381313 Fax 01325 380539
Owner *Newsquest (North East) Ltd (a Gannett company)*
Editor *Peter Barron*
Circulation 70,358

FOUNDED 1870. Freelance pieces welcome but telephone first to discuss submission.
   News Editor *Sarah Andrews* Interested in reports involving the North-East or North Yorkshire. Preferably phoned in.
   Features Editor *Chris Lloyd* Background pieces to topical news stories relevant to the area. Must be arranged with the features editor before submission of any material.
   Business Editor *Jonathan Jones*
   Sports Editor *Nick Loughlan*
   Payment and length by arrangement.

Derby

Derby Evening Telegraph

Northcliffe House, Meadow Road, Derby
DE1 2DW
☎01332 291111 Fax 01332 253027
Owner *Northcliffe Newspapers Group Ltd*
Editor *Keith Perch*
Circulation 60,691

Weekly business supplement.
   News Editor *Andy Wright*
   Features Editor/Women's Page
   Nigel Poulson
   Sports Editor *Steve Nicholson*
   Motoring Editor *Bob Maddox*

Doncaster

The Doncaster Star

40 Duke Street, Doncaster, South Yorkshire
DN1 3EA
☎01302 344001 Fax 01302 768340
Owner *Sheffield Newspapers Ltd*
Circulation 9,716

Editor/News Editor *Graham Walker*

All editorial material to be addressed to the editor.
  Deputy News Editor *Jane Cartledge*
  Sports Editor *Steve Hossack*
  Women's Page *Jane Stapleton*

Dundee
The Courier and Advertiser
80 Kingsway East, Dundee DD4 8SL
☎01382 223131 Fax 01382 454590
Email courier@dcthomson.co.uk
Website www.thecourier.co.uk

Owner *D. C. Thomson & Co. Ltd*
Editor *Adrian Arthur*
Circulation 95,203

Circulates in East Central Scotland. Features
occasionally accepted on a wide range of subjects, particularly local/Scottish interest –
including finance, insurance, agriculture,
motoring, modern homes, lifestyle and fitness.
Maximum length, 500 words.
  News Editor *Arliss Rhind*
  Features Editor/Women's Page *Shona
    Lorimer*
  Sports Editor *Graham Dey*

Evening Telegraph & Post
80 Kingsway East, Dundee DD4 8SL
☎01382 223131 Fax 01382 454590

Owner *D. C. Thomson & Co. Ltd*
Editor *Alan Proctor*
Circulation 31,309

Circulates in Tayside, Dundee and Fife. All
material should be addressed to the editor.

East Anglia
East Anglian Daily Times
See under *Ipswich*

Eastern Daily Press
See under *Norwich*

Edinburgh
Evening News
108 Holyrood Road, Edinburgh EH1 1YT
☎0131 620 8620 Fax 0131 620 8696

Owner *European Press Holdings Ltd*
Editor *John C. McLellan*
Circulation 90,000

FOUNDED 1873. Circulates in Edinburgh, Fife,
Central and Lothian. Coverage: entertainment,
gardening, motoring, shopping, fashion, health

and lifestyle, showbusiness. Occasional plat-
form pieces, features of topical and/or local
interest. Unsolicited feature material welcome.
Approach the appropriate editor in writing.
  Associate Editor (News) *David Lee*
  Associate Editor (Features) *Helen Martin*
  Sports Editor *Martin Dempster*
  Payment NUJ/house rates.

Exeter
Express & Echo
Heron Road, Sowton, Exeter, Devon EX2 7NF
☎01392 442211
Fax 01392 442294/442287 (editorial)
Email echonews@westcountrypublications.
co.uk Website www.thisisexeter.co.uk

Owner *Westcountry Publications Limited*
Editor *Steve Hall*
Circulation 30,978

Weekly supplements: *Business Week; Property
Echo; Wheels; Weekend Echo.*
  News Editor *Chris Styles*
  Features Editor/Women's Page *Sue Kemp*
  Sports Editor *Simon Mills*

Glasgow
Evening Times
195 Albion Street, Glasgow G1 1QP
☎0141 552 6255 Fax 0141 553 1355

Owner *Scottish Media Newspapers Ltd*
Editor *Charles McGhee*
Circulation 110,585

Circulates in Glasgow and the west of Scotland.
Supplements: *Job Search; Home Front; Woman;
Times Out* (leisure); *Times Out Weekend Extra.*
  News Editor *To be appointed*
  Features Editor *Russell Kyle*
  Sports Editor *David Stirling*
  Women's Editor *Agnes Stevenson*

The Herald (Glasgow)
See **National Newspapers**

Gloucester
The Citizen
St John's Lane, Gloucester GL1 2AY
☎01452 424442 Fax 01452 420664 (Editorial)

Owner *Northcliffe Newspapers Group Ltd*
Editor *Spencer Feeney*
Circulation 25,426

All editorial material to be addressed to the
News Editor *Gavin Curry*.

Gloucestershire Echo
See under *Cheltenham*

Greenock

Greenock Telegraph
2 Crawfurd Street, Greenock PA15 1LH
☎01475 726511 Fax 01475 783734
Owner *Clyde & Forth Press Ltd*
Editor *Ian Wilson*
Circulation 19,872

Circulates in Greenock, Port Glasgow, Gourock, Kilmacolm, Langbank, Bridge of Weir, Inverkip, Wemyss Bay, Skelmorlie, Largs. Unsolicited mss considered 'if they relate to the newspaper's general interests'. No fiction. All material to be addressed to the editor.

Grimsby

Grimsby Evening Telegraph
80 Cleethorpe Road, Grimsby, N. E. Lincs DN31 3EH
☎01472 360360 Fax 01472 372257
Email newsdesk@grimsbytelegraph.co.uk
Owner *Northcliffe Newspapers Group Ltd*
Editor *Peter Moore*
Circulation 71,167

Sister paper of the *Scunthorpe Evening Telegraph*. Unsolicited mss generally welcome. Approach in writing. No fiction. Monthly supplement: *Business Telegraph*. All material to be addressed to the **News Editor** *S. P. Richards*. Particularly welcomes hard news stories – approach in haste by telephone.
    Special Publications Editor *B. Farnsworth*

Guernsey

Guernsey Press & Star
Braye Road, Vale, Guernsey, Channel Islands GY1 3BW
☎01481 240240 Fax 01481 240235
Email newsroom@guernsey-press.com
Website www.guernsey-press.com
Owner *Guiton Group*
Editor *Nick Machon*
Circulation 16,000

Special pages include children's and women's interest, gardening and fashion.
    News Editor *James Falla*
    Sports Editor *Rob Batiste*
    Women's Page *Jackie Chappell*

Halifax

Evening Courier
PO Box 19, King Cross Street, Halifax, West Yorkshire HX1 2SF
☎01422 260200 Fax 01422 260341
Owner *Johnston Press Plc*
Editor *Edward Riley*
Circulation 29,000
    News Editor *John Kenealy*
    Features Editor *William Marshall*
    Sports Editor *Ian Rushworth*
    Women's Page *Diane Crabtree*

Hartlepool

Mail (Hartlepool)
New Clarence House, Wesley Square, Hartlepool TS24 8BX
☎01429 274441 Fax 01429 869024
Owner *Johnston Press Plc*
Editor *Harry Blackwood*
Circulation 24,263
    News Editor *Gavin Ledwith*
    Features Editor *Bernice Saltzer*
    Sports Editor *Roy Kelly*

Huddersfield

Huddersfield Daily Examiner
Queen Street South, Huddersfield, West Yorkshire HD1 2TD
☎01484 430000 Fax 01484 437789
Owner *Trinity Mirror Plc*
Editor *John Williams*
Circulation 35,218

Home improvement, home heating, weddings, dining out, motoring, fashion, services to trade and industry.
    Deputy Editor *Melvyn Briggs*
    Assistant Editor *John Bird*
    News Editor *Neil Atkinson*
    Features Editor *Andrew Flynn*
    Sports Editor *John Gledhill*
    Women's Page *Hilarie Stelfox*

Hull

Hull Daily Mail
Blundell's Corner, Beverley Road, Hull, North Humberside HU3 1XS
☎01482 327111 Fax 01482 584353
Owner *Northcliffe Newspapers Group Ltd*
Editor *John Meehan*
Circulation 88,000
    Head of News *Marc Astley*
    Women's Page *Richard Rae*

Ipswich
East Anglian Daily Times
Press House, 30 Lower Brook Street, Ipswich, Suffolk IP4 1AN
☎01473 230023 Fax 01473 211391
Email EADT@ecn.co.uk
Website www.suffolk.now.co.uk
Owner *Eastern Counties Newspapers Group Ltd*
Editor *Terry Hunt*
Circulation 46,008

FOUNDED 1874. Unsolicited mss generally not welcome; three or four received a week and almost none are used. Approach in writing in the first instance. No fiction. Supplements: Young Readers' section (Monday); Business (Tuesday); Job Quest (Wednesday); Property (Thursday); Motoring (Friday); Magazine (Saturday).
News Editor *Mark Hindle* Hard news stories involving East Anglia (Suffolk, Essex particularly) or individuals resident in the area are always of interest.
Features *Steve Hughes* (**Deputy Editor**) Mostly in-house, but will occasionally buy in when the subject is of strong Suffolk/East Anglian interest. Photo features preferred (extra payment). Special advertisement features are regularly run. Some opportunities here. Maximum 1000 words.
Sports Editor *Nick Garnham*
Women's Page *Victoria Hawkins*

Evening Star
30 Lower Brook Street, Ipswich, Suffolk IP4 1AN
☎01473 230023 Fax 01473 225296
Owner *Eastern Counties Newspaper Group*
Editor *Nigel Pickover*
Circulation 30,391
Deputy Editor (News) *Russell Cook*
Sports Editor *Mike Horne*

Jersey
Jersey Evening Post
PO Box 582, Jersey, Channel Islands JE4 8XQ
☎01534 611611 Fax 01534 611622
Email editorial@jerseyeveningpost.com
Website www.jerseyeveningpost.com
Owner *Jersey Evening Post Ltd*
Editor *Chris Bright*
Circulation 23,070

Special pages: gardening, motoring, property, boating, technology, young person's (16–25), women, food and drink, personal finance, rock reviews, health, business.

News Editor *Sue Le Ruez*
Features Editor *Richard Pedley*
Sports Editor *Ron Felton*

Kent
Kent Messenger
See under *Maidstone*

Kent Today
See under *Chatham*

Kettering
Evening Telegraph
Newspaper House, Ise Park, Rothwell Road, Kettering, Northamptonshire NN16 8GA
☎01536 506100 Fax 01536 506195
Email editor@
northamptonshireeveningtelegraph.co.uk
Website www.northamptonshireevening
telegraph.co.uk
Owner *Johnston Press Plc*
Managing Editor *David Rowell*
Circulation 33,346

Northamptonshire Business Guide (weekly); *Guide* supplement (Thursday/Saturday), featuring TV, gardening, videos, films, eating out; and a monthly supplement, *Home & Garden.*
News Editor *Nick Tite*
Sports Editor *Ian Davidson*

Lancashire
Lancashire Evening Post
See under *Preston*

Lancashire Evening Telegraph
See under *Blackburn*

Leamington Spa
Leamington Spa Courier
32 Hamilton Terrace, Leamington Spa, Warwickshire CV32 4LY
☎01926 888222 Fax 01926 339960
Email editorial@leamingtoncourier.co.uk
Website www.leamingtononline.co.uk
Owner *Central Counties Newspapers*
Editor *Martin Lawson*
Circulation 13,410

One of the Leamington Spa Courier Series which also includes the *Warwick Courier* and *Kenilworth Weekly News.* Unsolicited feature articles considered, particularly matter with a local angle. Telephone with idea first.
News Editor *Richard Parker*

Leeds

Yorkshire Evening Post
Wellington Street, Leeds, West Yorkshire
LS1 1RF
☎0113 2432701 Fax 0113 2388536

Owner *Regional Independent Media*
Editor *Neil Hodgkinson*
Circulation 100,596

Evening sister of the *Yorkshire Post*.
  News Editor *David Helliwell*
  Features Editor *Anne Pickles*
  Sports Editor *Martin Rose*
  Women's Page *Carmen Bruegmann*

Yorkshire Post
Wellington Street, Leeds, West Yorkshire
LS1 1RF
☎0113 2432701 Fax 0113 2388537

Owner *Regional Independent Media*
Editor *Tony Watson*
Circulation 75,836

A serious-minded, quality regional daily with a generally conservative outlook. Three or four unsolicited mss arrive each day; all will be considered but initial approach in writing preferred. All submissions should be addressed to the editor. No fiction, poetry or family histories.
  Head of Content *John Furbisher*
  Features Editor *Mick Hickling* Open to suggestions in all fields (though ordinarily commissioned from specialist writers).
  Sports Editor *Bill Bridge*
  Women's Page *Jill Armstrong*

Leicester

Leicester Mercury
St George Street, Leicester LE1 9FQ
☎0116 2512512 Fax 0116 2530645
Website www.thisisleicestershire.co.uk

Owner *Northcliffe Newspapers Group Ltd*
Editor *Nick Carter*
Circulation 108,793
  News Editor *Mary Williams*
  Features Editor *Alex Dawon*

Lincoln

Lincolnshire Echo
Brayford Wharf East, Lincoln LN5 7AT
☎01522 525252 Fax 01522 545759
Email editorecho@dial.pipex.com

Owner *Northcliffe Newspapers Group Ltd*
Editor *Michael Sassi*

Circulation 29,206

Best buys, holidays, motoring, dial-a-service, restaurants, sport, leisure, home improvement, record reviews, gardening corner, stars. All editorial material to be addressed to the editor.

Liverpool

Daily Post
PO Box 48, Old Hall Street, Liverpool L69 3EB
☎0151 227 2000 Fax 0151 236 4682
Email online@day-post.u-net.com

Owner *Liverpool Daily Post and Echo Ltd*
Editor *Alastair Machray*
Circulation 72,776

Unsolicited mss welcome. Receives about six a day. Approach in writing with an idea. No fiction. Local, national/international news, current affairs, profiles – with pictures. Maximum 800–1000 words.
  Features Editor *Andrew Forgrave*
  News Editor *Ian Lang*
  Sports Editor *Richard Williamson*
  Women's Page *Margaret Kitchen*

Liverpool Echo
PO Box 48, Old Hall Street, Liverpool L69 3EB
☎0151 227 2000 Fax 0151 236 4682

Owner *Liverpool Daily Post & Echo Ltd*
Editor *Mark Dickinson*
Circulation 157,999

One of the country's major regional dailies. Unsolicited mss welcome; initial approach with ideas in writing preferred.
  News Editor *Andrew Edwards*
  Features Editor *Andrew Forgrave*
  Sports Editor *Ken Rogers*
  Women's Editor *Susan Lee*

London

Evening Standard
Northcliffe House, 2 Derry Street, London
W8 5EE
☎020 7938 6000 Fax 020 7937 2648

Owner *Associated Newspapers/Lord Rothermere*
Editor *Max Hastings*
Circulation 450,000

Long-established evening paper, serving Londoners with both news and feature material. Genuine opportunities for London-based features. Produces a weekly colour supplement, *ES The Evening Standard Magazine*, a weekly listings magazine *Hot Tickets* and regular weekly supplements: *Just the Job* (Monday) and *Homes & Property* (Wednesday).

Deputy Editor *Andrew Bordiss*
Associate Editor (Features) *Nicola Jeal*
News Editor *Stephen Clackson*
Features Editor *Bernice Davison*
Sports Editor *Simon Greenberg*
Editor, ES *Mimi Spencer*
Editor, Hot Tickets *Mark Booker*

Maidstone

Kent Messenger

6 & 7 Middle Row, Maidstone, Kent
ME14 1TG
☎01622 695666 Fax 01622 757227
Email kentmessenger@thekmgroup.co.uk
Website www.kentonline.co.uk

Owner *Kent Messenger Group*
Editor *Simon Irwin*
Circulation 48,425

Very little freelance work is commissioned.

Manchester

Manchester Evening News

164 Deansgate, Manchester M60 2RD
☎0161 832 7200 Fax 0161 834 3814
Website www.manchesteronline.co.uk

Owner *Manchester Evening News Ltd*
Editor *Paul Horrocks*
Circulation 173,446

One of the country's major regional dailies. Initial approach in writing preferred. No fiction. *Property* (Tues); *Lifestyle* (Fri/Sat); *Holiday feature* (Sat).

News Editor *Lisa Roland*
Features Editor *Maggie Henfield* Regional news features, personality pieces and showbiz profiles considered. Maximum 1200 words.
Sports Editor *Peter Spencer*
Women's Page *Diane Cooke*
Payment based on house agreement rates.

Middlesbrough

Evening Gazette

Borough Road, Middlesbrough, Cleveland
TS1 3AZ
☎01642 234242 Fax 01642 249843

Owner *Trinity International Holdings plc*
Editor *Paul Robertson*
Circulation 69,000

Special pages: business, motoring, home, computing.

News Editor *Tony Beck*
Features Editor/Women's Page *Kathryn Armstrong*

Sports Editor *Allan Boughey*
Consumer *Michelle Ruane*
Health *Amanda Todd*
Councils *Sandy McKenzie*
Education *Karen Bell*

Mold

Evening Leader

Mold Business Park, Wrexham Road, Mold,
Clwyd CH7 1XY
☎01352 707707 Fax 01352 752180

Owner *North Wales Newspapers*
Editor *Reg Herbert*
Circulation 30,976

Circulates in Wrexham, Flintshire, Rhyl, Deeside and Chester. Special pages/features: motoring, travel, arts, women's, children's, photography, local housing, information and news for the disabled, music and entertainment.

Features Editor/Women's Page *Debra Greenhouse*
News Editors *Joanne Shone, Nick Bourne*
Sports Editor *Allister Syme*

Newcastle upon Tyne

Evening Chronicle

Thomson House, Groat Market, Newcastle upon Tyne, Tyne and Wear NE1 1ED
☎0191 232 7500 Fax 0191 232 2256
Website www.evening-chronicle.co.uk

Owner *Trinity Mirror Plc*
Editor *Alison Hastings*
Circulation 111,178

Receives a lot of unsolicited material, much of which is not used. Family issues, gardening, pop, fashion, cooking, consumer, films and entertainment guide, home improvements, motoring, property, angling, sport and holidays. Approach in writing with ideas.

News Editor *Mick Smith*
Features Limited opportunities due to full-time feature staff. Maximum 1000 words.
Sports Editor *Paul New*
Women's Interests *Kay Jordan*

The Journal

Thomson House, Groat Market, Newcastle upon Tyne, Tyne & Wear NE1 1ED
☎0191 232 7500
Fax 0191 232 2256/201 6044
Email jnl.newsdesk@ncjmedia.co.uk
Website www.the-journal.co.uk

Owner *Trinity Mirror Plc*

Editor *Gerard Henderson*
Circulation 51,936

Daily platforms include farming and business. Monthly full-colour business supplement: *The Journal Northern Business Magazine.*
Deputy Editor *Paul Robertson*
Sports Editor *Kevin Dinsdale*
Arts & Entertainment Editor *David Whetstone*
Environment Editor *Tony Henderson*
Business Editor *Peter Jackson*

Sunday Sun

Thomson House, Groat Market, Newcastle upon Tyne, Tyne & Wear NE1 1ED
☎0191 201 6330 Fax 0191 230 0238
Email petermontellier@sundaysun.co.uk
Owner *Trinity Mirror Plc*
Editor *Peter Montellier*
Circulation 112,918

All material should be addressed to the appropriate editor (phone to check), or to the editor.
Sports Editor *Dylan Younger*

Newport

South Wales Argus

Cardiff Road, Maesglas, Newport, Gwent NP9 1QW
☎01633 810000 Fax 01633 462202
Owner *Newscom Plc*
Editor *Gerry Keighley*
Circulation 30,644

Circulates in Newport, Gwent and surrounding areas.
News Editor *Nicole Garnon*
Features Editor/Women's Page *Lesley Williams*
Sports Editor *Rob Freeman*

Northampton

Chronicle and Echo

Upper Mounts, Northampton NN1 3HR
☎01604 467000 Fax 01604 467190
Owner *Northamptonshire Newspapers*
Editor *Mark Edwards*
Circulation 27,778

Unsolicited mss are 'not necessarily unwelcome but opportunities to use them are rare'. Some three or four arrive weekly. Approach in writing with an idea. No fiction. Supplements: *Sports Chronicle* (Monday); *Property Week* (Wednesday);

What's On Guide (Thursday); *Weekend Motors* (Friday).
News Editor *Richard Edmondson*
Features Editor/Women's Page *Jessica Pilkington*
Sports Editor *Steve Pitts*

Northern Ireland

Belfast Telegraph
See under *Belfast*

The Irish News
See under *Belfast*

Sunday Life
See under *Belfast*

Norfolk

Eastern Daily Press

Prospect House, Rouen Road, Norwich, Norfolk NR1 1RE
☎01603 628311 Fax 01603 612930
Website www.ecn.co.uk
Owner *Eastern Counties Newspapers*
Editor *Peter Franzen*
Circulation 78,647

Most pieces by commission only. Supplements: what's on (daily); motoring, business, property pages, women's interests, agriculture (all weekly); employment (twice-weekly); arts focus (monthly); plus horse and rider, boating, golf and wildlife; Saturday full colour magazine.
News Editor *Paul Durrant*
Features Editor *David Macaulay*
Sports Editor *David Thorpe*
Magazine Editor *Peter Waters*

Evening News

Prospect House, Rouen Road, Norwich, Norfolk NR1 1RE
☎01603 628311 Fax 01603 612930
Website www.ecn.co.uk
Owner *Eastern Counties Newspapers*
Editor *Bob Crawley*
Circulation 36,458

Includes special pages on local property, motoring, children's page, pop, fashion, arts, entertainments and TV, gardening, local music scene, home and family.
Assistant Editor *Roy Strowger*
Deputy Editor *Celia Sutton*
Features Editor *Derek James*

Nottingham

Evening Post Nottingham
Castle Wharf House, Nottingham NG1 7EU
☎0115 9482000 Fax 0115 9644032
Owner *Northcliffe Newspapers Group Ltd*
Editor *Graham Glen*
Circulation 97,000

Unsolicited mss occasionally used. Good local interest only. Maximum 800 words. No fiction. Send ideas in writing. Supplements: motoring, business, holidays and travel supplements; financial, employment and consumer pages.
   News Editor *Neil White*
   Deputy Editor *Jon Grubb*
   Sports Editor *Kevin Pick*

Oldham

Evening Chronicle
PO Box 47, Union Street, Oldham,
Lancashire OL1 1EQ
☎0161 633 2121 Fax 0161 652 2111
Email oec@compuserve.com
Owner *Hirst Kidd & Rennie Ltd*
Editor *Jim Williams*
Circulation 32,206

Motoring, food and wine, women's page, business page.
   News Editor *Mike Attenborough*
   Women's Page *Ralph Badham*

Oxford

Oxford Mail
Osney Mead, Oxford OX2 0EJ
☎01865 425262 Fax 01865 425554
Owner *Newsquest (Oxfordshire) Ltd*
Editor *Patrick Fleming*
Circulation 35,000

Unsolicited mss are considered but a great many unsuitable offerings are received. Approach in writing with an idea, rather than by phone. No fiction. All fees negotiable.

Paisley

Paisley Daily Express
14 New Street, Paisley PA1 1YA
☎0141 887 7911 Fax 0141 887 6254
Owner *Scottish & Universal Newspapers Ltd*
Editor *Norman Macdonald*
Circulation 9,067

Circulates in Paisley, Linwood, Renfrew, Johnstone, Elderslie, Neilston and Barrhead.

Unsolicited mss welcome only if of genuine local (Paisley) interest. The paper does not commission work, and will consider submitted material. Maximum 1000–1500 words. All submissions to the editor.
   News Editor *Anne Dalrymple*
   Sports Editor *Matthew Vallance*

Plymouth

Evening Herald
17 Brest Road, Derriford Business Park,
Derriford, Plymouth, Devon PL6 5AA
☎01752 765500 Fax 01752 765527
Email editor@thisisplymouth.co.uk
Website www.thisisplymouth.co.uk
Owner *Northcliffe Newspapers Group Ltd*
Editor *Rachael Campey*
Circulation 53,626

All editorial material to be addressed to the editor or the **News Editor** *Bill Martin*.

Sunday Independent
Burrington Way, Plymouth, Devon PL5 3LN
☎01752 206600 Fax 01752 206164
Owner *Newscom Plc*
Editor *Nikki Rowlands*
Circulation 38,958

Tabloid Sunday covering the whole of the West Country from Bristol to Weymouth and Land's End. News stories/tips, news features. All editorial should be addressed to the editor. Payment by arrangement.

Western Morning News
17 Brest Road, Derriford Business Park,
Derriford, Plymouth, Devon PL6 5AA
☎01752 765500 Fax 01752 765535
Owner *Northcliffe Newspapers Group Ltd*
Editor *Barrie Williams*
Circulation 53,050

Unsolicited mss welcome, but must be of topical and local interest and addressed to the **News Editor**, *Jason Clark*.
   Sports Editor *Rick Cowdery*

Portsmouth

The News
The News Centre, Hilsea, Portsmouth,
Hampshire PO2 9SX
☎023 9266 4488 Fax 023 9267 3363
Email newsdesk@thenews.co.uk
Website www.thenews.co.uk
Owner *Portsmouth Printing & Publishing Ltd*

Editor *Mike Gilson*
Circulation 73,161

Unsolicited mss not generally accepted. Approach by letter.

News Editor *Mary Williams*
Features Editor *Rachel Hughes* General subjects of S. E. Hants interest. Maximum 600 words. No fiction.
Sports Editor *Dave King* Sports background features. Maximum 600 words.

Preston
Lancashire Evening Post
Olivers Place, Eastway, Fulwood, Preston, Lancashire PR2 9ZA
☎01772 254841 Fax 01772 880173
Website www.lep.co.uk
Owner *Regional Independent Media*
Editor *Roger Borrell*
Circulation 48,831

Unsolicited mss are not generally welcome; many are received and not used. All ideas in writing to the editor.

Reading
Reading Evening Post
8 Tessa Road, Reading, Berkshire RG1 8NS
☎0118 9183000 Fax 0118 9599363
Email editorial@reading-epost.co.uk
Owner *Guardian Media Group*
Editor *Andy Murrill*
Circulation 23,802

Unsolicited mss welcome; one or two received every day. Fiction rarely used. Interested in local news features, human interest, well-researched investigations. Special sections include holidays & travel (Monday); food page (Tuesday); children's page (Tuesday); style page (Wednesday); business (Wednesday & Friday); motoring and motorcycling; gardening; rock music (Friday).

Scarborough
Scarborough Evening News
17–23 Aberdeen Walk, Scarborough, North Yorkshire YO11 1BB
☎01723 363636 Fax 01723 383825
Email editor@scarborough-news.demon.co.uk
Owner *Yorkshire Regional Newspapers Ltd*
Editor *David Penman*
Circulation 17,154

Special pages include property (Monday); motoring (Tuesday/Friday).

News Editor *Neil Pickford*
Motoring *Dennis Sissons*
Sports Editor *Charles Place*
All other material should be addressed to the editor.

Scotland
Daily Record (Glasgow)
See **National Newspapers**

Scotland on Sunday (Edinburgh)
See **National Newspapers**

The Scotsman (Edinburgh)
See **National Newspapers**

Sunday Herald (Glasgow)
See **National Newspapers**

Sunday Mail (Glasgow)
See **National Newspapers**

Sunday Post (Dundee)
See **National Newspapers**

Scunthorpe
Scunthorpe Evening Telegraph
Doncaster Road, Scunthorpe, N. E. Lincs DN15 7RQ
☎01724 273273 Fax 01724 273101
Owner *Northcliffe Newspapers Group Ltd*
Editor *Michelle Lalor*
Circulation 24,292

All correspondence should go to the **News Editor** *Lisa Wheaton.*

Sheffield
The Star
York Street, Sheffield, South Yorkshire S1 1PU
☎0114 2767676 Fax 0114 2725978
Owner *Sheffield Newspapers Ltd*
Editor *Peter Charlton*
Circulation 102,749

Unsolicited mss not welcome, unless topical and local.

News Editor *Bob Westerdale* Contributions only accepted from freelance news reporters if they relate to the area.
Features Editor *Jim Collins* Rarely requires outside features, unless on specialised subject.
Sports Editor *Martin Smith*
Women's Page *Jo Davison*
Payment negotiable.

Shropshire

Shropshire Star
See under *Telford*

South Shields

Gazette
Chapter Row, South Shields, Tyne & Wear
NE33 1BL
☎0191 455 4661 Fax 0191 456 8270
Website www.shields-gazette.co.uk
Owner *Northeast Press Ltd*
Editor *Rob Lawson*
Circulation 23,332
　News Editor *Gary Welford*
　Sports Editor *John Cornforth*
　Women's Page *Joy Yates*

Southampton

The Southern Daily Echo
Newspaper House, Test Lane, Redbridge,
Southampton, Hampshire SO16 9JX
☎023 8042 4777 Fax 023 8042 4770
Owner *Newscom Plc*
Editor *Ian Murray*
Circulation 60,343

Unsolicited mss 'tolerated'. Approach the editor in writing with strong ideas; staff supply almost all the material.

Stoke on Trent

The Sentinel
Sentinel House, Etruria, Stoke on Trent,
Staffordshire ST1 5SS
☎01782 602525 Fax 01782 280781
Owner *Staffordshire Sentinel Newspapers Ltd*
Editor *Sean Dooley*
Circulation 90,368

Weekly sports final supplement. All material should be sent to the **Head of Content** *Michael Wood*.

Sunderland

Sunderland Echo
Echo House, Pennywell, Sunderland, Tyne &
Wear SR4 9ER
☎0191 501 5800 Fax 0191 534 5975
Owner *Johnston Press Plc*
Group Editorial Director *Andrew Smith*
Circulation 58,397

All editorial material to be addressed to the **News Editor** *Patrick Lavelle*.

Swansea

South Wales Evening Post
Adelaide Street, Swansea, West Glamorgan
SA1 1QT
☎01792 510000 Fax 01792 514697
Email postbox@swwp.co.uk
Website www.thisissouthwales.co.uk
Owner *Northcliffe Newspapers Group Ltd*
Editor *George Edwards*
Circulation 63,856

Circulates throughout south west Wales.
　News Editor *Jonathan Isaacs*
　Features Editor *Andy Pearson*
　Sports Editor *David Evans*

Swindon

Evening Advertiser
100 Victoria Road, Swindon, Wilts SN1 3BE
☎01793 528144 Fax 01793 542434
Email editor@newswilts.co.uk
Website www.thisiswiltshire.co.uk
Owner *Newsquest (Wiltshire) Ltd*
Editor *Simon O'Neill*
Circulation 26,343

Copy and ideas invited but 'must be strongly related or relevant to the town of Swindon or the county of Wiltshire.' Little scope for freelance work. Fees vary depending on material.
　Deputy Editor *Pauline Leighton*
　News Editor *Mark Drew*
　Sports Editor *Matt Reeder*

Telford

Shropshire Star
Ketley, Telford, Shropshire TF1 4HU
☎01952 242424 Fax 01952 254605
Owner *Shropshire Newspapers Ltd*
Editor *Adrian Faber*
Circulation 89,619

No unsolicited mss; approach the editor with ideas in writing. No news or fiction.
　News Editor *Sarah-Jane Smith*
　Head of Supplements *Sharon Walters* Limited opportunities; uses mostly in-house or syndicated material. Maximum 1200 words.
　Sports Editor *Keith Harrison*

Torquay

Herald Express
Harmsworth House, Barton Hill Road,
Torquay, Devon TQ2 8JN
☎01803 676000 Fax 01803 676299/676228
Owner *Northcliffe Newspapers Group Ltd*

Editor *B. Hanrahan*
Circulation 30,174

Drive scene, property guide, *What's On Now* – leisure guide, Monday sports, special pages, rail trail, Saturday surgery, nature and conservation column. Supplements: *Gardening* (quarterly); *Visitors Guide* and *Antiques & Collectables* (fortnightly); *Devon Days Out* (every Saturday in summer and at Easter and May Bank Holidays). Unsolicited mss generally not welcome. All editorial material should be addressed to the editor in writing.

Wales

South Wales Argus
See under *Newport*

South Wales Echo
See under *Cardiff*

South Wales Evening Post
See under *Swansea*

Wales on Sunday
See under *Cardiff*

Western Mail
See under *Cardiff*

West of England

Express & Echo
See under *Exeter*

Western Daily Press
See under *Bristol*

Western Morning News
See under *Plymouth*

Weymouth

Dorset Evening Echo
Fleet House, Hampshire Road, Granby Industrial Estate, Weymouth, Dorset DT4 9XD
☎01305 830930 Fax 01305 830956

Owner *Newscom Plc*
Editor *David Murdock*
Circulation 20,430

Farming, by-gone days, films, arts, showbiz, brides, children's page, motoring, property, weekend leisure and entertainment including computers and gardening.
    News Editor *Paul Thomas*
    Sports Editor *Jack Wyllie*

Wolverhampton

Express & Star
Queen Street, Wolverhampton, West Midlands WV1 1ES
☎01902 313131 Fax 01902 319721

Owner *Midlands News Association*
Editor *Warren Wilson*
Circulation 182,146
    Deputy Editor *Richard Ewels*
    News Editor *John Bray*
    Features Editor *Jim Walsh*
    Sports Editor *Steve Gordos*
    Women's Page *Shirley Tart*

Worcester

Evening News
Berrow's House, Hylton Road, Worcester WR2 5JX
☎01905 748200 Fax 01905 748009

Owner *Newsquest (Midlands South) Ltd*
Editor *Andrew Martin*
Circulation 23,102

Local events (Tues); jobs/careers (Weds); property (Thurs); showbiz/what's on, motoring/Pulse pop page (Fri); holidays/what's on (Sat).
    News Editor *Tina Faulkner*
    Features/Women's Page *Mark Higgitt*
    Sports Editor *Paul Ricketts*

York

Evening Press
PO Box 29, 76–86 Walmgate, York YO1 9YN
☎01904 653051 Fax 01904 612853
Email editor@ycp.co.uk
Website www.thisisyork.co.uk

Owner *Newsquest Media Group (a Gannett co.)*
Editor *Elizabeth Page*
Circulation 42,074

Unsolicited mss not welcome, unless from journalists of proven ability. *Business Press Pages* (Tues), *Property Press* (Thurs), *Friday Night Fever* what's on (Fri), *8 Days* TV supplement (Sat).
    News Editor *Fran Clee*
    Picture Editor *Martin Oates*
    Sports Editor *Martin Jarred*
    Payment negotiable.

Yorkshire

Yorkshire Evening Post
See under *Leeds*

Yorkshire Post
See under *Leeds*

Magazines

Abraxas
57 Eastbourne Road, St Austell, Cornwall
PL25 4SU
☎01726 64975 Fax 01726 64975
Owner *Paul Newman*
Editors *Paul Newman, Pamela Smith-Rawnsley*
FOUNDED 1991. QUARTERLY incorporating
the *Colin Wilson Newsletter*. Unsolicited mss
welcome after a study of the magazine – initial
approach by phone or letter preferred.
    Features Essays, translations and reviews.
Welcomes provocative, lively articles on little-
known literary figures and new slants on psychology, existentialism and ideas. Maximum
length 2000 words. *Payment* nominal if at all.
    Fiction One story per issue, max. 2000
words. Favours compact, obsessional stories.
    Poetry Double-page spread per issue – slight
penchant for the surreal but open to most styles.
Payment free copy of magazine.

Acclaim
See **The New Writer**

Accountancy
40 Bernard Street, London WC1N 1LD
☎020 7833 3291 Fax 020 7833 2085
Owner *Institute of Chartered Accountants in*
   England and Wales
Editor *Brian Singleton-Green*
Circulation 64,505
FOUNDED 1889. MONTHLY. Written ideas welcome. **Features** *Brian Singleton-Green* Account-
ing/ tax/business-related articles of high technical content aimed at professional/managerial
readers. Maximum 2000 words.
    Payment by arrangement.

Accountancy Age
32–34 Broadwick Street, London W1A 2HG
☎020 7316 9000/Features: 020 7316 9611
Fax 020 7316 9250
Email accountancy_age@vnu.co.uk
Website www.accountancyage.com
Owner *VNU Business Publications*
Editor *Douglas Broom*
News Editor *Damian Wild* (020 7316 9237)
Circulation 79,085
FOUNDED 1969. WEEKLY. Unsolicited mss wel-
come. Ideas may be suggested in writing pro-

vided they are clearly thought out. **Features** *Liz
Loxton* Topics right across the accountancy, business and financial world. Maximum 2000 words.
    Payment negotiable.

Ace Tennis Magazine
9–11 North End Road, London W14 8ST
☎020 7605 8000 Fax 020 7602 2323
Email Dominic.Bliss@acemag.co.uk
Owner *Tennis GB*
Editor *Dominic Bliss*
Circulation 45,000
FOUNDED 1996. MONTHLY specialist tennis
magazine. News (250 words max.) and features
(2000 words max.). No unsolicited mss; send
feature synopses by fax in the first instance. No
tournament reports.
    Payment £150–200 per 1000 words.

Active Life
Lexicon, 1st Floor, 1–5 Clerkenwell Road,
London EC1M 5PA
☎020 7253 5775 Fax 020 7253 5676
Email activelife@lexicon-uk.com
Owner *Lexicon Editorial Group Services*
Editor *Helene Hodge*
Assistant to Editor *Claire Selsby*
FOUNDED 1990. BI-MONTHLY magazine aimed
at over 50s. General consumer interests including
travel, finance, property and leisure. Opportuni-
ties for freelancers in all departments, including
fiction. Approach in writing with synopsis of
ideas. Authors' notes available on receipt of s.a.e.

Acumen
See under **Poetry Magazines**

Aeroplane
IPC Magazines (IPC Country & Leisure
Media), King's Reach Tower, Stamford
Street, London SE1 9LS
☎020 7261 5849 Fax 020 7261 5269
Email aeroplane_monthly@ipc.co.uk
Owner *IPC Magazines Ltd*
Editor *Michael Oakey*
Circulation 38,000
FOUNDED 1973. MONTHLY. Historic aviation
and aircraft preservation. No modern aviation
unless very unusual; no poetry.
    News *Tony Harsmworth* Aircraft preservation

and historic aviation with good quality colour pictures (print or slide). 500 words max. *Payment* around £20 per item.

Features *Michael Oakey* Historic and preservation features written with authoritative knowledge of subject. 2500 words max. *Payment* £60 per 1000 words; £10–40 per picture used. Approach in writing in the first instance.

African Affairs

Dept of Historical & Cultural Studies, Goldsmiths College, University of London, New Cross, London SE14 6NW
☎020 7919 7486 Fax 020 7919 7398
Email afraf@compuserve.com
Owner *Royal African Society*
Editors *David Killingray, Stephen Ellis*
Circulation 2250

FOUNDED 1901. QUARTERLY learned journal publishing articles on recent political, social and economic developments in sub-Saharan countries. Also included are historical studies that illuminate current events in the continent. Unsolicited mss welcome. Max. 8000 words.

No payment.

Air International

PO Box 100, Stamford, Lincolnshire PE9 1XQ
☎01780 755131 Fax 01780 757261
Email English@keymags.demon.co.uk
Owner *Key Publishing Ltd*
Editor *Malcolm English*

FOUNDED 1971. MONTHLY. Civil and military aircraft magazine. Unsolicited mss welcome; initial approach by phone or in writing preferred.

AirForces Monthly

PO Box 100, Stamford, Lincolnshire PE9 1XQ
☎01780 755131 Fax 01780 757261
Email edafm@keymags.demon.co.uk
Owner *Key Publishing Ltd*
Editor *Alan Warnes*
Circulation 24,749

FOUNDED 1988. MONTHLY. Modern military aircraft magazine. Unsolicited mss welcome; initial approach by phone or in writing preferred.

Amateur Gardening

Westover House, West Quay Road, Poole, Dorset BH15 1JG
☎01202 440840 Fax 01202 440860
Owner *IPC Magazines Ltd*
Editor *Adrian Bishop*
Circulation 63,0111

FOUNDED 1884. WEEKLY. New contributions are welcome especially if they are topical and informative. All articles/news items should be supported by colour pictures.

Features Topical and practical gardening articles. Maximum 1000 words.

News Compiled and edited in-house generally but all stories welcomed.

Payment negotiable.

Amateur Photographer

King's Reach Tower, Stamford Street, London SE1 9LS
☎020 7261 5100 Fax 020 7261 5404
Owner *IPC Magazines Ltd*
Editor *Garry Coward-Williams*
Circulation 28,709

FOUNDED 1884. WEEKLY. For the competent amateur with a technical interest. Freelancers are used but writers should be aware that there is ordinarily no use for words without pictures.

Amateur Stage

Hampden House, 2 Weymouth Street, London W1N 3FD
☎020 7636 4343 Fax 020 7636 2323
Email cvtheatre@aol.com
Owner *Platform Publications Ltd*
Editor *Charles Vance*

Interested in contributions on: amateur premières, technical developments within the amateur forum and items relating to landmarks or anniversaries in the history of amateur societies. Approach in writing only (include s.a.e. for return of mss). *No payment.*

Ambit

See under **Poetry Magazines**

Amiga Format

30 Monmouth Street, Bath BA1 2AP
☎01225 442244 Fax 01225 732275
Email amformat@futurenet.co.uk
Owner *Future Publishing*
Editor *Ben Vost*
Circulation 13,264

FOUNDED 1988. MONTHLY. Specialist computer magazine dedicated to Commodore Amiga home computers, offering reviews, features and product information of specific interest to Amiga users. Unsolicited material welcome. Contact by phone with ideas.

News Amiga-specific exclusives and product information. Length 500–1000 words.

Features Computer-related features (i.e. CD-ROMs, games, virtual reality) with Amiga-specific value. Maximum 10,000 words.

Special Pages Hardware and software reviews. Maximum 3000 words.
Payment £100 per 1000 words.

Animal Action

Causeway, Horsham, West Sussex RH12 1HG
☎01403 264181 Fax 01403 241048
Email publications@rspca.org.uk
Website www.rspca.org.uk
Owner *RSPCA*
Editor *Michaela Miller*
Circulation 80,000

BI-MONTHLY RSPCA youth membership magazine. Articles are written in-house. Good-quality animal photographs welcome.

Animal Prints

Worthing Animal Aid, PO Box 4065,
Worthing, West Sussex BN11 3JL
☎01903 877144 Fax 01903 877144
Email WorthingAnimalAid@btinternet.com
Website www.rspca.org.uk
Owner *Worthing Animal Aid*
Editor *Lilian Taylor*
Circulation 350

FOUNDED 1999. QUARTERLY bulletin that aims advance the animal movement. Welcomes contributions that are well researched, subtly thought provoking and have the potential for stimulating discussion. Approach in writing.

The Antique Dealer and Collectors' Guide

PO Box 805, Greenwich, London SE10 8TD
☎020 8691 4820 Fax 020 8691 2489
Email antiquedealercollectorsguide@
    ukbusiness.com
Website www.antiquecollectorsguide.co.uk
Owner *Statuscourt Ltd*
Publisher *Philip Bartlam*
Circulation 12,500

FOUNDED 1946. MONTHLY. Covers all aspects of the antiques and fine art worlds. Unsolicited mss welcome.
Features Practical but readable articles on the history, design, authenticity, restoration and market aspects of antiques and fine art. Max. 2000 words. *Payment* £76 per 1000 words.
News *Philip Bartlam* Items on events, sales, museums, exhibitions, antique fairs and markets. Max. 300 words.

Antique Interiors International

162 Packington Street, Islington, London
N1 8RA
☎020 7359 6011 Fax 020 7359 6025

Owner *Antique Publications*
Editor-in-Chief *Alistair Hicks*
Managing Editor *Steven Pryke*
Circulation 22,000

FOUNDED 1986. QUARTERLY. Amusing coverage of antiques, art and interiors. Unsolicited mss not welcome. Approach by phone or in writing in the first instance. Interested in freelance contributions on international art news items.

Antiques & Art Independent

PO Box 1945, Comely Bank, Edinburgh
EH4 1AB
☎07000 765263 Fax 0131 332 4481
Email antiquesnews@hotmail.com
Website www.antiques-uk.co.uk
Owner *Gallery UK Ltd*
Publisher/Editor *Tony Keniston*
Circulation 21,000

FOUNDED 1997. BI-MONTHLY. Latest information for the British antiques and art trade, circulated to dealers and collectors in the UK. News, photographs, gossip and controversial views on all aspects of the fine art and antiques world welcome. Articles on antiques and the fine arts are not featured. Approach in writing with ideas.

Apollo Magazine

1 Castle Lane, London SW1E 6DR
☎020 7233 6640 Fax 020 7630 7791
Email editorial@apollomag.com
Owner *Paul Z. Josefowitz*
Editor *David Ekserdjian*

FOUNDED 1925. MONTHLY. Specialist articles on art and antiques, exhibition and book reviews, exhibition diary, information on dealers and auction houses. Unsolicited mss welcome. Interested in specialist, usually new research in fine arts, architecture and antiques. Not interested in crafts or practical art, photography or art after 1945.

Aquarist & Pondkeeper

Suite 4, Invicta Business Centre, Monument Way, Orbital Park, Ashford, Kent TN24 0HB
☎01233 500070 Fax 01233 500099
Email aandpeditor@btinternet.com
Owner *Inline Magazines Ltd*
Editor *Derek Lambert*
Circulation 20,000

FOUNDED 1924. MONTHLY. Covers all aspects of aquarium and pondkeeping: conservation, herpetology (study of reptiles and amphibians), news, reviews and aquatic plant culture. Unsolicited mss welcome. Ideas should be submitted in writing first.

Features Good opportunities for writers on any of the above topics or related areas. 1500–3000 words, plus illustrations. 'We have stocks in hand for up to two years, but new material and commissioned features will be published as and when relevant.' Average lead-in 4–6 months.
News Very few opportunities.

Architects' Journal
151 Rosebery Avenue, London EC1R 4GB
☎020 7505 6700 Fax 020 7505 6701
Owner *EMAP Construct*
Editor *Isabel Allen*
Circulation 18,000

WEEKLY trade magazine dealing with all aspects of the industry. No unsolicited mss. Approach in writing with ideas.

Architectural Design
John Wiley & Sons, 4th Floor, International House, Ealing Broadway Centre, London W5 5DB
☎020 8326 3800 Fax 020 8326 3801
Owner *John Wiley & Sons Ltd*
Editor *Maggie Toy*
Managing Editor *Helen Castle*
Senior Production Editor *Mariangela Palazzi-Williams*
Circulation 5,000

FOUNDED 1930. BI-MONTHLY. Sold as a book as well as a journal, *AD* charts theoretical and topical developments in architecture. Format consists of 112pp, the first part dedicated to a theme compiled by a specially commissioned guest-editor; the back section – AD+ – carries series and more current one-off articles. Unsolicited mss not welcome generally, though journalistic contributions will be considered for the back section.

The Architectural Review
151 Rosebery Avenue, London EC1R 4GB
☎020 7505 6725 Fax 020 7505 6701
Owner *EMAP Construct*
Editor *Peter Davey*
Circulation 23,208

MONTHLY professional magazine dealing with architecture and all aspects of design. No unsolicited mss. Approach in writing with ideas.

Arena
Block A, Exmouth House, Pine Street, London EC1R 0JL
☎020 7689 9999 Fax 020 7698 0901
Owner *Emap Elan Network*
Editor *Greg Williams*

Circulation 47,096

Style and general interest magazine for men. Intelligent feature articles and profiles. **Features** Fashion, lifestyle, film, television, politics, business, music, media, design, art, architecture and sport. *Payment* £200–250 per 1000 words.

Art & Craft
Villiers House, Clarendon Avenue, Leamington Spa, Warwickshire CV32 5PR
☎01926 887799 Fax 01926 883331
Owner *Scholastic Ltd*
Editor *Sian Morgan*
Circulation 15,000

FOUNDED 1936. MONTHLY aimed at a specialist market – the needs of primary school teachers, art coordinators and pupils. Ideas and synopses considered for commission.
Features The majority of contributors are primary school teachers with good art and craft skills and familiar with the curriculum.
News Handled by in-house staff. No opportunities.

Art Monthly
Suite 17, 26 Charing Cross Road, London WC2H 0DG
☎020 7240 0389 Fax 020 7497 0726
Email info@artmonthly.co.uk
Website www.artmonthly.co.uk
Owner *Brittania Art Publications*
Editor *Patricia Bickers*
Circulation 6000

FOUNDED 1976. TEN ISSUES YEARLY. News and features of relevance to those interested in modern and contemporary visual art. Unsolicited mss welcome. Contributions should be addressed to the deputy editor, accompanied by s.a.e.
Features Always commissioned. Interviews and articles of up to 1500 words on art theory, individual artists, contemporary art history and issues affecting the arts (e.g. funding and arts education). Exhibition reviews of 750–1000 words; book reviews of 750–1000 words.
News Brief reports (250–300 words) on art issues.
Payment negotiable.

The Art Newspaper
27-29 Vauxhall Grove, London SW8 1SY
☎020 7735 3331 Fax 020 7735 3332
Owner *Umberto Allemandi & Co. Publishing*
Editor *Anna Somers Cocks*
Circulation 22,000

FOUNDED 1990. ELEVEN ISSUES YEARLY. Tabloid

format with hard news on the international art market, news, museums, exhibitions, archaeology, conservation, books and current debate topics. Length 250–2000 words. No unsolicited mss. Approach with ideas in writing. Commissions only. *Payment* £120 per 1000 words.

The Artist

Caxton House, 63–65 High Street, Tenterden, Kent TN30 6BD
☎0158076 3673 Fax 0158076 5411
Website www.theartistmagazine.co.uk
Owner/Editor *Sally Bulgin*
Circulation 19,000

FOUNDED 1931. MONTHLY. Art journalists, artists, art tutors and writers with a good knowledge of art materials are invited to write to the editor with ideas for practical and informative features about art, materials, techniques and artists.

Artscene

Dean Clough Industrial Park, Halifax, West Yorkshire HX3 5AX
☎01422 322527 Fax 01422 322518
Owner *Yorkshire and Humberside Arts*
Editor *Victor Allen*
Circulation 25,000

FOUNDED 1973. MONTHLY. Listings magazine for Yorkshire and Humberside. No unsolicited mss. Approach by phone with ideas.

Features Profiles of artists (all media) and associated venues/organisers of events of interest. Topical relevance vital. Max. length 1500 words. *Payment* £100 per 1000 words.

News Artscene strives to bring journalistic values to arts coverage – all arts 'scoops' in the region are of interest. Max. length 500 words. *Payment* £100 per 1000 words.

Asian Times

148 Cambridge Heath Road, London E1 5QJ
☎020 7702 8012 Fax 020 7702 7937
Owner *Ethnic Media Group*
Editor *Nadeem Kahn*
Circulation 33,000

FOUNDED 1983. WEEKLY community paper for the Asian community in Britain. Interested in relevant general, local and international issues. Approach in writing with ideas for submission.

Athletics Weekly

13 Cavell Court, Lincoln Road, Peterborough, Cambridgeshire PE1 2RJ
☎01733 898440 Fax 01733 898441
Email results@athletics-weekly.co.uk

Owner *Descartes Publishing*
Editor *Nigel Walsh*
Circulation 14,000

FOUNDED 1945. WEEKLY Covers track and field, road, fell, cross-country, race walking, athletic features and sports politics.
News *Trevor Frecknall* Max. 600 words.
Features *Tony Ward* Max. 2000 words.
Special Pages *Allan Haines* Training, health and fitness. Max. 2000 words. Approach in writing.
Payment £70–100 per 1000 words.

Attitude

Northern & Shell Tower, City Harbour, London E14 9GL
☎020 7308 5090 Fax 020 7308 5075
Owner *Northern & Shell plc*
Editor *Adam Mattera*
Circulation 50,000

FOUNDED 1994. MONTHLY. Style magazine aimed primarily, but not exclusively, at gay men. Celebrity, fashion and cultural coverage. Brief summaries of proposed features, together with details of previously published work, should be sent by post or fax only. 'It sounds obvious, but anyone wanting to contribute to the magazine should read it first.'

The Author

84 Drayton Gardens, London SW10 9SB
☎020 7373 6642
Owner *The Society of Authors*
Editor *Derek Parker*
Manager *Kate Pool*
Circulation 8,500

FOUNDED 1890. QUARTERLY journal of **The Society of Authors**. Most articles are commissioned.

Autocar

60 Waldegrave Road, Teddington, Middlesex TW11 8LG
☎020 8943 5630 Fax 020 8267 5759
Email autocar@haynet.com
Owner *Haymarket Magazines Ltd*
Editor *Patrick Fuller*
Circulation 77,403

FOUNDED 1895. WEEKLY. All news stories, features, interviews, scoops, ideas, tip-offs and photographs welcome.
News *Chris Rosamond*
Payment negotiable.

B Magazine

17–18 Berners Street, London W1P 3DD
☎020 7664 6470   Fax 020 7436 2250
Email letters@bmagazine.co.uk
Owner *Attic Futura*
Editor *Gina Johnson*
Circulation 223,532

MONTHLY women's fashion and beauty magazine aimed at 18–26-year-olds. Will consider real-life stories, emotional issues. Ideas for features should be sent to *Sarah Maber*. No short stories or opinion pieces. Approach in writing.

Baby Magazine

WV Publications, 57–59 Rochester Place, London N1 9JY
☎020 7331 1000   Fax 020 7331 1225
Email danbrom@hotmail.com
Owner *Highbury House Communications*
Editor *Dan Bromage*
Circulation 79,000

MONTHLY. For parents-to-be and parents of children up to two years old. No unsolicited mss.

Features Send synopsis of feature with covering letter in the first instance. Unsolicited material is not returned.

Baby's Best Buys

WV Publications, 57–59 Rochester Place, London N1 9JY
☎020 7331 1000   Fax 020 7331 1241
Email danbrom@hotmail.com
Owner *Highbury House Communications*
Editor *Dan Bromage*

QUARTERLY. Comprehensive product testing for parenting equipment and maternity wear.

Babycare and Pregnancy

D. C. Thomson & Co. Ltd, 80 Kingsway East, Dundee DD4 8SL
☎01382 223131   Fax 01382 452491
Email baby@dcthomson.co.uk/mags/baby
Website www.dcthomson.co.uk/mags/baby
Owner *D. C. Thomson & Co. Ltd*
Editor *Irene K. Duncan*
Circulation 21,000

FOUNDED 1994. MONTHLY magazine on pregnancy, birth and babycare. Unsolicited mss on these topics welcome. Not interested in material relating to children over three years of age. Approach in writing or by phone.

Back Brain Recluse (BBR)

PO Box 625, Sheffield S1 3GY
Website www.bbr-online.com/magazine

Owner/Editor *Chris Reed*
Circulation 3000

Award-winning British fiction magazine which actively seeks new fiction that ignores genre pigeonholes. 'We tread the thin line between experimental speculative fiction and avant garde literary fiction. We strongly recommend familiarity with our guidelines for contributors, and with recent issues of *BBR*, before any material is submitted.' All correspondence must be accompanied by s.a.e. or international reply coupons; US$1 is an acceptable alternative to IRCs. If a response by e-mail is wanted, send disposable copy and no return postage.

Payment £10 per 1000 words.

Badminton

Connect Sports, 14 Woking Road, Cheadle Hulme, Cheshire SK8 6NZ
☎0161 486 6159   Fax 0161 488 4505
Owner *Mrs S. Ashton*
Editor *William Kings*

BI-MONTHLY. Specialist badminton magazine, with news, views, product information, equipment reviews, etc. Unsolicited material will be considered; phone first with an idea.

Features *William Kings/Sue Ashton* Open to approaches and likes to discuss ideas in the first instance. Interested in badminton-related articles on health, fitness, psychology, clothing, accessories, etc.

The Badminton Times

PO Box 3250, Wokingham, Berkshire RG40 4FR
☎0118 973 7744
Editor *Mr R. Richardson*

FOUNDED 1980. QUARTERLY. Events, players, fashion and footwear, rackets, facilities, technique and tactics.

Balance

British Diabetic Association, 10 Queen Anne Street, London W1M 0BD
☎020 7323 1531   Fax 020 7637 3644
Email balance@diabetes.org.uk
Owner *British Diabetic Association*
Editor *John Isitt*
Deputy Editor *Martin Cullen*
Circulation 200,000

FOUNDED 1935. BI-MONTHLY. Unsolicited mss are not accepted. Writers may submit a brief proposal in writing. Only topics relevant to diabetes will be considered.

Features *John Isitt* Medical, diet and lifestyle

features written by people with diabetes or with an interest and expert knowledge in the field. General features are mostly based on experience or personal observation. Maximum 1500 words. *Payment* NUJ rates.

News *Martin Cullen* Short pieces about activities relating to diabetes and the lifestyle of diabetics. Maximum 150 words. *Payment* varies.

The Banker
149 Tottenham Court Road, London W1P 9LL
☎020 7896 2507   Fax 020 7896 2586
Website www.thebanker.com

Owner *Financial Times Business*
Editor *Stephen Timewell*
Circulation 24,000

FOUNDED 1926. MONTHLY. News and features on banking, finance and capital markets world-wide and technology.

BBC Gardeners' World Magazine
Woodlands, 80 Wood Lane, London W12 0TT
☎020 8433 3959   Fax 020 8433 3986
Website www.gardenersworld.beeb.com

Owner *BBC Worldwide Publishing Ltd*
Editor *Adam Pasco*
Features Editor *Jodie Jones*
Circulation 321,670

FOUNDED 1991. MONTHLY. Gardening advice, ideas and inspiration. No unsolicited mss. Approach by phone or in writing with ideas – interested in features about exceptional small gardens. Also interested in any exciting new gardens showing good design and planting ideas. 'The magazine aims to be the first to bring news of new trends and developments, and always welcomes ideas from contributors.'

BBC Good Food
Woodlands, 80 Wood Lane, London W12 0TT
☎020 8433 2000   Fax 020 8433 3931
Website www.bbcworldwide.com

Owner *BBC Worldwide Ltd*
Editor *Orlando Murrin*
Circulation 291,416

FOUNDED 1989. MONTHLY food and drink magazine with television and radio links. No unsolicited mss.

BBC Homes & Antiques
Woodlands, 80 Wood Lane, London W12 0TT
☎020 8433 3490   Fax 020 8433 3867
Website www.bbcworldwide.com/
   homesandantiques

Owner *BBC Worldwide Publishing Ltd*

Editor *Judith Hall*
Circulation 200,426

FOUNDED 1993. MONTHLY traditional home interest magazine with a strong bias towards antiques and collectables. Opportunities for freelancers are limited; most features are commissioned from regular stable of contributors. No fiction, health and beauty, fashion or general showbusiness. Approach with ideas by phone or in writing.

Features *Caroline Wheater* At-home features: inspirational houses – people-led items. Commissions pieces on recce shots and cuttings. Guidelines are available on request. Celebrity features: 'at homes or favourite things'. Send cuttings of relevant published work. Maximum 1500 words.

Special Pages Regular feature – 'Home Thoughts'. Maximum 800 words.

Payment negotiable.

BBC Match of the Day Magazine
See **Match of the Day Magazine**

BBC Music Magazine
Room A1004, Woodlands, 80 Wood Lane, London W12 0TT
☎020 8433 2000   Fax 020 8433 3292
Email music.magazine@bbc.co.uk
Website www.bbcmusicmagazine.com

Owner *BBC Worldwide Publishing Ltd*
Editor *Helen Wallace*
Circulation 67,432 (UK edition)

FOUNDED 1992. MONTHLY. All areas of classical music. Not interested in unsolicited material. Approach with ideas only, by fax or in writing.

BBC Top Gear Magazine
Woodlands, 80 Wood Lane, London W12 0TT
☎020 8433 3716   Fax 020 8433 3754
Website www.topgear.com

Owner *BBC Worldwide Publishing Ltd*
Editor *Kevin Blick*
Circulation 184,000

FOUNDED 1993. MONTHLY companion magazine to the popular TV series. No unsolicited material as most features are commissioned.

BBC Wildlife Magazine
Broadcasting House, Whiteladies Road, Bristol BS8 2LR
☎0117 973 8402   Fax 0117 946 7075
Email wildlife.magazine@bbc.co.uk

Owner *BBC Worldwide Publishing Ltd*
Editor *Rosamund Kidman Cox*
Circulation 72,432

FOUNDED 1963 (formerly *Wildlife*, née *Animals*).
MONTHLY. Unsolicited mss generally not welcome.

Features Most features commissioned from writers with expert knowledge of wildlife or conservation subjects. Maximum 3500 words. *Payment* £200–450.

News Most news stories commissioned from known freelancers. Maximum 800 words. *Payment* £80–120

Bee World
18 North Road, Cardiff CF10 3DT
☎029 2037 2409 Fax 029 2066 5522
Email ibra@cf.ac.uk
Website www.cf.ack.uk/ibra/

Owner *International Bee Research Association*
Editor *Dr P. A. Munn*
Circulation 1700

FOUNDED 1919. QUARTERLY. High-quality factual journal, including peer-reviewed articles, with international readership. Features on apicultural science and technology. Unsolicited mss welcome but authors should write to the editor for guidelines before submitting mss.

Bella
H. Bauer Publishing, Shirley House,
25–27 Camden Road, London NW1 9LL
☎020 7241 8000 Fax 020 7241 8059

Owner *H. Bauer Publishing*
Editor-in-Chief *Jackie Highe*
Circulation 572,151

FOUNDED 1987. WEEKLY. Women's magazine specialising in real-life, human interest stories.

Features *Sue Ricketts* Contributions welcome for some sections of the magazine: readers' letters, 'Precious Moments', 'Blush with Bella' and 'Bella Rat'.

Fiction *Linda O'Byrne* Maximum 1200–2000 words. Send s.a.e. for guidelines.

Best
197 Marsh Wall, London E14 9SG
☎020 7519 5500 Fax 020 7519 5516

Owner *G & J (UK)*
Editor *Louise Court*
Circulation 471,735

FOUNDED 1987. WEEKLY women's magazine and stablemate of *Prima*. Multiple features, news, short stories on all topics of interest to women. Important for would-be contributors to study the magazine's style which differs from many other women's weeklies. Approach in writing with s.a.e.

Features Maximum 1500 words. No unsolicited mss.

Fiction Short story slot; unsolicited mss accepted. Maximum 1000 words. *Payment* negotiable.

Best of British
Ian Beacham Publishing, Bank Chambers, 27a Market Place, Market Deeping, Lincolnshire PE6 8EA
☎01778 342814

Owner *CMS Publishing*
Editor *Peter Kelly*

FOUNDED 1994. MONTHLY magazine celebrating all things British, both past and present. Study of the magazine is advised in the first instance. All preliminary approaches should be made in writing. No telephone calls, please.

Best Solutions
38 Broad Street, Earls Barton, Northamptonshire NN6 0ND
☎01635 522488 Fax 01635 522212

Owner *Grahame White*
Editor *Geoff Ellis*
Circulation 300,000

FOUNDED 1996. QUARTERLY business to business consultancy magazine. No unsolicited mss. 'Interested in articles (1000 words) for heads of substantial consultancy practices.' Approach in writing.

The Big Issue
236–240 Pentonville Road, London N1 9JY
☎020 7526 3200 Fax 020 7526 3201

Editor-in-Chief *A. John Bird*
Editor *Matthew Collin*
Deputy Editor *Andrew Davies*
Circulation 266,060

FOUNDED 1991. WEEKLY. An award-winning campaigning and street-wise general interest magazine sold in London, the Midlands, the North East and South of England. Separate regional editions sold in Manchester, Scotland, Wales, the South West and Ireland.

Features *Andrew Davies* Interviews, campaigns, comment, opinion and social issues reflecting a varied and informed audience. Balance includes social issues but mixed with arts and cultural features. Freelance writers used each week – commissioned from a variety of contributors. Best approach is to fax or post synopses to features editor with examples of work in the first instance. Maximum 1500 words. *Payment* £150 for 1000 words.

News *Gibby Zobel* Hard-hitting exclusive

stories with emphasis on social injustice aimed at national leaders.

Arts *Tina Jackson* Interested in comment, interviews and analysis ideas. Reviews written in-house. Send synopses to arts editor.

BIG!

Mappin House, 4 Winsley Street, London W1N 7AR
☎020 7436 1515 Fax 020 7312 8246
Email big@ecm.emap.com
Owner *EMAP Metro*
Editor *Kate Finnegan*
Circulation 93,044

FOUNDED 1990. FORTNIGHTLY celebrity/entertainment magazine for teenage girls. Interested in interviews with celebrities from the worlds of pop, film and television. 1500 words maximum; approach by phone in the first instance.

Bird Life Magazine

RSPB, The Lodge, Sandy, Bedfordshire SG19 2DL
☎01767 680551 Fax 01767 683262
Email derek.niemann@rspb.org.uk
Owner *Royal Society for the Protection of Birds*
Editor *Derek Niemann*
Circulation 90,000

FOUNDED 1965. BI-MONTHLY. Bird, wildlife and nature conservation for 8–12-year-olds (Young Ornithologist Club members). No unsolicited mss. No 'captive/animal welfare' articles.

Features *Derek Niemann* Unsolicited material is rarely used. 'Good transparencies to accompany articles help success.'

News *Derek Niemann* News releases welcome but news stories must relate to YOC members. Approach in writing in the first instance.

Birds

The Lodge, Sandy, Bedfordshire SG19 2DL
☎01767 680551 Fax 01767 683262
Owner *Royal Society for the Protection of Birds*
Editor *R. A. Hume*
Circulation 1 million

QUARTERLY magazine which covers not only wild birds but also wildlife and related conservation topics. No interest in features on pet birds or 'rescued' sick/injured/orphaned ones. Mss or ideas welcome. 'No captive birds, please.'

Birdwatch

3D/F Leroy House, 436 Essex Road, London N1 3QP
☎020 7704 9495 Fax 020 7704 2767
Website www.birdwatch.co.uk

Owner *Solo Publishing*
Editor *Dominic Mitchell*
Circulation 16,500

FOUNDED 1992. MONTHLY high-quality magazine featuring illustrated articles on all aspects of birds and birdwatching, especially in Britain. No unsolicited mss. Approach in writing with synopsis of 100 words maximum. Annual **Birdwatch Bird Book of the Year** award (see entry under **Prizes**).

Features *Dominic Mitchell* Unusual angles/personal accounts, if well-written. Articles of an educative or practical nature suited to the readership. Maximum 2000–3000 words.

Fiction *Dominic Mitchell* Very little opportunity although occasional short story published. Maximum 1500 words.

News *Tim Harris* Very rarely use external material.

Payment £40 per 1000 words.

Bizarre

John Brown Publishing, The New Boathouse, 136–142 Bramley Road, London W10 6SR
☎020 7565 3000 Fax 020 7565 3055
Email bizarre@johnbrown.co.uk
Website www.bizarremag.com
Owner *John Brown Publishing*
Editor *Joe Gardiner*
Circulation 120,534

FOUNDED 1997. MONTHLY magazine featuring amazing stories and images from around the world. No fiction, poetry, illustrations, short snippets. **Features** *Joe Gardiner* Particularly interested in global stories and celebrity interviews. Maximum 2500 words. Approach in writing *Payment* £120 per 1000 words.

Black Beauty & Hair

Hawker Consumer Publications Ltd, 13 Park House, 140 Battersea Park Road, London SW11 4NB
☎020 7720 2108 Fax 020 7498 3023
Email irene@hawkerpubs.demon.co.uk
Owner *Hawker Consumer Publications Ltd*
Editor *Irene Shelley*
Circulation 22,017

BI-MONTHLY with one annual special: *The Hairstyle Book* in October; and a *Bridal Supplement* in the April/May issue. Black hair and beauty magazine with emphasis on authoritative articles relating to hair, beauty, fashion, health and lifestyle. Unsolicited contributions welcome.

Features Beauty and fashion pieces welcome from writers with a sound knowledge of the Afro-Caribbean beauty scene plus bridal features. Minimum 1000 words.

Payment £100 per 1000 words.

Black Media Journal

PO Box 29629, London E8 2XG
☎020 7923 2270 Fax 020 7823 9773
Email blkmedj@aol.com

Owner *Claudine Boothe*
Editor *Sara Wajid*
Circulation 16,000

FOUNDED 1999. QUARTERLY arts and media critique on African-Caribbean and South Asian issues. Interested in writing, illustrations and photography.

News *Marc Wadsworth* News about the media and arts. **Features** *Sara Wajid* Critique of media and arts (dance, the Web, theatre, TV, literature, music, visual art, radio, print media). No fiction. Approach in writing or by e-mail.

Bliss Magazine

Endeavour House, 189 Shaftesbury Avenue, London WC2H 8JG
☎020 7208 3478 Fax 020 7208 3591
Email christina.reeves@ecm.emap.com

Owner *EMAP plc*
Editor *Kerry Parnell*
Circulation 287,796

FOUNDED 1995. MONTHLY teenage lifestyle magazine for girls. No unsolicited mss; 'call the deputy editor with an idea and then send it in.'

News *Marina Crook* Worldwide teenage news. Maximum 200 words. *Payment* £50–100.

Features *Maria Coole* Real life teenage stories with subjects willing to be photographed. Reports on teenage issues. Maximum 2000 words. *Payment* £350.

The Book Collector

PO Box 12426, London W11 3GW
☎020 7792 3492 Fax 020 7792 3492
Email info@thebookcollector.co.uk
Website www.thebookcollector.co.uk

Owner *The Collector Ltd*
Editor *Nicolas J. Barker*

FOUNDED 1950. QUARTERLY magazine on bibliography and the history of books, book-collecting, libraries and the book trade.

The Book Directory

'Ambleside', 52 Heaton Street, Brampton, Chesterfield, Derbyshire S40 3AQ
☎01246 230408

Owner/Editor *Ron Mihaly*

Circulation 2500 (quarterly)

FOUNDED 1997. QUARTERLY. Carries articles of a bibliographical nature, quarterly list of book fairs, auction news, for sale/wanted ads. Unsolicited mss and ideas welcome – but write first, please. Maximum 2000 words.

Payment Commissions: £15 per 1000 words.

Book World Magazine

2 Caversham Street, London SW3 4AH
☎020 7351 4995 Fax 020 7351 4995

Owner *Christchurch Publishers Ltd*
Editor *James Hughes*
Circulation 5,500

FOUNDED 1980. MONTHLY news and reviews for serious book collectors, librarians, anti-quarian and other booksellers. No unsolicited mss. Interested in material relevant to literature, art and book collecting. Send letter in the first instance.

Bookdealer

Suite 34, 26 Charing Cross Road, London WC2H 0DH
☎020 7240 5890 Fax 020 7379 7379

Editor *Barry Shaw*

WEEKLY trade paper which acts almost exclusively as a platform for people wishing to buy or sell rare/out-of-print books. Twelve-page editorial only; occasional articles and book reviews by regular freelance writers.

Books

39 Store Street, London WC1F 7DB
☎020 7692 2900 Fax 020 7419 2111

Editor *Liz Thomson*
Circulation 115,000

Formerly *Books and Bookmen*. Consumer magazine dealing chiefly with features about authors and reviews of books. Carries few commissioned pieces.

Payment negotiable.

The Bookseller

12 Dyott Street, London WC1A 1DF
☎020 7420 6000 Fax 020 7420 6103
Website www.theBookseller.com

Owner *J. Whitaker & Sons Ltd*
Editor *Nicholas Clee*

Trade journal of the publishing and book trade – the essential guide to what is being done to whom. Trade news and features, including special features, company news, publishing trends, etc. Unsolicited mss rarely used as most writing is either done in-house or commissioned from experts within the trade. Approach in writing first.

Features *Jenny Bell*
News *Ms Danuta Kean*

Boxing Monthly
40 Morpeth Road, London E9 7LD
☎020 8986 4141 Fax 020 8986 4145
Email bm@boxing-monthly.demon.co.uk

Owner *Topwave Ltd*
Editor *Glyn Leach*
Circulation 30,000

FOUNDED 1989. MONTHLY. International coverage of professional boxing; previews, reports and interviews. Unsolicited material welcome. Interested in small hall shows and grass-roots knowledge. No big fight reports. Approach in writing in the first instance.

Boyz
72 Holloway Road, London N7 8NZ
☎020 7296 6230 Fax 020 7296 0026
Email hudson@boyz.co.uk

Editor *David Hudson*
Circulation 55,000

FOUNDED 1994. WEEKLY entertainment and features magazine aimed at a gay readership covering clubs, fashion, TV, films, music, theatre, celebrities and the UK gay scene in general. Unsolicited mss are looked at but not often used.

Brides and Setting Up Home
Vogue House, Hanover Square, London W1R 0AD
☎020 7499 9080 Fax 020 7460 6369

Owner *Condé Nast Publications Ltd*
Editor *Sandra Boler*
Circulation 63,543

BI-MONTHLY. Much of the magazine is produced in-house, but a good, relevant feature on cakes, jewellery, music, flowers, etc. is always welcome. Maximum 1000 words. Prospective contributors should telephone with an idea in the first instance.

British Birds
Fountains, Park Lane, Blunham, Bedford MK44 3NJ
☎01767 640025 Fax 01767 640025

Owner *British Birds Ltd*
Editor *Dr J. T. R. Sharrock*
Circulation 8,000

FOUNDED 1907. MONTHLY ornithological journal. Features annual *Reports on Rare Birds in Great Britain*, bird news from official national correspondents throughout Europe and sponsored competitions for Bird Photograph of the Year, Bird Illustrator of the Year and Young Ornithologists of the Year. Unsolicited mss welcome from ornithologists only.

Features Well-researched, original material relating to Western Palearctic birds welcome. Maximum 6000 words.

News *Bob Scott/Wendy Dickson* Items ranging from conservation to humour. Maximum 200 words.

Payment only for photographs, drawings and paintings.

British Chess Magazine
The Chess Shop, 69 Masbro Road, London W14 0LS
☎020 7603 2877 Fax 020 7371 1477

Owner/Editor *Murray Chandler*

FOUNDED 1881. MONTHLY. Emphasis on tournaments, the history of chess and chess-related literature. Approach in writing with ideas. Unsolicited mss not welcome unless from qualified chess experts and players.

British Medical Journal
BMA House, Tavistock Square, London WC1H 9JR
☎020 7387 4499 Fax 020 7383 6418
Email editor@bmj.com
Website www.bmj.com

Owner *British Medical Association*
Editor *Professor Richard Smith*

Journal of the British Medical Association. No unsolicited material.

British Philatelic Bulletin
Royal Mail National, Royal London House, 2–14 Dunhill Row, London EC1Y 8HQ
☎020 7847 3321 Fax 020 7847 3359

Owner *Royal Mail*
Editor *John Holman*
Circulation 30,000

FOUNDED 1963. MONTHLY bulletin giving details of forthcoming British stamps, features on older stamps and postal history, and book reviews. Welcomes photographs of interesting, unusual or historic letter boxes.

Features Articles on all aspects of British philately. Maximum 1500 words.

News Reports on exhibitions and philatelic events. Maximum 500 words. Approach in writing in the first instance.

Payment £45 per 1000 words.

British Railway Modelling

The Maltings, West Street, Bourne,
Lincolnshire PE10 9PH
☎01778 391167 Fax 01778 393668
Email david.b@warners.co.uk
Website www.brmodelling.com
Owner *Warners Group Publications Plc*
Managing Editor *David Brown*
Deputy Editor *John Emerson*
Assistant Editor *Jarrod Cotter*
Circulation 17,594

FOUNDED 1993. MONTHLY. A general magazine
for the practising modeller. No unsolicited mss
but ideas are welcome. Interested in features on
quality models, from individual items to complete layouts. Approach in writing.
  Features Articles on practical elements of
the hobby, e.g. locomotive construction, kit
conversions, etc. Layout features and articles on
individual items which represent high standards
of the railway modelling art. Maximum length
6000 words (single feature). *Payment* up to £50
per published page.
  News News and reviews containing the
model railway trade, new products, etc. Maximum length 1000 words. *Payment* up to £50
per published page.

Broadcast

33-39 Bowling Green Lane, London
EC1R 0DA
☎020 7505 8014 Fax 020 7505 8050
Owner *EMAP Business Communications*
Editor *Lucy Rouse*
Circulation 14,297

FOUNDED 1960. WEEKLY. Opportunities for
freelance contributions. Write to the relevant
editor in the first instance.
  Features *Katy Elliott* Any broadcasting issue.
Maximum 1500 words.
  News *Tabitha Cole* Broadcasting news. Maxi-
mum 350 words.
  Payment £200 per 1000 words.

Brownie

17–19 Buckingham Palace Road, London
SW1W 0PT
☎020 7834 6242 Fax 020 7828 5791
Email brownie@guides.org.uk
Website www.guides.org.uk
Owner *The Guide Association*
Editor *Marion Thompson*
Circulation 30,000

FOUNDED 1962. MONTHLY. Aimed at Brownie
members aged 7–10.
  Articles Crafts and simple make-it-yourself
items using inexpensive or scrap materials.
  Fiction Brownie content an advantage. No
adventures involving unaccompanied children
in dangerous situations – day or night. Maximum 1000 words.
  Payment £50 per 1000 words pro rata.

The Burlington Magazine

14–16 Duke's Road, London WC1H 9AD
☎020 7388 1228 Fax 020 7388 1230
Owner *The Burlington Magazine Publications Ltd*
Editor *Caroline Elam*

FOUNDED 1903. MONTHLY. Unsolicited contributions welcome on the subject of art history
provided they are previously unpublished. All
preliminary approaches should be made in
writing.
  Exhibition Reviews Usually commissioned,
but occasionally unsolicited reviews are published if appropriate. Maximum 1000 words.
  Articles Maximum 4500 words. *Payment*
£100 (maximum).
  Shorter Notices Maximum 2000 words.
Payment £50 (maximum).

Bus and Coach Professional

56 Market Street, Wellington, Telford,
Shropshire TF1 1DT
☎01952 415334 Fax 01952 406762
Email editorial@busandcoach.com
Website www.busandcoach.com
Editorial Director *Steve Rooney*

MONTHLY magazine for executives and senior
managers in the bus and coach industry.
'Strong on news and features. Some opportunities for well-written freelance material if relevant to our requirement. Phone or e-mail
before submission.'

Business Brief

PO Box 582, Five Oaks, St Saviour, Jersey
JE4 8XQ
☎01534 611600 Fax 01534 611610
Email mspeditorial@mspublishing.com
Owner *MSP Publishing*
Editor *Peter Body*
Circulation 6,000

FOUNDED 1989. MONTHLY magazine covering
business developments in the Channel Islands
and how they affect the local market. Styles
itself as the magazine for business people rather
than just a magazine about business. Interested
in business-orientated articles only – 800 words
maximum. Approach the editor by telephone
initially. *Payment* £8 per 100 words.

Business Life

Haymarket House, 1 Oxendon Street,
London SW1Y 4EE
☎020 7925 2544 Fax 020 7321 2942

Owner *Premier Media Partners*
Editor *Sandra Harris*
Deputy Editor *Catherine Flanagan*
Circulation 193,000

TEN ISSUES YEARLY plus two double issues. Glossy business travel magazine with few opportunities for freelancers. Distributed on BA European routes, TAT and Deutsche BA only. Unsolicited mss not welcome. Approach with ideas in writing only.

Business Traveller

Russell Square House, 10–12 Russell Square,
London WC1B 5ED
☎020 7580 9898 Fax 020 7580 6676
Website www.btonline.co.uk

Owner *Perry Publications*
Editor-in-Chief *Julia Brookes*
Circulation 41,158

MONTHLY. Consumer publication. Opportunities exist for freelance writers but unsolicited contributions tend to be about leisure travel rather than business travel. Would-be contributors are advised to study the magazine or the website first. Approach in writing with ideas. *Payment varies.*

Camcorder User

57–59 Rochester Place, London NW1 9JU
☎020 7331 1000 Fax 020 7331 1242
Email camusermail@yahoo.co.uk

Owner *W. V. Publications*
Editor *Robert Hull*
Circulation 21,797

FOUNDED 1988. MONTHLY magazine dedicated to camcorders, with features on creative technique, shooting advice, new equipment, accessory round-ups and interesting applications on location. Unsolicited mss, illustrations and pictures welcome. *Payment negotiable.*

Campaign

22 Bute Gardens, London W6 7HN
☎020 8267 4683 Fax 020 8267 4914
Website www.campaignlive.com

Owner *Haymarket Publishing Ltd*
Editor *Caroline Marshall*
Circulation 17,700

FOUNDED 1968. WEEKLY. Lively magazine serving the advertising and related industries.

Freelance contributors are best advised to write in the first instance.
 Features Articles of 1500–2000 words.
 News Relevant news stories of up to 300 words.
 Payment negotiable.

Camping and Caravanning

Greenfields House, Westwood Way,
Coventry, Warwickshire CV4 8JH
☎024 7669 4995 Fax 024 7669 4886

Owner *Camping and Caravanning Club*
Editor *Peter Frost*
Circulation 152,882

FOUNDED 1901. MONTHLY. Interested in journalists with camping and caravanning knowledge. Write with ideas for features in the first instance. **Features** Outdoor pieces in general, plus items on specific regions of Britain. Maximum 1200 words. Illustrations to support text essential.

Camping Magazine

Star Brewery, Castle Ditch Lane, Lewes, East
Sussex BN7 1YJ
☎01273 477421 Fax 01273 477421

Owner *Warners Group Publications*
Editor *John Lloyd*

FOUNDED 1961. MONTHLY magazine with features on camping. Aims to reflect this enjoyment by encouraging readers to appreciate the outdoors and to pursue an active camping holiday, whether as a family in a frame tent or as a lightweight backpacker. Articles that have the flavour of the camping lifestyle without being necessarily expeditionary or arduous are always welcome. Study of the magazine is advised in the first instance. Ideas welcome. Contact editor by phone before sending mss.
 Payment negotiable.

Canal and Riverboat

Inter Regional House, 9 Thorpe Road,
Norwich, Norfolk NR1 1EP
☎01603 623856 Fax 01603 623856
Email chris@canalandriverboat.co.uk
Website www.canalandriverboat.co.uk

Owner *A. E. Morgan Publications Ltd*
Editor *Chris Cattrall*
Circulation 26,000

Covers all aspects of waterways, narrow boats and cruisers. Contributions welcome. Make initial approach in writing.
 Features *Chris Cattrall* Waterways, narrow boats and motor cruisers, cruising reports, practical advice, etc. Unusual ideas and personal

comments are particularly welcome. Maximum 2000 words. Articles should be supplied in PC Windows format disk. *Payment* around £50 per page.

News *Chris Cattrall* Items of up to 300 words welcome on the Inland Waterways System, plus photographs if possible. *Payment* £15.

Car Mechanics
Kelsey Publishing Ltd, PO Box 13, Westerham, Kent TN16 3WT
☎01959 541444 Fax 01959 541400
Email carmechanics@kelsey.co.uk
Owner *Kelsey Publishing*
Editor *Phil Weeden*
Circulation 35,000

MONTHLY. Practical guide to maintenance and repair of post–1978 cars for DIY and the motor trade. Unsolicited mss, with good-quality colour prints or transparencies, 'at sender's risk'. Ideas preferred. Initial approach by letter or phone welcome and strongly recommended, 'but please read a recent copy first for style'.

Features Good, technical, entertaining and well-researched material welcome, especially anything presenting complex matters clearly and simply.

Payment by arrangement ('but generous for the right material').

Caravan Life
Warners Group Publications plc, The Maltings, West Street, Bourne, Lincolnshire PH10 9PH
☎01778 391027 Fax 01778 423063
Editor *Stuart Craig*
Circulation 16,119

FOUNDED 1987. Magazine for experienced caravanners and enthusiasts providing practical and useful information and product evaluation. Opportunities for caravanning, relevant touring and travel material with good-quality colour photographs.

Caravan Magazine
Link House, Dingwall Avenue, Croydon, Surrey CR9 2TA
☎020 8686 2599 Fax 020 8781 6044
Website www.linkhouse.co.uk/caravan.html
Owner *IPC Magazines Ltd*
Editor *Rob McCabe*
Circulation 21,002

FOUNDED 1933. MONTHLY. Unsolicited mss welcome. Approach in writing with ideas. All correspondence should go direct to the editor.

Features Touring with strong caravan bias, technical/DIY features and how-to section.

Maximum 1500 words. *Payment* by arrangement.

Caribbean Times
148 Cambridge Heath Road, London E1 5QJ
☎020 7702 8012 Fax 020 7702 7937
Owner *Ethnic Media Group*
Editor *Michael Eboda*
Circulation 22,500

FOUNDED 1981. WEEKLY community paper for the African and Caribbean communities in Britain. Interested in general, local and international issues relevant to these communities. Approach in writing with ideas for submission.

Carmarthenshire Life
Swan House Publishing, Swan House, Bridge Street, Newcastle Emlyn, Carmarthenshire SA38 9DX
☎01239 710632 Fax 01239 710632
Owner *Swan House Publishing*
Editor *David Fielding*

FOUNDED 1995. BI-MONTHLY county magazine with articles on local history, issues, characters, off-beat stories with good colour or b&w photographs. No country diaries, short stories or poems. Most articles are commissioned from known freelancers but 'always prepared to consider ideas from new writers'. No mss. Send cuttings of previous work (published or not) and synopsis to the editor.

Cars and Car Conversions Magazine
Link House, Dingwall Avenue, Croydon, Surrey CR9 2TA
☎020 8686 2599 Fax 020 8781 1159
Owner *IPC Magazines Ltd*
Editor *Steve Bennett*
Circulation 34,928

FOUNDED 1963. MONTHLY. Unsolicited mss welcome but prospective contributors are advised to make initial contact in writing.

Features Technical articles on current motorsport and unusual sport-orientated road cars. Length by arrangement.

Payment negotiable.

Cat World
Avalon Court, Star Road, Partridge Green, West Sussex RH13 8RY
☎01403 711511 Fax 01403 711521
Email lisa@ashdown.co.uk
Owner *Ashdown Publishing Ltd*
Editor *Lisa Lidderdale*

Circulation 19,000

FOUNDED 1981. MONTHLY. Unsolicited mss welcome; initial approach in writing preferred.

Features Lively, first-hand experience features on every aspect of the cat. Breeding features and veterinary articles by acknowledged experts only. Maximum 1800 words.

News Short, concise, factual or humorous items concerning cats. Maximum 100 words.

Submissions on disk (MS Word) if possible, with accompanying hard copy and s.a.e. for return or by e-mail.

Catholic Gazette
The Chase Centre, 114 West Heath Road, London NW3 7TX
☎020 8458 3316 Fax 020 8905 5780
Email catholic.gazette@cms.org.uk
Website www.cms.org.uk/gazette

Owner *Catholic Missionary Society*
Editor *Peter Stanton*
Circulation 1600

FOUNDED 1910. MONTHLY Covers the work of the Catholic Missionary Society – evangelisation, scripture and prayer features. Interested in items on what is going on in the Catholic Church in England and Wales. Maximum 2000 words for features with *payment of £15* for first page and £10 thereafter. 'Rear Light' – personal comment page: maximum 400 words. *Payment* £15. Approach in writing.

Catholic Herald
Lamb's Passage, Bunhill Row, London EC1Y 8TQ
☎020 7588 3101 Fax 020 7256 9728
Email catholic@atlas.co.uk
Website www.catholicherald.co.uk

Editor *Dr William Oddie*
Deputy Editor *Luke Coppen*
Literary Editor *Damian Thompson*
Circulation 22,000

WEEKLY. Interested mainly in straight Catholic issues but also in general humanitarian matters, social policies, the Third World, the arts and books. *Payment* by arrangement.

Challenge
50 Loxwood Avenue, Worthing, West Sussex BN14 7RA
☎01903 824174 Fax 01903 824376

Owner *Challenge Publishing*
Editor *Donald Banks*
Circulation 70,000

FOUNDED 1958. MONTHLY Christian newspaper which welcomes contributions. No fiction. Send for sample copy of writers' guidelines in the first instance.

News Items of up to 500 words (preferably with pictures) 'showing God at work', and human interest photo stories. 'Churchy' items not wanted. Stories of professional sportsmen and musicians who are Christians always wanted but check first to see if their story has already been used.

Women's Page Relevant items of interest welcome.

Payment negotiable.

Chapman
4 Broughton Place, Edinburgh EH1 3RX
☎0131 557 2207 Fax 0131 556 9565
Email editor@chapman–pub.co.uk
Website www.chapman–pub.co.uk

Owner/Editor *Joy M. Hendry*
Circulation 2000

FOUNDED 1970. QUARTERLY. Scotland's quality literary magazine. Features poetry, short works of fiction, criticism, reviews and articles on theatre, politics, language and the arts. Unsolicited material welcome if accompanied by s.a.e. Approach in writing unless discussion is needed. Priority is given to full-time writers.

Features Topics of literary interest, especially Scottish literature, theatre, culture or politics. Maximum 5000 words.

Fiction Short stories, occasionally novel extracts if self-contained. Maximum 6000 words. *Payment* copies.

Special Pages Poetry, both UK and non-UK in translation (mainly, but not necessarily, European). *Payment* by negotiation.

Chat
King's Reach Tower, Stamford Street, London SE1 9LS
☎020 7261 6565 Fax 020 7261 6534
Website www.ipc.co.uk/pubs/chat.htm

Owner *IPC Connect Ltd*
Editor *Keith Kendrick*
Circulation 498,000

FOUNDED 1985. WEEKLY general interest women's magazine. Unsolicited mss considered; approach in writing with ideas. Not interested in contributors 'who have never bothered to read *Chat* and therefore don't know what type of magazine it is'.

Features *June Smith-Sheppard* Human interest and humour. Maximum 1000 words. *Payment* up to £600 maximum.

Fiction *Olwen Rice* Maximum 800 words.

Cheshire Life

2nd Floor, Oyston Mill, Strand Road,
Preston, Lancashire PR1 8UR
☎01772 722022 Fax 01772 736496
Owner *Life Magazines*
Editor *Patrick O'Neill*
Circulation 15,000

FOUNDED 1934. MONTHLY. Homes, gardens,
personalities, business, farming, conservation,
property, heritage, books, fashion, arts, science
– anything which has a Cheshire connection.

Child Education

Villiers House, Clarendon Avenue,
Leamington Spa, Warwickshire CV32 5PR
☎01926 887799 Fax 01926 883331
Owner *Scholastic Ltd*
Editor *Gill Moore*
Circulation 56,791

FOUNDED 1923. MONTHLY magazine aimed at
nursery, infant and first teachers. Articles from
teachers about education for 4–7-year age group
are welcome. Maximum 1200 words. Approach
in writing with synopsis. No unsolicited mss.

Choice

Kings Chambers, 39–41 Priestgate,
Peterborough, Cambridgeshire PE1 1FR
☎01733 555123 Fax 01733 427500
Email choice@bayardpresse.co.uk
Owner *Bayard Presse (UK) Ltd*
Editor *Sue Dobson*
Circulation 100,000

MONTHLY full-colour, lively and informative
magazine for people aged 50 plus which helps
them get the most out of their lives, time and
money after full-time work.
    Features Real-life stories, hobbies, interesting
(older) people, British heritage and countryside,
involving activities for active bodies and minds,
health, relationships, book/entertainment reviews. Unsolicited mss read (s.a.e. for return of
material); write with ideas and copies of cuttings
if new contributor. No phone calls, please.
    Rights/Money All items affecting the maga-
zine's readership are written by experts. Areas of
interest include pensions, state benefits, health,
finance, property, legal.
    Payment by arrangement.

Christian Herald

96 Dominion Road, Worthing, West Sussex
BN14 8JP
☎01903 821082 Fax 01903 821081
Email news@christianherald.org.uk
Website www.christianherald.org.uk

Owner *Christian Media Centre Ltd*
Editor *Russ Bravo*
Circulation 15,000

WEEKLY. Christian newspaper, evangelical and
interdenominational, for committed Christians.
News, bible-based comment and incisive
features. No poetry. Contributors' guidelines
available. *Payment* Christian Media rates.

Church Music Quarterly

Cleveland Lodge, Westhumble, Dorking,
Surrey RH5 6BW
☎01306 872800 Fax 01306 887260
Owner *Royal School of Church Music*
Acting Editor *Esther Jones*
Circulation 13,700

QUARTERLY. Contributions welcome. Phone
in the first instance.
    Features Articles on church music or related
subjects considered. Maximum 2000 words.
    Payment £60 per page.

Church of England Newspaper

10 Little College Street, London SW1P 3SH
☎020 7878 1545 Fax 020 7976 0783
Owner *Parliamentary Communications Ltd*
Editor *Colin Blakely*
Circulation 9,200

FOUNDED 1828. WEEKLY. Almost all material is
commissioned but unsolicited mss considered.
    Features *Claire Shelley* Preliminary enquiry
essential. Maximum 1200 words.
    News *Andrew Carey* Items must be sent
promptly and should have a church/Christian
relevance. Maximum 200–400 words.
    Payment negotiable.

Church Times

33 Upper Street, London N1 0PN
☎020 7359 4570 Fax 020 7226 3073
Email news@churchtimes.co.uk *or*
    features@churchtimes.co.uk
Website www.churchtimes.co.uk
Owner *Hymns Ancient & Modern*
Editor *Paul Handley*
Circulation 36,500

FOUNDED 1863. WEEKLY. Unsolicited mss considered.
    Features *Prudence Fay* Articles and pictures
(any format) on religious topics. Maximum 1600
words. *Payment* £100 per 1000 words.
    News *Helen Saxbee* Occasional reports (com-
missions only) and up-to-date photographs.
Payment by arrangement.

Classic Bike

20-22 Station Road, Kettering,
Northamptonshire NN15 7HH
☎01536 386777 Fax 01536 386782
Email classic.bike@econ.emap.com
Website www.motorcyclenews.com
Owner *EMAP Active Ltd*
Editor *Brian Crichton*
Circulation 50,000

FOUNDED 1978. MONTHLY Mainly pre-1972
classic motorcycles with a heavy bias to British
marques. Approach in writing.
    News Genuine news with good illustrations,
if possible, suitable for a global audience. Max.
500 words.
    Features British motorcycle industry inside
stories, technical features 'that can be understood
by all', German, Spanish and French machine
features, people. Max. 2000 words. **Special
Pages** How-to features, oddball machines, stunning pictures, features with a fresh slant.
    Payment £100 per 1000 words, plus pictures.

Classic Boat

Link House, Dingwall Avenue, Croydon,
Surrey CR9 2TA
☎020 8686 2599 Fax 020 8781 6535
Email cb@ipc.co.uk
Website www.classicboat.co.uk
Owner *IPC Magazines Ltd*
Editor *Nic Compton*
Circulation 19,138

FOUNDED 1987. MONTHLY. Traditional boats
and classic yachts old and new; maritime history. Unsolicited mss, particularly if supported
by good photos, are welcome. Sail and power
boat pieces considered. Approach in writing
with ideas. Interested in well-researched stories
on all nautical matters. News reports welcome.
Contributor's notes available (s.a.e.).
    Features Boatbuilding, history and design,
events, yachts and working boats. Material must
be well-informed and supported where possible
by good-quality or historic photo. Max. 3000
words. Classic is defined by excellence of design
and construction – the boat need not be old and
wooden! *Payment* £75-100 per published page.
    News New boats, restorations, events, boat-
builders, etc. Maximum 500 words. *Payment*
according to merit.

Classic Cars

EMAP Active, Homenene House, Orton
Centre, Peterborough PE2 5UW
☎01733 237111 Fax 01733 465857
Website www.classiccarsworld.co.uk
Owner *EMAP Active*
Editor *Mark Walton*
International Editor *Robert Coucher*
Circulation 86,177

FOUNDED 1973. MONTHLY international classic
car magazine containing entertaining and informative articles about classic cars, events and
associated personalities. Contributions welcome.

Classical Guitar

1 & 2 Vance Court, Trans Britannia Enterprise
Park, Blaydon on Tyne NE21 5NH
☎0191 414 9000 Fax 0191 414 9001
Email classicalguitar@ashleymark.co.uk
Website www.ashleymark.co.uk/
Owner *Ashley Mark Publishing Co.*
Editor *Colin Cooper*
FOUNDED 1982. MONTHLY.
    Features *Colin Cooper* Usually written by
staff writers. Maximum 1500 words. *Payment*
by arrangement.
    News *Thérèse Wassily Saba* Small paragraphs
and festival concert reports welcome. *No payment.*
    Reviews *Tim Panting* Concert reviews of up
to 250 words are usually written by staff
reviewers.

Classical Music

241 Shaftesbury Avenue, London
WC2H 8EH
☎020 7333 1742 Fax 020 7333 1769
Email classical.music@rhinegold.co.uk
Website www.rhinegold.co.uk
Owner *Rhinegold Publishing Ltd*
Editor *Keith Clarke*
FOUNDED 1976. FORTNIGHTLY. A specialist
magazine using precisely targeted news and
feature articles aimed at the music business. Most
material is commissioned but professionally written unsolicited mss are occasionally published.
Freelance contributors may approach in writing
with an idea but should familiarise themselves
beforehand with the style and market of the
magazine.
    Payment negotiable.

Classics

Berwick House, 8–10 Knoll Rise, Orpington,
Kent BR6 0PS
☎01689 887200 Fax 01689 838844
Email classics@splpublishing.co.uk
Owner *SPL*
Editor *Andrew Noakes*
FOUNDED 1997. MONTHLY how-to magazine

for classic car owners, featuring everything from repairing and restoring to buying, selling and enjoying all types of cars from the '50s to '80s. Includes vehicle comparison tests, price guide, practical advice and technical know-how from experts and owners, plus hundreds of readers' free ads.

Features Illustrated features on classic car maintenance, repair and restoration with strong technical content and emphasis on DIY.

News All classic car related news stories and topical photos.

Climber

PO Box 28, Altrincham, Cheshire
WA15 8FR
☎0161 608 0300 Fax 0161 608 0298
Owner *Media Ventures Group Plc*
Editor *Bernard Newman*

FOUNDED 1962. MONTHLY. Unsolicited mss welcome (they receive about ten a day). Ideas welcome.

Features Freelance features (accompanied by photographs) are accepted on climbing and mountaineering in the UK and abroad, but the standard of writing must be extremely high. Maximum 2000 words. *Payment* negotiable.

News No freelance opportunities as all items are handled in-house.

Club International

2 Archer Street, London W1V 8JJ
☎020 7292 8000 Fax 020 7734 5030
Email club@pr-org.co.uk
Owner *Paul Raymond*
Editor *Robert Swift*
Circulation 180,000

FOUNDED 1972. MONTHLY. Features and short humorous items aimed at young male readership aged 18–30.

Features Maximum 1000 words.
Shorts 200–750 words.
Payment negotiable.

Coin News

Token Publishing Ltd, 1 Orchard House, Duchy Road, Heathpark, Honiton, Devon EX14 1YT
☎01404 46972 Fax 01404 44788
Email info@coin-news.com
Website www.coin-news.com
Editor *J. W. Mussell*
Owners *J. W. Mussell, Carol Hartman*
Circulation 10,000

FOUNDED 1964. MONTHLY. Contributions wel-come. Approach by phone in the first instance.

Features Opportunity exists for well-informed authors 'who know the subject and do their homework'. Maximum 2500 words.
Payment £20 per 1000 words.

Comhairle

See **ignotus press** under **Small Presses**

Company

National Magazine House, 72 Broadwick Street, London W1V 2BP
☎020 7439 5000 Fax 020 7439 5117
Owner *National Magazine Co. Ltd*
Editor *Sam Baker*
Circulation 242,180

MONTHLY. Glossy women's magazine appealing to the independent and intelligent young woman. A good market for freelancers: 'We look for great newsy features relevant to young British women'. Keen to encourage bright, new, young talent, but uncommissioned material is rarely accepted. Feature outlines are the only sensible approach in the first instance. Maximum 1500–2000 words. Features to *Celia Duncan*, Features Editor.

Payment £250 per 1000 words.

Company Clothing Magazine

7 Holbrook Road, Leicester LE2 3LG
☎0116 270 4075 Fax 0116 270 0136
Owner *Company Clothing Information Services Ltd*
Editor *Leonie Barrie*
Circulation 13,000

Only UK magazine dedicated to the corporate clothing industry. Unsolicited mss welcome on any aspect of business clothing and workwear.

Compass Sport

Ballencrieff Cottage, Ballencrieff Toll, Bathgate, West Lothian EH48 4LD
☎01506 632728 Fax 01506 635444
Email pages@clara.net
Website home.clara.net/pages
Owner *Pages Editorial & Publishing Services*
Editor *Suse Coon*

BI-MONTHLY orienteering magazine covering all disciplines of the sport including mountain marathons, mountain bike O, ski O and trail O. Includes profiles and articles on relevant topics, with subsections on fixtures, junior news and mountain marathons which are compiled by sub-editors. Letters, puzzles and competition. Phone or e-mail to discuss content and timing.
Payment by arrangement.

Computer Arts Special

30 Monmouth Street, Bath BA1 2BW
☎01225 442244 Fax 01225 732361
Email garrick.webster@futurenet.co.uk
Website www.computerarts.co.uk
Owner *The Future Network*
Editor *Garrick Webster*

FOUNDED 1999. BI-MONTHLY The world of
computer arts – 3D, web design, photoshop,
digital video. No unsolicited mss. Interested in
tutorials, profiles, tips, software and hardware
reviews. Approach by post or e-mail.

Computer Weekly

Quadrant House, The Quadrant, Sutton,
Surrey SM2 5AS
☎020 8652 3122 Fax 020 8652 8979
Email computer.weekly@rbi.co.uk
Owner *Reed Business Information*
Editor *Karl Schneider*
Circulation 150,000

FOUNDED 1966. Freelance contributions welcome.
Features *Mark Lewis* Always looking for good
new writers with specialised industry knowledge.
Previews and show features on industry events
welcome. Maximum 1500 words.
News Some openings for regional or foreign
news items. Maximum 300 words.
Payment Up to £50 for stories/tips.

Computing, The IT Newspaper

32–34 Broadwick Street, London W1A 2HG
☎020 7316 9000 Fax 020 7316 9160
Email computing@vnu.co.uk
Website www.vnu.com
Owner *VNU Business Publications Ltd*
Editor *Douglas Hayward*
Deputy Editor *Gary Flood*
Circulation 135,000

FOUNDED 1973. WEEKLY newspaper for IT
professionals.
Associate Editor *Ian Stobie*
Features Editor *Helen Guyatt*
News *Tim Stammers*
Unsolicited technical articles welcome. Please
enclose s.a.e. for return.
Payment negotiable.

Condé Nast Traveller

Vogue House, Hanover Square, London
W1R 0AD
☎020 7499 9080 Fax 020 7493 3758
Email traveller@msmail.condenast.co.uk
Website www.cntraveller.co.uk
Owner *Condé Nast Publications*
Editor *Sarah Miller*
Circulation 70,000

FOUNDED 1997. Monthly travel magazine.
Proposals rather than completed mss preferred.
Approach in writing in the first instance. No
unsolicited photographs. 'The magazine has a
no freebie policy and no writing can be
accepted on the basis of a press or paid-for trip.'

Contemporary Review

PO Box 1242, Oxford OX1 4FJ
☎01865 201529 Fax 01865 201529
Email editorial@contemporaryreview.co.uk
Owner *Contemporary Review Co. Ltd*
Editor *Dr Richard Mullen*

FOUNDED 1866. MONTHLY. Covers international
affairs and politics, literature and the arts, history
and religion. No fiction. Max. 3000 words.
Literary Editor *Dr James Munson* Monthly
book section with reviews which are always
commissioned.
Payment £5 per page.

Cosmopolitan

National Magazine House, 72 Broadwick
Street, London W1V 2BP
☎020 7439 5000 Fax 020 7439 5016
Owner *National Magazine Co. Ltd*
Editor-in-Chief *Mandi Norwood*
Circulation 470,280

MONTHLY. Designed to appeal to the mid-
twenties, modern-minded female. Popular mix
of articles, with emphasis on relationships and
careers, and hard news. No fiction. Will rarely
use unsolicited mss but always on the look-out
for 'new writers with original and relevant
ideas and a strong voice'. Send short synopsis of
idea. All would-be writers should be familiar
with the magazine.
Payment about £250 per 1000 words.

Cotswold Life

Treaford House, 54 Lansdown Road,
Cheltenham, Gloucestershire GL51 6QB
☎01242 255334 Fax 01242 255116
Email info@cotswoldlife.co.uk
Owner *Loyalty & Conquest Communications Ltd*
Managing Editor *David MacDonald*
Circulation 10,000

FOUNDED 1968. MONTHLY. News and features
on life in the Cotswolds. Contributions welcome.
Features Interesting places and people,
reminiscences of Cotswold life in years gone

by, and historical features on any aspect of Cotswold life. Approach in writing in the first instance. Maximum 1500–2000 words.

Payment by negotiation after publication.

Counselling at Work

Association for Counselling at Work, Eastlands Court, St Peter's Road, Rugby, Warwickshire CV21 3QP
☎01788 335617 Fax 01788 335618
Email sula@cwcom.net

Owner *British Association for Counselling*
Editor *Ian Macwhinnie*
Circulation 1600

FOUNDED 1993. QUARTERLY official journal of the Association for Counselling at Work, a division of B.A.C. Looking for well-researched articles (500–1600 words) about *any* aspect of workplace counselling. Mss from those employed as counsellors or in welfare posts are particularly welcome. Photographs not accepted at present but that may change in the near future. No fiction or poetry. Send A4 s.a.e. for writer's guidelines and sample copy of the journal. *No payment.*

Country Homes and Interiors

King's Reach Tower, Stamford Street, London SE1 9LS
☎020 7261 6451 Fax 020 7261 6895

Owner *IPC Magazines Ltd*
Editor *Katherine Hadley*
Circulation 111,616

FOUNDED 1986. MONTHLY. The best approach for prospective contributors is with an idea in writing as unsolicited mss are not welcome.

Features *Jean Carr* Monthly personality interviews of interest to an intelligent, affluent readership (women and men), aged 25–44. Maximum 1200 words. Also hotel reviews, leisure pursuits and weekending pieces in England and abroad. Length 750 words.

Houses *Clare Wallace* Country-style homes with excellent design ideas. Length 1000 words. *Payment* negotiable.

Country Life

King's Reach Tower, Stamford Street, London SE1 9LS
☎020 7261 7058 Fax 020 7261 5139
Website www.countrylife.co.uk

Owner *IPC Magazines*
Editor *Clive Aslet*
Circulation 44,774

ESTABLISHED 1897. WEEKLY. Features articles which relate to architecture, countryside, wildlife, rural events, sports, arts, exhibitions, current

events, property and news articles of interest to town and country dwellers. Strong informed material rather than amateur enthusiasm. 'We regret we cannot be liable for the safe custody or return of any solicited or unsolicited materials.' *Payment* variable, depending on word length and picture size.

Country Living

National Magazine House, 72 Broadwick Street, London W1V 2BP
☎020 7439 5000 Fax 020 7439 5093

Owner *National Magazine Co. Ltd*
Editor *Susy Smith*
Circulation 150,047

Magazine aimed at country dwellers and town dwellers who love the countryside. Covers people, conservation, wildlife, houses (gardens and interiors) and country businesses. No unsolicited mss. *Payment* negotiable.

Country Smallholding

Broad Leys Publishing Company, Buriton House, Station Road, Newport, Saffron Walden, Essex CB11 3PL
☎01799 540922 Fax 01799 541367

Owners *D. and K. Thear*
Editor *Helen Sears*
Circulation 21,000

FOUNDED 1975. MONTHLY journal dealing with practical country living. Unsolicited mss welcome; around 30 are received each week. Articles should be detailed and practical, based on first-hand knowledge and experience of smallholding.

Country Sports

The Old Town Hall 367 Kennington Road, London SE1 4PT
☎020 7582 5432 Fax 020 7793 8484

Owner *Countryside Alliance*
Editor *Graham Downing*
Circulation 60,000

FOUNDED 1996. QUARTERLY magazine on country sports and conservation issues. No unsolicited mss.

Country Walking

Apex House, Oundle Road, Peterborough, Cambridgeshire PE2 9NP
☎01733 898100 Fax 01733 465070

Owner *EMAP Plc*
Editor *Lynne Maxwell*
Circulation 53,995

FOUNDED 1987. MONTHLY magazine containing

walks, features related to walking and things you see, country crafts, history, nature, photography, etc., plus pull-out walks guide containing 25+ routes every month. Very few unsolicited mss accepted. An original approach to subjects welcomed. Not interested in book or gear reviews, news cuttings or poor-quality pictures. Approach by phone with ideas.

Features *Michelle Daniel* Reader's story (maximum 800 words). Practical (200–600 words).

Special Pages 'Down your way' section walks. Accurately and recently researched walk and fact file. Points of interest along the way and pictures to illustrate. Please contact for guidelines (unsolicited submissions not often accepted for this section).

Payment not negotiable.

The Countryman

King's Reach Tower, Stamford Street, London SE1 9LS
☎020 7261 5000

Owner *IPC Magazines Ltd*
Editor *Tom Quinn*
Circulation 36,471

FOUNDED 1927. EIGHT ISSUES YEARLY. Unsolicited mss with s.a.e. welcome; about 120 received each week. Contributors are strongly advised to study the magazine's content and character in the first instance. Articles supplied with top quality illustrations (colour transparencies, archive b&w prints and line drawings) are far more likely to be used. No fiction. No hunting, shooting or fishing. Maximum article length 1500 words.

The Countryman's Weekly
(incorporating **Gamekeeper** and **Sporting Dog**)

Yelverton, Devon PL20 7PE
☎01822 855281 Fax 01822 855372

Publisher *Vic Gardner*
Features Editor *Kelly Gardner*

FOUNDED 1895. WEEKLY. Unsolicited material welcome. **Features** On any country sports topic. Maximum 1000 words. *Payment* rates available on request.

County

PO Box 2486, Cane End, Reading, Berkshire RG4 6YJ
☎0118 9724800 Fax 0118 9724900

Owners *Mr and Mrs Watts*
Editor *Mrs Ashlyn Watts*
Circulation 50,000

FOUNDED 1986. QUARTERLY lifestyle magazine featuring homes, interiors, gardening, fashion and beauty, motoring, leisure and dining. Welcomes unsolicited mss. All initial approaches should be made in writing.

The Cricketer International

Third Street, Langton Green, Tunbridge Wells, Kent TN3 0EN
☎01892 862551 Fax 01892 863755
Email editorial@cricketer.co.uk

Owner *Ben G. Brocklehurst*
Editor *Peter Perchard*
Circulation 40,000

FOUNDED 1921. MONTHLY. Unsolicited mss considered. Ideas in writing only. No initial discussions by phone. All correspondence should be addressed to the editor.

Crimewave

5 Martins Lane, Witcham, Ely, Cambridgeshire CB6 2LB
☎01353 777931
Email ttapress@aol.com
Website www.tta-press.freewire.co.uk

Owner *TTA Press*
Editor *Mat Coward*

FOUNDED 1998. QUARTERLY B5 colour magazine of crime fiction. 'The UK's only magazine specialising in crime short stories, publishing the very best from across the spectrum.' Every issue contains stories by authors who are household names in the crime fiction world but room is found for lesser known and unknown writers. *Taking Care of Frank* by Antony Mann, from *Crimewave 2*, won the **CWA/Macallan Short Story Dagger** award in 1999. Submissions welcome (not via e-mail) with appropriate return postage. Potential contributors are advised to study the magazine. Contracts exchanged upon acceptance. *Payment* on publication.

Cumbria and Lake District Magazine

Dalesman Publishing Co. Ltd, Stable Courtyard, Broughton Hall, Skipton, North Yorkshire BD23 3AE
☎01756 701381 Fax 01756 701326
Email editorial@dalesman.co.uk

Owner *Dalesman Publishing Co. Ltd*
Editor *Terry Fletcher*
Circulation 17,000

FOUNDED 1951. MONTHLY. County magazine of strong regional and countryside interest, focusing on the Lake District. Unsolicited mss welcome. Maximum 1500 words. Approach in writing or by phone with feature ideas.

Cycle Sport

Link House, Dingwall Avenue, Croydon CR9 2TA
☎020 8774 0828 Fax 020 8686 0947
Owner *IPC Magazines Ltd*
Editor *Luke Edwardes-Evans*
Circulation 23,299

FOUNDED 1993. MONTHLY magazine dedicated to professional cycle racing. Unsolicited ideas for features welcome.

Cycling Weekly

IPC Magazines Ltd, Link House, Dingwall Avenue, Croydon, Surrey CR9 2TA
☎020 8774 0703 Fax 020 8686 0947
Website www.ipc.co.uk/pubs/cyclweek.htm
Owner *IPC Magazines Ltd*
Editor *Robert Garbutt*
Circulation 31,735

FOUNDED 1891. WEEKLY. All aspects of cycle sport covered. Unsolicited mss and ideas for features welcome. Approach in writing with ideas. Fiction rarely used.

Features Cycle racing, technical material and related areas. Maximum 2000 words. Most work commissioned but interested in seeing new work. *Payment* around £60–120 per 1000 words (quality permitting).

News Short news pieces, local news, etc. Maximum 300 words. *Payment* £15 per story.

The Dalesman

Stable Courtyard, Broughton Hall, Skipton, North Yorkshire BD23 3AE
☎01756 701381 Fax 01756 701326
Email editorial@dalesman.co.uk
Owner *Dalesman Publishing Co. Ltd*
Editor *Terry Fletcher*
Circulation 51,000

FOUNDED 1939. Now the biggest-selling regional publication of its kind in the country. MONTHLY magazine with articles of specific Yorkshire interest. Unsolicited mss welcome; receives approximately ten per day. Initial approach in writing or by phone. Maximum 1500 words. *Payment* negotiable.

Dance Theatre Journal

Laban Centre London, Laurie Grove, London SE14 6NH
☎020 8692 4070 Fax 020 8694 8749
Owner *Laban Centre London*

Editor *Ian Bramley*
Circulation 2000

FOUNDED 1982. QUARTERLY. Interested in features on every aspect of the contemporary dance scene, particularly issues such as the funding policy for dance, critical assessments of choreographers' work and the latest developments in the various schools of contemporary dance. Unsolicited mss welcome. Length 1000–3000 words. *Payment* varies 'according to age and experience'.

The Dancing Times

Clerkenwell House, 45–47 Clerkenwell Green, London EC1R 0EB
☎020 7250 3006 Fax 020 7253 6679
Email DT@dancing-times.co.uk
Owner *The Dancing Times Ltd*
Editor *Mary Clarke*

FOUNDED 1910. MONTHLY. Freelance suggestions welcome from specialist dance writers and photographers only. Approach in writing.

Darts World

28 Arrol Road, Beckenham, Kent BR3 4PA
☎020 8650 6580 Fax 020 8654 4343
Owner *World Magazines Ltd*
Editor *A. J. Wood*
Circulation 24,500

Features Single articles or series on technique and instruction. Maximum 1200 words.

Fiction Short stories with darts theme. Maximum 1000 words.

News Tournament reports and general or personality news required. Maximum 800 words.

Payment negotiable.

Dateline Magazine

Pollet House, St Peter Port, Guernsey GY1 1WF
☎0870 766262 Fax 01481 735353
Email magazine@dateline.co.uk
Owner *Columbus Group plc*
Editor *Nicky Boult*
Circulation 7,000

FOUNDED 1976. MONTHLY magazine for single people. Unsolicited mss welcome.

Features Anything of interest to, or directly concerning, single people. Max. 2500 words.

News Items required at least six weeks ahead. Max. 2500 words.

Payment from £45 per 1000 words; £10 per illustration/picture used.

Day by Day

Woolacombe House, 141 Woolacombe Road, Blackheath, London SE3 8QP
☎020 8856 6249

Owner *Loverseed Press*
Editor *Patrick Richards*
Circulation 24,000

FOUNDED 1963. MONTHLY. News commentary and digest of national and international affairs, with reviews of the arts (books, plays, art exhibitions, films, opera, musicals) and county cricket and Test reports among regular slots. Unsolicited mss welcome (s.a.e. essential). Approach in writing with ideas. Contributors are advised to study the magazine in the first instance. (Specimen copy 90p.) UK subscription: £11.

News *Ronald Mallone* Interested in themes connected with non-violence and social justice only. Maximum 600 words.

Features No scope for freelance contributions here.

Fiction Very rarely published.

Poems *Michael Gibson* Short poems in line with editorial principles considered. Maximum 20 lines.

Payment negotiable.

Dazed & Confused

112 Old Street, London EC1V 1BD
☎020 7336 0766 Fax 020 7336 0966
Email dazed@confused.co.uk
Website www.confused.co.uk

Owner *Waddell Ltd*
Editor *Jefferson Hack*
Circulation 80,000

FOUNDED 1992. MONTHLY. Cutting edge fashion, music, art interviews and features. No unsolicited material. Approach in writing with ideas in the first instance.

Dead Things Magazine

12 Grace Avenue, Orford, Warrington, Cheshire WA2 8BT
☎0771 3283231
Email letters@deadthings.co.uk
Website www.deadthings.co.uk

Owner/Editor *D. Cowdall*

FOUNDED 1999. QUARTERLY magazine dedicated to horror fiction with the emphasis on horror humour. Short stories plus articles, interviews and competitions. No poetry. Submissions of up to 5000 words; 'send without query; needed all year round. Request our quidelines or see them on the website.' Approach by e-mail or post.

Decanter

583 Fulham Road, London SW6 5UA
☎020 7610 3929 Fax 020 7385 8444
Email editorial@decanter.com
Website www.decantermagazine.com

Editor *Susan Keevil*
Circulation 35,000

FOUNDED 1975. Glossy wines and spirits magazine. Unsolicited material welcome but an advance telephone call or faxed outline appreciated. No fiction.

News/Features All items and articles should concern wines, spirits, food and related subjects.

Derbyshire Life and Countryside

Heritage House, Lodge Lane, Derby DE1 3HE
☎01332 347087 Fax 01332 290688

Owner *B. C. Wood*
Editor *Vivienne Irish*
Circulation 11,957

FOUNDED 1931. MONTHLY county magazine for Derbyshire. Unsolicited mss and photographs of Derbyshire welcome, but written approach with ideas preferred.

Descent

51 Timbers Square, Roath, Cardiff CF24 3SH
☎029 2048 6557 Fax 029 2048 6557
Email descent@wildplaces.co.uk

Owner *Wild Places Publishing*
Editor *Chris Howes*
Assistant Editor *Judith Calford*

FOUNDED 1969. BI-MONTHLY magazine for cavers and mine enthusiasts. Submissions welcome from freelance contributors who can write accurately and knowledgeably on any aspect of caves, mines or underground structures.

Features General interest articles of under 1000 words welcome, as well as short foreign news reports, especially if supported by photographs/illustrations. Suitable topics include exploration (particularly British, both historical and modern), expeditions, equipment, techniques and regional British news. Max. 2000 words.

Payment on publication according to page area filled.

Desire

1 Fentiman Road, London SW8 1LD
☎020 7820 8844 Fax 020 7627 5808

Owner *Moondance Media Ltd*
Editor *Ian Jackson*

FOUNDED 1994. SIX ISSUES YEARLY. Britain's first erotic magazine for both women and men, celebrating sex and sensuality with a mix of articles, columns, features, reviews, interviews, fantasy and poetry (1000–2500 words).

For sample copy of magazine plus contributors' guidelines and rates, please enclose 4x first class stamps.

The Dial

77 Old Tiverton Road, Exeter, Devon
EX4 6NG
☎01392 213843 Fax 01392 213843
Owner *Hermitage Press*
Editor *John Evans*

FOUNDED 2000. QUARTERLY magazine aimed at professional downshifters, Thoreauvians and all individualists. Interested in articles on natural history, self-sufficiency and spiritual path; short fiction: relevant stories of quality. Nothing hip; no cool Britannia. Approach by post or fax. Maximum 2500 words. *Payment* £20.

Director

116 Pall Mall, London SW1Y 5ED
☎020 7766 8950 Fax 020 7766 8840
Editor *Joe Higgins*
Circulation 50,000

1991 Business Magazine of the Year. Published by The Director Publications Ltd. for members of the Institute of Directors. Wide range of features from political and business profiles and management thinking to employment and financial issues. Also book reviews. Regular contributors used. Send letter with synopsis/published samples rather than unsolicited mss. Strictly no 'lifestyle' writing. *Payment* negotiable.

Dirt Bike Rider (DBR)

Lancaster & Morecambe Newspapers Ltd, Victoria Street, Morecambe, Lancashire
LA4 4AG
Owner *L&M Newspapers Ltd*
Editor *Gary Pinchin*
Circulation 19,836

FOUNDED 1981. MONTHLY. Off-road dirt bikes (motocross, enduro and trials).

Disability Now

6 Market Road, London N7 9PW
☎020 7619 7323 Fax 020 7619 7331
Publisher *SCOPE* (Formerly The Spastics Society)
Editor *Mary Wilkinson*
Circulation 22,196

FOUNDED 1984. Leading MONTHLY newspaper for the disabled in the UK, for people with a wide range of physical disabilities, as well as their families, carers and relevant professionals. No unsolicited material but freelance contributions welcome. Approach in writing.

Features Covering new initiatives and services, personal experiences and general issues of interest to a wide national readership. Maximum 1200 words. Disabled contributors welcome.

News Maximum 300 words.

Special Pages Possible openings for cartoonists.

Payment by arrangement.

Disabled Motorist

DDMC, Cottingham Way, Thrapston, Northamptonshire NN14 4PL
☎01832 734724 Fax 01832 733816
Email ddme@ukonline.co.uk
Website www.ukonline.co.uk/ddmc
Owner *Disabled Drivers' Motor Club*
Editor *Lesley Browne*
Circulation 14,500+

BI-MONTHLY publication of the Disabled Drivers' Motor Club, an organisation which aims to promote and protect the interests and welfare of disabled people and help and encourage them in gaining increased mobility. Various discounts available for members; membership costs £10 p.a. (single), £15 (joint). The magazine includes information for members plus members' letters. Approach in writing with ideas. Unsolicited mss welcome.

Diva, lesbian life and style

Worldwide House, 116–134 Bayham Street, London NW1 0BA
☎020 7482 2576 Fax 020 7284 0329
Email diva@gaytimes.co.uk
Website www.prowler.co.uk
Owner *Millivres Prowler Group*
Editor *Gillian Rodgerson*

FOUNDED 1994. MONTHLY journal of lesbian news and culture. Welcomes news, features, short fiction and photographs. No poetry. Contact the news editor with news items and *Gillian Rodgerson* with features, fiction and photographs. First approach in writing.

Dog World

Somerfield House, Wotton Road, Ashford, Kent TN23 6LW
☎01233 621877 Fax 01233 645669
Owner *Dog World Ltd*
Editor *Simon Parsons*
Circulation 28,252

FOUNDED 1902. WEEKLY newspaper for people who are seriously interested in pedigree dogs.

Unsolicited mss occasionally considered but initial approach in writing preferred.

Features Well-researched historical items or items of unusual interest concerning dogs. Maximum 1000 words. Photographs of unusual 'doggy' situations occasionally of interest. *Payment* up to £50; photos £15.

News Freelance reports welcome on court cases and local government issues involving dogs.

The Dom Camillo Review

Casa Guareschi, 116 Gaywood Road, King's Lynn, Norfolk PE30 2PX
☎01553 762737

Owner *Il Cestino internazionale*
Editor *Dr David Willings*
Assistant Editor *Carol Downing*

FOUNDED 1998. QUARTERLY. Translations of Giovannino Guareschi's *Dom Camillo* stories and other short works, reproductions of his cartoons and commentary. Will consider articles (max. 1600 words), poems (max. 50 lines) and short stories in the Guareschi tradition; also articles on the cultural heritage of Italy (plus photographs). *Payment* by arrangement for articles; no payment for poetry.

Eastern Eye

148 Cambridge Heath Road, London E1 5QJ
☎020 7702 8012 Fax 020 7702 7937

Owner *Ethnic Media Group*
Editor *Nadeem Kahn*
Circulation 40,000

WEEKLY community paper for the Asian community in Britain. Interested in relevant general, local and international issues. Approach in writing with ideas for submission.

The Ecologist

Unit 18, Chelsea Wharf, 15 Lots Road, London SW10 0QJ
☎020 7351 3578 Fax 020 7351 3617
Email ecologist@gn.apc.org

Owner *Ecosystems Ltd*
Editor *Zac Goldsmith*
Deputy Editor *Paul Kingsnorth*
Circulation 15,000

FOUNDED 1970. MONTHLY. Unsolicited mss welcome but best approach is a brief (one-side, A4) proposal to the editor, outlining experience and background and summarising suggested article. Writers should study the magazine for style before submission.

Features Radical approach to political, economic, social and environmental issues, with an emphasis on rethinking the basic assumptions that underpin modern society. Articles of between 500 and 3000 words.
Payment £150 per 1000 words.

The Economist

25 St James's Street, London SW1A 1HG
☎020 7830 7000 Fax 020 7839 2968
Website www.economist.com

Owner *Pearson/individual shareholders*
Editor *Bill Emmott*
Circulation 696,000

FOUNDED 1843. WEEKLY. Worldwide circulation. Approaches should be made in writing to the editor. No unsolicited mss.

The Edge

65 Guinness Buildings, Fulham Palace Road, London W6 8BD
☎020 7460 9444
Email grahamevans@cwcom.net

Editor *Graham Evans*

BI-MONTHLY magazine. Looking for feature writers and reviewers: film (non-Hollywood/arts/mainstream), popular culture/books. Also requires imaginative fiction: modern SF/horror/urban fiction. Sample copy £2.95 (post-free, cheques payable to 'The Edge'). Writers' guidelines available for s.a.e.
Payment negotiable; fiction: £30 per 1000 words; non-fiction: £50–200 per piece.

Edinburgh Review

22A Buccleuch Place, Edinburgh
☎0131 651 1415

Owner *Edinburgh University Press*
Circulation 750

FOUNDED 1969. BIANNUAL. Articles and fiction on Scottish and international literary, cultural and philosophical themes. Unsolicited contributions are welcome (1600 are received each year), but prospective contributors are strongly advised to study the magazine first. Allow up to six months for a reply.

Features Interest will be shown in accessible articles on philosophy and its relationship to literature or visual art.

Fiction Scottish and international. Maximum 6000 words.

Electrical Times

Quadrant House, The Quadrant, Sutton, Surrey SM2 5AS
☎020 8652 3115 Fax 020 8652 8972

Owner *Reed Business Information*
Editor *Paul Doughty*

Circulation 12,900

FOUNDED 1891. MONTHLY. Aimed at electrical contractors, designers and installers. Unsolicited mss welcome but initial approach preferred.

Elle

Endeavour House, 189 Shaftesbury Avenue, London WC2H 8JG
☎020 7437 9011 Fax 020 7208 3599
Owner *EMAP Elan Publications*
Editor *Fiona McIntosh*
Circulation 210,076

FOUNDED 1985. MONTHLY fashion glossy. Prospective contributors should approach the relevant editor in writing in the first instance, including cuttings.
Features Maximum 2000 words.
First Word Short articles on current/cultural events, fashion and beauty. Maximum 500 words.
Payment about £250 per 1000 words.

Empire

Mappin House, 4 Winsley Street, London W1N 7AR
☎020 7436 1515 Fax 020 7312 8249
Website www.empireonline.co.uk
Owner *EMAP élan Network*
Editor *Emma Cochrane*
Circulation 165,778

FOUNDED 1989. Launched at the Cannes Film Festival. MONTHLY guide to the movies which aims to cover the world of films in a 'comprehensive, adult, intelligent and witty package'. Although most of *Empire* is devoted to films and the people behind them, it also looks at the developments and technology behind television and video plus music, multimedia and books. Wide selection of in-depth features and stories on all the main releases of the month, and reviews of over 100 films and videos. Contributions welcome but approach in writing first.
Features Behind-the-scenes features on films, humorous and factual features.
Payment by agreement.

The Engineer

50 Poland Street, London SW1V 4AX
☎020 7970 4106 Fax 020 7970 4189
Owner *Centaur Communications*
Editor *Paul Carslake*
Circulation 38,000

FOUNDED 1856. WEEKLY news magazine for the UK manufacturing industry.

Features Most outside contributions are commissioned but good ideas are always welcome. Maximum 2000 words.
News Scope for specialist regional freelancers, and for tip-offs. Maximum 500 words.
Technology Technology news from specialists, and tip-offs. Maximum 500 words.
Payment by arrangement.

The English Garden

Romsey Publishing Ltd, Glen House, Stag Place, London SW1E 5AQ
☎020 7233 9191 Fax 020 7630 8084
Email editorial@theenglishgarden.co.uk
Owner *Romsey Publishing Ltd*
Editor *Vanessa Berridge*
Circulation 103,845

FOUNDED 1996. MONTHLY. Features on beautiful gardens with practical ideas on design and planting. No unsolicited mss.
Features *Julia Watson* Maximum 1000–1200 words. Approach in writing in the first instance; send synopsis of 150 words with strong design and planting ideas, or sets of photographs of interesting gardens. 'No stately home or estate gardens with teams of gardeners.'

English Nature

English Nature, Northminster House, Peterborough, Cambridgeshire PE1 1UA
☎01733 455193 Fax 01733 455188
Email press@english-nature.org.uk
Website www.english-nature.org.uk
Owner *English Nature*
Editor *Alex Gearns*
Circulation 16,000

FOUNDED 1992. BI-MONTHLY magazine which explains the work of English Nature, the government adviser on wildlife and conservation policies. No unsolicited material.

Enigmatic Tales

117 Birchanger Lane, Birchanger, Hertfordshire CM23 5QF
Email michael@micksims.force9.co.uk
Website www.epress.force9.co.uk
Editors *Mick Sims, Len Maynard*

QUARTERLY illustrated anthology of supernatural stories and novellas of any length. Ghost stories, horror, psychological, traditional and modern. New writers and rare fiction from the past. Prefers submissions on disk, accompanied by hard copy or e-mail with Word file attachment. Enclose s.a.e. for any enquiries requiring a response. Full details and guidelines on the website. Also publishes *Enigmatic*

Novellas, a quarterly publication for longer pieces, *Enigmatic Variations*, and *Enigmatic Electronic*, a webzine exclusive to the Internet.
Payment free copy of relevant issue.

The Erotic Review

EPS, 4th Floor, 1 Maddox Street, London W1R 9WA
☎020 7437 8887 Fax 020 7437 3528
Email eros@eps.org.uk
Website www.eps.org.uk
Owner *Erotic Print Society*
Editor *Rowan Pelling*
Circulation 30,000

FOUNDED 1997. MONTHLY erotic literary magazine containing articles, humour, fiction, poetry and art work. Unsolicited material welcome. No pornography. Approach in writing in the first instance enclosing a brief sample of work and s.a.e.
Features Esoteric, humorous or real-life experiences. Maximum 2000 words. *Payment* £40–100. **Fiction** Erotic short stories. Maximum 2000 words. *Payment* £50–100.

ES (Evening Standard magazine)

See entry under **Regional Newspapers**

Esquire

National Magazine House, 72 Broadwick Street, London W1V 2BP
☎020 7439 5000 Fax 020 7312 3920
Owner *National Magazine Co. Ltd*
Editor *Peter Howarth*
Circulation 100,482

FOUNDED 1991. MONTHLY. Quality men's general interest magazine. No unsolicited mss or short stories.

Essentials

King's Reach Tower, Stamford Street, London SE1 9LS
☎020 7261 6970 Fax 020 7261 5262
Owner *IPC Magazines*
Editor *Karen Livermore*
Circulation 262,269

FOUNDED 1988. MONTHLY women's interest magazine. Unsolicited mss (not originals) welcome if accompanied by s.a.e. Initial approach in writing preferred. Prospective contributors should study the magazine thoroughly before submitting anything. No fiction.
Features Maximum 2000 words (double-spaced on A4).
Payment negotiable, but minimum £100 per 1000 words.

Essex Countryside

Griggs Farm, West Street, Coggeshall, Essex CO6 1NT
☎01376 563994 Fax 01376 562581
Email andy@countryside.demon.co.uk
Owner *Market Link Publishing Ltd*
Editor *Andy Tilbrook*
Circulation 17,000

FOUNDED 1952. MONTHLY. Unsolicited material of Essex interest welcome. No general interest material.
Features Countryside, culture and crafts in Essex. Maximum 1500 words.
Payment £40.

European Medical Journal

Publishing House, Trinity Place, Barnstaple, Devon EX32 9HJ
☎01271 328892 Fax 01271 328768
Email emj@vernoncoleman.com
Website www.vernoncoleman.com
Owner/Editor *Dr Vernon Coleman*
Circulation 21,000

FOUNDED 1991. MONTHLY critical medical review.

Eventing

See **Horse and Hound**

Evergreen

PO Box 52, Cheltenham, Gloucestershire GL50 1YQ
☎01242 577775 Fax 01242 222034
Editor *R. Faiers*
Circulation 75,000

FOUNDED 1985. QUARTERLY magazine featuring articles and poems about Britain. Unsolicited contributions welcome.
Features Britain's natural beauty, towns and villages, nostalgia, wildlife, traditions, odd customs, legends, folklore, crafts, etc. Length 250– 2000 words.
Payment £15 per 1000 words; poems £4.

Executive Woman

2 Chantry Place, Harrow, Middlesex HA3 6NY
☎020 8420 1210 Fax 020 8420 1691
Email info@execwoman.com
Website www.execwoman.com
Owner *Saleworld*
Editor *Angela Giveon*
Circulation 75,000

FOUNDED 1987. BI-MONTHLY magazine for female executives in the corporate field and female entrepreneurs.

Features New and interesting business issues and 'Women to Watch'. Health and conferencing, profiles, technology, beauty, fashion, training and arts items. Maximum 600–1200 words.

Legal/Financial Opportunities for lawyers/accountants to write on issues in their field. Maximum 600 words.

Payment negotiable.

Express on Sunday Magazine

See under **National Newspapers (Express on Sunday)**

The Face

2nd Floor, Block A, Exmouth House, Pine Street, London EC1R 0JL
☎020 7689 9999 Fax 020 7689 0300
Owner *EMAP Elan*
Editor *Johnny Davis*
Fashion Editor *Heathermary Jackson*
Circulation 61,341

FOUNDED 1980. Magazine of the style generation, concerned with who's what and what's cool. Profiles, interviews and stories. No fiction. Acquaintance with the 'voice' of *The Face* is essential before sending mss on spec.

Features *Alex Needham* New contributors should write to the features editor with their ideas. Maximum 3000 words. *Payment* £250 per 1000 words.

Diary No news stories.

Family Circle

King's Reach Tower, Stamford Street, London SE1 9LS
☎020 7261 5000 Fax 020 7261 5929
Owner *IPC Magazines Ltd*
Editor *Linda Gray*
Circulation 218,558

FOUNDED 1964. THIRTEEN ISSUES YEARLY. Little scope for freelancers as most material is produced in-house. Unsolicited material is rarely used, but it is considered. Prospective contributors are best advised to send written ideas to the relevant editor.

Style *Amanda Cooke*
Food and Wine *Corolla Weymouth*
Home *Lucy Searle*
Payment by arrangement.

Family Tree Magazine

61 Great Whyte, Ramsey, Huntingdon, Cambridgeshire PE17 1HL
☎01487 814050 Fax 01487 711361
Owner *Armstrong Boon & Marriott (Publishing)*
Editor *Sue Fearn*

Circulation 39,000

FOUNDED 1984. MONTHLY. News and features on matters of genealogy. Not interested in own family histories. Approach in writing with ideas. All material should be addressed to *Sue Fearn*.

Features Any genealogically related subject. Maximum 2400 words. No puzzles or fictional articles.

Payment £35 per 1000 words (news and features).

Farmers Weekly

Quadrant House, Sutton, Surrey SM2 5AS
☎020 8652 4911 Fax 020 8652 4005
Email farmers.weekly@rbi.co.uk
Website www.fwi.co.uk
Owner *Reed Business Information*
Editor *Stephen Howe*
Circulation 98,268

WEEKLY. 1996 Business Magazine of the Year. For practising farmers. Unsolicited mss considered.

Features A wide range of material relating to farmers' problems and interests: specific sections on arable and livestock farming, farm life, practical and general interest, machinery and business.

News General farming news.
Payment negotiable.

Farming News

Miller Freeman House, Sovereign Way, Tonbridge, Kent TN9 1RW
☎01732 364422 Fax 01732 377675
Owner *Miller Freeman plc*
Editor *Jim van den Bos*
Circulation 66,000

News of direct concern to farmers and the agricultural supply trade.

Fast Car

Berwick House, 8–10 Knoll Rise, Orpington, Kent BR6 0PS
☎01689 887200 Fax 01689 838844
Email fastcar@splpublishing.co.uk
Owner *SPL*
Editor *Daniel Lewis*
Circulation 93,447

FOUNDED 1987. THIRTEEN ISSUES YEARLY. Lad's magazine about perfomance tuning and modifying cars. Covers all aspects of this youth culture including the latest street styles and music. Features cars and their owners, product tests and in-car entertainment. Also includes a free reader ads section.

Features Innovative ideas in line with the above and in the *Fast Car* writing style. Generally four pages in length. No Kit-car features, race reports or road test reports of standard cars. Copy should be as concise as possible. *Payment* negotiable.

News Any item in line with the above.

FHM

Mappin House, 4 Winsley Street, London W1N 7AR
☎020 7436 1515 Fax 020 7312 8191
Website www.fhm.co.uk

Owner *EMAP Metro*
Editor *Anthony Noguera*
Circulation 702,514

FOUNDED in 1986 as a free fashion magazine, FHM evolved to become more male oriented but without much public acclaim until EMAP bought the title in 1994. Since then it has become the best-selling men's magazine in the UK covering all areas of men's lifestyle. Published MONTHLY. Unsolicited mss welcome; send to the deputy editor.

The Field

King's Reach Tower, Stamford Street, London SE1 9LS
☎020 7261 5198 Fax 020 7261 5358
Website www.thefield.co.uk

Owner *IPC Magazines*
Editor *Jonathan Young*
Circulation 33,379

FOUNDED 1853. MONTHLY magazine for those who are serious about the British countryside and its pleasures. Unsolicited mss (and transparencies) welcome but initial approach should be made in writing.

Features Exceptional work on any subject concerning the countryside. Most work tends to be commissioned.

Payment varies.

Film and Video Maker

594A Bolton Road, Pendlebury, Swinton, Manchester M27 4ET
☎0161 794 8282 Fax 0161 793 9696

Owner *Film Maker Publications*
Editor *Mrs Liz Donlan*
Circulation 2400

FOUNDED in the 1930s. BI-MONTHLY magazine of the Institute of Amateur Cinematographers. Reports, news and views of the Institute. Unsolicited mss welcome but all contributions are unpaid.

Film Review

Visual Imagination Ltd, 9 Blades Court, Deodar Road, London SW15 2NU
☎020 8875 1520 Fax 020 8875 1588
Website www.visimag.com

Owner *Visual Imagination Ltd*
Editor *Neil Corry*
Circulation 50,000

MONTHLY. Reviews, profiles, interviews and special reports on films. Unsolicited material considered.

Payment negotiable.

Fine Food Digest

PO Box 1525, Gillingham, Dorset SP8 5TA
☎01963 371271 Fax 01963 371270
Email bobfarrand@btinternet.com

Owner/Editor *Robert Farrand*
Circulation 4200

FOUNDED 1980. SIX ISSUES YEARLY. Serves the speciality food retail trade. Small budget for freelance material.

First Down

7–9 Rathbone Street, London W1P 1AF
☎020 7323 1988 Fax 020 7637 0862
Email firstdown@indmags.co.uk
Website www.first-down.co.uk

Owner *Independent Magazines (UK)Ltd*
Editor *Keith Webster*
Circulation 15,000

FOUNDED 1986. WEEKLY American football tabloid paper. Features and news. Welcomes contributions; approach in writing.

The First Word Bulletin

Calle Domingo Fernandez 5, Box 500, 28036 Madrid Spain
☎00 34 1 359 6418 Fax 00 34 1 320 8961
Email gw83@correo.interlink.es
Website www.interlink.es/peraso/first

Owner *The First Word Bulletin Associates*
Publisher/Editor *G. W. Amick*
Circulation 5000

FOUNDED 1995. QUARTERLY international magazine, printed in Madrid and distributed to the English speaking community worldwide. Welcomes articles on self-improvement, both mental and physical, also environmental problems and cures. Human interest, alternative medicine, fiction and non-fiction, nature stories, young adult and senior citizen retirement articles. 'No smut, pornography, love stories, detective stories, science fiction or horror.' 400 words maximum. Approach in writing with s.a.e. and IRCs. Disk submissions accepted; no submissions by e-mail. Contributors' guidelines cannot be e-mailed. *Payment* £30 maximum.

Fishing News
21 John Street, London WC1N 2BP
☎020 7505 3523 Fax 020 7831 9362
Website www.fishingnews.co.uk
Owner *Informa Group Plc*
Editor *Tim Oliver*
Circulation 13,000

FOUNDED 1913. WEEKLY. All aspects of the commercial fishing industry in the UK and Ireland. No unsolicited mss; telephone inquiry in the first instance. Maximum 600 words for news and 1500 words for features. *Payment* £100 per 1000 words.

Flight International
Quadrant House, The Quadrant, Sutton, Surrey SM2 5AS
☎020 8652 3882 Fax 020 8652 3840
Email flight.international@rbi.co.uk
Website www.flightinternational.co.
Owner *Reed Business Information*
Editor *Carol Reed*
Circulation 65,000

FOUNDED 1909. WEEKLY. International trade magazine for the aerospace industry, including civil, military and space. Unsolicited mss considered. Commissions preferred - phone with ideas and follow up with letter. E-mail, modem and disk submissions encouraged.

Features *Carol Reed* Technically informed articles and pieces on specific geographical areas with international appeal. Analytical, in-depth coverage required, preferably supported by interviews. Maximum 1800 words.

News *Andrew Chuter* Opportunities exist for news pieces from particular geographical areas on specific technical developments. Maximum 350 words.

Payment NUJ rates.

Flora International
The Fishing Lodge Studio, 77 Bulbridge Road, Wilton, Salisbury, Wiltshire SP2 0LE
☎01722 743207 Fax 01722 743207
Owner/Publisher *Maureen Foster*
Editor *Judith Blacklock*
Circulation 16,000

FOUNDED 1974. BI-MONTHLY magazine for flower arrangers and florists. Unsolicited mss welcome. Approach in writing with ideas. Not interested in general gardening articles.

Features Fully illustrated, preferably with b&w photos or illustrations/colour transparencies. Flower arranging, flower gardens and flowers. Floristry items written with practical knowledge and well illustrated are particularly welcome. Maximum 1000 words.

Profiles/Reviews Personality profiles and book reviews.

Payment £40 per 1000 words.

FlyPast
PO Box 100, Stamford, Lincolnshire PE9 1XQ
☎01780 755131 Fax 01780 757261
Email flypast@keymags.demon.co.uk
Owner *Key Publishing Ltd*
Editor *Ken Ellis*
Circulation 52,000

FOUNDED 1981. MONTHLY. Historic aviation and aviation heritage, mainly military, Second World War period up to c.1970. Unsolicited mss welcome.

Focus
See **British Science Fiction Association** under **Professional Associations**

For Women
Fantasy Publications, 4 Selsdon Way, London E14 9EL
☎020 7308 5090 Fax 020 7308 5075
Email ecoldwell@norshell.co.uk
Editor *Liz Beresford*
Circulation 60,000

FOUNDED 1992. SIX-WEEKLY magazine of erotic and sex interest for women – health and sex, erotic fiction and erotic photography. No homes and gardens articles. Approach in writing in the first instance. Send e-mail or s.a.e. for submission guidelines.

Features Relationships and sex. Maximum 2500 words. *Payment* £100 per 1000 words.

Fiction *Elizabeth Coldwell* Erotic short stories. Maximum 3000 words. *Payment* £150 total.

Fortean Times: The Journal of Strange Phenomena
PO Box 2409, London NW5 4NP
☎020 7485 5466 Fax 020 7485 5002
Email sieveking@forteantimes.com
Website www.forteantimes.com
Owners/Editors *Bob Rickard/Paul Sieveking*
Circulation 35,000

FOUNDED 1973. MONTHLY. Accounts of strange phenomena and experiences, curiosities, mysteries, prodigies and portents. Unsolicited mss welcome. Approach in writing with ideas. No fiction, poetry, rehashes or politics.

Features Well-researched and referenced material on current or historical mysteries, or first-hand accounts of oddities. Maximum 3000 words, preferably with good relevant photos/ illustrations.

News Concise copy with full source references essential.

Payment negotiable.

Foundation: The International Review of Science Fiction

c/o Dept. of History, University of Reading, Whiteknights, Reading, Berkshire RG6 6AA
☎0118 9263047 Fax 0118 9316440
Email e.f.james@reading.ac.uk

Owner *Science Fiction Foundation*
Editor *Professor Edward James*

THRICE-YEARLY publication devoted to the critical study of science fiction. *Payment* None.

France Magazine

Dormer House, Digbeth Street, Stow-on-the-Wold, Gloucestershire GL54 1BN
☎01451 833210 Fax 01451 833234
Email editorial@francemag.com
Website www.francemag.com

Owner *Centralhaven*
Editor *Philip Faiers*
Circulation 61,000

FOUNDED 1989. QUARTERLY magazine containing all things of interest to Francophiles – in English. Approach in writing in the first instance.

Freelance Market News

Sevendale House, 7 Dale Street, Manchester M1 1JB
☎0161 228 2362 Fax 0161 228 3533
Email fmn@writersbureau.com

Editor *Angela Cox*

MONTHLY. News and information on the freelance writers' market, both inland and overseas. Includes market information on competitions, seminars, courses, overseas openings, etc. Short articles (700 words maximum). Unsolicited contributions welcome.

Payment £35 per 1000 words.

The Freelance

NUJ, Acorn House, 314 Gray's Inn Road, London WC1X 8DP
☎020 7843 3706 Fax 020 7278 1812

MONTHLY published by the **National Union of Journalists**.

Garden Answers (incorporating Practical Gardening)

Apex House, Oundle Road, Peterborough, Cambridgeshire PE2 9NP
☎01733 898100 Fax 01733 466857

Owner *EMAP Active Ltd*
Editor *Jim Ward*
Circulation 192,000

FOUNDED 1982. MONTHLY. 'It is unlikely that unsolicited manuscripts will be used, as articles are usually commissioned and must be in the magazine style.' Prospective contributors should approach the editor in writing. Interested in hearing from gardening writers on any subject, whether flowers, fruit, vegetables, houseplants or greenhouse gardening.

Garden News

Apex House, Oundle Road, Peterborough, Cambridgeshire PE2 9NP
☎01733 898100 Fax 01733 898433

Owner *EMAP Active Publications Ltd*
Editor *Sarah Page*
Circulation 86,967

FOUNDED 1958. Britain's biggest-selling, full-colour gardening WEEKLY. News and advice on growing flowers, fruit and vegetables, plus colourful features on all aspects of gardening especially for the committed gardener. News and features welcome, especially if accompanied by top-quality photos or illustrations. Contact the editor before submitting any material.

The Garden, Journal of the Royal Horticultural Society

Apex House, Oundle Road, Peterborough, Cambridgeshire PE2 9NP
☎01733 898100 Fax 01733 466885
Email thegarden@rhs.org.uk
Website www.rhs.org.uk

Owner *The Royal Horticultural Society*
Editor *Ian Hodgson*
Circulation 270,000

FOUNDED 1866. MONTHLY journal of the Royal Horticultural Society. Covers all aspects of the art, science and practice of horticulture and garden making. 'Articles must have depth and substance'; approach by letter with a synopsis in the first instance. Maximum 2500 words.

Gardens Illustrated

John Brown Publishing Ltd, The New Boathouse, 136–142 Bramley Road, London W10 6SR
☎020 7565 3000 Fax 020 7565 3056

Owner *John Brown Publishing Ltd*
Editor *Rosie Atkins*
Circulation 40,236

FOUNDED 1993. TEN ISSUES YEARLY. 'Britain's fastest growing garden magazine' with a world-wide readership. The focus is on garden design, with a strong international flavour. Unsolicited mss are rarely used and it is best that prospective contributors approach the editor with ideas in writing, supported by photographs.

Gardens Made Easy

SPL, Berwick House, 8–10 Knoll Rise, Orpington, Kent BR6 0PS
☎01689 887200 Fax 01689 876438
Email email@splpublishing.co.uk

Owner *SPL Publishing*
Editor *Andrée Frieze*

LAUNCHED April 2000. Aimed at 30–55-year-olds 'who have been inspired by the recent boom in gardening' and want to improve the look of their own gardens.

Gargoyle Magazine

152 Harringay Road, London N15 3HL
☎020 8292 7350 Fax 020 7401 2055
Email gargoyle@ursarum.demon.co.uk

Owner *Paycock Press*
London Editor *Maja Prausnitz*
Assistant London Editor *Sandra Tharumalingam*
US Editors *Richard Peabody, Lucinda Ebersole*
Circulation 5000

FOUNDED 1976. BIANNUAL literary magazine dedicated to championing work by new poets and fiction writers alongside the more established, and aiming to bridge the American and European literary worlds. Unsolicited mss welcome, though some knowledge of *Gargoyle* is recommended before submission.
Payment one copy of relevant issue.

Gay Times

Worldwide House, 116–134 Bayham Street, London NW1 0BA
☎020 7482 2576 Fax 020 7284 0329
Website www.prowler.co.uk

Owner *Millivres Prowler Group*
Editor *Colin Richardson*
Circulation 57,000

Covers all aspects of gay life, plus general interest likely to appeal to the gay community, art reviews and news. Regular freelance writers used. Unsolicited contributions welcome.
Payment negotiable.

Gibbons Stamp Monthly

Stanley Gibbons, 5 Parkside, Ringwood, Hampshire BH24 3SH
☎01425 472363 Fax 01425 470247
Email gsm@stanleygibbons.co.uk
Website www.stanleygibbons.co.uk

Owner *Stanley Gibbons Ltd*
Editor *Hugh Jefferies*
Circulation 22,000

FOUNDED 1890. MONTHLY. News and features. Unsolicited mss welcome. Make initial approach in writing or by telephone to avoid disappointment.
  Features *Hugh Jefferies* Unsolicited material of specialised nature and general stamp features welcome. Max. 3000 words but longer pieces can be serialised. *Payment* £30–50 per 1000 words.
  News *Michael Briggs* Any philatelic news item. Max. 500 words. *No payment.*

Girl About Town

9 Rathbone Street, London W1P 1AF
☎020 7636 6651 Fax 020 7255 2352

Owner *Independent Magazines*
Editor-in-Chief *Bill Williamson*
News/Style Pages *Dee Pilgrim*
Circulation 85,000

FOUNDED 1972. Free WEEKLY magazine for women aged 16 to 26. Unsolicited mss may be considered. No fiction.
  Features Standards are 'exacting'. Commissions only. Some chance of unknown writers being commissioned. Maximum 1500 words. *Payment* negotiable.

Golf Monthly

King's Reach Tower, Stamford Street, London SE1 9LS
☎020 7261 7237 Fax 020 7261 7240

Owner *IPC Magazines Ltd*
Editor *Jane Carter*
Circulation 73,000

FOUNDED 1911. MONTHLY. Player profiles, golf instruction, general golf features and columns. Not interested in instruction material from outside contributors. Unsolicited mss welcome. Approach in writing with ideas.
  Features Maximum 1500–2000 words. *Payment* by arrangement.

Golf Weekly

Bretton Court, Bretton, Peterborough, Cambridgeshire PE3 8DZ
☎01733 264666 Fax 01733 465221
Email bob.warters@ecm.emap.com

Owner *EMAP Active Ltd*
Managing Editor *Bob Warters*
Circulation 20,000

FOUNDED 1890. WEEKLY. Unsolicited material welcome from full-time journalists only. 'Always looking for photographic and written news contributions.' For features, approach in writing in first instance; for news, fax or phone.
   Features Maximum 1500 words.
   News Maximum 300 words.
   Payment negotiable.

Golf World

Angel House, 338–346 Goswell Road,
London EC1V 7QP
☎01733 264666

Owner *EMAP Active Ltd*
Editor *Steve Prentice*
Circulation 85,181

FOUNDED 1962. MONTHLY. No unsolicited mss. Approach in writing with ideas.

Good Holiday Magazine

3A High Street, Esher, Surrey KT10 9RP
☎01372 468140   Fax 01372 470765
Email goodholiday@btinternet.com
Website www.good-holiday.com

Editor *John Hill*
Circulation 100,000

FOUNDED 1985. QUARTERLY aimed at better-off holiday-makers rather than travellers. Worldwide destinations including Europe and domestic. Any queries regarding work/commissioning must be in writing. Copy must be precise and well-researched – the price of everything from coffee and tea to major purchases are included along with exchange rates, etc.
   Payment negotiable.

Good Housekeeping

National Magazine House, 72 Broadwick
Street, London W1V 2BP
☎020 7439 5000   Fax 020 7439 5591
Website www.natmags.co.uk

Owner *National Magazine Co. Ltd*
Editor-in-Chief *Lindsay Nicholson*
Circulation 400,000

FOUNDED 1922. MONTHLY glossy. No unsolicited mss. Write with ideas in the first instance to the appropriate editor.
   Features *June Walton* Most work is commissioned but original ideas are always welcome. No ideas are discussed on the telephone. Send short synopsis, plus relevant cuttings, showing

previous examples of work published. No unsolicited mss.
   Entertainment *Kerry Fowler* Reviews and previews on film, television, theatre and art.

Good Housekeeping's Having a Baby

National Magazine House, 72 Broadwick
Street, London W1V 2BP
☎020 7439 5000   Fax 020 7439 5331
Email m.baby@natmags.co.uk
Website www.natmags.co.uk

Owner *National Magazine Co. Ltd*
Editor-in-Chief *Lindsay Nicholson*
Circulation 53,000

FOUNDED 1997. BI-MONTHLY glossy celebration of pregnancy, childbirth and early parenting. Also beauty, health, celebrity and real-life stories. No unsolicited mss.
   Features *Diane Kenwood* Interesting, unusual and original angles on all aspects of pregnancy, birth, early childhood and parenting. Send outline proposals. 'We are a small team; patience (or persistence) is required for a response.' Maximum 2000 words. *Payment* £300–450.

Good Motoring

Station Road, Forest Row, East Sussex
RH18 5EN
☎01342 825676   Fax 01342 824847
Email gem@gemrecovery.org.uk
Website www.roadsafety.org.uk

Owner *Guild of Experienced Motorists*
Editor *Derek Hainge*
Deputy Editor *John Taylor*
Circulation 52,000

FOUNDED 1932. QUARTERLY motoring, road safety and travel magazine. Occasional general features. 1500 words maximum. Prospective contributors should approach in writing only.

Good Ski Guide

3A High Street, Esher, Surrey KT10 9RP
☎01372 468140   Fax 01372 470765
Email goodskiguide@btinternet.com
Website www.goodskiguide.com

Editor *John Hill*
Circulation 79,654

FOUNDED 1976. QUARTERLY. Unsolicited mss welcome from writers with a knowledge of skiing and ski resorts. Prospective contributors are best advised to make initial contact in writing as ideas and work need to be seen before any discussion can take place. *Payment* negotiable.

The Goodlife Magazine

28 Coleherne Mews, London SW10 9EA
☎020 7373 7282 Fax 020 7373 3215

Owner/Editor *Eileen Spence-Moncrieff*
Circulation 37,502

FOUNDED 1988. Features on fashion, interiors, restaurants, theatre, social scene, health and beauty. No unsolicited mss.

GQ

Vogue House, Hanover Square, London
W1R 0AD
☎020 7499 9080 Fax 020 7495 1679
Website www.gq-magazine.co.uk

Owner *Condé Nast Publications Ltd*
Editor *Dylan Jones*
Circulation 141,162

FOUNDED 1988. MONTHLY. Men's style magazine. No unsolicited material. Write or fax with an idea in the first instance.

Granta

2–3 Hanover Yard, Noel Road, London
N1 8BE
☎020 7704 9776 Fax 020 7704 0474
Website www.granta.com

Editor *Ian Jack*
Deputy Editor *Liz Jobey*

QUARTERLY magazine of new writing, including fiction, autobiography, politics, history and reportage published in paperback book form. Highbrow, diverse and contemporary, with a thematic approach. Unsolicited mss (including fiction) considered. A lot of material is commissioned. Vital to read the magazine first to appreciate its very particular fusion of cultural and political interests. No reviews or news articles. No poetry. Access the website for submission guidelines.
Payment negotiable.

The Great Outdoors

See **TGO**

Guardian Weekend

See under **National Newspapers**
(The Guardian)

Guiding Magazine

17–19 Buckingham Palace Road, London
SW1W 0PT
☎020 7834 6242 Fax 020 7828 5791

Owner *The Guide Association*
Editor *Jan Clampett*
Circulation 28,000

FOUNDED 1914. MONTHLY. Unsolicited mss welcome provided topics relate to the Movement and/or women's role in society. Ideas in writing appreciated in first instance.
Activity Ideas Interesting, contemporary ideas and instructions for activities for girls aged 5 to 18+ to do during unit meetings – crafts, games (indoor/outdoor), etc.
Features Topics that can be useful in the Guide programme. 650–1200 words.
News Guide activities. Max. 100–150 words.
Payment £70 per 1000 words.

H&P Magazine
(formerly **Horse & Pony**)

Apex House, Oundle Road, Peterborough, Cambridgeshire PE2 9NP
☎01733 898100 Fax 01733 466843

Owner *EMAP Active Ltd*
Editor *Amanda Stevenson*
Circulation 54,260

For people who live, breath and have fun around horses. Readership mainly teenage females. Most writing produced in-house but well-targeted articles will always be considered.

Hair

King's Reach Tower, Stamford Street, London SE1 9LS
☎020 7261 6975 Fax 020 7261 7382

Owner *IPC Magazines Ltd*
Editor *Kate Barlow*
Circulation 152,602

FOUNDED 1977. BI-MONTHLY hair and beauty magazine. No unsolicited mss, but always interested in good photographs. Approach with ideas in writing. **Features** Fashion pieces on hair trends and styling advice. Maximum 1000 words. *Payment* negotiable.

Hairflair

Kimber House, 134–136 King Street, Hammersmith, London W6 0QU
☎020 8563 2266 Fax 020 8563 2299

Owner *James Kimber Publishing Ltd*
Editor *Rebecca Barnes*
Circulation 100,000

FOUNDED 1982. BI-MONTHLY. Original and interesting hair and beauty-related features written in a young, lively style to appeal to a readership aged 16–35 years. Unsolicited mss not welcome, although freelancers are used occasionally. **Features** Hair and beauty. Maximum 1500 words.
Payment negotiable.

Harpers & Queen

National Magazine House, 72 Broadwick Street, London W1V 2BP
☎020 7439 5000 Fax 020 7439 5506

Owner *National Magazine Co. Ltd*
Editor *Fiona Macpherson*
Deputy Editor *Anthony Gardner*
Circulation 91,101

MONTHLY. Up-market glossy combining the stylish and the streetwise. Approach in writing (not phone) with ideas.

Features *Lydia Slater* Ideas only in the first instance.

News Snippets welcome if very original.
Payment negotiable.

Health & Fitness Magazine

Nexus Media, Nexus House, Azalea Drive, Swanley, Kent BR8 8HY
☎01322 660070 Fax 01322 616319
Website www.hfonline.co.uk

Owner *Nexus Media*
Editor *Mary Comber*
Circulation 65,000

FOUNDED 1983. MONTHLY. Will consider ideas; approach in writing in the first instance.

Health Education

The Health Education Unit, Research and Graduate School of Education, University of Southampton, Southampton SO17 1BJ
☎023 8059 3707
Email skw@soton.ac.uk

Owner *MCB University Press*
Editor *Dr Katherine Weare*
Circulation 2000

FOUNDED 1992. SIX ISSUES YEARLY. Health education magazine with an emphasis on schools and young people. Professional readership.

Heat

Mappin House, 4 Winsley Street, London W1N 7AR
☎020 7436 1515 Fax 020 7817 8847
Website www.heatmagazine.co.uk

Owner *EMAP Elan Network*
Editor *Mark Frith*
Circulation 88,000

FOUNDED January 1999. WEEKLY entertainment magazine dealing with TV, film and radio information, fashion and features, with an emphasis on celebrity interviews and news. Targets 18- to 40-year-old readership, male and female. Articles written both in-house and by trusted freelancers. No unsolicited mss.

Hello!

Wellington House, 69–71 Upper Ground, London SE1 9PQ
☎020 7667 8700 Fax 020 7667 8716

Owner *Hola!* (Spain)
Editor *Maggie Koumi*
Circulation 495,349

WEEKLY. Owned by a Madrid-based publishing family, *Hello!* has grown faster than any other British magazine since its launch here in 1988 and continues to grow despite the recession. The magazine is printed in Madrid, with editorial offices both there and in London. Major colour features plus regular news pages. Although much of the material is provided by regulars, good proposals do stand a chance. Approach with ideas in the first instance. No unsolicited mss.

Features Interested in celebrity features, with a newsy angle, and exclusive interviews from generally unapproachable personalities.
Payment by arrangement.

Here's Health

Endeavour House, 189 Shaftesbury Avenue, London WC2H 8JG
☎020 7437 9011 Fax 020 7208 3583

Owner *EMAP Elan Publications*
Editor *Elaine Griffiths*
Circulation 37,502

FOUNDED 1956. MONTHLY. Full-colour magazine dealing with alternative medicine, nutrition, natural health, wholefoods, supplements, organics and the environment. Prospective contributors should bear in mind that this is a specialist magazine with a pronounced bias towards alternative/complementary medicine, using expert contributors on the whole.
Payment negotiable.

Heritage

Glen House, Stag Place, London SW1E 5AQ
☎020 7233 9191 Fax 020 7630 8084

Owner *Bulldog Magazines*
Editor *Richard Fairhurst*
Circulation 73,000

FOUNDED 1984. BI-MONTHLY. Interested in complete packages of written features with high-quality transparencies – words or pictures on their own also accepted. Not interested in poetry, fiction, nostalgia or non-British themes. Approach in writing with ideas.

Features British villages, tours, towns, castles, gardens, traditions, crafts, historical themes and people. Maximum length 1200 words.
Payment approx. £100 per 1000 words.

News Small pieces – usually picture stories in Diary section. Limited use. Maximum length 100–150 words. *Payment £20.*

Heritage Scotland
28 Charlotte Square, Edinburgh EH2 4ET
☎0131 243 9387 Fax 0131 243 9589

Owner *National Trust for Scotland*
Editor *Myra Sanderson*
Circulation 138,878

FOUNDED 1983. QUARTERLY magazine containing heritage/conservation features. No unsolicited mss.

Hi-Fi News & Record Review
Link House, Dingwall Avenue, Croydon, Surrey CR9 2TA
☎020 8686 2599 Fax 020 8781 6046

Owner *IPC Magazines Ltd*
Editor *Steve Harris*
Circulation 21,196

FOUNDED 1956. MONTHLY. Write in the first instance with suggestions based on knowledge of the magazine's style and subject. All articles must be written from an informed technical or enthusiast viewpoint. *Payment* negotiable, according to technical content.

High Life
Haymarket House, 1 Oxendon Street, London SW1Y 4EE
☎020 7925 2544 Fax 020 7321 2942
Email high_life@premiermp.com
Website www.premiermp.com

Owner *Premier Media Partners*
Editor *Mark Jones*
Circulation 295,000

FOUNDED 1973. MONTHLY glossy. British Airways in-flight magazine. Almost all the content is commissioned. No unsolicited mss. Few opportunities for freelancers.

History Today
20 Old Compton Street, London W1V 5PE
☎020 7534 8000 Fax 020 7534 8008
Email p.furtado@historytoday.com
Website www.historytoday.com

Owner *History Today Trust for the Advancement of Education*
Editor *Peter Furtado*
Circulation 29,269

FOUNDED 1951. MONTHLY General history and archaeology worldwide, history behind the headlines. Serious submissions only; no 'jokey' material. Approach by post or e-mail.

Home
SPL, Berwick House, 8–10 Knoll Rise, Orpington, Kent BR6 0PS
☎01689 887200 Fax 01689 896847
Email ksleeman@splpublishing.co.uk

Owner *Havas*
Editor *Sarah Giles*

MONTHLY magazine with ideas, information and inspiration for the home. Features include style, design, home products, gardens and cookery. Synopses and ideas welcome; approach in writing. No health and lifestyle articles.

Home & Country
104 New Kings Road, London SW6 4LY
☎020 7731 5777 Fax 020 7736 4061

Owner *National Federation of Women's Institutes*
Editor *Susan Seager*
Circulation 60,000

FOUNDED 1919. MONTHLY. Official full-colour journal of the Federation of Women's Institutes, containing articles on a wide range of subjects of interest to women. Strong environmental country slant with crafts and cookery plus gardening appearing every month. Unsolicited mss, photos and illustrations welcome.

Payment by arrangement.

Home & Family
Mary Sumner House, 24 Tufton Street, London SW1P 3RB
☎020 7222 5533 Fax 020 7222 1591

Owner *MU Enterprises Ltd*
Editor *Jill Worth*
Circulation 70,000

FOUNDED 1976. QUARTERLY. Unsolicited mss considered. No fiction or poetry. Features on family life, social problems, marriage, Christian faith, etc. Maximum 1000 words.
Payment 'modest'.

Homes & Gardens
King's Reach Tower, Stamford Street, London SE1 9LS
☎020 7261 5000 Fax 020 7261 6247

Owner *IPC Magazines Ltd*
Editor *Matthew Line*
Circulation 172,473

FOUNDED 1919. MONTHLY. Almost all published articles are specially commissioned. No fiction or poetry. Best to approach in writing with an idea, enclosing snapshots if appropriate.

Homes & Ideas
King's Reach Tower, Stamford Street,
London SE1 9LS
☎020 7261 7494 Fax 020 7261 7495
Owner *IPC Magazines Ltd*
Editor *Paula Woods*
Circulation 181,090

FOUNDED 1993. MONTHLY magazine for
homeowners looking for new styles and decorating techniques. No unsolicited mss; all work
is commissioned.

Horse & Pony
See **H&P Magazine**

Horse and Hound
King's Reach Tower, Stamford Street,
London SE1 9LS
☎020 7261 6315 Fax 020 7261 5429
Email jenny_sims@ipc.co.uk
Owner *IPC Magazines Ltd*
Editor *Arnold Garvey*
Circulation 70,000

FOUNDED 1884. WEEKLY. The oldest equestrian magazine on the market, now relaunched with modern make-up and colour
pictures throughout. Contains regular veterinary advice and instructional articles, as well as
authoritative news and comment on fox hunting, international and national showjumping,
horse trials, dressage, driving and endurance
riding. Also weekly racing and point-to-points,
breeding reports and articles. Regular books
and art reviews, and humorous articles and cartoons are frequently published. Plenty of
opportunities for freelancers. Unsolicited contributions welcome.
   Also publishes a sister monthly publication,
Eventing, which covers the sport of horse trials
comprehensively.
   Payment NUJ rates.

Horse and Rider
Haslemere House, Lower Street, Haslemere,
Surrey GU27 2PE
☎01428 651551 Fax 01428 653888
Email djm@djmurphy.co.uk
Website
www.equestrian.co.uk/horse_and_rider
Owner *D. J. Murphy (Publishers) Ltd*
Editor *Alison Bridge*
Assistant Editor *Sarah Muir*
Circulation 46,000

FOUNDED 1949. MONTHLY. Adult readership,
largely horse-owning. News and instructional

features, which make up the bulk of the magazine, are almost all commissioned. New contributors and unsolicited mss are occasionally used.
Approach the editor in writing with ideas.

Horticulture Week
174 Hammersmith Road, London W6 7JP
☎020 7413 4595 Fax 020 7413 4518
Owner *Haymarket Magazines Ltd*
Editor *Pete Weston*
Circulation 11,200

FOUNDED 1841. WEEKLY. Specialist magazine
involved in the supply of business-type information. No unsolicited mss. Approach in writing in first instance.
   Features No submissions without prior discussion. *Payment* negotiable.
   News *Richard Rhydderch* Information about
horticultural businesses – nurseries, garden centres, landscapers and parks departments in the
various regions of the UK. No gardening
stories.

House & Garden
Vogue House, Hanover Square, London
W1R 0AD
☎020 7499 9080 Fax 020 7629 2907
Owner *Condé Nast Publications Ltd*
Editor *Susan Crewe*
Circulation 150,414

FOUNDED 1947. MONTHLY. Most feature
material is produced in-house but occasional
specialist features are commissioned from qualified freelancers, mainly for the interiors, wine
and food sections and travel.
   Features *Liz Elliot* Suggestions for features,
preferably in the form of brief outlines of proposed subjects, will be considered.

House Beautiful
National Magazine House, 72 Broadwick
Street, London W1V 2BP
☎020 7439 5000 Fax 020 7439 5595
Owner *National Magazine Co. Ltd*
Editor *Libby Norman*
Circulation 222,468

FOUNDED 1989. MONTHLY. Lively magazine
offering sound, practical information and
plenty of inspiration for those who want to
make the most of where they live. Over 100
pages of easy-reading editorial. Regular features about decoration, DIY and home finance.
Approach in writing with synopses or ideas in
the first instance.

i-D Magazine

124 Tabernacle Street, London EC2A 4SA
☎020 7813 6170 Fax 020 7813 6179
Email editor@i-Dmagazine.co.uk

Owner *Levelprint*
Editor *Avril Mair*
Circulation 55,000

FOUNDED 1980. MONTHLY lifestyle magazine for both sexes with a fashion bias. International. Very hip. Does not accept unsolicited contributions but welcomes new ideas from the fields of fashion, music, clubs, art, film, technology, books, sport, etc. No fiction or poetry. 'We are always looking for freelance non-fiction writers with new or unusual ideas.' A different theme each issue – past themes include Green politics, taste, films, sex, love and loud dance music – means it is advisable to discuss feature ideas in the first instance.

Ideal Home

King's Reach Tower, Stamford Street, London SE1 9LS
☎020 7261 6505 Fax 020 7261 6697

Owner *IPC Magazines Ltd*
Editor-in-Chief *Isobel McKenzie-Price*
Circulation 254.427

FOUNDED 1920. MONTHLY glossy. Unsolicited feature articles are welcome if appropriate to the magazine. Prospective contributors wishing to submit ideas should do so in writing to the editor. No fiction.

Features Furnishing and decoration of houses, kitchens or bathrooms; interior design, soft furnishings, furniture and home improvements, lifestyle, travel, etc. Length to be discussed with editor.

Payment negotiable.

The Illustrated London News

20 Upper Ground, London SE1 9PF
☎020 7805 5562 Fax 020 7805 5911

Owner *James Sherwood*
Editor *Alison Booth*
Circulation 47,547

FOUNDED 1842. BIANNUAL: the Christmas and Summer issues, plus the occasional special issue to coincide with particular events. Although the *ILN* covers issues concerning the whole of the UK, its emphasis remains on the capital and its life. Travel, wine, restaurants, events, cultural and current affairs are all covered. There are few opportunities for freelancers but all unsolicited mss are read (receives about 20 a week). The best approach is with an idea in writing. Particularly interested in articles relating to events and developments in contemporary London, and about people working in the capital. All features are illustrated, so ideas with picture opportunities are particularly welcome.

Image Magazine

Upper Mounts, Northampton NN1 3HR
☎01604 231122 Fax 01604 233000

Owner *Northamptonshire Newspapers Ltd*
Editor *Ruth Supple*
Circulation 12,000

FOUNDED 1905. MONTHLY general interest regional magazine. No unsolicited mss. Initial approach by phone or in writing with ideas. No fiction.

Features Issues, personalities, businesses, etc. local to Northamptonshire, Bedfordshire, Buckinghamshire interest. Max. 500 words. *Payment* negotiable.

News No hard news as such, just monthly diary column.

Other Regulars on motoring, fashion, beauty, lifestyle, travel and horoscopes. Max. 500 words.

In Britain

Haymarket House, 1 Oxendon Street, London SW1Y 4EE
☎020 7925 2544 Fax 020 7976 1088
Email in_britain@premiermp.com

Owner *Premier Media Partners*
Editor *Andrea Spain*
Circulation 40,000

MONTHLY. Travel magazine of the British Tourist Authority. Articles vary from 1000 to 1500 words. Approach (by e-mail, if possible) with ideas and samples – not much opportunity for unsolicited work.

Independent Magazine

See under **National Newspapers (The Independent)**

Insurance Age

69–77 Paul Street, London EC2A 4LQ
☎020 7553 1668 Fax 020 7553 1151
Website www.insuranceage.com

Owner *Informa*
Editor *Rachel Gordon*
Circulation 20,000

FOUNDED 1979. MONTHLY publication circulated to insurance brokers. Covers general insurance (*not* life and pensions). No unsolicited mss. Interested in exclusive stories linked to the insurance broker market; no hi-tech or IT information material.

News *Luke Satchell* Maximum 400 words.
Features *Jane Bernstein* Maximum 800 words.
Payment negotiable.

Interzone:
Science Fiction & Fantasy
217 Preston Drove, Brighton, East Sussex
BN1 6FL
☎01273 504710
Website www.sfsite/interzone
Owner/Editor *David Pringle*
Circulation 10,000

FOUNDED 1982. MONTHLY magazine of science fiction and fantasy. Unsolicited mss are welcome 'from writers who have a knowledge of the magazine and its contents'. S.a.e. essential for return.

Fiction 2000–6000 words. *Payment* £30 per 1000 words.

Features Book/film reviews, interviews with writers and occasional short articles. Length by arrangement. *Payment* negotiable.

Investors Chronicle
Maple House, 149 Tottenham Court Road,
London W1P 9LL
☎020 7896 2525   Fax 020 7896 2054
Email ceri.jones@ft.com
Website www.investorschronicle.co.uk
Owner *Pearson*
Editor *Ceri Jones*
Commissioning Editor *Stephen Moore*
Circulation 63,000

FOUNDED 1860. WEEKLY. Opportunities for freelance contributors in the survey section only. All approaches should be made in writing. Over forty surveys are published each year on a wide variety of subjects, generally with a financial, business or investment emphasis. Copies of survey list and synopses of individual surveys are obtainable from the surveys editor.
Payment negotiable.

J17
Endeavour House, 189 Shaftesbury Avenue,
London WC2H 8JG
☎020 7208 3408   Fax 020 7208 3590
Owner *EMAP Elan Publications*
Editor *Sophie Wilson*
Circulation 230,190

FOUNDED 1983. MONTHLY. News, articles and quizzes of interest to girls aged 13–17. Ideas are sought in all areas. Prospective contributors should send ideas to the deputy editor.

Beauty *Lara Williamson*
Features/News *Sarra Manning*
Payment by arrangement.

Jane's Defence Weekly
Sentinel House, 163 Brighton Road,
Coulsdon, Surrey CR5 2YH
☎020 8700 3700   Fax 020 8763 1007
Email jdw@janes.co.uk
Website www.janes.com
Owner *Jane's Information Group*
Editor *Clifford Beal*
Circulation 25,492

FOUNDED 1984. WEEKLY. No unsolicited mss. Approach in writing with ideas in the first instance.

Features Current defence topics (politics, strategy, equipment, industry) of worldwide interest. No history pieces. Max. 2000 words.

Jazz Journal International
3 & 3A Forest Road, Loughton, Essex
IG10 1DR
☎020 8532 0456/0678   Fax 020 8532 0440
Owner *Jazz Journal Ltd*
Editor-in-Chief *Eddie Cook*
Circulation 9,000+

FOUNDED 1948. MONTHLY. A specialised jazz magazine, for record collectors, principally using expert contributors whose work is known to the editor. Unsolicited mss not welcome, with the exception of news material (for which no payment is made). It is not a gig guide, nor a free reference source for students.

Jersey Now
PO Box 582, Five Oaks, St Saviour, Jersey,
Channel Islands JE4 8XQ
☎01534 611743   Fax 01534 611610
Email mspeditorial@msppublishing.com
Owner *MSP Publishing*
Managing Editor *Peter Body*
Deputy Editor *Jane Delmer*
Circulation 10,000

FOUNDED 1987. QUARTERLY lifestyle magazine for Jersey covering homes, gardens, the arts, Jersey heritage, motoring, boating, fashion and technology. Upmarket glossy aimed at an informed and discerning readership and delivered free to the top ten thousand households in Jersey. Interested in Jersey-orientated articles only – 1200 words maximum. Approach the deputy editor initially.
Payment £10 per 100 words.

Jewish Chronicle
25 Furnival Street, London EC4A 1JT
☎020 7415 1500 Fax 020 7405 9040
Email jconline@jchron.co.uk
Owner *Kessler Foundation*
Editor *Edward J. Temko*
Circulation 50,000

WEEKLY. Unsolicited mss welcome if 'the specific interests of our readership are borne in mind by writers'. Approach in writing, except for urgent current news items. No fiction. Maximum 1500 words for all material.
> **Features** *Gerald Jacobs*
> **Leisure/Lifestyle** *Alan Montague*
> **Home News** *Barry Toberman*
> **Foreign News** *Jenni Frazer*
> **Supplements** *Angela Kiverstein*
> *Payment* negotiable.

Jewish Quarterly
PO Box 2078, London W1A 1JR
☎020 7629 5004 Fax 020 7629 5110
Publisher *Jewish Literary Trust Ltd*
Editor *Matthew Reisz*

FOUNDED 1953. QUARTERLY illustrated magazine featuring Jewish literature and fiction, politics, art, music, film, poetry, history, dance, community, autobiography, Hebrew, Yiddish, Israel and the Middle East, Judaism, interviews, Zionism, philosophy and holocaust studies. Features a major books and arts section. Unsolicited mss welcome but letter or phone call preferred in first instance.

Jewish Telegraph
Jewish Telegraph Group of Newspapers, 11 Park Hill, Bury Old Road, Prestwich, Manchester M25 0HH
☎0161 740 9321 Fax 0161 740 9325
Email editor@jewishtelegraph.com
Editor *Paul Harris*
Circulation 16,000

FOUNDED 1950. WEEKLY publication with local, national and international news and features. (Separate editions published for Manchester, Leeds, Liverpool and Glasgow.) Unsolicited features on Jewish humour and history welcome.

The Journal Magazines (Norfolk, Suffolk, Cambridgeshire)
The Old County School, Northgate Street, Bury St Edmunds, Suffolk IP33 1HP
☎01284 701190 Fax 01284 701680
Owner *Acorn Magazines Ltd*
Editor *Pippa Bastin*

Circulation 9000 each

FOUNDED 1990. MONTHLY magazines covering items of local interest – history, people, conservation, business, places, food and wine, fashion, homes and sport.
> **Features** 750–1250 words maximum, plus pictures. Approach the deputy editor by phone with ideas in the first instance.

Judaism Today: An Independent Journal of Jewish Thought
PO Box 16096, London N3 3WG
☎020 8346 1668 Fax 020 8346 1776
Email colsh@today.u-net.com
Owner *The Judaism Today Trust Limited*
Editor *Dr Colin Shindler*

FOUNDED 1994, the magazine aims to meet the need for an independent and open discussion of contemporary Jewish religious issues in a non-partisan forum that is reasoned, enlightened and tolerant. Unsolicited mss welcome but a letter or telephone call beforehand is preferred.

Just Seventeen
See **J17**

Kent Life
Datateam Publishing Ltd, London Road, Maidstone, Kent ME15 8LY
☎01622 687031 Fax 01622 757646
Publisher *Datateam Publishing Ltd*
Editor *Roderick Cooper*
Circulation 10,000

FOUNDED 1962. MONTHLY. Strong Kent interest plus fashion, food, books, wildlife, motoring, property, sport, interiors with local links. Unsolicited mss welcome. Interested in anything with a genuine Kent connection. No fiction or non-Kentish subjects. Approach in writing with ideas. Maximum length 1500 words.
> *Payment* negotiable.

The Lady
39–40 Bedford Street, London WC2E 9ER
☎020 7379 4717 Fax 020 7836 4620
Editor *Arline Usden*
Circulation 42,505

FOUNDED 1885. WEEKLY. Unsolicited mss are accepted provided they are not on the subject of politics or religion, or on topics covered by staff writers, i.e. fashion and beauty, health, cookery, household, gardening, finance and shopping.
> **Features** Well-researched pieces on British and foreign travel, historical subjects or events; interviews and profiles and other general interest

topics. Maximum 1000 words for illustrated articles; 900 words for one-page features; 450 words for first-person 'Viewpoint' pieces. All material should be addressed to the editor. Photographs supporting features may be supplied as colour transparencies or b&w prints.

Lakeland Walker
Cromwell Court, New Road, St Ives, Cambridgeshire PE17 4BG
Owner *Raven Marketing Group*
Editor *David Ogle*

FOUNDED 1996. BI-MONTHLY. News and features relating to the Lake District and walking in the area – wildlife, local history, places to visit, local transport. Maximum 1000–1500 words. Unsolicited material welcome.

Land Rover World
Link House, Dingwall Avenue, Croydon, Surrey CR9 2TA
☎020 8686 2599 Fax 020 8781 6042
Owner *Link House Magazines Ltd*
Editor *John Carroll*
Circulation 30,000

FOUNDED 1994. MONTHLY. Incorporates *Practical Land Rover World*. Unsolicited material welcome, especially if supported by high-quality illustrations.
  Features All articles with a Land Rover theme of interest. Potential contributors are strongly advised to examine previous issues before starting work.
  Payment negotiable.

Lexikon
PO Box 754, Stoke-on-Trent, Staffordshire ST1 4BU
☎01782 205060 Fax 01782 285331
Email enquiries@lexikon-publishing.co.uk
Website www.lexikon-publishing.co.uk
Senior Editor *Francis Anderson*
Poetry Editor *Alan Barrett*
Children's Editor *Roger Bradley*
Submissions email: submissions@ lexikon-publishing.co.uk

'Sharp, discerning prose, giving writers in the UK and abroad the opportunity to share their work and exchange new ideas.' Poetry, short stories, critical articles, book reviews plus regular competitions with cash prizes. 2000 words maximum for short stories; 60 lines maximum for poetry. Please enclose A4 s.a.e. with all submissions. Subscription (UK): £10 for 4 issues (annual); £15 (2 years). Call for overseas rates. Available in A4 print, on disk, on-line and (for the blind and visually impaired only) on audiocassette. *Payment* by arrangement.

Lexikon Online Newsletter
PO Box 754, Stoke-on-Trent, Staffordshire ST1 4BU
☎01782 205060
Email lexikon-subscribe@listbot.com
Website www.lexikon-publishing.co.uk
Editor *Francis Anderson*

Online free newsletter providing news and information to writers, editors and publishers. Includes top literary news stories from around the world, reviews, special features, market news and current competitions. Submissions welcome; non-fiction only. For free subscription, apply by e-mail.

Life&Soul Magazine
PO Box 119, Chipping Norton OX7 6GR
☎01993 832578 Fax 01993 832578
Email editor@lifeandsoul.com
Website www.lifeandsoul.com
Publisher *Karma Publishing Ltd*
Editor *Roy Stemman*
Circulation 3000

QUARTERLY. The only magazine in the world dealing with all aspects of reincarnation – from people who claim to recall their past lives spontaneously to those who have been regressed. It also examines other evidence for immortality, including near-death experiences and spirit communication.

Lincolnshire Life
County Life Ltd, PO Box 81, Lincoln LN1 1HD
☎01522 527127 Fax 01522 560035
Email editorial@lincolnshirelife.co.uk
Website www.lincolnshirelife.co.uk
Publisher *A. L. Robinson*
Executive Editor *Judy Theobald*
Circulation 10,000

FOUNDED 1961. MONTHLY county magazine featuring geographically relevant articles on local culture, history, personalities, etc. Maximum 1000–1500 words. Contributions supported by three or four good-quality photographs are always welcome. Approach in writing.
  Payment varies.

The List
14 High Street, Edinburgh EH1 1TE
☎0131 558 1191 Fax 0131 557 8500
Email editor@list.co.uk

Owner *The List Ltd*
Publisher *Robin Hodge*
Editor *Alan Morrison*
Circulation 17,500

FOUNDED 1985. FORTNIGHTLY. Events guide covering Glasgow and Edinburgh. Interviews and profiles of people working in film, theatre, music and the arts. Maximum 1200 words. No unsolicited mss. Phone with ideas. News material tends to be handled in-house.
Payment £100.

Literary Review
44 Lexington Street, London W1R 3LH
☎020 7437 9392 Fax 020 7734 1844
Owner *Namara Group*
Editor *Auberon Waugh*
Circulation 15,000

FOUNDED 1979. MONTHLY. Publishes book reviews (commissioned), features and articles on literary subjects. Prospective contributors are best advised to contact the editor in writing. Unsolicited mss not welcome. Runs a monthly competition, the Literary Review Grand Poetry Competition, on a given theme. Open to subscribers only. Details published in the magazine.
Payment varies.

Living France
Picture House Publishing, 9 High Street, Olney, Buckinghamshire MK46 4EB
☎01234 713203 Fax 01234 711507
Email livingfrance@easynet.co.uk
Website www.livingfrance.com
Editor *Trevor Yorke*

FOUNDED 1989. TEN ISSUES YEARLY. Francophile magazine catering for those with a passion for France, French culture and lifestyle. Covers all aspects of holidaying, living and working in France. Property section for those owning or wishing to buy a property in France. No unsolicited mss; approach in writing with an idea.

Loaded
King's Reach Tower, Stamford Street, London SE1 9LS
☎020 7261 5562 Fax 020 7261 5557
Email simon.guirao@ipc.co.uk
Website www.uploaded.com
Owner *IPC Magazines*
Editor *John Perry*
Circulation 371,548

FOUNDED 1994. MONTHLY men's lifestyle magazine featuring music, sport, sex, humour, travel, fashion, hard news and popular culture.

Will consider material which comes into these categories; approach in writing first. No fiction, poetry or articles on relationships.

Logos
5 Beechwood Drive, Marlow, Buckinghamshire SL7 2DH
☎01628 477577 Fax 01628 477577
Owner *Whurr Publishers Ltd*
Editor *Gordon Graham*
Associate Editor *Betty Graham*

FOUNDED 1990. QUARTERLY. Aims to 'deal in depth with issues which unite, divide, excite and concern the world of books,' with an international perspective. Each issue contains 6–8 articles of between 3500–7000 words. 'Logos is a professional forum, not a scholarly journal.' Suggestions and ideas for contributions are welcome, and should be addressed to the editor. 'Guidelines for Contributors' available. Contributors write from their experience as authors, publishers, booksellers, librarians, etc.
No payment.

London Hotel Magazine
28 Coleherne Mews, London SW10 9EA
☎020 373 7282 Fax 020 373 3215
Owner/Editor *Eileen Spence-Moncrieff*

FOUNDED 1995. Features on antiques, fashion, galleries, events and attractions, restaurants. Circulated to 107 major hotels.

London Magazine
30 Thurloe Place, London SW7 2HQ
☎020 7589 0618
Owner/Editor *Alan Ross*
Deputy Editor *Jane Rye*
Circulation 4500

FOUNDED 1954. BI-MONTHLY paperback journal providing an eclectic forum for literary talent, thanks to the dedication of Alan Ross. *The Times* once said that '*London Magazine* is far and away the most readable and level-headed, not to mention best value for money, of the literary magazines'. Today it boasts the publication of early works by the likes of William Boyd, Graham Swift and Ben Okri among others. The broad spectrum of interests includes art, memoirs, travel, poetry, criticism, theatre, music, cinema, short stories and essays, and book reviews. Unsolicited mss welcome; s.a.e. essential. About 150–200 unsolicited mss are received weekly.
   Fiction Maximum 5000 words.
   Payment £100 maximum.
   Annual Subscription £28.50 or $67.

London Review of Books

28 Little Russell Street, London WC1A 2HN
☎020 7209 1101 Fax 020 7209 1102
Owner *LRB Ltd*
Editor *Mary-Kay Wilmers*
Circulation 33,267

FOUNDED 1979. FORTNIGHTLY. Reviews, essays and articles on political, literary, cultural and scientific subjects. Also poetry. Unsolicited contributions welcome (approximately 50 received each week). No pieces under 2000 words. Contact the editor in writing. Please include s.a.e.
  Payment £150 per 1000 words; poems £75.

Looking Good

Upper Mounts, Northampton NN1 3HR
☎01604 231122 Fax 01604 233000
Owner *Northamptonshire Newspapers Ltd*
Editor *Ruth Supple*
Circulation 6000

FOUNDED 1984. QUARTERLY county lifestyle magazine of Northamptonshire. Contributions occasionally considered but majority of work is done in-house.

Looks

Endeavour House, 189 Shaftesbury Avenue, London WC2H 8JG
☎020 7437 9011 Fax 020 7208 3586
Owner *EMAP Elan Publications*
Editor *Margi Conklin*
Circulation 137,091

MONTHLY celebrity-led magazine for young women aged 16–24, with fashion, beauty and hair, as well as general interest features, interviews, giveaways, etc. Freelance writers are occasionally used in all areas of the magazine. Contact the editor with ideas.
  Payment varies.

M & E Design

Quadrant House, The Quadrant, Sutton, Surrey SM2 5AS
☎020 8652 3115 Fax 020 8652 8951
Email richard.simmonds@rbi.co.uk
Owner *Reed Business Information*
Editor-in-Chief *Paul Doughty*
Deputy Editor *Richard Simmonds*
Circulation 8,000

FOUNDED 1996. MONTHLY. Aimed at mechanical and electrical consulting engineers and designers. Would-be contributors should submit a 300-word synopsis via e-mail to the Deputy Editor.

Machine Knitting Monthly

PO Box 1479, Maidenhead, Berkshire SL6 8YX
☎01628 783080 Fax 01628 633250
Email rpa@surf3.net
Owner *RPA Publishing Ltd*
Editor *Anne Smith*

FOUNDED 1986. MONTHLY. Unsolicited mss considered 'as long as they are applicable to this specialist publication. We have our own regular contributors each month but we're always willing to look at new ideas from other writers.' Approach in writing in first instance.

Management Today

174 Hammersmith Road, London W6 7JP
☎020 7413 4566
Email management.today@haynet.com
Owner *Haymarket Business Publications Ltd*
Editor-in-Chief *Rufus Olins*
Circulation 97,976
General business topics and features. Ideas welcome. Send brief synopsis to the editor.
  Payment about £300 per 1000 words.

marie claire

2 Hatfields, London SE1 9PG
☎020 7261 5240 Fax 020 7261 5277
Owner *European Magazines Ltd*
Editor *Elizabeth A. Jones*
Circulation 450,213

FOUNDED 1988. MONTHLY. An intelligent glossy magazine for women, with strong international features and fashion. No unsolicited mss. Approach with ideas in writing. No fiction.
  Features *Judith Keeling* Detailed proposals for feature ideas should be accompanied by samples of previous work.

Market Newsletter

Focus House, 497 Green Lanes, London N13 4BP
☎020 8882 3315 Fax 020 8886 5174
Owner *Bureau of Freelance Photographers*
Editor *John Tracy*
Deputy Editor *Stewart Gibson*
Circulation 7,000

FOUNDED 1965. MONTHLY. Circulated to members of the Bureau of Freelance Photographers (annual membership fee: £40 UK; £55 Overseas). News of current markets – magazines, books, cards, calendars, etc – and the type of submissions (mainly photographs) they are currently looking for. Includes details of new magazine launches, publication revamps, etc. Also profiles of particular markets and photographers. Limited scope for non-members to contribute.

Marketing Week

12–26 Lexington Street, London W1R 4HQ
☎020 7970 4000 Fax 020 7970 6721
Email mw.editorial@chiron.co.uk
Website www.marketing-week.co.uk
Owner *Centaur Communications*
Editor *Stuart Smith*
Circulation 40,986

WEEKLY trade magazine of the marketing industry. Features on all aspects of the business, written in a newsy and up-to-the-minute style. Approach with ideas in the first instance.

Features *Joanne Flack*
Payment negotiable.

Match

Bretton Court, Bretton, Peterborough, Cambridgeshire PE3 8DZ
☎01733 260333 Fax 01733 465206
Website www.matchfacts.co.uk
Owner *EMAP Active Ltd*
Editor *Chris Hunt*
Circulation 145,749

FOUNDED 1979. WEEKLY. The UK's biggest-selling football magazine aimed at 10–15-year-olds. Most material is generated in-house by a strong news and features team. Some freelance material used if suitable. No submissions without prior consultation with editor, either by phone or in writing. Work experience placements often given to trainee journalists and students; the majority of staff are recruited through this route.

Features/News Good and original material is always considered. Maximum 500 words.
Payment negotiable.

Match of the Day Magazine

BBC Worldwide Ltd, Woodlands, 80 Wood Lane, London W12 0TT
☎020 8433 3170 Fax 020 8433 2898
Email tim.glynne-jones@bbc.co.uk
Website www.bbcworldwide.com
Owner *BBC Worldwide Publishing Ltd*
Editor *Tim Glynne-Jones*
Circulation 72,000

FOUNDED 1996. MONTHLY Football articles, interviews and opinion. No unsolicited mss. No opinion pieces. Approach in writing.

News *Nigel Matheson* Unusual story ideas welcome. Maximum 300 words. *Payment* £20–75.

Features *Tim Glynne-Jones* Ideas welcome. Maximum 2000 words. *Payment* £150 per 1000 words.

Matrix

See **British Science Fiction Association** under **Professional Associations**

Maxim

19 Bolsover Street, London W1P 7HJ
☎020 7917 3912 Fax 020 7917 7663
Owner *Dennis Publishing*
Editor *Tom Loxley*
Circulation 315,102

ESTABLISHED 1995. MONTHLY glossy men's lifestyle magazine featuring sex, travel, health, finance, motoring and fashion. No fiction or poetry. Approach in writing in the first instance, sending outlines of ideas only together with examples of published work. Some scope for first-person accounts.

Mayfair

2 Archer Street, Piccadilly Circus, London W1V 8JJ
☎020 7292 8000 Fax 020 7734 5030
Email mayfair@pr-org.co.uk
Owner *Paul Raymond Publications*
Editor *Steve Shields*
Circulation 331,760

FOUNDED 1966. THIRTEEN ISSUES YEARLY. Unsolicited material accepted if pertinent to the magazine and if accompanied by suitable illustrative material. 'We will *only* publish work if we can illustrate it.' Interested in features and humour aimed at men aged 20–30. For style, length, etc., writers are advised to study the magazine. 'No more romantic fiction, we beseech you!'

Mayfair Times

102 Mount Street, London W1X 5HF
☎020 7629 3378 Fax 020 7629 9303
Owner *Mayfair Times Ltd*
Editor *Stephen Goringe*
Circulation 20,000

FOUNDED 1985. MONTHLY. Features on Mayfair of interest to both residential and commercial readers. Unsolicited mss welcome.

Medal News

1 Orchard House, Duchy Road, Heathpark, Honiton, Devon EX14 1YT
☎01404 46972 Fax 01404 44788
Email info@medal-news.com
Website www.medal-news.com
Owners *J. W. Mussell, Carol Hartman*
Editor *John Sly*

Circulation 4500

FOUNDED 1989. MONTHLY. Unsolicited material welcome but initial approach by phone or in writing preferred.

Features 'Opportunities exist for well-informed authors who know the subject and do their homework.' Maximum 2500 words.

Payment £20 per 1000 words.

Media Week

Quantum House, 19 Scarbrook Road, Croydon, Surrey CR9 1LX
☎020 8565 4323 Fax 020 8565 4394
Email mweeked@qpp.co.uk
Website www.mediaweek.co.uk

Owner *Quantum*
Editor *Patrick Barrett*
Circulation 22,000

FOUNDED 1986. WEEKLY trade magazine. UK and international coverage on all aspects of commercial media. No unsolicited mss. Approach in writing with ideas.

Melody Maker

26th Floor, King's Reach Tower, Stamford Street, London SE1 9LS
☎020 7261 6229 Fax 020 7261 6706

Owner *IPC Magazines Ltd*
Editor *Mark Sutherland*
Circulation 37,881

FOUNDED 1926. WEEKLY. Freelance contributors used on this A4 magazine competitor of the *NME*. Opportunities exist in reviewing and features.

Features *Ian Watson* A large in-house team, plus around six regulars, produce most feature material.

Reviews *Daniel Booth* (Live), *Neil Mason* Sample reviews, whether published or not, welcome on pop, rock, soul, funk, etc.

Payment negotiable.

Men's Health

7–10 Chandos Street, London W1M 0AD
☎020 7291 6000 Fax 020 7291 6053

Owner *Rodale Press*
Editor *Simon Geller*
Circulation 233,653

FOUNDED 1994. MONTHLY men's healthy lifestyle magazine covering health, fitness, nutrition, stress and sex issues. No unsolicited mss; will consider ideas and synopses tailored to men's health. No fiction, celebrities, sportsmen or extreme sports. Approach in writing in the first instance.

MiniWorld Magazine

IPC Link House Division, Dingwall Avenue, Croydon, Surrey CR9 2TA
☎020 8774 0645 Fax 020 8781 6042
Email miniworld@ipc.co.uk
Website www.miniworld.co.uk

Owner *IPC Music and Sport Publishing*
Editor *Monty Watkins*
Circulation 37,122

FOUNDED 1991. MONTHLY car magazine devoted to the Mini. Unsolicited material welcome but prospective contributors are advised to contact the editor.

Features Maintenance, tuning, restoration, technical advice, classified, sport, readers' cars and social history of this cult car.

Payment negotiable.

Minx

Endeavour House, 189 Shaftesbury Avenue, London WC2H 8JG
☎020 7208 3428 Fax 020 7208 3323

Owner *EMAP*
Editor *Vanessa Thompson*
Circulation 123,278

FOUNDED 1996. MONTHLY lifestyle magazine for young women. Interested in receiving ideas for features; approach in writing in the first instance. No fiction.

Mizz

King's Reach Tower, Stamford Street, London SE1 9LS
☎020 7261 6319 Fax 020 7261 6032

Owner *IPC Magazines Ltd*
Editor *Lucie Tobin*
Circulation 130,254

FOUNDED 1985. FORTNIGHTLY magazine for the 10–14-year-old girl. Freelance articles welcome on real life, human interest stories and emotional issues. Also quizzes. All material should be addressed to the features editor.

Features *Chloe Thompson/Leslie Sinoway* Approach in writing, with synopsis, for feature copy; send sample writing with letter for general approach.

Fiction Maximum 1000 words.

Model Railway Collector

9 Mulberry Close, Whittlesay, Peterborough, Cambridgeshire PE7 1UL
☎01733 203749

Owner *Kelsey Publishing*
Editor *Peter Simpson*
Circulation 20,000

FOUNDED 1993. MONTHLY magazine which is the only national model railway magazine in the UK catering specifically for model railway collectors. Articles with good photographs or drawings on the subject of collecting or modelling are welcome but ideas should be discussed first with the editor.
Payment negotiable.

Mojo

Mappin House, 4 Winsley Street, London W1N 7AR
☎020 7436 1515 Fax 020 7312 8296
Email mojo@ecm.emap.com
Owner *EMAP-Metro*
Editor *Paul Trynka*
Circulation 75,365

FOUNDED 1993. MONTHLY magazine containing features, reviews and news stories about rock music and its influences. Receives about five mss per day. No poetry, think-pieces on dead rock stars or similar fan worship.
Features Amateur writers discouraged except as providers of source material, contacts, etc. *Payment* negotiable.
News All verifiable, relevant stories considered. *Payment* approx. £150 per 1000 words.
Reviews Write to Reviews Editor with relevant specimen material. *Payment* approx. £150 per 1000 words.

Moneywise

RD Publications Ltd, 11 Westferry Circus, Canary Wharf, London E14 4HE
☎020 7715 8465 Fax 020 7715 8725
Website www.moneywise.co.uk
Owner *Reader's Digest Association*
Acting Editor *Kathleen Hennessy*
Circulation 105,000

FOUNDED 1990. MONTHLY. Unsolicited mss with s.a.e. welcome but initial approach in writing preferred.

More!

Endeavour House, 189 Shaftesbury Avenue, London WC2H 8JG
☎020 7208 3165 Fax 020 7208 3595
Owner *EMAP Elan Publications*
Editor *Marina Gask*
Features Director *Julian Linley*
Editorial Enquiries *Ali Wick*
Circulation 300,194

FOUNDED 1988. FORTNIGHTLY women's magazine aimed at the working woman aged 18–24. Features on sex and relationships plus news. Most items are commissioned; approach

features editor with idea. Prospective contributors are strongly advised to study the magazine's style before submitting anything.

Mother and Baby

Greater London House, Hampstead Road, London NW1 7EJ
☎020 7874 0200
Owner *EMAP Elan Publications*
Editor *Rashmi Madan*
Circulation 80,200

FOUNDED 1956. MONTHLY. Welcomes suggestions for feature ideas about pregnancy, newborn basics, practical babycare, baby development and childcare subjects. Approaches may be made by telephone or in writing to the **Features Editor** *Tina Gough*.

Motor Boat and Yachting

IPC Country & Leisure Media Limited, King's Reach Tower, Stamford Street, London SE1 9LS
☎020 7261 5333 Fax 020 7261 5419
Email mby@ipc.co.uk
Website www.mby.com
Owner *IPC Magazines Ltd*
Editor *Alan Harper*
Circulation 20,444

FOUNDED 1904. MONTHLY for those interested in motor boats and motor cruising.
Features *Alan Harper* Cruising and practical features especially welcome. Illustrations/ photographs (mostly colour) are just as important as text. Maximum 3000 words. *Payment* from £100 per 1000 words or by arrangement.
News *Tom Isitt* Factual pieces. Maximum 200 words. *Payment* up to £50 per item.

Motorcaravan Motorhome Monthly (MMM)

PO Box 44, Totnes, Devon TQ9 5XB
Owner *Sanglier Publications Ltd*
Editor *Mike Jago*
Circulation 25,893

FOUNDED 1966. MONTHLY. 'There's no money in motorcaravan journalism but for those wishing to cut their first teeth ...' Unsolicited mss welcome if relevant, but ideas in writing preferred in first instance.
Features Caravan site reports. Maximum 500 words.
Travel Motorcaravanning trips (home and overseas). Maximum 2000 words.
News Short news items for miscellaneous pages. Maximum 200 words.
Fiction Must be motorcaravan-related and

include artwork/photos if possible. Maximum 2000 words.

Special pages DIY – modifications to motorcaravans. Maximum 1500 words.

Owner Reports Contributions welcome from motorcaravan owners. Contact the editor for requirements. Maximum 2000 words.

Payment varies.

Motorgliding and Gliding International

281 Queen Edith's Way, Cambridge CB1 9NH
☎01223 247725 Fax 01223 413793
Email bryce.smith@virgin.net
Website www.glidingmagazine.com

Owner *Soaring Society of America*
Editor *Gillian Bryce-Smith*

FOUNDED November 1998 for an international market concentrating entirely on motorgliding. Few opportunities for freelance writers. Now on the Internet as the first gliding magazine to be electronic only. *No payment.*

Ms London

7–9 Rathbone Street, London W1P 1AF
☎020 7636 6651

Owner *Independent Magazines*
Editor-in-Chief *Bill Williamson*
Circulation 85,000

FOUNDED 1968. WEEKLY. Aimed at working women in London, aged 18–35. No unsolicited mss.

Features Varied and topical, ranging from celebrity interviews to news issues, fashion, health, careers, relationships and homebuying. Approach in writing only with ideas in the first instance and enclose sample of published writing. Material should be London-angled, sharp or humorous and fairly sophisticated in content. Maximum 1500 words. *Payment* about £130 per 1000 words on publication.

News Handled in-house but follow-up feature ideas welcome.

Mslexia (For Women Who Write)

PO Box 656, Newcastle upon Tyne
NE99 2XD
☎0191 261 6656 Fax 0191 261 6636
Email postbag@mslexia.demon.co.uk
Website www.mslexia.co.uk

Owner *Mslexia Publications Limited*
Editor *Debbie Taylor*
Circulation 6000

FOUNDED 1997. QUARTERLY. Articles, advice, reviews, interviews, events for women writers plus new poetry and prose. Will consider fiction, poetry, features and letters but contributors *must* send for guidelines first. Approach in writing.

Multi-Storey

PO Box 62, Levenshulme, Manchester
M19 1TH

Editors *Finella Davenport, Bill Jones, Gary Parkinson*

FOUNDED 1999. BIANNUAL literary magazine. Book reviews, short stories, poetry, interviews, articles. 'We are pleased to accept new writing but would prefer that we are contacted in the first instance for guidelines as each magazine is themed.' **News** Max. 1000 words; **Features** Maximum 2000 words; **Fiction** Max. 3000 words. Send two hard copies and one on disk. Also interested in art work.

Music Week

8 Montague Close, London SE1 9UR
☎020 7620 3636 Fax 020 7407 7094

Owner *Miller Freeman Entertainment*
Editor-in-Chief *Steve Redmond*
Editor *Ajax Scott*
Circulation 13,900

Britain's only WEEKLY music business magazine. No unsolicited mss. Approach in writing with ideas.

Features *Ajax Scott* Analysis of specific music business events and trends.

News Music industry news only.

Musical Opinion

2 Princes Road, St Leonards on Sea,
East Sussex TN37 6EL
☎01424 715167 Fax 01424 712214
Email musical-opinion@cwcom.net
Website www.musicalopinion.co.uk

Owner *Musical Opinion Ltd*
Editor *Denby Richards*
Circulation 5000

FOUNDED 1877. QUARTERLY with four free supplements in intervening months. Classical music content, with topical features on music, musicians, festivals, etc., and reviews (concerts, festivals, opera, ballet, jazz, CDs, CD-ROMs, videos, books and printed music). International readership. No unsolicited mss; commissions only. Ideas always welcome though; approach by phone or fax, giving telephone number. It should be noted that topical material has to be submitted six months prior to events. Not interested in review material.

Payment negotiable.

My Weekly
80 Kingsway East, Dundee DD4 8SL
☎01382 223131 Fax 01382 452491
Email myweekly@dcthomson.co.uk
Owner *D. C. Thomson & Co. Ltd*
Editor *Harrison Watson*
Circulation 336,329

A traditional women's WEEKLY. D. C. Thomson has long had a policy of encouragement and help to new writers of promise. Ideas welcome. Approach in writing.

Features Particularly interested in human interest pieces (1000–1500 words) which by their very nature appeal to all age groups.

Fiction Three stories a week, ranging in content from the emotional to the off-beat and unexpected. 1500–4000 words. Also serials.

Payment negotiable.

The National Trust Magazine
36 Queen Anne's Gate, London SW1H 9AS
☎020 7222 9251 Fax 020 7222 5097
Owner *The National Trust*
Editor *Gaynor Aaltonen*
Circulation 1.34 million

FOUNDED 1968. THRICE-YEARLY. Conservation of historic houses, coast and countryside in England, Northern Ireland and Wales. No unsolicited mss. Approach in writing with ideas.

Natural World
Victory House, 14 Leicester Place, London WC2H 7QH
☎020 7306 0304 Fax 020 7306 0314
Owner *River Publishing Ltd*
Editor *Sarah-Jane Forder*
Circulation 178,000

FOUNDED 1981. THRICE-YEARLY. Unsolicited mss are not accepted. Ideas in writing preferred. No poetry.

Features Popular but accurate articles on British wildlife and the countryside, particularly projects associated with the local wildlife trusts. Maximum 1500 words.

News Interested in national wildlife conservation issues, particularly those involving local nature conservation or wildlife trusts. Maximum 300 words.

Payment negotiable.

The Naturalist
c/o University of Bradford, Bradford, West Yorkshire BD7 1DP
☎01274 234212 Fax 01274 234231
Email m.r.d.seaward@bradford.ac.uk
Owner *Yorkshire Naturalists' Union*
Editor *Prof. M. R. D. Seaward*
Circulation 5000

FOUNDED 1875. QUARTERLY. Natural history, biological and environmental sciences for a professional and amateur readership. Unsolicited mss and b&w illustrations welcome. Particularly interested in material – scientific papers – relating to the north of England.

No payment.

Nature
Porters South, 4–6 Crinan Street, London N1 9XW
☎020 7833 4000 Fax 020 7843 4595
Email nature@nature.com
Website www.nature.com
Owner *Macmillan Magazines Ltd*
Editor *Philip Campbell*
Circulation 61,000

Covers all fields of science, with articles and news on science policy only. No features. Little scope for freelance writers.

Needlecraft
30 Monmouth Street, Bath BA1 2BW
☎01225 442244 Fax 01225 732398
Email debora.bradley@futurenet.co.uk
Website www.thefuturenetwork.plc.uk
Owner *Future Publishing*
Editor *Debora Bradley*
Circulation 35,000

FOUNDED 1991. MONTHLY. Needlework projects with full instructions covering cross stitch, needlepoint, embroidery, patchwork, quilting and lace. Will consider ideas or sketches for projects covering any of the magazine's topics. Initial approaches should be made in writing.

Features on the needlecraft theme. Discuss ideas before sending complete mss. Maximum 1000 words.

Technical pages on 'how to' stitch, use different threads, etc. Only suitable for experienced writers.

Payment negotiable.

New Beacon
224 Great Portland Street, London W1N 6AA
☎020 7388 1266 Fax 020 7388 0945
Owner *Royal National Institute for the Blind*
Editor *Ann Lee*
Circulation 6000

FOUNDED 1917. MONTHLY (except August). Published in print, braille and on tape and disk. Unsolicited mss welcome. Approach with ideas in writing. Personal experiences by writers who have a visual impairment (partial sight or blindness), and authoritative items by professionals or volunteers working in the field of visual impairment welcome. Maximum 1500 words.

Payment negotiable.

New Humanist

Bradlaugh House, 47 Theobald's Road, London WC1X 8SP

☎020 7430 1371 Fax 020 7430 1271

Email jim.herrick@rationalist.org.uk

Owner *Rationalist Press Association*

Editor *Jim Herrick*

Circulation 1500

FOUNDED 1885. QUARTERLY. Unsolicited mss welcome. No fiction.

Features Articles with a humanist perspective welcome in the following fields: religion (critical), humanism, human rights, philosophy, current events, literature, history and science. 2000–4000 words. *Payment* nominal, but negotiable.

Book reviews 750–1000 words, by arrangement with the editor.

New Impact

Anser House, Courtyard Offices, 3 High Street, Marlow, Bucks SL7 1AX

☎01628 475570 Fax 01628 475570

Email curious@newimpact.co.uk

Website www.newimpact.co.uk

Owner *D. E. Sihera*

Editor *Elaine Sihera*

Features Editor *Mary Howe Clements*

Circulation 10,000

FOUNDED 1993. BI-MONTHLY. Celebrates diversity, enterprise and achievement from a minority ethnic perspective. Unsolicited mss welcome. Interested in training, arts, features, personal achievement, small business features, profiles of personalities especially for a multicultural audience. Promotes the British Diversity Awards each November and the Windrush Awards each June, the Diversity Associates Register (DIVAS), the Register of Diversity Managers among employers and the Annual Diversity UK Directory.

News Local training/business features – some opportunities. Maximum length 250 words. *Payment* negotiable.

Features Original, interesting pieces with a deliberate multicultural/diversity focus. Personal/professional successes and achievements welcome. Maximum length 1200 words. *Payment* negotiable.

Fiction Short stories, poems – especially

from minority writers. Not interested in romantic/sexual narratives. Maximum length 1500 words. *Payment* negotiable.

Special Pages Interviews with personalities – especially Asian, African Caribbean. Maximum length 1200 words. *Payment* negotiable.

New Internationalist

55 Rectory Road, Oxford OX4 1BW

☎01865 728181 Fax 01865 793152

Email ni@newint.org

Website www.newint.org/

Owner *New Internationalist Trust*

Co-Editors *Vanessa Baird, Chris Brazier, David Ransom, Nikki van der Gaag*

Circulation 70,000

Radical and broadly leftist in approach, but unaligned. Concerned with world poverty and global issues of peace and politics, feminism and environmentalism, with emphasis on the Third World. Difficult to use unsolicited material as they work to a theme each month and features are commissioned by the editor on that basis. The way in is to send examples of published or unpublished work; writers of interest are taken up. Unsolicited material for shorter articles could be used in the magazine's regular *Update* section.

New Musical Express

King's Reach Tower, Stamford Street, London SE1 9LS

☎020 7261 6472 Fax 020 7261 5185

Website www.nme.com

Owner *IPC Magazines Ltd*

Editor *Ben Knowles*

Circulation 100,093

Britain's best-selling musical WEEKLY. Freelancers used, but always for reviews in the first instance. Specialisation in areas of music (or film, which is also covered) is a help.

Reviews: Books/Film *John Mulvey* **LPs** *John Robinson* **Live** *James Oldham*. Send in examples of work, either published or specially written samples.

New Nation

148 Cambridge Heath Road, London E1 5QJ

☎020 7702 8012 Fax 020 7702 7937

Owner *Ethnic Media Group*

Editor *Michael Eboda*

Circulation 30,000

FOUNDED 1996. WEEKLY community paper for the Black community in Britain. Interested in relevant general, local and international issues. Approach in writing with ideas for submission.

New Scientist

1st Floor, 151 Wardour Street, London W1V 4BN

☎020 7331 2701 Fax 020 7331 2777

Owner *Reed Business Information Ltd*
Editor-in-Chief *Dr Alun Anderson*
Editor *Jeremy Webb*
Circulation 130,994

FOUNDED 1956. WEEKLY. No unsolicited mss. Approach with ideas – one A4-page synopsis – by fax.

Features *Gabriel Walker* Commissions only, but good ideas welcome. Max. 3500 words.

News *Daniel Clery* Mostly commissions, but ideas for specialist news welcome. Max. 1000 words.

Reviews *Maggie McDonald* Reviews are commissioned.

Forum *Richard Fifield* Unsolicited material welcome if of general/humorous interest and related to science. Maximum 1000 words.

Payment negotiable.

The New Shetlander

11 Mounthooly Street, Lerwick, Shetland ZE1 0BJ

☎01595 693816 Fax 01595 696787
Email shetland@zetnet.co.uk

Owner *Shetland Council of Social Service*
Editors *Alex Cluness, John Hunter*
Circulation 1900

FOUNDED 1947. QUARTERLY literary magazine containing short stories, essays, poetry, historical articles, literary criticism, political comment, arts and books. The magazine has two editors and an editorial committee who all look at submitted material. Interested in considering short stories, poetry, historical articles with a northern Scottish or Scandinavian flavour, literary pieces and articles on Shetland. As a rough guide, items should be between 1000 and 2000 words although longer mss are considered. Initial approach in writing, please.

Payment Complimentary copy.

New Statesman

Victoria Station House, 191 Victoria Street, London SW1E 5NE

☎020 7828 1232 Fax 020 7828 1881

Publisher *Spencer Neal*
Editor *Peter Wilby*
Deputy Editor *Cristina Odone*
Circulation 26,000

WEEKLY magazine, the result of a merger (1988) of *New Statesman* and *New Society*.

Coverage of news, book reviews, arts, current affairs, politics and social reportage. Unsolicited contributions with s.a.e. will be considered. No short stories.

Books *Jason Cowley*
Arts *Frances Stonor Saunders*

New Welsh Review

Chapter Arts Centre, Market Road, Cardiff CF5 1QE

☎029 2066 5529 Fax 029 2066 5529

Owner *New Welsh Review Ltd*
Editor *Robin Reeves*
Circulation 1000

FOUNDED 1988. QUARTERLY Welsh literary magazine in the English language. Welcomes material of literary and cultural interest to Welsh readers and those with an interest in Wales. Approach in writing in the first instance.

Features Max. 3000 words. *Payment* £25 per 1000 words.

Fiction Max. 5000 words. *Payment* £40–80 average.

News Max. 400 words. *Payment* £10–30.

New Woman

Endeavour House, 189 Shaftesbury Avenue, London WC2H 8JG

☎020 7437 9011 Fax 020 7208 3585
Website www.newwomanonline.co.uk

Owner *Hachette/EMAP Elan Ltd*
Editor *Jo Elvin*
Circulation 276,285

MONTHLY women's interest magazine. Winner of the PPA 'Magazine of the Year' award in 1998. Aimed at women aged 25–35. An 'entertaining, informative and intelligent' read. Main topics of interest include men, sex, love, health, careers, beauty and fashion. Uses mainly established freelancers but unsolicited ideas submitted in synopsis form will be considered. Welcomes ideas from male writers for humorous 'men's opinion' pieces.

Features/News *Margi Conklin* Articles must be original and look at subjects or issues from a new or unusual perspective.

Fashion *Corinna Kitchen*

The New Writer

PO Box 60, Cranbrook, Kent TN17 2ZR

☎01580 212626 Fax 01580 212041
Email thenewwriter@hotmail.com
Website www.tnwriter.free-online.co.uk

Publisher *Merric Davidson*
Editor *Suzanne Ruthven*

Poetry Editor *Abi Hughes-Edwards*

FOUNDED 1996. Published MONTHLY following the merger between *Acclaim* and *Quartos* magazines. TNW continues to offer practical 'nuts and bolts' advice on poetry and prose but with the emphasis on *forward-looking* articles and features on all aspects of the written word that demonstrate the writer's grasp of contemporary writing and current editorial/publishing policies. Plenty of news, views, competitions, reviews and regional gossip in the Newsletter section; writers' guidelines available with s.a.e.

Features Unsolicited mss welcome. Interested in lively, original articles on writing in its broadest sense. Approach with ideas in writing in the first instance. No material is returned unless accompanied by s.a.e. *Payment* £20 per 1000 words.

Fiction Publishes short-listed entries from guest writers and subscriber-only submissions. *Payment* £10 per story.

Poetry Unsolicited poetry welcome. Both short and long unpublished poems, providing they are original and interesting. *Payment* £3 per poem.

New Writing Scotland

Association for Scottish Literary Studies, c/o Department of Scottish History, 9 University Gardens, University of Glasgow G12 8QH
☎0141 330 5309 Fax 0141 330 5309
Email cmc@arts.gla.ac.uk
Website www.arts.gla.ac.uk/ScotLit/ASLS

Contact *Duncan Jones*

ANNUAL anthology of contemporary poetry and prose in English, Gaelic and Scots, produced by the **Association for Scottish Literary Studies** (see entry under **Professional Associations and Societies**). Will consider poetry, drama, short fiction or other creative prose but not full-length plays or novels, though self-contained extracts are acceptable. Maximum length of 3500 words is suggested. Send no more than two short stories and six poems. Submissions should be accompanied by two s.a.e.s (one for receipt, the other for return of mss). Mss, which must be sent by 31 January, should be typed, double-spaced, on one side of the paper only with the sheets secured at top left-hand corner. Mark with your name and address and, for prose, an approximate word count.

Newcastle Life

See **North East Times**

19

King's Reach Tower, Stamford Street, London SE1 9LS
☎020 7261 6410 Fax 020 7261 7634

Owner *IPC Magazines Ltd*
Editor *Samantha Warwick*
Circulation 126,606

FOUNDED 1968. MONTHLY women's magazine aimed at 16–24-year-olds. Aims for a 50/50 balance between fashion/lifestyle aspects and newsier, meatier material, e.g. women in prison, boys, abortion, etc. 40% of the magazine's feature material is commissioned, ordinarily from established freelancers. 'But we're always keen to see bold, original, vigorous writing from people just starting out.'

Features Approach in writing with ideas.

North East Times

Tattler House, Beech Avenue, Fawdon, Newcastle upon Tyne NE3 4LA
☎0191 284 4495 Fax 0191 285 9606
Email northeasttimes@onyxnet.co.uk

Owner *Chris Robinson (Publishing) Ltd*
Editor *Chris Robinson*
Circulation 10,000

MONTHLY county magazine incorporating *Newcastle Life*. No unsolicited mss. Approach with ideas in writing. Not interested in any material that is not applicable to ABC1 readers.

The North

See under **Poetry Magazines**

Now

King's Reach Tower, Stamford Street, London SE1 9LS
☎020 7261 6274

Owner *IPC Magazines Ltd*
Editor *Jane Ennis*
Circulation 396,303

FOUNDED 1996. WEEKLY magazine of celebrity gossip, news and topical features aimed at the working woman. Unlikely to use freelance contributions due to specialist content – e.g. exclusive showbiz interviews – but ideas will be considered. Approach in writing; no faxes.

Nursing Times

Greater London House, Hampstead Road, London NW1 7EJ
☎020 7874 0500 Fax 020 7874 0505

Owner *EMAP Healthcare*
Editor *Tricia Reid*
Circulation 80,670

A large proportion of *Nursing Times*' feature content is from unsolicited contributions sent on spec. Pieces on all aspects of nursing and health care, both practical and theoretical, written in a lively and contemporary way, are welcome. Commissions also.

Payment varies/NUJ rates apply to commissioned material from union members only.

OK! Magazine

The Northern & Shell Tower, City Harbour, London E14 9GL
☎020 7308 5091 Fax 020 7301 5082

Owner *Richard Desmond*
Editor *Martin Townsend*
Circulation 551,901

FOUNDED 1996. WEEKLY celebrity-based magazine. Welcomes interviews and pictures on well known personalities, and ideas for general features. Approach by phone or fax in the first instance.

The Oldie

45–46 Poland Street, London W1V 4AU
☎020 7734 2225 Fax 020 7734 2226
Email theoldie@theoldie.demon.co.uk
Website www.theoldie.co.uk

Owner *Oldie Publications Ltd*
Editor *Richard Ingrams*
Circulation 45,000

FOUNDED 1992. MONTHLY general interest magazine with a strong humorous slant for the older person. Submissions welcome; enclose s.a.e.

OLS (Open Learning Systems) News

11 Malford Grove, Gilwern, Abergavenny, Monmouthshire NP7 0RN
☎01873 830872
Email GSSE@zoo.co.uk

Owner/Editor *David P. Bosworth*
Circulation 300

FOUNDED 1980. QUARTERLY dealing with the application of open, flexible, distance learning and supported self-study at all educational/training levels. Interested in open-access learning and the application of educational technology to learning situations. Case studies particularly welcome. Not interested in theory of education alone, the emphasis is strictly on applied policies and trends.

Features Learning programmes (how they are organised); student/learner-eye views of educational and training programmes with an open-access approach. Sections on teleworking and lifelong learning. Approach the editor by e-mail or in writing.

No payment for 'news' items. Focus items will negotiate.

On the Ball

Moondance Publications, The Design Works, William Street, Gateshead, Tyne and Wear NE10 0JP
☎0191 420 8383 Fax 0191 420 4950

Owner *Moondance Publications Ltd*
Editor *Jennifer O'Neill*
Circulation 30,000

FOUNDED 1996. BI-MONTHLY. The only magazine for women football players. Contributions welcome.

Features *Jennifer O'Neill* International reports, player and team profiles, diet, health and fitness, tactics, training advice, play improvement; fundraising. 1500 words maximum.

News *Wilf Frith* Match reports, team news, transfers, injuries, results and fixtures. 600 words maximum.

Payment negotiable.

Opera

1A Mountgrove Road, London N5 2LU
☎020 7354 2700 Fax 020 7359 1037
Email operamag@clara.co.uk
Website www.opera.co.uk

Owner *Opera Magazine Ltd*
Editor *John Allison*
Circulation 11,500

FOUNDED 1950. MONTHLY review of the current opera scene. Almost all articles are commissioned and unsolicited mss are not welcome. All approaches should be made in writing.

Opera Now

241 Shaftesbury Avenue, London WC2H 8EH
☎020 7333 1740 Fax 020 7333 1769
Email opera.now@rhinegold.co.uk

Publisher *Rhinegold Publishing Ltd*
Editor-in-Chief *Ashutosh Khandekar*
Deputy Editor *Antonia Couling*
Assistant Editor *Matthew Peacock*

FOUNDED 1989. BI-MONTHLY. News, features and reviews aimed at those involved as well as those interested in opera. No unsolicited mss. All work is commissioned. Approach with ideas in writing.

Orbis

See under **Poetry Magazines**

Organic Gardening

PO Box 29, Minehead, Somerset TA24 6YY
☎01984 641212 Fax 01984 641212
Email organic.gardening@virgin.net
Editor *Gaby Bartai Bevan*
Circulation 20,000

FOUNDED 1988. MONTHLY. Articles and features on all aspects of gardening based on organic methods. Unsolicited material welcome; 800–2000 words for features and 100-300 for news items. Prefers 'hands-on' accounts of projects, problems, challenges and how they are dealt with. Approach in writing.
Payment by arrangement.

OS (Office Secretary) Magazine

Brookmead House, Thorney Leys Business Park, Witney, Oxfordshire OX8 7GE
☎01993 894500 Fax 01993 778884
Owner *Peebles Media Group*
Editor *Sarah Sheppard*
Circulation 50,000

FOUNDED 1986. QUARTERLY. Features articles of interest to secretaries and personal assistants aged 25–60. No unsolicited mss.
Features Informative pieces on technology and practices, office and employment-related topics. Length 1000 words.
Payment by negotiation.

Outcast

The Glass House, 42 Birch Grove, London W3 9SS
☎020 8354 0790 Fax 020 8248 9107
Email mail@outcastmagazine.co.uk
Website www.outcastmagazine.co.uk
Owner *Outcast Publishing Ltd*
Editor *Chris Morris*
Circulation 40,000

FOUNDED 1999. MONTHLY current affairs magazine aimed at the lesbian, gay and bisexual communities. Focuses on news, sexual politics and debate. Freelance contributions welcome.
News *Andy Armitage*
news@outcastmagazine.co.uk
Features *Emma Butcher*
emma@outcastmagazine.co.uk
Reviews *David Leddy*
david@outcastmagazine.co.uk
Payment nominal.

Palmtop Magazine

Palmtop Publications, PO Box 188, Bicester, Oxfordshire OX6 0GP
☎01869 249287 Fax 01869 246043
Email editor@palmtop.co.uk
Website www.palmtop.co.uk
Editor *Mr S. Clack*
Owners *Mr S. Clack, Miss R. A. Rolfe*
Circulation 12,000

FOUNDED 1994. BI-MONTHLY users' magazine for Psion hand-held computers. No unsolicited mss; approach by 'phone or e-mail in the first instance.

PC Format

Future Publishing, 30 Monmouth Street, Bath BA1 2BW
☎01225 442244 Fax 01225 732275
Email pcfmail@futurenet.co.uk
Website www.futurenet.co.uk
Owner *Future Publishing*
Editor *Dan Hutchinson*
Circulation 110,227

FOUNDED 1991. FOUR-WEEKLY magazine covering everything for the consumer PC – games, hardware, Internet creativity. Welcomes feature ideas in the first instance; approach by telephone or in writing.

Peakland Walker

33 Park Road, Bakewell, Derbyshire DE45 1AX
☎01629 812034 Fax 01629 812034
Email rolysmith@compuserve.com
Owner *MagMaker Ltd*
Editor *Roly Smith*

FOUNDED 1997. QUARTERLY. Predominantly walking, natural history and heritage, serving the Peak District National Park and surrounding area. Unsolicited material considered but telephone first. Maximum 1200 words.

Pembrokeshire Life

Swan House Publishing, Bridge Street, Newcastle Emlyn, Carmarthenshire SA38 9DX
☎01239 710632   Fax 01239 710632
Owner *Swan House Publishing*
Editor *David Fielding*

FOUNDED 1989. BI-MONTHLY county magazine with articles on local history, issues, characters, off-beat stories with good colour or b&w photographs. No country diaries, short stories, poems. Most articles are commissioned from known freelancers but 'always prepared to consider ideas from new writers'. No mss. Send cuttings of previous work (published or not) and synopsis to the editor.

People Management

Personnel Publications Limited, 17 Britton Street, London EC1M 5TP
☎020 7880 6200 Fax 020 7336 7635
Email editorial@peoplemanagement.co.uk
Website www.peoplemanagement.co.uk
Editor *Steve Crabb*
Circulation 90,000

FORTNIGHTLY magazine on human resources, industrial relations, employment issues, etc. Welcomes submissions but apply for 'Guidelines for Contributors' in the first instance; approach in writing. **Features** *Jane Pickard* **News** *Jennie Walsh* **Law at Work** *Jill Evans.*

The People's Friend

80 Kingsway East, Dundee DD4 8SL
☎01382 462276/223131 Fax 01382 452491
Owner *D. C. Thomson & Co. Ltd*
Editor *Sinclair Matheson*
Circulation 412,570

The *Friend* is basically a fiction magazine, with two serials and several short stories each week. FOUNDED in 1869, it has always prided itself on providing 'a good read for all the family'. All stories should be about ordinary, identifiable characters with the kind of problems the average reader can understand and sympathise with. 'We look for the romantic and emotional developments of characters, rather than an over-complicated or contrived plot. We regularly use period serials and, occasionally, mystery/adventure.' Guidelines on request with s.a.e.
Short Stories Can vary in length from 1000 words or less to as many as 4000.
Serials Long-run serials of 10–15 instalments or more preferred. Occasionally shorter.
Articles Short fillers welcome.
Payment on acceptance.

Period Living & Traditional Homes

Endeavour House, 189 Shaftesbury Avenue, London WC2H 8JG
☎020 7208 3507 Fax 020 7208 3597
Owner *EMAP Elan Ltd*
Editor *Garry Mason*
Circulation 86,098

FOUNDED 1992. Formed from the merger of *Period Living* and *Traditional Homes*. Covers interior decoration in a period style, period house profiles, traditional crafts, renovation of period properties.
Features *Pamela Shipkey*
Payment varies according to length/type of article.

Personal

See under **National Newspapers (Sunday Mirror)**

Personal Finance

Arnold House, 36–41 Holywell Lane, London EC2A 3SF
☎020 7827 5454 Fax 020 7827 0567
Owner *Charterhouse Communications plc*
Editor *Juliet Oxborrow*
Circulation 50,000

ESTABLISHED 1994. MONTHLY finance magazine.
Features All issues relating to personal finance, particularly investment, insurance, banking, mortgages, savings, borrowing, health care and pensions. No corporate articles or personnel issues. Write to the editor with ideas in the first instance. No unsolicited mss. *Payment* £190 per 1000 words.
News All items written in-house.

The Philosopher

Centre for Lifelong Learning, Newcastle University, Newcastle upon Tyne NE1 7RU
Website www.philsoc.freeserve.co.uk
Owner *The Philosophical Society*
Editor *Martin Cohen*

FOUNDED 1913. BIANNUAL journal of the Philosophical Society of Great Britain with an international readership made up of members, libraries and specialist booksellers. Wide range of interests, but leaning towards articles that present philosophical investigation which is relevant to the individual and to society in our modern era. Accessible to the non-specialist. Will consider articles and book reviews. Notes for Contributors available; send s.a.e. or see website.
As well as short philosophical papers, will accept:
News about lectures, conventions, philosophy groups. Ethical issues in the news. Maximum 1000 words.
Reviews of philosophy books (maximum 600 words); discussion articles of individual philosophers and their published works (maximum 2000 words).
Miscellaneous items, including graphics, of philosophical interest and/or merit.
Payment free copies.

Piano

241 Shaftesbury Avenue, London WC2H 8EH
☎020 7333 1724 Fax 020 7333 1769
Owner *Rhinegold Publishing*
Editor *Jeremy Siepmann*
Deputy Editor *Matthew Peacock*

Circulation 11,000

FOUNDED 1993. BI-MONTHLY magazine containing features, profiles, technical information, news, reviews of interest to those with a serious amateur or professional concern with pianos or their playing. No unsolicited material. Approach with ideas in writing only.

Picture Postcard Monthly
15 Debdale Lane, Keyworth, Nottingham NG12 5HT
☎0115 9374079 Fax 0115 9376197
Email reflections@argonet.co.uk
Website www.postcard.co.uk/ppm

Owners *Brian & Mary Lund*
Editor *Brian Lund*
Circulation 4000

FOUNDED 1978. MONTHLY. News, views, clubs, diary of fairs, sales, auctions, and well-researched postcard-related articles. Might be interested in general articles supported by postcards. Unsolicited mss welcome. Approach by phone or in writing with ideas.

Pilot
The Clock House, 28 Old Town, Clapham, London SW4 0LB
☎020 7498 2506 Fax 020 7498 6920
Email pilotmagazine@compuserve.com
Website www.pilotweb.co.uk

Owner/Editor *James Gilbert*
Circulation 29,358

FOUNDED 1968. MONTHLY magazine for private plane pilots. No staff writers; the entire magazine is written by freelancers – mostly regulars. Unsolicited mss welcome but ideas in writing preferred. Perusal of any issue of the magazine will reveal the type of material bought. 700 words of 'Advice to would-be contributors' sent on receipt of s.a.e. (mark envelope 'Advice').

Features *James Gilbert* Many articles are unsolicited personal experiences/travel accounts from pilots of private planes; good photo coverage is very important. Maximum 5000 words. *Payment* £100–700 (first rights). Photos £26 each.

News *Mike Jerram* Contributions need to be as short as possible. See *Pilot Notes* in the magazine.

Pink Paper
72 Holloway Road, London N7 8NZ
☎020 7296 6210 Fax 020 7957 0046
Email editorial@pinkpaper.co.uk

Owner *Chronos Group*
Editor *Justin Webb*
Circulation 55,079

FOUNDED 1987. WEEKLY. Only national newspaper for lesbians and gay men covering politics, social issues, health, the arts and all areas of concern to lesbian/gay people. Unsolicited mss welcome. Initial approach by phone with an idea preferred. Interested in profiles, reviews, in-depth features and short news pieces.

News Maximum 300 words.
Payment by arrangement.

Planet: The Welsh Internationalist
See **Planet** under **Small Presses**

Plays and Players Applause
Northway House, 1379 High Road, London N20 9LP
☎020 8343 9977 Fax 020 8343 7831

Owner *Mineco Designs*
Editor *Sandra Rennie*
Circulation 10,000

Theatre MONTHLY which publishes a mixture of news, reviews, reports and features on all the performing arts. Rarely uses unsolicited material but writers of talent are taken up. Almost all material is commissioned.

PN Review
See under **Poetry Magazines**

Poetry Ireland Review
See under **Poetry Magazines**

Poetry Review
See under **Poetry Magazines**

Poetry Scotland
See under **Poetry Magazines**

Poetry Wales
See under **Poetry Magazines**

Ponies Today
TP Publications Ltd, Barn Acre House, Saxtead Green, Suffolk IP13 9QJ
☎01354 741538 Fax 01728 685842

Owner *Today Magazines*
Editor *Charlotte Jarvis*

FOUNDED 1998. Magazine for adults who ride, show, breed and drive ponies, with the emphasis on native ponies. All topics relating to ponies covered with the slant on ponies not horses. Veterinary, breeding and driving articles welcome. Prize pony spot. Length 500–100 words; photos welcomed (and returned). Send for free sample copy; phone/write with ideas.
Payment 'modest at present'.

Pony

D. J. Murphy (Publishers) Ltd, Haslemere House, Lower Street, Haslemere, Surrey GU27 2PE
☎01428 651551 Fax 01428 653888
Owner *D. J. Murphy (Publishers) Ltd*
Editor *Janet Rising*
Assistant Editor *Nicky Moffatt*
Circulation 32,309

FOUNDED 1948. Lively MONTHLY aimed at 10–16-year-olds. News, instruction on riding, stable management, veterinary care, interviews. Approach in writing with an idea.
 Features welcome. Maximum 900 words.
 News Written in-house. Photographs and illustrations (serious/cartoon) welcome.
 Payment £65 per 1000 words.

Popular Crafts

Azalea Drive, Swanley, Kent BR8 8HU
☎01322 660070 Fax 01322 616319
Owner *Nexus Special Interests*
Editor *Debbie Moss*
Circulation 32,000

FOUNDED 1980. MONTHLY. Covers crafts of all kinds. Freelance contributions welcome – copy needs to be lively and interesting. Approach in writing with an outline of idea and photographs.
 Features Project-based under the following headings: Homecraft; Needlecraft; Popular Craft; Kidscraft; News and Columns. Any craft-related material including projects to make, with full instructions/patterns supplied in all cases; profiles of crafts people and news of craft group activities or successes by individual persons; articles on collecting crafts; personal experiences and anecdotes. *Payment* on publication.

PR Week

174 Hammersmith Road, London W6 7JP
☎020 7413 4520 Fax 020 7413 4509
Owner *Haymarket Business Publications Ltd*
Editor *Kate Nicholas*
Circulation 17,000

FOUNDED 1984. WEEKLY. Contributions accepted from experienced journalists. Approach in writing with an idea.
 Features *Maja Pawinska*
 News *David McCormack*
 Payment negotiable.

Practical Boat Owner

Westover House, West Quay Road, Poole, Dorset BH15 1JG
☎01202 440820 Fax 01202 440860
Website www.ipc.co.uk/pubs/pracboat.htm

Owner *IPC Magazines Ltd*
Editor *Rodger Witt*
Circulation 54,819

FOUNDED 1967. MONTHLY magazine of practical information for cruising boat owners. Receives about 1500 mss per year. Interested in hard facts about gear, equipment, pilotage and renovation, etc. from experienced yachtsmen.
 Features Technical articles about maintenance, restoration, modifications to cruising boats, power and sail up to 45ft, or reader reports on gear and equipment. European pilotage articles and cruising guides. Approach in writing with synopsis in the first instance. *Payment* negotiable.

Practical Caravan

60 Waldegrave Road, Teddington, Middlesex TW11 8LG
☎020 8267 5629 Fax 020 8267 5725
Email practicalcaravan@dial.pipex.com
Owner *Haymarket Magazines Ltd*
Editor *John Evans*
Circulation 47,037

FOUNDED 1967. MONTHLY. Contains caravan reviews, travel features, investigations, products, park reviews. Unsolicited mss welcome on travel relevant only to caravanning/touring vans. No motorcaravan or static van stories. Approach with ideas by phone or letter.
 Features *Rob McCabe* Must refer to caravanning, towing. Written in friendly, chatty manner. Features with pictures/transparencies welcome but not essential. Maximum length 2000 words. *Payment* negotiable (usually £120 per 1000 words).

Practical Fishkeeping

Apex House, Oundle Road, Peterborough, Cambridgeshire PE2 9NP
☎01733 898100 Fax 01733 898487
Email steve.windsor@ecm.emap.com
Owner *EMAP Apex Publications Ltd*
Managing Editor *Steve Windsor*
Circulation 30,000

MONTHLY. Practical articles on all aspects of fishkeeping. Unsolicited mss welcome. Approach in writing with ideas. Quality photographs of fish always welcome. No fiction or verse.

Practical Gardening
See **Garden Answers**

Practical Parenting

King's Reach Tower, Stamford Street, London SE1 9LS
☎020 7261 5058 Fax 020 7261 6542

Website www.ipc.co.uk/pubs/pracpare.htm
Owner *IPC Magazines Ltd*
Editor-in-Chief *Jayne Marsden*
Circulation 82,000

FOUNDED 1987. MONTHLY. Practical advice on pregnancy, birth, babycare and childcare up to five years. Submit ideas in writing with synopsis or send mss on spec. Interested in feature articles of up to 3000 words in length, and in readers' experiences/personal viewpoint pieces of between 750–1000 words. All material must be written for the magazine's specifically targeted audience and in-house style.
Payment negotiable.

Practical Photography
Apex House, Oundle Road, Peterborough, Cambridgeshire PE2 9NP
☎01733 898100 Fax 01733 466843
Owner *EMAP Active Publications Ltd*
Editor *William Cheung*
Circulation 77,654

THIRTEEN ISSUES YEARLY All types of photography, particularly technique-orientated pictures. No unsolicited mss. Preliminary approach may be made by telephone. Always interested in new ideas.
Features Anything relevant to the world of photography, but not 'the sort of feature produced by staff writers'. Features on technology and humour are two areas worth exploring. Bear in mind that there is a three-month lead-in time. Maximum 2000 words.
News Only 'hot' news applicable to a monthly magazine. Maximum 400 words.
Payment varies.

Practical Wireless
Arrowsmith Court, Station Approach, Broadstone, Dorset BH18 8PW
☎01202 659910 Fax 01202 659950
Email <name>@pwpublishing.ltd.uk
Website www.pwpublishing.ltd.uk
Owner *P.W. Publishing*
Editor *Rob Mannion*
Circulation 27,000

FOUNDED 1932. MONTHLY. News and features relating to amateur radio, radio construction and radio communications. Unsolicited mss welcome. Author's guidelines available (send s.a.e.). Approach by phone with ideas in the first instance. Copy should be supported where possible by artwork, either illustrations, diagrams or photographs.
Payment £54–70 per page.

Practical Woodworking
Nexus Media, Nexus House, Azalea Drive, Swanley, Kent BR8 8HU
☎01322 660070 Fax 01332 667633
Owner *Nexus Media Ltd*
Editor *Mark Chisholm*

FOUNDED 1965. MONTHLY. Contains articles relating to woodworking – projects, techniques, new products, tips, letters, etc. Unsolicited mss welcome. No fiction. Approach with ideas in writing or by phone.
News Anything related to woodworking. *Payment* £60 per published page.
Features Projects, techniques, etc. *Payment* £60–75 per published page.

Prediction
Link House, Dingwall Avenue, Croydon, Surrey CR9 2TA
☎020 8686 2599 Fax 020 8781 6044
Email prediction@ipc.co.uk
Owner *IPC Magazines Ltd*
Editor *Jo Logan*
Circulation 35,000

FOUNDED 1936. MONTHLY. Covering astrology and occult-related topics. Unsolicited material in these areas welcome (about 200–300 mss received every year). Writers' guidelines available on request.
Astrology Pieces, of either 750 words or 1500–2000 words, depending on number of charts, should be practical and of general interest. Charts and astro data should accompany them, especially if profiles.
Features *Jo Logan* Articles on mysteries of the earth, alternative medicine, psychical/occult experiences and phenomena are considered. 800–2000 words. *Payment* £25–100 and over.
News & Views Items of interest to readership welcome. Maximum 300 words. *No payment.*

Pregnancy Magazine
WV Publications, 57–59 Rochester Place, London N1 9JY
☎020 7331 1000 Fax 020 7331 1241
Email danbrom@hotmail.com
Owner *Highbury House Communications*
Editor *Dan Bromage*

BI-MONTHLY magazine for mothers-to-be, giving them the facts they need for successful pregnancy and birth.

Press Gazette
Quantum House, 19 Scarbrook Road, Croydon, Surrey CR9 1LX
☎020 8565 4200 Fax 020 8565 4395

Email pged@qpp.co.uk
Owner *Quantum*
Editor *Philippa Kennedy*
Deputy Editor *Jon Slattery*
Circulation 9,500

WEEKLY magazine for all journalists – in regional and national newspapers, magazines, broadcasting, and on-line – containing news, features and analysis of all areas of journalism, print and broadcasting. Unsolicited mss welcome; interested in profiles of magazines, broadcasting companies and news agencies, personality profiles, technical and current affairs relating to the world of journalism. Approach with ideas by phone, e-mail, fax or in writing.

Pride
Hamilton House, 55 Battersea Bridge Road, London SW11 3AX
☎020 7228 3110 Fax 020 7228 3129
Website www.pridemagazine.com
Owner *Carl Cushnie Junior*
Editor *Dionne St Hill*
Circulation 36,000

FOUNDED 1991. MONTHLY lifestyle magazine for black women with features, beauty, arts and fashion. No unsolicited material; approach in writing with ideas.
    Features Issues pertaining to the black community. 'Ideas and solicited mss are welcomed from new freelancers.' Maximum 2000 words. *Payment £200.* **Fiction** Publishes the occasional short story. Unsolicited mss welcome. Maximum 3000 words. *No payment.* **Beauty** Freelancers used for short features. Maximum 1000 words. *Payment 10 pence per word.*

Prima
197 Marsh Wall, London E14 9SG
☎020 7519 5500 Fax 020 7519 5514
Owner *Gruner & Jahr (UK)*
Editor *Maire Fahey*
Circulation 421,412

FOUNDED 1986. MONTHLY women's magazine.
    Features Coordinator *Verity Watkins* Mostly practical and written by specialists, or commissioned from known freelancers. Unsolicited mss not welcome.

Private Eye
6 Carlisle Street, London W1V 5RG
☎020 7437 4017 Fax 020 7437 0705
Email strobes@private-eye.co.uk
Owner *Pressdram*

Editor *Ian Hislop*
Circulation 181,437

FOUNDED 1961. FORTNIGHTLY satirical and investigative magazine. Prospective contributors are best advised to approach the editor in writing. News stories and feature ideas are always welcome, as are cartoons. All jokes written in-house. *Payment* in all cases is 'not great', and length of piece varies as appropriate.

Prospect
4 Bedford Square, London WC1B 3RA
☎020 7255 1281 Fax 020 7255 1279
Email publishing@prospect-magazine.co.uk
Website www.prospect-magazine.co.uk
Owner *Prospect Publishing Limited*
Editor *David Goodhart*
Circulation 20,000

FOUNDED 1995. MONTHLY. Essays, reviews and research on current/international affairs and cultural issues. No news features. Unsolicited contributions welcome, although more useful to approach in writing with ideas.

Psychic News
The Coach House, Stansted Hall, Stansted, Essex CM24 8UD
☎01279 817050 Fax 01279 817051
Owner *Psychic Press 1995 Ltd*
Editor *Lyn Guest de Swarte*
Circulation 40,000

FOUNDED 1932. *Psychic News* is the world's only WEEKLY spiritualist newspaper. It covers subjects such as psychic research, hauntings, ghosts, poltergeists, spiritual healing, survival after death, and paranormal gifts. Unsolicited material considered.

Publishing News
39 Store Street, London WC1E 7DB
☎020 7692 2900 Fax 020 7419 2111
Email mailbox@publishingnews.co.uk
Website www.publishingnews.co.uk
Editor *Rodney Burbeck*

WEEKLY newspaper of the book trade. Hardback and paperback reviews and extensive listings of new paperbacks and hardbacks. Interviews with leading personalities in the trade, authors, agents and features on specialist book areas.

Punch
Trevor House, 100 Brompton Road, London SW3 1ER
☎020 7225 6716 Fax 020 7225 6766
Email edit@punch.co.uk

Website www.punch.co.uk
Owner *Liberty Publishing*
Editor *James Steen*

FOUNDED in 1841 and RELAUNCHED in 1996. BI-WEEKLY investigative and gossip magazine. Ideas are welcome; telephone in the first instance. *Payment* negotiable.

Q

Mappin House, 4 Winsley Street, London W1N 7AR
☎020 7436 1515 Fax 020 7312 8247
Website www.qonline.co.uk
Owner *EMAP Metro Publications*
Editor *Mat Toor*
Circulation 211,229

FOUNDED 1986. MONTHLY. Glossy aimed at educated popular music enthusiasts of all ages. Few opportunities for freelance writers. Unsolicited mss are strongly discouraged. Prospective contributors should approach in writing only.

Quartos Magazine
See **The New Writer**

QWF Magazine
PO Box 1768, Rugby CV21 4ZA
☎01788 334302 Fax 01788 334302

Editor *Jo Good*

BI-MONTHLY small press magazine. FOUNDED in 1994, as a showcase for the best in women's short story writing – original and thought-provoking. Only considers stories that are previously unpublished and of less than 4000 words; articles must be less than 1000 words and of interest to the writer. Include covering letter, s.a.e. and brief biography with mss. Also runs script appraisal service and regular short story competitions. For further information and detailed guidelines for contributors, contact the editor at the address above.

Racing Post (incorporating **The Sporting Life**)
1 Canada Square, Canary Wharf, London E14 5AP
☎020 7293 3000 Fax 020 7293 3758
Email editor@racingpost.co.uk
Website www.racingpost.co.uk
Owner *Trinity Mirror Plc*
Editor *Alan Byrne*

FOUNDED 1986. DAILY horse racing paper with some general sport. In 1998, following an agreement between the owners of *The Sporting Life* and the *Racing Post*, the two papers merged.

Radio Times
80 Wood Lane, London W12 0TT
☎020 8433 3400 Fax 020 8433 3160
Email radio.times@bbc.co.uk
Website www.radiotimes.com
Owner *BBC Worldwide Limited*
Editor *Sue Robinson*
Deputy Editor *Liz Vercoe*
Circulation 1.34 million

WEEKLY. UK's leading broadcast listings magazine. The majority of material is provided by freelance and retained writers, but the topicality of the pieces means close consultation with editors is essential. Very unlikely to use unsolicited material. Detailed BBC, ITV, Channel 4, Channel 5 and satellite television and radio listings are accompanied by feature material relevant to the week's output. *Payment* by arrangement.

RAIL
Apex House, Oundle Road, Peterborough, Cambridgeshire PE2 9NP
☎01733 898100 Fax 01733 466859
Owner *EMAP Active Ltd*
Managing Editor *Nigel Harris*
Circulation 33,811

FOUNDED 1981. FORTNIGHTLY magazine dedicated to modern railway. News and features, and topical newsworthy events. Unsolicited mss welcome. Approach by phone with ideas. Not interested in personal journey reminiscences. No fiction.

Features By arrangement with the editor. All modern railway British subjects considered. Max. 2000 words. *Payment* varies/negotiable.

News Items welcomed, max. 500 words. *Payment* varies up to £100 per 1000 words.

Railway Gazette International
Quadrant House, Sutton, Surrey SM2 5AS
☎020 8652 8608 Fax 020 8652 3738
Website www.railwaygazette.com
Owner *Reed Business Information*
Editor *Murray Hughes*

FOUNDED 1835. MONTHLY magazine written for senior railway managers and engineers worldwide. 'No material for railway enthusiast publications.' Telephone to discuss ideas in the first instance.

The Railway Magazine
King's Reach Tower, Stamford Street, London SE1 9LS
☎020 7261 5533/5821 Fax 020 7261 5269
Email railway@ipc.co.uk

Website www.ipc.co.uk/pubs/railway.htm
Owner *IPC Magazines Ltd*
Editor *Nick Pigott*
Circulation 33,132

FOUNDED 1897. MONTHLY. Articles, photos and short news stories of a topical nature, covering modern railways, steam preservation and railway history, welcome. Maximum 2000 words, with sketch maps of routes, etc., where appropriate. Unsolicited mss welcome.
Payment negotiable.

The Rambler
1–5 Wandsworth Road, London SW8 2XX
☎020 7339 8500 Fax 020 7339 8501
Email ramblers@london.ramblers.org.uk
Owner *Ramblers' Association*
Editor *Paul Rees*
Circulation 128,000

QUARTERLY. Official magazine of the Ramblers' Association, available to members only. Unsolicited mss welcome. S.a.e. required for return.

Features Freelance features are invited on any aspect of walking in Britain. Length 450–650 words, preferably with good photographs. No general travel articles.

Reader's Digest
11 Westferry Circus, Canary Wharf, London E14 4HE
☎020 7715 8000 Fax 020 7715 8716
Website www.readersdigest.co.uk
Owner *Reader's Digest Association Ltd*
Editor-in-Chief *Russell Twisk*
Circulation 1.14 million

In theory, a good market for general interest features of around 2500 words. However, 'a tiny proportion' comes from freelance writers, all of which are specially commissioned. Toughening up its image with a move into investigative journalism. Opportunities exist for short humorous contributions to regular features – 'Life's Like That', 'Humour in Uniform'. Issues a helpful booklet called 'Writing for Reader's Digest' available by post at £4.50.
Payment up to £200.

The Reader
English Department, University of Liverpool, Liverpool L69 7ZR
Email readers@thereader.co.uk
Editor *Jane Davis*
Circulation 1200

FOUNDED 1997. BIANNUAL. Poetry, short fiction, literary articles and essays, thought, reviews,

recommendations. Contributions from internationally lauded and new voices. Welcomes articles/essays about reading, maximum 2000 words. *Payment* up to £50. Recommendations for good reading, maximum 1000 words. *Payment* £30 approx. Short stories, maximum 2500 words. *Payment* £50 approx. No theoretical style literary discourses. Approach in writing.

Record Collector
43–45 St Mary's Road, Ealing, London W5 5RQ
☎020 8579 1082 Fax 020 8566 2024
Managing Editor *Johnny Dean*
Editor *Andy Davis*

FOUNDED 1979. MONTHLY. Detailed, well-researched articles welcome on any aspect of record collecting or any collectable artist in the field of popular music (1950s–1990s), with complete discographies where appropriate. Unsolicited mss welcome. Approach with ideas by phone. *Payment* negotiable.

Red
Endeavour House, 189 Shaftesbury Avenue, London WC2H 8JG
☎020 7437 9011 Fax 020 7208 3218
Email alison.williams@ecm.emap.com
Owner *EMAP Elan Publications*
Editor *Sally Brampton*
Circulation 180,403

FOUNDED 1998. MONTHLY magazine aimed at the 30-something woman. Will consider material sent in 'on spec' but tends to rely on regular contributors.

Report
ATL, 7 Northumberland Street, London WC2N 5DA
☎020 7930 6441 Fax 020 7925 0529
Owner *Association of Teachers and Lecturers*
Editor *Heather Pinnell*
Circulation 160,000

FOUNDED 1978. EIGHT ISSUES YEARLY during academic terms. Contributions welcome. All submissions should go directly to the editor. Articles should be no more than 800 words and must be of practical interest to the classroom teacher and F. E. lecturers.

Resident Abroad
4th Floor, 149 Tottenham Court Road, London W1P 9LL
☎020 7896 2500 Fax 020 7896 2229
Owner *Financial Times Business*

Editor *Cristina Nordenstahl*
Circulation 16,577

FOUNDED 1979. MONTHLY magazine aimed at British expatriates. Unsolicited mss considered, if suitable to the interests of the readership.

Features Up to 1200 words on finance, property, employment opportunities and other topics likely to appeal to readership, such as living conditions in countries with substantial British expatriate populations. No 'lighthearted looks' at anything.

Fiction Rarely published, but exceptional, relevant stories (max. 1000 words) might be considered.

Payment negotiable.

Riding

Suite D, Barber House, Storeys Bar Road, Fengate, Peterborough, Cambridgeshire PE1 5YS
☎01733 555830 Fax 01733 555831

Owner *GreenShires Creative Colour Ltd*
Editor *Steve Moore*

Aimed at an adult, horse-owning audience. Most of the writers on *Riding* are freelance. Emphasis on non-practical and lifestyle-orientated features. New and authoritative writers always welcome. *Payment* negotiable.

Right Now!

PO Box 2085, London W1A 5SX
☎020 8692 7099 Fax 020 8692 7099
Email rightnow@compuserve.com
Website www.right-now.org

Owner *Right Now!*
Editor *Derek Turner*
Circulation 2800

FOUNDED 1993. QUARTERLY right-wing conservative commentary. Welcomes well-documented disputations, news stories and elegiac features about British heritage ('the more politically incorrect, the better!'). No fiction and poems, although exceptions may be made. Initial pproach in writing. *No payment.*

Rugby News

7–9 Rathbone Street, London W1P 1AF
☎020 7323 1944 Fax 020 7323 1943

Owner *Independent Magazines Ltd*
Editor *Graeme Gillespie*
Circulation 44,000

FOUNDED 1987. Contains news, views and features on the UK and the world rugby scene, with special emphasis on clubs, schools, fitness and coaching. Welcomes unsolicited material.

Rugby World

23rd Floor, King's Reach Tower, Stamford Street, London SE1 9LS
☎020 7261 6830 Fax 020 7261 5419
Website www.rugbyworld.com

Owner *IPC Magazines Ltd*
Editor *Paul Morgan*
Circulation 38,500

FOUNDED 1960. MONTHLY. Features of special rugby interest only. Unsolicited contributions welcome but s.a.e. essential for return of material. Prior approach by phone or in writing preferred.

Runner's World

7–10 Chandos Street, London W1M 0AD
☎020 7291 6000 Fax 020 7291 6080
Email rwedit@rodale.co.uk
Website www.runnersworld.co.uk

Owner *Rodale Press*
Editor *Steven Seaton*
Circulation 48,334

FOUNDED 1979. MONTHLY magazine giving practical advice on all areas of distance running including products and training, travel features, up-to-date athlete profiles and news. Personal running-related articles, famous people who run or off-beat travel articles are welcome. No elite athlete or training articles. Approach with ideas in writing in the first instance.

Running Fitness

Apex House, Oundle Road, Peterborough, Cambridgeshire PE2 9NP
☎01733 898100 Fax 01733 466859

Owner *EMAP Active Ltd*
Editor *Paul Larkins*
Circulation 26,075

FOUNDED 1985. MONTHLY. Instructional articles on running, fitness, and lifestyle, plus running-related activities and health.

Features Specialist knowledge an advantage. Opportunities are wide, but approach with ideas in first instance.

News Opportunities for people stories, especially if backed up by photographs.

Safeway Magazine

Redwood Publishing, 7 Saint Martin's Place, London WC2N 4HA
☎020 7747 0788 Fax 020 7747 0799

Editor *Julie Breck*

FOUNDED 1996. MONTHLY in-store magazine covering food and recipes, beauty, health, family life and ABC cardholder products. Regular freelancers are employed and although outside material is rarely used ideas will be considered for beauty, health, family life and humorous columns. Approach in writing in the first instance.

Saga Magazine
The Saga Building, Middelburg Square, Folkestone, Kent CT20 1AZ
☎01303 771523 Fax 01303 776699

Owner *Saga Publishing Ltd*
Editor *Paul Bach*
Circulation 1.02 million

FOUNDED 1984. MONTHLY. 'Saga Magazine sets out to celebrate the role of older people in society. It reflects their achievements, promotes their skills, protects their interests, and campaigns on their behalf. A warm personal approach, addressing the readership in an up-beat and positive manner, required.' It has a hard core of celebrated commentators/writers (e.g. Clement Freud, Keith Waterhouse) as regular contributors. Articles mostly commissioned or written in-house but exclusive celebrity interviews welcome if appropriate/relevant. Length 1000–1200 words (maximum 1600).

Sailing Today
30 Monmouth Street, Bath BA1 2BW
☎01225 442244 Fax 01225 732248
Email sailingtoday@futurenet.co.uk

Owner *Future Publishing*
Editor *John Kendall*
Deputy Editor *Rupert Holmes*
Development Editor *Keith Colwell*

FOUNDED 1997. MONTHLY practical magazine for cruising sailors. *Sailing Today* covers owning and buying a boat, equipment and products for sailing and is about improving readers' skills, boat maintenance and product tests. Most articles are commissioned but will consider practical features and cruise stories with photos. Approach by telephone or in writing in the first instance.

Sailing with Spirit
4 South View, Nether Heyford, Northampton NN7 3NH
☎01327 342566
Email tigger@gn.apc.org
Website www.gn.apc.org/tigger/sws.htm

Editor *Keith Beasley*
Circulation 2000

FOUNDED 1986. QUARTERLY holistic magazine for Northamptonshire. Contributors must have local connections and expertise or first-hand experience in matters spiritual, organic or 'green'.

Sainsbury's The Magazine
20 Upper Ground, London SE1 9PD
☎020 7633 0266 Fax 020 7401 9423

Owner *New Crane Publishing*
Editor *Michael Wynn Jones*
Consultant Food Editor *Delia Smith*
Circulation 382,386

FOUNDED 1993. MONTHLY featuring a main core of food and cookery, features, health, beauty, fashion, home, gardening and news. No unsolicited mss. Approach in writing with ideas only in the first instance.

The Salisbury Review
33 Canonbury Park South, London N1 2JW
☎020 7226 7791 Fax 020 7354 0383
Email salisbury-review@easynet.co.uk
Website easyweb.easynet.co.uk/ ~salisbury-review

Editor *Roger Scruton*
Managing Editor *Merrie Cave*
Circulation 1700

FOUNDED 1982. QUARTERLY magazine of conservative thought. Editorials and features from a right-wing viewpoint. Unsolicited material welcome.
  Features Maximum 4000 words.
  Reviews Maximum 1000 words.
  No payment.

Sci-Fright
Springbeach Press, 11 Vernon Close, Eastbourne, East Sussex BN23 6AN
Email sian@springbeachpress.freeserve.co.uk
Owner *Springbeach Press*
Editor *Sian Ross*

FOUNDED 1999. BIANNUAL magazine with fiction, features and some poetry in the following genres: science fiction, horror, fantasy, humour. No mainstream. Interested in fiction, features poetry and b&w artwork. No poems over 40 lines, colour artwork or 'tea-break' fiction. Write or e-mail with ideas; no submissions by e-mail.
  Payment copy of magazine.

Scotland on Sunday Magazine
See under **National Newspapers (Scotland on Sunday)**

The Scots Magazine
2 Albert Square, Dundee DD1 9QJ
☎01382 223131 Fax 01382 322214
Owner *D. C. Thomson & Co. Ltd*

Editor *John Methven*
Circulation 60,000

FOUNDED 1739. MONTHLY. Covers a wide field of Scottish interests ranging from personalities to wildlife, climbing, reminiscence, history and folklore. Outside contributions welcome; 'staff delighted to discuss in advance by letter'.

The Scottish Farmer

Caledonian Magazines Ltd, 6th Floor, 195 Albion Street, Glasgow G1 1QQ
☎0141 302 7700 Fax 0141 302 7799
Email info@calmags.co.uk *or* farmer@calmags.co.uk

Owner *Caledonian Magazines Ltd*
Editor *Alasdair Fletcher*
Circulation 22,000

FOUNDED 1893. WEEKLY. Farmer's magazine covering most aspects of Scottish agriculture. Unsolicited mss welcome. Approach with ideas in writing.

Features *Alasdair Fletcher* Technical articles on agriculture or farming units. 1000–2000 words.

News *John Duckworth* Factual news about farming developments, political, personal and technological. Maximum 800 words.

Weekend Family Pages Rural and craft topics.

Scottish Field

Special Publications, Royston House, Caroline Park, Edinburgh EH5 1QJ
☎0131 551 2942 Fax 0131 551 2938
Owner *Oban Times*
Editor *Archie Mackenzie*

FOUNDED 1903. MONTHLY. Scotland's quality lifestyle magazine. Unsolicited mss welcome but writers should study the magazine first.

Features Articles of general interest on Scotland and Scots abroad with good photographs or, preferably, colour slides. Approx 1000 words.

Payment negotiable.

Scottish Golfer

c/o The Scottish Golf Union, Drumoig, Leuchars, St Andrews, Fife KY16 0BE
☎01382 549500 Fax 01382 549510

Owner *Scottish Golf Union*
Editor *Martin Dempster*
Circulation 30,000

FOUNDED mid-1980s. MONTHLY. Features and results, in particular the men's events. No unsolicited mss. Approach in writing with ideas.

Scottish Home & Country

42A Heriot Row, Edinburgh EH3 6ES
☎0131 225 1724 Fax 0131 225 8129

Owner *Scottish Women's Rural Institutes*
Editor *Airlie Fleming*
Circulation 12,000

FOUNDED 1924. MONTHLY. Scottish or rural-related issues. Unsolicited mss welcome but reading time may be from 1–2 months. Commissions are rare and tend to go to established contributors only.

Scottish Rugby Magazine

First Press Publishing, Seventh Floor, 40 Anderston Quay, Glasgow G3 8DA
☎0141 242 1400 Fax 0141 242 1430

Editor *David Ferguson*
Circulation 19,200

FOUNDED 1990. MONTHLY. Features, club profiles, etc. Approach in writing with ideas.

Scouting Magazine

Baden Powell House, Queen's Gate, London SW7 5JS
☎020 7584 7030 Fax 020 7590 5124

Owner *The Scout Association*
Editor *Ron Crabb*
Circulation 30,000

MONTHLY magazine for adults connected to or interested in the Scouting movement. Interested in Scouting-related features only. No fiction. *Payment* by negotiation.

Screen

Gilmorehill Centre for Theatre, Film and Television, University of Glasgow, Glasgow G12 8QQ
☎0141 330 5035 Fax 0141 330 3515
Email screen@arts.gla.ac.uk

Publisher *Oxford University Press*
Editors *Annette Kuhn, John Caughie, Simon Frith, Norman King, Karen Lury, Jackie Stacey*
Editorial Assistant *Caroline Beven*
Circulation 1400

QUARTERLY refereed academic journal of film and television studies for a readership ranging from undergraduates to screen studies academics and media professionals. There are no specific qualifications for acceptance of articles. Straightforward film reviews are not normally published. Check the magazine's style and market in the first instance.

Screen International

33–39 Bowling Green Lane, London
EC1R 0DA
☎020 7505 8056 Fax 020 7505 8102
Owner *EMAP Business Communications*
Managing Editor *Leo barraclough*

International trade paper of the film, video and television industries. Expert freelance writers are occasionally used in all areas. No unsolicited mss. Approach with ideas in writing.
Features *Louise Tutt*
Payment negotiable on NUJ basis.

Sea Breezes

Units 28–30, Spring Valley Industrial Estate, Braddan, Isle of Man IM2 2QS
☎01624 626018 Fax 01624 661655
Owner *Print Centres*
Editor *Captain A. C. Douglas*
Circulation 15,000

FOUNDED 1919. MONTHLY. Covers virtually everything relating to ships and seamen. Unsolicited mss welcome; they should be thoroughly researched and accompanied by relevant photographs. No fiction, poetry, or anything which 'smacks of the romance of the sea'.
Features Factual tales of ships, seamen and the sea, Royal or Merchant Navy, sail or power, nautical history, shipping company histories, epic voyages, etc. 1000–4000 words. 'The most readily acceptable work will be that which shows it is clearly the result of first-hand experience or the product of extensive and accurate research.'
Payment £14 per page (about 800 words).

She Magazine

National Magazine House, 72 Broadwick Street, London W1V 2BP
☎020 7439 5000 Fax 020 7312 3981
Owner *National Magazine Co. Ltd*
Editor *Alison Pylkkanen*
Circulation 226,086

Glossy MONTHLY for the thirtysomething woman, addressing her needs as an individual, a partner and a parent. Talks to its readers in an intelligent, humorous and sympathetic way. Features should be about 1500 words long. Approach with ideas in writing. No unsolicited material. *Payment* NUJ rates.

Ships Monthly

IPC Country & Leisure Media Ltd, 222 Branston Road, Burton-upon-Trent, Staffordshire DE14 3BT
☎01283 542721 Fax 01283 546436
Email ShipsMonthly@compuserve.com
Owner *IPC Country & Leisure Media Ltd*
Editor *Iain Wakefield*
Circulation 22,000

FOUNDED 1966. MONTHLY magazine for ship enthusiasts. News, photographs and illustrated articles on all kinds of ships – mercantile and naval, sail and steam, past and present. No yachting. Most articles are commissioned; prospective contributors should telephone in the first instance.

Shoot Magazine

King's Reach Tower, Stamford Street, London SE1 9LS
☎020 7261 6287 Fax 020 7261 6019
Owner *IPC Magazines Ltd*
Editor *Andy Winter*
Circulation 71,352

FOUNDED 1969. WEEKLY football magazine. No unsolicited mss. Present ideas for news, features or colour photo-features to the editor by telephone.
Features Hard-hitting, topical and off-beat.
News Items welcome, especially exclusive gossip and transfer speculation. @para:*Payment* negotiable.

Shooting and Conservation (BASC)

Marford Mill, Rossett, Wrexham, Clwyd LL12 0HL
☎01244 573000 Fax 01244 573001
Owner *The British Association for Shooting and Conservation (BASC)*
Editor *Jeffrey Olstead*
Circulation 120,000

FOUR ISSUES PER YEAR. Good articles and stories on shooting, conservation and related areas are always sought although most material is produced in-house. Maximum 1500 words.
Payment negotiable.

Shooting Times & Country Magazine

King's Reach Tower, Stamford Street, London SE1 9LS
☎020 7261 6180 Fax 020 7261 7179
Owner *IPC Magazines Ltd*
Editor *Mark Hedges*
Circulation 27,435

FOUNDED 1882. WEEKLY. Covers shooting, fishing and related countryside topics. Unsolicited mss considered. *Payment* negotiable.

Shout Magazine

D. C. Thomson & Co., Albert Square, Dundee, Tayside DD1 9QJ
☎01382 223131 Fax 01382 200880
Email shout@dcthomson.co.uk
Owner *D. C. Thomson Publishers*
Editor *Maria T. Welch*
Circulation 126,794

FOUNDED 1993. FORTNIGHTLY Pop music, quizzes, beauty, fashion, soap features, emotional. Welcomes ideas for fiction, horoscope features and quizzes. Queries by telephone welcome.

Features *Lesley Macpherson* Write with ideas. Max. 1500 words. *Payment* varies.

Fiction *Maria Welch* Supernatural/spooky stories welcome. Max. 1500 words. *Payment* £100.

Shout!

PO Box YR46, Leeds, West Yorkshire LS9 6XG
☎0113 2485700 Fax 0113 2956097
Email editor@shoutmag.demon.co.uk
Website www.shoutmag.demon.co.uk
Owner/Editor *Mark Michalowski*
Circulation 7000

FOUNDED 1995. MONTHLY lesbian/gay and bisexual news, views, arts and scene for Yorkshire; lgb health and politics. Interested in reviews of Yorkshire lgb events, happenings, news, analysis – 300 to maximum 1000 words. No fiction, fashion or items with no reasonable relevance to Yorkshire and the north.

Payment £30 per 1000 words.

Shropshire Magazine

77 Wyle Cop, Shrewsbury, Shropshire SY1 1UT
☎01743 362175
Owner *Shropshire Newspapers Ltd*
Editor *Keith Parker*

FOUNDED 1950. MONTHLY. Unsolicited mss welcome but ideas in writing preferred.

Features Personalities, topical items, historical (e.g. family) of Shropshire; also general interest: homes, weddings, antiques, etc. Maximum 1000 words.

Payment negotiable 'but modest'.

Sight & Sound

British Film Institute, 21 Stephen Street, London W1P 2LN
☎020 7255 1444 Fax 020 7436 2327
Website www.bfi.org.uk/s&s/

Owner *British Film Institute*
Editor *Nick James*

FOUNDED 1932. MONTHLY. Topical and critical articles on international cinema, with regular columns from the USA and Europe. Length 1000–5000 words. Relevant photographs appreciated. Also book, film and video release reviews. Unsolicited material welcome. Approach in writing with ideas. *Payment* by arrangement.

The Sign

See **Hymns Ancient & Modern Ltd** under **UK Publishers**

Ski and Board

The White House, 57–63 Church Road, Wimbledon, London SW19 5SB
☎020 8410 2000 Fax 020 8410 2001
Email s&b@skiclub.co.uk
Website www.skiclub.co.uk
Owner *Ski Club of Great Britain*
Editor *Gill Williams*
Circulation 19,675

FOUNDED 1903. FOUR ISSUES YEARLY. Features from established ski/snowboard writers only.

The Skier and Snowboarder Magazine

1st Floor, Squires House, 205 High Street, West Wickham, Kent BR4 0PH
☎020 8777 4426 Fax 020 8777 8789
Owner *Mountain Marketing Ltd*
Editor *Frank Baldwin*
Circulation 20,000

Official magazine to the World Ski and Snowboard Association, UK. SEASONAL. From September to May. FIVE ISSUES YEARLY. Outside contributions welcome.

Features Various topics covered, including race reports, resort reports, fashion, equipment update, dry slope, school news, new products, health and safety. Crisp, tight, informative copy of 1000 words or less preferred.

News All aspects of skiing news covered. *Payment* negotiable.

Slimming

Endeavour House, 189 Shaftesbury Avenue, London WC2H 8JG
☎020 7437 9011 Fax 020 7434 0656
Owner *EMAP Elan Publications*
Editor *Juliette Kellow*
Circulation 106,029

FOUNDED 1969. ELEVEN ISSUES YEARLY. Leading magazine about slimming, diet and health.

Opportunities for freelance contributions on general health (diet-related); psychology related to health and fitness; celebrity interviews. It is best to approach with an idea in writing. *Payment* negotiable.

Smallholder

Hook House, Wimblington March, Cambridgeshire PE15 0QL
☎01354 741182 Fax 01354 741182
Owner *News Com*
Editor *Liz Wright*
Circulation 20,000

FOUNDED 1982. MONTHLY. Outside contributions welcome. Send for sample magazine and editorial schedule before submitting anything. Follow up with samples of work to the editor so that style can be assessed for suitability. No poetry or humorous but unfocused personal tales.

Features New writers always welcome, but must have high level of technical expertise – 'not textbook stuff'. Illustrations and photos welcomed and paid for. 750–1500 words.

News All agricultural and rural news welcome. Length 200–500 words.

Payment negotiable ('but modest').

Smash Hits

Mappin House, Winsley Street, London W1N 7AR
☎020 7436 1515 Fax 020 7636 5792
Owner *EMAP Metro Publications*
Editor *John McKie*
Circulation 241,530

FOUNDED 1979. FORTNIGHTLY. Top of the mid-teen market. Unsolicited mss are not accepted, but prospective contributors may approach in writing with ideas.

Snooker Scene

Cavalier House, 202 Hagley Road, Edgbaston, Birmingham B16 9PQ
☎0121 454 2931 Fax 0121 452 1822
Owner *Everton's News Agency*
Editor *Clive Everton*
Circulation 16,000

FOUNDED 1971. MONTHLY. No unsolicited mss. Approach in writing with an idea.

Somerset Magazine

23 Market Street, Crewkerne, Somerset TA18 7JU
☎01460 270000 Fax 01460 270022
Owner *Smart Print Publications Ltd*

Editor *Roy Smart*
Circulation 9000

FOUNDED 1991. MONTHLY magazine with features on any subject of interest (historical, geographical, arts, crafts) to people living in Somerset. Length 1000–1500 words, preferably with illustrations. Unsolicited mss welcome but initial approach in writing preferred. *Payment* negotiable.

The Spectator

56 Doughty Street, London WC1N 2LL
☎020 7405 1706 Fax 020 7242 0603
Email editor@spectator.co.uk
Website www.spectator.co.uk
Owner *The Spectator (1828) Ltd*
Editor *Boris Johnson*
Managing Editor *Stuart Reid*
Circulation 56,705

FOUNDED 1828. WEEKLY political and literary magazine. Prospective contributors should write in the first instance to the relevant editor. Unsolicited mss welcome, but no 'follow up' phone calls, please.

Books *Mark Amory*

Payment nominal.

The Sporting Life

See **Racing Post**

Springboard – Writing To Succeed

30 Orange Hill Road, Prestwich, Manchester M25 1LS
☎0161 773 5911
Email leobrooks@rammy.com
Owner/Editor *Leo Brooks*
Circulation 200

FOUNDED 1990. QUARTERLY. *Springboard* is not a market for writers but a forum from which they can find encouragement and help. Provides articles, news, market information, competition/folio news directed at helping writers to achieve success. Free to subscribers: a copy of *The Curate's Egg* – a collection of poetry submitted.

The Squash Times

PO Box 3250, Wokingham, Berkshire RG40 4FR
☎0118 9737744
Editor *Mr R. Richardson*

FOUNDED 1980. QUARTERLY. Events, players, news, fashion and footwear, rackets, facilities, technique and tactics.

Staffordshire Life

The Publishing Centre, Derby Street, Stafford
ST16 2DT
☎01785 257700 Fax 01785 253287
Email editor@stafforshirelife.co.uk
Owner *The Staffordshire Newsletter*
Editor *Philip Thurlow-Craig*
Circulation 20,000

FOUNDED 1982. TEN ISSUES YEARLY. Full-
colour county magazine devoted to Staffordshire, its surroundings and people. Contributions
welcome. Approach in writing with ideas.
   Features Maximum 1200 words.
   Fashion Copy must be supported by photographs.
   Payment NUJ rates.

The Stage (incorporating Television Today)

47 Bermondsey Street, London SE1 3XT
☎020 7403 1818 Fax 020 7357 9287
Email info@thestage.co.uk
Website www.thestage.co.uk
Owner *The Stage Newspaper Ltd*
Editor *Brian Attwood*
Circulation 41,190

FOUNDED 1880. WEEKLY. No unsolicited mss.
Prospective contributors should write with ideas
in the first instance.
   Features Preference for middle-market,
tabloid-style articles. 'Puff pieces', PR plugs and
extended production notes will not be considered. Maximum 800 words.
   News News stories from outside London
are always welcome. Maximum 300 words.
   Payment £100 per 1000 words.

Stamp Magazine

Link House, Dingwall Avenue, Croydon
CR9 2TA
☎020 8774 0772 Fax 020 8781 6044
Email stampmagazine@ipc.co.uk
Owner *IPC Magazines Ltd*
Editor *Steve Fairclough*
Circulation 12,000

FOUNDED 1934. MONTHLY news and features
on the world of stamp collecting from the past to
the present day. Interested in articles by experts
on particular countries or themes such as subject
matter illustrated on stamps – dogs, politics, etc.
Approach in writing.
   News *Kevin Molloy* News of latest stamp
issues or industry news. Maximum 500 words.

   Features *Steve Fairclough* Any features welcome on famous stamps, rarities, postmarks,
postal history, exhibitions, postcards, personal
collections, auctions. Must be illustrated with
colour images ('we can arrange for photography
of original stamps'). Maximum 2500 words, or
5000 for 2-part expert piece.
   Payment negotiable.

Stand Magazine

See under **Poetry Magazines**

Staple New Writing

See under **Poetry Magazines**

The Strad

7 St. John's Road, Harrow, Middlesex
HA1 2EE
☎020 8863 2020 Fax 020 8863 2444
Email thestrad@orpheuspublications.com
Website www.thestrad.com
Owner *Orpheus Publications Ltd*
Editor *Joanna Pieters*
Circulation 17,000

FOUNDED 1890. MONTHLY for classical string
musicians, makers and enthusiasts. Unsolicited
mss welcome 'though acknowledgement/return
not guaranteed'.
   Features Profiles of string players, teachers,
luthiers and musical instruments, also relevant
research. Maximum 2000 words.
   Reviews *Naomi Sadler, Peter Quantrill.*
   Payment £100 per 1000 words.

Suffolk and Norfolk Life

Barn Acre House, Saxtead Green, Suffolk
IP13 9QJ
☎01728 685832 Fax 01728 685842
Owner *Today Magazines Ltd*
Editor *Kevin Davis*
Circulation 17,000

FOUNDED 1989. MONTHLY. General interest,
local stories, historical, personalities, wine, travel,
food. Unsolicited mss welcome. Approach by
phone or in writing with ideas. Not interested in
anything which does not relate specifically to
East Anglia.
   Features *Kevin Davis* Maximum 1500 words,
with photos.
   News *Kevin Davis* Maximum 1000 words,
with photos.
   Special Pages *William Locks* Study the magazine for guidelines. Maximum 1500 words.
   Payment £25 (news); £30 (other).

Sugar Magazine

17 Berners Street, London W1P 3DD
☎020 7664 6440 Fax 020 7636 5055
Editor *Sarah Pyper*
Editorial Director *Lysanne Sampson*
Circulation 430,217

FOUNDED 1994. MONTHLY. Everything that might interest the teenage girl. No unsolicited mss. Will consider ideas or contacts for real-life features. No fiction. Approach in writing in the first instance.

Sunday Post Magazine

See under **National Newspapers (Sunday Post, Dundee)**

Sunday Times Magazine

See under **National Newspapers (The Sunday Times)**

Superbike Magazine

Link House, Dingwall Avenue, Croydon, Surrey CR9 2TA
☎020 8686 2599 Fax 020 8781 1164
Publisher *Grant Leonard*
Editor *John Cantlie*
Circulation 70,483

FOUNDED 1977. MONTHLY. Dedicated to all that is best and most exciting in the world of high-performance motorcycling. Unsolicited mss, synopses and ideas welcome.

Surrey County

Datateam Publishing Ltd, London Road, Maidstone, Kent ME15 8LY
☎01622 687031 Fax 01622 757646
Owner *Datateam Publishing Ltd*
Editor *Roderick Cooper*
Circulation 10,000

FOUNDED 1970. MONTHLY. Strong Surrey interest plus fashion, food, books, wildlife, motoring, property, sport, interiors with local links. Unsolicited mss welcome. Interested in anything with a genuine Surrey connection. No fiction or non-Surrey subjects. Approach in writing with ideas. Maximum length 1500 words. *Payment* negotiable.

Sussex Life

Baskerville Place, 28 Teville Road, Worthing, West Sussex BN11 1UG
☎01903 218719 Fax 01903 820193
Owner *Sussex Life Ltd*
Editor *Trudi Linscer*
Circulation 70,000

FOUNDED 1965. MONTHLY. Sussex and general interest magazine. Regular supplements on education, fashion, homes and gardens. Interested in investigative, journalistic pieces relevant to the area and celebrity profiles. Unsolicited mss, synopses and ideas in writing welcome. Min. 500 words. *Payment* £15 per 500 words and picture.

Swimming Times

14 Granby Street, Loughborough, Leicestershire LE11 3DU
☎01509 632207 Fax 01509 632213
Owner *Amateur Swimming Association*
Editor *P. Hassall*
Circulation 20,000

FOUNDED 1923. MONTHLY about competitive swimming and associated subjects. Unsolicited mss welcome.
  Features Technical articles on swimming, water polo, diving or synchronised swimming. Length and payment negotiable.

The Tablet

1 King Street Cloisters, Clifton Walk, London W6 0QZ
☎020 8748 8484 Fax 020 8748 1550
Email thetablet@tablet.co.uk
Owner *The Tablet Publishing Co Ltd*
Editor *John Wilkins*
Circulation 20,488

FOUNDED 1840. WEEKLY. Quality international Roman Catholic magazine featuring articles – political, social, cultural, theological or spiritual – of interest to concerned Christian laity and clergy. Unsolicited material welcome (1500 words) if relevant to magazine's style and market. All approaches should be made in writing.
  Payment from about £75.

Take a Break

Shirley House, 25–27 Camden Road, London NW1 9LL
☎020 7241 8000
Owner *H. Bauer*
Editor *John Dale*
Circulation 1.23 million

FOUNDED 1990. WEEKLY. True-life feature magazine. Approach with ideas in writing.
  News/Features Always on the look-out for good, true-life stories. Maximum 1200 words. *Payment* negotiable.
  Fiction Sharp, succinct stories which are well told and often with a twist at the end. All categories, provided it is relevant to the magazine's style and market. Maximum 1000 words. *Payment* negotiable.

Tatler

Vogue House, Hanover Square, London
W1R 0AD
☎020 7499 9080 Fax 020 7409 0451
Website www.tatler.co.uk

Owner *Condé Nast Publications Ltd*
Editor *Geordie Greig*
Circulation 85,185

Up-market glossy from the Condé Nast stable.
New writers should send in copies of either
published work or unpublished material; writers of promise will be taken up. The magazine
works largely on a commission basis: they are
unlikely to publish unsolicited features, but will
ask writers to work to specific projects.

Features *Lucy Yeomans*

Telegraph Magazine

See under **National Newspapers (The
Daily Telegraph)**

The Tennis Times

PO Box 3250, Wokingham, Berkshire
RG40 4FR
☎0118 9737744

Editor *Mr R. Richardson*

FOUNDED 1980. QUARTERLY. Events, players,
news, fashion and footwear, rackets, facilities,
technique and tactics.

TGO (The Great Outdoors)

195 Albion Street, Glasgow G1 1QP
☎0141 302 7700 Fax 0141 302 7799

Owner *Caledonian Magazines Ltd*
Editor *Cameron McNeish*
Circulation 22,000

FOUNDED 1978. MONTHLY. Deals with walking, backpacking and wild country topics.
Unsolicited mss are welcome.

Features Well-written and illustrated items
on relevant topics. Maximum 2500 words.
Colour photographs only, please.

News Short topical items (or photographs).
Maximum 300 words.

*Payment £200–300 for features; £10–20 for
news.*

that's life!

2nd Floor, 1–5 Maple Place, London W1P 5FX
☎020 7462 4700 Fax 020 7462 4741

Owner *H. Bauer Publishing Ltd*
Editor *Janice Turner*
Circulation 526,845

FOUNDED 1995. WEEKLY. True-life stories, puzzles, health, homes, parenting, cookery and fun.

Features *Karen Jones* Maximum 1600 words.
Payment £650.

Fiction *Emma Fabian* 1200 words. *Payment
£200–300.*

Theologia Cambrensis

Church in Wales Centre, Woodland Place,
Penarth, Cardiff CF64 2YQ
☎029 2070 5278 Fax 029 2071 2413

Owner *The Church in Wales*
Editor *Rev. Gareth Williams*

FOUNDED 1988. THRICE YEARLY. Concerned
exclusively with theology and news of theological interest. Includes religious poetry, letters and
book reviews (provided they have a scholarly
bias). No secular material. Unsolicited mss welcome. Approach in writing with ideas.

The Third Alternative

5 Martins Lane, Witcham, Ely,
Cambridgeshire CB6 2LB
☎01353 777931
Email ttapress@aol.com
Website www.tta-press.freewire.co.uk

Owner *TTA Press*
Editor *Andy Cox*

FOUNDED 1993. Quarterly A4 colour magazine
of horror, fantasy, science fiction and slipstream
fiction, plus interviews, profiles, comment, cinema and artwork. Publishes talented newcomers
alongside famous authors. Unsolicited mss welcome if accompanied by s.a.e. or International
Reply Coupons (no length restriction, but no
novels or serialisations). Queries and letters welcome via e-mail but submissions as hard copy
only. Potential contributors are advised to study
the magazine. Contracts are exchanged upon
acceptance; payment is upon publication.
Winner of several British Fantasy Awards. The
magazine is supported by **Eastern Arts** and the
Arts Council of England.

This England

PO Box 52, Cheltenham, Gloucestershire
GL50 1YQ
☎01242 577775 Fax 01242 222034

Owner *This England Ltd*
Editor *Roy Faiers*
Circulation 200,000

FOUNDED 1968. QUARTERLY, with a strong
overseas readership. Celebration of England and
all things English: famous people, natural
beauty, towns and villages, history, traditions,
customs and legends, crafts, etc. Generally a

rural basis, with the 'Forgetmenots' section publishing readers' recollections and nostalgia. Up to one hundred unsolicited pieces received each week. Unsolicited mss/ideas welcome. Length 250–2000 words. *Payment £25 per 1000 words.*

Time

Brettenham House, Lancaster Place, London WC2E 7TL
☎020 7499 4080 Fax 020 7322 1259
Owner *Time Warner, Inc.*
Editor (Europe, Middle East, Africa)
Christopher Redman
Circulation 5.46 million
FOUNDED 1923. WEEKLY current affairs and news magazine. There are few opportunities for freelancers on *Time* as almost all the magazine's content is written by staff members from various bureaux around the world. No unsolicited mss.

Time Out

Universal House, 251 Tottenham Court Road, London W1P 0AB
☎020 7813 3000 Fax 020 7813 6001
Website www.timeout.com
Publisher *Tony Elliott*
Editor *Laura Lee Davies*
Circulation 98,839
FOUNDED 1968. WEEKLY magazine of news and entertainment in London.
Features *Chris Hemblade* 'Usually written by staff writers or commissioned, but it's always worth submitting an idea by phone if particularly apt to the magazine.' Maximum 2500 words.
News *Ruth Bloomfield* Despite having a permanent team of staff news writers, sometimes willing to accept contributions from new journalists 'should their material be relevant to the issue'.
Payment £164 per 1000 words.

The Times Educational Supplement

Admiral House, 66–68 East Smithfield, London E1 9XY
☎020 7782 3000 Fax 020 7782 3200
Email editor@tes.co.uk *or* copy@tes.co.uk
Website www.tes.co.uk
Owner *News International*
Editor *Caroline St John-Brooks*
Circulation 141,779
FOUNDED 1910. WEEKLY. New contributors are welcome and should fax ideas on one sheet

of A4 for news, features or reviews.
Opinion *Caroline St John-Brooks, Jeremy Sutcliffe* 'Platform': a weekly slot for a well-informed and cogently argued viewpoint. Max. 1200 words. 'Another Voice': a shorter comment on an issue of the day by non-education professionals. Maximum 700 words.
School Management *Neil Levis*/**Governors** *Karen Thornton* Weekly pages on practical issues for school governors and managers. Maximum 800 words.
Research Focus *David Budge*
Further Education *Ian Nash* Includes training, college management and lifelong learning.
Friday A weekly magazine with *The TES* which includes: **Features** *Sarah Bayliss* Unsolicited features are rarely accepted but ideas are welcome accompanied by cuttings and/or c.v. Length 1000–2000 words. **Arts and Books** *Heather Neill* **Curriculum Materials** *Mary Cruickshank* **Talkback** *Jill Craven* Short, first person pieces, maximum 650 words, are welcome for consideration. Humour from teachers is encouraged, especially for the 'Thank God it's Friday' column. **You and Your Job** *Jill Craven*
Online (Computers in Education) *Merlin John* A magazine devoted to information and communications technology appearing with *The TES* nine times a year.
Curriculum Specials *Joyce Arnold* New termly magazines for subject teachers appearing with *The TES*. Subjects covered: science and technology (includes food, textiles, graphics), mathematics, English, music and arts, modern languages, humanities and special needs. Articles should relate to current educational practice. Age range covered is primary to sixth form. Maximum 600–800 words.
Special Issues Occasional pull-out magazine on topics including school management (*Bob Doe*), first appointments (*Jill Craven*), business links (*Ian Nash*), school visits –*Going Places* – (*Janette Wolf*).
Primary *Diane Hofkins* A monthly A4 glossy magazine published separately from *The TES*. Articles should aim to help teachers think about their work or provide ideas for teaching. Length no more than 1000 words. It is advisable to send in a proposal before submitting a completed article.
College Manager *Ian Nash* New monthly A4 glossy magazine published separately from *The TES*. Aimed at leaders and opinion formers in the further education sector. News, features, comment and opinion articles on all aspects of college life welcome. Length from 350 words (news) to 1000 maximum (features).

The Times Educational Supplement Scotland

Scott House, 10 South St Andrew Street, Edinburgh EH2 2AZ
☎0131 557 1133 Fax 0131 558 1155
Email scoted@tes.co.uk
Website www.tes.co.uk

Owner *TSL Education Ltd*
Editor *Willis Pickard*
Circulation 9000

FOUNDED 1965. WEEKLY. Unsolicited mss welcome.

Features Articles on education in Scotland. Maximum 1000 words.
News Items on education in Scotland. Maximum 600 words.

The Times Higher Education Supplement

Admiral House, 66–68 East Smithfield, London E1 9XY
☎020 7782 3000 Fax 020 7782 3300
Email editor@thes.co.uk
Website www.thes.co.uk

Owner *News International*
Editor *Auriol Stevens*
Circulation 28,300

FOUNDED 1971. WEEKLY. Unsolicited mss are welcome but most articles and *all* book reviews are commissioned. 'In most cases it is better to write, but in the case of news stories it is all right to phone.'

Books *Andrew Robinson*
Features *Sian Griffiths* Most articles are commissioned from academics in higher education.
News *Mary Cook* Freelance opportunities very occasionally.
Science *Steve Farrar*
Science Books *Andrew Robinson*
Foreign *David Jobbins*
Payment by negotiation.

The Times Literary Supplement

Admiral House, 66–68 East Smithfield, London E1W 1BX
☎020 7782 3000 Fax 020 7782 3100
Website www.the-tls.co.uk

Owner *Times Supplements*
Editor *Ferdinand Mount*
Circulation 34,500

FOUNDED 1902. WEEKLY review of literature. Contributors should approach in writing and be familiar with the general level of writing in the *TLS*.

Literary Discoveries *Alan Jenkins*
Poems *Mick Imlah*
News *Ferdinand Mount* News stories and general articles concerned with literature, publishing and new intellectual developments anywhere in the world. Length by arrangement.
Payment by arrangement.

Titbits

2 Caversham Street, London SW3 4AH
☎020 7351 4995 Fax 020 7351 4995

Owner *Sport Newspapers Ltd*
Editor *James Hughes*
Circulation 150,000

FOUNDED 1895. MONTHLY. Consumer magazine for men covering show business and general interests. Unsolicited mss and ideas in writing welcome. Maximum 3000 words. News, features, particularly photofeatures (colour), and fiction. *Payment* negotiable.

Today's Golfer

Bretton Court, Bretton, Peterborough, Cambridgeshire PE3 8DZ
☎01733 264666 Fax 01733 465248

Owner *EMAP Active Ltd*
Editor *Neil Pope*
Deputy Editor *John McKenzie*
Circulation 65,000

FOUNDED 1988. MONTHLY. Golf instruction, features, player profiles and news. Most features written in-house but unsolicited mss will be considered. Approach in writing with ideas. Not interested in instruction material from outside contributors.

Features/News *Kevin Brown* Opinion, player profiles and general golf-related features.

Top of the Pops Magazine

Room A1136, Woodlands, 80 Wood Lane, London W12 0TT
☎020 8433 3910 Fax 020 8433 2694
Website www.beeb.com/totp

Owner *BBC Worldwide Publishing*
Editor *Corinna Shaffer*
Circulation 368,700

FOUNDED 1995. MONTHLY teenage pop music magazine with a lighthearted and humorous approach. No unsolicited material apart from pop star interviews.

Total Film

99 Baker Street, London W1M 1FB
☎020 7317 2600 Fax 020 7317 2644
Email totalfilm@futurenet.co.uk

Owner *Future Publishing*
Editor *Matt Mueller*
Circulation 69,000

FOUNDED 1997. MONTHLY reviews-based movie magazine. Interested in ideas for features, not necessarily tied in to specific releases, and humour items. No reviews or interviews with celebrities/directors. Approach by post or e-mail.

Total Football

30 Monmouth Street, Bath BA1 2BW
☎01225 442244 Fax 01225 732248
Email gary.tipp@futurenet.co.uk
Owner *Future Publishing*
Editor *Gary Tipp*
Circulation 34,791

FOUNDED 1995. MONTHLY. News, features and reviews covering all aspects of domestic and international football. Contributions welcome.
  Features *Alex Murphy* New and interesting angles; particularly funny pieces and fan-based articles. 2000 words maximum. *Payment* negotiable.
  News *Alex Murphy* Unusual stories from all areas of the game – tabloid style. 500 words maximum. *Payment* £75 per 500 words.

Total Style

57–59 Rochester Place, London NW1 9JU
☎020 7331 1265 Fax 020 7331 1241
Email totalstyle@yahoo.com
Owner *WV Publications*
Editor *Georgina Hersey*

FOUNDED 1998. BI-MONTHLY. Welcomes informative features on beauty, hair and fashion, aimed at women aged 25–45. 1200–2000 words. *Payment* around £225 per feature, depending on length. Also, celebrity 'style' features and interviews. No fiction. Approach in writing in the first instance.

Town and Country Post

Bridge House, Blackden Lane, Goostrey, Cheshire CW4 8PZ
☎01477 534440/533403 Fax 01477 535756
Email post2001@aol.com
Owner *Hill Bros. (Leek) Ltd*
Editor *John Williams*
Circulation 28,000

FOUNDED 1981. MONTHLY. Local news and features on Cheshire. Very little freelance material is used. No unsolicited mss. Approach by telephone in the first instance.

Traditional Woodworking

The Well House, High Street, Burton on Trent, Staffordshire DE14 1JQ
☎01283 742950 Fax 01283 742966
Owner *Waterways World*
Editor *Alan Kidd*

FOUNDED 1988. MONTHLY. Features workshop projects, techniques, reviews of the latest woodworking tools and equipment, general articles on woodworking and furniture making.
  Features Technical features and furniture projects welcome. The latter must include drawings and cutting lists. A photograph of the piece is required before commissioning. *Payment* negotiable. Approach in writing in the first instance.

Trail

Apex House, Oundle Road, Peterborough, Cambridgeshire PE2 9NP
☎01733 898100 Fax 01733 465070
Owner *EMAP Active Publishing Ltd*
Editor *Victoria Tebbs*
Circulation 35,172

FOUNDED 1990. MONTHLY. Gear reports, where to walk and practical advice for the hillwalker and long distance walker. Inspirational reads on people and outdoor/walking issues. Health, fitness and injury prevention for high level walkers and outdoor lovers. Approach by phone or in writing in the first instance.
  Features *Guy Procter* Very limited requirement for overseas articles, 'written to our style'. Ask for guidelines. Maximum 2000 words.
  Limited requirement for guided walks articles. Specialist writers only. Ask for guidelines. Maximum 750–2000 words (depending on subject).
  Payment £80 per 1000 words.

Traveller

45–49 Brompton Road, London SW3 1DE
☎020 7589 0500 Fax 020 7581 1357
Email traveller@wexas.com
Website www.traveller.org.uk
Owner *Wexas International*
Editor *Jonathan Lorie*
Circulation 35,359

FOUNDED 1970. QUARTERLY.
  Features High quality, personal narratives of remarkable journeys. Articles should be off-beat, adventurous, authentic. No mainstream destinations. For guidelines, see Website. Articles must be accompanied by professional

quality, original slides. Freelance articles considered. Maximum 1600 words.
Payment £150 per 1000 words.

Trout Fisherman

EMAP Active Ltd, Bushfield House, Orton Centre, Peterborough, Cambridgeshire PE2 5UW
☎01733 237111 Fax 01733 465658
Owner *EMAP Active Ltd*
Editor *Chris Dawn*
Circulation 42,220

FOUNDED 1977. MONTHLY instructive magazine on trout fishing. Most of the articles are commissioned, but unsolicited mss and quality colour transparencies welcome.
Features Maximum 2500 words.
Payment varies.

Turkeys

PO Box 18, Bishopdale, Leyburn DL8 3YY
☎01969 663764 Fax 01969 663764
Owner *Fancy Fowl Publications Ltd*
Editor *Shirley Murdoch*
Circulation 2000

BI-MONTHLY publication aiming to deal with all aspects of turkey breeding, growing, processing and marketing at an international level. Specialist technical information from qualified contributors will always be considered. Length by arrangement. No unsolicited mss. Approach in writing with ideas, or by phone.
Payment £70 per 1000 words.

TVTimes

King's Reach Tower, Stamford Street, London SE1 9LS
☎020 7261 7000 Fax 020 7261 7777
Owner *IPC Magazines*
Editor *Peter Genower*
Circulation 790,999

FOUNDED 1955. WEEKLY magazine of listings and features serving the viewers of independent television, BBC, satellite and radio. Almost no freelance contributions used, except where the writer is known and trusted by the magazine. No unsolicited contributions.

Ulster Tatler

39 Boucher Road, Belfast BT12 6UT
☎028 9068 1371 Fax 028 9038 1915
Email ulstertat@aol.com
Website www.ulstertatler.com
Owner/Editor *Richard Sherry*
Circulation 15,000

FOUNDED 1965. MONTHLY. Articles of local interest and social functions appealing to Northern Ireland's ABC1 population. Welcomes unsolicited material; approach by phone or in writing in the first instance.
Features *Noreen Dorman* Max. 1500 words.
Fiction *Richard Sherry* Max. 3000 words.

The Universe

St James's Buildings, Oxford Street, Manchester M1 6FP
☎0161 236 8856 Fax 0161 236 9017
Website www.the-universe.net
Owner *Gabriel Communications Ltd*
Editor *Joe Kelly*
Circulation 80,000

Occasional use of new writers, but a substantial network of regular contributors already exists. Interested in a very wide range of material: all subjects which might bear on Christian life. Fiction not normally accepted. *Payment* negotiable.

Vector

See **British Science Fiction Association** under **Professional Associations**

The Vegan

Donald Watson House, 7 Battle Road, St Leonards on Sea, East Sussex TN37 7AA
☎01424 427393 Fax 01424 717064
Email richard@vegansociety.com
Website www.vegansociety.com
Owner *Vegan Society*
Editor *Richard Farhall*
Circulation 5000

FOUNDED 1944. QUARTERLY. Deals with the ecological, ethical and health aspects of veganism. Unsolicited mss welcome. Maximum 2000 words. *Payment* negotiable.

Verbatim The Language Quarterly

PO Box 156, Chearsley, Aylesbury, Buckinghamshire HP18 0DQ
☎01844 208474
Email verbatim.uk@tesco.net
Website www.verbatimmag.com
Owner *Word, Inc.*
Editor *Erin McKean*

FOUNDED 1974. QUARTERLY journal devoted to what is amusing, interesting and engaging about the English language and languages in general. Will consider unsolicited material but write for writer's guidelines in the first instance. For a sample copy of the magazine, send 50p (stamp or IRC).

Payment ranges from £20–300, 'depending on length, wit and other merit'.

Vintage Times

PhD Publishing, Navestock Hall, Navestock, Essex RM4 1HA

☎01708 370053

Owner *PhD Publishing*
Editor *David Hoppit*
Circulation 60,000

FOUNDED 1994. QUARTERLY lifestyle magazine 'for over-40s who have not quite given up hope of winning Wimbledon'. Preliminary approach by phone or in writing with ideas.

Vogue

Vogue House, Hanover Square, London W1R 0AD

☎020 7499 9080 Fax 020 7408 0559
Website www.vogue.co.uk

Owner *Condé Nast Publications Ltd*
Editor *Alexandra Shulman*
Circulation 202,668

Condé Nast Magazines tend to use known writers and commission what's needed, rather than using unsolicited mss. Contacts are useful.

Features *Justine Picardie* Upmarket general interest rather than 'women's'. Good proportion of highbrow art and literary articles, as well as travel, gardens, food, home interest and reviews.

The Voice Newspaper

370 Coldharbour Lane, Brixton, London SW9 8PL

☎020 7737 7377 Fax 020 7274 8994
Email mike.best@the-voice.co.uk
Website www.voice-online.co.uk

Owner *Val McCalla*
Editor-in-Chief *Mike Best*
Circulation 40,000

FOUNDED 1982. WEEKLY newspaper for the Afro Caribbean community. News, features, arts, reviews and special pull-out of jobs and sport. Open to ideas for features, news and arts items; approach in writing. *Payment* negotiable.

Voyager

Mediamark Publishing International, 11 Kingsway, London WC2B 6PH

☎020 7212 9000 Fax 020 7212 9001
Email info@mediamark.co.uk

Owner *Mediamark/British Midland Airways*

Editor *Howard Rombough*
Circulation 54,191

TEN ISSUES PER YEAR. In-flight magazine of British Midland Airways. European lifestyle features and profiles, plus British Midland information. No unsolicited mss. Approach in writing with ideas in the first instance. No destination travel articles.

The War Cry

101 Queen Victoria Street, London EC4P 4EP

☎020 7367 4900 Fax 020 7367 4710
Email warcry@salvationarmy.org.uk
Website www.salvationarmy.org.uk/warcry

Owner *The Salvation Army*
Editor *Major Nigel Bovey*
Circulation 80,000

FOUNDED 1879. WEEKLY magazine containing Christian comments on current issues. Unsolicited mss welcome if appropriate to contents. No fiction or poetry. Approach by phone with ideas.

News relating to Christian Church or social issues. Maximum length 500 words. *Payment* £20 per article.

Features Magazine-style articles of interest to the 'man/woman-in-the-street'. Maximum length 500 words. *Payment* £20 per article.

The Water Gardener

Somerfield House, Wotton Road, Ashford, Kent TN23 6LW

☎01233 621877 Fax 01233 645669
Email wg@dogworld.co.uk

Owner *Dog World Publishing*
Editor *Yvonne Rees*
Circulation 23,568

FOUNDED 1994. MONTHLY. Everything relevant to water gardening. Will consider photonews items and features on aspects of the subject; write with idea in the first instance. Maximum 2000 words. *Payment* by negotiation.

Waterways World

The Well House, High Street, Burton on Trent, Staffordshire DE14 1JQ

☎01283 742950 Fax 01283 742957
Email ww@wellhouse.easynet.co.uk

Owner *Waterways World Ltd*
Editor *Hugh Potter*
Circulation 22,408

FOUNDED 1972. MONTHLY magazine for inland waterway enthusiasts. Unsolicited mss welcome, provided the writer has a good knowledge of the subject. No fiction.

Features *Hugh Potter* Articles (preferably illustrated) on all aspects of inland waterways in Britain and abroad, including recreational and commercial boating on rivers and canals.
News *Chris Daniels* Maximum 500 words. *Payment* £37 per 1000 words.

Waymark

IPROW, PO Box 78, Skipton, North Yorkshire BD23 4UP
☎0115 9774961 Fax 07000 782319
Email comms@iprow.co.uk
Website www.iprow.co.uk
Editor *Clare Denby*
Circulation 1000

FOUNDED 1986. QUARTERLY journal of the Institute of Public Rights of Way Officers. Glossy, spot colour magazine for countryside access managers in England and Wales, employed throughout the public and private sectors. Available to non-members by subscription. Read by politicians, landowners, environmental lobbyists and countryside access users.
News Most produced in-house but some opportunities for original/off-beat items. Max. 500 words.
Features Ideas welcome on any topic broadly relating to the British countryside and public access to it. Controversial, thought provoking pieces readily considered. Max. 1750 words.
Special Pages Cartoons or brief humorous items on an access or countryside/environmental theme welcome. Send ideas in writing with s.a.e. initially.
Payment negotiable, up to £35.

Wedding and Home

King's Reach Tower, Stamford Street, London SE1 9LS
☎020 7261 7471 Fax 020 7261 7459
Email weddingandhome@ipc.co.uk
Owner *IPC Magazines Ltd*
Editor *Christine Hayes*
Circulation 44,269

FOUNDED 1985. BI-MONTHLY offering ideas and inspiration for women planning their wedding. Most features are written in-house or commissioned from known freelancers. Unsolicited mss are not welcome, but approaches may be made in writing.

Weekly News

Albert Square, Dundee DD1 9QJ
☎01382 223131 Fax 01382 201390
Owner *D. C. Thomson & Co. Ltd*

Editor *David Hishmurgh*
Circulation 206,302

FOUNDED 1855. WEEKLY. Newsy, family-orientated magazine designed to appeal to the busy housewife. 'We get a lot of unsolicited stuff and there is great loss of life among them.' Usually commissions, but writers of promise will be taken up. Series include showbiz, royals and television. No fiction. *Payment* negotiable.

West Lothian Life

Ballencrieff Cottage, Ballencrieff Toll, Bathgate, West Lothian EH48 4LD
☎01506 632728 Fax 01506 635444
Email pages@clara.net
Website home.clara.net/pages
Owner *Pages Editorial & Publishing Services*
Editor *Susan Coon*

QUARTERLY county magazine for people who live, work or have an interest in West Lothian. Includes three or four major features (1500 words) on successful people, businesses or initiatives. A local walk takes up the centre spread. Regular articles by experts on collectables, property, interior design, cookery and local gardening, plus news items, letters and a competition. Freelance writers used exclusively for main features. Phone first to discuss content and timing. *Payment* by arrangement.

What Car?

60 Waldegrave Road, Teddington, Middlesex TW11 8LG
☎020 8267 5688 Fax 020 8267 5750
Email whatcar@haynet.com
Website www.whatcar.co.uk
Owner *Haymarket Motoring Publications Ltd*
Editor *Steve Fowler*
Circulation 153,164

MONTHLY. The car buyer's bible, *What Car?* concentrates on road test comparisons of new cars, news and buying advice on used cars, as well as a strong consumer section. Some scope for freelancers. Testing is only offered to the few, and general articles on aspects of driving are only accepted from writers known and trusted by the magazine. No unsolicited mss.
Payment negotiable.

What Hi-Fi?

38–42 Hampton Road, Teddington, Middlesex TW11 0JE
☎020 8943 5000 Fax 020 8267 5019
Owner *Haymarket Magazines Ltd*
Publishing Director *Kevin Costello*

Editor *Andy Clough*
Circulation 75,000

FOUNDED 1976. MONTHLY. Features on hi-fi and new technology. No unsolicited contributions. Prior consultation with the editor essential.

Features General or more specific on hi-fi and new technology pertinent to the consumer electronics market.

Reviews Specific product reviews. All material is now generated by in-house staff. Freelance writing no longer accepted.

What Investment

Arnold House, 36–41 Holywell Lane, London EC2A 3SF
☎020 7827 5454 Fax 020 7827 0567

Owner *Charterhouse Communications*
Editor *Jane Sumpter*
Circulation 37,000

FOUNDED 1983. MONTHLY. Features articles on a variety of savings and investment matters. All approaches should be made in writing.

Features Length 1200–1500 words (maximum 2000).
Payment NUJ rates minimum.

What Mortgage

Arnold House, 36–41 Holywell Lane, London EC2A 3SF

Owner *Charterhouse Communications*
Editor *Lizzie Sparrow*
Circulation 25,000

FOUNDED 1982. MONTHLY magazine on property purchase and finance. No unsolicited material; prospective contributors may make initial contact with ideas either by telephone or in writing.

Features Up to 1500 words on related topics are considered. Particularly welcome are new angles, ideas or specialities relevant to mortgages.
Payment £175 per 1000 words.

What Satellite TV

WV Publications, 57–59 Rochester Place, London NW1 9JU
☎020 7331 1000 Fax 020 7331 1241
Email wvwhatsat@AOL.com
Website www.wotsat.com

Owner *WV Publications*
Editor *Geoff Bains*
Circulation 65,000

FOUNDED 1986. MONTHLY including news, technical information, equipment tests, programme background, listings. Contributions welcome – phone first.

Features *Geoff Bains* Unusual installations and users. In-depth guides to popular/cult shows. Technical tutorials.

News *Alex Lane* Industry and programming. 250 words maximum.

What's New in Building

City Reach, 5 Greenwich View Place, Millharbour, London E14 9NN
☎020 8861 6309 Fax 020 8861 6241

Owner *Miller Freeman plc*
Editor *Mark Pennington*
Circulation 31,496

MONTHLY. Specialist magazine covering new products for building. Unsolicited mss not generally welcome. The only freelance work available is rewriting press release material. This is offered on a monthly basis of 25–50 items of about 150 words each. *Payment* £5.25 per item.

What's On in London

180–182 Pentonville Road, London N1 9LB
☎020 7278 4393 Fax 020 7837 5838

Owner *E. G. Shaw*
Editor *Michael Darvell*
Circulation 40,000

FOUNDED 1935. WEEKLY entertainment-based guide and information magazine. Features, listings and reviews. Always interested in well-thought-out and well-presented mss. Articles should have London/Home Counties connection, except during the summer when they can be of much wider tourist/historic interest, relating to unusual traditions and events. Approach the editor by telephone in the first instance.

Features *Graham Hassell*
Art *Rosanna Negrotti*
Cinema *Marshall Julius*
Pop Music *Cheryl Freedman*
Classical Music *Michael Darvell*
Theatre *Sam Marlowe*
Events *John Coleman*
Payment by arrangement.

Wine

Quest Magazines Ltd., 6–8 Underwood Street, London N1 7JQ
☎020 7549 2572 Fax 020 7549 2550

Owner *Wilmington Publishing*
Editor *Susan Vumback Low*
Circulation 35,000

FOUNDED 1983. MONTHLY. No unsolicited mss.

News/Features Wine, food and food/wine-related travel stories. Prospective contributors should approach in writing.

Wisden Cricket Monthly

c/o The New Boathouse, 136–142 Bramley Road, London W10 6SR
☎020 7565 3000 Fax 020 7565 3077

Owner *Wisden Cricket Magazines Ltd*
Editor *Tim de Lisle*
Circulation 20,000

FOUNDED 1979. MONTHLY. Very few uncommissioned articles are used, but would-be contributors are not discouraged. Approach in writing. *Payment* varies.

Woman

IPC Connect Ltd, King's Reach Tower, Stamford Street, London SE1 9LS
☎020 7261 5000 Fax 020 7261 5997

Owner *IPC Magazines Ltd*
Editor *Carole Russell*
Circulation 670,241

FOUNDED 1937. WEEKLY. Long-running, popular women's magazine which boasts a readership of over 2.5 million. No unsolicited mss. Most work commissioned. Approach with ideas in writing.
    Features *Kate Corr* Maximum 1250 words.
    Books *Carole Russell*

Woman and Home

King's Reach Tower, Stamford Street, London SE1 9LS
☎020 7261 5176 Fax 020 7261 7346

Owner *IPC Magazines Ltd*
Editor *Sarah Kilby*
Circulation 295,225

FOUNDED 1926. MONTHLY. No unsolicited mss. Prospective contributors are advised to write with ideas, including photocopies of other published work or details of magazines to which they have contributed. S.a.e. essential for return of material. Most freelance work is specially commissioned.

Woman's Journal

King's Reach Tower, Stamford Street, London SE1 9LS
☎020 7261 6622 Fax 020 7261 7061

Owner *IPC Magazines Ltd*
Editor *Elsa McAlonan*
Circulation 110,762

FOUNDED 1927. MONTHLY. Original feature ideas on 30+ women and their lives welcome, with samples of previous work. Major features are generally commissioned. *Payment* negotiable.

Woman's Own

King's Reach Tower, Stamford Street, London SE1 9LS
☎020 7261 5474 Fax 020 7261 5346

Owner *IPC Magazines Ltd*
Editor *Ms Terry Tavner*
Circulation 569,019

FOUNDED 1932. WEEKLY. Prospective contributors should contact the features editor *in writing* in the first instance before making a submission. No unsolicited fiction.

Woman's Realm

King's Reach Tower, Stamford Street, London SE1 9LS
☎020 7261 5000
Fax 020 7261 5326/7678 (Features)

Owner *IPC Magazines Ltd*
Editor *Mary Frances*
Deputy Editor *Linda Belcher*
Circulation 179,345

FOUNDED 1958. WEEKLY. Some scope here for freelancers. Write to the appropriate editor.
    Features *Liz Jarvis* General, real-life and human interest. Unsolicited mss not accepted.
    Fiction Two short stories used every week, a one-pager (up to 1000 words), plus a longer one (2000 words). Unsolicited mss not accepted.

Woman's Weekly

King's Reach Tower, Stamford Street, London SE1 9LS
☎020 7261 6131 Fax 020 7261 6322

Owner *IPC Magazines Ltd*
Editor *Gilly Sinclair*
Deputy Editor *Geoffrey Palmer*
Circulation 547,953

FOUNDED 1911. Mass-market women's WEEKLY.
    Features Inspiring, positive human interest stories, especially first-hand experiences, of up to 1200 words. Freelancers used regularly but tend to be experienced magazine journalists. Synopses and ideas should be submitted in writing.
    Fiction *Gaynor Davies* Short stories 1000–2500 words; serials 12,000–30,000 words. Guidelines for serials: 'a strong emotional theme with a conflict not resolved until the end'; short stories should have warmth and originality.

Women's Health

WV Publications, 57–59 Rochester Place, London NW1 9JU
☎020 7331 1000 Fax 020 7331 1242
Email wvmags@compuserve.com

Owner *Highbury House Communications*
Editor *To be appointed*
Circulation 100,000

FOUNDED 1998. MONTHLY lifestyle magazine with a health twist, taking an irreverant approach. Aimed at ABC1 women of 25–45. No unsolicited mss. Interested in ideas for items with an unconventional angle on fitness, fashion and beauty. No alternative health articles. Approach in writing in the first instance.

Woodworker
Azalea Drive, Swanley, Kent BR8 8HU
☎01322 660070 Fax 01322 667633
Owner *Nexus Special Interests*
Editor *Mark Ramuz*
Circulation 45,000

FOUNDED 1901. MONTHLY. Contributions welcome; approach with ideas in writing.
   Features Articles on woodworking with good photo support appreciated. Max. 2000 words. *Payment* £40–60 per page.
   News Stories and photos (b&w) welcome. Max. 300 words. *Payment* £10–25 per story.

World Fishing
Nexus House, Swanley, Kent BR8 8HY
☎01322 660070 Fax 01322 616324
Owner *Nexus Media Ltd*
Editor *Mark Say*
Circulation 5800

FOUNDED 1952. MONTHLY. Unsolicited mss welcome; approach by phone or in writing with an idea.
   News/Features of a technical or commercial nature relating to the commercial fishing and fish processing industries worldwide. Maximum 1000 words.
   Payment by arrangement.

The World of Embroidery
PO Box 42B, East Molesley, Surrey KT8 9BB
☎020 8943 1229 Fax 020 8977 9882
Email magsmag@compuserve.com
Website www.embroidersguild.org.uk/
   worldofembroidery/
Owner *Embroiderers' Guild*
Editor *Maggie Grey*
Circulation 14,500

FOUNDED 1933. BI-MONTHLY. Features articles on embroidery techniques, historical and foreign embroidery, and contemporary artists' work with illustrations. Also reviews. Unsolicited mss welcome. Max. 1000 words. *Payment* negotiable.

The World of Interiors
Vogue House, Hanover Square, London W1R 0AD
☎020 7499 9080 Fax 020 7493 4013
Email interiors@msmail.condenast.co.uk
Website www.worldofinteriors.co.uk
Owner *Condé Nast Publications Ltd*
Editor *Min Hogg*
Circulation 70,128

FOUNDED 1981. MONTHLY. Best approach by fax or letter with an idea, preferably with reference snaps or guidebooks.
   Features *Sarah Howell* Most feature material is commissioned. 'Subjects tend to be found by us, but we are delighted to receive suggestions of interiors, archives, little-known museums, collections, etc. unpublished elsewhere, and would love to find new writers.'

World Soccer
King's Reach Tower, Stamford Street, London SE1 9LS
☎020 7261 5737 Fax 020 7261 7474
Website www.worldsoccer.com
Owner *IPC Magazines Ltd*
Editor *Gavin Hamilton*
Circulation 63,211

FOUNDED 1960. MONTHLY. Unsolicited material welcome but initial approach by phone or in writing preferred. News and features on world soccer.

World Wide Writers
Briggs House, 26 Commercial Road, Ashley Cross, Poole, Dorset BH14 0JR
☎01202 716043 Fax 01202 740995
Email writintl@globalnet.co.uk
Website www.users.globalnet.co.uk/~writintl
Owner *Writers International Ltd*
Editor *Frederick E. Smith*

FOUNDED 1996. BI-MONTHLY. Welcomes short stories which must be original and not previously published or broadcast. 2500–5000 words.

Writers' Forum
First Floor, Briggs House, 26 Commercial Road, Ashley Cross, Poole, Dorset BH14 0JR
☎01202 716043 Fax 01202 740995
Email writintl@globalnet.co.uk
Website www.users.globalnet.co.uk/~writintl
Owner *Writers International Ltd*
Editor *John Jenkins*
Circulation 25,000

FOUNDED 1993. BI-MONTHLY magazine covering all aspects of the craft of writing. Well written articles welcome. Write to the editor in the first instance.

Writers' News/Writing Magazine

PO Box 168, Wellington Street, Leeds, West Yorkshire LS1 1RF
☎0113 2388333 Fax 0113 2388330
Owner *Yorkshire Post Newspapers*
Editor *Derek Hudson*
Circulation 21,500(WN)/45,000(WM)

FOUNDED 1989. MONTHLY/BI-MONTHLY magazines containing news and advice for writers. *Writers News* is exclusive to mail-order members who also receive *Writing Magazine* which is available on newsstands. No poetry or general items on 'how to become a writer'. Receive 1000 mss each year. Approach in writing.

News Exclusive news stories of interest to writers. Maximum 350 words.

Features How-to articles of interest to professional writers. Maximum 2000 words.

Yachting Monthly

King's Reach Tower, Stamford Street, London SE1 9LS
☎020 7261 6040 Fax 020 7261 7555
Website www.yachtingmonthly.com
Owner *IPC Magazines Ltd*
Editor *Sarah Norbury*
Circulation 37,083

FOUNDED 1906. MONTHLY magazine for yachting enthusiasts. Unsolicited mss welcome, but many are received and not used. Prospective contributors should make initial contact in writing.

Features *Paul Gelder* A wide range of features concerned with maritime subjects and cruising under sail; well-researched and innovative material always welcome, especially if accompanied by colour transparencies. Maximum 2750 words. *Payment* £90–110 per 1000 words.

Yachting World

King's Reach Tower, Stamford Street, London SE1 9LS
☎020 7261 6800 Fax 020 7261 6818
Email yachting_world@ipc.co.uk
Website www.yachting-world.com
Owner *IPC Magazines Ltd*
Editor *Andrew Bray*
Circulation 34,316

FOUNDED 1894. MONTHLY with international coverage of yacht racing, cruising and yachting events. Will consider well researched and written sailing stories. Preliminary approaches should be by phone for news stories and in writing for features.
Payment by arrangement.

You – The Mail on Sunday Magazine

See under **National Newspapers (The Mail on Sunday)**

You and Your Wedding

Silver House, 31–35 Beak Street, London W1R 3LD
☎020 7437 2998 (Editorial)
Fax 020 7287 8655
Owner *AIM Publications Ltd*
Editor *Carole Hamilton*
Circulation 58,000

FOUNDED 1985. BI-MONTHLY. Anything relating to weddings, setting up home, and honeymoons. No unsolicited mss. Ideas may be submitted in writing only, especially travel features. No phone calls.

Young Writer

Glebe House, Weobley, Hereford HR4 8SD
☎01544 318901 Fax 01544 318901
Email youngwriter@enterprise.net
Website www.mystworld.com/youngwriter
Editor *Kate Jones*

Describing itself as 'The Magazine for Children with Something to Say', *Young Writer* is issued three times a year, at the back-to-school times of September, January and April. A forum for young people's writing – fiction and non-fiction, prose and poetry – the magazine is an introduction to independent writing for young writers aged 5–18.
Payment from £20 to £100 for freelance commissioned articles (these can be from adult writers).

Your Cat Magazine

Roebuck House, 33 Broad Street, Stamford, Lincolnshire PE9 1RB
☎01780 766199 Fax 01780 766416
Owner *EMAP Apex*
Editor *Sue Parslow*

FOUNDED 1994. MONTHLY magazine giving practical information on the care of cats and kittens, pedigree and non-pedigree, plus a wide range of general interest items on cats. Will consider 'true life' cat stories (maximum 900 words) and quality fiction. Send synopsis in the first instance. 'No articles written as though by a cat.'

Your Dog Magazine

Roebuck House, 33 Broad Street, Stamford, Lincolnshire PE9 1RB
☎01780 766199 Fax 01780 766416
Email sarahbpgroup@talk21.com
Owner *BPC (Stamford) Ltd*
Editor *Sarah Wright*
Circulation 26,000

FOUNDED 1995. MONTHLY Practical advice for pet dog owners. Will consider practical features and some personal experiences (no highly emotive pieces or fiction). Phone in the first instance.
   News Maximum 300–400 words; a lot of freelance material is used.
   Features Maximum 2500 words; limited opportunities.
   Payment negotiable.

Your Garden Magazine

IPC Magazines Ltd., Westover House, West Quay Road, Poole, Dorset BH15 1JG
☎01202 440870 Fax 01202 440860
Email yourgarden@ipc.co.uk
Owner *IPC Magazines Ltd*
Editor *Adrienne Wild*
Circulation 57,260

FOUNDED 1993. MONTHLY full colour glossy for all gardeners. Welcomes good, solid gardening advice that is well written and fun. Receives approx 50 mss per month but only five per cent are accepted. Always approach in writing in the first instance.
   Features Good leisure gardening features, preferably with a new slant. Small gardens only. Maximum 1000 words. Photographs welcome.
   Payment negotiable – all rights preferred.

Yours Magazine

Apex House, Oundle Road, Peterborough, Cambridgeshire PE2 9NP
☎01733 898100 Fax 01733 466863
Owner *EMAP Active Ltd*
Editor *Neil Patrick*
Circulation 311,000

FOUNDED 1973. MONTHLY plus four seasonal specials. Aimed at a readership aged 55 and over.
   Features Best approach by letter with outline in first instance. Maximum 1000 words.
   News Short, newsy items of interest to readership welcome. Length 300–500 words.

Fiction One or two short stories used in each issue.
Payment negotiable.

Zade

87 Micheldever Road, Whitchurch, Hampshire RG28 7JH
Email blake_100@hotmail.com
Website www.users.globalnet.co.uk/~theeps
Owner/Editor *Blake Evans-Pritchard*
Circulation 200

QUARTERLY literary magazine specialising in short stories. All genres welcome 'as long as they are well written and highly entertaining'. Length: 500–5000 words. New contributors welcome; send s.a.e. for guidelines or access the website. No poetry or articles. *Payment* £5 per story plus complimentary copy of the magazine.

ZENE

5 Martins Lane, Witcham, Ely, Cambridgeshire CB6 2LB
☎01353 777931
Email ttapress@aol.com
Website www.tta-press.freewire.co.uk
Owner *TTA Press*
Editor *Andy Cox*

FOUNDED 1994. BI-MONTHLY. Features detailed contributors' guidelines of international small press and semi-professional publications, plus varied articles, news, views, reviews and interviews.
   Features Unsolicited articles welcome on any aspect of small press publishing: market information, writing, editing, illustrating, interviews and reviews. All genres. Submissions should include adequate return postage. 'Please study the magazine: this will greatly enhance your chances of acceptance.'

Zest

National Magazine House, 72 Broadwick Street, London W1V 2BP
☎020 7439 5000 Fax 020 7439 5632
Email zest.mail@natmags.co.uk
Website www.natmags.co.uk
Owner *National Magazine Company*
Editor *Eve Cameron*
Features Editor *Linda Bird*

FOUNDED 1994. MONTHLY. Health, beauty, fitness, nutrition and general well-being. No unsolicited mss. Prefers ideas in synopsis form, approach in writing.

ZM

National Magazines, 50 Marshall Street,
London W1V 1LR
☎020 7439 5000 Fax 020 7439 5403
Owner *National Magazines*
Editor *Paul Colbert*

FOUNDED 1999. MONTHLY health and lifestyle
magazine for men. Interested in submissions
from authors who have taken time to study the
magazine. 'Three rules only: read the magazine; give us a feature idea that fits what the
magazine is about; don't give us an obvious
idea we've already covered – make it fresh, different and useful.' Approach in writing.

The Zone

13 Hazely Combe, Arreton, Isle of Wight
PO30 3AJ
☎01983 865668
Email pigasus.press@virgin.net *(correspondence
only)*
Website freespace.virgin.net/pigasus.press/
index.htm
Publisher *Pigasus Press*

Editor *Tony Lee*

FOUNDED 1994. BIANNUAL science fiction
magazine. Unsolicited mss welcome but writers
are advised to study recent issues and be familiar
with the content before sending material.
Contributors' guidelines and mail order details
available. (All correspondence must be accompanied by an s.a.e. or IRC.)

Fiction Original, imaginative science fiction
and fantasy (no supernatural horror), 1000–
5000 words. Prose-poems, 60–70 lines; genre
verse also appears in the SF poetry showcase,
but by invitation only.

Features Interviews with prominent SF
authors. Critical articles and essays on any
aspect or theme related to the SF/fantasy scene,
whether topical or retrospective, will be considered. Length 1000–10,000 words. Approach
in writing with ideas in the first instance.

Reviews Books, cinema, video and TV.
Reviews are usually commissioned but will
consider reviews of new SF and non-fiction
books. Length 300–500 words.

Payment Token £5 for stories and non-fiction
of over 2000 words; otherwise payment in copy
only.

Freelance Rates – Magazines

Freelance rates vary enormously. The following minimum rates, set by the National Union of Journalists, should be treated as guidelines. The NUJ has no power to enforce minimum rates on journals that do not recognise the Union. It is up to freelancers to negotiate the best deal they can.

Examples of NUJ categories for magazines:

Group A (over £13,000 per page of advertising)
Cosmopolitan, Hello!, Radio Times, TV Times, Woman, Woman's Own.

Group B (between £7000 and £13,000 per page of advertising)
The Economist, GQ, Loaded, marie claire, Q.

Group C (between £2500 and £7000 per page of advertising)
Accountancy Age, Architect's Journal, Music Week, The Spectator, Time Out.

Group D (less than £2500 per page of advertising or carry no advertising)
Nursing Times.

The following figures are the minimum rates which should be paid by magazines in the above groups for first use only:

Features (per 1000 words)
Group A	£400
Group B	£275
Group C	£225
Group D	£160

Cartoons (b&w)
	Group A	Group B & C	Group D
Minimum fee	£100	£80	£64
Feature strip (up to 4 frames)	£123	£107	£100

For colour, charge at least double these rates.

Crosswords
	Group A	Group B & C	Group D
15 × 15 squares and under	£160	£85	£64
Over 15 × 15 squares	£210	£125	£85

News Agencies

Associated Press News Agency

12 Norwich Street, London EC4A 1BP
☎020 7353 1515
Fax 020 7353 8118 (Newsdesk)

Material is either generated in-house or by regulars. Hires the occasional stringer. No unsolicited mss.

Dow Jones Newswires

10 Fleet Place, London EC4M 7QN
☎020 7842 9900 Fax 020 7842 9361

A real-time financial and business newswire operated by Dow Jones & Co., publishers of *The Wall Street Journal*. No unsolicited material.

National News Press and Photo Agency

109 Clifton Street, London EC2A 4LD
☎020 7684 3000 Fax 020 7684 3030

All press releases welcome. Most work is ordered or commissioned. Coverage includes courts, tribunals, conferences, general news, etc. – words and pictures – as well as PR.

Press Association Ltd

292 Vauxhall Bridge Road, London SW1V 1AE
☎020 7963 7000/7107 (Newsdesk)
Fax 020 7963 7192 (Newsdesk)
Email newsdesk@pa.press.net
Website www.pa.press.net

No unsolicited material. Most items are produced in-house though occasional outsiders may be used. A phone call to discuss specific material may lead somewhere 'but this is rare'.

Reuters

85 Fleet Street, London EC4P 4AJ
☎020 7250 1122

No unsolicited mss.

Solo Syndication Ltd

49–53 Kensington High Street, London W8 5ED
☎020 7376 2166 Fax 020 7938 3165

FOUNDED 1978. *Specialises* in worldwide newspaper syndication of photos, features and cartoons. Professional contributors only.

South Yorkshire Sport

6 Sharman Walk, Apperknowle, Sheffield, South Yorkshire S18 4BJ
☎01246 414767/07970 284848 (mobile)
Fax 01246 414767
Email Nicksport1@aol.com

Provides written/broadcast coverage of sport in the South Yorkshire area.

Space Press NA

Bridge House, Blackden Lane, Goostrey, Cheshire CW4 8PZ
☎01477 533403/534440 Fax 01477 535756
Email Scoop2001@aol.com
Website www.CountylifeOnline.com

FOUNDED 1972. Press and picture agency covering Cheshire and the North West, North Midlands, including Kutsford, Macclesfield, Congleton, Crewe and Nantwich, Wilmslow, Alderley Edge, serving national, regional and local press, TV and radio.

Screen Writing

Lynda La Plante

For writers trying to develop a career in screenwriting there are various 'self-help hints' that I believe are necessary. Obviously we begin with talent and I won't waste space dealing with that; let's just say you've got it and what you have to learn is that having it is one thing but getting it recognized is an entirely different matter.

It would be wonderful to think that all the hundreds of producers, agents, editors, television networks and film financiers spend their time searching for fresh blood. Sadly, this is more often not the case. It's not the writers they are hungry for, it's the new innovative ideas, i.e. the story. No plot has one strand; there is to every good screenplay a beginning, a middle and an end. Listen to someone tell a joke. You'll hear in a condensed form what I'm talking about; and when a punch line doesn't work nobody laughs! There are a lot of scripts with a great opening sequence but if they dribble into snooze-time midway forget it.

So, be it a comedy story or a dramatic theme, know its content backwards. Know the characters. In other words, know the situation you are writing. Don't grab at straws and think that is how a police officer would speak or that is what a doctor would say. Get your facts and research under your belt before you start.

If you have a query regarding a plot or character line, go to the source. I have never at any time faced a brick wall when asking for facts, be they from a prison, a police station, a mortuary or a kids' nursery school. Just ask.

Unpicking a story line because you discover your main character realistically could not be in the situation you have placed him or her in means extra work and rewriting. You want your product read, you want it bought, this is not a game but a career, and completing your well-researched, well-plotted script is not enough because you also want to get paid for it.

Stage, film or television scripts have a shelf life. Do not think your idea is not being written by someone else at exactly the same time as you are hammering away at the keyboard. Do not believe that twenty thousand other writers haven't read the newspaper headline that you think would make a great thriller. It's a scramble, because ideas, fresh, good ideas, are hard to come by and there are not only writers sniffing around but hundreds of producers looking to spot a brilliant idea too. Producers can commission an idea to be written and they are unlikely to pluck out an unknown author with no credits to write it if it's hot. Plus if they commission you to write, they pay you, so they also own the story at the end of the day!

So…that's the bad news. The good news is there is always space for you. No matter how hard it sounds. If you have a script that is good, it can move into the mainstream, but . . . now comes the tricky part; how do you get it not just read but produced, filmed and the money in the bank? In other words, how do you get the initial break?

In my opinion it's got something to do with luck, right time, right place. I've no doubt that someone will reject everything I have said and tell me that they sent a script in to a company who loved it, called them in, introduced them to a fantastic production team and their careers were made overnight. But let's look at the steps that I suggest you take to ensure that for starters your work gets through stage one; that means that someone in the business actually reads it.

1) The Agent. An unknown scriptwriter with no track record might find it tough to get representation even if he's the next Chekhov. Agents rarely have time to wade through unsolicited scripts; they have enough unemployed writers on their books submitting their own work, let alone the writers also submitting their work that they want read because they have been commissioned.

2) Without an agent, how do you get your work read? And, most importantly, read by someone in the right department? Personally, I do not think sending a complete script is good business sense. It is treatment time.

Learn how to present a treatment (a short abridged version of the plot). Next, do not make the mistake of sending it off to a major corporation in the hope that it will be read by the correct department...remember that all broadcasters and production companies have different departments: drama, series, mini-series, comedy half-hours, comedy series, and children's sections. So it is logical to *find out* who runs the right section for your story treatment.

Do not believe that if it goes to the Comedy Department they will look over it and pass it on to drama. There are thousands of ideas submitted every single day! And then there are the readers who plough through unsolicited documents. I have been in offices where the walls are lined with scripts, literally six feet high and with little likelihood of them ever making it onto the screen.

The key is to determine first what your product is. Secondly, find out who runs the department you believe your idea is suitable for. How? You pick up the phone and ask. Then, armed with the fact that Joe Bloggs runs the Drama Department, you send your treatment direct to him. If they are interested they will get you in for a meeting. You are now through the door.

3) The Pitch. Having worked on your treatment, and found out who to send it to, you now have the meeting. You will be asked to 'talk it over' – this is, in actual fact, big assessment time. They want to know if you are capable of writing it, for one. Two, you have to reassure them that they were correct

in bringing you in for the meeting. Know your product backwards. If they fire any questions at you regarding plot and characters, you must have the answers. It is sell time! And you now verbally sell it, you have to excite them . . . If you've passed stage two they will commission you to write the script. Your toe is well and truly through the door.

4) Delivery. Remember these people you met will have readers. Do not think you have the only script they have in development – they could have ten or twenty, or even more. Do not make the mistake of thinking you are home and dry. Readers read and they get used to a format, used to seeing how a script should be set out, and if your script is presented in an unprofessional manner, all screwed up with misspellings, typos and other errors, you'll irritate the reader.

   Also, get to know your marketplace in that meeting. The Finance Department will be working with set budgets and it's a big mistake if you have an avalanche, two helicopter crashes and five hundred extras in your first four scenes when you are working with limited funds.

   How do you know? Again, ask! Get hold of videos of past television shows, ask to see formatted scripts, get to understand the profession you are embarking on . . . In other words, start to get street smart and ready to deliver the goods.

5) If from this first script draft you get commissioned to write a whole series it means you've won round five. You are now sailing upwind and the proof of your idea being special, being worth taking a punt on, is entirely up to and down to you. By this time you'll get guidance and editorial assistance, and also just by having a commission you might try a few agents at the same time. You now having something to deal with . . . So they will get to read this new script – meet this new writer!

I hope that what I have written helps some; it may annoy others, but I have spent years perfecting my craft. I do not profess to be a great writer but I am a successful one, and it's been a tough, hard ride. I work in a very competitive field and to remain in the profession I love, I have become a professional. I encourage new writers in every possible way. I give writer's bursaries to colleges and universities and am always looking for new writers who have the dedication and preparation that I have forced upon myself. I try when possible to give confidence, because it is such a mainstay for a writer. Rejection is wounding, but you get used to it and you keep on going. Rejection can also be a learning curve; no matter how it hurts, every day I learn more.

   I know I have also been lucky. I know I have had some wonderful mentors but, in reality, I can also hand on heart say that my own determination made me constantly get up from the knocks. There is nothing like seeing your words come to life. In a way they are your dreams and you pictured them first in your head, and that is the only time they really belong to you entirely. By the time your script comes to the screen many hands and many voices have put their ten cents in, some good, some perhaps not so good, but I still get the same excitement on every project. It's a great career to fight for.

Lynda La Plante began her career as a television actress. When she turned to writing she made her breakthrough with the hit TV series Widows. *Her subsequent novels,* The Legacy, Bella Mafia, Entwined, Cold Shoulder, Cold Heart *and* Cold Blood, *have all been international bestsellers. She is one of Britain's most successful and prolific screenwriters, with the much-acclaimed* Prime Suspect *winning four awards, including a BAFTA.*

Television and Radio

BBC TV and Radio

Website www.bbc.co.uk

Greg Dyke, on taking over the reins from John Birt as Director-General in April 2000, announced organisational changes which place programme makers at the forefront of the new BBC structure. The BBC Broadcast and BBC Production directorates are to be broken up with three new divisions replacing BBC Production: Drama, Entertainment, Film and Children; Factual and Learning; and Sport. Four departments of what was BBC Broadcast are represented on the executive committee: TV; Radio; New Media; and Nations & Regions. The new structure and appointments will not be in place until October 2000 and cannot be reflected in the listing which follows.

Director-General *Greg Dyke*

TELEVISION

Director, Television *Mark Thompson*
Controller, BBC1 *Peter Salmon*
Controller, BBC2 *Jane Root*

RADIO

Director of Radio *Jenny Abramsky*
Controller, Radio 1 *Andy Parfitt*
Controller, Radio 2 *James Moir*
Controller, Radio 3 *Roger Wright*
Controller, Radio 4 *Helen Boaden*
Controller, Radio 5 Live *Bob Shennan*

Radio 1 is the popular music-based station; Radio 2 broadcasts popular light entertainment with celebrity presenters; Radio 3 is devoted to classical and contemporary music; Radio 4 is the main news and current affairs station while broadcasting a wide range of other programmes such as consumer matters, wildlife, science, gardening, etc. It also produces the bulk of drama, comedy, serials and readings. Radio 5 Live is the 24-hour news and sport station.

BBC News

BBC Television Centre, Wood Lane,
London W12 7RJ
☎020 8743 8000
Website www.bbc.co.uk/news

BBC News is the world's largest newsgathering organisation, with 2000 journalists, 250 foreign correspondents and 55 bureaux around the world. BBC News serves: BBC1, BBC2, Radios 1, 2, 3, 4 and 5 Live, BBC News 24, BBC Parliament, BBC World, BBC World Service, BBC Online, Ceefax.

Chief Executive, BBC News *Tony Hall*
Deputy Chief Executive *Richard Sambrook*
Head of TV News *Roger Mosey*

NEWS PROGRAMMES/CONTINUOUS NEWS
Executive Editor, Radio Daily Current Affairs *Anne Koch*
Executive Editor, Radio News *John Allen*
Editor, Today *Rod Liddle*
Editor, The World at One/World This Weekend/PM/Broadcasting House *Kevin Marsh*
Editor, Radio 1 News *Colin Hancock*
Editors, The World Tonight *Pru Keely, Jenni Russell*
Editor, 1 o'clock News *Jay Hunt*
Editor, 6 o'clock News *Mark Popescu*
Editor, 9 o'clock News *Jonathan Baker*
Editor, Newsnight *Sian Kevill*
Editor, Breakfast News *Andrew Thompson*
Editor, Breakfast With Frost *Barney Jones*

CONTINUOUS NEWS
Managing Editor, Radio Five Live *Bill Rogers*
Editor, World Service News Programmes *John Morrison*
Editor, Radio News Bulletins *Tim Bailey*
Editor, Global Sunday (Radio 5 Live) *Maria Balinska*
Editor, Late Night Live, Global Saturday, Up All Night (Radio 5 Live) *Robin Britten*
Commissioning Editor *Steve Kyte*
Editor, Ceefax *Paul Brannan*

Ceefax

Room 7013, BBC Television Centre, Wood Lane, London W12 7RJ
☎020 8576 1801

Subtitling

Room 1468, BBC White City, Wood Lane, London W12 7RJ
☎020 8752 7054/0141 339 8844 ext. 2128

A rapidly expanding service available via Ceefax page 888. Units based in both London and Glasgow.

BBC Arts and Classical Music

EM07 East Tower, BBC Television Centre, Wood Lane, London W12 9RJ
☎020 8225 6217/8576 1053
Fax 020 8749 9259

Acting Head of BBC Arts and Classical Music *Alex Graham*
Head of Classical Music (Radio) *Dr John Evans*
Head of Classical Music (Television) *Peter Maniura*
Editor, Arts Features *Keith Alexander*
Editor, Omnibus *Basil Comely*
Editor, Arena *Anthony Wall*
Executive Editor, Radio *John Boundy*

Television, radio and World Service production of Arts programmes such as *Omnibus*; *Arena*; *Review*; *Night Waves* and *Meridian*.

BBC Children's Programes

RB200, BBC Television Centre, Wood Lane, London W12 7RJ
☎020 8576 1916 Fax 020 8576 8122

Head of BBC Children's Programmes *Dot Prior*
Executive Producer, Children's Acquisitions *Theresa Plummer-Andrews*
Executive Producer, Children's Drama *Elaine Sperber*
Executive Producer, Entertainment *Chris Bellinger*
Executive Producer, News and Factual Programmes *Roy Milani*
Editor, Blue Peter *Steve Hocking*
Producer, Grange Hill *Jo Ward*
Editor, Live & Kicking *Angela Sharp*

BBC Documentaries and History

BBC White City: 201 Wood Lane, London W12 7TS
☎020 8752 6354 Fax 020 8752 6060

Head of BBC Documentaries and History, Television *Paul Hamann*
Editor, Inside Story *Olivia Lichtenstein*
Editor, Modern Times *Alex Holmes*
Editor, Reputations *Jenny Abbott*
Editor, Timewatch *Laurence Rees*

BBC Drama Production

TV
BBC Television Centre, Wood Lane, London W12 7RJ
☎020 8743 8000
Controller, BBC Drama *Susan Spindler*

Head of Serials *Jane Tranter*
Head of Series *Mal Young*
Head of Single Drama & Films *David Thompson*
Head of Development, Serials *Pippa Harris*
Head of Development, Serials *Serena Cullen*
Head of Development, Single Drama & Films *Tracey Scoffield*

RADIO

Broadcasting House, London W1A 1AA
☎020 7580 4468

Head of Radio Drama *Kate Rowland*
Executive Producer *Jeremy Mortimer*
Executive Producer *David Hunter*
Executive Producer (Manchester) *Sue Roberts*
Executive Producer (Birmingham)/ Editor, The Archers *Vanessa Whitburn*
Executive Producer (World Service Drama) *Gordon House*

BBC Drama's New Writing Initiative develops and nurtures new writing talent across BBC TV and Radio Drama and handles unsolicited scripts for Single TV dramas and radio drama. To be considered for one of the schemes run by the New Writing Initiative please send a sample full length drama script to: New Writing Initiative, Room 6059, BBC Broadcasting House, Portland Place, London W1A 1AA. For guidelines on unsolicited scripts please send a large s.a.e. to the same address.

BBC Drama Coordinator, New Writing Initiative *Lucy Hannah*

BBC Education Production

BBC White City, 201 Wood Lane, London W12 7TS
☎020 8752 5252

Head of BBC Education Production *Marilyn Wheatcroft*
Executive Producers, Schools *Clare Elstow, Geoff Marshall-Taylor, Sue Nott*
Executive Producer, Languages *David Wilson*
Managing Editor, World Service *David Thomas*
Executive Producer, Radio *Philip Sellars*
Executive Producer, Learning *Chris Palmer*

BBC OPEN UNIVERSITY PRODUCTION CENTRE
Walton Hall, Milton Keynes, MK7 6BH
☎01908 655544 Fax 01908 376324

Head of Production *Ian Rosenbloom*
Executive Producer, Online *Karen Chilton*

Television and radio production of schools and college programmes, language courses, education for adults, plus multimedia and audiovisual material in partnership with the Open University. The Learning Zone broadcasts education, training and information programmes on BBC2 from midnight during the week.

BBC Entertainment

BBC Television Centre, Wood Lane, London W12 7RJ
☎020 8743 8000
Controller, BBC Entertainment
  Paul Jackson
Head of Light Entertainment, Television
  David Young
Head of Comedy, Television *Geoffrey Perkins*
Head of Comedy Entertainment,
  Television *Jon Plowman*
Script Executive (Bi-media) *Bill Dare*
Editor, Radio Entertainment *John Pidgeon*
Producer, The News Huddlines *Carol Smith*

Programmes produced by BBC Entertainment range from *Shooting Stars* and *Jonathan Creek* on television to *Just a Minute*; *I'm Sorry I Haven't a Clue* and *The News Quiz* on Radio 4. Virtually every comic talent in Britain got their first break writing one-liners for topical comedy weeklies like Radio 2's *The News Huddlines* (currently paying about £10 for a 'quickie' – one- or two-liners). Ideas welcome; fax to Carol Smith on 020 7765 3839. Non-commissioned writers are welcome to attend an open meeting held in the main reception at Broadcasting House, Portland Place, London W1, every Tuesday at 1.00 pm, where ideas can be discussed with the production team of *The News Huddlines*.

BBC Features and Events

Room 4360, BBC White City Wood Lane, London W12 7TS
☎020 8752 5906 Fax 020 8752 5915
Head of BBC Features and Events
  Anne Morrison
Executive Editor, Radio *Graham Ellis*
Executive Producer, Crimewatch
  Seetha Kumar

Covers consumer affairs, major national events and informal education, producing television and radio programmes such as *Crimewatch*; *Watchdog*; *You and Yours*; *Holiday* and *Woman's Hour*.

BBC Music Entertainment

Western House, 99 Great Portland Street, London W1A 1AA
☎020 7765 5407
Head of BBC Music Entertainment
  Trevor Dann

Music production for television and radio, with programmes such as *Top of the Pops*, *Ozone* and *Later With Jools*, and coverage of events such as Glastonbury. Provides the majority of output for Radio 1 and Radio 2 as well as popular music programming for World Service.

BBC Religion

New Broadcasting House, Oxford Road, Manchester M60 1SJ
☎0161 200 2020 Fax 0161 244 3183
Head of Religious Broadcasting
  Rev. Ernest Rea

Regular programmes for television include *Songs of Praise*; *Everyman*; *Heart of the Matter*. Radio output includes *Good Morning Sunday*; *Sunday Half Hour*; *Choral Evensong*; *The Brains Trust*.

BBC Science

BBC White City, 201 Wood Lane, London W12 7TS
☎020 8752 5252
Head of BBC Science *Glenwyn Benson*
Editor, Tomorrow's World *Saul Nasse*
Editor, Horizon *John Lynch*
Editor, Living Proof *Michael Mosley*

Produces programmes such as *Animal Hospital* and *Tomorrow's World* for television and radio.

BBC Sport

BBC TV Centre, Wood Lane, London W12 7RJ
☎020 8624 9200
Deputy Head of Sport, Executive Editor,
  Football *Niall Sloane*

Sports news and commentaries across television and Radios 1, 4 and 5 Live, with the majority of output on Radio 5 Live. Regular programmes include *Sportsnight*; *Sports News*; *Sport on Five* and *Littlejohn* (presented by Richard Littlejohn).

BBC Birmingham

Broadcasting Centre, Pebble Mill Road, Birmingham B5 7QQ
☎0121 432 8888 Fax 0121 432 8634
Head of Regional and Local Programmes
  Roy Roberts
Editor, Newsgathering *Rod Beards*
Producers, Midlands Today *Charles Watkins,*
  Naomi Bishop
Series Producer, The Midlands Report
  Bob Jefford

Home of the Pebble Mill Studio. Output for the network includes: TV – *Going For a Song*;

Countryfile; Top Gear; Country Tracks; Dalziel and Pascoe; Call My Bluff; Gardener's World; Real Rooms. Radio – *The Archers; Shake, Rattle and Roll; Farming Today; Jazz Notes; Listen to the Band.* Openings exist for well-researched topical or local material.

BBC Birmingham serves opt-out stations in Nottingham and Norwich:

BBC East Midlands (Nottingham)

East Midlands Broadcasting Centre, London Road, Nottingham NG2 4UU
☎0115 9550500

Head of Regional and Local Programmes
   Craig Henderson
Head of Newsgathering *Emma Agnew*
Senior Producer, East Midlands Today
   Liz Howell

BBC East (Norwich)

St Catherine's Close, All Saint's Green, Norwich, Norfolk NR1 3ND
☎01603 619331

Head of Regional and Local Programmes
   David Holdsworth
Head of Newsgathering *Tim Bishop*
Poducers, Look East *Ian Kings, Roger Farrant*
Series Producer, Matter of Fact *Diana Hare*

BBC Bristol

Broadcasting House, Whiteladies Road, Bristol BS8 2LR
☎0117 9732211

Head of Features *Jeremy Gibson* (bi-media)
Head of Natural History Unit *Keith Scholey*
   (bi-media)

BBC Bristol is the home of the BBC's Natural History Unit, producing programmes such as *Wildlife on One; The Natural World; The Life of Birds;* and *The Really Wild Show* for BBC1 and BBC2. It also produces natural history programmes for Radio 4 and Radio 5 Live. The Features department produces a wide range of television programmes, including *999; Antiques Roadshow; 10x10; Picture This; Vets in Practice; War Walks* and *Under the Sun* in addition to radio programmes specialising in history, travel, literature and human interest features for Radio 4.

BBC Northern Ireland

Broadcasting House, Ormeau Avenue, Belfast BT2 8HQ
☎028 9033 8000
Website www.bbc.co.uk/northernireland

Controller *Patrick Loughrey*
Head of Broadcasting *Anna Carragher*

Head of Production *Paul Evans*
Head of News & Current Affairs
   Andrew Colman
Head of Drama *Robert Cooper*
Chief Producer, Sport *Terry Smyth*
Chief Producer, Music & Arts *David Byers*
Chief Producer, Youth & Community
   Fedelma Harkin
Chief Producer, Education/Irish
   Language Programmes *Kiaran Hegarty*
Chief Producer, Topical Programmes
   Bruce Batten
Chief Producer, Religion *Bert Tosh*

Regular television programmes include *Newsline 6.30; Hearts and Minds* and *Country Times.* Radio stations: BBC Radio Foyle and BBC Radio Ulster (see entries).

BBC Scotland

Broadcasting House, Queen Margaret Drive, Glasgow G12 8DG
☎0141 338 2000
Website www.bbc.co.uk/scotland

Controller *John McCormick*
Secretary *Mark Leishman*
Head of Production *Colin Cameron*
Head of Broadcast *Ken MacQuarrie*
Head of Drama *Barbara McKissack*
Head of News and Current Affairs
   Blair Jenkins
Head of Children's and Features *Liz Scott*
Head of Arts & Entertainment *Mike Bolland*
Head of Education and Religious
   Broadcasting *Andrew Barr*
Head of Sport *Neil Fraser*
Head of Programmes, North *Andrew Jones*
Head of Gaelic *Donalda MacKinnon*

Headquarters of BBC Scotland with centres in Aberdeen, Dundee, Edinburgh and Inverness. Regular programmes include *Reporting Scotland* and *Sportscene* on television and *Good Morning Scotland; Fred Macaulay* and *Storyline* on radio.

Aberdeen

Broadcasting House, Beechgrove Terrace, Aberdeen AB9 2ZT
☎01224 625233

News, plus some features, including the regular *Beechgrove Garden.* Second TV centre, also with regular radio broadcasting.

Dundee

Nethergate Centre, 66 Nethergate, Dundee DD1 4ER
☎01382 202481

News base only; contributors' studio.

Edinburgh
Broadcasting House, Queen Street, Edinburgh
EH2 1JF
☎0131 225 3131
Religious, arts and science programming base.
Bi-media news operation.

Inverness
7 Culduthel Road, Inverness 1V2 4AD
☎01463 720720
News features for Radio Scotland. HQ for Radio
Nan Gaidheal, the Gaelic radio service serving
most of Scotland (**Editor** *Ishbel MacLennan*).

BBC North/BBC North West/
BBC North East & Cumbria

The regional centres at Leeds, Manchester and
Newcastle make their own programmes on a
bi-media approach, each centre having its own
head of regional and local programmes.

BBC North (Leeds)
Broadcasting Centre, Woodhouse Lane,
Leeds, West Yorkshire LS2 9PX
☎0113 2441188
Head of Regional and Local Programmes
Colin Philpott
Editor, Newsgathering *Kate Watkins*
Producer, North of Westminster *Rod Jones*
Producer, Close Up North *Ian Cundall*
Producers, Look North *Denise Wallace,*
Paul Greenan

BBC North West (Manchester)
New Broadcasting House, Oxford Road,
Manchester M60 1SJ
☎0161 200 2020
Head of Regional and Local Programmes
Martin Brooks
Editor, Newsgathering *Barbara Metcalf*
Producers, Northwest Tonight
Tamsin O'Brien, Jim Clark
Producer, Close Up North *Deborah van Bishop*
Producer, Northwestminster *Liam Fogarty*

BBC North East & Cumbria
(Newcastle upon Tyne)
Broadcasting Centre, Barrack Road,
Newcastle Upon Tyne NE99 2NE
☎0191 232 1313
Head of Regional and Local Programmes
Olwyn Hocking
Editor, Newsgathering *Andrew Hartley*
Producers, Look North *Iain Williams,*
Andrew Lambert

Producer, North of Westminster
Michael Wild
Producers, Close Up North *Dave Morrison,*
Michael Wild

BBC Wales

Broadcasting House, Llandaff, Cardiff CF5 2YQ
☎029 2032 2000 Fax 029 2055 2973
Website www.bbc.co.uk/wales
Controller *Menna Richards*
Head of Production *John Geraint*
Head of Programmes (Welsh Language)
Gwynn Pritchard
Head of Programmes (English Language)
Dai Smith
Head of News & Current Affairs *Aled Eurig*
Head of Drama *Matthew Robinson*
Series Editor, Pobol y Cwm
Terry Dyddgen-Jones

Headquarters of BBC Wales, with regional
centres in Bangor, Aberystwyth, Carmarthen,
Wrexham and Swansea. BBC Wales television
produces up to 12 hours of English language
programmes a week, 12 hours in Welsh for
transmission on **S4C** and an increasing number
of hours on network services. Regular programmes include *Wales Today; Wales on Saturday*
and *Pobol y Cwm* (Welsh-language soap) on
television and *Good Morning Wales; Good
Evening Wales; Post Cyntaf* and *Post Prynhawn*
on radio.

Bangor
Broadcasting House, Meirion Road, Bangor,
Gwynedd LL57 2BY
☎01248 370880 Fax 01248 351443
Head of Centre *Marian Wyn Jones*

BBC West/BBC South/
BBC South West/BBC South East

The four regional television stations, BBC
West, BBC South, BBC South West and BBC
South East produce more than 1100 hours of
television each year, including the nightly news
magazine programmes, as well as regular 30-
minute local current affairs programmes and
parliamentary programmes. Each of the regions
operates a comprehensive local radio service
and all have a 'bi-media' approach – which
means that both radio and television share their
resources – as well as a range of correspondents
specialising in subjects like health, education,
business, local government, home affairs and
the environment.

BBC West (Bristol)

Broadcasting House, Whiteladies Road,
Bristol BS8 2LR
☎0117 9732211

Head of Regional and Local Programmes
Rhodri Talfan-Davies (Responsible for BBC
West [TV], BBC Radio Bristol, BBC
Somerset Sound, BBC Radio
Gloucestershire and BBC Wiltshire Sound)
Editor, Newsgathering *Ian Cameron*
Series Producer, Close Up West
James MacAlpine

BBC South (Southampton)

Broadcasting House, Havelock Road,
Southampton, Hampshire SO14 7PU
☎023 8022 6201

Head of Regional and Local Programmes
Eve Turner (Responsible for BBC South
[TV], BBC Radio Berkshire, BBC Radio
Oxford and BBC Radio Solent)
Editors, Newsgathering *Mia Costello,
Cathy Burnett*
Series Producer, Southern Eye *Peter Pitt*

BBC South West (Plymouth)

Broadcasting House, Seymour Road,
Mannamead, Plymouth, Devon PL3 5BD
☎01752 229201

Head of Regional and Local Programmes
Leo Devine (Responsible for BBC South
West [TV], BBC Radio Devon, BBC
Radio Cornwall, BBC Radio Guernsey and
BBC Radio Jersey)
Editor, Newsgathering *Roger Clark*
Editor, Current Affairs *Simon Willis*

BBC South East (Elstree)

Elstree Centre, Clarendon Road,
Borehamwood, Hertfordshire WD6 1JF
☎020 8953 6100

Head of Regional and Local Programmes
Jane Mote (Responsible for BBC South East
[TV], BBC Radio Kent, BBC Southern
Counties Radio and BBC London Live)
Editor, Newsgathering *Peter Solomons*
Executive Producer, First Sight *John Samson*

BBC World Service

PO Box 76, Bush House, Strand, London
WC2B 4PH
☎020 7240 3456 Fax 020 7557 1900
Website www.bbc.co.uk/worldservice
Chief Executive *Mark Byford*
**Director, World Service News &
  Programme Commissioning** *Bob Jobbins*

The World Service broadcasts in English and 42
other languages. The English service is round-
the-clock, with news and current affairs as the
main component. With over 140 million listeners, excluding countries where research is not
possible, it reaches a bigger audience than its five
closest competitors combined. The World
Service is increasingly available throughout the
world on local FM stations, via satellite and online as well as through short-wave frequencies.
Coverage includes world business, politics, peo-
ple/events/opinions, development issues, the
international scene, developments in science and
technology, sport, religion, music, drama, the
arts. BBC World Service broadcasting is financed
by a grant-in-aid voted by Parliament amounting
to £160.9 million for 2000/2001.

BBC Local Radio

BBC Local Radio

Henry Wood House, 3 & 6 Langham Place,
London W1A 1AA
☎020 7580 4468
Website www.bbc.co/england

There are 39 local BBC radio stations in England
transmitting on FM and medium wave. These
present local news, information and entertainment to local audiences and reflect the life of the
communities they serve. Each has its own newsroom which supplies local bulletins and national
news service. Many have specialist producers. A
comprehensive list of programmes for each is
unavailable and would soon be out of date. For
general information on programming, contact
the relevant station direct.

BBC Asian Network

BBC Pebble Mill, Birmingham B5 7SH
☎0121 432 8558 Fax 0121 432 8185
Email asian.network@bbc.co.uk
Website www.bbc.co.uk/england/asiannetwork
Also at: Epic House, Charles Street, Leicester
LE1 3SH
☎0116 2516688 Fax 0116 2532004
Managing Editor *Vijay Sharma*

Commenced broadcasting in November 1996
to a Midlands audience with programmes in
English, Bengali, Gujerati, Hindi, Punjabi and
Urdu.

BBC Radio Berkshire

PO Box 104.4, Reading, Berkshire RG94 8FH
☎0645 311444 Fax 0645 311555

Website www.bbc.co.uk/england/
radioberkshire/index.shtml

Editor *Phil Ashworth*

Restored to its original name in 2000 having been merged with BBC Radio Oxford in 1995 to create BBC Thames Valley.

BBC Radio Bristol

PO Box 194, Bristol BS99 7QT
☎0117 9741111 Fax 0117 9732549
Email radio.bristol@bbc.co.uk
Website www.bbc.co.uk/england/radiobristol

Managing Editor *Jenny Lacey*

Wide range of feature material used.

BBC Radio Cambridgeshire

PO Box 96, 104 Hills Road, Cambridge CB2 1LD
☎01223 259696 Fax 01223 460832
Email Cambs@bbc.co.uk
Website www.bbc.co.uk/radiocambridgeshire

Editor *Andrew Wilson*

Short stories are broadcast occasionally.

BBC Radio Cleveland

Broadcasting House, PO Box 95FM, Middlesbrough, Cleveland TS1 5DG
☎01642 225211 Fax 01642 211356
Email radio.cleveland@bbc.co.uk
Website www.bbc.co.uk/england/radiocleveland

Managing Editor *David Peel*

Material used is mainly local to Teesside, Co. Durham and North Yorkshire, and is almost exclusively news and current affairs.

BBC Radio Cornwall

Phoenix Wharf, Truro, Cornwall TR1 1UA
☎01872 275421 Fax 01872 275045
Email radio.cornwall@bbc.co.uk
Website www.bbc.co.uk/england/radiocornwall

Editor *Pauline Causey*

On air from 1983 serving Cornwall and the Isles of Scilly. The station broadcasts a news/talk format 18 hours a day on 103.9/95.2 FM. Chris Blount's afternoon programme includes interviews with local authors and arts-related features on Cornish themes.

BBC Coventry & Warwickshire

Holt Court, Greyfriars Road, Coventry CV1 2WR
☎024 7686 0086 Fax 024 7657 0100
Email coventry.warwickshire@bbc.co.uk

Website www.bbc.co.uk/england/coventrywarwickshire

Managing Editor *David Robey*
Senior Editor *Raj Ford*

News, current affairs, public service information and community involvement, relevant to its broadcast area: Coventry and Warwickshire. Occasionally uses the work of local writers, though cannot handle large volumes of unsolicited material. Any material commissioned will need to be strong in local interest and properly geared to broadcasting.

BBC Radio Cumbria

Annetwell Street, Carlisle, Cumbria CA3 8BB
☎01228 592444 Fax 01228 511195
Email radio.cumbria@bbc.co.uk
Website www.bbc.co.uk/england/radiocumbria

Editor *Nigel Dyson*

Occasional opportunities for plays and short stories are advertised on-air. No outlet for literary material with the exception of *Write Now*, a weekly 30-minute local writing programme broadcast on Sundays at 5.30 pm.

BBC Radio Cymru

Broadcasting House, Llandaff, Cardiff CF5 2YQ
☎029 2032 2000 Fax 029 2032 2506
Email radio.cymru@bbc.co.uk
Website www.bbc.co.uk/cymru/radio/index.shtml

Editor *Aled Glynne Davies*
Editor, Radio Cymru News *Wil Morgan*

Welsh and English-language programmes, including *Post Cyntaf*; *Jonsi a Nia*; *Chwaraeon* and *Gang Bangor*.

BBC Radio Derby

PO Box 269, Derby DE1 3HL
☎01332 361111 Fax 01332 290794
Email radio.derby@bbc.co.uk
Website www.bbc.co.uk/england/radioderby

Managing Editor *Mike Bettison*

News and information (the backbone of the station's output), local sports coverage, daily magazine and phone-ins, minority interest, Asian and African Caribbean weekly programmes.

BBC Radio Devon

PO Box 5, Broadcasting House, Seymour Rd, Mannamead, Plymouth, Devon PL1 1XT
☎01752 260323 Fax 01752 234599
Email radio.devon@bbc.co.uk
Website www.bbc.co.uk/england/radiodevon

Managing Editor *John Lilley*

On air since 1983. Short stories – up to 1000 words from local authors only – used weekly on the Sunday afternoon show (2.05 pm–3.30 pm). Contact *Becky Newell*.

BBC Essex

198 New London Road, Chelmsford, Essex CM2 9XB
☎01245 616000 Fax 01245 492983
Email essex@bbc.co.uk
Website www.bbc.co.uk/england/essex

Editor *Margaret Hyde*

Broadcasts local and regional programmes for 20 hours every day aimed at a mature audience. Programmes are a mix of news, interviews, expert contributors, phone-ins, sport and special interest such as gardening. *Write On* is an annual short story competition open to local writers.

BBC Radio Foyle

8 Northland Road, Londonderry BT48 7JD
☎028 7126 2244 Fax 028 7137 8666

Manager *Ana Leddy*
News Producers *Felicity McCall, Paul McFadden*
Arts/Book Reviews *Frank Galligan, Colum Arbuckle*
Features *Michael Bradley*

Radio Foyle broadcasts about seven hours of original material a day, seven days a week to the north west of Northern Ireland. Other programmes are transmitted simultaneously with Radio Ulster. The output ranges from news, sport, and current affairs to live music recordings and arts reviews.

BBC Radio Gloucestershire

London Road, Gloucester GL1 1SW
☎01452 308585 Fax 01452 306541
Email radio.gloucestershire@bbc.co.uk
Website www.bbc.co.uk/england/ radiogloucestershire

Managing Editor *Bob Lloyd-Smith*

News and information covering the large variety of interests and concerns in Gloucestershire. Leisure, sport and music, plus African-Caribbean and Asian interests. Regular book reviews and interviews with local authors.

BBC GLR

See **BBC London Live**

BBC GMR

PO Box 951, Oxford Road, Manchester M60 1SD
☎0161 200 2000 Fax 0161 236 5804
Email gmr@bbc.co.uk
Website www.bbc.co.uk/england/gmr

Managing Editor *Karen Hannah*
News Editor *Angela Clarke*
Programmes Editor *Lawrence Mann*

On air from 1970 as Radio Manchester. Became BBC GMR in 1988. One of the largest of the BBC local radio stations, broadcasting news, current affairs, phone-ins, help, advice and sport.

BBC Radio Guernsey

Commerce House, Les Banques, St Peter Port, Guernsey, Channel Islands GY1 2HS
☎01481 728977 Fax 01481 713557
Email radio.guernsey@bbc.co.uk
Website www.bbc.co.uk/england/ radioguernsey

Managing Editor *Denzil Dudley*

Opened with its sister station, BBC Radio Jersey, in March 1982. Broadcasts 65 hours of local programming a week.

BBC Hereford & Worcester

Hylton Road, Worcester WR2 5WW
☎01905 748485 Fax 01905 748006
Email bbc.hw@bbc.co.uk
Website www.bbc.co.uk/england/ herefordworcester

Also at: 43 Broad Street, Hereford HR4 9HH
☎01432 355252 Fax 01432 356446

Managing Editor *James Coghill*

Holds competitions on an occasional basis for short stories, plays or dramatised documentaries with a local flavour.

BBC Radio Humberside

9 Chapel Street, Hull, North Humberside HU1 3NU
☎01482 323232 Fax 01482 621403
Email radio.humberside@bbc.co.uk
Website www.bbc.co.uk/england/ radiohumberside

Editor *Helen Thomas*

On air since 1971. Occasionally broadcasts short stories by local writers and holds competitions for local amateur authors and playwrights.

BBC Radio Jersey

18 Parade Road, St Helier, Jersey, Channel Islands JE2 3PL
☎01534 870000 Fax 01534 732569

Email james.filleul@bbc.co.uk
Website www.bbc.co.uk/england/radiojersey
Managing Editor *Denzil Dudley*
Senior Producer *James Filleul*
Local news, current affairs and community items.

BBC Radio Kent
Sun Pier, Chatham, Kent ME4 4EZ
☎01634 830505 Fax 01634 830573
Email radio.kent@bbc.co.uk
Website www.bbc.co.uk/england/radiokent
Editor, Local Services *Steve Tabchini*
Occasional commissions made for local interest
documentaries and other one-off programmes.

BBC Radio Lancashire
Darwen Street, Blackburn, Lancashire
BB2 2EA
☎01254 262411 Fax 01254 680821
Email radio.lancashire@bbc.co.uk
Website www.bbc.co.uk/england/
radiolancashire
Editor *Steve Taylor*
Journalism-based radio station, interested in
interviews with local writers. Also *Lancashire
Arts*, 1.00 pm–3.00 pm on Sundays.

BBC Radio Leeds
Broadcasting House, Woodhouse Lane, Leeds,
West Yorkshire LS2 9PN
☎0113 2442131 Fax 0113 2420652
Email radio.leeds@bbc.co.uk
Website www.bbc.co.uk/england/radioleeds
Managing Editor *Ashley Peatfield*
One of the country's biggest local radio stations,
BBC Radio Leeds was also one of the first, com-
ing on air in the 1960s as something of an exper-
imental venture. The station is 'all talk', with a
comprehensive news, sport and information ser-
vice as the backbone of its daily output. BBC
Radio Leeds has been a regular finalist for the
title of Sony Regional Station of the Year. Has
also won two Gold Sonys for best presentation.

BBC Radio Leicester
Epic House, Charles Street, Leicester LE1 3SH
☎0116 2516688
Fax 0116 2513632/2511463 (News)
Email radio.leicester@bbc.co.uk
Website www.bbc.co.uk/england/
radioleicester
Managing Editor *Mark Shardlow*
The first local station in Britain. Concentrates
on speech-based programmes in the morning
and on a music/speech mix in the afternoon.

BBC Radio Lincolnshire
PO Box 219, Newport, Lincoln LN1 3XY
☎01522 511411 Fax 01522 511726
Email radio.lincolnshire@bbc.co.uk
Website www.bbc.co.uk/england/
radiolincolnshire
Managing Editor *Charlie Partridge*
Unsolicited material considered only if locally
relevant. Maximum 1000 words: straight narra-
tive preferred, ideally with a topical content.

BBC London Live
PO Box 94.9, London WC2B 4QH
☎020 7224 2424 Fax 020 7208 9210
Email glr@bbc.co.uk
Website www.bbc.co.uk/londonlive
Managing Editor *David Robey*
Assistant Editor (News) *Martin Shaw*
Assistant Editor (General Programmes)
Suzanne Gilfillan
Formerly Greater London Radio which was
launched in 1988. It broadcasts news, infor-
mation, travel bulletins, sport and music to
Greater London and the Home Counties.

BBC Radio Manchester
See **BBC GMR**

BBC Radio Merseyside
55 Paradise Street, Liverpool L1 3BP
☎0151 708 5500 Fax 0151 794 0988
Email radio.merseyside@bbc.co.uk
Website www.bbc.co.uk/england/
radiomerseyside
Editor *Mick Ord*
Write Now, a weekly 25-minute regional writers'
programme, is produced at Radio Merseyside
and also broadcast on BBC Radio Cumbria.
Short stories (maximum 1200 words), plus
poetry and features on writing. Contact *Jenny
Collins* by post at the address above.

BBC Radio Newcastle
Broadcasting Centre, Barrack Road,
Newcastle upon Tyne NE99 1RN
☎0191 232 4141
Email radio.newcastle@bbc.co.uk
Website www.bbc.co.uk/england/
radionewcastle
Editor *Sarah Drummond*
Senior Producer (Programmes) *Jon Harle*

BBC Radio Norfolk
Norfolk Tower, Surrey Street, Norwich,
Norfolk NR1 3PA
☎01603 617411 Fax 01603 633692

Email norfolk@bbc.co.uk
Website www.bbc.co.uk/england/radionorfolk
Editor *David Clayton*

Good local material welcome for features/documentaries, but must relate directly to Norfolk.

BBC Northampton

Broadcasting House, Abington Street,
Northampton NN1 2BH
☎01604 239100 Fax 01604 230709
Email northampton@bbc.co.uk
Website www.bbc.co.uk/england/
radionorthampton
Editor, Local Services *John Ryan*
Senior Broadcast Journalists *Sarah Foster,*
Matthew Price, Mike Day

Books of local interest are regularly featured. Authors and poets are interviewed on merit. Poems and short stories are reviewed occasionally, but not broadcast. Runs regular competitions for local writers.

BBC Radio Nottingham

London Road, Nottingham NG2 4UU
☎0115 9550500 Fax 0115 9021983
Email radio.nottingham@bbc.co.uk
Website www.bbc.co.uk/england/
radionottingham
Editor *Kate Squire*

Rarely broadcasts scripted pieces of any kind but interviews with authors form a regular part of the station's output.

BBC Radio Oxford

PO Box 95.2, Oxford OX2 7YL
☎0645 311444 Fax 0645 311555
Website www.bbc.co.uk/england/
radiooxford/index.shtml
Managing Editor *Phil Ashworth*

Restored to its original name in 2000 having been merged with BBC Radio Berkshire in 1995 to create BBC Thames Valley. No opportunities at present as the outlet for short stories has been discontinued for the time being though the station frequently carries interviews with authors and offers books as prizes.

BBC Radio Scotland (Dumfries)

Elmbank, Lover's Walk, Dumfries DG1 1NZ
☎01387 268008 Fax 01387 252568
Email dumfries@bbc.co.uk
Senior Producer *Glenn Cooksley*
News Editor *Willie Johnston*

Previously Radio Solway. The station mainly outputs news bulletins (four daily). Changes have seen the station become more of a production centre with programmes being made for Radio Scotland as well as BBC Radio 2 and 5 Live. Freelancers of a high standard, familiar with Radio Scotland, should contact the producer.

BBC Radio Scotland (Orkney)

Castle Street, Kirkwall, Orkney KW15 1DF
☎01856 873939 Fax 01856 872908
Senior Producer *John Fergusson*

Regular programmes include *Around Orkney* (weekday news programme) and *Bruck* (magazine programme).

BBC Radio Scotland (Selkirk)

Municipal Buildings, High Street, Selkirk
TD7 4JX
☎01750 21884 Fax 01750 22400
Senior Producer *Carol Wightman*

Formerly BBC Radio Tweed. Produces weekly international travel and holiday programme, *The Case for Packing.*

BBC Radio Shetland

Pitt Lane, Lerwick, Shetland ZE1 0DW
☎01595 694747 Fax 01595 694307
Senior Producer *Richard Whitaker*

Regular programmes include *Good Evening Shetland.* An occasional books programme highlights the activities of local writers and writers' groups.

BBC Radio Sheffield

Ashdell Grove, 60 Westbourne Road,
Sheffield S10 2QU
☎0114 2686185 Fax 0114 2664375
Email radio.sheffield@bbc.co.uk
Website www.bbc.co.uk/england/
radiosheffield
Acting Editor *Emma Gilliam*

Weekly feature, *Write On* (Tuesday, 10.30 am to 11.00 am).

BBC Radio Shropshire

2–4 Boscobel Drive, Shrewsbury, Shropshire
SY1 3TT
☎01743 248484 Fax 01743 271702
Email radio.shropshire@bbc.co.uk
Website www.bbc.co.uk/england/
radioshropshire
Editor *Tony Fish*

On air since 1985. Unsolicited literary material very rarely used, and then only if locally relevant.

BBC Radio Solent

Broadcasting House, Havelock Road,
Southampton, Hampshire SO14 7PW
☎023 8063 1311 Fax 023 8033 9648
Email radio.solent@bbc.co.uk
Website www.bbc.co.uk/england/radiosolent
Managing Editor *Chris Van Schaick*

BBC Somerset Sound

14 Paul Street, Taunton, Somerset TA1 3PF
☎01823 252437 Fax 01823 332539
Email richard.austin@bbc.co.uk
Website www.bbc.co.uk/england/
    radiobristol/index.shtml

Editor *Jenny Lacey*

Informal, speech-based programming, with
strong news and current affairs output and
regular local-interest features, including local
writing. Poetry and short stories on the *Adam
Thomas Programme*.

BBC Southern Counties Radio

Broadcasting Centre, Guildford, Surrey
GU2 5AP
☎01483 306306 Fax 01483 304952
Email southern.counties.radio@bbc.co.uk
Website www.bbc.co.uk/england/
    southerncounties

Managing Editor *Mike Hapgood*

Formerly known as BBC Radio Sussex and
Surrey. Regular programmes include three
individual breakfast shows: *Breakfast Live in
Brighton with Jo Anne Good/in Surrey with Adrian
Love/in Sussex with John Radford*.

BBC Radio Stoke

Cheapside, Hanley, Stoke on Trent,
Staffordshire ST1 1JJ
☎01782 208080 Fax 01782 289115
Email radio.stoke@bbc.co.uk
Website www.bbc.co.uk/england/radiostoke
Managing Editor *Mark Hurrell*

On air since 1968, one of the first eight 'experimental' BBC stations. Emphasis on news,
current affairs and local topics. Music represents
one fifth of output. Unsolicited material of local
interest is welcome – send to managing editor.

BBC Radio Suffolk

Broadcasting House, St Matthew's Street,
Ipswich, Suffolk IP1 3EP
☎01473 250000 Fax 01473 210887
Email suffolk@bbc.co.uk
Website www.bbc.co.uk/england/radiosuffolk
Managing Editor *Keith Beech*

Strongly speech-based, dealing with news,
current affairs, community issues, the arts, agriculture, commerce, travel, sport and leisure.
Programmes frequently carry interviews with
writers.

BBC Thames Valley

See **BBC Radio Berkshire**and **BBC Radio
Oxford**

BBC Three Counties Radio

PO Box 3CR, Hastings Street, Luton,
Bedfordshire LU1 5XL
☎01582 441000 Fax 01582 401467
Email 3cr@bbc.co.uk
Website www.bbc.co.uk/england/threecounties
Managing Editor *Mark Norman*

Encourages freelance contributions from the
community across a wide range of radio output, including interview and feature material.
The station *very* occasionally broadcasts drama.
Stringent local criteria are applied in selection.
Particularly interested in historical topics (five
minutes maximum).

BBC Radio Ulster

Broadcasting House, Ormeau Avenue, Belfast
BT2 8HQ
☎028 9033 8000 Fax 028 9033 8800

Head of Broadcasting *Anna Carragher*
Head of Production *Paul Evans*

Programmes broadcast from 6.30 am – midnight
weekdays and from 7.55 am – midnight at weekends. Radio Ulster has won seven Sony awards
in recent years. Programmes include: *Good
Morning Ulster*; *John Bennett*; *Gerry Anderson*; *Talk
Back*; *Just Jones*; *Evening Extra* and *Across the Line*.

BBC Radio Wales

Broadcasting House, Llandaff, Cardiff CF5 2YQ
☎029 2032 2000 Fax 029 2035 5960
Email radio.wales@bbc.co.uk
Website www.bbc.co.uk/wales/radio

Editor *Daniel Jones*
Editor, Radio Wales News *Geoff Williams*

Broadcasts regular news bulletins Monday to
Friday and until lunchtime on Saturday.
Programmes include *Good Morning Wales*; *Wales
at One*; *Adam Walton* and *The Weekenders*.

BBC Wiltshire Sound

Broadcasting House, Prospect Place, Swindon,
Wiltshire SN1 3RW
☎01793 513626 Fax 01793 513650
Email wiltshire.sound@bbc.co.uk

Website www.bbc.co.uk/england/
  wiltshiresound
Editor *Vernon Harwood*

Regular programmes include: *Shirley Ludford's
Saturday Show* (reviews, stories, author interviews); *James Morrison's* (weekday) *Morning Show.*

BBC Radio WM
PO Box 206, Birmingham B5 7SD
☎0121 432 9000 Fax 0121 472 3174
Email radio.wm@bbc.co.uk
Website www.bbc.co.uk/england/radiowm
Managing Editor *David Robey*

News, current affairs and entertainment station.

BBC Radio York
20 Bootham Row, York YO30 7BR
☎01904 641351 Fax 01904 610937
Email radio.york@bbc.co.uk
Website www.bbc.co.uk/england/radioyork
Editor *Barrie Stephenson*
Senior Broadcast Journalist *William Jenkyns*

A regular outlet for short stories of up to 10
minutes' duration. They must be locally written or based (i.e. North Yorkshire).

Independent Television

Anglia Television
Anglia House, Norwich, Norfolk NR1 3JG
☎01603 615151 Fax 01603 631032
Email angliatv@angliatv.co.uk
Website www.anglia.tv.co.uk

London office: 48 Leicester Square, London
WC2H 7FB
☎020 7389 8555 Fax 020 7930 8499

Managing Director *Graham Creelman*
Director of Programmes *Malcolm Allsop*
Controller of News *Guy Adams*

Anglia Television is a major producer of programmes for the ITV network, including
Trisha, Sunday Morning and *Survival.* Network
dramas for 1999 included: *Where the Heart Is*
and *Touching Evil.*

Border Television plc
Television Centre, Durranhill, Carlisle,
Cumbria CA1 3NT
☎01228 525101 Fax 01228 541384
Website www.border-tv.com

Chairman *James Graham OBE*
Head of Programmes *Neil Robinson*

Border's programming concentrates on docu-

mentaries rather than drama. Most scripts are
supplied in-house but occasionally there are
commissions. Apart from notes, writers should
not submit written work until their ideas have
been fully discussed.

Carlton Television
101 St Martin's Lane, London WC2N 4AZ
☎020 7240 4000 Fax 020 7240 4171
Website www.carltontv.co.uk
Chairman *Nigel Walmsley*
Chief Executive *Clive Jones*
Director of Programmes *Steve Hewlett*

Carlton Television, part of Carlton Communications Plc, holds three ITV licences: Carlton –
the weekday broadcaster for the London
region; Central – covering the east, west and
south Midlands; and West Country region.
Network drama includes *Peak Practice*;
Kavanagh QC and *Picking up the Pieces.* See also
Carlton Productions under **Film, TV and
Video Production Companies**.

Carlton Broadcasting, Central Region
Gas Street, Birmingham B1 2JT
☎0121 643 9898
Website www.centraltv.co.uk
Managing Director *Ian Squires*

Regular regional programmes include *Central
Weekend; Asian Eye; Heart of the Country; Back
to the Present.*

Carlton Broadcasting, West Country Region
Langage Science Park, Western Wood Way,
Plymouth, Devon PL7 5BG
☎01752 333333 Fax 01752 333444
Website www.carlton.com/westcountry
Managing Director *Mark Haskell*
Director of Programmes *Jane McCloskey*
Director of News & Current Affairs
  Brad Higgins

Came on air in January 1993. News, current
affairs, documentary and religious programming.
Regular programmes include *Westcountry Live;
The View From Here; Power Game.*

Channel 4
124 Horseferry Road, London SW1P 2TX
☎020 7396 4444 Fax 020 7306 8356
Website www.channel4.com
Director of Programmes *Tim Gardam*
Deputy Director of Programmes
  Karen Brown
Head of Film *Paul Webster*
Head of Entertainment *Kevin Lygo*

COMMISSIONING EDITORS
Independent Film & Video *Adam Barker*
Arts *Janey Walker*
Head of Drama and Animation *Gub Neal*
Entertainment *Caroline Leddy*
Documentaries *Peter Dale*
News & Current Affairs *David Lloyd*
Sport *Karen Brown*
Multicultural Programmes *Yasmin Anwar*
Religion & Features *Janice Hadlow*
Controller of Acquisition *June Dromgoole*

When Channel 4 started broadcasting as a national channel in November 1982, it was the first new TV service to be launched in Britain for 18 years. Under the 1981 Broadcasting Act it was required to cater for tastes and audiences not previously served by the other broadcast channels, and to provide a suitable proportion of educational programmes. Channel 4 does not make any of its own programmes; they are commissioned from independent production companies, from the ITV sector, or co-produced with other organisations. The role of the commissioning editors is to sift through proposals for programmes and see interesting projects through to broadcast. Regulated by the ITC.

Channel 5
22 Long Acre, London WC2E 9LY
☎020 7550 5555 Fax 020 7497 5222
Website www.channel5.co.uk

Chief Executive *David Elstein*
Director of Programmes *Dawn Airey*
Controller of Children's Programmes
    Nick Wilson
Controller of Features & Arts *Michael Attwell*
Controller of News, Current Affairs &
    Documentaries *Chris Shaw*
Controller of Drama *Corinne Hollingworth*

Channel 5 Broadcasting Ltd won the franchise for Britain's third commercial terrestrial television station in 1995 and came on air at the end of March 1997. Regular programmes include *Family Affairs* (Monday to Friday soap opera) and *Open House* (Gloria Hunniford's daytime magazine show), plus documentaries, drama, films, children's programmes, sport and entertainment.

Channel Television
The Television Centre, La Pouquelaye,
St Helier, Jersey, Channel Islands JE1 3ZD
☎01534 816816 Fax 01534 816817
Website www.channeltv.co.uk

Also at: Television House, Bulwer Avenue,
St Sampsons, Guernsey, Channel Islands
GY2 4LA ☎01481 41888 Fax 01481 41878

Chief Executive *John Henwood*
Managing Director *Michael Lucas*
Head of Programmes *Karen Rankine*
Head of Sales *Gordon De Ste Croix*
Head of Transmission & Resources
    Kevin Banner

Channel Television is the Independent Television broadcaster to the Channel Islands, serving 143,000 residents, most of whom live on the main islands, Jersey, Guernsey, Alderney and Sark. Channel Television has pushed forward the frontiers of community television on ITV. The station has a weekly reach of more than 94% with local programmes (in the region of six hours each week) at the heart of the ITV service to the islands.

GMTV
The London Television Centre, Upper
Ground, London SE1 9TT
☎020 7827 7000 Fax 020 7827 7249
Email talk2us@gmtv.co.uk
Website www.gmtv.co.uk

Managing Director *Christopher Stoddart*
Director of Programmes *Peter McHugh*
Managing Editor *John Scammell*
Executive Producer *Martin Frizell*

Winner of the national breakfast television franchise. Jointly owned by Media Group, Carlton Communications, Walt Disney Company and Granada Group. GMTV took over from TV-AM on 1 January 1993, with live programming from 6.00 am to 9.25 am. Regular news headlines, current affairs, topical features, showbiz and lifestyle, sports and business, quizzes and competitions, travel and weather reports. Launched its digital service, GMTV2, on 4 January 1999, with daily broadcasts from 6.00 am to 9.25 am. News reports, travel, health and lifestyle features, some simulcast with GMTV1. Children's programming on Saturdays.

Grampian Television Limited
Queen's Cross, Aberdeen AB15 4XJ
☎01224 846846 Fax 01224 846800
Website www.grampiantv.co.uk

Controller *Derrick Thomson*
Head of News *Henry Eagles*
Head of Current Affairs *Alan Cowie*

Extensive regional news and reports including farming, fishing and sports, interviews and leisure features, various light entertainment, Gaelic and religious programmes, and live coverage of the Scottish political, economic and industrial scene. Serves the area stretching from Fife to Shetland.

Regular programmes include *North Tonight; Scotland's Larder* and *Telefios.*

Granada Television

Quay Street, Manchester M60 9EA
☎0161 832 7211 Fax 0161 953 0283
Website www.granadatv.co.uk

Director of Programmes *Grant Mansfield*
Director of Production *Max Graesser*
**Director of Channel Programming, GTP/
 Controller of Lifestyle Programmes,
 GTV** *James Hunt*
Controller of Drama *Simon Lewis*
Controller of Factual Programmes
 Charles Tremayme
Controller of Comedy *Andy Harries*
Controller of Entertainment *Duncan Gray*

Opportunities for freelance writers are not great but mss from professional writers will be considered. All mss should be addressed to the head of scripts. Regular programmes include *Coronation Street; World in Action* and *This Morning.*

HTV Wales

Television Centre, Culverhouse Cross, Cardiff CF5 6XJ
☎029 2059 0590 Fax 029 2059 7183
Website www.htv.co.uk

Group Managing Director *Jeremy Payne*
Controller/Director of Programmes
 Ellis Owen

HTV (West)

Television Centre, Bath Road, Bristol BS4 3HG
☎0117 9722722 Fax 0117 9722400
Website: www.htvwest.com

Managing Director *Jeremy Payne*
Controller of Children's Programmes
 Dan Maddicott
Controller of Network Programmes
 Tom Archer
Director of Programmes, Partridge Films
 Michael Rosenberg

Drama, children's, factual and natural history programming is produced for national and international markets. Programmes include *Dog and Duck; Giants* and *Top Ten of Everything.* Now part of the UNM Group (United News and Media).

ITN (Independent Television News Ltd)

200 Gray's Inn Road, London WC1X 8XZ
☎020 7833 3000
Website www.itn.co.uk

Chief Executive *Stewart Purvis*
Editor-in-Chief *Richard Tait*
Editor, ITN News for ITV *Nigel Dacre*
Editor, Channel 4 News *Jim Gray*
Editor, Channel 5 News *Gary Rogers*

Provider of the main national and international news for ITV, Channel 4 and Channel 5 and radio news for IRN. Programmes on ITV: *Lunchtime News; Evening News; Nightly News; ITN Morning News,* plus regular news summaries, and three programmes a day at weekends. Programmes on Channel 4 include the in-depth news analysis programmes *Channel 4 News* and *The Big Breakfast News.* Programmes on Channel 5: *5 News Early; 5 News at Noon; 5 News* plus regular updates. ITN also provides *World News For Public Television* and has operating control of *Euronews,* Europe's only pan-European broadcaster.

LWT (London Weekend Television)

The London Television Centre, Upper Ground, London SE1 9LT
☎020 7620 1620
Website www.lwt.co.uk

Chief Operating Officer *Charles Allen*
Managing Director *Liam Hamilton*
Director of Programmes *Marcus Plantin*
Controller of Entertainment *Nigel Lythgoe*
Controller of Drama *Jo Wright*
Controller of Arts *Melvyn Bragg*
Controller of Factual Programmes *Jim Allen*

Makers of current affairs, entertainment and drama series such as *Blind Date; Surprise Surprise; The Knock; London's Burning* also *The South Bank Show* and *Jonathan Dimbleby.* Provides a large proportion of ITV's drama and light entertainment, and also for BSkyB and Channel 4.

Meridian Broadcasting

Television Centre, Southampton, Hampshire SO14 0PZ
☎023 8022 2555 Fax 023 8033 5050
Email viewerliaison@meridiantv.com
Website www.meridian.tv.co.uk

London office: Ludgate House, 245 Blackfriars Road, London SE1 9UY
☎020 7921 5000

Managing Director *Mary McAnally*
Controller of Broadcasting *Keith Razey*
Director of Programmes *Richard Simons*
Director of News Strategy *Jim Raven*

Meridian's refurbished studios in Southampton provide a base for network and regional productions. Regular regional programmes include the award-winning news service, *Meridian Tonight; Countryways* and *The Pier.*

S4C

Parc Ty Glas, Llanishen, Cardiff CF14 5DU
☎029 2074 7444 Fax 029 2075 4444
Email huw_jones@s4c.co.uk
Website www.s4c.co.uk

Chief Executive *Huw Jones*
Director of Programmes *Huw Eirug*

The Welsh 4th Channel, established by the Broadcasting Act 1980, is responsible for a schedule of Welsh and English programmes on the Fourth Channel in Wales. Known as S4C, the service is made up of about 30 hours per week of Welsh language programmes and more than 85 hours of English language output from Channel 4. Ten hours a week of the Welsh programmes are provided by the BBC; the remainder are purchased from HTV and independent producers. Drama, comedy and documentary are all part of S4C's programming. On its digital channel, S4C's Welsh language output is around 84 hours per week.

Scottish Television Ltd

Cowcaddens, Glasgow G2 3PR
☎0141 300 3000 Fax 0141 300 3030
Website www.stv.co.uk
London office: 20 Lincoln's Inn Field, London WC2A 3ED
☎020 7446 7000 Fax 020 7446 7010

Managing Director, Television Division
  Donald Emslie
Controller, Regional Programming
  Sandy Ross
Controller, Scottish Television *Scott Ferguson*
Controller of Drama *Philip Hinchcliffe*
Head of Features & Entertainment
  Agnes Wilkie
Senior News Producer *Paul McKinney*
Head of Sport & General Factual
  Programmes *Denis Mooney*

An increasing number of STV programmes such as *Taggart* and *McCallum* are now networked nationally. Programme coverage includes drama, religion, news, sport, outside broadcasts, special features, entertainment and the arts, education and Gaelic programmes. Produces many one-offs for ITV and Channel 4.

Teletext Ltd

101 Farm Lane, Fulham, London SW6 1QJ
☎020 7386 5000 Fax 020 7386 5002
Website www.teletext.co.uk

Managing Director *Mike Stewart*

Editor-in-Chief *John Sage*

On 1 January 1993, Teletext Ltd took over the electronic publishing service for both ITV and Channel 4. Transmits a wide range of news pages and features, including current affairs, sport, TV listings, weather, travel, holidays, finance, games, competitions, etc. Provides a regional service to each of the ITV regions.

Tyne Tees Television

Television Centre, Newcastle upon Tyne NE1 2AL
☎0191 261 0181 Fax 0191 261 2302
Email tyne.tees@granadamedia.com
Website www.granadamedia.com

Managing Director *Margaret Fay*
Director of Broadcasting *Graeme Thompson*
Head of Network Features *Malcolm Wright*
Editor, Current Affairs and Features
  Jane Bolesworth
Managing Editor, News *Graham Marples*
Head of Young People's Programmes
  Lesley Oakden
Head of Regional Affairs *Norma Hope*
Head of Sport *Roger Tames*

Programming covers religion, politics, news and current affairs, regional documentaries, business, entertainment, sport and arts. Regular programmes include *North East Tonight with Mike Neville* and *Around the House* (politics).

UTV (Ulster Television)

Havelock House, Ormeau Road, Belfast BT7 1EB
☎028 9032 8122 Fax 028 9024 6695
Website www.utvlive.com

Controller of Programming *Alan Bremner*
Head of News & Current Affairs
  Rob Morrison

Regular programmes on news and current affairs, politics, sport, education, music, light entertainment, arts, health and local culture.

Westcountry Television

See **Carlton Television**

Yorkshire Television

The Television Centre, Leeds, West Yorkshire LS3 1JS
☎0113 2438283 Fax 0113 2445107
Website www.granadamedia.com
London office: Global House, 96–108 Great Suffolk Street, London SE1 0BE
☎020 7578 4304 Fax 020 7578 4320

Chairman *Charles Allen*

Managing Director *Richard Gregory*
Director of Programmes, Yorkshire Tyne Tees Productions *John Whiston*
Controller of Drama, Yorkshire Tyne Tees Productions *Keith Richardson*
Controller of Drama, YTV *Carolyn Reynolds*
Controller of Comedy Drama and Drama Features *David Reynolds*
Controller of Factual Programmes *Chris Bryer*
Head of News & Current Affairs *Clare Morrow*
Deputy Controller of Children's, Granada Media Group *Patrick Titley*

Part of Granada Media Group. Drama series, situation comedies, film productions and long-running series like *Emmerdale* and *Heartbeat*. Always looking for strong writing in these areas, but prefers to find it through an agent. Documentary/current affairs material tends to be supplied by producers; opportunities in these areas are rare but adaptations of published work as a documentary subject are considered. In theory, opportunity exists within series, episode material. Best approach is through a good agent.

Cable and Satellite Television

Asianet

PO Box 38, Greenford, Middlesex UB3 7SP
☎020 8566 9000 Fax 020 8810 5555
Chief Executive *Dr Banad Viswanath*
Managing Director *Deepak Viswanath*

Broadcasting since September 1994, Asianet transmits entertainment to the Asian community 24 hours a day in English, Hindi, Gujarati, Punjabi, Bengali and Urdu.

British Sky Broadcasting Ltd (BSkyB)

Grant Way, Isleworth, Middlesex TW7 5QD
☎020 7705 3000 Fax 020 7705 3030
Website www.sky.co.uk
Chief Executive *Tony Ball*
Head of Programming *James Baker*
General Manager, Broadcasting *Richard Freudenstein*
Chief Executive, British Interactive Broadcasting *James Ackerman*

BSkyB programming is distributed via cable and DTH satellite to 6.88 million homes in the UK and Eire. Launched in 1989, Sky operates 13 wholly-owned and 10 joint venture channels.

With the launch of SkyDigital in 1998, opportunities increased for many of the joint venture channels to expand hours of transmission.

WHOLLY-OWNED SKY CHANNELS:
Sky Premier
Blockbusting action, comedy and romance, featuring recent box office hits.

Sky MovieMax
Contemporary hit movies, embracing all genres, from Hollywood's major studios.

Sky Cinema
Classic and popular movies from 70 years of cinema, including seasons and retrospectives.

Sky News
Award winning 24-hours news service with hourly bulletins and expert comment.

Sky One
The most frequently watched Sky channel with the accent on family entertainment.

Sky Sports 1/Sky Sports 2/Sky Sports 3
Over 1000 hours of sport a month, much of it exclusively live, across three channels including FA Carling Premiership football, England internationals, Rugby Union and golf.

Sky Travel
Magazine shows and documentaries.

.tv
Entertaining, informative and educational programming for experts and beginners.

MULTI-CHANNELS PACKAGES INCLUDE:
Sky One; Sky News; The Discovery Channel; The National Geographic Channel; MTV; VH-1; The History Channel; The Sci-Fi Channel; Nickelodeon; Fox Kids Network; The Children's Channel; The Computer Channel; UK Gold; Sky Soap; Sky Travel; UK Living; Granada Good Life; Granada Plus; Granada Men & Motors; The Paramount Comedy Channel; CNBC; EBN; Bravo; Sky Scottish; Challenge TV; CMT; Discovery Home & Leisure; QVC.

JOINT VENTURES:
National Geographic; Nickelodeon; Nick Jr; The History Channel; Paramount; QVC; MUTV; Music Choice Europe; [.tv]; Granada Breeze; Granada Men & Motors; Granada Plus; Sky Travel; Sky News Australia.

CNBC

10 Fleet Place, London EC4M 7QS
☎020 7653 9300 Fax 020 7653 9333
Email feedback@cnbceurope.com
Website www.cnbceurope.com

Managing Director *Marga McNally*

A service of NBC and Dow Jones. 24-hour European financial and corporate news broadcasting. Programmes include *Europe Today; Europe This Week; The Tonight Show With Jay Leno.*

Cable News Network International

CNN House, 19–22 Rathbone Place, London W1P 1DF
☎020 7637 6800   Fax 020 7637 6910
Website www.cnn.com

Bureau Chief *Tom Mintier*
Managing Director CNN Financial News Europe *Mike McCarthy*

LAUNCHED in 1985 as the international sister network to CNN. Wholly-owned subsidiary of Time Warner Inc. Distributes 24-hour news to more than 151 million households in more than 210 countries and territories. Nearly six hours of programming are originated and produced daily in London: *World News; World Business Today; Inside Europe; Artclub*, plus 18 two-minute business news updates.

L!VE TV

Ceased broadcasting on 5 November 1999.

MTV Networks Europe Inc

180 Oxford Street, London W1N 0DS
☎020 7284 7777   Fax 020 7284 7788
Website www.mtv.com

President & Chief Executive *Brent Hansen*

ESTABLISHED 1987. Europe's 24-hour music and youth entertainment channel, available on cable, via satellite and digitally. Transmitted from London in English across Europe.

NBC Europe

Unit 1/1, Harbour Yard, Chelsea Harbour, London SW10 0XD
☎020 7352 9205   Fax 020 7352 9628

Chairman *Patrick Cox*
Director of Programming *Bernhard Bertram*

24-hour European broad-based news, information and entertainment service in English, with additional programmes in German and advertisements in English and German.

Travel (Landmark Travel Channel)

66 Newman Street, London W1P 3LA
☎020 7636 5401   Fax 020 7636 6424
Website www.travelchannel.co.uk

Launched in February 1994. Broadcasts programmes and information on the world of travel. Destinations reports, lifestyle programmes plus food and drink, sport and leisure pursuits. Transmits from 7.00am to 1.00am throughout Europe and Africa.

National Commercial Radio

Classic FM

7 Swallow Place, London W1R 7AA
☎020 7343 9000   Fax 020 7344 2700
Website www.classicfm.com

Chief Executive *Ralph Bernard*
Programme Director *Roger Lewis*
Head of News *Darren Henley*

Classic FM, Britain's largest national commercial radio station, started broadcasting in September 1992. It plays accessible classical music 24 hours a day and broadcasts news, weather, travel, business information, political/celebrity/general interest talks, features and interviews. Classic has gone well beyond its expectations, attracting six million listeners a week. Winner of the 'Station of the Year' Sony Award in April 2000.

Digital One

7 Swallow Place, London W1R 7AA
☎020 7518 2620
Website www.ukdigitalradio.com

The UK's only national commercial digital radio network. Backed by radio group GWR and cable supplier ntl, Digital One began broadcasting on 15 November 1999 with five channels: Planet Rock (classic rock music), Core (teenage pop music), **Classic FM**, Talk Radio (now **TalkSport**) and **Virgin Radio**. Five more channels go on air in 2000, including Oneword Radio, dedicated solely to plays, books, comedy and reviews, broadcasting between 6.00 a.m. and midnight daily. The Digital One network broadcasts to over 69% of the UK population and is due to expand to 85% by 2002.

TalkSport

18 Hatfields, London SE1 8DJ
☎020 7959 7800
Website www.talksport.net

C.E.O. *Kelvin MacKenzie*
Programme Director *Bill Ridley*

Commenced broadcasting in February 1995 as Talk Radio UK. Re-launched January 2000 as

TalkSport, the UK's first sports radio station. Broadcasts 24 hours a day.

Virgin Radio
1 Golden Square, London W1R 4DJ
☎020 7434 1215 Fax 020 7434 1197
Website www.virginradio.com

Chief Executive *John Pearson*
Programme Director *Henry Owens*

'Ten great songs in a row every hour, all day.' Bought by Chris Evans' Ginger Media Group in December 1997 and acquired by the Scottish Media Group in March 2000.

Independent Local Radio

96.3 Aire FM/Magic 828
51 Burley Road, Leeds, West Yorkshire LS3 1LR
☎0113 2835500 Fax 0113 2835501
Website www.airefm.com

Programme Director *Adam Woodgate*

Music-based programming. 96.3 Aire FM caters for the 15–34-year-old listener while Magic 828 aims at the 25–44 age group with easy favourites.

Beacon FM/WABC Classic Gold
267 Tettenhall Road, Wolverhampton, West Midlands WV6 0DQ
☎01902 461000 Fax 01902 461299
Website www.beaconfm.com

Programme Director *Steve Martin*

Part of the GWR Group plc. No outlets for unsolicited literary material at present.

Big AM
See **Signal One**

Radio Borders
Tweedside Park, Tweedbank, Galashiels TD1 3TD
☎01896 759444 Fax 01896 759494
Website www.radioborders.co.uk

Programme Controller *Danny Gallagher*
Head of News *Gordon Brown*

Music-based station with local and national news.

Breeze
See **Essex FM**

Breeze 1521 AM
See **Mercury FM 102.7/Breeze 1521 AM**

BRMB-FM 96.4/1152 Capital Gold
Nine Brindley Place, 4 Cozells Square, Birmingham B1 2DJ
☎0121 245 5000 Fax 0121 245 5245
Website www.brmb.co.uk

Programme Controller *Paul Jackson*
News Editor *Gordon Davidson*

Music-based stations; no outlets for writers. Part of Capital Radio Plc.

Broadland 102/Classic Gold Amber
47–49 Colegate, Norwich, Norfolk NR3 1DB
☎01603 630621
Fax 01603 630892 (newsroom)
Website www.broadland102.co.uk

Programme Controller *Dave Brown*

Part of GWR Group plc. Popular music programmes and local news only.

1152 Capital Gold
See **BRMB-FM 96.4/1152 Capital Gold**

Capital Radio
30 Leicester Square, London WC2H 7LA
☎020 7766 6000 Fax 020 7766 6100
Website www.capitalfm.com

Group Programme Director *Richard Park*

Commenced broadcasting in October 1973 as the country's second commercial radio station (the first being **LBC**, launched a week earlier). Europe's largest commercial radio station. Main outlet is news and showbiz programme each weekday at 7.30 pm called *Drivetime Showtime*. This covers current affairs, showbiz, features and pop news, aimed at a young audience. The vast majority of material is generated in-house.

107.5 CAT FM
Regent Arcade, Cheltenham, Gloucestershire GL50 1JZ
☎01242 699555 Fax 01242 699666
Website www.catfm.co.uk

Programme Controller *Huw James*

Music-based programmes, broadcasting 24 hours a day.

Central FM Ltd
201–203 High Street, Falkirk FK1 1DU
☎01324 611164 Fax 01324 611168

Managing Director *Lewis Carnie*
Programme Controller *Tom Bell*

Broadcasts music, sport and local news to Central Scotland, 24 hours a day.

Century Radio

Century House, PO Box 100, Church Street, Gateshead NE8 2YY
☎0191 477 6666 Fax 0191 477 5660
Website www.centurynortheast.com

Programme Controller *John Caine*

Music, talk, news and interviews, 24 hours a day.

CFM

PO Box 964, Carlisle, Cumbria CA1 3NG
☎01228 818964 Fax 01228 819444
Email studio@cfmradio.com

Programme Controller *Simon Monk*
Head of Commercial Production *Peter White*
News Editor *Gill Garston*

Music, news and information station.

Channel 103 FM

6 Tunnell Street, St Helier, Jersey, Channel Islands JE2 4LU
☎01534 888103 Fax 01534 887799
Email chan103@itl.net
Website www.103fm.itl.net

Station Manager *Richard Johnson*

Music programmes, 24 hours a day.

Chiltern FM/Classic Gold 828

Chiltern Road, Dunstable, Bedfordshire LU6 1HQ
☎01582 676200
Fax 01582 676241 (newsroom)

Programme Controller, FM *Trevor James*
Programme Controller, Classic Gold 828
    Don Douglas

Part of the GWR Group plc. Music-based programmes, broadcasting 24 hours a day.

Classic Gold 1557 Northamptonshire

See **Northants 96/Classic Gold 1557 Northamptonshire**

Classic Gold Amber

See **Broadland 102**

Classic Gold GEM AM

See **96 TRENT FM/Classic Gold GEM AM**

Radio Clyde/Clyde 1 FM/Clyde 2

Clydebank Business Park, Clydebank G81 2RX
☎0141 565 2200 Fax 0141 565 2265
Website www.clydeonline.co.uk

Managing Director *Alex Dickson, OBE, AE, FRSA, FIMgt*

Programmes usually originate in-house or by commission. All documentary material is made in-house. Good local news items always considered. There are three book programmes presented by Alex Dickson each week on Clyde 2 at 10.05–10.30 pm: *Authors* (Monday) features author interviews while *Hardback Bookcase* (Tues) and *Paperback Bookcase* (Weds) review latest titles.

Cool FM

See **Downtown Radio**

Downtown Radio/Cool FM

Newtownards, Co. Down, Northern Ireland BT23 4ES
☎028 9181 5555 Fax 028 9181 5252
Email programmes@downtown.co.uk
Website www.downtown.co.uk

Programme Head *John Rosborough*

Downtown Radio first ran a highly successful short story competition in 1988, attracting over 400 stories. The competition is now an annual event and writers living within the station's transmission area are asked to submit material during the winter and early spring. The competition is promoted in association with Eason Shops. For further information, write to *Derek Ray* at the station.

Essex FM/Breeze

Radio House, Clifftown Road, Southend on Sea, Essex SS1 1SX
☎01702 333711 Fax 01702 345224
Website www.essexradio.co.uk

Programme Director *Paul Chantler*

Music-based stations. No real opportunities for writers' work as such, but will occasionally interview local authors of published books. Contact *Peter Stewart* (Head of News).

Forth AM/Forth FM

Forth House, Forth Street, Edinburgh EH1 3LF
☎0131 556 9255 Fax 0131 558 3277
Website www.forthonline.co.uk

Director of Programming *David Johnston*
News Editor *Paul Robertson*

News stories welcome from freelancers. Music-based programming.

FOX FM

Brush House, Pony Road, Cowley, Oxford OX4 2XR
☎01865 871000 Fax 01865 871037 (news)

Managing Director *Lyn Long*
Head of News *Dominic Cotter*

Backed by an impressive list of shareholders

including the Blackwell Group of Companies and Capital Radio Plc. No outlet for creative writing.

Galaxy 101

Millennium House, 26 Baldwin Street, Bristol BS1 1SE
☎0117 9010101 Fax 0117 9014666/ 9014555 (news & programmes)
Email newsdesk@galaxy101.co.uk

Programme Controller *John Dash*

Dance music, 24 hours a day. Occasionally features books about local places. Contact the Programme Controller in the first instance.

Galaxy 102.2

1 The Square, 111 Broad Street, Birmingham B15 1AS
☎0121 695 0000 Fax 0121 695 0055
Email mail@galaxy1022.co.uk

Managing Director *Paul Fairburn*
Programme Controller *Neil Greenslade*

Commenced broadcasting in January 1995 (as Choice FM) and re-branded Galaxy in January 1999. Today's dance and soul, news and information.

Gemini Radio FM/Classic Gold

Hawthorn House, Exeter Business Park, Exeter, Devon EX1 3QS
☎01392 444444 Fax 01392 444433

Programme Controller (FM) *Kevin Kane*
Programme Controller (AM) *Colin Slade*

Part of Orchard Media Group. Occasional outlets for poetry and short stories on the AM wavelength. Contact *Colin Slade.*

GWR FM (West)

PO Box 2000, The Watershed, Bristol BS99 7SN
☎0117 9843200 Fax 0117 9843202
Website www.gwrfm.musicradio.com

Programme Controller, GWR FM (West)
To be appointed

Very few opportunities. Almost all material originates in-house. Part of the GWR Group plc.

Hallam FM/Magic AM

Radio House, 900 Herries Road, Sheffield S6 1RH
☎0114 2853333 Fax 0114 2853159
Website www.hallamfm.co.uk

Programme Director *Anthony Gay*

Music, news and features, 24 hours a day.

100.7 Heart FM

1 The Square, 111 Broad Street, Birmingham B15 1AS
☎0121 695 0000 Fax 0121 695 0055
Email mail@heartfm.co.uk

Managing Director *Paul Fairburn*
Programme Director *Alan Carruthers*
Deputy Programme Director *Adrian Stewart*

Commenced broadcasting in September 1994. Music, regional news and information.

102.7 Hereward FM/ Classic Gold 1332 AM

PO Box 225, Queensgate Centre, Peterborough, Cambridgeshire PE1 1XJ
☎01733 460460 Fax 01733 281445

Programme Controller *Chris Pegg*

Part of GWR Group plc. Not usually any openings offered to writers as all material is compiled and presented by in-house staff.

FM 103 Horizon

Broadcast Centre, Crownhill, Milton Keynes, Buckinghamshire MK8 0AB
☎01908 269111 Fax 01908 564893
Website www.mkweb.co.uk

Programme Controller *Trevor Marshall*

Part of the GWR Group plc. Music and news.

Imagine FM

Regent House, 1st Floor, Heaton Lane, Stockport, Cheshire SK4 1BX
☎0161 285 4545 Fax 0161 285 1010
Email <recipient>@imaginefm.net

Programme Controller *Helen Bowden*

Strong local flavour to programmes. Part of the Wireless Group.

Invicta FM/Capital Gold

PO Box 100, Whitstable, Kent CT5 3QX
☎01227 772004 Fax 01227 771558
Website www.invictafm.com

Programme Controller *Luis Clark*

Music-based station, serving listeners in Kent. Part of Capital Radio Plc.

Island FM

12 Westerbrook, St Sampsons, Guernsey, Channel Islands GY2 4QQ
☎01481 242000 Fax 01481 249676
Website www.islandfm.guernsey.net

Managing Director *Kevin Stewart*

Music-based programming.

Isle of Wight Radio
Dodnor Park, Newport, Isle of Wight
PO30 5XE
☎01983 822557 Fax 01983 821690
Email news@iwradio.co.uk
Website www.iwradio.co.uk
Managing Director *Andy Shier*
Programme Director *Stuart McGinley*
Part of the Local Radio Company, Isle of Wight
Radio is the island's only radio station broadcasting local news, music and general entertainment.

Key 103
See **Piccadilly 1152**

LBC 1152 AM
See **News Direct 97.3 FM**

105.4 FM Leicester Sound
Granville House, Granville Road, Leicester
LE1 7RW
☎0116 2561300 Fax 0116 2561305
Managing Director *Phil Dixon*
Programme Controller *Steve Marsh*
Part of GWR Group plc. Predominantly a music
station. Very occasionally, unsolicited material of
local interest 'targeted at our particular audience'
may be broadcast.

1458 Lite AM
PO Box 1458, Quay West, Trafford Park,
Manchester M17 1FL
☎0161 872 1458 Fax 0161 872 0206
Head of Programming *Jeff Graham*
Head of Music *Paul Fairclough*
Music-based programmes, 24 hours a day.

Magic 1152AM
See **Metro FM/Magic 1152AM**

Magic 1161
See **Viking FM**

Magic 1548
See **Radio City Ltd**

Magic 828
See **96.3 Aire FM**

Magic AM
See **Hallam FM**

Marcher Gold
Marcher Sound Ltd., The Studios, Mold
Road, Wrexham LL11 4AF
☎01978 752202 Fax 01978 759701

Email kevin.howard@mfmradio.co.uk
Website www.marchergold.co.uk
Programme Controller *Kevin Howard*
Occasional features and advisory programmes.
Hour-long Welsh language broadcasts are aired
weekdays at 6.00 pm.

Medway FM
Berkeley House, 186 High Street, Rochester,
Kent ME1 1EY
☎01634 841111 Fax 01634 841122
Website www.medwayfm.com
Managing Director *Nick Jenkins*
Programme Director *Bob Le-Roi*
A wide range of music programming plus
news, views and local interest.

Mercia FM/Classic Gold 1359
Mercia Sound Ltd., Hertford Place, Coventry
CV1 3TT
☎024 7686 8200 Fax 024 7686 8202
Managing Director *Carlton Dale*
Programme Controller *Trevor Marshall*
Music-based station.

Mercury FM 102.7/ Breeze 1521 AM
The Stanley Centre, Kelvin Way, Manor
Royal, Crawley, West Sussex RH10 2SE
☎01293 519161 Fax 01293 560927
Website www.mercuryfm.co.uk
Programme Director *Paul Chantler*
Mercury FM plays contemporary music targeting 25–44 years. Breeze 1521 AM plays hits
from the '60s to '90s, targeting 35 years-plus.
Both services carry local, national and international news.

Metro FM/Magic 1152AM
Swalwell, Newcastle upon Tyne NE99 1BB
☎0191 420 0971 (Metro)/420 3040
(Magic) Fax 520191 488 0933
Website www.yournewcastle.com
Programme Director *Tony McKenzie*
Very few opportunities for writers, but phone-in programmes may interview relevant authors.

Minster FM
PO Box 123, Dunnington, York YO1 5ZX
☎01904 488888 Fax 01904 488811
Website www.minsterfm.co.uk
Managing Director *Lynn Bell*
Music, local news and sport.

Moray Firth Radio

PO Box 271, Scorguie Place, Inverness
IV3 8UJ
☎01463 224433 Fax 01463 243224
Email MFR@mfr.cuk.com

**Managing Director/Programme
  Controller** *Thomas Prag*
Programme Organiser *Ray Atkinson*
Book Reviews *May Marshall*

Book reviews every Monday afternoon at
2.20 pm.

News Direct 97.3 FM/
LBC 1152 AM

200 Gray's Inn Road, London WC1X 8XZ
☎020 7973 1152 Fax 020 7312 8470
(FM)/8565 (AM)
Email editor@lbc.co.uk *(LBC editorial queries)*
Website www.newsdirect.co.uk *and*
  www.lbc.co.uk

Director *Nicholas Wheeler*

News Direct 97.3 FM – 24-hour rolling news
station; LBC 1152 AM – commenced broadcasting in October 1973. News, views and entertainment for London.

Northants 96/Classic Gold 1557
Northamptonshire

19–21 St Edmunds Road, Northampton
NN1 5DY
☎01604 795600 Fax 01604 795601
Email reception@northants96.musicradio.com

Programme Controller *Mark Jeeves*

Music and news, 24 hours a day.

NorthSound Radio

45 King's Gate, Aberdeen AB15 4EL
☎01224 337000 Fax 01224 400003

Programme Controller *Rod Webster*

Features and music programmes 24 hours a day
including, mid-morning (9.00 am – midday),
Northsound 2 feature programme.

Ocean Radio

Radio House, Whittle Avenue, Segensworth
West, Fareham, Hampshire PO15 5SH
☎01489 589911 Fax 01489 589453
Email info@oceanradio.co.uk
Website www.oceanradiofm.com

Programme Controller *Mark Sadler*
Head of News *Jane Dancer*

Music-based programming only. Part of Capital
Radio Plc.

Orchard FM

Haygrove House, Shoreditch, Taunton,
Somerset TA3 7BT
☎01823 338448 Fax 01823 321611
Email bob@orchardfm.co.uk
Website www.orchardfm.co.uk

Programme Director *Steve Bulley*
News Editor *Alan Jennings.*

Music-based programming only.

Piccadilly 1152/Key 103

Castlequay, Castlefield, Manchester M15 4PR
☎0161 288 5000 Fax 0161 288 5001
Website www.key103fm.com

Programme Director *Dave Shearer*

Music-based programming with some opportunities for comedy writers.

Plymouth Sound Radio

Earl's Acre, Alma Road, Plymouth, Devon
PL3 4HX
☎01752 227272 Fax 01752 670730

Programme Controller *Peter Greig*

Music-based station. No outlets for writers.

Premier Radio

Glen House, Stag Place, London SW1E 5AG
☎020 7316 1300 Fax 020 7233 6706
Email premier@premier.org.uk
Website www.premier.org.uk

Managing Director *Peter Kerridge*

Broadcasts programmes that reflect the beliefs
and values of the Christian faith, 24 hours a day.

Q103.FM

PO Box 103, Vision Park, Chivers Way,
Histon, Cambridge CB4 9WW
☎01223 235255 Fax 01223 235161

Managing Director *Alistair Wayne*

Part of GWR Group plc. Music and news.

96.3 QFM

PO Box 96.3, Paisley PA1 2LG
☎0141 887 9630 Fax 0141 887 0963
Email sales@q-fm.demon.co.uk

Station Director *Janis Melville*
Programme Controller *Mark McKenzie*

Music-based programming plus local information and news.

Radio City Ltd/Magic 1548

8–10 Stanley Street, Liverpool L1 6AF
☎0151 227 5100 Fax 0151 471 0330
Website www.radiocity967.com

Managing Director *Sean Marley*
Programme Director *Richard Maddock*

Opportunities for writers are very few and far between as this is predominantly a music station.

Red Dragon FM/Capital Gold

Radio House, West Canal Wharf, Cardiff
CF1 5XL
☎029 2038 4041 Fax 029 2038 4014
Website www.reddragonfm.co.uk

Programme Controller *Andy Johnson*
News Editor *Andrew Jones*

Acquired by Capital Radio in 1998. Relocating autumn 2000. Music-based programming only.

Red Rose Radio

PO Box 301, St Paul's Square, Preston,
Lancashire PR1 1YE
☎01772 556301 Fax 01772 201917
Website www.redrose.demon.co.uk

Programme Director *Mike Bawden*

Music-based station. No outlets for writers.

Sabras Radio

Radio House, 63 Melton Road, Leicester
LE4 6PN
☎0116 2610666 Fax 0116 2667776
Email don@sabrasradio.com
Website www.sabrasradio.com

Programme Controller *Don Kotak*

Programmes for the Asian community, broadcasting 24 hours a day.

SCOT FM

Number 1 Albert Quay, Leith, Edinburgh
EH6 7DN
☎0131 554 6677 Fax 0131 554 2266

Managing Director *Mick Hall*
Programme Controller *Donny Hughes*

On air since September 1994. Broadcasts music and conversation to the central Scottish region.

Severn Sound FM/Classic Gold 774

Bridge Studios, Eastgate Centre, Gloucester
GL1 1SS
☎01452 313200 Fax 01452 313213

Managing Director *Penny Holton*

Part of the GWR Group plc. Music and news.

SGR FM 97.1/96.4

Alpha Business Park, Whitehouse Road,
Ipswich, Suffolk IP1 5LT
☎01473 461000 Fax 01473 241111 (newsdesk)
Website www.sgrfm.co.uk

Managing Director *Mike Stewart*
Programme Controller *Mark Pryke*

Music-based programming.

Signal One/Big AM

Stoke Road, Shelton, Stoke on Trent,
Staffordshire ST4 2SR
☎01782 747047
Fax 01782 744110/747777

Programme Controller (Signal One)
Mark Franklin
Programme Controller (Big AM)
Mark Chivers

Music-based station. No outlets for writers.
Part of the Wireless Group.

Southern FM

PO Box 2000, Brighton, East Sussex
BN41 2SS
☎01273 430111 Fax 01273 430098
Website www.southernfm.com

Programme Controller *Andrew Jeffries*
News Manager *Laurence King*

Music, news, entertainment and competitions.
Part of Capital Radio Plc.

Spectrum Radio

204–206 Queenstown Road, Battersea,
London SW8 3NR
☎020 7627 4433 Fax 020 7627 3409
Email spectrum@spectrum558am.co.uk
Website www.spectrum558am.co.uk

Managing Director *Paul Hogan*

Programmes for a broad spectrum of ethnic groups in London.

Spire FM

City Hall Studios, Malthouse Lane, Salisbury,
Wiltshire SP2 7QQ
☎01722 416644 Fax 01722 415102
Website www.spirefm.co.uk

Station Director *Gary Haberfield*

Music, news current affairs, quizzes and sport.
Won the Sony Award for the best local radio station in 1994 and 1996.

Sun FM 103.4

PO Box 1034, Sunderland, Tyne & Wear
SR5 2YL
☎0191 548 1034 Fax 0191 548 7171
Website www.sun-fm.com

Managing Director *Brian Lister*
Programme Controller *Ricky Durkin*

Music-based programmes only.

Sunrise Radio
Sunrise House, 30 Chapel Street, Bradford,
West Yorkshire BD1 5DN
☎01274 735043 Fax 01274 728534

**Programme Controller, Chief Executive
  & Chairman** *Usha Parmar*

Programmes for the Asian community in
Bradford. Part of the Sunrise Radio Group.

Sunshine 855
South Shropshire Communications Ltd.,
Sunshine House, Waterside, Ludlow,
Shropshire SY8 1PE
☎01584 873795 Fax 01584 875900

Operations Director *Austin Powell*
Programme Controller *Mark Edwards*

Music, news and information 24 hours a day.

Swansea Sound 1170 MW
Victoria Road, Gowerton, Swansea SA4 3AB
☎01792 511170 Fax 01792 511171
Email admin@swanseasound.co.uk
Website www.swanseasound.co.uk

Station and Programme Director
  Andy Griffiths
News Editor *Simon Thompson*

Interested in a wide variety of material, though
news items must be of local relevance. An exploratory letter is advisable.

Tay FM/Radio Tay AM
Radio Tay Ltd., PO Box 123, Dundee
DD1 9UF
☎01382 200800 Fax 01382 423252
Email tayfm@frh.co.uk *and* tayam@frh.co.uk

Managing Director *Sandy Wilkie*
Programme Director *Ally Ballingall*

Wholly-owned subsidiary of Scottish Radio
Holdings. Carries a 20-minute book programme
every Sunday evening, presented by Mabel
Adams. Unsolicited material is assessed. Short
stories and book reviews of local interest are welcome. Send to the programme director.

107.8FM Thames Radio
Brentham House, 45c High Street, Hampton
Wick, Kingston upon Thames, Surrey
KT1 4DG
☎020 8288 1300 Fax 020 8288 1312
Website www.thamesradio.co.uk

Station Manager *Mark Bond*
Programme Controller *Mark Walker*

Music-based programmes of current hits and
classic pop.

96 TRENT FM/
Classic Gold GEM AM
29–31 Castlegate, Nottingham NG1 7AP
☎0115 9527000 Fax 0115 9129302
Email admin@trentfm.musicradio.com

Managing Director *Chris Hughes*

Part of the GWR Group plc.

2CR-FM (Two Counties Radio)/
Classic Gold
5–7 Southcote Road, Bournemouth, Dorset
BH1 3LR
☎01202 259259 Fax 01202 255244
Website www.2crfm.co.uk

Programme Controller *Craig Morris*

Wholly-owned subsidiary of the GWR Group
plc. Serves Dorset and Hampshire. All reviews/
topicality/press releases to the Programme
Controller, 2CRFM at the address above.

2-Ten FM/Classic Gold
PO Box 2020, Reading, Berkshire RG31 7FG
☎0118 9454400 Fax 0118 9288456
Website www.2-tenfm.co.uk

Programme Controller *Tim Parker*

A subsidiary of the GWR Group plc. Music-
based programming.

Viking FM/Magic 1161
Commercial Road, Hull, North Humberside
HU1 2SG
☎01482 325141 Fax 01482 587067
Website www.vikingfm.co.uk *and*
www.magic1161.co.uk

Managing Director *Sue Timson*
Programme Controller *Andrew Robson*
News Co-ordinator *Christine Dexter*

Music-based programming. Part of the EMAP
Group.

WABC Classic Gold
See **Beacon Radio**

The Wave
Victoria Road, Gowerton, Swansea SA4 3AB
☎01792 511964 Fax 01792 511965
Email admin@thewave.co.uk
Website www.thewave.co.uk

Station and Programme Director
  Andy Griffiths
News Editor *Simon Thompson*

Music-based programming. See also **Swansea
Sound 1170 MW**.

Wessex FM

Radio House, Trinity Street, Dorchester,
Dorset DT1 1DJ
☎01305 250333 Fax 01305 250052
Website www.wessexfm.co.uk

Programme Manager *Stewart Smith*

Music, local news, information and features.
These include reviews of theatre, cinema, videos,
local music.

West Sound FM/West FM

Radio House, 54 Holmston Road, Ayr
KA7 3BE
☎01292 283662
Fax 01292 283665/262607 (news)
Website www.westfm.co.uk *and*
  www.west-sound.co.uk

Programme Controller *Gordon McArthur*

Music-based broadcasting.

102.4 Wish FM

Orrell Road, Wigan WN5 8HJ
☎01942 761024 Fax 01942 777694
Website www.wishfm.net

Programme Controllerr *John Evington*

Music-based programming plus news and
sport. Part of the Wireless Group.

Wyvern FM

5–6 Barbourne Terrace, Worcester
WR1 3JZ
☎01905 612212/746644 (newsroom)
Fax 01905 746637

Managing Director *Rhian Garbett-Edwards*
Programme Controller *Sasha French*

Part of the GWR Group plc since spring 1997.
Music-based programming.

Radio XL 1296 AM

KMS House, Bradford Street, Birmingham
B12 0JD
☎0121 753 5353 Fax 0121 753 3111

Station Manager *Barry Curtis*

Asian broadcasting for the West Midlands, 24
hours a day. Broadcasts *Love Express* featuring
love stories and poems. Writers should send
material to *Priya Kular.*

Freelance Rates – Broadcasting

Freelance rates vary enormously. The following minimum rates should be treated as guidelines. Most work can command higher fees from employers. It is up to freelancers to negotiate the best deal they can.

BBC Guidelines for Freelance Minimum Rates

BBC – Published Material
(negotiated by the Publishers Association and the Society of Authors)

Domestic Radio

Plays/prose (per minute)	£12.85
Prose for dramatisation (per minute)	£10.02
Poems (per half-minute)	£12.85
Prose translation (per minute)	£8.56

World Service Radio (English)

Plays/prose (per minute)	£6.43
Prose for dramatisation (per minute)	£5.02
Poems (per half-minute)	£6.43
Prose translation (per minute)	£4.29

Television

Prose (per minute)	£19.46
Poems (per half-minute)	£22.59

BBC Radio Drama
(negotiated by the Society of Authors and the Writers' Guild)
A beginner in radio drama should receive at least £42.57 per minute for an original drama script. For an established writer – one who has three or more plays to his credit – the minimum rate per minute is £64.80.

An attendance payment of £38.12 per production is paid to established writers. The rate per script for *The Archers* is £656.64.

Daily Serial minimum rates:
1) Where the storyline, characters, format, etc. are provided, the minimum fee is £523.50;
2) Where the overall format and structure are provided but the writer provides the storyline, some characters, etc. the minimum fee is £6692.50. (All fees cover one origination and one repeat.)

BBC Interviews and Talks
Interviews of up to 5 minutes (for the interviewer): £50; 5 to 8 minutes: £55; 8 to 10 minutes: £66.50.

Linked interviews: 1 interview £8; 2 interviews £107
Illustrated talks: £16 per minute.

Features/documentaries
Up to 7 minutes: £178.50; £25.50 per minute thereafter.

Independent Radio

News reports: £22.14 for the first 2 minutes; £7.38 per minute thereafter
(NUJ/CRCA agreement). *News copy*: £8.21 per item. *Day rates*: Exclusive
engagement of a freelance journalist: £77.10 per day; £38.54 per half day.

Research
TV organisations which hire freelancers to research programme items should
pay on a day rate which reflects the value of the work and the importance of the
programme concerned.

Presentation
In all broadcast media, presenters command higher fees than news journalists.
There is considerable variation in what is paid for presenting programmes and
videos, according to their audience and importance. Day rates with television
companies are usually about £140 – £160 a day.

Television Drama

For a 60-minute teleplay, the BBC will pay an established writer £7410 and a
beginner £4703. The corresponding figures for ITV are £9245 for the established writer and £6568 for a writer new to television but with a solid reputation in other literary areas. ITV also has a 'beginner' category with a payment
of £6568 for a 60-minute teleplay.

Day rates for attendance at read-throughs and rehearsals is £67 for the BBC
and £74.40 for ITV.

(*NB* ITV rates currently under negotiation)

Feature Films

The Writers' Guild and PACT agreement of 1992 (still being re-negotiated)
allows for a minimum guaranteed payment to the writer of £31,200 on a feature
film with a budget in excess of £2 million; £19,000 on a budget from
£750,000 to £2 million; £14,000 on a budget below £750,000. However,
many in the industry pay rates which take inflation into account and negotiate a
royalty provision for uses instead of fixed percentage payments.

Film, TV and Video Production Companies

Aardman
Gas Ferry Road, Bristol BS1 6UN
☎0117 9848485 Fax 0117 9848486
Website www.aardman.com
Head of Film & TV *Michael Rose*

FOUNDED 1972. Award-winning animation studio producing films, television series, videos and commercials. OUTPUT includes: *Rex the Runt; Morph Files; Creature Comforts; Wallace and Gromit.*

Absolutely Productions Ltd
8th Floor, Alhambra House, 27–31 Charing Cross Road, London WC2H 0AU
☎020 7930 3113 Fax 020 7930 4114
Email info@absolutely-uk.com
Website www.absolutely-uk.com
Executive Producer *Miles Bullough*

TV and film production company specialising in comedy and entertainment. OUTPUT *Absolutely* series 1–4 (Ch4); *mr don and mr george* (Ch4); *Squawkietalkie* (comedy wildlife programme for Ch4); *The Preventers* (ITV); *Scotland v England* (Ch4); *Barry Welsh is Coming* (HTV); *The Jack Docherty Show* (Ch5); *The Morwenna Banks Show* (Ch5); *Stressed Eric* (BBC2); *Armstrong & Miller* (Paramount/Ch4); *The Creatives* (BBC2); *Trigger Happy* (Ch4); *The Announcement* (Dakota Entertainment).

Abstract Images
117 Willoughby House, Barbican, London EC2Y 8BL
☎020 7638 5123
Email productions@abstract-images.co.uk
Contact *Howard Ross*

Television documentary and drama programming. OUTPUT includes *Balm in Gilead* (drama); *Bent* (drama); *God: For & Against* (documentary); *This Is a Man* (drama/doc). Encourages new writers; send synopsis in the first instance.

Acacia Productions Ltd
80 Weston Park, London N8 9Tb
☎020 8341 9392 Fax 020 8341 4879
Email acacia@dial.pipex.com
Website www.greenindex.co.uk

Contact *J. Edward Milner*

Producer of television and video documentaries; also corporates and programmes for educational charities. No unsolicited mss. OUTPUT includes a documentary series in association with TVE, London and NHK, Japan entitled *Last Plant Standing; A Farm in Uganda; Montserrat: Under the Volcano; Spirit of Trees* (8 progs.); *Vietnam: After the Fire.*

Acrobat Television
107 Wellington Road North, Stockport, Cheshire SK4 2LP
☎0161 477 9090 Fax 0161 477 9191
Email acrobat.television@btinternet.com
Contacts *Annabel Maudsley, Sarah Hunter*

Corporate video producer. OUTPUT includes instructional video for the British Association of Ski Instructors; corporate videos for Neilson Sailing, Hepworth Building Products, The Simon Group and First Choice Ski. No unsolicited mss.

Action Time Ltd
1 Heathcock Court, 415 Strand, London WC2R 0NS
☎020 7836 0505 Fax 020 7836 1122
Joint Managing Directors *Stephen Leahy, Trish Kinane*

Major producer and licenser of TV quiz and game entertainment shows such as *Catchphrase; Here's One I Made Earlier; Wipeout; Mr & Mrs; Men for Sale.* Action Time has co-production partners in Spain, Sweden, Denmark, Norway, Ireland and India.

Alomo Productions
1 Stephen Street, London W1P 1PJ
☎020 7691 6531 Fax 020 7691 6081

Part of the Pearson Group since 1996. Major producer of television drama and comedy. OUTPUT *Goodnight Sweetheart; Birds of a Feather; Love Hurts; The New Statesman; Grown Ups; Unfinished Business; Cry Wolf.* Scripts not welcome unless via agents but new writing is encouraged.

Anglo/Fortunato Films Ltd

170 Popes Lane, London W5 4NJ
☎020 8932 7676 Fax 020 8932 7491

Contact *Luciano Celentino*

Film, television and video producer of action comedy and psych-thriller drama. No unsolicited mss.

Antelope (UK) Ltd

29b Montague Street, London WC1B 5BH
☎020 7209 0099 Fax 020 7209 0098
Website www.antelope.co.uk

Managing Director *Mick Csáky*
Head of Non-Fiction *Krishan Arora*

Film, television and video productions for drama, documentary and corporate material. OUTPUT *Cyberspace* (ITV); *Brunch* (Ch5); *The Pier* (weekly arts and entertainment programme); *Placido Domingo* (ITV); *Baden Powell – The Boy Man*; *Howard Hughes – The Naked Emperor* (Ch4 'Secret Lives' series); *Hiroshima*. No unsolicited mss – 'we are not reading any new material at present'.

Apex Television Production & Facilities Ltd

Button End Studios, Harston, Cambridge CB2 5NX
☎01223 872900 Fax 01223 873092

Contact *Bernard Mulhern*

Video producer: drama, documentary, commercials and corporate. Largely corporate production for a wide range of international companies. Many drama-based training programmes and current-affairs orientated TV work. No scripts. All work is commissioned against a particular project.

Arena Films Ltd

2 Pelham Road, London SW19 1SX
☎020 8543 3990 Fax 020 8540 3992

Producer *David Conroy*

Film and TV drama. Scripts with some sort of European connection or tie-in particularly welcome.

Argus Video Productions

52 Church Street, Briston, Melton Constable, Norfolk NR24 2LE
☎01263 861152 Fax 01263 740025

Contact *Siri Taylor*

Producer of corporate, documentary and educational videos. OUTPUT includes *View & Do* series on leisure and hobby interests; *The Chainsaw*

Safety and *Relaxation* series; and *Moving Postcard Series on East Anglia*. No unsolicited mss.

Ariel Productions Ltd

Ealing Studios, Ealing Green, London W5 5EP
☎020 8567 6655 Fax 020 8758 8658

Producer *Otto Plaschkes*

Feature film and television producer. OUTPUT includes *Georgy Girl; Hopscotch; In Celebration; Butley; Doggin' Around*. Encourages new writers through involvement with the **National Film and Television School** and Screen Laboratory. No unsolicited mss.

Arlington Productions Limited

Pinewood Studios, Iver Heath, Buckinghamshire SL0 0NH
☎01753 651700 Fax 01753 656050

Television producer. Specialises in popular international drama, with *occasional* forays into other areas. 'We have an enviable reputation for encouraging new writers but only accept unsolicited submissions via agents.'

The Ashford Entertainment Corporation Ltd

182 Brighton Road, Coulsdon, Surrey CR5 2NF
☎020 8645 0667 Fax 020 8763 2558
Email info@ashford-entertainment.co.uk
Website www.ashford-entertainment.co.uk

Managing Director *Frazer Ashford*
Script Consultant *Clare Cameron*

FOUNDED in 1996 by award-winning film and TV producer Frazer Ashford whose credits include *Great Little Trains* (Mainline Television for Westcountry/Ch4, starring the late Willie Rushton); *Street Life* and *Make Yourself at Home* (both for WTV). Produces theatrical films and television – drama, lifestyle and documentaries. Happy to receive ideas for dramas and documentaries but submit a one-page synopsis only in the first instance, enclosing s.a.e. 'Be patient, allow up to four weeks for a reply. Be precise with the idea; specific details rather than vague thoughts. Attach a back-up sheet with credentials and supporting evidence, ie, can you ensure that your idea is feasible?'

Assembly Film and Television Ltd

Riverside Studios, Crisp Road, London W6 9RL
☎020 8237 1075 Fax 020 8237 1071
Email judithmurrell@riversidestudios.co.uk

Contacts *William Burdett-Coutts, Judith Murrell*

Television documentary producer. OUTPUT includes the Prudential Awards for the Arts, the London Comedy Festival, Ch4's Black Season and *In Exile: Sitcom*. Welcomes unsolicited mss. 'We are always interested in looking at new writers.'

Avalon Films
1 Rook's Farm Road, Yelland, Barnstaple, Devon EX31 3EQ
☎01271 860294 Fax 01271 860294

Joint Managing Directors *Robin Price, Andrew Vincent*
Script Executive *Teresa Collard*

Production company now specialising in horror/sci-fi/supernatural and fantasy films. A Hammer-style permanent team of genre writers, directors and stars now looking at projects for next three years. 'Always willing to encourage new writers and work with them to help refine their skills. Unsolicited material given serious consideration.' OUTPUT Feature films, 2000: *Star of Ill-Omen; Shadow of the Witch; The Psychic Detective; Campari for the Fishes; Stinger; H. Riger Haggard's 'Allan Quatermain Esq. – His Quest for the Holy Flower'*. TV: *Jack the Ripper – Visitor from the Grave; Lorna Doon; Black Beauty; Wilkie Collins Collection*.

Bamboo Film & TV Productions Ltd
15 Rochester Square, London NW1 9SA
☎020 7916 9353 Fax 020 7485 4692

Contacts *Rosemary Forgan, Natasha Sweeney*

Television documentary producer. OUTPUT includes *The Lost Gardens of Heligan; There's Something About a Covent Girl; Mushroom Magic*. No unsolicited mss; 'We do *not* do fiction/drama.'

Bazal
See **GMG Endemol Entertainment plc**

Beckmann Productions Ltd
Meadow Court, West Street, Ramsey, Isle of Man IM8 1AE
☎01624 816585 Fax 01624 816589
Email beckmann@enterprise.net
Website www.beckmangroup.co.uk

Contacts *Stuart Semark, Michael Souter*

Isle of Man-based company. Video and television documentary. OUTPUT *Practical Guide to Europe* (travel series); *Maestro* (12-part series on classical composers); *Ivory Orphans; Ages in History*.

Paul Berriff Productions Ltd
Cedar House, 53 Heads Lane, Hessle, East Yorkshire HU13 0JH
☎01482 641158 Fax 01482 649692
Email pberriff@aol.com

Contact *Paul Berriff*

Television documentary. OUTPUT *Rescue* (13-part documentary for ITV); *M25: The Magic Roundabout* ('First Tuesday'); *Animal Squad Undercover* (Ch4); *Evidence of Abuse* (BBC1 'Inside Story'); *Lessons of Darkness* (BBC2 'Fine Cut'); *The Nick* (Ch4 series); *Confrontation on E Wing* (BBC 'Everyman'); *Astronauts* (Ch4 series); *Streets of Fire* (Ch4 series); *Passport Control* ('Cutting Edge').

BFI Production
21 Stephen Street, London W1P 2LN
☎020 7255 1444 Fax 020 7580 9456
Website www.bfi.org.uk

Head of Production *Roger Shannon*

Originally part of the **British Film Institute**, BFI Production transferred to the new Film Council in April 2000. At the time of printing the new remit was still to be confirmed although it is likely to continue developing new talent and innovative fillm-making. Previous OUTPUT includes *Under the Skin; Sixth Happiness; Love Is the Devil; Beautiful People; I Could Read the Sky* as well as the New Directors short film scheme.

Black Coral Productions Ltd
2nd Floor, 241 High Street, London E17 7BH
☎020 8520 2830 Fax 020 8520 2358
Email bcp@coralmedia.co.uk
Website www.m4media.net

Contact *Lazell Daley*

Producer of drama and documentary film and television. Committed to the development of new writing with a particular interest in short and feature-length dramas. Offers a script consultancy service for which a fee is payable. Runs courses – see **Black Coral Training** under **Writers' Courses, Circles and Workshops**.

Blackbird Productions
Suite 115, The Plaza, 535 Kings Road, Chelsea, London SW10 0SZ
☎020 7352 4882 Fax 020 7351 3728

Contact *Sally Bell*

Television and video producer of documentary, corporate work; also commercials and sitcoms. OUTPUT includes *Wild Bunch* (sitcom). No unsolicited mss but will consider 2–3-page synopsis with 2–3 pages of script. 'Always enclose s.a.e., please.'

Blackstone Pictures Ltd

12 Avondale Park Road, London W11 4HL
☎020 7243 3565 Fax 020 7243 3564
Email mail@blaxpix.demon.co.uk
Contact *Christopher Davis*

Film, television and video documentary producer. OUTPUT includes *Rwanda, the Betrayal* (Ch4) and *Charles Manson, The Man Who Killed the Sixties*. No unsolicited mss.

Blackwatch Productions Limited

29 Otago Street, Kelvinbridge, Glasgow G12 8JJ
☎0141 341 0044 Fax 0141 341 0055
Email blackwatch@cqm.co.uk
Company Director *Nicola Black*
Research & Development Officer
  Heidi Proven

Film, television, video producer of drama and documentary programmes. OUTPUT incudes *Lightbox* (film drama) and, for Ch4: *Mirrorball* (music video series); *Documentary Lab* (documentary series); *Carry On Darkly* (documentary); *Post Mortem* (drama-doc series). Currently working with five new writers but does not welcome unsolicited mss.

Blue Heaven Productions Ltd

116 Great Portland Street, London W1N 5PG
☎020 7436 5552 Fax 020 7436 0888
Contact *Christine Benson*

Film and television drama and occasional documentary. OUTPUT *The Ruth Rendell Mysteries; Crime Story: Dear Roy, Love Gillian; Ready When You Are/Screen Challenge* (three series for Meridian Regional); *The Man who Made Husbands Jealous* (Anglia Television Entertainment/Blue Heaven). Scripts considered but treatments or ideas preferred in the first instance. New writing encouraged.

Bond Clarkson Russell Ltd

16 Trinity Churchyard, Guildford, Surrey GU1 3RR
☎01483 594000 Fax 01483 302732
Email bcr@bcr-marketing.co.uk
Contact *Peter Bond, Simon Kozak*

Corporate literature, contract magazine publisher and film, video and multi-media producer of a wide variety of material, including conference videos, for blue-chip companies in the main. No scripts. All work is commissioned.

Box Clever Productions

13 St James Street, London WC1N 3DP
☎020 7831 1811 Fax 020 7831 6606
Contact *Claire Walmsley*

Broadcast TV, film and video documentaries, specialising in current affairs. Sister company of Boxclever Communication Training, specialising in media interview skills, presentation and communication skills. OUTPUT documentaries for BBC and Ch4; corporate videos. No unsolicited scripts; outlines and proposals only.

British Lion
Screen Entertainment Ltd

Pinewood Studios, Iver, Buckinghamshire SL0 0NH
☎01753 651700 Fax 01753 656391
Chief Executive *Peter R. E. Snell*

Film production. OUTPUT has included *A Man for All Seasons; Treasure Island; A Prayer for the Dying; Lady Jane; The Crucifer of Blood; Death Train*. No unsolicited mss. Send synopses only.

Broadcast Communications

See **GMG Endemol Entertainment plc**

Bronco Films Ltd

The Producers Centre, 61 Holland Street, Glasgow G2 4NJ
☎0141 287 6817 Fax 0141 287 6815
Email broncofilm@btinternet.com
Contact *Peter Broughan*

Film, television and video drama. OUTPUT includes *Rob Roy* (feature film) and *Young Person's Guide to Becoming a Rock Star* (TV series). No unsolicited mss.

Buccaneer Films

5 Rainbow Court, Oxhey, Hertfordshire WD1 4RP
☎01923 254000 Fax 01923 254000
Contact *Michael Gosling*

Corporate video production and still photography specialists in education and sport. No unsolicited mss.

Bumper Films Ltd

Unit 15, Bridgwater Court, Weston-super-Mare BS24 9AY
☎01934 418961 Fax 01934 624494
Email bumper@ibm.net
Contact *John Walker*

Producer of children's model animations. OUTPUT includes, for BBC1: *Fireman Sam;*

Joshua Jones; Star Hill Ponies, and *Rocky Hollow* for TVAM/S4C. Welcomes unsolicited mss; 'We are always looking for new projects in pre-school area.'

Can Television & Marketing

Smitham House, 127 Brighton Road, Coulsdon, Surrey CR5 2NJ
☎020 8763 9444 Fax 020 8763 0762
Email cantv@compuserve.com

Contact *Philip Saben*

Television and video producer of corporate programmes and commercials for clients such as London Electricity and NatWest. No unsolicited mss.

Caravel Film Techniques Ltd

The Great Barn Studios, Cippenham Lane, Slough, Berkshire SL1 5AU
☎01753 534828 Fax 01753 571383

Contact *Anita See*

Film, video and TV: documentary, commercials and corporate. OUTPUT Promos for commercial TV, documentaries for BBC & ITV, sales and training material for corporate blue chip companies. No unsolicited scripts. Prepared to review mostly serious new writing.

Carey St. Productions

Unit 8, Utopia Village, 7 Chalcot Road, London NW1 8LH
☎020 7722 8225 Fax 020 7722 8254
Email office@careyst.co.uk

Contacts *Charlie Hamp, Genevieve Christie*

Film, television and video documentaries. OUTPUT includes drama-documentaries for the Discovery Channel. No unsolicited mss.

Carlton Productions

35–38 Portman Square, London W1H 0NU
☎020 7486 6688 Fax 020 7486 1132
Website www.carltontv.com

Director of Programmes *Steve Hewlett*
Director of Drama & Co-production
 Jonathan Powell
Controller of Entertainment *Mike Wells*
Controller of Factual Programmes *Polly Bide*
Controller of Comedy *Nick Symons*

Makers of independently produced TV drama for ITV. OUTPUT *She's Out; Kavanagh QC; Morse; Boon; Gone to the Dogs; The Guilty; Tanamera; Soldier, Soldier; Seekers; Sharpe; Peak Practice; Cadfael; Faith*. 'We try to use new writers on established long-running series.' Scripts welcome from experienced writers and agents only.

Carnival (Films & Theatre) Ltd

12 Raddington Road, Ladbroke Grove, London W10 5TG
☎020 8968 0968 Fax 020 8968 0155
Email info@carnival-films.co.uk
Website www.carnival-films.co.uk

Contact *Brian Eastman*

Film, TV and theatre producer. OUTPUT Film: *The Mill on the Floss* (BBC); *Firelight* (Hollywood Pictures/Wind Dancer Productions); *Up on the Roof* (Rank/Granada); *Shadowlands* (Savoy/Spelling); *In Hitler's Shadow* (Home Box Office); *Under Suspicion* (Columbia/Rank/LWT). Television: *Lucy Sullivan is Getting Married* (ITV); *The Tenth Kingdom* (Sky/NBC); *Agatha Christie's Poirot* (ITV/LWT/A&E); *Every Woman Knows a Secret* and *Oktober* (both for ITV Network Centre); *The Fragile Heart* (Ch4); *Crime Traveller* (BBC); *Bugs 1–4* (BBC); *Anna Lee* (LWT); *All or Nothing At All* (LWT); *Head Over Heels* (Carlton); *Jeeves & Wooster* I–IV (Granada); *Traffik* (Ch4); *Forever Green 1–3* (LWT); *Porterhouse Blue* (Ch4); *Blott on the Landscape* (BBC). Theatre: *What a Performance; Juno & the Paycock; Murder is Easy; Misery; Ghost Train; Map of the Heart; Shadowlands; Up on the Roof*.

Cartwn Cymru

Screen Centre, Llantrisant Road, Cardiff CF5 2PU
☎029 2057 5999 Fax 029 2057 5919

Contact *Naomi Jones*

Animation production company. OUTPUT includes *Toucan 'Tecs* (YTV/S4C); *Funnybones* (S4C/ BBC); *Turandot: Operavox* (S4C/BBC); *Testament: The Bible in Animation* (BBC2/S4C); *The Miracle Maker* (S4C/BBC/British Screen/Icon Entertainment International); *Faeries* (HIT Entertainment plc for CITV).

CCCSoho

PO Box 2903, London W1A 6BR
☎020 7450 4720 Fax 020 7399 9977

Head of Productions *Nicholas Crean*

Film and video, multimedia and graphic design: corporate and commercials. CLIENTS include Bovis; Camelot; De La Rue plc; Del Monte Foods International; East Midlands Electricity; Hill & Norton; Knowlton; Lloyds of London; Nationwide Building Society; P&O; M&C Saatchi; Samaritans. 'We are very keen to hear from new writers, but please send c.v.s rather than scripts.'

Celador

39 Long Acre, London WC2E 9JT
☎020 7240 8101 Fax 020 7497 9541
Email tvhits@celador.co.uk

Head of Entertainment *Colman Hutchinson*
Head of Comedy *Mike Whitehill*

Producers of TV comedy and light entertainment. OUTPUT *Who Wants to be a Millionaire; Winning Lines; Jo Brand's Commercial Breakdown; Jasper Carrott − Back to the Front.* '... interested in original non-derivative sitcom scripts and entertainment formats. Some broadcast experience would be helpful. But as a relatively small company our script-reading capacity is limited.'

Celtic Films Ltd

Room 21, Ground Floor, Government Buildings, Bromyard Avenue, London W3 7XH
☎020 8740 6880 Fax 020 8740 9755
Email celticfilms@compuserve.com

Contact *Muir Sutherland*

Film and television drama producer. OUTPUT includes 14 feature-length *Sharpe* TV films for Carlton and *A Life for a Life − The True Story of Stefan Kiszko* TV film for ITV. Supports new writing and welcomes unsolicited mss.

Central Office of Information Film & Video

Hercules Road, London SE1 7DU
☎020 7261 8667 Fax 020 7261 8776
Email graison@coi.gov.uk

Contact *Geoff Raison*

Film, video and TV: drama, documentary, commercials, corporate and public information films. OUTPUT includes government commercials and corporate information. No scripts. New writing commissioned as required.

Chain Production Limited

2 Clanricarde Gardens, London W2 4NA
☎020 7229 4277 Fax 020 7229 0861

Contact *Garwin Davison*

Theatrical feature and televison films. OUTPUT includes *Senso Unico* (feature, co-production with India and Italy); *The Protagonists* (feature). 'Actively looking for drama action thrillers for TV movie production with international partners.' Send treatments rather than complete mss.

Chameleon Television Ltd

Television House, 104 Kirkstall Road, Leeds, West Yorkshire LS3 1JS
☎0113 2444486 Fax 0113 2431267
Email allen@chamtv.demon.co.uk

Contacts *Allen Jewhurst, Kevin Sim, Anna Hall*

Film and television drama and documentary producer. OUTPUT includes *The Reckoning* (USA/Ch4); *Dunblane* (ITV); *Foul Play* (Ch5); *St Hildas* and *Rules of the Game* (both for Ch4); *Divorces From Hell* and *New Voices* (both for ITV). 'We have four dramas and one situation comedy in script development with ITV broadcasters.'

Channel X Communications Ltd

22 Stephenson Way, London NW1 2HD
☎020 7387 3874 Fax 020 7387 0738
Email mail@channelx.co.uk

Contact *Alan Marke*

FOUNDED 1986 by Jonathan Ross and Alan Marke to develop Ross's first series *The Last Resort.* Now producing comedy series and documentary. Actively developing narrative comedy and game shows. OUTPUT *Unpleasant World of Penn & Teller; XYZ; Jo Brand − Through The Cakehole; Sean's Show; The Smell of Reeves & Mortimer; Fantastic Facts; One for the Road; Funny Business; Shooting Stars; Barking; Food Fight; Johnny Vaughan Meets Madonna; Families at War; Leftfield; The Cooler; All Back to Mine* (Series 1); *Celebrities ... the truth; Comedy Cafe.*

Chatsworth Television Limited

97–99 Dean Street, London W1V 5RA
☎020 7734 4302 Fax 020 7437 3301
Email television@chatsworth-tv.co.uk

Managing Director *Malcolm Heyworth*

Drama, factual and entertainment television producer. Interested in contemporary and factually based series.

The Children's Film & Television Foundation Ltd

The John Maxwell Building, Elstree Film Studios, Shenley Road, Borehamwood, Hertfordshire WD6 1JG
☎020 8953 0844 Fax 020 8207 0860
Email annahome@cftf.onyxnet.co.uk

Chief Executive *Anna Home*

FOUNDED as the Children's Entertainment Film Division of J. Arthur Rank Organisation in 1944; then became the Children's Film Foundation Ltd. Film and television drama. OUTPUT *The Borrowers; Danny − the Champion of the World; The Circus Connection.* Unsolicited mss welcome.

Chromatose Films

9 Camberwell Grove, London SE5 8JA
☎020 7207 6413 Fax 020 7207 6413
Email E9COOOL@aol.com

Film and video producer of pop promos and 'shorts'.

Cinécosse

Riversfield Studios, Ellon, Aberdeenshire AB41 9EY

☎01358 722150 Fax 01358 720053

Email admin@cinecosse.co.uk

Website www.cinecosse.co.uk

Contact *Michael Marshall*

Television and video documentary and corporate productions. OUTPUT includes *Scotland's Larder* (Scottish/Grampian TV); safety and training videos for industry; tourism promotional and sales information. All scripts are commissioned; no unsolicited mss.

Cinema Verity Productions Ltd

11 Addison Avenue, London W11 4QS

☎020 7460 2777 Fax 020 7371 3329

Contact *Verity Lambert*

Leading television drama producer whose credits include *She's Out* by Lynda la Plante; *Class Act* by Michael Aitkens; *May to December* (BBC series); *Running Late* by Simon Gray (Screen 1). No unsolicited mss.

Circus Films
See **Elstree (Production) Co. Ltd.**

Claverdon Films Ltd

28 Narrow Street, London E14 8DQ

☎020 7702 8700 Fax 020 7702 8701

Contact *Tony Palmer, Michela Antonello*

Film and TV: drama and documentary. OUTPUT *Menuhin; Maria Callas; Testimony; In From the Cold; Pushkin; England, My England* (by John Osborne); *Kipling*. Unsolicited material is read, but please send a written outline first.

Cleveland Productions

5 Rainbow Court, Oxhey, Near Watford, Hertfordshire WD1 4RP

☎01923 254000 Fax 01923 254000

Contact *Michael Gosling*

Communications in sound and vision A/V production and still photography specialists in education and sport. No unsolicited mss.

Collingwood & Convergence Productions Ltd

10–14 Crown Street, Acton, London W3 8SB

☎020 8993 3666 Fax 020 8993 9595

Email info@crownstreet.co.uk

Producers *Christopher O'Hare, Terence Clegg, Tony Collingwood*

Head of Development *Helen Stroud*

Film and TV. Convergence Productions produces live action, drama documentaries; Tony Collingwood Productions specialises in children's animation. OUTPUT **Convergence**: *Theo* (2 film drama series); *Plastic Fantastic* (UK cosmetic surgery techniques, Ch5) and *David Starkey's Henry VIII* (Ch4 historical documentary). **Collingwood**: *Rarg* (award-winning animated film); 26 episodes of *Captain Zed and the Zee Zone* (ITV); *Daisy-Head Mayzie* (Dr Seuss animated series for Turner Network and Hanna-Barbera); *Animal Stories* (52 5-minute animated poems, ITV network). Unsolicited mss not welcome as ' we do not have the capacity to process the sheer weight of submissions this creates. We therefore tend to review material from individuals recommended to us through personal contact with agents or other industry professionals. We like to encourage new writing and have worked with new writers but our ability to do so is limited by our capacity for development. We can usually only consider taking on one project each year, as development/finance takes several years to put in place.'

Convergence Productions Ltd
See **Collingwood & Convergence Productions Ltd**

Cosgrove Hall Films

8 Albany Road, Chorlton–cum–Hardy, Manchester M21 0AW

☎0161 882 2500 Fax 0161 882 2556

Email animation@chf.co.uk

Contacts *Mark Hall, Iain Pelling*

Children's animation producer; film video and television. OUTPUT *Noddy* and *Rotten Ralph* (both BBC); *Lavender Castle* by Gerry Anderson; *The Fox Busters; Animal Shelf; Rocky & the Dodos*; Alison Uttley's *Little Grey Rabbit* (all children's ITV); Terry Pratchett's *Discworld* (Ch4). 'We try to select writers on a project-by-project basis.' Hosted the **Writers' Guild** workshop in 1998.

Judy Counihan Films
See **Dakota Films Ltd**

Creative Channel Ltd

Channel TV, Television Centre, St Helier, Jersey, Channel Islands JE1 3ZD

☎01534 816873 Fax 01534 816889

Email creative@channeltv.co.uk

Website www.channeltv.co.uk

Head of Creative Channel *Tim Ringsdore*
Production Manager *David Evans*

Part of the Channel Television Group. Producer of TV commercials and corporate material: information, promotional, sales, training and events coverage. OUTPUT *Exploring Guernsey* and *This is Jersey* (video souvenir travel guides); promotional videos for all types of businesses in the Channel Islands and throughout Europe; plus over 300 commercials a year. No unsolicited mss; new writing/scripts commissioned as required. Interested in hearing from local writers resident in the Channel Islands.

Creative Film Makers Ltd

Pottery Lane House, 34A Pottery Lane, London W11 4LZ
☎020 7229 5131 Fax 020 7229 4999

Contacts *Michael Seligman, Nicholas Seligman*

Corporate and sports documentaries, commercials and television programmes. OUTPUT *The World's Greatest Golfers*, plus various corporate and sports programmes for clients like Nestlé, Benson & Hedges, Wimpey, Bouygues. 'Always open to suggestions but have hardly ever received unsolicited material of any value.' Keen nevertheless to encourage new writers.

The Creative Partnership

13 Bateman Street, London W1V 5TB
☎020 7439 7762
Email sally@sohocp.co.uk

Contacts *Christopher Fowler, Jim Sturgeon*

'Europe's largest "one-stop shop" for advertising and marketing campaigns for the film and television industries.' Clients include most major and independent film companies. No scripts. 'We train new writers in-house, and find them from submitted c.v.s. All applicants must have previous commercial writing experience.' Freelance writers employed for special projects.

Cricket Ltd

Medius House, 63–69 New Oxford Street, London WC1A 1EA
☎020 7845 0300 Fax 020 7845 0303
Email team@cricket-ltd.co.uk
Website www.cricket-ltd.co.uk

Head of Production (Film & Video)
  Jonathan Freer
Art Director *Sally Marshall*

Film and video, live events and conferences, print and design. Communications solutions for business clients wishing to influence targeted external and internal audiences.'

Cromdale Films Ltd

12 St Paul's Road, London N1 2QN
☎020 7226 0178

Contact *Ian Lloyd*

Film, video and TV: drama and documentary. OUTPUT *The Face of Darkness* (feature film); *Drift to Dawn* (rock music drama); *The Overdue Treatment* (documentary); *Russia, The Last Red Summer* (documentary). Initial phone call advised before submission of scripts.

Crown Business Communications Ltd

United House, 9 Pembridge Road, London W11 3JY
☎020 7727 7272 Fax 020 7727 9940
Email clarkea@crownbc.com
Website www.crownbc.com

Contact *Alex Clarke*

Leading producer of moving image, live, design, on-/off-line communications for major corporate clients. 'Always interested in talented writers, especially with a sector journalism or Internet experience.'

Cutting Edge Productions Ltd

27 Erpingham Road, Putney, London SW15 1BE
☎020 8780 1476 Fax 020 8780 0102
Email norridge@globalnet.co.uk

Contact *Julian Norridge*

Corporate and documentary video and television. OUTPUT US series on evangelicalism, 'Dispatches' on US tobacco and government videos. No unsolicited mss; 'we commission all our writing to order but are open to ideas.'

Cwmni'r Castell Ltd

10 Garth Road, Colwyn Bay, Conwy LL29 8AF
☎01492 512349 Fax 01492 514235
Email castell@enterprise.net

Contact *Elwyn Vaughan Williams*

Television light entertainment and corporate video producer. OUTPUT includes four series with Welsh comedians and *Bob yn Ddau* ('Two by Two') – a daily quiz. Welcomes material from new comedy writers.

Dakota Films Ltd

12A Newburgh Street, London W1V 1LG
☎020 7287 4329 Fax 020 7287 2303
Email lila@dakotafilm.demon.co.uk

Head of Development *Lila Rawlings*

Managing Director *Judy Counihan*

Film and television drama. Feature films include: *Let Him Have It; Othello; Janice Beard: 45wpm.* Judy Counihan Films: *Before the Rain; Antonia's Line; Time to Love.* Currently developing a slate of 12 feature film and TV projects, including John Sayles' *Fade to Black*, and a number of projects by new writers. Interested in working with and encouraging new talent but does not consider unsolicited material.

Dareks Production House
58 Wickham Road, Beckenham, Kent
BR3 6RQ
☎020 8658 2012 Fax 020 8325 0629
Email dareks@dircon.co.uk

Contact *David Crossman*

Independent producer of corporate and broadcast television. 'We are interested in *short* (10–15 minute) narrative scripts.'

Devlin Morris Productions Ltd
97b West Bow, Edinburgh EH1 2JP
☎0131 226 7728 Fax 0131 226 6668
Email contact@devlinmorris-prod.sol.co.uk

Contacts *Morris Paton, Vivien Devlin*

New independent media production house encompassing international arts and travel writing as well as a range of drama, radio, film and television projects.

Direct Image Productions Ltd
PO Box 17, Kendal, Cumbria LA8 8BE
☎015395 68931 Fax 015395 68932
Email enquiries@directimageprod.
   demon.co.uk
Website www.directimageprod.co.uk

Co-directors *Chris Ware, Elaine Ware*

An independent broadcast and video production company FOUNDED over 25 years ago. Produces outdoor adventure and outdoor education video and book packages with its publishing arm, **Direct Image Publishing** (see entry under **UK Packagers**). Ideas for programmes for outdoor education and/or training welcome. Send letter and outline in the first instance.

Diverse Production Limited
Gorleston Street, London W14 8XS
☎020 7603 4567 Fax 020 7603 2148

Contacts *Roy Ackerman, Narinder Minhas*

Broadcast television production with experience in popular prime-time formats, strong documentaries (one-offs and series), investigative journalism, science, business and history films, travel series, arts and music, talk shows, schools and education. 'We have always been committed to editorial and visual originality.' Recent OUTPUT includes *Secret Lives; Omnibus; Cutting Edge; Equinox; Modern Times; Dispatches; Without Walls; Panorama; The Big Idea; Empires and Emperors* and the *Little Picture Show.*

DMS Films Ltd
369 Burnt Oak Broadway, Edgware,
Middlesex HA8 5XZ
☎020 8951 6060 Fax 020 8951 6050
Email danny@argonaut.com

Producer *Daniel San*

Film drama producer. OUTPUT includes *Understanding Jane; Hard Edge; Strangers.* Welcomes unsolicited screenplays.

Double-Band Films
Crescent Arts Centre, 2–4 University Road,
Belfast BT7 1NH
☎028 9024 3331 Fax 028 9023 6980
Email info@dbfilms.dnet.coluk

Contacts *Michael Hewitt, Dermot Lavery*

Documentary and drama programmes for film and television. Has specialised in documentary production for the past ten years (programmes include *Escobar's Own Goal* for Ch4) but moved into drama production with the short film *Still Life* in 1998.

Dragon Pictures
23 Golden Square, London W1R 3PA
☎020 7734 6307 Fax 020 7734 6202
Email info@dragonpictures.demon.co.uk

Contacts *Katie Goodson, Lucy Guard,
   Graham Broadbent*

Feature films, including *Welcome to Sarajevo; Gridlock'd; The Debt Collector; Splendor; A Texas Funeral.* Likes to encourage young talent but cannot consider unsolicited mss.

Drake A-V Video Ltd
89 St Fagans Road, Fairwater, Cardiff
CF5 3AE
☎029 2056 0333 Fax 029 2055 4909
Website www.drakegroup.co.uk

Contact *Ian Lewis*

Corporate A-V film and video, mostly promotional, training or educational. Scripts in these fields welcome. Other work includes interactive multimedia and CD-ROM production.

The Drama House Ltd

20 Chalcot Square, London NW1 8YA
☎020 7586 1000 Fax 020 7586 1345
Email drama.house@virgin.net
Website freespace.virgin.net/drama.house

Contact *Jack Emery*

Film and television producer. OUTPUT *Little White Lies* (BBC1); *Witness Against Hitler* (BBC1); *Suffer the Little Children* (BBC2 'Stages'). Scripts (synopses preferred) welcome but only read and returned if accompanied by full postage. Interested in developing contacts with new and established writers.

Charles Dunstan Communications Ltd

42 Wolseley Gardens, London W4 3LS
☎020 8994 2328 Fax 020 8994 2328

Contact *Charles Dunstan*

Producer of film, video and TV for documentary and corporate material. OUTPUT *Renewable Energy* for broadcast worldwide in *Inside Britain* series; National Power Annual Report video *The Electric Environment*. No unsolicited scripts.

Ealing Films Limited

Beaumont House, 8 Beaumont Road, Poole, Dorset BH13 7JJ
☎01202 706644 Fax 01202 706655
Email utopia8@compuserve.com

Managing Director *Eben Foggitt*
Head of Development *Anita Simpkins*

Film and television drama producer. Unsolicited mss welcome; 'we encourage new writers'.

East Anglian Productions

Studio House, 21–23 Walton Road, Frinton on Sea, Essex CO13 0AA
☎01255 676252 Fax 01255 850528

Contact *Ray Anderson*

Film, video and TV: drama and documentary, children's television, comedy, commercials and corporate.

Eden Productions Ltd

24 Belsize Lane, London NW3 5AB
☎020 7435 3242 Fax 020 7794 1519
Email jancis@cix.co.uk

Contacts *Nicholas Lander, Jancis Robinson*

Producer of *Jancis Robinson's Wine Course; Vintners' Tales with Jancis Robinson; Taste with Jancis Robinson* and wine training videos for British Airways. No unsolicited mss.

Edinburgh Film Productions

Traquair House, Innerleithen, Peeblesshire EH44 6PW
☎01968 672131 Fax 01968 672685

Contact *R. Crichton*

Film, TV drama and documentary. OUTPUT *Sara; Moonacre; Torch; Silent Mouse; The Curious Case of Santa Claus; The Stamp of Greatness*. No unsolicited scripts at present.

Elstree (Production) Co. Ltd

Shepperton Studios, Studios Road, Shepperton, Middlesex TW17 0QD
☎01932 572680/1 Fax 01932 572682

Contact *Greg Smith*

Produces feature films and TV drama. OUTPUT *Othello* (BBC); *Great Expectations* (Disney Channel); *Porgy & Bess* (with Trevor Nunn); *Old Curiosity Shop* (Disney Channel/RHI); *London Suite* (NBC/Hallmark); *Animal Farm* and *David Copperfield* (both for Hallmark/TNT). Co-owner of Circus Films with Trevor Nunn for feature film projects.

Excalibur Productions

13–15 Northgate, Heptonstall, West Yorkshire HX7 7ND
☎01422 843871 Fax 01422 843871

Contact *Jay Jones*

Most recent productions are medical documentaries such as an investigation into diabetes control sponsored by Bayer Diagnostics, collaborative literary and cultural projects such as *The Boys From Savoy* with David Glass, and corporates for clients such as South Yorkshire Supertram and Datacolor International. Interested in ideas, scripts and possible joint development for broadcast, sell-through and experimental arts.

Extreme International Limited

The Coach House, Ashford Lodge, Halstead, Essex CO9 2RR
☎01787 479000 Fax 01787 479111
Email xdream@xdream.co.uk

Contact *Alistair Gosling*

Film, television and video; drama and documentary. Unsolicited mss welcome.

Fairline Productions Ltd

15 Royal Terrace, Glasgow G3 7NY
☎0141 331 0077 Fax 0141 331 0066
Email fairprods@aol.com

Contact *Mandi Cragg*

Television and video producer of documentary

and corporate programmes and commercials. OUTPUT includes *Hooked*, a 15-part angling series (Discovery Channel) plus training and instructional videos for Forbo-Nairn Ltd, Royal Bank of Scotland, and Health & Safety Executive. No unsolicited scripts.

Farnham Film Company Ltd
34 Burnt Hill Road, Lower Bourne, Farnham, Surrey GU10 3LZ
☎01252 710313 Fax 01252 725855
Website www.farnfilm.com

Contact *Ian Lewis*

Television and film: children's drama and documentaries. Unsolicited mss usually welcome. Check website for current needs.

Farrant Partnership
429 Liverpool Road, London N7 8PR
☎020 7700 4647 Fax 020 7697 0224
Email farrant.stern@dial.pipex.com

Contact *James Farrant*

Corporate video productions.

Feelgood Fiction
49 Goldhawk Road, London W12 8QP
☎020 8746 2535 Fax 020 8740 6177
Email fiction_@msn.com

Contact *Laurence Bowen*

Producer of film and TV drama. Recent OUTPUT includes: *Badger Series 1&2*; *The Hello Girls*; *Stone, Scissors, Paper*; *Dual Balls* and *Painted Angels*.

Festival Film and Television Ltd
Festival House, Tranquil Passage, Blackheath, London SE3 0BJ
☎020 8297 9999 Fax 020 8297 1155

Contact *Ray Marshall*

Film and television drama. Production credits include: Catherine Cookson's *Tilly Trotter* and *The Secret*. Has produced 16 Cookson miniseries in the last nine years but 'our interests go beyond costume drama'. New writing is welcome as long as it is aimed at a particular audience and is realistic about expectations. Manuscripts must be presented professionally.

Film and General Productions Ltd
4 Bradbrook House, Studio Place, London SW1X 8EL
☎020 7235 4495 Fax 020 7245 9853

Contact *Clive Parsons*

Film and television drama. Feature films include *True Blue* and *Tea with Mussolini*. Also *Seesaw*

(ITV drama), *The Greatest Store in the World* (family drama, BBC) and *The Queen's Nose* (children's series, BBC). Interested in considering new writing but subject to prior telephone conversation.

Firehouse Productions
42 Glasshouse Street, London W1R 5RH
☎020 7439 2220 Fax 020 7439 2210
Email postie@hellofirehouse.com

Contacts *Julie-anne Edwards, Gavin Knight*

Corporate film and video programmes plus commercials and pop promos. OUTPUT includes corporate film for De Beers; British Airways in-flight commercial. No unsolicited mss.

First Creative Ltd
Belgrave Court, Caxton Road, Fulwood, Preston, Lancashire PR2 9PL
☎01772 651555 Fax 01772 651777
Email mail@firstcreative.com

Contact *M. Mulvihill*

Film, video and TV productions for documentary, corporate and multimedia material. Unsolicited scripts welcome. Open to new writing.

Fitting Images Ltd
The Studio, Henry VII Cottage, Pyrford Road, Pyrford Green, Woking, Surrey GU22 8UX
☎01932 343214 Fax 01932 343184
Email fitting_images@compuserve.com

Managing Director *Sue Fleetwood*

Promotional, training, medical/pharmaceutical; contacts from experienced writers of drama and comedy welcome. 'We are also interested in broadcast projects.'

Flashback Communication Ltd
25 McPhail Street, Glasgow G40 1DN
☎0141 554 6868 Fax 0141 554 6869

Contact *Giselle Scott*

Video and TV producer: documentary, corporate, training and education, and sell-throughs. OUTPUT includes dramatised training videos and TV programmes or inserts for the ITV network, BBC and stations worldwide. Proposals considered; no scripts. New talent encouraged. Interested in fresh ideas and effective style.

Flashback Television Limited
11 Bowling Green Lane, London EC1R 0BD
☎020 7490 8996 Fax 020 7490 5610
Email mailbox@flashbacktv.co.uk
Website www.flashbacktv.com

Contact *Timothy Ball*

Producer of documentaries and factual entertainment such as *Lost Gardens* and *Fork to Fork* (both for Ch4); and *Churchill and the President* (A&E).

Flick Films

15 Golden Square, London W1R 3AG
☎020 7734 7979 Fax 020 7287 9495
Email flickfilms@supanet.com
Website www.flickfilms.com

Contact *John Deery*

Producer of film drama, including *Conspiracy of Silence*, and *County Kilburn* (comedy-drama TV series). No unsolicited scripts.

Flicks Films Ltd

101 Wardour Street, London W1V 3TD
☎020 7734 4892 Fax 020 7287 2307

Managing Director/Producer *Terry Ward*

Film and video: children's animated series and specials. OUTPUT *The Mr Men; Little Miss; Bananaman; The Pondles; Nellie the Elephant; See How They Work With Dig and Dug; Timbuctoo*. Scripts specific to their needs will be considered. 'Always willing to read relevant material.'

Focus Films Ltd

The Rotunda Studios,
Rear of 116–118 Finchley Road,
London NW3 5HT
☎020 7435 9004 Fax 020 7431 3562
Email focus@pupix.demon.co.uk

Contacts *David Pupkewitz, Lisa Nicholson, Malcolm Kohll (Head of Development)*

Film and TV producer. OUTPUT *CrimeTime* (feature thriller); *Diary of a Sane Man* (experimental feature for Ch4); *Othello* (Ch4 drama); *Secret Society* (feature film). Projects in development include *The 51st State; 60°N; Sandmother; Cut and Paste; Barry*. No unsolicited scripts.

Mark Forstater Productions Ltd

27 Lonsdale Road, London NW6 6RA
☎020 7624 1123 Fax 020 7624 1124

Production *Mark Forstater*

Active in the selection, development and production of material for film and TV. OUTPUT *Monty Python and the Holy Grail; The Odd Job; The Grass is Singing; Xtro; Forbidden; Separation; The Fantasist; Shalom Joan Collins; The Silent Touch; Grushko; The Wolves of Willoughby Chase; Between the Devil and the Deep Blue Sea; Doing Rude Things*. No unsolicited scripts.

Friday Productions Ltd

23a St. Leonards Terrace, London
SW3 4QG
☎020 7730 0608 Fax 020 7730 0608

Contact *Georgina Abrahams*

Film and TV production for drama material. OUTPUT *Goggle Eyes; Harnessing Peacocks; The December Rose*. No unsolicited scripts. New writing encouraged especially from under-represented groups.

Full Moon Productions

16 Westbourne Gardens Lane, Glasgow
G12 9PB
☎0141 334 3591 Fax 0141 334 3591

Contact *Barry C. Paton*

Documentary and corporate videos. 'We are keen to explore drama production.' No unsolicited scripts; initial contact should be by letter. 'Interested in creative/commercial (i.e. broadcast) ideas that are new and innovative.'

Gabriela Productions Limited

51 Goldsmith Avenue, London W3 6HR
☎020 8993 3158 Fax 020 8993 8216
Email only4contact@yahoo.com

Contact *W. Starecki*

Film and television drama and documentary productions, including *Blooming Youth* and *Dog Eat Dog* for Ch4 and *Spider's Web* for Polish TV. Welcomes unsolicited mss.

Gaia Communications

Sanctuary House, 35 Harding Avenue,
Eastbourne, East Sussex BN22 8PL
☎01323 734809/727183 Fax 01323 734809
Email production@gaiacommunications.co.uk
Website www.gaiacommunications.co.uk

Producer *Robert Armstrong*
Script Editor *Loni Webb*

ESTABLISHED 1987. Video and TV corporate and documentary. OUTPUT *Discovering* (south east regional tourist and local knowledge series); *Holistic* (therapies and general information). 'Submissions must relate to our field of production; synopsis only on first contact.'

Gala International Ltd

25 Stamford Brook Road, London W6 0XJ
☎020 8741 4200 Fax 020 8741 2323

Producer *David Lindsay*

TV commercials, promos, film and TV documentaries.

John Gau Productions

15 St Albans Mansion, Kensington Court
Place, London W8 5QH
☎020 7938 1398   Fax 020 7938 1429

Contact *John Gau*

Documentaries and series for TV, plus corporate
video. OUTPUT includes *The Great Sell-Off*;
Reaching for the Skies; *The Power and The Glory*;
The Team – A Season With McLaren (all for
BBC2); *Korea* series (BBC1); *Voyager* (Central);
The Great Outdoors; *The Triumph of the Nerds*;
Glory of the Geeks; *Civil War – England's Fight For
Freedom* (all for Ch4); *Lights, Camera, Action!: A
Century of the Cinema* (ITV network). Open to
ideas from writers.

Noel Gay Television

1 Albion Court, Hammersmith, London
W6 0QT
☎020 8600 5200   Fax 020 8600 5222

Contact *Anne Mensah*

The association with Noel Gay (agency/
management, film production and music pub-
lishing) makes this one of the most securely
financed independents in the business. OUTPUT:
Hububb – Series 2 & 3 (BBC); *I-Camcorder* (Ch4);
Frank Stubbs Promotes (Carlton/ITV); *10%ers –
Series 2* (Carlton/ITV); *Call Up the Stars* (BBC1);
Smeg Outs (BBC video); *Les Bubb* (BBC
Scotland); *Red Dwarf* – Series 8; *Making of Red
Dwarf* (BBC video); *Dave Allen* (ITV); *Windrush*
(BBC2). Joint ventures and companies include a
partnership with Odyssey, a leading Indian commercials, film and TV producer, and the Noel
Gay Motion Picture Company, whose credits
include *Virtual Sexuality*; *Trainspotting* (with Ch4
and Figment Films), and *Killer Tongue*, a co-production with Iberoamericana. Other associate
NGTV companies are Grant Naylor Productions, Rose Bay Film Productions (see entry),
Pepper Productions and Brazen Husky. NGTV
is willing to accept unsolicited material from
writers but 1–2-page treatments only. No scripts,
please.

Global Vision Network (GVN) Ltd

Elstree Film Studios, Shenley Road,
Borehamwood, Hertfordshire WD6 1JG
☎020 8324 2333   Fax 020 8324 2700
Email info@gvn.co.uk
Website www.gvn.co.uk

Company Manager *Alex Prior*

Film, TV and video production: documentary,
corporate and children's computer-generated
imagery. OUTPUT includes educational and
science programming and now moving into
mainstream entertainment and film. 'Keen to
encourage and develop new material and writers; telephone or e-mail first.'

GMG Endemol Entertainment plc

46/47 Bedford Square, London WC1B 3DP
☎020 7462 9000   Fax 020 7462 9001

Chief Executive *Tom Barnicoat*
Creative Director *Peter Bazalgette*
Managing Director – Initial *Malcolm Gerrie*
Managing Director – Bazal *Nikki Cheetham*
Managing Director – Gem *Peter Christiansen*

GMG Endemol Entertainment (formerly known
as Broadcast Communications) is joint owned by
the Guardian Media Group and Dutch producer
Endemol Entertainment. One of Britain's largest
independent producers, GMG Endemol
Entertainment is responsible for over 1000 hours
of programming for all the UK's terrestrial networks as well as cable and satellite. It has two
production companies: Bazal, specialising in
leisure and lifestyle entertainment programming
and Initial, specialising in music, live event and
entertainment programming. Gem is the distribution arm of the company, handling full
exploitation of rights and brands.

GMT Productions Ltd

The Old Courthouse, 26A Church Street,
Bishop's Stortford, Hertfordshire CM23 2LY
☎01279 501622   Fax 01279 501644
Email patrick.wallis@virgin.net

Contacts *Patrick Wallis, Barney Broom*

Film, television and video: drama, documentary,
corporate and commercials. No unsolicited mss.

Goldcrest Films International Ltd

65–66 Dean Street, London W1V 6PL
☎020 7437 8696   Fax 020 7437 4448

Chairman *John Quested*
Contact *Bunmi Osoba*

FOUNDED in the late '70s. Formerly part of the
Brent Walker Leisure Group but independent
since 1990 following management buy-out led
by John Quested. The company's core activities are film production and worldwide distribution. Scripts via agents only.

The Good Film Company

2nd Floor, 14–15 D'Arblay Street, London
W1V 3FP
☎020 7734 1331   Fax 020 7734 2997

Contact *Yanina Barry*

Commercials and pop videos. CLIENTS include Hugo Boss, Cadbury's, Wella, National Express Coaches, Camel Cigarettes, Tunisian Tourist Board. No unsolicited mss.

Granada Film

The London Television Centre, Upper Ground, South Bank, London SE1 9LT
☎020 7737 8681 Fax 020 7737 8682

Contacts *Pippa Cross, Rebecca Hodgson*

Films and TV films. OUTPUT *My Left Foot; Jack & Sarah; Misadventures of Margaret; Girls Night; Rogue Trader.* No unsolicited scripts. Supportive of new writing but often hard to offer real help as Granada are developing mainstream commercial projects which usually requires some status in talent areas.

Granite Film & Television Productions Ltd

5 Hanover Yard, Noel Road, London N1 8BE
☎020 7354 3232 Fax 020 7354 0205
Email Research@Granite.co.uk

Contact *Simon Welfare*

Producer of television documentary programmes such as *Nicholas & Alexandra; Victoria & Albert* and *Arthur C. Clarke's Mysterious Universe.* No unsolicited mss.

Green Umbrella Ltd

The Production House, 147a St Michael's Hill, Bristol BS2 8DB
☎0117 9731729 Fax 0117 9467432
Email info@umbrella.co.uk
Website www.umbrella.co.uk

Television documentary maker and children's drama producer. OUTPUT includes episodes for *The Natural World, Wildlife on One* and original series such as *Living Europe* and *Triumph of Life.* Unsolicited treatments relating to natural history and science subjects are welcome.

Greenwich Films Ltd

Studio 2B1, The Old Seager Distillery, Brookmill Road, London SE8 4FT
☎020 8694 2211 Fax 020 8694 2971

Contact *Liza Brown, Development Dept.*

Film, television and video: drama. 'We welcome new writers, though as a small outfit we prefer to meet them through personal contacts as we do not have the resources to deal with too many enquiries. No unsolicited mss, just outlines, please.'

Hammer Film Productions Ltd

Elstree Film Studios, Borehamwood, Hertfordshire WD6 1JG
☎020 8207 4011 Fax 020 8905 1127

Contacts *Roy Skeggs, Graham Skeggs*

Television and feature films. No unsolicited scripts.

Hammerwood Film Productions

110 Trafalgar Road, Portslade, East Sussex BN41 1GS
☎01273 277333 Fax 01273 705451
Email filmangels@freenetname.co.uk
Website www.filmangel.co.uk

Contacts *Ralph Harvey, Petra Ginman*

Film, video and TV drama. OUTPUT *Maison d'Amour; Operation Pandora* (on-going TV series; episodes are invited); *Boadicea – Queen of the Iceni* (co-production with Pan-European Film Productions and Mirabilis Films). 2000 projects: *The Ghosthunter; A Symphony of Spies* (true stories of World War 2 espionage and resistance required); *Can You Kill a Dead Man?* Authors are recommended to access www.filmangel.co.uk (see also **Useful Websites at a Glance** listing).

Hartswood Films Ltd

Twickenham Studios, The Barons, St Margarets, Middlesex TW1 2AW
☎020 8607 8736 Fax 020 8607 8744

Contact *Elaine Cameron*

Film and TV production for drama and light entertainment. OUTPUT *Men Behaving Badly* (BBC, previously Thames); *Is It Legal?* (Ch4); *The English Wife* (Meridian); *A Woman's Guide to Adultery* (Carlton); *Wonderful You* (ITV, 4x documentaries).

Hat Trick Productions Ltd

10 Livonia Street, London W1V 3PH
☎020 7434 2451 Fax 020 7287 9791
Website www.hattrick.co.uk

Contact *Denise O'Donoghue*

Television programmes. OUTPUT includes *Clive Anderson All Talk; Small Potatoes; The Wilsons; The Peter Principle; Whatever You Want; Confessions; Drop the Dead Donkey; Father Ted; Game On; Have I Got News For You; If I Ruled the World; Room 101; Whose Line Is It Anyway?* The company's drama output includes: *A Very Open Prison; Boyz Unlimited; Crossing the Floor; Eleven Men Against Eleven; Gobble; Lord of Misrule; Mr White Goes to Westminster; Underworld; Sex 'n' Death.*

Head to Head Communication Ltd

The Hook, Plane Tree Crescent, Feltham,
Middlesex TW13 7AQ
☎020 8893 7766 Fax 020 8893 2777
Email amanda@hthc.co.uk

Contact *Amanda Anderson*

Producer of business and corporate communication programmes and events.

Healthcare Productions Limited

Unit 1.04 Bridge House, Three Mills, Three
Mill Lane, London E3 3DU
☎020 8980 9444 Fax 020 8980 1901
Email penny@healthcareprod.co.uk

Contact *Penny Webb*

Television and video: documentary and drama.
Produces training and educational material, in
text, video and CD-ROM, mostly health-
related, social care issues, law and marriage.

Jim Henson Productions Ltd

30 Oval Road, Camden, London NW1 7DE
☎020 7428 4000 Fax 020 7428 4001
Website www.henson.com *and*
www.muppets.com

Contacts *Angus Fletcher, Sophie Finston*

Feature films and TV: family entertainment and
children's. OUTPUT *Gulliver's Travels; Buddy;
Muppet Treasure Island; The Muppet Christmas
Carol; Muppets From Space; The Dark Crystal;
Labyrinth; The Witches* (films); *Dinosaurs* (ABC);
Muppet Tonight (BBC/Sky); *The Muppet Show*
(ITV); *The Storyteller* (Ch4/BBC); *Dr Seuss; The
Secret Life of Toys* (BBC); *The Animal Show*
(BBC); *Mopatop's Shop* (ITV); *Brats of the Lost
Nebula* (WB); *Farscape* (Sci-Fi/USA/BBC); *Bear
in the Big Blue House* (Disney Channel/Ch5); *Jim
Henson's Construction Site* (ITV). Scripts via agents
only.

Holmes Associates

38–42 Whitfield Street, London W1P 5RF
☎020 7813 4333 Fax 020 7637 9024

Contact *Andrew Holmes*

Prolific originator, producer and packager of
documentary, drama and music television and
films. OUTPUT has included *Prometheus* (Ch4
'Film on 4'); *The Shadow of Hiroshima* (Ch4
'Witness'); *The House of Bernarda Alba* (Ch4/
WNET/Amaya); *Piece of Cake* (drama mini-
series for LWT); *The Cormorant* (BBC/Screen 2);
*John Gielgud Looks Back; Rock Steady; Well Being;
Signals; Ideal Home?* (all Ch4); *Timeline* (with
MPT, TVE Spain & TRT Turkey); *Seven
Canticles of St Francis* (BBC2). Unsolicited film/

drama scripts will be considered but may take
some time for response.

Hourglass Pictures Ltd

117 Merton Road, Wimbledon, London
SW19 1ED
☎020 8540 8786 Fax 020 8542 6598
Email pictures@hourglass.co.uk
Website www.hourglass.co.uk

Director *Martin Chilcott*

Film and video: documentary, drama and commercials. OUTPUT includes television science
documentaries and educational programming.
Also health and social issues for the World
Health Organization and product information
for pharmaceutical companies. Open to new
writing.

Icon Films

4 West End, Somerset Street, Bristol BS2 8NE
☎0117 9248535 Fax 0117 9420386
Email info@iconfilms.co.uk
Website www.iconfilms.co.uk

Contact *Harry Marshall*

Film and TV documentaries. OUTPUT *The
Elephant Men* (WNET/Ch4); *The Living Edens
– Bhutan, The Last Shangri La* (ABC/Kane);
*Joanna Lumley in the Kingdom of the Thunder
Dragon* (BBC); *Lost Civilisations – Tibet* (Time
Life for NBC). Specialises in documentaries.
Open-minded to new filmmakers. Proposals
welcome.

Ideal Image Ltd

Cherrywood House, Crawley Down Road,
Felbridge, Surrey RH19 2PP
☎01342 300566 Fax 01342 312566

Contact *Alan Frost*

Producer of documentary and drama for film,
video, TV and corporate clients. OUTPUT *Just
Another Friday* (corporate drama); *Living in a
Box; The Future for Rupert*. No unsolicited
scripts.

Initial

See **GMG Endemol Entertainment plc**

Interesting Television Ltd

Oakslade Studios, Station Road, Hatton,
Warwickshire CV35 7LH
☎01926 844044 Fax 01926 844045

Senior Producer *John Pluck*

Producer of broadcast documentaries and
feature series on film and video for ITV and
BBC television. Currently looking towards

cable, satellite and home video to broaden its output. Ideas for TV documentaries particularly welcome. Send a treatment in the first instance, particularly if the subject is 'outside our area of current interest'. OUTPUT has included television programmes on heritage, antiques, gardening, science and industry; also projects on heritage, health and sports for the home video front.

Isis Productions

106 Hammersmith Grove, London W6 7HB
☎020 8748 3042 Fax 020 8748 3046

Directors *Nick de Grunwald, Jamie Rugge-Price*
Production Coordinator *Catriona Lawless*

Formed in 1991, Isis Productions focuses on the production of music and documentary programmes, and co-produces children's programmes under its Rocking Horse banner. OUTPUT Classic Albums (major international series on the making of the greatest records in rock history, including films on Grateful Dead, Stevie Wonder, Jimi Hendrix, Paul Simon, The Band); *Classic Albums II* (with films on Meat Loaf, The Who, Phil Collins, U2, Steely Dan, Bob Marley); *Energize!* (kids-in-sport magazine series for Westcountry TV); *Behind the Reporting Line* (behind-the-scenes look at foreign news gathering with Foreign Editor John Simpson for BBC2); *Dido and Aeneas* (film of Purcell's opera for BBC2/Thirteen WNET/ZDF-Arte/NVC Arts); *The Score* (classical music magazine series, co-produced with After Image for BBC2); *The Making of Sgt Pepper* (60-min film for Buena Vista International/LWT – winner of Grand Prix at MIDEM).

JAM Pictures and Jane Walmsley Productions

8 Hanover Street, London W1R 9HF
☎020 7290 2676 Fax 020 7290 2677
Email producers@jampix.com

Contacts *Jane Walmsley, Michael Braham*

JAM Pictures was FOUNDED in 1996 to produce drama for film, TV and stage. Projects include *Breakthrough* (feature co-production with Viacom Productions, Inc.); *One More Kiss* (feature, directed by Vadim Jean); *Bad Blood* (UK theatre tour); *Chalet Girls* (ITV sitcom). Jane Walmsley Productions, formed in 1985 by TV producer, writer and broadcaster, Jane Walmsley, has completed award-winning documentaries and features such as *Hot House People* (Ch4). No unsolicited mss. 'Letters can be sent to us, asking if we wish to see mss; we are very interested in quality material.'

Kaje Limited

Breck Lodge, Kniveton, Ashbourne, Derbyshire DE6 1JF
☎01335 343536 Fax 01335 345634
Email sales@unkajed.com
Website www.unkajed.com

Contact *Jamie Avery*

Television and video; documentary, commercials, corporate programming plus news and sport shorts for the cable TV channel – The Local Channel. No unsolicited mss. 'We like and encourage new writing from many sources for use in the fields we work in.'

KEO Films

Studio 2B, 151–157 City Road, London EC1V 1JH
☎020 7490 3580 Fax 020 7490 8419
Email keo@keofilms.com

Contact *Alethea Palmer*

Television documentaries and factual entertainment. OUTPUT includes BBC's 'QED': *The Maggot Mogul* and *Sleeping it Off*; plus *A Cook on the Wild Side*; *TV Dinners*; *Beast of the Amazon* ('Ends of the Earth' series) and *Big Snake*, all for Ch4. No unsolicited mss.

King Rollo Films Ltd

Dolphin Court, High Street, Honiton, Devon EX14 1HT
☎01404 45218 Fax 01404 45328
Email admin@kingrollofilms.co.uk

Contact *Clive Juster*

Film, video and TV: children's animated series. OUTPUT *Surprise, Surprise; It's My Birthday; Badger's Bring Something Party; How Many Days to My Birthday?; The Trouble With Jack; Bear's Birthday; Elephant Pie; Good Night, Sleep Tight; Go to Sleep; Get into Bed; I'm not Sleepy; Good Night Everyone; Little Princess Bedtime; Bedtime Story; Dad, I Can't Sleep; Spot and His Grandparents Visit the Carnival; Spot's Magical Christmas; Maisy; Philipp; Jakob; Elmer.* Generally works from existing published material 'although there will always be the odd exception'. Proposals in the first instance. No scripts.

Kingfisher Television Productions Ltd

Carlton Studios, Lenton Lane, Nottingham NG7 2NA
☎0115 9645262 Fax 0115 9645263

Contact *Tony Francis*

Broadcast television production.

Kismet Film Company

27–29 Berwick Street, London W1V 3RF
☎020 7734 9878 Fax 020 7734 9871
Email kismetfilms@dial.pipex.com
Producer *Michele Camarda*
Head of Development *Nicole Stott*
Development Assistant *Asha Radwan*

Feature films. OUTPUT includes *Photographing Fairies; This Year's Love; Wonderland* and *Born Romantic.* Welcomes screenplay mss. 'We are very supportive of new writing. The three films produced by Kismet have all been written by first-time feature film writers and we have several projects in development with exciting new playwrights and screenwriters.' Involved in workshops such as PAL Writer's Workshop, **Equinoxe Screenwriting Workshops** and North by Northwest.

Kudos Productions Limited

65 Great Portland Street, London W1N 5DH
☎020 7580 8686 Fax 020 7580 8787
Email reception@kudosproductions.co.uk
Head of Development *Howard Burch*

Film and television; drama and documentaries such as *Among Giants* (feature); *The Magician's House* (BBC1 series) and *Psychos* (Ch4 series). No unsolicited mss.

Lagan Pictures Ltd

21 Tullaghbrow, Tullaghgarley, Ballymena,
Co Antrim BT42 2LY
☎028 2563 9479/077 9852 8797
Fax 028 2563 9479
Producer/Director *Stephen Butcher*
Producer *Alison Grundle*

Film, video and TV: drama, documentary and corporate. OUTPUT *A Force Under Fire* (Ulster TV). In development: *Into the Bright Light of Day* (drama-doc); *The £10 Float* (feature film); *The Centre* (drama series). 'We are always interested in hearing from writers originating from or based in Northern Ireland or anyone with, preferably unstereotypical, projects relevant to Northern Ireland. We do not have the resources to deal with unsolicited mss, so please phone or write with a brief treatment/synopsis in the first instance.'

Landseer Film and Television Productions Ltd

140 Royal College Street, London NW1 0TA
☎020 7485 7333 Fax 020 7485 7573
Email landseerfilms@msn.com
Contact *Derek Bailey*

Film and video production: documentary, drama, music and arts, children's and current affairs. OUTPUT *Should Accidentally Fall* (BBC/Arts Council); *Nobody's Fool* ('South Bank Show' on Danny Kaye for LWT); *Gounod's Faust* (Ch4); *Swinger* (BBC2/Arts Council); *Auld Lang Syne* (BBC Scotland); *Nureyev Unzipped* (Ch4); *Retying the Knot – The Incredible String Band* (BBC Scotland); *Benjamin Zander* ('The Works', BBC2); *Zeffirelli* ('The South Bank Show', LWT); *The Judas Tree* (Ch4); *Death of a Legend – Frank Sinatra* ('South Bank Show' special); *Petula Clark* ('South Bank Show'); *Routes of Rock* (Carlton); *See You in Court* (BBC); *Bing Crosby* ('South Bank Show'); *Ballet Boyz* and *4Dance* (both for Ch4).

Lightarama Ltd

12a Wellfield Avenue, London N10 2EA
☎020 8444 8315 Fax 020 8444 8315
Contact *Alexis Key*

Video and TV production for commercials and corporate material and also special effects. No unsolicited scripts but c.v.s welcome. Interested in new and creative ideas.

Lilyville Productions Ltd

7 Lilyville Road, London SW6 5DP
☎020 7371 5940 Fax 020 7736 9431
Email tonycash@msn.com
Contact *Tony Cash*

Drama and documentaries for TV. OUTPUT *Poetry in Motion* (series for Ch4); 'South Bank Show': *Ben Elton* and *Vanessa Redgrave*; *Musique Enquête* (drama-based French language series, Ch4); *Landscape and Memory* (arts documentary series for the BBC); Jonathan Miller's production of the *St Matthew Passion* for the BBC; major documentary on the BeeGees for the *South Bank Show*. Scripts with an obvious application to TV may be considered. Interested in new writing for documentary programmes.

Limelight Entertainment

33 Newman Street, London W1P 3PD
☎020 7637 2529 Fax 020 7637 2538
Email limelight.management@virgin.net
Website www.limelightmanagement.com
Contacts *Linda Shanks, Frances Whitaker, Fiona Lindsay*

Television and video lifestyle programming. OUTPUT includes a 13-part cookery series for Carlton Food Network entitled *First Taste*. No unsolicited mss.

Little Dancer Ltd

Avonway, Naseby Road, London SE19 3JJ
☎020 8653 9343   Fax 020 8286 1722

Contacts *Robert Smith, Sue Townsend*

Television and cinema, both shorts and full-length features.

London Broadcast Ltd

Premier House, 77 Oxford Street, London
W1R 1RB
☎020 7439 1188   Fax 020 7659 2100

Chairman *Eric Peters*
Head of Development & Programming
  Michael Jacobs

Television and radio producer. Specialises in light entertainment, especially the talk show format. Producer of the St Patrick's Day Concert for worldwide television distribution. Also operates a training school for radio and television. Always on the lookout for new talent. Format ideas should be sent to Head of Programming.

London Scientific Films Ltd

Suckling's Yard, Church Street, Ware,
Hertfordshire SG12 9EN
☎01920 486602   Fax 01920 462206
Email lsf@compuserve.com

Contact *Mike Cockburn*

Film and video documentary and corporate programming. No unsolicited mss.

Lucida Productions

Studio 1A, 14 Havelock Walk, London
SE23 3HG
☎020 8699 5070   Fax 020 8699 5359

Contact *Paul Joyce*

Television and cinema: arts, adventure, current affairs, documentary, drama and music. OUTPUT has included *Motion and Emotion: The Films of Wim Wenders; Dirk Bogarde – By Myself; Sam Peckinpah – Man of Iron; Kris Kristofferson – Pilgrim; Wild One: Marlon Brando; Stanley Kubrick: 'The Invisible Man'.* Currently in development for documentary and drama projects.

Main Communications

Southgate Chambers, 37–39 Southgate Street,
Winchester, Hampshire SO23 9EH
☎01962 870680   Fax 01962 870699
Email main@main.co.uk

Contact *Eben Wilson*

Multimedia marketing, communications, electronic and publishing company for film, video and TV: drama, documentary and commercials. OUTPUT includes marketing communications, educational, professional and managerial distance learning, documentary programmes for broadcast TV and children's material. Interested in proposals for television programmes, and in ideas for video sell-throughs, interactive multimedia and business information texts and programming.

Malone Gill Productions Ltd

9–15 Neal Street, London WC2H 9PU
☎020 7460 4683   Fax 020 7460 4679
Email ikonic@compuserve.com

Contact *Georgina Denison*

Mainly documentary but also some drama. OUTPUT includes *The Face of Russia* (PBS); *Vermeer* ('South Bank Show'); *Highlanders* (ITV); *Storm Chasers; Nature Perfected;* and *The Feast of Christmas* (all for Ch4); *The Buried Mirror: Reflections on Spain and the New World* by Carlos Fuentes (BBC2/Discovery Channel). Approach by letter with proposal in the first instance.

Mike Mansfield Television Ltd

41–42 Berners Street, London W1P 3AA
☎020 7580 2581   Fax 020 7580 2582
Email mikemantv@aol.com

Contact *Mr Hilary McLaren*

Television for BBC, ITV, Ch4 and Ch5. OUTPUT includes *Viva Diva!* (Shirley Bassey music special) and *Jean Michel Jarre Pyramids New Year.*

Mars Productions Ltd

8 Clanricarde Gardens, London W2 4NA
☎020 7243 2750   Fax 020 7792 8584
Email mars.prod@virgin.net

Contact *Robert Marshall*

Television and video: history, arts and social documentaries. Robert Marshall teaches writing for television at BBC TV Training. 'Sometimes' welcomes unsolicited mss.

Bill Mason Films Ltd

Orchard House, Dell Quay, Chichester, West
Sussex PO20 7EE
☎01243 783558
Email bill.mason@argonet.co.uk

Contact *Bill Mason*

Film and video: documentaries only. OUTPUT *Racing Mercedes; The History of Motor Racing; The History of the Motor Car.* No need for outside writing; all material is written in-house. The emphasis is on automotive history.

Maverick Television

The Custard Factory, Gibb Street, Birmingham B9 4AA
☎0121 771 1812 Fax 0121 771 1550
Email maverick@mavericktv.co.uk
Website www.mavericktv.co.uk

Contact *Clare Welch*

FOUNDED 1994. High quality and innovative DVC programming in both documentary and drama. Expanding into light entertainment and more popular drama. OUTPUT includes *Trade Secrets* (BBC2); *Picture This: Accidental Hero* (BBC2); *Motherless Daughters*, *Highland Bollywood: Black Bag*; *Health Alert: My Teenage Menopause* and *Embarrassing Illnesses* (all for Ch4).

Maya Vision International Ltd

43 New Oxford Street, London WC1A 1BH
☎020 7836 1113 Fax 020 7836 5169

Contact *John Cranmer*

Film and TV: drama and documentary. OUTPUT *Saddam's Killing Fields* (for 'Viewpoint', Central TV); *3 Steps to Heaven* and *A Bit of Scarlet* (feature films for BFI/Ch4); *A Place in the Sun* and *North of Vortex* (drama for Ch4/Arts Council); *The Real History Show* (Ch4); *In the Footsteps of Alexander the Great* (BBC1 documentary); *Out* (several pieces for Ch4's lesbian and gay series). No unsolicited material; commissions only.

MBP TV

Saucelands Barn, Coolham, Horsham, West Sussex RH13 8QG
☎01403 741620 Fax 01403 741647
Email info@mbptv.com

Contact *Mark Jennings*

Maker of film and video specialising in programmes covering equestrianism and the countryside. No unsolicited scripts, but always looking for new writers who are fully acquainted with the subject.

MedSci Healthcare Communications

Stoke Grange, Fir Tree Avenue, Stoke Poges, Buckinghamshire SL2 4NN
☎01753 516644 Fax 01753 516965
Email kerry@medsci.co.uk

Contacts *Peter Fogarty, Kerry Williams*

Training programmes, interactive CD-based training, websites and medical video programmes for the pharmaceutical industry.

Melendez Films

1–17 Shaftesbury Avenue, London W1V 7RL
☎020 7434 0220 Fax 020 7434 3131

Contacts *Steven Melendez, Graeme Spurway*

Independent producers working with TV stations. Animated films aimed mainly at a family audience, produced largely for the American market, and prime-time network broadcasting. Also develops and produces feature films (eight so far). OUTPUT has included *Peanuts* (half-hour TV specials); *The Lion, the Witch and the Wardrobe; Babar the Elephant* (TV specials); *Dick Deadeye or Duty Done*, a rock musical based on Gilbert & Sullivan operettas. Synopses only, please. Enclose s.a.e. for return.

Mersey Television Company Ltd

Campus Manor, Childwall Abbey Road, Liverpool L16 0JP
☎0151 722 9122 Fax 0151 722 1969

Chairman *Prof. Phil Redmond*

The best known of the independents in the North of England. Makers of television drama. OUTPUT *Brookside; Hollyoaks* (both for Ch4).

Moonstone Films Ltd

5 Linkenholt Mansions, Stamford Brook Avenue, London W6 0YA
☎020 8846 8511 Fax 020 8846 8511
Email moonstone@connect-2.co.uk

Contacts *Tony Stark, Ingrid Geser*

Television documentaries such as *Arafat's Authority*, a critical look at the Palestinian authority in the West Bank and Gaza for the BBC. Unsolicited mss welcome.

The Morrison Company

302 Clive Court, Maida Vale, London W9 1SF
☎020 7289 7976 Fax 07092 256959
Email don@morrisonco.com
Website www.morrisonco.com

Contact *Don Morrison*

Film and video: drama, documentary and multimedia.

MW Entertainments Ltd

48 Dean Street, London W1V 5HL
☎020 7734 7707 Fax 020 7734 7727
Email development@michaelwhite.co.uk

Contact *Michael White*

High-output company whose credits include *Widow's Peak; White Mischief; Nuns on the Run* (co-production with HandMade Films Ltd); *The Comic Strip Series*. Also theatre projects, including *Fame; Me and Mamie O'Rourke; She Loves Me;*

Crazy for You. Contributions are passed by Michael White to a script reader for consideration; please send treatment/synopsis only.

Newgate Company

13 Dafford Street, Larkhall, Bath, Somerset
BA1 6SW
☎01225 318335

Contact *Jo Anderson*

A commonwealth of established actors, directors and playwrights, Newgate originally concerned itself solely with theatre writing (at the Bush, Stratford, Roundhouse, etc.). However, in the course of development, several productions fed into a list of ongoing drama for BBC TV/Ch4. Looking to develop this co-production strand for film, television and radio projects with other 'Indies'.

Northlight Productions Ltd

The Media Village, Grampian Television, Queen's Cross, Aberdeen AB15 4XJ
☎01224 646460 Fax 01224 646450
Email tv@northlight.co.uk
Website www.northlight.co.uk

Contact *Robert Sproul-Cran*

Film, video and TV: drama, documentary and corporate work. OUTPUT ranges from high-end corporate fund-raising videos for the National Museum of Scotland to *Anything But Temptation*, a feature film currently in development; *Calcutta Chronicles* (5-part documentary series for Ch4) and two schools series for Ch4. Scripts welcome. Has links with EAVE (European Audio-Visual Entrepreneurs) and Media.

Novus Communications Ltd

Spratton Lodge, Spratton, Northamptonshire
NN6 8LD
☎01604 821195 Fax 01604 821651
Email barrie@novus.ltd.uk
Website www.novus.ltd.uk

Contact *Barrie Goulding*

Documentary video producers. OUTPUT *Police Stop!* (reality programming); *Caught in the Act* (CCTV documentary); *The Seriously Funny Guide to Weddings* (starring Roy Barraclough and Nerys Hughes) and corporate videos for Ford and Barclays Bank. 'Always interested in new writing; telephone or e-mail first.'

ONtv (Oxford Network Television)

Larkhill House, PO Box 400, Abingdon, Oxford OX14 1FD
☎01235 537400 Fax 01235 530581
Email ON@oncomms-tv.co.uk

Website www.oncomms-tv.co.uk

Contact *Mrs Sharon Frost*

An independent production company FOUNDED in 1985 to produce high-quality factual programming, including science, current affairs, authored documentaries for television, as well as for corporate and heritage markets. OUTPUT Ch4's *Equinox*, *Dispatches* and *Short Stories*, plus BBC2's *Horizon.*

Open Media

The Mews Studio, 8 Addison Bridge Road, London W14 8XP

Contact *Annabel Anderson*

Broadcast television: OUTPUT *After Dark; The Secret Cabaret; James Randi Psychic Investigator; Opinions; Is This Your Life?; Don't Quote Me; Brave New World; The Talking Show; Natural Causes; Equinox; Dispatches.*

Open Road Films

38–42 Whitfield Street, London W1P 5RF
☎020 7813 4333 Fax 020 7637 9024

Contact *Andrew Holmes*

New company, formed by **Holmes Associates** to produce low budget feature films.

Orlando TV Productions

Up-the-Steps, Little Tew, Chipping Norton, Oxfordshire OX7 4JB
☎01608 683218 Fax 01608 683364
Email orlando.tv@btinternet.com

Contact *Mike Tomlinson*

Producer of TV documentaries, with science subjects as a specialisation. OUTPUT includes programmes for *Horizon* and *QED* (BBC). Approaches by established writers/journalists to discuss proposals for collaboration are welcome.

Orpheus Productions

6 Amyand Park Gardens, Twickenham, Middlesex TW1 3HS
☎020 8892 3172 Fax 020 8892 4821

Contact *Richard Taylor*

Television documentaries and corporate work. OUTPUT has included programmes for BBC Current Affairs, Music and Arts, and the African-Caribbean Unit as well as documentaries for the Shell Film Unit and Video Arts. Unsolicited scripts are welcomed with caution. 'We have a preference for visually stirring documentaries with quality writing of the more personal and idiosyncratic kind, not straight reportage.'

Outcast Production

474 Upper Richmond Road, London
SW15 5JG
☎020 8878 9486
Email 100613.3445@compuserve.com

Contact *Andreas Wisniewski*

Low-budget feature films. No unsolicited mss;
send synopsis or treatment only. 'We are actively
searching for and encouraging new writing.'

Ovation Productions

One Prince of Wales Passage, 117 Hampstead
Road, London NW1 3EF
☎020 7387 2342 Fax 020 7380 0404

Contact *John Plews*

Corporate video and conference scripts. Unsolicited mss not welcome. 'We talk to new writers
from time to time.' Ovation also runs the fringe
theatre, 'Upstairs at the Gatehouse' in Highgate,
north London, and welcomes new plays.

Oxford Scientific Films Ltd

Lower Road, Long Hanborough, Oxfordshire
OX8 8LL
☎01993 881881 Fax 01993 882808
Email enquiries@osf.uk.com
Website www.osf.uk.com

Commercials Division: 45–49 Mortimer
Street, London W1N 7TD
☎020 7323 0061 Fax 020 7323 0161

Chairman *Peter Clark*
Directors *Sean Morris, Nicholas Unsworth,
Suzanne Aitzetmuller*

Established media company with specialist
knowledge and expertise in award-winning
natural history films and science-based programmes. Film, video and TV: documentaries,
TV commercials, multimedia, and educational
films. Scripts welcome. Operates an extensive
stills and film footage library specialising in
wildlife and special effects (see entry under
Picture Libraries).

Pace Productions Ltd

12 The Green, Newport Pagnell,
Buckinghamshire MK16 0JW
☎01908 618767
Email chris@paceproductions.com
Website www.paceproductions.com

Contact *Chris Pettit*

Film and video: corporate and commercials.

Paladin Pictures Ltd

22 Ashchurch Grove, London W12 9BT
☎020 8740 1811 Fax 020 8740 7220

Contact *Clive Syddall*

Film and television: drama and documentary
programmes such as *Plague Wars* (mini series on
biological warfare, BBC1); *Dance Ballerina
Dance* with Deborah Bull (BBC2); *Purple Secret*
(Ch4's 'Secret History'). No unsolicited mss;
'send a letter with one-page outline of the
book to see if we are interested.' Specialises in
working with writers before their books are
published to enable TV tie-in.

Barry Palin Associates Ltd

143 Charing Cross Road, London WC2H 0EE
☎020 7478 4680 Fax 020 7478 4788
Email bpa@eurocentergroup.com

Contact *Barry Palin*

Film, video and TV production for drama, documentary, commercials and corporate material.
OUTPUT *Harmfulness of Tobacco* Anton Chekhov
short story – BAFTA Best Short Film Award-
winner (Ch4); Corporate: Philip Morris, York
International, Republic Bank of New York.

Panther Pictures Ltd

53 Montpelier Walk, London SW7 1JH
☎0976 256610 Fax 020 7589 1663
Email rsutton@lineone.net

Contact *Robert Sutton*

Feature films, including *Inside/Out*, a US/UK/
Canada/France co-production.

Paper Moon Productions

Wychwood House, Burchetts Green Lane,
Littlewick Green, Nr. Maidenhead, Berkshire
SL6 3QW
☎01628 829819 Fax 01628 825949
Email david@paper-moon.co.uk

Contact *David Haggas*

Television and video: medical and health education documentaries. OUTPUT includes *Shamans
and Science*, a medical documentary examining
the balance between drugs discovered in nature
and those synthesised in laboratories. Unsolicited
scripts welcome. Interested in new writing 'from
people who really understand television pro-
gramme-making'.

Parallax Pictures Ltd

7 Denmark Street, London WC2H 8LS
☎020 7836 1478 Fax 020 7497 8062

Contact *Sally Hibbin*

Feature films/television drama. OUTPUT *Riff-
Raff; Bad Behaviour; Raining Stones; Ladybird,
Ladybird; I.D.; Land and Freedom; The Englishman
Who Went up a Hill But Came Down a Mountain;*

Bliss; Jump the Gun; Carla's Song; The Governess; My Name Is Joe; Stand and Deliver; Dockers; Hold Back the Night.

Passion Pictures
25–27 Riding House Street, London
W1P 7PB
☎020 7323 9933 Fax 020 7323 9030
Email info@passion-pictures.com
Managing Director *Andrew Ruhemann*
Producer *Sophie Byrne*

Television commercials: Dairylea, Levi's and, for the BBC, the 3-minute *Future Generations.* Unsolicited mss welcome.

Pathé Pictures
14–17 Kent House, Market Place, London
W1N 8AR
☎020 7323 5151 Fax 020 7631 3568
Development Executive *Ruth McGance*
Development Assistant *Vicki Patterson*

Produces 4–6 theatrical feature films each year. Together with partners, Orange, Pathé Pictures has launched a screenwriting and promotion award aimed specifically at new writing talent (see entry under **Prizes**). 'We are pleased to consider all material that has representation from an agent or production company.'

PBF Motion Pictures
The Little Pickenhanger, Tuckey Grove, Ripley, Surrey GU23 6JG
☎01483 225179 Fax 01483 224118
Email peter@pbf.co.uk
Contact *Peter B. Fairbrass*

Film, video and TV: drama, documentary, commercials and corporate. Also televised chess series and chess videos. OUTPUT *Grandmaster Chess; Glue Sniffing; RN Special Services; Nightfrights* (night-time TV chiller series). CLIENTS include GEC-Marconi, Coca Cola, MoD, Marks & Spencer, various government departments, British Consulate. No scripts; send one-page synopsis only in the first instance. 'Good scripts which relate to current projects will be followed up, otherwise not, as PBF do not have the time to reply to proposals which do not interest them. Only good writing stands a chance.'

Pearson Television Ltd
1 Stephen Street, London W1P 1PJ
☎020 7691 6000 Fax 020 7691 6100
Website www.pearsontv.com
Chief Executive *Richard Eyre*
Chief Executive, UK Production *Alan Boyd*

Head of Entertainment *Richard Holloway*
Head of Comedy *Tony Charles*

UK's largest independent production and distribution company, owned by international media group, Pearson plc. Acquired Thames Television in 1993 (producer of *The Bill*) and Grundy Worldwide (*Neighbours*) in 1995. Further acquisitions were Witzend Productions (*Lovejoy*; *Tracey Ullman*) and **Alomo Productions** (see entry) in 1996. Major developments are expected in 2000 following the merger of Pearson Television and European commercial TV and radio broadcaster CLT-UFA.

Pelicula Films
59 Holland Street, Glasgow G2 4NJ
☎0141 287 9522 Fax 0141 287 9504
Contact *Mike Alexander*

Television producer. Makers of drama documentaries and music programmes for the BBC and Ch4. OUTPUT *As an Eilean (From the Island); The Trans-Atlantic Sessions 1 & 2; Nanci Griffith, Other Voices 2; Follow the Moonstone.*

Penumbra Productions Ltd
80 Brondesbury Road, London NW6 6RX
☎020 7328 4550 Fax 020 7328 3844
Email nazpenumbra@compuserve.com
Contact *H. O. Nazareth*

Film, video, TV and radio: drama, documentary and information videos on health, housing, arts and political documentaries. OUTPUT includes *Fugitive Pieces* (Radio 3 play); *Stories My Country Told Me* (BBC2, 'Arena'); *Repomen* (Ch4, 'Cutting Edge'). Send synopses only, preferably by e-mail. Keen to assist in the development of new writing but only interested in social issue-based material.

Photoplay Productions Ltd
21 Princess Road, London NW1 8JR
☎020 7722 2500 Fax 020 7722 6662
Email photoplay@compuserve.com
Contact *Patrick Stanbury*

Documentaries for film, television and video plus restoration of silent films and their theatrical presentation. OUTPUT includes *Cinema Europe: The Other Hollywood; Universal Horror; D. W. Griffith: Father of Film* and the 'Channel 4 Silents' series of silent film restoration, including *The Wedding March* and *The Iron Mask.* In production: *Lon Chaney, Man of 1000 Faces.* No unsolicited mss; 'we tend to create and write all our own programmes.'

Picardy Television

1 Park Circus, Glasgow G3 6AX
☎0141 333 1200 Fax 0141 332 6002
Email jr@picardy.co.uk
Website www.picardy.co.uk

Senior Producer *John Rocchiccioli*

Television and video: arts documentaries, training and promotional videos, education projects, multi-media productions, and TV and cinema commercials. Unsolicited mss welcome; 'keen to encourage new writing.'

Picture Palace Films Ltd

13 Egbert Street, London NW1 8LJ
☎020 7586 8763 Fax 020 7586 9048
Email picpalace@compuserve.com

Contact *Malcolm Craddock*

FOUNDED 1971. Leading independent producer of TV drama. OUTPUT *Extremely Dangerous* (4x1-hour for ITV for Northwestone Films); *A Life for A Life* (2-hour film for ITV); *Sharpe's Rifles* (14 2-hour films for Carlton TV); *Little Napoleons* (4-part comedy drama for Ch4); *The Orchid House* (4-part drama serial for Ch4); plus episodes of *Eurocops; Tandoori Nights; 4 Minutes; When Love Dies; Ping Pong* (feature film). Material must submitted through an agent.

Phil Pilley Productions

Ferryside, Felix Lane, Shepperton, Middlesex TW17 8NG
☎01932 702916 Fax 01932 702916
Email pilley@tinyworld.co.uk

Programmes for TV and video, mainly sports. Now specialising in sporting history books, particularly golf.

Planet 24 Ltd

195 Marsh Wall, London E14 9SG
☎020 7345 2424 Fax 020 7345 9400

Managing Director *Mary Durkan*

Television producer of light and factual entertainment, comedy, music, features and computer animation. Bought by Carlton Communications in April 1999. OUTPUT TV: *The Big Breakfast; The Word; The Messiah* (live recording); *Hotel Babylon; Gaytime TV; Delicious; Extra Time, Nothing But the Truth; Watercolour Challenge; Andi Meets ...; Richard Whiteley Unbriefed; The Richard Blackwood Show; A Family of My Own.*

Plantagenet Films Limited

Ard-Daraich Studio B, Ardgour, Nr Fort William, Inverness-shire PH33 7AB
☎01855 841248

Email plantagenet@amumby.globalnet.co.uk

Contact *Norrie Maclaren*

Film and television: documentary and drama programming such as *Dig* (gardening series for Ch4); various 'Dispatches' for Ch4 and 'Omnibus' for BBC. Keen to encourage and promote new writing; unsolicited mss welcome.

Platinum Film & TV Production Ltd

1b Murray Street, London NW1 9RE
☎020 7916 9091 Fax 020 7916 5238
Email terry@plat-tv.demon.co.uk

Contact *Terry Kelleher*

Television documentaries, including drama-documentary. OUTPUT *South Africa's Black Economy* (Ch4); *Murder at the Farm* (Thames TV); *The Biggest Robbery in the World* (major investigative true-crime drama-documentary for Carlton TV); *Dead Line* (original drama by Chilean-exiled writer, Ariel Dorfman, for Ch4). Scripts and format treatments welcome.

Pola Jones Associates Ltd

See entry under **Theatre Producers**

Portman Productions

167 Wardour Street, London W1V 3TA
☎020 7468 3400 Fax 020 7468 3499

Television drama. OUTPUT includes: *Gravy Train* and *Gravy Train Goes East; Downwardly Mobile; Famous Five Series; Rebecca; Coming Home; Nancherro.* Synopses in the first instance, please.

Portobello Pictures

14–15 D'Arblay Street, London W1V 3FP
☎020 7379 5566 Fax 020 7379 5599
Email portopics@aol.com

Contacts *Ed Whitmore, Tom Hooper*

Film drama, including *Mojo,* director, Jez Butterworth; *Kolya,* Jan Sverak; *The War Zone,* Tim Roth, plus BBC1's *Dalziel and Pascoe* (series 1–3).

Premiere Productions Ltd

3 Colville Place, London W1P 1HN
☎020 7255 1650

Contact *Henrietta Fudakowski*

Film and television. Currently looking for feature film or TV drama scripts, with a preference for stories with humour. No horror or sci fi. Return postage and list of credits essential.

Gavin Prime Television
Christmas House, 213 Chester Road, Castle Bromwich, Solihull, West Midlands B36 0ET
☎0121 749 7147

Contact *Gavin Prime*

Film and television: comedy, entertainment and animation. Welcomes unsolicited mss, 'depending on type.'

Prospect Pictures
Wandsworth Plain, London SW18 1ET
☎020 7636 1234 Fax 020 7636 1236

Contact *Tony McAvoy*

Drama, documentary and corporate video and TV. Actively looking for projects from new writers; 'using our development fund for new drama'. Welcomes treatments and synopses of scripts.

Red Rooster Film and Television Entertainment
14/15 D'Arblay Street, London W1V 3FP
☎020 7439 6969 Fax 020 7439 6767

Contacts *Mervyn Watson, Rachel Murrell*

TV drama. OUTPUT *Trust; The Alchemists; Deadly Summer; Beyond Fear; The Sculptress; Wilderness; Crocodile Shoes; Body & Soul.* Primarily interested in TV drama series. No unsolicited scripts.

Reel Movies Ltd
75 Wigmore Street, London W1H 9LH
☎020 7935 4674 Fax 020 7935 4417
Email dnm@mendoza.demon.com

Contacts *Matthew Wakefield, Debby Mendoza, John Hayes*

Commercials, title sequences (e.g. Alan Bleasdale's *G.B.H.*); party political broadcasts. Currently in pre-production on a feature-length comedy film. Unsolicited mss welcome but 'we'd rather receive work from experienced writers'. Material will not be returned without s.a.e. Involved with **Screenwriters' Workshop**.

Renaissance Films
34–35 Berwick Street, London W1V 3RF
☎020 7287 5190 Fax 020 7287 5191

Producer *Stephen Evans*
Head of Development *Caroline Wood*

Feature films: *The Luzhin Defense; The Wings of the Dove; The Madness of King George* (as Close Call Films); *Twelfth Night; Much Ado About Nothing; Peter's Friends; Henry V.* No unsolicited mss.

Renaissance Vision
256 Fakenham Road, Taverham, Norwich, Norfolk NR8 6QW
☎01603 260280 Fax 01603 864857

Contact *B. Gardner*

Video: full range of corporate work (training, sales, promotional, etc.). Producers of educational and special-interest video publications. Willing to consider good ideas and proposals.

Richmond Films & Television Ltd
5 Dean Street, London W1V 5RN
☎020 7734 9313 Fax 020 7287 2058
Email general@richmondfilms.com

Contact *Development Executive*

Film and TV: drama and comedy. OUTPUT *Press Gang; The Lodge; The Office; Wavelength; Privates.* '*No unsolicited scripts.* We will accept *two pages only* consisting of a brief treatment of your project (either screenplay or TV series) which includes its genre and its demographics. Please tell us also where the project has been submitted previously and what response you have had. *Your two pages will not be returned.*'

Rocking Horse
See **Isis Productions**

Rose Bay Film Productions
1 Albion Court, Albion Place, London W6 0QT
☎020 8600 5200 Fax 020 8600 5222
Email info@rosebay.co.uk

Contacts *Matthew Steiner, Simon Usiskin*

Associate company of **Noel Gay Television**. Film and TV production: entertainment and comedy. Unsolicited scripts welcome.

Brenda Rowe Productions
42 Wellington Park, Clifton, Bristol BS8 2UW
☎0117 9730390 Fax 0117 9738254
Email brenda@roweprod.demon.co.uk

Contact *Brenda Rowe*

Produces observational, investigative, current affairs TV documentaries, and training and promotional videos for business organisations. Open to new work; unsolicited mss welcome.

RS Productions
47 Laet Street, Newcastle upon Tyne NE29 6NN
☎0191 259 1184/0410 064632 (Mobile)
Fax 0191 259 1184
Email enquiries@rsproductions

Also at: 83–84 Berwick Street, London W1V 3PJ ☎020 7272 9771
Contact *Mark Lavender*

Feature films, television and video: drama, documentary and corporates. Documentaries include: *Shooting the Albatross* and *Moving Mountains* (both for ITV). Encourages new writers and directors; unsolicited mss welcome with one-page synopsis and s.a.e. for return.

Sands Films

119 Rotherhithe Street, London SE16 4NF ☎020 7231 2209 Fax 020 7231 2119

Contacts *Richard Goodwin, Christine Edzard, Olivier Stockman*

Film and TV drama. OUTPUT *Little Dorrit; The Fool; As You Like It; A Dangerous Man; The Long Day Closes; A Passage to India; The Kiss; Swan Princess; Berlioz; The Nutcracker; Seven Years in Tibet.* In development: *The Children's Midsummer Night's Dream.* No unsolicited scripts.

Scala Productions Ltd

15 Frith Street, London W1V 5TS ☎020 7734 7060 Fax 020 7437 3248
Email scalaprods@aol.com

Contacts *Nik Powell, Rachel Wood*

Production company set up by ex-Palace Productions Nik Powell and Stephen Woolley, who have an impressive list of credits including *Company of Wolves; Absolute Beginners; Mona Lisa; Scandal; Crying Game; Backbeat; Hollow Reed; Neon Bible.* Productions include: *24:7; Little Voice; Divorcing Jack; Welcome to Woop Woop; The Lost Son; History is Made at Night; The Last Yellow; Fanny and Elvis; The Last September; Five Seconds to Spare; Wild About Harry.* In development: *St Agnes' Stand; Jonathan Wild; Mort; Wise Children; Money; Brian Jones Project; Shang A Lang; A Single Shot; Last Orders.*

Scope Productions Ltd

Keppie House, 147 Blythswood Street, Glasgow G2 4EN ☎0141 332 7720 Fax 0141 332 1049

TV Commercials *Sharon Fullarton*
Corporate *Bill Gordon*

Corporate film and video; broadcast documentaries and sport; TV commercials. Unsolicited, realistic scripts/ideas welcome.

Screen First Ltd

The Studios, Funnells Farm, Down Street, Nutley, East Sussex TN22 3LG ☎01825 712034 Fax 01825 713511

Email info@screenfirst.co.uk

Contacts *M. Thomas, P. Madden*

Television dramas, documentaries, arts and animation programmes. Developing major drama series, feature films, animated specials and series. No unsolicited scripts.

Screen Ventures Ltd

49 Goodge Street, London W1P 1FB ☎020 7580 7448 Fax 020 7631 1265
Email sales@screenventures.com

Contacts *Christopher Mould, Caroline Furness*

Film and TV sales and production: documentary, music videos and drama. OUTPUT *Woodstock Diary; Vanessa Redgrave* (LWT 'South Bank Show'); *Mojo Working; Burma: Dying for Democracy* (Ch4); *Genet* (LWT 'South Bank Show'); *Dani Dares* (Ch4 series on strong women); *Pagad* (Ch4 news report).

Screenhouse Productions Ltd

378 Meanwood Road, Leeds, West Yorkshire LS7 2JF ☎0113 2392292 Fax 0113 2392293
Email info@screenhouse.co.uk
Website www.screenhouse.co.uk/screenhouse

Contacts *Paul Bader, Lisa Holdsworth*

Television documentary producer. OUTPUT includes six series of *Local Heroes*, factual programmes about the greats of science and two series of *Hart-Davis on History*, a magazine series about local history and how to become involved in historical research (both for BBC2), and a new history series for BBC Knowledge, *History Fix.* Welcomes unsolicited mss; 'we take each case on its merits'.

September Films

35 Beak Street, London W1R 3LD ☎020 7494 1884 Fax 020 7439 1194
Email september@septemberfilms.com
Head of Production *Elaine Day*
Head of Development *Kate Thompson*

Film and television drama and documentary programming. OUTPUT includes *Breathtaking* (feature film, Sky Pictures/IAC); *The Final Day* (ITV/Pearson); Eddie Irvine – the Inside Track (Ch4/Pearson); *Geri's World Walkabout* (BBC/Target); *The Lookalikes Agency; Soap Secrets; Snobs* (all for ITV/Meridian); *Reconstruction* (BSkyB). 'We are interested in developing a small number of projects with new writing talent.' Unsolicited mss welcome, 'in most instances'.

Serendipity Picture Company

Media Centre, Emma-Chris Way,
Abbeywood Park, Bristol BS34 7JU
☎0117 9066541 Fax 0117 9066542
Email tony@serendipitypictures.com

Contacts *Tony Yeadon, Nick Dance*

Television and video; corporate and documentary programming. Encourages new writing and will consider scripts.

Seventh House Films

1 Hall Farm Place, Bawburgh, Norwich,
Norfolk NR9 3LW
☎01603 749068 Fax 01603 749069
Email caflo.dunn@virgin.net

Contacts *Clive Dunn, Angela Rule*

Documentary for film, video and TV on subjects ranging from arts to history and science to social affairs. OUTPUT *The Last Fling* (life for a paralysed jump-jockey); *Dark Miracle* (an investigation into a near nuclear disaster in East Anglia); *A Pleasant Terror* (life and ghosts of M. R. James); *Piano Pieces* (musical excursion exploring different aspects of the piano); *Rockin' the Boat* (memories of pirate radio); *White Knuckles* (on the road with a travelling funfair); *King Romance* (life of Henry Rider Haggard); *A Drift of Angels* (three women and the price of art); *Bare Heaven* (the life and fiction of L. P. Hartley); *A Swell of the Soil* (life of Alfred Munnings); *Light Out of the Sky* (the art and life of Edward Seago). 'We welcome programme proposals with a view to collaborative co-production. Always interested in original and refreshing expressions for visual media.'

Sianco Cyf

7 Ffordd Segontiwm, Caernarfon, Gwynedd
LL55 2LL
☎01286 673436/0831 726111 (Mobile)
Fax 01286 673436
Email sian@treannedd.demon.co.uk

Contact *Siân Teifi*

Children's, youth and education programmes and children's drama.

SilentSound Films Ltd

Cambridge Court, Cambridge Road, Frinton
on Sea, Essex CO13 9HN
☎01255 676381 Fax 01255 676381
Email thj@silentsoundfilms.co.uk

Contact *Timothy Foster*

Active in European film co-production with mainstream connections in the USA. Special interest in developing new projects for live orchestral accompaniment. Also film musicals and documentaries on the arts. No unsolicited material.

Siriol Productions

3 Mount Stuart Square, Butetown, Cardiff
CF1 6RW
☎029 2048 8400 Fax 029 2048 5962
Email siriol@baynet.co.uk

Contact *Andrew Offiler*

Animated series, mainly for children. OUTPUT includes *Meeow*; *Hilltop Hospital*; *The Hurricanes*; *Tales of the Toothfairies*; *Billy the Cat*; *The Blobs*, as well as the feature films, *Under Milkwood* and *The Princess and the Goblin*. Write with ideas and sample script in the first instance.

Skyline Productions

10 Scotland Street, Edinburgh EH3 6PS
☎0131 557 4580 Fax 0131 556 4377
Email leslie@skyline.uk.com

Producer/Writer *Leslie Hills*

Film and television drama and documentary. Encourages new writers but telephone first before sending material.

Specific Films

25 Rathbone Street, London W1P 1AG
☎020 7580 7476 Fax 020 7494 2676
Email specificfilms@compuserve.com

Contacts *Michael Hamlyn, Christian Routh*

FOUNDED 1991. OUTPUT includes *Mr Reliable* (feature film co-produced by PolyGram and the AFFC); *The Adventures of Priscilla, Queen of the Desert*, full-length feature film co-produced with Latent Image (Australia) and financed by PolyGram and AFFC; *U2 Rattle and Hum*, full-length feature – part concert film/part cinema verité documentary; *Paws* (executive producer); *The Last Seduction 2* (Polygram); and numerous pop promos for major international artists.

Spectel Productions Ltd

1 Trethorns Court, Ludgvan, Penzance,
Cornwall TR20 8HE
☎01736 740989 Fax 01736 740989
Email Davidwebster@msn.com

Contact *David Webster*

Film and video: documentary and corporate; also video publishing. No unsolicited scripts.

Spellbound Productions Ltd

90 Cowdenbeath Path, Islington, London
N1 0LG
☎020 7713 8066 Fax 020 7713 8067

Contact *Paul Harris*

Specialises in feature films for cinema and drama for television. Keen to support and encourage new writing. Material will only be considered if in correct screenplay format and accompanied by s.a.e.

Spice Factory

81 The Promenade, Brighton, East Sussex BN10 8LS
☎01273 585275 Fax 01273 585304
Email sfactory@fastnet.co.uk

Contacts *Michael Cowan, Jason Piette*

Film and TV drama producers. OUTPUT *Pilgrim* (starring Ray Liotta); New Blood (Nick Moran and John Hurt); Sabotage (David Suchet and Stephen Fry). 'Always open to commercial scripts. We have worked with new writers such as Alberto Sciamma, Jonathan Newman and Jeremy Warding.' Is associated with North By Northwest Media Business School.

'Spoken' Image Ltd

Hewitt Street, Manchester M15 4GB
☎0161 236 7522 Fax 0161 236 0020
Email multimedia@spoken-image.com

Contacts *Geoff Allman, Steve Foster, Phil Griffin*

Film, video and TV production for documentary and corporate material. Specialises in high-quality brochures and reports, CD-ROMs, exhibitions, conferences, film and video production for broadcast, industry and commerce. Unsolicited scripts welcome. Interested in educational, and historical new writing, mainly for broadcast programmes.

Stirling Film & TV Productions Limited

137 University Street, Belfast BT7 1HP
☎028 9033 3848 Fax 028 9043 8644
Email Astirling@btinternet.com

Contact *Anne Stirling*

Producers of broadcast and corporate programming – documentary, sport, entertainment and magazine programmes.

Storm Film Productions Ltd

32–34 Great Marlborough Street, London W1V 1HA
☎020 7439 1616 Fax 020 7439 4477
Email sophie@stormfilms.freeserve.co.uk

Contact *Nic Auerbach*

Producer of commercials for clients such as British Airways and Shell. Unsolicited mss welcome.

Straight Forward Film & Television Productions Ltd

Ground Floor, Crescent House, 14 High Street, Holywood, Co. Down BT18 9AZ
☎028 9042 6298 Fax 028 9042 3384
Email enquiries@sforward.prestel.co.uk

Contacts *John Nicholson, Ian Kennedy*

Northern Ireland-based production company specialising in documentary, feature and lifestyle series. Unsolicited mss welcome. New work in drama and documentary fields welcome, particularly those with a strong Irish theme, contemporary or historical. OUTPUT *Close to Home* (Ch4 documentary on abortion laws in N. Ireland); *Greenfingers* (BBC/RTE gardening series); *Places Apart* (BBC Northern Ireland series); *The Last Colony* (Ch4 documentary on the Troubles); *Adventure Ireland* (BBC N. Ireland holiday series). In production: *Just Jones* (BBC Radio Ulster daily show); *Missing* (BBC N. Ireland documentary); *Awash With Colour* (20-part painting series, BBC N. Ireland/BBC Daytime); *School Challenge* (2nd series, BBC N. Ireland schools' quiz); *Conquering the Normans* (Ch4 Schools history of the Normans in Ireland); *Gift of the Gab* (Ch4 Schools, contemporary Irish writers).

Strawberry Productions Ltd

36 Priory Avenue, London W4 1TY
☎020 8994 4494 Fax 020 8742 7675

Contact *John Black*

Film, video and TV: drama and documentary; corporate and video publishing.

Sunset & Vine plc

30 Sackville Street, London W1X 1DB
☎020 7478 7300 Fax 020 7478 7403

Sports, children's and music programmes for television. No unsolicited mss. 'We hire freelancers only upon receipt of a commission.'

Swanlind Communication

Shippon Mill Studios, Pendeford Lane, Coven, Staffordshire WV9 5BD
☎01902 847111 Fax 01902 846333
Email comms@swanlind.co.uk
Website www.swanlind.co.uk

Chief Executive *Peter Stack*

Producer of business television, internal communication strategies, multimedia and conferences.

Sweetheart Films

15 Quennel Mansions, Weir Road, London SW12 0NQ
☎020 8673 3855

Producer *Karel Bata*

Low-to-medium budget feature films. No unsolicited mss; 'an introductory letter with, perhaps, a treatment and short extract would certainly receive consideration. We are constantly on the look-out for talent. Tip: study your craft!'

Table Top Productions

1 The Orchard, Chiswick, London W4 1JZ
☎020 8742 0507 Fax 020 8742 0507
Email a.rakoff@talk21.com

Contact *Alvin Rakoff*

TV and film. OUTPUT *Paradise Postponed* (TV mini-series); *A Voyage Round My Father; The First Olympics 1896; Dirty Tricks; A Dance to the Music of Time.* No unsolicited mss. Also Dancetime Ltd.

Talisman Films Limited

5 Addison Place, London W11 4RJ
☎020 7603 7474 Fax 020 7602 7422
Email email@talismanfilms.com

Contact *Richard Jackson*

Drama for film and TV: developing the full range of drama – TV series, serials and single films, as well as theatric features. 'We will only consider material submitted via literary agents.' Interested in supporting and encouraging new writing.

TalkBack Productions

36 Percy Street, London W1P 0LN
☎020 7323 9777 Fax 020 7637 5105
Email talkb@dial.pipex.com
Website www.talkback.co.uk

Managing Director *Peter Fincham*
Deputy Managing Director *Sally Debonnaire*

Independent TV production company set up in 1981 by Mel Smith and Griff Rhys Jones. Specialises in comedy, comedy drama and drama; lifestyle programmes. OUTPUT *Smith and Jones; Murder Most Horrid; Bonjour la Classe; Demob; The Day Today; Paris; Knowing Me Knowing You with Alan Patridge; Milner; Loose Talk; In Search of Happiness; They Think It's All Over; Never Mind the Buzzcocks; Brass Eye; House Doctor; She's Gotta Have It; Grand Designs.*

Tandem TV & Film Ltd

10 Bargrove Avenue, Hemel Hempstead, Hertfordshire HP1 1QP
☎01442 261576 Fax 01442 219250
Email info@tandemtv.com
Website www.tandemtv.com

Contact *Barbara Page*

Produces training videos, especially health and safety; construction and civil engineering documentaries; drama-doc life stories for satellite television; Christian church and charity documentary, training and promotional programmes. Welcomes unsolicited mss.

Teamwork Productions

Gate House, Walderton, Chichester, West Sussex PO18 9ED
☎023 9263 1384/0410 483149

Contact *Rob Widdows*

Video and TV producer of documentary, corporate and commercial work. OUTPUT includes motor racing coverage, motor sport productions and corporate motor sport videos. Good ideas will always be considered. No scripts.

Telemagination Ltd

Regency House, 1–4 Warwick Street, London W1R 5WA
☎020 7434 1551 Fax 020 7434 3344
Email mail@tmation.co.uk
Website www.telemagination.co.uk

Contact *Marion Edwards*

Producer of television animation. OUTPUT includes *The Animals of Farthing Wood; Noah's Island; Wiggly Park.* 'New writing welcome although please ask for a submissions letter before presenting any work.'

Televideo Productions

The Riverside, Furnival Road, Sheffield, South Yorkshire S4 7YH
☎0114 2491500 Fax 0114 2491505
Email gking@televideo.co.uk
Website www.televideo.co.uk

Contact *Graham King*

Video and television: TV news and sports coverage, documentary and corporate work; sell-through videos (distributed on own label). OUTPUT *The Premier Collection* (football club videos); varied sports coverage for cable, satellite and terrestrial broadcasters plus a wide range of corporate work from drama-based material to documentary.

Teliesyn

Chapter Arts Centre, Market Road, Canton, Cardiff CF5 1QE
☎029 2030 0876 Fax 029 2030 0877

Contact *Chris Davies*

Film and video: produces drama, documentary, music and social action in English and Welsh. Celtic Film Festival, BAFTA Cymru, Grierson and Indie award winner. OUTPUT *Branwen* (90 minute feature film for S4C); *Reel Truth* (drama doc series on the history of early film for S4C and Ch4); *Subway Cops and the Mole Kings* (Ch4); *Dragon's Song* (music series for schools, Ch4); *Codi Clawr Hanes II* (a second drama–doc series on women's history for S4C). Will consider unsolicited mss only if accompanied by synopsis and c.v. Encourages new writing wherever possible, in close association with a producer.

Tern Television Productions Ltd

73 Crown Street, Aberdeen AB11 6EX
☎01224 211123 Fax 01224 211199
Email office@terntv.u-net.com
Website www.terntv.u-net.com

Contacts *David Strachan, Gwyneth Hardy*

Broadcast, video, corporate and training. Specialises in factual entertainment. Currently developing drama. Unsolicited mss welcome.

Thames Television

See **Pearson Television Ltd**

Theatre of Comedy Company

See **Theatre Producers**

Tiger Aspect Productions Ltd

5 Soho Square, London W1V 5DE
☎020 7434 0672 Fax 020 7287 1448
Email general@tigeraspect.co.uk
Website www.tigeraspect.co.uk

Contact *Charles Brand*

Television producer for comedy, drama, documentary and entertainment. OUTPUT *Births, Marriages & Deaths; Kid in the Corner; Country House; Gimme Gimme Gimme; Harry Enfield & Chums; Howard Goodalls' Big Bangs; Playing the Field I, II & III; Streetmate I & II; Let Them Eat Cake; The Vicar of Dibley.* Only considers material submitted via an agent or from writers with a known track record.

Tonfedd

Hen Ysgol Aberpwll, Y Felinheli, Bangor, Gwynedd LL56 4JS
☎01248 671167 Fax 01248 671172
Email sharon@ff-eryri.demon.co.uk

Contact *Hefin Elis*

Light entertainment and music.

Alan Torjussen Productions Ltd

17 Heol Wen, Cardiff CF14 6EG
☎029 2062 4669 Fax 029 2062 4667

Contact *Alan Torjussen*

Film, video and TV production for drama, documentary, commercials and corporate material. Particularly interested in all types of documentary, education, schools and drama. Background includes work in the Welsh language. Unsolicited scripts now welcome; send details first. Particularly seeking ideas about Wales by Welsh writers (includes Welsh language scripts). Also original ideas for comedy and documentary/dramas.

Touch Productions Ltd

The Malt House Studios, Donhead St Mary, Dorset SP7 9DN
☎01747 828030 Fax 01747 828004
Email touch.productions@virgin.net

Contacts *Erica Wolfe-Murray, Malcolm Brinkworth*

Television documentaries such as *Simon Weston V; Flying Soldiers; Siege Doctors* (all for BBC); *The Good Life; The Surgery; Coast of Dreams; A French Affair; Watching the Detectives; Brown Babies* (all for Ch4); *Bionic Woman* (BBC1's 'QED'); *Dreamtown; Fame School* (both for Meridian). Unsolicited mss welcome.

Transatlantic Films Production and Distribution Company

Studio One, 3 Brackbury Road, London W6 0BE
☎020 8735 0505 Fax 020 8735 0605

Executive Producer *Revel Guest*

Producer of TV documentaries. OUTPUT *Horse Tales* (Discovery Channel); *History's Turning Points* (26x30-mins programmes on decisive moments in world history, The Learning Channel); *Greek Fire* (10x30-mins on Greek culture, Ch4); *Four American Composers* (4x1-hour, Ch4); *The Horse in Sport* (8x1-hour, Ch4); *A Year in the Life of Placido Domingo.* No unsolicited scripts. Interested in new writers to write 'the book of the series', e.g. for *Greek Fire* and *The Horse in Sport*, but not usually drama script writers.

TV Choice Ltd

22 Charing Cross Road, London WC2H 0HR
☎020 7379 0873 Fax 020 7379 0263
Email 101367.2325@compuserve.com
Website ourworld.compuserve.com/
    homepages/tvchoice

Contact *Norman Thomas*

Produces a range of educational videos for schools and colleges on subjects such as history, geography, business studies and economics. No unsolicited mss; send proposals only.

Twentieth Century Fox Film Co

Twentieth Century House, 31–32 Soho Square, London W1V 6AP
☎020 7437 7766 Fax 020 7734 3187

London office of the American giant.

Two Four Productions Limited

Quay West Studios, Old Newnham, Plymouth, Devon PL7 5BH
☎01752 345424 Fax 01752 344224
Email enq@twofour.co.uk
Website www.twofour.co.uk

Managing Director *Charles Wace*
Director of Broadcasting *Jill Lourie*

Specialises in factual and leisure programming for network and regional television; corporate presentations for national/international business and charities; and special interest videos for retail/mail order.

Tyburn Film Productions Limited

Pinewood Studios, Iver Heath, Buckinghamshire SL0 0NH
☎01753 651700 Fax 01753 656050

Feature films. Subsidiary of **Arlington Productions Limited**. No unsolicited submissions.

UBA Ltd

21 Alderville Road, London SW6 2EE
☎01984 623619 Fax 01984 623733

Contact *Peter Shaw*

Quality feature films and TV for an international market. OUTPUT *Windprints; The Lonely Passion of Judith Hearne* (co-production with HandMade Films Ltd); *Taffin; Castaway; Turtle Diary; Sweeney Todd; Keep the Aspidistra Flying*. In development: *Kinder Garden; Rebel Magic; No Man's Land*. Prepared to commission new writing whether adapted from another medium or based on a short outline/treatment. Concerned with the quality of the script (*Turtle Diary* was written by Harold Pinter) and breadth of appeal. 'Exploitation material' not welcome.

Umbrella Productions Ltd

56 Belmont Road, Kilmacolm PA13 4LN
☎01505 874985
Email david.muir51@virgin.net

Contact *David Muir*

Feature films and TV drama. OUTPUT includes *The Acid House* (feature film distributed by Ch4) and *Clean* (drama for Ch4). Unsolicited mss welcome. 'New writers should submit story outlines first with some sample dialogue.'

United Film and Television Productions

48 Leicester Square, London WC2H 7FB
☎020 7389 8555 Fax 020 7930 8499

Managing Director *John Willis*
Controller of Drama *Michele Buck*
Head of Drama Development *Tim Vaughan*

Television drama. OUTPUT *Hornblower* (4x120-min); *Walking on the Moon* by Martin Sadofski (drama-doc); *Touching Evil* (4x60-min, series III); *Where the Heart Is* (14x60-min, series III).

United Media Ltd

68 Berwick Street, London W1V 3PE
☎020 7287 2396 Fax 020 7287 2398
Email umedia@globalnet.co.uk

Contact *L. Patterson*

Film, video and TV: drama. OUTPUT *To the Lighthouse* (TV movie with BBC); *Jamaica Inn* (HTV mini-series); *The Krays* (feature film with Fugitive/Rank). Will only accept scripts if submitted by an agent or lawyer.

Vanson Productions

PO Box 16926, London SW18 3ZP
☎020 8874 4241 Fax 020 8874 3600
Email vansonproductions@btclick.com

Contact *Yvette Vanson*

OUTPUT *Doomwatch* by John Howlett and Ian McDonald (science drama with **Working Title Films** for Ch5); *The Murder of Stephen Lawrence* by Paul Greengrass (a film with Granada for ITV). In development, amongst others, *Cowboys & Angels* by Ian McDonald. First feature, *The Fanmaker*, developed with British Screen and directed by Tim Webber.

Vera Productions

66–68 Margaret Street, London W1N 7FL
☎020 7436 6116 Fax 020 7436 6117

Contact *Dee Branch*

Produces television comedy such as *Alistair McGowan's Big Impression*; *Jo Brand's Christmas Special*; *Rory Bremner* and *Mark Thomas*. Unsolicited material considered.

Video Enterprises

12 Barbers Wood Road, High Wycombe, Buckinghamshire HP12 4EP
☎01494 534144/0831 875216 (Mobile)
Fax 01494 534152
Email maurice@vident.u-net.com
Website www.vident.u-net.com

Contact *Maurice R. Fleisher*

Video and TV, mainly corporate: business and industrial training, promotional material and conferences. No unsolicited material 'but always ready to try out good new writers'.

Video Presentations
51 Daybrook Road, Wimbledon, London SW19 3DJ
☎020 8542 7721 Fax 020 8543 0855
Email jhvp@btinternet.com
Contact *John Holloway*

Corporate video. CLIENTS include the Post Office, IBM, British Gas, Freemans, Eastern Electricity.

W.O.W. Productions
26A Fordwych Road, London NW2 3TG
☎020 8830 5978 Fax 020 8830 5978
Email wow@dircon.co.uk
Contacts *Carl Schonfeld, Dom Rotheroe*

Film and television drama and documentary programming. OUTPUT includes *A Sarajevo Diary* (documentary) and *My Brother Rob* (feature). Welcomes unsolicited mss.

Brian Waddell Productions Ltd
Strand Studios, 5/7 Shore Road, Holywood, Co. Down BT18 9HX
☎028 9042 7646 Fax 028 9042 7922
Email bwpl@globalgateway.co.uk
Contacts *Brian Waddell*

Producer of a wide range of television programmes in leisure activities, the arts, music, children's, comedy, travel/adventure and documentaries. Currently developing several film and drama projects.

Wall to Wall Television
8–9 Spring Place, London NW5 3ER
☎020 7485 7424 Fax 020 7267 5292
Contact *Alex Graham*

Documentaries, features and drama. OUTPUT includes *Plotlands; It's Not Unusual; Nightmare: The Birth of Horror* (BBC); *Baby It's You; A Taste of the Times; Weekly Planet* (Ch4); *Our Boy* (BBC); *A Rather English Marriage* (BBC). Material is produced in-house; occasional outside ideas accepted. Continued expansion of drama production means more opportunities for writers.

Jane Walmsley Productions
See **JAM Pictures**

The Walnut Partnership
Crown House, Armley Road, Leeds, West Yorkshire LS12 2EJ
☎0113 2456913 Fax 0113 2439614
Email info@walnutpartnership.co.uk
Website www.walnutpartnership.co.uk
Contact *Geoff Penn*

A communications consultancy and video production company specialising in business communication. Clients include Yorkshire Electricity, HSBC, Clydesdale and Yorkshire Banks.

Walsh Bros. Limited
4 The Heights, London SE7 8JH
☎020 8858 5870/8854 5557
Fax 020 8858 6870
Producer/Director *John Walsh*
Producer/Head of Finance
   David Walsh, ACA
Producer/Head of Development
   Maura Walsh

Award-winning producers of drama documentaries and feature films. OUTPUT *Monarch* (feature film on the events on the eve of the death of King Henry VIII); *Boyz & Girlz*, (15-part documentary series); *Cowboyz & Cowgirlz* (US sequel to the first hit series); *Ray Harryhausen* (profile of the work of Hollywood special effects legend); *The Comedy Store* (behind-the-scenes view of the birthplace of alternative comedy); *The Sceptic & The Psychic; The Sleeper* and *A State of Mind* (film dramas).

Warner Sisters Film & TV Ltd
The Cottage, Pall Mall Deposit, 124 Barlby Road, London W10 6BL
☎020 8960 3550 Fax 020 8960 3880
Email Sisters@WarnerCine.com
Chief Executives *Lavinia Warner, Jane Wellesley, Anne-Marie Casey, Dorothy Viljoen*
FOUNDED 1984. Drama and comedy. TV and feature films. OUTPUT includes *Selling Hitler; Rides; Life's a Gas; She-Play; A Village Affair; Dangerous Lady; Dressing for Breakfast; The Spy that Caught a Cold; The Bite; Jilting Joe; The Jump; Lady Audley's Secret*. Developing a wide range of projects including *Mad Mary* (feature film) and *Rubicon* (international co-production).

Paul Weiland Film Company
14 Newburgh Street, London W1V 1LF
☎020 7287 6900 Fax 020 7434 0146
Email weiland@easynet.co.uk
Contact *Mary Francis*

Television commercials and pop promos.

Unsolicited mss sometimes welcome; 'we encourage new writing.'

Western Eye Business Television

Easton Business Centre, Felix Road, Easton, Bristol BS5 0HE
☎0117 9415854 Fax 0117 9415851

Contact *Steve Spencer*

Corporate video production for Royal Mail, Re-Solv, NACAB, Water Aid, BT. Looking for experienced writers in the above field.

Michael White Productions Ltd
See **MW Entertainments Ltd**

Windrush Productions Ltd

7 Woodlands Road, Moseley, Birmingham B13 4EH
☎0121 449 6439/07977 059378 (Mobile)
Fax 0121 449 6439

Contacts *Pogus Caesar, Shawn Caesar*

Television documentaries, including a multi-cultural series for Carlton TV (*Xpress and Respect*); *The A-Force* (BBC); *I'm Black in Britain* (Central TV); *Drumbeat* (Carlton). Also produces *Windrush E. Smith Show* (comedy) and Pogus Caesar's *Off the Hook* for BBC Radio Pebble Mill. Produces pop promos/corporate videos for a range of clients. Encourages new writing, especially from the regions. 'We try to seek scripts from writers interested in developing new Black fiction/comedy.' Runs courses for writers in conjunction with Birmingham Education Dept.

WitzEnd Productions
See **Pearson Television Ltd**

Working Title Films Ltd

Oxford House, 76 Oxford Street, London W1N 9FD
☎020 7307 3000 Fax 020 7307 3001/2/3

Co-Chairmen (Films) *Tim Bevan, Eric Fellner*
Head of Development (Films) *Debra Hayward*
Development Executive (Films) *Chris Clark*
Television *Simon Wright*

Feature films, TV drama; also family/children's entertainment and TV comedy. OUTPUT Films: *Notting Hill; Elizabeth; Hi Lo Country; Plunkett & Macleane; Bean; The Borrowers; The Matchmaker; Fargo; Dead Man Walking; French Kiss; Four Weddings and a Funeral; The Hudsucker Proxy; The Tall Guy; A World Apart; Wish You Were Here; My Beautiful Laundrette*.

Television: *More Tales of the City; Lano and Woodley; The Borrowers I & II; Armisted Maupin's Tales of the City; News Hounds; Echoes; Randall & Hopkirk Deceased; Doomwatch*. No unsolicited mss at present, but keen to encourage new writing nevertheless via New Writers Scheme - contact *Natascha Wharton*.

Worldview Pictures

Unit 10, Cameron House, 12 Castlehaven Road, London NW1 8QW
☎020 7916 4696 Fax 020 7916 1091
Email anyone@worldviewpictures.co.uk

Contacts *Stephen Trombley, Bruce Eadie*

Documentaries and series for television, plus theatrical. OUTPUT *A Death in the Family; Project X* (Dixcovery); *War and Civilization* (8x60-min for The Learning Channel); *Nuremberg* (Discovery/Ch4); *Raising Hell: The Life of A. J. Bannister; The Execution Protocol* (both for Discovery/BBC/France 2); *Drancy: A Concentration Camp in Paris; The Lynchburg Story* (both for Discovery/Ch4/France 2); *99% Woman* (France 2).

Worthwhile Productions Ltd

16 Biddulph Road, London W6 1JB
☎020 7266 9166 Fax 020 7266 9166

Contact *Jeremy Wootliff*

Feature films, video; documentary, corporate and commercials. Unsolicited mss welcome.

Wortman Productions UK

48 Chiswick Staithe, London W4 3TP
☎020 8994 8886/0976 805976 (Mobile)

Producer *Neville Wortman*

Film, video and TV production for drama, documentary, commercials and corporate material. OUTPUT *House in the Country* John Julius Norwich (ITV series); *Ellington* (jazz series); *Celebration Theatre Company for the Young – The Winter's Tale; Copland's Century* (documentary on Aaron Copland); *Florence Nightingale* (film drama in development). Open to new writing but preferably from agents; single page outline and couple of pages of dialogue.

Wot Films & Television Ltd

Suite 3, 44 Mortimer Street, London W1N 7DG
☎020 7323 5901 Fax 020 7323 5903

Contacts *Jackie Thomas, Nick Fleming*

Television and video drama plus a film in development. Welcomes unsolicited mss.

The Writers Studio – a division of Screen Production Associates Ltd

☎020 7267 9953 Fax 020 7267 9953

Contacts *Piers Jackson, Nicholas McInerny*

Feature films. OUTPUT includes *The 4th Man; The Truth Game; Black Badge; The Case; Mothball City*. No unsolicited mss. Send preliminary letter outlining project (only movie screenplays) and c.v.

Yoda Productions Ltd

Brooklands Cottage, Guildford Road, Westcott, Dorking, Surrey RH4 3LB

☎01306 886916 Fax 01306 889352

Email gail@yodaproductions.co.uk

Contact *Gail Lowe*

Medical, scientific, technical marketing and promotional, training videos and multimedia. No unsolicited mss.

Yoyo Films

79 Dean Street, London W1V 5HA

☎020 7642 8954 Fax 020 7737 3901

Email yoyofilms@compuserve.com

Contact *Laurens Postma*

Film, television and video; drama and documentary. Unsolicited mss welcome; 'looking for new writing all the time.'

Zenith Entertainment Plc

43–45 Dorset Street, London W1H 4AB

☎020 7224 2440 Fax 020 7224 3194

Email general@zenith-entertainment.co.uk

Script Executive *Ming Ho*

Feature films and TV drama. OUTPUT Films: Todd Haynes' *Velvet Goldmine; Wisdom of Crocodiles*; Nicole Holofcener's *Walking and Talking*. Television: *Hamish Macbeth; Rhodes; Bodyguards; The Uninvited; Bomber*. No unsolicited scripts.

Theatre Producers

Actors Touring Company
Alford House, Aveline Street, London
SE11 5DQ
☎020 7735 8311
Fax 020 7735 1031 attn. ATC
Email atc@cwcom.net
Artistic Director *Nick Philippou*

'Actors Touring Company takes old stories and works with living writers to produce new theatre.' Collaborations with writers are based on adaptation and/or translation work and unsolicited mss will only be considered in this category. 'We endeavour to read mss but do not have the resources to do so quickly.' As a small-scale company, all plays must have a cast of six or less.

Almeida Theatre Company
Almeida Street, Islington, London N1 1TA
☎020 7226 7432 Fax 020 7704 9581
Website www.almeida.co.uk
Artistic Directors *Ian McDiarmid,*
Jonathan Kent

FOUNDED 1980. Now in its eleventh year as a full-time producing theatre, presenting a year-round theatre and music programme in which international writers, composers, performers, directors and designers are invited to work with British artists on challenging new and classical works. Previous productions: *Galileo; Moonlight; The School for Wives; Hamlet; Tartuffe; Who's Afraid of Virginia Woolf; Ivanov; The Government Inspector; Naked; The Judas Kiss; The Iceman Cometh; The Jew of Malta; Celebration; The Room; Richard II; Coriolanus.* No unsolicited mss: 'our producing programme is very limited and linked to individual directors and actors'.

Alternative Theatre Company Ltd
Bush Theatre, Shepherds Bush Green,
London W12 8QD
☎020 7602 3703 Fax 020 7602 7614
Email thebush@dircon.co.uk
Literary Manager *Tim Fountain*

FOUNDED 1972. Trading as The Bush Theatre. Produces nine plays a year (principally British) including up to three visiting companies also producing new work: 'we are a writer's theatre'. Previous productions: *Kiss of the*

Spiderwoman Manuel Puig; *Raping the Gold* Lucy Gannon; *The Wexford Trilogy* Billy Roche; *Love and Understanding* Joe Penhall; *This Limetree Bower* Conor McPherson; *Discopigs* Enda Walsh; *The Pitchfork Disney* Philip Ridley; *Caravan* Helen Blakeman; *Beautiful Thing* Jonathan Harvey; *Killer Joe* Tracy Letts; *Shang-a-Lang* Catherine Johnson; *Howie the Rookie* Mark O'Rowe. Scripts are read by a team of associates, then discussed with the management, a process which takes about three months. The theatre offers a small number of commissions, recommissions to ensure further drafts on promising plays, and a guarantee against royalties so writers are not financially penalised even though the plays are produced in a small house. Writers should send scripts with small s.a.e. for acknowledgement and large s.a.e. for return of script.

Yvonne Arnaud Theatre
Millbrook, Guildford, Surrey GU1 3UX
☎01483 440077 Fax 01483 564071
Contact *James Barber*

Credits include: *Alarms and Excursions* Michael Frayn; *Tom and Clem* Stephen Churchett; *Life Support* Simon Gray; *Equally Divided* Ronald Harwood; *Comic Potential* Alan Ayckbourn; *The Prisoner of Second Avenue* Neil Simon; *A Passionate Woman* Kay Mellor; *Indian Ink* Tom Stoppard; *Home* David Storey; *Cellmates* Simon Gray; *Letter of Resignation* Hugh Whitemore; *Quartet* Ronald Harwood.

Birmingham Repertory Theatre
Centenary Square, Broad Street, Birmingham
B1 2EP
☎0121 245 2000 Fax 0121 245 2100
Website www.birmingham-rep.co.uk
Artistic Director *Bill Alexander*
Associate Artistic Director *Tony Clark*
Associate Director *Indher Rubasingham*
Literary Manager *Ben Payne*
Literary Officer *Caroline Jester*

The Birmingham Repertory Theatre aims to provide a platform for the best work from new writers from both within and beyond the West Midlands region along with a programme which also includes classics and 'discovery' plays. The Rep is committed to a policy of integrated casting and to the production of new work which reflects the diversity of contemporary experience. The commissioning of new plays takes place across the full range of the theatre's activities: in the Main House, The Door (which is a dedicated new writing space) and on tour to community venues in the region. 'Writers are advised that the Rep is very unlikely to produce an unsolicited script. We usually assess unsolicited submissions on the basis of whether it indicates a writer with whom the theatre may be interested in working. The theatre runs a programme of writers' attachments every year in addition to its commissioning policy and maintains close links with *Stagecoach* (the regional writers' training agency) and the **MA in Playwriting Studies** at the University of Birmingham.' For more information contact the Literary Officer.

Black Theatre Co-op
See **Nitro**

Bootleg Theatre Company
23 Burgess Green, Bishopdown, Salisbury, Wiltshire SP1 3El
☎01722 421476

Contact *Colin Burden*

FOUNDED 1984. Tries to encompass as wide an audience as possible and has a tendency towards plays with socially relevant themes. A good bet for new writing since unsolicited mss are very welcome. 'Our policy is to produce new and/or rarely seen plays and anything received is given the most serious consideration.' Actively seeks to obtain grants to commission new writers for the company. Productions include: *Hanging Hanratty* by Michael Burnham – both a London run and film version; *The Boys Are Back in Town* Trevor Suthers; *The Truth About Blokes*; *A Rainy Night in Soho*; *Hardman*.

Borderline Theatre
Darlington New Church, North Harbour Street, Ayr KA8 8AA
☎01292 281010 Fax 01292 263825
Email <name>@borderlinetheatre.co.uk
Website www.borderlinetheatre.co.uk

Artistic Director *Leslie Finlay*
Chief Executive *Eddie Jackson*

FOUNDED 1974. Borderline is one of Scotland's leading touring companies. Committed to new writing, it tours an innovative programme of new plays and radical adaptations/translations of classic texts in an accessible and entertaining style. Tours to main-house theatres and small venues throughout Scotland. 2000/2001 productions include the world premières of *The Angels' Share* by Chris Dolan, *Indian Summer* A. L. Kennedy and *The Prince and the Pilot* Anita Sullivan. Writers under commission include Nicola McCartney, Chris Dolan, A. L. Kennedy and Anita Sullivan. Previous writers have included Dario Fo, Liz Lochhead, Roald Dahl and John Byrne. Borderline is also committed to commissioning and touring new plays for young people. Send synopsis with cast size in the first instance.

Bright Ltd
1–2 Henrietta Street, London WC2E 8PS
☎020 7379 7474 Fax 020 7379 8484
Email guy@g-c-a.co.uk

Contacts *Guy Chapman, Paul Spyker*

Performs to young audiences with innovative, experimental theatre. Productions include: *Shopping and Fucking*; *Love Upon the Throne*; *Crave*; *Disco Pigs*. Welcomes unsolicited mss; interested in modern issues, exciting boundary-pushing work.

Bristol Old Vic Company
Theatre Royal, King Street, Bristol BS1 4ED
☎0117 9493993 Fax 0117 9493996
Email the.bristol.old.vic@cableinet.co.uk

Bristol Old Vic is committed to the commissioning and production of new writing in the Theatre Royal (650 seats). Plays must have enough popular appeal to attract an audience of significant size. The theatre will read and report on unsolicited scripts, and asks for a fee of £15 per script to cover the payments to readers. 'We also seek to attract emerging talent to the Basement, a profit-share venue (50 seats) committed to producing one-act plays by un-proven writers. Plays for the Basement will be read free of charge although no report can be provided. At present we rarely produce in the New Vic Studio (150 seats) but often receive productions of new plays from visiting companies.'

Bush Theatre
See **Alternative Theatre Company Ltd**

Carnival (Films & Theatre) Ltd
See entry under **Film, TV and Video Production Companies**

Chester Gateway Theatre Trust Ltd
Hamilton Place, Chester, Cheshire CH1 2BH
☎01244 344238 Fax 01244 317277
Website www.gateway-theatre.org

Artistic Director *Deborah Shaw*

FOUNDED 1968. 440-seater, fairly intimate auditorium. Committed to producing at least one new play a year along with a balanced programme of classics, contemporary plays, Christmas adaptations and re-discoveries (e.g. Noël Coward's *The Young Idea*). Recent premières by Keith Waterhouse, Mick Martin, Dino Aristidou. Also busy Education and Access Department which occasionally commissions work. Writers' group meets fortnightly.

Citizens Theatre
Gorbals, Glasgow G5 9DS
☎0141 429 5561 Fax 0141 429 7374
Artistic Director *Giles Havergal*

No formal new play policy. The theatre has a play reader but opportunities to do new work are limited.

Clwyd Theatr Cymru
Mold, Flintshire CH7 1YA
☎01352 756331 Fax 01352 758323
Email drama@celtic.co.uk
Website www.clwyd-theatr-cymru.co.uk
Literary Manager *William James*

Theatre of the Year 1998–99 (Barclays/TMA), Clwyd Theatr Cymru produces a season of plays each year performed in repertoire by a resident company, along with tours throughout Wales (in English and Welsh). Plays are a mix of classics, revivals, contemporary drama and new writing. Recent new writing includes: *The Journey of Mary Kelly* Sian Evans; *Rape of the Fair Country*, *Hosts of Rebecca* and *Song of the Earth* all adapt. Manon Eames; *The Changelings* Gregg Cullen; *Celf* by Yasmina Reza, trans. Manon Eames; *Flora's War* Tim Baker. Plays by Welsh writers or with Welsh themes will be considered.

Michael Codron Plays Ltd
Aldwych Theatre Offices, Aldwych, London WC2B 4DF
☎020 7240 8291 Fax 020 7240 8467
General Manager *Paul O'Leary*

Michael Codron Plays Ltd manages the Aldwych Theatre in London's West End. The plays it produces don't necessarily go into the Aldwych, but always tend to be big-time West End fare. Previous productions: *Copenhagen; The Invention of Love; Hapgood; Uncle Vanya; The Sneeze; Rise and Fall of Little Voice; Arcadia; Dead Funny*. No particular rule of thumb on subject matter or treatment. The acid test is whether 'something appeals to Michael'. Straight plays rather than musicals.

Colchester Mercury Theatre Limited
Balkerne Gate, Colchester, Essex CO1 1PT
☎01206 577006 Fax 01206 769607
Email mercury.theatre@virgin.net
Artistic Producer *Gregory Floy*
Associate Director *Adrian Stokes*

Producing theatre with a wide-ranging audience. Unsolicited scripts welcome. The theatre has a free playwright's group for adults with a serious commitment to writing plays.

The Coliseum, Oldham
Fairbottom Street, Oldham, Lancashire OL1 3SW
☎0161 624 1731 Fax 0161 624 5318
Chief Executive *Kenneth Alan Taylor*

The policy of the Coliseum is to present high quality work that is unashamedly 'popular'. Has a special interest in new work that has a Northern flavour, however this does not rule out other plays. Unsolicited scripts are all read but will only be returned if a s.a.e. is included.

Contact Theatre Company
Oxford Road, Manchester M15 6JA
☎0161 274 3434 Fax 0161 273 6286
Artistic Director *John E. McGrath*

FOUNDED 1972. Plays to a young audience (up to 25). New productions have included: *Rupert Street Lonely Hearts Club* Jonathan Harvey; *Tell Me* Matthew Dunster (both world premières). Contact the company for detailed guidelines for writers.

Crucible Theatre
55 Norfolk Street, Sheffield S1 1DA
☎0114 2495999 Fax 0114 2496003
Contact *Artistic Director*

'Most of the new work we present will be the result of commissions or a prolonged exchange of ideas and script development with writers in whom we have expressed an interest. However, we are interested in all new work and offer a free script reading service for unsolicited scripts and are also happy to respond to synopses or outline ideas. NB We do not offer readers' reports. Please ring or send s.a.e. for full details of script reading service.'

Cwmni Theatr Gwynedd
Deiniol Road, Bangor, Gwynedd LL57 2TL
☎01248 351707 Fax 01248 351915
Email theatr@globalnet.co.uk
Artistic Director *Siân Summers*

FOUNDED 1984. A mainstream company, performing in major theatres on the Welsh circuit. Welsh-language work only at present. Classic Welsh plays, translations of European repertoire and new work, including adaptations from novels. New Welsh work always welcome; works in English considered if appropriate for translation (i.e. dealing with issues relevant to Wales). 'We are keen to discuss projects with established writers and offer commissions where possible.'

Derby Playhouse
Eagle Centre, Derby DE1 2NF
☎01332 363271 Fax 01332 294412
Website www.derbyplayhouse.demon.co.uk
Artistic Director *Mark Clements*

Derby Playhouse is interested in new work and has produced several world premières over the last year. 'We have a discrete commissioning budget but already have several projects under way. Due to the amount of scripts we receive, we now ask writers to send a letter accompanied by a synopsis of the play, a résumé of writing experience and any ten pages of the script they wish to submit. We will then determine whether we think it is suitable for the Playhouse, in which case we will ask for a full script.' Writers are welcome to send details of rehearsed readings and productions as an alternative means of introducing the theatre to their work.

Druid Theatre Company
Druid Lane, Galway, Republic of Ireland
☎00 353 91 568660 Fax 00 353 91 563109
Contact *Literary Manager*

FOUNDED 1975. Plays to a wide-ranging audience, urban and rural, from young adults to the elderly. National and international theatre with an emphasis on new Irish work, though contemporary European theatre is commonplace in the repertoire. Currently has six writers under commission and is commissioning more. Enclose s.a.e. for return of scripts.

The Dukes Playhouse Ltd
Moor Lane, Lancaster LA1 1QE
☎01524 67461 Fax 01524 846817
Administrative Director *Amanda Belcham*

FOUNDED 1971. The only producing house in Lancashire. Wide target market for cinema and theatre. Plays in a 320-seater end-on auditorium and in a 174-seater in-the-round studio. In the summer months open-air promenade performances are held in Williamson Park. Also, community based Youth Arts Centre.

Dundee Repertory Theatre
Tay Square, Dundee DD1 1PB
☎01382 227684 Fax 01382 228609
Artistic Director *Hamish Glen*

FOUNDED 1939. Plays to a varied audience. Translations and adaptations of classics, and new local plays. Most new work is commissioned. Interested in contemporary plays in translation and in new Scottish writing. No scripts except by prior arrangement.

Eastern Angles Theatre Company
Sir John Mills Theatre, Gatacre Road, Ipswich, Suffolk IP1 2LQ
☎01473 218202 Fax 01473 250954
Email admin@eastsernangles.freeserve.co.uk
Contact *Ivan Cutting*

FOUNDED 1982. Plays to a rural audience for the most part. New work only: some commissioned, some devised by the company, some researched documentaries. Unsolicited mss welcome from regional writers. 'We are always keen to develop and produce new writing, especially that which is germane to a rural area.'

Edinburgh Royal Lyceum Theatre
See **Royal Lyceum Theatre Company**

English Stage Company Ltd
See **Royal Court Theatre**

English Touring Theatre
New Century Building, Hill Street, Crewe CW1 2BX
☎01270 501800 Fax 01270 501888
Email admin@englishtouringtheatre.co.uk
Artistic Director *Stephen Unwin*

FOUNDED 1993. National touring company visiting middle-scale receiving houses and arts centres throughout England. Mostly mainstream. Largely classical programme, but with increasing interest to tour one modern English play per year. Strong commitment to Education and Community Outreach work. No unsolicited mss.

Everyman Theatre
5–9 Hope Street, Liverpool L1 9BH
☎0151 708 0338 Fax 0151 709 0398
Contact *Literary Manager*

Merged administration with the Liverpool Playhouse in 2000 to produce plays for both theatres. Offers a script-reading service and commissions new work.

Robert Fox Ltd

6 Beauchamp Place, London SW3 1NG
☎020 7584 6855 Fax 020 7225 1638
Contact *Robert Fox*

Producer and co-producer of work suitable for West End production. Current production: *The Lady in the Van* by Alan Bennett. Previous productions: *Another Country; Chess; Lettice and Lovage; Burn This; When She Danced; The Ride Down Mount Morgan; The Importance of Being Earnest; The Seagull; Goosepimples; Vita & Virginia; The Weekend; Three Tall Women; Skylight; Who's Afraid of Virginia Woolf; Masterclass; A Delicate Balance; Amy's View; Closer.* Scripts, while usually by established playwrights, are always read.

Gate Theatre Company Ltd

11 Pembridge Road, London W11 3HQ
☎020 7229 5387 Fax 020 7221 6055
Literary Manager *Katherine Mendelsohn*

FOUNDED 1979. Plays to a mixed, London-wide audience, depending on production. Aims to produce British premières of plays which originate from abroad and translations of neglected classics. Most work is with translators. Recent productions: *Marathon* by Edoardo Erba; *The Odyssey* by Peter Oswald. Positively encourages writers from abroad to send in scripts or translations. Most unsolicited scripts are read but it is extremely unlikely that new British, Irish or North American plays will have any future at the theatre due to emphasis on plays translated from foreign languages. The Gate does not welcome primary anglophone material and will not read these plays. Always enclose s.a.e. if play needs returning.

Graeae Theatre Company

Interchange Studios, Dalby Street, London NW5 3NQ
☎020 7267 1959 Fax 020 7267 2703
Email graeae@dircon.co.uk
Minicom 020 7267 3164
Artistic Director *Jenny Sealey*
Administrative Director *Kevin Dunn*

Europe's premier theatre company of disabled people, the company tours nationally and internationally with innovative theatre productions highlighting both historical and contemporary disabled experience. Graeae also runs Forum Theatre and educational programmes available to schools, youth clubs and day centres nationally, provides vocational training in theatre arts (including playwriting). Unsolicited scripts – from disabled writers – welcome. New work examining disability issues is commissioned.

Hampstead Theatre

Swiss Cottage Centre, Avenue Road, London NW3 3EX
☎020 7722 9224 Fax 020 7722 3860
Literary Manager *Ben Jancovich*

Produces new plays and the occasional modern classic. Scripts are intially assessed by a team of script readers and their responses are shared with management in monthly script meetings. The literary manager and/or artistic director then read and consider many submissions in more detail. It can therefore take 2–3 months to reach a decision. Writers produced in the past ten years include: Marguerite Duras, Terry Eagleton, Brad Fraser, Michael Frayn, Brian Friel, William Gaminara, Beth Henley, Stephen Jeffreys, Terry Johnson, Tony Kushner, Doug Lucie, Frank McGuinness, Rona Munro, Jennifer Phillips, Stephen Poliakoff, Philip Ridley, Martin Sherman, Shelagh Stephenson and Timberlake Wertenbaker.

Harrogate Theatre Company

Oxford Street, Harrogate, North Yorkshire HG1 1QF
☎01423 502710 Fax 01423 563205
Contact *Artistic Director/Executive Director*

FOUNDED 1950. Describes its audience as 'eclectic, all ages and looking for innovation'. Previous productions: *The Marriage of Figaro* (commissioned adaptation of Beaumarchais, Mozart, Da Ponte); *Barber of Seville* (commissioned translation and adaptation of Beaumarchais, Rossini and Sterbini); *School for Wives; The Baltimore Waltz* Paula Vogel (European première); *Hot 'n' Throbbing* Paula Vogel (European première); *My Children! My Africa!; Wings* (Kopit, Lunden & Perlman European première); new adaptations of *The Government Inspector* and *The Turn of the Screw; Marisol* Jose Rivera; *Lulu* Angela Carter (world première); *Skylight* David Hare. Always struggling to produce new work. The studio theatre was reopened in 1998 for small-scale productions including *White Lies* and *Mercy Killing* by Robert Shearman.

The Hiss & Boo Company

1 Nyes Hill, Wineham Lane, Bolney, West Sussex RH17 5SD
Fax 01444 882057
Email hissboo@msn.com
Website www.hissboo.co.uk

Contact *Ian Liston*

Particularly interested in new thrillers, comedy thrillers, comedy and melodrama – must be commercial full-length plays. Also interested in plays/plays with music for children. No one-acts. Previous productions: *Sleighrider; Beauty and the Beast; An Ideal Husband; Mr Men's Magical Island; Mr Men and the Space Pirates; Nunsense; Corpse!; Groucho: A Life in Revue; See How They Run; Christmas Cat and the Pudding Pirates; Pinocchio.* 'We are keen on revue-type shows and compilation shows but *not* tribute-type performances.' No unsolicited scripts; no telephone calls. Send synopsis and introductory letter in the first instance.

Hull Truck Theatre Company

Spring Street, Hull HU2 8RW
☎01482 224800 Fax 01482 581182

General Manager *Joanne Gower*

John Godber, of *Teechers, Bouncers, Up 'n' Under* fame, the artistic director of this high-profile Northern company since 1984, has very much dominated the scene in the past with his own successful plays. The emphasis is still on new writing but Godber's work continues to be toured extensively. Most new plays are commissioned. Previous productions: *Dead Fish* Gordon Steel; *Off Out* and *Fish and Leather* both by Gill Adams; *Happy Families* John Godber. The company receives a large number of unsolicited scripts but cannot guarantee a quick response. Bear in mind the artistic policy of Hull Truck, which is 'accessibility and popularity'. In general they are not interested in musicals, or in plays with casts of more than eight.

Stephen Joseph Theatre

Westborough, Scarborough, North Yorkshire YO11 1JW
☎01723 370540 Fax 01723 360506

Artistic Director *Alan Ayckbourn*
Literary Manager *Laura Harvey*

A two-auditoria complex housing a 165-seat end stage theatre/cinema (the McCarthy) and a 400-seat theatre-in-the-round (the Round). Positive policy on new work. For obvious reasons, Alan Ayckbourn's work features quite strongly but a new writing programme ensures plays from other sources are also actively encouraged. Previous première productions include: *Woman in Black* (adapt. Stephen Mallatratt); *Neville's Island* and *Larkin with Women* Tim Firth; *All Things Considered* Ben Brown; *A Listening Heaven* Torben Betts; *Penny Blue* Vanessa Brooks; *Perfect Pitch* John Godber. Plays should have a strong

narrative and be accessible and inventive. Submit to *Laura Harvey* enclosing an s.a.e. for return of mss.

Bill Kenwright Ltd

BKL House, 106 Harrow Road, London W2 1RR
☎020 7446 6200 Fax 020 7446 6222

Contact *Bill Kenwright*

Presents both revivals and new shows for West End and touring theatres. Although new work tends to be by established playwrights, this does not preclude or prejudice new plays from new playwrights. Scripts should be addressed to Bill Kenwright with a covering letter and s.a.e. 'We have enormous amounts of scripts sent to us although we very rarely produce unsolicited work. Scripts are read systematically. Please do not phone; the return of your script or contact with you will take place in time.'

Komedia

Gardner Street, North Lane, Brighton, East Sussex BN1 1UN
☎01273 647101 Fax 01273 647102
Email komedia@dircon.co.uk
Website www.komedia.dircon.co.uk

Contact *David Lavender*

FOUNDED in 1994, Komedia promotes, produces and presents new work. Mss of new plays welcome.

Leeds Playhouse

See **West Yorkshire Playhouse**

Leicester Haymarket Theatre

Belgrave Gate, Leicester LE1 3YQ
☎0116 2530021 Fax 0116 2513310
Website www.leicester-haymarket-theatre.co.uk

Artistic Director *Paul Kerryson*

'We aim for a balanced programme of original and established works.' Recent productions include: *Edward II* with Eddie Izzard and *King Lear* with Kathryn Hunter as Lear. A script-reading panel has been established, and new writing is welcome. An Asian initiative has been set up to promote Asian work and Asian practitioners. Future productions include a new commission for Clare McIntyre, a new play by David Greer, the British première of Sondheim's *Sunday in the Park with George* and the première of *Airport 2000*. There is also a full studio season and programme of activity for the outreach and education department, including youth theatre and community tours.

Library Theatre Company

St Peter's Square, Manchester M2 5PD
☎0161 234 1913 Fax 0161 228 6481
Email ltc@libraries.manchester.gov.uk
Website www.libtheatreco.org.uk

Artistic Director *Christopher Honer*

Produces new and contemporary work, as well as occasional classics. No unsolicited mss. Send outline of the nature of the script first. Encourages new writing through the commissioning of new plays and through a programme of rehearsed readings to help writers' development.

Live Theatre Company

7/8 Trinity Chare, Newcastle upon Tyne NE1 3DF
☎0191 261 2694 Fax 0191 232 2224

Artistic Director *Max Roberts*

FOUNDED 1973. Produces shows at its newly refurbished 200-seat venue, and also tours regionally and nationally. Company policy is to produce work that is rooted in the culture of the region, particularly for those who do not normally get involved in the arts. The company is particularly interested in promoting new writing. As well as full-scale productions the company organises workshops, rehearsed readings and other new writing activities. The company also enjoys a close relationship with New Writing North. Productions include: *Up and Running* Phil Woods; *Buffalo Girls* by Karin Young; *Two* Jim Cartwright; *Cabaret*, and an ambitious cycle of plays – *Twelve Tales of Tyneside* – which involved 12 writers; *Falling Together* Tom Hadaway; *Cooking With Elvis* Lee Hall; *Bones* Peter Straughan; *Laughter When We're Dead* Sean O'Brien.

Liverpool Everyman and Liverpool Playhouse

See **Everyman Theatre**

London Bubble Theatre Company

3–5 Elephant Lane, London SE16 4JD
☎020 7237 4434 Fax 020 7231 2366
Email peth@londonbubble.org.uk
Website www.londonbubble.org.uk

Artistic Director *Jonathan Petherbridge*

Produces workshops, plays and events for a mixed audience of theatregoers and non-theatregoers, wide-ranging in terms of age, culture and class. Previous productions: *Dealing With Feelings; The Lower Depths; Ali Baba and the Forty Thieves.* Unsolicited mss welcome but

'our reading service is extremely limited and there can be a considerable wait before we can give a response'. Produces at least one new show a year which is invariably commissioned.

Lyric Theatre Hammersmith

King Street, London W6 0QL
☎020 8741 0824 Fax 020 8741 5965
Email enquiries@lyric.co.uk
Website www.lyric.co.uk

Directors *Sue Storr, Simon Mellor*

The main theatre stages an eclectic programme of new and revived classics with a particular interest in music theatre. Interested in developing projects with writers, translators and adaptors. The Lyric does not accept unsolicited scripts. No longer able to produce in its 110-seat studio owing to reduced funding but the venue continues to host work, including new, by some of the best touring companies in the country.

MAC – The Centre for Birmingham

Cannon Hill Park, Birmingham B12 9QH
☎0121 440 4221 Fax 0121 446 4372
Website
www.birminghamarts.org.uk/mac.html

Director *Dorothy Wilson*

MAC is a theatre and music-theatre producer, commissioning 3–5 scripts each year and presenting new writing. Home of the Geese Theatre Company, Sampad South Asian Arts, Stan's Café Theatre Company and a host of other arts/performance-related organisations based in Birmingham. Details on Geese available from the Centre.

Cameron Mackintosh

1 Bedford Square, London WC1B 3RA
☎020 7637 8866 Fax 020 7436 2683

Musical producer. His productions include *Oliver!; Little Shop of Horrors; Side by Side by Sondheim; Cats; Les Misérables; Phantom of the Opera; Miss Saigon.* Unsolicited scripts are read and considered (there is no literary manager, however) but new projects are rarely taken on.

Made In Wales

Chapter, Market Road, Canton, Cardiff CF5 1QE
☎029 2034 4737 Fax 029 2034 4738
Email madein.wales@virgin.net

Artistic Director *Jeff Teare*
Associate Director *Rebecca Gould*

FOUNDED 1982. Made In Wales is Wales' leading new writing development and production company. It has produced nearly 50 new plays, recently not only in Wales but also Ireland and England with a prospective Australian production in development. Runs various development programmes and workshops and offers a free script-reading service. Three recently produced scripts have been published by Parthian Books under the title, *New Welsh Drama*. 'Made In Wales is particularly concerned to develop and present work reflecting our multicultural society.'

Man in the Moon Theatre Ltd
392 Kings Road, Chelsea, London SW3 5UZ
☎020 7351 5701 Fax 020 7351 1873
Email manmoon@netcomuk.co.uk
Executive Director *Leigh Shine*
Literary Manager *Nick Eisen*
General Manager *John Downs*

FOUNDED 1982. Fringe theatre. In 1996, awarded the Guinness Ingenuity Award for creativity and innovation. Often tries to fit new plays into seasons such as 'Nationalism' and 'Family Values' and very keen to do rehearsed readings. Unsolicited scripts welcome; 'interested in submissions from first-time writers or writers in the initial stages of their career'. Particularly keen to consider plays which challenge the relationship between performer and audience. No unfinished scripts or treatments.

Manchester Library Theatre
See **Library Theatre Company**

Midland Arts Centre
See **MAC - The Centre for Birmingham**

N.T.C. Touring Theatre Company
The Playhouse, Bondgate Without, Alnwick, Northumberland NE66 1PQ
☎01665 602586 Fax 01665 605837
Email info@ntc.connectfree.co.uk
Contact *Gillian Hambleton*
Administrator *Anna Flood*

FOUNDED 1978. Formerly Northumberland Theatre Company. Winner of one of only two drama production franchises in the Northern region. Predominantly rural, small-scale touring company, playing to village halls and community centres throughout the Northern region, the Scottish Borders and countrywide. Productions range from established classics to new work and popular comedies, but must be appropriate to their audience. Unsolicited scripts welcome but are unlikely to be produced. All scripts are read and returned with constructive criticism within six months. Writers whose style is of interest may then be commissioned. The company encourages new writing and commissions when possible. Financial constraints restrict casting to a *maximum* of five.

New Vic Theatre
Etruria Road, Newcastle under Lyme, Staffordshire ST5 0JG
☎01782 717954 Fax 01782 712885
Artistic Director *Gwenda Hughes*

The New Vic is a purpose-built theatre-in-the-round. Plays to a fairly broad-based audience which tends to vary from one production to another. A high proportion are not regular theatre-goers and new writing has been one of the main ways of contacting new audiences. Synopses preferred to unsolicited scripts.

Newpalm Productions
26 Cavendish Avenue, London N3 3QN
☎020 8349 0802 Fax 020 8346 8257
Contact *Phil Compton*

Rarely produces new plays (*As Is* by William M. Hoffman, which came from Broadway to the Half Moon Theatre, was an exception to this). National tours of productions such as *Peter Pan (The Musical); Noises Off, Seven Brides for Seven Brothers* and *Rebecca*, at regional repertory theatres, are more typical examples of Newpalm's work. Unsolicited mss, both plays and musicals, are, however, welcome; scripts are preferable to synopses.

Nitro
6 Brewery Road, London N7 9NH
☎020 7609 1331 Fax 020 7609 1221
Email black.theatreco-op@virgin.net
Artistic Director *Felix Cross*

FOUNDED 1978. Formerly Black Theatre Co-op. Plays to a mixed audience, approximately 65% female. Usually tours nationally twice a year. 'Committed in the first instance to new writing by Black British writers and work which relates to the Black culture and experience throughout the Diaspora, although anything considered.' Unsolicited mss welcome.

Northcott Theatre
Stocker Road, Exeter, Devon EX4 4QB
☎01392 223999 Fax 01392 499641
Artistic Director *Ben Crocker*

FOUNDED 1967. The Northcott is the Southwest's principal subsidised repertory theatre, situated on the University of Exeter campus. Describes its audience as 'geographically diverse, with a core audience of AB1s (40–60 age range)'. Continually looking to broaden the base of its audience profile, targeting younger and/or non-mainstream theatregoers. Aims to develop, promote and produce quality new writing which reflects the life of the region and addresses the audience it serves. Generally works on a commission basis but occasionally options existing new work. Unsolicited mss welcome – current turnaround on script-reading service approximately three months and no mss can be returned unless a correct value s.a.e. is included with the original submission.

Northern Stage

Newcastle Playhouse, Barras Bridge, Newcastle upon Tyne NE1 7RH
☎0191 232 3366 Fax 0191 261 8093
Email directors@northernstage.com
Website www.northernstage.co.uk

Artistic Director *Alan Lyddiard*

A contemporary performance company whose trademarks are a strongly visual and physical style, international influences, appeal to young people and strongly linked programmes of community work. As likely to produce devised work as conventional new writing. Before submitting unsolicited scripts, please contact *Ed Robson*, Associate Director.

Norwich Puppet Theatre

St James, Whitefriars, Norwich, Norfolk NR3 1TN
☎01603 615564 Fax 01603 617578
Email norpuppet@hotmail.com
Website www.geocities.com/norwichpuppets

Artistic Director *Luis Boy*
General Manager *Ian Woods*

Plays to a young audience (aged 3–12) but developing shows for adult audiences interested in puppetry. All year round programme plus tours to schools and arts venues. Unsolicited mss welcome if relevant.

Nottingham Playhouse

Nottingham Theatre Trust, Wellington Circus, Nottingham NG1 5AF
☎0115 9474361 Fax 0115 9475759

Artistic Director *Giles Croft*

Aims to make innovation popular, and present the best of world theatre, working closely with the communities of Nottingham and Nottinghamshire. Unsolicited mss will be read. It normally takes about six months, however,

and 'we have never yet produced an unsolicited script. All our plays have to achieve a minimum of 60 per cent audiences in a 732-seat theatre. We have no studio.'

Nottingham Playhouse Roundabout Theatre in Education

Wellington Circus, Nottingham NG1 5AF
☎0115 9474361 Fax 0115 9539055
Email admin@roundabout.org.uk

Contact *Andrew Breakwell*

FOUNDED 1973. Theatre-in-Education company of the **Nottingham Playhouse**. Plays to a young audience aged 5–18 years of age. Some programmes are devised or adapted in-house, many are commissioned. Unable to resource the adequate response required for unsolicited scripts. 'We are committed to the encouragement of new writing as and when resources permit.'

Nuffield Theatre

University Road, Southampton, Hampshire SO17 1TR
☎023 8031 5500 Fax 023 8031 5511

Artistic Director *Patrick Sandford*
Script Executive *To be appointed*

Well known as a good bet for new playwrights, the Nuffield gets an awful lot of scripts. They do a couple of new main stage plays every season. Previous productions: *Exchange* by Yri Trifonov (trans. Michael Frayn) which transferred to the Vaudeville Theatre; *The Floating Light Bulb* Woody Allen (British première); new plays by Claire Luckham: *Dogspot; The Dramatic Attitudes of Miss Fanny Kemble;* and by Claire Tomalin: *The Winter Wife*. Open-minded about subject and style, producing musicals as well as straight plays. Also opportunities for some small-scale fringe work. Scripts preferred to synopses in the case of writers new to theatre. All will, eventually, be read 'but please be patient. We do not have a large team of paid readers. We read everything ourselves.'

Octagon Theatre Trust Ltd

Howell Croft South, Bolton, Lancashire BL1 1SB
☎01204 529407 Fax 01204 380110

Executive Director *Simon Stallworthy*

FOUNDED 1967. The Octagon Theatre has pursued a dynamic policy of commissioning new plays in recent years. These have been by both established writers such as Paul Abbott, Tom Elliott, Henry Livings and Les Smith as well as new and emerging writers through partnerships with organisations such as **North West Playwrights** and the national new writing company **Paines Plough**. Whilst there is no prescriptive 'house style' at the Octagon, the theatre is nevertheless keen to encourage the development of writers from the North West region, telling stories that will resonate with the local audience. Unfortunately, the theatre does not have a resident literary manager or readers and is therefore unable to read and respond to unsolicited scripts.

Orange Tree Theatre

1 Clarence Street, Richmond, Surrey TW9 2SA
☎020 8940 0141 Fax 020 8332 0369
Artistic Director *Sam Walters*

One of those theatre venues just out of London which are good for new writing, both full-scale productions and rehearsed readings. Main house productions from January 2000: *Winner Takes All* Georges Feydeau; *Hurting* David Lewis; *A Wife Without a Smile* Arthur Pinero; *Sperm Wars* David Lewis; *The House Among the Stars* Michel Tremblay; *Lips Together, Teeth Apart* Terrence McNally; *The Way of the World* William Congreve; *Low Flying Aircraft* Jane Coles; *The Last Thrash* David Cregan; *The Cassilis Engagement* St John Hankin. Unsolicited mss are read, but patience (and s.a.e.) required.

Out of Joint

20–24 Eden Grove, London N7 8EA
☎020 7609 0207 Fax 020 7609 0203
Email ojo@outofjoint.demon.co.uk
Director *Max Stafford-Clark*
Producer *Graham Cowley*
Literary Manager *Lee White*

FOUNDED 1993. Award-winning theatre company with new writing central to its policy. Produces new plays which reflect society and its concerns, placing an emphasis on education activity to attract young audiences. Welcomes unsolicited mss. Productions include: *Blue Heart* Caryl Churchill; *Our Lady of Sligo* and *The Steward of Christendom* Sebastian Barry; *Shopping and Fucking* and *Some Explicit Polaroids* Mark Ravenhill; *Drummers* Simon Bennett.

Oxford Stage Company

131 High Street, Oxford OX1 4DH
☎01865 723238 Fax 01865 790625
Website www.oxfordstage.co.uk
Artistic Director *Dominic Dromgoole*

A middle-scale touring company producing established and new plays. At least one new play or new adaptation a year. Due to forthcoming projects not considering unsolicited scripts at present.

Paines Plough – New Writing New Theatre

4th Floor, 43 Aldwych, London WC2B 4DA
☎020 7240 4533 Fax 020 7240 4534
Email paines.plough@dial.pipex.com
Artistic Director *Vicky Featherstone*
Literary Manager *Jessica Dromgoole*

Tours new plays nationally. Works with writers to develop their skills and voices through courses, workshops and a free script-reading service. Provides a supportive environment for commissioned writers to push themselves and challenge their craft. Welcomes new full-length scripts from UK writers. For script-reading service send two s.a.e.s for acknowledgement and return of script.

Palace Theatre, Watford

Clarendon Road, Watford, Hertfordshire WD1 1JZ
☎01923 235455 Fax 01923 819664
Contact *Artistic Director*

An important part of artistic and cultural policy is the active commissioning of new plays. Previous productions: *Diplomatic Wives* Louise Page; *Over A Barrel* Stephen Bill; *The Marriage of Figaro*; *The Barber of Seville* (adapt. Ranjit Bolt); Jon Canter's *The Baby*; *Borders of Paradise* by Sharman Macdonald; *Elton John's Glasses* by David Farr (winner of the 1997 Writers' Guild Best Regional Play award); *The Talented Mr Ripley* by Phyllis Nagy; *The Dark* by Jonathan Holloway and *The Late Middle Classes* by Simon Gray. Also supports local writers with workshops, play readings and script development.

Perth Repertory Theatre Ltd

185 High Street, Perth PH1 5UW
☎01738 472700 Fax 01738 624576
Email theatre@perth.org.uk
Website www.perth.org.uk/perth/theatre.htm
Artistic Director *Michael Winter*
General Manager *Paul Hackett*

FOUNDED 1935. Combination of one- to four-weekly repertoire of plays and musicals, incoming tours, studio productions and local out-touring. Unsolicited mss are read when time permits, but the timetable for return of scripts is lengthy. New plays staged by the company are usually commissioned under the SAC scheme.

Plymouth Theatre Royal
See **Theatre Royal**

Pola Jones Associates Ltd
14 Dean Street, London W1V 5AH
☎020 7439 1165 Fax 020 7437 3994
Contact *André Ptaszynski*
FOUNDED 1982. Comedy, musicals and sitcoms preferred. Previous productions have included: *Tommy*; *Crazy For You*; *Me and My Girl*; *Return To The Forbidden Planet*; *Chicago*; *West Side Story*; *From A Jack To A King*; *Spend Spend Spend*; *Fosse*. Also produces comedy for TV: *Tygo Road; Joking Apart; Chalk; Hidden Camera Show*. Unsolicited scripts welcome.

Polka Theatre for Children
240 The Broadway, Wimbledon, London SW19 1SB
☎020 8542 4258 Fax 020 8542 7723
Email polkatheatre@dial.pipex.com
Website www.polkatheatre.com
Artistic Director *Vicky Ireland*
Administrator *Stephen Midlane*
FOUNDED in 1967 and moved into its Wimbledon base in 1979. Leading children's theatre committed to commissioning and producing new plays. Programmes are planned two years ahead and at least three new plays are commissioned each year. 'Because of our specialist needs and fixed budgets, all our scripts are commissioned from established writers with whom we work very closely. Writers are selected via recommendation and previous work. We do not perform unsolicited scripts. Potential new writers' work is read and discussed on a regular basis; thus we constantly add to our pool of interesting and interested writers.'

Praxis Theatre Company Ltd
24 Wykeham Road, London NW4 2SU
☎020 8203 1916 Fax 020 8203 1916
Email praxisco@globalnet.co.uk
Website www.users.globalnet.co.uk/~praxisco
Artistic Director *Sharon Kennet*
FOUNDED 1993. Performs to a mixed European audience, 'crossing the divide between text-based theatre and visual theatre'. No unsolicited mss. Previous productions: *Seed*; *My Brother Whom I Love*; *The Sacred Penman*.

Queen's Theatre, Hornchurch
Billet Lane, Hornchurch, Essex RM11 1QT
☎01708 456118 Fax 01708 452348
Email info@queens-theatre.co.uk
Artistic Director *Bob Carlton*
The Queen's Theatre is a 500-seat producing theatre in the London Borough of Havering and within the M25. ESTABLISHED in 1953, the theatre has been located in its present building since 1975 and produces up to nine in-house productions per year, including pantomime. The Queen's has re-established a permanent core company of actor/musicians under the artistic leadership of Bob Carlton. Aims to produce distinctive and accessible performances in an identifiable house style focused upon actor/musician shows but, in addition, embraces straight plays, classics and comedies. 'New play/musical submissions are welcome and will be read and given a report.' Each year there is a large-scale community play commissioned from a local writer culminating in a summer event beside the theatre.

The Really Useful Group Ltd
22 Tower Street, London WC2H 9NS
☎020 7240 0880 Fax 020 7240 1204
Website www.reallyuseful.com

Commercial/West End theatre producers whose output has included *Jesus Christ Superstar; Sunset Boulevard; Joseph and the Amazing Technicolor Dreamcoat; Cats; Phantom of the Opera; Starlight Express; Daisy Pulls It Off; Lend Me a Tenor; Arturo Ui* and *Aspects of Love*.

Red Ladder Theatre Company
3 St Peter's Buildings, York Street, Leeds, West Yorkshire LS9 8AJ
☎0113 2455311 Fax 0113 2455351
Email wendy@redladder.co.uk
Artistic Director/Literary Manager
   Wendy Harris
Administrator *Janis Smyth*
FOUNDED 1968. Commissioning company touring 2–3 shows a year with a strong commitment to new work and new writers. Aimed at an audience of young people aged between 14–25 years who have little or no access to theatre. Performances held in youth clubs and similar venues where young people choose to meet. Recent productions: *Last Night* John Binnie; *Crush* Rosy Fordham; *Wise Guys* by Philip Osment, a co-production with Theatre Centre. The company has scripts in development with Mike Kenny and Noël Greig. While unsolicited scripts are not discouraged, the company is particularly keen to enter into a dialogue with writers with regard to creating new work for young people.'

Red Shift Theatre Company

TRG2 Trowbray House, 108 Weston Street,
London SE1 3QB
☎020 7378 9787　Fax 020 7378 9789
Email rstc@dircon.co.uk
Website www.rstc.dircon.co.uk

Contact *Jonathan Holloway, Artistic Director*
General Manager *Sophie Elliott*

FOUNDED 1982. Small-scale touring company
which plays to a theatre-literate audience.
Unlikely to produce an unsolicited script as
most work is commissioned. Welcomes contact with writers – 'we try to see their work'
– and receipt of c.v.s and treatments.
Occasionally runs workshops bringing new
scripts, writers and actors together. These can
develop links with a reservoir of writers who
may feed the company. Interested in new plays
with subject matter which is accessible to a
broad audience and concerns issues of importance; also new translations and adaptations.
1999–2000 production: *Hamlet: First Cut*, a
new version of the First Folio 'Hamlet'.

Ridiculusmus

10F Owen O'Cork Mill, Beersbridge Road,
Belfast BT5 5DX
☎028 9046 0630　Fax 028 9046 0620
Email Ridiculusmus@altavista.net
Website www.ridiculu.dircon.co.uk

Artistic Directors *Jon Hough, David Woods*

FOUNDED 1992. Touring company which
plays to a wide range of audiences. Productions
have included adaptations of *Three Men In a
Boat; The Third Policeman; At Swim Two Birds*
and original work: *The Exhibitionists; Yes, Yes,
Yes* and *Say Nothing*. Unsolicited scripts welcome but not political drama.

Royal Court Theatre/ English Stage Company Ltd

Sloane Square, London SW1W 8AS
☎020 7565 5050
Fax 020 7565 5002 (Literary office)
Website www.royalcourttheatre.com

Literary Manager *Graham Whybrow*

The English Stage Company was founded by
George Devine in 1956 to put on new plays.
John Osborne, John Arden, Arnold Wesker,
Edward Bond, Caryl Churchill, Howard
Barker and Michael Hastings are all writers this
theatre has discovered. Christopher Hampton
and David Hare have worked here in the literary department. 'The aim of the Royal Court
is to develop and perform the best in new writing for the theatre, encouraging writers from
all sections of society to address the problems
and possibilities of our times.'

Royal Exchange Theatre Company

St Ann's Square, Manchester M2 7DH
☎0161 833 9333　Fax 0161 832 0881
Website www.royalexchange.co.uk

Literary Manager *Sarah Frankcom*

FOUNDED 1976. The Royal Exchange has
developed a new writing policy which it finds
is attracting a younger audience to the theatre.
The company has produced new plays by
Shelagh Stephenson, Brad Fraser, Simon
Burke, Jim Cartwright, Peter Barnes and Alex
Finlayson. Also English and foreign classics,
modern classics, adaptations and new musicals.
The Royal Exchange receives 500–2000 scripts
a year. These are read by Sarah Frankcom and a
team of experienced readers. Only a tiny percentage is suitable, but a number of plays are
commissioned each year.

Royal Lyceum Theatre Company

Grindlay Street, Edinburgh EH3 9AX
☎0131 248 4800　Fax 0131 228 3955

Artistic Director *Kenny Ireland*
Administration Manager *Ruth Butterworth*
External Affairs Manager *Sadie McKinlay*

FOUNDED 1965. Repertory theatre which plays
to a mixed urban Scottish audience. Produces
classic, contemporary and new plays. Would
like to stage more new plays, especially
Scottish. No full-time literary staff to provide
reports on submitted scripts.

Royal National Theatre

South Bank, London SE1 9PX
☎020 7452 3333　Fax 020 7452 3350
Website www.nt-online.org

Literary Manager *Jack Bradley*

The majority of the National's new plays come
about as a result of direct commission or from
existing contacts with playwrights. There is no
quota for new work, though so far more than a
third of plays presented have been the work of
living playwrights. Writers new to the theatre
would need to be of exceptional talent to be
successful with a script here, though the Royal
National Theatre Studio helps a limited number of playwrights, through readings, workshops and discussions. In some cases a new play
is presented for a shorter-than-usual run in the
Cottesloe Theatre. Scripts considered (send
s.a.e).

Royal Shakespeare Company

Literary Office, Barbican Centre, London
EC2Y 8BQ
☎020 7382 2303 Fax 020 7382 2320
Website www.rsc.org.uk/
Artistic Director *Adrian Noble*
Literary Manager *Simon Reade*

The RSC is a classical theatre company based
in Stratford upon Avon, bringing its repertoire
into London at the Barbican Theatre for six
months of the year, and with residencies in
Newcastle and Plymouth. It also tours extensively – nationally and internationally.

As well as Shakespeare, English classics and
foreign classics in translation, new plays coun-
terpoint the RSC's repertory, especially those
which celebrate language. 'The literary department is proactive rather than reactive and seeks
out the plays and playwrights it wishes to commission. It will read all translations of classic
foreign works submitted, or of contemporary
works where the original writer and/or translator is known. It is unable to read unsolicited
work from less established writers. It can only
return scripts if an s.a.e. is enclosed with submission.'

7:84 Theatre Company Scotland

333 Woodlands Road, Glasgow G3 6NG
☎0141 334 6686 Fax 0141 334 3369
Email 7.84-theatre@btinternet.com
Artistic Director *Iain Reekie*
General Manager *Tessa Rennie*

FOUNDED 1973. One of Scotland's foremost
touring theatre companies committed to producing work that addresses current social, cultural and political issues. Recent productions
include commissions by Scottish playwrights
such as Stephen Greenhorn (*Dissent*); David
Greig (*Caledonia Dreaming*) and the Scottish
premières of Tony Kushner's *Angels in America*
and Athol Fugard's *Valley Song*. 'The company
is committed to a new writing policy that
encourages and develops writers at every level
of experience, to get new voices and strong
messages on to the stage.' Although happy to
read unsolicited scripts, 'it would be impossible
to respond in detail to everything that we
receive ... we simply do not have the resources
to make this possible'. New writing development has always been central to 7:84's core
activity and has included Summer Schools and
the 7:84 Writers Group. The company continues to be committed to this work and its
development.

Shared Experience Theatre

The Soho Laundry, 9 Dufours Place, London
W1V 1FE
☎020 7434 9248 Fax 020 7287 8763
Email admin@setheatre.co.uk
Joint Artistic Directors *Nancy Meckler,*
   Polly Teale

FOUNDED 1975. Varied audience depending on
venue, since this is a touring company. Recent
productions have included: *The Birthday Party*
Harold Pinter; *Sweet Sessions* Paul Godfrey;
Anna Karenina (adapt. Helen Edmundson);
Trilby & Svengali (adapt. David Fielder); *Mill on
the Floss* (adapt. Helen Edmundson); *The Danube*
Maria Irene Fornes; *Desire Under the Elms*
Eugene O'Neill; *War and Peace* (adapt. Helen
Edmundson); *The Tempest* William Shakespeare;
Jane Eyre (adapt. Polly Teale); *I Am Yours* Judith
Thompson; *The House of Bernarda Alba* (trans.
Rona Munro); *Mother Courage* (trans. Lee Hall).
No unsolicited mss. Primarily not a new writing
company but 'we are interested in innovative
new scripts'.

Sherman Theatre Company

Senghennydd Road, Cardiff CF24 4YE
☎029 2064 6901 Fax 029 2064 6902
Artistic Director *Phil Clark*

FOUNDED 1973. Theatre for Young People,
with main house and studio. Encourages new
writing; has produced 82 new plays in the last ten
years. Previous productions (all new plays)
include: *Incognito* Tracy Spottiswoode; *The
Colour of Light* Sheila Yeger; *A Woman at Risk*
Peter Tinniswood; *Something Beginning With ...*
Brendan Murray; *Chasing Harrison Ford* Keiron
Self; *Break, My Heart* Arnold Wesker. The company has presented four seasons of six new plays
live on stage and broadcast on BBC Radio
Wales, and four series of one-act lunchtime plays
on stage and then filmed for HTV Wales.
Priority will be given to Wales-based writers.

Show of Strength

Hebron House, Sion Road, Bedminster,
Bristol BS3 3BD
☎0117 9021356 Fax 0117 9021330
Artistic Director *Sheila Hannon*

FOUNDED 1986. Plays to an informal, younger
than average audience. Aims to stage at least one
new play each season with a preference for work
from Bristol and the South West. Will read
unsolicited scripts but a lack of funding means
they are unable to provide written reports.

Interested in full-length stage plays; 'we are undeterred by large casts'. OUTPUT *A Busy Day* Fanny Burney; *A Man and Some Women* Githa Sowerby; *Blue Murder* Peter Nichols and *Rough Music* James Wilson (both world premières). Also, three rehearsed readings of new work each season.

Snap People's Theatre Trust
Unit A, 2 The Causeway, Bishop's Stortford, Hertfordshire CM23 2Ej
☎01279 836200 Fax 01279 501472
Contacts *Andy Graham, Mike Wood*
FOUNDED 1979. Plays to young people (5–11; 12–19), and to the thirty-something-plus age group. Classic adaptations and new writing. Writers may submit unsolicited material. New writing is encouraged and should involve, be written for or by young people. 'Projects should reflect the writer's own beliefs, be thought-provoking, challenging and accessible.'

Soho Theatre Company
21 Dean Street, London W1V 6NE
☎020 7287 5060 Fax 020 7287 5061
Email writer@sohotheatre.com
Website www.sohotheatre.com
Artistic Director *Abigail Morris*
Literary Manager *Paul Sirett*
Dedicated to new writing, the company has an extensive research and development programme consisting of a free script reading service, workshops and readings. Also runs many courses for new writers. The company produces around four plays a year. Previous productions include: *Angels and Saints* Jessica Townsend, joint winner of the 1998 Peggy Ramsay Award; *Jump Mr Malinoff Jump* Toby Whithouse, winner of the 1998 Verity Bargate Award; *Gabriel* Moira Buffini, winner of the 1996 LWT Award; *Brothers of the Brush* Jimmy Murphy; *Kindertransporte* Diane Samuels. Runs the **Verity Bargate Award**, a biennial competition (see entry under **Prizes**).

Sphinx Theatre Company
25 Short Street, London SE1 8LJ
☎020 7401 9993 Fax 020 7401 9995
Email sphinxtheatre@demon.co.uk
Artistic Director *Sue Parrish*
General Manager *Amanda Rigali*
FOUNDED 1973. Tours new plays by women nationally to small and mid-scale venues. Synopses and ideas are welcome.

The Steam Industry
Finborough Theatre, 118 Finborough Road, London SW10 9ED
☎020 7244 7439 Fax 020 7835 1853
Artistic Director *Phil Willmott*
Director, Finborough Theatre
   Neil McPherson
Since June 1994, the Finborough Theatre has been a base for The Steam Industry who produce in and out of the building. Their output is diverse and prolific and includes a high percentage of new writing alongside radical adaptations of classics and musicals. The space is also available for a number of hires per year and the hire fee is sometimes negotiable to encourage innovative work. Unsolicited scripts are welcome but due to minimal resources it can take up to six months to respond. Send s.a.e. with material. The company regularly workshops new scripts at Monday-night play-readings and has developed new work by writers such as Chris Lee, Anthony Neilson, Naomi Wallace, Conor McPherson, Tony Marchant, Diane Samuels and Mark Ravenhill.

Swan Theatre
The Moors, Worcester WR1 3EF
☎01905 726969 Fax 01905 723738
Artistic Director *Jenny Stephens*
Repertory company producing a wide range of plays to a mixed audience coming largely from the City of Worcester and the county of Hereford and Worcester. A writing group meets at the theatre. Unsolicited scripts are discouraged.

Swansea Little Theatre Ltd
Dylan Thomas Theatre, Maritime Quarter, Gloucester Place, Swansea, West Glamorgan SA1 1TY
☎01792 473238
Contact *Annalie Williams* (Chair, Artistic Committee)
A wide variety of plays, from pantomime to the classics. New writing encouraged. New plays considered by the Artistic Committee.

Talawa Theatre Company Ltd
23/25 Great Sutton Street, London EC1V 0DN
☎020 7251 6644 Fax 020 7251 5969
Email hq@talawa.com
Website www.talawa.com
Artistic Director *Yvonne Brewster*
General Manager *Anthony Corriette*

FOUNDED 1985. Plays to an ABC audience of 60% black, 40% white across a wide age range depending upon the nature of productions and targeting. Previous productions include all-black performances of *The Importance of Being Earnest* and *Antony and Cleopatra*; plus Jamaican pantomime *Arawak Gold; The Gods Are Not to Blame; The Road* Wole Soyinka; *Beef, No Chicken* Derek Walcott; *Flying West* Pearl Cleage; *Othello* William Shakespeare. Restricted to new work from Black writers only. Occasional commissions, though these tend to go to established writers. 'Interested in the innovative, the modern classic with special reference to the African diasporic experience.' Runs a Black script development project. Talawa is funded by the **London Arts Board** (for three years).

Theatre Absolute

57–61 Corporation Street, Coventry
CV1 1GQ
☎024 7625 7380 Fax 024 7655 0680
Email julia@theatreabsolute.demon.co.uk
Website www.theatreabsolute.demon.co.uk
Artistic Director/Writer *Chris O'Connell*
Producer *Julia Negus*

FOUNDED 1992. An independent theatre company which commissions, produces and tours new plays which are based on a strong narrative text and aimed at audiences aged 15 and upwards. Productions: *Big Burger Chronicles; She's Electric; Car*, winner of an Edinburgh Fringe First Award 1999 and a *Time Out* Live Award – Best New Play on the Fringe 1999. Alongside the Belgrade Theatre, the company also runs The Writing House, a script development scheme funded by the National Lottery.

Theatre of Comedy Company

210 Shaftesbury Avenue, London WC2H 8DP
☎020 7379 3345 Fax 020 7836 8181
Creative Director *Richard Porter*

FOUNDED 1983 to produce new work as well as classics and revivals. Interested in strong comedy in the widest sense – Chekhov comes under the definition as does farce. Also has a light entertainment division, developing new scripts for television, namely situation comedy and series.

Theatre Royal, Plymouth

Royal Parade, Plymouth, Devon PL1 2TR
☎01752 668282 Fax 01752 225892
Email d.prescott@theatreroyal.demon.co.uk
Artistic Director *Simon Stokes*
Artistic Associate *David Prescott*

Stages small-, middle- and large-scale drama including musicals and music theatre. Commissions and produces new plays. Unsolicited scripts are read and responded to.

Theatre Royal Stratford East

Gerry Raffles Square, London E15 1BN
☎020 8534 7374 Fax 020 8534 8381
Associate Director *Kerry Michael*

Lively East London theatre, catering for a very mixed audience, both local and London-wide. Produces plays, musicals, youth theatre and local community plays/events, all of which is new work. Special interest in Asian and Black British work. New initiatives include developing contemporary British musicals. Unsolicited scripts which are fully completed and have never been produced are welcome. NB The theatre is closed for refurbishment and is developing work for its reopening in 2001.

Theatre Royal Windsor

Windsor, Berkshire SL4 1PS
☎01753 863444 Fax 01753 831673
Email info@theatreroyalwindsor.co.uk
Website www.kenwright.com
Executive Producer *Bill Kenwright*
Executive Director *Mark Piper*

Plays to a middle-class, West End-type audience. Produces thirteen plays a year and 'would be disappointed to do fewer than two new plays in a year; always hope to do half a dozen'. Modern classics, thrillers, comedy and farce. Only interested in scripts along these lines.

Theatre Workshop Edinburgh

34 Hamilton Place, Edinburgh EH3 5AX
☎0131 225 7942 Fax 0131 220 0112
Artistic Director *Robert Rae*

Plays to a young, broad-based audience with much of the work targeted towards particular groups or communities. OUTPUT has included adaptations of Gogol's *The Nose* and Aharon Appelfeld's *Badenheim 1939* – two community performance projects. Particularly interested in new work for children and young people. Frequently engages writers for collaborative/devised projects. Commissions a significant amount of new writing for a wide range of contexts, from large-cast community plays to small-scale professional tours. Favours writers based in Scotland, producing material relevant to a contemporary Scottish audience. Member of Scottish Script Centre to whom it refers senders of unsolicited scripts.

Tiebreak Touring Theatre

Heartsease High School, Marryat Road,
Norwich, Norfolk NR7 9DF
☎01603 435209 Fax 01603 435184
Email tie.break@virgin.net
Website freespace.virgin.net/tie.break

Artistic Director *David Farmer*

FOUNDED 1981. Specialises in high-quality theatre for children and young people, touring
schools, youth centres, museums and festivals.
Productions: *Fast Eddy; Breaking the Rules; George
Speaks; Frog and Toad; Love Bites; Singing in the
Rainforest; Boadicea – The Movie; Dinosaurs on Ice;
The Invisible Boy; My Friend Willy; The Ugly
Duckling; Almost Human.* New writing encouraged. Interested in low-budget, small-cast material only. School, educational and socially relevant
material of special interest. Scripts welcome.

Torch Theatre

St Peter's Road, Milford Haven,
Pembrokeshire SA73 2BU
☎01646 694192 Fax 01646 698919
Email torchtheatre@cwcom.net
Website www.torchtheatre.org

Artistic Director *Peter Doran*

FOUNDED 1976. Plays to a mixed audience hard
to attract to new work on the whole.
Committed to new work but financing has
become somewhat prohibitive. Small-cast pieces
with broad appeal welcome. Previous productions: *Frankie and Tommy; School for Wives; Tess of
the d'Urbervilles.* The repertoire runs from
Ayckbourn to Friel. Scripts sometimes welcome.

Traverse Theatre

Cambridge Street, Edinburgh EH1 2ED
☎0131 228 3223 Fax 0131 229 8443
Email john@traverse.co.uk
Website www.traverse.co.uk

Artistic Director *Philip Howard*
Literary Director *John Tiffany*
Literary Associate *Katherine Mendelsohn*
Literary Assistant *Hannah Rye*

The Traverse is Scotland's new writing theatre,
with a particular commitment to producing
new Scottish plays. However, it also has a
strong international programme of work in
translation and visiting companies. Previous
productions: *King of the Fields* Stuart Paterson;
The Speculator David Greig; *The Juju Girl*
Aileen Ritchie; *Perfect Days* Liz Lochhead.
Unsolicited scripts accepted only after an initial
phone call or letter to *Hannah Rye*, Literary
Assistant.

Trestle Theatre Company

Birch Centre, Hill End Lane, St Albans,
Hertfordshire AL4 0RA
☎01727 850950 Fax 01727 855558

Artistic Director *Toby Wilsher*

FOUNDED 1981. Physical, mask theatre for
mostly student-based audiences (18–36 years).
From 2000 working with a writer-in-residence
to create new writing for physical/visual theatre. No unsolicited scripts.

Tricycle Theatre

269 Kilburn High Road, London NW6 7JR
☎020 7372 6611 Fax 020 7328 0795

Artistic Director *Nicolas Kent*

FOUNDED 1980. Plays to a very mixed audience,
in terms of both culture and class. Previous productions: *Pecong* Steve Carter; *A Love Song for
Ulster* Bill Morrison; *Three Hotels* Jon Robin
Baitz; *Nuremberg* adapt. from transcripts of the
trials by Richard Norton-Taylor; *Srebrenica*
adapt. Nicolas Kent; *The Stephen Lawrence
Enquiry – The Colour of Justice* adapt. from the
enquiry transcripts by Richard Norton-Taylor.
New writing welcome from women and ethnic
minorities (particularly Black, Asian and Irish).
Looks for a strong narrative drive with popular
appeal, not 'studio' plays. Can only return scripts
if postage coupons or s.a.e. are enclosed with
original submission.

Tron Theatre Company

63 Trongate, Glasgow G1 5HB
☎0141 552 3748 Fax 0141 552 6657
Email neil@tron.co.uk
Website www.tron.co.uk

General Manager *Neil Murray*

FOUNDED 1981. Plays to a broad cross-section of
Glasgow and beyond, including international
tours. Recent productions: *Sea Urchins* Sharman
Macdonald; *Mate in Three* Vittorio Franceschi;
Good C. P. Taylor; *Macbeth*; *Lavochkin-5* (*La Funf
in der Luft*) Alexei Shipenko, trans. Iain
Heggie/Irina Brown; *Further Than the Furthest
Thing* Zinnie Harris (co-production with the
Royal National Theatre). Interested in ambitious
plays by UK and international writers. No unso-
licited mss.

The Unearthly Theatre Company

150 Havelock Street, Preston, Lancashire
PR1 7NJ
☎01772 886003 Fax 01772 250556
Email moship@msn.com

Contacts *James Miley, Gary Nixon, Michael Moss*

FOUNDED 1997. A new company operating from the University of Central Lancashire. Produces three plays a year, both contemporary and period. OUTPUT includes a new adaption of *Fall of the House of Usher* and a highly successful production of *Our Boys*. Material is welcome; approach should be made in writing, enclosing an s.a.e. to ensure a response.

Unicorn Theatre for Children
St Mark's Studios, Chillingworth Road, London N7 8QJ
☎020 7700 0702 Fax 020 7700 3870
Email <name>@unicorntheatre.com
Website www.unicorntheatre.com
Artistic Director *Tony Graham*

FOUNDED 1947 as a touring company, and was resident at the Arts Theatre from 1967 until April 1999 when it moved to the Pleasance Theatre in north London. Plays mainly to children between the ages of 4–12. Previous productions: *The Lost Child* by Mike Kenny; *Cinderella, Hansel and Gretel* by Stuart Paterson; *Jemima Puddleduck and her Friends* adapt. by Adrian Mitchell; *Something Beginning With ...* by Brendan Murray; *Fairytaleheart* by Philip Ridley. New work in 2000 from Pomme Clayton, Charles Way and David Wood.

Upstairs at the Gatehouse
See **Ovation Productions** under **Film, TV and Video Production Companies**

Charles Vance Productions
Hampden House, 2 Weymouth Street, London W1N 3FD
☎020 7636 4343 Fax 020 7636 2323
Email cvtheatre@aol.com
Contact *Charles Vance, Jill Streatfeild*

In the market for medium-scale touring productions and summer-season plays. Hardly any new work and no commissions but writing of promise stands a good chance of being passed on to someone who might be interested in it. Occasional try-outs for new work in the Sidmouth repertory theatre. Send s.a.e. for return of mss.

Warehouse Theatre
Dingwall Road, Croydon CR0 2NF
☎020 8681 1257 Fax 020 8688 6699
Email warehous@dircon.co.uk
Website www.warehousetheatre.co.uk
Artistic Director *Ted Craig*

South London's new writing theatre (adjacent to East Croydon railway station) seats 100–120 and produces up to six new plays a year. Also co-produces with, and hosts, selected touring companies who share the theatre's commitment to new work. Continually building upon a tradition of discovering and nurturing new writers, with activities including a monthly writers' workshop and the annual **International Playwriting Festival**. Also hosts youth theatre workshops and Saturday morning children's theatre. Previous productions: *Iona Rain* by Peter Moffat and *Fat Janet is Dead* by Simon Smith (both past winners of the International Playwriting Festival); *The Blue Garden* Peter Moffat; *Coming Up* James Martin Charlton and M. G. 'Monk' Lewis; *The Castle Spectre* edited by Phil Willmott; *Dick Barton Special Agent* and *Dick Barton and the Curse of the Pharaoh's Tomb* Phil Willmott. Unsolicited scripts welcome but it is more advisable to submit plays through the theatre's International Playwriting Festival.

Watford Palace Theatre
See **Palace Theatre**

West Yorkshire Playhouse
Playhouse Square, Leeds, West Yorkshire LS2 7UP
☎0113 2137800 Fax 0113 2137250
Website www.wyp.co.uk

Committed to programming new writing as part of its overall policy. Before sending an unsolicited script please phone or write. The Playhouse does readings and workshops on new plays with writers from all over Britain and also has strong links with local writers and Yorkshire Playwrights. Premières include: *A Passionate Woman* Kay Mellor; *Fathers Day* Maureen Lawrence; *The Beatification of Area Boy* Wole Soyinka; *The Winter Guest* Sharman Macdonald; *You'll Have Had Your Hole* Irvine Welsh.

Whirligig Theatre
14 Belvedere Drive, Wimbledon, London SW19 7BY
☎020 8947 1732 Fax 020 8879 7648
Email whirligig-theatre@virgin.net
Contact *David Wood*

One play a year in major theatre venues, usually a musical for primary school audiences and weekend family groups. Interested in scripts which exploit the theatrical nature of children's tastes. Previous productions: *The See-Saw Tree; The Selfish Shellfish; The Gingerbread Man; The Old Man of Lochnagar; The Ideal Gnome Expedition; Save the Human; Dreams of Anne Frank; Babe, the Sheep-Pig*.

Michael White Productions Ltd

See **MW Entertainments Ltd** under **Film, TV and Video Production Companies**

White Bear Theatre Club

138 Kennington Park Road, London SE11 4DJ
Administration: 3 Dante Road, Kennington, London SE11 4RB
☎020 7793 9193 Fax 020 7293 9193

Contact *Michael Kingsbury*
Administrator *Julia Parr*

FOUNDED 1988. OUTPUT primarily new work for an audience aged 20–35. Unsolicited scripts welcome, particularly new work with a keen eye on contemporary issues, though not agitprop. Holds readings throughout the year. *Absolution* by Robert Sherwood was nominated by the Writers' Guild for 'Best Fringe Play'.

Windsor Theatre Royal

See **Theatre Royal Windsor**

The Young Vic

66 The Cut, London SE1 8LZ
☎020 7633 0133   Fax 020 7928 1585

Artistic Director *David Lan*

FOUNDED 1970. The Young Vic produces adventurous and demanding work for an audience with a youthful spirit. The main house is one of London's most exciting spaces and seats up to 500. In addition, a smaller, entirely flexible space, The Young Vic Studio, seats 100 and is used for experiment, performance, rehearsals and installations. NB Future policy on submissions uncertain at the time of going to press as new artistic director, David Lan, was not due to take over from Tim Supple until July 2000.

Freelance Rates – Subsidised Repertory Theatres (excluding Scotland)

The following minimum rates were negotiated by the Writers' Guild and Theatrical Management Association and are set out under the TMA/Writers Agreement.

Theatres are graded by a 'middle range salary level' (MRSL), worked out by dividing the 'total basic salaries' paid by the total number of 'actor weeks' in the year.

	MRSL 1	MRSL 2	MRSL 3
Commissioned Play			
Commission payment	£3,266	£2,672	£2,079
Delivery payment	£1,485	£1,187	£1,187
Acceptance payment	£1,485	£1,187	£1,187
Total payment	*£6,236*	*£5,046*	*£4,453*
Non-Commissioned Play			
Delivery payment	£4,752	£3,859	£3,265
Acceptance payment	£1,485	£1,187	£1,187
Total payment	*£6,237*	*£5,046*	*£4,452*
Rehearsal Attendance	£43.83	£38.45	£35.44

Options

UK (excluding West End)	£1,853
West End/USA	£3,089
Rest of the World (English speaking productions)	£2,471

Festivals

Aberystwyth International Poetry Festival & Summer School

Aberystwyth Arts Centre, Penglais, Aberystwyth SY23 3DE
☎01970 622889/622883
Email lla@aber.ac.uk

FOUNDED 1996. Annual week-long festival. Previous guest writers have included Jack Mapanje, Jo Shapcott and Menna Elfyn. Also Summer School courses 'for anyone who enjoys writing – young or old, from published poets to beginners'.

Aldeburgh Poetry Festival

Reading Room Yard, The Street, Brockdish, Diss, Norfolk IP21 4JZ
☎01379 668345 Fax 01379 668844
Festival Director *Naomi Jaffa*

Now in its twelfth year, an annual international festival of contemporary poetry held over one weekend each November in Aldeburgh and attracting large audiences. Regular features include a four-week residency leading up to the festival, poetry readings, children's event, workshops, public masterclass, lecture, performance spot and the festival prize for the year's best first collection (see entry under **Prizes**).

Arundel Festival

The Arundel Festival Society Ltd, The Mary Gate, Arundel, West Sussex BN18 9AT
☎01903 883690/Textphone: 01903 889900 Fax 01903 884243
Email arundel.festival@argonet.co.uk
Website www.argonet.co.uk/arundel.festival
Coordinator *Victoria Moles*

Annual ten-day summer festival (25 August to 3 September in 2000). Events include small-scale theatre, open-air theatre in Arundel Castle, concerts with internationally known artists, jazz, visual arts and active fringe.

Aspects Literature Festival

North Down Borough Council, Tower House, 34 Quay Street, Bangor BT20 5ED
☎01247 278032 Fax 01247 467744
Festival Director *Kenneth Irvine*
Administrator *Paula Clamp*

FOUNDED 1992. 'Ireland's Premier Literary Festival' is held at the end of September (26th –

30th in 2000) and celebrates the richness and diversity of living Irish writers with occasional special features on past generations. It draws upon all disciplines – fiction (of all types), poetry, theatre, non-fiction, cinema, song-writing, etc. It also includes a day of writing for young readers and sends writers to visit local schools during the festival. Highlights of recent festivals include appearances by Bernard MacLaverty, Marion Keyes, Alice Taylor, Frank Delaney, Seamus Heaney, Brian Keenan, Fergal Keane.

Bath Fringe Festival

The Bell, 103 Walcot Street, Bath BA1 5BW
☎01225 480079 Fax 01225 427441
Chair *John Wood*

FOUNDED 1981. Complementing the international music festival, the Fringe presents theatre, poetry, jazz, blues, comedy, cabaret, street performance and more in venues, parks and streets of Bath during late May and early June.

Bath Literature Festival

5 Broad Street, Bath BA1 5LJ
☎01225 462231 Fax 01225 445551
Director *Tim Joss*
Contact *Rachel Cottam (Head of Literature)*

FOUNDED 1995. Annual festival (3–11 March in 2001). Wide range of debates, performances, storytelling, author discussions and workshops. 2000 saw the inauguration of a Virtual Festival, running alongside and interacting with the 'real' Festival. The Virtual Festival featured online debates, critical commentary, chatrooms, a major collaborative writing project, an online poetry jam and games. Previous guests have included Andrew Motion, Edward Fox, Susie Orbach, Helen Dunmore, Richard Ingrams and Prue Leith.

Belfast Festival at Queen's

Festival House, 25 College Gardens, Belfast BT9 6BS
☎028 9066 7687 Fax 028 9066 3733
Email festival@qub.ac.uk
Website www.qub.ac.uk/festival
Executive Director *Robert Agnew*

FOUNDED 1964. Annual three-week festival held in the autumn (27 October to 12 November in 2000). Organised by Queen's University in association with the **Arts Council of Northern Ireland**, the festival covers a wide variety of events, including literature. Programme available in September.

Between the Lines – Belfast Literary Festival

Crescent Arts Centre, 2–4 University Road, Belfast BT7 1NH
☎028 9024 2338 Fax 028 9024 6748
Email info@crescentarts.org
Website www.crescentarts.org

Festival Director *Louise Emerson*

FOUNDED 1998. Annual 7–10-day international event held in March. Features readings, workshops, open platforms, quizzes and performance. All genres covered: playwriting, prose, poetry, screenwriting, etc. and special events for children. Previous guests include Patricia Duncker, Carol Shields, Ian Rankin, Jean Binta Breeze, Jamie McKendrick, Fay Weldon, Ali Smith. Telephone to join free mailing list.

Beyond the Border International Storytelling Festival

St Donats Arts Centre, St Donats Castle, Vale of Glamorgan CF61 1WF
☎01446 799100 Fax 01446 799101

Festival Directors *David Ambrose, Ben Haggarty*

FOUNDED 1993. Annual event held over the first weekend in July when storytellers from around the world gather in the grounds of a medieval cliff-top castle. Features formal and informal story sessions, ballad singing, story-walks, folk and world music, dance and a full programme of events for children.

Book Now!

Langholm Lodge, 146 Petersham Road, Richmond, Surrey TW10 6UX
☎020 8831 6138 Fax 020 8891 7787
Email n.cutting@richmond.gov.uk
Website www.richmond.gov.uk/leisure

Director *Nigel Cutting*

FOUNDED 1992. Annual festival which runs throughout the month of November, administered by the Arts Section of Richmond Council. Principal focus is on poetry and serious fiction, but events also cover biography, writing for theatre, children's writing. Programme includes readings, discussions, workshops, debates, exhibitions, schools events. Writers to appear at past festivals include A. S. Byatt, Penelope Lively, Benjamin Zephaniah, Sir Dirk Bogarde,

Roger McGough, Rose Tremain, John Mortimer and Sean Hughes.

Bradford Festival

The Wool Exchange, Hustlergate, Bradford, West Yorkshire BD1 1RE
☎01274 309199 Fax 01274 724213
Email info@bradfordfestival.yorks.com
Website www.bradfordfestival.yorks.com

Directors *Mark Fielding, Allan Brack*

FOUNDED 1987. May to July for six weeks. The 'largest, award-winning annual community arts festival in the country'. Includes the Literature Festival coordinated by Bradford Libraries' Reader to Reader Project; contact *Tom Palmer* (☎01274 754096; email tom.palmer@bradford.gov.uk).

Brighton Festival

Festival Office, 12a Pavilion Buildings, Castle Square, Brighton, East Sussex BN1 1EE
☎01273 700747 Fax 01273 707505
Email info@brighton-festival.org.uk
Website www.brighton-festival.org.uk

Contact *General Manager*

FOUNDED 1967. For 24 days every May, Brighton hosts England's largest mixed arts festival. Music, dance, theatre, film, opera, literature, comedy and exhibitions. Literary enquiries will be passed to the literature officer. Deadline October for following May.

Bristol Poetry Festival

The Poetry Can, Unit 11, 20–22 Hepburn Road, Bristol BS2 8UD
☎0117 9426976 Fax 0117 9441478
Email festival@poetrycan.demon.co.uk
Website www.poetrycan.demon.co.uk

Festival Director *Hester Cockcroft*

FOUNDED 1996. Annual festival taking place across the city throughout October. A celebration of the best in contemporary poetry, from readings and performances to cabaret and multimedia. Local, national and international poetry is showcased and explored in all its manifestations, with events for everyone including performances and workshops, competitions and exhibitions, public poetry interventions, community work and cross art form and digital projects. Telephone for further details.

Broadstairs Dickens Festival

8 Stone Road, Broadstairs, Kent CT10 1DY
☎01843 601364

Organiser *Priscilla Foot*

FOUNDED 1937 to commemorate the 100th anniversary of Charles Dickens' first visit to Broadstairs in 1837, which he continued to visit until 1859. The Festival lasts for eight days and events include an opening gala entertainment of words and music, a parade, a performance of a Dickens play (*David Copperfield* in 2000), a garden party, duels, melodramas, Dickens readings, a Victorian cricket match, Victorian sea bathing, talks, music hall, three-day Victorian country fair. Costumed Dickensian ladies in crinolines with top-hatted escorts promenade during the week.

Bury St Edmunds Festival

Borough Offices, Angel Hill, Bury St Edmunds, Suffolk IP33 1XB
☎01284 756933/4 Fax 01284 756932
Email kevin.appleby@burybo.stedsbc.gov.uk
Website www.stedmundsbury.gov.uk/buryfest

Contact *Kevin Appleby, Festival Manager*

FOUNDED 1986. ANNUAL 17-day spring festival in various venues throughout this historic East Anglian town and outlying areas. Programme features orchestral concerts, chamber music, jazz, world music, drama, dance, comedy and exhibitions. 2000 highlights included James Galway, the London Mozart Players, the Royal Liverpool Philharmonic Orchestra, The Black Dyke Band, Ken Russell and BBC Music Live.

Buxton Festival

5 The Square, Buxton, Derbyshire SK17 6AZ
☎01298 70395 Fax 01298 72289
Email www.buxtonfestival.co.uk

Contact *General Manager*

FOUNDED 1979. Annual two-week festival held in July. Rarely performed operas are staged in Buxton Opera House and the programme is complemented by a wide variety of other musical events, including recitals, Young Artists series, festival masses, chamber music and cabarets. Also, the Buxton Jazz Festival.

Canterbury Festival

Christ Church Gate, The Precincts, Canterbury, Kent CT1 2EE
☎01227 452853 Fax 01227 781830
Email jo@canterburyfestival.co.uk

Festival Director *Mark Deller*

FOUNDED 1984. Annual two-week festival held in October. A mixed programme of events including talks by visiting authors, readings and storytelling, walks, concerts in the cathedral, jazz, masterclasses, drama, visual arts, opera, film, cabaret and dance.

The Cheltenham Festival of Literature

Town Hall, Imperial Square, Cheltenham, Gloucestershire GL50 1QA
☎01242 521621 Fax 01242 256457
Email sarahsm@cheltenham.gov.uk
Website www.cheltenhamfestivals.co.uk

Festival Organiser *Sarah Smyth*

FOUNDED 1949. Annual festival held in October. The first purely literary festival of its kind, this festival has over the past decade developed from an essentially local event into the largest and most popular in Europe. A wide range of events including talks and lectures, poetry readings, novelists in conversation, exhibitions, discussions and a large bookshop.

Chester Literature Festival

8 Abbey Square, Chester CH1 2HU
☎01244 319985 Fax 01244 341200

Chairman *John Elsley*

FOUNDED 1989. Annual festival always held in early October. Events include international and nationally known writers, as well as events by local literary groups. There is a Literary Lunch, events for children, workshops, competitions, etc. Free mailing list.

Chichester Festivities

Canon Gate House, South Street, Chichester, West Sussex PO19 1PU
☎01243 785718 Fax 01243 528356

Festival Administrator *Amanda Sharp*

FOUNDED in 1975 to celebrate the 900th anniversary of Chichester Cathedral, which remains the principal venue for concerts (classical and jazz) and lectures. Subsequently became an annual event, now in its 26th year. Events also include chamber recitals, literary talks, comedy, exhibitions, films, theatre and outdoor events in other venues, notably Goodwood House and Racecourse, the latter the setting for a military tattoo and fireworks spectacular.

City Voice - a festival of words

Library HQ, 32 York Road, Leeds, West Yorkshire LS9 8TD
☎0113 2143341 Fax 0113 2143339
Email jane.stubbs@leeds.gov.uk

Festival Director *Sean Burn*

FOUNDED in 1997 by the Leeds **Word Arena** and Leeds Library & Information Services, City Voice focuses on new writing and reading and is held at the beginning of June. Strongly, but not exclusively, features commissioned new writing by Leeds-based writers. Previous events have included a commissioned sculpture based on readings, workshops for writing tutors and open spots in libraries. Visiting authors to-date include Jean Binta Breeze, Patricia Duncker and Courttia Newland. Call to join free mailing list.

Dartington Literary Festival
See **Ways With Words**

Dorchester Festival
Dorchester Arts Centre, School Lane, The Grove, Dorchester, Dorset DT1 1XR
☎01305 266926 Fax 01305 261589
Contact *Artistic Director*
FOUNDED 1996. A biennial four-day festival over early May Bank Holiday weekend (next to be held in 2002) which includes performing, media and visual arts, with associated educational and community projects in the three weeks around the Festival. Includes a wide range of events, in many venues, for all age groups, including some literature and poetry.

Dublin Writers' Festival
Irish Writers' Centre, 19 Parnell Square, Dublin 1, Republic of Ireland
☎00 353 1 872 1302
Website www.writerscentre.ie

Biennial festival held in September. Features conference sessions, public interviews, debates, readings and exhibitions, with some of the world's leading authors in attendance.

Dumfries and Galloway Arts Festival
Gracefield Arts Centre, 28 Edinburgh Road, Dumfries DG1 1JQ
☎01387 260447
Festival Organiser *Beryl Jago*
FOUNDED 1980. Annual week-long festival held at the end of May with a variety of events including classical and folk music, theatre, dance, literary events and exhibitions.

Durham Literary Festival
Durham City Arts, Byland Lodge, Hawthorn Terrace, Durham City DH1 4TD
☎0191 301 8245 Fax 0191 301 8821
Website www.durhamcityarts.demon.co.uk
Contact *The Director*
FOUNDED 1989. Annual 2–3-week festival held

in June at various locations in the city. Workshops, plus performances, cabaret, and other events.

Edinburgh International Book Festival
Scottish Book Centre, 137 Dundee Street, Edinburgh EH11 1BG
☎0131 228 5444 Fax 0131 228 4333
Email admin@edbookfest.co.uk
Website www.edbookfest.co.uk
Director *Faith Liddell*
FOUNDED 1983. Europe's largest and liveliest public book event, now taking place on an annual basis. Held during the first fortnight of the Edinburgh International Festival, it presents an extensive programme for both adults and children including discussions, readings, lectures, demonstrations and workshops.

Exeter Festival
Festival Office, Civic Centre, Exeter, Devon EX1 1JN
☎01392 265200 Fax 01392 265366
Website www.thisisexeter.co.uk
Festival Organiser *Lesley Maynard*
FOUNDED 1980. Annual two-week summer festival with a variety of events including concerts, theatre, dance and exhibitions.

Grayshott and Hindhead Literary Festival
Little Nutcombe, Portsmouth Road, Hindhead, Surrey GU26 6AQ
☎01428 606689 Fax 01428 605665
Festival Organiser *Denise McCulloch*
FOUNDED 1995. Annual festival which runs over a weekend in mid-September. Although there will not be a festival in 2000, it is hoped it will take place in 2001. The programme features a mix of workshops, lectures and presentations covering classic and contemporary literature and poetry, travel, comedy, creative and script writing and children's/family events.

Greenwich & Docklands International Festival
6 College Approach, London SE10 9HY
☎020 8305 1818 Fax 020 8305 1188
Email info@festival.org
Website www.festival.org
Director *Bradley Hemmings*
FOUNDED 1970. Annual summer festival. Features a wide variety of events, including

world music, theatre, dance, classical music, jazz, comedy, art, literature and free open-air events.

Guildford Book Festival
c/o Arts Office, University of Surrey, Guildford, Surrey GU2 5XH
☎01483 879167 Fax 01483 300803
Email s.wallach@surrey.ac.uk
Website www.guildford.org.uk
Book Festival Organiser *Glenis Pycraft*

FOUNDED 1990. A ten-day celebration of books and writing held annually, during the autumn half-term, throughout the town. The programme includes literary lunches, poetry readings, a writer-in-residence, children's events, the Annual University Poetry Lecture, writing workshops and competitions, and bookshop events.

Hallam Literature Festival and Book Fair
School of Cultural Studies, Sheffield Hallam University, 32 Colegiate Crescent Campus, Sheffield S10 2BP
☎0114 2252228 Fax 0114 2254403
Festival Coordinator *E. A. Markham*

FOUNDED 1997. The second festival, held in 1999, featured critics and literary journalists reflecting the range of the university's Creative Writing programme, book launches, stage readings of new plays, poetry readings, discussions on the short story and televised debates between writers. The next festival is to be held in 2001.

Haringey Literature Festival
Haringey Arts Council, The Chocolate Factory, Unit 104 Building B, Clarendon Road, London N22 6XJ
☎020 8365 7500 Fax 020 8365 8686
Festival Organiser *Dana Captainino*

FOUNDED 1995. Annual festival which runs from March to October. The programme is a mixture of poetry and literature in the form of readings, discussions, workshops and masterclasses. Writers who have appeared at past festivals include: Anna Pavord, Louis de Bernières, Nick Hornby, Blake Morrison, Bernice Rubens, James Kelman, Jean Binta Breeze, Beryl Bainbridge and Deborah Moggach.

Harrogate International Festival
1 Victoria Avenue, Harrogate, North Yorkshire HG1 1EQ
☎01423 562303 Fax 01423 521264
Email info@harrogate-festival.org.uk

Website www.harrogate-festival.org.uk
Festival Director *William Culver Dodds*
Administrator *Fiona Goh*

FOUNDED 1966. Annual two-week festival at the end of July and beginning of August. Events include international symphony orchestras, chamber concerts, ballet, celebrity recitals, contemporary dance, opera, drama, jazz, comedy plus an international street theatre festival.

Hastings International Poetry Festival
'The Snoring Cat, 136 Harold Road, Hastings, East Sussex TN35 5NN
Contact *Josephine Austin*

FOUNDED 1968. Annual weekend poetry festival held in November in the Marina Pavilion in St Leonards-on-Sea. Runs the Hastings National Poetry Competition; entry forms available from the address above.

Hay Children's Festival of the Arts
15 Knowle Avenue, Burley, Leeds, West Yorkshire LS4 2PQ
☎0113 2304661 Fax 0113 2304661
Email caroline.wylie@virgin.net
Website www.hay-on-wye.co.uk/cfestival
Festival Director *Caroline Wylie*

FOUNDED 1994. Annual four-day festival of the arts in Hay-on-Wye for children aged 3–14 years presenting a unique programme of arts workshops, visiting best-selling authors and children's theatre. Brochure/booking form available mid-April.

The Hay Festival
See **The Sunday Times Hay Festival**

Huddersfield Poetry Festival
The Word Hoard, Kirklees Media Centre, 7 Northumberland Street, Huddersfield, West Yorkshire HD1 1RL
☎01484 452070 Fax 01484 455049
Email hoard@zoo.co.uk

Twice-yearly event consisting of a spring season in March/April of around four/six events combined with a participatory multi-arts collaborative project; and four days of writing workshops and performances in October exploring particular themes. Also occasional one-off events. Though very interested in local writers, the festival has a cosmopolitan outlook and features related performing arts including music, theatre and the visual arts.

Hull Literature Festival

City Arts, Central Library, Albion Street,
Kingston upon Hull HU1 3TF
☎01482 616875/6 Fax 01482 616827
Contact *City Arts Unit*
FOUNDED 1992. Annual festival running in
November.

Ilkley Literature Festival

The Manor House, Ilkley, West Yorkshire
LS29 9DT
☎01943 601210 Fax 01943 817079
Email ilf@pop3.poptel.org.uk
Director *Dominic Gregory*
FOUNDED 1973. Major literature festival in the
north with events running throughout the
year. Large-scale festival in autumn each year.
Runs an open poetry competition. Telephone
to join free mailing list.

The International Festival of Mountaineering Literature

Bretton Hall College of the University of
Leeds, West Bretton, Wakefield, West
Yorkshire WF4 4LG
☎01924 830261 Fax 01924 832040
Email tgifford@bretton.ac.uk
Director *Terry Gifford*
FOUNDED 1987. Annual one-day festival held
at the end of November celebrating recent
books, commissioning new writing, overviews
of national literatures, debates of issues, discussion with Chair of Judges of the adjudication of
the annual **Boardman Tasker Award** for the
best mountaineering book of the year.
Announces the winner of the festival writing
competition run in conjunction with *High*
magazine. Write to join free mailing list.

International Playwriting Festival

Warehouse Theatre, Dingwall Road,
Croydon CR0 2NF
☎020 8681 1257 Fax 020 8688 6699
Email warehous@dircon.co.uk
Website www.warehousetheatre.co.uk
Acting Festival Administrator *Carolyn Braby*
FOUNDED 1985. Annual competition for full-
length unperformed plays, judged by a panel of
theatre professionals. Finalists given rehearsed
readings during the festival week in November.
Entries welcome from all parts of the world.
Scripts plus two s.a.e.s (one script-sized) should
reach the theatre by the end of June, accompanied by an entry form (available from the
theatre). Previous winners produced at the

theatre: Kevin Hood *Beached*; Guy Jenkin
Fighting for the Dunghill; James Martin Charlton
Fat Souls; Ellen Fox *Conversations with George
Sandburgh After a Solo Flight Across the Atlantic*;
Peter Moffat *Iona Rain*; Dino Mahoney *YoYo*;
Simon Smith *Fat Janet is Dead*; Dominic McHale
The Resurrectionists. 'Shares plays with our partner
festival in Italy, the Premio Candoni Arta Terme.

Kent Literature Festival

The Metropole Arts Centre, The Leas,
Folkestone, Kent CT20 2LS
☎01303 255070
Festival Director *Ann Fearey*
FOUNDED 1980. Annual week-long festival
held at the end of September which aims to
bring the best in modern writing to a large
audience. Visiting authors and dramatic presentations are a regular feature along with readings, workshops and talks. Also runs the **Kent
Short Story Competition**.

King's Lynn, The Fiction Festival

19 Tuesday Market Place, King's Lynn,
Norfolk PE30 1JW
☎01553 691661 (office hours) or 761919
Fax 01553 691779
Contact *Anthony Ellis*
FOUNDED 1989. Annual weekend festival held
in March. Over the weekend there are readings
and discussions, attended by guest writers of
which there are usually eight. Guests at the 2000
festival included Beryl Bainbridge, Paul Bailey,
Malcolm Bradbury, Abdulrazak Gurnah, Peter
Benson, Antonia Logue, Ann Harries.

King's Lynn, The Poetry Festival

19 Tuesday Market Place, King's Lynn,
Norfolk PE30 1JW
☎01553 691661 (office hours) or 761919
Fax 01553 691779
Contact *Anthony Ellis*
FOUNDED 1985. Annual weekend festival held
at the end of September (22–24 in 2000), with
guest poets (usually eight). Previous guests have
included Carol Ann Duffy, Paul Durcan,
Gavin Ewart, Peter Porter, Stephen Spender.
Events include readings and discussion panels
and the presentation of the King's Lynn
Award; current Laureate is Kit Wright.

Lancaster LitFest

Sun Street Studios, 23–29 Sun Street,
Lancaster LA1 1ET
☎01524 62166 Fax 01524 841216
Email info@lancslitfest.demon.co.uk

Website www.folly.co.uk/litfest

FOUNDED 1978. Regional Literature Development Agency, organising workshops, readings, residencies, publications. Year-round programme of literature-based events and annual festival in October featuring a wide range of writers from the UK and overseas. Organises annual poetry competition with winners receiving cash prizes and anthology publication.

Ledbury Poetry Festival

Town Council Offices, Church Lane, Ledbury, Herefordshire HR8 1DH
☎01531 634156
Email prog@ledburypoetryfestival.freeserve. co.uk
Website www.ledburypoetfest.org.uk
Contact *Alan Lloyd*

FOUNDED 1997. Annual ten-day festival held in July. Includes readings, discussions, workshops, exhibitions, music and walks. There are also writers in residence at local schools and residential homes, a national poetry competition and the Town Party. Past guests have included Andrew Motion, Benjamin Zephaniah, Simon Armitage, Roger McGough, John Hegley and Germaine Greer. Full programme available in May.

Leicester Literature Festival

See **Words Out**

Lichfield International Arts Festival

7 The Close, Lichfield, Staffordshire WS13 7LD
☎01543 306270 Fax 01543 306274
Email lichfieldfest@lichfield-arts.org.uk
Website www.lichfieldfestival.org
Festival Director *Paul Spicer*

FOUNDED 1982. Annual July festival with events taking place in the 13th century Cathedral, the Civic Hall, Guildhall and Hawksyard Priory as well as various country churches and outdoor venues. Mainly music but also includes poetry reading events and poetry reading competition for schools; talks and lectures. Being the birthplace of Samuel Johnson, a literary festival is planned for 2002.

City of London Festival

230 Bishopsgate, London EC2M 4HW
☎020 7377 0540 Fax 020 7377 1972
Email admin@colf.org
Website www.colf.org.uk
Director *Michael MacLeod*

FOUNDED 1962. Annual three-week festival held in June and July. Features over fifty classical and popular music events alongside poetry and prose readings, street theatre and open-air extravaganzas, in some of the most outstanding performance spaces in the world.

London Festival of Literature

See **The Word – The London Festival of Literature**

London New Play Festival

Diorama Arts Centre, 34 Osnaburgh Street, London NW1 3ND
☎020 7209 2326 Fax 020 7916 5282
Email lnpf@reverb.co.uk
Website come.to/lnpf
Artistic Director *Phil Setren*
Administrator *Chris Cooke*
Education Director *Christopher Preston*

FOUNDED 1989. Annual festival of new writing. The 1999 season featured two full productions and four rehearsed readings at the Finborough Theatre, workshops at the Diorama Arts Centre and a West End Platform season at the Gielgud Theatre, Shaftesbury Avenue. Open to full-length and one-act plays which are assessed for originality, form, etc. by a reading committee. Deadline for scripts according to festival dates – call Festival Office for information. LNPF Writing School – one-day workshops, courses and dramaturgy sessions held throughout the year. For full details check the website.

Ludlow Festival

Castle Square, Ludlow, Shropshire SY8 1AY
☎01584 875070 Fax 01584 877673
Contact *Festival Administrator*

FOUNDED 1959. Annual two-week festival held in the last week of June and first week of July with an open-air Shakespeare production held at Ludlow Castle and a varied programme of events including recitals, opera, dance, popular and classical concerts, literary and historical lectures.

Manchester Festival of Writing

Manchester Central Library, St Peter's Square, Manchester M2 5PD
☎0161 234 1981
Email janem@libraries.manchester.gov.uk
Contact *Jane Mathieson*

FOUNDED 1990. An annual event organised by Manchester Libraries and Commonword community publishers. It consists of a short programme of practical writing workshops on specific themes/genres run by well-known writers. Attendance at all workshops is free to Manchester residents.

Manchester Poetry Festival

2nd Floor, Enterprise House, 15 Whitworth Street West, Manchester M1 5WG
☎0161 907 0031 Fax 0161 907 0032
Email mpf@dial.pipex.com
Contact *Richard Michael*

Held in the autumn (5–14 October in 2000), the Festival aims to bring the world's best poets to Manchester and promote Manchester poets to the rest of the world. Includes workshops and events for children.

Mole Valley Literature and Media Festival

Mole Valley Leisure Services, Pippbrook, Dorking, Surrey RH4 1SJ
☎01273 478943 Fax 01273 478943
Email jo@koenig48.freeserve.com
Festival Coordinator *Jo König*

A festival which celebrates literary talent both past and present throughout the Mole Valley. Includes film fair, a programme of readings, workshops, exhibitions, storytelling, performance poetry, children's and young people's events. Dedicated to encouraging, promoting and developing literature in its broadest sense. Initiates sustainable literary projects for all the community.

National Eisteddfod of Wales

40 Parc Ty Glas, Llanishen, Cardiff CF14 5WU
☎029 2076 3777 Fax 029 2076 3737
Website www.eisteddfod.org.uk

The National Eisteddfod, held in August, is the largest arts festival in Wales, attracting over 170,000 visitors during the week-long celebration of more than 800 years of tradition. Competitions, bardic ceremonies and concerts.

National Student Drama Festival

See **University College, Scarborough** under **Writers' Courses**

Norfolk and Norwich Festival

42–58 St George's Street, Norwich, Norfolk NR3 1AB
☎01603 614921 Fax 01603 632303
Email info@nnfest.demon.co.uk
Website www.nnfest.demon.co.uk
Festival Director *Peter Bolton*

FOUNDED 1772, this performing arts festival is the second oldest in the UK. Held annually in October, the festival includes talks by writers along with poetry and storytelling events.

North East Lincolnshire Literature Festival

Arts Development, North East Lincolnshire Council, Knoll Street, Cleethorpes, Lincolnshire DN35 8LN
☎01472 323007 Fax 01472 323005
Festival Programmer *Lynne Conlan*

FOUNDED 1997. Annual themed festival held in February/March. Reflecting the heritage of the area, the festival aims to make literature accessible to all ages and abilities through a varied and unusual programme. In 2000 the Festival was entitled 'Time and Tide'. Guests included Barnsley Football Club's Poet in Residence, Ian McMillan, Joyce Dunbar and John Mortimer. Events featured poetry readings, workshops and children's events.

Northern Children's Book Festival

Information North, Bolbec Hall, Westgate Road, Newcastle upon Tyne NE1 1SE
☎0191 232 0877 Fax 0191 232 0804
Email ce24@dial.pipex.com

FOUNDED 1984. Annual two-week festival during November. Events in schools and libraries for children in the North East region. One Saturday during the festival sees the staging of a large book event hosted by one of the local authorities involved. Publications include books on holding your own book week such as: *Celebrating the North East*; *Getting the Show On the Road* and *Read On, Write On*.

Off the Page Literature Festival

County Library Support Services, Glaisdale Parkway, Nottingham NG8 4GP
☎0115 9854242 Fax 0115 9286400
Contact *Pam Middleton*

Author visits held twice a year, aimed at making authors accessible to readers. In June 2000 it was at Mansfield Library and the theme was sport. A series of visits will take place in the autumn at Nottingham Central Library when the authors will be Veronica Stallwood, Katie Fforde, Beryl Kingston and Patricia Wendorf.

Off the Shelf Literature Festival

Central Library, Surrey Street, Sheffield S1 1XZ
☎0114 2734716/4400 Fax 0114 2735009
Email off-the-shelf@pop3.poptel.org.uk
Festival Organisers *Maria de Souza, Susan Walker*

FOUNDED 1992. Annual two-week festival held during the last fortnight in October. Lively and diverse mix of readings, workshops, children's events, storytelling and competitions. Previous guests have included Bill Bryson, Irvine Welsh, Benjamin Zephaniah, Terry Pratchett, Michael Palin and Carol Ann Duffy.

Oxford Literary Festival

301 Woodstock Road, Oxford OX2 7NY
☎01865 514149 Fax 01865 514804

Directors *Sally Dunsmore, Angela Prysor-Jones*

FOUNDED 1997. Annual three-day festival held two weekends prior to Easter. Authors speaking about their books, covering a wide variety of writing: fiction, poetry, biography, travel, food, gardening, children's art. Previous guests have included William Boyd, Andrew Motion, Candia McWilliam, Beryl Bainbridge, Sophie Grigson, Jamie McKendrick, Bernard O'Donoghue, Philip Pullman and Korky Paul.

The Round Festival

c/o Word And Action (Dorset), 61 West Borough, Wimborne, Dorset BH12 1LX
☎01202 883197 Fax 01202 881061

Contact *Kate Wood*

FOUNDED 1990. International festival of theatre-in-the-round offering a variety of workshops and performances celebrating and exploring the form. Programme includes performances and playreading in the round.

Royal Court Young Writers Programme

Royal Court Theatre, Sloane Square, London SW1W 8AS
☎020 7565 5050 Fax 020 7565 5001

Associate Director *Ola Animashawin*

Open to young people up to the age of 26. The festival focuses on the process of playwriting and is open to young writers all over the country. Intensive work on the final draft of plays precedes production at the Royal Court Theatre Upstairs. 'We are always looking for scripts for theatrical production (not film scripts).'

Rye Festival

PO Box 33, Rye, East Sussex TN31 7YB
☎01797 224982

Artistic Director *David Willison*

FOUNDED 1972. Annual two-week September event, plus short winter series. Variety of events with strong emphasis on literature

(nominated by the *Independent on Sunday* as one of ten best British festivals), classical and modern music, visual arts, workshops and masterclasses. Write or phone to join free mailing list.

Salisbury Festival

Festival Office, 75 New Street, Salisbury, Wiltshire SP1 2PH
☎01722 323883 Fax 01722 410552

Director *Helen Marriage*

FOUNDED 1972. Annual festival held at the end of May/beginning of June, including classical music, theatre, jazz, exhibitions.

Scottish Young Playwrights Festival

6th Floor, Gordon Chambers, 90 Mitchell Street, Glasgow G1 3NQ
☎0141 221 5127 Fax 0141 221 9123
Email admin@scottishyouththeatre.freeserve.co.uk
Website www.scottishyouththeatre.freeserve.co.uk

Artistic Director *Mary McCluskey*

The Scottish Young Playwrights project operates throughout Scotland. In every region an experienced theatre practitioner runs regular young writers' workshops aimed at developing the best possible scripts from initial ideas. A representative selection of scripts is then selected to form a showcase. The festival is mounted in conjunction with the Royal Scottish Academy of Music and Drama. Scripts will be workshopped, revised and developed culminating in an evening presentation. Scripts are welcome throughout the year from young people aged 15–25 who are native Scots and/or resident in Scotland; synopses of unfinished scripts also considered. No restriction on style, content or intended media, but work must be original and unperformed. Further details from address above.

Stratford-upon-Avon Poetry Festival

The Shakespeare Centre, Henley Street, Stratford-upon-Avon, Warwickshire CV37 6QW
☎01789 204016 Fax 01789 296083
Email director@shakespeare.org.uk

Festival Director *Roger Pringle*

FOUNDED 1953. Annual festival held on Sunday evenings during July and August. Readings by poets and professional actors.

The Sunday Times Hay Festival

Festival Office, Hay-on-Wye HR3 5BX
☎01497 821217 Fax 01497 821066
Website www.litfest.co.uk

Festival Director *Peter Florence*

FOUNDED 1988. Annual May festival sponsored by *The Sunday Times*. Guests have included Salman Rushdie, Toni Morrison, Stephen Fry, Joseph Heller, Carlos Fuentes, Maya Angelou, Amos Oz, Arthur Miller.

Swansea Festivals

Dylan Thomas Centre, Somerset Place, Swansea SA1 1RR
☎01792 463980 Fax 01792 463993
Email dylan.thomas@cableol.uk
Website www.dylanthomas.org

Contact *David Woolley*

Wordplay (2–7 October): sixth annual festival of literature and arts for young people; The Dylan Thomas Celebration (27 Oct to 9 Nov), two weeks of performances, talks, lectures, films, music, poetry, exhibitions and celebrity guests.

Swindon Festival of Literature

Lower Shaw Farm, Shaw, Swindon, Wiltshire SN5 9PJ
☎01793 771080 Fax 01793 771080
Website www.swindonlink.com

Festival Director *Matt Holland*

FOUNDED 1994. Annual festival held in May. Commences with 'Dawn Chorus' in Lawn Woods at sunrise on May Day and includes writing workshops, short story competition, the Clive Brain Memorial Lecture and the Swindon Poetry Slam.

Warwick & Leamington Festival

Warwick Arts Society, Northgate, Warwick CV34 4JL
☎01926 410747 Fax 01926 407606

Festival Director *Richard Phillips*

FOUNDED 1980. Annual festival lasting 12 days in the first half of July. Basically a chamber and early music festival, with some open-air, large-scale concerts in Warwick Castle, the Festival also promotes plays by Shakespeare in historical settings. Large-scale education programme. Interested in increasing its literary content, both in performances and workshops.

Ways with Words

Droridge Farm, Dartington, Totnes, Devon TQ9 6JQ
☎01803 867311 Fax 01803 863688

Email wwwords@globalnet.co.uk
Website www.users.globalnet.co.uk/
~wwwords

Festival Director *Kay Dunbar*

Ways with Words runs a major literature festival at Dartington Hall in south Devon for ten days in July each year. Features over 200 writers giving lectures, readings, interviews, discussions, performances, masterclasses and workshops.

Ways with Words also runs Wordplay, a young people's and community book festival in Devon, as well as literary weekends in Southwold, Bury St Edmunds (Suffolk) and York, plus writing, reading and painting courses in the UK and abroad.

Wellington Literary Festival

Civic Offices, Tan Bank, Wellington, Telford, Shropshire TF1 1LX
☎01952 222935 Fax 01952 222936

Contact *Derrick Drew*

FOUNDED 1997. Annual festival held throughout October. Events include story telling, writers' forum, 'Pints and Poetry', children's poetry competition, story competition, theatre review and guest speakers.

Wells Festival of Literature

Tower House, St Andrew Street, Wells, Somerset BA5 2UN
☎01749 673385
Website www.somersite.co.uk/wellsfest.htm

Contact *Pamela Egan*

FOUNDED 1992. Annual weekend-plus festival held at the end of October. Main venue is the historic, moated Bishop's Palace. A wide range of speakers caters for different tastes in reading; previous guests: Douglas Hurd, Eric Newby, Elizabeth Jennings, P. D. James, Simon Jenkins, Barbara Trapido. Short story and poetry competitions are run in conjunction with the Festival.

Wimborne Poetry Festival

Word And Action (Dorset), 61 West Borough, Wimborne, Dorset BT2 1LX
☎01202 883197 Fax 01202 881061
Email wordandaction@wanda.demon.co.uk

Contact *Anne Jennings*

Bi-annual festival of poetry readings, performances and workshops. Culminates in an open-air poetry fair with guest poets, stalls and quizzes. Events vary each festival and aim to involve the whole community both on a local scale and nationally.

The Word – The London Festival of Literature

245 St John Street, London EC1V 4NB
☎020 7837 2555 Fax 020 7278 0480
Email admin@theword.org.uk
Website www.theword.org.uk

Director *Peter Florence*

FOUNDED 1999. Annual ten-day carnival celebration of the written and spoken word, featuring the best contemporary writing in every medium. (22 September to 1 October in 2000.) Campaign and programme of competitions, conversations, debates, fairs, films, lectures, masterclasses, plays, readings, receptions, workshops featuring hundreds of writers, musicians and artists. Guest writers at the first Festival (held in March): Margaret Atwood, Chinua Achebe, Joseph Heller, Shirley Hughes, Hanif Kureishi, Doris Lessing, Armistead Maupin, Ian McEwan, Terry Pratchett, Edward Said, Wole Soyinka, Derek Walcott and Benjamin Zephaniah.

Wordplay

See **Swansea Festivals**

Words Out – Leicester Literature Festival

Leicester City Council, Arts and Leisure, Block A, New Walk Centre, Welford Place, Leicester LE1 6ZG
☎0116 2527337

Literature Development Officer
Ms Anu Singh

Bi-annual festival held in October. A mixture of author events, workshops, profiles of community arts and spotlights on local writing Held in a range of community/library/arts venues around the city.

European Publishers

Austria

Springer-Verlag KG
PO Box 89, A–1200 Vienna
☎00 43 1 3302415 Fax 00 43 1 3302426
FOUNDED 1924. *Publishes* anthropology, architecture, art, business, chemistry, computer science, communications, electronics, economics, education, interior design, environmental studies, engineering, law, maths, dentistry, medicine, nursing, philosophy, physics, psychology, technology and general science.

Verlag Carl Ueberreuter
Postfach 306, A–1091 Vienna
☎00 43 1 404440 Fax 00 43 1 404445
FOUNDED 1548. *Publishes* fiction and general non-fiction: art, government, history, economics, political science, general science, science fiction, fantasy, music and dance.

Paul Zsolnay Verlag GmbH
Postfach 142, A–1041 Vienna
☎00 43 1 50576610 Fax 00 43 1 50576610
FOUNDED 1923. *Publishes* biography, fiction, general non-fiction, history, poetry.

Belgium

Brepols NV
Steenweg op Tielen 68, 2300 Turnhout
☎00 32 14 402500 Fax 00 32 14 428919
FOUNDED 1796. *Publishes* art, architecture, interior design, history, religion.

Facet NV
Willem Linnigstr 13, 2060 Antwerp
☎00 32 3 2274028 Fax 00 32 3 2273792
FOUNDED 1986. *Publishes* children's books.

Uitgeverij Lannoo NV
Kasteelstr 97, B-8700 Tielt
☎00 32 51 424211 Fax 00 32 51 401152
FOUNDED 1909. *Publishes* general non-fiction, art, biography, economics, gardening, health, history, management, nutrition, photography, poetry, government, political science, religion, travel.

Standaard Uitgeverij
Belgiëlei 147a, 2018 Antwerp
☎00 32 3 2857200 Fax 00 32 3 2857299
FOUNDED 1919. *Publishes* education, fiction, humour.

Denmark

Forlaget Apostrof ApS
Postboks 2580, DK–2100 Copenhagen
☎00 45 39 208420 Fax 00 45 39 208453
FOUNDED 1980. *Publishes* essays, fiction, literature, literary criticism, humour, general non-fiction, psychology, psychiatry.

Aschehoug Dansk Forlag A/S
Landemaerket 8, DK–1119 Copenhagen K
☎00 45 33 305522 Fax 00 45 33 305822
Website www.aschehoug.dk
FOUNDED 1977. Part of the Egmont Group. *Publishes* fiction, biography, cookery, health, how-to, maritime and nutrition.

Borgens Forlag A/S
Valbygardsvej 33, DK–2500 Valby
☎00 45 36 462100 Fax 00 45 36 441488
FOUNDED 1948. *Publishes* fiction, literature, literary criticism, general non-fiction, art, crafts, education, environmental studies, essays, games, gay and lesbian, hobbies, health, nutrition, music, dance, philosophy, poetry, psychology, psychiatry, religion.

Egmont Lademann A/S
Gerdasgade 37, DK–2500 Valby
☎00 45 36 156600 Fax 00 45 36 441162
Website www.egmont.com
FOUNDED 1954. *Publishes* general non-fiction.

Egmont Wangel AS
Gerdasgade 37, DK–1795 Valby
☎00 45 36 156600 Fax 00 45 36 441162
Website www.egmont.com
FOUNDED 1946. *Publishes* fiction and management.

Forum Publishers
Snaregade 4, DK–1205 Copenhagen K
☎00 45 33 147714 Fax 00 45 33 147791
FOUNDED 1940. *Publishes* fiction and mysteries.

GEC Gads Forlags Aktieselskab
Vimmelskaftet 32, DK–1161 Copenhagen K
☎00 45 33 150558 Fax 00 45 33 110800
FOUNDED 1855. *Publishes* general non-fiction, biological sciences, cookery, crafts, games, economics, education, English as a second language, environmental studies, gardening, history, maths, natural history, physics, plants, travel.

Gyldendalske Boghandel-Nordisk Forlag A/S
Klareboderne 3, DK–1001 Copenhagen K
☎00 45 33 110775 Fax 00 45 33 110323
Website www.gyldendal.dk
FOUNDED 1770. *Publishes* fiction, art, biography, dance, dentistry, education, history, how-to, medicine, music, poetry, nursing, philosophy, psychology, psychiatry, general and social sciences, sociology.

Hekla Forlag
Valbygaardsvej 33, DK–2500 Valby
☎00 45 36 462100 Fax 00 45 36 441488
FOUNDED 1979. *Publishes* general fiction and non-fiction.

Høst & Søns Publishers Ltd
PO Box 2212, DK–1018 Copenhagen
☎00 45 33 382888 Fax 00 45 33 382898
FOUNDED 1836. *Publishes* fiction, crafts, environmental studies, games, hobbies, regional interests, travel.

Lindhardt og Ringhof
Kristianiagade 14, DK–2100 Copenhagen
☎00 45 33 695000 Fax 00 45 33 436520
FOUNDED 1971. *Publishes* fiction and general non-fiction.

Munksgaard International Publishers Ltd
PO Box 2148, DK–1016 Copenhagen K
☎00 45 77 333333 Fax 00 45 77 333377
Email headoffice@munksgaard.dk
Website www.munksgaard.dk
FOUNDED 1917. *Publishes* dentistry, medicine, nursing, psychology, psychiatry, general science.

Nyt Nordisk Forlag Arnold Busck A/S
Købmagergade 49, DK–1150 Copenhagen K
☎00 45 33 733575 Fax 00 45 33 733576
FOUNDED 1896. *Publishes* fiction, art, biography, dance, dentistry, history, how-to, music, philosophy, religion, medicine, nursing, psychology, psychiatry, general and social sciences, sociology.

Politikens Forlag A/S
Vestergade 26, DK–1456 Copenhagen K
☎00 45 33 470707 Fax 00 45 33 470708
FOUNDED 1946. *Publishes* general non-fiction, art, crafts, dance, history, games, hobbies, how-to, music, natural history, sport, travel.

Samlerens Forlag A/S
Snaregade 4, DK–1205 Copenhagen K
☎00 45 33 131023 Fax 00 45 33 144314
FOUNDED 1942. *Publishes* essays, fiction, government, history, literature, literary criticism, political science.

Det Schønbergske Forlag
Landemaerket 5, DK–1119 Copenhagen K
☎00 45 33 113066 Fax 00 45 33 330045
FOUNDED 1857. *Publishes* art, biography, fiction, history, humour, philosophy, poetry, psychology, psychiatry, travel

Spektrum Forlagsaktieselskab
Snaregade 4, DK–1205 Copenhagen K
☎00 45 33 147714 Fax 00 45 33 147791
FOUNDED 1990. *Publishes* general non-fiction.

Tiderne Skifter Forlag A/S
Pilestraede 51/5, DK–1001 Copenhagen K
☎00 45 33 325772 Fax 00 45 33 144205
FOUNDED 1979. *Publishes* fiction, literature and literary criticism, essays, ethnicity, photography, behavioural sciences.

Finland

Gummerus Publishers
PO Box 2, SF–00131 Helsinki
☎00 358 9 584301 Fax 00 358 9 58430200
FOUNDED 1872. *Publishes* fiction and general non-fiction.

Karisto Oy
PO Box 102, SF–13101 Hämeenlinna
☎00 358 3 6161551 Fax 00 358 3 6161565
FOUNDED 1900. *Publishes* fiction and general non-fiction.

Kirjayhtymä Oy
PO Box 409, SF–00101 Helsinki
☎00 358 9 6937641 Fax 00 358 9 69376366
FOUNDED 1958. *Publishes* fiction and general non-fiction.

Otava Publishing Co. Ltd
PO Box 134, SF–00121 Helsinki
☎00 358 9 19961 Fax 00 358 9 643136

FOUNDED 1890. *Publishes* fiction, general non-fiction, how-to.

Werner Söderström Osakeyhtiö (WSOY)
PO Box 222, SF–00121 Helsinki
☎00 358 9 61681 Fax 00 358 9 6168405
FOUNDED 1878. *Publishes* fiction, general non-fiction, education.

Tammi Publishers
PO Box 410, SF–00101 Helsinki
☎00 358 9 6937621 Fax 00 358 9 69376266
FOUNDED 1943. *Publishes* fiction, general non-fiction.

France
Editions Arthaud SA
26 rue Racine, F–75006 Paris Cedex 06
☎00 33 1 4051 3008 Fax 00 33 1 4325 0118
FOUNDED 1890. Imprint of **Flammarion SA**.
Publishes art, history, literature, literary criticism, essays, sport, travel.

Editions Belfond
12 avenue d'Italie, F–75627 Paris
☎00 33 1 4416 0500 Fax 00 33 1 4416 0506
FOUNDED 1963. *Publishes* fiction, literature, literary criticism, essays, mysteries, romance, poetry, general non-fiction, art, biography, dance, health, history, how-to, music, nutrition.

Editions Bordas
21 rue du Montparnasse BP50,
F–75006 Paris Cedex 06
☎00 33 1 4439 4400 Fax 00 33 1 4439 4343
FOUNDED 1946. *Publishes* education and general non-fiction.

Editions Calmann-Lévy SA
3 rue Auber, F–75009 Paris
☎00 33 1 4742 3833 Fax 00 33 1 4742 7781
FOUNDED 1836. *Publishes* fiction, science fiction, fantasy, biography, history, humour, philosophy, psychology, psychiatry, social sciences, sociology, sport, economics.

Editions Denoël Sàrl
9 rue du Cherche-Midi, F–75006 Paris
☎00 33 1 4439 7373 Fax 00 33 1 4439 7390
FOUNDED 1932. *Publishes* art, economics, fiction, science fiction, fantasy, government, history, philosophy, political science, psychology, psychiatry.

Librairie Arthème Fayard
75 rue des Saints-Pères, F-75278 Paris Cedex 06
☎00 33 1 4549 8200 Fax 00 33 1 4222 4017
FOUNDED 1854. *Publishes* biography, fiction, history, dance, music, philosophy, religion, social sciences, sociology, general science, technology.

Flammarion SA
26 rue Racine, F–75006 Paris Cedex 06
☎00 33 1 4051 3008 Fax 00 33 1 4325 0118
FOUNDED 1875. *Publishes* general fiction and non-fiction, art, architecture, gardening, plants, interior design, literature, literary criticism, essays, medicine, nursing, dentistry, wine and spirits.

Editions Gallimard
5 rue Sébastien-Bottin,
F–75007 Paris Cedex 07
☎00 33 1 4054 1457 Fax 00 33 1 4954 1451
FOUNDED 1911. *Publishes* fiction, poetry, art, biography, dance, history, music, philosophy.

Société des Editions Grasset et Fasquelle
61 rue des Saints-Pères, F–75006 Paris
☎00 33 1 4439 2200 Fax 00 33 1 4222 6418
FOUNDED 1907. *Publishes* fiction and general non-fiction, essays, literature, literary criticism, philosophy.

Hachette Livre
43 quai de Grenelle, F–75905 Paris Cedex 15
☎00 33 1 4392 3000 Fax 00 33 1 4392 3030
FOUNDED 1826. *Publishes* fiction and general non-fiction, architecture and interior design, art, economics, education, general engineering, government, history, language and linguistics, political science, philosophy, general science, self-help, social sciences, sociology, sport, travel.

Editions Robert Laffont Fixot, Seghers, Julliard
24 ave Marceau, F–75008 Paris Cedex 08
☎00 33 1 5367 1400 Fax 00 33 1 5367 1414
FOUNDED 1941. *Publishes* fiction and non-fiction.

Librairie Larousse
21 rue de Montparnasse,
F–75298 Paris Cedex 06
☎00 33 1 4439 4400 Fax 00 33 1 4439 4107
FOUNDED 1852. *Publishes* general and social sciences, sociology, language arts, linguistics, technology.

Editions Jean-Claude Lattès

17 rue Jacob, F–75006 Paris
☎00 33 1 4441 7400 Fax 00 33 1 4325 3047
FOUNDED 1968. *Publishes* fiction and general non-fiction, biography, religion.

Les Editions Magnard Sàrl

20 rue Berbier-du-Mets,
F–75647 Paris Cedex 13
☎00 33 1 4408 8585 Fax 00 33 1 4408 4979
FOUNDED 1933. *Publishes* education.

Michelin et Cie (Services de Tourisme)

46 ave de Breteuil, F–75324 Paris Cedex 07
☎00 33 1 4566 1234 Fax 00 33 1 4566 1163
FOUNDED 1900. *Publishes* travel.

Les Editions de Minuit SA

7 rue Bernard-Palissy, F–75006 Paris
☎00 33 1 4439 3920 Fax 00 33 1 4544 8236
FOUNDED 1942. *Publishes* fiction, essays, literature, literary criticism, philosophy, social science, sociology.

Fernand Nathan

9 rue Méchain, F–75676 Paris
☎00 33 1 4587 5000 Fax 00 33 1 4331 2169
FOUNDED 1881. *Publishes* education, history, philosophy, psychology, psychiatry, general and social sciences, sociology.

Presses de la Cité

12 ave d'Italie, F–75627 Paris
☎00 33 1 4416 0500 Fax 00 33 1 4416 0505
FOUNDED 1947. Imprint of **Editions Belfond**. *Publishes* fiction and general non-fiction, science fiction, fantasy, biography, mysteries.

Presses Universitaires de France (PUF)

12 rue Jean-de-Beauvais, F–75005 Paris 06
☎00 33 1 4326 2216 Fax 00 33 1 4354 2633
Website www.puf.com
FOUNDED 1921. *Publishes* art, biography, dance, dentistry, government, general engineering, geography, geology, history, law, medicine, music, nursing, philosophy, psychology, psychiatry, religion, political and social sciences, sociology.

Editions du Seuil

27 rue Jacob, F–75006 Paris
☎00 33 1 4046 5050 Fax 00 33 1 4329 0829
FOUNDED 1935. *Publishes* fiction, literature, literary criticism, essays, poetry, art, biography, dance, government, history, how-to, music, photography, philosophy, psychology, psychiatry, religion, general and social sciences, sociology.

Les Editions de la Table Ronde

7 rue Corneille, F–75006 Paris
☎00 33 1 4046 7070 Fax 00 33 1 4046 7101
FOUNDED 1944. *Publishes* fiction and general non-fiction, biography, history, psychology, psychiatry, religion.

Librairie Vuibert

20 rue Berbier-du-Mets, F–75647 Paris
☎00 33 1 4408 4900 Fax 00 33 1 4408 4929
FOUNDED 1877. *Publishes* biological and earth sciences, chemistry, chemical engineering, economics, law, mathematics, physics.

Germany

Verlag C. H. Beck (OHG)

Postfach 400340, 80703 Munich
☎00 49 89 381890 Fax 00 49 89 38189398
FOUNDED 1763. *Publishes* general non-fiction, anthropology, archaeology, art, dance, economics, essays, history, language, law, linguistics, literature, literary criticism, music, philosophy, social sciences, sociology, theology.

C. Bertelsmann Verlag GmbH

Postfach 800360, 81603 Munich
☎00 49 89 431890 Fax 00 49 89 43189440
FOUNDED 1835. *Publishes* fiction and general non-fiction, government and political science.

Carlsen Verlag GmbH

Postfach 500380, 22703 Hamburg
☎00 49 40 3910090 Fax 00 49 40 39100962
FOUNDED 1953. *Publishes* humour and general non-fiction.

Deutscher Taschenbuch Verlag GmbH & Co. KG (dtv)

Postfach 400422, 80704 Munich
☎00 49 89 38167-0 Fax 00 49 89 346428
FOUNDED 1961. *Publishes* fiction and general non-fiction; art, astronomy, biography, child care and development, cookery, computer science, dance, education, government, history, how-to, music, poetry, psychiatry, psychology, philosophy, political science, religion, medicine, dentistry, nursing, social sciences, literature, literary criticism, essays, humour, travel.

Droemersche Verlagsanstalt Th. Knaur Nachfolger

Postfach 800480, 81604 Munich

☎00 49 89 92710 Fax 00 49 89 9271168

FOUNDED 1901. *Publishes* fiction, general non-fiction, cookery, how-to, self-help, travel and general science.

Econ-Verlag GmbH

Postfach 300321, 40403 Düsseldorf

☎00 49 211 43596 Fax 00 49 211 4359768

FOUNDED 1950. *Publishes* general non-fiction and fiction, economics, general science.

Falken-Verlag GmbH

Postfach 1120, 65521 Niederhausen

☎00 49 6127 7020 Fax 00 49 6127 702133

FOUNDED 1923. *Publishes* crafts, cookery, education, games, gardening, health, history, hobbies, how-to, humour, nutrition, photography, sport.

S Fischer Verlag GmbH

Postfach 700355, 60553 Frankfurt am Main

☎00 49 69 60620 Fax 00 49 69 6062214

FOUNDED 1886. Part of the Holtzbrinck Group. *Publishes* fiction, general non-fiction, essays, literature, literary criticism.

Carl Hanser Verlag

Postfach 860420, 81631 Munich

☎00 49 89 998300 Fax 00 49 89 99830460

Email info@hanser.de

Website www.hanser.de

Managing Director, Non-Fiction
  Wolfgang Beisler
Managing Director, Fiction *Michael Krüger*

FOUNDED in 1928 in Munich. *Publishes* international and German contemporary literature; classics, anthropology, non-fiction on social sciences and the arts; children's and juveniles; specialist books on engineering, natural science, plastics, computers and computer science, economics and management, dentistry. *Subsidiaries* **Paul Zsolnay Verlag**, Vienna; Sanssouci Verlag, Zurich; Verlag Nagel & Kimche, Zurich; Fachbuchverlag Leipzig, Leipzig; Hanser Gardner Publications, Cincinatti.

Wilhelm Heyne Verlag

Postfach 201204, 80333 Munich

☎00 49 89 286350 Fax 00 49 89 2800943

FOUNDED 1934. *Publishes* fiction, mystery, romance, humour, science fiction, fantasy, astrology, biography, cookery, film, history, how-to, occult, psychology, psychiatry, video.

Hoffmann und Campe Verlag

Postfach 130444, 20139 Hamburg

☎00 49 40 441880 Fax 00 49 40 44188-290

FOUNDED 1781. *Publishes* fiction and general non-fiction; art, biography, dance, history, music, poetry, philosophy, psychology, psychiatry, general science, social sciences, sociology.

Verlagsgruppe Georg von Holtzbrinck GmbH

Gansheidestrasse 26, 70184 Stuttgart

☎00 49 711 21500 Fax 00 49 711 2150269

FOUNDED 1948. One of the world's largest publishing groups with 12 book publishing houses and 40 imprints. Also publishes the newspapers, *Handelsblatt* and *Die Zeit*.

Ernst Klett Verlag GmbH

Postfach 106016, 70049 Stuttgart

☎00 49 711 66720 Fax 00 49 711 628053

FOUNDED 1897. *Publishes* education, career development, geography, geology.

Gustav Lübbe Verlag GmbH

Postfach 200127, 51431 Bergisch Gladbach

☎00 49 2202 1210 Fax 00 49 2202 121920

FOUNDED 1963. *Publishes* fiction and general non-fiction, archaeology, biography, history, how-to.

Mosaik Verlag GmbH

Postfach 800360, 81673 Munich 80

☎00 49 89 431890 Fax 00 49 89 43189743

Publishes animals, antiques, architecture and interior design, child care and development, cookery, crafts, economics, finance, career development, film, gardening, games, hobbies, health, house and home, human relations, nutrition, pets, self-help, sport, video, wine and spirits, women's studies.

Pestalozzi-Verlag Graphische Gesellschaft mbH

Am Pestalozziring 14, 91058 Erlangen

☎00 49 9131 60600 Fax 00 49 9131 773090

FOUNDED 1844. *Publishes* crafts, games, hobbies.

Rowohlt Taschenbuch Verlag GmbH

Postfach 1349, 21453 Reinbeck

☎00 49 40 72720 Fax 00 49 40 7272319

FOUNDED 1953. *Publishes* fiction and general non-fiction; archaeology, art, computer science, crafts, education, essays, games and hobbies, gay and lesbian, government, history, literature, literary criticism, philosophy, psychology, psychiatry, religion, general science, social sciences, sociology.

Springer-Verlag GmbH & Co KG
Postfach 311340, 10643 Berlin
☎00 49 30 827870 Fax 00 49 30 8214091

FOUNDED 1842. *Publishes* agriculture, architecture and interior design, astronomy, behavioural sciences, business, biological sciences, chemical engineering, chemistry, civil engineering, computer science, dentistry, economics, finance, geography, geology, health, nutrition, library and information sciences, management, marketing, mechanical engineering, electronics, electrical engineering, general engineering, physical sciences, earth sciences, environmental studies, law, mathematics, medicine, nursing, psychology, psychiatry, physics, general science, technology.

Suhrkamp Verlag
Postfach 101945, 60019 Frankfurt am Main
☎00 49 69 756010 Fax 00 49 69 75601314

FOUNDED 1950. *Publishes* biography, fiction, philosophy, poetry, psychology, psychiatry, general science.

SV-Hüthig Fachinformation GmbH
Sendlingerstr 8, 80331 Munich
☎00 49 89 2183620 Fax 00 49 89 21838490

Formed by the merger of Süddeutscher Verlag and Hüthig in 1998, SV-Hüthig Fachinformation is Germany's fourth largest professional publisher.

Benedict Taschen Verlag GmbH
Hohenzollernring 53, 50672 Cologne
☎00 49 221 201800 Fax 00 49 221 254919

FOUNDED 1980. *Publishes* photography, art, architecture and interior design.

K. Thienemanns Verlag
Blumenstr 36, 70182 Stuttgart
☎00 49 711 210550 Fax 00 49 711 2105539

FOUNDED 1849. *Publishes* fiction and general non-fiction.

Ullstein Buchverlage GmbH & Co KG
Charlottenstr 13, 10969 Berlin
☎00 49 30 25913500 Fax 00 49 30 25913570

FOUNDED 1903. *Publishes* fiction and general non-fiction, romance, mysteries, architecture and interior design, art, biography, dance, film,

video, education, essays, ethnology, geography, geology, government, health, history, how-to, humour, literature, literary criticism, maritime, military science, music, nutrition, poetry, political science, general science, social sciences, sociology, travel.

WEKA Firmengruppe GmbH & Co KG
Postfach 1180, 86425 Kissing
☎00 49 8233 230 Fax 00 49 8233 23195

FOUNDED 1973. Germany's largest professional publisher. *Publishes* architecture and interior design, business, career development, civil engineering, general engineering, how-to, electrical engineering, outdoor recreation, communications, management, mechanical engineering, medicine, nursing and dentistry, law, technology, environmental studies, behavioural sciences.

Italy

Adelphi Edizioni SpA
Via S. Giovanni sul Muro 14, 20121 Milan
☎00 39 02 72000975 Fax 00 39 02 89010337

FOUNDED 1962. *Publishes* fiction, art, biography, dance, music, philosophy, psychology, psychiatry, religion, general science.

Bompiana
Via Mecenate 91, 20138 Milan
☎00 39 02 50951 Fax 00 39 02 50952058

FOUNDED 1929. *Publishes* fiction and general non-fiction, art, drama, theatre and general science.

Bulzoni Editore SRL (Le Edizioni Universitarie d'Italia)
Via Dei Liburni 14, 00185 Rome
☎00 39 06 4455207 Fax 00 39 06 4450355

FOUNDED 1969. *Publishes* fiction, literature, literary criticism, essays, art, drama, general engineering, film, law, language, linguistics, philosophy, general science, social sciences, sociology, theatre, video.

Nuova Casa Editrice Licinio Cappelli GEM srl
Via Farini 14, 40124 Bologna
☎00 39 051 239060 Fax 00 39 051 239286

FOUNDED 1851. *Publishes* fiction, art, biography, drama, film, government, history, music and dance, medicine, nursing, dentistry, philosophy, poetry, political science, psychology, psychiatry, religion, general science, social sciences, sociology, theatre, video.

Garzanti Editore
Via Newton 18A, 20148 Milan
☎00 39 02 487941 Fax 00 39 02 76009233
FOUNDED 1861. *Publishes* fiction, literature, literary criticism, essays, art, biography, history, poetry, government, political science.

Giunti Publishing Group
Via Bolognese 165, 50139 Florence
☎00 39 055 66791 Fax 00 39 055 6679298
FOUNDED 1840. *Publishes* fiction, literature, literary criticism, essays, art, chemistry, chemical engineering, education, history, how-to, language arts, linguistics, mathematics, psychology, psychiatry, general science. Italian publishers of National Geographical Society books.

Gremese Editore SRL
Via Agnelli 88, 00151 Rome
☎00 39 06 65740507 Fax 00 39 06 65740509
FOUNDED 1978. *Publishes* fiction and non-fiction; art, astrology, cookery, crafts, dance, drama, environmental studies, fashion, games, hobbies, essays, literature, literary criticism, music, occult, parapsychology, photography, sport, travel, theatre, film, video, radio.

Longanesi & C
Corso Italia 13, 20122 Milan
☎00 39 02 8692640 Fax 00 39 02 72000306
FOUNDED 1946. *Publishes* fiction, art, biography, dance, history, how-to, medicine, nursing, dentistry, music, philosophy, psychology, psychiatry, religion, general and social sciences, sociology.

Arnoldo Mondadori Editore SpA
Via Mondadori, 20090 Segrate (Milan)
☎00 39 02 75421 Fax 00 39 02 75422302
FOUNDED 1907. *Publishes* fiction, mystery, romance, art, biography, dance, dentistry, history, how-to, medicine, music, poetry, philosophy, psychology, psychiatry, religion, nursing, general science, education.

Società Editrice Il Mulino
Str Maggiore 37, 40125 Bologna
☎00 39 051 256011 Fax 00 39 051 256034
FOUNDED 1954. *Publishes* dance, drama, economics, government, history, law, language, linguistics, music, philosophy, political science, psychology, psychiatry, social sciences, sociology, theatre.

Gruppo Ugo Mursia Editore SpA
Via Tadino 29, 20124 Milan
☎00 39 02 29403030
Fax 00 39 02 29400165
FOUNDED 1922. *Publishes* fiction, poetry, art, biography, education, history, maritime, philosophy, religion, sport, general and social sciences, sociology.

RCS Libri SpA
Via Mecenate 91, 20138 Milan
☎00 39 02 50952918
Fax 00 39 02 50952638
FOUNDED 1945. *Publishes* art, crafts, dance, business, games, hobbies, history, music, medicine, nursing, dentistry, outdoor recreation, general science.

Societa Editrice Internazionale – SEI
Corso Regina Margherita 176, 10152 Turin
☎00 39 011 52271 Fax 00 39 011 5211320
FOUNDED 1908. *Publishes* literature, literary criticism, essays, education, geography, geology, history, mathematics, philosophy, physics, religion, psychology, psychiatry.

Sonzogno
Via Mecenate 91, 20138 Milan
☎00 39 02 50951 Fax 00 39 02 5065361
FOUNDED 1818. *Publishes* fiction, mysteries, and general non-fiction.

Sperling e Kupfer Editori SpA
Via Borgonuovo 24, 20121 Milan
☎00 39 02 290341 Fax 00 39 02 6590290
FOUNDED 1899. *Publishes* fiction and general non-fiction, biography, economics, health, how-to, management, nutrition, general science, sport, travel.

Sugarco Edizioni SRL
Via Fermi 9, 21040 Carnago (Varese)
☎00 39 0331 985511
Fax 00 39 0331 985385
FOUNDED 1956. *Publishes* fiction, biography, history, how-to, philosophy.

Todariana Editrice
Via Gardone 29, 20139 Milan
☎00 39 02 56812953 Fax 00 39 02 55213405
FOUNDED 1967. *Publishes* fiction, poetry, science fiction, fantasy, literature, literary criticism, essays, language arts, linguistics, psychology, psychiatry, social sciences, sociology, travel.

The Netherlands

Addison Wesley Longman Publishers BV
Concertgebouwplein 25,
1071 LM Amsterdam
☎00 31 20 575 5800
Fax 00 31 20 664 5334
FOUNDED 1942. *Publishes* education, business, computer science, economics, management, technology.

A.W. Bruna Uitgevers BV
Postbus 40203, 3504 AA Utrecht
☎00 31 30 2470411 Fax 00 31 30 2410018
FOUNDED 1868. *Publishes* fiction and general non-fiction; computer science, history, philosophy, psychology, psychiatry, general and social science, sociology.

Uitgeverij BZZTÔH
Laan van Meerdervoort 10,
2517 AJ Gravenhage
☎00 31 70 3632934 Fax 00 31 70 3631932
FOUNDED 1970. *Publishes* fiction, mysteries, general non-fiction, animals, astrology, biography, cookery, dance, humour, music, occult, pets, religion (Buddhist), romance, travel.

Elsevier Science BV
PO Box 2400, 1000 CK Amsterdam
☎00 31 20 5862911 Fax 00 31 20 5862843
FOUNDED 1946. Parent company: Reed Elsevier. *Publishes* sciences (all fields), medicine, nursing, dentistry, economics, engineering (computer, chemical and general), mathematics, physics, technology.

Uitgeverij Hollandia BV
Postbus 70, 3740 AB Baarn
☎00 31 35 5418941 Fax 00 31 35 5421917
FOUNDED 1899. *Publishes* fiction, maritime, travel.

Uitgeversmaatschappij J. H. Kok BV
PO Box 5019, 8260 GA Kampen
☎00 31 38 3392555 Fax 00 31 38 3327331
FOUNDED 1894. *Publishes* fiction, poetry, history, religion, general and social sciences, sociology.

M & P Publishing House
Postbus 170, 3990 DD Houten
☎00 31 30 6377736 Fax 00 31 30 6377764
FOUNDED 1974. *Publishes* general non-fiction.

Meulenhoff & Co BV
Prins Hendriklaan 56, 1075 BE Amsterdam
☎00 31 20 5244310 Fax 00 31 20 6387376
FOUNDED 1895. *Publishes* international co-productions, fiction and general non-fiction. Specialises in Dutch and translated literature.

Uitgeverij Het Spectrum BV
Postbus 2073, 3500 GB Utrecht
☎00 31 30 2650650
Fax 00 31 30 2620850
FOUNDED 1935. *Publishes* science fiction, fantasy, literature, literary criticism, essays, mystery, criminology, general non-fiction, computer science, history, astrology, occult, management, environmental studies, travel.

Time-Life Books BV
Ottho Heldringstr 5, 1066 AZ Amsterdam
☎00 31 20 5104371 Fax 00 31 20 6176594
Publishes art, archaeology, astronomy, cookery, gardening, plants, history, how-to, health and nutrition, house and home, mystery.

Unieboek BV
Postbus 170, 3995 DB Houten
☎00 31 30 6377660 Fax 00 31 30 6377600
FOUNDED 1891. *Publishes* fiction, general non-fiction, architecture and interior design, government, political science, literature, literary criticism, essays, archaeology, cookery, history.

Uniepers BV
Postbus 69, 1390 AB Abcoude
☎00 31 294 285111 Fax 00 31 294 283013
FOUNDED 1961. *Publishes* (mostly in co-editions) antiques, anthropology, archaeology, architecture and interior design, art, culture, dance, history, music, nature, natural history.

Veen Uitgevers Groep
Postbus 14095, 3508 SC Utrecht
☎00 31 30 2349211 Fax 00 31 20 2349208
FOUNDED 1887. Part of Wolters Kluwer Trade Publishing. *Publishes* general non-fiction, fiction, essays, Dutch and foreign literature, literary criticism, travel, business,

Wolters Kluwer NV
PO Box 75248, 1070 AE Amsterdam
☎00 31 20 6070400
Fax 00 31 20 6070490
FOUNDED 1889. *Publishes* education, medical, technical encyclopedias, trade books and journals, law and taxation, periodicals.

Norway

H. Aschehoug & Co (W. Nygaard) A/S

Postboks 363, 0102 Sentrum, Oslo
☎00 47 22 400400 Fax 00 47 22 206395
FOUNDED 1872. *Publishes* fiction and general non-fiction, general and social science, sociology.

J. W. Cappelens Forlag A/S

Postboks 350, 0101 Sentrum, Oslo
☎00 47 22 365000 Fax 00 47 22 365040
FOUNDED 1829. *Publishes* fiction, general non-fiction, religion.

N. W. Damm og Søn A/S

Postboks 1755, Vika, 0122 Oslo
☎00 47 22 471100 Fax 00 47 22 360874
FOUNDED 1845. *Publishes* fiction and general non-fiction.

Ex Libris Forlag A/S

Postboks 2130, Grünerløkka, 0505 Oslo
☎00 47 22 384450 Fax 00 47 22 385160
FOUNDED 1982. *Publishes* cookery, health, nutrition, humour, human relations, publishing and book trade reference.

Gyldendal Norsk Forlag A/S

Postboks 6860, 0130 St Olaf, Oslo
☎00 47 22 034100 Fax 00 47 22 034105
FOUNDED 1925. *Publishes* fiction, science fiction, fantasy, art, dance, biography, government, political science, history, how-to, music, social sciences, sociology, poetry, philosophy, psychology, psychiatry, religion.

Hjemmets Bokforlag AS

Postboks 1755, Vika, N-0055 Oslo
☎00 47 22 471000 Fax 00 47 22 471098
FOUNDED 1969. *Publishes* fiction and general non-fiction.

NKS-Forlaget

Postboks 5853, 0308 Oslo
☎00 47 22 596000 Fax 00 47 22 596300
Website www.nks.no
FOUNDED 1971. *Publishes* accountancy, childcare and development, English as a second language, health, nutrition, mathematics, natural history, general and social sciences, sociology.

Tiden Norsk Forlag

PO Box 8813, Youngstorget, 0028 Oslo
☎00 47 22 007100 Fax 00 46 22 426458
FOUNDED 1933. *Publishes* fiction, general non-fiction; essays, literature, literary criticism, science fiction, fantasy, management.

Portugal

Bertrand Editora Lda

Rua Anchieta 29, 1200 Lisbon
☎00 351 1 3420084 Fax 00 351 1 3479728
FOUNDED 1727. *Publishes* art, essays, literature, literary criticism, social sciences, sociology.

Editorial Caminho SARL

Al Santo Antonio dos Capuchos 6B, 1100 Lisbon
☎00 351 1 3152683 Fax 00 351 1 534346
FOUNDED 1977. *Publishes* fiction, government, political science.

Livraria Civilizacão (Américo Fraga Lamares & Ca Lda)

Rua Alberto Aires de Gouveia 27, 4000 Porto
☎00 351 2 6062286 Fax 00 351 2 312382
FOUNDED 1921. *Publishes* fiction, art, economics, history, social and political science, government, sociology.

Publicações Dom Quixote Lda

Rua Luciano Cordeiro 116-2, 1098 Lisbon
☎00 351 1 3158079 Fax 00 351 1 3574595
FOUNDED 1965. *Publishes* fiction, poetry, education, history, philosophy, general and social sciences, sociology.

Publicações Europa–America Lda

Apdo 8, Estrada Lisbon-Sintra Km 14, 2726 Mem Martins Cedex
☎00 351 1 9211461 Fax 00 351 1 9217940
FOUNDED 1945. *Publishes* fiction, poetry, art, biography, dance, education, general engineering, history, how-to, music, philosophy, medicine, nursing, dentistry, psychology, psychiatry, general and social sciences, sociology, technology.

Gradiva – Publicações Lda

Rua Almeida e Sousa 21–r/c Esq, 1399–041 Lisbon
☎00 351 1 3974067 Fax 00 351 1 3953471
Website www.gravida.frt
FOUNDED 1981. *Publishes* fiction, literature, literary criticism, essays, science fiction, fantasy, romance, anthropology, astronomy, archaeology, behavioural and biological science, communications, computer science, crafts, education, games, hobbies, economics, general

engineering, geography, geology, natural history, history, humour, environmental studies, human relations, management, philosophy, general science.

Livros Horizonte Lda
Rua Chagas 17 – 1 Dto, 1200 Lisbon
☎00 351 1 3466917 Fax 00 351 1 3426921

FOUNDED 1953. *Publishes* art, education, history, psychology, psychiatry, social sciences, sociology.

Editorial Verbo SA
Rua Carlos Testa 1–2, 1000 Lisbon
☎00 351 1 3562121 Fax 00 351 1 3865396

FOUNDED 1959. *Publishes* education, history, general science.

Spain
Editorial Alhambra SA
Fernandez de la Hoz 9, 28010 Madrid
☎00 349 1 5940020 Fax 00 349 1 5941280

FOUNDED 1942. *Publishes* art, education, history, language arts, linguistics, medicine and nursing, dentistry, general science, psychology, psychiatry, philosophy.

Alianza Editorial SA
Juan Ignacio Luca de Tena 15, 28027 Madrid
☎00 349 1 7416600 Fax 00 349 1 3207480

FOUNDED 1965. *Publishes* fiction, poetry, art, history, mathematics, dance, music, philosophy, government, political and social sciences, sociology, general science.

Ediciones Anaya SA
Juan Ignacio Luca de Tena 15, 28027 Madrid
☎00 349 1 3938800 Fax 00 349 1 7426631

FOUNDED 1959. *Publishes* education.

Editorial Don Quijote
Compãs del Porvenir 6, 41013 Seville
☎00 349 5 4235080

FOUNDED 1981. *Publishes* fiction, literature, literary criticism, poetry, essays, drama, theatre, history.

EDHASA (Editora y Distribuidora Hispano – Americana SA)
Av Diagonal 519–521, 08029 Barcelona
☎00 349 3 4949720 Fax 00 349 3 4194584

FOUNDED 1946. *Publishes* fiction, literature, literary criticism, essays, history.

Editorial Espasa-Calpe SA
Apdo 547, Carretera de Irún Km 12, 200, 28080 Madrid
☎00 349 1 358 9689 Fax 00 349 1 358 9364

FOUNDED 1925. *Publishes* fiction, science fiction, fantasy, English as a second language, general non-fiction, art, child care and development, cookery, biography, essays, history, literature, literary criticism, self-help, social sciences, sociology.

Ediciones Grijalbo SA
Aragò 385, 08013 Barcelona
☎00 349 3 4587000 Fax 00 349 3 4580495

FOUNDED 1942. *Publishes* fiction, general non-fiction, art, biography, history, government, political science, philosophy, psychology, psychiatry, religion, social sciences, sociology, technology.

Grijalbo Mondadori SA
Aragó 385, 08013 Barcelona
☎00 349 3 4767100 Fax 00 349 3 4767121

FOUNDED 1962. *Publishes* fiction, general non-fiction, archaeology, economics, essays, history, human relations, literature, literary criticism.

Grupo Editorial CEAC SA
C/Peru 164, 08020 Barcelona
☎00 349 3 3075004 Fax 00 349 3 2660067

Publishes education, technology, science fiction, fantasy.

Ediciones Hiperión SL
Calle Salustiano Olózaga 14, 28001 Madrid
☎00 349 1 5576015 Fax 00 349 1 4358690

FOUNDED 1976. *Publishes* literature, literary criticism, essays, poetry, religion (Islamic and Jewish).

Editorial Luis Vives (Edelvives)
C/Xaudaró 25, 28034 Madrid
☎00 349 1 3344883 Fax 00 349 1 3344893

FOUNDED 1890. *Publishes* education.

Editorial Molino
Calabria 166 baixos, 08015 Barcelona
☎00 349 3 2260625 Fax 00 349 3 2266998

FOUNDED 1933. *Publishes* cookery, education, sport, fiction.

Editorial Planeta SA
Córsega 273–279, 08008 Barcelona
☎00 349 3 4154100 Fax 00 349 3 2173850

FOUNDED 1952. *Publishes* fiction and general non-fiction.

Plaza y Janés Editores SA
Enrique Granados 86–88, 08008 Barcelona
☎00 349 3 4151100 Fax 00 349 3 4156976
FOUNDED 1959. *Publishes* fiction and general non-fiction.

Santillana SA
Elfo 32, 28027 Madrid
☎00 349 1 3224500 Fax 00 349 1 3224475
FOUNDED 1964. *Publishes* fiction, essays, literature, literary criticism, travel.

Editorial Seix Barral SA
Córsega 270, Apdo 5023, 08008 Barcelona
☎00 349 3 2186400 Fax 00 349 3 2184773
FOUNDED 1945. *Publishes* fiction, poetry, drama, theatre.

Tusquets Editores
Cesare Cantù 8, 08023 Barcelona
☎00 349 3 2530400 Fax 00 349 3 4176703
FOUNDED 1969. *Publishes* fiction, biography, essays, literature, literary criticism, general science.

Ediciones Versal SA
Calabria 108, 08015 Barcelona
☎00 349 3 3257404 Fax 00 349 3 4236898
FOUNDED 1984. *Publishes* general non-fiction, biography, literature, literary criticism, essays.

Sweden

Albert Bonniers Förlag AB
Box 3159, S-103 63 Stockholm
☎00 46 8 6968620 Fax 00 46 8 6968359
FOUNDED 1837. *Publishes* fiction and general non-fiction.

Bokförlaget Bra Böcker AB
Södra Vägen, S-26380 Höganäs
☎00 46 42 339000 Fax 00 46 42 330504
FOUNDED 1965. *Publishes* fiction, geography, geology, history.

Brombergs Bokförlag AB
Box 12886, S-112 98 Stockholm
☎00 46 8 6503390 Fax 00 46 8 56262085
FOUNDED 1973. *Publishes* fiction, general non-fiction, government, political science, general science.

Bokförlaget Forum AB
PO Box 70321, S-107 23 Stockholm
☎00 46 8 6968440 Fax 00 46 8 6968368

FOUNDED 1944. *Publishes* fiction and general non-fiction.

Bokförlaget Natur och Kultur
Box 27323, S-102 54 Stockholm
☎00 46 8 4538600 Fax 00 46 8 4538790
FOUNDED 1922. *Publishes* fiction and general non-fiction, biography, history, psychology, psychiatry, general science.

Norstedts Förlag AB
Box 2052, S-103 12 Stockholm
☎00 46 8 7893000 Fax 00 46 8 7893038
FOUNDED 1823. *Publishes* fiction and general non-fiction.

AB Rabén och Sjögren Bokförlag
PO Box 2052, S-103 12 Stockholm
☎00 46 8 7893000 Fax 00 46 8 7893052
Website www.raben.se
FOUNDED 1942. *Publishes* fiction and general non-fiction.

Richters Förlag AB
Ostra Förstadsgatan 46, 205 75 Malmö
☎00 46 40 380600 Fax 00 46 40 933708
FOUNDED 1942. *Publishes* fiction.

B Wählströms Bokförlag AB
Box 30022, S-104 25 Stockholm
☎00 46 8 6198600 Fax 00 46 8 6189761
FOUNDED 1911. *Publishes* fiction and general non-fiction.

Switzerland

Arche Verlag AG, Raabe und Vitali
Postfach 8030, CH-8030 Zurich
☎00 41 1 2522410 Fax 00 41 1 2611115
FOUNDED 1944. *Publishes* literature and literary criticism, essays, biography, fiction, poetry, music, dance, travel.

Artemis Verlags AG
Munstergasse 9, CH-8001 Zurich
☎00 41 1 2521100 Fax 00 41 1 2624792
FOUNDED 1943. *Publishes* art, architecture and interior design, biography, history, philosophy, political science, government, travel.

Diogenes Verlag AG
Sprecherstr 8, CH-8032 Zurich
☎00 41 1 2528111 Fax 00 41 1 2528407
FOUNDED 1952. *Publishes* fiction, essays, litera-

ture, literary criticism, mysteries, art, drama, theatre, philosophy.

Langenscheidt AG Zürich-Zug
Postfach 326, CH-8021 Zurich
☎00 41 1 2115000 Fax 00 41 1 2122149

Part of Langenscheidt Group, Germany. *Publishes* language arts and linguistics.

Larousse (Suisse) SA
3 Route du Grand-Mont,
CH-1052 Le Mont-sur-Lausanne
☎00 41 21 24797

Publishes dictionaries, reference and textbooks. Part of **Librairie Larousse**, France.

Neptun-Verlag
Fidlerstr, Postfach 171, CH-8272 Ermatingen
☎00 41 72 642020 Fax 00 41 72 642023

FOUNDED 1946. *Publishes* history and travel.

Orell Füssli Verlag
Dietzingerstrasse 3, CH-8036 Zurich
☎00 41 1 2113630 Fax 00 41 1 4667412
Website www.orellfuessli-verlag.ch

FOUNDED 1519. *Publishes* art, biography, eco-

nomics, education, geography, geology, history, how-to.

Editions Payot Lausanne
18 ave de la Gare, CP 529, CH-1001 Lausanne
☎00 41 21 3290264 Fax 00 41 21 3290266

FOUNDED 1875. *Publishes* general non-fiction, anthropology, archaeology, architecture and interior design, dance, education, history, law, medicine, nursing, dentistry, music, philosophy, literature, literary criticism, essays, general science, social sciences and sociology.

Sauerländer AG
Laurenzenvorstadt 89, CH-5001 Aarau
☎00 41 62 8368626 Fax 00 41 62 8245780

FOUNDED 1807. *Publishes* biography, education, history, poetry, medicine, nursing, dentistry, general science, social sciences, sociology.

Scherz Verlag AG
Theaterplatz 4–6, CH-3000 Berne 7
☎00 41 31 3277117 Fax 00 41 31 3277171

FOUNDED 1939. *Publishes* fiction and general non-fiction; biography, history, psychology, psychiatry, philosophy, parapsychology.

European TV Companies

Austria

ORF (Österreichisher Rundfunk)
Würzburggasse 30, A–1136 Vienna
☎00 43 1 87 8780 Fax 00 43 1 87 8783766
Website www.orf.at

Belgium

Radio-Télévision Belge de la Communauté Française (RTBF)
Boulevard Auguste Reyers 52,
B–1044 Brussels
☎00 32 2 737 2111 Fax 00 32 2 737 2556
Website www.rtbf.be

Vlaamse Radio en Televisieomroep (VRT)
Reyerslaan 52, B–1043 Brussels
☎00 32 2 741 3111 Fax 00 32 2 739 9351
Email info@vrt.be
Website www.vrt.be

Vlaamse Televisie Maatschappij (VTM) (cable)
Medialaan 1, B–1800 Vilvoorde
☎00 32 2 255 3211 Fax 00 32 2 252 5141
Email info@vtm.be
Website www.vtm.be

Denmark

Danmarks Radio–TV
TV Byen, DK–2860 Søborg
☎00 45 35 20 3040 Fax 00 45 35 20 3023
Website www.dr.dk

TV Danmark
Indiakaj 12, DK–2100 Copenhagen 0,
Denmark
☎00 45 35 43 0522 Fax 00 45 35 43 0655

TV–2 Danmark
Rugaardsvej 25, DK–5100 Odense C
☎00 45 65 91 1244 Fax 00 45 65 91 3322
Website www.tv2.dk

Finland

MTV3 Finland
Ilmalantori 2, SF–00240 Helsinki
☎00 358 9 15001 Fax 00 358 9 1500707
Website www.mtv3.fi

Yleisradio Oy (YLE)
PO Box 00024 Yleisradio,
SF–00240 Helsinki
☎00 358 9 14801 Fax 00 358 9 14803391
Website www.yle.fi

France

Canal + (pay TV)
85–89 quai André Citroën,
75711 Paris Cedex 15
☎00 33 1 44 25 10 00
Fax 00 33 1 44 25 12 34
Website www.cplus.fr

La Cinquième
18 rue Horace-Vernet, 92136 Issey Les
Moulineaux
☎00 33 1 41 46 55 55
Fax 00 33 1 41 08 02 22
Website www.lacenquieme.fr

France Télévision (France 2/ France 3)
7 Esplanade Henri de France, Paris Cedex 15
☎00 33 1 56 22 42 42(France 2)/
30 30 (France 3)
Website www.france2.fr and france3.fr

M6 (Métropole Télévision)
89 ave Charles de Gaulle, 92575 Neuilly-sur-
Seine
☎00 33 1 41 92 66 66
Website www.m6.fr

RFO (Radio Télévision Française d'Outre-mer)
5 ave du Recteur Poincaré, 75782 Paris
☎00 33 1 42 15 71 00 Fax 00 33 1 42 15 74 37
Website www.rfo.fr

La Sept/Arte (cable & satellite)
8 rue Marceau, 92785 Issy les Moulineaux
Cedex 9
☎00 33 1 55 00 77 77
Fax 00 33 1 55 00 77 00
Website www.lasept-arte.fr

TF1 (Télévision Française 1)
1 quai du Pont du Jour, 92656 Boulogne
☎00 33 1 41 41 12 34
Fax 00 33 1 41 41 28 40
Website www.tf1.fr

Germany

ARD – Das Erste
ARD Büro, Bertramstr 8, 60320 Frankfurt am
Main
☎00 49 69 59 0607 Fax 00 49 69 15 52075
Website www.ard.de

ZDF (Zweites Deutsches Fernsehen)
Postfach 4040, 55100 Mainz
☎00 49 61 31 70 2050
Fax 00 49 61 31 70 2052
Website www.zdf.de

Ireland

Radio Telefis Éireann (RTE – RTE 1)
Donnybrook, Dublin 4
☎00 353 1 208 3111 Fax 00 353 1 208 3080
Website www.rte.ie

Teilefis na Gaelige
Baile na hAbhann, Co Na Gaillimhe
☎00 353 91 505050 Fax 00 353 91 505021
Website www.tg4.ie

Italy

RAI (RadioTelevisione Italiana)
Viale Mazzini 14, 00195 Rome
☎00 39 06 38781 Fax 00 39 06 3226070
Website www.rai.it

Tele piu' (pay TV)
Via Piranesi 44/a, 20137 Milan
☎00 39 02 700 271 Fax 00 39 02 700 27201

The Netherlands

AVRO (Algemene Omroep Vereniging)
Postbus 2, 1200 JA Hilversum
☎00 31 35 671 79 11 Fax 00 31 35 671 74 39
Website www.omroep.nl/avro

IKON
Postbus 10009, 1201 DA Hilversum
☎00 31 35 672 72 72 Fax 00 31 35 621 51 00
Website www.omroep.nl/ikon

NCRV (Nederlandse Christelijke Radio Vereniging)
Postbus 25000, 1202 HB Hilversum
☎00 31 35 671 99 11 Fax 00 31 35 671 92 85
Website www.ncrv.nl

NOS (Nederlandse Omroep Stichting)
Postbus 26600, 1202 JT Hilversum
☎00 31 35 677 92 22 Fax 00 31 35 624 20 23
Website www.omroep.nl/nos

NPS (Nederlandse Programma Stichting)
Postbus 29000, 1202 MA Hilversum
☎00 31 35 677 93 33 Fax 00 31 35 677 4959
Email publiek@nps.nl
Website www.omroep.nl/nps

TROS (Televisie en Radio Omroep Stichting)
Postbus 28450, 1202 LL Hilversum
☎00 31 35 671 57 15 Fax 00 31 35 671 52 36
Website www.omroep.nl/tros

VARA
Postbus 175, 1200 AD Hilversum
☎00 31 35 671 19 11 Fax 00 31 35 671 13 33
Website www.omroep.nl/vara

VPRO
Postbus 11, 1200 JC Hilversum
☎00 31 35 671 29 11 Fax 00 31 35 671 22 54

Norway

NRK (Norsk Rikskringkasting)
Bjørnstjerne Bjørnsons Plass 1, N–0340 Oslo
☎00 47 23 04 7000
Website www.nrk.no

TVNorge
Sagveien 17, N–0459 Oslo 4
☎00 47 22 38 7800 Fax 00 47 22 35 1000

TV2
Postboks 2, N–5002 Bergen
☎00 47 55 90 8070 Fax 00 47 55 90 8090

Portugal
Radiotelevisão Portuguesa (RTP)
Av 5 de Outubro 197, 1050–054 Lisbon
☎00 351 21 794 7000
Email rtp@rtp.pt
Website www.rtp.pt

TVI (Televisão Independente)
Rua Mário Castelhano 40, Queluz de Baixo,
2749–502 Barcarena
☎00 351 21 434 7500
Fax 00 351 21 434 7654
Website www.tvi.pt

Spain
RTVE (RadioTelevision Española)
Edificio Prado del Rey, E–28223 Madrid
☎00 349 1 581 5404
Fax 00 349 1 581 5412
Website www.rtve.es

TVE (Televisión Española, SA)
C/ Alcalde Saénz de Baranda 92,
28036 Madrid
☎00 349 1 346 4000
Fax 00 349 1 346 8533
Website www.tve.es

Sweden
Sveriges Television
Oxenstiernsgatan 26–34, S–10510 Stockholm
☎00 46 8 784 0000 Fax 00 46 8 784 1500
Website www.svt.se

TV4
Storangskroken 10, S–11579 Stockholm
☎00 46 8 459 4000 Fax 00 46 8 459 4444
Website www.tv4.se

Switzerland
RTR (Radio Television Rumantscha) (Romansch language TV)
Via du Teater 1, CH–7002 Cuira
☎00 41 81 255 7575 Fax 00 41 81 255 7500

RTSI (Radiotelevisione svizzera di lingua Italiana) (Italian language TV)
Casella postale, CH–6903 Lugarno
☎00 41 91 803 51 11 Fax 00 41 91 803 5355
Email info@rtsi
Website www.rtsi.ch

SRG SSR idée suisse (Swiss Broadcasting Corp.)
Giacomettistr 3, CH–3000 Berne15
☎00 41 31 350 91 11 Fax 00 41 31 350 92 56
Website tora.sri.ch/gd

SF DRS (Schweizer Fernsehen) (German language TV)
Fernsehenstrasse 1–4, CH–8052 Zurich
☎00 41 1 305 66 11 Fax 00 41 1 305 56 60
Email sfdrs@sfdrs
Website www.sfdrs.ch

TSR (Télévision Suisse Romande)
Quai Ernest Ansermet 20, CH–1211 Geneva 8
☎00 41 22 708 99 11 Fax 00 41 22 708 98 00
Website www.tsr.ch

Ich bin ein Frankfürter

Barry Turner roams the world's premier book fair

Every author should do it at least once. The expense is out of all proportion to the pleasure, but think of it as a learning experience and you won't be disappointed. Yes, it's the Frankfurt Book Fair, the annual autumn jamboree that brings together everybody who is anybody in world publishing. It has been going strong for over half a century and shows no sign of giving ground to younger rivals like the London Book Fair. Frankfurt outclasses them all, with close on 7,000 exhibitors trading rights on some 400,000 titles.

It is a far cry from the early years when one of Germany's post-war economic miracle workers had the bright idea of disassociating Frankfurt's exhibition centre from memories of the more demonstrable elements of the Third Reich. Services were rudimentary, to put it mildly. As late as the mid-sixties, as I recall less than fondly, the Book Fair was nothing so much as an endurance test. In the hall where the biggest crowds congregated, the lack of air conditioning produced an atmosphere so suffocating as to lead to intimations of an early demise. There was a simple choice of refreshments, hot dogs or hamburgers – assuming you didn't collapse with hunger before you got to the head of the queue.

Now it is all *Vorsprung durch Technik*. The world's largest marketplace for books has also become the world's largest marketplace for electronic media. The exhibition rights catalogue listing titles from 75 countries with the people responsible for them is published as a book, online and as a CD-ROM. The display area has expanded to close on 200,000 square metres. A complex system of moving walkways and a reliably timed bus service save on leg power. (In the old days, you could walk for miles without seeming to get anywhere.) There is even a train that whizzes from the exhibition to the city centre.

Though Germany claims the preponderance of exhibitors, the Book Fair is very much an Anglo-American event. Hall 8, where American and British publishers congregate, is like happy hour in a crush bar. By contrast, Hall 9, which is populated by Dutch and Scandinavian publishers, many of them leaders in their subjects, has more than enough room to move. Elsewhere, it is not unusual to find the exhibitors outnumbering visitors.

Authors? I thought you would never ask. Frankfurt is the best place to see at first-hand where publishers are heading, and that has to be of value to anyone who makes a living from writing.

The dominant feature of last year's Frankfurt was the ever-increasing might of the publishing conglomerates. OK, so you don't have to go to Germany to find that out, but the evidence of how fast and far events are moving comes as a surprise. When I first went to Frankfurt, the Macmillan stand was the responsibility of the European sales manager. He carried it from London in the back of his

Volkswagen and put the thing together the evening before the Fair opened. Now it must take an HGV and trailer to move the kit. Wandering the maze of literary display erected by Random House, say, or HarperCollins is to lose all sense of direction. So many books; so many editors eager to sell rights to books; so many eager supplicants queuing up to talk business. The contrast with the smaller publishers who often share space could not be more acute. There is nothing quite so sad as an expectant young editor sitting alone at one of those dinky tables, hoping against all the odds that one of the big boys will show an interest in his modest selection of titles.

Is it all worth it? It can be if a big enough deal is secured. But that, of course, begs the question. The story of every Frankfurt is of huge excitement over a few hot properties which may or may not realize their potential. Two years ago Little Brown, a canny investor if ever there was one, forked out £250,000 for a novel called *Ladies Man*. When last heard of, it had sold less than 1,500 copies. On the other hand, Transworld confounded the cynics with a successful £360,000 bid for *The Horse Whisperer* which then went to Dell Delacorte for over £3 million and to Hollywood for £2 million.

There are books sold at Frankfurt which exist only in a publisher's or agent's imagination. Everybody remembers the let-down of Elton John's autobiography, which attracted offers of up to £6 million until the star said thanks but no thanks. The agent, Giles Gordon, who is blessed with more creativity than most authors, tells the story of the Sean Connery coup that wasn't. Giles had the notion that a Connery biography would be popular. And so it proved. Wherever he went he was followed by publishers waving chequebooks. Only trouble was, Giles had not cleared his great idea with Mr Connery. Result – the book has still to be written.

Not all Frankfurt business is mega-business. Of the steady plodders who do well out of the Fair, the biggest single group must be the publishers of illustrated books. Everywhere you go at Frankfurt, there are stands promoting the latest large-format, colourful volumes on everything from modern design to DIY. You can understand why. Advances in technology combined with the dramatic savings achieved by printing in the Far East have brought down the price of illustrated books to a level that is attractive to the bookshop browser. At the same time, picture quality has improved enormously. Add to this that many illustrated books have international appeal and so lend themselves to multilingual co-editions, and the attraction to writers in search of steady income becomes apparent. Much of the business is done by packagers who tend to drive a hard bargain with their contributors but with increasing demand for writing talent the balance is shifting in favour of the author.

Occasionally, a publisher will analyse the cost of Frankfurt and the return on the investment. Nearly always, the hard figures are depressing. A big publisher will spend £100,000-plus on a week at the Book Fair, taking into account exhibition space, travel and hotel bills and those splendid parties held to impress competitors. You have to sell an awful lot of books to get back that sort of money. But then what publisher jealous of his reputation can afford not to go to Frankfurt? To be seen at the Book Fair is to be taken seriously; to stay away . . . the publisher shudders and pays up.

Authors who assert that the money they help to earn could be better spent should take comfort from a story that has gone the rounds for many years to show that publishers are forever prudent. It is said that during the week of the Book Fair, the prostitutes of Frankfurt take their holidays. One interpretation of this phenomenon is that publishing has more than a sufficiency of consenting adults. A subtler explanation is that publishers prefer to have sex with each other or with agents or even with authors, if they get lucky, because like all successful enterprises, it combines the minimum risk with the lowest possible overhead.

The 52nd Frankfurt Book Fair will be held on 18–23 October 2000. For more information access the Web site on www.frankfurt-book-fair.com

US Publishers

International Reply Coupons (IRCs)
For return postage, send IRCs, available from post offices. Letters, 60 pence; mss according to weight.

ABC–CLIO
PO Box 1911, Santa Barbara CA 93117–1911
☎001 805 968 1911 Fax 001 805 685 9685
Email library@abc-clio.com
Website www.abc-clio.com
Vice-President/Publisher *Rolf A Janke*

FOUNDED 1955. *Publishes* reference, mythology, political science, current world issues, social sciences, humanities, literature, cultural anthropology, sport, multimedia. No unsolicited mss; synopses and ideas welcome.
Royalties paid annually. *UK subsidiary* **ABC-Clio Ltd**, Oxford.

Abingdon Press
201 Eighth Avenue South, Box 801, Nashville TN 37202–0801
☎001 615 749 6404 Fax 001 615 749 6512
Editorial Director *Harriett Jane Olson*

Publishes non-fiction: religious (lay and professional), children's religious and academic texts. Over 100 titles a year. Approach in writing only with synopsis and samples. IRCs essential.

Harry N. Abrams, Inc.
100 Fifth Avenue, New York NY 10011
☎001 212 206 7715 Fax 001 212 645 8437
CEO/President/Editor-in-Chief
Paul Gottlieb

FOUNDED 1950. *Publishes* illustrated books: art, architecture, nature, entertainment and children's. No fiction. Submit completed mss (no dot matrix), together with sample illustrations.

Academy Chicago Publishers
363 W. Erie Street, Chicago IL 60610
☎001 312 751 7300 Fax 001 312 751 7306
Email academy363@aol.com
Website www.academychicago.com
Senior Editor *Anita Miller*

FOUNDED 1975. *Publishes* quality mainstream fiction; non-fiction: history, biography. No romance, children's, young adult, religious, sexist or avant-garde. Send first three consecu-

tive chapters with synopsis only, accompanied by IRCs.
Royalties paid twice-yearly. *Distributed* in the UK and Europe by Gazelle, Lancaster.

Ace/Putnam
See **Penguin Putnam Inc.**

Adams Media Corporation
260 Center Street, Holbrook MA 02343
☎001 781 767 8100 Fax 001 781 767 0994
Website www.adamsmedia.com
Editor-in-Chief *Edward Walters*

FOUNDED 1980. *Publishes* general non-fiction: careers, business, personal finance, relationships, parenting and maternity, self-improvement, reference, cooking, sports, games and humour. Ideas welcome but publisher will not respond to or return unsolicited material unless interested.

Addison Wesley Longman Pearson Education Publishing Group
1185 Avenue of the Americas, New York, NY 10036
☎001 212 782 3352 Fax 001 212 782 3313
Website www.awl.com
Editorial Director *Richard Wohl*

One of the world's largest educational publishers of books, multimedia and learning programmes.

University of Alabama Press
Box 870380, Tuscaloosa AL 35487
☎001 205 348 5180 Fax 001 205 348 9201
Director *Nicole Mitchell*

FOUNDED 1945. *Publishes* American history, southern history and culture, American religious history; Latin American history, American/southeastern archaeology, mesoamerican archaeology, thenohistory, American literature and criticism, rhetoric and communication, literary journalism, African-American studies, Native American studies, women's studies, Judaic studies, public administration, theatre, natural history and environmental studies, regional studies of Alabama and the southern states. Submissions are not invited in poetry, fiction or drama. About 50 titles a year.

Aladdin Books
See **Simon & Schuster Children's Publishing**

University of Alaska Press
1st Floor, Gruening Building,
PO Box 756240, University of Alaska,
Fairbanks AK 99775–6240
☎001 907 474 5831 Fax 001 907 474 5502
Email fypress@uaf.edu
Website www.uaf.edu/uapress

Manager *Debbie Gonzalez*
Managing Editor *Carla Helfferich*
Acquisitions *Pam Odom*

Traces its origins back to 1927 but was relatively dormant until the early 1980s. *Publishes* scholarly works about Alaska and the North Pacific rim, with a special emphasis on circumpolar regions. 5–10 titles a year. No fiction or poetry.

DIVISIONS
Ramuson Library Historical Translation Series *Marvin Falk*; **Oral Biography Series** *William Schneider*; **Monograph Series** *Carla Helfferich*; **Classic Reprint Series** *Terrence Cole*; **Lanternlight Library** Informal non-fiction covering Northern interest. Unsolicited mss, synopses and ideas welcome.

Allen Lane The Penguin Press
See **Penguin Putnam Inc.**

AMACOM Books
1601 Broadway, New York NY 10019–7406
☎001 212 586 8100 Fax 001 212 903 8083
Email hkennedy@amanet.org
Website www.amanet.org

President & Publisher *Harold V. Kennedy*

Owned by American Management Association. *Publishes* business books only, including general management, business communications, sales and marketing, finance, computers and information systems, human resource management and training, career/personal growth skills, research development, project management and manufacturing, quality/customer service titles. 65–70 titles a year. Proposals welcome.
Royalties paid twice-yearly.

Anvil
See **Krieger Publishing Co.**

Archway Paperbacks
See **Pocket Books**

University of Arizona Press
1230 North Park Avenue, Suite 102, Tucson AZ 85719–4140
☎001 520 621 1441 Fax 001 520 621 8899
Website www.uapress.arizona.edu

Director *Christine Szuter*

FOUNDED 1959. *Publishes* academic non-fiction, particularly with a regional/cultural link, plus Native-American and Hispanic literature. About 50 titles a year.

Arkana
See **Penguin Putnam Inc.**

University of Arkansas Press
McIlroy House, 201 Ozark Avenue,
Fayetteville AR 72701
☎001 501 575 3246 Fax 001 501 575 6044

Director *Lawrence J. Malley*

FOUNDED 1980. *Publishes* scholarly monographs, poetry and general trade including biography, etc. Particularly interested at present in scholarly works in history, politics and literary criticism. About 30 titles a year.
Royalties paid annually.

Aspect
See **Warner Books Inc.**

Atheneum Books for Young Readers
See **Simon & Schuster Children's Publishing**

Atlantic Monthly Press
See **Grove/Atlantic Inc**

AUP (Associated University Presses)
AUP New Jersey titles are handled in the UK by **Golden Cockerel Press** (see entry under **UK Publishers**).

Avery Publishing Group, Inc.
120 Old Broadway, Garden City Park,
New York NY 11040
☎001 516 741 2155 Fax 001 516 742 1892
Email info@averypublishing.com
Website www.averypublishing.com

President *Rudy Shur*

FOUNDED 1976. *Publishes* professional and trade books, specialising in childbirth education, health, self-help, nutrition, business, history,

psychiatry, how-to, government; college text-books in history, science, mathematics, military science and history, technology, social science. About 50 titles a year. No unsolicited mss; synopses and ideas welcome if accompanied by s.a.e.
Royalties paid twice-yearly.

Avon Books

1350 Avenue of the Americas, New York NY 10019
☎001 212 261 6800 Fax 001 212 261 6895
Website www.avonbooks.com

Senior Vice President/Publisher *Lou Aronica*

FOUNDED 1941. A division of the Hearst Corporation. *Publishes* hardcover; trade and mass-market paperback reprints and originals including fiction, non-fiction, adult, juvenile and young adult. 500 titles a year. Submit query letter and sample chapter.

Baker Book House

PO Box 6287, Grand Rapids MI 49516–6287
☎001 616 676 9185 Fax 001 616 676 9573
Website www.bakerbooks.com

President *Dwight Baker*
Director of Publications *Don Stevenson*

FOUNDED 1939. Began life as a used-book store and began publishing in earnest in the 1950s, primarily serving the evangelical Christian market. About 165 titles a year. Additional information for authors on Website.

DIVISIONS/IMPRINTS
Baker Books *Publishes* religious non-fiction and fiction, Bible reference, professional (pastors and church leaders) books, children's books. About 80 titles a year. Proposals welcome (request guidelines, specifying non-fiction, fiction, professional or children's).
   Baker Academic *Jim Kinney Publishes* college/seminary textbooks, religious reference books, biblical studies monographs. About 30 titles a year. Proposals welcome (guidelines available on request). No unsolicited mss. **Fleming H. Revell** *Linda Holland* FOUNDED 1870. A family-owned business until 1978, Revell was one of the first Christian publishers to take the step into secular publishing. Joined Baker Book House in 1992. *Publishes* adult fiction and non-fiction for evangelical Christians. About 45 titles a year. Synopses and ideas welcome.
   Chosen Books *Jane Campbell* FOUNDED 1971; joined Baker Book House in 1992. *Publishes* charismatic adult non-fiction for evangelical Christians. About 10 titles a year. Synopses or ideas welcome.
Royalties paid twice-yearly.

Ballantine Publishing Group

201 East 50th Street, New York NY 10022
☎001 212 572 2688 Fax 001 212 940 7580
Website www.randomhouse.com

President/Publisher *Gina Centrello*

FOUNDED 1952. A division of **Random House, Inc.** since 1973. *Publishes* fiction and non-fiction, science fiction.
   DIVISIONS/IMPRINTS **Ballantine Books**; **Del Rey**; **Fawcett Books**; **Ivy**; **Library of Contemporary Thought**; **One World**; **Wellspring**.

Banner Books

See **University Press of Mississippi**

Bantam Dell Publishing Group

1540 Broadway, New York NY 10036
☎001 212 782 5000 Fax 001 212 302 7985

President/Publisher *Irwyn Applebaum*

FOUNDED 1945. The largest mass market paperback publisher in the USA. A division of **Random House, Inc.** *Publishes* general commercial fiction and non-fiction, young readers and children's.

DIVISIONS/IMPRINTS
Bantam Hardcover; **Bantam Mass Market**; **Bantam Trade Paperback**; **Crimeline**; **Delacorte Press**; **Dell**; **Delta**; **Dial Press**; **DTP**; **Island**; **Domain**; **Fanfare**; **Spectra**;

Barron's Educational Series, Inc.

250 Wireless Boulevard, Hauppauge NY 11788
☎001 516 434 3311 Fax 001 516 434 3723
Email info@barronseduc.com
Website www.barronseduc.com

President *Manuel H. Barron*
Managing Editor *Grace Freedson*

FOUNDED 1942. *Publishes* adult non-fiction, children's fiction and non-fiction, test preparation materials and language materials, cookbooks, pets, hobbies, sport, photography, health, business, law, computers, travel, business, art and painting. No adult fiction. 150 titles a year. Unsolicited mss, synopses and ideas for books welcome.
Royalties paid twice-yearly.

Beacon Press

25 Beacon Street, Boston MA 02108
☎001 617 742 2110 Fax 001 617 723 3097
Website www.beacon.org

Director *Helene Atwan*

Publishes general non-fiction. About 85 titles a

year. Does not accept unsolicited mss. For further information, refer to Website page.

Beech Tree Books
See **William Morrow & Co., Inc.**

Berkley Books
See **Penguin Putnam Inc.**

H. & R. Block
See **Simon & Schuster Trade Division**

Boulevard
See **Penguin Putnam Inc.**

Boyds Mills Press
815 Church Street, Honesdale PA 18431
☎001 570 253 1164 Fax 001 570 253 0179
Website www.boydsmillspress.com
Publisher *Kent Brown Jr*
Editorial Director *Larry Rosler*

A subsidiary of Highlights for Children, Inc. FOUNDED 1990 as a publisher of children's trade books. *Publishes* children's fiction, nonfiction and poetry. About 50 titles a year. Unsolicited mss, synopses and ideas for books welcome. No romance or fantasy novels.
Royalties paid twice-yearly.

Bradford Books
See **The MIT Press**

Brassey's, Inc.
22841 Quicksilver Drive, Dulles WA 20166
☎001 703 661 1562 Fax 001 703 661 1547
Email djacobs@bookintl.com
Publisher *Don McKeon*
Assistant Editor *Donald Jacobs*

FOUNDED 1983. *Publishes* non-fiction titles on topics of history (especially military history), world and US affairs, US foreign policy, defence, intelligence, biography, transport (especially automobiles) and sports. About 50 titles a year. No unsolicited mss; synopses and ideas welcome.
Royalties paid annually.

Broadway Books
See **Doubleday Broadway Publishing Group**

University of California Press
2120 Berkeley Way, Berkeley CA 94720
☎001 510 642 4247 Fax 001 510 643 7127
Director *James H. Clark*

Publishes scholarly and scientific non-fiction; some fiction and poetry in translation. Preliminary letter with outline preferred.

Carol Publishing Group
120 Enterprise Avenue, Secaucus NJ 07094
☎001 201 866 0490 Fax 001 201 866 8159
Publisher *Steven Schragis*

FOUNDED 1989. *Publishes* some fiction but mostly non-fiction: biography and autobiography, history, science, humour, how-to, illustrated and self-help.

Carolrhoda Books, Inc.
241 First Avenue North, Minneapolis MN 55401
☎001 612 332 3344 Fax 001 612 332 7615
Submissions Editor *Rebecca Poole*

Publishes children's: nature, biography, history, beginners' readers, world cultures, photo essays and historical fiction. Please send s.a.e. for author guidelines, making sure guideline requests are clearly marked on the envelope or they will be returned. 'We are *only* accepting submissions twice a year – from March 1–31 and October 1–31. Submissions postmarked with other dates will be returned unopened. Also, only submissions with s.a.e. will receive a response.'

Chapman & Hall
See **Kluwer Academic Publishers**

Charlesbridge Publishing
85 Main Street, Watertown MA 02472
☎001 617 926 0329 Fax 001 617 926 5720
Email books@charlesbridge.com
Website www.charlesbridge.com
Chairman *Brent Farmer*
Managing Editor *Elena Dworkin Wright*

FOUNDED 1980 as an educational publisher focusing on teaching reading and math processes. *Publishes* children's educational programmes, non-fiction picture books and multicultural fiction for 3–12-year-olds. Also publishes mathematical stories, *Maths Adventures*, as well as other trade fiction, in picture-book format. Complete mss or proposals welcome with self-addressed envelope and IRCs. Unsolicited mss accepted but submissions must be exclusive. Responses are sent within three months.

University of Chicago Press
5801 South Ellis Avenue, Fourth Floor, Chicago IL 60637–1496
☎001 773 702 7700 Fax 001 773 702 9756
Website www.press.uchicago.edu

FOUNDED 1891. *Publishes* academic non-fiction only.

Children's Press
See **Grolier, Incorporated**

Chosen Books
See **Baker Book House**

Chronicle Books
85 Second Street, Sixth Floor, San Francisco CA 94105
☎001 415 537 3730 Fax 001 415 437 4450
Website www.chroniclebooks.com
President/Publisher *Jack Jensen*
Managing Editor *Dean Burrell*
FOUNDED 1966. Division of Chronicle Publishing Co. *Publishes* fiction and non-fiction and children's books. Also stationery and gift items. About 200 titles a year. Query or submit outline/synopsis and sample chapters and artwork.
Royalties paid twice-yearly.

Clarkson Potter
See **Crown Publishing Group**

Cliff Street Books
See **HarperCollins Publishers, Inc.**

Copper Beech Books
See **The Millbrook Press, Inc.**

Crimeline
See **Bantam Dell Publishing Group**

Crown Publishing Group
201 East 50th Street, New York NY 10022
☎001 212 572 2409 Fax 001 212 940 7408
Website www.randomhouse.com
President/Publisher *Chip Gibson*
FOUNDED 1933. Division of **Random House, Inc.** *Publishes* popular trade fiction and non-fiction.
IMPRINTS **Clarkson Potter** *Lauren Shakely*; **Harmony**; **Three Rivers Press** *Linda Loewenthal*; **Crown** *Steve Ross*; **Times Books** (see entry).

Currency
See **Doubleday Broadway Publishing Group**

DAW Books, Inc.
375 Hudson Street, 3rd Floor, New York NY 10014–3658
☎001 212 366 2096/Submissions: 366 2095
Fax 001 212 366 2090
Email daw@penguinputnam.com
Website www.dawbooks.com

Publishers *Elizabeth R. Wollheim, Sheila E. Gilbert*
Submissions Editor *Peter Stampfel*
FOUNDED 1971 by Donald and Elsie Wollheim as the first mass-market publisher devoted to science fiction and fantasy. *Publishes* science fiction/fantasy, and some horror. No short stories, anthology ideas or non-fiction. Unsolicited mss, synopses and ideas for books welcome. About 36 titles a year.
Royalties paid twice-yearly.

Dearborn Financial Publishing, Inc.
155 N. Wacker Drive, Chicago IL 60606–1719
☎001 312 836 4400 Fax 001 312 836 1021
President *Dennis Blitz*
FOUNDED 1967. A niche publisher serving the financial services industries. *Publishes* real estate, insurance, financial planning, securities, commodities, investments, banking, professional education, motivation and reference titles, investment reference and how-to books for the consumer (personal finance, real estate) and small business owner. About 150 titles a year.
DIVISIONS/IMPRINTS   **Trade/Professional** *Cynthia Zigmund*; **Securities Training** *Mark Emmons*; **Insurance** *Dan Trombley*; **Textbook: Real Estate Education Company** *Carol Luitjens*; **Commodity Trend Service** *Dennis Blitz*. Unsolicited mss, synopses and ideas welcome.
Royalties paid twice-yearly.

Del Rey
See **Ballantine Publishing Group**

Delacorte
See **Bantam Dell Publishing Group**

Dell
See **Bantam Dell Publishing Group**

Delta
See **Bantam Dell Publishing Group**

Michael di Capua Books
See **HarperCollins Publishers, Inc.**

Dial Books for Young Readers
345 Hudson Street, New York NY 10014–3657
☎001 212 366 2800
Queries *Submissions Coordinator*
FOUNDED 1961. A division of Penguin Putnam Books for Young Readers. *Publishes* children's books, including picture books, beginning

readers, fiction and non-fiction for middle grade and young adults. 150 titles a year.

IMPRINTS Hardcover only: **Dial Books for Young Readers**; **Dial Easy-to-Read**. No unsolicited mss accepted; query letters with return postage only.

Royalties paid twice-yearly.

Dial Press
See **Bantam Dell Publishing Group**

Domain
See **Bantam Dell Publishing Group**

Doubleday Broadway Publishing Group
1540 Broadway, New York NY 10036
☎001 212 782 9000 Fax 001 212 302 7985
Website www.randomhouse.com

President & Publisher *Stephen Rubin*

The Doubleday Broadway Publishing Group, a division of **Random House, Inc.** was formed by a merger of Doubleday and Broadway Books in 1999. *Publishes* fiction and non-fiction.

DIVISION/IMPRINTS **Broadway Books**; **Currency**; **Doubleday**; **Doubleday Religious Publishing**; **Doubleday/Image**; **Main Street Books**; **Nan A. Talese**.

Lisa Drew Books
See **Simon & Schuster Trade Division**

DTP
See **Bantam Dell Publishing Group**

Thomas Dunne Books
See **St Martin's Press LLC**

Sanford J. Durst Publications
11 Clinton Avenue, Rockville Centre, New York NY 11570
☎001 516 766 4444 Fax 001 516 766 4520

Owner *Sanford J. Durst*

FOUNDED 1975. *Publishes* non-fiction: numismatic and related, philatelic, legal and art. Also children's books. About 12 titles a year.

Royalties paid twice-yearly.

Dushkin/McGraw-Hill
See **The McGraw-Hill Companies, Inc.**

Dutton/Dutton's Children's Books
See **Penguin Putnam Inc**

Eaglebrook
See **William Morrow & Co., Inc.**

Edge Books
See **Henry Holt & Co LLC**

William B. Eerdmans Publishing Co.
255 Jefferson Avenue SE, Grand Rapids MI 49503
☎001 616 459 4591 Fax 001 616 459 6540
Email sales@eerdmans.com

President *William B. Eerdmans Jr*
Vice President/Editor-in-Chief *Jon Pott*

FOUNDED 1911 as a theological and reference publisher. Gradually began publishing in other genres with authors like C. S. Lewis, Dorothy Sayers and Malcolm Muggeridge on its lists. *Publishes* religious: theology, biblical studies, ethical and social concern, social criticism and children's, religious history, religion and literature. 120 titles in 1999.

DIVISIONS **Children's** *Judy Zylstra*; **Other** *Jon Pott*. Unsolicited mss, synopses and ideas welcome.

Royalties paid twice-yearly.

M. Evans & Co., Inc.
216 East 49th Street, New York NY 10017
☎001 212 688 2810 Fax 001 212 486 4544
Email mevans@sprynet.com

President *George C. de Kay*

FOUNDED 1954 as a packager. Began publishing in 1962. Best known for its popular psychology and health books, with titles like *Body Language*, *Open Marriage*, *Pain Erasure* and *Aerobics*. *Publishes* general non-fiction and fiction. About 30 titles a year. No unsolicited mss; query first. Synopses and ideas welcome.

Royalties paid twice-yearly.

Everyman's Library
See **Random House, Inc.**

Faber & Faber, Inc.
19 Union Square West, New York NY 1003
☎001 212 741 6900 Fax 001 212 633 9385

FOUNDED 1976. A division of **Farrar, Straus & Giroux, Inc.** *Publishes* fiction and non-fiction for adults. No unsolicited mss.

Royalties paid twice-yearly.

Facts On File, Inc.
11 Penn Plaza, New York NY 10001
☎001 212 967 8800 Fax 001 212 967 9196

President *Mark McDonnell*
Publisher *Laurie E. Likoff*

Started life in the early 1940s with News Digest

subscription series to libraries. Began publishing on specific subjects with the Checkmark Books series and developed its current reference and trade book programme in the 1970s. *Publishes* general trade, young adult trade and academic reference for the school and library markets. *Specialises* in single subject encyclopedias. About 135 titles a year. No fiction, cookery or popular non-fiction.

DIVISIONS **General Reference** *Laurie Likoff*; **Academic Reference** *Owen Lancer*; **Adult Trade** *James Chambers*; **Young Adult & US History***Nicole Bowen*; **Electronic Publishing** *James Housley*; **Literary Studies** *Anne Savarese*. Unsolicited synopses and ideas welcome; no mss. Send query letter in the first instance.

Royalties paid twice-yearly.

Fanfare
See **Bantam Dell Publishing Group**

Farrar, Straus & Giroux, Inc.
19 Union Square West, New York NY 10003
☎001 212 741 6900 Fax 001 212 741 6973
President/CEO *Roger W. Straus III*
Executive Vice-President/Editor-in-Chief *Jonathan Galassi*

FOUNDED 1946. *Publishes* general fiction, non-fiction, juveniles. About 190 titles a year.

DIVISIONS **Children's Books** *Margaret Ferguson Publishes* fiction and non-fiction, books and novels for children and young adults. Approximately 100 titles a year. Submit synopsis and sample chapters (copies of artwork/photographs as part of package). **Hill & Wang** *Elisabeth Sifton*.

IMPRINTS **MIRASOL Libros Juveniles**; **Noonday Press** *Elisabeth Dyssegaard*; **North Point Press**; **Sunburst Books**.

Fawcett Books
See **Ballantine Publishing Group**

Donald I. Fine
See **Penguin Putnam Inc.**

Fireside
See **Simon & Schuster Trade Division**

Fodor's Travel Publications
See **Random House, Inc.**

Forge
See **St Martin's Press LLC**

The Free Press
See **Simon & Schuster Trade Division**

Samuel French, Inc.
45 West 25th Street, New York
NY 10010–2751
☎001 212 206 8990 Fax 001 212 206 1429
Website www.samuelfrench.com
Editor *Lawrence Harbison*

FOUNDED 1830. *Publishes* plays in paperback: Broadway and off-Broadway hits, light comedies, mysteries, one-act plays and plays for young audiences. Unsolicited mss welcome. No synopses.

Royalties paid annually (books); twice-yearly (amateur productions); monthly (professional productions). *Overseas associates* in London, Toronto and Sydney.

The Globe Pequot Press
PO Box 480, Guildford CT 06437
☎001 203 458 4500 Fax 001 203 458 4604
President *Linda Kennedy*
Associate Publisher *Michael K. Urban*

Publishes regional and international travel, how-to, personal finance, and outdoor recreation. Also publishes the *Recommended Country Inns* guides. About 200 titles a year. Unsolicited mss, synopses and ideas welcome, particularly for travel and outdoor recreation books.

Royalties paid.

Great Source Education Group
See **Houghton Mifflin Co.**

Greenwillow Books
See **William Morrow & Co., Inc.**

Griffin
See **St Martin's Press LLC**

Grolier, Incorporated
90 Sherman Turnpike, Danbury CT 06816
☎001 203 797 3500 Fax 001 203 797 3197
Website www.grolier.com
President *Brian Beckwith*

FOUNDED 1895. *Publishes* juvenile non-fiction, encyclopedias, speciality reference sets, children's fiction and picture books. About 600 titles a year.

DIVISIONS/IMPRINTS **Children's Press**; **Grolier Educational**; **Grolier Interactive**; **Grolier Reference**; **Orchard Books**; **Franklin Watts** (see entry).

Grosset & Dunlap/Grosset Putnam
See **Penguin Putnam Inc**

Grove/Atlantic Inc.

841 Broadway, New York NY 10003–4793
☎001 212 614 7850 Fax 001 212 614 7886
President/Publisher *Morgan Entrekin*
Managing Editor *Michael Hornburg*
FOUNDED 1952. *Publishes* general fiction and
non-fiction. IMPRINTS **Atlantic Monthly
Press**; **Grove Press**.

Gulliver Books

See **Harcourt Children's Books Division**

Harcourt Children's Books Division

525 B Street, Suite 1900, San Diego
CA 92101–4495
☎001 619 231 6616 Fax 001 619 699 6777
Vice President/Publisher *Louise Pelan*

A division of Harcourt Inc. *Publishes* fiction,
poetry and non-fiction covering a wide range
of subjects: biography, environment and ecol-
ogy, history, travel, science and current affairs
for children and young adults. About 175 titles
a year.
   IMPRINTS **Gulliver Books**; **Harcourt
Children's Books**; **Harcourt Paperbacks**;
Odyssey Paperbacks Novels; **Red Wagon
Books** For ages 6 months to 3 years; **Voyager
Paperbacks** Picture books; **Silver Whistle**.
No unsolicited mss.

Harlequin Historicals

See **Silhouette Books**

Harmony

See **Crown Publishing Group**

HarperCollins Publishers, Inc.

10 East 53rd Street, New York NY 10022
☎001 212 207 7000 Fax 001 212 207 7797
Website www.harpercollins.com
President/Chief Executive Officer
   Jane Friedman
FOUNDED 1817. Owned by News Corporation.
Publishes general fiction, non-fiction and college
textbooks in hardcover, trade paperback and
mass-market formats. No unsolicited material.
   DIVISIONS/IMPRINTS **Adult Trade**; **Harper-
Reference**;   **HarperCollins Children's
Books**; **HarperPaperbacks**; **HarperBusiness**;
HarperPerennial; **HarperPrism**; **Harper-
Audio/Caedmon**; **Cliff Street Books**;
Michael di Capua Books; **Regan Books**.
   SUBSIDIARY **Zondervan Publishing House**
(see entry).

Harvard University Press

79 Garden Street, Cambridge MA 02138
☎001 617 495 2611 Fax 001 617 496 4677
Editor-in-Chief *Aida D. Donald*

Publishes scholarly non-fiction only: general
interest, literature, science and behaviour, social
science, history, humanities, psychology, political science, sociology, economics, law, business,
classics, religion, cultural studies, philosophy, history of science, history of nature, African-
American studies. 135 new titles a year and
80–90 paperbacks. Free book catalogue available.

Hearst Books

See **William Morrow & Co., Inc.**

Hill & Wang

See **Farrar, Straus & Giroux, Inc.**

Hippocrene Books, Inc.

171 Madison Avenue, New York NY 10016
☎001 212 685 4371 Fax 001 212 779 9338
Website www.hippocrenebooks.com
President/Editorial Director
   George Blagowidow

FOUNDED 1971. *Publishes* general non-fiction
and reference books. Particularly strong on
foreign language dictionaries, language studies,
military history and international cookbooks.
No fiction. Send brief summary, table of contents and one chapter for appraisal. S.a.e. essential for response. For manuscript return include
sufficient postage cover (IRCs).

Holiday House, Inc.

425 Madison Avenue, New York NY 10017
☎001 212 688 0085 Fax 001 212 421 6134
Vice President/Editor-in-Chief
   Regina Griffin
Publishes children's general fiction and non-fiction (pre-school to secondary). About 50 titles
a year. Send query letters only. IRCs for reply
must be included.

Henry Holt & Co LLC

115 West 18th Street, New York NY 10011
☎001 212 886 9200 Fax 001 212 633 0748
President/Publisher *John Sterling*
Senior Editor, Adult Trade *David Sobel*
**Executive Editor, Books for Young
   Readers** *Nina Ignatowicz*
FOUNDED in 1866, Henry Holt is one of the
oldest publishers in the United States. Part of
Holtzbrinck Publishing Holdings. *Publishes* fic-
tion, by both American and international

authors, biographies, and books on history and politics, ecology and psychology. 230 titles a year. DIVISIONS/IMPRINTS **Adult Trade**; **Books for Young Readers**; **Edge Books**; **John Macrae Books** *John Macrae*; **Bill Martin Jr Books**; **Metropolitan Books** *Sara Bershtel*; **Owl Books**; **Red Feather Books**.

Houghton Mifflin Co.

222 Berkeley Street, Boston MA 02116–3764
☎001 617 351 5000 Fax 001 617 351 1125
Website www.hmco.com

Contact *Submissions Editor*

FOUNDED 1832. *Publishes* literary fiction and general non-fiction, including autobiography, biography and history. Also school and college textbooks; children's fiction and non-fiction. Average 100 titles a year. Queries only for adult material; synopsis, outline and sample chapters for children's non-fiction; complete mss for children's fiction. IRCs required with all submissions/queries.

DIVISIONS/SUBSIDIARY COMPANIES **Great Source Education Group**; **Houghton Mifflin College Division**; **Houghton Mifflin School Division**; **Houghton Mifflin Trade & Reference Division**; **McDougal Littell Inc.**; **The Riverside Publishing Co.**; **Sunburst Technology** (multimedia and video).

HP Books

See **Penguin Putnam Inc.**

Hudson River Editions

See **Simon & Schuster Trade Division**

University of Illinois Press

1325 South Oak Street, Champaign IL 61820–6903
☎001 217 333 0950 Fax 001 217 244 8082
Email uipress@uillinois.edu
Website www.press.uillinois.edu

Editorial Director *Willis Regier*

Publishes non-fiction, scholarly and general, with special interest in Americana, women's studies, African–American studies, American music and regional books. About 140–150 titles a year.

Image

See **Doubleday Broadway Publishing Group**

Indiana University Press

601 North Morton Street, Bloomington IN 42404–3797
☎001 812 855 4203 Fax 001 812 855 8507

Email iupress@indiana.edu
Website www.indiana.edu/~iupress

Director *Peter-John Leone*

Publishes scholarly non-fiction in the following subject areas: African studies, anthropology, Asian studies, Afro-American studies, environment and ecology, film, folklore, history, Jewish studies, literary criticism, medical ethics, Middle East studies, military, music, paleontology, philanthropy, philosophy, politics, religion, semiotics, Russian and East European studies, Victorian studies, women's studies. Query in writing in first instance.

University of Iowa Press

Kuhl House, 119 West Park Road, Iowa City IA 52242
☎001 319 335 2000 Fax 001 319 335 2055
Website www.uiowa.edu/~uipress

Director *Holly Carver*

FOUNDED 1969 as a small scholarly press publishing about five books a year. Now publishing about 35 a year in a variety of scholarly fields, plus local interest, short stories, autobiography and poetry. No unsolicited mss; query first. Unsolicited ideas and synopses welcome.

Royalties paid annually.

Iowa State University Press

2121 South State Avenue, Ames IA 50010
☎001 515 292 0140 Fax 001 515 292 3348
Email vanhouten@isupress.edu
Website www.isupress.edu

Editor-in-Chief *Gretchen Van Houten*

FOUNDED 1934 as an offshoot of the university's journalism department. *Publishes* scholarly books and textbooks, agriculture, aeronautics, environmental studies, regional history, journalism, and veterinary medicine.

Royalties paid annually; sometimes twice-yearly.

Irwin/McGraw-Hill

See **The McGraw-Hill Companies, Inc.**

Island

See **Bantam Dell Publishing Group**

Ivy

See **Ballantine Publishing Group**

Jove

See **Penguin Putnam Inc.**

University Press of Kansas

2501 West 15th Street, Lawrence
KS 66049–3905
☎001 785 864 4154 Fax 001 785 864 4586
Email mail@newpress.upress.ukans.edu
Website www.kansaspress.ku.edu
Director *Fred M. Woodward*
FOUNDED 1946. Became the publishing arm
for all six state universities in Kansas in 1976.
Publishes scholarly books in American history,
women's studies, presidential studies, social and
political philosophy, political science, military
history and environmental. About 50 titles a
year. Proposals welcome.
Royalties paid annually.

Jean Karl Books

See **Simon & Schuster Children's
Publishing**

Kent State University Press

Kent OH 44242–0001
☎001 330 672 7913 Fax 001 330 672 3104
Director *John T. Hubbell*
Editor-in-Chief *Joanna Hildebrand Craig*
FOUNDED 1965. *Publishes* scholarly works in
history and biography, literary studies and general non-fiction. 25–30 titles a year. Queries
welcome; no mss.
Royalties paid annually.

Kluwer Academic Publishers

101 Philip Drive, Norwell MA 02061
☎001 781 871 6600 Fax 001 781 871 6528
Email kluwer@wkap.com
President *Jeff Smith*
Managing Editor *Claire Stanton*
FOUNDED 1946. *Publishes* scholarly scientific
books and journals. Over 300 titles a year.
Queries only.
IMPRINTS **Kluwer Academic Publishers/
Plenum Publishers**; **Chapman & Hall**
Science and technology.

Knopf Publishing Group

See **Random House, Inc.**

Krieger Publishing Co.

PO Box 9542, Melbourne FL 32902–9542
☎001 407 724 9542 Fax 001 407 951 3671
Email info@krieger-pub.com
Website www.web4u.com/krieger-publishing
Chairman *Robert E. Krieger*
President *Donald E. Krieger*
Vice-President *Maxine D. Krieger*

FOUNDED 1970. *Publishes* science, education,
geology, ecology, social sciences, humanities,
history, mathematics, psychology, chemistry,
space science, technology and engineering.
IMPRINTS/SERIES **Anvil**; **Orbit**; **Open
Forum**; **Exploring Community History**;
Professional Practices; **Public History**. Unsolicited mss welcome. Not interested in syn-
opses/ideas or trade type titles.
Royalties paid yearly.

Lanternlight Library

See **University of Alaska Press**

Lehigh University Press

See **Golden Cockerel Press** under **UK
Publishers**

Lerner Publications Co. (A division of Lerner Publishing Group)

241 First Avenue North, Minneapolis
MN 55401
☎001 612 332 3344 Fax 001 612 332 7615
Website www.lernerbooks.com
Submissions Editor *Jennifer Zimian*

Publishes primarily non-fiction for readers of all
grade levels. List includes titles encompassing
nature, geography, natural and physical science,
current events, ancient and modern history,
world art, special interest, sports, world cultures
and numerous biography series. Some young
adult and middle grade fiction. No alphabet,
puzzle, song or text books, religious subject
matter or plays. Submissions are accepted in the
months of March and October *only*. Work
received in any other month will be returned
unopened. S.a.e. required for authors who wish
to have their material returned. Please allow two
to six months for a response. No phone calls.

Library of Contemporary Thought

See **Ballantine Publishing Group**

Little Simon

See **Simon & Schuster Children's
Publishing**

Little, Brown and Company .

3 Center Plaza, Boston MA 02108–2084
☎001 617 227 0730
Website www.littlebrown.com
Vice-President/Publisher, Children's
   John Keller
**Vice-President/Editor-in-Chief,
   Children's** *Maria Modugno*
Subsidiary of Time Warner Trade Publishing.

FOUNDED 1837. *Publishes* fiction and non-fiction; cookbooks, biographies, drama, history, mysteries, poetry, art, photography, reference, science, sport, travel and juvenile. No unsolicited mss. Query letter in the first instance.

Living Language
See **Random House, Inc.**

Llewellyn Publications
PO Box 64383, St Paul MN 55164–0383
☎001 612 291 1970 Fax 001 612 291 1908
Email nancym@llewellyn.com
Website www.llewellyn.com

President/Publisher *Carl L. Weschcke*
Acquisitions Manager *Nancy J. Mostad*

Division of Llewellyn Worldwide Ltd. FOUNDED 1901. *Publishes* self-help and how-to: astrology, alternative health, tantra, Fortean studies, tarot, yoga, Santeria, dream studies, metaphysics, magic, witchcraft, herbalism, shamanism, organic gardening, women's spirituality, graphology, palmistry, parapsychology. Also fiction with an authentic magical or metaphysical theme. About 100 titles a year. Unsolicited mss welcome; proposals preferred. IRCs essential in all cases.

Lothrop, Lee & Shepard
See **William Morrow and Co., Inc.**

Louisiana State University Press
Baton Rouge LA 70893
☎001 225 388 6295 Fax 001 225 388 6461

Director *L. E. Phillabaum*

Publishes non-fiction: Southern history, American history, Southern literary criticism, American literary criticism, biography, political science, music (jazz) and Latin American studies. About 80 titles a year. Send IRCs for mss guidelines.

Love Inspired
See **Silhouette Books**

The Lyons Press
123 West 18th Street, Sixth Floor, New York
NY 10011
☎001 212 620 9580 Fax 001 212 929 1836
Website www.lyonspress.com

President/Publisher *Tony Lyons*
Editor-in-Chief *Bryan Oettel*

FOUNDED 1978. *Publishes* general fiction and non-fiction; outdoor, natural history, sports, gardening and angling titles, plus cookery,

woodwork and art. About 120 titles a year. No unsolicited mss; synopses and ideas welcome.
Royalties paid twice-yearly.

McDougal Littell Inc.
See **Houghton Mifflin Co.**

Margaret K. McElderry Books
See **Simon & Schuster Children's Publishing**

McFarland & Company, Inc., Publishers
PO Box 611, Jefferson NC 28640
☎001 336 246 4460 Fax 001 336 246 5018
Email info@mcfarlandpub.com
Website www.mcfarlandpub.com

President/Editor-in-Chief *Robert Franklin*
Vice President *Rhonda Herman*
Senior Editor *Steve Wilson*
Editors *Virginia Tobiassen, Marty McGee*

FOUNDED 1979. A library reference and upper-end speciality market press publishing scholarly books in many fields: international studies, performing arts, popular culture, sports, automotive history, women's studies, music and fine arts, chess, history and librarianship. *Specialises* in general reference. Especially strong in cinema studies. No fiction, poetry, children's, New Age or inspirational/devotional works. About 170 titles a year. No unsolicited mss; send query letter first. Synopses and ideas welcome.
Royalties paid annually.

The McGraw-Hill Companies, Inc.
1221 Avenue of the Americas, New York
NY 10020
☎001 212 512 2000
Website www.mcgrawhill.com

President/CEO *Harold McGraw III*
Contact *Submissions Editor*

FOUNDED 1873. US parent of the UK-based **McGraw-Hill Publishing Company**. *Publishes* a wide range of educational, professional, business, science, engineering and computing books.
DIVISIONS **Educational & Professional Publishing Group; Professional Book Group; Science, Technology & Medical Group; Electronic Publishing; Computer Book Group; College; Dushkin/McGraw-Hill; McGraw-Hill International Marine; Irwin/McGraw-Hill; Osborne/McGraw-Hill; WCB/McGraw-Hill.**

John Macrae Books
See **Henry Holt & Co LLC**

Magic Attic Press
See **The Millbrook Press, Inc.**

Main Street Books
See **Doubleday Broadway Publishing Group**

Bill Martin Jr Books
See **Henry Holt & Co LLC**

University of Massachusetts Press
PO Box 429, Amherst MA 01004–0429
☎001 413 545 2217 Fax 001 413 545 1226
Website www.umass.edu/umpress
Director *Bruce Wilcox*
Senior Editor *Clark Dougan*

FOUNDED 1964. *Publishes* scholarly, general interest, African-American, ethnic, women's and gender studies, cultural criticism, architecture and environmental design, literary criticism, poetry, philosophy, biography, history. Unsolicited mss considered but query letter preferred in the first instance. Synopses and ideas welcome. 40 titles a year.
Royalties paid annually.

Mentor
See **Penguin Putnam Inc.**

Meridian
See **Penguin Putnam Inc.**

Metropolitan Books
See **Henry Holt & Co LLC**

The University of Michigan Press
PO Box 1104, 839 Greene Street, Ann Arbor MI 48106
☎001 734 764 4388 Fax 001 734 615 1540
Email um.press@umich.edu
Website www.press.umich.edu/
Director *Colin Day*

FOUNDED 1930. *Publishes* non-fiction, text-books, literary criticism, theatre, economics, political science, history, classics, anthropology, law studies, women's studies, English as a second language.
Royalties paid twice-yearly.

The Millbrook Press, Inc.
2 Old New Milford Road, PO Box 335, Brookfield CT 06804
☎001 203 740 2220 Fax 001 203 775 5643
Website www.millbrookpress.com

School/Library Publisher *Jean Reynolds*
Trade Publisher *Judy Korman*
Managing Editor *Colleen Seibert*

FOUNDED 1989. *Publishes* mainly non-fiction, children's and young adult, for trade, school and public library. About 120 titles a year. IMPRINTS **Copper Beech Books**; **Twenty-First Century Books**; **Magic Attic Press**.
Royalties paid twice-yearly.

Minotaur
See **St Martin's Press, Inc.**

Minstrel Books
See **Pocket Books**

MIRASOL Libros Juveniles
See **Farrar, Straus & Giroux, Inc.**

University Press of Mississippi
3825 Ridgewood Road, Jackson MS 39211–6492
☎001 601 432 6205 Fax 001 601 432 6217
Email press@ihl.state.ms.us
Website www.upress.state.ms.us
Director/Editor-in-Chief *Seetha Srinivasan*

FOUNDED 1970. Non-profit book publisher partially supported by the eight State universities. *Publishes* scholarly and trade titles in literature, history, American culture, Southern culture, African-American, women's studies, popular culture, folklife, ethnic, performance, art and photography, and other liberal arts. About 50 titles a year.
IMPRINTS **Muscadine Books** *Craig Gill* Regional trade titles. **Banner Books** Paperback reprints of significant fiction and non-fiction. Send letter of enquiry, prospectus, table of contents and sample chapter prior to submission of full mss.
Royalties paid annually. *Represented* worldwide. UK representatives: **Roundhouse Publishing Group**.

University of Missouri Press
2910 LeMone Boulevard, Columbia MO 65201–8227
☎001 573 882 7641 Fax 001 573 884 4498
Website www.system.missouri.edu/upress
Director/Editor-in-Chief *Beverly Jarrett*

Publishes academic: history, literary criticism, intellectual history and related humanities disciplines and short stories – usually four volumes a year. Best approach is by letter. Send one short story for consideration, and synopses for academic work. About 55 titles a year.

The MIT Press

5 Cambridge Ctr., Cambridge MA 02142
☎001 617 253 5646 Fax 001 617 258 6779
Website www.mitpress.mit.edu

Editor-in-Chief *Laurence Cohen*

FOUNDED 1961. *Publishes* sophisticated scholarly and professional technical books, including computer science, artificial intelligence, economics, finance, architecture, cognitive science, neuroscience, environmental studies, linguistics and philosophy. IMPRINT **Bradford Books**.

The Modern Library

See **Random House, Inc.**

Monograph Series

See **University of Alaska Press**

William Morrow & Co., Inc.

1350 Avenue of the Americas, New York
NY 10019
☎001 212 261 6500 Fax 001 212 261 6549

Vice-President/Editor-in-Chief
Betty Kelly
Executive Editor, Adult Books
Henry Ferris

FOUNDED 1926. *Publishes* fiction, biography and general non-fiction. Approach in writing only. No unsolicited mss or proposals for adult books. Proposals read only if submitted through a literary agent. About 600 titles a year.

IMPRINTS
Hearst Books *Jacqueline Deval* VP/Publisher, *Elizabeth Rice* Editorial Director; **Quill Trade Paperbacks** *Toni Sciarra* Executive Editor; **Morrow Junior Books** *Barbara Lalicki* Snr. VP/Publisher, *Meredith Charpentier* Executive Editor; **Lothrop, Lee & Shepard** *Susan Pearson* VP/Editor-in-Chief; **Greenwillow Books** *Susan Hirschman* Snr. VP/Editor-in-Chief, *Virginia Duncan* Executive Editor; **Eaglebrook** *Joann Davis*; **Mulberry Books/Beech Tree Books** (trade paperbacks) *Paulette Kaufmann* VP/Editor-in-Chief; **Rob Weisbach Books** *Rob Weisbach*.

MTV Books

See **Pocket Books**

Mulberry Books

See **William Morrow and Co., Inc.**

Muscadine Books

See **University Press of Mississippi**

Mysterious Press

See **Warner Books Inc.**

NAL

See **Penguin Putnam, Inc.**

University of Nevada Press

MS 166, Reno NV 89557–0076
☎001 775 784 6573 Fax 001 775 784 6200

Director *Ronald Latimer*
Editor-in-Chief *Margaret Dalrymple*

FOUNDED 1960. *Publishes* scholarly and popular books; serious fiction, Native American studies, natural history, Western Americana, Basque studies and regional studies. About 40 titles a year including reprints. Unsolicited material welcome if it fits in with areas published, or offers a 'new and exciting' direction.
Royalties paid twice-yearly.

University Press of New England

23 South Main Street, Hanover
NH 03755–2055
☎001 603 643 7100 Fax 001 603 643 1540
Website www.university.press@dartmouth.edu

Director & Acquisitions Editor
Richard Abel
Editorial Director *Philip Pochoda*

FOUNDED 1970. A scholarly book publisher sponsored by six institutions of higher education in the region: Brandeis, Dartmouth, Middlebury, Tufts, Wesleyan and the University of New Hampshire. *Publishes* general and scholarly non-fiction; plus poetry through the Wesleyan Poetry Series and Hardscrabble Books fiction of New England. About 75 titles a year. Unsolicited material welcome.
Royalties paid annually. *Overseas associates:* UK – University Presses Marketing; Europe – Trevor Brown Associates.

University of New Mexico Press

1720 Lomas Boulevard NE, Albuquerque
NM 87131–1591
☎001 505 277 2346 Fax 001 505 277 9270
Website www.unmpress.com

Director *Elizabeth C. Hadas*
Editor *Larry Durwood Ball*

Publishes scholarly and regional books. No fiction, how-to, children's, humour, self-help, technical or textbooks. 60 titles in 1999.

Noonday Press

See **Farrar, Straus & Giroux, Inc.**

North Point Press

See **Farrar, Straus & Giroux, Inc.**

University of North Texas Press
PO Box 311336, Denton TX 76203–1336
☎001 940 565 2142 Fax 001 940 565 4590
Email vick@unt.edu
Website www.unt.edu/untpress
Director *Frances B. Vick*

FOUNDED 1987. *Publishes* folklore, regional
interest, contemporary, social issues, history,
military, women's issues, writing and publishing
reference. Publishes the Vassar Miller Poetry
Prize winner each year. About 14 titles a year.
No unsolicited mss. Approach by letter in the
first instance. Synopses and ideas welcome.
Royalties paid annually.

W. W. Norton & Company, Inc.
500 Fifth Avenue, New York NY 10110–0017
☎001 212 354 5500 Fax 001 212 869 0856
Website www.wwnorton.com
Vice-President/Managing Editor
Nancy K. Palmquist

FOUNDED 1923. *Publishes* fiction and non-
fiction, college textbooks and professional
books. About 300 titles a year.

NTC/Contemporary Publishing Group
4255 West Touhy Avenue, Lincolnwood
IL 60646–1975
☎001 847 679 5500 Fax 001 847 679 2494
Vice-President/Publisher *John Nolan*

FOUNDED 1947. *Publishes* general adult non-
fiction and education books. About 800 titles a
year. Submissions require s.a.e. for response.

Odyssey Paperbacks
See **Harcourt Children's Books Division**

University of Oklahoma Press
1005 Asp Avenue, Norman OK 73019–6051
☎001 405 325 2000 Fax 001 405 325 4000
Website www.ou.edu/oupress
Director *John N. Drayton*

FOUNDED 1928. *Publishes* general scholarly non-
fiction only: American Indian studies, history of
American West, classical studies, literary theory
and criticism, anthropology, archaeology, natural
history, political science and women's studies.
About 100 titles a year.

One World
See **Ballantine Publishing Group**

Onyx
See **Penguin Putnam Inc.**

Open Forum
See **Krieger Publishing Co.**

Orbit
See **Krieger Publishing Co.**

Orchard Books
See **Grolier, Incorporated**

Osborne/McGraw Hill
See **The McGraw-Hill Companies, Inc.**

Owl Books
See **Henry Holt & Co LLC**

Pantheon
See **Random House, Inc.**

Paper Star
See **Penguin Putnam Inc**

Paragon House
2700 University Avenue, Suite 200, St Paul
MN 55114–1016
☎001 651 644 3087 Fax 001 651 644 0997
Email paragon@paragonhouse.com
Website www.paragonhouse.com
Executive Director *Gordon L. Anderson*

FOUNDED 1982. *Publishes* non-fiction: reference
and academic. Subjects include history, religion,
philosophy, spirituality, Jewish interest, political
science, international relations, psychology.
Royalties paid twice-yearly.

Pelican Publishing Company
Box 3110, Gretna LA 70054–3110
☎001 504 368 1175
Website www.pelicanpub.com
Editor-in-Chief *Nina Kooij*

Publishes general non-fiction: popular history,
cookbooks, travel, art, business, children's, editorial cartoon, architecture, golf, Scottish interest, collectibles guides and motivational.
About 70 titles a year. Initial enquiries required
for all submissions.

Pelion Press
See **The Rosen Publishing Group, Inc.**

Penguin Putnam Inc.
375 Hudson Street, New York NY 10014
☎001 212 366 2000 Fax 001 212 366 2666
Email online@penguinputnam.com
Website www.penguinputnam.com
Chairman/CEO, The Penguin Group
Michael Lynton

President *Phyllis Grann*

Penguin Putnam is a division of the Penguin Group, which is owned by Pearson plc. The group is the second-largest trade book publisher in the world. *Publishes* fiction and non-fiction in hardback and paperback; adult and children's. About 2500 titles a year.

PENGUIN GROUP IMPRINTS
Hardback: **Penguin Studio**; **Dutton**; **Viking**; **Donald I. Fine**; **Allen Lane The Penguin Press**; **DAW Books, Inc.** (see entry); Paperback: **Penguin**; **Plume**; **Signet/Signet Classics**; **Onyx**; **Roc**; **Topaz**; **Mentor**; **Meridian**; **Arkana**.

CHILDREN'S DIVISION: **Dial Books for Young Readers** (see entry); **Puffin**; **Dutton's Children's Books**; **Viking Children's Books**; **Grosset & Dunlap**; **NAL**; **Frederick Warne**.

PUTNAM BERKLEY IMPRINTS
Hardback: **G. P. Putnam's Sons** (see entry); **Riverhead Books**; **Jeremy P. Tarcher**; **Grosset/Putnam**; **Ace/Putnam**; **Boulevard**; **Putnam**; **Price Stern Sloan**; Paperbacks: **Berkley Books**; **Jove**; **Perigee**; **Prime Crime**; **HP Books**;

CHILDREN'S DIVISION: **Philomel Books**; **Grosset & Dunlap**; **Wee Sing**; **Paper Star**.

Royalties paid twice-yearly.

University of Pennsylvania Press
4200 Pine Street, Philadelphia PA 19104–4011
☎001 215 898 6261 Fax 001 215 898 0404
Website www.upenn.edu/pennpress

Director *Eric Halpern*

FOUNDED 1890. *Publishes* serious non-fiction: scholarly, reference, professional, textbooks and semi-popular trade. No original fiction or poetry. About 75 titles a year. No unsolicited mss but synopses and ideas for books welcome.
Royalties paid annually.

Perigee
See **Penguin Putnam Inc.**

Philomel Books
See **Penguin Putnam Inc.**

Picador USA
See **St Martin's Press, Inc.**

Players Press
PO Box 1132, Studio City CA 91614-0132
☎001 818 789 4980

Chairman *William-Alan Landes*
Managing Director *Chris Cordero*

FOUNDED 1965 as a publisher of plays; now publishes across the entire range of performing arts: plays, musicals, theatre, film, cinema, television, costume, puppetry, plus technical theatre and cinema material. 60 titles in 1999. No unsolicited mss; synopses/ideas welcome. Send query letter.
Royalties paid twice-yearly. *Overseas subsidiaries* in Canada, Australia and the UK.

Plenum Publishers
See **Kluwer Academic Publishers**

Plume
See **Penguin Putnam Inc.**

Pocket Books
1230 Avenue of the Americas, New York NY 10020
☎001 212 698 7000 Fax 001 212 698 7439

President/Publisher *Judith Curr*

FOUNDED 1939. A division of Simon & Schuster Consumer Group. *Publishes* trade paperbacks and hardcovers; mass-market, reprints and originals.
IMPRINTS **Archway Paperbacks**; **Minstrel Books**; **Pocket Books/Pocket Star Books/Pocket Pulse**; **Washington Square Press**; **MTV Books**.

PowerKids Press
See **The Rosen Publishing Group, Inc.**

Price Stern Sloan
See **Penguin Putnam Inc**

Prime Crime
See **Penguin Putnam Inc.**

Princeton Review
See **Random House, Inc.**

Professional Practices
See **Krieger Publishing Co.**

Public History
See **Krieger Publishing Co.**

Puffin
See **Penguin Putnam Inc**

G. P. Putnam's Sons
345 Hudson Street, New York NY 10014
☎001 212 414 3600

President/Publisher *Nancy Paulsen*
Senior Editor *Kathy Dawson*

A children's book division of Penguin Putnam Books for Young Readers, a member of

Penguin Putnam Inc. *Publishes* picture books, middle-grade fiction and young adult fiction.

Quill Trade Paperbacks
See **William Morrow and Co., Inc.**

Rand McNally
PO Box 7600, Chicago IL 60680
☎001 847 329 8100 Fax 001 847 673 0539
Website www.randmcnally.com
President/CEO *Henry J. Feinberg*
FOUNDED 1856. *Publishes* world atlases and maps, road atlases of North America and Europe, city and state maps of the United States and Canada, educational wall maps, atlases and globes, plus children's products. Includes electronic multimedia products.

Random House, Inc.
1540 Broadway, New York NY 10036
☎001 212 751 2600 Fax 001 212 572 8700
Website www.randomhouse.com
Chairman/Chief Executive Officer
Peter Olson
FOUNDED 1925. The world's largest English-language general trade book publisher. A division of the Bertelsmann Book Group AG, one of the foremost media companies in the world. The reach of Random House, Inc. is global with subsidiaries and affiliated companies in Canada, the UK, Australia, New Zealand and South Africa. Through **Random House International**, the books published by the imprints of Random House, Inc. are sold in virtually every country in the world. Submissions via agents preferred.

DIVISIONS/IMPRINTS
Ballantine Publishing Group (see entry); **Bantam Dell Publishing Group** (see entry); **Crown Publishing Group** (see entry); **Doubleday Broadway Publishing Group** (see entry); **Knopf Publishing Group** (including **Everyman's Library, Knopf, Pantheon/ Schocken** and **Vintage Anchor**) FOUNDED 1915. Fiction and non-fiction; **Random House Audio Publishing Group**; **Random House Children's Media Group** (including **Random House, Knopf, Bantam, Crown, Delacorte** and **Doubleday Books for Young Readers, Children's Television Workshop Books** and **Random House Home Video**); **Random House Diversified Publishing Group** (including **Random House Large Print Publishing** and **Random House Value Publishing**); **Random House Information Group** (including **Fodor's Travel**

Publications, Living Language, Princeton Review and **Random House Reference & Information Publishing**); **Random House Trade Publishing Group** (including **Random House Trade Books, Villard** and **The Modern Library**).
Royalties paid twice-yearly.

Rawson Associates
See **Simon & Schuster Trade Division**

Reader's Digest Association, Inc
Reader's Digest Road, Pleasantville,
NY 10570–7000
☎001 914 238 1000 Fax 001 914 238 4559
Website www.readersdigest.com
Chairman/CEO *Thomas Ryder*
Publishes cooking, DIY, health, gardeing, children's books; videos and magazines.

Red Feather Books
See **Henry Holt & Co LLC**

Red Wagon Books
See **Harcourt Children's Books Division**

Regan Books
See **HarperCollins Publishers, Inc.**

Fleming H. Revell
See **Baker Book House**

Riverhead Books
See **Penguin Putnam Inc.**

The Riverside Publishing Co.
See **Houghton Mifflin Co.**

Roc
See **Penguin Putnam Inc.**

The Rosen Publishing Group, Inc.
29 East 21st Street, New York NY 10010
☎001 212 777 3017 Fax 001 212 777 0277
President *Roger Rosen*
Associate Editor, PowerKids Press
Gina Strazzabosco-Hayn
Editorial Director *Erin Hovanec*
FOUNDED 1950. *Publishes* non-fiction books (supplementary to the curriculum, reference and self-help) for a young adult audience. Reading levels are years 7–12, 4–6 (books for teens with literacy problems), and 5–9. Areas of interest include careers, self-esteem, sexuality, personal safety, science, sport, African studies, Holocaust studies and a wide variety of other multicultural titles. About 180 titles a year.

IMPRINTS
Pelion Press Music titles; **PowerKids Press** Non-fiction books for Reception up to Year 4 that are supplementary to the curriculum. Subjects include conflict resolution, character building, health, safety, drug abuse prevention, history, self-help, religion and multicultural titles. 144 titles a year. For all imprints, write with outline and sample chapters.

Rutgers University Press

100 Joyce Kilmer Avenue, Piscataway
NJ 08854–8099
☎001 732 445 7762 Fax 001 732 445 7039
Editor-in-Chief *Leslie Mitchner*

FOUNDED 1936. *Publishes* scholarly books, regional and social sciences. Unsolicited mss, synopses and ideas for books welcome. No original fiction or poetry. About 90 titles a year.
Royalties paid annually.

St Martin's Press LLC

175 Fifth Avenue, New York NY 10010
☎001 212 674 5151 Fax 001 212 420 9314
Email inquiries@stmartins.com
Website www.stmartins.com
President (Holtzbrinck) *John Sargent*
President/Publisher (Trade Division)
Sally Richardson

FOUNDED 1952. A subsidiary of **Macmillan Publishers** (UK), St Martin's Press made its name and fortune by importing raw talent from the UK to the States and has continued to buy heavily in the UK. *Publishes* general fiction, especially mysteries and crime; and adult non-fiction: history, self-help, political science, travel, biography, scholarly, popular reference, college textbooks.

IMPRINTS **Picador USA**; **Griffin** (Trade paperbacks); **St Martin's Paperbacks** (Mass market); **Thomas Dunne Books**; **Minotaur**; **Tor**; **Truman Talley Books**; **Forge**.

Scarecrow Press, Inc.

4720 Boston Way, Lanham Maryland 20706
☎001 301 459 3366 Fax 001 301 459 2118
Website www.scarecrowpress.com
Associate Publisher *Shirley Lambert*

FOUNDED 1950 as a short-run publisher of library reference books. Acquired by **University Press of America, Inc.** in 1995 which is now part of Rowman and Littlefield Publishers, Inc. *Publishes* reference, scholarly and monographs (all levels) for libraries. Reference books in all areas except sciences, specialising in the performing arts, music, cinema and library science. About 165 titles a year. Publisher for the Society of American Archivists, Children's Literature Association, Institute of Jazz Studies of Rutgers – the State University of New Jersey, the American Theological Library Association. Also publisher of *VOYA* (Voice of Youth Advocates); six issues a year. Unsolicited mss welcome but material will not be returned unless requested and accompanied by return postage. Unsolicited synopses and ideas for books welcome. Send submissions to *Katie Regen*, Associate Editor (e-mail kregen@scarecrowpress.com)
Royalties paid annually.

Schocken
See **Random House, Inc.**

Scholastic, Inc.

555 Broadway, New York NY 10012–3999
☎001 212 343 6100 Fax 001 212 343 6390
Website www.scholastic.com/
Executive Vice President
Barbara Marcus
Senior Vice-President/Publisher
Jean Feiwel

FOUNDED 1920. The world's largest publisher and distributor of children's books in the English language. Acquired Grolier from the French Lagardere Group in April 2000. *Publishes* picture books and fiction for middle grade (8–12-year-olds) and young adults: family, friendship, humour, fantasy, mystery and school stories. Also non-fiction: biography, reference and multicultural subjects. About 500 titles a year. Does not accept unsolicited mss or queries unless the author is represented by an agent or has been published previously in book form.

Anne Schwartz Books
See **Simon & Schuster Children's Publishing**

Scott Foresman

1900 E Lake Avenue, Glenview
IL 60025–2086
☎001 847 729 3000 Fax 001 847 486 3999
President, Scott Foresman *Paul McFall*

FOUNDED 1896. *Publishes* elementary education materials. No unsolicited material.

Scribner
See **Simon & Schuster Trade Division**

Signet/Signet Classics
See **Penguin Putnam Inc.**

Silhouette Books

300 East 42nd Street, New York NY 10017
☎001 212 682 6080 Fax 001 212 682 4539
Editorial Director *Tara Gavin*

FOUNDED 1979 as an imprint of **Simon & Schuster** and was acquired by a wholly owned subsidiary of Toronto-based Harlequin Enterprises Ltd in 1984. *Publishes* category, contemporary romance fiction and historical romance fiction only. Over 360 titles a year across a number of imprints.

IMPRINTS **Silhouette Romance** *Mary Theresa Hussey*; **Silhouette Desire** *Joan Marlow Golan*; **Silhouette Special Edition** *Karen Taylor Richman*; **Silhouette Intimate Moments** *Leslie Wainger*; **Harlequin Historicals** *Tracy Farrell*; **Steeple Hill** *Tracy Farrell*. Imprint, launched in 1997, **Love Inspired** publishes a line of inspirational contemporary romances with stories designed to 'lift readers' spirits and gladden their hearts'. No unsolicited mss. Submit query letter in the first instance or write for detailed submission guidelines/tip sheets.

Royalties paid twice-yearly. *Overseas associates* worldwide.

Silver Whistle

See **Harcourt Children's Books Division**

Simon & Schuster Children's Publishing

1230 Avenue of the Americas, New York NY 10020
☎001 212 698 7200
President/Publisher *Rick Richter*

A division of the Simon & Schuster Consumer Group. *Publishes* pre-school to young adult, picture books, hardcover and paperback fiction, non-fiction, trade, library and mass-market titles. About 480 titles a year.

IMPRINTS
Aladdin Books *Ellen Krieger* Picture books, paperback fiction and non-fiction reprints and originals, and limited series for ages pre-school to young adult; **Atheneum Books for Young Readers** *Jonathan Lanman* Picture books, hardcover fiction and non-fiction books across all genres for ages three to young adult. Two lines within this imprint are **Jean Karl Books** quality fantasy-fiction and **Anne Schwartz Books** distinct picture books and high-quality fiction; **Little Simon** *Alison Weir* Mass-market novelty books (pop-ups, board books, colouring & activity) and merchandise (book and audiocassette) for ages birth through eight; **Margaret K.**

McElderry Books *Margaret K. McElderry* Picture books, hardcover fiction and non-fiction trade books for children ages three to young adult; **Simon & Schuster Books for Young Readers** *Stephanie Owens Lurie* Picture books, hardcover fiction and non-fiction for children ages three to young adult. **Simon Spotlight** *Jennifer Koch* New imprint devoted exclusively to children's media tie-ins and licensed properties.

For submissions to all imprints: send envelope (US size 10) for guidelines, attention: *Manuscript Submissions Guidelines*.

Simon & Schuster Trade Division (Division of Simon & Schuster, Inc)

1230 Avenue of the Americas, New York NY 10020
☎001 212 698 7000 Fax 001 212 698 7007
Website www.simonsays.com
President/Publisher *Carolyn K. Reidy*

Publishes fiction and non-fiction.

DIVISIONS **The Free Press** *Paula Barker Duffy* VP & Publisher, *Elizabeth Maguire* VP & Editorial Director; **Fireside/Touchstone** *Mark Gompertz* VP & Publisher, *Trish Todd* VP & Editor-in-Chief; **Scribner** *Susan Moldow* VP & Publisher, *Nan Graham* VP & Editor-in-Chief; **Simon and Schuster** *David Rosenthal* VP & Publisher, *Michael V. Korda* Senior VP & Editor-in-Chief; **Trade Paperbacks** *Mark Gompertz* VP & Publisher, *Trish Todd* VP & Editor-in-Chief.

IMPRINTS **H. & R. Block**; **Lisa Drew Books**; **Fireside**; **The Free Press**; **Free Press Paperbacks**; **Hudson River Editions**; **Rawson Associates**; **Scribner**; **Scribner Classics**; **Scribner Paperback Fiction**; **S&S Libros eñ Espanol**; **Simon & Schuster**; **Touchstone**. No unsolicited mss.

Royalties paid twice-yearly.

Simon Spotlight

See **Simon & Schuster Children's Publishing**

Southern Illinois University Press

PO Box 3697, Carbondale IL 62902–3697
☎001 618 453 2281 Fax 001 618 453 1221
Director *John F. Stetter*

FOUNDED 1956. *Publishes* scholarly and general interest non-fiction books and educational materials. 50 titles a year.

Royalties paid annually.

Spectra

See **Bantam Dell Publishing Group**

Stackpole Books

5067 Ritter Road, Mechanicsburg
PA 17055
☎001 717 796 0411 Fax 001 717 796 0412
Email sales@stackpolebooks.com
Website www.stackpolebooks.com
President *David Ritter*
Vice President/Editorial Director
Judith Schnell

FOUNDED 1933. *Publishes* outdoor sports, fishing, nature, photography, military reference, history, PA Books. 75 titles in 1999.
Royalties paid twice-yearly.

Stanford University Press

Stanford CA 94305-2235
☎001 650 723 9434 Fax 001 650 725 3457
Director *Norris Pope*

Publishes non-fiction: scholarly works in all areas of the humanities, social sciences, history and literature. About 120 titles a year. No unsolicited mss; query in writing first.

Steeple Hill

See **Silhouette Books**

Sterling Publishing Co. Inc.

387 Park Avenue South, 5th Floor,
New York NY 10016–8810
☎001 212 532 7160 Fax 001 212 213 2495
Email s.magnuson@sterlingpub.com
Website www.sterlingpub.com
President *Lincoln Boehm*
Executive Vice-President *Charles Nurnberg*
Vice President/Editorial *Steven Magnuson*

FOUNDED 1949. *Publishes* non-fiction: reference and information books, science, nature, arts and crafts, architecture, home improvement, history, photography, children's humour, complementary health, wine and food, social sciences, sports, music, psychology, New Age, occult, woodworking, pets, hobbies, gardening, puzzles and games. 800 titles in 1999.

Sunburst Books

See **Farrar, Straus & Giroux, Inc.**

Sunburst Technology

See **Houghton Mifflin Co.**

Susquehanna University Press

See **Golden Cockerel Press** under **UK Publishers**

Syracuse University Press

621 Skytop Road, Suite 110, Syracuse
NY 13244–5290
☎001 315 443 5534 Fax 001 315 443 5545
Director *Robert Mandel*

FOUNDED 1943. *Publishes* scholarly books in: contemporary Middle East studies, international affairs, Irish studies, Iroquois studies, women and religion, Jewish studies, peace studies. About 70 titles a year. Also co-publishes with a number of organisations such as the American University of Beirut. No unsolicited mss. Send query letter with IRCs.
Royalties paid annually.

Nan A. Talese

See **Doubleday Broadway Publishing Group**

Jeremy P. Tarcher

See **Penguin Putnam Inc**

Temple University Press

1601 N. Broad Street, 083–42, Philadelphia
PA 19122–6099
☎001 215 204 8787 Fax 001 215 204 4719
Email tempress@astro.ocis.temple.edu
Website www.temple.edu/tempress
Editor-in-Chief *Janet M. Francendese*

FOUNDED 1969. *Publishes* scholarly non-fiction: American history, Latin American studies, gay and lesbian studies, Asian American studies, ethnic studies, anthropology, law, cultural studies, sociology, women's studies, health care and disability, public policy, labour studies, urban studies, American studies and African American studies, ethnomusicology, Latino studies, political science, film, media and television studies, music, education, religion, animals and culture, baseball history. About 60 titles a year. Authors generally academics. Letter of inquiry with brief outline. Include fax/email address.

University of Tennessee Press

293 Communications Building, Knoxville
TN 37996
☎001 865 974 3321 Fax 001 865 974 3724
Managing Editor *Stan Ivester*

FOUNDED in 1940. *Publishes* scholarly and regional non-fiction.
Royalties paid annually.

University of Texas Press

PO Box 7819, Austin TX 78713-7819
☎001 512 471 7233/Editorial: 471 4278
Fax 001 512 320 0668
Website www.utexas.edu/utpress/
Director *Joanna Hitchcock*
Assistant Director/Editor-in-Chief
Theresa J. May

Publishes scholarly and regional non-fiction:
anthropology, Old and New World archaeology, art, architecture, classics, environmental
studies, film and media studies, geography, language studies, literary modernism; Latin Ameri-
can/Latino/Mexican American/Middle Eastern/
Native American studies, natural history and
ornithology, regional books (Texas and the
southwest), women's studies. Unsolicited material welcome in above subject areas only. About
90 titles a year and 12 journals.
Royalties paid annually.

Three Rivers Press

See **Crown Publishing Group**

Time-Life Inc.

2000 Duke Street, Alexandria VA 22314
☎001 703 838 7000 Fax 001 703 838 7225
President/Chief Executive/Chairman
George Artandi

FOUNDED 1961. Subsidiary of Time Warner
Inc. *Publishes* non-fiction: cooking, food,
gardening, health, history, home maintenance,
nature, science. No unsolicited mss. About 300
titles a year.
    DIVISIONS/IMPRINTS **Time-Life Books**;
Time-Life Education; **Time-Life International**; **Time-Trade Publishing**.

Times Books

201 East 50th Street, New York NY 10022
☎001 212 572 2170 Fax 001 212 940 7464
Vice-President/Publisher *Carie Freimuth*

FOUNDED 1959. A division of **Crown
Publishing Group**. *Publishes* general non-fiction and consumer reference. Unsolicited mss
not considered. Letter essential.

Topaz

See **Penguin Putnam Inc.**

Tor

See **St Martin's Press LLC**

Touchstone

See **Simon & Schuster Trade Division**

Truman Talley Books

See **St Martin's Press LLC**

Twenty-First Century Books

See **The Millbrook Press, Inc.**

Tyndale House Publishers, Inc.

351 Executive Drive, Carol Stream IL 60188
☎001 630 668 8300 Fax 001 630 668 8311
Chairman *Kenneth N. Taylor*
President *Mark D. Taylor*

FOUNDED 1962 by Kenneth Taylor. Non-
denominational religious publisher of around
200 titles a year for the evangelical Christian
market. Books cover a wide range of categories
from home and family to inspirational, theology,
doctrine, Bibles, general reference and fiction.
Also produces video material, calendars and
audio books for the same market. No poetry.
No unsolicited mss; they will be returned
unread. Synopses and ideas considered. Send
query letter summarising contents of books and
length. Include a brief biography, detailed outline and sample chapters. IRCs essential for
response or return of material. No audio cassettes, disks or video tapes in lieu of mss.
Response time around 6–12 weeks. No phone
calls or e-mail submissions. Send s.a.e. for free
catalogue and full submission guidelines.
Royalties paid annually.

University Press of America, Inc.

4720 Boston Way, Lanham MD 20706
☎001 301 459 3366 Fax 001 301 459 2118
Website www.univpress.com
Publisher *James E. Lyons*

FOUNDED 1974. *Publishes* scholarly mono-
graphs, college and graduate level textbooks.
No children's, elementary or high school.
About 450 titles a year. Submit outline or
request proposal questionnaire.
Royalties paid annually.

Viking/Viking Children's Books

See **Penguin Putnam Inc**

Villard

See **Random House, Inc.**

Vintage Anchor

See **Random House, Inc.**

Voyager Paperbacks

See **Harcourt Children's Books Division**

J. Weston Walch, Publisher

321 Valley Street, PO Box 658, Portland
ME 04104-0658
☎001 207 772 2846 Fax 001 207 772 3105
Website www.walch.com

President *John Thoreson*
Editor-in-Chief *Lisa French*

FOUNDED 1927. *Publishes* supplementary educational materials for secondary schools across a wide range of subjects, including English/language arts, literacy, special needs, mathematics, social studies, science and school-to-career. Always interested in ideas from secondary school teachers who develop materials in the classroom. Proposal letters, synopses and ideas welcome.
Royalties paid twice-yearly.

Walker & Co.

435 Hudson Street, New York NY 10014
☎001 212 727 8300 Fax 001 212 727 0984

Contact *Submissions Editor*

FOUNDED 1959. *Publishes* mystery, children's and non-fiction. Please contact the following editors in advance before sending any material to be sure of their interest, then follow up as instructed: **Mystery** *Michael Seidman* 65–70,000 words. Send first three chapters and two-page synopsis. **Trade Non-fiction** *George Gibson* Permission and documentation must be available with mss. Submit prospectus first, with sample chapters and marketing analysis. **Books for Young Readers** *Emily Easton* Fiction and non-fiction. Query before sending non-fiction proposals. Especially interested in young science and picture books, historical and contemporary fiction for middle grades and young adults.

Frederick Warne

See **Penguin Putnam Inc**

Warner Books Inc.

1271 Avenue of the Americas, New York
NY 10020
☎001 212 522 7200 Fax 001 212 522 7991

Senior Vice-President/Publisher *Jamie Rabb*
Associate Publisher *Les Pockell*

FOUNDED 1961. A subsidiary of Time Warner Trade Publishing. *Publishes* fiction and non-fiction, audio books, gift books. About 230 titles a year.
IMPRINTS **Aspect** *Betsy Mitchell*; **Mysterious Press** *William Malloy*; **Time Warner Audio Books**; **Warner Vision**. Query or submit outline with sample chapters and letter.

Washington Square Press

See **Pocket Books**

Washington State University Press

PO Box 645910, Pullman WA 99164-5910
☎001 509 335 3518 Fax 001 509 335 8568
Website www.publications.wsu.edu/wsupress

Director *Thomas H. Sanders*

FOUNDED 1928. Revitalised in 1984. *Publishes* hardcover originals, trade paperbacks and reprints, mainly on the history, prehistory, culture, politics and natural history of the Northwest United States (Washington, Idaho, Oregon, Montana, Alaska) and British Columbia. Works that focus on national topics or other regions may also be considered if they have a Northwest connection. 8–10 titles a year. Unsolicited mss and queries welcome.
Royalties paid annually.

Franklin Watts Inc.

90 Sherman Turnpike, Danbury CT 06816
☎001 203 797 3500 Fax 001 203 797 6986

Vice President/Publisher *John W. Selfridge*
Executive Editor *Mark Friedman*

FOUNDED 1942 and acquired by **Grolier** in 1975. *Publishes* non-fiction: curriculum-based material for ages 5–18 across a wide range of subjects, including history, social sciences, natural and physical sciences, health and medicine, biography. Over 100 titles a year. No unsolicited mss. Synopses and ideas considered. Address samples to 'Submissions' and include IRCs if response required. Be prepared for a three-month turnaround.
Royalties paid twice-yearly.

WCB/McGraw-Hill

See **The McGraw-Hill Companies, Inc.**

Wee Sing

See **Penguin Putnam Inc**

Rob Weisbach Books

See **William Morrow & Co., Inc.**

Wellspring

See **Ballantine Publishing Group**

John Wiley & Sons Inc.

605 Third Avenue, New York NY 10158
☎001 212 850 6000 Fax 001 212 850 6088
Website www.wiley.com

Chief Executive Officer *William J. Pesce*

FOUNDED 1807. *Publishes* professional and trade

books in the following fields: culinary arts and hospitality, architecture/design, business technology, accounting, psychology, engineering and general interest. Educational products: the sciences, mathematics, engineering, accounting, business, teacher education, modern languages, religion. Scientific, technical and medical publishers of journals, encyclopedias, available in print and electronic media.

Zondervan Publishing House

5300 Patterson Avenue SE, Grand Rapids MI 49530

☎001 616 698 6900 Fax 001 616 698 3421

President/Chief Executive *Bruce E. Ryskamp*

FOUNDED 1931. Subsidiary of **HarperCollins Publishers, Inc.** *Publishes* Protestant religion, Bibles, books, audio & video, computer software, calendars and speciality items.

US Agents

Adler & Robin Books, Inc.

3000 Connecticut Avenue, NW, Suite 317,
Washington DC 20008
☎001 202 986 9275 Fax 001 202 986 9485
Email adlerbooks@adlerbooks.com
President/Agent *Bill Adler Jr*
Senior Agents *Martha Kaufman Amitay, Laura
    Belt, Djana Pearson Morris*
Editor *Tracy Quinn*
FOUNDED 1988. *Handles* computer books and
non-fiction. Unsolicited synopses and queries
welcome with s.a.e. Send letter with outline or
proposal and sample chapters if possible. Elec-
tronic submissions accepted. No reading fee.
Commission Home 15%; UK 20%.

AMG – Renaissance

9465 Wilshire Boulevard, Beverly Hills
CA 90212
☎001 310 860 8000 Fax 001 310 860 8100
President *Joel Gotler*
Literary Associates *Alan Nevins, Irv
    Schwartz, Judi Farkas, Michael Prevett*
FOUNDED 1934. Fiction and non-fiction; film
and TV rights. No unsolicited mss. Send query
letter with IRCs in the first instance. No reading fee. *Commission* Home 10–15%.

Marcia Amsterdam Agency

Suite 9A, 41 West 82nd Street, New York
NY 10024–5613
☎001 212 873 4945
Contact *Marcia Amsterdam*
FOUNDED 1969. *Specialises* in mainstream fiction,
horror, suspense, humour, young adult, TV and
film scripts. No poetry, books for the 8–10 age
group or how-to. No unsolicited mss. First
approach by letter only and enclose IRCs. No
reading fee for outlines and synopses. *Commission*
Home 15%; Dramatic 10%; Foreign 20%.

Bart Andrews & Associates Inc

7510 Sunset Boulevard, Suite 100, Los
Angeles CA 90046–3418
☎001 310 271 9916
Contact *Bart Andrews*

FOUNDED 1982. General non-fiction: show
business, biography and autobiography, film
books, trivia, TV and nostalgia. No scripts. No
fiction, poetry, children's or science. No books
of less than major commercial potential.
Specialises in working with celebrities on autobiographies. No unsolicited mss. 'Send a brilliant
letter (with IRCs for response) extolling your
manuscript's virtues. Sell me!' No reading fee.
Commission Home & Translation 15%. *Overseas
associates* **Abner Stein**, London.

Joseph Anthony Agency

15 Locust Court Road, 20 Mays Landing,
New Jersey NJ 08330
☎001 609 625 7608
Contact *Joseph Anthony*
FOUNDED 1964. *Handles* all types of novel and
scripts for TV: 2-hour mini-series, screenplays
and ½-hour sitcoms. No poetry, short stories
or pornography. *Specialises* in action, romance
and detective novels. Last sale to **Silhouette
Books** by writer Karen Alaire. Unsolicited mss
welcome. Enclose return postage (US money
order or US cheque). Send query first. Reading fee charged to new writers: novels $85;
screenplays $100. Signatory of the Writer's
Guild of America. *Commission* Home 15%;
Dramatic & Translation 20%.

Malaga Baldi Literary Agency

204 84th Street, Suite 3C, New York
NY 10024
☎001 212 579 5075 Fax 001 212 579 5078
Email MBALDI@aol.com
Contact *Malaga Baldi*
FOUNDED 1986. *Handles* quality fiction and
non-fiction. No scripts. No westerns, men's
adventure, science fiction/fantasy, romance,
how-to, young adult or children's. Writers of
fiction should send query letter describing the
novel plus IRCs. Allow ten weeks *minimum* for
response. For non-fiction, approach in writing
with a proposal, table of contents and two sample chapters. No reading fee. *Commission* 15%.
Overseas associates **Abner Stein**, UK; Japan Uni.

The Balkin Agency, Inc.★

PO Box 222, Amherst MA 01004
☎001 413 548 9835 Fax 001 413 548 9836

Contact *Richard Balkin*

FOUNDED 1973. *Handles* adult non-fiction only. No reading fee for outlines and synopses. *Commission* Home 15%; Foreign 20%.

Meredith Bernstein Literary Agency, Inc.★

2112 Broadway, Suite 503A, New York NY 10023
☎001 212 799 1007 Fax 001 212 799 1145

Contacts *Meredith Bernstein, Elizabeth Cavanaugh*

FOUNDED 1981. *Handles* fiction (women's and men's), mysteries, romance, and non-fiction (women's issues, personal memoirs, parenting, psychology, business, spirituality, science, travel, fashion, inspiration and humour). 'Always interested in new ideas, voices and other original projects. We are looking for mainstream fiction, psychological suspense, medical thrillers, love stories (but not romances).' Not taking on any unpublished romance writers at present. *Commission* Home & Dramatic 15%; Translation 20%. *Overseas associates* **Abner Stein**, UK; Lennart Sane, Holland, Scandinavia and Spanish language; Thomas Schluck, Germany; Bardon Chinese Media Agency; William Miller, Japan; Frederique Porretta, France; Agenzia Letteraria, Italy.

Reid Boates Literary Agency

PO Box 328, Pittstown NJ 08867-0328
☎001 908 730 8523 Fax 001 908 730 8931
Email rboatesla@aol.com

Contact *Reid Boates*

FOUNDED 1985. *Handles* general fiction and non-fiction. No scripts. No science fiction, fantasy, romance, western, gothic, personal memoirs, children's or young adult. Enquire by letter with IRCs in first instance. No reading fee. *Commission* Home & Dramatic 15%; Translation 20%. *Overseas associates* Michael Meller, UK & Germany; Kyoshi Asano, Japan; Raquel de la Concha, Spanish languages; Eliane Baristi, France.

Georges Borchardt, Inc.★

136 East 57th Street, New York NY 10022
☎001 212 753 5785 Fax 001 212 838 6518

FOUNDED 1967. Works mostly with established/published authors. *Specialises* in fiction,

biography, and general non-fiction of unusual interest. Unsolicited mss not read. *Commission* Home, UK, Dramatic 15%; Translation 20%. *UK associates* **Sheil Land Associates Ltd** (Richard Scott Simon), London.

Brandt & Brandt Literary Agents, Inc.★

1501 Broadway, New York NY 10036
☎001 212 840 5760 Fax 001 212 840 5776

Contacts *Carl D. Brandt, Gail Hochman, Marianne Merola, Charles Schlessiger*

FOUNDED 1914. *Handles* non-fiction and fiction. No poetry or children's books. No unsolicited mss. Approach by letter describing background and ambitions. No reading fee. *Commission* Home & Dramatic 15%; Foreign 20%. *UK associates* **A. M. Heath & Co. Ltd**.

Pema Browne Ltd

HCR Box 104B, Neversink NY 12765
☎001 914 985 2936 Fax 001 914 985 7635

Contacts *Pema Browne, Perry Browne*

FOUNDED 1966. ('Pema rhymes with Emma.') *Handles* mass-market mainstream and hardcover fiction: romance, men's adventure, business, humour, children's picture books and young adult; non-fiction: how-to and reference. No unsolicited mss; send query letter with IRCs. No fax queries. Also handles illustrators' work. *Commission* Home 15%; Translation 20%; Dramatic 10%; Overseas authors 20%.

Sheree Bykofsky Associates, Inc.★

16 West 36th Street, 13th Floor, New York NY 10018
☎001 212 244 4144

Contact *Sheree Bykofsky*

FOUNDED 1985. *Handles* adult fiction and non-fiction. No scripts. No children's, young adult, horror, science fiction, romance, westerns, occult or supernatural. No unsolicited mss. Send query letter first with brief synopsis or outline and writing sample (1–3 pp) for fiction. IRCs essential for reply or return of material. No phone calls. No reading fee. *Commission* Home 15%; UK (including sub-agent's fee) 25%.

Maria Carvainis Agency, Inc.★

235 West End Avenue, New York NY 10023
☎001 212 580 1559 Fax 001 212 877 3486

Contact *Maria Carvainis*

FOUNDED 1977. *Handles* fiction: literary and mainstream, contemporary women's, mystery, suspense, fantasy, historical, children's and young adult novels; non-fiction: business, finance, women's issues, political and film biography, medicine, psychology and popular science. No film scripts unless from writers with established credits. No science fiction. No unsolicited mss; they will be returned unread. Queries only, with IRCs for response. No reading fee. *Commission* Domestic & Dramatic 15%; Translation 20%.

Martha Casselman, Literary Agent★
PO Box 342, Calistoga CA 94515
☎001 707 942 4341

Contact *Martha Casselman*

FOUNDED 1979. *Handles* all types of non-fiction. No fiction at present. Main interests: food/cookery, biography, current affairs, popular sociology. No scripts, textbooks, poetry, coming-of-age fiction or science fiction. Especially interested in cookery with an appeal to the American market for possible co-publication in UK. Send queries and brief summary, with return postage. No mss. If you do not wish return of material, please state so. Also include, where applicable, any material on previous publications, reviews, brief biography. No proposals via fax. No reading fee. *Commission* Home 15%.

The Catalog Literary Agency
PO Box 2964, Vancouver WA 98668
☎001 360 694 8531

Contact *Douglas Storey*

FOUNDED 1986. *Handles* popular, professional and textbook material in all subjects, especially business, health, money, science, technology, computers, electronics and women's interests; also how-to, self-help, mainstream fiction and children's non-fiction. No genre fiction. No scripts, articles, screenplays, plays, poetry or short stories. No reading fee. No unsolicited mss. Query with an outline and sample chapters and include IRCs. *Commission* 15%.

Linda Chester & Associates
Rockefeller Center, 630 Fifth Avenue, New York NY 10111
☎001 212 218 3350 Fax 001 212 218 3343

Contact *Joanna Pulcini*

FOUNDED 1978. *Handles* literary and commercial fiction and non-fiction in all subjects. No scripts, children's or textbooks. No unsolicited mss. No reading fee for solicited material. *Commission* Home & Dramatic 15%; Translation 25%.

Clausen, Mays & Tahan Literary Agency
249 West 34th Street, Suite 605, New York NY 10001
☎001 212 239 4343 Fax 001 212 239 5248
Email cmtassist@aol.com

Contacts *Stedman Mays, Mary M. Tahan*

Handles non-fiction work such as memoirs, biography, true crime, true stories, how-to, psychology, spirituality, relationships, style, health/nutrition, fashion/beauty, women's issues, humour and cookbooks. Some fiction. Send query letter only. Include IRCs. *UK associates* **David Grossman Literary Agency Ltd**.

Hy Cohen Literary Agency Ltd
PO Box 43770, Up. Montclair NJ 07043
☎001 973 783 9494 Fax 001 973 783 9867
Email cogency@home.com

President *Hy Cohen*

FOUNDED 1975. Fiction and non-fiction. No scripts. Unsolicited mss welcome, but synopsis with sample 100 pp preferred. IRCs essential. No reading fee. *Commission* Home & Dramatic 10%; Foreign 20%. *Overseas associates* **Abner Stein**, UK.

Ruth Cohen, Inc.★
Box 7626, Menlo Park CA 94025
☎001 650 854 2054

President *Ruth Cohen*

FOUNDED 1982. Works mostly with established/published authors but will consider new writers. *Specialises* in high-quality mystery and women's fiction, plus historical romance. No poetry, short stories or film scripts. No unsolicited mss. Send opening 10 pp with synopsis. Include enough IRCs for return postage or *materials will not be returned*. No reading fee. *Commission* Home & Dramatic 15%; Foreign 20%.

Frances Collin Literary Agent★
PO Box 33, Wayne PA 19087–0033
☎001 610 254 0555 Fax 001 610 254 5029

Contact *Frances Collin*

FOUNDED 1948. Successor to Marie Rodell. *Handles* general fiction and non-fiction. No scripts. No unsolicited mss. Send query letter only, with IRCs for reply, for the attention of *Marsha Kear*. No reading fee. Rarely accepts non-professional writers or writers not represented in the UK. *Overseas associates* worldwide.

Don Congdon Associates, Inc.★
156 Fifth Avenue, Suite 625, New York
NY 10010–7002
☎001 212 645 1229 Fax 001 212 727 2688

Contacts *Don Congdon, Michael Congdon,*
Susan Ramer

FOUNDED 1983. *Handles* fiction and non-fiction. No academic, technical, romantic fiction, or scripts. No unsolicited mss. Approach by letter in the first instance. No reading fee. *Commission* Home 10%; UK & Translation 19%. *Overseas associates* **The Marsh Agency** (Italy, Germany, Spain, Portugal, Latin America); **Abner Stein** (UK); Michelle Lapautre (France); Tuttle Mori Agency (Japan); **Andrew Nurnberg** (Eastern Europe); Lennart Sane (Scandinavia and The Netherlands).

Richard Curtis Associates, Inc.
171 East 74th Street, Second Floor,
New York NY 10021
☎001 212 772 7363 Fax 001 212 772 7393
Email shackwkorth@curtisagency.com
Website www.curtisagency.com

Contact *Richard Curtis*

FOUNDED 1969. *Handles* genre and mainstream fiction, plus commercial non-fiction. No scripts. *Specialises* in electronic rights and multimedia.

Curtis Brown Ltd★
10 Astor Place, New York NY 10003
☎001 212 473 5400

Book Rights *Laura Blake Peterson, Ellen*
Geiger, Peter L. Ginsberg, Emilie Jacobson,
Ginger Knowlton, Perry Knowlton, Marilyn E.
Marlow, Andrew Pope, Clyde Taylor, Maureen
Walters, Mitchell Walters
Film, TV, Audio Rights *Timothy Knowlton,*
Edwin Wintle
Translation *Dave Barbor*

FOUNDED 1914. *Handles* general fiction and non-fiction. Also some scripts for film, TV and theatre. No unsolicited mss; queries only, with IRCs for reply. No reading fee. *Overseas associates* Representatives in all major foreign countries.

Joan Daves Agency
21 West 26th Street, New York
NY 10010-1003
☎001 212 685 2663 Fax 001 212 685 1781

Director *Jennifer Lyons*

FOUNDED 1952. Literary fiction and non-fiction. No romance or textbooks. No scripts. Send query letter in the first instance. 'A detailed synopsis seems valuable only for non-fiction work. Material submitted should specify the author's background, publishing credits and similar pertinent information.' No reading fee. *Commission* Home 15%; Dramatic 10–25%; Foreign 20%.

Sandra Dijkstra Literary Agency★
PMB 515, 1155 Camino Del Mar, Del Mar
CA 92104–3115
☎001 858 755 3115 Fax 001 858 792 1494

Contact *Sandra Zane*

FOUNDED 1981. *Handles* quality and commercial non-fiction and fiction, including some genre fiction. No scripts. No westerns, contemporary romance or poetry. Willing to look at children's projects. *Specialises* in quality fiction, mystery/thrillers, psychology, self-help, science, health, business, memoirs, biography. Dedicated to promoting new and original voices and ideas. For fiction: send brief synopsis (one page) and first 50 pages; for non-fiction: send proposal with overview, chapter outline, author biog. and two sample chapters. All submissions should be accompanied by IRCs. No reading fee. *Commission* Home 15%; Translation 20%. *Overseas associates* **Abner Stein**, UK; Ursula Bender, Agence Hoffman, Germany; Monica Heyum, Scandinavia; Luigi Bernabo, Italy; M. Casanovas, Spain; Caroline Van Gelderen, Netherlands; M. Kling (La Nouvelle Agence), France; William Miller, The English Agency, Japan.

Jane Dystel Literary Management★
One Union Square West, Suite 904, New
York NY 10003
☎001 212 627 9100 Fax 001 212 627 9313
Website www.dystel.com

Contacts *Jane Dystel, Miriam Goderich, Todd*
Keithley, Jo Fagan, Kyung Cho, Stacey Glick

FOUNDED 1991. *Handles* non-fiction and fiction. *Specialises* in politics, history, biography, cookbooks, current affairs, celebrities, commercial and literary fiction. No reading fee.

Educational Design Services, Inc.
PO Box 253, Wantagh NY 11793
☎001 718 539 4107/516 221 0995
Email linder.eds@juno.com *or*
edselzer@aol.com

President *Bertram Linder*
Vice President *Edwin Selzer*

FOUNDED 1979. *Specialises* in educational material and textbooks for sale to school markets. IRCs must accompany submissions. *Commission* Home 15%; Foreign 25%.

Elek International Rights Agents

457 Broome Street, New York NY 10013
☎001 212 431 9368 Fax 001 212 966 5768
Website www.theliteraryagency.com

Contact *Lauren Mactas*

FOUNDED 1979. *Handles* adult non-fiction and
children's picture books. No scripts, fiction, psychology, New Age, poetry, short stories or autobiography. No unsolicited mss; send letter of
enquiry with IRCs for reply; include résumé,
credentials, brief synopsis. No reading fee.
Commission Home 15%; Dramatic & Foreign
20%.

Ann Elmo Agency, Inc.★

60 East 42nd Street, New York NY 10165
☎001 212 661 2880/1 Fax 001 212 661 2883

Contacts *Lettie Lee, Mari Cronin,*
Andree Abecassis

FOUNDED in the 1940s. *Handles* literary and
romantic fiction, mysteries and mainstream; also
non-fiction in all subjects, including biography
and self-help. Some children's (8–12-year-olds).
Query letter with outline of project in the first
instance. No reading fee. *Commission* Home
15–20%. *Overseas associates* **John Johnson Ltd,**
UK.

ForthWrite Literary Agency & Speakers Bureau

23852 W. Pacific Coast Highway, Suite 701,
Malibu CA 90265
☎001 310 456 5698 Fax 001 310 456 6589

Contact *Wendy Keller*

FOUNDED 1988. *Specialises* in non-fiction: biography, business (marketing, finance, management and sales), alternative health, cookery,
gardening, nature, popular psychology, history,
self-help, home and health, crafts, computer,
how-to, animal care by experts known in the
field. Handles electronic, foreign (translation and
distribution) and resale rights for previously published books. Send query letter with IRCs. No
reading fee. *Commission* Foreign 20%.

Robert A. Freedman Dramatic Agency, Inc.★

Suite 2310, 1501 Broadway, New York
NY 10036
☎001 212 840 5760

President *Robert A. Freedman*
Vice President *Selma Luttinger*

FOUNDED 1928 as Brandt & Brandt Dramatic
Department, Inc. Took its present name in 1984.
Works mostly with established authors. *Specialises*
in plays, film and TV scripts. Unsolicited mss not
read. *Commission* Dramatic 10%.

Max Gartenberg, Literary Agent

521 Fifth Avenue, Suite 1700, New York
NY 10175
☎001 212 860 8451 Fax 001 973 535 5033
Email gartenbook@hotmail.com

Contact *Max Gartenberg*

FOUNDED 1954. Works mostly with established/
published authors. *Specialises* in non-fiction and
trade fiction. Query first. *Commission* Home &
Dramatic 10%; 15% on initial sale, 10% thereafter; Foreign 15/20%.

Gelfman Schneider Literary Agents, Inc.★

250 West 57th Street, Suite 2515, New York
NY 10107
☎001 212 245 1993 Fax 001 212 245 8678

Contacts *Deborah Schneider, Jane Gelfman*

FOUNDED 1919 (London), 1980 (New York).
Formerly John Farquharson Ltd. Works mostly
with established/published authors. *Specialises*
in general trade fiction and non-fiction. No
poetry, short stories or screenplays. No reading
fee for outlines. Submissions must be accompanied by IRCs. *Commission* Home 15%;
Dramatic 15%; Foreign 20%. *Overseas associates*
Curtis Brown Group Ltd, UK.

The Sebastian Gibson Agency

PO Box 13350, Palm Desert
CA 92255–3350
☎001 760 322 2446 Fax 001 760 322 3857

Contact *Sebastian Gibson*

FOUNDED 1994. *Handles* all categories of fiction; psychological thrillers, historical novels,
mysteries/suspense, action/adventure, crime/
police, medical dramas. Also non-fiction written by celebrities, cookbooks or photography,
children's and juvenile books. No poetry, textbooks, essays, short stories, child development,
how-to, gardening, erotic, autobiography,
drug recovery, religious books or scripts. 'We
are constantly seeking something fresh and new
with novel plot lines or a story told in a way
that has never been told before. Grab our
imagination and you may grab the imagination
of a publisher as well.' No reading fee. Send
query letter, synopsis and first three chapters
with IRCs. No phone calls, faxes or e-mail.
Commission Home 10%; Overseas & Translation 20%; Film & Ancilliary Rights 15%.

Sanford J. Greenburger Associates, Inc.★

15th Floor, 55 Fifth Avenue, New York NY 10003
☎001 212 206 5600 Fax 001 212 463 8718
Website www.greenburger.com

Contacts *Heide Lange, Faith Hamlin, Beth Vesel, Theresa Park*

Handles fiction and non-fiction. No unsolicited mss. First approach with query letter, sample chapter and synopsis. No reading fee.

The Charlotte Gusay Literary Agency

10532 Blythe Avenue, Los Angeles CA 90064
☎001 310 559 0831 Fax 001 310 559 2639

Contact *Charlotte Gusay*

FOUNDED 1988. *Handles* fiction, both literary and commercial, plus non-fiction: children's and adult humour, parenting, gardening, women's and men's issues, feminism, psychology, memoirs, biography, travel. No science fiction, horror, short pieces or collections of stories. No unsolicited mss; send query letter first, then if your material is requested, send succinct outline and first three sample chapters for fiction, or proposal for non-fiction. No response without IRCs. No reading fee. *Commission* Home 15%; Dramatic 10%; Translation & Foreign 25%.

Joy Harris Literary Agency, Inc.★

156 Fifth Avenue, Suite 617, New York NY 10010
☎001 212 924 6269 Fax 001 212 924 6609
Email JHLitAgent@aol.com

Contacts *Joy Harris, Stephanie Abou, Leslie Daniels*

Handles adult non-fiction and fiction. No unsolicited mss. Query letter in the first instance. No reading fee. *Commission* Home & Dramatic 15%; Foreign 20%. *Overseas associates* Michael Meller, Germany; **Abner Stein**, UK; Roberto Santachiara, Italy; The English Agency, Japan; **Andrew Nurnberg Associates**, rest of the territories.

John Hawkins & Associates, Inc.★

71 West 23rd Street, Suite 1600, New York NY 10010
☎001 212 807 7040 Fax 001 212 807 9555

Contacts *John Hawkins, William Reiss*

FOUNDED 1893. *Handles* film and TV rights. No unsolicited mss; send queries with 1–3-page outline and one-page c.v. IRCs necessary for response. No reading fee. *Commission* Apply for rates.

The Jeff Herman Agency, LLC

332 Bleecker Street, Suite 6–31, New York NY 10014
☎001 212 941 0540 Fax 001 212 941 0614
Email jeff@jeffherman.com
Website www.jeffherman.com

Contact *Jeffrey H. Herman*

Handles all areas of non-fiction, textbooks and reference. No scripts. No unsolicited mss. Query letter with IRCs in the first instance. No reading fee. Jeff Herman publishes a useful reference guide to the book trade called *The Writer's Guide to Book Editors, Publishers & Literary Agents* (Prima). *Commission* Home 15%; Translation 10%.

Susan Herner Rights Agency, Inc.

PO Box 303, Scarsdale NY 10583
☎001 914 725 8967 Fax 001 914 725 8969

Contacts *Susan N. Herner, Sue P. Yuen*

FOUNDED 1987. Adult fiction and non-fiction in all areas. No children's books. *Handles* film and TV rights and software. Send query letter with outline and sample chapters. No reading fee. *Commission* Home 15%; Dramatic & Translation 20%. *Overseas associates* **David Grossman Literary Agency Ltd**, UK.

Frederick Hill Associates

1842 Union Street, San Francisco CA 94123
☎001 415 921 2910 Fax 001 415 921 2802

Contacts *Fred Hill, Bonnie Nadell, Irene Moore*

FOUNDED 1979. General fiction and non-fiction. No scripts. Send query letter detailing past publishing history if any. IRCs required. *Commission* Home & Dramatic 15%; Foreign 20%. *Overseas associates* **Mary Clemmey Literary Agency**, UK.

Hull House Literary Agency

240 East 82nd Street, New York NY 10028
☎001 212 988 0725 Fax 001 212 794 8758

President *David Stewart Hull*
Associate *Lydia Mortimer*

FOUNDED 1987. *Handles* commercial fiction, mystery, biography, military history. No scripts, poetry, short stories, romance, science fiction and fantasy, children's or young adult. No unsolicited mss; send single-page letter describing project briefly, together with short biographical note and list of previous publications if any. IRCs essential. No reading fee. *Commission* Home 15%; Translation 20%.

IMG Literary

825 Seventh Avenue, New York NY 10019
☎001 212 489 5400 Fax 001 212 246 1118
Contact *David Chalfant (Vice President)*

FOUNDED 1986. A wholly-owned subsidiary of IMG, The Mark McCormack Group of Companies. *Handles* non-fiction and fiction. No science fiction, fantasy, poetry or photography. No scripts. Query first. Submissions should include brief synopsis (typed), sample chapters (50 pp maximum), publishing history, etc. *Commission* Home & Dramatic 15%; Foreign 20%. *Overseas associates* worldwide.

Kidde, Hoyt & Picard Literary Agency★

333 East 51st Street, New York NY 10022
☎001 212 755 9461/9465
Fax 001 212 223 2501
Chief Associate *Katharine Kidde*
Associate *Laura Langlie*

FOUNDED 1981. *Specialises* in mainstream and literary fiction, romantic fiction (historical and contemporary), and quality non-fiction in humanities and social sciences (biography, history, current affairs, the arts). No reading fee. Query first, include s.a.e. *Commission* 15%.

Kirchoff/Wohlberg, Inc.★

866 United Nations Plaza, Suite 525,
New York NY 10017
☎001 212 644 2020 Fax 001 212 223 4387
Authors' Representative
Elizabeth Pulitzer-Voges

FOUNDED 1930. *Handles* books for children and young adults, specialising in children's picture books. No adult material. No scripts for TV, radio, film or theatre. Send letter of enquiry with synopsis or outline and IRCs for reply or return. No reading fee.

Paul Kohner, Inc.

9300 Wilshire Boulevard, Suite 555, Beverly Hills CA 90212
☎001 310 550 1060 Fax 001 310 276 1083
Contacts *Pearl Wexler, Stephen Moore, Deborah Obad, Lorianne Hall*

FOUNDED 1938. *Handles* a broad range of books for subsidiary rights sales to film and TV. Few direct placements with publishers as film and TV scripts are the major part of the business. *Specialises* in true crime, biography and history. Non-fiction preferred to fiction for the TV market but anything 'we feel has strong potential' will be considered. No short stories, poetry, science fiction or gothic. Unsolicited material will be returned unread, if accompanied by s.a.e. Approach via a third-party reference or send query letter with professional résumé. No reading fee. *Commission* Home & Dramatic 10%; Publishing 15%.

Barbara S. Kouts, Literary Agent★

PO Box 560, Bellport NY 11713
☎001 516 286 1278 Fax 001 516 286 1538
Contact *Barbara S. Kouts*

FOUNDED 1980. *Handles* fiction, non-fiction and children's. No romance, science fiction or scripts. No unsolicited mss. Query letter in the first instance. No reading fee. *Commission* Home 10%; Foreign 20%.

Peter Lampack Agency, Inc.

551 Fifth Avenue, Suite 1613, New York NY 10176
☎001 212 687 9106 Fax 001 212 687 9109
Contact *Loren Soeiro*

FOUNDED in 1977. *Handles* commercial fiction: male action and adventure, contemporary relationships, historical, mysteries and suspense, literary fiction; also non-fiction from recognised experts in a given field, plus biographies, autobiographies. Also handles theatrical, motion picture, and TV rights from book properties. No original scripts or screenplays, series or episodic material. Best approach by letter in first instance. No reply without s.a.e. 'We will respond within three weeks and invite the submission of manuscripts which we would like to examine.' No reading fee. No unsolicited mss. *Commission* Home & Dramatic 15%; Translation & UK 20%.

The Lazear Agency, Inc.

800 Washington Avenue N., Suite 660, Minneapolis MN 55401
☎001 612 332 8640 Fax 001 612 332 4648
Contacts *Christi Cardenas, Jonathon Lazear, Wendy Lazear, Neil Ross, Anne Blackstone, Tanya Cromey*

FOUNDED 1984. *Handles* fiction: mysteries, suspense, young adult and literary; also true crime, addiction recovery, biography, travel, business, and scripts for film and TV, CD-ROM, broad band interactive television. Children's books from previously published writers. No poetry or stage plays. Approach by letter, with description of mss, short autobiography and IRCs. No reading fee. *Commission* Home & Dramatic 15%; Translation 20%.

Ellen Levine, Literary Agency, Inc.★

Suite 1801, 15 East 26th Street, New York NY 10010-1505
☎001 212 899 0620 Fax 001 212 725 4501

Contacts *Diana Finch, Elizabeth Kaplan, Louise Quayle, Ellen Levine*

FOUNDED 1980. *Handles* all types of books. No scripts. No unsolicited mss, nor any other material unless requested. No telephone calls. First approach by letter; send US postage or IRCs for reply, otherwise material not returned. No reading fee. *Commission* Home 15%; Foreign 20%. *UK Associates* **A. M. Heath & Co. Ltd** .

Literary & Creative Artists Agency★

3543 Albemarle Street NW, Washington DC 20008
☎001 202 362 4688 Fax 001 202 362 8875
Website www.lca.com

Contacts *Muriel G. Nellis, Jane F. Roberts, Leslie Toussaint*

FOUNDED 1981. *Specialises* in a broad range of general non-fiction. No poetry, pornography, academic or educational textbooks. No unsolicited mss; query letter in the first instance. Include IRCs for response. No reading fee. *Commission* Home 15%; Dramatic 20%; Translation 20–25%.

Sterling Lord Literistic, Inc.

65 Bleecker Street, New York NY 10012
☎001 212 780 6050 Fax 001 212 780 6095

Contacts *Peter Matson, Sterling Lord*

FOUNDED 1979. *Handles* all genres, fiction and non-fiction, plus scripts for TV and film. No unsolicited mss. Prefers letter outlining all non-fiction. No reading fee. *Commission* Home 15%; UK & Translation 20%.

Richard P. McDonough, Literary Agent

34 Pinewood, Irvine CA 92604
☎001 949 654 5480 Fax 001 949 654 5481
Email cestmoi@msn.com

Contact *Richard P. McDonough*

FOUNDED 1986. General non-fiction and literary fiction. No genre fiction. No unsolicited mss; query first and include IRCs. No reading fee. *Commission* 15%.

McIntosh & Otis, Inc.★

353 Lexington Avenue, New York NY 10016
☎001 212 687 7400 Fax 001 212 687 6894

President *Eugene H. Winick*
Adult Books *Sam Pinkus, Sean Farrell, Whitney Calam*
Children's *Dorothy Markinko, Tracey Adams*
Motion Picture/Television *Evva Pryor*

FOUNDED 1928. Adult and juvenile literary fiction and non-fiction. No textbooks or scripts. No unsolicited mss. Query letter indicating nature of the work plus details of background. IRCs for response. No reading fee. *Commission* Home & Dramatic 15%; Foreign 20%. *UK Associates* **A. M. Heath & Co. Ltd**, London.

The Evan Marshall Agency★

6 Tristam Place, Pine Brook NJ 07058–9445
☎001 973 882 1122 Fax 001 973 882 3099
Email evanmarshall@TheNovelist.com
Website www.TheNovelist.com

Contact *Evan Marshall*

FOUNDED 1987. *Handles* general adult fiction. No unsolicited mss; send query letter first. *Commission* Home 15%; UK & Translation 20%.

Mews Books Ltd

c/o Sidney B. Kramer, 20 Bluewater Hill, Westport CT 06880
☎001 203 227 1836 Fax 001 203 227 1144
Email mewsbooks@aol.com (initial contact only; submission by regular mail)

Contacts *Sidney B. Kramer, Fran Pollak*

FOUNDED 1970. *Handles* adult fiction and non-fiction, children's, pre-school and young adult. No scripts, short stories or novellas (unless by established authors). *Specialises* in cookery, medical, health and nutrition, scientific non-fiction, children's and young adult. Unsolicited material welcome. Presentation must be professional and should include summary of plot/characters, one or two sample chapters, personal credentials and brief on target market, all suitable for forwarding to a publisher. No reading fee. If material is accepted, agency asks $350 circulation fee (4–5 publishers), which will be applied against commissions (waived for published authors). Charges for photocopying, postage expenses, telephone calls and other direct costs. Principal agent is an attorney and former publisher (a founder of Bantam Books). Offers consultation service through which writers can get advice on a contract or on publishing problems. *Commission* Home 15%; Film & Translation 20%. *Overseas associates* **Abner Stein**, UK.

Maureen Moran Agency
PO Box 20191, Parkwest Station, New York NY 10025
☎001 212 222 3838 Fax 001 212 531 3464
Email maureenm@erols.com
Contact *Maureen Moran*

Formerly Donald MacCampbell, Inc. *Handles* novels only. No scripts, non-fiction, science fiction, westerns or suspense. *Specialises* in romance. No unsolicited mss; approach by letter. No reading fee. *Commission* US Book Sales 10%; First Novels US 15%.

Howard Morhaim Literary Agency★
841 Broadway, Suite 604, New York NY 10003
☎001 212 529 4433 Fax 001 212 995 1112
Contact *Howard Morhaim*

FOUNDED 1979. *Handles* general adult fiction and non-fiction. No scripts. No children's or young adult material, poetry or religious. No unsolicited mss. Send query letter with synopsis and sample chapters for fiction; query letter with outline or proposal for non-fiction. No reading fee. *Commission* Home 15%; UK & Translation 20%. *Overseas associates* worldwide.

Henry Morrison, Inc.
PO Box 235, Bedford Hills NY 10507
☎001 914 666 3500 Fax 001 914 241 7846
Contact *Henry Morrison*

FOUNDED 1965. *Handles* general fiction, crime and science fiction, and non-fiction. No scripts unless by established writers. Unsolicited material welcome; but send query letter with outline (1–5 pp) in the first instance. No reading fee. *Commission* Home 15%; UK & Translation 25%.

Ruth Nathan Agency
53 East 34th Street, Suite 207, New York NY 10016
☎001 212 481 1185 Fax 001 212 481 1185

FOUNDED 1984. *Specialises* in illustrated books, fine art & decorative arts, historical fiction with emphasis on Middle Ages, true crime, showbiz. Query first. No unsolicited mss. No reading fee. *Commission* 15%.

B. K. Nelson Literary Agency
139 S. Beverly Hills Drive, Site 323, Beverly Hills CA 90212
☎001 310 858 7006 Fax 001 310 858 7967
Website www.cmonline.com/bknelson
President *Bonita K. Nelson*

FOUNDED 1979. *Specialises* in business, self-help, how-to, political, autobiography, celebrity biography. Major motion picture and TV documentary success. No unsolicited mss. Letter of inquiry. Reading fee charged. *Commission* 20%. Lecture Bureau for Authors founded 1994; Foreign Rights Catalogue established 1995; BK Nelson Infomercial Marketing Co. 1996, primarily for authors and endorsements, and Red Pepper Productions for motion picture production in 1998.

New England Publishing Associates, Inc.★
Box 5, Chester CT 06412
☎001 860 345 7323 Fax 001 860 345 3660
Email nepa@nepa.com
Website www.nepa.com
Contacts *Elizabeth Frost-Knappman, Edward W. Knappman, Kris Schiavi, Ron Formica*

FOUNDED 1983. *Handles* non-fiction and (clients only) fiction. *Specialises* in current affairs, history, science, women's studies, reference, psychology, politics, biography, true crime. No textbooks or anthologies. No scripts. Unsolicited mss considered but query letter or phone call preferred first. No reading fee. *Commission* Home 15%. *Overseas associates* throughout Europe and Japan; Scott-Ferris, UK. Dramatic rights: Joe Gotler, Los Angeles.

Richard Parks Agency★
138 East 16th Street, Suite 5B, New York NY 10003
☎001 212 254 9067
Contact *Richard Parks*

FOUNDED 1989. *Handles* general trade fiction and non-fiction: literary novels, mysteries and thrillers, commercial fiction, science fiction, biography, pop culture, psychology, self-help, parenting, medical, cooking, gardening, etc. No scripts. No technical or academic. No unsolicited mss. Fiction read by referral only. No reading fee. *Commission* Home 15%; UK & Translation 20%. *Overseas associates* **The Marsh Agency**, **Barbara Levy Literary Agency**.

James Peter Associates, Inc.★
PO Box 772, Tenafly NJ 07670
☎001 201 568 0760 Fax 001 201 568 2959
Contact *Bert Holtje*

FOUNDED 1971. Non-fiction only. 'Many of our authors are historians, psychologists, physicians – all are writing trade books for general readers.' No scripts. No fiction or children's books. *Specialises* in history, popular culture, business, health, biography and politics. No unsolicited mss. Send query letter first with brief project outline, samples and biographical information. No reading fee. *Commission* 15%.

Alison J. Picard Literary Agent
PO Box 2000, Cotuit MA 02635
☎001 508 477 7192 Fax 001 508 420 0762
Email ajpicard@aol.com

Contact *Alison Picard*

FOUNDED 1985. *Handles* mainstream and literary fiction, contemporary and historical romance, children's and young adult, mysteries and thrillers; plus non-fiction. No short stories unless suitable for major national publications, and no poetry. Rarely any science fiction and fantasy. Particularly interested in expanding non-fiction titles. Approach with written query. No reading fee. *Commission* 15%. *Overseas associates* **A. M. Heath & Co. Ltd**, UK.

Pinder Lane & Garon-Brooke Associates Ltd★
159 West 53rd Street, Suite 14–E, New York NY 10019
☎001 212 489 0880 Fax 001 212 489 7104

Owner Agents *Dick Duane, Robert Thixton*
Vice President *Jean Free*
Agent *Nancy Coffey*

FOUNDED 1951. Fiction and non-fiction. No category romance, westerns or mysteries. No unsolicited mss. First approach by query letter. No reading fee. *Commission* Home 15%; Dramatic 10–15%; Foreign 30%. *Overseas associates* **Abner Stein**, UK; Translation: Bernard Kurman.

PMA Literary & Film Management, Inc.
Box 1817, Old Chelsea Sta., New York NY 10011
☎001 212 929 1222 Fax 001 212 206 0238
Email pmalitfilm@aol.com
Website www.pmalitfilm.com

President *Peter Miller*
Vice President *Delin Cormeny*
Associate *Elaine Gartneri*

FOUNDED 1976. Commercial fiction, non-fiction and screenplays. *Specialises* in books with motion picture and television potential, and in true crime. No poetry, pornography, non-commercial or academic. No unsolicited mss. Approach by letter with one-page synopsis. *Commission* Home 15%; Dramatic 10–15%; Foreign 20–25%.

Susan Ann Protter Literary Agent★
110 West 40th Street, Suite 1408, New York NY 10018–3616
☎001 212 840 0480

Contact *Susan Protter*

FOUNDED 1971. *Handles* general fiction, mysteries, thrillers, science fiction and fantasy; non-fiction: history, general reference, biography, true crime, science, health and parenting. No romance, poetry, westerns, religious, children's or sport manuals. No scripts. First approach with letter, including IRCs. No reading fee. *Commission* Home & Dramatic 15%; Foreign 25%. *Overseas associates* **Abner Stein**, UK; agents in all major markets.

Quicksilver Books, Literary Agents
50 Wilson Street, Hartsdale NY 10530
☎001 914 946 8748

President *Bob Silverstein*

FOUNDED 1973. *Handles* literary fiction and mainstream commercial fiction: blockbuster, suspense, thriller, contemporary, mystery and historical; and general non-fiction, including self-help, psychology, holistic healing, ecology, environmental, biography, fact crime, New Age, health, nutrition, enlightened wisdom and spirituality. No scripts, science fiction and fantasy, pornographic, children's or romance. UK material being submitted must have universal appeal for the US market. Unsolicited material welcome but must be accompanied by IRCs for response, together with biographical details, covering letter, etc. No reading fee. *Commission* Home & Dramatic 15%; Translation 20%.

Helen Rees Literary Agency★
123 N. Washington Street, 5th Floor, Boston MA 02114
☎001 617 723 5232 ext 233
Fax 001 617 723 5211
Email wwhelen@aol.com *or*
 joanmax@aol.com *or*
 brifkind@mediaone.com

Contact *Joan Mazmanian*
Associate *Barbara Rifkind*

FOUNDED 1982. *Specialises* in books on health and business; also handles biography, autobiography and history; quality fiction. No scholarly, academic or technical books. No scripts, science fiction, children's, poetry, photography, short stories, cooking. No unsolicited mss. Send query letter with IRCs. No reading fee. *Commission* Home 15%; Foreign 20%.

Rights Unlimited, Inc.★

101 West 55th Street, Suite 2D, New York
NY 10019
☎001 212 246 0900 Fax 001 212 246 2114

Contact *Bernard Kurman*

FOUNDED 1985. *Handles* adult fiction, non-fiction. No scripts, poetry, short stories, educational or literary works. Unsolicited mss welcome; query letter with synopsis preferred in the first instance. No reading fee. *Commission* Home 15%; Translation 20%.

Rosenstone/Wender★

3 East 48th Street, 4th Floor, New York
NY 10017
☎001 212 832 8330 Fax 001 212 759 4524

Contacts *Phyllis Wender, Susan Perlman Cohen, Sonia E. Pabley*

FOUNDED 1981. *Handles* fiction, non-fiction, children's, and scripts for film, TV and theatre. No material for radio. No unsolicited mss. Send letter outlining the project, credits, etc. No reading fee. *Commission* Home 15%; Dramatic 10%; Foreign 20%. *Overseas associates* La Nouvelle Agence, France; Andrew Nurnberg, Netherlands; The English Agency, Japan; Mohrbooks, Germany; Ole Licht, Scandinavia.

Jane Rotrosen Agency LLC★

318 East 51st Street, New York NY 10022
☎001 212 593 4330 Fax 001 212 935 6985

Contacts *Meg Ruley, Andrea Cirillo, Ruth Kagle, Stephanie Tade*

Handles commercial fiction: romance, horror, mysteries, thrillers and fantasy and popular non-fiction. No scripts, educational, professional or belles lettres. No unsolicited mss; send query letter in the first instance. No reading fee. *Commission* Home 15%; UK & Translation 20%. *Overseas associates* worldwide and film agents on the West Coast.

Victoria Sanders Literary Agency★

241 Avenue of the Americas, Suite 11H,
New York NY 10014
☎001 212 633 8811 Fax 001 212 633 0525

Contacts *Victoria Sanders, Diane Dickensheid*

FOUNDED 1993. *Handles* general trade fiction and non-fiction, plus ancillary film and television rights. *Commission* Home & Dramatic 15%; Translation 20%.

Sandum & Associates

144 East 84th Street, New York NY 10028
☎001 212 737 2011

Contact *Howard E. Sandum*

FOUNDED 1987. *Handles* all categories of general adult non-fiction, plus occasional fiction. No scripts. No children's, poetry or short stories. No unsolicited mss. Third-party referral preferred but direct approach by letter, with synopsis, brief biography and IRCs, is accepted. No reading fee. *Commission* Home & Dramatic 15%; Translation & Foreign 20%. *Overseas associates* Scott Ferris Associates.

Jack Scagnetti Talent & Literary Agency

5118 Vineland Avenue, Suite 102, North
Hollywood CA 91601
☎001 818 762 3871

Contact *Jack Scagnetti*

FOUNDED 1974. Works mostly with established/published authors. *Handles* non-fiction, fiction, film and TV scripts. No reading fees. *Commission* Home & Dramatic 10% (scripts), 15% (books); Foreign 15%.

Schiavone Literary Agency, Inc.

236 Trails End, West Palm Beach
FL 33413–2135
☎001 561 966 9294 Fax 001 561 966 9294
Email profschia@aol.com

President *James Schiavone*

FOUNDED 1997. *Handles* fiction and non-fiction (all genres). *Specialises* in biography, autobiography, celebrity memoirs. No poetry or scripts. No unsolicited mss; send query with brief biog-sketch, synopsis, outline and sample chapters (enclose IRCs). No reading fee. *Commission* Home 15%; Foreign & Translation 20%. *Overseas associates* in Europe.

Susan Schulman, A Literary Agency★

454 West 44th Street, New York NY 10036
☎001 212 713 1633/4/5
Fax 001 212 581 8830
Email schulman@aol.com
Website www.susan.schulman.com

Submissions Editor (Books) *Christine Maren*
Submissions Editor (Plays) *Brian Leifest*

FOUNDED 1979. *Specialises* in non-fiction of all types but particularly in psychology-based self-help for men, women and families. Other interests include business, the social sciences, biography, language and linguistics. Fiction interests include contemporary fiction, including women's, mysteries, historical and thrillers 'with a cutting edge'. Always looking for 'something original and fresh'. No unsolicited mss. Query first, including outline and three sample chapters with IRCs. No reading fee. Represents properties for film and television, and works with agents in appropriate territories for translation rights. *Commission* Home & Dramatic 15%; Translation 20%. *Overseas associates* Plays: **Rosica Colin Ltd** and **The Agency Ltd**, UK; Children's books: Marilyn Malin, UK, Commercial fiction: **MBA Literary Agents**, UK.

Shapiro-Lichtman-Stein Talent Agency

8827 Beverly Boulevard, Los Angeles
CA 90048
☎001 310 859 8877 Fax 001 310 859 7153

FOUNDED 1969. Works mostly with established/published authors. *Handles* film and TV scripts. Unsolicited mss will not be read. *Commission* Home & Dramatic 10%; Foreign 20%.

The Shepard Agency

Premier National Bank Building, Suite 3,
1525 Rt. 22, Brewster NY 10509
☎001 914 279 2900/3236
Fax 001 914 279 3239
Email shepard-ldi@mindspring.com

Contacts *Jean Shepard, Lance Shepard*

FOUNDED 1987. *Handles* non-fiction: business, food, self-help and travel; some fiction: adult, children's and young adult and the occasional script. No pornography. *Specialises* in business. Send query letter, table of contents, sample chapters and IRCs for response. No reading fee. *Commission* Home & Dramatic 15%; Translation 20%.

Lee Shore Agency Ltd

The Sterling Building, 440 Friday Road,
Pittsburgh PA 15209
☎001 412 821 0440 Fax 001 412 821 6099
Email LeeShore1@aol.com
Website www.leeshoreagency.com

Contacts *Jennifer Piemme, Patricia Reuscher*

FOUNDED 1988. *Handles* non-fiction, including textbooks, and mass-market fiction: horror, romance, mystery, westerns, science fiction. Also some young adult and, more recently, screenplays. *Specialises* in New Age, self-help, how-to and quality fiction. No children's. No unsolicited mss. Send IRCs for guidelines before submitting work. Reading fee charged. *Commission* Home 15%; Dramatic 20%.

Bobbe Siegel Literary Agency

41 West 83rd Street, New York NY 10024
☎001 212 877 4985 Fax 001 212 877 4985

Contact *Bobbe Siegel*

FOUNDED 1975. Works mostly with established/published authors. *Specialises* in literary fiction, detective, suspense, historical, fantasy, biography, how-to, women's interest, fitness, health, beauty, sports, pop psychology. No scripts. No cookbooks, crafts, children's, short stories or humour. First approach with letter including IRCs for response. No reading fee. Critiques given if the writer is taken on for representation. *Commission* Home 15%; Dramatic & Foreign 20%. (Foreign/Dramatic split 50/50 with sub-agent.) Also handles foreign rights for many US agents. *Overseas associates* in various countries, including **John Pawsey** in the UK.

Michael Snell Literary Agency

PO Box 1206, Truro MA 02666–1206
☎001 508 349 3718

President *Michael Snell*
Vice President *Patricia Smith*

FOUNDED 1980. Adult non-fiction, especially science, business and women's issues. *Specialises* in business and computer books (professional and reference to popular trade how-to); general how-to and self-help on all topics, from diet and exercise to parenting, relationships, health, sex, psychology and personal finance, plus literary and suspense fiction. No unsolicited mss. Send outline and sample chapter with return postage for reply. No reading fee for outlines. Brochure available on how to write a book proposal. Author of *From Book Idea to Bestseller*, published by Prima. Rewriting, developmental editing, collaborating and ghostwriting services available on a fee basis. Send IRCs. *Commission* Home 15%.

Southern Writers

Magee Building, 3004 Jackson Street, Suite A,
Alexandria LA 71301–4745
☎001 318 445 6550 Fax 001 318 445 6650

President *Emilie Griffin*

FOUNDED 1979. *Handles* fiction and non-fiction of general interest. No scripts, short stories, poetry, autobiography or articles. No unsolicited mss. Approach in writing with query. Reading fee charged to authors unpublished in the field. *Commission* Home 15%; Dramatic & Translation 20%.

The Spieler Agency

154 West 57th Street, Room 135, New York NY 10019

☎001 212 757 4439 Fax 001 212 333 2019

The Spieler Agency/West, 1328 Sixth Street, #3, Berkeley, CA 94710

☎001 510 528 2616 Fax 001 510 528 8117

Contacts *Joseph Spieler, Lisa M. Ross, John Thornton, Ada Muellner* (New York); *Victoria Shoemaker* (Berkeley)

FOUNDED 1980. *Handles* literary fiction and non-fiction. No how-to or genre romance. *Specialises* in history, science, ecology, social issues and business. No scripts. Approach in writing with IRCs. No reading fee. *Commission* Home 15%; Translation 20%. *Overseas associates* **Abner Stein, The Marsh Agency**, UK.

Philip G. Spitzer Literary Agency★

50 Talmage Farm Lane, East Hampton NY 11937

☎001 516 329 3650 Fax 001 516 329 3651

Contact *Philip Spitzer*

FOUNDED 1969. Works mostly with established/published authors. *Specialises* in general non-fiction and fiction – thrillers. No reading fee for outlines. *Commission* Home & Dramatic 15%; Foreign 20%.

Lyle Steele & Co. Ltd
Literary Agents

511 East 73rd Street, Suite 6, New York NY 10021

☎001 212 288 2981

President *Lyle Steele*

FOUNDED 1985. *Handles* general non-fiction and category fiction. Also North American rights to titles published by major English publishers. No scripts unless derived from books already being handled. No romance. No unsolicited mss; query with IRCs in first instance. No reading fee. *Commission* 10%. *Overseas associates* worldwide.

Gloria Stern Agency (Hollywood)

12535 Chandler Boulevard, Suite 3, North Hollywood CA 91607

☎001 818 508 6296 Fax 001 818 508 6296

Contact *Gloria Stern*

FOUNDED 1984. *Handles* film scripts, genre (romance, detective, thriller and sci-fi) and mainstream fiction; electronic media. Accepts interactive material, games and electronic data. 'No books containing gratuitous violence.' Approach with letter, biography and synopsis.

Reading fee charged by the hour. *Commission* Home 15%; Offshore 20%.

Gunther Stuhlmann
Author's Representative

PO Box 276, Becket MA 01223

☎001 413 623 5170

Contacts *Gunther Stuhlmann, Barbara Ward*

FOUNDED 1954. *Handles* literary fiction, biography and serious non-fiction. No film/TV scripts unless from established clients. No short stories, detective, romance, adventure, poetry, technical or computers. Query first with IRCs, including sample chapters and synopsis of project. '*We take on few new clients.*' No reading fee. *Commission* Home 10%; Foreign 15%; Translation 20%.

The Tantleff Office★

375 Greenwich Street, Suite 603, New York NY 10013

☎001 212 941 3939 Fax 001 212 941 3948

Contacts (scripts) *Jack Tantleff, Jill Bock, Charmaine Ferenczi, John B. Santoianni*

FOUNDED 1986. *Handles* primarily scripts for theatre, film and TV, and represents actors. Does not handle books. No unsolicited mss; queries only. No reading fee. *Commission* 10%.

2M Communications Ltd

121 West 27th Street, Suite 601, New York NY 10001

☎001 212 741 1509 Fax 001 212 691 4460

Contact *Madeleine Morel*

FOUNDED 1982. *Handles* non-fiction only: everything from pop psychology and health to cookery books, biographies and pop culture. No scripts. No fiction, children's, computers or science. No unsolicited mss; send letter with sample pages and IRCs. No reading fee. *Commission* Home & Dramatic 15%; Translation 20%. *Overseas associates* Thomas Schluck Agency, Germany; Asano Agency, Japan; EAIS, France; Living Literary Agency, Italy; Nueva Agencia Literaria Internacional, Spain.

Van der Leun & Associates

22 Division Street, Easton CT 06612

☎001 203 259 4897

Contact *Patricia Van der Leun*

FOUNDED 1984. *Handles* fiction and non-fiction. No scripts. No science fiction, fantasy, romance. *Specialises* in art and architecture, science, biography and fiction. No unsolicited mss; query first, with proposal and short biography. No reading fee. *Commission* 15%. *Overseas associates* **Abner**

Stein, UK; Michelle Lapautre, France; English Agency, Japan; Carmen Balcells, Spain; Lucia Riff, South America; Susanna Zevi, Italy.

Wales Literary Agency, Inc.*
108 Hayes Street, Seattle WA 98109
☎001 206 284 7114 Fax 001 206 284 0190
Email waleslit@aol.com
Contacts *Elizabeth Wales, Nancy Shawn*

FOUNDED 1988. *Handles* quality fiction and non-fiction. No genre fiction, westerns, romance, science fiction or horror. Special interest in 'Pacific Rim', West Coast, and Pacific Northwest stories. No unsolicited mss; send query letter with publication list and writing sample. No reading fee. No e-mail queries longer than one page. *Commission* Home 15%; Dramatic & Translation 20%.

John A. Ware Literary Agency
392 Central Park West, New York NY 10025
☎001 212 866 4733 Fax 001 212 866 4734
Contact *John Ware*

FOUNDED 1978. *Specialises* in non-fiction: biography, history, current affairs, investigative journalism, science, inside looks at phenomena, medicine and psychology (academic credentials required). Also handles literary fiction, mysteries/thrillers, sport, oral history, Americana and folklore. Unsolicited mss not read. Send query letter first with IRCs to cover return postage. No reading fee. *Commission* Home & Dramatic 15%; Foreign 20%.

Waterside Productions, Inc.
2191 San Elijo Avenue, Cardiff by the Sea CA 92007–839
☎001 760 632 9190 Fax 001 760 632 9295
Email bgladstone@compuserve.com
Contact *William Gladstone*

FOUNDED 1982. *Handles* general non-fiction: computers and technology, psychology, science, business, sports. All types of multimedia. No unsolicited mss; send query letter. No reading fee. *Commission* Home 15%; Dramatic 20%; Translation 25%. *Overseas associates* Serafina Clarke, UK; Asano Agency, Japan; Ulla Lohren, Sweden; Ruth Liepman, Germany; Vera Le Marie, EAIS, France; Bardon Chinese Media Agency, China; Grandi & Vitali, Italy; DRT, Korea; Mercedes Casanovas, Spain.

Watkins Loomis Agency, Inc.
133 East 35th Street, Suite 1, New York NY 10016
☎001 212 532 0080 Fax 001 212 889 0506

Contact *Katherine Fausset*

FOUNDED 1904. *Handles* fiction and non-fiction. No scripts for film, radio, TV or theatre. No science fiction, fantasy or horror. No reading fee. No unsolicited mss. Approach in writing with enquiry or proposal and s.a.e. *Commission* Home 15%; UK & Translation 20%. *Overseas associates* **Abner Stein**; **The Marsh Agency**, UK.

Wecksler-Incomco
170 West End Avenue, New York NY 10023
☎001 212 787 2239 Fax 001 212 496 7035
Contacts *Sally Wecksler, Joann Amparan*

FOUNDED 1971. *Handles* literary fiction and non-fiction: business, reference, biographies, performing arts and heavily illustrated books. Send queries only. No unsolicited mss. No submissions by fax or e-mail; hard copy only. No reading fee. Foreign rights. *Commission* Home 15%; Translation & UK 20%.

Cherry Weiner Literary Agency
28 Kipling Way, Manalapan NJ 07726
☎001 732 446 2096 Fax 001 732 792 0506
Contact *Cherry Weiner*

FOUNDED 1977. *Handles* more or less all types of genre fiction: science fiction and fantasy, romance, mystery, westerns. No scripts. No non-fiction. No unsolicited mss. No submissions except through referral. No reading fee. *Commission* 15%. *Overseas associates* **Abner Stein**, UK; Thomas Schluck, Germany; International Editors Inc., Spain; Prava Prevodi Agency (Eastern Europe), Serbia; Elaine Benisti Agency, France; Borderline Literary Agency, Italy; Nucihan Kesim Literary Agency, Turkey; English Agency (Japan) Ltd; Alex Korzhenevski Agency, Russia; Renaissance Media – movie agent. Also dealing with various e-book publishers.

Wieser & Wieser, Inc.
25 East 21st Street, New York NY 10010
☎001 212 260 0860 Fax 001 212 505 7186
Contacts *Olga B. Wieser, Jake Elwell*

FOUNDED 1976. Works mostly with established/published authors. *Specialises* in literary and mainstream fiction, serious and popular historical fiction, and general non-fiction: business, finance, aviation, sports, photography, cookbooks, travel and popular medicine. No poetry, children's, science fiction or religious. No unsolicited mss. First approach by letter with IRCs. No reading fee for outlines. *Commission* Home & Dramatic 15%; Foreign 20%.

Ann Wright Representatives

165 West 46th Street, Suite 1105, New York NY 10036–2501

☎001 212 764 6770 Fax 001 212 764 5125

Contact *Dan Wright*

FOUNDED 1961. *Specialises* in screenplays for film and TV. Also handles novels, drama and fiction. No academic, scientific or scholarly. Approach by letter; no reply without IRCs. Include outline and credits only. New film and TV writers encouraged. No reading fee. Signatory to the Writers Guild of America Agreement. *Commission* Home – varies according to current trend (10–20%); Dramatic 10% of gross.

Writers House, Inc.★

21 West 26th Street, New York NY 10010

☎001 212 685 2400 Fax 001 212 685 1781

Contacts *Albert Zuckerman, Amy Berkower,* *Merrilee Heifetz, Susan Cohen, Susan Ginsburg, Fran Lebowitz, Karen Solem, Robin Rue, John Hodgman, Simon Lipskar, Steven Malk*

FOUNDED 1974. *Handles* all types of fiction, including children's and young adult, plus narrative non-fiction: history, biography, popular science, pop and rock culture. *Specialises* in popular fiction, women's novels, thrillers and children's. Represents novelisation rights for film producers such as New Line Cinema. No scripts. No professional or scholarly. For consideration of unsolicited mss, send letter of enquiry, 'explaining why your book is wonderful, briefly what it's about and outlining your writing background'. No reading fee. *Commission* Home & Dramatic 15%; Foreign 20%. Albert Zuckerman is author of *Writing the Blockbuster Novel*, published by **Little, Brown & Co.** and **Warner Paperbacks**.

US Media Contacts in the UK

ABC News Intercontinental Inc.
3 Queen Caroline Street, Mail Code 2303,
London W6 9PE
☎020 8222 5000 Fax 020 8222 5020
**Bureau Chief & Director of News
Coverage, Europe, Middle East &
Africa** *Rex Granum*

Alaska Journal of Commerce
16 Cavaye Place, London SW10 9PT
☎0702 0924480 Fax 0702 0924482
Bureau Chief *Robert Gould*

The Associated Press
12 Norwich Street, London EC4A 1BP
☎020 7353 1515 Fax 020 7353 8118
Chief of Bureau/Managing Director
Myron L. Belkind

The Baltimore Sun
11 Kensington Court Place, London
W8 5BJ
☎020 7460 2200 Fax 020 7460 2211
Bureau Chief *Bill Glauber*

Bloomberg Business News
City Gate House, 39–45 Finsbury Square,
London EC2A 1PQ
☎020 7330 7500 Fax 020 7392 6666
London Bureau Chief *Marybeth Berger*

Boston Globe
61 Cholmeley Crescent, Highgate, London
N6 5EX
☎020 8341 0126 Fax 020 8374 7631
Bureau Chief *Kevin Cullen*

Bridge News
Winchmore House, 15 Fetter Lane, London
EC4A 1BW
☎020 7842 4000 Fax 020 7583 5032
Managing Editor, Western Europe
Timothy Penn

Business Week
1 Albemarle Street, London W1X 3HF
☎020 7491 8985 Fax 020 7409 7152
Bureau Chief *Stanley Reed*

Cable News Network Inc. (CNN)
CNN House, 19–22 Rathbone Place, London
W1P 1DF
☎020 7637 6800 Fax 020 7637 6868
Bureau Chief *Thomas Mintier*

CBC Television and Radio
43/51 Great Titchfield Street, London
W1P 8DD
☎020 7412 9200 Fax 020 7637 1892
London Bureau Manager *Sue Phillips*

CBS News
68 Knightsbridge, London SW1X 7LL
☎020 7581 4801 Fax 020 7581 4431
Vice President/Bureau Chief *John Paxson*

Chicago Tribune Press Service
169 Piccadilly, London W1V 9DD
☎020 7499 8769 Fax 020 7499 8781
Chief European Correspondent *Ray Moseley*

CNBC
3 Shortlands, Hammersmith, London W6 8HX
☎020 8600 6380 Fax 020 8600 6390
Bureau Chief *Karen Nye*

Cox Newspapers
PO Box 75, East Horsley, Surrey KT24 6WA
☎01372 452279 Fax 01372 450530
Correspondent *Bert Roughton Jr.*

Dallas Morning News
35 Rusthall Avenue, London W4 1BW
☎020 8994 3248 Fax 020 8994 9438
European Bureau Chief *Gregory Katz*

Dow Jones Newswires
10 Fleet Place, Limeburner Lane, London
EC4M 7QN
☎020 7842 9300 Fax 020 7832 9599
**Managing Director and Senior Editor,
International News** *Arjen Bongard*

Fairchild Publications
of New York
20 Shorts Gardens, London WC2H 9AU
☎020 7240 0420 Fax 020 7240 0290
Bureau Chief *James Fallon*

Forbes Magazine
10 Rotherwick Road, London NW11 7DA
☎020 8455 0463 Fax 020 8455 0512
European Bureau Chief *Richard C. Morais*

Fox News Channel
6 Centaurs Business Park, Grant Way,
Isleworth, Middlesex TW7 5QD
☎020 7805 7143 Fax 020 7805 7140
Bureau Chief *Scott Norvell*

The Globe and Mail
43–51 Great Titchfield Street, London
W1P 8DD
☎020 7323 0449 Fax 020 7323 0428
European Correspondent *Alan Freeman*

International Herald Tribune
40 Marsh Wall, London E14 9TP
☎020 7510 5718 Fax 020 7987 3470
London Correspondent *Tom Buerkle*
(See entry under **National Newspapers**)

Los Angeles Times
150 Brompton Road, London SW3 1HX
☎020 7823 7315 Fax 020 7823 7308
Bureau Chief *Marjorie Miller*

Market News International
167 Fleet Street, 8th Floor, London EC4A 2EA
☎020 7353 4462 Fax 020 7353 9122
Deputy Bureau Chief *Ralph Johnston*

National Public Radio
Room G-10 East Wing, Bush House, Strand,
London WC2B 4PH
☎020 7557 1089 Fax 020 7379 6486
Bureau Chief *Julie McCarthy*

NBC News Worldwide Inc.
4th Floor, 3 Shortlands, Hammersmith,
London W6 8HX
☎020 7637 8655 Fax 020 7636 2628
Bureau Chief *Chris Hampson*

The New York Times
66 Buckingham Gate, London SW1E 6AU
☎020 7799 5050 Fax 020 7799 2962
Chief Correspondent *William Hoge*

Newsweek
18 Park Street, London W1Y 4HH
☎020 7629 8361 Fax 020 7408 1403
Bureau Chief *Stryker McGuire*

People Magazine
Brettenham House, Lancaster Place, London
WC2E 7TL
☎020 7322 1134 Fax 020 7322 1125
Bureau Chief *Bryan Alexander*

Philadelphia Inquirer
17 Overstone Road, London W6 0AA
☎020 8846 8054 Fax 020 8741 8849
Correspondent *Fawn Vrazo*

Reader's Digest Association Ltd
11 Westferry Circus, Canary Wharf, London
E14 4HE
☎020 7715 8046 Fax 020 7715 8716
Editor-in-Chief, British Edition
Russell Twisk
(See entries under **UK Publishers** and
Magazines)

Time Magazine
Brettenham House, Lancaster Place, London
WC2E 7TL
☎020 7499 4080 Fax 020 7322 1230
Bureau Chief *Jef McAllister*
(See entry under **Magazines**)

USA Today
69 New Oxford Street, London
WC1A 1DG
☎020 7559 5859 Fax 020 7559 5895
Chief of European Correspondents
David Lynch

Voice of America
International Press Centre, 76 Shoe Lane,
London EC4A 3JB
☎020 7410 0960 Fax 020 7410 0966
Bureau Chief/Senior Editor *Jack Huizenga*

Wall Street Journal
10 Fleet Place, Limeburner Lane, London
EC4M 7RB
☎020 7832 9200 Fax 020 7832 9201
London Bureau Chief *Gregory Steinmetz*

Washington Post
18 Park Street, London W1Y 4HH
☎020 7629 8958 Fax 020 7629 8950
Bureau Chief *T. R. Reid*

Commonwealth Publishers

Australia

ACER Press
19 Prospect Hill Road, Camberwell,
Victoria 3124
☎00 61 3 9277 5555 Fax 00 61 3 9277 5678
FOUNDED 1930. *Publishes* Education, human
relations, psychology, psychiatry.

Addison Wesley Longman Australia Pty Ltd
95 Coventry Street, South Melbourne
Victoria 3205
☎00 61 3 9697 0633 Fax 00 61 3 9699 2041
Email awlaus@awl.com.au
Website www.awl.com.au
FOUNDED 1972. Australia's largest educational
publisher.

Allen & Unwin Pty Ltd
PO Box 8500, St Leonards, Sydney,
NSW 1590
☎00 61 2 8425 0100 Fax 00 61 2 9906 2218
Website www.allen.unwin.com.au
FOUNDED 1976. *Publishes* general non-fiction,
art, Asian studies, business, cookery, earth sciences, economics, education, fiction, gay and
lesbian, government, political science, health
and nutrition, history, industrial relations, literature, literary criticism, essays, general science.

Edward Arnold (Australia) Pty Ltd
PO Box 885, Kew, Victoria 3101
☎00 61 3 859 9011 Fax 00 61 3 859 9141
FOUNDED 1966. Part of Hodder & Stoughton
(Australia) Pty Ltd. *Publishes* general non-
fiction: accountancy, Asian studies, career development, computer science, cookery, geography,
geology, government, political science, health
and nutrition, law, mathematics, psychology and
psychiatry, technology.

Blackwell Science Pty Ltd
PO Box 378, South Carlton, Victoria 3053
☎00 61 3 9347 0300 Fax 00 61 3 9347 5552
FOUNDED 1971. Part of **Blackwell Science
Ltd**, UK. *Publishes* general science, medicine,
nursing, dentistry, engineering, computer science, mathematics, physical sciences, physics,
psychology, psychiatry.

Butterworths
PO Box 345, North Ryde, NSW 2113
☎00 61 2 9335 3444 Fax 00 61 2 9335 4655
FOUNDED 1910. A division of Reed International Books Australia Pty Ltd. *Publishes*
accountancy, business and law.

Choice Books
57 Carrington Road, Marrickville, NSW 2204
☎00 61 2 9577 3333 Fax 00 61 2 9577 3222
FOUNDED 1960. *Publishes* architecture and interior design, house and home, self-help, health
and nutrition, travel.

Currency Press Pty Ltd
PO Box 2287, Strawberry Hills, NSW 2012
☎00 61 2 9332 1300 Fax 00 61 2 9319 3649
Website www.currency.com.au
FOUNDED 1971. Performing arts publisher –
drama, theatre, music, dance, film and video.

Dangaroo Press
PO Box 93, New Lambton, NSW 2305
☎00 61 4 954 5938 Fax 00 61 4 954 6531
FOUNDED 1978. *Publishes* general non-fiction,
art, literature and literary criticism, essays,
poetry, social sciences, women's studies.

E. J. Dwyer (Australia) Pty Ltd
Locked Bag 71, Alexandria, NSW 2015
☎00 61 2 9550 2355 Fax 00 61 2 9519 3218
FOUNDED 1904. *Publishes* self-help, marketing,
social sciences, sociology, religion, theology.

Harcourt Australia Pty Ltd
Locked Bag 16, St Peters, NSW 2204
☎00 61 2 9517 8999 Fax 00 61 2 9517 2249
FOUNDED 1972. *Publishes* business, education,
general science, medicine, nursing, dentistry,
psychology, psychiatry, veterinary science,
social sciences, mathematics.

HarperCollins Publishers (Australia) Pty Ltd
PO Box 321, Pymble, NSW 2073
☎00 61 2 9952 5000 Fax 00 61 2 9952 5600
Owner *HarperCollins Publishers Group*
FOUNDED 1872. *Publishes* fiction and general
non-fiction, biography, children's, gardening,

humour, political science, regional interests, literature and literary criticism, essays, women's studies. DIVISIONS **General Illustrated Non-fiction** *Alison Presley*; **Children's** *Brian Cook*; **Mass Market Non-fiction** *Carolyn Walsh*.

Hodder Headline Australia
Level 22, 201 Kent Street, Sydney, NSW 2000
☎00 61 2 8248 0800 Fax 00 61 2 8248 0810
Owner Hodder & Stoughton Ltd (UK)
FOUNDED 1958. *Publishes* general non-fiction and fiction (adult and children's), education.

Hyland House Publishing Pty Ltd
387–389 Clarendon Street, South Melbourne, Victoria 3205
☎00 61 3 9696 9065 Fax 00 61 3 9696 9064
FOUNDED 1976. *Publishes* general non-fiction, Asian studies, cookery, crafts, games and hobbies, animals, pets, essays, fiction, gardening, literature and literary criticism.

Jacaranda Wiley Ltd
PO Box 1226, Milton, Queensland 4064
☎00 61 7 3699 7565 Fax 00 61 7 3859 9715
Owner John Wiley & Sons Inc. (USA)
FOUNDED 1954. *Publishes* general non-fiction and education books.

Thomas C. Lothian Pty Ltd
11 Munro Street, Port Melbourne, Victoria 3027
☎00 61 3 9645 1544 Fax 00 61 3 9646 4882
FOUNDED 1888. *Publishes* general non-fiction: business, health and nutrition, New Age, self-help.

Macmillan Education Australia Pty Ltd
107 Moray Street, Melbourne, Victoria 3205
☎00 61 3 9646 6100 Fax 00 61 3 9646 5946
FOUNDED 1896. *Publishes* accountancy, economics, education, geography, geology, government, political science, history, management, mathematics, physics, general science, social sciences, sociology.

McGraw-Hill Book Company Australia Pty Ltd
PO Box 239, Roseville, NSW 2069
☎00 61 2 9417 4288 Fax 00 61 2 9417 8872
Owner McGraw-Hill Inc. (USA)
FOUNDED 1964. *Publishes* accountancy, edu-

cation, health and nutrition, advertising, aviation, anthropology, architecture and interior design, art, chemistry, child care and development, computer science, criminology, economics, electronics, electrical engineering, general engineering, English as a second language, environmental studies, film and video, geology, geography, journalism, industrial relations, linguistics, management, maritime, mathematics, mechanical engineering, medicine, nursing, dentistry, philosophy, photography, physics, psychology, psychiatry, sport, social sciences and sociology.

Melbourne University Press
PO Box 278, Carlton, South Victoria 3053
☎00 61 3 9347 3455 Fax 00 61 3 9349 2527
FOUNDED 1922. *Publishes* general non-fiction, biography, essays, history, literature and literary criticism, natural history, psychology, psychiatry, travel.

Openbook Publishing
PO Box 1368J, Adelaide, SA 5001
☎00 61 8 8223 5468 Fax 00 61 8 8223 4552
FOUNDED 1913. *Publishes* religious and educational books.

Pan Macmillan Pty Ltd
PO Box 124, Chippendale, NSW 2008
☎00 61 2 9318 0111 Fax 00 61 2 9319 3438
Owner *Macmillan Publishers Ltd (UK)*
FOUNDED 1983. *Publishes* essays, fiction, literature and literary criticism.

Penguin Books Australia Ltd
PO Box 157, Ringwood, Victoria 3134
☎00 61 3 9871 2400 Fax 00 61 3 9870 9618
FOUNDED 1946. *Publishes* general non-fiction and fiction; biography, cookery, humour, literature and literary criticism, essays, science fiction and fantasy, self-help, travel.

University of Queensland Press
PO Box 42, St Lucia, Queensland 4067
☎00 61 7 3365 2127 Fax 00 61 7 3365 7579
FOUNDED 1948. *Publishes* general non-fiction and fiction, literature and literary criticism, essays, poetry, biography, history, sport, travel.

Random House Australia Pty Ltd
20 Alfred Street, First Floor, Milsons Point, NSW 2062
☎00 61 2 9954 9966 Fax 00 61 2 9954 4562
Website www.randomhouse.com.au
Publishes fiction and non-fiction.

Reader's Digest (Australia) Pty Ltd

PO Box 4353, Sydney, NSW 2001
☎00 61 2 9690 6492 Fax 00 61 2 9690 6390

FOUNDED 1946. Associate company of **Reader's Digest Association, Inc.** (USA). Educational publisher.

Reed Books Australia

20 Alfred Street, First Floor, Milsons Point, NSW 2061
☎00 61 2 9954 9966
Fax 00 61 2 9954 4562

Owner *Random House*

FOUNDED 1967. *Publishes* fiction and general non-fiction.

Reed Educational & Professional Publishing Australia

22 Salmon Street, Port Melbourne, Victoria 3207
☎00 61 3 9245 7111
Fax 00 61 3 9245 7333

FOUNDED 1982. *Publishes* art, chemical engineering, environmental studies, geography, geology, health and nutrition, history, mathematics, physics.

Scholastic Australia Pty Limited

PO Box 579, Gosford, NSW 2250
☎00 61 24 328 3555
Fax 00 61 24 323 3827

Owner *Scholastic, Inc. (USA)*

FOUNDED 1968. *Publishes* education titles.

Science Press

Fitzroy & Chapel Streets, Marrickville, NSW 2204
☎00 61 2 9516 1122 Fax 00 61 2 9550 1915
FOUNDED 1945. Educational publisher.

Simon & Schuster Australia

PO Box 507, East Roseville, NSW 2069
☎00 61 2 9417 3255 Fax 00 61 2 9417 3188
FOUNDED 1987. Part of **Simon & Schuster Consumer Group**, USA. *Publishes* general non-fiction.

Transworld Publishers Pty Ltd

Private Bag 12, Neutral Bay, NSW 2089
☎00 61 2 9908 4366 Fax 00 61 2 9953 8563

Owner *Bertelsmann AG (Germany)*

FOUNDED 1980. *Publishes* non-fiction and fiction – romance, science fiction, fantasy, humour, health and nutrition, self-help.

University of Western Australia Press

The University of Western Australia, Nedlands, WA 6009
☎00 61 8 9380 3182 Fax 00 61 8 9380 1027

FOUNDED 1954. *Publishes* general non-fiction, essays, literature and literary criticism, history, social sciences and sociology, natural history, autobiography.

Canada

Addison Wesley Longman Canada

PO Box 491002, Don Mills, Ontario M3C 2T8
☎001 416 447 5101 Fax 001 416 443 0948
Website www.awl.ca

FOUNDED 1967. Fourth-largest educational publisher in Canada. Acquired HarperCollins' educational list in 1997. Publishes in English and French.

Arnold Publishing Ltd

11016 127th Street, Edmonton, Alberta T5M 0T2
☎001 780 454 7477
Website www.arnold.ca

FOUNDED 1967. Educational textbooks and CD-ROMS.

Butterworths Canada

75 Clegg Road, Markham, Ontario L6G 1A1
☎001 905 479 2665 Fax 001 905 479 2826
Website www.butterworths.ca

FOUNDED 1912. Division of Reed Elsevier plc. *Publishes* law books, CD-ROMs, journals, newsletters, law reports and newspapers.

Canada Publishing Corp

164 Commander Boulevard, Scarborough, Ontario M1S 3C7
☎001 416 293 8141 Fax 001 416 293 9009
FOUNDED 1844. *Publishes* fiction, non-fiction and school textbooks.

Canadian Scholars' Press, Inc

180 Bloor Street W, Suite 1202, Toronto, Ontario M5S 2V6
☎001 416 929 2774 Fax 001 416 929 1926
Email info@cspi.org
Website www.cspi.org
FOUNDED 1987. *Publishes* scholarly books in English and French.

Fenn Publishing Co Ltd
34 Nixon Road, Bolton, Ontario L7E 1W2
☎001 905 951 6600 Fax 001 905 951 6601
Website www.hbfenn.com
FOUNDED 1977. *Publishes* fiction and non-fiction, children's.

Fitzhenry & Whiteside Limited
195 Allstate Parkway, Markham,
Ontario L3R 4T8
☎001 905 477 9700 Fax 001 905 477 9179
Email godwit@fitzhenry.ca
Website www.fitzhenry.ca
FOUNDED 1966. *Publishes* reference and children's books; educational material.

Golden Books Publishing (Canada) Inc
73 Water Street N., No 501, Cambridge,
Ontario N1R 5X2
☎001 519 623 3590 Fax 001 519 623 3598
FOUNDED 1942. *Publishes* (in English and French) juvenile and adult books, Bibles, cookery, crafts, gardening.

Harcourt Canada Ltd
55 Horner Avenue, Toronto,
Ontario M8Z 4X6
☎001 416 255 4491 Fax 001 416 255 4046
Website www.harcourtcanada.com
Publishes educational material.

HarperCollins Publishers Limited
55 Avenue Road, Suite 2900, Hazelton Lanes,
Toronto, Ontario M5R 3L2
☎001 416 975 9334 Fax 001 416 975 9884
Website www.harpercanada.com
FOUNDED 1989. *Publishes* fiction and non-fiction, children's and religious.

Irwin Publishing
325 Humber College Blvd., Toronto,
Ontario M9W 7C3
☎001 416 798 0424 Fax 001 416 798 1384
Email irwin@irwin-pub.com
Website www.irwin-pub.com
FOUNDED 1945. *Publishes* (in English and French) educational.

ITP Nelson
1120 Birchmount Road, Scarborough,
Ontario M1K 5G4
☎001 416 752 9100 Fax 001 416 752 9646
Website www.nelson.com/nelson.html
FOUNDED 1914. Division of Thomson Canada Ltd. *Publishes* educational, professional, reference.

Macmillan Canada
99 Yorkville Avenue, Suite 400, Toronto,
Ontario M5R 3K5
☎001 416 963 8830 Fax 001 416 923 4821
FOUNDED 1905. Division of Canada Publishing Corp. *Publishes* fiction and non-fiction.

McClelland & Stewart Inc
481 University Avenue, Suite 900, Toronto,
Ontario M5G 2E9
☎001 416 598 1114 Fax 001 416 598 7764
Website www.mcclelland.com
FOUNDED 1906. *Publishes* fiction and non-fiction, poetry.

McGill–Queen's University Press
3430 McTavish Street, Montreal,
Quebec H3A 1X9
☎001 514 398 3750 Fax 001 514 398 4333
Website www.mcgill.ca/mqupress
FOUNDED 1969. *Publishes* (in English and French) scholarly and non-fiction.

McGraw-Hill Ryerson Ltd
300 Water Street, Whitby,
Ontario L1N 9B6
☎001 905 430 5000 Fax 001 905 430 5020
Website www.mcgrawhill.ca
FOUNDED 1944. Subsidiary of the McGraw-Hill Companies. *Publishes* education, professional and general trade.

New Star Books Ltd
107–3477 Commercial Street, Vancouver,
BC V5N 4E8
☎001 604 738 9429 Fax 001 604 738 9332
Email newstar@pinc.com
FOUNDED 1974. *Publishes* social issues and current affairs, fiction, literature, history, international politics, labour, feminist, gay and lesbian studies.

Penguin Books Canada Ltd
10 Alcorn Avenue, Suite 300, Toronto,
Ontario M4V 3B2
☎001 416 925 2249 Fax 001 416 925 0068
Email oper@penguin.ca
Website www.penguin.ca
FOUNDED 1974. *Publishes* fiction and non-fiction books and audio cassettes.

Prentice Hall Canada
1870 Birchmount Road, Scarborough,
Ontario M1P 2J7
☎001 416 293 3621 Fax 001 416 299 2529
Website www.phcanada.com

FOUNDED 1960. *Publishes* education, textbooks, reference and non-fiction.

Random House of Canada
2775 Matheson Blvd. East, Mississauga, Ontario L4W 4P7
☎001 905 624 0672 Fax 001 905 624 6217
FOUNDED 1944. *Publishes* fiction and non-fiction and children's.

Scholastic Canada Ltd
175 Hillmount Road, Markham, Ontario L6C 1Z7
☎001 905 887 7323 Fax 001 905 883 4113
Website www.scholastic.ca
FOUNDED 1957. *Publishes* (in English and French) children's books and educational material.

Tundra Books Inc
481 University Avenue, Suite 802, Toronto, Ontario M5G 2E9
☎001 416 598 4786 Fax 001 416 598 0247
FOUNDED 1967. Division of McClelland & Stewart Inc. *Publishes* (in English and French) juvenile and art books.

John Wiley & Sons Canada Ltd
22 Worcester Road, Etobicoke, Ontario M9W 1L1
☎001 416 236 4433 Fax 001 416 236 4447
Website www.wiley.com
FOUNDED 1968. *Publishes* professional, reference and textbooks.

Women's Press
517 College Street. Suite 302, Toronto, Ontario M6G 4A2
☎001 416 921 2425 Fax 001 416 921 4428
FOUNDED 1972. *Publishes* social issues, non-fiction, fiction and children's.

India

Addison Wesley Longman Pte Ltd
90 New Raidhani Enclave, Ground Floor, Delhi 110 092
☎00 91 11 2059850 Fax 00 91 11 2059852
Website www.awl.com
Owned by Addison Wesley Longman USA. Educational publishers.

Affiliated East West Press Pvt Ltd
104 Nirmal Tower, 26 Barakhamba Road, New Delhi 110 001
☎00 91 11 331 5398 Fax 00 91 11 326 0538

FOUNDED 1962. *Publishes* Aeronautics, aviation, agriculture, anthropology, biological sciences, chemistry, engineering (chemical, civil, electrical, mechanical), computer science, economics, electronics, mathematics, microcomputers, physical sciences, physics, general science, veterinary science, women's studies.

Arnold Heinman Publishers (India) Pvt Ltd
AB-9, 1st Floor, Safdarjang Enclave, New Delhi 110 029
☎00 91 11 688 3422 Fax 00 91 11 687 7571
Associate company of **Edward Arnold (Publishers) Ltd**, UK. *Publishes* fiction, poetry, essays, literature, literary criticism, art, general engineering, government, political science, philosophy, religion, medicine, nursing and dentistry, social sciences and sociology.

S. Chand & Co Ltd
Ram Nagar, PO Box 5733, New Delhi 110 055
☎00 91 11 777 208011 Fax 00 91 11 777 7446
FOUNDED 1917. *Publishes* art, business, economics, government, political science, medicine, nursing, dentistry, philosophy, general science, technology.

Current Books
Round West, Trichur 680 001
☎00 91 487 335642 Fax 00 91 487 335660
FOUNDED 1952. *Publishes* fiction and general non-fiction.

General Book Depot
PO Box 1220, 1691 Nai Sarak, Delhi 110 006
☎00 91 11 326 3695 Fax 00 91 11 294 0861
FOUNDED 1936. *Publishes* general non-fiction; business, career development, how-to, English as a second language, language arts, linguistics, self-help, travel.

HarperCollins Publishers India Pty Ltd
7/61 Ansari Road, Daryaganj, New Delhi 110 002
☎00 91 11 327 8586 Fax 00 91 11 327 7294
Publishes fiction, poetry, biography and education.

Hind Pocket Books Private Ltd
18–19 Dilshad Garden Road, Delhi 110 095
☎00 91 11 202 046 Fax 00 91 11 228 332
Publishes fiction and general non-fiction; biography, how-to and self-help.

Jaico Publishing House

121–125 Mahatma Gandhi Road,
Mumbai 400 023

☎00 91 22 267 6702 Fax 00 91 22 204 1673

FOUNDED 1945. *Publishes* biography, languages, linguistics, nutrition, cookery, law, criminology, astrology, occult, philosophy, religion, general engineering, economics, humour, history, political science, government, psychology, psychiatry.

Macmillan India

315/316 Raheja Chambers, 12 Museum Road, Bangalore 560 001

☎00 91 80 558 7878 Fax 00 91 80 558 8713

FOUNDED 1903. *Publishes* fiction, engineering (chemical and general), science (computer and general), history, philosophy, chemistry, medicine, nursing and dentistry, psychiatry, psychology, biological sciences, mathematics, social sciences, sociology, government, political science, management.

Munshiram Manoharlal Publishers Pvt Ltd

PO Box 5715, New Delhi 110 055

☎00 91 11 777 3650 Fax 00 91 11 751 2745

FOUNDED 1952. *Publishes* art, architecture and interior design, anthropology, archaeology, astrology, occult, religion (Buddhist, Hindu, Islamic), philosophy, history, language arts and linguistics, music, dance, drama, theatre, Asian studies.

National Book Trust India

India A–5, Green Park, New Delhi 110 016

☎00 91 11 664 9962 Fax 00 91 11 685 1795

FOUNDED 1957. *Publishes* human relations and foreign countries.

National Publishing House

23 Daryaganj, New Delhi 110 002

☎00 91 11 327 4161

FOUNDED 1950. *Publishes* human relations, ethnicity, social sciences and sociology.

Orient Longman Ltd

3–6–272 Himayat Nagar, Hyderabad 500 029

☎00 91 40 322 4294 Fax 00 91 40 322 2900

FOUNDED 1948. *Publishes* fiction and general non-fiction; business, biography, biological sciences, chemistry, chemical and electrical engineering, child care and development, civil engineering, computer and general science, cookery, crafts, games, hobbies, economics, education, electronics, English as a second language, environmental studies, genealogy, geography, geology, government and political science, history, literature, literary criticism, essays, management, mathematics, medicine, nursing and dentistry, philosophy, physics, religion (Hindu), social sciences, sociology, travel, women's studies.

Oxford University Press

PO Box 43, New Delhi 110 001

☎00 91 11 202 1029 Fax 00 91 11 373 2312

FOUNDED 1912. *Publishes* business, biography, developing countries, economics, history, literature, literary criticism, essays, philosophy, religion (Hindu), sociology, natural history, politics, cultural studies, gender studies, ecology, science and medicine.

Rajpal & Sons

Madarasa Road, Kashmere Gate, Delhi 110 006

☎00 91 11 296 3904 Fax 00 91 11 296 7791

FOUNDED 1891. *Publishes* fiction, literature, literary criticism, essays, human relations, general science.

Scholastic India (Pvt) Ltd

29 Udyog Vihar, Phase-1, Gurgaon 122 016 (Haryana)

☎00 91 12 434 6824 Fax 00 91 12 434 6825

Email scholasticindia@scholastic.com

FOUNDED 1997. Owned by **Scholastic, Inc.**, USA. Educational publishers.

Tata McGraw-Hill Publishing Co Ltd

4/12 Asaf Ali Road, 3rd Floor,
New Delhi 110 002

☎00 91 11 278 251 Fax 00 91 11 327 8253

FOUNDED 1970. Parent company **The McGraw Hill Companies**, USA. *Publishes* general engineering and science, business, social sciences, sociology and management.

Vidyarthi Mithram Press

Baker Road, Kottayam 686 001

☎00 91 481 563 281 Fax 00 91 481 562 616

FOUNDED 1928. *Publishes* child care and development, cookery, drama and theatre, economics, biography, biological sciences, chemistry and chemical engineering, computer science.

A. H. Wheeler & Co Ltd

411 Surya Kiran Building, 19 K G Marg,
New Delhi 110 001

☎00 91 11 331 2629 Fax 00 91 11 335 7798

FOUNDED 1879. *Publishes* computer science,

behavioural sciences, accountancy, advertising, business, career development, civil engineering, communications.

New Zealand

Addison Wesley Longman New Zealand Ltd

Private Bag 102908, North Shore Mail Centre, Glenfield, Auckland 10
☎00 64 9 444 4968 Fax 00 64 9 444 4957
FOUNDED 1968. Educational publishers.

Butterworths of New Zealand Ltd

CPO Box 472, Wellington 1
☎00 64 4 385 1479 Fax 00 64 4 385 1598
FOUNDED 1914. *Publishes* accountancy, business, law and taxation.

Canterbury University Press

University of Canterbury, Private Bag 4800, Christchurch
☎00 64 3 348 2009 Fax 00 64 3 364 2999
FOUNDED 1960. *Publishes* general non-fiction; biography, biological sciences, history, Maori and Pacific studies.

The Caxton Press

PO Box 25088, Christchurch
☎00 64 3 366 8516 Fax 00 64 3 365 7840
FOUNDED 1935. *Publishes* general non-fiction; biography, gardening and plants.

Century Hutchinson Group New Zealand Ltd

POB 40086, North Shore Mail Centre, Glenfield, Auckland 10
☎00 64 9 444 7197 Fax 00 64 9 444 7524
FOUNDED 1977. *Publishes* fiction and general non-fiction. Parent company **Random House, Inc**, USA.

HarperCollins Publishers (New Zealand) Ltd

PO Box 1, Auckland
☎00 64 9 443 9400 Fax 00 64 9 443 9403
Website www.harpercollins.co.nz
FOUNDED 1888. *Publishes* fiction, art, humour, natural history, biography, gardening, sport, travel, self-help.

Hodder Moa Beckett Publishers Ltd

PO Box 3858, Auckland
☎00 64 9 444 3640 Fax 00 64 9 444 3646

FOUNDED 1971. Owned by **Hodder Headline Ltd**, UK. *Publishes* fiction and general non-fiction, biography.

University of Otago Press

PO Box 56, Dunedin
☎00 64 3 479 8807 Fax 00 64 3 479 8385
Email university.press@otago.ac.nz
FOUNDED 1958. *Publishes* fiction, essays, literature, literary criticism, history, education, biography, anthropology, natural history, environmental studies, government and political science.

Random House New Zealand

See **Century Hutchinson Group New Zealand Ltd**

Reed Publishing (NZ) Ltd

Private Bag 34901, Birkenhead, Auckland 10
☎00 64 9 480 4950 Fax 00 64 9 419 4999
Website www.reed.co.nz
FOUNDED 1988. *Publishes* fiction and general non-fiction, biography, cookery, history, natural history, regional interests, travel.

Scholastic New Zealand Ltd

Private Bag 94407, Greenmount, Auckland
☎00 64 9 274 8112 Fax 00 64 9 274 1730
FOUNDED 1962. Owned by **Scholastic, Inc.**, USA. Educational publishers.

Southern Press Ltd

R D 1, Porirua 50134
☎00 64 4 233 1899 Fax 00 64 4 239 9835
FOUNDED 1971. *Publishes* aviation, aeronautics, maritime, transport, technology, mechanical and civil engineering, archaeology.

Tandem Press

PO Box 34272, Birkenhead, Auckland 10
☎00 64 9 480 1452 Fax 00 64 9 480 1455
FOUNDED 1990. *Publishes* fiction and general non-fiction; cookery, business, alternative, ethnicity, health and nutrition, photography, psychology, psychiatry, self-help, women's studies.

Victoria University Press

PO Box 600, Wellington
☎00 64 4 496 6580 Fax 00 64 4 496 6581
Website www.vup.vuw.ac.nz
FOUNDED 1979. *Publishes* government, political science, essays, poetry, literature, literary criticism, drama, theatre, history, social sciences and sociology, anthropology, language and linguistics, law, architecture and interior design.

Viking Sevenseas NZ Ltd
PO Box 152, Paraparaumu, Wellington
☎00 64 4 297 1990 Fax 00 64 4 297 2040
FOUNDED 1963. *Publishes* general non-fiction;
astrology, occult, health and nutrition, medicine, nursing and dentistry, ethnicity.

South Africa
Books of Africa (Pty) Ltd
PO Box 1516, Capetown 8000
☎00 27 21 888316 Fax 00 27 21 888316
FOUNDED 1962. *Publishes* biography, history,
ethnicity and art.

Butterworths South Africa
PO Box 792, Durban 4000
☎00 27 31 294247 Fax 00 27 31 286350
Owned by Butterworths UK. *Publishes* general
science, medicine, nursing and dentistry, economics, education, law.

Flesch Financial Publications (Pty) Ltd
PO Box 3473, Cape Town 8000
☎00 27 21 461 7472
Fax 00 27 21 461 3758
FOUNDED 1966. *Publishes* aviation, aeronautics,
maritime, animals, pets, business.

Heinemann Publishers (Pty) Ltd
PO Box 781940, Sandown 21461,
Johannesburg
☎00 27 11 784 8619
Fax 00 27 11 322 8615
FOUNDED 1986. Parent company: **Reed
Educational & Professional Publishing**,
UK. *Publishes* economics, education, English as
a second language, mathematics, mechanical
engineering.

Maskew Miller Longman (Pty) Ltd
PO Box 396, Cape Town 8000
☎00 27 21 531 7750
Fax 00 27 21 531 4049
FOUNDED 1893. *Publishes* education, language
arts and linguistics.

University of Natal Press
PB X01, Scottsville, Pietermaritzburg 3209
☎00 27 331 260 5226 Fax 00 27 331 260 5801
FOUNDED 1947. *Publishes* essays, literature and
literary criticism, natural history, history,
women's studies.

Oxford University Press Southern Africa
PO Box 12119, N1 City 7463
☎00 27 21 595 4400 Fax 00 27 21 595 4430
FOUNDED 1915. Academic publishers. Parent
company: **Oxford University Press**, UK.

Ravan Press (Pty) Ltd
PO Box 145, Randburg, Johannesburg 2125
☎00 27 11 789 7636 Fax 00 27 11 789 7653
FOUNDED 1972. Part of Hodder & Stoughton
Educational South Africa. *Publishes* fiction and
general non-fiction; anthropology, biography,
business, economics, education, environmental
studies, ethnicity, government, political science, history, labour and industrial relations,
management, music, dance, social studies and
sociology, women's studies.

Shuter & Shooter (Pty) Ltd
PO Box 109, Pietermaritzburg 3200
☎00 27 331 427419 Fax 00 27 331 943096
FOUNDED 1925. *Publishes* general non-fiction;
biography, history, ethnicity, general science,
technology, social sciences and sociology.

Struik Publishers (Pty) Ltd
PO Box 1144, Cape Town 8000
☎00 27 21 216740 Fax 00 27 21 4624379
FOUNDED 1962. *Publishes* child care and development, cookery, gardening, environmental
studies, natural history.

Witwatersrand University Press
PO Wits, Johannesburg 2050
☎00 27 11 484 5907 Fax 00 27 11 484 5971
FOUNDED 1922. *Publishes* essays, literature and
literary criticism, drama, theatre, history, business, anthropology, archaeology, natural history,
religion (Jewish), medicine, nursing and dentistry.

Professional Associations and Societies

ABSW
See **Association of British Science Writers**

Academi (Yr Academi Gymreig)
3rd Floor, Mount Stuart House, Mount Stuart Square, Cardiff CF10 6DQ
☎029 2047 2266 Fax 029 2049 2930
Email post@academi.org
Website www.academi.org
North Wales office: TŷNewydd, Llanystumdwy, Criccieth, Gwynedd LL52 0LW
☎01766 522817
E-mail: academi.gog@dial.pipex.com
Chief Executive *Peter Finch*

Academi is the trading name of Yr Academi Gymreig , the national society of Welsh writers. The Society exists to promote the literature of Wales. Yr Academi Gymreig was FOUNDED in 1959 as an association of Welsh language writers. An English language section was established in 1968. Membership, for those who have made a significant contribution to the literature of Wales, is by invitation. Membership currently stands at 400. The Academi runs courses, competitions (including the **Cardiff International Poetry Competition**), conferences, tours by authors, festivals and represents the interests of Welsh writers and Welsh writing both inside Wales and beyond. Its publications include *Taliesin*, a quarterly literary journal in the Welsh language, *The Oxford Companion to the Literature of Wales*, *The Welsh Academy English-Welsh Dictionary*, and a variety of translated works.

In 1998 the Academi won the franchise from the Arts Council of Wales to run the Welsh National Literature Promotion Agency. The new, much enlarged organisation now administers a variety of schemes including Writers on Tour, Writers Residencies and a number of literature development projects. It promotes an annual literary festival alternating between North and South Wales, runs its own programme of literary activity and publishes *A470*, a bi-monthly literature information magazine. The Academi is also in receipt of a lottery grant to publish the first Welsh National Encyclopedia. This is expected to be ready towards the end of 2003.

Those with an interest in literature in Wales can become an associate of the Academi (which carries a range of benefits). Rates are £15 p.a. (waged); £7.50 (unwaged).

ALCS
See **Authors' Licensing & Collecting Society**

Alliance of Literary Societies
22 Belmont Crescent, Havant, Hampshire PO9 3PU
☎023 9247 5855 Fax 08700 560330
Email rosemary@sndc.demon.co.uk
Website www.sndc.demon.co.uk/als.htm
President *Gabriel Woolf*
Honorary Secretary *Mrs Rosemary Culley*

FOUNDED 1974. Aims to help and support its 80+ member societies and, when necessary, to act as a pressure group. Produces a handbook which holds useful information that is deemed important for the successful running of a literary society. It also contains details of the member societies and events to publicise them to the ALS members and the wider public.

Arts & Business (A&B)
Nutmeg House, 60 Gainsford Street, Butlers Wharf, London SE1 2NY
☎020 7378 8143 Fax 020 7407 7527
Email head.office@AandB.org.uk
Website www.AandB.org.uk

Arts & Business (formerly the Association for Business Sponsorship of the Arts) exists to promote and encourage partnerships between the private sector and the arts, to their mutual benefit and to that of the community at large. It provides a wide range of services to over 300 business members as well as to 600 arts organisations and museums through the Development Forum. To enable individual business people to share their skills, Arts & Business manages the Arthur Andersen Skills Bank and the NatWest Board Bank schemes. On behalf of the Department for Culture, Media and Sport and the Department of Education for Northern Ireland, it manages the Arts & Business New Partners Programme, an incentive programme for new and established sponsors of the arts. Increasingly, Arts & Business is working with forward-looking businesses to determine the future of business/arts partnerships through its Creative Forum. With the support of its Patron, HRH The Prince of Wales, it is exploring and developing new ways for business, the arts and society to interact. Runs its programmes from London and through a network of offices nationwide.

Arvon Foundation

Totleigh Barton, Sheepwash, Beaworthy, Devon EX21 5NS
☎01409 231338 Fax 01409 231338
Email t-barton@arvonfoundation.org
Website www.arvonfoundation.org

Lumb Bank, Heptonstall, Hebden Bridge, West Yorkshire HX7 6DF
☎01422 843714 Fax 01422 843714
Email l-bank@arvonfoundation.org

Moniack Mhor, Teavarran, Kiltarlity, Beauly, Inverness-shire IV4 7HT
☎01463 741675
Email m-mhor@arvonfoundation.org

President *Terry Hands*
Chairman *Sir Robin Chichester-Clark*
National Director *David Pease*

FOUNDED 1968. Offers people of any age (over 16) and any background the opportunity to live and work with professional writers. Four-and-a-half-day residential courses are held throughout the year at Arvon's three centres, covering poetry, fiction, drama, writing for children, songwriting and the performing arts. A number of bursaries towards the cost of course fees are available for those on low incomes, the unemployed, students and pensioners. Runs a biennial poetry competition (see entry under **Prizes**).

Association for Business Sponsorship of the Arts (ABSA)

See **Arts & Business**

Association for Scottish Literary Studies

c/o Department of Scottish History, 9 University Gardens, University of Glasgow, Glasgow G12 8QH
☎0141 330 5309 Fax 0141 330 5309
Email cmc@arts.gla.ac.uk
Website www.arts.gla.ac.uk/ScotLit/ASLS

Contact *Duncan Jones*
Subscription £33 (Individual);
    £61 (Institutional)

FOUNDED 1970. ASLS is an educational charity promoting the languages and literature of Scotland. *Publishes* works of Scottish literature; essays, monographs and journals; and *Scotnotes*, a series of comprehensive study guides to major Scottish writers. Also produces *New Writing Scotland*, an annual anthology of contemporary poetry and prose in English, Gaelic and Scots (see entry under **Magazines**).

Association of American Correspondents in London

12 Norwich Street, London EC4A 1BP
☎020 7353 1515 Fax 020 7936 2229

Contact *Sandra Marshall*
Subscription £90 (Organisations)

FOUNDED 1919 to serve the professional interests of its member organisations, promote social co-operation among them, and maintain the ethical standards of the profession. (An extra £30 is charged for each department of an organisation requiring a separate listing in the Association's handbook.)

Association of American Publishers, Inc

71 Fifth Avenue, 2nd Floor, New York, NY 10003–3004 USA
☎001 212 255 0200 Fax 001 212 255 7007
Website www.publishers.org

Also at: 50 f Street, NW, Washington, DC 20001–1564
☎001 202 347 3375 Fax 001 202 347 3690

Contact *Tom McKee*

FOUNDED 1970. For information about subscription rates and membership, contact the Association's website.

Association of Authors' Agents

c/o Curtis Brown Group Ltd, 4th Floor, Haymarket House, 28/29 Haymarket, London SW1Y 4SP
☎020 7396 6600 Fax 020 7396 0110/1
Email jlloyd@curtisbrown.co.uk
Website www.agentsassoc.co.uk

President *Jonathan Lloyd*
Membership £50 p.a.

FOUNDED 1974. Membership voluntary. The AAA maintains a code of practice, provides a forum for discussion, and represents its members in issues affecting the profession. For a full list of members visit the AAA website.

Association of Authors' Representatives

PO Box 237201, Ansonia Station, New York, NY 10023 USA
☎001 212 252 3695

Email aarinc@mindspring.com
Website www.aar-online.org
Administrative Secretary *Leslie Carroll*
FOUNDED in 1991 through the merger of the Society of Authors' Representatives and the Independent Literary Agents Association. Membership of this US organisation is restricted to agents of at least two years' operation. Provides information, education and support for its members and works to protect their best interests.

Association of British Editors
See **Society of Editors**

Association of British Science Writers (ABSW)
23 Savile Row, London W1X 2NB
☎020 7439 1205 Fax 020 7973 3051
Email absw@absw-demon.co.uk
Administrator *Barbara Drillsma*
Membership £35 p.a.; £30 (Associate); £5 (Student)
ABSW has played a central role in improving the standards of science journalism in the UK over the last 40 years. The Association seeks to improve standards by means of networking, lectures and organised visits to institutional laboratories and industrial research centres. Puts members in touch with major projects in the field and with experts worldwide. A member of the European Union of Science Journalists' Associations, ABSW is able to offer heavily subsidised places on visits to research centres in most other European countries, and hosts reciprocal visits to Britain by European journalists. Membership open to those who are considered to be *bona fide* science writers/editors, or their film/TV/radio equivalents, who earn a substantial part of their income by promoting public interest in and understanding of science. Runs the administration and judging of the **Glaxo Science Writers' Awards**, for outstanding science journalism in newspapers, journals and broadcasting.

Association of Christian Writers
73 Lodge Hill Road, Farnham, Surrey
GU10 3RB
☎01252 715746 Fax 01252 715746
Email christian-writers@dial.pipex.com
Website dspace.dial.pipex.com/christian-writers
Administrator *Mr W. G. Crawford*
Subscription £17 (Including Overseas); £15 (Direct debit)
FOUNDED in 1971 'to inspire and equip men and women to use their talents and skills with integrity to devise, write and market excellent material which comes from a Christian worldview. In this way we seek to be an influence for good and for God in this generation.' *Publishes* a quarterly magazine. Runs three training events each year, biennial conference, competitions, postal workshops, area groups, prayer support and manuscript criticism. Charity No. 1069839.

Association of Freelance Journalists
5 Beacon Flats, Kings Haye Road, Wellington, Telford, Shropshire TF1 1RG
Fax 0870 0882750 Email afj_UK@Yahoo.com
Website members.tripod.com/~media_2/afj.html
Founding President *Martin Scholes*
Subscription £30 p.a.
Offers membership to all who work in the field of journalism but especially local correspondents, stringers, freelance journalists, news photographers, those at the beginning of their careers or long established. Also welcomes those who make a modest income writing for the specialist press or who self-publish; who have written for a hobby but now wish to make a career of their writing. Members receive a regular newsletters, a laminated press card, a free postal/e-mail advice service, the opportunity to network with other members (through the newsletter and a special Internet service) and editors who contact the AFJ. There are discounts on products and services, including the AFJ writing course.

Association of Freelance Writers
Sevendale House, 7 Dale Street, Manchester
M1 1JB
☎0161 228 2362 Fax 0161 228 3533
Email fmn@writersbureau.com
Contact *Angela Cox*
Subscription £29 p.a.
FOUNDED in 1995 to help and advise new and established freelance writers. Members receive a copy of *Freelance Market News* each month which gives news, views and the latest advice and guidelines about publications at home and abroad. Other benefits include one free appraisal of prose or poetry each year, reduced entry to **The Writers Bureau** writing competition, reduced fees for writing seminars and discounts on books for writers.

Association of Golf Writers
106 Byng Drive, Potters Bar, Hertfordshire
EN6 1UJ
☎01707 654112 Fax 01707 654112
Honorary Secretary *Mark Garrod*

FOUNDED 1938. Aims to cooperate with golfing bodies to ensure best possible working conditions.

Association of Illustrators

1–5 Beehive Place, London SW9 7QR
☎020 7733 9155 Fax 020 7733 1199

Contact *Samantha Taylor*

FOUNDED 1973 to promote illustration and illustrators' rights, and encourage professional standards. The AOI is a non-profit-making trade association dedicated to its members, to protecting their interests and promoting their work. Talks, seminars, a newsletter, regional groups, legal and portfolio advice as well as a number of related publications such as *Rights, The Illustrator's Guide to Professional Practice* and *Survive, The Illustrator's Guide to a Professional Career.*

Association of Independent Libraries

Leeds Library, 18 Commercial Street, Leeds, West Yorkshire LS1 6AL
☎01132 453071

Chairman *Geoffrey Forster*

Established to 'further the advancement, conservation and restoration of a little-known but important living portion of our cultural heritage'. Members include the **London Library, Devon & Exeter Institution, Linen Hall Library** and **Plymouth Proprietary Library**.

Association of Learned and Professional Society Publishers

South House, The Street, Clapham, Worthing, West Sussex BN13 3UU
☎01903 871686 Fax 01903 871457
Email sec-gen@alpsp.org.uk
Website www.alpsp.org.uk

Secretary-General *Sally Morris*
Administrator *Eileen Storrie*
Editor, Learned Publishing *Michele Benjamin*

FOUNDED 1972 to foster the publishing activities of learned societies and academic and professional bodies. Membership is limited to such organisations, those publishing on behalf of member organisations and those closely associated with the work of academic publishers.

Association of Scottish Motoring Writers

c/o Scottish and Universal Newspapers, 5/15 Bank Street, Airdrie ML6 6AF
☎01236 748048 Fax 01236 748098

Secretary *John Murdoch*

Subscription £45 (Full); £25 (Associate)

FOUNDED 1961. Aims to co-ordinate the activities of, and provide shared facilities for, motoring writers resident in Scotland. Membership is by invitation only.

Australian Copyright Council

245 Chalmers Street, Redfern, NSW 2016 Australia
☎00 61 29318 1788 Fax 00 61 29698 3536
Email info@copyright.org.au
Website www.copyright.org.au

Contact *Customer Service*

FOUNDED 1968. The Council's activities and services include a range of publications, organising and speaking about copyright at seminars, research, consultancies and free legal advice. Aims include assistance for copyright owners to exercise their rights effectively, raising awareness about the importance of copyright, and seeing changes to the law of copyright.

Author-Publisher Network

SKS, St Aldhelm, 20 Paul Street, Frome, Somerset BA11 1DX
☎01373 451777
Website www.author.co.uk

Chairman *Clive Brown*
Administrator *Vicky Knowles*
Subscription £15 (p.a.)

FOUNDED 1993. The association aims to provide an active forum for writers publishing their own work. An information network of ideas and opportunities for self-publishers. Explores the business and technology of writing and publishing. Regular newsletter, supplements, seminars and workshops, etc.

Authors North

c/o The Society of Authors, 84 Drayton Gardens, London SW10 9SB
☎020 7373 6642

Secretary *Colin Shelbourn*

A group within the **Society of Authors** which organises meetings for members living in the North of England.

Authors' Club

40 Dover Street, London W1X 3RB
☎020 7499 8581 Fax 020 7409 0913

Secretary *Mrs Ann de la Grange*

FOUNDED in 1891 by Sir Walter Besant, the Authors' Club welcomes as members writers, agents, publishers, critics, journalists, academics and anyone involved with literature. Administers the **Authors' Club Best First Novel Award**; **Sir Banister Fletcher Award** and organises regular talks and dinners with well-known guest speakers. Membership fee: apply to secretary.

Authors' Licensing & Collecting Society (ALCS)

Marlborough Court, 14–18 Holborn, London EC1N 2LE
☎020 7395 0600 Fax 020 7395 0660
Email alcs@alcs.co.uk
Website www.alcs.co.uk
Chief Executive *Dafydd Wyn Phillips*
Subscription £7.50 incl. VAT (UK; free to members of **Society of Authors**, **Writers' Guild, NUJ, BAJ** and **CIOJ**); £7.50 (EU residents); £10 (Overseas)

FOUNDED 1977. The British collecting society for all writers and their heirs, ALCS is a non-profit organisation whose principle purpose is to ensure that hard-to-collect revenues due to authors are efficiently collected and speedily distributed. Established to give assistance to writers in their battle to make a better living through the protection and exploitation of collective rights, ALCS has distributed some £32m. to British writers since its creation. On joining, members license ALCS to administer on their behalf those rights which an author is unable to exercise as an individual or which are best handled on a collective basis. Chief among these are: photocopying, cable retransmission (including the fees for BBC Prime and BBC World Service programming), rental and lending rights (but not British Public Lending Right), off-air recording, electronic rights, the performing right and public reception of broadcasts. The society is a prime resource and a leading authority on copyright matters and writers' collective interests. It maintains a watching brief on all matters affecting copyright both in Britain and abroad, making representations to UK government authorities and the EU. Consult the ALCS website or contact the office for application forms and further information.

BACB

See **British Association of Communicators in Business**

BAFTA (British Academy of Film and Television Arts)

195 Piccadilly, London W1V 0LN
☎020 7734 0022 Fax 020 7734 1792
Website www.bafta.org
Subscription £165 p.a. (Over 30); £80 p.a. (Under 30); £85 p.a. (Country); £75 p.a.

(Overseas); £50 (Initial entry fee); £89 (Guest card)

FOUNDED 1947. Membership limited to 'those who have made a creative contribution to the industry' over a minimum period of three years. Nominees must be proposed and seconded by two existing BAFTA members. Best known for its annual awards ceremonies, now held separately for film, television, craft, children's programmes and interactive entertainment, the Academy runs a full programme of screenings, seminars, masterclasses, debates, lectures, etc. It also actively supports training and educational projects.

Also, BAFTA Scotland, BAFTA Wales, BAFTA North, BAFTA LA, BAFTA East Coast (USA) run separate programmes and, in the case of Scotland, Wales and the North, hold their own awards.

BAPLA (British Association of Picture Libraries and Agencies)

18 Vine Hill, London EC1R 5DZ
☎020 7713 1780 Fax 020 7713 1211
Email bapla@bapla.org.uk
Website www.bapla.org.uk

Represents the interests of the British picture library industry. Works on UK and worldwide levels on such issues as copyright and technology. Offers researchers free telephone referrals from its database and through its website. With access to 350 million images through its membership, BAPLA is a good place to start. *Publishes* a *Directory*, a definitive guide to UK picture libraries and a quarterly magazine, *Light Box*.

The Bibliographical Society

c/o The Wellcome Institute Library, 183 Euston Road, London NW1 2BE
☎020 7611 7244 Fax 020 7611 8703
Email jm93@dial.pipex.com
President *D. J. McKitterick*
Honorary Secretary *D. Pearson*
Subscription £33 p.a.

Aims to promote and encourage the study and research of historical, analytical, descriptive and textual bibliography, and the history of printing, publishing, bookselling, bookbinding and collecting; to hold meetings at which papers are read and discussed; to print and publish works concerned with bibliography; to form a bibliographical library. Awards grants and bursaries for bibliographical research. *Publishes* a quarterly magazine called *The Library*.

Book Packagers Association

8 St John's Road, Saxmundham, Suffolk
IP17 1BE
☎01728 604204 Fax 01728 604029
Treasurer *Charles Perkins*
Subscription £150 p.a.; £75 (Associate);
£100 (Overseas)

Aims to provide members with a forum for the exchange of information, to improve the image of packaging and to represent the interests of members. Activities include meetings, seminars, the provision of standard contracts and a stand at the London Book Fair.

Book Trust

Book House, 45 East Hill, London
SW18 2QZ
☎020 8516 2977 Fax 020 8516 2978
Chief Executive *Chris Meade*
Subscription £25 p.a.; £28 (Overseas)

FOUNDED 1925. Book Trust, the independent educational charity promoting books and reading, includes Young Book Trust (formerly Children's Book Foundation). The Trust offers a book information service (free to the public); administers many literary prizes (including the **Booker**); carries out surveys, *publishes* useful reference books and resource materials; houses a children's book reference library, and promotes children's books through activities like Children's Book Week.

Booksellers Association of the UK & Ireland Ltd

Minster House, 272 Vauxhall Bridge Road,
London SW1V 1BA
☎020 7834 5477 Fax 020 7834 8812
Email mail@booksellers.org.uk
Website www.booksellers.org.uk
Chief Executive *Tim Godfray*

FOUNDED 1895. The BA helps 3,300 independent, chain and multiple members to sell more books, reduce costs and improve efficiency. It represents members' interests to the UK Government, European Commission, publishers, authors and others in the trade as well as offering marketing assistance, running training courses, conferences, seminars and exhibitions. Together with **The Publishers Association**, coordinates World Book Day. *Publishes* directories, catalogues, surveys and various other publications connected with the book trade and administers the **Whitbread Book Awards** and the **Samuel Johnson Prize for Non-fiction**.

The British Academy of Composers and Songwriters

2nd Floor, Music House, 25–27 Berners
Street, London W1P 3DB
☎020 7636 2929 Fax 020 7636 2212
Chief Executive *Chris Green*

The Academy represents the interests of music writers of all genres, providing advice on professional and artistic matters. *Publishes* quarterly magazine, *The Works*. Administers the annual Ivor Novello Awards.

British Academy of Film and Television Arts

See **BAFTA**

British Association of Communicators in Business (BACB)

42 Borough High Street, London SE1 1XW
☎020 7378 7139 Fax 020 7387 7140
Email bacb@globalnet.co.uk
Website www.bacb.org
Membership Secretary *Linda McCrea*

FOUNDED 1949. The Association aims to be the 'market leader for those involved in corporate media management and practice by providing professional, authoritative, dynamic, supportive and innovative services'.

British Association of Journalists

88 Fleet Street, London EC4Y 1PJ
☎020 7353 3003 Fax 020 7353 2310
General Secretary *Steve Turner*
Subscription National newspaper staff, national
broadcasting staff, national news agency staff:
£12.50 a month. Other seniors, including
magazine journalists, PRs and freelancers
whose majority income comes from
journalism: £7.50 a month. Journalists under
24: £5 a month. Trainee journalists: Free.

FOUNDED 1992. Aims to protect and promote the industrial and professional interests of journalists.

British Association of Picture Libraries and Agencies

See **BAPLA**

British Centre for Literary Translation

University of East Anglia, Norwich, Norfolk
NR4 7TJ
☎01603 592134/593262 Fax 01603 592737

Email p.bush@uea.ac.uk
Website www.literarytranslation.com
Contact *Dr Peter Bush*

FOUNDED 1989. Aims to promote literary translation and the status of the literary translator by working in the UK and overseas with translator associations and centres (e.g. European network of Translation Centres), cultural policy-makers, teachers and researchers of literary translation, Regional Arts Boards, publishers and the media, libraries and schools. Activities, mostly in collaboration with other organisations, include conferences (e.g. ITI biennial colloquia on literary translation) and seminars, workshops and readings. With European and other funding, BCLT runs a translator-in-residence programme for translators to spend one calendar month in Norwich. *Publishes* proceedings and reports of its activities where possible and a newsletter; website in conjunction with the **British Council**.

British Copyright Council

Copyright House, 29–33 Berners Street, London W1P 4AA
☎01986 788230 Fax 01986 788847
Email copyright@bcc2.demon.co.uk
Contact *Janet Ibbotson*

Works for the national and international acceptance of copyright and acts as a lobby/watchdog organisation on behalf of creators, publishers and performers on copyright and associated matters. Publications include *Guide to the Law of Copyright and Rights in Performances in the UK; Photocopying from Books and Journals*. An umbrella organisation which does not deal with individual enquiries.

The British Council

10 Spring Gardens, London SW1A 2BN
☎020 7930 8466/7389 4268 (Press Office)
Fax 020 7839 6347
Website www.britishcouncil.org
Head of Literature *Dr Alastair Niven*

The British Council promotes Britain abroad. It provides access to British ideas, expertise and experience in education, the English language, literature and the arts, science and technology and governance. Works in 110 countries running a mix of offices, libraries, resource centres and English teaching operations.

British Equestrian Writers' Association

Priory House, Station Road, Swavesey, Cambridge CB4 5QJ
☎01954 232084 Fax 01954 231362

Contact *Gillian Newsum*
Subscription £15

FOUNDED 1973. Aims to further the interests of equestrian sport and improve, wherever possible, the working conditions of the equestrian press. Membership is by invitation of the committee. Candidates for membership must be nominated and seconded by full members and receive a majority vote of the committee.

British Film Commission

10 Little Portland Street, London W1N 5DF
☎020 7224 5000 Fax 020 7224 1013
Email info@britfilmcom.co.uk
Website www.britfilmcom.co.uk
Head of Marketing *Krysia Rozanska*

FOUNDED in 1991, the BFC is now part of the newly formed Film Council, funded through the Department for Culture, Media and Sport. Its remit is to promote the United Kingdom as an international production centre, to encourage the use of British artists and technicians, technical services, facilities and locations, and to provide wide-ranging support to those filming and contemplating filming in the UK.

British Film Institute

21 Stephen Street, London W1P 2LN
☎020 7255 1444 Fax 020 7436 7950
Website www.bfi.org.uk
Chair *Joan Bakewell, CBE*
Director *Jon Teckman*
24-hour *bfi* events line: 0870 240 4050

'The *bfi* offers opportunities to experience, enjoy and discover more about the world of film and television.' Its three main departments are: *bfi* Education, comprising the *bfi* National LIbrary, *bfi* Publishing, *Sight and Sound* magazine and *bfi* Education Projects, which encourages life-long learing about the moving image; *bfi* Exhibition, which runs the National Film Theatre on London's South Bank and the annual London Film Festival, and supports local cinemas and film festivals UK-wide; and *bfi* Collections, which preserves the UK's moving image heritage and promotes access to it through a variety of means, including film, video and DVD releases and touring exhibitions. The *bfi* also runs the *bfi* London IMAX® Cinema at Waterloo, featuring the UK's largest screen.

British Guild of Beer Writers

15 Sollershott West, Letchworth, Hertfordshire SG6 3PU
☎01462 685844 Fax 01462 685783
Email bsb@tccnet.co.uk

Secretary *Barry Bremner*
Subscription £40 p.a.

FOUNDED 1988. Aims to improve standards in beer writing and at the same time extend public knowledge of beers and brewing. *Publishes* a directory of members with details of their publications and their particular areas of interest; this is then circulated to newspapers, magazines, trade press and broadcasting organisations. As part of the plan to improve writing standards and to achieve a higher profile for beer, the Guild offers annual awards, The Gold and Silver Tankard Awards, to writers and broadcasters judged to have made the most valuable contribution towards this end in their work. Meetings are held regularly.

British Guild of Travel Writers

Springfield, Hangersley Hill, Ringwood,
Hampshire BH24 3JN
☎01425 470946

Chairman *Martin Roberts*
Honorary Secretary *Adele Evans*
Subscription £75 p.a.

The professional association of travel writers, broadcasters, photographers and editors which aims to serve its members' professional interests by acting as a forum for debate, discussion and 'networking'. The Guild *publishes* an annual Year Book giving full details of all its members, holds monthly meetings and has a monthly newsletter. Members are required to earn the majority of their income from travel reporting.

British Science Fiction Association

1 Long Row Close, Everdon, Daventry,
Northants NN11 3BE
☎01327 361661
Email bsfa@enterprise.net

Membership Secretary *Paul Billinger*
Subscription £21 p.a. (reduction for unwaged)

FOUNDED originally in 1958 by a group of authors, readers, publishers and booksellers interested in science fiction. With a worldwide membership, the Association aims to promote the reading, writing and publishing of science fiction and to encourage SF fans to maintain contact with each other. Also offers postal writers workshop, a magazine chain and an information service. *Publishes Matrix* bi-monthly newsletter with comment and opinions, news of conventions, etc. Contributions from members welcomed; *Vector* bi-monthly critical journal – reviews of books and magazines; *Focus* bi-annual magazine with articles, original fiction and letters column. For further information,

contact the Membership Secretary at the above address or on e-mail.

British Screen Finance

14–17 Wells Mews, London W1P 3FL
☎020 7323 9080   Fax 020 7323 0092
Contacts *Simon Perry, Jenny Borgars*

A private company aided by government grant; shareholders are the Film Council, Channel 4, Granada and United Artists. Exists to invest in British films specifically intended for cinema release in the UK and worldwide. Divided into two functions: project development (contact *Jenny Borgars*), and production investment (contact *Simon Perry*). British Screen also manages the European Co-production Fund which exists to support feature films co-produced by the UK with other European countries. British Screen develops around 40 projects per year, and has invested in 125 British feature film productions in the last ten years.

British Society of Comedy Writers

61 Parry Road, Ashmore Park,
Wolverhampton, West Midlands WV11 2PS
☎01902 722729   Fax 01902 722729
Email comedy@qwertyuiop.co.uk
Website www.qwertyuiop.co.uk/comedy
Contact *Ken Rock*

FOUNDED 1999. The Society aims to develop good practice and professionalism among comedy writers while bringing together the best creative professionals, and working to standards of excellence agreed with the light entertainment industry. Offers a network of industry contacts and a range of products, services and training initiatives.

British Society of Magazine Editors (BSME)

137 Hale Lane, Edgware, Middlesex HA8 9QP
☎020 8906 4664   Fax 020 8959 2137
Email bsme@cix.co.uk
Contact *Gill Branston*

Holds regular industry forums and events as well as an annual awards dinner.

Broadcasting Press Guild

Tiverton, The Ridge, Woking, Surrey
GU22 7EQ
☎01483 764895   Fax 01483 765882
Membership Secretary *Richard Last*
Subscription £15 p.a.

FOUNDED 1973 to promote the professional interests of journalists specialising in writing or broadcasting about the media. Organises monthly lunches addressed by leading industry figures, and annual TV and radio awards. Membership by invitation.

BSME
See **British Society of Magazine Editors**

Bureau of Freelance Photographers
Focus House, 497 Green Lanes, London N13 4BP
☎020 8882 3315 Fax 020 8886 5174
Email bfplondon@x-stream.co.uk
Membership Secretary *Kelly Wood*
Subscription £40 p.a. (UK);
  £50 p.a. (Overseas)

FOUNDED 1965. Assists members in selling their pictures through monthly *Market Newsletter* and offers advisory, legal assistance and other services.

Campaign for Press and Broadcasting Freedom
8 Cynthia Street, London N1 9JF
☎020 7278 4430 Fax 020 7837 8868
Email freepress@cpbf.demon.co.uk
Website www.cpbf.demon.co.uk
Subscription £15 p.a. (concessions available); £25 p.a. (Institutions/ Organisations)

Broadly based pressure group working for more accountable and accessible media in Britain. Advises on right of reply and takes up the issue of the portrayal of minorities. Members receive *Free Press* (bi-monthly), discounts on publications and news of campaign progress.

Canadian Authors Association
National Office: Box 419, 320 South Shores Road, Campbellford, ON K0L 1L0 Canada
☎001 705 653 0323 Fax 001 705 653 0593
Email canauth@redden.on.ca
Website www.CanAuthors.org
Administrator *Alec McEachern*

FOUNDED 1921. The CAA 'has expanded from a group of published authors concerned with protection of their own property to one that now includes those not yet published who want protection of what they might eventually produce and who need help producing it.' The Association has branches across the country providing support to local members in the form of advice, local contests, publications and writers' circles. *Publishes National Newsletter* and *The Canadian Writers' Guide.*

Canadian Publishers' Council
250 Merton Street, Suite 203, Toronto, Ontario M4S 1B1 Canada
☎001 416 322 7011 Fax 001 416 322 6999
Email pubadmin@pubcouncil.ca
Website www.pubcouncil.ca
Executive Director, External Relations
  Jacqueline Hushion

FOUNDED 1910. Trade association of English-language publishers which represents the domestic and international interests of member companies.

The Caravan Writers' Guild
13 Grovelands Avenue, Hitchin, Hertfordshire SG4 0QT
☎01462 432877 Fax 01462 632548
Email doug.king@ukgateway.net
Membership Secretary *D. King*
Subscription £5 Joining fee plus £15 p.a.

Guild for writers active in the specialist fields of caravan and camping journalism.

Careers Writers' Association
71 Wimborne Road, Colehill, Wimborne, Dorset BH21 2RP
☎01202 880320 Fax 01202 880320
Email Barbara.Buffton@wsmail.co.uk
Membership Secretary *Barbara Buffton*

FOUNDED 1979. An association of professional careers writers whose work meets its high standards of accuracy and impartiality. It provides a network for members to exchange information and experience and holds meetings on topics of interest to its members. Forges links with organisations that share related interests and maintains regular contact with national education and training bodies, government agencies and publishers. 'The association can provide a list of its members to organisations that require high standards of careers writing.'

Centreprise Literature Development Project
136–138 Kingsland High Street, London E8 2NS
☎020 7254 9362, exts. 211 & 214
Fax 020 7923 1951
Website www.centrepriseuk.freeserve.co.uk
Contacts *Catherine Johnson, Eva Lewin*

FOUNDED 1971. 'Centreprise has been at the forefront of community writing and publishing for nearly 30 years', making writing accessible to all the community. Although no longer a publisher it continues to nuture new writers with its New Writing and Black Literature Development Projects. CLDP offers creative writing courses, book discussion groups, and advice and information for writers. Offers links to other readers, writers and writers' organisations; produces *Calabash*, a thrice-yearly free newsletter for Black and Asian writers.

Chartered Institute of Journalists

2 Dock Offices, Surrey Quays Road, London SE16 2XU
☎020 7252 1187   Fax 020 7232 2302
General Secretary *Christopher Underwood*
Subscription £150
FOUNDED 1884. The Institute is concerned with professional journalistic standards and with safeguarding the freedom of the media. It is open to writers, broadcasters and journalists (including self-employed) in all media. Affiliate membership (£110) is available to part-time or occasional practitioners and to overseas journalists who can join the Institute's International Division. Members also belong to the IOJ (TU), an independent trade union which protects, advises and represents them in their employment or freelance work; negotiates on their behalf and provides legal assistance and support. The IOJ (TU) is a certificated independent trade union which represents members' interests in the workplace, and is also a constituent member of the National Council in the Training of Journalists, the Independent Unions Training Council and the **British Copyright Council**.

Children's Book Circle

c/o Victoria Library, Buckingham Palace Road, London SW1W 9UD
☎020 7641 4253   Fax 020 7641 2181
Email j.d.douglas@hotmail.com
Membership Secretary *Jonathan Douglas*
The Children's Book Circle provides a discussion forum for anybody involved with children's books. Monthly meetings are addressed by a panel of invited speakers and topics focus on current and controversial issues. Administers the **Eleanor Farjeon Award**.

Children's Book Foundation

See **Book Trust**

Circle of Wine Writers

29 Rowan Road, London W6 7DT
☎020 8741 9589

Membership £35 p.a.
FOUNDED 1962. Open to all *bona fide* authors, broadcasters, journalists and photographers currently being published, as well as lecturers and tutors, all of whom are professionally engaged in communicating about wines and spirits. Aims to improve the standard of writing, broadcasting and lecturing about wines, spirits and beers; to contribute to the growing knowledge and interest in wine; to promote wines and spirits of quality and to comment adversely on faulty products or dubious practices; to establish and maintain good relations with the news media and the wine trade; to provide members with a strong voice with which to promote their views; to provide a programme of workshops, meetings, talks and tastings.

Cleveland Arts

Third Floor, Melrose House, Melrose Street, Middlesbrough TS1 2HZ
☎01642 264651   Fax 01642 264955
Website www.clevelandarts.org
Contact *Buzzwords Development Worker*
Not one of the Regional Arts Boards, Cleveland Arts is an independent arts development agency working in the areas of Middlesbrough, Stockton on Tees, Hartlepool and Redcar & Cleveland. The company works in partnership with local authorities, public agencies, the business sector, schools, colleges, individuals and organisations to coordinate, promote and develop the arts – crafts, film, video, photography, music, drama, dance, literature, public arts, disability, Black arts, community arts. Buzzwords is the literature development unit which promotes writing classes, reading promotions, poetry readings and residencies, issues a free newsletter and assists local publishers and writers.

Clé, The Irish Book Publishers' Association

43/44 Temple Bar, Dublin 2, Republic of Ireland
☎00 353 1 6706393   Fax 00 353 1 6706642
Email cle@iol.ie
President *John Murphy*
Executive Director *Orla Martin*
FOUNDED 1970 to promote Irish publishing, protect members' interests and train the industry.

Comedy Writers' Association UK

44 Cherry Avenue, Swanley, Kent BR8 7DU
Also at: 41 Lyme Grove, Longview, Huyton L36 8BN
Honorary President *Ken Dodd*
Chair & Marketing Information Officer
Jenny Roche

Email: marknich@vossnet.co.uk
orJ@roche46.freeserve.co.uk

FOUNDED 1981 to assist and promote the work of comedy writers, the Association has grown to become the largest group of independent comedy writers in the UK. Holds annual and one-day seminars. Members receive a monthly newsletter and regular market opportunities.

Comhairle nan Leabhraichean/ The Gaelic Books Council

22 Mansfield Street, Glasgow G11 5QP
☎0141 337 6211 Fax 0141 353 0515
Email fios@gaelicbooks.demon.co.uk
Chairman *Boyd Robertson*
Director *Ian MacDonald*

FOUNDED 1968 and now a charitable company with its own bookshop. Encourages and promotes Gaelic publishing by giving grants to publishers and writers; providing editorial and word-processing services; retailing Gaelic books; producing a catalogue of all Gaelic books in print and answering enquiries about them; mounting occasional literary evenings and training courses.

Commercial Radio Companies Association

77 Shaftesbury Avenue, London W1V 7AD
☎020 7306 2603 Fax 020 7470 0062
Email info@crca.co.uk
Chairman *Lord Eatwell*
Chief Executive *Paul Brown*
Operations Director *Rachell Fox*
Public Affairs Manager *Nick Irvine*

The CRCA is the trade body for the independent radio stations. It represents members' interests to Government, the **Radio Authority**, trade unions, copyright organisations and other bodies.

Copyright Advice and Anti-Piracy Hotline

Unit 7, Victory Business Centre, Worton Road, Isleworth, Middlesex TW7 6DB
☎0845 6034567 Fax 020 8847 5947
Email contact@copyright-info.org
Website www.copyright-info.org
Copyright Line Administrator *Jo Holcroft*

FOUNDED 1999 to offer advice and information to anyone who wants to use film, music and software copyrights. The Hotline also helps the public and law enforcement agencies to identify and report piracy, and the intellectual property industries to monitor infringements and co-ordinate

their responses. (See also the **Federation Against Copyright Theft (FACT) Limited**.)

The Copyright Licensing Agency Ltd

90 Tottenham Court Road, London W1P 0LP
☎020 7631 5555 Fax 020 7631 5500
Email cla@cla.co.uk
Website www.cla.co.uk
Chief Executive *Peter Shepherd*

FOUNDED 1982 by the **Authors' Licensing and Collecting Society (ALCS)** and the **Publishers Licensing Society Ltd (PLS)**, the CLA administers collectively photocopying and other copying rights that it is uneconomic for writers and publishers to administer for themselves. The Agency issues collective and transactional licences, and the fees it collects, after the deduction of its operating costs, are distributed at regular intervals to authors and publishers via their respective societies (i.e. ALCS or PLS). Since 1986, CLA has distributed approximately £70 million.

Council for British Archaeology

Bowes Morrell House, 111 Walmgate, York YO1 2WA
☎01904 671417 Fax 01904 671384
Email archaeology@compuserve.com
Website www.britarch.ac.uk
Information Officer *Mike Heyworth*

FOUNDED 1944 to represent and promote archaeology at all levels. Its aims are to improve the public's awareness in and understanding of Britain's past; to carry out research; to survey, guide and promote the teaching of archaeology at all levels of education; to publish a wide range of academic, educational, general and bibliographical works (see **CBA Publishing** under **UK Publishers**).

Council of Academic and Professional Publishers

See **The Publishers Association**

Crime Writers' Association (CWA)

PO Box 6939, Kings Heath, Birmingham B14 7LT
Website www.twbooks.co.uk/cwa/cwa.html
Secretary *Judith Cutler*
Membership £40 (Town); £35 (Country)

Full membership is limited to professional crime writers, but publishers, literary agents, booksellers, etc. who specialise in crime, are eligible for Associate membership. The

Association has regional chapters throughout the country, including Scotland. Meetings are held regularly in central London, with informative talks frequently given by police, scenes of crime officers, lawyers, etc., and a weekend conference is held annually in different parts of the country. Produces a monthly newsletter for members called *Red Herrings* and presents various annual awards (see **Prizes**).

The Critics' Circle
c/o The Stage (incorporating Television Today), 47 Bermondsey Street, London SE1 3XT
☎020 7403 1818 ext 148 (Catherine Cooper)
Fax 020 7357 9287
President *George Perry*
Honorary General Secretary *Charles Hedges*
Subscription £18 p.a.

Membership by invitation only. Aims to uphold and promote the art of criticism (and the commercial rates of pay thereof) and preserve the interests of its members: professionals involved in criticism of film, drama, music and dance.

Department for Culture, Media and Sport
2–4 Cockspur Street, London SW1Y 5DH
☎020 7211 6000 Fax 020 7211 6270
Senior Press Officer, Arts *Toby Sargent*

The Department for Culture, Media and Sport has responsibilities for Government policies relating to the arts, museums and galleries, public libraries, sport, broadcasting, Press standards, the built heritage, the film and music industries, tourism and the National Lottery. It funds the **Arts Council**, national museums and galleries, the **British Library** (including the new library building at St Pancras), the Public Lending Right and the Royal Commission on Historical Manuscripts. It is responsible within Government for the public library service in England, and for library and information matters generally, where they are not the responsibility of other departments.

Directory & Database Publishers Association
PO Box 23034, London W6 0RJ
☎020 8846 9707
Website www.directory-publisher.co.uk
Contact *Rosemary Pettit*
Subscription £120 – £1200 p.a.

FOUNDED 1970 to promote the interests of *bona fide* directory and database publishers and protect the public from disreputable and fraudulent practices. The objectives of the Association are to maintain a code of professional practice to safeguard public interest; to raise the standard and status of directory publishing throughout the UK; to promote business directories as a medium for advertising; to protect the legal and statutory interests of directory publishers; to foster bonds of common interest among responsible directory publishers and to provide for the exchange of technical, commercial and management information between members. Meetings, seminars, conference, newsletter, awards, fairs.

Drama Association of Wales
The Old Library Building, Singleton Road, Splott, Cardiff CF24 2ET
☎029 2045 2200 Fax 029 2045 2277
Email aled.daw@virgin.net
Contact *Teresa Hennessy*

Runs a large playscript lending library; holds an annual playwriting competition (see entry under **Prizes**); offers a script-reading service (£10 per script) which usually takes three months from receipt of play to issue of reports. From plays submitted to the reading service, selected scripts are considered for publication of a short run (250–750 copies). Writers receive a percentage of the cover price on sales and a percentage of the performance fee.

Edinburgh Bibliographical Society
Edinburgh University Library, George Square, Edinburgh EH8 9LJ
☎0131 650 3412 Fax 0131 650 6863
Treasurer *Peter Freshwater*
Subscription £10; £15 (Institution); £5 (Students)

FOUNDED 1890. Organises lectures on bibliographical topics and visits to libraries. *Publishes* a biennial journal called *Transactions*, which is free to members, and other occasional publications.

Educational Publishers Council
See **The Publishers Association**

Electronic Publishers' Forum
See **The Publishers Association**

The English Association
University of Leicester, University Road, Leicester LE1 7RH
☎0116 252 3982 Fax 0116 252 2301
Email engassoc@le.ac.uk
Website www.le.ac.uk/engassoc/

Chief Executive *Helen Lucas*

FOUNDED 1906 to promote understanding and appreciation of the English language and its literatures. Activities include sponsoring a number of publications and organising lectures and conferences for teachers, plus annual sixth-form conferences. Publications include *Year's Work in Critical and Cultural Theory, English, Use of English, English 4–11, Essays and Studies* and *Year's Work in English Studies.*

ETmA (Educational Television & Media Association)

37 Monkgate, York YO3 7PB
☎01904 639212 Fax 01904 639212
Email josie.key@etma.u–net.com
Website www.etma.org.uk

Administrator *Josie Key*

The ETmA is a 'dynamic association' comprising a wide variety of users of television and other electronic media in education. Annual awards scheme (video competition), annual conferences. New members always welcome. CPD scheme.

Federation Against Copyright Theft (FACT) Limited

Unit 7, Victory Business Centre, Worton Road, Isleworth, Middlesex TW7 6DB
☎020 8568 6646 Fax 020 8560 6364

Director General *Reginald Dixon*
Company Secretary *David Lowe*
Field Operations Supervisor *Robert Melrose*

FOUNDED in 1999, FACT is an investigative organisation funded by its members to combat counterfeiting piracy and misuse of their products. It assists all law enforcement authorities and will undertake private criminal prosecutions wherever possible. Membership is made up of major companies in the British and American film, video and television industries.

Federation of Entertainment Unions

1 Highfield, Twyford, Nr Winchester, Hampshire SO21 1QR
☎01962 713134 Fax 01962 713288
Email harris@interalpha.co.uk

Secretary *Steve Harris*

Plenary meetings six times annually and meetings of the Film and Electronic Media Committee six times annually on alternate months. Additionally, there are Training & European Committees. Represents the following unions: British Actors' Equity Association; Broadcasting Entertainment Cinematograph and Theatre Union; Musicians' Union; AEEU; **National Union of Journalists**; **The Writers' Guild of Great Britain.**

The Federation of Worker Writers and Community Publishers (FWWCP)

67 The Boulevard, Stoke on Trent ST6 6BD
☎01782 822327 Fax 01782 822327
Email fwwcp@cwcom.net
Website www.fwwcp.mcmail.com

Administrator/Coordinator *Tim Diggles*

The FWWCP is a federation of writing groups who are committed to writing and publishing based on working-class experience and creativity. The FWWCP is the membership's collective national voice and has for some time been given funding by the **Arts Council**. Founded in 1976, it comprises around 60 member groups, each one with its own identity, reflecting its community and membership. They represent over 5000 people who regularly (often weekly) meet to offer constructive criticism, produce books and tapes, perform and share skills, offering creative and critical support. There are writers' workshops of long standing; adult literacy organisations; groups working mainly in oral and local history; groups and local networks of writers who come together to publish, train or perform; groups with a specific remit to further the aims of a section of the community such as the homeless or disabled. Although diverse in nature, member organisations share the aim to make writing and publishing accessible to people and encourage them to take an active, cooperative and democratic role in writing, performing and publishing. The main activities include training days and weekends to learn and share skills, a quarterly magazine, a quarterly broadsheet of members' writing, a major annual festival of writing and networking between member organisations. The FWWCP has published a number of anthologies and is willing to work with other organisations on publishing projects. Membership is open only to groups but individuals will be put in touch with groups which can help them, and become friends of the Federation. Contact the address above for an information leaflet.

Foreign Press Association in London

11 Carlton House Terrace, London SW1Y 5AJ
☎020 7930 0445 Fax 020 7925 0469

Contacts *Davina Crole, Catherine Flury*
Membership (not incl. VAT) £124 p.a.
  (Full); £115 (Associate Journalists);
  £172 (Associate Non-Journalists)

FOUNDED 1888. Non-profit-making service association for foreign correspondents based in London, providing a variety of press-related services.

The Gaelic Books Council
See **Comhairle nan Leabhraichean**

The Garden Writers' Guild
c/o Institute of Horticulture, 14/15 Belgrave Square, London SW1X 8PS
☎020 7245 6943
Email gwg@horticulture.org.uk
Website www.gardenwriters.co.uk
Contact *Angela Clarke*
Subscription £30; (£25 to Institute of Horticulture members); £40 (Associate members)

FOUNDED 1990. Aims to raise the quality of gardening communication, to help members operate efficiently and profitably, to improve liaison between garden communicators and the horticultural industry. Administers an annual awards scheme. Operates a mailing service and organises press briefing days.

General Practitioner Writers' Association
West Carnliath, Strathtay, Perthshire PH9 0PG
☎01887 840380
Contact *Professor F. M. Hull (President & Journal Editor)*
Subscription £30 p.a.; £40 (Joint)

FOUNDED in 1986 and expanding rapidly in membership and influence. Exists to promote and improve professional and lay writing activities within and for general practice. Open to doctors and other health professionals especially those working in the field of general practice; also to professional journalists writing on anything pertaining to general practice. Keen to develop input from interested parties who work mainly outside the profession. Regular workshops held around Britain. *Publishes* a twice-yearly journal (*The GP Writer*), anthologies and books from members, and a register of members and their writing interests.

Guild of Agricultural Journalists
Charnwood, 47 Court Meadow, Rotherfield, East Sussex TN6 3LQ
☎01892 853187 Fax 01892 853551
Email don.gomery@farmline.com
Honorary General Secretary *Don Gomery*
Subscription £30 p.a.

FOUNDED 1944 to promote a high professional standard among journalists who specialise in agriculture, horticulture and allied subjects. Represents members' interests with representative bodies in the industry; provides a forum through meetings and social activities for members to meet eminent people in the industry; maintains contact with associations of agricultural journalists overseas; promotes schemes for the education of members and for the provision of suitable entrants into agricultural journalism.

Guild of Editors
See **Society of Editors**

The Guild of Erotic Writers
CTCK PO Box 8431, Deptford, London SE8 4BP
Contact *Elizabeth Coldwell*
Subscription £10 p.a. (cheques made payable to CTCK)

FOUNDED 1995. Aims to provide a network for all authors of erotic fiction, both published and unpublished and to promote erotica as a valid form of writing. Members receive quarterly newsletters and a tip sheet on getting work accepted, together with discounts on conferences and events, and a manuscript-reading service (also available to non-members at 'very competitive rates' – short stories £4.50 for members, £7 non-members).

The Guild of Food Writers
48 Crabtree Lane, London SW6 6LW
☎020 7610 1180 Fax 020 7610 0299
Email gfw@gfw.co.uk
Administrator *Christina Thomas*
Subscription £70

FOUNDED 1985. The objects of the Guild include: 'to bring together professional food writers including journalists, broadcasters and authors, to print and issue an annual list of members, to extend the range of members' knowledge and experience by arranging discussions, tastings and visits, and to encourage the development of new writers by every means including competitions and awards. The Guild aims to contribute to the growth of public interest in, and knowledge of, the subject of food and to campaign for improvements in the quality of food.'

Guild of Motoring Writers
30 The Cravens, Smallfield, Surrey RH6 9QS
☎01342 843294 Fax 01342 844093
General Secretary *Sharon Scott-Fairweather*
FOUNDED 1944. Represents members' interests

and provides a forum for members to exchange information.

Horror Writers Association

UK Contact: 24 Pearl Road, Walthamstow, London E17 4QZ
Email hwa@horror.org
Website www.horror.org
US Contact: HWA Membership, PO Box 50577, Palo Alto, CA 94303, USA
☎001 650 322 4610

Contact (UK) *Jo Fletcher*

FOUNDED 1987. World-wide organisation of writers and publishers dedicated to promoting the interests of writers of horror and dark fantasy. *Publishes* a bi-monthly newsletter, issues e-mail bulletins, gives access to lists of horror agents, reviewers and bookstores; and keys to the 'Members Only' area of the HWA website. Presents the annual **Bram Stoker Awards** (see entry under **Prizes**).

HTML Writers Guild

Email membership-questions@hwg.org
Website www.hwg.org

FOUNDED in 1994 by a small group of HTML writers, the Guild is an international organisation for Internet designers with over 100,000 members world-wide and is open to anyone with an interest in the craft of web design. Provides extensive resources through the Guild website, mailing lists. Online classes to support members' efforts from the professional designer to the hobbyist designing a homepage. Various levels of membership available.

HWA

See **Horror Writers Association**

Independent Publishers Guild

PO Box 93, Royston, Hertfordshire SG8 5GH
☎01763 247014   Fax 01763 246293
Email sheila@ipg.uk.com

Secretary *Sheila Bounford*
Subscription approx. £75 p.a.

FOUNDED 1962. Membership open to independent publishers, packagers and suppliers, i.e. professionals in allied fields. Regular meetings, conferences, seminars, mailings and a quarterly bulletin.

Independent Television Association

See **ITV Network Ltd**

Independent Television Commission (ITC)

33 Foley Street, London W1P 7LB
☎020 7255 3000   Fax 020 7306 7800
Website www.itc.org.uk

Chief Executive *Peter Rogers*

The ITC issues licences and regulates commercial television in the UK; maintains standards of the programmes which appear plus advertising and technical quality. Complaints against the service are investigated by the Commission which frequently publishes its findings and it is empowered to impose penalties on licensees that do not comply with their licence conditions.

Independent Theatre Council

12 The Leathermarket, Weston Street, London SE1 3ER
☎020 7403 1727   Fax 020 7403 1745

Contact *Charlotte Jones*

The management association and representative body for small/middle-scale theatres (up to around 450 seats) and touring theatre companies. Negotiates contracts and has established standard agreements with Equity on behalf of all professionals working in the theatre. Negotiations with the **Theatre Writers' Union** and the **Writers' Guild** for a contractual agreement covering rights and fee structure for playwrights were concluded in 1991. Terms and conditions were renegotiated and updated in September 1998. Copies of the minimum terms agreement can be obtained from the Writers' Guild. *Publishes* a booklet, *A Practical Guide for Writers and Companies* (£3.50 plus p&p), giving guidance to writers on how to submit scripts to theatres and guidance to theatres on how to deal with them.

Institute of Copywriting

Honeycombe House, Bagley, Wedmore BS28 4TD
☎01934 713563   Fax 01934 713492
Email copy@inst.org
Website ds.dial.pipex.com/institute/copy.htm

Secretary *Alex Middleton*

FOUNDED 1991 to promote copywriters and copywriting (writing publicity material). Maintains a code of practice. Membership is open to students as well as experienced practitioners. Runs training courses (see entry under **Writers' Courses**). Has a list of approved copywriters. Answers queries relating to copywriting. Contact the Institute for a free booklet.

Institute of Linguists

Saxon House, 48 Southwark Street, London
SE1 1UN
☎020 7940 3100 Fax 020 7940 3101
Email info@iol.org.uk
Website www.iol.org.uk
Chief Executive Officer *Henry Pavlovich*
Marketing Manager *Stephen Eden*

FOUNDED 1910. Professional association for translators, interpreters and trainers; examining body for languages at degree level and above for vocational purposes; IOL manages the National Register of Public Service Interpreters. Subscription rates on application. The Institute's limited company, Language Services Ltd, provides customised assessments of language-oriented requirements, skills, etc.

Institute of Publishing

Unit 17G Shrub Hill Industrial Estate,
Worcester WR4 9EL
☎01905 613869 Fax 01905 613869
Email rosiethom@compuserve.com
Website www.instpublishing.org.uk

Secretary *Rosie Thom*

Launched at the London Book Fair in March 2000, the Institute aims to promote a programme of educational training, research and development, the introduction of a code of practice for publishers and the development of qualifications based on occupational standards. *Publishes* bulletins, handbooks and reports, and organises seminars and conferences.

Institute of Translation and Interpreting (ITI)

377 City Road, London EC1V 1ND
☎020 7713 7600 Fax 020 7713 7650
Email info@iti.org.uk
Website www.iti.org.uk

FOUNDED 1986. The ITI is a professional association of translators and interpreters aiming to promote the highest standards in translating and interpreting. It has strong corporate membership and runs professional development courses and conferences, sometimes in conjunction with its language, regional and subject network. Membership is open to those with a genuine and proven involvement in translation and interpreting (including students). ITI's Directory of Members, its bi-monthly Bulletin and other publications are available from the Secretariat. The Secretariat offers a free referral service whereby enquirers can be given the names of suitable members for any interpreting/translating assignment. ITI is a full and active member of FIT (International Federation of Translators).

International Association of Puzzle Writers

42 Brigstocke Terrace, Ryde, Isle of Wight
PO33 2PD
☎01983 811688

Contact *Dr Jeremy Sims*
Membership fee £25 p.a.

FOUNDED 1966 for writers of brainteasing puzzles, crosswords and word games, and for designers of games in general. Enquiries from publishers seeking material welcome. Aims to provide support and information and to promote the art of puzzle writing and games design to publishers, games manufacturers and the general public. *Publishes* bi-monthly newsletter – contributions welcome. Members must have e-mail. For further information, send s.a.e. to the above address.

Irish Book Publishers' Association

See **Clé**

Irish Copyright Licensing Agency Ltd

19 Parnell Square, Dublin 1, Republic of
Ireland
☎00 353 1 872 9202 Fax 00 353 1 872 2035
Email icla@esatlink.com

Executive Director *Orla O'Sullivan*

FOUNDED 1992 by writers and publishers in Ireland to provide a scheme through which rights holders can give permission, and users of copyright material can obtain permission, to copy.

Irish Translators' Association

Irish Writers' Centre, 19 Parnell Square,
Dublin 1 Republic of Ireland
☎00 353 1 285 9137 Fax 00 353 1 872 6282
Email translation@eircom.net
Website homepage.eircom.net/~translation

Honorary Secretary *Miriam Lee*
Subscription £IR 20 p.a. (Ordinary); £IR8 (Students, Unwaged, Pensioners, Members of affiliated organisations); Professional membership by application to Professional Membership Committee only

FOUNDED 1986. The Association is for all translators: technical, commercial, literary and cultural, both written and spoken. It is also for those with an interest in translation such as teachers and students. Provides legal advice to members, issues a register of translators and *publishes* a quarterly newsletter, *Translation Ireland*.

Irish Writers' Union

Irish Writers' Centre, 19 Parnell Square,
Dublin 1 Republic of Ireland
☎00 353 1 872 1302
Fax 00 353 1 872 6282
Secretary *Sheila Barrett*
Subscription £30 p.a.
FOUNDED 1986 to promote the interests and
protect the rights of writers in Ireland.

ISBN Agency

12 Dyott Street, London WC1A 1DF
☎020 7420 6008 (9.00 am to 2.00 pm)
Fax 020 7836 4342
Email isbn@whitaker.co.uk
Website www.whitaker.co.uk/information.htm

The UK Standard Book Numbering Agency is
the national ISBN agency, responsible for
assigning ISBN prefixes to publishers based in
the UK or Republic of Ireland. Its services
include advising publishers on the correct
implementation of the ISBN system and maintaining a database of publishers and their prefixes, as well as providing technical advice and
assistance to publishers and the booktrade on all
aspects of ISBN usage.

Isle of Man Authors

24 Laurys Avenue, Ramsey, Isle of Man
IM8 2HE
☎01624 815634
Secretary *Mrs Beryl Sandwell*
Subscription £5 p.a.
An association of writers living on the Isle of
Man, which has links with the **Society of
Authors**.

ITC

See **Independent Television Commission**

ITI

See **Institute of Translation and
Interpreting**

ITV Network Ltd.

200 Gray's Inn Road, London WC1X 8HF
☎020 7843 8000 Fax 020 7843 8158
Website www.itv.co.uk
Director of Programmes *David Liddiment*
The ITV Network Ltd., wholly owned by the
ITV companies, independently commissions
and schedules the television programmes

which are shown across the ITV network. As a
successor to the Independent Television
Association, it also provides a range of services
to the ITV companies where a common
approach is required.

IVCA (International Visual Communication Association)

(Relocating to new offices, summer 2000;
check website for address)
Website www.ivca.org
Chief Executive *Wayne Drew*
The IVCA is a professional association representing the interests of the users and suppliers
of visual communications. In particular it pursues the interests of producers, commissioners
and manufacturers involved in the non-broadcast and independent facilities industries and
also business event companies. It represents all
sizes of company and freelance individuals,
offering information and advice services, publications, a professional network, special interest
groups, a magazine and a variety of events
including the UK's Film and Video Communications Festival.

The Library Association

7 Ridgmount Street, London WC1E 7AE
☎020 7255 0500 Fax 020 7255 0501
Email info@la-hq.org.uk
Website www.la-hq.org.uk
Chief Executive *Bob McKee*
The professional body for librarians and information managers, with 25,000 individual and
institutional members. **Library Association
Publishing** produces 30–35 new titles each
year and has over 250 in print. The *LA Record*
is the monthly magazine for members. Further
information from Information Services, The
Library Association.

The Media Society

56 Roseneath Road, London SW11 6AQ
Contact *Peter Dannheisser*
Subscription £25 p.a.; £10 Entry fee
FOUNDED 1973. A registered charity which
aims to provide a forum for the exchange of
knowledge and opinion between those in public and political life, the professions, industry
and education. Meetings (about 10 a year) usually take the form of luncheons and dinners in
London with invited speakers. The society also
acts as a 'think tank' and submits evidence and
observations to royal commissions, select committees and review bodies.

Medical Journalists' Association

101 Cambridge Gardens, London W10 6JE
☎020 8968 1614   Fax 020 8968 7910
Chairman *John Illman*
Honorary Secretary *Sue Lowell*
Subscription £30 p.a.

FOUNDED 1967. Aims to improve the quality and practice of medical and health journalism and to improve relationships and understanding between medical and health journalists and the health and medical professions. Regular meetings with senior figures in medicine and medico politics; teach-ins on particular subjects to help journalists with background information; weekend symposium for members with people who have newsworthy stories in the field; awards for medical journalists offered by various commercial sponsors, plus MJA's own award financed by members. *Publishes* a detailed directory of members and freelances and two-monthly newsletter.

Medical Writers' Group & Medical Awards

The Society of Authors, 84 Drayton Gardens, London SW10 9SB
☎020 7373 6642   Fax 020 7373 5768
Email authorsoc@writers.org.uk
Contact *Dorothy Wright*

FOUNDED 1980. A specialist group within the **Society of Authors** offering advice and help to authors of medical books. Administers Medical Prizes.

National Association of Writers Groups

The Arts Centre, Biddick Lane, Washington, Tyne & Wear NE38 2AB
☎0191 416 9751   Fax 0191 431 1263
Contact *Brian Lister*

FOUNDED 1995 with the object of furthering the interests of writers' groups throughout the UK. A registered charity, No: 1059047, NAWG is strictly non-sectarian and non-political. *Publishes* a bi-monthly newsletter, distributed to member groups; gives free entry to competitions for group anthologies, poetry, short stories, articles, novels and sketches; holds an annual open festival of writing with 40 workshops, seminars, individual surgeries led by professional, high-profile writers. Membership is open to all writers' groups – there are no restrictions or qualifications required for joining; 120 groups are affiliated to-date.

National Association of Writers in Education

PO Box 1, Sheriff Hutton, York YO60 7YU
☎01653 618429   Fax 01653 618429
Email paul@nawe.co.uk
Website www.nawe.co.uk
Contact *Paul Munden*
Subscription £12 p.a.

FOUNDED 1991. Aims to promote the contribution of living writers to education and to encourage both the practice and the critical appreciation of creative writing. Has over 500 members. Organises national conferences and training courses. A directory of over 1200 writers who work in schools, colleges and the community is available on-line. *Publishes* a magazine, *Writing in Education*, issued free to members three times per year.

National Campaign for the Arts

Pegasus House, 37–43 Sackville Street, London W1X 1DB
☎020 7333 0375   Fax 020 7333 0660
Email nca@artscampaign.org.uk
Director *Victoria Todd*

FOUNDED 1984 to represent the cultural sector in Britain and to make sure that the problems facing the arts are properly put to Government, at local and national level. The NCA is an independent body relying on finance from its members. Involved in all issues which affect the arts: public finance, education, broadcasting and media affairs, the fight against censorship, the rights of artists, the place of the arts on the public agenda and structures for supporting culture. Membership open to all arts organisations (except government agencies) and to individuals. Literature subscriptions available.

National Literacy Trust

Swire House, 59 Buckingham Gate, London SW1E 6AS
☎020 7828 2435   Fax 020 7931 9986
Email contact@literacytrust.org.uk
Website www.literacytrust.org.uk
Director *Neil McClelland*

FOUNDED 1993. A registered charity (No: 1015539) which aims to make 'an independent, strategic contribution to the creation of a society in which all can enjoy the appropriate skills, confidence and pleasures of literacy to support their educational, economic, social and cultural goals.' Maintains an extensive website with literacy issues, research news and a searchable database detailing literacy practice nationwide; promotes and facilitates literacy partnerships; organises an annual conference, courses and training events; *publishes* quarterly magazine, *Literacy Today* (the Educational Publishing Company, subscription £16). Organised the National Year of Reading 1998–99 and is coordinating the National Reading Campaign. It also runs Reading Is Fundamental, UK which provides books free to children.

National Small Press Centre
See **Organisations of Interest to Poets**

National Union of Journalists
Acorn House, 314 Gray's Inn Road, London WC1X 8DP
☎020 7278 7916 Fax 020 7837 8143
Email acorn.house@nuj.org.uk
Website www.gn.apc.org/media/
General Secretary *John Foster*
Subscription £148.50 p.a. (Freelance) or 1% of annual income if lower; minimum contribution £57.75

Represents journalists in all sectors of publishing, print and broadcast. Responsible for wages and conditions agreements which apply across the industry. Provides advice and representation for its members, as well as administering unemployment and other benefits. *Publishes* various guides and magazines: *Freelance Directory, Fees Guide, The Journalist* and *The Freelance* (see entry under **Magazines**).

New Playwrights Trust
See **Writernet**

New Producers Alliance (NPA)
9 Bourlet Close, London W1P 7PJ
☎020 7580 2480 Fax 020 7580 2484
Email admin@npa.org.uk
Website www.newproducer.co.uk
FOUNDED 1993; current membership of over 1300. Aims to encourage the production of commercial feature films for an international audience and to educate and inform feature film producers, writers and directors. The NPA is an independent networking organisation providing members with access to contacts, free legal advice and general help regarding film production. *Publishes* a monthly newsletter and organises meetings, workshops and seminars. The NPA also actively lobbies for better access to funds for first- and second-time film makers. The NPA does not produce films so please do not send scripts or treatments.

The New SF Alliance (NSFA)
c/o BBR Magazine, PO Box 625, Sheffield, South Yorkshire S1 3GY
Website www.bbr-online.com/writers
Contact *Chris Reed*
FOUNDED 1989. Committed to supporting the work of new writers and artists by promoting independent and small press publications worldwide. 'Help with finding the right market for your material by providing a mail-order service which allows you to sample magazines, and various publications including *Zene* magazine and *Scavenger's Newsletter* which feature the latest market news and tips.'

New Writing North
7/8 Trinity Chare, Quayside, Newcastle upon Tyne NE1 3DF
☎0191 232 9991 Fax 0191 230 1883
Email subtext.nwn@virgin.net
Director *Claire Malcolm*
Administrator *John McGagh*

New Writing North is the literature development agency for the **Northern Arts** region and offers many useful services to writers, organising events, readings and courses. NWN produces writing guides and a regular magazine with literary news, events and opportunities. Administers the Northern Playwriting Panel (aiding new drama) and the Northern Writers' Awards, which include tailored development packages (mentoring and financial help). NWN has strong links with the post of Northern Literary Fellow – Jo Shapcott is the present incumbent – and organised a workshop group with her to aid northern poets at a midpoint in their careers. NWN also programmes the **Durham Literature Festival**.

The Newspaper Society
Bloomsbury House, 74–77 Great Russell Street, London WC1B 3DA
☎020 7636 7014 Fax 020 7631 5119
Email ns@newspapersoc.org.uk
Website www.newspapersoc.org.uk
Director *David Newell*
FOUNDED in 1836, the Newspaper Society is the voice of Britain's regional and local newspapers. It represents and promotes the interests of over 1300 regional daily and weekly, paid for and free, titles. The range of activities and services provided by the Society can be split into two broad areas: marketing and lobbying. Holds a series of conferences and seminars each year and runs the annual Local Newspaper Week.

NPA

See **New Producers Alliance**

NSFA

See **The New SF Alliance**

Outdoor Writers' Guild

PO Box 520, Bamber Bridge, Preston,
Lancashire PR5 8LF
☎01772 696732 Fax 01772 696732
Secretary *Terry Marsh*
Subscription £45p.a.; Joining fee £10

FOUNDED 1980 to promote, encourage and
assist the development and maintenance of professional standards among those involved in all
aspects of outdoor journalism. Membership is
not limited to writers but includes other outstanding professional media practitioners in the
outdoor world such as broadcasters, photographers, filmmakers, editors, publishers and illustrators. *Publishes* a quarterly journal, *Bootprint*,
and an annual *Directory* (£25; free to members)
as well as guidelines, codes of practice and
advice notes. Presents six Awards for Excellence.

PACT (Producers Alliance for Cinema and Television)

45 Mortimer Street, London W1N 7TD
☎020 7331 6000 Fax 020 7331 6700
Email enquiries@pact.co.uk
Website www.pact.co.uk
Chief Executive *Shaun Williams*
Membership Officer *David Alan Mills*

FOUNDED 1991. PACT is the trade association of
the UK independent television and feature film
production sector and is a key contact point for
foreign producers seeking British co-production,
co-finance partners and distributors. Works for
producers in the industry at every level and operates a members' regional network throughout
the UK with a divisional office in Scotland.
Membership services include: a dedicated industrial relations unit; discounted legal advice;
a varied calendar of events; business advice;
representation at international film and television
markets; a comprehensive research programme;
various publications: a monthly magazine, an
annual members' directory; affiliation with
European and international producers' organisations; extensive information and production
advice. Lobbies actively with broadcasters,
financiers and governments to ensure that the
producer's voice is heard and understood in
Britain and Europe on all matters affecting the
film and television industry.

PAPA

See **The Professional Authors' and Publishers' Association**

PEN

152–156 Kentish Town Road, London
NW1 9QB
☎020 7267 9444 Fax 020 7267 9304
Email enquiries@pen.org.uk
Website www.pen.org.uk
Director *Diana Reich*
Membership £40 (London/Overseas);
£35 (members living over 50 miles from
London)

English PEN is part of International PEN, a
worldwide association of published writers
which fights for freedom of expression and
speaks out for writers who are imprisoned or
harassed for criticising their governments or
publishing other unpopular views. FOUNDED in
London in 1921, International PEN now consists of 130 centres in almost 100 countries. PEN
originally stood for poets, essayists and novelists,
but membership is now open to published playwrights, editors, translators and journalists. A
programme of talks and discussions is supplemented by a twice-yearly mailing and annual
congress at one of the centre countries.

Performing Right Society

29–33 Berners Street, London W1P 4AA
☎020 7580 5544 Fax 020 7306 4455
Email info@prs.co.uk
Website www.prs.co.uk

Collects and distributes royalties arising from the
performance and broadcast of copyright music
on behalf of its composer, lyricist and music
publisher members and members of affiliated
societies worldwide.

Periodical Publishers Association (PPA)

Queens House, 28 Kingsway, London
WC2B 6JR
☎020 7404 4166 Fax 020 7404 4167
Email info1@ppa.co.uk
Website www.ppa.co.uk
Contact *Daska Davis*

FOUNDED 1913 to promote and protect the
interests of magazine publishers in the UK.

The Personal Managers' Association Ltd

1 Summer Road, East Molesey, Surrey
KT8 9LX
☎020 8398 9796 Fax 020 8398 9796

Co-chairs *Marc Berlin, Tim Corrie*
Secretary *Angela Adler*
Subscription £250 p.a.

An association of artists' and dramatists' agents (membership not open to individuals). Monthly meetings for exchange of information and discussion. Maintains a code of conduct and acts as a lobby when necessary. Applicants screened. A high proportion of play agents are members of the PMA.

The Picture Research Association

Head Office: 2 Culver Drive, Oxted, Surrey RH8 9HP
☎01883 730123   Fax 01883 730144
Email pra@lippmann.co.uk
Chair *Charlotte Lippmann*
Subscription Members: Introductory £40; Full £50; Associate £45. Magazine only: £25 p.a. quarterly

FOUNDED 1977 as the Society of Picture Researchers & Editors. The Picture Research Association is a professional body for picture researchers, managers, picture editors and all those involved in the research, management and supply of visual material to all forms of the media. The Association's main aims are to promote the interests and specific skills of its members internationally; to promote and maintain professional standards; to bring together those involved in the research and publication of visual material; to provide a forum for the exchange of information and to provide guidance to its members. Free advisory service for members, regular meetings, quarterly magazine, monthly newsletter and Freelance Register.

Player–Playwrights

9 Hillfield Park, London N10 3QT
☎020 8883 0371
Email P-P@dial.pipex.com
President *Jack Rosenthal*
Contact *Peter Thompson* (at the above address)
Subscription £10 (Joining fee); £6 p.a. thereafter, plus £1 per attendance

FOUNDED 1948. A society giving opportunity for writers new to stage, radio and television, as well as others finding difficulty in achieving results, to work with writers established in those media. At weekly meetings (7.45 pm to 10.00 pm, Mondays, St Augustine's Hall, Queen's Gate, London SW7), members' scripts are read or performed by actor members and afterwards assessed and dissected in general discussion. Newcomers and new acting members are always welcome.

PLS

See **Publishers Licensing Society Ltd**

PMA

See **The Personal Managers' Association Ltd**

Poetry Book Society

See **Organisations of Interest to Poets**

Poetry Ireland

See **Organisations of Interest to Poets**

The Poetry Society

See **Organisations of Interest to Poets**

Private Libraries Association

16 Brampton Grove, Kenton, Harrow, Middlesex HA3 8LG
☎020 8907 6802   Fax 020 8907 6802
Email Frank@plantage.demon.co.uk
Honorary Secretary *Frank Broomhead*
Membership £25 p.a.

FOUNDED 1956. An international society of book collectors. The Association's objectives are to promote and encourage the awareness of the benefits of book ownership, and the study of books, their production, and ownership; to publish works concerned with this, particularly those which are not commercially profitable, to hold meetings at which papers on cognate subjects can be read and discussed. Lectures and exhibitions are open to non-members.

Producers Alliance for Cinema and Television

See **PACT**

The Professional Authors' and Publishers' Association (PAPA)

292 Kennington Road, London SE11 4LD
☎020 7582 1477   Fax 020 7582 4084
Email papa@newmillennium.demon.co.uk
Website www.newmillennium.demon.co.uk
Contacts *Tom Deegan, Andy Dempsey*

FOUNDED 1993 to provide self-publishing authors with an imprint, a book production, promotion and marketing service, thereby enabling them to avoid exploitation by so-called 'subsidy' or 'partnership' publishers. Authors using the Association's New Millenium imprint own the stock of books and receive the greater proportion of the profits on book sales.

The Publishers Association

1 Kingsway, London WC2B 6XF
☎020 7565 7474 Fax 020 7836 4543
Email mail@publishers.org.uk
Website www.publishers.org.uk

Chief Executive *Ronnie Williams, OBE*

The national UK trade association for books, learned journals, and electronic publications, with around 200 member companies in the industry. Very much a trade body representing the industry to Government and the European Commission, and providing services to publishers. *Publishes* the *Directory of Publishing* in association with **Cassell**. Also home of the Educational Publishers Council (school books), PA's International Division (BDCI), the Council of Academic and Professional Publishers, and the Electronic Publishers' Forum.

Publishers' Association of South Africa

PO Box 22640, Fish Hoek 7974 South Africa
☎00 27 21 7827677 Fax 00 27 21 7827679
Email pasa@publishsa.co.za
Website www.publishsa.co.za

FOUNDED in 1992 to represent publishing in South Africa, a small but key industry sector. With a membership of over 120 companies, the Association includes commercial organisations, university presses, one-person privately-owned publishers as well as importers and distributors.

Publishers Licensing Society Ltd

5 Dryden Street, Covent Garden, London WC2E 9NW
☎020 7829 8486 Fax 020 7829 8488
Email pls@dial.pipex.com
Website www.pls.org.uk

Chief Executive *Jens Bammel*
Manager *Caroline Elmslie*

FOUNDED in 1981, the PLS obtains mandates from publishers which grant PLS the authority to license photocopying of pages from published works. Some licences for digitisation of printed works are available. PLS aims to maximise revenue from licences for mandating publishers and to expand the range and repertoire of mandated publishers available to licence holders. It supports the **Copyright Licensing Agency (CLA)** in its efforts to increase the number of legitimate users through the issuing of licences and vigorously pursues any infringements of copyright works belonging to rights' holders.

Publishers Publicity Circle

65 Airedale Avenue, London W4 2NN
☎020 8994 1881
Email ppc-@lineone.net

Contact *Heather White*

Enables book publicists from both publishing houses and freelance PR agencies to meet and share information regularly. Meetings, held monthly in central London, provide a forum for press journalists, television and radio researchers and producers to meet publicists collectively. A directory of the PPC membership is published each year and distributed to over 2500 media contacts.

The Queen's English Society

Fernwood, Nightingales, West Chiltington, Pulborough, West Sussex RH20 2QT
☎01798 813001

Honorary Membership Secretary *David Ellis*
Subscription £10p.a.; £12 p.a. (Joint); £100 (Life)

FOUNDED in 1972 to promote and uphold the use of good English and to encourage the enjoyment of the language. Holds regular meetings to which speakers are invited, an annual luncheon and *publishes* a quarterly journal, *Quest*, for which original articles are welcome.

Radio Authority

Holbrook House, 14 Great Queen Street, London WC2B 5DG
☎020 7430 2724 Fax 020 7405 7062
Website www.radioauthority.org.uk

The Radio Authority plans frequencies, awards licences, regulates programming and advertising, and plays an active role in the discussion and formulation of policies which affect the Independent Radio industry and its listeners. The Authority also licenses digital radio services. The national commercial digital radio service was launched on 15 November 1999. The number of Independent Radio stations, now over 240, continues to increase with new licences being advertised on a regular basis.

The Romantic Novelists' Association

48 Southampton Road, Fareham, Hampshire PO16 7DY
☎01329 822196 Fax 01329 825248

Contact *Karen King*
Subscription Full & Associate: £28 p.a.; £33 (Overseas, non-EU); New Writers: £63; £68 (Overseas, non-EU)

Membership is open to published writers of romantic fiction (modern or historical), or those who have had two or more full-length serials published. Associate membership is open to publishers, editors, literary agents, booksellers, librarians and others having a close connection with novel writing and publishing. Membership, in the New Writers' Scheme, is available to writers who have not yet had a full-length novel published. New Writers must submit a manuscript each year. The mss receive a report from experienced published members and the reading fee is included in the subscription of £55. Meetings are held in London and the regions with interesting guest speakers. The *RNA News* is published quarterly and issued free to members. The Association makes two annual awards: **The Major Award** for the Romantic Novel of the Year, and **The New Writers Award** for the best published novel by a new writer.

Royal Festival Hall Literature Office

Performing Arts Department, Royal Festival Hall,, London SE1 8XX
☎020 7921 0906 Fax 020 7928 2049
Email shoare@rfh.org.uk
Website www.sbc.org.uk

Head of Literature *Ruth Borthwick*

The Royal Festival Hall presents a year-round literature programme covering all aspects of writing. Regular series range from New Voices to Fiction International and there is a biennial Poetry International Festival. Literature events are now programmed in the Voice Box, Purcell Room and Queen Elizabeth Hall. To join the free mailing list, phone 020 7921 0971 or email: Literature&Talk@rfh.org.uk

Royal Society of Literature

c/o The Royal Literary Fund, 3 Johnson's Court, off Fleet Street, London EC4A 3EA
☎020 7353 7411 Fax 020 7353 7422
Email RSLit@aol.com
Website www.rslit.org

President *Lord Jenkins of Hillhead*
Subscription £30 p.a.

FOUNDED 1820. Membership by application to the Secretary. Fellowships are conferred by the Society on the proposal of two Fellows. Membership benefits include lectures, discussion meetings and poetry readings in the Society's rooms. Lecturers have included Patrick Leigh Fermor, Seamus Heaney, Richard Holmes, John Mortimer and Tom Stoppard. Presents the

W. H. Heinemann Award and the **Winifred Holtby Prize**.

Royal Television Society

Holborn Hall, 100 Gray's Inn Road, London WC1X 8AL
☎020 7430 1000 Fax 020 7430 0924
Email royaltvsociety@btinternet.com
Website www.rts.org.uk

Subscription £62 p.a.

FOUNDED 1927. Covers all disciplines involved in the television industry. Provides a forum for debate and conferences on technical, social and cultural aspects of the medium. Presents various awards including journalism, programmes, technology, design and commercials. *Publishes Television Magazine* nine times a year for members and subscribers.

Science Fiction Foundation

Membership Secretary: 33 Brookview Drive, Keyworth, Nottingham NG12 5JN
Email ambutler@enterprise.net
Website www.liv.ac.uk/~asawyer/sffchome.html

Contact *Andrew M. Butler*

The SFF is a national academic body for the furtherance of science fiction studies. *Publishes* a thrice-yearly magazine, *Foundation* (see entry under **Magazines**), which features academic articles and reviews of new fiction. It also has a reference library (see entry under **Library Services**), housed at Liverpool University.

Scottish Book Trust

The Scottish Book Centre, 137 Dundee Street, Edinburgh EH11 1BG
☎0131 229 3663 Fax 0131 228 4293
Email scottish.book.trust@dial.pipex.com
Website www.scottishbooktrust.com

Contact *Lindsey Fraser*

FOUNDED 1956. Scottish Book Trust works with schools, libraries, writers, artists, publishers, bookshops and individuals to promote the pleasures of reading to people of all ages. It provides a book information service which draws on the children's reference library (a copy of every children's book published in the previous twelve months) and a range of press cuttings on Scottish literary themes. Scottish Book Trust administers **The Fidler Award** and the **Scottish Writer of the Year Award**; and *publishes* guides to Scottish books and writers, both adult and children's. It administers the *Writers in Scotland* scheme and produces a range of posters and literary guides.

Scottish Daily Newspaper Society

48 Palmerston Place, Edinburgh EH12 5DE
☎0131 220 4353 Fax 0131 220 4344
Email info@sdns.org.uk

Director *Mr J. B. Raeburn*

FOUNDED 1915. Trade association representing publishers of Scottish daily and Sunday newspapers.

Scottish Library Association

Scottish Centre for Information & Library Services, 1 John Street, Hamilton, Strathclyde ML3 7EU
☎01698 458888 Fax 01698 458899
Email sla@amlibs.co.uk
Website www.slainte.org.uk

Director *Robert Craig*

FOUNDED 1908 to bring together everyone engaged in or interested in library work in Scotland. The Association has over 2300 members, covering all aspects of library and information work. Its main aims are the promotion of library services and the qualifications and status of librarians.

Scottish Newspaper Publishers Association

48 Palmerston Place, Edinburgh EH12 5DE
☎0131 220 4353 Fax 0131 220 4344
Email info@snpa.org.uk
Website www.snpa.org.uk

Director *Mr J. B. Raeburn*

FOUNDED around 1905. The representative body for the publishers of paid-for weekly and associated free newspapers in Scotland. Represents the interests of the industry to government, public and other bodies and provides a range of services including marketing of *The Scottish Weekly Press*, industrial relations, and education and training. It is an active supporter of the Press Complaints Commission.

Scottish Print Employers Federation

48 Palmerston Place, Edinburgh EH12 5DE
☎0131 220 4353 Fax 0131 220 4344
Email info@spef.org.uk
Website www.spef.org.uk

Director *Mr J. B. Raeburn*

FOUNDED 1910. Employers' organisation and trade association for the Scottish printing industry. Represents the interests of the industry to government, public and other bodies and provides a range of services including industrial relations. Negotiates a national wages and con-ditions agreement with the Graphical, Paper and Media Union, as well as education, training and commercial activities. The Federation is a member of Intergraf, the international confederation for employers' associations in the printing industry. In this capacity its views are channelled on the increasing number of matters affecting print businesses emanating from the European Union.

Scottish Publishers Association

Scottish Book Centre, 137 Dundee Street, Edinburgh EH11 1BG
☎0131 228 6866 Fax 0131 228 3220
Email enquiries@scottishbooks.org
Website www.scottishbooks.org

Director *Lorraine Fannin*
Marketing Manager *Alison Rae*
SBMG/Training *Allan Shanks*
Administrator *Davinder Bedi*

The Association represents over 70 Scottish publishers, from multinationals to very small presses, in a number of capacities, but primarily in the cooperative promotion and marketing of their books. The SPA also acts as an information and advice centre for both the trade and general public. *Publishes* seasonal catalogues, membership lists, the annual *Directory of Publishing in Scotland* and regular newsletters. Represents members at international book fairs; runs an extensive training programme in publishing skills; carries out market research; and encourages export initiatives. Also provides administrative back-up for the Scottish Book Marketing Group, a cooperative venture with Scottish booksellers.

Society for Children's Book Writers & Illustrators

134 Glasgow Road, Perth PE2 0LX
British Isles Regional Advisor
Natascha Biebow
Assistant Regional Advisor *Elizabeth Wein*
(at address above)

FOUNDED in 1968 by a group of Los Angeles-based writers, the Society acts as a network for the exchange of knowledge between writers, illustrators, editors, publishers, agents and others involved with literature for young people. With a membership of over 10,000 worldwide, it is the largest organisation of its kind in the world. Holds an annual national conference plus a number of regional ones, *publishes* a bi-monthly newsletter and awards grants for works in progress. The Golden Kite Award, which is presented annually, is for best fiction and non-fiction books. For membership enquiries, contact *Elizabeth Wein* at the address above.

The Society of Authors

84 Drayton Gardens, London SW10 9SB
☎020 7373 6642 Fax 020 7373 5768
Email authorsoc@writers.org.uk
Website www.writers.org.uk/society

General Secretary *Mark Le Fanu*
Subscription £70/75 p.a.

FOUNDED 1884. The Society of Authors is an independent trade union with some 6500 members. It advises on negotiations with publishers, broadcasting organisations, theatre managers and film companies; assists with complaints and takes action for breach of contract, copyright infringement, etc. Together with the **Writers' Guild**, the Society has played a major role in advancing the Minimum Terms Agreement for authors. Among the Society's publications are *The Author* (a quarterly journal) and the *Quick Guides* series to various aspects of writing (all free of charge to members). Other services include vetting of contracts, emergency funds for writers, and various special discounts. There are groups within the Society for scriptwriters, children's writers and illustrators, educational writers, medical writers and translators. Authors under 35 or over 65, not earning a significant income from their writing, may apply for lower subscription rates. Contact the Society for a free booklet and a copy of *The Author*.

The Society of Authors in Scotland

Bonnyton House, Arbirlot, Angus DD11 2PY
☎01241 874131 Fax 01241 874131
Email eileen@ramsaye.freeserve.co.uk

Secretary *Eileen Ramsay*

The Scottish branch of the **Society of Authors**, which organises business meetings, social and bookshop events throughout Scotland.

Society of Civil Service Authors

4 Top Street, Wing, Nr Oakham, Rutland LE15 8SE

Membership Secretary *Mrs Joan Hykin*
Subscription £15 p.a.

FOUNDED 1935. Aims to encourage authorship by present and past members of the Civil Service and to provide opportunities for social and cultural relationships between civil servants who are authors or who aspire to be authors. Annual competitions, open to members only, are held for short stories, poetry, sonnets, travel articles,

humour, etc. Members receive *The Civil Service Author*, a quarterly magazine. Occasional meetings in London, one or two weekends outside London.

Society of Editors

University Centre, Granta Place, Mill Lane, Cambridge CB2 1RU
☎01223 304080 Fax 01223 304090
Email society@ukeditors.com
Website www.ukeditors.com

Executive Director *Bob Satchwell*

Formed by a merger of the Association of British Editors and the Guild of Editors, the Society of Editors has nearly 500 members in national, regional and local newspapers, broadcasting, new media, journalism education and media law. Campaigns for media freedom and self-regulation. For further information contact *Bob Satchwell* at the address above or on pager number 07625 155366.

Society of Freelance Editors and Proofreaders (SFEP)

Mermaid House, 1 Mermaid Court, London SE1 1HR
☎020 7403 5141 Fax 020 7407 1193
Email admin@sfep.demon.co.uk
Website www.sfep.org.uk

Chair *Kathleen Lyle*
Vice-chair *Naomi Laredo*
Secretary *Katie Lewis*
Subscription £60 p.a. (Individuals) plus £20 joining fee; Corporate membership available

FOUNDED 1988 in response to the growing number of freelance editors and their increasing importance to the publishing industry. Aims to promote high editorial standards by disseminating information through advice and training, and to achieve recognition of the professional status of its members. The Society also supports moves towards recognised standards of training and qualifications, and is currently putting in place accredited and registered membership of SFEP.

Society of Indexers

Globe Centre, Penistone Road, Sheffield, South Yorkshire S6 3AE
☎0114 2813060 Fax 0114 2813061
Email admin@socind.demon.co.uk
Website www.socind.demon.co.uk

Secretary *Liza Weinkove*
Administrator *Wendy Burrow*
Subscription £40 p.a.; £60 (Institutions)

FOUNDED 1957. *Publishes The Indexer* (bi-annual, April and October) and a quarterly newsletter. Issues an annual list of members and *Indexers Available (IA)*, which lists members and their subject expertise. In addition, the Society runs an open-learning course entitled *Training in Indexing* and recommends rates of pay (currently £14.50 per hour).

Society of Picture Researchers & Editors

See **The Picture Research Association**

Society of Women Writers and Journalists

110 Whitehall Road, London E4 6DW
☎020 8529 0886
Email swwriters@aol.com
Honorary Secretary *Jean Hawkes*
Subscription £30 (Town); £25 (Country); £20 (Overseas). £10 Joining fee
FOUNDED 1894. The first of its kind to be run as an association of women engaged in journalism. Aims to encourage literary achievement, uphold professional standards, and establish social contacts with other writers. Lectures given at monthly lunchtime meetings. Offers advice to members and has regular seminars, etc. *Publishes* a quarterly society journal, *The Woman Journalist*.

Society of Young Publishers

12 Dyott Street, London WC1A 1DF
Website www.thesyp.demon.co.uk
Subscription £20 p.a.; £15 (Student/unwaged)

Provides facilities whereby members can increase their knowledge and widen their experience of all aspects of publishing, and holds regular social events. Open to those in related occupations, with associate membership available for over-35s. *Publishes* a monthly newsletter called *Inprint* and holds meetings on the last Wednesday of each month at the **Publishers Association**. Please enclose an s.a.e. when writing to the Society.

Spoken Word Publishing Association (SWPA)

2 Richmond Road, Basingstoke, Hampshire RG21 5NX
☎01256 358343 Fax 01256 816578
Email lynne.powell@virgin.net
Website www.swpa.org.uk
Chairman *Anna Hopkins*
Secretary *Lynne Powell*

FOUNDED 1994. SWPA is the UK trade association for the spoken word industry with membership open to all those involved in the publishing of spoken word audio. *Publishes SWPA Resources Directory* available from the address above.

Sports Writers' Association of Great Britain

c/o Sport England External Affairs, 16 Upper Woburn Place, London WC1H 0QP
☎020 7273 1789 Fax 020 7383 0273
Subscription £23.50 p.a. incl. VAT (London); £11.75 (Regional)

FOUNDED 1948 to promote and maintain a high professional standard among journalists who specialise in sport in all its branches and to serve members' interests. *Publishes* a quarterly bulletin for members and promotes jointly with Sport England the annual British Sports Journalism Awards and the Sports Photographer of the Year award.

SWPA

See **Spoken Word Publishing Association**

Theatre Writers' Union

See **The Writers' Guild of Great Britain**

The Translators Association

84 Drayton Gardens, London SW10 9SB
☎020 7373 6642 Fax 020 7373 5768
Email authorsoc@writers.org.uk
Secretary *Dorothy Wright*

FOUNDED 1958 as a subsidiary group within the **Society of Authors** to deal exclusively with the special problems of literary translators into the English language. Members are entitled to all the benefits and services of the Association, in addition to those of the Society, without extra charge. These include free legal and general advice and assistance on all matters relating to translators' work, including the vetting of contracts and information about improvements in rates of remuneration. Membership is normally confined to translators who have had their work published in volume or serial form or produced in this country for stage, television or radio. Translators of work for industrial firms or government departments are in certain cases admitted to membership if their work, though not on general sale, is published by the organisation commissioning the work. The Association administers several prizes for translators of published work (see **Prizes**) and maintains a database to enable members' details to be supplied to publishers who are seeking a translator for a particular work.

Voice of the Listener and Viewer (VLV)

101 Kings Drive, Gravesend, Kent DA12 5BQ
☎01474 352835 Fax 01474 351112
Email vlv@btinternet.com

VLV represents the citizen and consumer interest and is an independent, non-profit-making society working to ensure independence, quality and diversity in broadcasting. VLV is the only consumer body speaking for listeners and viewers on the full range of broadcasting issues. VLV is funded by its members and is free from sectarian, commercial and political affiliations. Holds public lectures, seminars and conferences, and has frequent contact with MPs, civil servants, the BBC and independent broadcasters, regulators, academics and other consumer groups. VLV has responded to all parliamentary and public enquiries on broadcasting since 1984 and to all consultation documents issued by the ITC and Radio Authority since 1990. The VLV does not handle complaints.

W.A.T.C.H.

See **Writers and their Copyright Holders**

Welsh Academy

See **Academi**

Welsh Books Council (Cyngor Llyfrau Cymru)

Castell Brychan, Aberystwyth, Ceredigion SY23 2JB
☎01970 624151 Fax 01970 625385
Email castellbrychan@cllc.org.uk
Website www.cllc.org.uk *and*
www.gwales.com

Director *Gwerfyl Pierce Jones*
Head of Editorial Department
  Dewi Morris Jones

FOUNDED 1961 to stimulate interest in Welsh literature and to support authors. The Council distributes the government grant for Welsh language publications and promotes and fosters all aspects of both Welsh and Welsh-interest book production. Its Editorial, Design, Marketing and Children's Books departments and wholesale distribution centre offer central services to publishers in Wales. Writers in Welsh and English are welcome to approach the Editorial Department for advice on how to get their manuscripts published.

Welsh Union of Writers

13 Tyn–y–Coed Road, Pentyrch, Cardiff CF15 9NP
Email wuw@btinternet.com
Secretary *Jean Henderson*
Subscription £15 p.a. (Full); £5 (Associate); £5 Joining fee

FOUNDED 1982. Independent union. Full membership by application to persons born or working in Wales with at least one publication in a quality journal or other outlet. Associate membership now available for other interested supporters. (*Membership Secretary:* Alison Dudeney, 197 Barry Road, Barry CF62 9BG.) Lobbies for writing in Wales, represents members in disputes; annual conference and occasional events, publications and twice-yearly newsletter.

Women in Publishing

c/o The Publishers Association, 1 Kingsway, 3rd Floor, Strand, London WC2B 6XF
Website www.cyberiacafe.net/wip/
Contact *Information Officer*
Membership £20 p.a. (Individuals); £15 (unwaged); £25 (if paid for by company)

Aims to promote the status of women working within the publishing industry and related trades, to encourage networking, and to provide training for career and personal development. Meetings (with panels of speakers) held on the second Wednesday of the month at the **Publishers Association** at 6.30 pm. Monthly newsletter *WiPlash* and *Women in Publishing Directory*.

Women Writers Network (WWN)

23 Prospect Road, London NW2 2JU
☎020 7794 5861
Membership Secretary *Cathy Smith*
Subscription £35 p.a. (Full); £25 p.a. (Overseas); £20 p.a. ('Newsletter only' UK membership)

FOUNDED 1985. Provides a forum for the exchange of information, support, career and networking opportunities for working women writers. Meetings, seminars, excursions, newsletter and directory. Full membership includes free admission to monthly meetings, a directory of members and a monthly newsletter. Details from the Membership Secretary.

Word Arena, Leeds

Library HQ, 32 York Road, Leeds, West Yorkshire LS8 7SJ
☎0113 2143341 Fax 0113 2143339
Email sean.burn@leeds.gov.uk

Manager *Sean Burn*

Leeds Word Arena is funded by Leeds City Council as the Literature Development Agency for the city. Provides a year-round programme of projects supporting reader and writer development, including residencies, commissions, events as well as support, advice and advocacy for Leeds-based writers, readers and publishers. Runs an annual literary festival, **City Voice**, (see entry under **Festivals**) in the first two weeks of June.

Writernet

Interchange Studios, 15 Dalby Street, London NW5 3NQ

☎020 7284 2818 Fax 020 7482 5292

Email npt@easynet.co.uk

Executive Director *Jonathan Meth*

Subscription (information on rates available by post)

Writernet (formerly the New Playwrights Trust) is the national research and development organisation for writing for all forms of live and recorded performance. *Publishes* a range of information pertinent to writers on all aspects of development and production in the form of pamphlets, and a six-weekly journal which also includes articles and interviews on aesthetic and practical issues. Writernet also runs a script-reading service and a link service between writers and producers, organises seminars and conducts research projects. The latter includes research into the use of bilingual techniques in playwriting (*Two Tongues*), documentation of training programmes for writers (*Going Black Under the Skin*) and an investigation of the relationship between live art and writing (*Writing Live*).

Writers and their Copyright Holders (W.A.T.C.H.)

The Library, The University of Reading, PO Box 223, Whiteknights, Reading, Berkshire RG6 6AE

☎0118 9318783 Fax 0118 9316636

Website www.lib.utexas.edu/hrc/watch.html

Contact *Dr David Sutton*

FOUNDED 1994. Provides an on-line database of information about the copyright holders of literary authors. The database is available free of charge on the Internet and the Web. W.A.T.C.H. is the successor project to the Location Register of English Literary Manuscripts and Letters, and continues to deal with location register enquiries.

The Writers' Guild of Great Britain

430 Edgware Road, London W2 1EH

☎020 7723 8074 Fax 020 7706 2413

Email postie@wggb.demon.co.uk

Website www.writers.org.uk/guild

Acting General Secretary *Jacob Ecclestone*

Annual subscription 1% of that part of the author's income earned in the areas in which the Guild operates, with a basic subscription of £100 and a maximum of £950

FOUNDED 1959. The Writers' Guild is the writers' trade union, affiliated to the TUC. It represents writers in film, radio, television, theatre and publishing. The Guild has negotiated agreements on which writers' contracts are based with the BBC, Independent Television companies, and **PACT** (the Producers' Alliance for Cinema and Television). Those agreements are regularly renegotiated, both in terms of finance and conditions. In 1997, the Guild membership joined with that of the Theatre Writers' Union to create a new, more powerful union.

In 1979, together with the Theatre Writers' Union, the Guild negotiated the first ever industrial agreement for theatre writers, the TNC Agreement, which covers the **Royal National Theatre**, the **Royal Shakespeare Company**, and the **English Stage Company**. Further agreements have been negotiated with the Theatrical Management Association which covers regional theatre and the **Independent Theatre Council**, the organisation which covers small theatres and the Fringe.

The Guild initiated a campaign over ten years ago which achieved the first ever publishing agreement for writers with the publisher W. H. Allen. Jointly with the **Society of Authors**, that campaign has continued and most years see new agreements with more publishers. Perhaps the most important breakthrough came with **Penguin** on 20 July 1990. The Guild now also has agreements covering **HarperCollins**, **Random House Group**, **Transworld** and others.

The Guild regularly provides individual help and advice to members on contracts, conditions of work, and matters which affect a member's life as a professional writer. Members are given the opportunity of meeting at craft meetings, which are held on a regular basis throughout the year. Writers can apply for Full Membership if they have one piece of written work for which payment has been received under a contract with terms not less than those negotiated by the Guild. Writers who do not qualify for Full

Membership can apply for Candidate Membership. This is open to all those who wish to be involved in writing but have not yet had work published. The subscription fee for this is £50.

Yachting Journalists' Association

3 Friars Lane, Maldon, Essex CM9 6AG
☎01621 855943/0468 962936(mobile)
Fax 01621 852212
Email petercookyja@compuserve.com
Website www.yja.co.uk
Honorary Secretary *Peter Cook*
Subscription £30 p.a.

To further the interest of yachting, sail and power, and to provide support and assistance to journalists in the field; current membership is just over 260 with 23 from overseas. A handbook, listing details of members and subscribing PR organisations, press facility recommendations, forthcoming events and other useful information, is published annually in December at a cost to non-members and non-advertisers of £10. Information for inclusion should be submitted by the end of August. The YJA organises the Yachtsman of the Year and Young Sailor of the Year Awards, that form part of the British Nautical Awards, presented annually at the beginning of January on the first Friday of the London International Boat Show.

Yr Academi Gymreig
See **Academi**

Copyright in the Age of Advanced Technology

The latest fuss over copyright centres on a scheme launched by Simon & Schuster, followed by Macmillan and Wiley, to 'keep works of academic value in print on a permanent basis' by printing on demand. The drawback, from an author's point of view, is that while under current rules if a book goes out of print for more than eight weeks the copyright in the text reverts to the author, this print-on-demand initiative could be used by a publisher to hold on to those rights. The issue will doubtless be decided eventually by combat between expensive lawyers. Meanwhile, we can only wonder at the further confusion over who owns what created by the new technology. In the Far East it is reckoned that over 90 per cent of all videocassettes sold are pirated. Unauthorised printing of books in China, Russia and a motley of smaller nations is said to be depriving British publishers and their authors of £200 million a year. As for the photocopier, it is now responsible for some 300 billion pages of illegally reproduced material.

What is to be done?

If it is any comfort, copyright holders have legislation on their side. Until recently, British copyright lasted for fifty years beyond the author's death. Now, courtesy of the European Community, it is seventy years. There is support too for efforts to secure a decent return from those who would readily exploit an author's work without paying for it. Photocopying used to be a licence to save money. Hardly anyone thought twice before reproducing articles, chapters from books or even a whole book without reference to the copyright holder. Today, the **Authors' Licensing and Collecting Society** (ALCS) has forged agreements with education and commerce on a licensing scheme for reprographic rights. Whether or not a similar scheme can be applied to electronic rights depends largely on developing an effective policing system. Reports are already filtering through the technological grapevine of new metering systems which will allow publishers to monitor and record the use of their information on the Internet and other networks. In early 1997, the World Intellectual Property Organisation, the UN's agency responsible for administering copyright conventions, required member states to outlaw devices aimed at bypassing technical measures to prevent unauthorised copying.

Meanwhile, there is much that the individual writer can do to guard against the free use of what is, or what might turn out to be, a valuable property. The starting point is the small print of a contract. Any publisher who offers a deal that is dependent on exclusive rights must be regarded with suspicion. It is likely that he has no intention of paying the author a single penny beyond a basic fee or royalty. This is what happens to contributors to academic and specialist journals, who are invariably asked to assign their copyright as a condition of publication.

Even those who make a living out of writing and are skilled in the devious ways of publishing can lose out simply by ignoring the subsidiary clauses of a contract or, if reading them, by not realising the long-term implications.

Once surrendered, copyright cannot be retrieved. As Nicola Solomon, a lawyer specialising in copyright law, warns, 'an assignment of copyright is binding . . . it is not contingent on an agreed fee or royalties being paid. If a publisher fails to pay, your only remedy . . . is to sue for the unpaid debt but you will not be able to regain copyright.'

There may well be occasions when the surrender of copyright is justified. A writer who works to order, adapting material provided for a company training course, say, or a sponsored history to be used as a promotional tool, would be pushing his luck to argue for more than a set fee.

On occasion, it is not altogether clear who it is that has first claim to copyright. The most obvious example is the journalist – say, a columnist whose by-line appears twice-weekly in a national newspaper. If he is on the payroll, with all the rights and responsibilities of an employee, then copyright on his articles is assumed to belong to his employer – 'unless otherwise agreed'. In other words, if the journalist is a self-assertive type who is ready to bargain with his editor he may well emerge with a contract which secures his copyright beyond the first printing. A scribe with less muscle might prefer to rely on his editor's sense of decency in handing over a share of any supplementary fees. As a general rule, those who commission work invariably demand exclusive copyright, including syndication rights. This applies to freelancers, who, technically speaking, are entitled to copyright, as well as to regular employees. The journalists' unions urge members to resist but the need to make a living in a highly competitive market weakens the resolve of all but the star turns.

Film and television

In late 1992 the European Commission's Rental and Lending Directive declared the 'author' of a film to have the right to '"equitable" remuneration'. But who is the 'author'? Under British law, he is generally assumed to be the producer, an interpretation which naturally offends writers and directors. The European Community, on the other hand, takes its lead from France, where the primary author of a film is the director while others, including the scriptwriter, can be named as co-authors. Producers have tried to frustrate the change, threatening expensive legal action, but in late 1996 Parliament gave the go-ahead for scriptwriters and authors whose work has been filmed or broadcast to receive payments for the rental of their works. Checking who owes what to whom is made easier by signing up with the ALCS, which acts as a collecting agency on behalf of its members.

Problems remain, however. Lending is horrendously difficult to control. It has been known for years that the loss of income attributed to domestic sound and video recorders runs into billions. With the advance of technology, the problem is bound to worsen. Before long we will have video on demand, an almost limitless choice of programming available to any home at a push of the remote control. Imagine what that will do to undermine copyright.

Extent of copyright

In most books a copyright notice appears on one of the front pages. In its simplest form this is the symbol © followed by the name of the copyright owner and the year of first publication. The assertion of copyright may be emphasised by the phrase 'All rights reserved', and in case there are any lingering doubts the reader may be warned that 'No part of this publication may be reproduced or transmitted in any form or by any means without permission'.

But this is to overstate the case. In principle, a quotation of a 'substantial' extract from a copyright work or for any quotation of copyright material, however short, for an anthology must be approved by the publishers of the original work. But there is no fixed rule on what constitutes a substantial extract. In any case, even a lengthy quotation from a copyright work may not be an infringement if it is 'fair dealing . . . for purposes of criticism or review'. Much depends on the standing of the writer being quoted. If he is a world-famous author he or his heirs are liable to take a tougher line than, say, the copyright holder of an esoteric work of limited circulation. The families of literary giants are notoriously stingy. In granting permission to quote they are liable to charge hefty fees or, if the applicant is at all suspect, a biographer who is liable to do the dirt on a revered memory, for example, to refuse to cooperate in any way. For this, if for no other reason, an author who needs permission to quote should deal with the matter at an early stage. Last-minute requests just before a book goes to press can lead to crisis if fees are too high or if permission is refused.

A contract must specify the territory permissions will cover. The difference between British Commonwealth and the world can be a yawning gap in costs. Some publishers have a standard letter for clearing permissions which may help to speed up negotiations. But Rights Departments are notoriously slow in responding to requests from individuals who are unclear as to what they want or who give the impression of writing in on spec.

Difficulties can arise when the identity of a copyright holder is unclear. The publisher of the relevant book may have gone out of business or been absorbed into a conglomerate, leaving no records of the original imprint. Detective work can be yet more convoluted when it comes to unpublished works. When copyright holders are hard to trace, the likeliest source of help is the **Writers and their Copyright Holders** project, otherwise known as WATCH. A joint enterprise of the universities of Texas and Reading, WATCH has created a database of English-language authors whose papers are housed in archives and manuscript repositories. The database is available free of charge on the Internet.

If, despite best efforts, a copyright owner cannot be found, there are two options; either to cut the extract or to press ahead with publication in the hope that if the copyright holder does find out he will not object or will not demand an outrageous fee. The risk can be minimised by an open acknowledgement that every effort to satisfy the law has been made.

Anthology and quotation rates

Prose
The rate suggested by the **Society of Authors** and the **Publishers Association** is £120–146 per 1,000 words for world rights. The rate for the UK and Commonwealth or the USA alone is usually half of the world rate, and for an individual country, one quarter of the world rate. Where an extract is complete in itself (e.g. a chapter or short story) publishers sometimes charge an additional fee at half the rate applicable for 1,000 words. This scale generally covers one edition only. An additional fee may be payable if the material is used in a reset or offset edition or in a new format or new binding (e.g. a paperback edition) and will certainly be required if the publisher of an anthology sub-licenses publication rights to another publisher.

Fees vary according to the importance of the author quoted, the proportion of the original work that the user intends to quote and its value to the author or publisher requesting permission. The expected size of the print run should also be taken into consideration. Fees for quotations in scholarly works with print runs of under 1,000 copies are usually charged at half the normal rate.

Poetry
The world rate for anthology publication is a minimum fee of £90–120 for the first 10 lines; thereafter £2.10–2.30 per line for the next 20 lines and £1.30–1.50 a line subsequently, but the rates for established poets may well be significantly higher. The rate for the UK and Commonwealth or the USA alone is usually half of the world rate.

Moral rights

With the 1988 Copyright Designs and Patents Act, the European concept of 'moral rights' was introduced into British law. The most basic is the right of paternity, which entitles authors to be credited as the creators of their work. However, paternity must be asserted in writing and is not retrospective. No right of paternity attaches to authors of computer programs or to writers who create works as part of their employment or journalists or as contributors to a 'collective work' such as an encyclopaedia, dictionary or year book.

A second moral right is that of integrity. In theory, this opens the way to force-ful objections to any 'derogatory treatment' if derogatory amounts to 'distortion or mutilation . . . or is otherwise prejudicial to the honour or reputation of the author'. Miscorrection of grammar by an illiterate editor does not qualify. In the absence of test cases it seems that a book would have to be savaged beyond recognition for an injunction to be granted.

Those most likely to have their right of integrity infringed are film directors (specifically mentioned in the 1988 Act) and visual artists who might, for example, suffer the attentions of an airbrusher. For those in the writing trade, the Society of Authors urges 'locking the stable door before the horse bolts by ensuring that your contract does not permit the publishers to make significant editorial changes without your agreement', though with the virtual abandonment of hard copy in favour of disks, changes can be introduced without the author noticing – until it is too late.

Moral rights may 'be waived by written agreement or with the consent of the author'. There are cases where the concession is justified. For example, a ghost writer who has chosen to be anonymous may reasonably be expected to waive moral rights.

Titles and trademarks

Technically, there is no copyright in a title. But where a title is inseparable from the work of a particular author, proceedings for 'passing off' are likely to be successful. Everything depends on the nature of the rival works, the methods by which they are exploited and the extent to which the title is essentially distinctive.

The risks of causing offence multiply when a unique image is involved. Mickey Mouse, Thomas the Tank Engine, and the *Mr Men* characters created by Roger Hargreaves (60 million books sold to date) are examples of registered trademarks that protect against literary and other predators. The interesting feature of trademarks is that, unlike copyright, they go on for ever. The Coca-Cola and Kodak marks, for example, are well over 100 years old.

In theory it should be easier to preserve copyright in fictional characters than on titles. But in broadcasting a frequent source of dispute is the lifting of characters from one series to another when there are two or more writers involved. Sometimes royalties are paid; other times, not. Production companies are liable to take possession of fictional characters unless their originators make a fuss.

The singularity of letters

The copyright status of a letter is something of a curiosity. The actual document belongs to the recipient, but the copyright remains with the writer, and after death to the writer's estate. This has caused difficulty for some biographers who have assumed that it is the owners of letters who are empowered to give permission to quote from them. This only applies if the writer has assigned copyright. Even then, the way may not be smooth. Witness the frustration of Eric Jacobs, the biographer of Sir Kingsley Amis, who found himself unable to quote from letters written by the novelist because the Bodleian Library, which has the bulk of the Amis papers, would not concede any part of the copyright Sir Kingsley had invested in them. The matter was resolved only when the letter-writer himself requested permission to quote from his own correspondence.

Copyright in lectures and speeches

Even if a speaker talks without notes, copyright exists in a lecture as soon as it is recorded (in writing or otherwise) but not until then. The copyright belongs to the person who spoke the words, whether or not the recording was made by, or with the permission of, the speaker. There is one important exception: when a record of spoken words is made to report current events.

Copyright on ideas

Writers trying to sell ideas should start on the assumption that it is almost impossible to stake an exclusive claim. So much unsolicited material comes the way of publishers and script departments the duplication of ideas is inevitable.

Frequent complaints of plagiarism have led publishers and production companies to point out the risks whenever they acknowledge an unsolicited synopsis or script, warning correspondents, 'it is often the case that we are currently considering or have already considered ideas that may be similar to your own'.

In America the studios are now so worried about being sued that any writer offering an idea or script must sign a document waiving rights.

A writer who is nervous of the attention of rivals is best advised to maintain a certain reticence in dealings with the media. He should resist the urge to give out all his best ideas at an expensive lunch or in a brain-storming session with an ever so friendly producer. It is flattering to be invited to hold forth but the experience can be costly unless there is an up-front fee.

At the same time, remember that there is no such thing as an entirely original plot. To succeed in an action for infringement of copyright on an idea or on the bare bones of a plot, the copying of 'a combination or series of dramatic events' must be very close indeed. Proceedings have failed because incidents common to two works have been stock incidents or revolving around stock characters common to many works.

Two years ago a Californian judge threw out a $100 million copyright infringement suit filed by two New Zealand playwrights against the producers of *The Full Monty*. The playwrights claimed the film closely resembled their ten-year-old play, *Ladies Night*. The late Hughie Green unsuccessfully fought a court battle to stop New Zealand producers making a show he claimed was a version of *Opportunity Knocks*. Since little of his original idea was ever committed to paper his claim was too difficult to prove.

For any queries on British copyright contact: The Copyright Directorate, The Patent Office, Harmsworth House, 13–15 Bouverie Street, London EC4Y 8DP (☎020 7596 6513; Fax 020 7596 6526; Email copyright@patent.gov.uk; Website www.patent.gov.uk).

The WATCH Website is at www.lib.utexas.edu/hrc/watch.html (see entry under **Professional Associations and Societies***).*

Copyright information may be sent to Dr David Sutton, director of research projects in the University of Reading Library, at d.c.sutton@reading.ac.uk or the Library, University of Reading, PO Box 223, Whiteknights, Reading RG6 6AE.

Literary Societies

Most literary societies exist on a shoestring budget; it is a good idea to enclose an A5 s.a.e. with all correspondence needing a reply.

Margery Allingham Society

2B High Green, Winchelsea, East Sussex
TN36 4HB
☎01797 222363 Fax 01797 222363
Contact *Mrs Pamela Bruxner*
Subscription £8 p.a.

FOUNDED 1988 to promote interest in and study of the works of Margery Allingham. The Society *publishes* two issues of the newsletter, *The Bottle Street Gazette*, per year. Contributions welcome. Two social events a year. Open membership.

Jane Austen Society

Carton House, Redwood Lane, Medstead, Alton, Hampshire GU34 5PE
☎01420 562469 Fax 01420 562469
Email janeaustensoc@freeuk.com
Website www.janeaustensociety.org.uk
Honorary Secretary *Susan McCartan*
Subscription UK: £10 (Annual);
£15 (Joint); £30 (Corporate); £150 (Life);
Overseas: £12 (Annual); £18 (Joint);
£33 (Corporate); £180 (Life)

FOUNDED 1940 to promote interest in and enjoyment of Jane Austen's novels and letters. The society has branches in Bath & Bristol, Midlands, London, Oxford, Kent and Hampshire. There are independent Societies in North America and Australia.

The Baskerville Hounds

6 Bramham Moor, Hill Head, Fareham, Hampshire PO14 3RU
☎01329 667325
Chairman *Philip Weller*
Subscription £6 p.a.

FOUNDED 1989. An international Sherlock Holmes society specialising solely in studies of *The Hound of the Baskervilles* and its Dartmoor associations. *Publishes* a quarterly newsletter, an annual journal and specialist monographs. It also organises many social functions, usually on Dartmoor. Open membership.

The Beckford Society

15 Healey Street, London NW1 8SR
☎020 7267 7750 Fax 01985 213239
Email Sidney.Blackmore@btinternet.com
Secretary *Sidney Blackmore*
Subscription £10 (min.) p.a.

FOUNDED 1995 to promote an interest in the life and works of William Beckford (1760–1844) and his circle. Encourages Beckford studies and scholarship through exhibitions, lectures and publications, including an annual journal, *The Beckford Journal*, and occasional newsletters.

Thomas Lovell Beddoes Society

11 Laund Nook, Belper, Derbyshire
DE56 1GY
☎01773 828066 Fax 01773 828066
Email tlbeddoes@tlbeddoes.force9.co.uk
Chairman *John Lovell Beddoes*
Secretary *Judith Higgens*

Formed to research the life, times and work of poet Thomas Lovell Beddoes (1803–1849), encourage relevant publications, further the reading and appreciation of his works by a wider public and liaise with other groups and organisations. *Publishes* an annual newsletter.

Arnold Bennett Society

106 Scotia Road, Burslem, Stoke on Trent
ST6 4ET
☎01782 816311
Secretary *Mrs Jean Potter*
Subscription £6 (Single); £7 (Family);
£5 (unwaged)

Aims to promote interest in the life and works of 'Five Towns' author Arnold Bennett and other North Staffordshire writers. Annual dinner. Regular functions in and around Burslem. Quarterly newsletter. Open membership.

E. F. Benson Society

The Old Coach House, High Street, Rye, East Sussex TN31 7JF
☎01797 223114
Secretary *Allan Downend*

Subscription £7.50 (UK/Europe); £12.50 (Overseas)

FOUNDED 1985 to promote the life and work of E. F. Benson and the Benson family. Organises social and literary events, exhibitions, talks and Benson interest walks in Rye. *Publishes* a quarterly newsletter and annual journal, *The Dodo*, postcards and reprints of E. F. Benson articles and short stories. Holds an archive which includes the Seckersen Collection (transcriptions of the Benson collection at the Bodleian Library in Oxford).

E. F. Benson/The Tilling Society

5 Friars Bank, Pett Road, Guestling, Hastings, East Sussex TN35 4EJ Fax 01424 813237

Contact *Cynthia Reavell*

Subscription Full starting membership (members receive all back newsletters) £26 (UK); £30 (Overseas); or Annual Membership (members receive only current year's newsletters) £8 (UK); £10 (Overseas).

FOUNDED 1982 for the exchange of news, information and speculation about E. F. Benson, his works and, in particular, his *Mapp & Lucia* novels. Readings, talks and substantial biannual newsletter. Annual get-together in Rye/ 'Tilling'. Acts as a clearing house for every sort of news and activity concerning E. F. Benson.

The Betjeman Society

35 Eaton Court, Boxgrove Avenue, Guildford, Surrey GU1 1XH
☎01483 560882

Honorary Secretary *John Heald*

Subscription £7 (Individual); £9 (Family); £3 (Student); £2 extra each category for Overseas members

Aims to promote the study and appreciation of the work and life of Sir John Betjeman. Annual programme includes poetry readings, lectures, discussions, visits to places associated with Betjeman, and various social events. Meetings are held in London and other centres. Regular newsletter and annual journal, *The Betjemanian*.

The Bewick Society

National Trust, Scots Gap, Morpeth, Northumberland NE1 8ST

Chairman *Kenneth McConkey*

Subscription £7 p.a.

FOUNDED 1988 to promote an interest in the life and work of Thomas Bewick, wood-engraver and naturalist (1753–1828). Organises related events and meetings, and is associated with the Bewick birthplace museum.

Birmingham Central Literary Association

c/o Birmingham & Midland Institute, Margaret Street, Birmingham B3 3DS
☎0121 236 3591

Contact *The Honorary Secretary*

Holds fortnightly meetings at the Birmingham Midland Institute to discuss the lives and work of authors and poets. Holds an annual dinner to celebrate Shakespeare's birthday.

The George Borrow Society

The Gables, 112 Irchester Road, Rushden, Northants NN10 9XQ
☎01933 312965 Fax 01933 312965
Email eibj2077@xerp934.freeserve.co.uk
Website www.lefant.freeserve.co.uk/gb.htm

President *Sir Angus Fraser, KCB TD*

Honorary Secretary *Dr James H. Reading*

Honorary Treasurer *Mrs Ena R. J. Reading*

Chairman/Editor *George Borrow Bulletin: Dr Ann M. Ridler*, St Mary's Cottage, 61 Thame Road, Warborough, Wallingford, Oxford OX10 7EA
☎01865 858379 Fax 01865 858575
Email 113250.1724@compuserve.com

Subscription £10 p.a.

FOUNDED 1991 to promote knowledge of the life and works of George Borrow (1803–81), traveller, linguist and writer. The Society holds biennial conferences (with published proceedings) and informal intermediate gatherings, all at places associated with Borrow. *Publishes* the *George Borrow Bulletin* twice yearly, a newsletter containing scholarly articles, publications relating to Borrow, reports of past events and news of forthcoming events. Member of the **Alliance of Literary Societies** and corporate associate member of the Centre of East Anglian Studies (CEAS) at the University of East Anglia, Norwich (Borrow's home city for many years).

Elinor Brent-Dyer

See **Friends of the Chalet School**

British Fantasy Society

201 Reddish Road, South Reddish, Stockport, Cheshire SK5 7HR
☎0161 476 5368 (after 6pm)
Email faliol@yahoo.com
Website www.herebedragons.co.uk/bfs

President *Ramsey Campbell*

Vice-President *Jan Ward*

Secretary *Robert Parkinson*

Subscription from £20 p.a. (apply to Secretary.)

FOUNDED 1971 for devotees of fantasy, horror and related fields in literature, art and the cinema. *Publishes* a regular newsletter with information and reviews of new books and films, plus related fiction and non-fiction magazines. Annual conference at which the **British Fantasy Awards** are presented. These awards are voted on by the membership and are not an open competition.

The Brontë Society

Brontë Parsonage Museum, Haworth, Keighley, West Yorkshire BD22 8DR
☎01535 642323 Fax 01535 647131
Email bronte@bronte.prestel.co.uk
Website www.bronte.org.uk

Contact *Membership Secretary*
Subscription £18 p.a. (UK/Europe);
£7.50 (Student); £5 (Junior – up to age 14);
£27 (Overseas); Joint subscriptions and life membership also available

FOUNDED 1893. Aims and activities include the preservation of manuscripts and other objects related to or connected with the Brontë family, and the maintenance and development of the museum and library at Haworth. The society holds regular meetings, lectures and exhibitions; and *publishes* information relating to the family, a biannual society journal *Transactions* and a biannual *Gazette*. Freelance contributions for either publication should be sent to the Publications Secretary at the address above.

The Browning Society

163 Wembley Hill Road, Wembley Park, Middlesex HA9 8EL
☎020 8904 8401

Honorary Secretary *Ralph Ensz*
Subscription £15 p.a.

FOUNDED 1969 to promote an interest in the lives and poetry of Robert and Elizabeth Barrett Browning. Meetings are arranged in the London area, one of which occurs in December at Westminster Abbey to commemorate Robert Browning's death.

The John Buchan Society

'Greenmantle', Ingles Hill, Ashby-de-la-Zouch LE65 2TF
☎01530 416969

Secretary *Kenneth Hillier*
Subscription £10 (Full/Overseas);
£4 (Associate); £6 (Junior);
£20 (Corporate); £90 (Life)

To perpetuate the memory of John Buchan and to promote a wider understanding of his life and works. Holds regular meetings and social gatherings, *publishes* a journal, and liaises with the John Buchan Centre at Broughton in the Scottish borders.

The Burns Federation

The Dick Institute, Elmbank Avenue, Kilmarnock, Strathclyde KA1 3BU
☎01563 572469 Fax 01563 572469
Email robertburnsfederation@kilmarnock26. freeserve.co.uk

Chief Executive *Shirley Bell*
Subscription £20 p.a.(Individual);
£25 (Family); £40 (Club subscription)

FOUNDED 1885 to encourage interest in the life and work of Robert Burns and keep alive the old Scottish Tongue. The Society's interests go beyond Burns himself in its commitment to the development of Scottish literature, music and arts in general. *Publishes* the quarterly *Burns Chronicle/Burnsian*.

The Byron Society

Byron House, 6 Gertrude Street, London SW10 0JN
☎020 7352 5112

Honorary Director, Byron Society
Mrs Elma Dangerfield OBE
Subscription £20 p.a.

Also: Newstead Abbey Byron Society, Newstead Abbey, Newstead Abbey Park, Nottingham NG15 8GE ☎01623 797392

Contact *Mrs Maureen Crisp*

FOUNDED 1876; revived in 1971. Aims to promote knowledge and discussion of Lord Byron's life and works, and those of his contemporaries, through lectures, readings, concerts, performances and international conferences. *Publishes* annually in April *The Byron Journal*, a scholarly journal – £5 plus £1.75 postage.

Randolph Caldecott Society

Clatterwick House, Little Leigh, Northwich, Cheshire CW8 4RJ
☎01606 891303 (day)/781731 (evening)

Honorary Secretary *Kenneth N. Oultram*
Subscription £7–£10 p.a.

FOUNDED 1983 to promote the life and work of artist/book illustrator Randolph Caldecott. Meetings held in the spring and autumn in Caldecott's birthplace, Chester. Guest speakers, outings, newsletter, exchanges with the society's American counterpart. (Caldecott died and was buried in St Augustine, Florida.) A medal in his memory is awarded annually in the US for children's book illustration.

The Carlyle Society, Edinburgh

Dept of English Literature, The University of Edinburgh, David Hume Tower, George Square, Edinburgh EH8 9JX
Fax 0131 650 6898
Email ian.campbell@ed.ac.uk
Contact *The President*
Subscription £2 p.a.; £10 (Life); $20 (US)

FOUNDED 1929 to examine the lives of Thomas Carlyle and his wife Jane, his writings, contemporaries, and influences. Meetings are held about six times a year and occasional papers are published annually. Enquiries should be addressed to the President of the Society at the address above or to the Secretary at 16a Blackford Road, Edinburgh EH9 2DS.

Lewis Carroll Society

69 Cromwell Road, Hertford, Hertfordshire SG13 7DP
☎01992 584530
Email alanwhite@tesco.net
Website aznet.co.uk/LCS
Secretary *Alan White*
Subscription Individual: £13 (UK); £15 (Europe); £17 (Outside Europe); £10 (Retired rate); £2 (Additional family members); Institutions: £26 (UK); £28 (Europe); £30 (Outside Europe)

FOUNDED 1969 to bring together people with an interest in Charles Dodgson and promote research into his life and works. *Publishes* bi-annual journal *The Carrollian*, featuring scholarly articles and reviews; a newsletter (*Bandersnatch*) which reports on Carrollian events and the Society's activities; and *The Lewis Carroll Review*, a book reviewing journal. Regular meetings held in London with lectures, talks, outings, etc.

Lewis Carroll Society (Daresbury)

Clatterwick House, Little Leigh, Northwich, Cheshire CW8 4RJ
☎01606 891303 (day)/781731 (evening)
Honorary Secretary *Kenneth N. Oultram*
Subscription £5 p.a.

FOUNDED 1970. To promote the life and work of Charles Dodgson, author of the world-famous *Alice's Adventures*. Holds regular meetings in the spring and autumn in Carroll's birthplace, Daresbury, in Cheshire. Guest speakers, theatre visits and a newsletter. Appoints annually a 10-year-old 'Alice' who is available for public engagements.

Friends of the Chalet School

4 Rock Terrace, Coleford, Bath, Somerset BA3 5NF
☎01373 812705 Fax 01373 813517
Email focs@rockterrace.co.uk
Website www.rockterrace.demon.co.uk/FOCS
Contacts *Ann Mackie-Hunter, Clarissa Cridland*
Subscription £7.50 p.a.; £6 (Under-18); Outside UK: details on application

FOUNDED 1989 to promote the works of Elinor Brent-Dyer. The society has members worldwide; *publishes* four magazines a year and runs a lending library.

The Raymond Chandler Society

6 Barkers Road, Nether Edge, Sheffield S7 1SE
☎0114 255 6302 Fax 0114 255 6302
Email william.adamson@zsp.uni-ulm.de
UK Contact *Simon Beckett*
Subscription £15 p.a. (£7 concessions)

Although based in Germany, the Society has an international membership. Its foremost concerns are with Raymond Chandler's works and his influence and reception within a historical and contemporary context, but it is also concerned with the genre of the 'crime novel' in general. Presents the 'Marlowe' awards (see entry under **Prizes**). *Publishes* the *Chandler Yearbook*, a scholarly publication containing reviews and articles on crime writing in both English and German. The Society attends international conferences such as 'Dead on Deansgate' and 'Bouchercon', and organises the Chandler Symposium, usually held in Ulm, Germany in July.

The Chesterton Society UK

11 Lawrence Leys, Bloxham, Near Banbury, Oxfordshire OX15 4NU
☎01295 720869/07747 786428 (mobile)
Honorary Secretary *Robert Hughes, KHS*
Subscription £12.50 p.a.

FOUNDED 1964 to promote the ideas and writings of G. K. Chesterton.

The Children's Books History Society

25 Field Way, Hoddesdon, Hertfordshire EN11 0QN
☎01992 464885 Fax 01992 464885
Email cbhs@abcgarrett.demon.co.uk
Membership Secretary *Mrs Pat Garrett*
Subscription £10 p.a. (UK/Europe)

ESTABLISHED 1969. Aims to promote an appreciation of children's books and to study their history, bibliography and literary content. The Society holds approximately six meetings per year in London and a summer meeting to a collection, or to a location with a children's book connection. Three substantial newsletters issued annually, also an occasional paper. The Society constitutes the British branch of the Friends of the Osborne and Lillian H. Smith Collections in Toronto, Canada, and also liaises with the **Library Association**. In 1990, the Society established its biennial Harvey Darton Award for a book, published in English, which extends our knowledge of some aspect of British children's literature of the past. 1998 joint-winners: John Goldthwaite *The Natural History of Make-Believe* and Peter Newbolt *G. A. Henty 1832–1902*.

The John Clare Society

The Stables, 1a West Street, Helpston, Peterborough PE6 7DU
☎01733 252678
Websites: uzone.virgin.net/linda.curry/
    jclaresociety.htm *and* human.ntu.ac.uk/clare
Honorary Secretary *Peter Moyse*
Subscription £9.50 (Individual);
    £12.50 (Joint); £7.50 (Fully Retired);
    £9.50 (Joint Retired);
    £10 (Group/Library); £3 (Student, Full-time); £12.50 sterling draft/$25 (Overseas)

FOUNDED 1981 to promote a wider appreciation of the life and works of the poet John Clare (1793–1864). Organises an annual festival in Helpston in July; arranges exhibitions, poetry readings and conferences; and *publishes* an annual society journal and quarterly newsletter.

The Friends of Coleridge

87 Richmond Road, Montpelier, Bristol BS6 5EP
☎0117 9426366
Email 113223.2774@compuserve.com
Membership Secretary *Shirley Watters*
Editor (Coleridge Bulletin) *Graham Davidson*
Subscription £10 (UK);
    £15 or £20 (Overseas)

FOUNDED in 1987 to advance knowledge about the life, work and times of Samuel Taylor Coleridge and his circle, and to support his Nether Stowey Cottage, with the National Trust, as a centre of Coleridge interest. Holds study weekends and a biennial international academic conference. *Publishes* the *Coleridge Bulletin* biannually. Short academic articles on

Coleridge-related topics may be sent to the editor at the address above.

Wilkie Collins Society

47 Hereford Road, Acton, London W3 9JW
Email paul@wilkiecollins.org
Website www.wilkiecollins.org
Chairman *Andrew Gasson*
Membership Secretary *Paul Lewis*
Subscription £8.50 (UK); £12.50 (US/
    outside Europe – remittance must be made
    in UK sterling)

FOUNDED 1980 to provide information on and promote interest in the life and works of Wilkie Collins, one of the first English novelists to deal with the detection of crime. *The Woman in White* appeared in 1860 and *The Moonstone* in 1868. *Publishes* newsletters, reprints of Collins' work and an annual academic journal.

The Arthur Conan Doyle Society

PO Box 1360, Ashcroft, British Columbia Canada V0K 1A0
☎001 250 453 2045 Fax 001 250 453 2075
Email ashtree@ash-tree.bc.ca
Website www.ash-tree.bc.ca/acdsocy.html
Joint Organisers *Christopher Roden,*
    Barbara Roden
Membership Contact *R. Dixon-Smith*, 59
    Stonefield, Bar Hill, Cambridge CB3 8TE
Subscription £16 (UK); £16 (Overseas);
    Family rates available

FOUNDED 1989 to promote the study and discussion of the life and works of Sir Arthur Conan Doyle. Occasional meetings, functions and visits. *Publishes* a biannual journal together with reprints of Conan Doyle's writings.

The Rhys Davies Trust

10 Heol Don, Whitchurch, Cardiff CF14 2AU
☎029 2062 3359 Fax 029 2052 9202
Contact *Meic Stephens*

FOUNDED 1990 to perpetuate the literary reputation of Welsh writer, Rhys Davies (1901–78), and to foster Welsh writing in English. Organises competitions in association with other bodies such as **The Welsh Academy**, puts up plaques on buildings associated with Welsh writers, offers grant-aid for book production, etc.

The Dickens Fellowship

48 Doughty Street, London WC1N 2LF
☎020 7405 2127 Fax 020 7831 5175
Joint Honorary General Secretaries *Mrs*
    Thelma Grove, Dr Tony Williams

Subscription £5 (First year); £8.50 (Renewal)
FOUNDED 1902. The Society's particular aims and objectives are: to bring together lovers of Charles Dickens; to spread the message of Dickens, his love of humanity ('the keynote of all his work'); to remedy social injustice for the poor and oppressed; to assist in the preservation of material and buildings associated with Dickens. Annual conference. *Publishes* journal called *The Dickensian* (available at special rate to members) and organises a full programme of lectures, discussions, visits and conducted walks throughout the year. Branches worldwide.

Early English Text Society

Christ Church, Oxford OX1 1DP
Fax 01865 286581
Executive Secretary *R. F. S. Hamer*
(at address above)
Editorial Secretary *Dr H. L. Spencer*
(at Exeter College, Oxford OX1 3DP)
Membership Secretary *Dr W. E. J. Collier*
(at Buffers Cottage, Station Road, Hope, Derbyshire S33 2RR)
Subscription £15 p.a. (UK); $30 (US); $35 (Canada)

FOUNDED 1864. Concerned with the publication of early English texts. Members receive annual publications (one or two a year) or may select titles from the backlist in lieu.

The George Eliot Fellowship

71 Stepping Stones Road, Coventry, Warwickshire CV5 8JT
☎024 7659 2231
Contact *Mrs Kathleen Adams*
Subscription £10 p.a.; £100 (Life); Concessions for pensioners

FOUNDED 1930. Exists to honour George Eliot and promote interest in her life and works. Readings, memorial lecture, birthday luncheon and functions. Issues a quarterly newsletter and an annual journal. Awards an annual prize for a George Eliot essay.

Folly (Fans of Light Literature for the Young)

21 Warwick Road, Pokesdown, Bournemouth, Dorset BH7 6JW
☎01202 432562 Fax 01202 460059
Email folly@sims.abel.co.uk
Contact *Mrs Sue Sims*
Subscription £7.50 p.a. (UK); £9 (Europe); £11 (Worldwide)

FOUNDED 1990 to promote interest in a wide variety of children's authors – with a bias towards writers of girls' books and school stories. *Publishes* three magazines a year.

The Franco-Midland Hardware Company

6 Bramham Moor, Hill Head, Fareham, Hampshire PO14 3RU
☎01329 667325
Email franco.midland@btinternet.com
Website www.btinternet.com/~sherlock.fmhc
Chairman *Philip Weller*
Subscription £15 p.a.

FOUNDED 1989. 'The world's leading Sherlock Holmes correspondence study group and the most active Holmesian society in Britain.' *Publishes* biannual journal, a biannual news magazine and two individual case studies as a subscription package. Also publishes at least four specialist monographs a year. It provides certificated self-study courses and organises monthly functions at Holmes-associated locations. Open membership.

The Friends of Shandy Hall (The Laurence Sterne Trust)

Shandy Hall, Coxwold, York YO61 4AD
☎01347 868465 Fax 01347 868465
Website www.let.ruu.n1/~PeterdeVoogd/shandean.html
Honorary Secretary *Mrs J. Monkman*
Subscription £7 (Annual); £70 (Life)

Promotes interest in the works of Laurence Sterne and aims to preserve the house in which they were created (open to the public). *Publishes* annual journal *The Shandean*. Annual memorial lecture is delivered at Shandy Hall each summer.

The Gaskell Society

Far Yew Tree House, Over Tabley, Knutsford, Cheshire WA16 0HN
☎01565 634668
Email JoanLeach@aol.com
Website www.gaskellsociety.cwc.net
Honorary Secretary *Joan Leach*
Subscription £8 p.a.; £12 (Corporate & Overseas)

FOUNDED 1985 to promote and encourage the study and appreciation of the life and works of Elizabeth Cleghorn Gaskell. Meetings held in Knutsford, Manchester and London; residential study weekends and visits; annual journal and biannual newsletter. On alternate years holds either a residential weekend conference or overseas visit.

The Ghost Story Society

PO Box 1360, Ashcroft, British Columbia
Canada V0K 1A0
☎001 250 453 2045 Fax 001 250 453 2075
Email ashtree@ash-tree.bc.ca
Website www.ash-tree.bc.ca/gss.html
Joint Organisers *Barbara Roden, Christopher Roden*
Subscription UK: £14.50 (Surface mail)/
£16 (Airmail); $25 (US); $31 (Canadian)

FOUNDED 1988. Devoted mainly to supernatural fiction in the literary tradition of M. R. James, Walter de la Mare, Algernon Blackwood, E. F. Benson, A. N. L. Murphy, R. H. Malden, etc. *Publishes* a thrice-yearly journal, *All Hallows*, which includes new fiction in the genre and non-fiction of relevance to the genre.

Graham Greene Birthplace Trust

Rhenigidale, Ivy House Lane, Berkhamsted,
Hertfordshire HP4 2PP
☎01442 865158
Email KSherw9100@aol.com
Website www.zyworld.com/GGBT/home
Secretary *Ken Sherwood*
Subscription £7 (UK, £18 for 3 years);
£9 (Europe, £22); £12 (RoW, £30)

FOUNDED on 2 October 1997, the 93rd anniversary of Graham Greene's birth, to promote the appreciation and study of his works. *Publishes* a newsletter and occasional papers. Organises the Graham Greene Festival.

Rider Haggard Appreciation Society

27 Deneholm, Whitley Bay, Tyne & Wear
NE25 9AU
☎0191 252 4516 Fax 0191 252 4516
Email 106251.3413@compuserve.com
Contact *Roger Allen*
Subscription £8 p.a. (UK); £10 (Overseas)

FOUNDED 1985 to promote appreciation of the life and works of Sir Henry Rider Haggard, English novelist, 1856–1925. News/books exchange, and meetings every two years.

James Hanley Network

Old School House, George Green Road,
George Green, Wexham, Buckinghamshire
SL3 6BJ
☎01753 578632
Email gostick@altavista.net
Website www.jameshanley.mcmail.com/
index.htm
Network Coordinator *Chris Gostick*

An informal international association FOUNDED in 1997 for all those interested in exploring and publicising the works and contribution to literature of the novelist and dramatist James Hanley (1901–1985). *Publishes* an annual newsletter and more formal publications. Occasional conferences are planned for the future. All enquiries welcome.

The Thomas Hardy Society

PO Box 1438, Dorchester, Dorset DT1 1YH
☎01305 251501 Fax 01305 251501
Honorary Secretary *Mrs Olive Blackburn*
Subscription £12 (Individual); £16
(Corporate); £15 (Individual Overseas);
£20 (Corporate Overseas)

FOUNDED 1967 to promote the reading and study of the works and life of Thomas Hardy. Thrice-yearly journal, events and a biennial conference.

The Henty Society

Old Foxes, Kelshall, Royston, Hertfordshire
SG8 9SE
☎01763 287208
Honorary Secretary *Mrs Ann J. King*
Subscription £13 p.a. (UK); £16 (Overseas)

FOUNDED 1977 to study the life and work of George Alfred Henty, and to publish research, bibliographical data and lesser-known works, namely short stories. Organises conferences and social gatherings in the UK and Canada, and *publishes* quarterly bulletins to members. Published in 1996: *G. A. Henty (1832–1902) a Bibliographical Study* by Peter Newbolt.

Sherlock Holmes Society (Northern Musgraves)

Fairbank, Beck Lane, Bingley, West Yorkshire
BD16 4DN
☎01274 563426
Contacts *John Hall, Anne Jordan*
Subscription £17 p.a. (UK)

FOUNDED 1987 to promote enjoyment and study of Sir Arthur Conan Doyle's Sherlock Holmes through publications and meetings. One of the largest Sherlock Holmes societies in Great Britain. Honorary members include Bert Coules, Richard Lancelyn Green, Edward Hardwicke, Michael Williams, Clive Merrison and Douglas Wilmer. Past honorary members: Dame Jean Conan Doyle, Peter Cushing and Jeremy Brett. Open membership. Lectures, presentations and consultation on matters relating to Holmes and Conan Doyle available.

Sherlock Holmes

See **The Franco-Midland Hardware Company**

Hopkins Society

35 Manor Park, Gloddaeth Avenue, Llandudno LL30 2SE
☎01492 878334
Email carolinemay@hopkinsoc.freeserve.co.uk
Contact *Ambrose Boothby*
Subscription £7 p.a. (UK); £10 (Overseas)

FOUNDED 1990 to celebrate the life and work of Gerard Manley Hopkins; to inform members of any publications, courses or events about the poet. Holds an annual lecture on Hopkins in the spring; produces two newsletters a year; sponsors and organises educational projects based on Hopkins' life and works.

Housman Society

80 New Road, Bromsgrove, Worcestershire B60 2LA
☎01527 874136 Fax 01527 837274
Email jimpage@btinternet.com
Website www.knowledge.co.uk/housman/
Contact *Jim Page*
Subscription £10 (UK); £12.50 (Overseas)

FOUNDED 1973 to promote knowledge and appreciation of the lives and work of A. E. Housman and other members of his family, and to promote the cause of literature and poetry. Sponsors a lecture at the **Sunday Times Hay Festival** each year under the title of 'The Name and Nature of Poetry'. *Publishes* an annual journal and biannual newsletter.

W. W. Jacobs Appreciation Society

3 Roman Road, Southwick, West Sussex BN42 4TP
☎01273 871017 Fax 01273 871017
Contact *A. R. James*

FOUNDED 1988 to encourage and promote the enjoyment of the works of W. W. Jacobs, and stimulate research into his life and works. *Publishes* a quarterly newsletter free to those who send s.a.e. (9 × 4ins). Contributions welcome but no payment. Preferred length: 600–1200 words. No subscription charge. Biography, bibliography, directories of plays and films are available for purchase, including *W. W. Jacobs*, a biography published in 1999, price £12, post paid.

Richard Jefferies Society

Eidsvoll, Bedwells Heath, Boars Hill, Oxford OX1 5JE
☎01865 735678

Honorary Secretary *Lady Phyllis Treitel*
Membership Secretary *Mrs Margaret Evans*
Subscription £7 p.a. (Individual); £8 (Joint); Life membership for those over 50

FOUNDED 1950 to promote understanding of the work of Richard Jefferies, nature/country writer, novelist and mystic (1848–87). Produces newsletters, reports and an annual journal; organises talks, discussions and readings. Library and archives. Assists in maintaining the museum in Jefferies' birthplace at Coate near Swindon. Membership applications should be sent to *Margaret Evans*, 23 Hardwell Close, Grove, Nr Wantage, Oxon OX12 0BN.

Jerome K. Jerome Society

c/o Fraser Wood, Mayo and Pinson, 15/16 Lichfield Street, Walsall, West Midlands WS1 1TS
☎01922 629000 Fax 01922 721065
Email tonygray@fraserwood.demon.co.uk
Honorary Secretary *Tony Gray*
Subscription £7 p.a. (Ordinary);
£25 (Corporate); £6 (Joint); £2.50 (Under 21/Over 65)

FOUNDED 1984 to stimulate interest in Jerome K. Jerome's life and works (1859–1927). One of the Society's principal activities is the support of a small museum in the author's birthplace, Walsall. Meetings, lectures, events and a twice-yearly newsletter *Idle Thoughts*. Annual dinner in Walsall near Jerome's birth date (2nd May).

The Captain W. E. Johns Appreciation Society

Nottingham meeting: Wendover, Windy Harbour Lane, Bromley Cross, Bolton, Lancashire BL7 9AP
☎01204 306051
Contacts *Mrs A. Thompson (Nottingham), Joy Tilley (Hertford)*
Hertford meeting: 8 Holmes Close, Castlefields, Stafford ST16 1AR

Society for the appreciation of W. E. Johns, creator of Biggles. Meets twice a year in Nottingham and Hertford. See contacts above.

Johnson Society

Johnson Birthplace Museum, Breadmarket Street, Lichfield, Staffordshire WS13 6LG
☎01543 264972
Hon. General Secretary *Mrs Norma Hooper*
Subscription £7.50 p.a.; £10 (Joint)

FOUNDED 1910 to encourage the study of the

life, works and times of Samuel Johnson (1709–1784) and his contemporaries. The Society is committed to the preservation of the Johnson Birthplace Museum and Johnson memorials.

Johnson Society of London
255 Baring Road, Grove Park, London
SE12 0BQ
☎020 8851 0173
Email JSL@nbbl.demon.co.uk
Website www.nbbl.demon.co.uk/index.html
Honorary Secretary *Mrs Z. E. O'Donnell*
Subscription £10 p.a.; £12.50 (Joint)

FOUNDED 1928 to promote the knowledge and appreciation of Dr Samuel Johnson and his works. *Publishes* an annual journal, *New Rambler* and occasional newsletter. Regular meetings from October to April in the Vestry Hall of St Edmund the King, Lombard Street in London on the second Saturday of each month, and a commemoration ceremony around the anniversary of Johnson's death (December) held in Westminster Abbey.

The Just William Society
18 Colthill Crescent, Milltimber, Aberdeen
AB131 0EG
☎01224 732513
Secretary *Charles Wilson*
Treasurer *Phil Woolley*
Subscription £7 p.a. (UK); £10 (Overseas); £5 (Juvenile/Student); £15 (Family)

FOUNDED 1994 to further knowledge of Richmal Crompton's *William* and *Jimmy* books. An annual 'William' meeting is held in April, although this is not currently organised by the Society. The Honorary President of the Society is Richmal Crompton's niece, Richmal Ashbee.

The Keats–Shelley Memorial Association (Inc)
(Registered office): 1 Lewis Road, Radford Semele, Warwickshire CV31 1UB
Contact *Honorary Secretary* (at 1 Satchwell Walk, Royal Priors, Leamington Spa, Warwickshire CV32 4QE
☎01926 427400 Fax 01926 335133)
Subscription £10 p.a.; £100 (Life)

FOUNDED 1909 to promote appreciation of the works of Keats and Shelley, and their contemporaries. One of the Society's main tasks is the preservation of 26 Piazza di Spagna in Rome as a memorial to the British Romantic poets in Italy, particularly Keats and Shelley. *Publishes* an annual review of Romantic Studies called the *Keats-*

Shelley Review, arranges events and lectures for Friends and promotes bursaries and competitive writing on Romantic Studies. The review is edited by *Angus Graham-Campbell*, c/o Eton College, Windsor, Berkshire SL4 6EA.

The Kenny/Naughton Society
Box No 2000, Aghamore, Ballyhaunis, Co Mayo Republic of Ireland
Chairman *Paul W. D. Rogers*

FOUNDED in 1993 to commemorate two writers who had links with Aghamore: P. D. Kenny, who wrote under the pseudonym 'Pat' and Bill Naughton, best known as the author of *Alfie*. Holds an annual school over the October bank holiday weekend which includes lectures, drama, debate and the **Bill Naughton Short Story Competition** (see entry under **Prizes**).

Kent & Sussex Poetry Society
23 Arundel Road, Tunbridge Wells, Kent
TN1 1TB
☎01892 530438 Fax 01892 522502
Email walter.scape@which.net
Honorary Secretary *Joyce Walter*
Subscription £10 p.a. (Full); £6 (Concessionary – country members living farther afield, senior citizens, under-16s, unemployed)

FOUNDED 1946 to promote the enjoyment of poetry. Monthly meetings are held in Tunbridge Wells, including readings by major poets, a monthly workshop and an annual writing retreat week. *Publishes* an annual folio of members' work based on Members' Competition, adjudicated and commented upon by a major poet, and runs an Open Poetry Competition (see entry under **Prizes**) annually.

The Kilvert Society
The Old Forge, Kinnersley, Hereford
HR3 6QB
☎01544 327426
Secretary *Mr M. Sharp*
Subscription £6 p.a.; £60 (Life)

FOUNDED 1948 to foster an interest in the Diary, the diarist and the countryside he loved. *Publishes* three newsletters each year; during the summer holds three weekends of walks, commemoration services and talks.

The Kipling Society
Tree Cottage, 2 Brownleaf Road, Brighton, East Sussex BN2 6LB
☎01273 303719 Fax 01273 303719
Email kipling@fastmedia.demon.co.uk
Website www.kipling.org.uk

Honorary Secretary *Mr J. W. Michael Smith*
Subscription £20 p.a.

FOUNDED 1927. The Society's main activities are: maintaining a specialised library in London; answering enquiries from the public (schools, publishers, writers and the media); arranging a regular programme of lectures, especially in London and in Sussex, and an annual luncheon with guest speaker; maintaining a small museum and reference at The Grange, in Rottingdean near Brighton; issuing a quarterly journal. (For the Kipling mailbox discussion list, e-mail to: mailbase@mailbase.ac.uk and send following message: 'join rudyard-kipling' then sign your name.) This is a literary society for all who enjoy the prose and verse of Rudyard Kipling (1865–1936) and are interested in his life and times. Please contact the Secretary by letter, telephone, fax or e-mail for further information (brownleaf@btinternet.com).

The Kitley Trust
Toadstone Cottage, Edge View, Litton, Derbyshire SK17 8QU
☎01298 871564
Email stottie2@waitrose.com

Contact *Rosie Ford*

FOUNDED 1990 by a teacher in Sheffield to promote the art of creative writing, in memory of her mother, Jessie Kitley. Activities include: biannual poetry competitions; a 'Get Poetry' day (distribution of children's poems in shopping malls); annual sponsorship of a writer for a school; campaigns; organising conferences for writers and teachers of writing. Funds are provided by donations and profits (if any) from competitions.

Charles Lamb Society
BM Elia, London WC1N 3XX
Subscription £12 p.a. (Single); £18 (Joint & Corporate); US$28 (Overseas Personal); US$42 (Overseas Corporate)

FOUNDED 1935 to promote the study of the life, works and times of English essayist Charles Lamb (1775–1834). Holds regular monthly meetings and lectures in London and organises society events over the summer. Annual luncheon in February. *Publishes* a quarterly bulletin, *The Charles Lamb Bulletin*. Contributions of Elian interest are welcomed by the editor *Rick Tomlinson* at 669 South Monroe Street, Decatur, Illinois 62522–3225, USA (Email kublakhan@poboxes.com). Membership applications should be sent to the box number address above. The Society's library is housed in the **Guildhall**

Library, Aldermanbury, London EC2P 2EJ. Requests to consult printed sources must be made 48 hours in advance by letter to the Principal Reference Librarian, in person at the Printed Books Enquiry Desk or by telephone (020 7332 1868/1870). Member of the **Alliance of Literary Societies**. Registered Charity No: 803222.

Lancashire Authors' Association
Heatherslade, 5 Quakerfields, Westhoughton, Bolton, Lancashire BL5 2BJ
☎01942 791390
Email eholt@cwctv.net

General Secretary *Eric Holt*
Subscription £9 p.a.; £12 (Joint); £1 (Junior)

FOUNDED 1909 for writers and lovers of Lancashire literature and history. Aims to foster and stimulate interest in Lancashire history and literature as well as in the preservation of the Lancashire dialect. Meets four times a year on Saturday at various locations. *Publishes* a quarterly journal called *The Record* which is issued free to members and holds eight annual competitions (open to members only) for both verse and prose. Comprehensive library with access for research to members.

The Philip Larkin Society
c/o Department of English, The University of Hull, Hull HU6 7RX
☎01482 847930 Fax 01482 465641
Email j.booth@english.hull.ac.uk

Contact *Dr James Booth*
Subscription £18 (Full rate); £12 (Unwaged/ Senior Citizen); £8 (Student)

FOUNDED in 1995 to promote awareness of the life and work of Philip Larkin (1922–1985) and his literary contemporaries; to bring together all those who admire Larkin's work as a poet, writer and librarian; to bring about publications on all things Larkinesque. Organises a programme of events ranging from lectures to rambles exploring the countryside of Larkin's schooldays.

The D. H. Lawrence Society
24 Briarwood Avenue, Nottingham NG3 6JQ
☎0115 9503008

Secretary *Ron Faulks*
Subscription £10; £9 (Concession); £11 (Joint); £12 (European); £15 (RoW)

FOUNDED 1974 to increase knowledge and the appreciation of the life and works of D. H. Lawrence. Monthly meetings, addressed by guest speakers, are held in the library at

Eastwood (birthplace of DHL). Organises visits to places of interest in the surrounding countryside, supports the activities of the D. H. Lawrence Centre at Nottingham University, and has close links with DHL Societies worldwide. *Publishes* two newsletters and one journal each year, free to members.

The T. E. Lawrence Society

PO Box 728, Oxford OX2 6YP
Website www.telawrence.org
Contact *Gigi Horsfield*
Subscription £15 (UK); £20 (Overseas)

FOUNDED 1985 as a non-profit making, educational, registered charity to advance awareness of the life and work of Thomas Edward Lawrence and to promote research into his life and work. *Publishes* four newsletters and two journals per year. A biennial symposium is held, usually in Oxford, to bring members together to share both academic and social interests. The Society encourages the formation of regional groups of which, currently, there are seven: three in England (Northwest, London, Dorset), one in Europe (Netherlands), two in the USA (Eastern and Western States) and one in Japan.

The Leamington Literary Society

15 Church Hill, Leamington Spa,
Warwickshire CV32 5AZ
☎01926 425733
Honorary Secretary *Mrs Margaret Watkins*
Subscription £10 p.a.

FOUNDED 1912 to promote the study and appreciation of literature and the arts. Holds regular meetings every second Tuesday of the month (except August) at the Royal Pump Rooms, Leamington Spa. The Society has published various books of local interest.

Lewes Monday Literary Club

c/o 12 Little East Street, Lewes, East Sussex
BN7 2NU
☎01273 472658
Email cm@aubrey1626.freeserve.co.uk
Contact *Mrs Christine Mason*
Subscription £15 p.a.; £3 (Guest, per meeting)

FOUNDED in 1948 for the promotion and enjoyment of literature. Seven meetings are held during the winter on the last Monday of each month (from October to April) at the White Hart Hotel in Lewes. The Club attracts speakers of the highest quality and a balance between all forms of literature is aimed for. Guests are welcome to attend meetings.

Wyndham Lewis Society

18 Coltsfoot Road, Ware, Hertfordshire
SG12 7NW Email sam_brown@lineone.net
Contact *Mrs Sam Brown*
Subscription £10 p.a. (UK/Europe); £12 p.a. (Institutions); US$25 (Rest of World); US$30 (Institutions, RoW) – all cheques payable to the Wyndham Lewis Society

FOUNDED 1974 to promote recognition of the value of Lewis's works and encourage scholarly research on the man, his painting and his writing. *Publishes* inaccessible Lewis writings; the annual society journal (*The Wyndham Lewis Annual*) plus two newsletters; and reproduces Lewis's paintings.

The Friends of Arthur Machen

Clemendy Cottage, 14 New Market Street,
Usk, Gwent NP5 1AT
☎01291 672869
Email adrian@machensoc.demon.co.uk
Website www.machensoc.demon.co.uk/welcome.htm
Contact *Godfrey Brangham*
Subscription £15 p.a. (UK); £18 (US)

FOUNDED 1998. (Formerly the Arthur Machen Society.) Promotes a wider readership of Arthur Machen and a greater understanding of his life and work. Members receive hardback journals (*Faunus*) and newsletters (*Machenalia*). 'While stocks last, new members also receive a hardback book, *Precious Balms*.'

The John Masefield Society

The Frith, Ledbury, Herefordshire HR8 1LW
☎01531 631647   Fax 01531 631647
Email petercarter@btinternet.com
Website www.ucl.ac.uk/~uczzpwe/jms6.htm
Chairman *Peter Carter*
Subscription £5 p.a. (Individual); £8 (Family, Institutions, Libraries)' £10 (Overseas); £2.50 (Junior, Student)

FOUNDED in 1992 to stimulate the appreciation of and interest in the life and works of John Masefield (Poet Laureate 1930–1967). The Society is based in Ledbury, the Herefordshire market town of his birth and holds various public events in addition to publishing a journal and occasional papers.

William Morris Society

Kelmscott House, 26 Upper Mall,
Hammersmith, London W6 9TA
☎020 8741 3735
Contact *Helen Elletson*

Subscription £13.50 p.a.

FOUNDED 1953 to promote interest in the life, work and ideas of William Morris (1834–1896), English poet and craftsman.

The Neil Munro Society
8 Briar Road, Kirkintilloch, Glasgow
G66 3SA
☎0141 776 4280
Email brian@bdosborne.demon.co.uk
Secretary *Brian D. Osborne*
Subscription £8 (Annual); £9 (Family);
    £5 (Unwaged); £15 (Institutional)

FOUNDED in 1996 to encourage interest in the works of Neil Munro (1863–1930), the Scottish novelist, short story writer, poet and journalist. An annual programme of meetings is held in Glasgow and Munro's home-town of Inveraray. *Publishes ParaGraphs*, a twice-yearly magazine, sponsors reprints of Munro's work and is developing a Munro archive.

Bill Naughton
See **The Kenny/Naughton Society**

Violet Needham Society
c/o 19 Ashburnham Place, London
SE10 8TZ
☎020 8692 4562
Honorary Secretary *R. H. A. Cheffins*
Subscription £6 p.a. (UK & Europe);
    £9 (outside Europe)

FOUNDED 1985 to celebrate the work of children's author Violet Needham and stimulate critical awareness of her work. *Publishes* thrice-yearly *Souvenir*, the Society journal with an accompanying newsletter; organises meetings and excursions to places associated with the author and her books. The journal includes articles about other children's writers of the 1940s and '50s and on ruritanian fiction. Contributions welcome.

The Edith Nesbit Society
73 Brookehowse Road, London SE6 3TH
Chairman *Nicholas Reed*
Secretary *Margaret McCarthy*
Subscription £5 p.a.; £7.50 (Joint);
    £50 (Life)

FOUNDED in 1996 to celebrate the life and work of Edith Nesbit (1858–1924), best known as the author of *The Railway Children*. The Society's activities include a regular newsletter, booklets, talks and visits to relevant places.

The Wilfred Owen Association
17 Belmont, Shrewsbury, Shropshire
SY1 1TE
☎01743 235904
Website www.wilfred.owen.mcmail.com
Chairman *Helen McPhail*
Subscription Adults £4 (£6 Overseas);
    £2 (Senior Citizens/Students/Unemployed);
    £10 (Groups/Institutions)

FOUNDED 1989 to commemorate the life and works of Wilfred Owen by promoting readings, visits, talks and performances relating to Owen and his work, and supporting appropriate academic and creative projects. Membership is international with 600 members. *Publishes* a newsletter twice a year. Speakers are available for schools or clubs, etc.

The Elsie Jeanette Oxenham Appreciation Society
32 Tadfield Road, Romsey, Hampshire
SO51 5AJ
☎01794 517149 Fax 01794 517149
Email abbey@bufobooks.demon.co.uk
Websites: ds.dial.pipex.com/ct/ejo.html *and*
www.bufobooks.demon.co.uk/abbeylnk.htm
Contact *Ms Ruth Allen (Editor, The Abbey Chronicle)*
Subscription £6 p.a.; enquire for Overseas rates

FOUNDED 1989 to promote the works of Elsie J. Oxenham. Publishes a newsletter for members, *The Abbey Chronicle*, three times a year.

Thomas Paine Society
43 Wellington Gardens, Selsey, West Sussex
PO20 0RF
☎01243 605730
President *The Rt. Hon. Michael Foot*
Honorary Secretary/Treasurer *Eric Paine* (at address above)
Subscription (Minimum) £10 p.a. (UK);
    $20 (Overseas); £5 (Unwaged/Pensioners/Students)

FOUNDED 1963 to promote the life and work of Thomas Paine, and continues to expound his ideals. Meetings, newsletters, lectures and research assistance. Membership badge. The Society has members worldwide and keeps in touch with American and French Thomas Paine associations. *Publishes* magazine, *Bulletin*, twice yearly (Editor: R. W. Morrell, 43 Eugene Gardens, Nottingham NG2 3LF) and holds occasional exhibitions and talks on Paine's life.

Mervyn Peake Society

2 Mount Park Road, Ealing, London
W5 2RP
☎020 8566 9307 Fax 020 8991 0559
Email 101367.1376@compuserve.com
Contact *Frank Surry*
Subscription £12 p.a. (UK & Europe);
£5 (Students/OAP/Unwaged);
£12 (Institutions); £14 (RoW); £16
(Institutions overseas)

FOUNDED 1975 to promote a wider understanding of Mervyn Peake's achievements as novelist, poet, painter and illustrator. Membership is open to all, irrespective of native language or country of residence. *Publishes The Mervyn Peake Review* annually and the *MPS Newsletter* quarterly. AGM held annually.

The John Polidori Literary Society

City Lights Magazine, PO Box 7068,
Nottingham NG16 4HX
Founder & President *Franklin Charles Bishop*
Subscription £30 p.a.

FOUNDED 1990 to promote and encourage appreciation of the life and works of John William Polidori MD (1795–1821) – novelist, poet, tragedian, philosopher, diarist, essayist, reviewer, traveller and one of the youngest students to obtain a medical degree (at the age of 19). He was one-time intimate of the leading figures in the Romantic movement and travelling companion and private physician to Lord Byron. He was a pivotal figure in the infamous Villa Diodati ghost story sessions in which he assisted Mary Shelley in the creation of her *Frankenstein* tale. Polidori introduced into literature the enduring icon of the vampire portrayed as an aristocratic, handsome seducer with his seminal work *The Vampyre – A Tale*, published in 1819. Polidori was honoured in 1998 by the erection of a City of Westminster Plaque at his birthplace – 38 Great Pulteney Street, Westminster, London – by the Italian ambassador. The Society issues unique publications of the rare works of Polidori. International membership in Italy, USA, Canada and Spain.

The Beatrix Potter Society

Administration Office, Resources for Business,
South Park Road, Macclesfield SK11 6SH
☎01625 267880 Fax 01625 267879
Email bps@resources.demon.co.uk
Subscription UK: £10 p.a. (Individual);
£15 (Institution); Overseas: £15 (or US$25/
Can./ Aust.$30, Individual); £22 (US$35/

Can./Aust.$47, Institution)

FOUNDED 1980 to promote the study and appreciation of the life and works of Beatrix Potter (1866–1943). Potter was not only the author of *The Tale of Peter Rabbit* and other classics of children's literature; she was also a landscape and natural history artist, diarist, farmer and conservationist, and was responsible for the preservation of large areas of the Lake District through her gifts to the National Trust. The Society upholds and protects the integrity of the inimitable and unique work of the lady, her aims and bequests. Holds regular talks and meetings in London with visits to places connected with Beatrix Potter. Biennial International Study Conferences are held in the UK and occasionally in the USA. The Society has an active publishing programme.

The Powys Society

The Old School House, George Green Road,
George Green, Wexham, Buckinghamshire
SL3 6BJ
☎01753 578632
Email gostick@altavista.net
Website www.iaehv.nl/users/tklijn/pws/
powys.htm
Honorary Secretary *Chris Gostick*
Subscription £13.50 (UK); £16 (Overseas);
£6 (Students)

The Society (with a membership of 350) aims to promote public education and recognition of the writings, thought and contribution to the arts of the Powys family; particularly of John Cowper, Theodore and Llewelyn, but also of the other members of the family and their close associates. The Society holds two major collections of Powys published works, letters, manuscripts and memorabilia. *Publishes* the *Powys Society Newsletter* in April, June and November and *The Powys Journal* in August. Organises an annual conference as well as lectures and meetings in Powys places.

The Queen's English Society

Fernwood, Nightingales, West Chiltington,
Pulborough, West Sussex RH20 2QT
☎01798 813001
Membership Secretary *David Ellis*
Subscription £10 p.a. (Ordinary);
£12 (Family/Corporate); £100 (Life
member); reduced rates available for
students and long-term unemployed

FOUNDED to promote and uphold the use of good English and to encourage the enjoyment of the language. 'The Society aims to defend the precision, subtlety and marvellous richness of our language against debasement, ambiguity and other forms of misuse.' *Publishes* a monthly journal, *Quest*.

The Arthur Ransome Society Ltd

Abbot Hall Art Gallery, Kirkland, Kendal, Cumbria LA9 5AL
☎01539 722464 Fax 01539 722494
Website www.arthur-ransome.org/ar
Chairman *Roger Wardale*
Secretary *Bill Janes*
Subscription £5 (Junior); £10 (Student); £15 (Adult); £20 (Family); £40 (Corporate); Overseas: £5 (Junior); £20 (Adult); £25 (Family)

FOUNDED 1990 to celebrate the life and promote the works and ideas of Arthur Ransome, author of the world-famous *Swallows and Amazons* titles for children and biographer of Oscar Wilde. TARS seeks to encourage children and adults to engage in adventurous pursuits, to educate the public about Ransome and his works, and to sponsor research into his literary works and life.

The Followers of Rupert

31 Whiteley, Windsor, Berkshire SL4 5PJ
☎01753 865562
Email followersofrupert@hotmail.com
Membership Secretary *Mrs Shirley Reeves*
Subscription UK: £9.50; £11.50 (Joint); Europe, airmail: £10.50 (Individual); £12.50 (Joint); Worldwide, airmail: £12.50 (Individual); £14.50 (Joint)

FOUNDED in 1983. The Society caters for the growing interest in the Rupert Bear stories, past, present and future. *Publishes* the *Nutwood Newsletter* quarterly which gives up-to-date news of Rupert and information on Society activities. A national get-together of members – the Followers Annual – is held during the autumn.

The Ruskin Society (affiliated to The Ruskin Foundation)

49 Hallam Street, London W1N 5LN
☎020 7580 1894
Honorary Secretary *Dr Cynthia. J. Gamble*
Honorary Treasurer *The Hon. Mrs Catherine Edwards*
Subscription £10 p.a. (payable on January 1st)

FOUNDED in 1997 to encourage a wider understanding of John Ruskin and his contemporaries. Organises lectures and events which seek not only to explain to the public at large the nature of Ruskin's theories but also to place these in a modern context. Promotes and organises publications and exhibitions in conjunction with the Ruskin Foundation.

The Ruskin Society of London

351 Woodstock Road, Oxford OX2 7NX
☎01865 310987/515962 Fax 01865 240448
Honorary Secretary *Miss O. E. Forbes-Madden*
Subscription £10 p.a.

FOUNDED 1986 to promote interest in John Ruskin (1819–1900) and his contemporaries. All aspects of Ruskinia are introduced. Functions are held in London. *Publishes* the annual *Ruskin Gazette*, a journal concerned with Ruskin's influence.

The Malcolm Saville Society

10 Bilford Road, Worcester WR3 8QA
Email mystery@witchend.demon.co.uk
General Secretary *Mark O'Hanlon*
Subscription £7.50 p.a. (UK); £12 (Overseas)

FOUNDED in 1994 to remember and promote interest in the work of the popular children's author. Regular social activities, booksearch, library, contact directory and three magazines per year.

The Dorothy L. Sayers Society

Rose Cottage, Malthouse Lane, Hurstpierpoint, West Sussex BN6 9JY
☎01273 833444 Fax 01273 835988
Website www.sayers.org.uk
Contact *Christopher Dean*
Subscription £14 p.a.; US$28 p.a.

FOUNDED 1976 to promote the study of the life, works and thoughts of Dorothy Sayers; to encourage the performance of her plays and publication of her books and books about her; to preserve original material and provide assistance to researchers. Acts as a forum and information centre, providing material for study purposes which would otherwise be unavailable. Annual seminars and other meetings. Co-founder of the Dorothy L. Sayers Centre in Witham. *Publishes* bi-monthly bulletin, annual proceedings and other papers.

The Bernard Shaw Information & Research Service

Yearnshaw House, 5 Singret Place, Cowley, Uxbridge, Middlesex UB8 2NU
Email gbshaw@georgebernardshaw.net
Website www.georgebernardshaw.net
Contact *Diane S. Uttley*

ESTABLISHED in 1997 by writer and Shaw specialist Diane S. Uttley who was custodian of and lived in the writer's home, Shaw's Corner, from 1989 to 1997. The service is used by enthusiasts and academics; literary, theatrical and biographical.

The Shaw Society

51 Farmfield Road, Downham, Bromley, Kent BR1 4NF
☎020 8697 3619 Fax 020 8697 3619
Honorary Secretary *Ms Barbara Smoker*
Subscription £12 p.a. (Individual);
    £18 (Joint)

FOUNDED 1941 to promote interest in the life and works of G. Bernard Shaw. Meetings are held on the last Friday of every month (except July, August and December) at Conway Hall, Red Lion Square, London WC1 (6.30pm for 7pm) at which speakers are invited to talk on some aspect of Shaw's life or works. Monthly playreadings are held on the first Friday of each month (except August). A 'Birthday Tribute' is held at Shaw's Corner, Ayot St Lawrence in Hertfordshire, on the weekend nearest to Shaw's birthday (26th July). *Publishes* a quarterly newsletter and a magazine, *The Shavian*, which appears approximately every nine months. (No payment for contributors.)

The Robert Southey Society

1 Lewis Terrace, Abergarwed, Neath SA11 4DL
☎01639 711480
Contact *Robert King*
Subscription £10 p.a.

FOUNDED 1990 to promote the work of Robert Southey. *Publishes* an annual newsletter and arranges talks on his life and work. Open membership.

The Laurence Sterne Trust

See **The Friends of Shandy Hall**

Robert Louis Stevenson Club

37 Lauder Road, Edinburgh EH9 1UE
☎0131 667 6256 Fax 0131 662 0353
Email mbeanconferences@compuserve.com
Contact *Margaret Bean, MA*
Subscription £15 p.a.; £100 (Life)

FOUNDED in 1920 to foster interest in Robert Louis Stevenson's life and works. The Club organises an annual lunch and other events. *Publishes RLS Club News* three times a year.

The R. S. Surtees Society

Manor Farm House, Nunney, Near Frome, Somerset BA11 4NJ
☎01373 836937 Fax 01373 836574
Email 101657.673@compuserve.com
Website www.clique.co.uk/r.s.surteessociety
Contact *Orders and Membership Secretary*
Subscription £10

FOUNDED 1979 to republish the works of R. S. Surtees and others.

The Tennyson Society

Central Library, Free School Lane, Lincoln LN2 1EZ
☎01522 552862 Fax 01522 552858
Email kathleenjefferson@lincolnshire.gov.uk
Honorary Secretary *Miss K. Jefferson*
Subscription £8 p.a. (Individual);
    £10 (Family); £15 (Corporate);
    £125 (Life)

FOUNDED 1960. An international society with membership worldwide. Exists to promote the study and understanding of the life and work of Alfred, Lord Tennyson. The Society is concerned with the work of the Tennyson Research Centre, 'probably the most significant collection of mss, family papers and books in the world'. *Publishes* annually the *Tennyson Research Bulletin*, which contains articles and critical reviews; and organises lectures, visits and seminars. Annual memorial service at Somersby in Lincolnshire.

The Dylan Thomas Society of Great Britain

Llwyncelyn, Upland Arms, Carmarthen, Carmarthenshire SA32 8DX
☎01267 233742
Contact *J. Rodney Hughes*
Subscription £5 (Individual); £8 (2 adults from same household)

FOUNDED 1977 to foster an understanding of the work of Dylan Thomas and to extend members' awareness of other 20th century writers, especially Welsh writers in English. Meetings take place monthly, mainly in Swansea.

The Edward Thomas Fellowship

Butlers Cottage, Halswell House, Goathurst, Bridgwater, Somerset TA5 2DH
☎01278 662856
Secretary *Richard Emeny*
Subscription £7 p.a. (Single); £10 p.a. (Joint)

FOUNDED 1980 to perpetuate and promote the memory of Edward Thomas and to encourage an appreciation of his life and work. The Fellowship holds a commemorative birthday walk on the Sunday nearest the poet's birthday, 3 March; issues newsletters and holds various events.

The Tolkien Society

65 Wentworth Crescent, Ash Vale, Surrey GU12 5LF Fax 0870 0525569
Email membership@tolkiensociety.org
Website www.tolkiensociety.org
Membership Secretary *Trevor Reynolds*
Subscription £20 p.a. (UK); £22 (Overseas)

An international organisation which aims to encourage and further interest in the life and works of the late Professor J. R. R. Tolkien, CBE, author of *The Hobbit* and *Lord of the Rings*. Current membership stands at 620. *Publishes Mallorn* annually and *Amon Hen* bi-monthly.

The Trollope Society

9A North Street, Clapham, London SW4 0HN
☎020 7720 6789 Fax 020 7978 1815
Contacts *John Letts, Phyllis Eden*

FOUNDED 1987 to study and promote Anthony Trollope's works. Linked with the publication of the first complete uniform edition of his novels.

Edgar Wallace Society

Kohlbergsgracht 40, 6462 CD Kerkrade, The Netherlands
☎00 31 455 67 0070 Fax 00 31 455 67 0060
Organiser *K. J. Hinz*
Subscription £15 p.a.; £10 (Senior Citizens/ Students); Overseas: £20; £15 (Senior Citizens/Students)

FOUNDED 1969 by Wallace's daughter, Penelope, to bring together all who have an interest in Edgar Wallace. Members receive a brief biography of Edgar by Penelope Wallace, with a complete list of all published book titles. A quarterly newsletter, *Crimson Circle*, is published in February, May, August and November.

The Walmsley Society

April Cottage, No 1 Brand Road, Hampden Park, Eastbourne, East Sussex BN22 9PX
☎01323 506447
Email walmsley@haughshw.demon.co.uk
Honorary Secretary *Fred Lane*
Subscription £8 p.a.; £10 (Family);
£7 (Students/Senior Citizens);
£15 (Overseas, £25 for 2 years)

FOUNDED 1985 to promote interest in the art and writings of Ulric and Leo Walmsley. Two annual meetings – one held in Robin Hood's Bay on East Yorkshire coast, spiritual home of the author Leo Walmsley. The Society also seeks to foster appreciation of the work of his father Ulric Walmsley. *Publishes* a journal twice-yearly and newsletters, and is involved in other publications which benefit the aims of the Society.

Sylvia Townsend Warner Society

2 Vicarage Lane, Dorchester, Dorset DT1 1LH
☎01305 266028
Email tartarus@pavilion.co.uk
Contact *Eileen Johnson*
Website: www.freepages.pavilion.net/users/ tartarus/warner1.htm
Subscription £10 p.a.; $20 (Overseas)

FOUNDED in 2000 to promote a wider readership and better understanding of the writings of Sylvia Townsend Warner.

Mary Webb Society

8 The Knowle, Willaston, Neston, South Wirral CH64 1TA
Website www.wlv.ac.uk/~me1927/ mwebb.html/
Secretary *Sue Higginbotham*
Subscription £7.50 p.a.

FOUNDED 1972. Attracts members from the UK and overseas who are devotees of the literature of Mary Webb and of the beautiful Shropshire countryside of her novels. *Publishes* annual journal in September, organises summer schools in various locations related to the authoress's life and works. Archives; lectures; tours arranged for individuals and groups.

H. G. Wells Society

49 Beckingthorpe Drive, Bottesford, Nottingham NG13 0DN
Website www.rdg.ac.uk/~lhsjamse/wells/wells.htm
Honorary Secretary *J. R. Hammond*
Subscription £16 (UK/EU); £19 (Overseas); £20 (Corporate); £10 (Concessions)

FOUNDED 1960 to promote an interest in and appreciation of the life, work and thought of Herbert George Wells. *Publishes The Wellsian* (annual) and *The H. G. Wells Newsletter* (bi-annual). Organises meetings and conferences.

The Charles Williams Society

3 The Rise, Islip, Kidlington, Oxfordshire OX5 2TG
Email rsturch@compuserve.com
Contact *Honorary Secretary*

FOUNDED 1975 to promote interest in, and

provide a means for the exchange of views and information on the life and work of Charles Walter Stansby Williams (1886–1945).

The Henry Williamson Society

16 Doran Drive, Redhill, Surrey RH1 6AX
☎01737 763228
Website www.hwsoc.org.uk
Membership Secretary *Mrs Margaret Murphy*
Subscription £12 p.a.; £15 (Family);
£5 (Students)

FOUNDED 1980 to encourage, by all appropriate means, a wider readership and deeper understanding of the literary heritage left by the 20th-century English writer Henry Williamson (1895–1977). *Publishes* annual journal.

The P. G. Wodehouse Society

16 Herbert Street, Plaistow, London E13 8BE
Website www.eclipse.co.uk/wodehouse
Membership Secretary *Helen Murphy*
Subscription £15 p.a.

Relaunched in May 1997 to advance the genius of P. G. Wodehouse. Publications include the *Wooster Source* quarterly journal and the *By The Way* newsletter. Regular national/international group meetings (members in most countries throughout the world). Society patrons include Rt. Hon. Tony Blair MP, Sir Edward Cazelet (Wodehouse's grandson) and Stephen Fry.

The Virginia Woolf Society of Great Britain

c/o 69 Rope Street, London SE16 7TF
☎020 7394 1050
Email snclarke@talk21.com
Website orlando.jp.org/vwsgb/
Contact *Stuart N. Clarke*
Subscription £12 p.a.; £15 (Overseas)

FOUNDED 1998 to promote interest in the life and work of Virginia Woolf, author, essayist and diarist. The Society's activities include trips away, walks, reading groups and talks. *Publishes* a literary journal, *Virginia Woolf Bulletin* three times a year.

WW2 HMSO PPBKS Society

3 Roman Road, Southwick, West Sussex BN42 4TP
☎01273 871017   Fax 01273 871017
Contact *A. R. James*
Subscription £2 p.a.

FOUNDED 1994 to encourage collectors and to promote research into HMSO's World War II series of paperbacks. Most were written by well-

known authors, though in many cases anonymously. *Publishes* bi-monthly newsletter (send s.a.e. 9×4″). Contributions of 600–1200 words welcome, but no payment. Available for purchase: Collectors' Guide, £5; bibliography, £3; handbook, *Informing the People*, £10.

The Yeats Society Sligo

Yeats Memorial Building, Douglas Hyde Bridge, Sligo Republic of Ireland
☎00 353 71 42693   Fax 00 353 71 42780
Email yeatsoity@eircom.net
Website www.itsligo.ie/yeats/yeats.html
Director *Marian F. Quinn*
Subscription £15 (Single); £25 (Couple);
£100 (Corporate); £10 (Overseas)

FOUNDED in 1958 to promote the heritage of W. B. Yeats and the Yeats family. Attractions include continuous updated Yeats exhibitions for public viewing, annual Yeats International Summer School in August and Yeats Winter School in January. The Yeats Summer Festival is held each August and lectures are held in the winter and spring, sponsored by the Institute of Technology, Sligo. *Publishes* a newsletter and organises year-round events/programmes in arts, culture, education for writers' groups, poetry/drama groups, etc.

Yorkshire Dialect Society

51 Stepney Avenue, Scarborough, North Yorkshire YO12 5BW
Secretary *Michael Park*
Subscription £7 p.a.

FOUNDED 1897 to promote interest in and preserve a record of the Yorkshire dialect. *Publishes* dialect verse and prose writing. Two journals to members annually. Details of publications are available from the Librarian, YDS, School of English, University of Leeds, Leeds, West Yorkshire LS2 9JT.

Francis Brett Young Society

92 Gower Road, Halesowen, West Midlands B62 9BT
☎0121 422 8969
Honorary Secretary *Mrs Jean Hadley*
Subscription £7 p.a. (Individuals); £10
(Couples sharing a journal); £5 (Students);
£7 (Organisations/Overseas); £70 (Life);
£100 (Joint, Life)

FOUNDED 1979. Aims to provide a forum for those interested in the life and works of English novelist Francis Brett Young and to collate research on him. Promotes lectures, exhibitions and readings; *publishes* a regular newsletter.

Arts Councils and Regional Arts Boards

The Arts Council of England

14 Great Peter Street, London SW1P 3NQ
☎020 7333 0100/Minicom: 020 7973 6564
Fax 020 7973 6590
Email enquiries@artscouncil.org.uk
Website www.artscouncil.org.uk

Chairman *Gerry Robinson*
Chief Executive *Peter Hewitt*

The Arts Council of England is undergoing a substantial change of role and function which aims to serve the arts, artists and audiences more effectively. One of the imperatives guiding this change is the belief that arts activity should be funded as close to its source as possible. This will result in the devolution of Development Fund monies to Regional Arts Boards and, where appropriate, the delegation of Arts Council funded organisations to Regional Arts Boards.

For details of funding available in 2000/2001, please contact the Information Department, ☎020 7973 6517 or e-mail.

The Irish Arts Council/
An Chomhairle Ealaion

70 Merrion Square, Dublin 2
☎00 353 1 6180200 Fax 00 353 1 6761302

Literature Officer *Sinead MacAodha*

The Irish Arts Council has programmes under six headings to assist in the area of literature and book promotion: a) Writers; b) Literary Organisations; c) Publishers; d) Literary Magazines; e) Participation Programmes; f) Literary Events and Festivals. It also gives a number of annual bursaries (see **Arts Council Literature Bursaries, Ireland** under **Bursaries, Fellowships and Grants**).

The Arts Council of
Northern Ireland

MacNeice House, 77 Malone Road, Belfast BT9 6AQ
☎028 9038 5200 Fax 028 9066 1715

Literature Arts Officer *John Brown*

Funds book production by established publishers, programmes of readings, literary festivals, writers-in-residence schemes and literary maga-zines and periodicals. Occasional schools pro-grammes and anthologies of children's writing are produced. Annual awards and bursaries for writers are available. Holds information also on various groups associated with local arts, work-shops and courses.

Scottish Arts Council

12 Manor Place, Edinburgh EH3 7DD
☎0131 226 6051 Fax 0131 225 9833
Email administrator@scottisharts.org.uk
Website www.sac.org.uk

Chairman *Magnus Linklater*
Director *Tessa Jackson*
Literature Director *Jenny Brown*
Literature Officer *Gavin Wallace*
Literature Secretary *Catherine Allan*

Principal channel for government funding of the arts in Scotland. The Scottish Arts Council (SAC) is funded by the Scottish Executive. It aims to develop and improve the knowledge, understanding and practice of the arts, and to increase their accessibility throughout Scotland. It offers around 1300 grants a year to artists and arts organisations concerned with the visual arts, dance and mime, drama, literature, music, festi-vals and traditional, ethnic and community arts. It is also a distributor of National Lottery funds to the arts in Scotland. SAC's support for Scottish-based writers with a track record of publication includes bursaries, writing and trans-lation fellowships (see entries under **Bursaries, Fellowships and Grants**). Information offered includes lists of literary awards, literary maga-zines, agents and publishers.

The Arts Council of Wales

Museum Place, Cardiff CF1 3NX
☎029 2037 6500 Fax 029 2022 1447
Website www.ccc-acw.org.uk

Senior Literature Officer *Tony Bianchi*
Senior Officer: Dance and Drama
  Anna Holmes

Funds literary magazines and book production; *Writers on Tour* and bursary schemes; **Welsh Academy**, **Welsh Books Council**, **Hay-on-Wye Literature Festival** and **Tŷ Newydd Writers' Centre** at Cricieth; also children's literature, annual awards and translation projects. The Council aims to develop theatrical experience among Wales-based writers through a variety of schemes – in particular, by funding writers on year-long attachments.

English Regional Arts Boards
5 City Road, Winchester, Hampshire SO23 8SD
☎01962 851063 Fax 01962 842033
Email info@erab.org.uk
Website www.arts.org.uk
Chief Executive *Christopher Gordon*
Assistant *Carolyn Nixson*

English Regional Arts Boards is the representative body for the 10 Regional Arts Boards (RABs) in England. Its Winchester secretariat provides project management, services and information for the members, and acts on their behalf in appropriate circumstances. Scotland, Northern Ireland and Wales have their own Arts Councils. The three former Welsh Regional Arts Associations are now absorbed into the Arts Council of Wales. RABs are support and development agencies for the arts in the regions. Policies are developed in response to regional demand, and to assist new initiatives in areas of perceived need; they may vary from region to region. The RABs are now responsible for the distribution of Arts Council Lottery funding for capital and revenue projects under £100,000.

SUPPORT FOR WRITERS
All the Regional Arts Boards offer support for professional creative writers through a range of grants, awards, advice, information and contacts. Interested writers should contact the Board in whose region they live or access the RAB pages on the website.

East Midlands Arts
Mountfields House, Epinal Way, Loughborough, Leicestershire LE11 0QE
☎01509 218292 Fax 01509 262214
Email info@ema-arts.co.uk
Literature Officer *Sue Stewart*
Drama Officer *Helen Flach*

Covers Leicestershire, Rutland, Lincolnshire, Nottinghamshire, Derbyshire (excluding the High Peak district) and Northamptonshire. A comprehensive information service for regional writers includes an extensive *Writers' Information Pack*, with details of local groups, workshops, residential writing retreats, publishers and publishing information, regional magazines which offer a market for work, advice on approaching the media, on unions, courses and grants. Also

available is a directory of writers, primarily to aid people wishing to organise workshops, readings or writer's attachments. Writers' awards are granted for work on a specific project – all forms of writing are eligible except for local history and biography. Writing for the theatre can come under the aegis of both Literature and Drama. A list of writers' groups is available, plus *Foreword*, the literature newsletter.

Eastern Arts Board
Cherry Hinton Hall, Cambridge CB1 4DW
☎01223 215355 Fax 01223 248075
Literature Officer *Emma Drew*
Drama Officer *Alan Orme*
Cinema & Broadcast Media Officer
  Martin Ayres

Covers Bedfordshire, Cambridgeshire, Essex, Hertfordshire, Norfolk and Suffolk. Policy emphasises quality and access. Support is given to publishers and literature promoters based in the EAB region, also to projects which develop audiences for literature performances and publishing, including electronic media. Bursaries are offered annually to individual published writers. Supplies lists of literary groups, workshops, local writing courses and writers working in the educational sector. Also provides advice on applying for National Lottery funds.

London Arts Board
Elme House, 3rd Floor, 133 Long Acre, London WC2E 9AF
☎020 7240 1313 Fax 020 7670 2400
Literature Administrator *Sarah Sanders*
Drama Administrator *Vicky Reece*

The London Arts Board is the Regional Arts Board for the Capital, covering the 32 boroughs and the City of London. Potential applicants for support for literature and other arts projects should contact the Board for information.

North West Arts Board
Manchester House, 22 Bridge Street, Manchester M3 3AB
☎0161 834 6644 Fax 0161 834 6969
Email nwarts-info@mcrl.poptel.org.uk
Arts Officer – Literature *Bronwen Williams*
  (E-mail: bwilliams@nwarts.co.uk)
Arts Officer – Drama *Ian Tabbron*
  (Email itabbron@nwarts.co.uk)

NWAB covers Cheshire, Greater Manchester, Merseyside, Lancashire and the High Peak district of Derbyshire. Offers financial assistance to a great variety of organisations and individuals through a number of schemes, including

Writers' Bursaries, Residencies and Placements and the Live Writing scheme. NWAB publishes a directory of local writers groups, a directory of writers and a range of information covering topics such as performance and publishing. For further details please contact the Literature or Drama Departments.

Northern Arts Board

9–10 Osborne Terrace, Jesmond, Newcastle upon Tyne NE2 1NZ
☎0191 281 6334 Fax 0191 281 3276
Email nab@norab.demon.co.uk
Website www.poptel/org.uk/arts/
Head of Film, Media and Literature
  Janice Campbell

Covers Cumbria, Durham, Northumberland, Teesside and Tyne and Wear, and was the first regional arts association in the country to be set up by local authorities. It supports both organisations and writers and aims to stimulate public interest in artistic events. The Northern Writers Awards scheme is operated through **New Writing North** (see entry under **Professional Associations and Societies**). Northern Arts also has a film/TV script development fund operated through the Northern Production Fund. A separate scheme for playwrights is operated by the Northern Playwrights Society. Northern Arts makes drama awards to producers only. Also funds writers' residencies, and has a fund for publications. Contact list of regional groups available.

South East Arts

Union House, Eridge Road, Tunbridge Wells, Kent TN4 8HF
☎01892 507200 Fax 01892 549383
Email info@seab.co.
Website www.arts.org.uk
Literature Officer *Suzy Joinson*
Drama Officer *Judith Hibberd*

Covers Kent, Surrey, East Sussex, West Sussex, Brighton and Hove and Medway (excluding the London boroughs). Grant schemes accessible to all art forms in the areas of new work, presentation of work and venue development. Awards for individuals include training bursaries and writers' awards schemes. The literature programme aims to raise the profile of contemporary literature in the region and encourage creative writing and reading development projects. Priorities include live literature, writers and readers in residence and training bursaries for writers resident in the region. A regular feature on literature appears in the *Arts News* newsletter.

South West Arts

Bradninch Place, Gandy Street, Exeter, Devon EX4 3LS
☎01392 218188 Fax 01392 413554
Email info@swa.co.uk
Website www.swa.co.uk
Director of Visual Arts and Media
  David Drake
Visual Arts and Media Administrator
  Sara Williams

Covers Cornwall, Devon, Dorset (excluding Bournemouth, Christchurch and Poole), Gloucestershire, Somerset and the unitary authorities of Bristol, Bath and North East Somerset, South Gloucestershire, North Somerset, Torbay and Plymouth. The central theme running through the Board's aims are 'promoting quality and developing audiences for new work'. Specific policies aim to support the development and promotion of new writing and performance work in all areas of contemporary literature and published arts. There is direct investment in small presses and magazine publishers, literary festivals, writer residencies and training and marketing bursaries for individual writers. There is also a commitment to supporting the development of new writing in the performing arts.

Southern Arts

13 St Clement Street, Winchester, Hampshire SO23 9DQ
☎01962 855099 Fax 01962 861186
Email info@southernarts.co.uk
Literature Officer *Keiren Phelan*
Film, Video & Broadcasting Officer
  Jane Gerson
Theatre Officer *Nic Young*

Covers Berkshire, Buckinghamshire, Hampshire, the Isle of Wight, Oxfordshire, Wiltshire and South East Dorset. The Literature Department funds fiction and poetry readings, festivals, magazines, bursaries, a literature prize, publications, residencies and a scheme which subsidises writers working in education and the community.

West Midlands Arts

82 Granville Street, Birmingham B1 2LH
☎0121 631 3121 Fax 0121 643 7239
Website www.arts.org.uk/directory/regions/
  west-mid
Literature Officer *Adrian Johnson*

There are special criteria across the art forms, so contact the Information Office for details of

Creative Ambition Awards for writers (eight application dates throughout the year) and other schemes as well as for the *Reading (Correspondence Mss Advice) Service*. There are contact lists of writers, storytellers, writing groups, etc. WMA supports the regional publication, *Raw Edge Magazine*: contact PO Box 4867, Birmingham B3 3HD, the Virtual Literature Centre for the West Midlands (and beyond) called 'Lit-net' (www.lit-net.org) and the major storytelling and poetry festivals in Shropshire and Ledbury respectively.

Yorkshire Arts

21 Bond Street, Dewsbury, West Yorkshire WF13 1AY
☎01924 455555 Fax 01924 466522
Email <firstname.surname>.yha@artsfb.org.uk
Website www.arts.org.uk
Literature Officer *Steve Dearden*
Drama Officer *David Bown*

Administrator *Jill Leahy*

'Libraries, publishing houses, local authorities and the education service all make major contributions to the support of literature. Recognising the resources these agencies command, Yorkshire Arts actively seeks ways of acting in partnership with them, while at the same time retaining its particular responsibility for the living writer and the promotion of activities currently outside the scope of these agencies.' Funding goes to **Yorkshire Art Circus** (community publishing); poetry publishers **Arc Publications** and **Smith/ Doorstop**; *Live Writing* and *Writing Development* are schemes which subsidise projects where a professional writer is employed as a performer or tutor. Support is also given to Ilkley, Hull, Huddersfield and Sheffield Literature Festivals. YA offers a bursary scheme for writers; holds lists of workshops and writers' groups throughout the region. *Publishes* an on-line directory of writers and *writeANGLES*, bi-monthly newsletter. Contact the Administrator.

Writers' Courses, Circles and Workshops

Courses (listed under country and county)

ENGLAND

Berkshire

University of Reading
Department of Continuing Education,
London Road, Reading, Berkshire RG1 5AQ
☎0118 9318347

An expanding programme of creative writing courses, includes *Life into Fiction; Getting Started; Poetry Workshop; Writers Helping Writers* (with **Southern Arts**' help, includes visits from well-known writers); *Writing Fiction; Publishing Poetry; Adventures in Writing; Scriptwriting; Becoming Independent*. There is also a support group for teachers of creative writing, a public lecture by a writer and a reading by students of their work, various Saturday workshops. Tutors include science fiction writer Brian Stableford, novelist Leslie Wilson and poets Jane Draycott, Elizabeth James and Susan Utting. Fees vary depending on length of course; concessions available.

Buckinghamshire

Missenden Abbey Continuing Education
Chilterns Consortium, The Misbourne Centre, Great Missenden, Buckinghamshire HP16 0BN
☎01494 862904 Fax 01494 890087
Email enquiries@missendenabbey.ac.uk
Website www.aredu.org.uk/missendenabbey

Residential and non-residential weekend workshops and summer school. Programmes have included *Writing Magazine Articles and Getting Them Published; Writing for Television and Radio; A Creative Approach to Non-Fiction Writing; Writing Poetry*. Missenden Abbey is a member of the Adult Residential Colleges Association.

National Film & Television School
Beaconsfield Studios, Station Road,
Beaconsfield, Buckinghamshire HP9 1LG
☎01494 671234 Fax 01494 674042
Email admin@nftsfilm-tv.ac.uk
Website www.nftsfilm-tv.ac.uk

Intensive, one-year, full-time screenwriting course for people with established writing skills but little or no experience of writing for the screen. One-year, part-time course for people with some screenwriting experience, ready to focus on feature script development. Courses also develop an understanding of the practical stages involved in the making of film and television drama. Range of work covers comedy, TV series and serials, short-film, adaptation and narrative. The ability to collaborate successfully is developed through exercises and projects shared with students in other specialisations. 'We encourage the formation of working partnerships which will continue after graduation.'

The Writers' Workshop
The Wash House, Meadowsweet, 16 Church Walk, Lent Green, Burnham,
Buckinghamshire SL1 7AR
☎01442 871004 Fax 01442 871004
Email word_shop@hotmail.com

The Writers' Workshop runs regular daytime classes in creative writing and offers professional assessments and guidance, over three 10-week terms per year. Published writers and beginners are equally welcome.

Cambridgeshire

National Extension College
18 Brooklands Avenue, Cambridge CB2 2HN
☎01223 450200 Fax 01223 313586
Website www.nec.ac.uk

Runs a number of home-study courses on writing. Courses include: *Essential Editing; Creative Writing; Writing for Money; Copywriting; Essential Desktop Publishing; Essential Design*. Contact the NEC for copy of the *Guide to Courses* which includes details of fees.

PMA Training
PMA House, Free Church Passage, St Ives,
Cambridgeshire PE17 4AY
☎01480 300653 Fax 01480 496022
Email admin@pma-group.com
Website www.pma-group.co.uk

One-/two-/three-day editorial, PR, design and publishing courses held in central London. High-powered, intensive courses run by Fleet Street journalists and magazine editors. Courses include: *News-Writing; Writing and Surviving as a Freelance; Feature Writing; Investigative Reporting; Basic Writing Skills*. Fees range from £150 to £600 plus VAT. Special rates for freelances.

Cheshire

The College of Technical Authorship – Distance Learning Course

The College of Technical Authorship, PO Box 7, Cheadle, Cheshire SK8 3BY
☎0161 437 4235 Fax 0161 437 4235
Email crossley@coltecha.u-net.com
Website www.colltecha.com

Distance learning courses for City & Guilds Tech 536, Part 1, Technical Communication Techniques, and Part 2, Technical Authorship. Individual tuition by correspondence and fax; includes some practical work done at home. A member of the British Association for Open Learning. Contact: *John Crossley*, DipDistEd, DipM, MCIM, FISTC, LCGI.

Cornwall

Brackenside House

Brackenside House, Polperro, Cornwall PL13 2RU
☎01503 273074 Fax 01503 273148
Email DavidMHinds@AfterStroke.fsbusiness.co.uk
Website www.AfterStroke.fsbusiness.co.uk

A series of weekend and mid-week residential courses in the historic Cornish village of Polperro, facilitated by David M. Hinds, author of *After Stroke*. The course, which is supported by senior academic staff, advises writers how to get their first book published and follows up the progress of individual writers. All-inclusive residential fees range from £350 to £850.

Cumbria

Higham Hall College

Bassenthwaite Lake, Cockermouth, Cumbria CA13 9SH
☎01768 776276 Fax 01768 776013

Winter and summer residential courses. Programme has included *Prose, Poetry and Painting*. Detailed brochure available.

Derbyshire

Losehill Hall

Peak District National Park Centre, Castleton, Hope Valley, Derbyshire S33 8WB
☎01433 620373 Fax 01433 620346
Email leisure.losehill@peakdistrict-npa.gov.uk
Website www.peakdistrict.org

Weekend residential creative writing courses set in the Peak District National Park. Suitable for both beginners and experienced writers. Brochure available.

Real Writers

PO Box 170, Chesterfield, Derbyshire S40 1FE
☎01246 238492 Fax 01246 238492
Email realwrtrs@aol.com
Website www.turtledesign.com/RealWriters/

Correspondence service with personal tuition from working writers. In addition to the support and appraisal service, runs an annual short story competition. Send s.a.e. for details.

University of Derby

Student Information Centre, Kedleston Road, Derby DE22 1GB
☎01332 622236 Fax 01332 622754
Email J.Bains@derby.ac.uk (prospectus requests only)
Website www.derby.ac.uk

Contact *Graham Parker*
With upwards of 300 students, *Experience of Writing* runs 21 modules as part of the undergraduate degree programme. These include: *Storytelling, Poetry, Playwriting, Writing for TV and Radio, Screenwriting, The Short Story, Journalism, Writing for Children*. The courses are all led by practising writers. The University has extended its creative writing provision with the MA in *Narrative Writing*, now in its third year.

Writers' Summer School, Swanwick

The Hayes, Swanwick, Derbyshire
Email contact@wss.org.uk
Website www.wss.org.uk
A week-long summer school of informal talks and discussion groups, forums, panels, quizzes, competitions, and 'a lot of fun'. Open to everyone, from absolute beginners to published authors. Held in August from Saturday to Friday morning. Cost (2000) £200+, all inclusive. Contact the Secretary, *Brenda Courtie* at PO Box 5532, Heanor, Derbyshire DE75 7YF (☎07050 630949).

Devon

Dartington College of Arts

Totnes, Devon TQ9 6EJ
☎01803 862224 Fax 01803 863569
Email c.bergvall@dartington.ac.uk *or*
  registry@dartington.ac.uk
Website www.dartington.ac.uk

BA(Hons) course in *Performance Writing*: exploratory approach to writing as it relates to performance. The course is part of a performance arts programme which encourages interdisciplinary work with Arts Management, Music, Theatre, Visual Performance. The programme includes a range of elective modules in digital media and emerging art forms which are available to all students. Contact Subject Director, Performance Writing: *Caroline Bergvall.*

Exeter Phoenix

Bradninch Place, Gandy Street, Exeter, Devon
EX4 3LS
☎01392 667055 Fax 01392 667599
Website www.exeterphoenix.org.uk

Exeter Phoenix has regular literature events, focusing on readings by living poets and other writers and is often linked to aspects of a wider performance programme. Tutors in a wide range of writing skills run classes and workshops, listed in the brochure of Phoenix activities.

University of Exeter

Exeter, Devon EX4 4QW
☎01392 264580

BA(Hons) in *Drama* with a third-year option in *Playwriting.* Contact *Professor Peter Thomson.*

Dorset

Bournemouth University

School of Media Arts and Communication,
Poole House, Talbot Campus, Fern Barrow,
Poole, Dorset BH12 5BB
☎01202 595553 Fax 01202 595530

Three-year, full-time BA(Hons) course in *Scriptwriting for Film and Television.* Contact *Sue Sykes*, Programme Administrator.

Essex

National Council for the Training of Journalists

Latton Bush Centre, Southern Way, Harlow,
Essex CM18 7BL
☎01279 430009 Fax 01279 438008
Email NCTJ@itecharlow.co.uk

Website www.itecharlow.co.uk/nctj/
For details of journalism courses, both full-time and via distance learning, please write to the NCTJ enclosing a large s.a.e.

Gloucestershire

Chrysalis – The Poet In You

5 Oxford Terrace, Uplands, Stroud,
Gloucestershire GL5 1TW
☎01453 759436

Offers courses, workshops and one-to-one sessions. The course consists of Part 1, 'for those who feel drawn to reading more poetry as well as wanting to start to write their own', and Part 2, 'a more advanced course designed for those who are already writing and who want to go more deeply into its process and technique'. Brochure available from the address above.

Hampshire

Highbury College, Portsmouth

Dovercourt Road, Cosham, Portsmouth,
Hampshire PO6 2SA
☎023 9238 3131 Fax 023 9237 8382

Courses include: one-year *Pre-entry Magazine Journalism*, run under the auspices of the Periodicals Training Council; 20-week *Pre-entry Newspaper Journalism* course, run under the auspices of the National Council for Training of Journalists; one-year Post-Graduate Diploma in *Broadcasting Journalism*, run under the auspices of the Broadcast Journalism Training Council. Contact the Secretary, ☎023 9231 3287.

King Alfred's College

Winchester, Hampshire SO22 4NR
☎01962 841515 Fax 01962 842280
Website www.wkac.ac.uk

Three-year degree course in *Drama, Theatre and Television Studies*, including *Writing for Devised Community Theatre* and *Writing for Television Documentary.* Contact the Admissions Office (☎01962 827262). MA course in *Theatre for Development* – one year, full-time course with major project overseas or in the UK. MA course in *Writing for Children* available on either a one- or two-year basis. Enquiries: Admissions Officer (☎01962 827235).

University of Southampton New College

The Avenue, Southampton SO17 1BG
☎023 8059 7261 Fax 023 8059 7271
Email vah@soton.ac.uk

Creative writing courses and writers' workshops. Courses are held in local/regional centres.

Hertfordshire

West Herts College
School of Media Communications,
Hempstead Road, Watford, Hertfordshire
WD1 3EZ
☎01923 812654 (Admissions)

The 24-week postgraduate course in *Journalism, Radio and Advertising: Writing and Practice* covers two options: *Writing for Print* and *Writing for Radio*. The college also offers a postgraduate diploma in *Publishing* with an option in *Multimedia Publishing*. Contact the Admissions Secretary on the number above.

Kent

University of Kent at Canterbury
Unit for Part-time Study, Keynes College,
Canterbury, Kent CT2 7NP
☎01227 823507 Fax 01227 458745
Website www.ukc.ac.uk/registry/UPS

Certificate course in *Practical Writing* and *Imaginative Writing*. 20-week course in *Creative Writing*. Contact the Information Office.

Lancashire

Alston Hall College
Alston Lane, Longridge, Preston, Lancashire
PR3 3BP
☎01772 784661 Fax 01772 785835
Email alston.hall@ed.lancscc.gov.uk
Website www.alstonhall.u-net.com

Holds regular day-long creative writing workshops, also weekend residential courses. Brochure available.

Edge Hill College of Higher Education
St Helen's Road, Ormskirk, Lancashire
L39 4QP
☎01695 575171

Offers a two-year, part-time MA in *Writing Studies*. Combines advanced-level writers' workshops with closely related courses in the poetics of writing and contemporary writing in English. There is also provision for MPhil- and PhD-level research in writing and poetics. A full range of creative writing courses is available at undergraduate level, in poetry and fiction writing

which may be taken as part of a modular BA. Contact *Dr R. Sheppard*.

Lancaster University
Department of Creative Writing, Lonsdale
College, Bailrigg, Lancaster LA1 4YN
☎01524 594169 Fax 01524 843934
Email L.Anderson@lancaster.ac.uk

Offers practical graduate and undergraduate courses in writing fiction, poetry and scripts. All based on group workshops – students' work-in-progress is circulated and discussed. Visiting writers have included: Carol Ann Duffy, Kazuo Ishiguro, Bernard MacLaverty, David Pownall. Contact *Linda Anderson* for details.

The Written Word
43 Green Lane, Beaumont, Lancaster
LA1 2ES
☎01524 35215 Fax 01524 35215
Email steve@ashton01.freeserve.co.uk

Contact *Steve Ashton*
Postal course in all categories of short and full-length non-fiction work, with an emphasis on writing magazine feature articles and getting them published. Personal tuition from a working professional with 15 years' experience. £195 fee includes comprehensive course book plus detailed guidance and feedback on eight realistic assignments. Also, script evaluation service (£45 for articles, £95 for three chapters plus the synopsis of a book). Send for information leaflet.

Leicestershire

Leicester Adult Education College, Writing School
2 Wellington Street, Leicester LE1 6HL
☎0116 2334343 Fax 0116 2334344
Email admin@leicester-adult-ed.ac.uk
Website www.leicester-adult-ed.ac.uk

Offers a wide range of creative writing and journalism courses throughout the year. The programme offers a mix of critical workshops and short craft courses. Specialises in supporting new and more experienced writers through to publication and has strong links with local media. Manuscript appraisal is available by post for short stories and articles. Occasional masterclasses and talks. Visiting writers have included Melvyn Bragg, Simon Brett, John Harvey, Roy Hattersley, Susan Hill, Rose Impey, Graham Joyce, Deric Longden, Simon Armitage and Andrew Motion. For course information and advice, contact *Valerie Moore*.

London

Black Coral Training
2nd Floor, 241 High Street, London E17 7BH
☎020 8520 2830
Email bctraining@coralmedia.co.uk
Website www.black-coral.com
ScriptCity at Black Coral provides creative and professional training in screenwriting and story editing skills for writers, readers and script editors. *Do the Write Thing*: for writers new to the screen; *Reading Room*: professional development for script readers; *Final Edition*: foundation and advanced training for script editors and producers; *Write Out Loud*: performance strand for producers, writers and directors wishing to see their scripts read by actors; *New Perspectives*: 10-month intensive script development programme in association with professional editors and incorporating workshops and masterclasses. Prices from around £100 to £500, concessions available; call course administrator for full details.

The Central School of Speech and Drama
Embassy Theatre, Eton Avenue, London NW3 3HY
☎020 7722 8183   Fax 020 7722 4132
MA in *Advanced Theatre Practice*. One-year, full-time course aimed at providing a grounding in principal areas of professional theatre practice – *Writing, Dramaturgy, Directing, Performance, Puppetry* and *Design*, with an emphasis on collaboration between the various strands. 'The writing and dramaturgy strands are particularly suitable for those wishing to work in a lively and stimulating atmosphere creating, with other practitioners, new work for the theatre.' Prospectus available. Writing/dramaturgy tutor: *Nick Wood*.

The City Literary Institute
Humanities Dept, Stukeley Street, London WC2B 5LJ
☎020 7430 0542   Fax 020 7405 3347
The Writing School offers a wide range of courses from *Playwriting* and *Writing for Children* to *Autobiographical Writing* and *Writing Short Stories*. The Department offers information and advice during term time.

City University
Northampton Square, London EC1V 0HB
☎020 7477 8268   Fax 020 7477 8256
Website www.city.ac.uk/conted.ofa.htm
Creative writing classes include: *Writer's Workshop; Wordshop* (poetry); *Writing Comedy;*

Playwright's Workshop; Writing Freelance Articles for Newspapers; Women Writer's Workshop; Creative Writing; Fiction Short and Long; Feature Journalism; Writing for Children. Contact: Courses for Adults.

The Complete Creative Writing Course at the Groucho Club
☎020 7249 3711   Fax 020 7248 3711
Email maggie.j@cwcom.net
Contact *Maggie Hamand*
Courses of ten two-hour sessions held at the Groucho Club in Soho, starting in January, April and September, Monday or Saturday afternoons, 2.30 –4.30 pm. Beginners and advanced courses offered. Each week looks at a different aspect of fiction writing and includes stimulating exercises, discussion and weekly homework. The tutors are novelists Maggie Hamand and Henrietta Soames. £180 for whole course.

The Drill Hall
16 Chenies Street, London WC1B 7EX
☎020 7631 1353   Fax 020 7631 4468
Email admin@drillhall.co.uk
Holds a number of writing classes and workshops. Regular tutors include Carol Burns and Peter Carty. Writers interested in *Writing for Performance* may also be interested in Claire Dowie and Colin Watkey's *Stand-Up Theatre Workshop*. Call for brochure on 020 7631 5107.

LNPF Writing School
See **London New Play Festival** under **Festivals**

London College of Printing
Elephant & Castle, London SE1 6SB
☎020 7514 7667
Website www.linst.ac.uk/lcp/dali
Courses in journalism. Short courses run by DALI (Developments at the London Institute) at the Elephant & Castle address above: *Guide to Magazine Writing/News Writing/Feature Writing/ Freelance Journalism/Proof Reading/Subbing on the Screen; Sub-editing*. Also offers two-day specialist journalism courses in food writing, travel writing, writing for the music press, sports journalism and fashion writing. For individuals and companies there are 'tailor-made training' services. Prospectus and information leaflets available; ☎020 7514 6770.

London School of Journalism
22 Upbrook Mews, London W2 3HG
☎020 7706 3790   Fax 020 7706 3780
Email info@lsjournalism.com

Website www.home-study.com

Correspondence courses with an individual and personal approach. Students remain with the same tutor throughout their course. Options include: *Short Story Writing; Writing for Children; Poetry; Freelance Journalism; Improve Your English; English for Business; Journalism and Newswriting*. Fees vary but range from £215 for *Enjoying English Literature* to £395 for *Journalism and Newswriting*. Contact the Student Administration Office at the address above.

Middlesex University

School of Humanities and Cultural Studies, White Hart Lane, London N17 8HR
☎020 8362 5941 Fax 020 8362 6878
Email admissions@mdx.ac.uk

Undergraduate courses (full-time, part-time, associate) for those interested in writing, publishing and the media. Writing & Publishing Studies includes *Editing* and *Marketing* (contact *Juliet Gardiner* ☎020 8362 6041); BA(Hons) Writing Programme includes *Journalism, Scriptwriting* and *Narrative* and *Poetry Workshops* (contact *Susanna Gladwin* ☎020 8362 5379).

MA in *Writing* (full-time, part-time; day and evening classes) includes a specialist strand in Asian and Black British writing, approaches to the short story and novel; lectures and workshops from established writers.

University of Surrey Roehampton

Department of Drama: Theatre, Film and Television, Roehampton Lane, London SW15 5PU
☎020 8392 3230 Fax 020 8392 3289
Email j.ridgman@roehampton.ac.uk
Website www.roehampton.ac.uk

Three-year BA(Hons) programmes in *Drama and Theatre Studies* and *Film and Television Studies* include courses on writing for stage and screen. Contact: *Jeremy Ridgman*.

University of Westminster

Harrow Campus, Watford Road, Harrow, Middlesex HA1 3TP
☎020 7911 5903 Fax 020 7911 5955
Email barrata@wmin.ac.uk
Website www.wmin.ac.uk

Part-time evening MAs available in *Journalism, Film and TV, Photography*.

Greater Manchester

Manchester Metropolitan University – The Writing School

Department of English, Geoffrey Manton Building, Rosamond Street West, off Oxford Road, Manchester M15 6LL
☎0161 247 1732/1 Fax 0161 247 6345

Closely associated with **Carcanet Press Ltd** and *PN Review*, offers three principal 'routes' for students to follow: *Poetry; The Novel*; and *Biography and Autobiography*. A key feature of the programme is regular readings, lectures, workshops and masterclasses by writers, publishers, producers, booksellers, librarians and agents. Tutors include Simon Armitage, Carol Ann Duffy, Sophie Hannah, Jacqueline Roy and Jeffrey Wainwright. Course convenor: *Michael Schmidt*.

University of Manchester

Department of English & American Studies, Arts Building, Oxford Road, Manchester M13 9PL
☎0161 275 3144 Fax 0161 275 3256
Email novel@man.ac.uk

Offers a one-year MA in *Novel Writing*.

University of Salford

Postgraduate Admissions, Dept. of Media & Performance, Adelphi Building, Peru Street, Salford, Greater Manchester M3 6EQ
☎0161 295 6027
Website www.salford.ac.uk

MA in *Television and Radio Scriptwriting*. Two-year, part-time course taught by professional writers and producers. Also offers a number of masterclasses with leading figures in the radio and television industry.

Password Training Ltd

23 New Mount Street, Manchester M4 4DE
☎0161 953 4071 Fax 0161 953 4001

Prrovides training for publishers, writers' groups and individuals in Internet publishing, planning, production, design, marketing, costing and distribution. Clients: the Federation of Worker Writers and Community Publishers, The Arts Council, Regional Arts Boards, Yorkshire Art Circus and Corridor Community Press. For further details, contact *Claire Turner*.

The Writers Bureau

Sevendale House, 7 Dale Street, Manchester M1 1JB
☎0161 228 2362 Fax 0161 236 9440
Email advisory@writersbureau.com

Website www.writersbureau.com

Comprehensive home-study writing course with personal tuition service from professional writers (fee: £249). Fiction, non-fiction, articles, short stories, novels, TV, radio and drama all covered in detail. Trial period, guarantee and no time limits. ODLQC accredited. Quote Ref. EH20. Free enquiry line: 0800 856 2008

The Writers Bureau College of Journalism

Address etc as The Writers Bureau above
Home-study course covering all aspects of journalism. Real-life assignments assessed by qualified tutors with the emphasis on getting into print and enjoying the financial rewards. Comprises 28 modules and three handbooks with special introductory offers. Ref: EHJ20. Free enquiry line: 0800 298 7008.

The Writers College

Address etc as The Writers Bureau above
The Art of Writing Poetry Course from The Writers Bureau sister college. A home-study course with a more 'recreational' emphasis. The 60,000-word course has 17 modules and lets you complete six written assignments for tutorial evaluation. Fees: £99. Quote Ref. EHP20. Free enquiry line: 0800 856 2008.

Merseyside

University of Liverpool

Centre for Continuing Education,
19 Abercromby Square, Liverpool L69 7ZG
☎0151 794 6900 (24 hours)
Fax 0151 794 2544

Courses include: *Introduction to Creative Writing; The Short Story and the Novel; Introduction to Writing Poetry; Introduction to Scripting for Radio and Television; Introduction to Writing Journalism; Science Fiction and Fantasy; Travel Writing; Biography and Autobiography; Writing for Children; Songwriting; Popular Music Journalism; Theatre Playwrights Workshop; Scripting Situation Comedy; Screenwriting: Film and Television; Scriptwriting for Women.* Most courses are run in the evening over 10 or 20 weeks but there are some linked Saturday and weekday courses on offer. Students have the option of accreditation towards a university award in Creative Writing. Some of the above courses are also part of the university's part-time Flexible Degree pathway (Comb. Hons., Arts). No pre-entry qualifications required. Fees vary with concessions for the unwaged and those in receipt of benefit. For fur-

ther information and/or copy of current prospectus, phone or write to *Keith Birch*, Head of Creative Arts (address as above).

Norfolk

University of East Anglia

School of English & American Studies, Norwich, Norfolk NR4 7TJ
☎01603 593262 Fax 01603 593799
Email a.o.davies@uea.ac.uk

UEA has a history of concern with contemporary literary culture. Among its MA programmes is one in *Creative Writing*, Stream 1: Prose Fiction; Stream 2: Poetry; Stream 3: Scriptwriting.

Nottinghamshire

The Nottingham Trent University

Humanities Faculty Office (Post Graduate Studies), Clifton Lane, Nottingham NG11 8NS
☎0115 9486335 Fax 0115 9486339
Email amanda.samuels@ntu.ac.uk
Website human.ntu.ac.uk/pg/courses/
    writing.html

MA in *Writing*. Hands-on and workshop-based, the course concentrates primarily on the practice and production of writing. A choice of options from *Fiction*, *Poetry* and *Life-Writing* (which includes *Feature* and *Travel Writing*). Assignments and a dissertation of your writing to complete for award of degree. No formal exams. Staff are all established writers. Current visiting professors: Peter Porter, Michele Roberts and Miranda Seymour. Also a full programme of visiting speakers. Study either full-time (three evenings per week) or part-time (two evenings per week over two years). Further details and application forms from *Amanda Samuels*, Postgraduate Administrator from the address above.

Somerset

Bath Spa University College

Newton Park, Bath BA2 9BN
☎01225 875875 Fax 01225 875444
Email enquiries@bathspa.ac.uk

Postgraduate Diploma/MA in *Creative Writing*. A course for creative writers wanting to develop their work. Teaching is by published writers in the novel, poetry, short stories and scriptwriting. In recent years, several students from this course have received contracts from publishers for novels, awards for poetry and short stories and have had work produced on

BBC Radio. Contact Admissions Officer, *Clare Brandram Jones* for details.

Institute of Copywriting

Honeycombe House, Bagley, Wedmore, Somerset BS28 4TD
☎01934 713563 Fax 01934 713492
Email copy@inst.org
Website ds.dial.pipex.com/institute/copy.htm

Comprehensive home-study course covering all aspects of copywriting, including advice on becoming a self-employed copywriter. Each student has a personal tutor who is an experienced copywriter and who provides detailed feedback on the student's assignments.

University of Bristol

Department of English, 3/5 Woodland Road, Bristol BS8 1TB
☎0117 954 6969 Fax 0117 928 8860
Email rowena.fowler@bris.ac.uk
Website www.bris.ac.uk/Depts/English-ce_creat.html

Courses: *Women and Writing*, for women who write or would like to begin to write (poetry, fiction, non-fiction, journals) and various other writing courses for the general public. *Certificate in Creative Writing* and *Certificate in Creative Writing for Theraputic Purposes*. Detailed brochure available.

Staffordshire

Keele University

The Centre for Continuing and Professional Education, Keele University, (Freepost ST1666), Newcastle under Lyme, Staffordshire ST5 5BG
☎01782 583436

Weekend courses on literature and creative writing. The 1999 programme included fiction writing and writing for children. Also runs study days where major novelists or poets read and discuss their work.

Surrey

Royal Holloway

University of London, Egham Hill, Egham, Surrey TW20 0EX
☎01784 443922 Fax 01784 431018
Email drama@rhbnc.ac.uk

Three-year BA course in *Theatre Studies* during which playwriting can be studied as an option in the second or third year. Contact *Dan Rebellato* or *David Wiles*.

University of Surrey

School of Educational Studies, University of Surrey, Guildford, Surrey GU2 5XH
☎01483 876172 Fax 01483 259522

The Open Access Continuing Education programme includes several *Creative Writing* courses, held at the University, the Guildford Institute and throughout the county. The courses carry credits and can build to a *Certificate in Creative Writing*, equivalent to completion of the first year of an undergraduate degree. For details contact the Enrolment Secretary or *Dr Brian Crossley FRSA*, Lecturer and Subject Leader in Creative Writing.

Sussex

University College Chichester

Bishop Otter Campus, College Lane, Chichester, West Sussex PO19 4PE
☎01243 816000 Fax 01243 816080

Offers Postgraduate Certificate/Diploma/MA in *Creative Writing*. Contact *Stephanie Norgate*, Route Leader, MA in Creative Writing, for details.

The Earnley Concourse

Earnley, Chichester, West Sussex PO20 7JL
☎01243 670392 Fax 01243 670832
Email info@earnley.co.uk
Website www.earnley.co.uk

Offers a range of residential and non-residential courses throughout the year. Previous programme has included *Writing for Publication; You Can Sell What You Write*. Brochure available.

University of Sussex

Centre for Continuing Education, Education Development Building, Falmer, Brighton, East Sussex BN1 9RG
☎01273 678537 Fax 01273 678848
Email y.d.barnes@sussex.ac.uk
Website www.sussex.ac.uk

Postgraduate Diploma in *Dramatic Writing*: the student is treated as a commissioned writer working in theatre, TV, radio or film with professional directors and actors. Includes workshops, masterclasses and a residential weekend. One-year, part-time. Convenor: *Richard Crane*. Certificate in *Creative Writing*: short fiction, novel and poetry for imaginative writers. One-year, part-time. Convenor: *Richard Crane*. Postgraduate Diploma in *Creative Writing and Personal Development*: for writers working in care services and self exploration. Convenor: *Celia Hunt*. Contact for all courses: *Yvonne Barnes*.

Tyne & Wear

University of Newcastle upon Tyne

Centre for Lifelong Learning, Newcastle upon Tyne NE1 7RU
☎0191 222 5680

Writing-related courses include: *Writing From the Inside Out; Dramatic Writing for Film, TV and Radio; Writing Workshops.* Contact the Secretary, Adult Education Programme.

Warwickshire

University of Warwick

Open Studies, Continuing Education Department, Coventry, Warwickshire CV4 7AL
☎024 7652 3831
Email k.rainsley@warwick.ac.uk *or*
l.downs@warwick.ac.uk

Creative writing courses held at the university or in regional centres. Subjects include: *Starting to Write; Prose and Poetry Writing; Writing for Radio; Screenwriting for Beginners.* A one-year certificate in *Creative Writing* is available.

Focus on Fiction

PO Box 1768, Hillmorton, Rugby CV21 4ZA
☎01788 334302
Email FocusOnFiction@aol.com
Correspondence course with one-to-one tuition from professional published writers and literary agents. Offers support, encouragement, contacts and advice. Registration fee includes personal organiser with over 400 pages of advice, tips and course notes. A small fee is then paid with each item sent in for appraisal. Covers all genres of fiction writing: writing for women's magazines, science fiction, horror, crime, erotica, writing for children and teenagers, fantasy and caters for all levels of ability. Also runs an annual short story competition, The Focus on Fiction Short Story Competition, closing date 30 November; send s.a.e. for details.

West Midlands

Sandwell College

Smethwick Campus, Crocketts Lane, Smethwick B66 3BU
☎0121 556 6000

Creative writing courses held afternoons/evenings, from September to July. General courses covering short stories, poetry, autobiography, etc. Also women's writing courses. Contact *Tony Martin*.

University of Birmingham

School of Continuing Studies, Edgbaston, Birmingham B15 2TT
☎0121 414 5607/7259 Fax 0121 414 5619

Certificate of Higher Education in *Creative Writing* – two years, part-time in Birmingham and Worcester. Day and weekend classes, including creative writing, literature, theatre are held at locations throughout Birmingham, the West Midlands, Herefordshire, Worcestershire and Shropshire. Course brochures are available from the above address. Please specify which course you are interested in. The University also offers an MPhil in *Playwriting Studies* established by playwright David Edgar in 1989. Contact *April Di Angelis*, Course Director at the Department of Drama and Theatre Arts (☎0121 414 5790).

Wiltshire

Marlborough College Summer School

Marlborough, Wiltshire SN8 1PA
☎01672 892388/9 Fax 01672 892476
Email summer.school@marlboroughcollege.
wilts.sch.uk

Summer School with literature and creative writing included in its programme. Caters for residential and day students. Brochure available giving full details and prices.

Yorkshire

Hull College

Queen's Gardens, Hull, East Yorkshire HU1 3DG
☎01482 329943 Fax 01482 219079

Offers part-time day/evening writing courses in *Novel Writing* and *Short Story Writing*, at Hull College, Park Street Centre. Courses begin each academic term. Writers are encouraged to contribute stories for a collection. Contact: *Gwynneth Yates.*

University of Leeds

Springfield Mount, Leeds, West Yorkshire LS2 9JT
Email r.k.o'rourke@leeds.ac.uk
Also at: Adult Education Centre, 37 Harrow Road, Middlesbrough, Cleveland, TS5 5NT
☎01642 814987

Creative writing courses held throughout Cleveland, North and West Yorkshire in the autumn, spring and summer terms. These are held weekly and as non-residential summer schools. Courses carrying undergraduate credit are part-time and offered in a range of subjects, at beginners, intermediate and advanced levels. Professional development courses for writers and Writing Development Workers which carry post-graduate credit are also offered. Contact *Rebecca O'Rourke* for details.

The Northern Film School

Leeds Metropolitan University, 2 Queen Square, Leeds, West Yorkshire LS2 8AF
☎0113 2831900 Fax 0113 2831901
Email nfs@lmu.ac.uk
Website www.lmu.ac.uk/hen/aad/nfs

Offers a Postgraduate Diploma/MA course in *Fiction Screenwriting*. Full-time or part-time. Its graduates are working on *The Bill*, *Family Affairs*, *Coronation Street*, three features and other professional projects. Contact: *Alby James*.

Open College of the Arts

Houndhill, Worsbrough, Barnsley, South Yorkshire S70 6TU
☎01226 730495 Fax 01226 730838
Email open.arts@ukonline.co.uk
Website www.oca-uk.com

The OCA correspondence course, *Starting to Write*, offers help and stimulus from experienced writers/tutors. Emphasis is on personal development rather than commercial genre. Subsequent levels available include specialist poetry, fiction and autobiographical writing courses. OCA's *Creative Reading* course helps student writers understand how readers interact with their writing. OCA writing courses are accredited to the University of Glamorgan. Prospectus and guide to courses available on request.

Sheffield Hallam University

School of Cultural Studies, Sheffield Hallam University, Collegiate Crescent, Sheffield S10 2BP
☎0114 2254408 Fax 0114 2254363

Offers MA in *Creative Writing* (one-year, full-time; also part-time).

University College Bretton Hall

School of English, Faculty of Arts, University College Bretton Hall, West Bretton, Wakefield, West Yorkshire WF4 4LG
☎01924 830261 Fax 01924 832006
Email rwatson@bretton.ac.uk

Offers one-year full-time/two-year part-time MA course in *Creative Writing* designed for competent though not necessarily published writers. Contact *Rob Watson* for details.

University College, Scarborough

North Riding College, Filey Road, Scarborough, North Yorkshire YO11 3AZ
☎01723 362392 Fax 01723 362392
Website www.ucscarb.ac.uk

BA Single Honours and Combined Honours Degrees in *Theatre Studies* incorporates *Writing for Performance* and *Writing for Theatre*. Contact: *Helen Iball*. University College Scarborough also works closely with the Stephen Joseph Theatre and its artistic director Alan Ayckbourn. The theatre sustains a policy for staging new writers. (See entry under **Theatre Producers**.) The College hosts the annual National Student Drama Festival which includes the International Student Playscript Competition (details from The National Information Centre for Student Drama at UCS; email: nsdf@ucscarb.ac.uk).

University of Sheffield

Division of Adult Continuing Education, 196–198 West Street, Sheffield S1 4ET
☎0114 2227000 Fax 0114 2227001

Creative writing courses and workshops.

IRELAND

Dingle Writing Courses Ltd

Ballintlea, Ventry, Co. Kerry, Republic of Ireland
☎00 353 66 9159052 Fax 00 353 66 9159052
Email dinglewc@iol.ie
Website www.iol.ie~dinglewc

A summer and autumn programme of weekend and five-day residential courses for beginners and experienced writers alike. Tutored by professional writers the courses take place in 'an inspirational setting overlooking Inch strand'. The programme includes poetry, fiction, starting to write and writing for theatre as well as special themed courses.

Past tutors have included Jennifer Johnston, Paul Durcan, Mary O'Malley, Leland Bardwell and Graham Mort. Writing courses for schools are also available. Brochures and further information available from directors, *Abigail Joffe* or *Nicholas McLachlan* at the address above.

University of Dublin (Trinity College)

Graduates Studies Office, Arts Building, Trinity College, Dublin 2, Republic of Ireland
☎00 353 1 608 1166 Fax 00 353 1 671 2821
Email evansd@tcd.ie

Offers an MPhil *Creative Writing* course. A one-year, full-time course intended for students who are seriously committed to writing, are practising, or prospective authors. Contact Admissions at the address above.

Queen's University of Belfast

Institute of Continuing Education, Belfast, BT7 1NN
☎028 9027 3323
Email ice@qub.ac.uk
Website www.qub.ac.uk/ice

Courses have included *Creative Writing* and *Writing for Profit*.

University of Ulster

Short Course Unit, Room 17C21, University of Ulster, Belfast BT37 0QB
☎028 9036 5131   Fax 028 9036 6060

Creative writing course/workshop, usually held in the autumn and spring terms. Concessions available. Contact the Administrative Officer.

SCOTLAND

University of Aberdeen

Centre for Continuing Education, Regent Building, Regent Walk, Aberdeen AB24 3FX
☎01224 272449   Fax 01224 272478
Email evening-classes@abdn.ac.uk

Creative writing evening class held weekly, taught by published author. Participants may join at any time.

University of Dundee

Institute for Education and Lifelong Learning, Nethergate, Dundee DD1 4HN
☎01382 344128   Fax 01382 221057
Email k.mackle@dundee.ac.uk

Various creative writing courses held at the University and elsewhere in Dundee, Perthshire and Angus. Detailed course brochure available.

Edinburgh University

Centre for Continuing Education, 11 Buccleuch Place, Edinburgh EH8 9LW
☎0131 650 4400   Fax 0131 667 6097
Email cce@ed.ac.uk
Website www.cce.ed.ac.uk

Several writing-orientated courses and summer schools. Beginners welcome. Intensive two-week course in *Playwriting* is held in July, culminating in a rehearsed reading by professional actors and recorded on video for participants to take away. Free tuition in word-processing and use of computer room. Course brochure available.

University of Glasgow

Department of Adult and Continuing Education, 59 Oakfield Avenue, Glasgow G12 8LW
☎0141 330 4032/4394 (Brochure/Enquiries)
Fax 0141 330 3525

Runs writers' workshops and courses at all levels; all friendly and informal. Daytime and evening meetings. Tutors are all experienced published writers in various fields.

University of St Andrews

School of English, The University, St Andrews, Fife KY16 9AL
☎01334 462666   Fax 01334 462655
Website www.st-andrews.ac.uk

Offers postgraduate study in *Creative Writing*. Candidates choose two topics from: *Fiction: The Novel; Craft and Technique in Poetry* and all take the *Short Story* module.

7:84 Summer School

See **7:84 Theatre Company Scotland** under **Theatre Producers**

WALES

Tŷ Newydd Writers' Centre

Llanystumdwy, Criccieth, Gwynedd LL52 0LW
☎01766 522811   Fax 01766 523095
Email tynewydd@dial.pipex.com

Residential writers' centre set up by the Taliesin Trust with the support of the **Arts Council of Wales** to encourage and promote writing in both English and Welsh. Most courses run from Monday evening to Saturday morning. Each course has two tutors and takes a maximum of 16 participants. The centre offers a wide range of specific courses for writers at all levels of experience. Early booking essential. Fee £330 (single)/£305 (twin-bedded) inclusive. People on low incomes may be eligible for a grant or bursary. Course leaflet available. (See also **Organisations of Interest to Poets**.)

University of Glamorgan

Treforest, Pontypridd CF37 1DL
☎01443 482551

MPhil in *Writing* – a two-year part-time Masters

degree for writers of fiction and poets. ESTABLISHED 1993. Contact *Professor Tony Curtis* at the School of Humanities and Social Sciences.

Also, BA in Theatre and Media Drama. Modules include *Scriptwriting: Theatre, Radio, TV and Video.* Contact *Steven Blandford.*

University of Wales, Bangor

Department of English, College Road, Bangor LL57 2DG
☎01248 382102 Fax 01248 382102

Email els029@bangor.ac.uk *or*
DevelopmentCentr@netscape.net

New MA *Creative Studies (Creative Writing)* programme offers writers the chance to develop their work. Also coming on stream: MA *Creative Studies (Film)* and MA *Creative Studies (Media and Journalism).* The Development Centre for the Creative and Performing Arts at the University of Wales, Bangor, is the location of the UK national database on creative writing education and the well-known UK research programme: Creative Writing in Universities and Colleges.

Circles and Workshops

Directory of Writers' Circles

Oldacre, Horderns Park Road, Chapel-en-le-Frith, High Peak SK23 9SY
☎01298 812305
Email jillie@cix.co.uk
Website www.cix.co.uk/~oldacre/

Comprehensive directory of writers' circles, containing contacts and addresses of more than 600 groups and circles meeting throughout the country. Some overseas entries too. Available from *Jill Dick* at the address above; £5 post free.

Annual Writers' Conference Winchester

'Chinook', Southdown Road, Winchester, Hampshire SO21 2BY
☎01962 712307
Email WriterConf@aol.com
Website www.gmp.co.uk/writers/conference

Conference Director *Barbara Large*

Having grown over the past 20 years from a creative writing workshop, this event is now the foremost writers' conference in the country, attracting international authors, playwrights, poets, agents and editors who give workshops, mini courses, editor appointments, lectures and seminars to help writers harness their creativity and develop technical skills. 15 writing competitions are attached to the conference. All first-place winners are published in *The Best of* series annually. The 2001 Conference will be held over the weekend of 29 June to 1 July at King Alfred's University College, Winchester, with workshops from 2–6 July. The Bookfair offers delegates a wide choice of exhibits including Internet author services, publishers, booksellers, printers and associations.

Ayr Writers' Club

Wallace Tower, High Street, Ayr
Contact *May Stevenson* (on 01292 263 7900)

FOUNDED in 1970, this well-established writers' club is strong on encouraging its members towards achieving success in various genres and many of them have been published. Meetings are held every Wednesday from September to April at 7.30 pm. These take the form of club nights and workshops at which published authors are invited to speak once a month. A library of books on the mechanics of writing is available free to members.

Carmarthern Writers' Circle

Lower Carfan, Tavernspite, Whitland, Pembrokeshire SA34 0NP
☎01994 240441

Contact *Jenny White*

FOUNDED 1989. The Circle meets on the second Monday of every month upstairs at the Queen's Hotel in Carmarthen. Both beginners and experienced writers are welcome. Activities include competitions, workshops and 'poets and pints' evenings. More information available from the address above.

Children's Novel Writers' Folio

See **Short Story Writers' Folio**

Chiltern Writers' Group

Marsh Green House, Bassetsbury Lane, High Wycombe HP11 1QY
☎01494 451654

Contact *Diana Atkinson*

Invites writers, publishers, editors and agents to speak at its monthly meetings at Wendover

Public Library. Regular newsletter and competitions. Annual subscription: £15; concessions: £10. Non-members meeting: £3.

The Cotswold Writers' Circle

Dar-es-Salaam, Beeches Park, Hampton Fields, Minchinhampton, Gloucestershire GL6 9BA
☎01453 882912

Honorary Treasurer *Charles Hooker*

The Circle meets fortnightly during the day (10.30 am to 12.30 pm) in Cirencester. Circle activities include organising and running two competitions (one international – closing date 31 January 2001; details from the address above), publishing an anthology of Circle work, organising a writing workshop, etc. The Circle is now in its 15th year and its patron is Elizabeth Webster. Contact *Charles Hooker* for details of the activities.

Cumbrian Literary Group

'Calgarth', The Brow, Flimby, Maryport, Cumbria CA15 8TD
☎01900 813444

President *George Bott*
Secretary *Joyce E. Fisher*

FOUNDED in 1946 to provide a meeting place for readers and writers in Cumbria. The Group meets once a month (April to November), usually in Windermere. Invites speakers to meetings and holds annual competitions for poetry and prose. *Publishes Bookshelf* magazine. *Subscription* £8 p.a. Contact *Joyce E Fisher* at the address above for details.

'Sean Dorman' Manuscript Society

Cherry Trees, Crosemere Road, Cockshutt, Ellesmere, Shropshire SY12 0JP
☎01939 270293

FOUNDED 1957. The Society provides mutual help among writers and aspiring writers in England, Wales and Scotland. By means of circulating manuscript parcels, members receive constructive criticism of their own work and read and comment on the work of others. Each 'Circulator' has up to nine participants and members' contributions may be in any medium: short stories, chapters of a novel, poetry, magazine articles, etc. Members may join two such circulators if they wish. Each circulator has a technical section and a letters section in which friendly communication between members is encouraged, and all are of a general nature apart from one, specialising in mss for the Christian

market. Full details and application forms available on receipt of s.a.e. Subscription: £6.50 p.a.

East Anglian Writers

52 Riverside Road, Norwich, Norfolk NR1 1SR
☎01603 629088 Fax 01603 629088
Email anthony.vivis@tesco.net

Contact *Anthony Vivis*

A group of over 80 professional writers living in Norfolk and Suffolk. Informal pub meetings, occasional speakers' evenings and contact point for professional writers new to the area.

Electronic Manuscript Exchange

Email MSExch@aol.com

A group of serious not-yet-published authors who send and critique each other's work by email. All kinds of fiction accepted. The only requirement is to give as well as receive feedback. Email for membership details.

Equinoxe Screenwriting Workshops

Association Equinoxe, 4 Square du Roule, 75008 Paris France
☎00 33 1 5353 4488 Fax 00 33 1 5353 4489
Email equinoxef@aol.com

FOUNDED 1993, with Jeanne Moreau as president, to promote screenwriting and to establish a link between European and American film production. In association with Canal+, Sony Pictures Entertainment and Media Programme of the EU, Equinoxe supports young writers of all nationalities by creating a screenwriting community capable of appealing to an international audience. Open to selected professional screenwriters able to speak English or French fluently. To-date, Equinoxe has helped 140 European and American authors to perfect and promote scripts. 40 of these have been brought to the screen and several are in production. Contact *Claire Dubert* for further information.

Euroscript

Suffolk House, 1–8 Whitfield Place, London W1P 5SF
☎020 7387 5880 Fax 020 7387 5880
Email euroscript@netmatters.co.uk
Website www.euroscript.co.uk

Euroscript, a Media programme of the EU to advance European scriptwriting, is a distance training project working in EU languages. It develops screenplays, reads, selects and promotes scripts, writers and writer/producer teams. Also runs workshops and supports writers' groups.

Two story competitions per year: deadlines 30 April and 31 October. Write or access the website for further information.

Gay Authors Workshop

BM Box 5700, London WC1N 3XX
☎020 8520 5223

Contact *Kathryn Byrd*

Established 1978 to encourage and support gay and lesbian writers. Regular meetings and a newsletter. The publishing arm – Paradise Press – considers high quality fiction from GAW members only.

Historical Novel Folio

17 Purbeck Heights, Mount Road, Parkstone, Poole, Dorset BH14 0QP
☎01202 741897

Contact *Doris Myall-Harris*

An independent postal workshop – single folio dealing with any period before World War II. Send s.a.e. for details.

The International Inkwell

See entry under **Miscellany**

Kops and Ryan Advanced Playwriting Workshops

41B Canfield Gardens, London NW6 3JL
☎020 7624 2940

Tutors *Bernard Kops, Tom Ryan*

Three ten-week terms per year beginning in September. Students may join course any term. Workshops on Tuesday, 7–10 pm or Thursday, 7–10 pm, or Saturday, 2–5 pm. Small groups. Focus on structure, character, language, meaning and style through written and improvised exercises; reading scenes from students' current work; and readings of full-length plays. Two actors attend each session. Also, instruction in film technique and private tutorials. Call for details.

London Writer Circle

Flat D, 49 Christchurch Street, London SW3 4AS
☎020 7351 6377
Email wendy.stickler@org.uk

FOUNDED 1924. Aims to help and encourage writers of all grades. Monthly evening meetings with well-known speakers on aspects of literature and journalism, and workshops for short story writing, poetry and feature writing. Occasional social events and quarterly magazine. Subscription: £20 (London); £10 (Country); £6 (Overseas). Contact: *Pamela Birley*.

NWP (North West Playwrights)

18 St Margaret's Chambers, 5 Newton Street, Manchester M1 1HL
☎0161 237 1978 Fax 0161 237 1978

FOUNDED 1982. Award-winning organisation whose aim is to develop and promote new theatre writing. Operates a script-reading service, classes and script development scheme and *The Lowdown* newsletter. Services available to writers in the region only.

QueenSpark Books

See entry under **Small Presses**

Screenwriters' Workshop

Suffolk House, 1–8 Whitfield Place, London W1P 5SF
☎020 7387 5511 Fax 020 7387 5511
Website www.lsw.org.uk

ESTABLISHED 1983. Formerly London Screenwriters Workshop, the SW is open to writers from all over Britain and Europe. The Workshop is an educational charity whose aim is to help writers into the film and TV industries. Many high-profile members. Offers a rolling programme of tuition, networking and events including guest speakers and showcasing opportunities. Membership: £30 p.a. Runs *Feedback* – a script-reading service with reduced rates for members. (Contact K. Way, ☎020 8520 9103.)

Scribo

1/31 Hamilton Road, Boscombe, Bournemouth, Dorset BH1 4EQ
☎01202 302533

Contact *K. S. P. A. Sylvester*

Scribo (established for more than 20 years) is a postal workshop for novelists. Mss criticism foilos cover fantasy/sci-fi, crime/thrillers, mainstream, women's fiction, literary. Forums offer information, discussion on all topics relating to writing and literature. No annual subscription. £5 joining fee only. Full details from the address above; enclose s.a.e., please.

Short Story Writers' Folio/ Children's Novel Writers' Folio

5 Park Road, Brading, Sandown, Isle of Wight PO36 0HU
☎01983 407697
Email dawn.wortley-nott@lineone.net

Contact *Mrs Dawn Wortley-Nott*

Postal workshops – members receive constructive criticism of their work and read and offer advice on fellow members' contributions. Send an s.a.e. for further details.

Society of Sussex Authors

Bookends, Lewes Road, Horsted Keynes, Haywards Heath, West Sussex RH17 7DP
☎01825 790755 Fax 01825 790755

Contact *Michael Legat*

FOUNDED 1968 to promote the interests of its members and of literature, particularly within the Sussex area. Regular meetings and exchange of information; plus social events. Membership restricted to writers who live in Sussex and who have had at least one book commercially published, or other writings used professionally. Meetings are held six times a year in Lewes. Annual subscription: £10.

The South and Mid-Wales Association of Writers (SAMWAW)

c/o I.M.C. Consulting Group, Denham House, Lambourne Crescent, Cardiff CF14 5ZW
☎029 2076 1170 Fax 029 2076 1304

Contact *Julian Rosser*

FOUNDED 1971 to foster the art and craft of writing in all its forms. Provides a common meeting ground for writers, critics, editors, adjudicators from all over the UK and abroad. Organises an annual residential weekend conference and a day seminar in May and October respectively. Holds competitions, two for members only and two which are open to the public, in addition to **The Mathew Prichard Award for Short Story Writing** (see entry under **Prizes**). Subscription: £7 (Single); £12 (Joint).

South Eastern Writers' Association

114 Church Road, Harold Wood, Romford, Essex RM3 0SD
☎01708 703479

President *Marion Hough*
Secretary *Janice Grande*

FOUNDED 1989 to bring together experienced and novice writers in an informal atmosphere. Non-profit-making, the Association holds an annual residential weekend each spring at Bulphan, Essex. Free workshops and discussion groups included in the overall cost. Previous guest speakers: Simon Brett, Bernard Cornwell, Deric Longden, Maureen Lipman, Terry Pratchett, Jack Rosenthal. Contact the secretary at the address above for details.

South Manchester Writer's Workshop

c/o Didsbury Methodist Church Hall, Sandhurst Road, Didsbury, Manchester M20
☎0161 431 4717 Email Philcave@aol.com
Website www.manchester-writers.freeserve. co.uk

Contact *Philip Caveney*

The Workshop, which has been running for around 20 years, provides a lively and informative forum where writers at all levels of their craft can meet to read and discuss their work. Meetings held every Tuesday, 7.30–9.30 pm. The first session is free and thereafter a small charge (currently £1.50) is made. Write or access the website for more details.

Southport Writers' Circle

40 Pilkington Road, Southport, Merseyside PR8 6PD

Contact *Marjorie Harriman*

Runs a poetry competition (see entry under **Prizes**).

Southwest Scriptwriters

☎0117 9020788 Fax 0117 9021473
Website www.southwest-scriptwriters.co.uk

FOUNDED 1994 to offer encouragement and advice to those writing for stage, screen, radio and TV in the region. The group, which attracts professional writers, enthusiasts and students, meets regularly at the Theatre Royal, Bristol to read aloud and provide critical feedback on members' work, discuss writing technique and exchange market information. Lucy Catherine, writer-in-residence at the Bristol Old Vic, acts as Honorary President. Subscription: £5 p.a. Contact the Secretary, *John Colborn* for details.

Speakeasy – Milton Keynes Writers' Group

46 Wealdstone Place, Springfield, Milton Keynes MK6 3JG
☎01908 663860
Email martinbrocklebank@ukgateway.net

Contact *Martin Brocklebank*

Invites lovers of the written and spoken word to their monthly meetings on the first Friday of each month, 7.45 pm. Full and varied programme including Local Writers Nights where work can be read and performed. Also runs Annual Open Creative Writing competitions. Phone, email or send s.a.e. for details to address above.

Sussex Playwrights' Club

2 Brunswick Mews, Hove, East Sussex
BN3 1HD
☎01273 730106

Secretary *Dennis Evans*

FOUNDED 1935. Aims to encourage the writing of plays for stage, radio and TV by giving monthly dramatic readings of members' work by experienced actors, mainly from local drama groups. Gives constructive, critical suggestions as to how work might be improved, and suggests possible marketing. Membership is not confined to writers but to all who are interested in theatre in all its forms, and all members are invited to take part in such discussions. Guests are always welcome at a nominal £1. Meetings held at New Venture Theatre, Bedford Place, Brighton, East Sussex. Subscription: £5 p.a. Contact the Secretary for details.

Ver Poets

Haycroft, 61–63 Chiswell Green Lane,
St Albans, Hertfordshire AL2 3AL
☎01727 867005

Chairman *Ray Badman*
Editor/Organiser *May Badman*

FOUNDED 1966 to promote poetry and to help poets. With postal and local members, holds meetings in St Albans; runs a poetry bookstall for members' books and publications from other groups; publishes members' work in anthologies and organises poetry competitions, including the annual **Ver Poets Open** competition. Gives help and advice whenever they are sought and makes information available to members about other poetry groups, events and opportunities for publication. Membership: £12.50 p.a.; £15 or US$30 (Overseas).

West Country Writers' Association

Malvern View, Garway Hill, Hereford
HR2 8EZ
President *Christopher Fry*
Honorary Secretary *Mrs Anne Double*

FOUNDED 1951 in the interest of published authors with an interest in the West Country. Meets to discuss news and views and to listen to talks. Conference and newsletters. Annual subscription: £10 p.a.

Workers' Educational Association

National Office: Temple House, 17 Victoria Park Square, London E2 9PB
☎020 8983 1515 Fax 020 8983 4840
Email info@wea.org.uk

Website www.wea.org.uk

FOUNDED in 1903, the WEA is a voluntary body with members drawn from all walks of life. It runs writing courses and workshops throughout the country and all courses are open to everyone. Branches in most towns and many villages, with 13 district offices in England and one in Scotland. Contact your district WEA office for courses in your region. All correspondence should be addressed to the District Secretary.

Cheshire, Merseyside & West Lancashire: 7/8 Bluecoat Chambers, School Lane, Liverpool L1 3BX (☎0151 709 8023)

Eastern: Botolph House, 17 Botolph Lane, Cambridge CB2 3RE (☎01223 350978)

East Midlands: 39 Mapperley Road, Mapperley Park, Nottingham NG3 5AQ (☎0115 9628400)

London: 4 Luke Street, London EC2A 4NT (☎020 7388 7261/7387 8966)

Northern: 51 Grainger Street, Newcastle upon Tyne NE1 5JE (☎0191 232 3957)

North Western: 4th Floor, Crawford House, University Precinct Centre, Oxford Road, Manchester M13 9GH (☎0161 273 7652)

South Eastern: 4 Castle Hill, Rochester, Kent ME1 1QQ (☎01634 842140)

South Western: Martin's Gate Annexe, Bretonside, Plymouth, Devon PL4 0AT (☎01752 664989)

Thames & Solent: 6 Brewer Street, Oxford OX1 1QN (☎01865 246270)

Western: 40 Morse Road, Redfield, Bristol BS5 9LB (☎01179 351764)

West Mercia: 78–80 Sherlock Street, Birmingham B5 6LT (☎0121 666 6101)

Yorkshire North: 6 Woodhouse Square, Leeds, W. Yorkshire LS3 1AD (☎01132 453304)

Yorkshire South: Chantry Buildings, 6–20 Corporation Street, Rotherham S60 1NG (☎01709 837001)

Scottish Association: Riddle's Court, 322 Lawnmarket, Edinburgh EH1 2PG (☎0131 226 3456)

Writers in Oxford

41 Kingston Road, Oxford OX2 6RH
☎01865 513844 Fax 01865 510017

FOUNDED 1992. Open to published authors, playwrights, poets and journalists. Linked to the **Society of Authors** but organised locally. Arranges a programme of meetings, seminars and social functions. Publishes newsletter, *The Oxford Writer*. Subscription: £15 p.a. Contact the Secretary, *Maggie Black* for details.

Yorkshire Playwrights
3 Trinity Road, Scarborough, North Yorkshire YO11 2TD
☎01723 367449 Fax 01723 367449
Email ScarTam@aol.com
Website www.poptel.org.uk/unholy/yp

FOUNDED 1989 out of an initiative by Jude Kelly and William Weston of the **West Yorkshire Playhouse**. A group of professional writers of plays for stage, TV and radio whose aims are to encourage the writing and performance of new plays in Yorkshire. Open to any writers living in Yorkshire who are members, preferably, of the **Writers' Guild**, or the **Society of Authors**. Contact the Administrator, *Ian Watson* for an information sheet.

Watching your Language:
The Libel Risks of Free Speech

The wild excesses of the court battle between Mohammed Al Fayed and Neil Hamilton seemed to confirm the popular view that the libel laws were designed for general entertainment. But the laughter faded when David Irving sued the American historian Deborah Lipstadt for branding him a 'Holocaust-denier'. Irving tried to promote himself as a victim of censorship, arguing that Lipstadt and her publisher, Penguin, were part of a wider media conspiracy preventing him from having his say. In the event, the court decided that it was Irving who was the enemy of free speech in that he was trying to stop Lipstadt from expressing a sincerely held opinion. Quite apart from the human rights issue, the interest for authors was in Penguin's readiness to foot the legal bill, conservatively estimated to be in the region of £2 million.

Publishers are not always so ready to dash to the barricades. Typically, a publishing contract includes a warranty clause which entitles the publisher to be indemnified by the author against damages and costs if any part of the work turns out to be libellous. It will be interesting to see if, after Penguin's good example, any publisher dares to enforce a warranty clause. The assumption has to be that where the publisher has not been deliberately misled, he has to stand by his author. Up to a point, that is.

Publishers have been made nervous knowing that the risks of encountering a libel action have increased substantially with the extension of 'no win, no fee' litigation to all claims for damages. It is already commonplace to hear solicitors advertising on commercial radio for prospective clients to come forward. Allowing actions to be funded by solicitors working for a success fee is bound to appeal to the easily offended. Even if a loony case fails to get to court, a cost-conscious publisher may choose to play safe by amending a text to a point where it loses its cutting edge and thus its sales appeal. It is not unknown for an entire book to be jettisoned to save on lawyers' bills.

Peter Marsh, a barrister specialising in defamation, offers these tips for writers about to embark on a controversial project.

If the subject or subjects of critical comment are still alive, beware; if you are writing a book about real-life incidents but have changed names to avoid identification, take extreme care in the choice of names for your characters; remember that damage to a person's reputation can be caused by innuendo. For example, to write of someone that most people thought he was taking advantage of the Inland Revenue may suggest some improper and unethical practice. If a living person is going to be the subject of comment which is expressly or implicitly derogatory, make absolutely sure your facts are correct and can be substantiated. Otherwise, your publisher is going to be propelled into the courtroom naked of a defence.

Recent changes in the libel laws were intended to simplify what had become a hideously complex and expensive process. Until recently, for example, it was hard to escape from a libel by arguing that it was committed unintentionally. A claimant had no need to prove that you intended to discredit him or even that he had been harmed by whatever you wrote. All that was necessary was to show that a hurt to reputation had been suffered. The 'offer to make amends' (by fulsome apology, for example) was available but was hedged by technicalities.

Now, under the 1996 Defamation Act, the rules have been tightened to allow for a speedy and relatively inexpensive resolution of disputes. If there was no intention to defame, expensive litigation can be avoided by offering a published apology, a sum in compensation and a settlement of costs. If the amount to be paid cannot be agreed mutually a judge can make an order.

There is a downside, as Daniel Eilon, a solicitor with Campbell Hooper, points out: 'The offer of amends is not so much a defence as an orderly surrender. If you use it, you cannot plead any of the other recognised defences such as justification, fair comment, privilege and innocent dissemination.'

So what if you are in fighting mood? It is a complete defence to prove that a statement, however defamatory, is true in substance and in fact. The trouble with pleading justification, however, is that every significant detail of a statement must be proved to be true, a hard trick to pull.

Another line of defence is to prove that the words complained of are fair comment on a matter of public interest. The defence will fail if the defendant is shown to have been actuated by malice (merely disliking the plaintiff is insufficient) or the facts on which he based the comment were untrue. But fair comment allows for critics to do their worst. For over a century it has been the rule that 'Every latitude must be given to opinion and to prejudice . . . Mere exaggeration, or even gross exaggeration, would not make the comment unfair.'

Privilege covers 'fair and accurate' reports of public judicial proceedings while innocent dissemination applies only to distributors (not authors, editors or publishers). To rely on this defence, a defendant must show that he has taken reasonable care in relation to the publication of the statement; had no reason to believe that he was contributing to the publication of a defamatory statement; and had no effective control over the maker of the statement. This defence came into force in 1996 and was aimed at protecting booksellers. But there is a catch. It now appears that by putting responsibility on 'agents' of author, editor and publisher, a bookseller might still be prosecuted because a court could argue that he has 'contributed to the publication of a defamatory statement'.

To choose any one of these defences is to cut off any line of retreat. There can be no resort to an offer to make amends.

Since 1996, the time limit for starting an action for defamation has been cut from three years to one (except in Scotland), thus curbing the use of 'gagging writs' such as those used by the late Robert Maxwell. There is a new summary procedure under which every defamation claim can come before a judge at an early stage. The judge assesses whether the claim is suitable for summary disposal, or whether it should go for trial, with or without a jury. He has power to award damages up to £10,000. This makes it easier for an ordinary citizen to seek redress against a rich opponent who, otherwise, is liable to keep a trial going as long as possible in the hope that a plaintiff will run out of patience and money.

There is some hope that the lid has been put on outrageous libel awards now that the Court of Appeal can provide guidelines. Many reformers would go further. They want the responsibility of a jury to be limited to saying whether damages should be substantial, moderate, nominal or contemptuous. The judge would then decide on the appropriate figure. A useful compromise would compel juries to explain their calculations. As Lord Donaldson has observed, 'having to give reasons puts a substantial premium on ensuring that the head rules the heart'.

Is there anything to be said for those who bring libel actions? John Mortimer, who has defended in numerous libel actions, denounces what he still believes to be an 'arcane and hideously expensive branch of the law' and advises 'if anyone insults you forget about it as quickly as possible'.

As for those who are unable to keep out of the courts, the best advice comes from Tom Crone in his book *Law and the Media*. The libel litigant, he says, must possess two prime qualities – 'a strong nerve and a deep pocket'.

Miscellany

Arjay Research
20 Rookery View, Little Thurrock, Grays,
Essex RM17 6AS
☎01375 372199 Fax 01375 372199
Email RogWJ@aol.com
Contact *Roger W. Jordan*

All aspects of international merchant shipping
and naval research undertaken by former shipping archivist and editor. Extensive maritime
library and comprehensive databases on *inter
alia* ships wrecked/lost and passenger and cruise
ships. Terms by arrangement.

Authors' Research Services
32 Oak Village, London NW5 4QN
☎020 7284 4316 Fax 020 7284 4316
Email rmwindser@aol.com
Contact *Richard Wright*

Research and document supply service, particularly to authors, academics and others without
easy access to London libraries and sources of
information. Also indexing of books and journals. Rates negotiable.

Book Affairs Ltd
74 Lee Road, Perivale, Middlesex UB6 7DB
Email enquiries@BookAffairs.com
Website www.BookAffairs.com
Directors *Rohail Ahmad, Samar Ahmad*

FOUNDED 1999. Website for new authors; fiction only. Material is vetted initially for literary
quality then complete manuscripts are made
available on the website. Readers can download
and read the books for free and submit reviews,
in particular their opinion as to whether the
book should be published or not. Reader-
approved books are then placed in a separate
section for consideration by publishers and conventional literary agents. See website for details.

Brooks Krikler Research
455 Finchley Road, London NW3 6HN
☎020 7431 9886 Fax 020 7431 9887
Email bkr@pictures.demon.co.uk
Contact *Emma Krikler*

Provides a full picture-research service to publishers and the media. Books, magazines, advertising, CD-ROM and multimedia, brochures,
video and computer games manufacturers and
designers. The service includes finding, editing

and providing images, negotiating all reproduction charges inclusive of full copyright clearance.
Has special arrangements with photographic
libraries worldwide and a variety of photographers can undertake commissioned work. An
online service is available with all requests.

Combrógos
10 Heol Don, Whitchurch, Cardiff CF14 2AU
☎029 2062 3359 Fax 029 2052 9202
Contact *Meic Stephens*

FOUNDED 1990. Arts and media research, editorial services, specialising in books about Wales or
by Welsh authors. 'Encyclopaedic knowledge of
Welsh history, language, literature and culture.'

Copyplus
Hadnock Road, Monmouth NP5 3NQ
☎01600 772600 Fax 01600 712896
Email info@copyplus.demon.co.uk
Contact *Peter T. Wilson*

Advice and technical assistance to poets, writers
and organisations that wish to self-publish.
Specialises in bespoke publications with print
runs as low as 25 copies.

The International Inkwell, a writers' retreat
Cafe du Livre, Rue de la Mairie,
11170 Montolieu, Aude France
☎00 33 468 248117
Email cafedulivre@aol.com
Website www.cafedulivre.com
Also: 96 Edith Grove, Chelsea, London SW10
☎01304 369799 Fax 020 7352 3951
Contact *Lucia Stuart*

Set in the French medieval village of Montolieu,
which boasts 14 bookshops to a population of
800, The International Inkwell rents rooms for
writers. Open from June to September, groups
are welcome for writing courses, reading weeks
or forums. For further details contact *Lucia Stuart*
at the address in France from May to September
or the London address from November to April.

The Literary Consultancy
PO Box 12939, London N8 9WA
☎020 8372 3922 Fax 020 8372 3922
Email swifttlc@dircon.co.uk
Website www.literaryconsultancy.co.uk

Contact *Rebecca Swift*

Founded by former publishers to offer an editorial service and advice for aspiring writers. Will provide an appraisal of fiction, poetry and most categories of non-fiction. Charges from £40 for a short story to £300 for a full ms of 300 pages.

Murder Files

Marienau, Brimley Road, Bovey Tracey, Devon TQ13 9DH
☎01626 833487 Fax 01626 835797
Email ukmurders@bigfoot.com
Website www.bigfoot.com/@ukmurders

Contact *Paul Williams*

Crime writer and researcher specialising in UK murders. Can provide information on thousands of well-known and less well-known cases dating from 1400. Copies of press cuttings relating to murder available for cases from 1920 onwards. Service available to general enquirers, writers, TV, radio, video, etc. Rates on application.

Netcontent

42 Brigstocke Terrace, Ryde, Isle of Wight PO33 2PD
☎0870 7415802 Fax 0870 4589985
Email netcontent@cyber-hospital.co.uk

Contacts *Dr Jeremy Sims, Dr Sean Radford*

FOUNDED 1999 to develop content for both paper-based and web-based publishers. Has access to over 200 writers. Provides content for magazines, newspapers and websites across a broad range of subjects including quizzes, puzzles, crosswords, health, travel, entertainment and information technology.

New Authors Showcase

Rivendell, Kingsgate, Torquay, Devon TQ2 8QA
☎01803 326617
Email james@newauthors.org.uk
Website www.newauthors.org.uk

Contact *Barrie E. James*

FOUNDED 1997. An Internet site for new writers and poets to display their work to publishers. No unsolicited mss. First approach by sending s.a.e.

Ormrod Research Services

Weeping Birch, Burwash, East Sussex TN19 7HG
☎01435 882541 Fax 01435 882541

Contact *Richard Ormrod*

ESTABLISHED 1982. Comprehensive research service: literary, historical, academic, biographical, commercial. Verbal quotations available.

Roger Palmer Limited, Media Contracts

Antonia House, 262 Holloway Road, London N7 6NE
☎020 7697 8989 Fax 020 7697 8877
Email contracts@rogerpalmer.co.uk

Contact *Peter Palmer*

ESTABLISHED 1993. Drafts, advises on and negotiates all media contracts (on a regular or *ad hoc* basis) for publishers, literary and merchandising agents, authors, packagers, charities and others. Manages and operates clients' complete contracts functions, undertakes contractual audits, devises contracts and permissions systems, advises on copyright and related issues and provides training and seminars on an individual or group basis. Extensive private client list, with special rates for members of the **Society of Authors** and the **Writers' Guild**.

Patent Research

Dachsteinstr. 12a, D–81825 Munich, Germany
☎00 49 89 430 7833

Contact *Gerhard Everwyn*

All world, historical patents for researchers, authors, archives, museums and publishers. Rates on application.

Teral Research Services

45 Forest View Road, Moordown, Bournemouth, Dorset BH9 3BH
☎01202 516834 Fax 01202 516834

Contact *Terry C. Treadwell*

All aspects of research undertaken but specialises in all military, aviation, naval and defence subjects, both past and present. Extensive book and photographic library, including one of the best collections of World War One aviation photographs. Terms by arrangement.

Melanie Wilson

Ten Steps, Church Street, Seagrave LE12 7LT
☎01509 812806 Fax 01509 812334
Email MelanieWilson@bigfoot.com

Contact *Melanie Wilson*

Comprehensive research service for books, magazines, newspapers, documentaries, films, radio, education, TV drama. Includes free worldwide booksearch service and groundwork for factual basis for all media presentations, particularly in historical research, costume and textiles, crafts, food and cooking, weapons and uniforms, traditional storytelling, past technology, living history displays and exhibitions.

Press Cuttings Agencies

The Broadcast Monitoring Company

89½ Worship Street, London EC2A 2BF
☎020 7377 1742 Fax 020 7377 6103
Website www.bmc.co.uk

Television, radio, national and European press monitoring agency. Cuttings from national and all major European press available seven days a week, with early morning delivery. Also monitoring of all news and current affairs programmes – national, international and satellite. Retrospective research service and free telephone notification. Sponsorship evaluation from all media sources.

Clipserver.com

Newserve House, Singer Street, London EC2A 4BQ
☎020 7959 1200 Fax 020 7959 1201
Email infor@clipserver.com
Website www.clipserver.com

Contact *Gary Forrest*

Offers an overnight national press monitoring service with same day, early morning delivery. Also coverage of European and regional papers, and weekly/monthly business/trade magazines. Rates on application.

Durrants Press Cuttings Ltd

Discovery House, 28–42 Banner Street, London EC1Y 8QE
☎020 7674 0200 Fax 020 7674 0222
Website www.durrants.co.uk

Wide coverage of all print media sectors; foreign press in association with agencies abroad; current affairs and news programmes from UK broadcast media. High speed, early morning press cuttings from the national press. Overnight delivery via courier to most areas or first-class mail. Well presented, laser printed, A4 cuttings. Rates on application.

International Press-Cutting Bureau

224–236 Walworth Road, London SE17 1JE
☎020 7708 2113 Fax 020 7701 4489
Email rpodro@aol.com

Contact *Robert Podro*

Covers national, provincial, trade, technical and magazine press. Cuttings are normally sent twice weekly by first-class post and there are no additional service charges or reading fees. Subscriptions for 100 and 250 cuttings are valid for six months. 100 cuttings, £246.75, including VAT; 250, £528.75.

Press Express

3rd Floor, 53—56 Great Sutton Street, London EC1V 0DE
☎020 7689 0123 Fax 020 7251 1412

Contact *Charles Stuart-Hunt*

High-speed overnight press cuttings.

Romeike & Curtice

Hale House, 290—296 Green Lanes, London N13 5TP
☎0800 289543 Fax 020 8882 6716
Email info@romeike.com
Website www.romeike.com

Contact *Mary Michael*

Monitors national and international dailies and Sundays, provincial papers, consumer magazines, trade and technical journals, teletext services as well as national radio and TV networks. Back research, advertising checking and Internet monitoring are also available.

We Find It (Press Clippings)

103 South Parade, Belfast BT7 2GN
☎028 9064 6008 Fax 028 9064 6008

Contact *Avril Forsythe*

Specialises in Northern Ireland press and magazines, both national and provincial. Rates on application.

Bursaries, Fellowships and Grants

Aosdána

An Chomhairle Ealaíon (The Irish Arts Council), 70 Merrion Square, Dublin 2, Republic of Ireland

☎00 353 1 6180252 Fax 00 353 1 6761302

Website www.artscouncil.ie

Registrar of Aosdána *Patricia Quinn*

Assistant Registrar *Dermot McLaughlin*

Aosdána is an affiliation of creative artists engaged in literature, music and the visual arts, and consists of not more than 200 artists who have gained a reputation for achievement and distinction. Membership is by competitive sponsored selection and is open to Irish citizens or residents only. Members are eligible to receive an annuity for a five-year term to assist them in pursuing their art full-time.

Award IR£8720 (annuity).

Arts Council Literature Bursaries, Ireland

An Chomhairle Ealaíon (The Irish Arts Council), 70 Merrion Square, Dublin 2, Republic of Ireland

☎00 353 1 6180252 Fax 00 353 1 6761302

Website www.artscouncil.ie

Literature Officer *Sinéad Mac Aodha*

Bursaries in literature awarded to creative writers of fiction, poetry and drama in Irish and English to enable concentration on, or completion of, specific projects. A limited number of bursaries may also be given to non-fiction projects. Open to Irish citizens or residents only. Final entry date 19 May.

Award IR£3000–£8000 (£10,000–16,000 over two years).

Arts Council Theatre Writing Bursaries

Arts Council of England, 14 Great Peter Street, London SW1P 3NQ

☎020 7973 6431 Fax 020 7973 6983

Email jemima.lee@artscouncil.org.uk

Website www.artscouncil.org.uk

Contact *Jemima Lee*

Intended to provide experienced playwrights with an opportunity to research and develop a play for the theatre independently of financial pressures and free from the need to write for a particular market. Bursaries are also available for theatre translation projects. Writers must be resident in England. Writers resident in Wales, Scotland or Northern Ireland should approach their own Arts Council.

Award £5500.

The Authors' Contingency Fund

The Society of Authors, 84 Drayton Gardens, London SW10 9SB

☎020 7373 6642 Fax 020 7373 5768

This fund makes modest grants to published authors who find themselves in sudden financial difficulties. Contact the **Society of Authors** for an information sheet and application form.

The Authors' Foundation

The Society of Authors, 84 Drayton Gardens, London SW10 9SB

☎020 7373 6642 Fax 020 7373 5768

Grants to writers whose publisher's advance is insufficient to cover the costs of research involved. Application by letter to The Authors' Foundation giving details, in confidence, of the advance and royalties, together with the reasons for needing additional funding. Grants are sometimes given even if there is no commitment by a publisher, so long as the applicant has had a book published and the new work will almost certainly be published. About £50,000 is distributed each year. Contact the **Society of Authors** for an information sheet. Final entry dates 30 April and 30 October.

The K. Blundell Trust

The Society of Authors, 84 Drayton Gardens, London SW10 9SB

☎020 7373 6642 Fax 020 7373 5768

Grants to writers whose publisher's advance is insufficient to cover the costs of research. Author must be under 40, has to submit a copy of his/her previous book and the work must 'contribute to the greater understanding of existing social and economic organisation'. Application by letter. Contact the **Society of Authors** for an information sheet. Final entry dates 30 April and 30 October.

Alfred Bradley Bursary Award

c/o Network Radio Drama, BBC North,
Room 2104, New Broadcasting House,
Oxford Road, Manchester M60 1SJ
☎0161 244 4260 Fax 0161 244 4248
Email wils.wilson@bbc.co.uk

Contact *Wils Wilson*

ESTABLISHED 1992. Biennial award in commemoration of the life and work of the distinguished radio producer Alfred Bradley. Aims to encourage and develop new writing talent in the BBC North region. There is a change of focus for each award; the theme for the 2000 award is Comedy Drama/Sitcom. Entrants must live or work in the North region. The award is given to help authors to pursue a career in writing for radio. Support and guidance is given from regional BBC radio producers. Previous winners: Lee Hall, Mandy Precious, Peter Stranghan.

Award Up to £6000 over two years.

British Academy Small Personal Research Grants

10 Carlton House Terrace, London SW1Y 5AH
☎020 7969 5200 Fax 020 7969 5300

Contact *Assistant Secretary, Research Grants*

Quarterly award to further original creative research at postdoctoral level in the humanities and social sciences. Entrants must no longer be registered for postgraduate study, and must be resident in the UK. Final entry dates end of September, November, February and April.

Award maximum £5000.

Cholmondeley Awards

The Society of Authors, 84 Drayton Gardens, London SW10 9SB
☎020 7373 6642 Fax 020 7373 5768

FOUNDED 1965 by the late Dowager Marchioness of Cholmondeley. Annual honorary awards to recognise the achievement and distinction of individual poets. 1999 winners: Vicki Feaver, Geoffrey Hill, Elma Mitchell, Sheenagh Pugh.

Award (total) £8000.

The Economist/Richard Casement Internship

The Economist, 25 St James's Street, London SW1A 1HG
☎020 7830 7000
Website www.economist.com

Contact *Science Editor (re. Casement Internship)*

For an aspiring journalist under 25 to spend three months in the summer writing for *The Economist* about science and technology. Applicants should write a letter of introduction along with an article of approximately 600 words suitable for inclusion in the Science and Technology Section. Competition details usually announced in the magazine late January or early February and 4–5 weeks allowed for application.

European Jewish Publication Society

PO Box 19948, London N3 3ZJ
☎020 8346 1668 Fax 020 8346 1776
Email cs@ejps.org.uk
Website www.ejps.org.uk

Contact *Dr Colin Shindler*

ESTABLISHED in 1995 to help fund the publication of books of European Jewish interest which would otherwise remain unpublished. Helps with the marketing, distribution and promotion of such books. Publishers who may be interested in publishing works of Jewish interest should approach the Society with a proposal and manuscript in the first instance. Books which have been supported include: *The Vanished Shtetl* Stanislav Brunstein; *Tidings from Zion* Jennifer Glynn; *Botchki* David Zagier; *Just One More Dance* Ernest Levy.

Grant £3000 (maximum)

Fulbright Awards

The Fulbright Commission, Fulbright House, 62 Doughty Street, London WC1N 2LS
☎020 7404 6880 Fax 020 7404 6834
Website www.fulbright.co.uk

Contact *Programme Director*

The Fulbright Commission has a number of scholarships given at postgraduate level and above, open to any field (science and the arts) of study/research to be undertaken in the USA. Length of award is typically an academic year. Application deadline for postgraduate awards is usually late October/early November of preceding year of study; and mid-March/early April for distinguished scholar awards. Further details and application forms are available on the website. Alternatively, send A4 envelope with sufficient postage for 100g with a covering letter explaining which level of award is of interest.

Fulton Fellowship

David Fulton (Publishers) Ltd, Ormond House, 26/27 Boswell Street, London WC1N 3JD
☎020 7405 5606 Fax 020 7831 4840
Email david.fulton@fultonbooks.co.uk

Website www.fultonbooks.co.uk
Chairman and Publisher *David Fulton*
Managing Director *David Hill*

The Fulton Fellowship in Special Education was ESTABLISHED in 1995 with The Centre for the Study of Special Education, Westminster College, Oxford. The Fellowship, worth £2000, has been extended to offer schools as well as individual teachers the chance to share work their staff have done or are doing collaboratively through written publication to a wider audience. 2000 Fellow: Mordaunt School, Southampton.

The Tony Godwin Award
The Tony Godwin Memorial Trust,
c/o Laurence Pollinger Limited, 18 Maddox Street, London W1R 0EU
☎020 7629 9761 Fax 020 7629 9765
Email info@tgmt.org.uk
Website www.tgmt.org.uk
Contact *Lesley Hadcroft*
Chairman *Iain Brown* (020 7627 4244)

Biennial award established to commemorate the life of Tony Godwin, a prominent publisher in the 1960s/70s. Open to all young people (under 35 years old) who are UK nationals and working, or intending to work, in publishing. The award provides the recipient with the means to spend at least one month as the guest of an American publishing house in order to learn about international publishing. The recipient is expected to submit a report upon return to the UK. Final entry date for next award: 1 February, 2001. Previous winners: George Lucas (Hodder), Richard Scrivener (Penguin), Fiona Stewart (HarperCollins).
  Award Bursary of approx. US$5000.

Eric Gregory Trust Fund
The Society of Authors, 84 Drayton Gardens, London SW10 9SB
☎020 7373 6642 Fax 020 7373 5768

Annual competitive awards of varying amounts are made each year for the encouragement of young poets under the age of 30 who can show that they are likely to benefit from an opportunity to give more time to writing. Open only to British-born subjects resident in the UK. Final entry date, 31 October. Contact the **Society of Authors** for further information. 1999 winners: Ross Cogan, Matthew Hollis, Helen Ivory, Andrew Pidoux, Owen Sheers, Dan Wyke.
  Award (total) £21,000.

The Guardian Research Fellowship
Nuffield College, Oxford OX1 1NF
☎01865 278520 Fax 01865 278676
Contact *Warden's Secretary*

One-year fellowship endowed by the Scott Trust, owner of *The Guardian*, to give someone working in the media the chance to put their experience into a new perspective, publish the outcome and give a *Guardian* lecture. Applications welcomed from journalists and management members, in newspapers, periodicals or broadcasting. Research or study proposals should be directly related to experience of working in the media. Accommodation and meals in college will be provided and a stipend. Advertised biennially in November.

Hawthornden Castle Fellowship
Hawthornden Castle, The International Retreat for Writers, Lasswade, Midlothian EH18 1EG
☎0131 440 2180
Administrator *Dr Kusnetz*

ESTABLISHED 1982 to provide a peaceful setting where published writers can work without disturbance. The Retreat houses five writers at a time, who are known as Hawthornden Fellows. Writers from any part of the world may apply for the fellowships. No monetary assistance is given, nor any contribution to travelling expenses, but once arrived at Hawthornden, the writer is the guest of the Retreat. Applications on forms provided must be made by the end of September for the following calendar year. Previous winners include: Les Murray, Alasdair Gray, Helen Vendler, Olive Senior, Hilary Spurling.

Francis Head Bequest
The Society of Authors, 84 Drayton Gardens, London SW10 9SB
☎020 7373 6642 Fax 020 7373 5768

Provides grants to published British authors over the age of 35 who need financial help during a period of illness, disablement or temporary financial crisis. Contact the **Society of Authors** for an information sheeet and application form.

Ralph Lewis Award
University of Sussex Library, Brighton, East Sussex BN1 9QL
☎01273 678158 Fax 01273 678441

ESTABLISHED 1985. Occasional award set up by Ralph Lewis, a Brighton author and art collector who left money to fund awards for promising manuscripts which would not otherwise be published. The award is given in the form of a grant to a UK-based publisher in respect of an agreed three-year programme of publication of literary works by new authors or by established authors using new styles or forms. No direct applications from writers. Previous winners: **Peterloo Poets** (1989–91); **Serpent's Tail** (1992–94); **Stride Publications** (1997–99).

London Arts Board: Publishing New Writing Fund

London Arts Board, Elme House, 133 Long Acre, London WC2E 9AF
☎020 7240 1313 Fax 020 7670 2400
Email sarah.sanders@lonab.co.uk

Aims to support and develop small presses and literary magazines in the publishing of new or under-represented fiction and poetry. This fund is open only to groups for whom publishing is a central activity. Deadline for applications is in August. Contact the Literature Administrator for further details and an application form.

Macaulay Fellowship

An Chomhairle Ealaíon (The Irish Arts Council), 70 Merrion Square, Dublin 2, Republic of Ireland
☎00 353 1 6180252 Fax 00 353 1 6761302

Literature Officer *Sinéad Mac Aodha*

To further the liberal education of a young creative artist. Candidates for this triennial award must be under 30 on 30 June, or 35 in exceptional circumstances, and must be Irish citizens or residents. The Fellowship is offered on rotation between Music, Visual Arts and Literature (Visual Arts in 2000).
Award IR£3500.

The John Masefield Memorial Trust

The Society of Authors, 84 Drayton Gardens, London SW10 9SB
☎020 7373 6642 Fax 020 7373 5768

This trust makes occasional grants to professional poets (or their immediate dependants) who are faced with sudden financial problems. Contact the **Society of Authors** for an information sheet and application form.

Somerset Maugham Trust Fund

The Society of Authors, 84 Drayton Gardens, London SW10 9SB
☎020 7373 6642 Fax 020 7373 5768

The annual awards arising from this Fund are designed to encourage young writers to travel and to acquaint themselves with other countries.

Candidates must be under 35 and their publishers must submit a published literary work in volume form in English. They must be British subjects by birth. Final entry date 31 December. Presentation in June. 1999 winners: Andrea Ashworth *Once in a House on Fire*; Paul Farley *The Boy From the Chemist is Here to See You*; Giles Foden *The Last King of Scotland*; Jonathan Freedland *Bring Home the Revolution*.
Awards £3000 each.

The Airey Neave Trust

40 Charles Street, London W1X 7PB
☎020 7495 0554 Fax 020 7491 1118

Contact *Hannah Scott*

INITIATED 1989. Annual research fellowships for up to three years – towards a book or paper – for serious research connected with national and international law, and human freedom. Must be attached to a particular university in Britain. Interested applicants should come forward with ideas, preferably before March in any year.

New London Writers Awards

London Arts Board, Elme House, 133 Long Acre, London WC2E 9AF
☎020 7240 1313 Fax 020 7670 2400
Email sarah.sanders@lonab.co.uk

Contact *Sarah Sanders*

ESTABLISHED 1993/94. Five bursaries, of £4000 each, are awarded annually to London writers. Application form available from the address above. Final entry date: 12 January 2001. The five winners in 1998/99 were Daphne Rock, Luke Sutherland, Judith Bryan, Alex Wheatle and Simon Lewis.

Newspaper Press Fund

Dickens House, 35 Wathen Road, Dorking, Surrey RH4 1JY
☎01306 887511 Fax 01306 888212

Director/Secretary *David Ilott*

Aims to relieve distress among journalists and their dependants. Limited help available to non-member journalists. Continuous and/or occasional financial grants; also retirement homes for eligible beneficiaries. Further information and subscription details available from the Secretary or via the Reuter Foundation website on: www.foundation.reuters.com.npf

Northern Arts Literary Fellowship

Northern Arts, 10 Osborne Terrace, Jesmond, Newcastle upon Tyne NE2 1NZ
☎0191 281 6334 Fax 0191 281 3276

Contact *Film, Media & Literature Department*

A competitive fellowship in association with the Universities of Durham and Newcastle upon Tyne. Contact Northern Arts for details.

Northern Playwriting Panel
See **New Writing North** under **Professional Associations and Societies**

Northern Writers' Awards
See **New Writing North** under **Professional Associations and Societies**

The PAWS (Public Awareness of Science) Drama Script Fund
The PAWS Office, OMNI Communications, Osborne House, 111 Bartholomew Road, London NW5 2BJ
☎020 7267 2555 Fax 020 7482 2394

Contacts *Barrie Whatley, Andrew Millington*

ESTABLISHED 1994. Annual award aimed at encouraging television scriptwriters to include science and engineering scenarios in their work. Grants (currently £2000) are given to selected writers to develop their script ideas into full treatments; prizes are awarded for the best of these treatments. The PAWS Fund holds meetings enabling writers to meet scientists and engineers and also offers a contacts service to put writers in 'one-to-one' contact with specialists who can help them develop their ideas. See also **The PAWS Midas Prize** under **Prizes**.

Pearson Playwrights' Scheme
3 Burlington Gardens, London W1X 1LE

Administrator *Jack Andrews*

Awards four bursaries to playwrights annually, each worth £5000. Applicants must be sponsored by a theatre which then submits the play for consideration by a panel. Each award allows the playwright a twelve-month attachment. Applications invited via theatres in September 2000. For up-to-date information, contact *Jack Andrews* (☎020 8943 2250).

The Margaret Rhondda Award
The Society of Authors, 84 Drayton Gardens, London SW10 9SB
☎020 7373 6642 Fax 020 7373 5768

Competitive award given to a woman writer as a grant-in-aid towards the expenses of a research project in journalism. Contact the **Society of Authors** for an information sheet.

Triennial (next awarded: 2002). Final entry date 31 December 2001.
Award approx. £1000.

The Royal Literary Fund
3 Johnson's Court, off Fleet Street, London EC4A 3EA
☎020 7353 7150 Fax 020 7353 1350

Secretary *Eileen Gunn*

Grants and pensions are awarded to published authors in financial need, or to their dependants. Examples of author's works are needed for assessment by Committee. Write for further details and application form.

Scottish Arts Council Book Awards
Scottish Arts Council, 12 Manor Place, Edinburgh EH3 7DD
☎0131 226 6051 Fax 0131 240 2575
Email gavin.wallace@scottisharts.org.uk

Literature Officer *Gavin Wallace*

Four awards of £1000 each are made in both spring and autumn. Preference is given to literary fiction and verse, but literary non-fiction is also considered. Authors should be Scottish or resident in Scotland, but books of Scottish interest by other authors are eligible for consideration. Books by Scottish writers for children are eligible for three new annual awards. Publishers should apply for further information.

Scottish Arts Council Writers' Bursaries
Scottish Arts Council, 12 Manor Place, Edinburgh EH3 7DD
☎0131 226 6051 Fax 0131 240 2575
Email jenny.brown@scottisharts.org.uk

Contact *Jenny Brown, Literature Director*

A limited number of bursaries – of between £1000 and £10,000 – are offered to enable professional writers, including writers for children, to devote more time to writing. Priority is given to writers of fiction and verse, but writers of literary non-fiction are also considered. Application normally open only to writers who have been living and working in Scotland for at least two years.

Southern Arts Writer's Award
13 St Clement Street, Winchester, Hampshire SO23 9DQ
☎01962 855099 Fax 01962 861186

Contact *Literature Officer*

Offers annual awards of £3000 each to two published writers living in the region to assist a specific project. Awards can be used to cover a period of unpaid leave while writing from home, to finance necessary research and travel, or to purchase equipment. Final entry date: October – please contact for date nearer the time.

Laurence Stern Fellowship

Department of Journalism, City University, Northampton Square, London EC1V 0HB
☎020 7477 8224 Fax 020 7477 8594
Website www.city.ac.uk/journalism
Contact *Bob Jones*

FOUNDED 1980. Awarded to a young journalist experienced enough to work on national stories. It gives them the chance to work on the national desk of the *Washington Post*. Benjamin Bradlee, the *Post*'s Vice-President-at-Large, selects from a shortlist drawn up in March/April. 1999 winner: Will Woodward. Full details available on the website.

David Thomas Prize

The Financial Times (W), 1 Southwark Bridge, London SE1 9HL
☎020 7873 3000 Fax 020 7873 3924
Managing Editor *John Ridding*

FOUNDED 1991. Annual award in memory of David Thomas, *FT* journalist killed on assignment in Kuwait in April 1991, whose 'life was characterised by original and radical thinking coupled with a search for new subjects and orthodoxies to challenge'. The award will provide an annual study/travel grant to enable the recipient to take a career break to explore a theme in the fields of industrial policy, Third World development or the environment. Entrants may be of any nationality; age limits vary. A given theme which changes from year to year is announced in the early autumn. Entrants should submit up to 800 words on the theme, together with a brief c.v. and proposal outlining how the award could be used to explore the theme further. Award winners will be required to write an essay of 1500–2000 words at the end of the study period which will be considered for publication in the newspaper. Final entry date end December/early January.
Prize £3000 travel grant.

Tom-Gallon Trust

The Society of Authors, 84 Drayton Gardens, London SW10 9SB
☎020 7373 6642 Fax 020 7373 5768

A biennial award is made from the Trust Fund to fiction writers of limited means who have had at least one short story accepted for publication. Authors wishing to enter should send a list of their already published fiction, giving the name of the publisher or periodical in each case and the approximate date of publication; one short story; a brief statement of their financial position; an undertaking that they intend to devote a substantial amount of time to the writing of fiction as soon as they are financially able to do so; their date of birth; and s.a.e.s for acknowledgement and for the return of work submitted. Final entry date 20 September 2000.
Award £1000.

The Betty Trask Awards

The Society of Authors, 84 Drayton Gardens, London SW10 9SB
☎020 7373 6642 Fax 020 7373 5768

These annual awards are for authors who are under 35 and Commonwealth citizens, awarded on the strength of a first novel (published or unpublished) of a traditional or romantic nature. The awards must be used for a period or periods of foreign travel. Final entry date 31 January. Contact the **Society of Authors** for an information sheet. 1999 winners: Elliot Perlman *Three Dollars*; Catherine Chidgey *In a Fishbone Church*; Giles Foden *The Last King of Scotland*; Dennis Bock *Olympia*; Rajeev Balasubramanyam *In Beautiful Disguises*; Sarah Waters *Tipping the Velvet*.
Award (total) £23,500.

The Travelling Scholarships

The Society of Authors, 84 Drayton Gardens, London SW10 9SB
☎020 7373 6642 Fax 020 7373 5768

Annual honorary grants to established British writers. 1999 winners: Julia Blackburn, David Hart, David Mitchell.
Award (total) £6000.

UEA Writing Fellowship

University of East Anglia, University Plain, Norwich, Norfolk NR4 7TJ
☎01603 592734 Fax 01603 593522
Director of Personnel & Registry Services *J. R. L. Beck*

ESTABLISHED 1971. Awarded to a writer of established reputation in any field for a period of six months, January to end June. The duties of the Fellowship are discussed at an interview. It is assumed that one activity will be the pursuit of the Fellow's own writing. In addition the Fellow will be expected to (a) offer an under-graduate creative writing workshop in the School of English and American Studies during the Spring semester; (b) make contact with groups around the county. An office and some limited secretarial assistance will be provided, and some additional funds will be available to help the Fellow with the activities described above. Applications for the fellowship should be lodged with the Director of Personnel & Registry Services in the autumn; candidates should submit at least two examples of recent work. Previous winner: Bridget O'Connor.

Award £7000 plus free flat on campus.

Gwyn Alf Williams Memorial Award

Academi, 3rd Floor, Mount Stuart House, Mount Stuart Square, Cardiff CF10 6DQ
☎029 2047 2266 Fax 029 2049 2930
Website www.academi.org

Annual research award commemorating the life and work of Gwyn Alf Williams, the distin-guished Welsh historian and writer. Proposals submitted should be for a work of historical non-fiction, in English or Welsh. The recipient of the award will be expected to produce a piece of work of Welsh interest comprising 10,000 to 20,000 words. Entry details available from the Academi. 1998 winner: Sally Parkin for research into the social history of witchcraft in Wales.

Prizes

ABSW/Glaxo Science Writers' Awards

Association of British Science Writers,
23 Savile Row, London W1X 2NB
☎020 7439 1205 Fax 020 7973 3051

ABSW Administrator *Barbara Drillsma*

A series of annual awards for outstanding science journalism in newspapers, journals and broadcasting.

J. R. Ackerley Prize

English Centre of International PEN,
152–156 Kentish Town Road, London
NW1 9QB
☎020 7267 9444 Fax 020 7267 9304
Email enquiries@pen.org.uk
Website www.pen.org.uk

Commemorating the novelist/autobiographer J. R. Ackerley, this prize is awarded for a literary autobiography, written in English and published in the year preceding the award. Entry restricted to nominations from the Ackerley Trustees only ('please do not submit books'). 2000 winner: Mark Frankland *Child of My Time.*

Acorn-Rukeyser Chapbook Contest

Mekler & Deahl, Publishers, 237 Prospect
Street South, Hamilton, Ontario, Canada
L8M 2Z6
☎001 905 312 1779 Fax 001 905 312 8285
Email meklerdeahl@globalserve.net
Website www.meklerdeahl.com

Contacts *James Deahl, Gilda Mekler*

ESTABLISHED in 1996, this annual award is named after the poets Milton Acorn and Muriel Rukeyser in order to honour their achievements as populist poets. Poets may enter as many as 30 poems for a fee of £5. Final entry date: 31 October. Contact the above address for a copy of the rules or access the website.

Prizes 1st and 2nd, (US) $100 and publication of the manuscript.

Age Concern Book of the Year
See **The Seebohm Trophy**

Aldeburgh Poetry Festival Prize

Reading Room Yard, The Street, Brockdish,
Diss, Norfolk IP21 4JZ
☎01379 668345 Fax 01379 668844

Contact *Naomi Jaffa*

ESTABLISHED 1989 by the Aldeburgh Poetry Trust. Sponsored by the Aldeburgh Bookshop for the best first collection published in Britain or the Republic of Ireland in the preceding twelve months. Open to any first collection of poetry of at least 40 pp. Final entry date: 1 October. Previous winners include: Donald Atkinson, Susan Wicks, Gwyneth Lewis, Glyn Wright, Robin Robertson, Tamar Yoseloff.

Prize £500, plus an invitation to read at the following year's festival.

Alexander Prize

Royal Historical Society, University College
London, Gower Street, London WC1E 6BT
☎020 7387 7532 Fax 020 7387 7532

Contact *Literary Director*

Awarded for a historical essay of not more than 8000 words. Competitors may choose their own subject for the essay. Closing date: 1 November.

Prize £250 or a silver medal.

An Duais don bhFilíocht i nGaeilge

An Chomhairle Ealaíon (The Irish Arts
Council), 70 Merrion Square, Dublin 2,
Republic of Ireland
☎00 353 1 6180252 Fax 00 353 1 6761302

Literature Officer *Sinéad Mac Aodha*

Triennial award for the best book of Irish poetry. Works must have been published in the Irish language in the preceding three years. Next award in 2001.

Prize £3000.

Hans Christian Andersen Awards

IBBY, Nonnenweg 12, Postfach CH-4003,
Basel, Switzerland
☎00 41 61 272 2917 Fax 00 41 61 272 2757
Email ibby@eye.ch
Website www.ibby.org

Executive Director *Leena Maissen*

The highest international prizes for children's literature: The Hans Christian Andersen Award for

Writing ESTABLISHED 1956; The Hans Christian Andersen Award for Illustration ESTABLISHED 1966. Candidates are nominated by National Sections of IBBY (The International Board on Books for Young People). Biennial prizes are awarded, in even-numbered years, to an author and an illustrator whose body of work has made a lasting contribution to children's literature. 2000 winners: Award for Writing: Ana Maria Machado (Brazil); Award for Illustration: Anthony Browne (UK).

Award Gold medals.

Angus Book Award

Angus Council Cultural Services, County Buildings, Forfar DD8 3WF
☎01307 473256 Fax 01307 462590

Contact *Norman Atkinson* (Director of Cultural Services)

ESTABLISHED 1995. Designed to try to help teenagers develop an interest in and enthusiasm for reading. Eligible books are read and voted on by third-year schoolchildren in all eight Angus secondary schools. 1999 winner: Tim Bowler *River Boy*.

Prize £250 cheque, plus trophy in the form of a replica Pictish stone.

Annual Theatre Book Prize

See **The Society for Theatre Research Annual Theatre Book Prize**

Arts Council Children's Award

Arts Council of England, 14 Great Peter Street, London SW1P 3NQ
☎020 7973 6431 Fax 020 7973 6983
Email jemima,lee@artscouncil.org.uk
Website www.artscouncil.org.uk

Contact *Theatre Writing Section*

A new annual award for playwrights who write for children. The plays, which must have been produced professionally, should be suitable for children up to the age of 12 and be at least 45 minutes long. The playwright must be resident in England. Contact the Theatre Writing Section for full details and application form.

Award £6000.

Arvon Foundation International Poetry Competition

11 Westbourne Crescent, London W2 3DB
☎020 7262 2788 Fax 020 7262 4004
Email london@arvonfoundation.org
Website www.arvonfoundation.org

Contact *David Pease*

ESTABLISHED 1980. Biennial competition (next in 2002) for poems written in English and not previously broadcast or published. There are no restrictions on the number of lines, themes, age of entrants or nationality. No limit to the number of entries. Entry fee: £5 per poem. Previous winners: Paul Farley *Laws of Gravity*; Don Paterson *A Private Bottling*.

Prize (1st) £5000 and £5000 worth of other prizes sponsored by Duncan Lawrie Limited.

Asher Prize

See **Medical Book Awards**

Authors' Club First Novel Award

Authors' Club, 40 Dover Street, London W1X 3RB
☎020 7499 8581 Fax 020 7409 0913

Contact *Mrs Ann de la Grange*

ESTABLISHED 1954. This award is made for the most promising work published in Britain by a British author, and is presented at a dinner held at the Authors' Club in April. Entries for the award are accepted from publishers by the end of November of the year in question and must be full-length – short stories are not eligible. 1999 winner: Jackie Kay *Trumpet*.

Award £750.

The Aventis Prizes for Science Books

COPUS, c/o The Royal Society, 6 Carlton House Terrace, London SW1Y 5AG
☎020 7451 2581 Fax 020 7451 2693

Contact *Anna Link*

ESTABLISHED 1988 by COPUS (Committee on the Public Understanding of Science) with the Science Museum. Sponsored by Aventis. Annual awards for popular non-fiction science and technology books judged to contribute most to people's understanding of science. Books must have first been written in the English language and must have been published in the UK in the calendar year 1 January - 31 December 2000. The prizes, totalling £30,000, are divided between two categories: the Aventis Prize awarded for a book for general readership, and the Junior Prize for books written primarily for young people. Final entry date: January. 1999 winners: Paul Hoffman *The Man Who Loved Only Numbers*; Kirsteen Rogers *The Usborne Complete Book of the Microscope* (Junior Prize).

Prizes Aventis Prize £10,000; Junior Prize £10,000; £1000 for every shortlisted author.

BAAL Book Prize

BAAL Publications Secretary, Centre for Language & Communication, Cardiff University, PO Box 94, Cardiff CF10 3XB
☎029 2087 4243 Fax 029 2087 4242
Email sarangi@cardiff.ac.uk

Contact *Dr Srikant Sarangi*

Annual award made by the British Association for Applied Linguistics to an outstanding book in the field of applied linguistics. Final entry at the end of Oct/Nov. Nominations from publishers only. Previous winners: Susan Berk-Seligson *The Bilingual Courtroom*; Joshua A. Fishman *Reversing Language Shift*; Deborah Cameron *Verbal Hygiene*; Marco Jacquemet *Credibility in Court*; Ana Celia Zentella *Growing Up Bilingual*; Colin Baker and Sylvia Prys Jones *Encyclopedia of Bilingualism and Bilingual Education*.

Barclays Bank Prize

See **Lakeland Book of the Year Awards**

Verity Bargate Award

The Soho Theatre Company, 21 Dean Street, London W1V 6NE
☎020 7287 5060 Fax 020 7287 5061
Email writers@sohotheatre.com

Contact *Sara Murray, Literary Manager*

The award was set up to commemorate the late Verity Bargate, founder and director of the **Soho Theatre Company**. This national award is presented biennially for a new and unperformed play (next in 2002). To go on the mailing list, please send s.a.e. to Sara Murray or email. Previous winners include: Fraser Grace, Lyndon Morgans, Adrian Pagan, Diane Samuels, Judy Upton and Toby Whithouse.

The Herb Barrett Award

Mekler & Deahl, Publishers, 237 Prospect Street South, Hamilton, Ontario, Canada L8M 2Z6
☎001 905 312 1779 Fax 001 905 312 8285
Email meklerdeahl@globalserve.net
Website www.meklerdeahl.com

Contact *James Deahl*

ESTABLISHED in 1996, this annual award is named in honour of Herb Barrett, founder of the Hamilton Chapter of the Canadian Poetry Association. Poets may enter up to 10 haiku for a fee of £5. Final entry date: 30 November. Contact the address above for a copy of the rules or access the website.

Prize (US) $200, $100 and $50; anthology publication for the winners and all other worthy entries.

H. E. Bates Short Story Competition

See **Words & Pictures Literary & Photographic Competition**

BBC Wildlife Magazine Awards for Nature Writing

BBC Wildlife Magazine, Broadcasting House, Whiteladies Road, Bristol BS8 2LR
☎0117 9738402 Fax 0117 9467075
Email wildlife.magazine@bbc.co.uk

Contact *Nina Epton*

Annual competition for professional and amateur writers. Entries (no longer than 1000 words) should be based on personal observations of, or thoughts about, nature – general or specific. The entry form appears in the magazine; closing date varies.

Prizes Winner: £500 plus publication in the magazine; runners-up: cash prizes plus publication; two young writers' awards.

BBC Wildlife Magazine Poetry Awards

PO Box 229, Bristol BS99 7JN
☎0117 9738402 Fax 0117 9467075
Email wildlife.magazine@bbc.co.uk

Contact *Nina Epton*

Annual award for a poem, the subject of which must be the natural world and/or our relationship with it. Entrants may submit one poem only of no more than 50 lines with the entry form which appears in the magazine. Closing date for entries varies from year to year.

Prizes Poet of the Year: £500, publication in the magazine, plus reading of the poem on Radio 4's *Poetry Please*; runners-up: cash prizes plus publication in the magazine; four young poets awards.

David Berry Prize

Royal Historical Society, University College London, Gower Street, London WC1E 6BT
☎020 7387 7532 Fax 020 7387 7532

Annual award for an essay of not more than 10,000 words on Scottish history. Candidates may select any subject from the relevant period, providing it has been submitted to, and approved by, the Council of the Royal Historical Society. Closing date: 31 October.

Prize £250.

Besterman/McColvin Medal

See **The Library Association Besterman/McColvin Medal**

The BFC Mother Goose Award

Books for Children, Brettenham House,
Lancaster Place, London WC2E 7TL
☎020 7322 1423 Fax 020 7322 1488

Contact *Editorial Coordinator*

ESTABLISHED 1979. Annual award for the most
exciting newcomer to British children's book
illustration. 1999 winner: Niamh Sharkey *The
Gigantic Turnip* and *Tales of Wisdom and Wonder*.
Prize £1000, plus Golden Egg trophy.

Birdwatch Bird Book of the Year

c/o Birdwatch Magazine, 3D/F Leroy House,
436 Essex Road, Islington, London N1 3QP
☎020 7704 9495

Contact *Dominic Mitchell*

ESTABLISHED in 1992 to acknowledge excellence in ornithological publishing – an increasingly large market with a high turnover.
Annual award. Entries, from publishers, must
offer an original and comprehensive treatment
of their particular ornithological subject matter
and must have a broad appeal to British-based
readers. 1999 winner: *The Handbook of Bird
Identification for Europe and the Western Palearctic*
Mark Beaman and Steve Madge.

James Tait Black Memorial Prizes

University of Edinburgh, David Hume
Tower, George Square, Edinburgh EH8 9JX
☎0131 650 3619 Fax 0131 650 6898

Contact *Department of English Literature*

ESTABLISHED 1918 in memory of a partner of
the publishing firm of **A. & C. Black Ltd**. Two
prizes, one for biography and one for fiction.
Closing date for submissions: 30 September.
Each prize is awarded for a book published in
Britain in the previous twelve months. Prize
winners are announced in December each year.
1999 winners: Kathryn Hughes *George Eliot: The
Last Victorian*; Timothy Mo *Renegade or Halo²*.
Prizes £3000 each.

The Robert Bloomfield Awards for Rustic Poetry

Hilton House (Publishers), Hilton House,
39 Long John Hill, Norwich, Norfolk
NR1 2JP
☎01603 449845

Contact *Michael K. Moore*

Annual competition to publicise the works of
the Suffolk poet and to promote descriptive
poetry with a rural theme, drawing attention to
the wonders of nature in the British and Irish
countryside and emphasising the necessity for
protecting the environment and wildlife. Entry
forms available from 2 January on receipt of s.a.e.
or IRC. Closing date: 30 September. Previous
winners: Frances Winfield, Lynne Wycherley,
J. Anthony Rock, Maxine Symons.
  Cash *prizes* £200; £100; £50 cash. All winners, runners-up and commended poets
receive complimentary copy of awards booklet
containing their winning poems. The three
main winners are also published in *Advance! –
Poetry Quarterly*

Boardman Tasker Award

14 Pine Lodge, Dairyground Road, Bramhall,
Stockport, Cheshire SK7 2HS
☎0161 439 4624 Fax 0161 439 4624

Contact *Dorothy Boardman*

ESTABLISHED 1983, this award is given for a work
of fiction, non-fiction or poetry, whose central
theme is concerned with the mountain environment and which can be said to have made an
outstanding contribution to mountain literature.
Authors of any nationality are eligible, but the
book must have been published or distributed in
the UK for the first time between 1 November
1998 and 31 October 1999. Entries from publishers only. 1999 winner: Paul Pritchard *The
Totem Pole and a whole new adventure*.
Prize £2000 (at Trustees' discretion).

Booker Prize for Fiction

Book Trust, Book House, 45 East Hill,
London SW18 2QZ
☎020 8516 2973 Fax 020 8516 2978
Email sandra@booktrust.org.uk
Website www.booktrust.org.uk

Contact *Sandra Vince*

The leading British literary prize, set up in 1968
by Booker McConnell Ltd, with the intention of
rewarding merit, raising the stature of the author
in the eyes of the public and increasing the sale of
the books. The announcement of the winner has
been televised live since 1981, and all books on
the shortlist experience a substantial increase in
sales. Eligible novels must be written in English
by a citizen of Britain, the Commonwealth, the
Republic of Ireland or South Africa, and must be
published in the UK for the first time between
1 October and 30 September of the year of
the prize. Self-published books are no longer
accepted. Entries are accepted from UK publishers who may each submit not more than two
novels within the appropriate scheduled publication dates. The judges may also ask for certain
other eligible novels to be submitted to them.
Annual award. 1999 winner: J. M. Coetzee

Disgrace. Previous winners include: Ian McEwan *Amsterdam*; Arundhati Roy *God of Small Things*; Graham Swift *Last Orders*; Pat Barker *The Ghost Road*; James Kelman *How Late It Was, How Late*; Roddy Doyle *Paddy Clarke Ha, Ha, Ha*.

Prize £20,000 winner; £1000, shortlist.

Author of the Year Award
Booksellers Association Ltd

Booksellers Association Ltd, 272 Vauxhall Bridge Road, London SW1V 1BA
☎020 7834 5477 Fax 020 7834 8812

Contact *Denise Bayat*

Founded as part of the BA Annual Conference to involve authors more closely in the event. Authors must be British or Irish. Not an award open to entry but voted on by the BA's membership. 1999 winner: J. K. Rowling.

Award £1000 plus trophy.

Border Television Prize
See **Lakeland Book of the Year Awards**

The BP Natural World Book Prize

Book Trust, Book House, 45 East Hill, London SW18 2QZ
☎020 8516 2973 Fax 020 8516 2978
Email sandra@booktrust.org.uk
Website www.booktrust.org.uk

Contact *Sandra Vince*

ESTABLISHED in 1996 as an amalgamation of the Natural World Book Prize (the magazine of the Wildlife Trusts) and the BP Conservation Book Prize. Award for a book on creative conservation of the environment. Entries from UK publishers only. 1999 winner: Steve Jones *Almost Like a Whale*.

Prizes (1st) £5000; Runner-up: £1000.

The Branford Boase Award

18 Grosvenor Road, Portswood, Southampton, Hampshire SO17 1RT
☎023 8055 5057
Email locol@compuserve.com
Website www.henriettabranford.co.uk

Administrator *Lois Beeson*

ESTABLISHED in 2000 in memory of children's novelist, Henrietta Branford and editor and publisher, Wendy Boase. To be awarded annually to encourage and celebrate the most promising novel by a new writer of children's books, while at the same time highlighting the importance of the editor in nurturing new talent.

Award £1000.

The Bridport Prize

Bridport Arts Centre, South Street, Bridport, Dorset DT6 3NR
☎01308 427183 Fax 01308 459166
Website www.wdi.co.uk/arts

Contact *Competition Secretary*

Annual competition for poetry and short story writing. Unpublished work only, written in English. Winning stories are read by literary agent (**A. M. Heath**), the winning poems are put forward to *Poetry Review* and the **Forward Prize** and an anthology of winning entries is published. Final entry date: 30 June. Send s.a.e. for entry forms.

Prizes £2500, £1000 & £500 in each category, plus various supplementary prizes.

Katharine Briggs Folklore Award

The Folklore Society, University College London, Gower Street, London WC1E 6BT
☎020 7387 5894

Contact *The Convenor*

ESTABLISHED 1982. An annual award in November for the book, published in Britain and Ireland between 1 June and 30 May in the previous calendar year, which has made the most distinguished non-fiction contribution to folklore studies. Intended to encourage serious research in the field which Katharine Briggs did so much to establish. The term folklore studies is interpreted broadly to include all aspects of traditional and popular culture, narrative, belief, custom and folk arts.

Prize £50, plus engraved goblet.

British Book Awards

Publishing News, 39 Store Street, London WC1E 7DB
☎020 7692 2900 Fax 020 7419 2111
Email mailbox@publishingnews.co.uk
Website www.publishingnews.co.uk

ESTABLISHED 1988. Viewed by the book trade as the one to win, 'The Nibbies' are presented annually in February. The awards are made in various categories. Each winner receives the prestigious Nibbie and the awards are presented to those who have made the most impact in the book trade during the previous year. Previous winners have included: J. K. Rowling, Spike Milligan, Louis de Bernières, Alan Bennett, Salman Rushdie, Dava Sobel, Sebastian Faulks, Books etc., Waterstone's, Ottakar's, and the publishers **Transworld**, **Fourth Estate**, **Little Brown** and **Random House**. For further information contact: Merric Davidson, 12 Priors

Heath, Goudhurst, Cranbrook, Kent TN17 2RE (☎/Fax 01580 212041).

British Comparative Literature Association/British Centre for Literary Translation Competition

School of Modern Language, Linguistics and Translation Studies, University of East Anglia, Norwich, Norfolk NR4 7TJ
Email JBoase-Beier@uea.ac.uk
Website www.bcla.org/trancomp.htm
Competition Organiser *Dr Jean Boase-Beier*

ESTABLISHED 1983. Annual competition open to unpublished literary translations from all languages. Maximum submission 25 pages.

Prizes (1st) £350; (2nd) £200; (3rd) £100; plus publication for all winning entries in the Association's annual journal *Comparative Criticism* (**Cambridge University Press**). Other entries may receive commendations.

British Fantasy Awards

201 Reddish Road, South Reddish, Stockport, Cheshire SK5 7HR
☎0161 476 5368 (after 6.00 pm)
Email faliol@yahoo.com
Website www.herebedragons.co.uk/bfs
Secretary *Robert Parkinson*

Awarded by the **British Fantasy Society** by members at its annual conference for Best Novel and Best Short Story categories, among others. Not an open competition. Previous winners include: Ramsey Campbell, Dan Simmonds, Michael Marshall Smith, Thomas Ligotti.

British Press Awards

Press Gazette, Quantum House, 19 Scarbrook Road, Croydon, Surrey CR9 1LX
☎020 8565 4200 Fax 020 8565 4395

'The Oscars of British journalism.' Open to all British morning and Sunday newspapers sold nationally and news agencies. March event. Run by *Press Gazette*.

British Science Fiction (Association) Award

The Bungalow, 27 Lower Evingar Road, Whitchurch, Hampshire RG28 7EY
☎01256 893253
Email awards@sandman.enterprise-plc
Award Administrator *Chris Hill*

ESTABLISHED 1966. The BSFA awards a trophy each year in three categories – novel, short fiction and artwork – published in the preceding year. Previous winners: Ken Macleod *The Sky*

Road (novel); Eric Brown *Hunting the Slarque* (short fiction); Jim Burns *Darwinia* (artwork).

British Sports Journalism Awards

See **Sports Writers' Association of Great Britain** under **Professional Associations and Societies**

James Cameron Award

City University, Department of Journalism, Northampton Square, London EC1V 0HB
☎020 7477 8221 Fax 020 7477 8594
Contact *The Administrator*

Annual award for journalism to a reporter of any nationality, working for the British media, whose work is judged to have contributed most during the year to the continuance of the Cameron tradition. Administered by the City University Department of Journalism. 1999 winner: Anne Lesley, *Daily Mail*.

The Canongate Prize

Canongate Books, 14 High Street, Edinburgh EH1 1TE
☎0131 557 5111 Fax 0131 557 5211
Email info@canongate.co.uk
Website www.canongate-prize.com

FOUNDED in 1999 by **Canongate Books** and Waterstone's to stimulate innovative new prose writing. The theme of the 2000 competition is 'Sin'. Submissions must be previously unpublished. All styles and genres (e.g. short story, reportage, essay or sketch) may be submitted; length 2000–5000 words. Closing date: 31 August. Leaflet available from the address above or access the website for further details.

Prizes 15 winners receive £2000 each plus publication in the Canongate Prize anthology.

Cardiff International Poetry Competition

PO Box 438, Cardiff CF1 6YA
☎029 2047 2266 Fax 029 2049 2930
Email post@academi.org
Website www.academi.org
Contact *Peter Finch*

ESTABLISHED 1986. An annual competition for unpublished poems in English of up to 50 lines. Closing date in December.

Prize (total) £5000.

Carey Award

Society of Indexers, Globe Centre, Penistone Road, Sheffield, South Yorkshire S6 3AE
☎0114 2813060 Fax 0114 2813061

Email admin@socind.demon.co.uk
Website www.socind.demon.co.uk
Secretary *Liza Weinkove*
A private award made by the Society to a member who has given outstanding services to indexing. The recipient is selected by Council with no recommendations considered from elsewhere.

Carnegie Medal
See **The Library Association Carnegie Medal**

The Raymond Chandler Society's 'Marlowe' Award for Best International Crime Novel
Heidenheimerstr. 106, 89075 Ulm, Germany
☎0114 255 6302 (UK contact)
0114 255 6302
Email william.adamson@zsp.uni-ulm.de
Contact *Simon Beckett (UK), Dr William R. Adamson (Germany)*
ESTABLISHED 1991. Annual award to the best English language crime novel. Awards also for best German language crime novel and best German language crime short story. Entry details from UK contact number. Submissions direct to the Society. Previous international 'Marlowe' winners include: Sara Paretsky, Minette Walters, Michael Connelly, Liza Cody, George P. Pelecanos.

Sid Chaplin Short Story Competition
Shildon Town Council, Civic Centre Square, Shildon, Co Durham DL4 1AH
☎01388 772563 Fax 01388 775227
Contact *Mrs J. M. Stafford*
FOUNDED 1986. Annual themed short story competition (1999 theme was The Millennium). Maximum 3000 words; £2 entrance fee (Juniors free). All stories must be unpublished and not broadcast and/or performed. Application forms available from September 2000. Closing date: 31 December. *Prizes* (1st) £300; (2nd) £150; (3rd) £75; (Junior) £50.

Children's Book Award
The Federation of Children's Book Groups, The Old Malt House, Aldbourne, Wiltshire SN8 2DW
☎01672 540629 Fax 01672 541280
Coordinator *Marianne Adey*
ESTABLISHED 1980. Awarded annually for best book of fiction suitable for children. Unique in that it is judged by the children themselves. Previous winners include: Dick King-Smith *Harriet's Hare*; Ian Strachan *The Boy in the Bubble*; Mick Inkpen *Threadbear*; Robert Swindells *Room 13*; Elizabeth Laird *Kiss the Dust*; Jaqueline Wilson *The Suitcase Kid* and *Double Act*; J. K. Rowling *Harry Potter and the Philosopher's Stone*.
Award A silver and oak sculpture made by Graham Stewart and Tim Stead, plus portfolio of letters, drawings and comments from the children who took part in the judging; category winners receive silver bowls designed by the same artists and portfolios.

Children's Book Circle Eleanor Farjeon Award
See **Eleanor Farjeon Award**

The Children's Laureate
18 Grosvenor Road, Portswood, Southampton, Hampshire SO17 1RT
☎023 8055 5057
Email locol@compuserve.com
Website www.waterstones.co.uk
Administrator *Lois Beeson*
ESTABLISHED 1998. Sponsored by Waterstone's, the Laureate is awarded biennially to an eminent British writer or illustrator of children's books both in celebration of a lifetime's achievement and to highlight the role of children's book creators in making the readers of the future. The first Children's Laureate was awarded in 1999 to writer and illustrator Quentin Blake.
Award Medal and £10,000.

Arthur C. Clarke Award for Science Fiction
60 Bournemouth Road, Folkestone, Kent CT19 5AZ
☎01303 252939 Fax 01303 252939
Email clarke@appomattox.demon.co.uk
Administrator *Paul Kincaid*
ESTABLISHED 1986. The Arthur C. Clarke Award is given annually to the best science fiction novel with first UK publication in the previous calendar year. Both hardcover and paperback books qualify. Made possible by a generous donation from Arthur C. Clarke, this award is selected by a rotating panel of judges nominated by the **British Science Fiction Association**, the **Science Fiction Foundation** and the Science Museum. 1999 winner: Tricia Sullivan *Dreaming in Smoke*.
Award £1000 plus trophy.

The Cló Iar-Chonnachta Literary Award

Cló Iar-Chonnachta Teo, Indreabhán, Conamara, Co. Galway Republic of Ireland
☎00 353 91 593307 Fax 00 353 91 593362
Website www.wombat.cic.ie

Editor *Róisín Ní Mhianàinn*

An annual prize for a newly written and unpublished work in the Irish language. Awarded in 1999 for the best collection of poems or long play and in 2000 for the best novel. Last date of entry for 2001 Award (short stories): 17 December 2000. 1999 winner: Liam ó Muirthile for his poetry collection, *Walking Time*.
Prize IR£5000.

David Cohen British Literature Prize

Arts Council of Great Britain, 14 Great Peter Street, London SW1P 3NQ
☎020 7333 0100 Fax 020 7973 6520

Literature Director *Gary McKeone*
Literature Assistant *Liz Graham*

ESTABLISHED 1993. By far the most valuable literature prize in Britain, the British Literature Prize, launched by the **Arts Council**, is awarded biennially. Anyone is eligible to suggest candidates and the award recognises writers who use the English language and who are British citizens, encompassing dramatists as well as novelists, poets and essayists. The prize is for a lifetime's achievement rather than a single play or book and is donated by the David Cohen Family Charitable Trust in association with Coutts Bank. Set up in 1980 by David Cohen, general practitioner and son of a property developer, the Trust has helped composers, choreographers, dancers, poets, playwrights and actors. The Council is providing a further £10,000 to enable the winner to commission new work, with the dual aim of encouraging young writers and readers. 1999 winner: William Trevor. Previous winners: Dame Muriel Spark., Harold Pinter, V. S. Naipaul.
Award £30,000, plus £10,000 towards new work.

The Commonwealth Writers Prize

Book Trust, Book House, 45 East Hill, London SW18 2QZ
☎020 8516 2973 Fax 020 8516 2978
Email sandra@booktrust.org.uk
Website www.booktrust.org.uk

Contact *Sandra Vince*

ESTABLISHED 1987. An annual award to reward and encourage the upsurge of new Commonwealth fiction. Any work of prose or fiction is eligible, i.e. a novel or collection of short stories. No drama or poetry. The work must be written in English by a citizen of the Commonwealth and be first published in the year before its entry for the prize. Entries must be submitted by the publisher to the region of the writer's Commonwealth citizenship. The four regions are: Africa, Eurasia, S. E. Asia and South Pacific, Caribbean and Canada. 1999 winners: Murray Bail *Eucalyptus* (Best Book); Kerri Sakamoto *The Electrical Field* (Best First Book).
Prizes £10,000 for Best Book; £3000 for Best First Book; 8 prizes of £1000 for each best and first best book in four regions.

The Thomas Cook/*Daily Telegraph* Travel Book Award

Thomas Cook Publishing, PO Box 227, Peterborough PE3 6PU
☎01733 503566 Fax 01733 503596
Email joan.lee@thomascook.com

Contact *Joan Lee, Publishing*

FOUNDED in 1980 by The Thomas Cook Group. Annual award given to the author of the book, published (in the English language) in the previous year, which most inspires the reader to want to travel. Submissions by publishers only. 1999 winner: Philip Marsden *The Spirit-Wrestlers*.
Award £7500.

The Duff Cooper Prize

54 St Maur Road, London SW6 4DP
☎020 7736 3729 Fax 020 7731 7638

Contact *Artemis Cooper*

An annual award for a literary work of biography, history, politics or poetry, published by a recognised publisher (member of **Publishers Association**) during the previous 12 months. The book must be submitted by the publisher, not the author. Financed by the interest from a trust fund commemorating Duff Cooper, first Viscount Norwich (1890–1954). 1999 winner: Adam Hochschild *King Leopold's Ghost*.
Prize £3000.

Rose Mary Crawshay Prize

The British Academy, 10 Carlton House Terrace, London SW1Y 5AX
☎020 7969 5200 Fax 020 7969 5300
Website www.britac.ac.uk

Contact *British Academy Secretary*

ESTABLISHED 1888 by Rose Mary Crawshay, this

prize is given for a historical or critical work by a woman of any nationality on English literature, with particular preference for a work on Keats, Byron or Shelley. The work must have been published in the preceding three years.

Prizes Normally two of around £500 each.

Crime Writers' Association (Cartier Diamond Dagger)

PO Box 6939, Kings Heath, Birmingham B14 7LT

Contact *The Secretary*

An annual award for a lifetime's oustanding contribution to the genre. 2000 winner: Peter Lovesey.

Crime Writers' Association (The CWA Ellis Peters Historical Dagger)

PO Box 6939, Kings Heath, Birmingham B14 7LT

Contact *The Secretary*

ESTABLISHED 1999. Annual award for the best historical crime novel. Nominations from publishers only. 2000 winner: Gillian Linscott *Absent Friends*.

Award Dagger, plus cheque.

Crime Writers' Association (John Creasey Memorial Dagger for Best First Crime Novel)

PO Box 6939, Kings Heath, Birmingham B14 7LT

Contact *The Secretary*

ESTABLISHED 1973 following the death of crime writer John Creasey, founder of the **Crime Writers' Association**. This award, sponsored by **Chivers Press**, is given annually for the best crime novel by an author who has not previously published a full-length work of fiction. Nominations from publishers only. 1999 winner: Dan Fesperman *Lie in the Dark*.

Award Dagger, plus cheque.

Crime Writers' Association (The CWA/The Macallan Gold Dagger for Non-Fiction)

PO Box 6939, Kings Heath, Birmingham B14 7LT

Contact *The Secretary*

Annual award for the best non-fiction crime book published during the year. Nominations from publishers only. 1999 winner: Brian Cathcart *The Case of Stephen Lawrence*.

Award Dagger, plus cheque (sum varies).

Crime Writers' Association (The CWA/The Macallan Gold and Silver Daggers for Fiction)

PO Box 6939, Kings Heath, Birmingham B14 7LT

Contact *The Secretary*

Two annual awards for the best crime fiction published during the year. Nominations for Gold Dagger from publishers only. 1999 winners: Robert Wilson *A Small Death in Lisbon* (Gold); Adrian Mathews *Vienna Blood* (Silver).

Award Dagger, plus cheque (sum varies).

Crime Writers' Association (The CWA/The Macallan Short Story Dagger)

PO Box 6939, Kings Heath, Birmingham B14 7LT

Contact *The Secretary*

ESTABLISHED 1993. An award for a published crime story. Publishers should submit three copies of the story by 30 September. 1999 winner: Antony Mann *Taking Care of Frank T.*

Prize Dagger, plus cheque.

Curtis Brown Prize

Curtis Brown Group Ltd, Haymarket House, 28/29 Haymarket, London SW1Y 4SP
☎020 7396 6600 Fax 020 7396 0110
Email cb@curtisbrown.co.uk

Contact *Giles Gordon (GilesG@CurtisBrown.co.uk)*

ESTABLISHED 1998. Annual prize for the best novel, in the opinion of Curtis Brown, written by a student on the MA in Novel Writing programme run by the University of Manchester. Open to all those not currently represented by a literary agent or under contract to a publisher.

Prize £1000. (Curtis Brown reserves the right to offer to act as literary agent to the winner.)

Harvey Darton Award

See **The Children's Books History Society** under **Literary Societies**

Hunter Davies Prize

See **Lakeland Book of the Year Awards**

Isaac & Tamara Deutscher Memorial Prize

School of African and Asian Studies, University of Sussex, Brighton, East Sussex BN1 9RH
☎01273 606755

Email J.P.Rosenberg@Sussex.ac.uk

Secretary *Dr Justin Rosenberg*

An annual award in recognition of, and as an encouragement to, outstanding research in or about the Marxist tradition. Made to the author of an essay or full-scale work published or in manuscript. Final entry date 1 May.

Award £250.

George Devine Award

17A South Villas, London NW1 9BS
☎020 7267 9793

Contact *Christine Smith*

Annual award for a promising new playwright writing for the stage in memory of George Devine, artistic director of the **Royal Court Theatre**, who died in 1965. The play, which can be of any length, does not need to have been produced. Send two copies of the script, plus outline of work, to Christine Smith by the end of March. Information leaflet available.

Prize £7500.

Denis Devlin Memorial Award for Poetry

An Chomhairle Ealaíon (The Irish Arts Council), 70 Merrion Square, Dublin 2, Republic of Ireland
☎00 353 1 6180252   Fax 00 353 1 6761302

Literature Officer *Sinéad Mac Aodha*

Triennial award for the best book of poetry in English by an Irish poet, published in the preceding three years. Next award 2001.

Award £1500.

Drama Association of Wales Playwriting Competition

The Old Library, Singleton Road, Splott, Cardiff CF24 2ET
☎029 2045 2200   Fax 029 2045 2277
Email aled.daw@virgin.net

Contact *Teresa Hennessy*

Annual competition held to promote the writing of one-act plays in English and Welsh of between 20 and 45 minutes' playing time. The theme of the competition is changed each year (the 2000 title was *Fallen Idols*). Application forms from the address above.

Prizes awarded for Best Play for an All Female Cast; Best Play in the Welsh Language; Best Play for a Children's/Youth Cast; Best Author Under 25; Best Adult Play; Best Overall Play.

Eccles Prize

Columbia Business School, 834 Uris Hall, 3022 Broadway, New York NY 10027, USA
☎001 212 854 2747   Fax 001 212 854 3050

Contact *Office of Public Affairs*

ESTABLISHED 1986 by Spencer F. Eccles in commemoration of his uncle, George S. Eccles, a 1922 graduate of the Business School. Annual award for excellence in economic writing. One of the US's most prestigious book prizes. Books must have a business theme and be written for a general audience. Previous winners: *The Warburgs* Ron Chernow; *A Stream of Windows: Unsettling Reflections on Trade, Immigration and Democracy* Jagdish Bhagwati.

The T.S. Eliot Prize

The Poetry Book Society, Book House, 45 East Hill, London SW18 2QZ
☎020 8870 8403/8874 6361/8877 1615 (24hr answerphone)

Contact *Clare Brown, Director*

ESTABLISHED 1993. Annual award named after T. S. Eliot, one of the founders of the **Poetry Book Society**. Open to books of new poetry published in the UK and Republic of Ireland during the year and over 32 pages in length. At least 75 per cent of the collection must be previously unpublished in book form. Final entry date is in August. Previous winners: Ciaran Carson *First Language*; Paul Muldoon *The Annals of Chile* ; Mark Doty *My Alexandria*; Les Murray *Subhuman Redneck Poems*; Don Paterson *God's Gift to Women*; Ted Hughes *Birthday Letters*; Hugo Williams *Billy's Rain*.

The Encore Award

The Society of Authors, 84 Drayton Gardens, London SW10 9SB
☎020 7373 6642   Fax 020 7373 5768

ESTABLISHED 1990. Awarded for the best second published novel of the year. Final entry date 30 November. Details from the **Society of Authors**. 1999 winner: Christina Koning *Undiscovered Country*.

Prize (total) £7500.

Envoi Poetry Competition

Envoi, 44 Rudyard Road, Biddulph Moor, Stoke on Trent, Staffordshire ST8 7JN
☎01782 517892

Contact *Roger Elkin*

Run by *Envoi* poetry magazine. Competitions are featured regularly, with prizes of £200, plus three annual subscriptions to *Envoi*. Winning poems along with full adjudication report are published. Send s.a.e. to Competition Secretary, 17 Millcroft, Bishops Stortford, Hertfordshire CM23 2BP.

Euroscript

See entry under **Writers' Courses, Circles and Workshops**

Exeter International Poetry Prize

See **Exeter Phoenix** under **Writers' Courses, Circles and Workshops**

Geoffrey Faber Memorial Prize

Faber & Faber Ltd, 3 Queen Square, London WC1N 3AU
☎020 7465 0045 Fax 020 7465 0034

ESTABLISHED 1963 as a memorial to the founder and first chairman of **Faber & Faber**, this prize is awarded in alternate years for the volume of verse and the volume of prose fiction published in the UK in the preceding two years, which is judged to be of greatest literary merit. Authors must be under 40 at the time of publication and citizens of the UK, Commonwealth, Republic of Ireland or South Africa. 1999 winner: Gavin Kramer *Shopping*.
  Prize £1000.

Eleanor Farjeon Award

c/o Children's Book Circle, The Watts Publishing Group, 96 Leonard Street, London EC2A 4XD
☎020 7739 2929 Fax 020 7739 2118

Contact *Susan Barry*

This award, named in memory of the much-loved children's writer, is for distinguished services to children's books either in this country or overseas, and may be given to a librarian, teacher, publisher, bookseller, author, artist, reviewer, television producer, etc. Nominations from members of the **Children's Book Circle**. 1999 winner: *Klaus Flugge*.
  Award £750.

The Fidler Award

c/o Scottish Book Trust, The Scottish Book Centre, 137 Dundee Street, Edinburgh EH11 1BG
☎0131 229 3663 Fax 0131 228 4293
Email scottish.book.trust@dial.pipex.com
Website www.scottishbooktrust.com

Sponsored by Hodder Children's Books for an unpublished novel for children aged 8–12, to encourage authors new to writing for this age group. The award is administered by **Scottish Book Trust**. Authors should not previously have had a novel published for this age group. Final entry date: end October. Previous winners: Theresa Breslin *Simon's Challenge*; Catherine McPhail *Run Zan Run*; Mark Leyland *Slate Mountain*; Thomas Bloor *The Memory Prisoner*.
  Award £1000, plus publication.

Fish (Publishing) Short Story Prize

Fish Publishing, Durrus, Bantry, Co Cork
Republic of Ireland
☎00 353 27 61246
Email fishpublishing@eircom.net
Website www.sleeping-giant.ie/fishpublishing

Contacts *Clem Cairns, Jula Walton*

ESTABLISHED 1994. Annual international award which aims to discover, encourage and publish exciting new literary talent. Stories of 5000 words maximum which have not been published previously may be entered. An entry fee of £8 is charged for the first entry and £5 per subsequent entry. (£5 for pensioners, unemployed and full-time students.) Closing date: 30 November. Previous winners: Molly McCloskey *The Stranger*; Karl Iagnemma *Dog Days*; Richard O'Reilly *Scrap Magic*. Honorary Patrons: Roddy Doyle, Dermot Healy and Frank McCourt.
  Prize £1000; the best 15 stories are published in an anthology.

Sir Banister Fletcher Award

Authors' Club, 40 Dover Street, London W1X 3RB
☎020 7499 8581 Fax 020 7409 0913

Contact *Mrs Ann de la Grange*

This award was created by Sir Bannister Fletcher, who was president of the **Authors' Club** for many years. The prize is presented annually for the best book on architecture or the fine arts published in the preceding year. Submissions: Fletcher Award Committee, RIBA, 66 Portland Place, London W1N 4AD. Previous winners: Richard Weston *Alvar Aalto*; Dr Megan Aldrich *Gothic Revival*; Professor Thomas Markus *Building and Power*; John Onians *Bearers of Meaning: Classical Orders in Antiquity*; Sir Michael Levey *Giambattista Tiepolo: His Life and Art;* John Allan *Berthold Lubetkin – Architecture and The Tradition of Progress*; Professor David Watkin *Sir John Soane, Enlightenment Thought and the Royal Academy*.
  Award £750.

The John Florio Prize

See **The Translators Association Awards**

The Focus on Fiction Short Story Competition

See **Focus on Fiction** under **Writers' Courses, Circles and Workshops**

The Forward Prizes for Poetry

Colman Getty PR, Carrington House, 126–130 Regent Street, London W1R 5FE
☎020 7439 1783   Fax 020 7439 1784

Contacts *Liz Sich, Margot Weale*

ESTABLISHED 1992. Three awards: the Forward Prize for Best Collection, the Waterstone's Prize for Best First Collection and the Tolman Cunard Prize for Best Single Poem which is not already part of an anthology or collection. All entries must be published in the UK or Eire and submitted by poetry publishers (collections) or newspaper and magazine editors (single poems). Individual entries of poets' own work are not accepted. 1999 winners: Jo Shapcott, Nick Drake, Robert Minhinnick.

Prizes £10,000 for best collection; £5000 for best first collection; £1000 for best single poem.

The Frogmore Poetry Prize

42 Morehall Avenue, Folkestone, Kent CT19 4EF
Contact *Jeremy Page*

ESTABLISHED 1987. Awarded annually and sponsored by the Frogmore Foundation. The winning poem, runners-up and short-listed entries are all published in the magazine. Previous winners have been: David Satherley, Caroline Price, Bill Headdon, John Latham, Diane Brown, Tobias Hill, Mario Petrucci, Gina Wilson, Ross Cogan, Joan Benner.

Prize The winner receives 100 guineas and a life subscription to the biannual literary magazine, *The Frogmore Papers*.

David Gemmell Cup Short Story Competition

Hastings Writers' Group, 39 Emmanuel Road, Hastings, East Sussex TN34 3LB
Contact *Mrs R. Bartholomew*

ESTABLISHED 1988. Annual award to encourage writers of short fiction (1500 words) resident in East and West Sussex, Kent, Surrey, London and London boroughs. Final entry date: end of August. Please send s.a.e. for rules and entry form (essential). The competition is organised by Hastings Writers' Group and prizes are presented by judge and patron David Gemmell. 1999 winner: Barry Mercer.

Prizes (1st) £250 plus David Gemmell Cup;
(2nd) £150; (3rd) £100; (4th) £50; (5th) £30; (6th) £20.

The Gladstone History Book Prize

Royal Historical Society, University College London, Gower Street, London WC1E 6BT
☎020 7387 7532   Fax 020 7387 7532

Contact *Executive Secretary*

ESTABLISHED 1998. Annual award for the best new work on any historical subject which is not primarily related to British history, published in the UK in the preceding calendar year. The book must be the author's first (solely written) history book and be an original and scholarly work of historical research. Closing date: 31 December 2000.

Prize £1000.

Glaxo Science Writers' Awards

See **ABSW/Glaxo Science Writers' Awards**

Glenfiddich Food & Drink Awards

4 Bedford Square, London WC1B 3RA
☎020 7255 1100   Fax 020 7631 0602

Known as the 'Cooker Bookers' or the 'Oscars' of the gastronomic world, the awards aim to recognise excellence in writing, publishing and broadcasting on the subjects of food and drink. There are 12 category winners from work published or broadcast in the UK and the Republic of Ireland. 2000 winners: Drink Book: *The Wines of California* Stephen Brook; Food Writer: Michael Bateman for work in *Condé Nast Traveller*; Magazine Cookery Writer: Ruth Watson for work in *Sainsbury's The Magazine*; Television Programme: *The Naked Chef*, presented by Jamie Oliver and produced by Pat Llewellyn for Optomen Television, BBC2; Radio Programme: *The Melting Pot – Food from the Balkans* presented by Tom Jaine, produced by Jessica Mitchell for BBC Radio 4; Visual Work: Peter Williams for work in *The Guardian Weekend*; Drink Writer: Andrew Jefford for work in the *Evening Standard*; Food Book: *Sally Clarke's Book – Recipes from a restaurant, shop & bakery* Sally Clarke; Newspaper Cookery Writer: Simon Hopkinson for work in *The Independent Magazine*; Regional Writer: John McKenna for work in *The Irish Times*; Restaurant Critic: Nicholas Lander for work in *Condé Nast Traveller* and *FT Weekend*; Wine Writer: Anthony Rose for work in *The Independent Weekend Review*; Special Award: Alan Davidson for *The Oxford Companion to Food*; 2000 Glenfiddich Trophy Winner: Tom Jaine.

Award Overall winner (chosen from the category winners) £3000, plus the Glenfiddich Trophy (which is held for one year); category winners £800 each, plus a case of Glenfiddich Single Malt Scotch Whisky.

Golden Kite Award
See **Society for Children's Book Writers & Illustrators** under **Professional Associations and Societies**

The Phillip Good Memorial Prize
QWF Magazine, PO Box 1768, Rugby CV21 4ZA
Email qwfmagazine@hotmail.com
Contact *Competition Secretary*

ESTABLISHED in 1997, the competition is run by *QWF Magazine* and a percentage of the entry fee goes to the Brain Research Trust. The prize commemorates the memory of Phillip Good (late husband of *QWF* editor, Jo Good) and is for short stories of less than 5000 words in any style or genre (except children's). Open entry. Entrants may request in-depth critique of their stories for an extra fee. For entry forms send s.a.e. to the address above.

Prizes (total) at least £525 plus free subscription to *QWF Magazine*; also book prizes and publication for winning authors.

Edgar Graham Book Prize
c/o Department of Geography, School of Oriental and African Studies, Thornhaugh Street, Russell Square, London WC1H 0XG
☎020 7898 4750 Fax 020 7898 4599
Contact *The Secretary*

ESTABLISHED 1984. Biennial award in memory of Edgar Graham. Aims to encourage research work in Third World agricultural and industrial development. Open to published works of original scholarship on agricultural and/or industrial development in Asia and/or Africa. No edited volumes. Next award 2002.

Prize £1500.

Kate Greenaway Medal
See **The Library Association Kate Greenaway Medal**

The Guardian Children's Fiction Award
The Guardian, 119 Farringdon Road, London EC1R 3ER
☎020 7239 9694 Fax 020 7713 4366
Children's Book Editor *Julia Eccleshare*

ESTABLISHED 1967. Annual award for an out-standing work of fiction for children aged seven and over by a British or Commonwealth author, first published in the UK in the preceding year, excluding picture books. Final entry date: mid-December. No application form necessary. 2000 winner: Jacqueline Wilson *The Illustrated Mum*. Previous winners: Susan Price *The Sterkarm Handshake*; Henrietta Branford *Fire, Bed and Bone*; Melvin Burgess *Junk*; Lesley Howarth *MapHead*; Rachel Anderson *Paper Faces*; Hilary McKay *The Exiles*; William Mayne *Low Tide*; Sylvia Waugh *The Mennyms*; Philip Pullman *Dark Materials I: Northern Lights*.

Award £1500.

The Guardian First Book Award
The Guardian, 119 Farringdon Road, London EC1R 3ER
☎020 7239 9694 Fax 020 7713 4366
Contact *Literary Editor*

ESTABLISHED 1999. Annual award for a first time author published in English in the UK. All genres eligible, apart from academic, guidebooks, children's, educational, manuals, reprints and TV, radio and film tie-ins. 1999 winner: Philip Gourevitch *We Wish to Inform You That Tomorrow We Will be Killed With Our Families*.

Award £10,000, plus *Guardian/Observer* advertising package and £1000 endowment of books to UK school of winner's choice.

Guild of Food Writers Awards
48 Crabtree Lane, London SW6 6LW
☎020 7610 1180 Fax 020 7610 0299
Email awards@gfw.co.uk
Website www.gfw.co.uk
Contact *Christina Thomas*

ESTABLISHED 1985. Annual awards in recognition of outstanding achievement in all areas in which food writers work and have influence. Entry is not restricted to members of the Guild. Entry form available from the address above. 1999 winners: Special Award for a lifetime achievement in food writing: Liz Burn; Michael Smith Award: Sybil Kapoor *Simply British*; Jeremy Round Award: Regina Sexton *A Little History of Irish Food*; Food Book of the Year: Jeffrey Steingarten *The Man Who Ate Everything*; Cookery Book of the Year: Madhur Jaffrey *World Vegetarian*; Recipe Writer of the Year: Jennifer John; Food Journalist of the Year: Manisha Gambhir Harkins for articles in *The Master's Table*; Cookery Journalist of the Year: Brian Glover for work in *Food & Travel*; Food Broadcast of the Year: Nigel Slater and Kudos Productions for *Nigel Slater's Real Food*.

Hastings National Poetry Competition

See **Hastings International Poetry Festival** under **Festivals**

W. H. Heinemann Award

c/o The Royal Literary Fund, 3 Johnson's Court, off Fleet Street, London EC4A 3EA
☎020 7353 7411 Fax 020 7353 7422
Email RSlit@aol.com
Website www.rslit.org

ESTABLISHED 1945. Works of any kind of literature may be submitted by publishers under this award, which aims to encourage genuine contributions to literature. Books must be written in the English language and have been published in the previous year; translations are not eligible for consideration nor are single poems, nor collections of pieces by more than one author, nor may individuals put forward their own work. Preference tends to be given to publications which are unlikely to command large sales: poetry, biography, criticism, philosophy, history. Publishers must contact the Secretary for details of how to submit works. Final entry date: 15 December. Up to three awards may be given. Previous winner: Richard Holmes *Coleridge: Darker Reflections*.
Prize £5000.

Felicia Hemans Prize for Lyrical Poetry

University of Liverpool, PO Box 147, Liverpool, Merseyside L69 3BX
☎0151 794 2458 Fax 0151 794 2454
Email wilderc@liv.ac.uk
Contact *The Registrar*

ESTABLISHED 1899. Annual award for published or unpublished verse. Open to past or present members and students of the University of Liverpool. One poem per entrant only. Closing date 1 May.
Prize £30.

Heywood Hill Literary Prize

10 Curzon Street, London W1Y 7FJ
☎020 7629 0647
Contact *John Saumarez Smith*

ESTABLISHED 1995 by the Duke of Devonshire to reward a lifetime's contribution to the enjoyment of books. Three judges chosen annually. No applications are necessary for this award. 1999 winner: Jane Gardam.
Prize £12,500.

William Hill Sports Book of the Year

Greenside House, Station Road, Wood Green, London N22 4TP
☎020 8918 3731 Fax 020 8918 3728
Contact *Graham Sharpe*

ESTABLISHED 1989. Annual award introduced by Graham Sharpe of bookmakers William Hill. Sponsored by William Hill and thus dubbed the 'bookie' prize, it is the first, and only, Sports Book of the Year award. Final entry date: September. 1999 winner: Sir Derek Birley *A Social History of English Cricket*.
Prize (reviewed annually) £10,000 package including £8000 cash, hand-bound copy, £1000 free bet. Runners-up prizes.

Hilton House Poet of the Year/ Open Competitions

Hilton House (Publishers), Hilton House, 39 Long John Hill, Norwich, Norfolk NR1 2JP
☎01603 449845
Contact *Michael K. Moore*

ESTABLISHED 1995. Annual awards to promote interest in poetry and to encourage high standards. Unpublished poems only, of up to 40 lines; no limit to number of entries. Entrants for all competitions must apply for rules and entry forms. Final entry dates: 31 March (Poet of the Year); 31 August (Open Competition); 30 November (Spiritual Competition). Previous winners: David Rogers, Andrew Farmer, Allister Fraser MBE, Beryl Fleming, Paul Hampton, Phil Powley, Wolfgang Somery.
Cash *prizes* £200; £100; £50. All winners, runners-up and commended poets receive complimentary copy of awards booklet containing their winning poems. The three winners in each competition are also published in *Advance! – Poetry Quaterly*.

Calvin & Rose G. Hoffman Prize

King's School, Canterbury, Kent CT1 2ES
☎01227 595501
Contact *The Headmaster*

Annual award for distinguished publication on Christopher Marlowe, established by the late Calvin Hoffman, author of *The Man Who was Shakespeare* (1955) as a memorial to himself and his wife. For unpublished works of at least 5000 words written in English for their scholarly contribution to the study of Christopher Marlowe and his relationship to William Shakespeare. Final entry date: 1 September. 1999 winner: Prof. Ken Cartwright.

Winifred Holtby Prize

Royal Society of Literature, 1 Hyde Park Gardens, London W2 2LT
☎020 7353 7411 Fax 020 7353 7422
Email RSlit@aol.com
Website www.rslit@org

ESTABLISHED 1966 by Vera Brittain who gave a sum of money to the RSL to provide an annual prize in honour of Winifred Holtby who died at the age of 37. Administered by the **Royal Society of Literature**. The prize is for the best regional novel of the year written in the English language. The writer must be of British or Irish nationality, or a citizen of the Commonwealth. Translations, unless made by the author himself of his own work, are not eligible. If in any year it is considered that no regional novel is of sufficient merit the prize money may be awarded to an author, qualified as aforesaid, of a literary work of non-fiction or poetry, concerning a regional subject. Publishers are invited to submit works published during the current year and must contact the Secretary for details. Final entry date: 15 December. Previous winners: Eden Robinson *Traplines*; Rohinton Mistry *A Fine Balance*; Giles Foden *The Last King of Scotland*. *Prize* £1000.

L. Ron Hubbard's Writers of the Future Contest

PO Box 218, East Grinstead, West Sussex RH19 4GH
Contest Administrator *Andrea Grant-Webb*

ESTABLISHED 1984 by L. Ron Hubbard to encourage new and amateur writers of science fiction, fantasy and horror. Quarterly awards with an annual grand prize. Entrants must submit a short story of up to 10,000 words, or a novelette less than 17,000 words, which must not have been published previously. The contest is open only to those who have not been published professionally. Previous winners: Roge Gregory, Malcolm Twigg, Janet Martin, Alan Smale, Ken Rand. Send s.a.e. for entry form.

Prizes (1st) £640, (2nd) £480 and (3rd) £320 each quarter; Annual Grand Prize: £2500. All winners are awarded a trip to the annual L. Ron Hubbard Achievement Awards which include a series of professional writers' workshops, and are published in the *L. Ron Hubbard Presents Writers of the Future* anthology.

Ilkley Literature Festival Poetry Competition

See **Ilkley Literature Festival** under **Festivals**

The Richard Imison Memorial Award

The Society of Authors, 84 Drayton Gardens, London SW10 9SB
☎020 7373 6642 Fax 020 7373 5768
Contact *The Secretary, The Broadcasting Committee*

Annual award established 'to perpetuate the memory of Richard Imison, to acknowledge the encouragement he gave to writers working in the medium of radio, and in memory of the support and friendship he invariably offered writers in general, and radio writers in particular'. Administered by the **Society of Authors** and generally sponsored by the Peggy Ramsay Foundation, the purpose is 'to encourage new talent and high standards in writing for radio by selecting the radio drama by a writer new to radio which, in the opinion of the judges, is the best of those submitted.' An adaptation for radio of a piece originally written for the stage, television or film is not eligible. Any radio drama first transmitted in the UK between 1 January and 31 December by a writer or writers new to radio, is eligible, provided the work is an original piece for radio and it is the first dramatic work by the writer(s) that has been broadcast. Submission may be made by any party to the production in the form of two copies of an audio cassette (not-returnable) accompanied by a nomination form. 1999 winner: Ben Cooper *Skin Deep*. *Prize* £1500.

The International IMPAC Dublin Literary Award

Dublin City Public Libraries, Administrative Headquarters, Cumberland House, Fenian Street, Dublin 2 Republic of Ireland
☎00 353 1 6619000 Fax 00 353 1 6761628
Email dubaward@iol.ie
Website www.iol.ie/~dubcilib

ESTABLISHED 1995. Sponsored by Dublin Corporation and a US-based productivity improvement firm, IMPAC, this prize is awarded for a work of fiction written and published in the English language or written in a language other than English and published in English translation. Initial nominations are made by municipal public libraries in major and capital cities worldwide, each library putting forward up to three books to the international panel of judges in Dublin. 2000 winner: Nicola Barker *Wide Open*.

Prize IR£100,000 (if the winning book is in English translation, prize is shared IR£75,000 to the author and IR£25,000 to the translator).

International Reading Association Literacy Award

International Reading Association, 800 Barksdale Road, PO Box 8139, Newark, Delaware 19714-8139 USA
☎001 302 731 1600   Fax 001 302 731 1057

Executive Director *Alan E. Farstrup*

The International Reading Association is a non-profit education organisation devoted to improving reading instruction and promoting literacy worldwide. In addition to the US $15,000 award presented each year on International Literacy Day (September 8), the organisation gives more than 25 awards in recognition of achievement in reading research, writing for children, media coverage of literacy, and literacy instruction.

International Student Playscript Competition

See **University College, Scarborough** under **Writers' Courses, Circles and Workshops**

Irish Times International Fiction Prize

The Irish Times Ltd, 10–16 D'Olier Street, Dublin 2, Republic of Ireland
☎00 353 1 679 2022   Fax 00 353 1 670 9383

Administrator, Book Prizes *Gerard Cavanagh*

FOUNDED 1989. Biennial award to the author of a work of fiction written in the English language and published in Ireland, the UK or the US in the two years of the award. Next award to be announced in autumn 2001. Books are nominated by literary critics and editors only. Previous winners: J. M. Coetzee *The Master of Petersburg*; E. Annie Proulx *The Shipping News*; Norman Rush *Mating*; Louis Begley *Wartime Lies*; Seamus Deane *Reading in the Dark*.
Prize IR£7500.

Irish Times Irish Literature Prizes

The Irish Times Ltd, 10–16 D'Olier Street, Dublin 2, Republic of Ireland
☎00 353 1 679 2022   Fax 00 353 1 670 9383

Administrator, Book Prizes *Gerard Cavanagh*

FOUNDED 1989. Biennial prizes awarded in four different categories: fiction (a novel, novella or collection of short stories), non-fiction prose (history, biography, autobiography, criticism, politics, sociological interest, travel, current affairs and belles-lettres), poetry (collection or a long poem or a sequence of poems, or a revised/updated edition of a previously pub-lished selection/collection) and (since 1999) for a work in the Irish language (fiction, poetry or non-fiction). The author must have been born in Ireland or be an Irish citizen, but may live in any part of the world. Books are nominated by literary editors and critics, and are then called in from publishers. Previous winners: Paddy Devlin *Straight Left* (non-fiction); Kathleen Ferguson *A Maid's Tale* (fiction); Robert Greacen *Collected Poems*; Brian Keenan *An Evil Cradling*; John MacKenna *The Fallen and Other Stories*.
Prizes IR£5000 each category.

Jennings Brothers Prize

See **Lakeland Book of the Year Awards**

Jewish Quarterly Literary Prizes

PO Box 2078, London W1A 1JR
☎020 7629 5004   Fax 020 7629 5110

Contact *Gerald Don*

Formerly the H. H. Wingate Prize. Annual awards (one for fiction and one for non-fiction) for works which best stimulate an interest in and awareness of themes of Jewish interest. Books must have been published in the UK in the year of the award and be written in English by an author resident in Britain, the Commonwealth, Israel, Republic of Ireland or South Africa. 2000 winners: Howard Jacobson *The Mighty Walzer*; Wladyslaw Szpilman *The Pianist*. Previous winners: Anne Michaels *Fugitive Pieces*; Claudia Roden *The Book of Jewish Food*; Dorit Rabinyan *Persian Brides*; Edith Velmans *Edith's Book*; Clive Sinclair *The Lady With the Laptop*; W. G. Sebald *The Emigrants*.
Prizes Fiction: £4000; Non-fiction: £3000.

The Samuel Johnson Prize for Non-fiction

The Booksellers Association, Minster House, 272 Vauxhall Bridge Road, London SW1V 1BA
☎020 7834 5477   Fax 020 7834 8812
Email 100437.2261@compuserve.com

Contact *Gill Cronin*

ESTABLISHED 1998. Annual prize sponsored by an anonymous retired British businessman to reward the best of non-fiction. Eligible categories include the arts, autobiography, biography, business, commerce, current affairs, history, natural history, popular science, religion, sport and travel. Entries submitted by publishers only. 1999 winner: Antony Beevor *Stalingrad*.
Prize £30,000; £2500 to each shortlisted author.

Mary Vaughan Jones Award

Cyngor Llyfrau Cymru (Welsh Books
Council), Castell Brychan, Aberystwyth,
Dyfed SY23 2JB
☎01970 624151 Fax 01970 625385
Email castellbrychan@cllc.org.uk
Website www.wbc.org.uk

Contact *The Administrator*

Triennial award for distinguished services in
the field of children's literature in Wales over a
considerable period of time.

Award Silver trophy.

Keats–Shelley Prize

Keats–Shelley Memorial Association,
117 Cheyne Walk, London SW10 0ES
☎020 7352 2180 Fax 020 7352 6705
Website www.demon.co.uk.heritage/
   Keats.House.Rome

Contact *Harriet Cullen*

ESTABLISHED 1998. Annual award to promote
the study and appreciation of Keats and Shelley,
especially in the universities, and of creative writing inspired by the younger Romantic poets.
Sponsored by **The Folio Society**. Two categories: essay and poem; open to all ages and
nationalities. Previous winners: Sarah Wootton,
Rukmini Maria Callimachi, James Burton, Cate
Parish.

Prize £3000 distributed between the winners of the two categories.

Kent & Sussex Poetry Society Open Competition

13 Ruscombe Close, Southborough,
Tunbridge Wells, Kent TN4 0SG
☎01892 543862

Chairman *Clive R. Eastwood*

Annual competition. Entry fee: £3 per poem,
maximum 40 lines.

Prizes (total) £1000.

Kent Short Story Competition

Kent Literature Festival, The Metropole Arts
Centre, The Leas, Folkestone, Kent
CT20 2LS
☎01303 255070

Contact *Ann Fearey*

ESTABLISHED 1992. For a short story of up to
3000 words by anyone over the age of 16.
Sponsored by Midland Bank and supported by
Saga and Shepway District Council. Send s.a.e.
for entry forms, available from March.

Prizes (1st) £350; (2nd) £175; (3rd) £100.

Kraszna-Krausz Book Awards

122 Fawnbrake Avenue, London SE24 0BZ
☎020 7738 6701 Fax 020 7738 6701
Email k-k@dial.pipex.com
Website www.editor.net/k-k

Administrator *Andrea Livingstone*

ESTABLISHED 1985. Annual award to encourage
and recognise oustanding achievements in the
publishing and writing of books on the art, practice, history and technology of photography and
the moving image (film, television, video and
related screen media). Books in any language,
published worldwide, are eligible. Entries must
be submitted by publishers only. Prizes for books
on still photography alternate annually with
those for books on the moving image (2000:
photography). Previous winners include: James
Naremore *More than Night: Film Noir in its
Contexts*; R. W. Burns *Television: An International
History of the Formative Years*; Herbert Molderings
Umbo: Otto Umbehr 1902–1980; Ann Thomas
(ed.) *Beauty of Another Order: Photography in
Science*.

Prizes £5000 in each of the main categories;
£1000 special commendations.

Lakeland Book of the Year Awards

Cumbria Tourist Board, Ashleigh, Holly
Road, Windermere, Cumbria LA23 2AQ
☎015394 44444 Fax 015394 44041
Email mail@cumbria-tourist-board.co.uk

Contact *Sheila Lindsay*

Seven annual awards set up by Cumbrian author
Hunter Davies and the Cumbria Tourist Board.
The **Hunter Davies Prize** was established in
1984 and is awarded for the book which best
helps visitors or residents enjoy a greater love or
understanding of any aspect of life in Cumbria
and the Lake District. In 1993 three awards were
established with funding from the private sector:
the **Tullie House Prize** is for the book which
best helps develop a greater appreciation of the
built and/or natural environment of Cumbria;
the **Barclays Bank Prize** is for the best small
book on any aspect of Cumbrian life, its people
or culture; and the **Border Television Prize** is
for the book which best illustrates the beauty and
character of Cumbria. A new award was established in 1997: the **Jennings Brothers Prize** for
the best small book or guide book, and a further
two prizes in 1999: the **Ron Sands Prize** for
the best book on a cultural theme; and the **Titus
Wilson Prize** for the best research and book.
Final entry date mid-March. 1999 winners:
Hunter Davies Prize/Tullie House Prize: Gil and
Pat Hitchon *Sam Bough RSA – The Rivers in*

Bohemia; Barclays Bank Prize: Cedric Robinson *Sand Pilot of Morecambe Bay*; Border Television Prize: Denis Perriam and David Ramshaw *Carlisle Citadel Station*; Jennings Brothers Prize: Mary Scott-Parker *Silloth*; Ron Sands Prize: Anne Johnson *Leaping Niagara*; Titus Wilson Prize: Bob Orrell and Margaret Vincent *Lakeland Monuments (Book 1 – North)*.

Prize £100 and certificate.

Lancashire County Library/NWB Children's Book of the Year Award

Lancashire County Library Headquarters, County Hall, PO Box 61, Preston, Lancashire PR1 8RJ
☎01772 264040 Fax 01772 264043
Manager, Young People's Service
Jean Wolstenholme

ESTABLISHED 1986. Annual award, presented in June and sponsored by the National Westminster Bank for a work of original fiction suitable for 11–14-year-olds. The winner is chosen by 13–14-year-old secondary school pupils in Lancashire. Books must have been published between 1 September and 31 August in the year of the award and authors must be UK residents. Final entry date: 1 September each year. Recent winners: Elizabeth Hawkins *The Sea of Peril*; Elizabeth Laird *Jay*. 1999 winner: Nigel Hinton *Out of the Darkness*. To celebrate the tenth anniversary of the award, all previous winners were judged for the 'Books Across Europe Award'. Ian Strachan's *The Boy in the Bubble* was voted the overall winner.

Prize £500 plus engraved glass decanter.

The Library Association Besterman/McColvin Medal

7 Ridgmount Street, London WC1E 7AE
☎020 7255 0650 Fax 020 7255 0501

Annual award for an outstanding reference work first published in the UK during the preceding year. Consists of two categories: printed and electronic. Works eligible for consideration include: encyclopedias, general and special dictionaries; annuals, yearbooks and directories; handbooks and compendia of data; atlases. Nominations are invited from members of **The Library Association**, publishers and others.

The Library Association Carnegie Medal

7 Ridgmount Street, London WC1E 7AE
☎020 7255 0650 Fax 020 7255 0501

ESTABLISHED 1936. Presented for an outstanding book for children written in English and first published in the UK during the preceding year. This award is not necessarily restricted to books of an imaginative nature. 1998 winner: David Almond *Skellig*.

Award Medal.

The Library Association Kate Greenaway Medal

7 Ridgmount Street, London WC1E 7AE
☎020 7255 0650 Fax 020 7255 0501

ESTABLISHED 1955. Presented annually for the most distinguished work in the illustration of children's books first published in the UK during the preceding year. 1998 winner: Helen Cooper *Pumpkin Soup*.

Award Medal. The Colin Mears Award (£5000 cash) is given annually to the winner of the Kate Greenaway Medal.

The Library Association Walford Award

7 Ridgmount Street, London WC1E 7AE
☎020 7255 0650 Fax 020 7255 0501

Awarded to an individual who has made a sustained and continual contribution to British bibliography over a period of years. The nominee need not be resident in the UK. The award is named after Dr A. J. Walford, a bibliograper of international repute. Previous winners include: Prof. Stanley Wells, Prof. J. D. Pearson and Prof. R. C. Alston.

Award Cash prize and certificate.

The Library Association Wheatley Medal

7 Ridgmount Street, London WC1E 7AE
☎020 7255 0650 Fax 020 7255 0501

ESTABLISHED 1962. Annual award for an outstanding index first published in the UK during the preceding three years. Whole work must have originated in the UK and recommendations for the award are invited from members of **The Library Association**, the **Society of Indexers**, publishers and others. Previous winners include: Elizabeth Moys *British Tax Encyclopedia*; Paul Nash *The World of Environment 1972–1992*; Richard Raper *The Works of Charles Darwin*.

Award Medal.

Lichfield Prize

c/o Tourist Information Centre, Donegal House, Bore Street, Lichfield, Staffordshire WS13 6NE
☎01543 308209 Fax 01543 308211
Email prize@lichfield-tourist.co.uk
Website www.lichfield-tourist.co.uk

Contact *Mrs Alison Bessey* (at Lichfield District Council on 01543 308000)

ESTABLISHED 1988. Biennial award initiated by Lichfield District Council to coincide with the Lichfield Festival. Run in conjunction with James Redshaw Booksellers of Lichfield and Prize co-sponsors, **Hodder & Stoughton** publishers. Awarded for a previously unpublished novel based upon the geographical area of Lichfield district, contemporary or historical, but not futuristic. Previous winners include: Stephen Booth *The Only Dead Thing*; Anthony Clarke *Ordeal at Lichfield*. Next award 2001. Final entry date in April of award year.

Prize £5000, plus possible publication.

Literary Review Grand Poetry Competition

See *Literary Review* under **Magazines**

The London Writers Competition

Room 224a, The Town Hall, Wandsworth High Street, London SW18 2PU
☎020 8871 8711 Fax 020 8871 8712
Email arts@wandsworth.gov.uk
Website www.wandsworth.gov.uk

Contact *Wandsworth Arts Office*

Arranged by Wandsworth Borough Council in association with Waterstone's. Annual competition, open to all writers of 16 or over who live, work or study in the Greater London area. Work must not have been published previously. There are three sections: poetry, short story and play.

Prizes £1000 for each section, with a first prize of £600. Poetry and story winners are published and the winning play is produced in a London venue.

Longman-History Today Book of the Year Award

c/o History Today, 20 Old Compton Street, London W1V 5PE
☎020 7534 8000

Contacts *Peter Furtado, Marion Soldan*

ESTABLISHED 1993. Annual award set up as joint initiative between *History Today* magazine and the publisher Longman (**Pearson Education**) to mark the past links between the two organisations, to encourage new writers, and to promote a wider public understanding of, and enthusiasm for, the study and publication of history. Submissions are made by publishers only. 1999 winner: Amanda Vickery *The Gentleman's Daughter: Women's Lives in Georgian England*.

Prize £1000 (see *History Today* from July 2000).

Sir William Lyons Award

The Guild of Motoring Writers, 30 The Cravens, Smallfield, Surrey RH6 9QS
☎01342 843294 Fax 01342 844093

Contact *Sharon Scott-Fairweather*

An annual competitive award to encourage young people in automotive journalism and to foster interests in motoring and the motor industry. Entrance by two essays and interview with Awards Committee. Applicants must be British, aged 17–23 and resident in UK. Final entry date 31 August. Presentation date in December.

Award £1000 plus trophy.

The Macallan/Scotland on Sunday Short Story Competition

Scotland on Sunday, 108 Holyrood Road, Edinburgh EH8 8AS
☎0131 620 8480 Fax 0131 523 0316

Contact *Rosemary Goring*

ESTABLISHED 1990. Annual competition to recognise the best in new Scottish writing. Stories are accepted from those who were born or are living in Scotland, or from Scots living abroad. Up to three stories per applicant permitted. Maximum 3000 words per story. Final entry date in March. The top 20 entries are published in a book in conjunction with the **Scottish Arts Council**. Previous winners: Alan Spence, Ali Smith, Chris Dolan, Michael Faber, Anne Donovan.

Prizes 1st £6000; 2nd £1000; four runners-up receive £500 each. Winning story is published in *Scotland on Sunday* and four of six shortlisted will be broadcast on BBC Radio Scotland.

McColvin Medal

See **The Library Association Besterman/McColvin Medal**

W. J. M. Mackenzie Book Prize

Political Studies Association, Department of Politics, University of Newcastle, Newcastle upon Tyne NE1 7RU
☎0191 222 8021 Fax 0191 222 5069

PSA Executive Director *Jack Arthurs*

ESTABLISHED 1987. Annual award to best work of political science published in the UK during the previous year. Submissions from publishers only. Final entry date in June. 1999 winner: Prof. Christoper Hood *The Art of the State – Culture, Rhetoric and Public Management*.

Prize £100, plus dinner.

McKitterick Prize

Society of Authors, 84 Drayton Gardens,
London SW10 9SB
☎020 7373 6642 Fax 020 7373 5768

Contact *Awards Secretary*

Annual award for a full-length novel in the
English language, first published in the UK or
unpublished. Open to writers over 40 who have
not had any novel published other than the one
submitted (excluding works for children).
Closing date 16 December. 1999 winner:
Magnus Mills *The Restraint of Beasts*.
Prize £4000.

Enid McLeod Prize

Franco-British Society, Room 623, Linen Hall,
162–168 Regent Street, London W1R 5TB
☎020 7734 0815 Fax 020 7734 0815

Executive Secretary *Mrs Kate Brayn*

ESTABLISHED 1982. Annual award to the author
of the work of literature published in the UK
which, in the opinion of the judges, has contributed most to Franco-British understanding.
Any full-length work written in English by a
citizen of the UK, Commonwealth, Republic of
Ireland, Pakistan, Bangladesh and South Africa.
No English translation of a book written originally in any other language will be considered.
Nominations from publishers for books published between 1 January and 31 December of
the year of the prize. 1999 winner: Reverend
Canon Ian Dunlop *Louis XIV*.
Prize Cheque.

Macmillan Prize for a Children's Picture Book

Macmillan Children's Books, 25 Eccleston
Place, London SW1W 9NF
☎020 7881 8000 Fax 020 7881 8001

Contact *Marketing Dept., Macmillan
Children's Books*

Set up in order to stimulate new work from
young illustrators in art schools, and to help
them start their professional lives. Fiction or
non-fiction. **Macmillan** have the option to
publish any of the prize winners.
Prizes (1st) £1000; (2nd) £500; (3rd) £250.

Macmillan Silver PEN Award

The English Centre of International PEN,
152–156 Kentish Town Road, London
NW1 9QB
☎020 7267 9444 Fax 020 7267 9304
Email enquiries@pen.org.uk
Website www.pen.org.uk

Sponsored by **Macmillan Publishers**. An
annual award for a volume of short stories written in English by a British author and published
in the UK in the year preceding the prize.
Nominations by the PEN Executive Committee
only. Please do not submit books. 2000 winner:
Cressida Connolly *The Happiest Days*.
Prize £500, plus silver pen.

The Mail on Sunday Novel Competition

Postal box address changes each year (see below)

Annual award ESTABLISHED 1983. Judges look
for a story/character that springs to life in the
'tantalising opening 50–150 words of a novel'.
Details of the competition, including the postal
box address, are published in *The Mail on
Sunday* in July/August. Previous winners: Jude
Rodger, Nicola Richardson, Michael Ryan,
Kate Spencer, Karen Martin, Pat Simpson.
Awards (1st) £400 book tokens and a weekend writing course at the **Arvon Foundation**;
(2nd) £300 tokens; (3rd) £200 tokens; three
further prizes of £150 tokens each.

The Mail on Sunday/ John Llewellyn Rhys Prize

Book Trust, Book House, 45 East Hill,
London SW18 2QZ
☎020 8516 2973 Fax 020 8516 2978
Email sandra@booktrust.org.uk
Website www.booktrust.org.uk

Contact *Sandra Vince*

ESTABLISHED 1942. An annual young writer's
award for a memorable work of any kind.
Entrants must be under the age of 35 at the time
of publication; books must have been published
in the UK in the year of the award. The author
must be a citizen of Britain or the Common-
wealth, writing in English. 1999 winner: Peter
Ho Davis *The Ugliest House in the World*.
Previous winners: Phil Whitaker *Eclipse of the
Sun*; Matthew Kneale *Sweet Thames*; Jason
Goodwin *On Foot to the Golden Horn*, Melanie
McGrath *Motel Nirvana*.
Prize (1st) £5000; £500 for shortlisted entries.

Marches Literary Prize

48 Erw Wen, Welshpool, Powys SY21 7HL
Contact *Competition Secretary*

ESTABLISHED 1998. Annual award which aims
to use surplus funds from the prize to support
charities with a literacy bias. In 1999, £1000
was presented to the Royal National College
for the Blind in Hereford to purchase library
resources. Open competition for short stories

of 2000 words maximum and poems of not more than 50 lines, of any genre. Entry fee: £3. Closing date: 31 March. Entry forms available from the Secretary.

Prizes for both categories: £200 (1st); £100 (2nd); £50 (3rd).

Marsh Award for Children's Literature in Translation

National Centre for Research in Children's Literature, University of Surrey Roehampton, Digby Stuart College, Roehampton Lane, London SW15 5PH
☎020 8392 3008 Fax 020 8392 3031

Contact *Dr Gillian Lathey*

ESTABLISHED 1995 and sponsored by the Marsh Christian Trust, the award aims to encourage translation of foreign children's books into English. It is a biennial award (next award: 2001), open to British translators of books for 4–16-year-olds, published in the UK by a British publisher. Any category will be considered with the exception of encyclopedias and reference books. No electronic books. First winner: Anthea Bell *A Dog's Life* by Christine Nostlinger. 1999 winner: Patricia Crampton for her translation of *The Final Journey* by Gudrun Pausewang.

Prize £750.

Marsh Biography Award

The English-Speaking Union, Dartmouth House, 37 Charles Street, London W1X 8AB
☎020 7493 3328 Fax 020 7495 6108
Email lucy_passmore@esu.org
Website www.esu.org

Contact *Lucy Passmore*

A biennial award for the most significant biography published over a two-year period by a British publisher. Next award October 2001. 1999 winner: Richard Holmes *Coleridge: Darker Reflections*. Previous winners: Jim Ring *Erskine Childers*; Selina Hastings *Evelyn Waugh*; Patrick Marnham *The Man Who Wasn't Maigret*; Hugh and Mirabel Cecil *Clever Hearts*.

Award £3500, plus silver trophy presented at a dinner.

Kurt Maschler Award

Book Trust, Book House, 45 East Hill, London SW18 2QZ
☎020 8516 2973 Fax 020 8516 2978
Email sandra@booktrust.org.uk
Website www.booktrust.org.uk

Contact *Sandra Vince*

ESTABLISHED 1982. Annual award for 'a work of imagination in the children's field in which

text and illustration are of excellence and so presented that each enhances, yet balances the other'. Books published in the current year in the UK by a British author and/or artist, or by someone resident for ten years, are eligible. 1999 winner: Helen Oxenbury's *Lewis Carrol's Alice's Adventures in Wonderland*. Previous winner: Anthony Browne *Voices in the Park*.

Award £1000 plus bronze Emil trophy.

Colin Mears Award

See **Library Association Kate Greenaway Medal**

Medical Book Awards

The Society of Authors, 84 Drayton Gardens, London SW10 9SB
☎020 7373 6642 Fax 020 7373 5768

Contact *Dorothy Wright*

Annual awards in six categories: basic book, advanced author book, advanced edited book, medical history, Asher Prize for a first textbook, dental book, published in the UK in the year preceding the awards. Previous winners: Basic Book: *Uveitis: An Illustrated Manual*; Advanced Authored: *The Autonomic Nervous System and its Effectors* and *McAlpine's Multiple Sclerosis, 3rd ed.* (joint winners); Advanced Multi-Contributor: *Pediatric Neurosurgery* and *Imaging in Oncology* (joint winners); ; Medical History: *Erasmus Darwin: A Life of Unequalled Achievement*; Asher Prize: *Obstetrics and Gynaecology*; Dental Prize: *Maxillofacial Surgery*.

Prizes £1000 (each medical category); £500 (dental category).

Mere Literary Festival Open Competition

'Lawrences', Old Hollow, Mere, Wiltshire BA12 6EG
☎01747 860475

Contact *Mrs Adrienne Howell (Events Organiser)*

Annual open competition which alternates between short stories and poetry. The winners are announced at the Mere Literary Festival during the second week of October. The 2001 competition is for poetry with a closing date for entries in July. For further details, including entry fees and form, contact the address above from 1 March with s.a.e.

Cash prizes

Meyer-Whitworth Award

Arts Council of England, 14 Great Peter Street, London SW1P 3NQ
☎020 7973 6431 Fax 020 7973 6983

Email jemima.lee@artscouncil.org.uk
Website www.artscouncil.org.uk

Contact *Jemima Lee*

In 1908 the movement for a National Theatre joined forces with that to create a memorial to William Shakespeare. The result was the Shakespeare Memorial National Theatre Committee, the embodiment of the campaign for a National Theatre. This award, bearing the name of but two protagonists in the movement, has been established to commemorate all those who worked for the SMNT. Endowed by residual funds of the SMNT, the award is intended to help further the careers of UK playwrights who are not yet established, and to draw contemporary theatre writers to the public's attention. The award is given to the writer whose play most nearly satisfies the following criteria: a play which embodies Geoffrey Whitworth's dictum that 'drama is important in so far as it reveals the truth about the relationships of human beings with each other and the world at large'; a play which shows promise of a developing new talent; a play in which the writing is of individual quality. Nominations from professional theatre companies. Plays must have been written in the English language and produced professionally in the UK in the 12 months preceding the award. Candidates will have had no more than two of their plays professionally produced.
Award £8000.

MIND Book of the Year/ Allen Lane Award

Granta House, 15–19 Broadway, London E15 4BQ
☎020 8519 2122 Fax 020 8522 1725

ESTABLISHED 1981. Annual award, in memory of Sir Allen Lane, for the author of a book published in the current year (fiction or non-fiction), which furthers public understanding of mental health problems. 1999 winner: Linda Grant *Remind Me Who I Am, Again*.

The Mitchell Prize for Art History/ The Eric Mitchell Prize

c/o The Burlington Magazine, 14–16 Duke's Road, London WC1H 9AD
☎020 7388 8157 Fax 020 7388 1230

Executive Director *Caroline Elam*

ESTABLISHED 1977 by art collector, philanthropist and businessman, Jan Mitchell, to draw attention to exceptional achievements in the history of art. Consists of two prizes: The Mitchell Prize, given for an outstanding and original contribution to the study and understanding of visual arts, and The Eric Mitchell Prize, given for the most outstanding first book in this field. The prizes are awarded to authors of books in English that have been published in the previous 12 months. Books are submitted by publishers before the end of February. Previous winners: Mitchell Prize: *Nicolas Poussin* Elizabeth Cropper and Charles Dempsey; The Eric Mitchell Prize: *The Triumph of Vulcan* Suzanne Brown Butters.
Prizes $15,000 (Mitchell Prize); $5000 (Eric Mitchell Prize)

Scott Moncrieff Prize
See **The Translators Association Awards**

The Montagu of Beaulieu Trophy

Guild of Motoring Writers, 30 The Cravens, Smallfield, Surrey RH6 9QS
☎01342 843294 Fax 01342 844093

Contact *Sharon Scott-Fairweather*

First presented by Lord Montagu on the occasion of the opening of the National Motor Museum at Beaulieu in 1972. Awarded annually to a member of the **Guild of Motoring Writers** who, in the opinion of the nominated jury, has made the greatest contribution to recording in the English language the history of motoring or motor cycling in a published book or article, film, television or radio script, or research manuscript available to the public.
Prize Trophy.

Brian Moore Short Story Award

Creative Writers' Network, 15 Church Street, Belfast BT1 1ER
☎028 9031 2361 Fax 028 9043 4669
Email mmooney.cwn@virgin.net

Contact *The Development Officer*

ESTABLISHED 1996. Annual competition to encourage short fiction in Northern Ireland. Final entry date in September; full details available from May. 'Entries of a more adventurous or experimental nature are especially welcome.' In 1999 five winners shared a prize fund of £1000.

Mother Goose Award
See **The BFC Mother Goose Award**

Shiva Naipaul Memorial Prize

The Spectator, 56 Doughty Street, London WC1N 2LL
☎020 7405 1706 Fax 020 7242 0603

Contact *Emma Bagnall*

ESTABLISHED 1985. Annual prize given to an

English language writer of any nationality under the age of 35 for an essay of not more than 4000 words describing a culture alien to the writer. Final entry date is 30 April. Previous winner: Philip MacCann.
Prize £3000.

NASEN Special Educational Needs Book Awards

The Educational Publishers Council, The Publishers Association, 1 Kingsway, London WC2B 6XF
☎020 7565 7474 Fax 020 7836 4543
Email mail@publishers.org.uk
Website www.publishers.org.uk

ESTABLISHED 1992. Organised by the National Association for Special Education Needs (NASEN) and the Educational Publishers Council. Two awards: The Children's Book Award, for the book that most successfully provides a positive image of children with special needs; The Academic Book Award celebrates the work of authors and editors who have made an outstanding contribution to the theory and practice of special education. Books must have been published in the UK within the year preceding the award. 1999 winners: James Riordan *Sweet Clarinet* (Children's); Nicola Grove *Literature For All* and Christina Tilstone, Lani Florian and Richard Rose (eds.) *Promoting Inclusive Practice* (Academic).
Prize £500.

National Poetry Competition (in association with BT)

The Poetry Society, 22 Betterton Street, London WC2H 9BU
☎020 7420 9880 Fax 020 7240 4818
Email poetrysoc@dial.pipex.com
Website www.poetrysoc.com

Contact *Competition Organiser (WH)*

One of Britain's major open poetry competitions. Closing date: 31 October. Poems on any theme, up to 40 lines. For rules and entry form send s.a.e. to the Competition Organiser at the address above.
Prizes (1st) £5000; (2nd) £1000; (3rd) £500; plus 10 commendations of £50. From 1999–2001 there will be six additional prizes courtesy of British Telecommunications plc.

Bill Naughton Short Story Competition

Box No. 2000, Aghamore, Ballyhaunis, Co. Mayo Republic of Ireland
Organised by the **Kenny/Naughton Society**

(see entry under **Literary Societies**). Stories may be on any topic and no more than 2500 words in length. All work must be unpublished; typed scripts only with no name or address appearing on the work. Entry fee: £3 per story (£1.50 unwaged); three stories may be submitted for the price of two. Closing date: 1 September 2000.
Prizes £150 (1st); £100 (2nd); £50 (3rd).

Nestlé Smarties Book Prize

Book Trust, Book House, 45 East Hill, London SW18 2QZ
☎020 8516 2973 Fax 020 8516 2978
Email sandra@booktrust.org.uk
Website www.booktrust.org.uk

Contact *Sandra Vince*

ESTABLISHED 1985 to encourage high standards and stimulate interest in books for children, this prize is given for a children's book (fiction), written in English by a citizen of the UK or an author resident in the UK, and published in the UK in the year ending 31 October. There are three age-group categories: 5 and under, 6–8 and 9–11. 1999 winners: *The Gruffalo* Julia Donaldson, illus. Axel Scheffler (5 and under, gold); *Snow White and the Seven Aliens* Lawrence Anholt, illus. Arthur Robins (6–8, gold); *Harry Potter and the Prisoner of Azkaban* J. K. Rowling (9–11, gold).
Prizes in each category: £2500 (gold); £1000 (silver); £500 (bronze).

The New Writer Poetry Prizes

The New Writer, PO Box 60, Cranbrook, Kent TN17 2ZR
☎01580 212626 Fax 01580 212041
Email thenewwriter@hotmail.com
Website www.tnwriter.free-online.co.uk

Contact *Merric Davidson*

ESTABLISHED 1997. Annual award founded by *The New Writer* poetry editor and poet, Abi Hughes-Edwards. Open to all poets writing in the English language for an original, previously unpublished poem or collection of six to ten poems. Final entry date: 20 November. Previous winners: Mark Granier, Ros Barber, Celia de Fréine, John Hilton.
Prizes Up to 20 prizes from £20 to £600 plus publication in collection.

No Love Lost Poetry Anthology Contest

See **SEEDS International Poetry Chapbook Anthology Contest**

Nobel Prize

The Nobel Foundation, PO Box 5232, 102
45 Stockholm Sweden
☎00 46 8 663 0920   Fax 00 46 8 660 3847
Website www.nobel.se

Contact *Information Section*

Awarded yearly for outstanding achievement in
physics, chemistry, physiology or medicine, literature and peace. FOUNDED by Alfred Nobel, a
chemist who proved his creative ability by
inventing dynamite. In general, individuals cannot nominate someone for a Nobel Prize. The
rules vary from prize to prize but the following
are eligible to do so for Literature: members of
the Swedish Academy and of other academies,
institutions and societies similar to it in constitu-
tion and purpose; professors of literature and of
linguistics at universities or colleges; Nobel
Laureates in Literature; presidents of authors'
organisations which are representative of the literary production in their respective countries.
British winners of the literature prize, first
granted in 1901, include Rudyard Kipling, John
Galsworthy and Winston Churchill. Recent
winners: Seamus Heaney; Camilio Jose Cela
(Spain); Octavio Paz (Mexico); Nadine
Gordimer (South Africa); Derek Walcott (St
Lucia); Toni Morrison (USA); Kenzaburo Oe
(Japan); Wislawa Szymborska (Poland); Dario Fo
(Italy); José Saramago (Portugal). Nobel Laureate
in Literature 1999: Günter Grass (Germany) .
Prize 1999: SEK7,900,000 (about £600,000),
increasing each year to cover inflation.

The Noma Award for Publishing Africa

PO Box 128, Witney, Oxfordshire OX8 5XU
☎01993 775235   Fax 01993 709265
Email maryljay@aol.com

Contact *Mary Jay, Secretary to the Managing
Committee*

ESTABLISHED 1979. Annual award, founded by
the late Shoichi Noma, President of Kodansha
Ltd, Tokyo, to encourage the publication of
works by African writers and scholars in Africa.
Award is for an outstanding book, published in
Africa by an African writer, in three categories:
scholarly and academic; literature and creative
writing; children's books. Entries, by publishers
only, by 28 February for a title published in the
previous year. Max. three entries per publisher.
Previous winners: Kitia Touré *Destins Parallèles*;
A. Adu Boahen *Mfantsipim and the Making of
Ghana: A Centenary History 1876–1976*; Peter
Adwok Nyaba *The Politics of Liberation in South
Sudan; An Insider's View*; Djibril Samb *L'intépre-*

*tation des rêves dans la région Sénégambienne. Suivi de
la clef des songes de la Sénégambie, de l'Egypte
pharaonique et de la tradition islamique.*
Prize US$10,000 and presentation plaque.

C. B. Oldman Prize

Aberdeen University Library, Queen Mother
Library, Meston Walk, Aberdeen AB24 3UE
☎01224 272592   Fax 01224 487048
Email r.turbet@abdn.ac.uk

Contact *Richard Turbet*

ESTABLISHED 1989 by the International Association of Music Libraries, UK Branch. Annual
award for best book of music bibliography,
librarianship or reference published the year
before last (i.e. books published in 1999 considered for the 2001 prize). Previous winners:
Michael Twyman, Andrew Ashbee, Michael
Talbot, Donald Clarke, John Parkinson, John
Wagstaff, Stanley Sadie, William Waterhouse,
Richard Turbet.
Prize £150.

Open Window Poetry Anthology Contest

See **SEEDS International Poetry
Chapbook Anthology Contest**

Orange Prize for Fiction

Book Trust, 45 East Hill, London SW18 2QZ
☎020 8516 2973   Fax 020 8516 2978
Email sandra@booktrust.org.uk
Website www.booktrust.org.uk

Contact *Sandra Vince*

ESTABLISHED 1996. Annual award founded by a
group of senior women in publishing to 'create
the opportunity for more women to be rewarded for their work and to be better known
by the reading public'. Awarded for a full-length
novel written in English by a woman of any
nationality, and published in the UK between
1 April and 31 March of the following year.
1999 winner: Suzanne Berne *Crime in the
Neighbourhood.*
Prize £30,000 and a work of art (a limited
edition bronze figurine to be known as 'The
Bessie' in acknowledgement of anonymous prize
endowment).

Orange Prize for Screenwriting/ Pathé Production Prize

Pathé Pictures, 14–17 Kent House, London
W1N 8AR
☎020 7323 5151   Fax 020 7462 4417

Contact *Clova McCallum*

ESTABLISHED 1999. Together with partners, Orange, Pathé Pictures has launched a two-tier screenwriting and promotion award aimed specifically at new writing talent. The Orange Prize for Screenwriting and the Pathé Production Prize undertakes to find three feature-length scripts by new writers each year. Winners will receive a cash prize and go into development at Pathé, after which one script will be chosen for production and distribution throughout the UK. First winners: Bernard Wright *Frankie's Come Back*; Clive Bradley *Priceless*; Sara Sugarman *Pavarotti in Dad's Room*.

The Orwell Prize

Specialist Conferences Ltd, 21 The Lodge, Kensington Park Gardens, London W11 3HA
☎020 7727 9732 Fax 020 7221 5187
Contact *Maxine Vlieland*

Jointly ESTABLISHED in 1993 by the George Orwell Memorial Fund and the *Political Quarterly* to encourage and reward writing in the spirit of Orwell's 'What I have most wanted to do ... is to make political writing into an art'. Two categories: book or pamphlet; newspaper and/or articles, features, columns, or sustained reportage on a theme. Submissions by editors, publishers or authors. Previous winners: Polly Toynbee (journalism); Lady Hollis (book).
Prizes £1000 for each category.

Outposts Poetry Competition

Outposts, 22 Whitewell Road, Frome, Somerset BA11 4EL
☎01373 466653
Contact *Roland John*

Annual competition for an unpublished poem of not more than 60 lines run by **Hippopotamus Press**.
Prizes (1st) £500, (2nd) £200, (3rd) £100.

OWG Awards for Excellence

Outdoor Writers' Guild, PO Box 520, Bamber Bridge, Preston, Lancashire PR5 8LF
☎01772 696732 Fax 01772 696732
Contact *Terry Marsh*

ESTABLISHED 1980. Annual award by the **Outdoor Writers' Guild** to raise the standard of outdoor writing, journalism and broadcasting. Winning categories include guidebook, outdoor book, feature (one-off), feature (regular), photography, technical report. Open to OWG members only. Final entry date: March.

Catherine Pakenham Award

The Sunday Telegraph, 1 Canada Square, Canary Wharf, London E14 5DT
☎020 7538 6847 Fax 020 7513 2512
Contact *Melanie Tuppen*

ESTABLISHED in 1970, the award is designed to ecourage women journalists as they embark on their careers. Open to women aged 18–25 who have had at least one piece of work published, however small. 2000 winner: Laura Barton.
Award £1000 and a writing commission with one of the Telegraph publications; three runner-up prizes of £200 each.

The Parker Romantic Novel of the Year

The Old Bakehouse, 36 Eastgate, Hallaton, Market Harborough, Leicester LE16 8UB
☎01858 555602
Award Organiser *Anthea Kenyon*

ESTABLISHED 1960. Formerly known as the Romantic Novelists' Association Major Award. Sponsorship for the 2001 award is by Parker Pen. Annual award for the best romantic novel of the year, open to non-members as well as members of the **Romantic Novelists' Association**. Novels must be published between specified dates. Authors must be based in the UK unless members of the RNA. 2000 winner: Maureen Lee *Dancing in the Park*. Contact the Organiser for entry form.
Award £5000.

The PAWS (Public Awareness of Science) Midas Prize

The PAWS Office, OMNI Communications, Osborne House, 111 Bartholomew Road, London NW5 2BJ
☎020 7267 2555/voice mail: 020 7428 0961
Fax 020 7482 2394
Contacts *Barrie Whatley, Andrew Millington*

ESTABLISHED 1998. Annual prize awarded to the writer and producer of the best television drama, first transmitted in the year up to the end of October, that bears in a significant way on science or engineering. The drama may be a single play or an episode of a series, serial or soap. It need not be centred on a science or engineering theme, though clearly it can be. The context and quality of the drama and the audience size weigh alongside the science in making the Award. To enter a programme or suggest that a programme should be entered, contact the PAWS office above. 1999 winner: episode of *Silent Witness*.
Prize £5000.

Peer Poetry Competition

26(wh) Arlington House, Bath Street, Bath,
Somerset BA1 1QN
☎01225 445298

Contact *Paul Amphlett*

Winners are chosen by poets and subscribers to
Peer Poetry magazine. The two winning collections are published by *Peer Poetry* which prints all
qualifying entries. 'No size limits, eclectic range,
for 30–35 poets.' Send for information sheet
which includes entry form. No entry fee for
existing annual subscribers. New submissions:
£4.50 for a complete group of poems comprising approximately 200 lines, 1000 words, presented double-column, single sides, name and
address on top line of reverse. Closing dates: end
April/October. Two s.a.e.s, A5 size, required.
Magazine subscription £12 for two issues, incl.
p&p (UK), single issue £7. Enclose list of poems.

PEN Awards

See **Macmillan Silver PEN Award**; **The
Stern Silver PEN Non-Fiction Award**

Peterloo Poets Open Poetry Competition

The Old Chapel, Sand Lane, Calstock,
Cornwall PL18 9QX
☎01822 833473

Contact *Lynn Chambers*

ESTABLISHED 1986. Annual competition for
unpublished English language poems of not
more than 40 lines. Final entry date 1 March.
Send s.a.e. for rules and entry form. Previous
winners: John Watts, David Craig, Rodney
Pybus, Debjani Chatterjee, Donald Atkinson,
Romesh Gunesekera, Shafi Ahmed, Anna
Crowe, Carol Ann Duffy, Mimi Khalvati, John
Lyons, M. R. Peacocke, Alison Pryde, Carol
Shergold, David Simon, Maureen Wilkinson,
Chris Woods.
Prize £2000 (1st); £1000 (2nd); £500 (3rd);
£100 (4th); plus 10 prizes of £50.

Poetry Business Competition

The Studio, Byram Arcade, Westgate,
Huddersfield, West Yorkshire HD1 1ND
☎01484 434840 Fax 01484 426566
Email edit@poetrybusiness.co.uk
Website www.poetrybusiness.co.uk

Contact *The Competition Administrator*

ESTABLISHED 1986. Annual award which aims
to discover and publish new writers. Entrants
should submit a manuscript of poems. Winners
will have their work published by the **Poetry**
Business under the Smith/Doorstop imprint.
Final entry date: end of October. Previous
winners include: Pauline Stainer, Michael
Laskey, Mimi Khalvati, David Morley, Julia
Casterton, Liz Cashdan, Moniza Alvi, Selima
Hill. Send s.a.e. for full details.
Prize Publication of full collection; runners-
up have pamphlets; 20 complimentary copies.
Also cash prize (£1000) to be shared equally
between all winners.

Poetry Life Poetry Competition

1 Blue Ball Corner, Water Lane, Winchester,
Hampshire SO23 0ER
Email adrian.bishop@virgin.net
Website freespace.virgin.net/poetry.life/
Contact *Adrian Bishop*

ESTABLISHED 1993. Open competition for original poems in any style which have not been published in a book. Maximum length of 80 lines.
Entry fee of £3 per poem. Send s.a.e. for details.
Prize £500 (1st); £100 (2nd); £50 each (3rd
& 4th).

The Poetry Society's National Poetry Competition

See **National Poetry Competition**

Peter Pook Humorous Novel Competition

See **Emissary Publishing** under **UK
Publishers**

The Portico Prize

The Portico Library, 57 Mosley Street,
Manchester M2 3HY
☎0161 236 6785 Fax 0161 236 6803

Contact *Miss Emma Marigliano*

ESTABLISHED 1985. Administered by the
Portico Library in Manchester. Biennial award
for a work of fiction or non-fiction published
between the two closing dates. Set wholly or
mainly in the North-West of England, including Cumbria and the High Peak District of
Derbyshire. Previous winners include: John
Stalker *Stalker*; Alan Hankinson *Coleridge Walks
the Fells*; Jenny Uglow *Elizabeth Gaskell: A
Habit of Stories.*
Prize £3000.

The Dennis Potter Screenwriting Award

BBC2 Awards, BBC Broadcasting House,
Whiteladies Road, Bristol BS8 2LR
☎0117 9747586
Email BBC2Awards@bbc.co.uk

BBC2 Awards Editor *Jeremy Howe*

Annual award ESTABLISHED in 1995 in memory of the late television playwright to 'nurture and encourage the work of new writers of talent and personal vision'. The winning drama is screened as part of a BBC2 Awards programme in November. Submissions should be made through a BBC TV drama producer or an independent production company. For further information contact the editor of BBC2 Awards.

The Premio Valle Inclán
See **The Translators Association Awards**

The Mathew Prichard Award for Short Story Writing
2 Rhododendron Close, The Greenways, Cyn Coed, Cardiff CF23 7HS
Competition Organiser *Philip Beynon*

ESTABLISHED 1996 to provide sponsorship and promote Wales and its writers. Competition open to all writers in English; the final entry date is 1 March each year.
Prizes A total of £2000.

Pulitzer Prizes
The Pulitzer Prize Board, 709 Journalism, Columbia University, New York NY 10027, USA
☎001 212 854 3841/2
Website www.pulitzer.org

Awards for journalism in US newspapers, and for published literature, drama and music by American nationals. Deadlines: 1 February (journalism); 1 March (music); 1 March (drama); 1 July for books published between 1 Jan–30 June, and 1 Nov for books published between 1 July–31 Dec (literature). Previous winners include: Michael Cunningham *The Hours*; A. Scott Berg *Lindbergh*; Mark Strand *Blizzard of One*; John McPhee *Annals of the Former World*.

Real Writers
PO Box 170, Chesterfield, Derbyshire S40 1FE
☎01246 238492 Fax 01246 238492
Email realwrtrs@aol.com
Website www.turtledesign.com/RealWriters/

ESTABLISHED 1994. Annual short story competition. Closing date: 30 September. Entry fee: £5. Optional critiques. Entry forms, rules and further details available from the address above; send s.a.e. for details.
Prize (1st) £1000.

Trevor Reese Memorial Prize
Institute of Commonwealth Studies, University of London, 28 Russell Square, London WC1B 5DS
☎020 7862 8844 Fax 020 7862 8820
Contact *Events & Publicity Officer*

ESTABLISHED 1979 with the proceeds of contributions to a memorial fund to Dr Trevor Reese, Reader in Commonwealth Studies at the Institute and a distinguished scholar of imperial history (d.1976). Biennial award (next award 2002) for a scholarly work, usually by a single author, in the field of Imperial and Commonwealth History published in the preceding two academic years. All correspondence relating to the prize should be marked 'Trevor Reese Memorial Prize'.
Prize £1000.

Regional Press Awards
Press Gazette, Quantum House, 19 Scarbrook Road, Croydon, Surrey CR9 1LX
☎020 8565 4463 Fax 020 8565 4462

Comprehensive range of journalist and newspaper awards for the regional press. Five newspapers of the year, by circulation and frequency, and a full list of journalism categories. Open to all regional journalists, whether freelance or staff. July event. Run by the *Press Gazette*.

Renault UK Journalist of the Year Award
Guild of Motoring Writers, 30 The Cravens, Smallfield, Surrey RH6 9QS
☎01342 843294 Fax 01342 844093
Contact *Sharon Scott-Fairweather*

Originally the Pierre Dreyfus Award and ESTABLISHED 1977. Awarded annually by Renault UK Ltd in honour of Pierre Dreyfus, president director general of Renault 1955–75, to the member of the **Guild of Motoring Writers** who is judged to have made the most outstanding journalistic effort during the year.
Prize (1st) £1500, plus trophy.

John Llewellyn Rhys Prize
See **The Mail on Sunday/John Llewellyn Rhys Prize**

Rio Tinto David Watt Memorial Prize
Rio Tinto plc, 6 St James's Square, London SW1Y 4LD
☎020 7930 2399 Fax 020 7930 3249
Contact *The Administrator*

INITIATED in 1987 to commemorate the life and work of David Watt. Annual award, open to writers currently engaged in writing for English language newspapers and journals, on international and national political affairs. The winners are judged as having made 'outstanding contributions towards the clarification of political issues – whether international or national – and the promotion of their greater understanding'. Entries must have been published during the year preceding the award. Final entry date 31 March. The 1999 winner was Charles Leadbetter for his article 'Goodbye, Inland Revenue', published in *The New Statesman*.
Prize £5000.

Romantic Novelists' Association Major Award
See **The Parker Romantic Novel of the Year**

Rooney Prize for Irish Literature
Rooney Prize, Strathin, Templecarrig, Delgany, Co. Wicklow, Republic of Ireland
☎00 353 1 287 4769   Fax 00 353 1 287 2595

Contacts *Jim Sherwin, Grainne Davis*

ESTABLISHED 1976. Annual award to encourage young Irish writing to develop and continue. Authors must be Irish, under 40 and published. A non-competitive award with no application procedure.
Prize IR£5000.

Royal Economic Society Prize
c/o University of York, York YO10 5DD
☎01904 433575   Fax 01904 433575

Contact *Prof. Mike Wickens*

Annual award for the best article published in *The Economic Journal*. Open to members of the Royal Economic Society only. Previous winners: Drs O. P. Attanasio & Guglielmo Weber; Prof. M. H. Pesaran; Prof. J. Pemberton.
Prize £3000.

Royal Society of Literature Awards
See **Winifred Holtby Memorial Prize** and **W. H. Heinemann Prize**

Runciman Award
Anglo-Hellenic League, c/o The Hellenic Centre, 16–18 Paddington Street, London W1M 4AS
☎020 7486 9410

Contact *The Administrator*

ESTABLISHED 1985. Annual award, sponsored by the National Bank of Greece. Founded by the Anglo-Hellenic League to promote Anglo-Greek understanding and friendship, for a work wholly or mainly about some aspect of Greece or the Hellenic scene, which has been published in its first English edition in the UK during the previous year and listed in Whitaker's *Books in Print*. Named after Sir Steven Runciman, former chairman of the Anglo-Hellenic League. The Award may be given for a work of fiction, drama or non-fiction; concerned academically or not with the history of any period; biography or autobiography, the arts, archaeology; a guide book or a translation from the Greek of any period. Final entry date in February; award presented in May/June. Previous winners include: *The Cassell Dictionary of Classical Mythology* Dr Jenny March; *The Empire of Manuel I Kommenos 1143–1180* Paul Magdalino; *Crete: the Battle and the Resistance* Antony Beevor; *A Concise History of Greece* Richard Clogg; *An Introduction to Modern Greek Literature* Roderick Beaton; *The Diffusion of Classical Art in Antiquity* Sir John Boardman; *Siren Feasts* Andrew Dalby; *Painting the Soul: Icons, Death Masks and Shrouds* Robin Cormack.
Awards of at least £2000.

Sagittarius Prize
Society of Authors, 84 Drayton Gardens, London SW10 9SB
☎020 7373 6642   Fax 020 7373 5768

ESTABLISHED 1990. For first published novel by an author over the age of 60. Final entry date: mid-December. Full details available from the **Society of Authors**. 1999 winner: Ingrid Man *The Danube Testament*.
Prize £2000.

Sainsbury's Baby Book Award
Book Trust, Book House, 45 East Hill, London SW18 2QZ
☎020 8516 2973   Fax 020 8516 2978
Email sandra@booktrust.org.uk
Website www.booktrust.org.uk

Contact *Sandra Vince*

ESTABLISHED 1999. A new annual award, set up by **Book Trust** with sponsorship from Sainsbury's, for the best book for a baby under one year old, published in the UK. 1999 winner: Helen Oxenbury *Tickle, Tickle*.
Prize £2000 and trophy to the winner; certificate and trophy to the winning publisher.

The Saltire Literary Awards
Saltire Society, 9 Fountain Close, 22 High Street, Edinburgh EH1 1TF
☎0131 556 1836   Fax 0131 557 1675

Administrator *Kathleen Munro*

ESTABLISHED 1982. Annual awards, one for Book of the Year, the other for Best First Book by an author publishing for the first time. Open to any author of Scottish descent or living in Scotland, or to anyone who has written a book which deals with either the work and life of a Scot or with a Scottish problem, event or situation. Nominations are invited from editors of leading newspapers, magazines and periodicals. Previous winners: The Scotsman/ Saltire Scottish Book of the Year: George Bruce *Pursuits*; The Post Office/Saltire Best First Book: Michael Faber *Some Rain Must Fall*.

Prizes £5000 (Scottish Book); £1500 (First Book).

Sandburg-Livesay Anthology Contest

Mekler & Deahl, Publishers, 237 Prospect Street South, Hamilton, Ontario, Canada L8M 2Z6
☎001 905 312 1779 Fax 001 905 312 8285
Email meklerdeahl@globalserve.net
Website www.meklerdeahl.com

Contacts *James Deahl, Gilda Mekler*

FOUNDED 1996. Annual award named after the poets Carl Sandburg and Dorothy Livesay to honour their achievement as populist poets. Up to ten poems may be entered for a fee of £6. A copy of the rules is available from the above address or from the website. Final entry date: 31 October.

Prizes (1st) US$250; (2nd) US$150; (3rd) US$100; anthology publication for the winners and all other worthy entries.

Aileen and Albert Sanders Memorial Trophy

3 Alledge Drive, Woodford NN14 4JQ
Contact *Ivan Sanders*

Annual poetry competition. Entry fee: £5 for up to two poems, £10 for up to five (maximum per competitor). Rules and entry forms available from the address above; enclose s.a.e. 1999 winner: K. V. Skene.

Prizes 1st £500 plus trophy and certificate; nine runners-up prizes and certificates.

Ron Sands Prize

See **Lakeland Book of the Year Awards**

The Biennial Sasakawa Prize

British Haiku Society, Sinodun, Shalford, Braintree, Essex CM7 5HN
☎01371 851097 Fax 01371 851097

Contact *David Cobb*

ESTABLISHED 1999. Biennial prize (next in 2001) for original contributions in the field of haikai (haiku and related genres). Open to entrants domiciled in either the UK or Japan. Closing date: 31 December 2001. Entry details available from the British Haiku Society at the address above.

Prize £2500, partly in the form of a return air ticket to Japan (or to the UK for a Japanese winner).

Schlegel-Tieck Prize

See **The Translators Association Awards**

Scottish Arts Council Children's Book Awards

Scottish Arts Council, 12 Manor Place, Edinburgh EH3 7DD
☎0131 226 6051 Fax 0131 240 2575
Email jenny.brown@scottisharts.org.uk

Literature Director *Jenny Brown*

A number of awards are given annually (spring) to authors of published books in recognition of high standards in children's fiction or non-fiction from new or established writers. Awards are made in three categories: picture books for children, books aimed at 6–9 years, and books aimed at 10+ years. Authors should be Scottish or resident in Scotland, or books must be of Scottish interest. Applications from publishers only. 2000 winners: Debi Gliori *Mr Bear's New Baby*; Judith O'Neill *Whirlwind*; Julie Bertagna *Soundtrack*; Margaret Ryan and illus. Priscilla Lamont *The Queen's Birthday Hat*; Richard Brassey and Stewart Ross *The Story of Scotland*.

Award £1000 each.

Scottish Arts Council Creative Scotland Awards

Scottish Arts Council, 12 Manor Pace, Edinburgh EH3 7DD
☎0131 240 2443
Email help.desk@scottisharts.org.uk

Contact *Help Desk*

Fourteen awards available to artists in Scotland with a demonstrable and substantial record of achievement in their artform, covering a wide range, including architecture, crafts, design and fashion, dance, film and video, literature, music (from rock to classical), photography, theatre and the visual arts.

Awards each worth £25,000.

Scottish Book of the Year
See **The Saltire Literary Awards**

Scottish Historical Book of the Year in Memory of Agnes Mure Mackenzie
The Saltire Society, 9 Fountain Close, 22 High Street, Edinburgh EH1 1TF
☎0131 556 1836 Fax 0131 557 1675
Website www.saltire-society.demon.co.uk
Administrator *Kathleen Munro*

ESTABLISHED 1965. Annual award in memory of the late Dr Agnes Mure Mackenzie for a published work of distinguished Scottish historical research of scholarly importance (including intellectual history and the history of science). Editions of texts are not eligible. Nominations are invited and should be sent to the Administrator. Previous winner: William Ferguson *The Identity of the Scottish Nation*.

Prize Bound and inscribed copy of the winning publication.

The Scottish Writer of the Year Award
c/o Scottish Book Trust, The Scottish Book Centre, 137 Dundee Street, Edinburgh EH11 1BG
☎0131 229 3663 Fax 0131 228 4293
Email scottish.book.trust@dial.pipex.com
Website www.webpost.net/bts

Contact *Kathryn Ross*

ESTABLISHED 1987. Awarded for the best substantial work of an imaginative nature, including TV and radio scripts and writing for children (for 8–16 years), first published, performed, filmed or transmitted between 1st August and 31st July. Writers born in Scotland, or who have Scottish parents, or who have been resident in Scotland for a considerable period, or who take Scotland as their inspiration are all eligible. Submissions accepted in English, Scots or Gaelic. Recent winners: Janice Galloway, Edwin Morgan and James Kelman.

Prize £10,000, plus £1,000 to each of the other four shortlisted writers.

SCSE Book Prizes
Institute of Education, University of London, 20 Bedford Way, London WC1H 0AL
☎020 7580 1122 Fax 020 7612 6330

Contact *Professor G. Grace*

Annual awards given by the Standing Conference on Studies in Education for the best book on education published during the preceding year and for the best book by a new author. Nomination by members of the Standing Conference and publishers.
Prizes £1000 and £500.

The Seebohm Trophy – Age Concern Book of the Year
1268 London Road, London SW16 4ER
☎020 8765 7200/8765 7456

Contacts *Vinnette Marshall, Jane Marsh*

ESTABLISHED 1995. Annual award in memory of the late Lord Seebohm, former President of Age Concern England. Awarded to the author and publisher of a non-fiction title published in the previous calendar year which, in the opinion of the judges, is most successful in promoting the well-being and understanding of older people. The award was suspended in 2000 and is under review at present.

SEEDS International Poetry Chapbook Anthology Contest
Hidden Brook Press, 412–701 King Street West, Toronto, Ontario Canada M5V 2W7
Email writers@pathcom.com
Website www.hiddenbrookpress.com/ homepage.htm

Biannual international poetry competition. Electronic and hard copy submissions are required. Send three poems, of any style, theme or length, with name, address, phone number and email address on the back of each sheet. Send with fee (US$13 for submissions outside of Canada) and follow this with submission by email (no attachments). Closing dates: 1 May and 1 October. *Prizes* $100 (1st); $50 (2nd); $25 (3rd); all prize winners are published in the *SEEDS* International Chapbook Anthology and website.

(Also organises two further international anthology contests: No Love Lost and The Open Window. Access website for details.)

Bernard Shaw Translation Prize
See **The Translators Association Awards**

Signal Poetry for Children Award
Thimble Press, Lockwood, Station Road, South Woodchester, Stroud, Gloucestershire GL5 5EQ
☎01453 873716/872208 Fax 01453 878599

Contact *Nancy Chambers*

This award is given annually for particular excellence in one of the following areas: single-poet collections published for children; poetry anthologies published for children; the body of work of a contemporary poet; critical or educational activity promoting poetry for children. All books for children published in Britain are eligible regardless of the original country of publication. Unpublished work is not eligible. Previous winners include: Helen Dunmore *Secrets*; Roger McGough *Bad, Bad Cats*.

Award Substantial article-citation in each May issue of the journal *Signal*; certificate designed by Michael Harvey.

André Simon Memorial Fund Book Awards

5 Sion Hill Place, Bath BA1 5SJ
☎01225 336305 Fax 01225 421862

Contact *Tessa Hayward*

ESTABLISHED 1978. Three awards given annually for the best book on drink, best on food and special commendation in either. Previous winners: Ken Hom *Easy Family Dishes*; Max Allen *Red and White*; Stephen Brook *Pauillac* (special commendation).

Awards £2000 (best books); £1000 (special commendation); £200 to shortlisted books.

WHSmith Book Prize

WH Smith Group PLC, Nations House, 103 Wigmore Street, London W1H 0WH
☎020 7409 3222 Fax 020 7514 9635
Website www.whsmithgroup.com

Contact *Corporate Affairs*

Newly-established prize – first award to be made in 2001 – to celebrate all forms of excellence in book publishing with categories such as 'new author', 'lifestyle' and 'children's book of the year'. A panel of judges for each category will select its own short list with the general public being invited to vote for the winner.

WHSmith's Thumping Good Read Award

WH Smith PLC, Greenbridge Road, Swindon, Wiltshire SN3 3LD
☎01793 616161 Fax 01793 562590

Contact *Victoria Seymour*

ESTABLISHED 1992 to promote new writers of popular fiction. Books must have been published in the twelve months preceding the award. Submissions, made by publishers, are judged by a panel of customers to be the most un-put-down-able from a shortlist of six. 1999 winner: Lee Child *The Killing Floor*.

Award £5000.

The Society for Theatre Research Annual Theatre Book Prize

c/o The Theatre Museum, 1e Tavistock Street, London WC2E 7PA
☎01304 379179
Email e.cottis@btinternet.com
Website www.unl.ac.uk/str

ESTABLISHED 1997. Annual award for books, in English, of original research into any aspect of the history and technique of the British Theatre. Not restricted to authors of British nationality nor books solely from British publishers. No submissions; independent judges rely on their personal observations during the year. 1999 winner: Ian McIntyre *Garrick*.

Award £400.

Sony Radio Awards

Alan Zafer & Associates, 47–48 Chagford Street, London NW1 6EB
☎020 7723 0106 Fax 020 7724 6163
Email zafer@compuserve.com
Website www.radioawards.org

Contact *The Secretariat*

ESTABLISHED 1981 by the **Society of Authors**. Sponsored by Sony and presented in association with the Radio Academy. Annual awards to recognise excellence in radio broadcasting. Entries must have been broadcast in the UK between 1 January and 31 December in the year preceding the award. The categories for the awards are reviewed each year.

Southern Arts Literature Prize

Southern Arts, 13 St Clement Street, Winchester, Hampshire SO23 9DQ
☎01962 855099 Fax 01962 861186

Contact *Literature Officer*

ESTABLISHED 1991, this prize is awarded annually to an author living in the **Southern Arts** region for the most promising work of prose or poetry published during the year. The 2000 prize will be for poetry. The 1999 prize, awarded for fiction, went to Sunetra Gupta for *A Sin of Colour*.

Prize £1000, plus a craft commission to the value of £600.

Southport Writers' Circle Poetry Competition

32 Dover Road, Southport, Merseyside PR8 4TB

Contact *Mrs Hilary Tinsley*

For previously unpublished work. Entry fee: £2 per poem, plus £1 for each subsequent entry, or £5 for three. Open category (any subject, any form) and humorous category; maximum 40 lines. Closing date: end April. Poems must be entered under a pseudonym, accompanied by a sealed envelope marked with the pseudonym and title of poem, containing s.a.e. Entries must be typed on A4 paper and be accompanied by the appropriate fee payable to Southport Writers' Circle. No application form is required. Envelopes should be marked 'Poetry Competition'. Postal enquiries only. No calls.

Prizes (1st) £150; (2nd) £75; five runners-up of £10 in each category.

Stand Magazine Poetry Competition

Haltwhistle House, George Street, Newcastle upon Tyne NE4 7JL
☎0191 273 3280
Website www.saturn.vcu.edu/~dlatane/ stand.html

Contact *Linda Goldsmith*

Biennial award for poems written in English and not yet published, broadcast or under consideration elsewhere. Next award 2001. Send s.a.e. for entry form.

Prize (total) £2500.

Stand Magazine Short Story Competition

Haltwhistle House, George Street, Newcastle upon Tyne NE4 9JL
☎0191 273 3280
Website
www.saturn.vcu.edu/~dlatane/stand.html

Contact *Linda Goldsmith*

Biennial award for short stories written in English and not yet published, broadcast or under consideration elsewhere. Next award 2001. Send s.a.e. for entry form.

Prize (total) £2500.

The Stern Silver PEN Non-Fiction Award

English Centre of International PEN, 152–156 Kentish Town Road, London NW1 9QB
☎020 7267 9444 Fax 020 7267 9304
Email enquiries@pen.org.uk
Website www.pen.org.uk

ESTABLISHED 1986 and sponsored, from 1997, by the family of James Stern in memory of their father. An annual award for an outstanding work of non-fiction written in English and published in England in the year preceding the prize.

Nominations by the PEN Executive Committee only. Please do not submit books. 2000 winner: Andrew Roberts *Salisbury; Victorian Titan.*

Prize £1000, plus silver pen.

Bram Stoker Awards for Superior Achievement

Horror Writers Association, PO Box 50577, Palo Alto, CA 94303 USA
☎001 650 322 4610
Email hwa@horror.org
Website www.horror.org

Contact *Nancy Etchemendy*

FOUNDED 1988 and named in honour of Bram Stoker, author of *Dracula*. Presented annually by the **Horror Writers Association** (HWA) for works of horror first published in the English language during their year of publication. HWA members recommend works for consideration in eleven categories: novel, first novel, short fiction, long fiction, fiction collection, anthology, non-fiction, illustrated narrative, screenplay, work for young readers, and other media. In addition, Lifetime Achievement Stokers are occasionally presented to individuals whose entire body of work has substantially influenced horror.

Sunday Times Award for Small Publishers

Independent Publishers Guild, PO Box 93, Royston, Hertfordshire SG8 5GH
☎01763 247014 Fax 01763 246293
Email sheila@ipg.uk.com

Contact *Sheila Bounford*

ESTABLISHED 1988, the first winner was **Fourth Estate**. Open to any publisher producing between five and forty titles a year, which must primarily be original titles, not reprints. Entrants are invited to submit their catalogues for the last twelve months, together with two representative titles. Award presented at the London Book Fair. 2000 winner: **Carcanet Press**. Previous winners: **Profile Books**; **Nick Hern Books**; **Tarquin Publications**; **Ellipsis**; **Bradt Publications**.

Sunday Times Writer of the Year Award

The Sunday Times, 1 Pennington Street, London E1 9XW
☎020 7782 5770 Fax 020 7782 5798

ESTABLISHED 1987. Annual award to fiction and non-fiction writers. The panel consists of *Sunday Times* journalists, publishers and other figures from the book world. Previous winners:

Anthony Burgess, Seamus Heaney, Stephen Hawking, Ruth Rendell, Muriel Spark, William Trevor, Martin Amis, Ted Hughes, Harold Pinter, Tom Wolfe. No applications; prize at the discretion of the Literary Editor.

Sunday Times Young Writer of the Year Award

The Society of Authors, 84 Drayton Gardens, London SW10 9SB
☎020 7373 6642 Fax 020 7373 5768
Contact *Awards Secretary*

ESTABLISHED 1991. Annual award given on the strength of the promise shown by a full-length published work of fiction, non-fiction, poetry or drama. Entrants must be British citizens, resident in Britain and under the age of 35 at the closing date of 31 December. The work must be by one author, in the English language, and published in Britain during the 12 months prior to the closing date. Full details available from the **Society of Authors**. 1999 winner: Paul Farley *The Boy From the Chemist is Here to See You.*
Prize £5000.

Tabla Poetry Competition

Department of English, University of Britsol, 3–5 Woodland Road, Bristol BS8 1TB
Fax 0117 9288860
Email stephen.james@bristol.ac.uk
Website www.bris.ac.uk/tabla
Contact *Stephen James*

ESTABLISHED 1991. Annual award for poems of any length which have not been published or broadcast. Minimum age of entrants must be 16. Final entry date: 20 September. No poems by e-mail, please. Winning and other selected entries are published, alongside leading names, in the annual *Tabla Book of New Verse*. Previous winners: Paul F. Cowlan, Philip Gross.
Prizes £500 (1st); £200 (2nd); 3 runners-up, £100 each.

The Talkies

15 Prescott Place, London SW4 6BS
☎020 7819 1111 Fax 020 7819 1122/33
Email info@squareonepublishing.co.uk
Contacts *Peter Dean, Sean King, Samantha Warren*

Annual award ESTABLISHED in 1995 by *Talking Business* magazine to recognise the best in spoken word publishing, production, design and retailing. There are 20 awards with the 'Talkie of the Year' being picked from the winners of all the categories. Contact *Talking Business* for entry form. Final entry date: late July. Previous Talkie of the Year winners: *Alan Bennett Diaries*; *This Sceptred Isle*; *Spoonface Steinberg*; *Ambush at Fort Bragg*; *Talking Heads 2.*
Prizes Framed certificate for all winners, plus trophy for Best Reader and Talkie of the Year.

Reginald Taylor and Lord Fletcher Essay Prize

Journal of the British Archaeological Association, Institute of Archaelogy, 36 Beaumont Street, Oxford OX1 2PG
Contact *Dr Martin Henig*

A biennial prize, in memory of the late E. Reginald Taylor and of Lord Fletcher, for the best unpublished essay, not exceeding 7500 words, on a subject of archaeological, art history or antiquarian interest within the period from the Roman era to AD 1830. The essay should show *original* research on its chosen subject, and the author will be invited to read the essay before the Association. The essay may be published in the journal of the Association if approved by the Editorial Committee. Closing date for entries is 1 June 2002. All enquiries by post please. No phone calls. Send s.a.e. for details.
Prize £300 and a medal.

The Teixeira Gomes Prize

See **The Translators Association Awards**

David Thomas Prize

See entry under **Bursaries, Fellowships and Grants**

Anne Tibble Poetry Competition

See **Words & Pictures Literary & Photographic Competition**

The Times Educational Supplement Book Awards

Times Educational Supplement, Admiral House, 66–68 East Smithfield, London E1 9XY
☎020 7782 3000 Fax 020 7782 3200
Email friday@tes.co.uk
Website www.tes.co.uk
Contact *Awards Administrator*

ESTABLISHED 1973. The Awards are under review at present.

The Tir Na N-Og Award

Cyngor Llyfrau Cymru (Welsh Books Council), Castell Brychan, Aberystwyth, Dyfed SY23 2JB
☎01970 624151 Fax 01970 625385
Email castellbrychan@cllc.org.uk
Website www.wbc.org.uk

An annual award given to the best original book published for children in the year prior to the announcement. There are three categories: Best Welsh Fiction; Best Welsh Non-fiction; Best English Book with an authentic Welsh background.

Awards £1000 (each category).

TLS/Blackwells Poetry Competition

Times Literary Supplement, Admiral House, 66–68 East Smithfield, London E1 9XY
☎020 7782 3000

Contact *Mick Imlah (Poetry Editor, TLS)*

ESTABLISHED 1997. Annual open competition. Final entry date: 30 November. 1999 winner: Matthew Francis.

Prizes £2000; three runners-up £500 each.

Marten Toonder Award

An Chomhairle Ealaíon (The Irish Arts Council), 70 Merrion Square, Dublin 2, Republic of Ireland
☎00 353 1 6180200 Fax 00 353 1 6761302

Music Officer *Maura Eaton*

The award, made possible by Dutch artist Marten Toonder, honours established artists in music, literature and the visual arts. In 2000 the award was made to a composer; in 2001 it will be for literature; the visual arts in 2002 and music in 2003. Applicants should enclose a detailed c.v. as well as a CD or tape recording of their work. The standard application form for individuals should be used and is available on request.

Award 9000 Euros/IR£7088.

The Translators Association Awards

The Translators Association, 84 Drayton Gardens, London SW10 9SB
☎020 7373 6642 Fax 020 7373 5768

Contact *Dorothy Wright*

Various awards for published translations into English from Dutch and Flemish (The Vondel Translation Prize), French (Scott Moncrieff Prize), German (Schlegel-Tieck Prize), Italian (The John Florio Prize), Portuguese (The Teixeira Gomes Prize), Spanish (The Premio Valle Inclán), Swedish (Bernard Shaw Translation Prize) and Japanese (Sasakawa Prize). Contact the **Translators Association** for full details.

The Betty Trask Prize

See entry under **Bursaries, Fellowships and Grants**

Travelex Travel Writers' Awards

Travelex UK Limited, 65 Kingsway, London WC2B 6TD
☎020 7405 7200 Fax 020 7404 1005

ESTABLISHED in 1993 to reward excellence in UK travel journalism. An overall winner is selected from the eight category winners. These cover national daily newspaper, national Sunday newspaper, regional newspaper, trade press, consumer magazine, radio, television and guidebook. Previous winners: Michael Palin, Alan Whicker.

Prizes £1500 and special crystal trophy; £500 and crystal trophy for each category winner.

The Trewithen Poetry Prize

Chy-an-Dour, Trewithen Moor, Stithians, Truro, Cornwall TR3 7DU

Contact *Competition Secretary*

ESTABLISHED 1995 in order to promote poetry with a rural theme. Entry forms available from the address above (enclose s.a.e.). Closing date: 31 October. Entry fee of £3 for first poem, £1.75 for subsequent entries. Previous winners include: Elizabeth Rapp, David Smart, Ann Drysdale, Roger Elkin.

Prizes (total) £800 plus publication in *The Trewithen Chapbook.*

Tullie House Prize

See **Lakeland Book of the Year Awards**

UNESCO Prize for Children's and Young People's Literature in the Service of Tolerance

Division of Creativity, Cultural Industries and Copyright, UNESCO, 1 rue Miollis, 75732–Paris Cedex 15 France
☎00 33 1 45 68 43 40
Fax 00 33 1 45 68 55 95
Email m.bulos@unesco.org

Contact *Ms Maha Bulos*

The UNESCO Prize is awarded every two years in recognition of works for the young that 'best embody the concepts and ideals of tolerance and peace, and promote mutual understanding based on respect for other people and cultures'. The works may be novels, collections of short stories or illustrated picture books, and fall within two categories: for children up to the age of 12 and for young people aged 13 to 18. Submissions by publishers only. The 2001 awards will be presented during the Bologna Children's Book Fair in Italy.

Prizes US$8000 in each category.

The V. B. Poetry Prize

20 Clifton House, Club Row, London E2 7HB
Email LOOKLEARN@aol.com
Website www.looklearn.com

Contact *Nicholas Morgan*

Annual open competition for original single un-published poems, any style, maximum length 40 lines. Entry fee: £3 for first two poems, £1.50 for each additional. Closing date: 31 March 2001. Send s.a.e. for full details and entry form.

Prize £400 (1st), £150 (2nd), £50 (3rd). Winning poems will be published on the Look and Learn Productions' website.

Ver Poets Open Competition

Haycroft, 61–63 Chiswell Green Lane, St Albans, Hertfordshire AL2 3AL
☎01727 867005

Contact *May Badman*

Various competitions are organised by **Ver Poets**, the main one being the annual Open for unpublished poems of no more than 30 lines written in English. Entry fee: £2.50 per poem. Entries must be made under a pseudo-nym, with name and address on form or sepa-rate sheet. Two copies of poems typed on A4 white paper. *Vision On*, the anthology of win-ning and selected poems, and the adjudicators' report are normally available from mid-June. Final entry date: 30 April. Back numbers of the anthology are available for £2, post-free.

Prizes (1st) £500; (2nd) £300; two runners-up £100.

Vogue Talent Contest

Vogue, Vogue House, Hanover Square, London W1R 0AD
☎020 7499 9080 Fax 020 7408 0559

Contact *Frances Bentley*

ESTABLISHED 1951. Annual award for young writers and journalists (under 25 on 1 January in the year of the contest). Final entry date is in April. Entrants must write three pieces of jour-nalism on given subjects.

Prizes £1000, plus a month's paid work experience with *Vogue*; (2nd) £500.

The Vondel Translation Prize

See **The Translators Association Awards**

Wadsworth Prize for Business History

Business Archives Council, 101 Whitechapel High Street, London E1 7RE
☎020 7247 0024 Fax 020 7422 0026

Chairman *Mrs Lenore Symons*

ESTABLISHED 1978. Annual award for the best book published on British business history. Previous winners: Niall Ferguson *The World's Banker: The History of the House of Rothschild*; Dr Richard Saville *Bank of Scotland, A History 1695–1995*; Dr T. R. Gourvish and Dr R. Wilson *The British Brewing Industry: A History*.

Prize £500.

Arts Council of Wales Book of the Year Awards

Arts Council of Wales, Museum Place, Cardiff CF10 3NX
☎029 2037 6500 Fax 029 2022 1447

Contact *Tony Bianchi*

Annual non-competitive prizes awarded for works of exceptional literary merit written by Welsh authors (by birth or residence), published in Welsh or English during the previous calendar year. There is one major prize in English, the Book of the Year Award, and one major prize in Welsh, Gwobr Llyfr y Flwyddyn. Shortlists of three titles in each language are announced in April; winners announced in May. 1999 win-ners: Emyr Humphreys *The Gift of a Daughter*; Bobi Jones *Ysbryd y Cwylym*.

Prizes £3000 (each); £1000 to each of four runners-up.

Walford Award

See **The Library Association Walford Award**

The Harri Webb Prize

10 Heol Don, Whitchurch, Cardiff CF14 2AU
☎029 2062 3359 Fax 029 2052 9202

Contact *Meic Stephens*

ESTABLISHED 1995. Annual award to com-memorate the Welsh poet, Harri Webb (1920–94), for a single poem in any of the cat-egories in which he wrote: ballad, satire, song, polemic or a first collection of poems. The poems are chosen by three adjudicators; no submissions. 1998 winner: David Hughes.

Prize £100/£200.

The Weidenfeld Translation Prize

European Humanities Research Centre, The Queen's College, Oxford OX1 4AW
☎01865 279183/244701 Fax 01865 790819
Email david.constantine@queens.ox.ac.uk

Contact *The Fellows' Secretary or David Constantine*

ESTABLISHED in 1996 by publisher Lord

Weidenfeld to encourage good translation into English. Annual award to the translator(s) of a work of fiction, poetry or drama written in any living European language. Submissions from publishers only. For further information, contact Dr David Constantine at the Queen's College address above. 1999 winner: Jonathan Galassi for his translation of *Collected Poems 1920–54* by Eugenio Montale.
Prize £1000.

The Wellcome Trust Prize

Consultation and Education Dept., The Wellcome Trust, 210 Euston Road, London NW1 2BE
☎020 7611 7221 Fax 020 7611 8269
Email r.birse@wellcome.ac.uk
Website www.wellcome.ac.uk

Contact *Ruth Birse*

ESTABLISHED 1997. Biennial award for a book that 'will educate, captivate and inspire the non-specialist lay reader', to be written by a professional life scientist who is unpublished and resident in the UK or Ireland. Contact the Wellcome Trust for rules and guidelines or visit the website. The winning book will be published by **Weidenfeld & Nicolson**. Previous winners: Dr Guy Brown, Prof. Chris McManus.
Prize £25,000 (in four instalments, depending on progress of the book)

Wellington Town Council Award

Civic Offices, Tan Bank, Wellington, Telford, Shropshire TF1 1LX
☎01952 222935 Fax 01952 222936

Contacts *Martin Scholes, Derrick Drew*

ESTABLISHED 1995. Annual short story competition to promote the ancient town of Wellington, now part of the Wellington annual literary festival. Open to all for a minimum fee of £2.50; prizes are sponsored so all entry fee monies go to charity. 1999 winners: G. Reynolds (Overall winner); Austin Ford (Best Shropshire Entry); Pippa McCathie (Best Story for Children).
Prizes Trophies and money.

Wheatley Medal

See **The Library Association Wheatley Medal**

Whitbread Book Awards

Minster House, 272 Vauxhall Bridge Road, London SW1V 1BA
☎020 7834 5477 Fax 020 7834 8812

Contact *Gillian Cronin*

ESTABLISHED 1971. Publishers are invited to submit books for this annual competition designed for writers who have been resident in Great Britain or the Republic of Ireland for three years or more. The awards are made in two stages. First, four category award winners are selected: novel, first novel, biography and poetry. A shortlist of four books is selected for the Whitbread Children's Book of the Year. A final panel of nine judges selects the winning children's book which then competes alongside the other four winners for the title of Whitbread Book of the Year. 1999 winners: J. K. Rowling *Harry Potter and the Prisoner of Azkaban* (children's); Rose Tremain *Music and Silence* (novel); Tim Lott *White City Blue* (first novel); David Cairns *Berlioz Volume 2* (biography); Seamus Heaney *Beowulf* (poetry and overall winner).
Awards £21,000 (Book of the Year); £3500 (all category winners).

Whitfield Prize

Royal Historical Society, University College London, Gower Street, London WC1E 6BT
☎020 7387 7532 Fax 020 7387 7532

Contact *Executive Secretary*

ESTABLISHED 1977. An annual award for the best new work within a field of British history, published in the UK in the preceding calendar year. The book must be the author's first (solely written) history book and be an original and scholarly work of historical research. Final entry date: 31 December. 1999 winner: Amanda Vickery *The Gentleman's Daughter: Women's Lives in Georgian England*.
Prize £1000.

John Whiting Award

Arts Council of England, 14 Great Peter Street, London SW1P 3NQ
☎020 7973 6431 Fax 020 7973 6983
Email jemima.lee@artscouncil.org.uk
Website www.artscouncil.org.uk

Contact *John Johnston*

FOUNDED 1965. Annual award to commemorate the life and work of the playwright John Whiting (*The Devils, A Penny for a Song*). Any writer who has received during the previous two calendar years an award through the **Arts Council's Theatre Writing Schemes** or who has had a première production by a theatre company in receipt of annual subsidy is eligible to apply. Awarded to the writer whose play most nearly satisfies the following criteria: a play in which the writing is of special quality; a play of

relevance and importance to contemporary life; a play of potential value to the British theatre. Closing date for entries: 5 January 2001.
Prize £6000.

Alfred and Mary Wilkins International £2000 Prize Memorial Poetry Competition

Birmingham & Midland Institute, 9 Margaret Street, Birmingham B3 3BS
☎0121 236 3591 Fax 0121 212 4577
Administrator *Mr P. A. Fisher*

An annual competition for an unpublished poem, not exceeding 40 lines, written in English by an author over the age of 15. The poem should not have been entered for any other poetry competition.
Prizes (total) £2000.

Titus Wilson Prize
See **Lakeland Book of the Year Awards**

H. H. Wingate Prize
See **Jewish Quarterly Literary Prizes**

Wolf Web
PO Box 136, Norwich, Norfolk NR3 3NJ
☎01603 440944 Fax 01603 440940
Contact *Tricia Frances*

Sayana Wolf Trust publishes *Wolf Web Quarterly* and runs one poetry competiton annually. Unpublished poems only on the theme of 'wolf'. All profits go to the work of The Sayana Wolf Trust who fund personal development, educational and community projects for British and North American children and adults. For more details, send s.a.e. to the above address.
Prizes One-year's membership to Wolf Web.

Wolfson History Prizes
Wolfson Foundation, 8 Queen Anne Street, London W1M 9LD
☎020 7323 5730 Fax 020 7323 3241
Contact *Executive Secretary*

ESTABLISHED 1972. An award made annually to authors of published historical works, with the object of encouraging historians to communicate with general readers as well as with their professional colleagues. Previous winners include: Antony Beevor *Stalingrad*; Fiona MacCarthy *William Morris*; John G. C. Rohl *The Kaiser and His Court: Wilhelm II and the Government of Germany*; Lord Skidelsky *John Maynard Keynes: The Economist as Saviour 1920–1937*. 1999 win-

ner: Amanda Vickery *The Gentleman's Daughter: Women's Lives in Georgian England*.
Prizes vary each year.

The David T. K. Wong Short Story Prize
International PEN, 9/10 Charterhouse Buildings, Goswell Road, London EC1M 7AT
☎020 7253 4308 Fax 020 7253 5711
Contact *Gilly Vincent*

ESTABLISHED 2000. An international, biannual prize to promote literary excellence in the form of the short story written in English. Unpublished stories are welcome from writers worldwide, as long as their entries are submitted via their local PEN Centre and incorporate one or more of International PEN's ideals as set out in its Charter. Writers in those few countries without a PEN Centre can be directed to the nearest appropriate centre by International PEN.
Prize £7500 (1st).

Words & Pictures Literary & Photographic Competition
Events Team, Directorate of Community Services, Northampton Borough Council, Cliftonville House, Bedford Road, Northampton NN4 7NR
☎01604 238791 Fax 01604 238577
Email events@northampton.gov.uk

A combination of four competitions: National Literary Competition; Short Story Competition for the H. E. Bates Prize; Poetry Competition for the Anne Tibble Prize; and National Photographic Competition. Short stories must not be of more than 2000 words and poems not exceed 20 lines. Entries should be typed on one side of the paper only; entry fee of £4 per competition. Send s.a.e. for full details and entry form.

World Wide Writers Award
Suite 22, Ashley Business Centre, Briggs House, Commercial Road, Poole, Dorset BH14 0JR
☎01202 716043 Fax 01202 740995
Email writintl@globalnet.co.uk
Website www.users.globalnet.co.uk/~wrtintl
Contacts *John Jenkins, Mary Hogarth*

ESTABLISHED 1997. Quarterly and annual competitions for original, unpublished short stories of between 2500 and 5000 words. Entries are published in *World Wide Writers* magazine. Entry fee of £6. Closing dates: end of January, March, June and September. Previous winners:

Sally Zigmond, Shirley Nunes, Judi Moore, Gerald Phillipson, Brian Dixon, L. Morgana Braveraven. *Prize* £3000 and an annual trophy.

The Writers Bureau Poetry and Short Story Competition

The Writers Bureau, Sevendale House, 7 Dale Street, Manchester M1 1JB
☎0161 228 2362 Fax 0161 228 3533
Email compent@writersbureau.com
Website www.writersbureau.com

Competition Secretary *Angela Cox*

ESTABLISHED 1994. Annual award. Poems should be no longer than 40 lines and short stories no more than 2000 words. £4 entry fee. Closing date: 31 July 2001.

Prizes in each category: £1000 (1st); £400 (2nd); £200 (3rd); £100 (4th); £50 (5th).

Yorkshire Post Book of the Year Award

Yorkshire Post, PO Box 168, Wellington Street, Leeds, West Yorkshire LS1 1RF
☎0113 2432701 ext 1704 Fax 0113 2388909

Contact *Margaret Brown*

An annual award for the book (either fiction or non-fiction) which, in the opinion of the judges, is the best work published in the preceding year. Closing date: 31 December. Previous winner: John Ehrman *The Younger Pitt, Vol. III: The Consuming Struggle.*

Prize £1200.

Young Science Writer Award

The Daily Telegraph, 1 Canada Square, Canary Wharf, London E14 5DT
☎020 7538 6960

Contact *Amelia Watson-Steele*

ESTABLISHED 1987, this award is designed to bridge the gap between science and writing, challenging the writer to come up with a piece of no more than 700 words that is friendly, informative and, above all, understandable. Open to two age groups: 16–19 and 20–28.

Award Winners and runners-up receive cash prizes and have the opportunity to have their pieces published on the science pages of *The Daily Telegraph*. The winner in each category also gets an all expenses paid trip to the USA for the 2001 meeting of the American Association for the Advancement of Science and an invitation to meet Britain's most distinguished scientists at the British Association's Festival of Science.

PLR at 21

David Whitaker

Twenty-one years ago, in 1979, Parliament passed the act which brought Public Lending Right into being. In February of this year Dr James Parker, the Registrar of PLR, sent out the seventeenth annual payment, of just over £4 million, to eligible authors. Had successive arts ministers managed to keep their end up against the Treasury, which has allowed inflation to erode PLR's original modest stipend, the sum would have been £7 million.

But, putting that caveat to one side, it has to be said that the British PLR scheme is the best constructed and most efficiently run of the seventeen schemes that exist throughout the world. That there are so few reflects the fact that rewarding authors for the loans of their books through a public library service is not usually seen as a government priority. This may change during the present decade, at least in Europe, as member states try to implement the 1992 Directive on Rental and Lending.

However, authors will not be holding their breath. It took twenty-eight years to get the PLR Act on to the statute books in Britain. The struggle began on 3 February 1951 with a modest proposal in the *Bookseller* that circulating libraries should pay authors a halfpenny each time their books were lent to subscribers. The novelist John Brophy took the idea further. As Michael Holroyd records in *Whose Loan is it Anyway?* Brophy argued that users of public libraries would not object to paying a penny – 'less than the cost of half a cigarette', as he put it then – as a royalty to the author of the book being borrowed. And thus was born 'Brophy's penny', which was the unofficial title of the campaign for public lending right in the fifties.

It was a long and acrimonious campaign. When, finally, it was successful, the late Lord Goodman said, 'It seems to me as plain as the nose on my face that it is a social wrong to allow a book . . . to be borrowed from a public library without any payment, of any kind, to the living author. A great deal of sophistry has been wasted obscuring this simple situation.' Another view had been expressed earlier that the proposals were 'phoney in conception, ill-considered in policy and substantially unworkable in practice. It also involves a significant misapplication of public money.' It was the second view which, for years, had seemed to prevail. Its proponents were not only many leaders of the library profession, to their lasting shame, but a number of vocal politicians. Indeed, even as late as 1979 three MPs, Moate, Sproate and English – infamous in PLR annals – tried to scupper the PLR bill by a filibuster.

Other opponents were at the Treasury. Solicitors there refused to accept the concept of a right, allied to or part of property right, existing in something which had been written down and turned into a book, continuing with the author after that book had been bought for the purpose of lending. They applied their minds to rubbishing it, but failed. By the 1970s the leading polemicist for the authors was the late Brigid Brophy, novelist daughter of John Brophy. Treasury solicitors took positions, made judgements, and allowed these to become public. Unfailingly, Brigid Brophy blew to pieces all of the intellectual pretensions of their positions. She had both a fine mind and a wicked wit.

Among other heroes of the time were Lord (Ted) Willis, Elizabeth Thomas, Michael Holroyd, Francis King and, crucially, Maureen Duffy. A close ally of Brophy, she it was who realised that technology in the book and library world might be far enough advanced for there to be a fully computerised scheme which, using extensive sampling, could give a statistically reputable picture of all book loans throughout the country. The building blocks for this were the International Standard Book Number (ISBN) which at that time was nineteen years old; computer lists of the bibliographical details of the majority of books held in the public library systems, mostly with ISBNs; and a sufficient number of computer systems recording loans in libraries to provide a valid national sample.

But to know that a system is possible is one thing, to create it is quite another. The job of making it all work fell to John Sumsion who was appointed first Registrar of Public Lending Right late in 1981. He was an unlikely, but inspired choice. The huge volume of data to be processed required systems that had to be purpose built. Premises had to be found, and staffed for tasks which had never been done before. Procedures had to be invented, forms created and staff imbued with that sense of service and impeccable courtesy which has become the hallmark of the Registry. Negotiations had to take place with library authorities to install new, or updated systems for recording loans. Sampling techniques had to be finalised and methods of grossing up devised and agreed upon. And all of this with authors' organisations on one side, and some civil servants on the other, waiting for something, anything, to go wrong. The choice fell on a man who had spent his whole working life in the boot and shoe trade. He did it superbly well.

A simplified description of the scheme is that eligible authors register their books by ISBN; periodically during the year selected libraries send to PLR computer tapes which record the ISBNs and the number of loans made of the books to which they related; PLR attaches the ISBNs and number of loans to the details of the authors who have registered them; annually the grand total of eligible loans is divided into the sum of money available for distribution, to arrive at the year's 'rate per loan'. Each registered author's total of loans is then multiplied by the rate per loan, bibliographical details are added to what has been until that time a numerical record, and the author gets a print-out and a cheque. The print-out provides a view of a book's popularity in the public library service which cannot be got in any other way and has been widely welcomed.

Eligible authors are those resident in Britain or Germany (which has a reciprocal agreement with Britain). Some 30,000 have registered their interests in 305,000 books since PLR began. In 1999 loans data was collected from a sample of just under 400 libraries in thirty library authorities. The sample was over 10 per cent. The rate per loan was 2.18 pence and the total distributed was £4.2 million. The maximum annual payment to any author is £6000 and 102 authors were on the maximum for the February 2000 payments. The minimum payment is £5, and all payments which would be below that threshold are put back into the fund. The amount put back because of the upper threshold of £6000 was £470,949; the amount put back because of the lower threshold was £15,206.

As the PLR offices collect details of *all* loans, not just those of registered authors, the Registrar's annual report makes fascinating reading for the overview it gives of national tastes. The five most borrowed 'classic' authors in the twelve months to June 1999 were Ernest Hemingway, Beatrix Potter, A. A. Milne, Daphne du Maurier and J. R. R. Tolkien. The five most borrowed living authors who write for adults were Danielle Steel, Dick Francis, Josephine Cox, Jack Higgins and Ruth Rendell. R. L. Stine, the Ahlbergs, Roald Dahl, Enid Blyton (still) and Ann M. Martin headed the children's lists. Loans of children's books accounted for 29 per cent of all loans made, and ten of the top twenty most popular authors in public libraries write for children. The late Catherine Cookson, who died in 1998, was the most borrowed author of all, as she had been every year since PLR began counting.

What of the future? The PLR office plans to move away from processing tapes from libraries and towards receiving data by electronic links. It also hopes to have direct access to library catalogues to resolve queries over loans data such as problematic ISBNs. Internet access for authors to the PLR database is on the agenda. The provision of a 'PLR Direct' system – registration by telephone – may be provided but not all authors polled last year believed that this would be an enhancement: 'You'd become like the building societies. People would hate you. And the tinkly music. And being on hold. And paper is more efficient than people give it credit for . . . Paper spreads work out. It doesn't kill authors to do the work. They're *writers* after all', was a sample comment.

There is modest optimism over funding. Arts Minister Alan Howarth welcomed the 2000 results by saying, 'The PLR scheme is central to the government's plans for culture and literacy. It underpins the work of libraries, encourages creativity and develops talent.' Such a positive statement, made in a year of huge fiscal surplus, can only be a cause for hope, particularly as the money needed to bring PLR back to its proper total is, in government terms, miniscule.

The Minister's Advisory Committee for PLR, now chaired by Michael Holroyd, has been pushing for years for reference books to be included. As reference books cannot be removed from libraries there are no loans, and it is not practicable to count the number of times they are consulted. However, in Sweden there is a scheme, partly based on numbers of copies purchased, which might now be emulated here and which would go some way to righting an injustice. There has long been an acceptance that school and academic libraries should be included in PLR legislation. Sadly, neither sector is structured in a way which would make its inclusion economic and, in schools, library computer systems remain the exception. This is an area where little progress is expected in the next five years.

The extension of British PLR to all EU countries may come about in a much shorter time. The Advisory Committee has recommended that authors resident in the EU be able to qualify from 1 July 2000, with first payments to be made in February 2002. This would put right the anomaly that British authors resident elsewhere in Europe are ineligible, correct what is probably a breach of the Treaty of Rome, and set a good example. There would be a tactical benefit to British authors if Britain were to show the way, although the absolute purity of British motives might reasonably be doubted across the Channel: large numbers of books by British authors are found in continental libraries; comparatively few books by continental authors are found here.

Where compensation for loans of non-book material is concerned, there is little positive news. The Copyright and Related Rights Regulations, of 1996, provide a means for authors and other rights holders – artists and performers in, and producers of sound and video recordings, as well as directors of films – to authorise or prohibit lending of their products by public libraries. As PLR existed well before these regulations came into being, and as authors get some modest recompense for loans, the government of the day excepted books from the provisions. Audio books are not excepted. The pressure from authors of books which become audio books, and which are widely borrowed, to qualify for PLR, has been cleverly diverted by a decision of the ministry for the arts to pass this hot potato to the newly formed Museums, Libraries and Archives Commission. MLAC will be asked to recommend how to deal with non-book materials under the Copyright and Related Rights Regulations, and with other copyright issues facing public library services. Authors who will remember the twenty-eight-year struggle for PLR, and who note that the MLAC board has on it few creators of content, will be pessimistic about there being any rapid out-come.

David Whitaker, former chairman of Whitakers, was a member of the Registrar's Advisory Committee from 1983 to 1989, and chairman of the Minister's Advisory Committee from 1989 to 1993.

Whose Loan is it Anyway? (Registrar of Public Lending Right, 1999, £4; ISBN 0 952 52914 9)

Lending and Copying: Authors' Rewards

The number of writers on the PLR register is close to 30,000. With just £5.05 million available for distribution at a rate of 2.18p per loan, over a third of recipients got less than £100 and another third nothing at all. The government has hinted at a modest increase in funding but little is now heard of rewarding authors of reference books which are consulted but rarely taken out on loan or of applying PLR to talking books or loans from school and university libraries.

There is better news from the Authors' Licensing & Collecting Society, which collects and redistributes payments for photocopying, cable retransmission and electronic exploitation. The reason is that the ALCS is not tied down by government. The money it has for distribution – some £8 million in the 1999/2000 financial year – increases along with its scope as a collecting agency.

In the early days the ALCS acted as the link with VG Wort, the German collecting agency, which paid over fees collected for British authors whose books were borrowed from German libraries. Soon it was the turn of scriptwriters to benefit, this time from cable retransmission throughout Benelux. By the early 1990s, ALCS was receiving money from BBC World Service programmes shown in Europe and from radio transmissions to the Benelux countries and to Ireland.

But the biggest boost to revenue came from licensing deals on photocopying. While income from broadcast sources continues to grow (educational 'off-air' recording where schools are licensed to record programmes for later use is now on the list) photocopying money accounts for 65 per cent of ALCS income. This is hardly surprising when it is estimated that worldwide some 300 billion photocopies of copyright material are made every year.

Recent initiatives include a scheme allowing authors 'equitable remuneration' for the rental of videos and other recordings of their work, an agreement with the Newspaper Licensing Agency to receive on behalf of freelance journalists a share of revenues from the photocopying of newspapers and a licensing deal on the creation, storage and use of digital versions of printed works.

Membership of the ALCS is via one of the writers' organisations. If, say, you are a member of the Society of Authors you automatically belong to the ALCS and will profit accordingly. On the other hand, it is as well to register items of work as they become available to the public. Not all media promoters hand over fees willingly. Every bit of additional information gathered by the ALCS helps it to become more effective as a policing as well as a collecting agency.

PLR application forms and details can be obtained from the Registrar of Public Lending

Right: Richard House, Sorbonne Close, Stockton-on-Tees TS17 6DA (☎01642 604699; Fax 01642 615641; Email registrar@plr.octacon.co.uk; Website www.earl. org.uk/partners/plr/index.html)

The Authors' Licensing & Collecting Society (ALCS) is at Marlborough Court, 14–18 Holborn, London EC1N 2LE (☎020 7395 0600; Fax 020 7395 0660; Email alcs@alcs.co.uk; Web site www.alcs.co.uk)

Library Services

Aberdeen Central Library

Rosemount Viaduct, Aberdeen AB25 1GW
☎01224 652500 Fax 01224 641985

Open 9.00 am to 7.00 pm Monday to
Thursday; 9.00 am to 5.00 pm Friday
(Reference & Local Studies: 9.00 am to
8.00 pm); 9.00 am to 5.00 pm Saturday.
Branch library opening times vary.

Open access
General reference and loans. Books, pamphlets, periodicals and newspapers; videos, CDs
and cassettes; arts equipment lending service;
DTP, Internet and WP for public access; photographs of the Aberdeen area; census records,
maps; on-line database, patents and standards.
The library offers special services to housebound
readers. Non-resident administrative fee for
audiovisual and lending services.

Armitt Library

Ambleside, Cumbria LA22 9BL
☎015394 31212 Fax 015394 31313

Open 10.00 am to 12.30 pm and 1.30 pm to
4.00 pm Monday to Friday.

Free access (To view original material please
give prior notice)
A small but unique reference library of rare
books, manuscripts, pictures, antiquarian prints
and museum items, mainly about the Lake
District. It includes early guidebooks and topographical works, books and papers relating to
Ruskin, H. Martineau, Charlotte Mason and
others; fine art including work by W. Green,
J. B. Pyne, John Harden, K. Schwitters, and
Victorian photographs by Herbert Bell; also a
major collection of Beatrix Potter's scientific
watercolour drawings and microscope studies.
Museum and Exhibition open seven days per
week from 10.00 am to 5.00 pm. Entry fee.

The Athenaeum, Liverpool

Church Alley, Liverpool L1 3DD
☎0151 709 7770 Fax 0151 709 0418
Email library @athena.force9.net
Website www.athena.force9.co.uk

Open 9.00 am to 4.00 pm Monday to Friday

Access To club members; researchers by application only
General collection, with books dating from

the 15th century, now concentrated mainly on
local history with a long run of Liverpool directories and guides. *Special collections* Liverpool
playbills; William Roscoe; Blanco White;
Robert Gladstone; 18th-century plays; 19th-century economic pamphlets; the Norris books;
bibles; Yorkshire and other genealogy. Some
original drawings, portraits, topographical material and local maps.

Bank of England Information Centre

Threadneedle Street, London EC2R 8AH
☎020 7601 4715 Fax 020 7601 4356

Open 9.30 am to 5.30 pm Monday to Friday

Access For research workers by prior arrangement only, when material is not readily available elsewhere
50,000 volumes of books and periodicals.
3000 periodicals taken. UK and overseas coverage of banking, finance and economics. *Special
collections* Central bank reports; UK 17–19th-century economic tracts; Government reports in
the field of banking.

Barbican Library

Barbican Centre, London EC2Y 8DS
☎020 7638 0569 Fax 020 7638 2249
Email barbicanlib@corpoflondon.gov.uk

Open 9.30 am to 5.30 pm Monday,
Wednesday, Thursday, Friday; 9.30 am to
7.30 pm Tuesday; 9.30 am to 12.30 pm
Saturday

Open access
Situated on Level 2 of the Barbican Centre,
this is the Corporation of London's largest lending library. Limited study facilities are available.
In addition to a large general lending department, the library seeks to reflect the Centre's
emphasis on the arts and includes strong collections (including videos and CD-ROMs), on
painting, sculpture, theatre, cinema and ballet,
as well as a large music library with books,
scores and CDs (sound recording loans available
at a small charge). Also houses the City's main
children's library and has special collections on
finance, natural resources, conservation, socialism and the history of London. Service available
for housebound readers. A literature events
programme is organised by the Library which

supplements and provides cross-arts planning opportunities with the Barbican Centre artistic programme.

Barnsley Public Library
Central Library, Shambles Street, Barnsley, South Yorkshire S70 2JF
☎01226 773930 Fax 01226 773955
Email Librarian@Barnsley.ac.uk
Website bmbc-online/internet-site/educat/libraries/index.html
Open Lending & Reference: 9.30 am to 7.00 pm Monday and Wednesday; 9.30 am to 5.30 pm Tuesday and Friday; 9.30 am to 4.00 pm Saturday. Please telephone to check hours of other departments.

Open access
General library, lending and reference. Archive collection of family history and local firms; local studies: coal mining, local authors, Yorkshire and Barnsley; European Business Information Unit; large junior library. (Specialist departments are closed on certain weekday evenings and Saturday afternoons.)

BBC Written Archives Centre
Peppard Road, Caversham Park, Reading, Berkshire RG4 8TZ
☎0118 946 9280/1/2 Fax 0118 946 1145
Email wac.enquiries@bbc.co.uk
Contact *Jacqueline Kavanagh*
Open 9.30 am to 5.30 pm Monday to Friday
Access For reference, by appointment only on Wednesday to Friday.

Holds the written records of the BBC, including internal papers from 1922 to 1974 and published material to date. 20th century biography, social history, popular culture and broadcasting. Charges for certain services.

Bedford Central Library
Harpur Street, Bedford MK40 1PG
☎01234 350931/270102 (Reference Library)
Fax 01234 342163
Open 9.30 am to 7.00 pm Monday and Wednesday; 9.30 am to 5.30 pm Tuesday, Thursday, Friday; 9.30 am to 5.00 pm Saturday

Open access
Lending library with a wide range of stock, including books, music (CDs and cassettes), audio books and videos; reference and information library, children's library, local history library, Internet facilities and gallery.

Belfast Public Libraries: Central Library
Royal Avenue, Belfast BT1 1EA
☎028 9024 3233 Fax 028 9033 2819
Email info@libraries.belfast-elb.gov.uk
Open 9.30 am to 8.00 pm Monday and Thursday; 9.30 am to 5.30 pm Tuesday, Wednesday, Friday; 9.30 am to 1.00 pm Saturday

Open access To lending libraries; reference libraries by application only

Over two million volumes for lending and reference. *Special collections* United Nations/UNESCO depository; complete British Patent Collection; Northern Ireland Newspaper Library; British and Irish government publications. The Central Library offers the following reference departments: General Reference; Irish and Local Studies; Business and Law; Electronic Information Services; Fine Arts, Language and Literature; Music and Recorded Sound. The lending library, supported by twenty branch libraries and two mobile libraries, offers special services to hospitals, prisons and housebound readers.

BFI National Library
21 Stephen Street, London W1P 2LN
☎020 7255 1444 Fax 020 7436 2338
Email library@bfi.org.uk
Website www.bfi.org.uk
Open 10.30 am to 5.30 pm Monday and Friday; 10.30 am to 8.00 pm Tuesday and Thursday; 1.00 pm to 8.00 pm Wednesday; Telephone Enquiry Service operates from 10.00 am to 5.00 pm
Access For reference only; annual and limited day membership available

The world's largest collection of information on film and television including periodicals, cuttings, scripts, related documentation, personal papers. Information available through SIFT (Summary of Information on Film and Television).

Birmingham and Midland Institute
9 Margaret Street, Birmingham B3 3BS
☎0121 236 3591 Fax 0121 212 4577
Administrator & General Secretary
Philip Fisher
Access For research, to students (loans restricted to members)
ESTABLISHED 1855. Later merged with the Birmingham Library (now renamed the Priestley Library), which was founded in 1779. The

Priestley Library specialises in the humanities, with approximately 100,000 volumes in stock. Founder member of the **Association of Independent Libraries**. Meeting-place of many affiliated societies including many devoted to poetry and literature.

Birmingham Library Services

Central Library, Chamberlain Square,
Birmingham B3 3HQ
☎0121 303 4511
Website www.birmingham.gov.uk

Open 9.00 am to 8.00 pm Monday to Friday;
9.00 am to 5.00 pm Saturday

Over a million volumes. *Research collections* include the Shakespeare Library; War Poetry Collection; Parker Collection of Children's Books and Games; Johnson Collection; Milton Collection; Cervantes Collections; Early and Fine Printing Collection (including the William Ridler Collection of Fine Printing); Joseph Priestley Collection; Loudon Collection; Railway Collection; Wingate Bett Transport Ticket Collection; Labour, Trade Union and Co-operative Collections. Photographic Archives: Sir John Benjamin Stone; Francis Bedford; Francis Frith; Warwickshire Photographic Survey; Boulton and Watt Archive; Charles Parker Archive; Birmingham Repertory Theatre Archive and Sir Barry Jackson Library; Local Studies (Birmingham); Patents Collection; Song Sheets Collection; Oberammergau Festival Collection.

Bradford Central Library

Princes Way, Bradford, West Yorkshire
BD1 1NN
☎01274 753600 Fax 01274 395108
Email public.libraries@bradford.gov.uk

Open 9.00 am to 7.30 pm Monday to Friday;
9.00 am to 5.00 pm Saturday

Open access

Wide range of books and media loan services. Comprehensive reference and information services, including major local history collections and specialised business information service. Bradford Libraries runs *Reader2Reader*, a ground-breaking, reader-centred literature development project.

Brighton Central Library

Vantage Point, New England Street, Brighton,
East Sussex BN1 2GW
☎01273 290800 Fax 01273 296951

Local Studies Library: Church Street,
Brighton BN1 2UE

Open 10.00 am to 7.00 pm Monday to Friday (closed Wednesday); 10.00 am to 4.00 pm Saturday

Access Limited stock on open access; all material for reference use only

FOUNDED 1869, the library has a large stock covering most subjects. Specialisations include art and antiques, history of Brighton and Sussex, family history, local illustrations, TSO, business and large bequests of antiquarian books and ecclesiastical history.

Bristol Central Library

College Green, Bristol BS1 5TL
☎0117 9037200 Fax 0117 9221081

Open 9.30 am to 7.30 pm Monday, Tuesday and Thursday; 9.30 am to 5.00 pm Wednesday, Friday and Saturday

Open access

Lending, reference, art, music, commerce and local studies are particularly strong.

British Architectural Library

Royal Institute of British Architects,
66 Portland Place, London W1N 4AD
☎020 7580 5533 Fax 020 7631 1802
Email bal@inst.riba.org
Website www.architecture.com

Members' Information Line (Premium rate): 0906 302 0444; Public Information Line (Premium rate): 0906 302 0400

Open 1.30 pm to 5.00 pm Monday; 10.00 am to 7.00 pm Tuesday and Thursday; 10.00 am to 5.00 pm Wednesday and Friday; 10.00 am to 1.30 pm Saturday

Access Free to RIBA members; non-members must buy a day ticket (£10/£5 concessions, but on Tuesdays and Thursdays between 5.00 –7.00 pm and Saturdays £5/£2.50); subscriber membership available (write for details); loans available to RIBA and library members only

Collection of books, drawings, manuscripts, photographs and periodicals. All aspects of architecture, current and historical. Material both technical and aesthetic, covering related fields including: interior design, landscape architecture, topography, the construction industry and applied arts. Brochure available; queries by telephone, letter or in person. Charge for research (min. charge £30).

The British Library

Admission to St Pancras Reading Rooms

The British Library does not provide access to all those who request admission to use its research facilities but operates an admissions policy which grants access to those who need to use the collection because they cannot find the material they require in other libraries.

Admission is by interview and applicants are required to demonstrate that they need access to the reading rooms because: (a) material they need to consult is not available elsewhere; (b) their work or studies require the facilities of a large research library; (c) they need access to the Library's public records.

For further information, contact Reader Admissions Office, The British Library, 96 Euston Road, London NW1 2DB (Email reader-admissions@bl.uk ☎020 7412 7677 Fax 020 7412 7794)

British Library Business Information Service (BIS)

96 Euston Road, London NW1 2DB
Email business-information@bl.uk
Website www.bl.uk
Free enquiry service: ☎020 7412 7977
Fax 020 7412 945

Priced enquiry service: ☎020 7412 7457
Fax 020 7412 7453

Open 10.00 am to 8.00 pm Monday; 9.30 am to 8.00 pm Tuesday to Thursday; 9.30 am to 5.00 pm Friday and Saturday; closed for public holidays

Access Pass required for access

BIS holds the most comprehensive collection of business information literature in the UK. This includes market research reports and journals, directories, company annual reports, trade and business journals, house journals, trade literature and CD-ROM services.

British Library Early Printed Collections

96 Euston Road, London NW1 2DB
☎020 7412 7673 Fax 020 7412 7577
Email rare-books@bl.uk
Website www.bl.uk

Open 10.00 am to 8.00 pm Monday; 9.30 am to 8.00 pm Tuesday to Thursday; 9.30 am to 5.00 pm Friday and Saturday; closed for public holidays

Access By British Library reader's pass

General enquiries about reader services and advance reservations: ☎020 7412 7676 Fax 020 7412 7609 Email reader-services-enquiries@bl.uk

The Early Printed Collections Department, which is an integral part of British Library Reader Services and Collection Development,

selects, acquires, researches and provides access to material in the humanities collections printed in the British Isles to 1914 and in Western European languages before 1851. The collections are available in the Rare Books and Music Reading Room at St Pancras which also functions as the focus for the British Library's extensive collection of humanities microforms.

Further information about Early Printed Collections can be found at the British Library website.

British Library Humanities Reading Room

96 Euston Road, London NW1 2DB
☎020 7412 7676 Fax 020 7412 7609
Email reader-services-enquiries@bl.uk
Website www.bl.uk

Open 9.30 am to 6.00 pm Monday; 9.30 am to 8.00 pm Tuesday, Wednesday, Thursday; 9.30 am to 5.00 pm Friday and Saturday; closed for public holidays

Access By British Library reader's pass

This reading room is the focus for the Library's modern collections service in the humanities. It is on two levels, Humanities 1 and Humanities 2 and provides access to the Library's comprehensive collections of books and periodicals in all subjects in the humanities and social sciences and in all languages apart from Oriental. These collections are not available for browsing at the shelf. Material is held in closed access storage and needs to be identified and ordered from store using an on-line catalogue. A selective open access collection on most humanities subjects can be found in Humanities 1 whilst in Humanities 2 there are open access reference works relating to periodicals and theses, to recorded sound and to librarianship and information science.

To access British Library catalogues, go to the website at opac97.bl.uk

British Library Manuscript Collections

96 Euston Road, London NW1 2DB
☎020 7412 7513 Fax 020 7412 7745
Email mss@bl.uk
Website www.bl.uk

Open 10.00 am to 5.00 pm Monday; 9.30 am to 5.00 pm Tuesday to Saturday; closed for public holidays

Access Reading facilities only, by British Library reader's pass; a written letter of recommendation is required for certain categories of material

Two useful publications *Index of Manuscripts in the British Library,* Cambridge 1984–6, 10 vols and *The British Library: Guide to the Catalogues and Indexes of the Department of Manuscripts,* M. A. E. Nickson, help guide the researcher through this collection of manuscripts dating from Ancient Greece to the present day. Around 300,000 mss, charters, papyri and seals are housed here.

For information on British Library collections and services and to access British Library catalogues, including the Manuscripts online catalogues, visit the website.

British Library Map Library

96 Euston Road, London NW1 2DB
☎020 7412 7702   Fax 020 7412 7780
Email maps@bl.uk
Website www.bl.uk

Open 9.30 am to 5.00 pm Monday to Saturday; closed for public holidays

Access By British Library reader's pass
A collection of two million maps, charts and globes with particular reference to the history of British cartography. Maps for all parts of the world in a wide range of scales and dates, including the most comprehensive collection of Ordnance Survey maps and plans. *Special collections* King George III Topographical Collection and Maritime Collection, and the Crace Collection of maps and plans of London.

For information on British Library collections and services, visit the website.

To access main British Library catalogues, go to the website at opac97.bl.uk (NB Map Library catalogue on CD-ROM; not yet available on-line.)

British Library Music Collections

96 Euston Road, London NW1 2DP
☎020 7412 7772   Fax 020 7412 7751
Email music-collections@bl.uk
Website www.bl.uk

Open 10.00 am to 8.00 pm Monday; 9.30 am to 8.00 pm Tuesday to Thursday; 9.30 am to 5.00 pm Friday and Saturday; closed for public holidays

Access By British Library reader's pass
Special collections The Royal Music Library (containing almost all Handel's surviving autograph scores) and the Paul Hirsch Music Library. Also a large collection (about one and a quarter million items) of printed music and about 100,000 items of manuscript music, both British and foreign.

For information on British Library collections and services, visit the website.

To access British Library catalogues, go to the website at opac97.bl.uk (NB Only the current music catalogue – printed music acquired after 1980 – is available through the Internet. The retrospective music catalogues and the catalogues of manuscripts are not yet available on-line.)

British Library National Sound Archive

96 Euston Road, London NW1 2DB
☎020 7412 7440   Fax 020 7412 7441
Email nsa@bl.uk
Website www.bl.uk/collections/sound-archive

Open 10.00 am to 8.00 pm Monday; 9.30 am to 8.00 pm Tuesday to Thursday; 9.30 am to 5.00 pm Friday and Saturday; closed for public holidays

Listening service (by appointment)

Northern Listening Service:
British Library Document Supply Centre, Boston Spa, West Yorkshire: 9.15 am to 4.30 pm Monday to Friday

Open access
An archive of over 1,000,000 discs and more than 185,000 tape recordings, including all types of music, oral history, drama, wildlife, selected BBC broadcasts and BBC Sound Archive material. Produces a thrice-yearly newsletter, *Playback.*

For information on British Library National Sound Archive collections and services, visit the website.

To access British Library catalogues, go to the website at opac97.bl.uk

British Library Newspaper Library

Colindale Avenue, London NW9 5HE
☎020 7412 7353   Fax 020 7412 7379
Email newspaper@bl.uk
Website www.bl.uk/collections/newspaper

Open 10.00 am to 4.45 pm Monday to Saturday (last newspaper issue 4.15 pm); closed for public holidays

Access By British Library reader's pass or Newspaper Library pass (available from and valid only for Colindale)
Major collections of English provincial, Scottish, Welsh, Irish, Commonwealth and selected overseas foreign newspapers from *c.*1700 are housed here. Some earlier holdings are also available. London newspapers from 1801 and many weekly and fortnightly periodicals are also in stock. (London newspapers pre-dating 1801 are housed at the new library building in St Pancras – 96 Euston Road, NW1 2DB – though

many are available at Colindale Avenue on microfilm.) Readers are advised to check availability of material in advance.

For information on British Library Newspaper Library collections and services, visit the website.

British Library Oriental and India Office Collections

96 Euston Road, London NW1 2DB
☎020 7412 7873 Fax 020 7412 7641
Email oioc-enquiries@bl.uk
Website www.bl.uk

Open 10.00 am to 5.00 pm Monday; 9.30 am to 5.00 pm Tuesday to Saturday; closed for public holidays

Open access By British Library reader's pass (identification required)

A comprehensive collection of printed volumes and manuscripts in the languages of North Africa, the Near and Middle East and all of Asia, plus records of the East India Company and British government in India until 1947. Also prints, drawings and paintings by British artists of India.

For information on British Library collections and services, visit the website.

To access British Library catalogues, go to the website at opac97.bl.uk

British Library Science, Technology and Business

96 Euston Road, London NW1 2DB
☎020 7412 7494/7496 (General Enquiries)
  Fax 020 7412 7495
Email scitech@bl.uk
Website www.bl.uk

British/EPO patent equiries: 020 7412 7919

Business enquiries: 020 7412 7454/7977
(Business quick enquiry line available 9.00 am to 5.00 pm Monday to Friday)

Open 10.00 am to 8.00 pm Monday; 9.30 am to 8.00 pm Tuesday to Thursday; 9.30 am to 5.00 pm Friday and Saturday; closed for public holidays

Engineering, business information on companies, markets and products, physical science and technologies. British, European and Patent Co-operation Treaty patents and trade marks.

For information on British Library collections and services, visit the website.

To access British Library catalogues go to the website at opac97.bl.uk

British Library Social Policy Information Service

96 Euston Road, London NW1 2DB
☎020 7412 7536 Fax 020 7412 7761
Website www.bl.uk/services/sris/spis.html

Open 10.00 am to 8.00 pm Monday; 9.30 am to 8.00 pm Tuesday to Thursday; 9.30 am to 5.00 pm Friday and Saturday; closed for public holidays

Access By British Library reader's pass

Provides an information service on social policy, public administration, and current and international affairs, and access to current and historical official publications from all countries and intergovernmental bodies, including House of Commons sessional papers, UK legislation, UK electoral registers, up-to-date reference books on official publications and on the social sciences, a major collection of statistics and a browsing collection of recent social science books and periodicals. Also offers a priced research service providing literature surveys, current awareness and topic briefings for clients on demand.

To access British Library catalogues, go to the website at opac97.bl.uk

British Museum Department of Ethnography Library

6 Burlington Gardens, London W1X 2EX
☎020 7323 8031 Fax 020 7323 8013

Open 10.00 am to 4.45 pm Monday to Friday

Access By ticket-holders only. Tickets are given to scholars and postgraduate students, with special privileges accorded to Fellows of the Royal Anthropological Institute. Reference tickets are issued to *bona fide* researchers provided that the material is not available elsewhere. Undergraduates are admitted only if engaged in a research project

In 1976 the important library of the Royal Anthropological Institute (RAI) was donated to the Department of Ethnography Library and the RAI continues to support the library with donations of books and periodicals.

The collection consists of books (120,000), periodicals (1000 current titles), congress reports, newsletters, maps, microforms, manuscripts. It covers every aspect of anthropology: cultural anthropology (notably material culture and the arts), archaeology, biological anthropology and linguistics, together with such related fields as history, sociology, description and travel. Geographically the collection's scope is worldwide. Particular strengths are in the British Commonwealth, Eastern Europe and the Americas. Mesoamerica is well represented as the library holds the Sir John Eric Thompson (1898– 1970) collection.

British Psychological Society Library

c/o Psychology Library, University of London, Senate House, Malet Street, London WC1E 7HU
☎020 7862 8451/8461 Fax 020 7862 8480
Email ull@ull.ac.uk

Open Term-time: 9.00 am to 9.00 pm Monday to Thursday; 9.00 am to 6.30 pm Friday; 9.30 am to 5.30 pm Saturday (Holidays: 9.00 am to 6.00 pm Monday to Friday; 9.30 am to 5.30 pm Saturday)

Access Members only; Non-members £7 day ticket

Reference library, containing the British Psychological Society collection of periodicals – over 140 current titles housed alongside the University of London's collection of books and journals. Largely for academic research. General queries referred to Swiss Cottage Library in London which has a very good psychology collection.

Bromley Central Library

London Borough of Bromley - Leisure & Community Services, High Street, Bromley, Kent BR1 1EX
☎020 8460 9955 Fax 020 8313 9975
Email info@cenlibbr1.freeserve.co.uk
Website www.bromley.gov.uk

Open 9.30 am to 6.00 pm Monday, Wednesday, Friday; 9.30 am to 8.00 pm Tuesday and Thursday; 9.30 am to 5.00 pm Saturday

Open access

A large selection of fiction and non-fiction books for loan, both adult and children's. Also videos, CDs, cassettes, language courses, open learning packs for hire. Other facilities include a business information service (email bromley.bis @dial.pipex.com), CD-ROM, computer hire, Internet, local studies library, 'Upfront' teenage section, large reference library with photocopying, fax, microfiche and film facilities and specialist 'Healthpoint', 'Signpost' – online community information and 'Careerpoint' sections. Specialist collections include: H. G. Wells, Walter de la Mare, Crystal Palace, The Harlow Bequest, and the history and geography of Asia, America, Australasia and the Polar regions.

CAA Library and Information Centre

Aviation House, Gatwick Airport, West Sussex RH6 0YR
☎01293 573725 Fax 01293 573181

Open 9.30 am to 4.30 pm Monday to Friday; 10.00 am to 4.30 pm first Wednesday of the month

Open access

Books, periodicals and reports on air transport, air traffic control, electronics, radar and computing.

Cambridge Central Library (Reference Library & Information Service)

7 Lion Yard, Cambridge CB2 3QD
☎01223 712000 Fax 01223 712018
Email cambridge.central.library@camcnty. gov.uk
Website www.camcnty.gov.uk/library/ index.html

Open 9.30 am to 7.00 pm Monday and Thursday; 9.30 am to 5.00 pm Tuesday, Friday, Saturday; 12 noon to 7.00 pm Wednesday

Open access

Large stock of books, periodicals, newspapers, maps, plus comprehensive collection of directories and annuals covering UK, Europe and the world. Microfilm and fiche reading and printing services. On-line access to news and business databases. News databases on CD-ROM; Internet access. Monochrome and colour photocopiers.

Camomile Street Library

12–20 Camomile Street, London EC3A 7EX
☎020 7247 8895 Fax 020 7377 2972

Open 9.30 am to 5.30 pm Monday to Friday

Open access

Corporation of London lending library. Wide range of fiction and non-fiction books and language courses on cassette, foreign fiction, paperbacks, maps and guides for travel at home and abroad, children's books, a selection of large print, and collections of music CDs and of videos.

Cardiff Central Library

Frederick Street, St David's Link, Cardiff CF10 2DU
☎029 2038 2116 Fax 029 2087 1599
Email robboddy@hotmail.com

Open 9.00 am to 6.00 pm Monday, Tuesday,

Wednesday, Friday; 9.00 am to 7.00 pm
Thursday; 9.00 am to 5.30 pm Saturday

General lending library with the following departments: leisure, music, children's, local studies, information, science and humanities.

Carmarthen Public Library

St Peter's Street, Carmarthen SA31 1LN
☎01267 224830 Fax 01267 221839

Open 9.30 am to 7.00 pm Monday, Tuesday, Wednesday Friday; 9.30 am to 5.00 pm Thursday and Saturday

Open access
Comprehensive range of fiction, non-fiction, children's books and reference works in English and in Welsh. Large local history library. Free Internet access and CD-ROM facilities. Large Print books, books on tape, CDs, cassettes, and videos available for loan.

Catholic Central Library

Lancing Street, London NW1 1ND
☎020 7383 4333 Fax 020 7388 6675
Email librarian@catholic-library.demon.co.uk
Website www.catholic-library.demon.co.uk

Open 10.30 am to 5.00 pm Monday, Tuesday, Thursday, Friday; 10.30 am to 7.00 pm Wednesday

Open access For reference (non-members must sign in; loans restricted to members)
Contains books, many not readily available elsewhere, on theology, religions worldwide, scripture and the history of churches of all denominations.

The Centre for the Study of Cartoons and Caricature

See entry under **Picture Libraries**

City Business Library

1 Brewers Hall Garden, London EC2V 5BX
☎020 7332 1812 Fax 020 7332 1847
☎0171 480 7638 (recorded information)

Open 9.30 am to 5.00 pm Monday to Friday

Open access
Local authority public reference library run by the Corporation of London. Books, pamphlets, periodicals and newspapers of current business interest, mostly financial. Aims to satisfy the day-to-day information needs of the City's business community, and in so doing has become one of the leading public resource centres in Britain in its field. Strong collection of directories for both the UK and overseas, plus companies information, market research sources, management, law,

banking, insurance, statistics and investment. No academic journals or textbooks.

Commonwealth Institute

Commonwealth Resource Centre, Kensington High Street, London W8 6NQ
☎020 7603 4535 Fax 020 7602 7374
Email info@commonwealth.org
Website www.commonwealth.org.uk

Open 10.00 am to 4.00 pm Monday to Saturday

Open Access to the public. Loan service available on an annual subscription basis (£10 p.a.)
The Commonwealth Literature Library includes fiction, poems, drama and critical writings. *Special collection* Books and periodicals on the 54 Commonwealth countries. Also a collection of directories and reference books on the Commonwealth and information on arts, geography, history and literature, cultural organisations and bibliography.

Commonwealth Secretariat Library

Marlborough House, Pall Mall, London SW1Y 5HX
☎020 7747 6164/5/6 Fax 020 7747 6168
Email library@commonwealth.int
Website www.thecommonwealth.org

Open 9.15 am to 5.00 pm Monday to Friday

Access For reference only, by appointment
Extensive reference source concerned with economy, development, trade, production and industry of Commonwealth countries; also human resources including women, youth, health, management and education.

Corporation of London Libraries

See **Barbican Library; Camomile Street Library; City Business Library; Guildhall**

Coventry Central Library

Smithford Way, Coventry, Warwickshire CV1 1FY
☎024 7683 2314 Fax 024 7683 2440
Email covinfo@discover.co.uk

Open 9.00 am to 8.00 pm Monday, Tuesday, Thursday; 9.30 am to 8.00 pm Wednesday; 9.00 am to 5.00 pm Friday; 9.00 am to 4.30 pm Saturday

Open access
Located in the middle of the city's main shopping centre. Approximately 120,000 items (books, cassettes and CDs) for loan; plus reference collection of business information and local history. *Special collections* Cycling and motor

industries; George Eliot; Angela Brazil; Tom Mann Collection (trade union and labour studies); local newspapers on microfilm from 1740 onwards. Over 300 periodicals taken. 'Peoplelink' community information database available.

Derby Central Library

Wardwick, Derby DE1 1HS
☎01332 255398 Fax 01332 369570

Open 10.00 am to 7.00 pm Monday, Tuesday, Thursday, Friday; 10.00 am to 1.00 pm Wednesday and Saturday

LOCAL STUDIES LIBRARY
25B Irongate, Derby DE1 3GL
☎01332 255393

Open 10.00 am to 7.00 pm Monday and Tuesday; 10.00 am to 5.00 pm Wednesday, Thursday, Friday; 10.00 am to 1.00 pm Saturday

Open access
General library for lending, information and Children's Services. The Central Library also houses specialist private libraries: Derbyshire Archaeological Society; Derby Philatelic Society. The Local Studies Library houses the largest multimedia collection of resources in existence relating to Derby and Derbyshire. The collection includes mss deeds, family papers, business records including the Derby Canal Company, Derby Board of Guardians and the Derby China Factory.

Devon & Exeter Institution Library

7 Cathedral Close, Exeter, Devon EX1 1EZ
☎01392 251017
Email M.Midgley@exeter.ac.uk
Website www.ex.ac.uk/library/devonex.html

Open 9.00 am to 5.00 pm Monday to Friday

Access Members only (Temporary membership available)
FOUNDED 1813. Administered by Exeter University Library. Contains over 36,000 volumes, including long runs of 19th-century journals, theology, history, topography, early science, biography and literature. A large and growing collection of books, journals, newspapers, prints and maps relating to the South West.

Doncaster Libraries and Information Services

Central Library, Waterdale, Doncaster, South Yorkshire DN1 3JE
☎01302 734305 Fax 01302 369749

Open 9.30 am to 6.00 pm Monday; 9.00 am

to 6.00 pm Tuesday to Friday; 9.00 am to 4.00 pm Saturday

Open access
Books, cassettes, CDs, videos, picture loans. Reading aids unit for people with visual handicap; activities for children during school holidays, including visits by authors, etc. Occasional funding available to support literature activities. Also reference library.

Dorchester Library (part of Dorset County Library)

Colliton Park, Dorchester, Dorset DT1 1XJ
☎01305 224440 (lending)/224448 (reference)
Fax 01305 266120

Open 10.00 am to 7.00 pm Monday; 9.30 am to 7.00 pm Tuesday, Wednesday, Friday; 9.30 am to 5.00 pm Thursday; 9.00 am to 4.00 pm Saturday

Open access
General lending and reference library, including Local Studies Collection, special collections on Thomas Hardy, the Powys Family and William Barnes. Periodicals, children's library, CD-ROMs, free Internet access and video lending service.

Dundee Central Library

The Wellgate, Dundee DD1 1DB
☎01382 434318 Fax 01382 434642

Open Lending Departments: 9.30 am to 7.00 pm Monday, Tuesday, Thursday, Friday; 10.00 am to 7.00 pm Wednesday; 9.30 am to 5.00 pm Saturday. General Reference Department: 9.30 am to 9.00 pm Monday, Tuesday, Thursday, Friday; 10.00 am to 9.00 pm Wednesday; 9.30 am to 9.00 pm Saturday. Local History Department: 9.30 am to 5.00 pm Monday, Tuesday, Friday, Saturday; 10.00 am to 7.00 pm Wednesday; 9.30 am to 7.00 pm Thursday.

Access Reference services available to all; lending services to those who live, work, study or were educated within Dundee City
Adult lending, reference and children's services. Art, music, audio and video lending services. Free Internet access. Schools service (Agency). Housebound and mobile services. *Special collections*: The Wighton Collection of National Music; The Wilson Photographic Collection; The Lamb Collection.

English Nature

Northminster House, Peterborough, Cambridgeshire PE1 1UA
☎01733 455000 Fax 01733 568834

Email enquiries@english-nature.org.uk
Website www.english-nature.org.uk

Open 8.30 am to 5.00 pm Monday to
Thursday; 8.30 am to 4.30 pm Friday;

Access To *bona fide* students only. Telephone
library for appointment on 01733 455094

Information on nature conservation, nature
reserves, SSSIs, planning, legislation, etc. English
Nature is the government-funded body whose
purpose is to promote the conservation of
England's wildlife and natural features.

Equal Opportunities Commission Library

Overseas House, Quay Street, Manchester
M3 3HN
☎0161 838 8343 Fax 0161 834 0805
Website www.eoc.org.uk

Open 10.00 am to 12.00 pm & 2.00 pm to
4.00 pm Monday to Friday

Access For reference

Books and journals on equal opportunities
and gender issues. Equal Opportunities
Commission publications.

Essex County Council Libraries

County Library Headquarters, Goldlay
Gardens, Chelmsford, Essex CM2 0EW
☎01245 284981 Fax 01245 492780
Email essexlib@essexcc.gov.uk
Website www.essexcc.gov.uk

Essex County Council Libraries has 74 static
libraries throughout Essex as well as 13 mobile
libraries and three special-needs mobiles. Services
to the public include books, newspapers, periodicals, CDs, cassettes, videos, pictures, CD-ROM
and Internet access as well as postal cassettes for
the blind and subtitled videos. Specialist subjects
and collections are listed below at the relevant
library.

Chelmsford Library

PO Box 882, Market Road, Chelmsford,
Essex CM1 1LH
☎01245 492758 Fax 01245 492536

Open: 9.00 am to 7.00 pm Monday to Friday;
9.00 am to 5.00 pm Saturday; 1.00 pm to
4.00 pm Sunday

Science and technology, business information
and social sciences.

Colchester Library

Trinity Square, Colchester, Essex CO1 1JB
☎01206 245900 Fax 01206 245901

Open: 9.00 am to 7.30 pm Monday, Tuesday,
Wednesday, Friday; 9.00 am to 5.00 pm

Thursday and Saturday; 1.00 pm to 4.00 pm
Sunday

Local studies, music scores and education.
Harsnett collection (early theological works 16/
17th-century); Castle collection (18th-century
subscription library); Cunnington collection;
Margaret Lazell collection; Taylor collection.

Harlow Library

The High, Harlow, Essex CM20 1HA
☎01279 413772 Fax 01279 424612

Open: 9.00 am to 7.00 pm Monday to Friday;
9.00 am to 5.00 pm Saturday; 1.00 pm to
4.00 pm Sunday

Fiction, language and literature. Sir John Newson
Memorial collection; Maurice Hughes Memorial
collection.

Loughton Library

Traps Hill, Loughton, Essex IG10 1HD
☎020 8502 0181 Fax 020 8508 5041

Open: 9.30 am to 7.00 pm Monday, Tuesday,
Wednesday, Friday; 9.30 am to 1.30 pm
Thursday; 9.00 am to 5.00 pm Saturday;
1.00 pm to 4.00 pm Sunday

National Jazz Foundation Archive.

Saffron Walden Library

2 King Street, Saffron Walden, Essex CB10 1ES
☎01799 523178 Fax 01799 513642

Open: 9.00 am to 7.00 pm Monday, Tuesday,
Thursday, Friday; 9.00 am to 5.00 pm
Saturday; 1.00 pm to 4.00 pm Sunday
(closed Wednesday)

Victorian studies collection.

Witham Library

18 Newland Street, Witham, Essex CM8 2AQ
☎01376 519625 Fax 01376 501913

Open: 9.00 am to 7.00 pm Monday, Tuesday,
Thursday, Friday; 9.00 am to 5.00 pm
Saturday (closed Wednesday)

Drama. Dorothy L. Sayers and Maskell collections.

The Fawcett Library

London Guildhall University, Calcutta House,
Old Castle Street, London E1 7NT
☎020 7320 1189 Fax 020 7320 1188
Email fawcett@lgu.ac.uk
Website www.lgu.ac.uk/fawcett

Open University term-time: 10.15 am to
8.30 pm Monday; 9.00 am to 8.30 pm
Wednesday; 9.00 am to 5.00 pm Thursday
and Friday. During University vacation:
9.00 am to 5.00 pm Monday, Wednesday
to Friday

Open access Members of staff and students at London Guildhall University and to *bona fide* researchers employed in higher education institutions funded by the (UK) Funding Councils and DENI. Otherwise, full membership including limited borrowing rights £30, or £7 for full-time students and the unwaged. Day fee (reference only) £3, or £1.50 for students and the unwaged. Bring a student ID card or similar to claim concessionary rate and two passport-type photographs if intending to join as an annual member

The Fawcett Library, national research library for women's history, is the UK's oldest and most comprehensive research library on all aspects of women in society, with both historical and contemporary coverage. The Library includes materials on feminism, work, education, health, the family, law, arts, sciences, technology, language, sexuality, fashion and the home. The main emphasis is on Britain but many other countries are represented, especially the Commonwealth and the Third World. Established in 1926 as the library of the London Society of Women's Service (formerly Suffrage), a non-militant organisation led by Millicent Fawcett. In 1953 the Society was renamed after her and the library became the Fawcett Library.

Collections include: women's suffrage, work, education; women and the church, the law, sport, art, music; abortion, prostitution. Mostly British materials but some American, Commonwealth and European works. Books, journals, pamphlets, archives, photographs, posters, postcards, audiovisual materials, artefacts, scrapbooks, albums and press cuttings dating mainly from the 19th century although some materials date from the 17th century.

The Fawcett Library will close in its present premises in December 2000 and re-open in April 2001 in the National Library of Women, also in Old Castle Street, London E1 7NT. Intending readers are advised to check with the Library by telephone, email, fax, letter, via the website or in person, about detailed opening arrangements nearer the time. The National Library of Women will include a reading room, exhibition gallery, café, education areas and a conference room, and will be the cultural and research centre for anyone interested in women's lives and achievements.

Foreign and Commonwealth Office Library

King Charles Street, London SW1A 2AH
☎020 7270 3925 Fax 020 7270 3270
Website www.fco.gov.uk

Access By appointment only

An extensive stock of books, pamphlets and other reference material on all aspects of historical, socio-economic and political subjects relating to countries covered by the Foreign and Commonwealth Office. Particularly strong on colonial history, early works on travel, and photograph collections, mainly of Commonwealth countries and former colonies, *c.* 1850s–1960s.

Forestry Commission Library

Forest Research Station, Alice Holt Lodge, Wrecclesham, Farnham, Surrey GU10 4LH
☎01420 22255 Fax 01420 23653
Email library@forestry.gov.uk
Website www.forestry.gov.uk

Open 9.00 am to 5.00 pm Monday to Thursday; 9.00 am to 4.30 pm Friday

Access By appointment for personal visits

Approximately 20,000 books on forestry and arboriculture, plus 500 current journals. CD-ROMS include TREECD (1939 onwards). Offers a Research Advisory Service for advice and enquiries on forestry (☎01402 23000) with a charge for consultations and diagnosis of tree problems exceeding ten minutes.

French Institute Library

17 Queensberry Place, London SW7 2DT
☎020 7838 2144 Fax 020 7838 2145
Email library@ambrinsie.ambafrance.org.uk

Open 12.00 noon to 7.00 pm Tuesday to Friday; 12 noon to 6.00 pm Saturday

Open access For reference and consultation (loans restricted to members)

A collection of over 40,000 volumes mainly centred on French cultural interests with special emphasis on language, literature and history. Books in French and English. Collection of 2000 videos; 250 periodicals; 2000 CDs (French music); 200 CD-ROMs; Children's library (8000 books); also a special collection about 'France Libre'. Inter-library loans; quick information service; Internet access. Group visits on request.

John Frost Newspapers

8 Monks Avenue, Barnet, Hertfordshire EN5 1DB
☎020 8440 3159 Fax 020 8440 3159

Contacts *John Frost, Andrew Frost*

A collection of 70,000 original newspapers (1630 to the present day) and 100,000 press cuttings available, on loan, for research and rostrum/stills work (TV documentaries, book and magazine publishers and audiovisual presen-

tations). Historic events, politics, sports, royalty, crime, wars, personalities, etc., plus many
in-depth files.

Gloucestershire County Library Arts & Museums Service

Quayside House, Shire Hall, Gloucester
GL1 2HY
☎01452 425020 Fax 01452 425042
Email gclams@gloscc.gov.uk
Website www.gloscc.gov.uk

Open access
The service includes 39 local libraries – call the
number above for opening hours; and six mobile
libraries – ☎01452 425039 for timetable/route
enquiries. The website (GlosNet) includes library
catalogue and book renewal facility.

Goethe-Institut Library

50 Princes Gate, Exhibition Road, London
SW7 2PH
☎020 7596 4040 Fax 020 7594 0230
Email Library@London.goethe.org
Website www.goethe.de/london

Librarian *Marilen Daum*

Open 12.00 am to 8.00 pm Monday to
Thursday; 11.00 am to 5.00 pm Saturday

Library specialising in German literature and
books/audiovisual material on German culture
and history: 25,000 books (4800 of them in
English), 140 periodicals, 14 newspapers, 2800
audiovisual media (including 1000 videos),
selected press clippings on German affairs from
the German and UK press, information service,
photocopier, video facility. Also German language teaching material for teachers and students of German.

Greater London Record Office

See **London Metropolitan Archives**

Guildford Institute of University of Surrey Library

Ward Street, Guildford, Surrey GU1 4LH
☎01483 562142
Email c.miles@surrey.ac.uk

Librarian *Clare Miles*

Open 10.00 am to 3.00 pm Tuesday,
Thursday, Friday; 10.00 am to 4.30 pm
Wednesday

Open access To members only but open to
enquirers for research purposes
FOUNDED 1834. Some 12,000 volumes of
which 7500 were printed before the First World
War. The remaining stock consists of recently

published works of fiction, biography and travel.
Newspapers and periodicals also available. *Special
collections* include an almost complete run of the
Illustrated London News from 1843–1906, a col-
lection of Victorian scrapbooks, and about 400
photos and other pictures relating to the
Institute's history and the town of Guildford.
Publishes Library newsletter twice-yearly.

Guildhall Library

Aldermanbury, London EC2P 2EJ
☎See below Fax 020 7600 3384
Website www.corpoflondon.gov.uk

Access For reference (but much of the material is kept in storage areas and is supplied to
readers on request; proof of identity is required
for consultation of certain categories of stock)
Part of the Corporation of London libraries.
Seeks to provide a basic general reference service
but its major strength, acknowledged worldwide, is in its historical collections. The library is
divided into three sections, each with its own
catalogues and enquiry desks. These are: Printed
Books; Manuscripts; the Print Room.

PRINTED BOOKS
Open 9.30 am to 5 pm Monday to Saturday
excluding Saturdays preceding Bank
Holidays ☎020 7332 1868/1870

Strong on all aspects of London history, with
wide holdings of English history, topography and
genealogy, including local directories, poll books
and parish register transcripts. Also good collections of English statutes, law reports, parliamentary debates and journals, and House of
Commons papers. Home of several important
collections deposited by London institutions: the
Marine collection of the Corporation of Lloyd's,
the Stock Exchange's historical files of reports
and prospectuses, the Clockmakers' Company
library and museum, the Gardeners' Company,
Fletchers' Company, the Institute of Masters of
Wine, International Wine and Food Society and
Gresham College.

MANUSCRIPTS
Open 9.30 am to 4.45 pm Monday to
Saturday (no requests for records after
4.30 pm) NB closes on Saturdays preceding
Bank Holidays; check for details
☎020 7332 1863 Email manuscripts.
guildhall@ms.corpoflondon.gov.uk
Website ihr.sas.ac.uk/gh/

The official repository for historical records relating to the City of London (except those of the
Corporation of London itself, which are housed
at the Corporation Records Office). Records

date from the 11th century to the present day. They include archives of most of the City's parishes, wards and livery companies, and of many individuals, families, estates, schools, societies and other institutions, notably the Diocese of London and St Paul's Cathedral, as well as the largest collection of business archives in any public repository in the UK. Although mainly of City interest, holdings include material for the London area as a whole and beyond.

PRINT ROOM
Open 9.30 am to 5.00 pm Monday to Friday
☎020 7332 1839
Email john.fisher@ms. corpoflondon.gov.uk
Website collage.nhil.com

An unrivalled collection of prints and drawings relating to London and the adjacent counties. Emphasis is on topography, but there are strong collections of portraits and satirical prints. The map collection includes maps of the capital from the mid-16th century to the present day and various classes of Ordnance Survey maps. Other material includes photographs, theatre bills and programmes, trade cards, book plates and playing cards as well as a sizeable collection of Old Master prints. Over 30,000 items have been digitally imaged on Collage, including topographical prints, some maps, a small number of photographs and all the Guildhall art collection.

Free, *limited* enquiry service available. Also a fee-based service for in-depth research – ☎020 7332 1854 Fax 020 7600 3384 Email search. guildhall@corpoflondon.gov.uk website www. cityoflondon.gov.uk/search_guildhall

Guille–Alles Library
Market Street, St Peter Port, Guernsey, Channel Islands GY1 1HB
☎01481 720392 Fax 01481 712425

Open 9.00 am to 5.00 pm Monday, Thursday, Friday, Saturday; 10.00 am to 5.00 pm Tuesday; 9.00 am to 8.00 pm Wednesday

Open access For residents; payment of returnable deposit by visitors. Music CD collection: £10 for two-year subscription
Lending, reference and information services.

Herefordshire Libraries and Information Service
Shirehall, Hereford HR1 2HY
☎01432 359830 Fax 01432 260744

Open Opening hours vary in the libraries across the county

Access Information and reference services

open to anyone; loans to members only (membership criteria: resident, being educated, working, or an elector in the county or neighbouring authorities; temporary membership to visitors. Proof of identity and address required)

Information service, reference and lending libraries. Non-fiction and fiction for all age groups, including normal and large print, spoken word cassettes, sound recordings (CD and cassette), videos, maps, local history, CD-ROMs at Hereford and Leominster Libraries. *Special collections* Cidermaking; Beekeeping; Alfred Watkins; John Masefield; Pilley.

University of Hertfordshire Library
College Lane, Hatfield, Hertfordshire AL10 9AD
☎01707 284678 Fax 01707 284670
Website www.herts.ac.uk/lis/

Open Term-time: 24 hours a day from 8.00 am Monday to 11.00 pm Saturday; 11.00 am to 11.00 pm Sunday; Vacation: 8.30 am to 10.00 pm Monday to Friday; 11.00 am to 6.00 pm Saturday

Access For reference use of printed collections
Volumes and journals in science technology and social science, including law, across all five of the university's campuses. There are four other site libraries: at the Business School at Hertford, at the Watford campus near Radlett (education and humanities), at the Art & Design building in Hatfield and at the Law School in St Albans. Desk research, postal interlibrary loans and consultancy undertaken by HERTIS Information and Research Unit which is based at Hatfield and has capacity for up to 300 subscribing companies and organisations.

HERTIS
See **University of Hertfordshire Library**

Highgate Literary and Scientific Institution Library
11 South Grove, London N6 6BS
☎020 8340 3343 Fax 020 8340 5632
Email admin@hlsi.demon.co.uk

Open 10.00 am to 5.00 pm Tuesday to Friday; 10.00 am to 4.00 pm Saturday (closed Sunday and Monday)

Annual membership £40 (individual); £63 (household)
25,000 volumes of general fiction and non-fiction, with a children's section and extensive local archives. *Special collections* on local history, London, and local poets Samuel Taylor Coleridge and John Betjeman.

Highland Libraries, The Highland Council, Cultural and Leisure Services

Library Support Unit, 31A Harbour Road, Inverness IV1 1UA
☎01463 235713 Fax 01463 236986
Email libraries@highland.gov.uk
Website www.highland.gov.uk

Open Library opening hours vary to suit local needs. Contact Administration and support services for details (8.00 am to 6.00 pm Monday to Friday)

Open access
Comprehensive range of lending and reference stock: books, pamphlets, periodicals, newspapers, compact discs, audio and video cassettes, maps, census records, genealogical records, photographs, educational materials, etc. Highland Libraries provides the public library service throughout the Highlands with a network of 42 static and 12 mobile libraries.

Holborn Library

32–38 Theobalds Road, London WC1X 8PA
☎020 7974 6345/6

Open 10.00 am to 7.00 pm Monday and Thursday; 10.00 am to 6.00 pm Tuesday and Friday; 10.00 am to 5.00 pm Saturday (closed all day Wednesday)

Open access
London Borough of Camden public library. Includes a law collection and the London Borough of Camden Local Studies and Archive Centre.

Sherlock Holmes Collection (Westminster)

Marylebone Library, Marylebone Road, London NW1 5PS
☎020 7641 1206 Fax 020 7641 1019
Email c.cooke@dial.pipex.com
Website www.westminster.gov.uk/el/libarch/
services/special/sherlock.html

Open 9.30 am to 8.00 pm Monday, Tuesday, Thursday, Friday; 10.00 am to 8.00 pm Wednesday; Closed Saturday and Sunday (unless by prior arrangement)

Telephone for access By appointment only
Located in Westminster's Marylebone Library. An extensive collection of material from all over the world, covering Sherlock Holmes and Sir Arthur Conan Doyle. Books, pamphlets, journals, newspaper cuttings and photos, much of which is otherwise unavailable in this country. Some background material.

Imperial College Central Library
See **Science Museum Library**

Imperial War Museum

Department of Printed Books, Lambeth Road, London SE1 6HZ
☎020 7416 5000 Fax 020 7416 5374

Open 10.00 am to 5.00 pm Monday to Saturday (restricted service Saturday; closed on Bank Holiday Saturdays and last two full weeks of November for annual stock check)

Access For reference (but at least 24 hours' notice must be given for intended visits)
A large collection of material on 20th-century life with detailed coverage of the world wars and other conflicts. Books, pamphlets and periodicals, including many produced for short periods in unlikely wartime settings; also maps, biographies, privately printed memoirs, and foreign language material. Additional research material available in the following departments: Art, Documents, Exhibits and Firearms, Film, Sound Records, Photographs. Active publishing programme based on reprints of rare books held in library. Catalogue available.

Instituto Cervantes

102 Eaton Square, London SW1W 9AN
☎020 7235 0324 Fax 020 7235 0329
Email biblon@cervantes.es

Open 12.30 pm to 6.30 pm Monday; 9.30 am to 6.30 pm Tuesday to Thursday; 9.30 am to 5.00 pm Friday; 9.30 am to 1.30 pm Saturday

Open access For reference and lending
Spanish literature, history, art, philosophy. The library houses a collection of books, periodicals, videos, slides, tapes, CDs, cassettes, films and CD-ROMs specialising entirely in Spain and Latin America.

Italian Institute Library

39 Belgrave Square, London SW1X 8NX
☎020 7235 1461 Fax 020 7235 4618
Email maria.dangels@italcultur.org.uk
Website www.italcultur.org.uk

Open 10.00 am to 1.00 pm and 2.00 pm to 5.00 pm Monday to Friday

Open access For reference
A collection of over 21,000 volumes relating to all aspects of Italian culture. Texts are mostly in Italian, with some in English.

Jersey Library
Halkett Place, St Helier, Jersey JE2 4WH
☎01534 59991 (lending)/59992 (reference)
Fax 01534 69444
Email piano@itl.net
Website www.itl.net/vc/europe/jersey/
education/library/index.html

Open 9.30 am to 5.30 pm Monday,
Wednesday, Thursday, Friday; 9.30 am to
7.30 pm Tuesday; 9.30 am to 4.00 pm
Saturday

Open access
Books, periodicals, newspapers, CDs, cassettes,
CD-ROMs, videos, microfilm, specialised local
studies collection, public Internet access.

Kent County Central Library
Kent County Council Arts & Libraries,
Springfield, Maidstone, Kent ME14 2LH
☎01622 696511 Fax 01622 753338

Open 9.30 am to 5.30 pm Monday,
Wednesday, Friday; 9.30 am to 6.00 pm
Tuesday; 9.30 am to 7.00 pm Thursday;
10.00 am to 5.00 pm Saturday

Open access
50,000 volumes available on the floor of the
library plus 250,000 volumes of non-fiction,
mostly academic, available on request to staff.
English literature, poetry, classical literature,
drama (including play sets), music (including
music sets). Strong, too, in sociology, art history, business information and government
publications. Loans to all who live or work in
Kent; those who do not may consult stock for
reference or arrange loans via their own local
library service.

Lansdowne Library
Meyrick Road, Bournemouth, Dorset BH1 3DJ
☎01202 556603 Fax 01202 291781

Open 10.00 am to 7.00 pm Monday; 9.30 am
to 7.00 pm Tuesday, Thursday, Friday; 9.30
am to 5.00 pm Wednesday; 9.00 am to 1.00
pm Saturday

Open access
Main library for Bournemouth with separate
lending, music and reference departments, the
latter including Bournemouth Local Studies
Collection. Collection of government publications; children's section, periodicals.

The Law Society
113 Chancery Lane, London WC2A 1PL
☎0870 6062511 Fax 020 7831 1687
Website www.lawsociety.org.uk

Open 9.00 am to 5.00 pm with out-of-hours
answerphone back-up

Access Library restricted to solicitors/members
Provides all information about solicitors, the
legal profession in general, law reform issues, etc.

Leeds Central Library
Calverley Street, Leeds, West Yorkshire
LS1 3AB
☎0113 2478274 Fax 0113 2478426
Website www.leeds.gov.uk/libraries

Open 9.00 am to 8.00 pm Monday and
Wednesday; 9.00 am to 5.30 pm Tuesday
and Friday; 9.30 am to 5.30 pm Thursday;
10.00 am to 5.00 pm Saturday

Open access to lending libraries; Reference
material on request
Lending Library covering all subjects. ☎
as above.
Music Library contains scores, books,
video and audio. ☎0113 2478273
Information for Business Library holds
company information, market research, statistics, directories, journals and computer-based
information. Email information.for.business@
leeds.gov.uk ☎0113 2478265
Art Library (in Art Gallery) has a major
collection of material on fine and applied arts.
☎0113 2478247
Local Studies Library contains an extensive
collection on Leeds and Yorkshire, including
maps, books, pamphlets, local newspapers, illustrations and playbills. Census returns for the
whole of Yorkshire also available. International
Genealogical Index and parish registers. ☎0113
2478290 Email local.studies @leeds.gov.uk
Research & Study Library with over
270,000 volumes, including extensive files of
newspapers and periodicals plus all government
publications since 1960. *Special collections* include
military history, Judaic, early gardening books,
and mountaineering. ☎0113 2478282/3 Email
research.and.studies@leeds.gov.uk
Leeds City Libraries has an extensive network of 65 branch and mobile libraries.

Leeds Library
18 Commercial Street, Leeds, West Yorkshire
LS1 6AL
☎0113 2453071 Fax 0113 2438218

Open 9.00 am to 5.00 pm Monday to Friday

Access To members; research use upon application to the librarian
FOUNDED 1768. Contains over 120,000 books
and periodicals from the 15th century to the present day. *Special collections* include Reformation

pamphlets, Civil War tracts, Victorian and Edwardian children's books and fiction, European language material, spiritualism and psychical research, plus local material.

Lincoln Central Library
Free School Lane, Lincoln LN2 1EZ
☎01522 510800 Fax 01522 535882

Open 9.30 am to 7.00 pm Monday to Friday; 9.30 am to 4.00 pm Saturday

Open access to the library; appointment required for the Tennyson Research Centre
Lending and reference library. Special collections include Lincolnshire local history (printed and published material, photographs, maps, directories and census data) and the Tennyson Research Centre (contact *Susan Gates*).

Linen Hall Library
17 Donegall Square North, Belfast BT1 5GB
☎028 9032 1707 Fax 028 9043 8586
Email info@linenhall.com

Librarian *John Gray*

Open 9.30 am to 5.30 pm Monday to Friday; 9.30 am to 4.00 pm Saturday

Open access For reference (loans restricted to members)
FOUNDED 1788. Holdss about 200,000 books. Major Irish and local studies collections, including the Northern Ireland Political Collection (about 140,000 items).

Literary & Philosophical Society of Newcastle upon Tyne
23 Westgate Road, Newcastle upon Tyne NE1 1SE
☎0191 232 0192 Fax 0191 261 2885

Librarian *Elizabeth A. Pescod*

Open 9.30 am to 7.00 pm Monday, Wednesday, Thursday, Friday; 9.30 am to 8.00 pm Tuesday; 9.30 am to 1.00 pm Saturday

Access Members; research facilities for *bona fide* scholars on application to the Librarian
200-year-old library of 140,000 volumes, periodicals (including 130 current titles), classical music on vinyl recordings and CD, plus a collection of scores. A programme of lectures and recitals provided. Recent publications include: *The Reverend William Turner: Dissent and Reform in Georgian Newcastle upon Tyne* Stephen Harbottle; *History of the Literary and Philosophical Society of Newcastle upon Tyne, Vol. 2 (1896–1989)* Charles Parish; *Bicentenary Lectures 1993* ed. John Philipson.

Liverpool City Libraries
William Brown Street, Liverpool LE3 8EW
☎0151 233 5829 Fax 0151 233 5886
Email central@lvpublib.demon.co.uk

Open 9.00 am to 7.30 pm Monday to Thursday; 9.00 am to 5.00 pm Friday; 10.00 am to 4.00 pm Saturday

Open access
Humanities Reference Library Total stock in excess of 120,000 volumes and 24,000 maps, plus book plates, prints and autographed letters. *Special collections* Walter Crane and Edward Lear illustrations, Kolmscott Press, Audubon.
Business and Technology Reference Library Extensive stock dealing with all aspects of science, commerce and technology, including British and European standards and patents and trade directories.
Audio Visual Library Extensive stock relating to all aspects of music. Includes 128,000 volumes and music scores, 18,500 records, and over 3000 cassettes and CDs. *Special collections* Carl Rosa Opera Company Collection and Earl of Sefton's early printed piano music.
Record Office and Local History Department Printed and audiovisual material relating to Liverpool, Merseyside, Lancashire and Cheshire, together with archive material mainly on Liverpool. Some restrictions on access, with 30-year rule applying to archives.

The London Institute – London College of Printing: Library and Learning Resources
Elephant and Castle, London SE1 6SB
☎020 7514 6527 Fax 020 7514 6597
Website www.linst.ac.uk/library

Access By arrangement
Library and Learning Resources operates from the two sites of the college at: Elephant & Castle and Back Hill (Clerkenwell). Books, periodicals, slides, CD-ROMs, videos and computer software on all aspects of the art of the book, printing, management, film/photography, graphic arts, plus retailing. *Special collections* Private Press books and the history and development of printing and books.

The London Library
14 St James's Square, London SW1Y 4LG
☎020 7930 7705 Fax 020 7766 4766
Email membership@londonlibrary.co.uk
Website www.londonlibrary.co.uk

Librarian *Mr A. S. Bell*

Open 9.30 am to 5.30 pm Monday to Saturday (Thursday till 7.30 pm)

Access For members only (£150 p.a., 2000)

With over a million books and 8400 members, The London Library 'is the most distinguished private library in the world; probably the largest, certainly the best loved'. Founded in 1841, it is a registered charity and wholly independent of public funding. Its permanent collection embraces most European languages as well as English. Its subject range is predominantly within the humanities, with emphasis on literature, history, fine and applied art, architecture, bibliography, philosophy, religion, and topography and travel. Some 6000–7000 titles are added yearly. Most of the stock is on open shelves to which members have free access. Members may take out up to 10 volumes; 15 if they live more than 20 miles from the Library. The comfortable Reading Room has an annexe for users of personal computers. There are photocopiers, CD-ROM workstations, free access to the Internet, and the Library also offers a postal loans service.

Prospective members are required to submit a refereed application form in advance of admission, but there is at present no waiting list for membership. The London Library Trust may make grants to those who are unable to afford the full annual fee; details on application.

London Metropolitan Archives

40 Northampton Road, London EC1R 0HB
☎020 7332 3820 Fax 020 7833 9136
Email ask.lma@corpoflondon.gov.uk
Website
www.cityoflondon.gov.uk/archives/lma
Minicom 020 7278 8703

Open 9.30 am to 4.45 pm Monday, Wednesday, Friday; 9.30 pm to 7.30 pm Tuesday and Thursday

Access For reference only

Formerly, the Greater London Record Office Library. Covers all aspects of the life and development of London, specialising in the history and organisation of local government in general, and London in particular. Books on London history and topography, covering many subjects. Also London directories dating back to 1677, plus other source material including Acts of Parliament, Hansard reports, statistical returns, atlases, yearbooks and many complete sets of newspapers and magazines.

Lord Louis Library

Orchard Street, Newport, Isle of Wight
PO30 1LL
☎01983 527655/823800 (Reference Library)
Fax 01983 825972
Email reflib@llouis.demon.co.uk

Open 9.30 am to 5.30 pm Monday to Friday (Saturday till 5.00 pm)

Open access

General adult and junior fiction and non-fiction collections; local history collection and periodicals. Also the county's main reference library.

Manchester Central Library

St Peters Square, Manchester M2 5PD
☎0161 234 1900 Fax 0161 234 1963
Email mclib@libraries.manchester.gov.uk
Website www.manchester.gov.uk/mccdlt/index.htm

Open 10.00 am to 8.00 pm Monday to Thursday; 10.00 am to 5.00 pm Friday and Saturday; Commercial and European Units: 10.00 am to 6.00 pm Monday to Thursday; 10.00 am to 5.00 pm Friday and Saturday

Open access

One of the country's leading reference libraries with extensive collections covering all subjects. Departments include: Commercial, European, Technical, Social Sciences, Arts, Music, Local Studies, Chinese, General Readers, Language & Literature. Large lending stock and VIP (visually impaired) service available.

Marylebone Library (Westminster)

See **Sherlock Holmes Collection**

Ministry of Agriculture, Fisheries and Food

Nobel House, 17 Smith Square, London
SW1P 3JR
☎020 7238 3000 Fax 020 7238 6591

MAFF Helpline 0645 335577 (local call rate) – general contact point which can provide information on the work of MAFF, either directly or by referring callers to appropriate contacts. Available 9.00 am to 5.00 pm Monday to Friday (excluding Bank Holidays)

Open 9.30 am to 5.00 pm Monday to Friday

Access For reference (but at least 24 hours notice must be given for intended visits)

Large stock of volumes on temperate agriculture.

The Mitchell Library

North Street, Glasgow G3 7DN
☎0141 287 2999 Fax 0141 287 2815
Website www.libarch.glasgow.gov.uk

Open 9.00 am to 8.00 pm Monday to Thursday; 9.00 am to 5.00 pm Friday and Saturday

Open access

Europe's largest public reference library with stock of over 1,200,000 volumes. It subscribes to 46 newspapers and more than 2000 periodicals. There are collections in microform, records, tapes and videos, as well as CD-ROMs, illustrations, photographs, postcards, etc.

The library is divided into a number of subject departments including the Arts department which contains a number of special collections, e.g. the Robert Burns Collection (5000 vols) the Scottish Poetry Collection (12,000 items) and the Scottish Drama Collection (1650 items).

Morrab Library

Morrab House, Morrab Gardens, Penzance, Cornwall TR18 4DA
☎01736 364474
Librarian L. Lowdon, BA,ALA
Open 10.00 am to 4.00 pm Tuesday to Friday; 10.00 am to 1.00 pm Saturday

Access Non-members may use the library for a small daily fee, but may not borrow books

Formerly known as the Penzance Library. An independent subscription lending library of over 60,000 volumes covering virtually all subjects except modern science and technology, with large collections on history, literature and religion. There is a comprehensive Cornish collection of books, newspapers and manuscripts including the Borlase letters; a West Cornwall photographic archive; many runs of 18th- and 19th-century periodicals; a collection of over 2000 books published before 1800.

National Library of Scotland

George IV Bridge, Edinburgh EH1 1EW
☎0131 226 4531   Fax 0131 622 4803
Email enquiries@nls.uk
Website www.nls.uk
Open Main Reading Room: 9.30 am to 8.30 pm Monday, Tuesday, Thursday, Friday; 10.00 am to 8.30 pm Wednesday; 9.30 am to 1.00 pm Saturday. Map Library: 9.30 am to 5.00 pm Monday, Tuesday, Thursday, Friday; 10.00 am to 5.00 pm Wednesday; 9.30 am to 1.00 pm Saturday. Scottish Science Library: 9.30 am to 5.00 pm Monday, Tuesday, Thursday, Friday; 10.00 am to 8.30 pm Wednesday.

Access To reading rooms and Map Library, for research not easily done elsewhere, by reader's ticket

Collection of over seven million volumes. The library receives all British and Irish publications. Large stock of newspapers and periodicals. Many special collections, including early Scottish books, theology, polar studies, baking, phrenology and liturgies. Also large collections of maps, music and manuscripts including personal archives of notable Scottish persons.

National Library of Wales

Aberystwyth, Ceredigion SY23 3BU
☎01970 632800   Fax 01970 615709
Website www.llgc.org.uk
Open 9.30 am to 6.00 pm Monday to Friday; 9.30 am to 5.00 pm Saturday (closed Bank Holidays and first week of October)

Access To reading rooms by reader's ticket, available on application. Open acess to regular exhibition programme and to permanent exhibition 'The Treasures of the Nation'

Collection of over four million books and including large collections of periodicals, maps, manuscripts and audiovisual material. Particular emphasis on humanities in printed foreign material, and on Wales and other Celtic areas in all collections.

National Library of Women

See **The Fawcett Library**

National Meteorological Library and Archive

London Road, Bracknell, Berkshire RG12 2SZ
☎01344 854841   Fax 01344 854840
Email metlib@meto.gov.uk
Open Library & Archive: 8.30 am to 4.30 pm Monday to Friday; Archive closed between 1.00 pm and 2.00 pm

Access By Visitor's Pass available from the reception desk; advance notice of a planned visit is appreciated

The major repository of most of the important literature on the subjects of meteorology, climatology and related sciences from the 16th century to the present day. The Library houses a collection of books, journals, articles and scientific papers, plus published climatological data from many parts of the world. The Technical Archive (The Scott Building, Sterling Centre, Eastern Road, Bracknell, Berks RG12 2PW, ☎01344 855960; Fax 01344 855961) holds the document collection of meteorological data and charts from England, Wales and British overseas bases, including ships' weather logs. Records from Scotland are stored in Edinburgh and those from Northern Ireland in Belfast.

The Natural History Museum Library

Cromwell Road, London SW7 5BD
☎020 7942 5460 Fax 020 7942 5559
Email library@nhm.ac.uk
Website www.nhm.ac.uk/info/library/
index.html

Open 10.00 am to 4.30 pm Monday to Friday

Access To *bona fide* researchers, by reader's ticket on presentation of identification (telephone first to make an appointment)

The library is in five sections: general; botany; zoology; entomology; earth sciences. The subdepartment of ornithology is housed at the Zoological Museum, Akeman Street, Tring, Herts HP23 6AP (☎01442 834181). Resources available include books, journals, maps, manuscripts, drawings and photographs covering all aspects of natural history, including palaeontology and mineralogy, from the 14th century to the present day. Also archives and historical collection on the museum itself.

Newcastle upon Tyne City Library

Princess Square, Newcastle upon Tyne
NE99 1DX
☎0191 277 4100 Fax 0191 277 4168

Open 9.30 am to 8.00 pm Monday and
Thursday; 9.30 am to 5.00 pm Tuesday,
Wednesday, Friday; 9.00 am to 5.00 pm
Saturday

Open access
Extensive local studies collection, including newspapers, illustrations and genealogy. Also business, science, humanities and arts, open learning resource centre, marketing advice centre. Patents advice centre.

Norfolk Library & Information Service

Norfolk and Norwich Central Library,
Central Lending Service, 71 Ber Street,
Norwich, Norfolk NR1 3AD
☎01603 215215
Website www.norfolk.gov.uk/council/
departments/lis/libhome.htm

Central Reference & Information Service and Norfolk Studies

Gildengate House, Upper Green Lane,
Norwich, Norfolk NR3 1AX
☎01603 215222 Fax 01603 215258

Open Lending Library, Reference and
Information Service and Norfolk Studies:
10.00 am to 8.00 pm Monday to Friday;
9.00 am to 5.00 pm Saturday

Open access
Reference and lending library with wide range of stock for loan, including books, recorded music, music scores, plays and videos. Houses the 2nd Air Division Memorial Library and has a strong Local Studies Library. Extensive range of reference stock including business information. On-line database and CD-ROM services. Public fax and colour photocopying, access to the Internet. Information brokerage provides in-depth research services.

Northamptonshire Libraries & Information Service

Library HQ, PO Box 216, John Dryden House,
8–10 The Lakes, Northampton NN4 7DD
☎01604 236236 Fax 01604 237937

Since 1991, the Libraries and Information Service have run two to three programmes of literary events for adults each year. Programmes so far have included visiting authors, poetry readings, workshops and other events and activities. The programmes are supported by regular touring fiction displays, writers' advice sessions and dedicated notice boards in libraries across the county.

Northumberland Central Library

The Willows, Morpeth, Northumberland
NE61 1TA
☎01670 534518/534514 Fax 01670 534513

Open 10.00 am to 8.00 pm Monday,
Tuesday, Wednesday, Friday; 9.30 am to
12.30 pm Saturday (closed Thursday)

Open access
Books, periodicals, newspapers, cassettes, CDs, video, microcomputers, CD-ROMs, Internet access, prints, microforms, vocal scores, playsets, community resource equipment. *Special collections* **Northern Poetry Library**: 15,000 volumes of modern poetry (see entry under **Organisations of Interest to Poets**); Cinema: comprehensive collection of about 5000 volumes covering all aspects of the cinema; Family History.

Nottingham Central Library

Angel Row, Nottingham NG1 6HP
☎0115 9152828 Fax 0115 9152840

Open 9.30 am to 7.00 pm Monday to Friday;
9.00 am to 1.00 pm Saturday

Open access
General public lending library: business information, online information, the arts, local studies, religion, community languages, litera-

ture. Videos, periodicals, spoken word, recorded music, CD-ROM service – textual information on CD-ROM on public access machines. Internet on public access. *Special collection* on D. H. Lawrence. Extensive back-up reserve stocks. Drama and music sets for loan to groups. Art gallery – contemporary exhibitions; coffee shop.

Nottingham Subscription Library Ltd
Bromley House, Angel Row, Nottingham NG1 6HL
☎0115 9473134
Librarian *Julia Wilson*
Open 9.30 am to 5.00 pm Monday to Friday; also first Saturday of each month from 10.00 am to 12.30 pm
Access For members only
FOUNDED 1816. Collection of 30,000 books including local history, topography, biography, travel and fiction.

Office for National Statistics
The Library, 1 Drummond Gate, London SW1V 2QQ
☎020 7533 6262 Fax 020 7533 6261
Email info@ons.gov.uk
Website www.ons.gov.uk
Also at: The Library, Government Buildings, Cardiff Road, Newport NP10 8XG
01633 812973 Fax 01633 812599
Open 9.30 am to 4.30 pm (London); 10.00 am to 4.30 pm (Newport) Monday to Friday
All published Census data from 1801 onwards for the UK. Population and health statistics from 1837 onwards. Some foreign censuses and statistics (incomplete; most are out-housed and require one week's notice for retrieval). International statistics (WHO, UN, etc). Government Social Survey reports, 1941 onwards. Wide range of other government statistical publications, business and economic statistics, Eurostat publications. Small stock of books on demography, vital registration, epidemology, survey methodology, census taking. Newport library collection consists mainly of economic statistics, including the main statistical publications of government departments.

Orkney Library
Laing Street, Kirkwall, Orkney KW15 1NW
☎01856 873166 Fax 01856 875260
Email orkey.library@ork.gov.uk
Open 9.00 am to 8.00 pm Monday to Friday; 9.00 am to 5.00 pm Saturday. Archives:

9.00 am to 1.00 pm and 2.00 pm to 4.45 pm Monday to Friday
Open access
Local studies collection. Archive includes sound and photographic departments.

Oxford Central Library
Westgate, Oxford OX1 1DJ
☎01865 815549 Fax 01865 721694
Open Call 01865 815509 for details
General lending and reference library including the Centre for Oxfordshire Studies. Also periodicals, audio visual materials, music library, children's library and Business Information Point.

PA News Library
292 Vauxhall Bridge Road, London SW1V 1AE
☎020 7963 7012 Fax 020 7963 7065
Website www.pa.press.net
Open 8.00 am to 8.00 pm Monday to Friday; 8.00 am to 6.00 pm Saturday; 9.00 am to 5.00 pm Sunday
Open access
PA News, the 24-hour national news and information group, offers public access to its press cutting archive. Covering a wide range of subjects, the library includes over 14 million cuttings dating back to 1928. Personal callers welcome or research undertaken by in-house staff.

Penzance Library
See **Morrab Library**

City of Plymouth Library and Information Services
Central Library, Drake Circus, Plymouth, Devon PL4 8AL
☎01752 385905
Website www.plymouth.gov.uk/star/library.htm
Open access
CENTRAL LIBRARY LENDING DEPARTMENTS:
Lending ☎01752 385912
Children's Department ☎01752 385916
Music & Drama Department ☎01752 385914 Email music@plymouth.gov.uk
Open 9.30 am to 7.00 pm Monday and Friday; 9.30 am to 5.30 pm Tuesday, Wednesday, Thursday; 9.30 am to 4.00 pm Saturday

The Lending departments offer books on all subjects; language courses on cassette and foreign language books; the Holcenberg Jewish Collection; books on music and musicians, drama and theatre; music parts and sets of music parts; play sets; videos; song index; cassettes and CDs.

CENTRAL LIBRARY REFERENCE
DEPARTMENTS:
Reference ☎01752 385907/8
Email ref@plymouth.gov.uk
Business Information ☎01752 385906
Email keyinfo@plymouth.gov.uk
**Local Studies & Naval History
Department** ☎01752 385909
Email localstudies@plymouth.gov.uk

Open 9.00 am to 7.00 pm Monday to Friday; 9.00 am to 4.00 pm Saturday

The Reference departments include an extensive collection of Ordnance Survey maps and town guides; community and census information; marketing and statistical information; Patents and British Standards; books on every aspect of Plymouth; naval history; Mormon Index on microfilm; Baring Gould manuscript of 'Folk Songs of the West'.

Plymouth Proprietary Library

Alton Terrace, 111 North Hill, Plymouth, Devon PL4 8JY
☎01752 660515

Librarian *John R. Smith*

Open Monday to Saturday from 9.30 am (closing time varies)

Access To members; visitors by appointment only

FOUNDED 1810. Contains approximately 17,000 volumes of mainly 20th-century work. Member of the **Association of Independent Libraries**.

The Poetry Library

See entry under **Organisations of Interest to Poets**

Polish Library

238–246 King Street, London W6 0RF
☎020 8741 0474 Fax 020 8741 7724

Open 10.00 am to 8.00 pm Monday and Wednesday; 10.00 am to 5.00 pm Friday; 10.00 am to 1.00 pm Saturday (library closed Tuesday and Thursday)

Access For reference to all interested in Polish affairs; limited loans to members and *bona fide* scholars only through inter-library loans

Books, pamphlets, periodicals, maps, music, photographs on all aspects of Polish history and culture. *Special collections* Emigré publications; Joseph Conrad and related works; Polish underground publications; bookplates.

Poole Central Library

Dolphin Centre, Poole, Dorset BH15 1QE
☎01202 673910 Fax 01202 670253
Email poolelendlib@hotmail.com

Open 10.00 am to 7.00 pm Monday; 9.30 am to 7.00 pm Tuesday to Friday; 9.00 am to 1.00 pm Saturday

Open access

General lending and reference library, including Healthpoint health information centre, business information, children's library, periodicals and newspapers.

Press Association Library

See **PA News Library**

Harry Price Library of Magical Literature

University of London Library, Senate House, Malet Street, London WC1E 7HU
☎020 7862 8470 Fax 020 7862 8480
Website www.ull.ac.uk

Open 9.30 am to 6.00 pm Monday to Friday; 9.30 am to 1.00 pm, 2.00 pm to 5.15 pm Saturday (by prior appointment only); Monday evenings in term time (by prior appointment only)

Restricted access For reference only, restricted to members of the University and *bona fide* researchers (apply in writing); items must be requested from, and consulted in, the Special Collections Reading Room

Over 14,000 volumes and pamphlets on psychic phenomena and pseudo-phenomena; books relating to spiritualism and its history, to hypnotism, telepathy, astrology, conjuring and quackery.

Public Record Office

Ruskin Avenue, Kew, Richmond, Surrey TW9 4DU
☎020 8876 3444 Fax 020 8878 8905
Email enquiry@pro.gov.uk
Website www.pro.gov.uk

Also at: The Family Record Centre, 1 Myddleton Street, London EC1R 1UW

Open 9.00 am to 5.00 pm Monday, Wednesday, Friday; 10.00 am to 7.00 pm Tuesday; 9.00 am to 7.00 pm Thursday; 9.30 am to 5.00 pm Saturday

Access For reference, by reader's ticket, available free of charge on production of proof of identity (UK citizens: banker's card or driving licence; non-UK: passport or national identity card. Telephone for further information)

Over 168 kilometres of shelving house the national repository of records of central Government in the UK and law courts of England and Wales, which extend in time from the 11th–20th century. Medieval records and the records of the State Paper Office from the early 16th–late 18th century, plus the records of the Privy Council Office and the Lord Chamberlain's and Lord Steward's departments. Modern government department records, together with those of the Copyright Office dating mostly from the late 18th century. Under the Public Records Act, records are normally only open to inspection when they are 30 years old.

Reading Central Library

Abbey Square, Reading, Berkshire RG1 3BQ
☎0118 901 5955 Fax 0118 901 5954
Email
reading.borough.libraries@reading.gov.uk

Open 9.30 am to 5.00 pm Monday and Wednesday; 9.30 am to 7.00 pm Tuesday, Thursday, Friday; 9.30 am to 4.00 pm Saturday

Open access
Lending library; reference library; local studies library, bringing together every aspect of the local environment and human activity in Berkshire; business library; music and drama library. Special collections: Mary Russell Mitford; local illustrations.

Public meeting room available.

Religious Society of Friends Library

Friends House, 173 Euston Road, London NW1 2BJ
☎020 7663 1135 Fax 020 7663 1001
Email library@quaker.org.uk
Website www.quaker.org.uk

Open 1.00 pm to 5.00 pm Monday, Tuesday, Thursday, Friday; 10.00 am to 5.00 pm Wednesday

Open access A letter of introduction from someone in good standing is required for researchers who are not members of the Society

Quaker history, thought and activities from the 17th century onwards. Supporting collections on peace, anti-slavery and other subjects in which Quakers have maintained long-standing interest. Also archives and manuscripts relating to the Society of Friends.

Richmond Central Reference Library

Old Town Hall, Whittaker Avenue, Richmond, Surrey TW9 1TP
☎020 8940 5529 Fax 020 8940 6899
Email reference.services@richmond.gov.uk

Open 10.00 am to 6.00 pm Monday, Thursday, Friday (Tuesday till 1.00 pm; Wednesday till 8.00 pm and Saturday till 5.00 pm)

Open access
General reference library serving the needs of local residents and organisations. Internet access and online databases for public use.

Royal Anthropological Institute Library
See **British Museum Department of Ethnography Library**

Royal Geographical Society Library (with the Institute of British Geographers)

1 Kensington Gore, London SW7 2AR
☎020 7591 3040 Fax 020 7591 3001
Email library@rgs.org
Website www.rgs.org

Open 11.00 am to 5.00 pm Monday to Friday

Access to the library and reading rooms restricted to use by Fellows and members. Visitors strictly by appointment. There is a charge of £15 per person per day, with a reduction of £5 for those who are unwaged or in full-time education

Books and periodicals on geography, topography, cartography, voyages and travels. The Map Room houses map and chart sheets, atlases and RGS-sponsored expedition reports. Photographs on travel and exploration are housed in the picture library, for which an appointment is necessary. (See entry under **Picture Libraries**.)

Royal Society Library

6 Carlton House Terrace, London SW1Y 5AG
☎020 7451 2606 Fax 020 7930 2170
Website www.royalsoc.ac.uk

Open 10.00 am to 5.00 pm Monday to Friday

Access For research only, to *bona fide* researchers; contact the Library in advance of first visit

History of science, scientists' biographies, science policy reports, and publications of international scientific unions and national academies from all over the world.

RSA (Royal Society for the Encouragement of Arts, Manufactures & Commerce)

8 John Adam Street, London WC2N 6EZ
☎020 7930 5115 Fax 020 7839 5805
Email library@rsa-uk.demon.co.uk
Website www.rsa.org.uk
Curator *Susan Bennett*
Open Research Library: 9.30 am to 1.00 pm
Monday to Friday and 2.00pm to 5.00 pm
Wednesdays only; Fellows Library: 9.30 am
to 5.00 pm Monday to Friday

Access to Fellows of RSA; by application and
appointment to non-Fellows (contact *Julie
Cranage* Library Services Coordinator, ☎020
7451 6874)
Archives of the Society since 1754. A collection of approximately 5000 volumes; international exhibition material.

Royal Society of Medicine Library

1 Wimpole Street, London W1M 8AE
☎020 7290 2940 Fax 020 7290 2939
Email library@roysocmed.ac.uk
Website www.roysocmed.ac.uk
Director of Information Services *Ian Snowley*
Head of Customer Services *Sheron Burton*
Open 9.00 am to 8.30 pm Monday to Friday;
10.00 am to 5.00 pm Saturday

Access For reference only, on introduction by
Fellow of the Society (temporary membership
is available to non-members; £10 per day; £25
per week; £75 per month)
Books and periodicals on general medicine,
biochemistry and biomedical science. Extensive
historical material and portrait collection.

Royal Statistical Society Library

University College London, Gower Street,
London WC1E 6BT
☎020 7387 7050 Fax 020 7679 7373
Email library@ucl.ac.uk
Website www.ucl.ac.uk/Library
Open 8.45 am to 10.30 pm Monday to
Thursday; 8.45 am to 7.00 pm Friday;
9.30 am to 4.30 Saturday

Access RSS Fellows registered with University
College London Library
Statistics (theory and methodology), mathe-
matical statistics, applied statistics, econometrics.

Science Fiction Foundation Research Library

Liverpool University Library, PO Box 123,
Liverpool L69 3DA

☎0151 794 2696/2733 Fax 0151 794 2681
Email asawyer@liverpool.ac.uk
Website www.liv.ac.uk/~sawyer/
sffchome.html
Contact *Andy Sawyer*
Access For research, by appointment only
(telephone first)
This is the largest collection outside the US of
science fiction and related material – including
autobiographies and critical works. *Special collection* Runs of 'pulp' magazines dating back to the
1920s. Foreign-language material (including a
large Russian collection), and the papers of the
Flat Earth Society. The collection also features a
growing range of archive and manuscript material, including the Eric Frank Russell archive.
The University of Liverpool also holds the Olaf
Stapledon and John Wyndham archives.

Science Museum Library

Imperial College Road, London SW7 5NH
☎020 7942 4242 Fax 020 7942 4243
Email smlinfo@nmsi.ac.uk
Website www.nmsi.ac.uk/library
Open 9.30 am to 9.00 pm Monday to Friday
(closes 5.30 pm outside academic terms);
9.30 am to 5.30 pm Saturday

Open access Reference only; no loans
National library for the history and public
understanding of science and technology, with a
large collection of source material. Operates
jointly with Imperial College Central Library.

Scottish Poetry Library

See entry under **Organisations of Interest
to Poets**

Sheffield Libraries, Archives and Information

Central Library, Surrey Street, Sheffield S1 1XZ
☎0114 273 4711 Fax 0114 2735009

Sheffield Archives
52 Shoreham Street, Sheffield S1 4SP
☎0114 2039395 Fax 0114 2039398
Email sheffield.archives@dial.pipex.com
Open 9.30 am to 5.30 pm Monday to
Thursday; 9.00 am to 1.00 pm and 2.00 pm
to 4.30 pm Saturday (documents should be
ordered by 5.00 pm Thursday for Saturday)

Access By reader's pass
Holds documents relating to Sheffield and
South Yorkshire, dating from the 12th century
to the present day, including records of the City
Council, churches, businesses, landed estates,
families and individuals, institutions and societies.

Arts and Social Sciences Reference Service
☎0114 2734747/8

Open 10.00 am to 8.00 pm Monday; 9.30 am to 5.30 pm Tuesday and Friday; 9.30 am to 8.00 pm Wednesday; 9.30 am to 4.30 pm Saturday (closed Thursday)

Access For reference only
A comprehensive collection of books, periodicals and newspapers covering all aspects of arts (excluding music) and social sciences.

Music and Video Service
☎0114 2734733

Open as for Arts and Social Sciences above

Access For reference (loans to ticket holders only)
An extensive range of books, CDs, cassettes, scores, etc. related to music. Also a video cassette loan service.

Local Studies Service ☎0114 2734753

Open as for Arts & Social Sciences above (except Wednesday 9.30 am to 5.30 pm)

Access For reference
Extensive material covering all aspects of Sheffield and its population, including maps, photos and videos.

Business, Science and Technology Reference Services
☎0114 2734736/7 or 2734742

Open as for Arts & Social Sciences above

Access For reference only
Extensive coverage of science and technology as well as commerce and commercial law. British patents and British and European standards with emphasis on metals. Hosts the World Metal Index. The business section holds a large stock of business and trade directories, plus overseas telephone directories and reference works with business emphasis.

Sheffield Information Service
☎0114 2734760/1 or 2734712
Fax 0114 2757111
Email nd54@dial.pipex.com
Website dis.shef.ac.uk/help_yourself

Open 10.00 am to 5.30 pm Monday; 9.30 am to 5.30 pm Tuesday, Wednesday, Friday; 9.30 am to 4.30 pm Saturday (closed Thursday)

Full local information service covering all aspects of the Sheffield community and a generalist advice service on a sessional basis.

Children's and Young People's Library Service
☎0114 2734734

Open 10.30 am to 5.00 pm Monday and Friday; 1.00 pm to 5.00 pm Tuesday and Wednesday; 9.30 am to 4.30 pm Saturday (closed Thursday)

Books, spoken word sets, videos; under-five play area; teenage reference section; readings and promotions; storytime sessions.

Sports Library
☎0114 2735929
Email sports.library@dial.pipex.com

Open 10.00 am to 1.00 pm and 2.00 pm to 6.00 pm Monday and Wednesday; 10.00 pm to 1.00 pm and 2.00 pm to 4.30 pm Tuesday and Friday (closed Thursday and Saturday)

Information on all aspects of sport and physical recreation including sports medicine, physiologoy, nutrition, coaching, recreation management, sports history. Special collection on mountaineering.

Shetland Library
Lower Hillhead, Lerwick, Shetland ZE1 0EL
☎01595 693868 Fax 01595 694430
Email info@shetland-library.gov.uk
Website www.shetland-library.gov.uk

Open 10.00 am to 7.00 pm Monday, Wednesday, Friday; 10.00 am to 5.00 pm Tuesday, Thursday, Saturday

General lending and reference library; extensive local interest collection including complete set of *The Shetland Times, The Shetland News* and other local newspapers on microfilm and many old and rare books; audio collection including talking books/newspapers. Junior room for children. Disabled access and Housebound Readers Service (delivery to reader's home). Mobile library services to rural areas. Open Learning Service. Same day photocopying service. Publishing programme of books in dialect, history, literature.

Shoe Lane Library
Hill House, Little New Street, London EC4A 3JR
☎020 7583 7178

Open 9.30 am to 5.30 pm Monday, Wednesday, Thursday, Friday; 9.30 am to 6.30 pm Tuesday

Open access
Corporation of London general lending

library, with a comprehensive stock of 50,000 volumes, most of which are on display.

Shrewsbury Library

Castlegates, Shrewsbury, Shropshire SY1 2AS
☎01743 255300 Fax 01743 255309
Email shrewsbury.library@shropshire-cc.gov.uk
Website www.shropshire-cc.gov.uk/library.nsf

Open 9.30 am to 5.00 pm Monday and Wednesday; 9.30 am to 1.00 pm Thursday; 9.30 am to 7.30 pm Tuesday and Friday; 9.30 am to 4.00 pm Saturday

Open access
Largest public lending library in Shropshire. Books, cassettes, CDs, talking books, videos, language courses. Open Learning, homework and study centre with public use computers for word processing, CD-ROMs and Internet access. Strong music, literature and art book collection. Reference and local studies provision in adjacent buildings.

Spanish Institute Library

See **Instituto Cervantes**

St Bride Printing Library

Bride Lane, London EC4Y 8EE
☎020 7353 4660 Fax 020 7583 7073

Open 9.30 am to 5.30 pm Monday to Friday

Open access
Corporation of London public reference library. Appointments advisable for consultation of special collections. Every aspect of printing and related matters: publishing and bookselling, newspapers and magazines, graphic design, calligraphy and type, papermaking, bookbinding. One of the world's largest specialist collections in its field, with over 40,000 volumes, over 3000 periodicals (200 current titles), and extensive collection of drawings, manuscripts, prospectuses, patents and materials for printing and typefounding. Noted for its comprehensive holdings of historical and early technical literature.

Suffolk County Council Libraries & Heritage

St Andrew House, County Hall, St Helens Street, Ipswich, Suffolk IP4 1LJ
☎01473 584564 Fax 01473 584549
E-mail (general enquiries) infolink@libher.suffolk.gov.uk
Website www.suffolkcc.gov.uk/libraries_and_heritage/

Open Details on application. Major libraries open six days a week

Access A single user registration card gives access to the lending service of 42 libraries across the county

Full range of lending and reference services. Free public access to the Internet and multimedia CD-ROMs in all libraries. Catalogue with self-service facilities for registered borrowers available on the website. *Special collections* include Suffolk Archives and Local History Collection; Benjamin Britten Collection; Edward Fitzgerald Collection; Seckford Collection and Racing Collection (Newmarket). The Suffolk Infolink service gives details of local groups and societies and is available in libraries throughout the county.

Sunderland City Library and Arts Centre

28–30 Fawcett Street, Sunderland, Tyne & Wear SR1 1RE
☎0191 514 1235 Fax 0191 514 8444

Open 9.30 am to 7.30 pm Monday and Wednesday; 9.30 am to 5.00 pm Tuesday, Thursday, Friday; 9.30 am to 4.00 pm Saturday

The city's main library for lending and reference services. Local studies and children's sections, plus Sound and Vision department (CDs, cassettes, videos, CD-ROMs, talking books). The City of Sunderland also maintains community libraries of varying size, offering a range of services, plus mobile libraries. A Books on Wheels service is available to housebound readers; the Schools Library Service serves teachers and schools. Two writers' groups meet at the City Library and Arts Centre: Janus Writers, every Wednesday, 1.30 pm to 3.30 pm. Tuesday Writers, every Tuesday, 7.30 pm to 9.30 pm.

Swansea Central Reference Library

Alexandra Road, Swansea SA1 5DX
☎01792 516753/516757 Fax 01792 615759
Email swanlib@demon.co.uk

Open 9.00 am to 7.00 pm Monday, Tuesday, Wednesday, Friday; 9.00 am to 5.00 pm Thursday and Saturday. The library has a lending service but hours tend to be shorter – check in advance (Tel 01792 516750/1).

Access For reference only (Local Studies closed access: items must be requested on forms provided)
General reference material (approx. 100,000 volumes); also British standards, statutes, company information, maps, European Community information. Local studies: comprehensive collections on Wales; Swansea & Gower; Dylan

Thomas. Local maps, periodicals, illustrations, local newspapers from 1804. B&w and colour photocopying facilities, access to the Internet and microfilm/microfiche copying facility.

Swiss Cottage Central Library

88 Avenue Road, London NW3 3HA
☎020 7413 6533

Open 10.00 am to 7.00 pm Monday and Thursday; 10.00 am to 6.00 pm Tuesday, Wednesday, Friday; 10.00 am to 5.00 pm Saturday

Open access
Over 300,000 volumes in the lending and reference libraries and 300 periodicals (200 current titles). Home of the London Borough of Camden's Information and Reference Services.

Theatre Museum Library & Archive

1e Tavistock Street, London WC2E 7PA
☎020 7943 4700 Fax 020 7943 4777
Website www.theatremuseum.vam.ac.uk

Open 10.30 am to 4.30 pm Tuesday to Friday

Access By appointment only
The Theatre Museum was founded as a separate department of the Victoria & Albert Museum in 1974 and moved to its own building in Covent Garden in 1987. The museum (open Tuesday to Sunday 11.00 am to 7.00 pm) houses permanent displays, temporary exhibitions, a studio theatre, and organises a programme of special events, performances, lectures, guided visits and workshops. The library houses the UK's largest performing arts research collections, including books, photographs, designs, engravings, programmes, press cuttings, etc. All the performing arts are covered but strengths are in the areas of theatre, dance, musical theatre and stage design. The Theatre Museum has acquired much of the British Theatre Association's library and is providing reference access to its collections of play texts and critical works.

Thurrock Council Leisure, Libraries & Cultural Services Department

Grays Library, Orsett Road, Grays, Essex RM17 5DX
☎01375 383611 Fax 01375 370806
Virtual Enquiry Desk:
acairns@thurrock.gov.uk

Open 9.00 am to 7.00 pm Monday, Tuesday, Thursday; 9.00 am to 5.00 pm Wednesday,

Friday, Saturday; branch library opening times vary

Open access
General library lending and reference through nine libraries and a mobile library. Services include books, magazines, newspapers, audiocassettes, CDs, videos, pictures and language courses. Large collection of Thurrock materials. Internet and word processing.

Truro Library

Union Place, Pydar Street, Truro, Cornwall TR1 1EP
☎01872 279205 (lending)/272702 (reference)

Open 9.30 am to 5.00 pm Monday to Thursday; 9.30 am to 7.00 pm Friday; 9.00 am to 4.00 pm Saturday

Books, cassettes, CDs and videos for loan through branch or mobile networks. Reference collection. *Special collections* on local studies.

United Nations Information Centre

Millbank Tower (21st Floor), 21–24 Millbank, London SW1P 4QH
☎020 7630 1981 Fax 020 7976 6478
Email info@uniclondon.org
Website www.unitednations.org.uk

Open Library: 9.00 am to 1.00 pm and 2.00 pm to 5.30 pm Monday to Thursday

Open access By appointment only
A full stock of official publications and documentation from the United Nations.

Western Isles Libraries

Public Library, 19 Cromwell Street, Stornoway, Isle of Lewis HS1 2DA
☎01851 703064 Fax 01851 708676

Open 10.00 am to 5.00 pm Monday to Thursday; 10.00 am to 7.00 pm Friday; 10.00 am to 5.00 pm Saturday

Open access
General public library stock, plus local history and Gaelic collections including maps, printed music, cassettes and CDs; census records and Council minutes; music collection (cassettes). Branch libraries on the isles of Barra, Benbecula, Harris and Lewis.

City of Westminster Archives Centre

10 St Ann's Street, London SW1P 2DE
☎020 7641 5180 Fax 020 7641 5179

Open 9.30 am to 7.00 pm Tuesday, Thursday, Friday; 9.30 am to 9.00 pm

Wesdnesday; 9.30 am to 5.00 pm Saturday (closed Monday)

Access For reference

Comprehensive coverage of the history of Westminster and selective coverage of general London history. 22,000 books, together with a large stock of maps, prints, photographs, and theatre programmes.

Westminster Music Library

Victoria Library, 160 Buckingham Palace Road, London SW1W 9UD
☎020 7641 4292 Fax 020 7641 4281
Email westmuslib@dial.pipex.com
Website www.earl.org.uk/music/westminster/ composers

Open 11.00 pm to 7.00 pm Monday to Friday; 10 am to 5.00 pm Saturday

Open access

Located at Victoria Library, this is the largest public music library in the South of England, with extensive coverage of all aspects of music, including books, periodicals and printed scores. No recorded material, notated only. Lending library includes a small collection of CDs, cassettes and videos.

Westminster Reference Library

35 St Martin's Street, London WC2H 7HP
☎020 7641 4640
Website www.westminster.gov.uk/el/libarch/ index.html

General Reference & Performing Arts:
☎020 7641 4636
Art & Design: ☎020 7641 4638
Business and Official Publications:
☎020 7641 4634

Open 10.00 am to 8.00 pm Monday to Friday; 10.00 am to 5.00 pm Saturday

Access For reference only

A general reference library with emphasis on the following: Art & Design – fine and decorative arts, architecture, graphics and design; Performing Arts – theatre, cinema, radio, television and dance; Official Publications – major collection of HMSO publications from 1947, plus parliamentary papers dating back to 1906; Business – UK directories, trade directories, company and market data; Official EU Depository Library – carries official EU material; Periodicals – long files of many titles. One working day's notice is required for government documents, some monographs and most older periodicals.

The Wiener Library

4 Devonshire Street, London W1N 2BH
☎020 7636 7247 Fax 020 7436 6428
Email lib@wl.u-net.com
Website wienerlibrary.co.uk

Open 10.00 am to 5.30 pm Monday to Friday

Access By letter of introduction (readers needing to use the Library for any length of time should become members)

Private library – one of the leading research centres on European history since the First World War, with special reference to the era of totalitarianism and to Jewish affairs. Founded by Dr Alfred Wiener in Amsterdam in 1933, it holds material that is not available elsewhere. Books, periodicals, press archives, documents, pamphlets, leaflets and brochures. Much of the material can be consulted on microfilm.

Vaughan Williams Memorial Library

English Folk Dance and Song Society, Cecil Sharp House, 2 Regent's Park Road, London NW1 7AY
☎020 7485 2206 ext. 207 & 208
Fax 020 7284 0523
Email library@efdss.org
Website www.efdss.org

Open 9.30 am to 5.30 pm Tuesday to Friday; 10.00 am to 4.00 pm 1st & 3rd Saturday (sometimes closed between 1.00 pm and 2.00 pm)

Access For reference to the general public, on payment of a daily fee; members may borrow books and use the library free of charge

A multimedia collection: books, periodicals, manuscripts, tapes, records, CDs, films, videos. Mostly British traditional culture and how this has developed around the world. Some foreign language material, and some books in English about foreign cultures. Also, the history of the English Folk Dance and Song Society.

Dr Williams's Library

14 Gordon Square, London WC1H 0AG
☎020 7387 3727 Fax 020 7388 1142

Open 10.00 am to 5.00 pm Monday, Wednesday, Friday; 10.00 am to 6.30 pm Tuesday and Thursday

Open access To reading room (loans restricted to subscribers). Visitors required to supply identification.

Annual subscription £10; ministers of religion and certain students £5

Primarily a library of theology, religion and

ecclesiastical history. Also philosophy, history (English and Byzantine). Particularly important for the study of English Nonconformity. Trustees of Dr William's Library manage the Congregational Library on behalf of the Memorial Hall Trustees.

Wolverhampton Central Library
Snow Hill, Wolverhampton WV1 3AX
☎01902 552025 (lending)/552026 (reference)
Fax 01902 552024

Open 9.00 am to 7.00 pm Monday to Thursday; 9.00 am to 5.00 pm Friday and Saturday

Archives & Local Studies Collection
42–50 Snow Hill, Wolverhampton WV2 4AB
☎01902 552480

Open 10.00 am to 5.00 pm Monday, Tuesday, Friday, 1st and 3rd Saturday of each month; 10.00 am to 7.00 pm Wednesday; closed Thursday

General lending and reference libraries, plus children's library. Also audiovisual library holding cassettes, CDs, videos and music scores. Internet access.

Worcestershire Libraries and Information Service
Cultural Services, County Hall, Spetchley Road, Worcester WR5 2NP
☎01905 766231 Fax 01905 766240
Website www.worcestershire.gov.uk/cwis

Open Opening hours vary in the 22 libraries and mobile libraries covering the county; all full-time libraries open at least one evening a week until 7.00 pm or 8.00 pm, and on Saturday until 1 pm; 8 largest libraries open until 4.00 pm on Saturday; part-time libraries vary

Access Information and reference services open to anyone; loans to members only (membership criteria: resident, being educated, working, or an elector in the county or neighbouring authorities; temporary membership to visitors. Proof of identity and address required. No charge for membership or for borrowing books.)

Information service, and reference and lending libraries. Non-fiction and fiction for all age groups, including normal and large print, spoken word cassettes, sound recordings (CD, cassette, some vinyl), videos, maps, local history, CD-ROMs for reference at main libraries, free public Internet access in all libraries. *Special collections* Carpets and Textiles; Needles & Needlemaking; Stuart Period; A. E. Housman.

York Central Library
Museum Street, York YO1 7DS
☎01904 655631 Fax 01904 611025

Lending Library
Open 9.30 am to 8.00 pm Monday, Tuesday, Friday; 9.30 am to 5.30 pm Wednesday and Thursday; 9.30 am to 4.00 pm Saturday

General lending library including videos, CDs, music cassettes, audio books and children's storytapes.

Reference Library
Open 9.00 am to 8.00 pm Monday, Tuesday, Wednesday, Friday; 9.00 am to 5.30 pm Thursday; 9.00 am to 4.00 pm Saturday

General reference library; organisations database; local studies library for York and surrounding area; business information service; microfilm/fiche readers for national and local newspapers; census returns and family history resource; general reference collection. Maintains strong links with other local history resource centres, namely the Borthwick Institute, York City Archive and York Minster Library. CD-ROM and Internet facilities.

Young Book Trust Children's Reference Library
Book House, 45 East Hill, London SW18 2QZ
☎020 8516 2985 Fax 020 8516 2978

Open 9.00 am to 5.00 pm Monday to Friday (by appointment only)

Access For reference only

A comprehensive collection of children's literature, related books and periodicals. Aims to hold most of all children's titles published within the last two years. An information service covers all aspects of children's literature, including profiles of authors and illustrators. Reading room facilities.

Zoological Society Library
Regent's Park, London NW1 4RY
☎020 7449 6293 Fax 020 7586 5743
Email library@zsl.org
Website ww.zsl.org

Open 9.30 am to 5.30 pm Monday to Friday

Access To members and staff; non-members by application and on payment of fee

160,000 volumes on zoology including 5000 journals (1300 current) and a wide range of books on animals and particular habitats. Slide collection available and many historic zoological prints.

Picture Libraries

A–Z Botanical Collection Ltd
192 Goswell Road, London EC1V 7DT
☎020 7253 0991 Fax 020 7253 0992
Website www.a-z.picture-library.com
Contact *James Wakefield*
300,000 transparencies, specialising in plants and related subjects.

Acme
See **Popperfoto**

Action Plus
54–58 Tanner Street, London SE1 3PH
☎020 7403 1558 Fax 020 7403 1526
Email info@actionplus.co.uk
Specialist sports and action library with a vast comprehensive collection of small-format colour and b&w images covering all aspects of over 300 professional and amateur sports from around the world. As well as personalities, events, venues, etc, also covers themes such as success, celebration, dejection, teamwork, effort and exhaustion. Offers same-day despatch of pictures or alternatively, clients with modem or ISDN links can receive digital images direct.

Lesley & Roy Adkins Picture Library
Longstone Lodge, Aller, Langport, Somerset TA10 0QT
☎01458 250075 Fax 01458 250858
Email Adkins_Archaeology@compuserve.com
Colour coverage of archaeology, heritage and related subjects in the UK, Europe, Egypt and Turkey. Subjects include towns, villages, housing, landscape and countryside, churches, temples, castles, monasteries, art and architecture, gravestones and tombs, and antiquarian views. No service charge if pictures are used.

The Advertising Archive Limited
45 Lyndale Avenue, London NW2 2QB
☎020 7435 6540 Fax 020 7794 6584
Email suzanne@advertisingarchives.co.uk
Website www.advertisingarchives.co.uk
Contact *Suzanne or Larry Viner*
With over one million images, the largest collection of British and American press ads and magazine cover illustrations in Europe. Material from 1870 to the present day. Visitors by appointment. Research undertaken; rapid service, competitive rates. Exclusive UK agents for *Saturday Evening Post* cover illustrations including artwork of Norman Rockwell and Josef Leyendecker.

AKG London Ltd, The Arts and History Picture Library
4 Melbray Mews, 158 Hurlingham Road, London SW6 3NS
☎020 7610 6103 Fax 020 7610 6125
Email enquiries@akg-london.co.uk
Website www.akg-london.co.uk
Contact *Julia Engelhardt*
Collection of 180,000 images with computerised access to ten million more kept in the Berlin AKG Library. *Specialises* in art, archaeology, history, topography, music, personalities and film.

Bryan & Cherry Alexander Photography
Higher Cottage, Manston, Sturminster Newton, Dorset DT10 1EZ
☎01258 473006 Fax 01258 473333
Email alexander@arcticphoto.co.uk
Website www.arcticphoto.co.uk
Contact *Cherry Alexander*
Arctic and Antarctic specialists; indigenous peoples, wildlife and science in polar regions; Norway, Iceland, Siberia and Alaska.

Allsport (UK) Ltd
3 Greenlea Park, Prince George's Road, London SW19 2JD
☎020 8685 1010 Fax 020 8648 5240
Email lmartin@allsport.co.uk
Website www.allsport.com
Contact *Lee Martin*
A large specialist library with six million colour transparencies, covering 140 different sports and top sports personalities. Represented in 27 countries worldwide. Digital wiring facilities through Macintosh picture desk. Online digital archive access available via ISDN and Internet.

Alvey & Towers
Enterprise House, Ashby Road, Coalville, Leicestershire LE67 3LA
☎01530 450011 Fax 01530 450011
Email alveytower@aol.com
Website members.aol.com/alveytower

Contact *Emma Rowen*

Houses two separate collections; one covering the modern railway industry and all related supporting industries, the other features a more general 'lifestyle' collection with the emphasis on people and day-to-day living plus a substantial selection of transport images.

Andalucia Slide Library
Apto 499, Estepona, Malaga 29 680, Spain
☎00 34 952 793647 Fax 00 34 952 793647
Email info@andalucia.com
Website www.andalucia.com

Contact *Chris Chaplow*

Specialist library covering all aspects of Spain and Spanish life and culture. Cities, white villages, landscapes, festivals, art, gastronomy, leisure, tourism. Commissions undertaken.

Andes Press Agency
26 Padbury Court, London E2 7EH
☎020 7613 5417 Fax 020 7739 3159
Email photos@andespress.demon.co.uk

Contacts *Val Baker, Carlos Reyes*

80,000 colour transparencies and 300,000 b&w, specialising in social documentary, world religions, Latin America and Britain.

Heather Angel/Natural Visions
Highways, 6 Vicarage Hill, Farnham, Surrey GU9 8HJ
☎01252 716700 Fax 01252 727464
Email hangel@naturalvisions.co.uk
Website www.naturalvisions.co.uk

Contact *Valerie West*

Constantly expanding worldwide natural history, wildlife and landscapes: polar regions; tropical rainforest flora and fauna; all species of plants and animals in natural habitats from Africa, Asia (notably China and Malaysia), Australasia, South America and USA; urban wildlife; pollution; biodiversity; global warming. Also gardens and cultivated flowers. Transparencies only loaned to publishers after contract exchanged with author.

Ansel Adams
See **Corbis Images**

Aquarius Library
PO Box 5, Hastings, East Sussex TN34 1HR
☎01424 721196 Fax 01424 717704
Email aquarius.lib@clara.net

Contact *David Corkill*

Over one million images specialising in cinema past and present, television, pop music, ballet, opera, theatre, etc. The library includes various American showbiz collections. Film stills date back to the beginning of the century. Interested in film stills, the older the better. Current material is supplied by own suppliers.

Aquila Wildlife Images
PO Box 1, Studley, Warwickshire B80 7JG
☎01527 852357 Fax 01527 857507

Natural history library specialising in birds, British and European wildlife, North America, Africa and Australia, environmental subjects, farming, habitats and related subjects, domestic animals and pets.

Arcaid
The Factory, 2 Acre Road, Kingston upon Thames, Surrey KT2 6EF
☎020 8546 4352 Fax 020 8541 5230
Email arcaid@arcaid.co.uk
Website www.arcaid.co.uk

The built environment, historic and contemporary architecture and interior design by leading architectural photographers. Covers international and British subjects, single images and series, with background information. Visitors welcome by appointment. Commissions undertaken.

Architectural Association Photo Library
36 Bedford Square, London WC1B 3ES
☎020 7887 4078 Fax 020 7414 0782

Contacts *Valerie Bennett, Sarah Farmer, Anna Jury*

100,000 35mm transparencies on architecture, historical and contemporary. Archive of large-format b&w negatives from the 1920s and 1930s.

Ardea London Ltd
35 Brodrick Road, London SW17 7DX
☎020 8672 2067 Fax 020 8672 8787
Email ardea@ardea.co.uk

Specialist natural history photographic library supplying original transparencies of animals, birds, plants, fish, reptiles and amphibians in their natural habitat worldwide and domestic pets. Coverage includes landscapes, conservation and environmental images.

Art Directors & Trip Photo Library
57 Burdon Lane, Cheam, Surrey SM2 7BY
☎020 8642 3593/8661 7104
Fax 020 8395 7230
Email images@tripphoto.demon.co.uk
Website www.tripphoto.demon.co.uk

Contacts *Helene Rogers, Bob Turner*

Englarged newly-merged library with over 750,000 images. Extensive coverage of all lifestyles, countries, religion, peoples, etc. Backgrounds a speciality. Catalogues available free to professionals.

Artbank Illustration Library

8 Woodcroft Avenue, London NW7 2AG
☎020 8906 2288 Fax 020 8906 2289
Email info@artbank.com
Website www.artbank.com

Illustration and art library holding thousands of images by many renowned contemporary illustrators. Large-format transparencies. Catalogue available on faxed request. Represents a diverse group of UK and American illustrators for commissioned work. Portfolios available for viewing.

Aspect Picture Library Ltd

40 Rostrevor Road, London SW6 5AD
☎020 7736 1998/7731 7362
Fax 020 7731 7362
Email Aspect.Ldn@btinternet.com
Website www.aspect-picture-library.co.uk

Colour and b&w worldwide coverage of countries, events, industry and travel, with large files on art, namely paintings, space, China and the Middle East.

Audio Visual Services

Imperial College School of Medicine at St Mary's, London W2 1PG
☎020 7886 1739 Fax 020 7724 7349

Contact B. Tallon

Colour and b&w, mostly 35mm colour. Clinical medicine, contemporary and historical, including HIV-AIDS material and history of penicillin. Also surgical and scientific illustrations. Commissions undertaken.

Australia Pictures

28 Sheen Common Drive, Richmond TW10 5BN
☎020 8898 0150/8876 3637
Fax 020 8898 0150/8876 3637

Contact John Miles

Collection of 4000 transparencies covering all aspects of Australia: Aboriginal people, paintings, Ayers Rock, Kakadu, Tasmania, underwater, reefs, Arnhem Land, Sydney. Also Africa, Middle East and Asia.

Aviation Images – Mark Wagner

42B Queens Road, London SW19 8LR
☎020 8944 5225 Fax 020 8944 5335
Email mark.wagner@aviation-images.com

Website www.aviation-images.com

Contact Mark Wagner

250,000+ aviation images, civil and military, technical and generic. Mark Wagner is the photographer for *Flight International* magazine. Member of **BAPLA** and RAeS.

Aviation Photographs International

15 Downs View Road, Swindon, Wiltshire SN3 1NS
☎01793 497179 Fax 01793 434030

The 250,000 photographs comprise a comprehensive coverage of army, naval and airforce hardware ranging from early pistols to the latest ships. Extensive coverage of military and civil aviation includes modern together with many air-to-air views of vintage/warbird types. Collections available on disk. Commissions undertaken for additional photography and research.

Aviation Picture Library

116 The Avenue, St Stephens, West Ealing, London W13 8JX
☎020 8566 7712 Fax 020 8566 7714
Email avpix@avnet.co.uk

Contacts Austin John Brown, Chris Savill

Specialists in the aviation field but also a general library which includes travel, architecture, transport, landscapes and skyscapes. *Special collections*: aircraft and all aspects of the aviation industry, including the archival collection of John Stroud; aerial obliques of Europe, USA, Caribbean and West Africa; architectural and town planning. Commissions undertaken on the ground and in the air.

Axel Poignant Archive

115 Bedford Court Mansions, Bedford Avenue, London WC1B 3AG
☎020 7636 2555 Fax 020 7636 2555
Email Rpoignant@aol.com

Contact Roslyn Poignant

Anthropological and ethnographic subjects, especially Australia and the South Pacific. Also Scandinavia (early history and mythology), Sicily and England.

Barnaby's Picture Library

Barnaby House, 19 Rathbone Street, London W1P 1AF ☎020 7636 6128
Fax 020 7637 4317
Email barnabyspicturelibrary@ukbusiness.com
Website www.ukbusiness.com/
    barnabyspicturelibrary

Contact *John Buckland*

Colour and b&w coverage of a wide range of subjects: nature, transport, industry and historical, including a collection on Hitler. Etchings throughout history.

Barnardos Photographic and Film Archive

Tanners Lane, Barkingside, Ilford, Essex IG6 1QG
☎020 8550 8822   Fax 020 8550 0429

Contact *John Kirkham*

Specialises in social history (1874 to present day), child care, education, war years, emigration/migration. Half a million prints, slides, negatives. Images are mainly b&w, colour since late 1940s/early '50s. Archive of 200 films dating back to 1905. Visitors by appointment Mon–Fri 9.30 am to 4.30 pm.

Colin Baxter Photography Limited

Woodlands Industrial Estate, Grantown-on-Spey PH26 3NA
☎01479 873999   Fax 01479 873888
Email colin.baxter@zetnet.co.uk

Contacts *Colin B. Kirkwood* (Marketing), *Mike Rensner* (Editorial)

Over 50,000 images specialising in Scotland. Also the Lake District, Yorkshire, the Cotswolds, France, Iceland and a special collection on Charles Rennie Mackintosh's work. *Publishes* books, calendars, postcards and greetings cards on landscape, cityscape and natural history containing images which are primarily, but not exclusively, Colin Baxter's. Also publishers of the *Worldlife Library* of natural history books.

BBC Natural History Unit Picture Library

Broadcasting House, Whiteladies Road, Bristol BS8 2LR
☎0117 9746720   Fax 0117 9238166
Email nhu.picture.library@bbc.co.uk
Website www.bbcwild.com

Contacts *Helen Gilks, Sue Fogden*

A collection of 80,000 transparencies of wildlife from around the world, especially animal portraits and behaviour. Other subjects covered include plants, landscapes, environmental issues and photos relating to the making of the Natural History Unit's films. Wildlife sound recordings and film footage also available.

The Photographic Library Beamish, The North of England Open Air Museum

Beamish, The North of England Open Air Museum, Beamish, County Durham DH9 0RG
☎01207 231811   Fax 01207 290933
Email museum@beamish.org.uk
Website www.beamish.org.uk

Keeper of Resource Collections *Jim Lawson*

Comprehensive collection; images relate to the North East of England and cover agricultural, industrial, topography, advertising and shop scenes, people at work and play. Also on laser disk for rapid searching. Visitors by appointment weekdays.

Francis Bedford

See **Birmingham Library Services** under **Library Services**

Ivan J. Belcher Colour Picture Library

57 Gibson Close, Abingdon, Oxfordshire OX14 1XS
☎01235 521524   Fax 01235 521524

Extensive colour picture library specialising in top-quality medium-format transparencies depicting the British scene. Particular emphasis on tourist, holiday and heritage locations, including famous cities, towns, picturesque harbours, rivers, canals, castles, cottages, rural scenes and traditions photographed throughout the seasons. Mainly of recent origin, and constantly updated.

Andrew Besley PhotoLibrary

'Trenerth Barton', Fraddam, Near Hayle, Cornwall TR27 5EP
☎01736 850086   Fax 01736 850086
Email bes.pix@btinternet.com
Website www.andrewbesley-photolibrary.co.uk

Contact *Andrew Besley*

Specialist library of 20,000 images of West Country faces, places and moods.

Bettmann Archive

See **Corbis Images**

BFI Stills, Posters and Designs

British Film Institute, 21 Stephen Street, London W1P 2LN
☎020 7957 4797   Fax 020 7323 9260
Website www.bfi.org.uk

Holds images from more than 60,000 films and TV programmes on seven million b&w prints and over 500,000 colour transparencies. A further 20,000 files hold portraits of film and TV personalities and cover related general subjects such as studios, equipment, awards. Also holds original posters and set and costume designs. Visitors welcome by appointment only (from 11.00 am to 4.00 pm, Tuesday to Thursday).

Blackwoods Picture Library
See **Geoslides Photography**

Anthony Blake Photo Library
54 Hill Rise, Richmond, Surrey TW10 6UB
☎020 8940 7583 Fax 020 8948 1224
Email info@abpl.co.uk
Website ww.abpl.co.uk

'Europe's premier source' of food- and wine-related images, from the farm and the vineyard to the plate and the bottle. Cooking and kitchens, top chefs and restaurants, country trades and markets, worldwide travel with an extensive Italian section. Many recipes available to accompany transparencies. Free brochure available.

Peter Boardman Collection
See **Chris Bonnington Picture Library**

Boats & Boating Features (Keith Pritchard)
9 High Street, Southwell, Portland, Dorset DT5 2EH
☎01305 861006/0771 2483775
Fax 0870 0569019
Email boats@boating-features.demon.co.uk
Website www.boating-features.demon.co.uk

Contact *Keith Pritchard*

Images of over 300 kinds of craft: historic and modern boats up to 100ft, boating events, people and places in Britain and overseas.

Chris Bonington Picture Library
Badger Hill, Nether Row, Hesket Newmarket, Wigton, Cumbria CA7 8LA
☎016974 78286 Fax 016974 78238
Email frances@bonington.com
Website www.bonington.com

Contact *Frances Daltrey*

Based on the personal collection of climber and author Chris Bonington and his extensive travels and mountaineering achievements; also work by Doug Scott and other climbers, including the Peter Boardman and Joe Tasker Collections. Full coverage of the world's mountains, from British hills to Everest, depicting expedition planning and management stages, the approach march showing inhabitants of the area, flora and fauna, local architecture and climbing action shots on some of the world's highest mountains.

Boulton and Watt Archive
See **Birmingham Library Services** under **Library Services**

The Bridgeman Art Library
17–19 Garway Road, London W2 4PH
☎020 7727 4065 Fax 020 7792 8509
Email info@bridgeman.co.uk
Website www.bridgeman.co.uk

Head of Marketing *Vivienne Wheeler*

Fine art photo archive acting as an agent to more than 1000 museums, galleries and picture owners around the world. Large-format colour transparencies of private collections, artists, paintings, sculptures, prints, manuscripts, antiquities and the decorative arts. The Library is currently expanding at the rate of 500 new images each week and has offices in Paris and New York. Collections represented by the library include the British Library, the National Galleries of Scotland, the National Library of Australia, and the National Gallery of South Africa. Fully searchable catalogue online and printed catalogue available.

British Library Reproductions
British Library, 96 Euston Road, London NW1 2DB
☎020 7412 7614 Fax 020 7412 7771
Email bl-repro@bl.uk
Website www.bl.uk

Twelve million books and approximately five million other items available for photography, microfilming or photocopying by Library staff. Specialist subjects include illuminated manuscripts, stamps, music, maps, botanical and zoological illustration, portraits of historical figures, history of India and South East Asia. All copies should be ordered as far in advance as possible. However, a picture library service is available for photographs for commercial reproduction which enables orders to be processed more quickly. The picture library has a small but unique collection of colour and b&w images mainly covering royalty, religion, medieval life and world maps plus a selection of natural history. Customers are welcome to visit the collection.

Brooklands Museum Picture Library
Brooklands Museum, Brooklands Road, Weybridge, Surrey KT13 0QN
☎01932 857381 Fax 01932 855465

Contacts *John Pulford (Curator of Collections), Julian Temple (Curator of Aviation)*

About 40,000 b&w and colour prints and slides. Subjects include: Brooklands Motor Racing 1907–1939; British aviation and aerospace 1908–present day – particularly BAC, Hawker, Sopwith and Vickers aircraft built at Brooklands.

Hamish Brown Scottish Photographic

26 Kirkcaldy Road, Burntisland, Fife KY3 9HQ
☎01592 873546

Contact *Hamish M. Brown*

Colour and b&w coverage of most topics and areas of Scotland (sites, historic, buildings, landscape, mountains), also travel and mountains abroad, Ireland and Morocco. Commissions undertaken.

Simon Brown, Nature and Landscape Photographer

36 Sandymount Road, Wath–Upon–Dearne, Rotherham, South Yorkshire S63 7AE
☎01709 874322/07769 684656 (mobile)
Fax 01709 874322
Email simon_l.brown@virgin.net
Website freespace.virgin.net/simon_l.brown

Contact *Simon Brown*

Over 30,000 images of the landscape and nature of the British Isles with particular emphasis on the Peak District and Northumberland. Images tend more to monochrome landscape and documentary with colour shots of wild flowers. Current projects are Coast, a study of the British coastline, living with public transport and the Sheffield climbing scene. Self publishers welcome; full research service in life sciences, history, photography and moutaineering.

Camera Press

21 Queen Elizabeth Street, London SE1 2PD
☎020 7378 1300 Fax 020 7278 5126

Quality studio images of celebrities, photofeatures, news, personality portraits, humour, royals, fashion and beauty.

Camera Ways Ltd Picture Library

Court View, Stonebridge Green Road, Egerton, Ashford, Kent TN27 9AN
☎01233 756454
Email derek@cameraways.co.uk

Contacts *Derek, Caryl*

Founded by award-winning film-maker and photographer, Derek Budd, the digital scanned library specialises in rural activities and natural history. It contains 35mm and 6x4.5mm, colour and b&w images as well as 16mm film and video footage on Beta SP and digital Betacam formats. Coverage includes: wildlife habitats, flora and fauna of Britain and Europe, traditional country crafts and people, village scenes, landscapes, gardens, coastal and aquatic life, dinosaurs, aerial surveys, storm damage and M.O.D. reserves. Commissions undertaken in all aspects of commercial multi-media photography, 16mm film, broadcast and corporate video production.

Capital Pictures

49–51 Central Street, London EC1V 8AB
☎020 7253 1122 Fax 020 7253 1414
Email sales@capitalpictures.demon.co.uk

Contact *Phil Loftus*

500,000 images. *Specialises* in photographs of famous people from the worlds of showbusiness, rock and pop, television, politics, royalty and film stills.

The Casement Collection

Erin Lodge, Jigs Lane South, Warfield, Berkshire RG42 3DR
☎01344 302067 Fax 01344 303158
Website www.btinternet.com/~jackcasement

Colour and b&w travel library, strong on North America and the Gulf. Not just beaches and palm trees. Based on Jack Casement's collection. Digitised images available.

The Centre for the Study of Cartoons and Caricature

The Templeman Library, University of Kent at Canterbury, Canterbury, Kent CT2 7NU
☎01227 823127 Fax 01227 823127
Email N.P.Hiley@ukc.ac.uk *or*
    J.M.Newton@ukc.ac.uk
Website libservb.ukc.ac.uk/cartoons/

Contacts *Dr Nicholas Hiley, Jane Newton*

A national research archive of over 85,000 20th century cartoons and caricatures, supported by a library of books, papers, journals, catalogues and assorted ephemera. A computer database provides quick and easy catalogued access. A source for exhibitions and displays as well as a picture library service. *Specialises* in historical, political and social cartoons from British newspapers.

CEPHAS Picture Library

Hurst House, 157 Walton Road, East Molesey, Surrey KT8 0DX
☎020 8979 8647 Fax 020 8224 8095
Email pictures@cephas.co.uk
Website www.cephas.co.uk

The wine industry and vineyards of the world is the subject on which Cephas has made its reputation. 100,000 images, mainly original 6 × 7″s, make this the most comprehensive and up-to-date archive in Britain. Almost all wine-producing countries and all aspects of the industry are covered in depth. Spirits, beer and cider also included. A major food and drink collection now also exists, through preparation and cooking, to eating and drinking.

Giles Chapman Library

3A Peacock Yard, Iliffe Street, London SE17 3LH
☎020 7708 5818 Fax 020 7703 8209

Contact *Giles Chapman*

Around 100,000 colour and b&w images of cars and motoring, from 1945 to the present day. No research fees.

Christel Clear Marine Photography

Roselea, Church Lane, Awbridge, Near Romsey, Hampshire SO51 0HN
☎01794 341081 Fax 01794 340890
Email christel.clear@btinternet.com
Website www.christelclear.com

Contacts *Nigel Dowden, Christel Dowden*

Over 70,000 images on 35mm and 645 transparency: yachting and boating from Grand Prix sailing to small dinghies, cruising locations and harbours. Recent additions include angling, fly fishing and travel. Visitors by appointment.

Christian Aid Photo Section

PO Box 100, London SE1 7RT
☎020 7523 2235 Fax 020 7620 0719

Pictures are mainly from Africa, Asia and Latin America, relating to small-scale, community-based programmes. Mostly development themes: agriculture, health, education, urban and rural life.

Christie's Images Ltd

1 Langley Lane, London SW8 1TH
☎020 7582 1282 Fax 020 7582 5632
Email imageslondon@christies.com
Website www.christies.com/christiesimages/

Contact *Emma Strouts*

The UK's largest fine art photo library. 150,000 images of fine and decorative art. An extensive list of subjects is covered through paintings, drawings and prints of all periods as well as silver, ceramics, jewellery, sculpture, textiles and many other decorative and collectable items. Staff will search files and database to locate specific requests or supply a selection for consideration. Visits by appointment. Search fee.

Chrysalis Picture Library

8 Blenheim Court, Brewery Road, London N7 9NT
☎020 7700 7799 Fax 020 7700 3918/3572
Email tforshaw@chrysalisbooks.co.uk

Contact *Terry Forshaw*

Approximately 250,000 images, colour and b&w, of American history, collectables, cookery, crafts, military, natural history, space and transport.

The Cinema Museum

The Master's House, Old Lambeth Workhouse, off Renfrew Road, London SE11 4TH
☎020 7840 2200 Fax 020 7840 2299
Email martin@cinemamuseum.org.uk

Colour and b&w coverage (including stills) of the motion picture industry throughout its history, including the Ronald Grant Archive. Smaller collections on theatre, variety, television and popular music.

John Cleare/Mountain Camera

Hill Cottage, Fonthill Gifford, Salisbury, Wiltshire SP3 6QW
☎01747 820320 Fax 01747 820320
Email cleare@btinternet.com

Colour and b&w coverage of mountains and wild places, climbing, ski-touring, trekking, expeditions, wilderness travel, landscapes, people and geographical features from all continents. *Specialises* in the Himalaya, Andes, Antarctic, Alps and the British countryside, and a range of topics from reindeer in Lapland to camels in Australia, from whitewater rafting in Utah to ski-mountaineering in China. Commissions and consultancy work undertaken. Researchers welcome by appointment. Member of **BAPLA** and the **OWG**.

The Clifton Archive

71 Broadmead Road, Folkestone, Kent CT19 5AW
☎01303 850524 Fax 01303 850524

Contact *Alan Clifton*

Established in 1956 by photographer Alan Clifton. A collection of 300,000 b&w 35mm negatives and 200,000 colour 35mm transparencies which includes a large travel section and over 500 personalities.

Close-Up Picture Library
14 Burnham Wood, Fareham, Hampshire
PO16 7UD
☎01329 239053
Director *David Stent*

Specialises in the close-up angle of all aspects of life: people, places, animal and bird-life and the environment in general. Also a wide range of pictures covering travel in Europe and the Orient, multicultural, ethnic and educational issues. Photographers with quality material always welcome: no minimum initial submission; 50% commission on 35mm.

Stephanie Colasanti
38 Hillside Court, 409 Finchley Road,
London NW3 6HQ
☎020 7435 3695 Fax 020 7435 9995
Email stephani@photosource.co.uk
Website www.photosource.co.uk/
   photosource/stephanie

Colour coverage of Europe, Africa, Asia, United Arab Emirates, the Caribbean, USA, Australia, New Zealand, the Pacific Islands and South America: people, animals, towns, agriculture, landscapes, carnivals, markets, archaeology, religion and ancient civilisations. Travel assignments undertaken. Medium-format transparencies (54mm).

Michael Cole Camerawork
The Coach House, 27 The Avenue,
Beckenham, Kent BR3 2DP
☎020 8658 6120 Fax 020 8658 6120
Website www.tennisphotos.com
Contacts *Michael Cole, Derrick Bentley*

Probably the largest and most comprehensive collection of tennis pictures in the world. Over 50 years' coverage of Wimbledon Championships. M.C.C. incorporates the tennis archives of Le Roye Productions, established in 1945.

Collections
13 Woodberry Crescent, London N10 1PJ
☎020 8883 0083 Fax 020 8883 9215
Email collections@btinternet.com
Contact *Brian Shuel*

Extensive coverage of the British and Ireland from the Shetlands to the Channel Islands, and Connemara to East Anglia, including people, traditional customs, workers, religions and pastimes, as well as places both well known and obscure, and an extensive collection of 'things'. Includes the landscapes of Fay Godwin. Visitors are welcome but please make an appointment.

Comstock Photolibrary
21 Chelsea Wharf, 15 Lots Road, London
SW10 0QJ
☎020 7351 4448 Fax 020 7352 8414
Email info@comstock.co.uk
Website www.comstock.co.uk
Contact *Julie Steinberg*

Extensive coverage of business, people, industry, science, futuristic, world travel, landscapes, medical and natural history. Also desktop photography and CD-ROM. Free catalogues on request. Access to over four million images.

Concannon Golf History Library
11 Cheyne Gardens, Westcliff, Bournemouth,
Dorset BH4 8AS
☎01202 766145
Email chrisdale@newsfactory.net
Contact *Dale Concannon*

Private collection of historic golfing images 1750–1950. Players, courses, Ryder Cup, Open Championship, golf architecture, memorabilia, US golf. Specialist advice. Commissions undertaken.

Corbis Images
12 Regents Wharf, All Saints Street, London
N1 9RL
☎020 7843 4444 Fax 020 7278 1408
Email info@uk.corbis.com
Website www.corbisimages.com
Contact *Anna Calvert*

A unique and comprehensive resource containing more than 65 million images, with over 2.1 million of them available online. The images come from professional photographers, museums, cultural institutions and public and private collections worldwide, including images from the Bettmann Archive, Ansel Adams, Lynn Goldsmith, the Turnley Collection and Hulton Deutsch. Subjects include history, travel, celebrities, events, science, world art and cultures. Free catalogues are available or register for a free password to search, save and order online.

Sylvia Cordaiy Photo Library
45 Rotherstone, Devizes, Wiltshire SN10 2DD
☎01380 728327 Fax 01380 728328
Email sylviacordaiy@compuserve.com
Website www.sylvia-cordaiy.com

Over 150 countries on file from the obscure to main stock images – Africa, North, Central and South America, Asia, Atlantic, Indian and Pacific Ocean islands, Australasia, Europe, polar regions. Covers travel, architecture, ancient civilisations, people worldwide, environment, wildlife, natural history, Antarctica, domestic pets, livestock, marine biology, veterinary treatment, equestrian, ornithology, flowers. UK files cover cities, towns villages, coastal and rural scenes, London. Transport, railways, shipping and aircraft (military and civilian). Aerial photography. Backgrounds and abstracts. Also the Paul Kaye B/W archive.

Country Collections
Unit 9, Ditton Priors Trading Estate, Bridgnorth, Shropshire WV16 6SS
☎01746 712533/861330

Contact *Robert Foster*

Small select collection of colour transparencies specialising in sundials, Celtic culture, villages, churches and ancient monuments. Assignments undertaken.

Country Images Picture Library
27 Camwood, Bamber Bridge, Preston, Lancashire PR5 8LA
☎01772 321243 Fax 01772 321243
Email terrymarsh@countrymatters.demon. co.uk

Contact *Terry Marsh*

35mm and 645 colour coverage of landscapes and countryside features generally throughout the UK (Cumbria, North Yorkshire, Lancashire, southern Scotland, Isle of Skye, Wales, Cornwall), France (Alps, Pyrenees, Provence) and Australia. Commissions undertaken.

Country Life Picture Library
King's Reach Tower, Stamford Street, London SE1 9LS
☎020 7261 6337 Fax 020 7261 6216

Contact *Camilla Costello*

Over 150,000 b&w negatives dating back to 1897, and 15,000 colour transparencies. Country houses, stately homes, churches and town houses in Britain and abroad, interiors of architectural interest (ceilings, fireplaces, furniture, paintings, sculpture), and exteriors showing many landscaped gardens, sporting and social events, crafts, people and animals. Visitors by appointment. Open Tuesday to Friday.

Philip Craven Worldwide Photo-Library
Surrey Studios, 21 Nork Way, Nork, Banstead, Surrey SM7 1PB
☎01252 627233 Fax 01252 812399

Contact *Eve Horan*

Extensive coverage of British scenes, cities, villages, English countryside, gardens, historic buildings and wildlife. Worldwide travel and wildlife subjects on medium- and large-format transparencies.

CTC Picture Library
CTC Ltd, Longfield, Midhurst Road, Fernhurst, Haslemere, Surrey GU27 3HA
☎01428 661441 Fax 01428 641071
Email ctcpub@globalnet.co.uk
Website ctcreate@globalnet.co.uk

Contact *Neil Crighton*

One of the biggest specialist libraries in the UK with 250,000 slides covering world and UK agriculture, horticulture, and environmental subjects. Also a small section on travel.

Cumbria Picture Library
See **Eric Whitehead Photography**

Sue Cunningham Photographic
56 Chatham Road, Kingston upon Thames, Surrey KT1 3AA
☎020 8541 3024 Fax 020 8541 5388
Email pictures@scphotographic.com
Website www.scphotographic.com

Extensive coverage of many geographical areas: South America (especially Brazil), Eastern Europe from the Baltic to the Balkans, various African countries, Western Europe including the UK. Colour and b&w. Member of **BAPLA**.

Dalton–Watson Collection
See **The Ludvigsen Library Limited**

James Davis Travel Photography
65 Brighton Road, Shoreham, West Sussex BN43 6RE
☎01273 452252 Fax 01273 440116
Email eyeubiquitous@msn.com

Travel collection: people, places, emotive scenes and tourism. Constantly updated by James Davis and a team of photographers, both at home and abroad. Same-day service available.

The Defence Picture Library
Sherwell House, 54 Staddiscombe Road, Plymouth, Devon PL9 9NB
☎01752 401800 Fax 01752 402800
Email picdesk@defencepictures.demon.co.uk
Website www.defencepictures.demon.co.uk

Contacts *David Reynolds, Jessica Kelly, James Rowlands, Andrew Chittock*

Leading source of military photography covering all areas of the UK Armed Forces, supported by a research agency of facts and figures. More than 450,000 images with a significant number on CD-ROM. Campaigns in Aden, the Falklands, Ulster, the Gulf and Kosovo. Specialist collections include the Chinese Armed Forces, US Special Forces, military units of Italy, Spain and France. Visitors welcome by appointment.

Douglas Dickins Photo Library

2 Wessex Gardens, Golders Green, London NW11 9RT
☎020 8455 6221

Sole Proprietor *Douglas Dickens, FRPS*

Worldwide colour and b&w coverage, specialising in Asia, particularly India, Indonesia and Japan. Meeting educational requirements on landscape, archaeology, history, religions, customs, people and folklore.

C M Dixon

The Orchard, Marley Lane, Kingston, Canterbury, Kent CT4 6JH
☎01227 830075 Fax 01227 831135

Colour coverage of ancient civilisations, archaeology and art, ethnology, mythology, world religion, museum objects, geography, geology, meteorology, landscapes, people and places from many countries including most of Europe, former USSR, Ethiopia, Iceland, Jordan, Morocco, Sri Lanka, Tunisia, Turkey, Egypt, Uzbekistan.

Dominic Photography

4B Moore Park Road, London SW6 2JT
☎020 7381 0007 Fax 020 7381 0008

Contacts *Zoë Dominic, Catherine Ashmore*

Colour and b&w coverage of the entertainment world from 1957 onwards: dance, opera, theatre, ballet, musicals and personalities.

Philip Dunn Picture Library

'Seaside', 2 South Street, Garlieston, Newton Stewart DG8 8BH
☎01988 600611/08605 23599 (mobile)
Email philip.dunn@btinternet.com
Website www.photoactive.co.uk

Contact *Philip Dunn*

Constantly expanding collection of some 75,000 b&w/colour images of travel, people, activities and places in Britain and overseas. Commissions undertaken.

E&E Picture Library – Ecclesiastical and Eccentricities

Beggars Roost, Woolpack Hill, Brabourne Lees, Near Ashford, Kent TN25 6RR

☎01303 812608 Fax 01303 812608
Email isobel@picture-library.freeserve.co.uk
Website www.picture-library.freeserve.co.uk

Contact *Isobel Sinden*

80,000 colour images of ecclesiastical buildings, clergy, ceremony, burial/funerals, English curiosities, 'Biblelands', buildings, wind and water festivals.

Patrick Eagar Photography

5 Ennerdale Road, Kew Gardens, Surrey TW9 3PG
☎020 8940 9269 Fax 020 8332 1229
Email patrickeager@compuserve.com

Colour and b&w coverage of cricket from 1965. Test matches, overseas tours and all aspects of the sport. Also a constantly expanding wine library of vineyards, grapes, cellars and winemakers of France, Italy, Germany, Lebanon, Australia, New Zealand, South Africa, UK. Digital photograph transmission by ISDN and modem.

Ecoscene

The Oasts, Headley Lane, Passfield, Liphook, Hampshire GU30 7RX
☎01428 751056 Fax 01428 751057
Email sally@ecoscene.com
Website www.ecoscene.com

Contact *Sally Morgan*

Expanding colour library of over 80,000 transparencies specialising in all aspects of the environment: pollution, conservation, recycling, restoration, natural history, habitats, education, landscapes, industry and agriculture. All parts of the globe are covered with specialist collections covering Antarctica, Australia, North America. Sally Morgan, who runs the library, is a professional ecologist and expert source of information on all environmental topics. Photographic and writing commissions undertaken. Images delivered by post, on CD-ROM, by email and ISDN.

Edifice

14 Doughty Street, London WC1N 2PL
☎020 7242 0740 Fax 020 7267 3632
Email info@edificephoto.com
Website www.edificephoto.com

Contacts *Philippa Lewis, Gillian Darley*

Colour coverage of architecture, buildings of all possible descriptions, gardens, urban and rural landscape. *Specialises* in details of ornament, period style and material. British Isles, USA, Africa, Europe and Japan all covered. Detailed list available, visits by appointment.

Edinburgh Photographic Library
14 Carscube Terrace, Edinburgh EH12 6BQ
☎0131 337 7615 Fax 0131 337 0303
Email epl@mercat.co.uk
Website www.mercat.co.uk

Contact *James Young*

15,000 transparencies of Scotland: cities, towns and villages, castles, bridges, scenery, mountains, lochs, activities, wildlife, traditional industries. Visitors by appointment only.

English Heritage Photo Library
23 Savile Row, London W1X 1AB
☎020 7973 3338/9 Fax 020 7973 3027
Email celia.sterne@english-heritage.org.uk

Contact *Celia Sterne*

Images of English castles, abbeys, houses, gardens, Roman remains, ancient monuments, battlefields, industrial and post-war buildings, interiors, paintings, artifacts, architectural details, conservation, archaeology.

Mary Evans Picture Library
59 Tranquil Vale, Blackheath, London SE3 0BS
☎020 8318 0034 Fax 020 8852 7211
Email lib@mepl.co.uk
Website www.mepl.co.uk

Collection of historical illustrations documenting social, political, cultural, technical, geographical and biographical themes from ancient times to the recent past (up to mid-20th century). Photographs, prints and ephemera backed by large book and magazine collection. Many special collections including Sigmund Freud, the **Fawcett Library** (women's rights), the paranormal, the Meledin Collection (20th-century Russian history) and individual photographers such as Roger Mayne and Grace Robertson. Brochure sent on request. Compilers of the *Picture Researcher's Handbook*, published every three years by Pira International.

Express Newspapers Syndication
Ludgate House, 245 Blackfriars Road, London SE1 9UX
☎020 7922 7884 Fax 020 7922 7871
Email christian.oakley-white@express.co.uk

Manager *Jamie Maskey*

Two million images updated daily, with strong collections on personalities, royalty, showbiz, sport, fashion, nostalgia and events. Electronic transmission available. Daily news and feature service.

Eye Ubiquitous
65 Brighton Road, Shoreham, East Sussex BN43 6RE
☎01273 440113 Fax 01273 440116
Email eyeubiquitous@msn.com

Contact *Paul Seheult*

General stock specialising in social documentary worldwide, including the work of Tim Page, and now incorporating the **James Davis Travel** library (see entry).

Falklands Pictorial
Vision House, 16 Broadfield Road, Heeley, Sheffield, South Yorkshire S8 0XJ
☎0114 2589299 Fax 0114 2550113

Colour and b&w photographs showing all aspects of Falklands life from 1880 to the present day.

Famous Pictures & Features Agency
13 Harwood Road, London SW6 4QP
☎020 7731 9333 Fax 020 7731 9330
Email info@famous.uk.com
Website www.famous.uk.com

Pictures and features agency with a growing library of interviews and colour transparencies dating back to 1985. Portrait, party and concert shots of rock and pop stars plus international entertainers, film and TV celebrities. The library is supplied by a team of photographers and journalists from the UK and around the world, keeping it up-to-date on a daily basis.

ffotograff
10 Kyveilog Street, Pontcanna, Cardiff CF1 9JA
☎029 2023 6879 Fax 029 2022 9326

Contact *Patricia Aithie*

Library and agency specialising in travel, exploration, the arts, architecture, traditional culture, archaeology and landscape. Based in Wales but specialising in the Middle and Far East; Yemen and Wales are unusually strong aspects of the library. Churches and cathedrals of Britain and Crusader castles. Abstract paintings and detailed photographic textures suitable for book covers. Digital transfer by ISDN and modem available.

Financial Times Pictures
1 Southwark Bridge, London SE1 9HL
☎020 7873 3671 Fax 020 7873 4606
Email richard.pigden@ft.com

Photographs from around the world ranging from personalities in business, politics and the arts, people at work and other human interests and activities. 'FT Graphics are outstanding in their ability to make complex issues comprehensible.' Delivery via modem, ISDN or email.

Fine Art Photographic Library Ltd
2A Milner Street, London SW3 2PU
☎020 7589 3127 Fax 020 7584 1944
Contact Linda Hammerbeck

Over 20,000 large-format transparencies, with a specialist collection of 19th-century paintings.

Fire-Pix International
68 Arkles Lane, Anfield, Liverpool,
Merseyside L4 2SP
☎0151 260 0111/0777 5930419 (mobile)
Fax 0151 250 0111
Email info@firepix.com
Website www.firepixint.demon.co.uk
Contact Tony Myers

The UK's only fire photo library. 17,000 images of fire-related subjects, firefighters, fire equipment manufacturers. Website contains 16 different categories from historical fire to abstract flame. Member of **BAPLA**.

Fogden Wildlife Photos
Basement, 10 Bellevue, Bristol BS8 1DA
☎0117 923 8849 Fax 0117 923 8543
Email susan.fogden@virgin.net
Contact Susan Fogden

Natural history collection, with special reference to rain forests and deserts. Emphasis on quality rather than quantity; growing collection of around 10,000 images.

Food Features
Farnham Forge, 5 Upper Church Lane,
Farnham, Surrey GU9 7DW
☎01252 735240 Fax 01252 735242
Email frontdesk@foodpix.co.uk
Website www.foodpix.co.uk
Contacts Steve Moss, Alex Barker

Specialised high-quality food and drink photography, features and tested recipes. Clients' specific requirements can be incorporated into regular shooting schedules.

Ron & Christine Foord Colour Picture Library
155B City Way, Rochester, Kent ME1 2BE
☎01634 847348 Fax 01634 847348

Specialist library with over 1000 species of British and European wild flowers, plus garden flowers, trees, indoor plants, pests and diseases,

mosses, lichen, cacti and the majority of larger British insects.

Forest Life Picture Library
231 Corstorphine Road, Edinburgh EH12 7AT
☎0131 314 6411 Fax 0131 314 6285
Email n.campbell@forestry.gov.uk
Contacts Douglas Green, Neill Campbell

Official image bank of the Forestry Commission, the library provides a single source for all aspects of forest and woodland management. The comprehensive subject list includes tree species, scenic landscapes, employment, wildlife, flora and fauna, conservation, sport and leisure.

Werner Forman Archive Ltd
36 Camden Square, London NW1 9XA
☎020 7267 1034 Fax 020 7267 6026
Email wfa@btinternet.com
Website www.btinternet.com/~wfa

Colour and b&w coverage of ancient civilisations, oriental and primitive societies around the world. A number of rare collections. Subject lists available.

Format Photographers
19 Arlington Way, London EC1R 1UY
☎020 7833 0292 Fax 020 7833 0381
Email format@formatphotogs.demon.co.uk
Contact Maggie Murray

Over 100,000 documentary images in colour and b&w covering education, health, disability and women's issues in the UK and abroad.

Formula One Pictures
29 Merlin Close, Waltham Abbey, Essex
EN9 3NG
☎01992 787800 Fax 01992 714366
Email jt@f1pictures.com
Website www.f1pictures.com
Contacts John Townsend, Erika Townsend

500,000 35mm colour slides, b&w and colour negatives of all aspects of Formula One grand prix racing including driver profiles and portraits.

Robert Forsythe Picture Library
16 Lime Grove, Prudhoe, Northumberland
NE42 6PR
☎01661 834511 Fax 01661 834511
Email robert@forsythe.demon.co.uk
Website www.forsythe.demon.co.uk/
Contacts Robert Forsythe, Fiona Forsythe

25,000 transparencies of industrial and transport heritage; plus a unique collection of 50,000 items of related publicity ephemera from 1945. Image finding service available. Robert Forsythe is a transport/industrial heritage historian and consultant. Nationwide coverage, particularly strong on Northern Britain. A bibliography of published material is available.

Fortean Picture Library

Henblas, Mwrog Street, Ruthin LL15 1LG
☎01824 707278 Fax 01824 705324
Email janet.bord@forteanpix.demon.co.uk
Website www.forteanpix.demon.co.uk/

Contact *Janet Bord*

30,000 colour and 45,000 b&w images: mysteries and strange phenomena worldwide, including ghosts, UFOs, witchcraft and monsters; also antiquities, folklore and mythology. Subject list available.

The Fotomas Index

12 Pickhurst Rise, West Wickham, Kent BR4 0AL
☎020 8776 2772 Fax 020 8776 2236/2772

Contact *John Freeman*

General historical collection, mostly pre-1900. Subjects include London, topography, art, satirical, social and political history. Large portrait section.

The Francis Frith Collection

Frith's Barn, Teffont, Salisbury, Wiltshire SP3 5QP
☎01722 716376 Fax 01722 716881
Email john_buck@francisfrith.com
Website www.francisfrith.com

Contact *John Buck*

330,000 b&w and sepia photographs of British topography from 1860 to 1969 depicting 7000 British towns and villages.

John Frost Newspapers

See entry under **Library Services**

Andrew N. Gagg's Photo Flora

Town House Two, Fordbank Court, Henwick Road, Worcester WR2 5PF
☎01905 748515
Email gagg@cwcom.net
Website www.gagg.mcmail.com/ photoflora.htm

Specialist in British and European wild plants, flowers, ferns, grasses, trees, shrubs, etc. with colour coverage of most British and many European species (rare and common) and habitats; also travel in India, Sri Lanka, Nepal, Egypt, China, Mexico, Thailand and Tibet.

Galaxy Picture Library

1 Milverton Drive, Ickenham, Uxbridge, Middlesex UB10 8PP
☎01895 637463 Fax 01895 623277
Email galaxypix@compuserve.com
Website ourworld.compuserve.com/ homepages/galaxypix

Contact *Robin Scagell*

Specialises in astronomy, space, telescopes, observatories, the sky, clouds and sunsets. Composites of foregrounds, stars, moon and planets prepared to commission. Editorial service available.

Garden and Wildlife Matters Photo Library

'Marlham', Henley's Down, Battle, East Sussex TN33 9BN
☎01424 830566 Fax 01424 830224
Email gardens@ftech.co.uk
Website web.ftech.net/~gardens

Contact *Dr John Feltwell*

Collection of 110,000 6 ×4″ and 35mm images. General gardening techniques and design; cottage gardens and USA designer gardens. 8000 species of garden plants and over 1000 species of trees. Flowers, wild and house plants, trees and crops. Environmental, ecological and conservation pictures, including sea, air, noise and freshwater pollution, SE Asian and Central and South American rainforests; Eastern Europe, Mediterranean. Recycling, agriculture, forestry, horticulture and oblique aerial habitat shots from Europe and USA. High-quality images required. Digital images supplied worldwide by ISDN.

The Garden Picture Library

Unit 12, Ransome's Dock, 35 Parkgate Road, London SW11 4NP
☎020 7228 4332 Fax 020 7924 3267
Email info@gardenpicture.com
Website www.gardenpicture.com

Contact *Sally Wood*

'Our inspirational images of gardens, plants and gardening offer plenty of scope for writers looking for original ideas to write about.' Special collections include al fresco food, floral graphics and the still life photography of Linda Burgess. From individual stock photos to complete features, photographers submit material from the UK, Europe, USA and Australia on 35mm and medium formats. In-house picture research can be undertaken on request. Visitors to the library are welcome by appointment and copies of promotional literature are available on request.

Ed Geldard Picture Collection

9 Sunderland Bridge Village, Durham
DH6 5HB
☎0191 378 2592

Contact *Ed Geldard*

Approximately 15,000 colour transparencies and b&w negs, all by Ed Geldard, specialising in mountain landscapes: particularly in the Lake District; and the Yorkshire limestone areas, from valley to summit. Commissions undertaken. Books published: *Wainwright's Tour of the Lake District* and *Wainwright in the Limestone Dales* and *The Lake District*.

Genesis Space Photo Library

Greenbanks, Robins Hill, Raleigh, Bideford, Devon EX39 3PA
☎01237 471960 Fax 01237 472060
Email tim@spaceport.co.uk
Website www.spaceport.co.uk

Contact *Tim Furniss*

Contemporary and historical colour and b&w spaceflight collection including rockets, space-craft, spacemen, Earth, moon and planets. Stock list available on request.

Geo Aerial Photography

4 Christian Fields, London SW16 3JZ
☎020 8764 6292/0115 9819418
Fax 020 8764 6292/0115 9815474/9819418
Email geo.aerial@geo-group.demon.co.uk

Contact *Kelly White*

Established 1990 and now a growing collection of aerial oblique photographs from the UK, Scandinavia, Asia and Africa – landscapes, buildings, industrial sites, etc. Commissions undertaken.

GeoScience Features

6 Orchard Drive, Wye, Kent TN25 5AU
☎01233 812707 Fax 01233 812707
Email gsf@geoscience.demon.co.uk
Website www.geoscience.demon.co.uk

Fully computerised and comprehensive library containing the world's principal source of volcanic phenomena. Extensive collections, providing scientific detail with technical quality, of rocks, minerals, fossils, microsections of botanical and animal tissues, animals, biology, birds, botany, chemistry, earth science, ecology, environment, geology, geography, habitats, landscapes, macro/microbiology, peoples, sky, weather, wildlife and zoology. Over 300,000 original colour transparencies in medium- and 35mm-format. Subject lists and CD-ROM catalogue available on application. Incorporates the RIDA photolibrary.

Geoslides Photography

4 Christian Fields, London SW16 3JZ
☎020 8764 6292
Fax020 8764 6292/0115 9819418
Email geoslides@geo-group.demon.co.uk

Contact *John Douglas*

Established in 1968. Landscape and human interest subjects from the Arctic, Antarctica, Scandinavia, UK, Africa (south of Sahara), Middle East, Asia (south and southeast); also Australia, via Blackwoods Picture Library. Also specialist collections of images from British India (the Raj) and Boer War.

Getty Images (incorporating Tony Stone Images & The Hulton Getty Collection)

101 Bayham Street, London NW1 0AG
☎020 7544 3333 Fax 020 7544 3334
Email info@getty-images.com
Website www.tonystone.co.uk

Contact *Sales Dept.*

With over 15 million images, the collection is the largest picture resource in Europe with images from ancient history through the early years of photography up to the present day. As well as many old newspaper archives, the extensive contemporary collections cover lifestyles, travel, science, business.

Lynn Goldsmith

See **Corbis Images**

Martin and Dorothy Grace

40 Clipstone Avenue, Mapperley, Nottingham NG3 5JZ
☎0115 9208248 Fax 0115 9626802
Email graces@lineone.net

Colour coverage of Britain's natural history, specialising in trees, shrubs and wild flowers. Also ferns, birds and butterflies, habitats, landscapes, ecology.

Ronald Grant Archive

See **The Cinema Museum**

Sally and Richard Greenhill

357 Liverpool Road, London N1 1NL
☎020 7607 8549 Fax 020 7607 7151
Email rg@shadow.org.uk
Website www.shadow.org.uk/photolibrary

Photo Librarian *Denise Lalonde*

Social documentary photography in colour and b&w of working lives: pregnancy and birth, child development, education, work, old people, medical, urban. Also modern China 1971 to the present; most London statues. Some material from Borneo, USA, India, Israel, Philippines and Sri Lanka.

V. K. Guy Ltd

Silver Birches, Troutbeck, Windermere, Cumbria LA23 1PN
☎015394 33519 Fax 015394 32971

Contacts *Vic Guy, Pauline Guy, Mike Guy, Paul Guy, Nicola Guy*

British landscapes and architectural heritage. 20,000 5 × 4″ transparencies, suitable for tourism brochures, calendars, etc. Colour catalogue available.

Angela Hampton 'Family Life Picture Library'

Holly Tree House, The Street, Walberton, Arundel, West Sussex BN18 0PH
☎01243 555952/07880 550653 (mobile)
Fax 01243 555952

Contact *Angela Hampton*

Over 50,000 transparencies on all aspects of contemporary lifestyle, including pregnancy, childbirth, babies, children, parenting, behaviour, education, medical, holidays, pets, family life, relationships, teenagers, women and men's health, over-50's and retirement. Also comprehensive stock on domestic and farm animal life. Isle of Wight travel pictures in 35mm. Commissions undertaken. Offers fully illustrated text packages on most subjects and welcomes ideas for collaboration from writers with proven, successful background.

Tom Hanley

61 Stephendale Road, London SW6 2LT
☎020 7731 3525 Fax 020 7731 3525
Email Tomhanley@londonoffice.co.uk
Website www.eoffers.com

Colour and b&w coverage of London, England, Europe, Canada, India, the Philippines, Brazil, China, Japan, Korea, Taiwan, the Seychelles, Cayman Islands, USA. Also pop artists of the '60s, First World War trenches, removal of London Bridge to America, and much more. Current preoccupation with Greece, Turkey, Spain and Egypt, ancient and modern.

Robert Harding Picture Library

58–59 Great Marlborough Street, London W1V 1DD
☎020 7478 4000 Fax 020 7631 1070
Email info@robertharding.com
Website www.robertharding.com

A leading source of stock photography with over two million colour images covering a wide range of subjects – worldwide travel and culture, geography and landscapes, people and lifestyle, architecture, business and industry, medicine, sports, food and drink. Can supply images as transparencies, on CD or ISDN. Visitors welcome; telephone or visit the website.

Dennis Hardley Photography, Scottish Photo Library

Rosslynn, Benderloch, Oban, Argyll PA37 1ST
☎01631 720434 Fax 01631 720434
Email dennishardley@sol.co.uk

Contacts *Dennis Hardley, Tony Hardley*
Websites www.scottishphotographic.com *and* www.englishphotographic.com
ESTABLISHED 1974. About 30,000 images (6x7, 6x9 format colour transparencies) of Scotland: castles, historic, scenic landscapes, islands, transport, etc. Also English views – Liverpool, Chester, Bath, Weston Super Mare, Sussex, Somerset and Cambridge.

Jim Henderson Photographer & Publisher

Crooktree, Kincardine O'Neil, Aboyne, Aberdeenshire AB34 4JD
☎01339 882149 Fax 01339 882149
Email JHende7868@aol.com
Website www.sldirect.co.uk/jhenderson/

Contact *Jim Henderson, AMPA, ARPS*

Scenic and general activity coverage of the north east Scotland/Grampian region and Highlands for tourist, holiday and activity illustration. Specialist collection of over 100 Aurora Borealis displays from 1989–1999 in Grampian and co-author of *The Aurora* (pub. 1997). Large collection of recent images of Egypt: Cairo through to Abu-Simbel. Commissions undertaken.

Heritage and Natural History Photographic Library

37 Plainwood Close, Summersdale, Chichester, West Sussex PO19 4YB
☎01243 533822 Fax 01243 533822

Contact *Dr John B. Free*

Specialises in insects (particularly bees and beekeeping), tropical and temperate agriculture and crops, archaeology and history worldwide.

John Heseltine Picture Library

Mill Studio, Frogmarsh Mill, South Woodchester, Gloucestershire GL5 5ET
☎01453 873792 Fax 01453 873793
Email Johnhes@aol.com
Website www.heseltine.co.uk

Contact *John Heseltine*

Over 100,000 colour transparencies of landscapes, architecture, food and travel with particular emphasis on Italy and the UK.

Christopher Hill Photographic Library

17 Clarence Street, Belfast BT2 8DY
☎028 9024 5038 Fax 028 9023 1942
Email ChrisHillPhotographic@btinternet.com
Website www.scenic-ireland.com

Contact *Christopher Hill*

A comprehensive collection of landscapes of Northern Ireland, from Belfast to the Giant's Causeway, updated daily. Images of farming, food and industry. 'We will endeavour to supply images overnight.'

Hobbs Golf Collection

5 Winston Way, New Ridley, Stocksfield, Northumberland NE43 7RF
☎01661 842933 Fax 01661 842933
Email hobbs.golf@btinternet.com

Contact *Michael Hobbs*

Specialist golf collection: players, courses, art, memorabilia and historical topics (1300–present). 40,000+ images – mainly 35mm colour transparencies and b&w prints. Commissions undertaken. Author of 30 golf books.

David Hoffman Photo Library

21 Norman Grove, London E3 5EG
☎020 8981 5041 Fax 020 8980 2041
Email info:hoffmanphotos.demon.co.uk
Website www.hoffmanphotos.demon.co.uk

Contact *David Hoffman*

Commissioned photography and stock library with a strong emphasis on social issues built up from 35mm journalistic and documentary work dating from the late 1970s. Files on drugs and drug use, policing, disorder, riots, major strikes, youth protest, homelessness, housing, environmental demonstrations and events, waste disposal, alternative energy, industry and pollution. Wide range of images especially from UK and Europe but also USA, Canada,

Venezuela and Thailand. General files on topical issues and current affairs plus specialist files from leisure cycling to local authority services.

Holt Studios International Ltd

The Courtyard, 24 High Street, Hungerford, Berkshire RG17 0NF
☎01488 683523 Fax 01488 683511
Email library@holt-studios.co.uk
Website www.holt-studios.co.uk

Director *Nigel Cattlin*

Specialist photo library covering world agriculture, horticulture, gardens and gardening from pictorial and technical aspects. Worldwide assignments undertaken.

The Bill Hopkins Collection

See **The Special Photographers Library**

Houghton's Horses/Kit Houghton Photography

Radlet Cottage, Spaxton, Bridgwater, Somerset TA5 1DE
☎01278 671362 Fax 01278 671739
Email kit@enterprise.net

Contacts *Kit Houghton, Debbie Cook*

Specialist equestrian library of over 200,000 transparencies on all aspects of the horse world, with images ranging from the romantic to the practical, step-by-step instructional and competition pictures in all equestrian disciplines worldwide. Online picture delivery with ISDN facility.

Houses and Interiors

192 Goswell Road, London EC1V 7DT
☎020 7253 0991 Fax 020 7253 0992

Manager *Victoria Norman*

Stylish house interiors and exteriors, home dossiers, renovations, architectural details, interior design, gardens, houseplants and cookery. Also step-by-step photographic sequences of DIY subjects and gardening techniques. Large format and 35mm. Member of **BAPLA**.

Chris Howes/Wild Places Photography

51 Timbers Square, Roath, Cardiff CF24 3SH
☎029 2048 6557 Fax 029 2048 6557
Email photos@wildplaces.co.uk

Contacts *Chris Howes, Judith Calford*

Expanding collection of over 50,000 colour transparencies and b&w prints covering travel, topography and natural history worldwide, plus action sports such as climbing. *Specialist areas* include caves, caving and mines (with historical coverage using engravings and early photographs), wildlife, landscapes and the environment, including pollution and conservation. Europe (including Britain), USA, Africa and Australia are all well represented within the collection. Commissions undertaken.

Hulton Deutsch
See **Corbis Images**

The Hulton Getty Picture Collection
See **Getty Images**

Huntley Film Archive
78 Mildmay Park, Islington, London N1 4PR
☎020 7923 0990 Fax 020 7241 4929
Email films@huntleyarchives.com
Website www.huntleyarchives.com

Contact *Amanda Huntley*

Originally a private collection, the library is now a comprehensive archive of rare and vintage documentary film dating from 1895. 30,000–35,000 films on all subjects of a documentary nature, plus 50,000 feature film stills. Hollywood and the British film studios plus a television archive of rare stills and films.

Jacqui Hurst
66 Richford Street, Hammersmith, London W6 7HP
☎020 8743 2315/07970 781336 (mobile)
Fax 020 8735 0382

Contact *Jacqui Hurst*

A specialist library of traditional and contemporary designers and crafts, regional food producers and markets. The photos form illustrated essays of how something is made and finish with a still life of the completed object. The collection is always being extended and a list is available on request. Commissions undertaken.

Hutchison Picture Library
118B Holland Park Avenue, London W11 4UA
☎020 7229 2743 Fax 020 7792 0259
Email library@hutchisonpic.demon.co.uk

Worldwide contemporary images from the straight-forward to the esoteric and quirky. With over half a million documentary colour photographs on file and more than 200 photographers continually adding new work, this is an ever-growing resource covering people, places, customs and faiths, agriculture, industry and transport. *Special collections* include the environ-ment and climate, family life (including pregnancy and birth), ethnic minorities worldwide (including Disappearing World archive), conventional and alternative medicine, and music around the world. Search service available.

Illustrated London News Picture Library
20 Upper Ground, London SE1 9PF
☎020 7805 5585 Fax 020 7805 5905
Email iln.pictures@seacontainers.com

Engravings, photographs and illustrations from 1842 to the present day, taken from magazines published by Illustrated Newspapers: *Illustrated London News; Graphic; Sphere; Tatler; Sketch; Illustrated Sporting and Dramatic News; Illustrated War News 1914–18; Bystander; Britannia & Eve.* Social history, London, Industrial Revolution, wars, travel. Brochure available. Visitors by appointment.

The Image Bank
17 Conway Street, London W1P 6EE
☎020 7312 0300 Fax 020 7391 9111
Website www.imagebank.co.uk

4 Jordan Street, Manchester M15 4PY
☎0161 236 9226 Fax 0161 236 8723

57 Melville Street, Edinburgh EH3 7HL
☎0131 225 1770 Fax 0131 225 1660

11 Upper Mount Street, Dublin 2
☎00 353 1 676 0872 Fax 00 353 1 676 0873

Contact, London *Jo Rees*
Contact, Manchester *Rowan Young*
Contact, Edinburgh *Roddy McRae*
Contact, Dublin *Brid Harrington*

Contemporary and archival stock photography, illustration and footage with over 20 million constantly updated images. Visit and search the full digital library or call for free catalogue.

Images Colour Library/ Landscape Only
Ramillies House, 1–2 Ramillies Street, London W1V 1DF
☎020 7734 7344 Fax 020 7287 3933

15/17 High Court Lane, The Calls, Leeds, West Yorkshire LS2 7EU
☎0113 2433389 Fax 0113 2425605

A general contemporary library specialising in top-quality advertising, editorial and travel photography. Catalogues available. Visitors welcome. Also holds the Landscape Only collection featuring the work of top photographers Charlie Waite, Nick Meers, Joe Cornish and many others.

Images of Africa Photobank

11 The Windings, Lichfield, Staffordshire
WS13 7EX
☎01543 262898 Fax 01543 417154
Email info@imagesofafrica.co.uk

Contact *Jacquie Shipton*
Owner *David Keith Jones, FRPS*

Over 135,000 images covering 14 African
countries: Botswana, Egypt, Ethiopia, Kenya,
Malawi, Namibia, Rwanda, South Africa,
Swaziland, Tanzania, Uganda, Zaire, Zambia
and Zimbabwe. 'Probably the best collection
of photographs of Kenya in Europe.' Wide
range of topics covered. Particularly strong on
African wildlife with over 80 species of mammals including many sequences showing action
and behaviour. Popular animals like lions and
elephants are covered in encyclopedic detail.
More than 100 species of birds and many reptiles are included. Other strengths include
National Parks & Reserves, natural beauty,
tourism facilities, traditional and modern people. Most work is by David Keith Jones, FRPS;
several other photographers are represented.
Colour brochure available.

Images of India

See **Link Picture Library**

Imperial War Museum Photograph Archive

All Saints Annexe, Austral Street, London
SE1 4SL
☎020 7416 5333 Fax 020 7416 5355
Email photos@iwm.org.uk
Website www.iwm.org.uk

A national archive of over six million photographs illustrating all aspects of 20th century
conflict. Emphasis on the two world wars but
includes material from other conflicts involving
Britain and the Commonwealth. Majority of
material is b&w, although holdings of colour
material increases with more recent conflicts.
Visitors welcome by appointment, Mon–Fri,
10.00 am. to 5.00 pm.

International Photobank

Loscombe Barn Farmhouse, West Knighton,
Dorchester, Dorset DT2 8LS
☎01305 854145 Fax 01305 853065

Over 360,000 transparencies, mostly medium-
format. Colour coverage of travel subjects:
places, people, folklore, events. Assignments
undertaken for guide books and brochure photography.

The Isle of Wight Photo Library

The Old Rectory, Calbourne, Isle of Wight
PO30 4JE
☎01983 531247 Fax 01983 531253

Contact *The Librarian*

Stock material represents all that is best on the
Isle of Wight – landscapes, seascapes, architecture, gardens, boats.

Robbie Jack Photography

45 Church Road, Hanwell, London W7 3BD
☎020 8567 9616 Fax 020 8567 9616
Email rjackphoto@aol.com

Contact *Robbie Jack*

Built up over the last 17 years, the library contains over 300,000 colour transparencies of the
performing arts – theatre, dance, opera and
music. Includes West End shows, the RSC and
Royal National Theatre productions, English
National Opera and Royal Opera. The dance
section contains images of the Royal Ballet,
English National Ballet, the Rambert Dance
Company, plus many foreign companies. Also
holds the largest selection of colour material from
the Edinburgh International Festival. Researchers are welcome to visit by appointment.

Jayawardene Travel Photo Library

7A Napier Road, Wembley, Middlesex
HA0 4UA
☎020 8902 3588 Fax 020 8902 7114
Email rjayawarde@aol.com
Website members.aol.com/rjayawarde

Contact *Rohith Jayawardene*

170,000 colour transparencies of travel and
travel-related subjects, covering countries worldwide. Most places have been photographed in
depth, with more than 600 images per destination. Shot in 35mm and medium format and
regularly updated. Commissions undertaken.
Contributing photographers welcome (please
telephone first) – minimum initial submission:
200 transparencies.

Trevor Jones Thoroughbred Photography

The Hornbeams, 2 The Street, Worlington,
Suffolk IP28 8RU
☎01638 713944 Fax 01638 713945
Email trevorjones@thorobredphoto.co.uk

Contacts *Trevor Jones, Gill Jones*

Extensive library of high-quality colour transparencies depicting all aspects of thoroughbred
horse racing dating from 1987. Major group
races, English classics, studs, stallions, mares and

foals, early morning scenes, personalities, jockeys, trainers and prominent owners. Also international work: USA Breeders Cup, Arc de Triomphe, French Classics, Irish Derby, Dubai racing scene, Japan Cup and Hokkaido stud farms; and more unusual scenes such as racing on the sands at low tide, Ireland, and on the frozen lake at St Moritz. Visitors by appointment.

Katz Pictures

Zetland House, 5–25 Scrutton Street, London EC2A 4HJ
☎020 7377 5888   Fax 020 7613 1274
Email katzpictures@katzpictures.com

Contact *Alyson Whalley*

Contains an extensive collection of colour and b&w material covering a multitude of subjects from around the world – business, environment, industry, lifestyles, politics plus celebrity portraits from the entertainment world. Also Hollywood portraits and film stills dating back to the twenties. Represents *Life* and *Time* magazines for syndication in the UK and can offer a complete selection of material spanning over 50 years; also the Mansell Collection.

David King Collection

90 St Pauls Road, London N1 2QP
☎020 7226 0149   Fax 020 7354 8264

Contact *David King*

250,000 b&w original and copy photographs and colour transparencies of historical and present-day images. Russian history and the Soviet Union from 1900 to the fall of Khrushchev; the lives of Lenin, Trotsky and Stalin; the Tzars, Russo-Japanese War, 1917 Revolution, World War I, Red Army, the Great Purges, Great Patriotic War, etc. Special collections on China, Eastern Europe, the Weimar Republic, John Heartfield, American labour struggles, Spanish Civil War. Open to qualified researchers by appointment, Monday to Friday, 10.00 am – 6.00 pm. Staff will undertake research; negotiable fee for long projects. David King's latest photographic book, *The Commissar Vanishes*, documents the falsification of photographs and art in Stalin's Russia.

The Kobal Collection

4th Floor, 184 Drummond Street, London NW1 3HP
☎020 7383 0011   Fax 020 7383 0044

Colour and b&w coverage of Hollywood films: portraits, stills, publicity shots, posters, ephemera. Visitors by appointment.

Kos Picture Source Ltd

7 Spice Court, Ivory Square, Plantation Wharf, London SW11 3UE
☎020 7801 0044   Fax 020 7801 0055
Email images@kospictures.com
Website www.kospictures.com

Specialists in water-related images including international yacht racing and cruising, classic boats and superyachts, and extensive range of watersports. Also worldwide travel including seascapes, beach scenes, underwater photography and the weather.

La Casa Photos

PO Box One, Newtown, Powys SY16 2WP
☎01686 621421   Fax 01686 621421
Email lacasa@clara.net
Website www.lacasa.clara.net

Contact *Mike Slater*

Specialist collection of photo-art images, abstract colour and form; close-up nature photography. Available as transparencies and also supplied as prints, including framed prints of any size.

Landscape Only
See **Images Colour Library**

Frank Lane Picture Agency Ltd

Pages Green House, Wetheringsett, Stowmarket, Suffolk IP14 5QA
☎01728 860789   Fax 01728 860222
Email pictures@flpa-images.co.uk
Website www.flpa-images.co.uk

Colour and b&w coverage of natural history, environment, pets and weather. Represents Sunset from France, Foto Natura from Holland and works closely with Eric and David Hosking, plus 270 freelance photographers.

Last Resort Picture Library

Manvers Studios, 12 Ollerton Road, Tuxford, Newark, Nottinghamshire NG22 0LF
☎01777 870166   Fax 01777 871739
Email LRPL@dmimaging.co.uk
Website www.dmimaging.co.uk

Contact *Jo Makin*

Images of agriculture, architecture, education, landscape, industry, food, people at work, computing and new technology. Images cover a wide variety of areas rather than specialising, ranging from the everyday to the obscure.

LAT Photographic

Somerset House, Somerset Road, Teddington TW11 8RU
☎020 8251 3000   Fax 020 8251 3001

Email digital@latphoto.co.uk
Website www.latphoto.co.uk

Motor sport collection of over seven million images dating from 1920 to the present day.

André Laubier Picture Library

4 St James Park, Bath BA1 2SS
☎01225 420688 Fax 01225 420688

Extensive library of photographs from 1935 to the present day in 35mm- and medium-format. Main subjects: archaeology and architecture, art and artists (wood carving, sculptures, contemporary glass), botany, historical buildings, sites and events, landscapes, nature, leisure sports, events, experimental artwork and photography, people and travel. Substantial stock of many other subjects including: birds, buildings and cities, folklore, food and drink, gardens, transport. Special collection: Images d'Europe (Austria, Britain, France, Greece, Italy, Spain, Turkey, former Yugoslavia, S.W. Ireland and Norway). Private collection: World War II to D-Day. List available on request. Photo assignments, artwork, design, line drawings undertaken. Correspondence welcome in English, French or German.

Lebrecht Music Collection

58b Carlton Hill, London NW8 0ES
☎020 7625 5341/7372 8233
Fax 020 7625 5341
Email pictures@lebrecht.co.uk
Website www.lebrecht.co.uk

Contact Elbie Lebrecht

50,000 prints and transparencies covering classical music, from antiquity to 21st century minimalists. Instruments, opera singers, concert halls and opera houses, composers and musicians.

The Erich Lessing Archive of Fine Art & Culture

c/o AKG London Ltd, The Arts and History Picture Library, 5 Melbray Mews, 158 Hurlingham Road, London SW6 3NS
☎020 7610 6103 Fax 020 7610 6125
Email enquiries@akg-london.co.uk
Website www.akg-london.co.uk

Computerised archive of large-format transparencies depicting the contents of many of the world's finest art galleries as well as ancient archaeological and biblical sites. CD-ROM available. Represented by AKG London Ltd.

Life File Ltd

76 Streathbourne Road, London SW17 8QY
☎020 8767 8832 Fax 020 8672 8879
Website simontaylor@attglobal.net

Contact Simon Taylor

300,000 images of people and places, lifestyles, industry, environmental issues, natural history and customs, from Afghanistan to Zimbabwe. Stocks most of the major tourist destinations throughout the world, including the UK.

Lindley Library, Royal Horticultural Society

80 Vincent Square, London SW1P 2PE
☎020 7821 3603 Fax 020 7828 3022

Contact Jennifer Vine

18,000 original drawings and approx. 8000 books with hand-coloured plates of botanical illustrations. Appointment is absolutely essential; all photography is done by own photographer.

Link Picture Library

33 Greyhound Road, London W6 8NH
☎020 7381 2261/2433 Fax 020 7385 6244
Email lib@linkpics.demon.co.uk
Website www.linkphotographers.com

Contacts Orde Eliason

100,000 images of South Africa, India, China, Vietnam and Israel. A more general collection of colour transparencies from 100 countries worldwide. Link Picture Library and its partner, Images of India, has an international network and can source material not in its file from Japan, USA, Holland, Scandinavia, Germany and South Africa. Original photographic commissions undertaken.

London Aerial Photo Library

PO Box 25, Ashwellthorpe, Norwich, Norfolk NR16 1HL
☎01508 488320 Fax 01508 488282
Email aerialphotos@btinternet.com
Website www.londonaerial.co.uk

Contact Sandy Stockwell

80,000 colour negatives of aerial photographs covering most of Britain, with particular emphasis on London and surrounding counties. No search fee. Photocopies of library prints are supplied free of charge to enquirers. Welcomes enquiries in respect of either general subjects or specific sites and buildings.

The London Film Archive

78 Mildmay Park, Islington, London N1 4PR
☎020 7923 4074 Fax 020 7241 4929
Email info@londonfilmarchive.org
Website www.londonfilmarchive.org

Contact Robert Dewar

Archive which concentrates on all aspects of

commercial, political and social life in the City and suburbs of London. The collection is primarily a film collection but also has stills, glass plate negatives, posters, advertising and documents of London interest.

London Metropolitan Archives

40 Northampton Road, London EC1R 0HB
☎020 7332 3820 Fax 020 7833 9136
Email ask.lma@corpoflondon.gov.uk
Website
www.cityoflondon.gov.uk/archives/lma

Contact *The Senior Librarian*

Approximately 500,000 images of London, mostly topographical and architectural. Subjects include education, local authority housing, transport, the Thames, parks, churches, hospitals, war damage, pubs, theatres and cinemas. Also major redevelopments like the South Bank, The City, Covent Garden and Docklands.

London Transport Museum Photographic Library

39 Wellington Street, London WC2E 7BB
☎020 7379 6344 Fax 020 7565 7252
Website www.ltmuseum.co.uk

Contacts *Hugh Robertson, Simon Murphy, Martin Harrison-Putnam*

Around 100,000 b&w images from the 1860s and 10,000 colour images from c.1975. *Specialist collections* Poster archive, Underground construction, corporate design and architecture, street scenes, London Transport during the war. Collection available for viewing by appointment on Monday and Tuesday. No loans system but prints and transparences can be purchased.

Lonely Planet Images

See **Lonely Planet Publications** under **UK Publishers**

The Ludvigsen Library Limited

73 Collier Street, London N1 9BE
☎020 7837 1700 Fax 020 7837 1776
Email library@ludvigsen.com
Website www.ludvigsen.com

Contact *Paul Parker*

Approximately 400,000 images (both b&w and many colour transparencies) of automobiles and motorsport, from 1920s through 1980s. Glass plate negatives from the early 1900s; Formula One, Le Mans, motor car shows, vintage, antique and classic cars from all countries. Includes the Dalton-Watson Collection and

noted photographers such as John Dugdale, Edward Eves, Peter Keen, Max le Grand, Karl Ludvigsen, Rodolfo Mailander, Ove Nielsen, Stanley Rosenthall and others. Extensive information research facilities for writers and publishers.

MacQuitty International Photographic Collection

7 Elm Lodge, River Gardens, Stevenage Road, London SW6 6NZ
☎020 7385 5606 Fax 020 7385 5606
Email miranda.macquitty@btinternet.com

Contact *Dr Miranda MacQuitty*

Colour and b&w collection on aspects of life in over 70 countries: dancing, music, religion, death, archaeology, buildings, transport, food, drink, nature. Visitors by appointment.

Magnum Photos Ltd

Moreland Buildings, 2nd Floor, 5 Old Street, London EC1V 9HL
☎020 7490 1771 Fax 020 7608 0020
Email magnum@magnumphotos.co.uk
Website www.magnumphotos.com

Head of Library *Hamish Crooks*

FOUNDED 1947 by Cartier Bresson, George Rodger, Robert Capa and David 'Chim' Seymour. Represents over 50 of the world's leading photo-journalists. Coverage of all major world events from the Spanish Civil War to present day. Also a large collection of personalities.

The Raymond Mander & Joe Mitchenson Theatre Collection

The Mansion, Beckenham Place Park, Beckenham, Kent BR3 2BP
☎020 8658 7725 Fax 020 8663 0313

Contact *Richard Mangan*

Enormous collection covering all aspects of the theatre: plays, actors, dramatists, music hall, theatres, singers, composers, etc. Visitors welcome by appointment.

Mansell Collection

See **Katz Pictures**

S & O Mathews Photography

The Old Rectory, Calbourne, Isle of Wight PO30 4JE
☎01983 531247 Fax 01983 531253

Library of colour transparencies of gardens, plants and landscapes.

Institution of Mechanical Engineers
1 Birdcage Walk, London SW1H 9JJ
☎020 7973 1265 Fax 020 7222 4557
Email k_moore@imeche.org.uk
Website www.imeche.org.uk
Senior Librarian & Archivist *Keith Moore*

Historical and contemporary images on mechanical engineering. Open 9.15 am to 5.30 pm, Mon. to Fri. Telephone for appointment.

Medimage
32 Brooklyn Road, Coventry CV1 4JT
☎024 7666 8562 Fax 024 7666 8562
Email chambersking@clara.co.uk
Contacts *Anthony King, Catherine King*

Medium format colour transparencies of Mediterranean countries covering a wide range of subjects – agriculture, archaeology, architecture, arts, crafts, education, festivals, flora, geography, history, industry, landscapes, markets, recreation, seascapes, sports and transport. The collection is added to on a regular basis and photographic commissions are undertaken. No search fees. Pictures by other photographers not accepted.

Meledin Collection
See **Mary Evans Picture Library**

Lee Miller Archives
Farley Farm House, Chiddingly, Near Lewes, East Sussex BN8 6HW
☎01825 872691 Fax 01825 872733
Email archives@leemiller.co.uk
Website www.leemiller.co.uk

The work of Lee Miller (1907–77). As a photojournalist she covered the war in Europe from early in 1944 to VE Day with further reporting from the Balkans. Collection includes photographic portraits of prominent Surrealist artists: Ernst, Eluard, Miró, Picasso, Penrose, Tanning, Carrington, and others. Surrealist and contemporary art, poets and writers, fashion, the Middle East, Egypt, the Balkans in the 1930s, London during the Blitz, war in Europe and the liberation of Dachau and Buchenwald.

Mirror Syndication International
22nd Floor, 1 Canada Square, Canary Wharf, London E14 5AP
☎020 7293 3700 Fax 020 7293 2712
Email desk@mirpix.com
Website www.mirrorpix.com
Managing Director *Frank Walker*

Major photo library specialising in current affairs, personalities, royalty, sport, pop and glamour, plus extensive British and world travel pictures. Major motion picture archive up to 1965. Agents for Mirror Group Newspapers. Syndicator of photos and text for news/features.

Monitor Syndication
17 Old Street, London EC1V 9HL
☎020 7253 7071 Fax 020 7250 0966

Colour and b&w coverage of leading international personalities. Politics, entertainment, royals, judicial, commerce, religion, trade unions, well-known buildings. Also an archive library dating back to 1840, and a specialist file on Lotus cars. Syndication to international, national and local media.

Moroccan Scapes
Seend Park, Seend, Wiltshire SN12 6NZ
☎01380 828533 Fax 01380 828630
Email chris@morocco-travel.com
Contact *Chris Lawrence*

Specialist collection of Moroccan material: scenery, towns, people, markets and places, plus the Atlas Mountains. Over 16,000 images.

Motoring Picture Library
National Motor Museum, Beaulieu, Hampshire SO42 7ZN
☎01590 614656 Fax 01590 612655
Email nmmt@compuserve.com
Contact *Jonathan Day*

Three-quarters of a million b&w images, plus 80,000 colour transparencies covering all forms of motoring history from the 1880s to the present day. Commissions undertaken. Own studio.

Mountain Camera
See **John Cleare**

Moving Image Communications
61 Great Titchfield Street, London W1P 7FL
☎020 7580 3300 Fax 020 7580 2242
Email mail@milibrary.com
Website www.milibrary.com
Contact *Patrick Smith*

Over 11,350 hours of quality archive and contemporary footage, including: RSPB Film Library; TVAM Archive 1983–92, Leo & Mandy Dickinson Action & Adventure Sports Archive, The Lonely Planet (TV travel series); Shark Bay Films (tropical and sub-aqua); British Tourist Authority – BTA (1930 to present-day); TIDA Public Information Films (BTA's predecessory); Buff Films (aviation archive/NATO planes and ships); Drummer Films (travel classics, 1950–70); British Airways; Universal Newsreels (1950s-60s); Medical Technology; The Freud Archive (1930–39); Natural World; Stockshots (timelapse, cityscapes, land and seascapes, chroma-key); Space Exploration (NASA); WPA Film Library (America's most extensive film library).

Museum of Antiquities Picture Library

University and Society of Antiquaries of Newcastle upon Tyne, Newcastle upon Tyne NE1 7RU
☎0191 222 7846 Fax 0191 222 8561
Email m.o.antiquities@ncl.ac.uk
Website www.ncl.ac.uk/antiquities

Contact *Lindsay Allason-Jones*

25,000 images, mostly b&w, of special collections including: Hadrian's Wall Archive (b&ws taken over the last 100 years); Gertrude Bell Archive (during her travels in the Near East, 1900–26); and aerial photographs of archaeological sites in the North of England. Visitors welcome by appointment.

Museum of London Picture Library

150 London Wall, London EC2Y 5HN
☎020 7814 5604 Fax 020 7600 1058
Email picturelib@museumoflondon.org.uk

The Museum of London Picture Library tells the story of London from its earliest settlers to the present day. Suffragettes: photographs and memorabilia; Museum Objects: gallery and reserve collections – Prehistoric, Roman, Saxon, Medieval, Stuart, Georgian, Victorian, London Now; Photographs: social history of the capital – working life, East End, inter-war years, the Blitz, post-war; Prints and Caricatures: political and social satire, architecture; Paintings: dating from the 17th century, portraits, landscapes, cityscapes.

National Galleries of Scotland Picture Library

The Dean Gallery, Belford Road, Edinburgh EH4 3DS
☎0131 624 6258/6260 Fax 0131 623 7135
Email picture.library@natgalscot.ac.uk

Contacts *Deborah Hunter, Helen Nicoll*

Over 30,000 b&w and several thousand images in colour of works of art from the Renaissance to present day. Specialist subjects cover fine art (painting, sculpture, drawing), portraits, Scottish, historical, still life, photography and landscape. Colour leaflet, scale of charges and application forms available on request.

National Maritime Museum Picture Library

Greenwich, London SE10 9NF
☎020 8312 6631/6704 Fax 020 8312 6533
Website www.nmm.ac.uk

Contacts *David Taylor, Eleanor Heron*

Over three million maritime-related images and artefacts, including oil paintings from the 16th century to present day, prints and drawings, historic photographs, plans of ships built in the UK since the beginning of the 18th century, models, rare maps and charts, instruments, etc. Over 50,000 items in the collection are now photographed and with the Historic Photographs Collection form the basis of the library's stock.

National Medical Slide Bank

See **Wellcome Trust Medical Photographic Library**

National Meteorological Library and Archive

See entry under **Library Services**

National Monuments Record

National Monuments Record Centre, Kemble Drive, Swindon, Wiltshire SN2 2GZ
☎01793 414600 Fax 01793 414606
Email info@rchme.gov.uk
Website www.english-heritage.org.uk

The first stop for photographs and information on England's heritage. Over 12 million photographs, documents and drawings are held. English architecture from the first days of photography to the present, air photographs covering every inch of England from the first days of flying to the present, and archaeological sites. The record is now the public archive of English Heritage and includes the material gathered by the Royal Commission on the Historical Monuments of England in its 90-year history. The London office specialises in the architecture of the capital city – for more information phone 020 7208 8200.

National Portrait Gallery Picture Library

St Martin's Place, London WC2H 0HE
☎020 7312 2473/4/5/6 Fax 020 7312 2464
Email picturelibrary@npg.org.uk
Website www.npg.org.uk

Contact *Tom Morgan*

Access to over 700,000 portraits of famous British men and women dating from the middle ages to the present. Images can be searched and viewed on the website.

National Railway Museum Picture Library

Leeman Road, York YO26 4XJ
☎01904 621261 Fax 01904 611112
Email nrm@nmsi.ac.uk
Website www.nrm.org.uk

1.5 million images, mainly b&w, covering every aspect of railways from 1866 to the present day. Visitors by appointment.

The National Trust Photo Library

36 Queen Anne's Gate, London SW1H 9AS
☎020 7447 6788/9 Fax 020 7447 6767
Email photolibrary@ntrust.org.uk
Website www.nationaltrust.org.uk/photolibrary

Contact *Ed Gibbons*

Collection of mixed-format transparencies covering landscape and coastline throughout England, Wales and Northern Ireland; also architecture, interiors, gardens, paintings and conservation, plus a new collection of wildlife photographs. Award-winning brochure available on request. Profits from the picture library are reinvested in continuing the work of the Trust.

Natural History Museum Picture Library

Cromwell Road, London SW7 5BD
☎020 7938 9122 Fax 020 7938 9169
Email nhmpl@nhm.ac.uk
Website www.nhm.ac.uk/images

Contacts *Gwyneth Campling, Lodvina Mascarenhas*

12,000 large-format transparencies on natural history and related subjects: extinct animals, dinosaurs, fossils, anthropology, minerals, gemstones, fauna and flora. No wildlife pictures but many images of historic natural history art. Commissions of museum specimens undertaken.

Natural History Photographic Agency

See **NHPA**

Natural Science Photos

33 Woodland Drive, Watford, Hertfordshire WD1 3BY
☎01923 245265 Fax 01923 246067

Colour coverage of natural history subjects worldwide. The work of some 150 photographers, it includes angling, animals, birds, reptiles, amphibia, fish, insects and other invertebrates, habitats, plants, fungi, geography, weather, scenics, horticulture, agriculture, farm animals and registered dog breeds. Researched by experienced scientists Peter and Sondra Ward. Visits by appointment. Commissions undertaken.

Nature Photographers Ltd

West Wit, New Road, Little London, Tadley, Hampshire RG26 5EU
☎01256 850661 Fax 01256 851157
Email nature.photos@clara.net

Contact *Dr Paul Sterry*

Over 150,000 images on worldwide natural history and environmental subjects. The library is run by a trained biologist and experienced author on his subject.

Peter Newark's Pictures

3 Barton Buildings, Queen Square, Bath BA1 2JR
☎01225 334213 Fax 01225 480554

Over one million images covering world history from ancient times to the present day. Includes an extensive military collection of photographs, paintings and illustrations. Also a special collection on American history covering Colonial times, exploration, social, political and the Wild West and Native-Americans in particular. Subject list available. Visitors welcome by appointment.

NHPA (Natural History Photographic Agency)

Little Tye, 57 High Street, Ardingly, West Sussex RH17 6TB
☎01444 892514 Fax 01444 892168
Email nhpa@nhpa.co.uk
Website www.nhpa.co.uk

Library Manager *Tim Harris*

Extensive coverage on all aspects of natural history – animals, plants, landscapes, environmental issues, gardens and pets. 120 photographers worldwide provide a steady input of high-quality transparencies. Specialist files include the unique high-speed photography of Stephen Dalton, extensive coverage of African and American wildlife, also rainforests, marine life and the polar regions. UK agents for the ANT collection of Australasian material. Loans are generally made direct to publishers; individual writers must request material via their publisher.

NRSC – Air Photo Group

Arthur Street, Barwell, Leicestershire LE9 8GZ

☎01455 849227 Fax 01455 841785

Contact *Joanne Burchnall*

Leading supplier of earth observation data, including satellite imagery, aerial photography and airborne remote sensing.

Odhams Periodicals Library

See **Popperfoto**

Only Horses Picture Agency

27 Greenway Gardens, Greenford, Middlesex UB6 9TU

☎020 8578 9047 Fax 020 8575 7244

Colour and b&w coverage of all aspects of the horse. Foaling, retirement, racing, show jumping, eventing, veterinary, polo, breeds, personalities.

Open University Photo Library

Room 163 A Block, Walton Hall, Milton Keynes MK7 6AA

☎01908 658408 Fax 01908 653313

Contact *Debbie Nicholls-Brien*

Education, industry and social welfare collection. 65,000 mainly b&w images dating from the early 1970s.

Oxford Picture Library

15 Curtis Yard, North Hinksey Lane, Oxford OX2 0LX

☎01865 723404 Fax 01865 725294

Email chris.andrews@virgin.net

Website www.chris-andrews-publications.co.uk

Contacts *Annabel Webb, Chris Andrews, Angus Palmer*

Specialist collection on Oxford: the city, university and colleges, events, people, spires and shires; the Cotswolds, architecture and landscape from Stratford-upon-Avon to Bath; the Thames and Chilterns, including Henley on Thames and Windsor; Channel Islands, especially Guernsey and Sark. Aerial views of all areas specified above. General collection includes wildlife, trees, plants, clouds, sun, sky, water and teddy bears. Commissions undertaken.

Oxford Scientific Films Photo Library

Lower Road, Long Hanborough, Oxfordshire OX8 8LL

☎01993 881881 Fax 01993 882808

Email photo.library@osf.uk.com

Website www.osf.uk.com

Senior Account Manager *Suzanne Aitzetmuller*

Account Managers *Tim Stentiford, Rebecca Warren*

Collection of 300,000 colour transparencies of wildlife and natural science images supplied by over 300 photographers worldwide, covering all aspects of wildlife plus landscapes, weather, seasons, plants, environment, anthropology, habitats, industry, space, creative textures and backgrounds, and geology. Macro and micro photography. UK agents for Animals Animals, USA, Okapia, Germany and Dinodia, India. Research by experienced researchers for specialist and creative briefs. Visits welcome, by appointment.

PA News Photo Library

PA News Centre, 292 Vauxhall Bridge Road, London SW1V 1AE

☎020 7963 7038/7039 Fax 020 7963 7066

Email paphotos.research@pa.press.net

Website www.pa.press.net/info/paphotos/main.html

PA News, the 24-hour national news and information group, offers public access to its photographic archives. Photographs, dating from 1890 to the present day, cover everything from news and sport to entertainment and royalty, with around 50 new pictures added daily. Personal callers welcome (10.00 am to 4.00 pm weekdays) or research undertaken by in-house staff.

PAL (Performing Arts Library)

First Floor, Production House, 25 Hackney Road, London E2 7NX

☎020 7749 4850 Fax 020 7749 4858

Email performingartspics@pobox.com

Website www.PerformingArtsLibrary.co.uk

Continually updated specialist image collection covering classical music, opera, theatre, musicals, instruments, festivals, venues, circus, ballet and contemporary dance. Almost one million images from late 19th century onwards. Please phone, fax or email to make a selection.

Hugh Palmer

Knapp House, Shenington, Near Banbury, Oxfordshire OX15 6NE

☎01295 670433 Fax 01295 670709

Email hupalmer@msn.com

Extensive coverage of gardens from Britain and Europe, as well as rural landscapes and architecture. Medium-format transparencies from numerous specialist commissions for books and magazines.

Panos Pictures
1 Chapel Court, Borough High Street, London SE1 1HH
☎020 7234 0010 Fax 020 7357 0094
Email pics@panos.co.uk
Website www.panos.co.uk
Documentary colour and b&w library specialising in Third World and Eastern Europe, with emphasis on environment and development issues. Leaflet available. Fifty per cent of all profits from this library go to the Panos Institute to further its work in international sustainable development.

Papilio Natural History & Travel Library
44 Palestine Grove, Merton, London SW19 2QN
☎020 8687 2202 Fax 020 8640 2011
Email justine@papilio.demon.co.uk
Website www.papilio.demon.co.uk
Contacts *Robert Pickett, Justine Bowler*

Over 100,000 colour transparencies of natural history, including birds, animals, insects, flowers, plants, fungi and landscapes; plus travel worldwide including people, places and cultures. Commissions undertaken. Colour catalogue and digital slide show on disk available; call for further information. Visits by appointment only.

Charles Parker Archive
See **Birmingham Library Services** under **Library Services**

Ann & Bury Peerless Picture Library
St David's, 22 King's Avenue, Minnis Bay, Birchington-on-Sea, Kent CT7 9QL
☎01843 841428 Fax 01843 848321
Contacts *Ann or Bury Peerless*

Specialist collection on world religions: Hinduism, Buddhism, Jainism, Christianity, Islam, Sikhism. Geographical areas covered: India, Afghanistan (Bamiyan Valley of the Buddhas), Pakistan, Bangladesh, Sri Lanka, Cambodia (Angkor Wat), Java (Borobudur), Bali, Thailand, Russia, Republic of China, Spain, Poland, Uzbekistan (Samarkand and Bukhara), Vietnam. 10,000 35mm colour transparencies.

Performing Arts Library
See **PAL**

Photo Resources
The Orchard, Marley Lane, Kingston, Canterbury, Kent CT4 6JH
☎01227 830075 Fax 01227 831135
Colour and b&w coverage of archaeology, art, ancient art, ethnology, mythology, world religion, museum objects.

Photofusion
17A Electric Lane, London SW9 8LA
☎020 7738 5774 Fax 020 7738 5509
Email library@photofusion.org
Website www.photofusion.org
Contact *Liz Somerville*

Colour and b&w coverage of contemporary social issues including babies and children, disability, education, the elderly, environment, family, health, housing, homelessness, people and work. Brochure available.

The Photographers' Library
81A Endell Street, London WC2H 9AJ
☎020 7836 5591 Fax 020 7379 4650
Email info@photographerslibrary.com
Covers people, lifestyles, commerce, holiday people, travel destinations, industry, landscapes, health. Brochure available.

The Photolibrary Wales
Bro-nant, Church Road, Pentyrch, Cardiff CF15 9QG
☎029 2089 0311 Fax 029 2089 2650
Email info@photo-lib-wales.co.uk
Website www.photo-lib-wales.co.uk
Contacts *Steve Benbow, Kate Benbow*

50,000 colour transparences covering all areas and subjects of Wales. Represents the work of 140 photographers, living and working in Wales.

Photos Horticultural
169 Valley Road, Ipswich, Suffolk IP1 4PJ
☎01473 257329 Fax 01473 233974
Email library@photos.keme.co.uk
Website www.photos-horticultural.co.uk
Wide coverage of gardens and all aspects of gardening from library established in 1968. Now incorporates the Kenneth Scowen Collection. 'Extensive travelling ensures the best material from around the world is on file.'.

PictureBank Photo Library Ltd
Parman House, 30–36 Fife Road, Kingston upon Thames, Surrey KT1 1SY
☎020 8547 2344 Fax 020 8974 5652
Over 400,000 colour transparencies covering

people, travel and scenic (UK and world), moods (sunsets, seascapes, deserts, etc.), industry and technology, environments and general. Commissions undertaken. Visitors welcome. Member of **BAPLA**. New material on medium/large format welcome.

Pictures Colour Library

4th Floor, The Italian Building, 41 Dockhead, London SE1 2BS
☎020 7252 3300 Fax 020 7252 3345
Email Researcher@PicturesColourLibrary.
  co.uk
Website www.PicturesColourLibrary.co.uk

Travel and travel-related images depicting lifestyles and cultures, people and places, attitudes and environments from around the world, including a comprehensive section on Great Britain.

H. G. Ponting

See **Popperfoto**

Popperfoto

The Old Mill, Overstone Farm, Overstone, Northampton NN6 0AB
☎01604 670670 Fax 01604 670635
Email popperfoto@msn.com
Website www.popperfoto.com

Home to over 14 million images, covering 150 years of photographic history. Renowned for its archival material, a world-famous sports library and stock photography. Popperfoto's credit line includes Reuters, Bob Thomas Sports Photography, UPI, Acme, INP, Planet, Paul Popper, Exclusive News Agency, Victory Archive, Odhams Periodicals Library, Illustrated, Harris Picture Agency, and H. G. Ponting which holds the Scott 1910–1912 Antarctic expedition. Colour from 1940, b&w from 1870 to the present. Major subjects covered worldwide include events, personalities, wars, royalty, sport, politics, transport, crime, history and social conditions. Material available on the same day to clients throughout the world. Mac-desk available. Researchers welcome by appointment. Free catalogue available.

PPL Photo Agency Ltd

Bookers Yard, The Street, Walberton, Arundel, West Sussex BN18 0PF
☎01243 555561 Fax 01243 555562
Email ppl@mistral.co.uk
Website www.pplmedia.com

Contacts *Barry Pickthall, Dave Giles, Lynne Fox*

Two million pictures of sailing and boating, watersports, travel, water and coastal scenes.

British Steel Multimedia Library – all aspects of steel and steel making. Construction, science and technology, transport, mining and industry.

Premaphotos Wildlife

Amberstone, 1 Kirland Road, Bodmin, Cornwall PL30 5JQ
☎01208 78258 Fax 01208 72302
Email premaphotos@compuserve.com
Website www.premaphotos.co.uk

Contact *Jean Preston-Mafham, Library Manager*

Natural history worldwide. Subjects include flowering and non-flowering plants, fungi, slime moulds, fruits and seeds, galls, leaf mines, seashore life, mammals, birds, reptiles, amphibians, insects, spiders, habitats, scenery and cultivated cacti. Commissions undertaken. Visitors welcome. 'Make sure your name is on our mailing list to receive regular, colourful mailers.'

Professional Sport UK Ltd

18–19 Shaftesbury Quay, Hertford, Hertfordshire SG14 1SF
☎01992 505000 Fax 01992 505020
Email pictures@prosport.co.uk
Website www.prosport.co.uk

Photographic coverage of tennis, soccer, athletics, golf, cricket, rugby, winter sports and many minor sports. Major international events including the Olympic Games, World Cup soccer and all Grand Slam tennis events. Also news and feature material supplied worldwide. Computerised library with in-house processing and studio facilities; photo transmission services available for editorial and advertising.

Public Record Office
Image Library

Ruskin Avenue, Kew, Richmond, Surrey TW9 4DU
☎020 8392 5225 Fax 020 8392 5266
Email image-library@pro.gov.uk

Contacts *Paul Johnson, Hugh Alexander*

British and colonial history from the Domesday Book to the 1960s, shown in photography, maps, illuminations, posters, advertisements, textiles and original manuscripts. Approximately 30,000 5 ×4″ and 35mm colour transparencies and b&w negatives. Open: 9.00 am to 5.30 pm, Monday to Friday.

Punch Cartoon Library

Trevor House, 100 Brompton Road, London SW3 1ER
☎020 7225 6710/6711 Fax 020 7225 6712
Email library@punch.co.uk

Owner *Liberty Publishing*
Library Manager *Miranda Taylor*

Gives access to the 500,000 cartoons published in *Punch* magazine between 1841–1992. The library has a 500+ subject listing and can search on any topic. Social history, politics, fashion, fads, famous people and more by the world's most famous cartoonists, including Tenniel, du Maurier, Pont, Fougasse, E. H. Shepard and Emett.

PWA International Ltd

City Gate House, 399–425 Eastern Avenue, Gants Hill, Ilford, Essex IG2 6LR
☎020 8518 2057 Fax 020 8518 2241
Email pwaint@dircon.co.uk

Contact *Terry Allen*

Leading comprehensive library of story illustrations comprising work by some of the UK's best-known illustrators, including book covers and magazines. Also over half a million images of beauty, cookery and craft.

Railfotos

Millbrook House Ltd., Unit 1, Oldbury Business Centre, Pound Road, Oldbury, West Midlands B68 8NA
☎0121 544 2970 Fax 0121 253 6836 (quote Millbrook House)

One of the largest specialist libraries dealing comprehensively with railway subjects worldwide. Colour and b&w dating from the turn of the century to present day. Up-to-date material on UK, South America and Far East. Visitors by appointment.

Redferns Music Picture Library

7 Bramley Road, London W10 6SZ
☎020 7792 9914 Fax 020 7792 0921
Email info@redferns.com
Website www.redferns.com

Music picture library covering every aspect of popular music from 1920's jazz to present day. Over 12,000 artists on file plus other subjects including musical instruments, recording studios, crowd scenes, festivals, etc. Brochure available.

Remote Source

See **Royal Geographical Society Picture Library**

Retna Pictures Ltd

Ground Floor, 53–56 Great Sutton Street, London EC1V 0DG
☎020 7608 4800 Fax 020 7608 4805
Email london@retna.com

Colour and b&w coverage of international rock and pop performers, actors, actresses, entertainers and celebrities. Also a general stock library covering a wide range of subjects, including travel, people, sport and leisure, flora and fauna, and the environment.

Retrograph Nostalgia Archive Ltd

164 Kensington Park Road, London W11 2ER
☎020 7727 9378 Fax 020 7229 3395
Email MBreese999@aol.com
Website www.Retrograph.com

Contact *Jilliana Ranicar-Breese*

'Number One for nostalgia!' A vast archive of commercial and decorative art (1860–1960). Worldwide labels and packaging for food, wine, chocolate, soap, perfume, cigars and cigarettes; fine art and commercial art journals, fashion and lifestyle magazines, posters, Victorian greetings cards, scraps, Christmas cards, Edwardian postcards, wallpaper and gift-wrap sample books, music sheets, folios of decorative design and ornament – Art Nouveau and Deco; hotel, airline and shipping labels; memorabilia, tourism, leisure, food and drink, transport and entertainment. Lasers for book dummies, packaging, mock-ups, film/TV action props. Colour brochure on request. Picture research service. Design consultancy service. Victorian-style montages conceived, designed and styled (RetroMontages).

Rex Features Ltd

18 Vine Hill, London EC1R 5DX
☎020 7278 7294 Fax 020 7696 0974
Website www.rexpix.co.uk

Established in the 1950s. Colour and b&w coverage of news, politics, personalities, show business, glamour, humour, art, medicine, science, landscapes, royalty, etc.

Royal Air Force Museum

Grahame Park Way, Hendon, London NW9 5LL
☎020 8205 2266 Fax 020 8200 1751
Email christine.gregory@rafmuseum.org.uk

Contact *Christine Gregory*

About a quarter of a million images, mostly b&w, with around 1500 colour in all formats, on the history of aviation. Particularly strong on the activities of the Royal Air Force from the 1870s to 1970s. Researchers are requested to enquire in writing only.

The Royal Collection

Windsor Castle, Windsor, Berks SL4 1NJ
☎01753 868286 Fax 01753 620046

Contact *Shruti Patel*

Photographic material of items in the Royal Collection, particularly oil paintings, drawings and watercolours, works of art, and interiors and exteriors of royal residences. 35,000 colour transparencies plus 25,000 b&w negatives.

Royal Geographical Society Picture Library

1 Kensington Gore, London SW7 2AR
☎020 7591 3060 Fax 020 7591 3061
Website www.rgs.org/picturelibrary

Contact *Joanna Scadden*

A strong source of geographical and historical images, both archival and modern, showing the world through the eyes of photographers and explorers dating from the 1830s to the present day. The Remote Source Collection provides up-to-date transparencies from around the world, highlighting aspects of cultural activity, environmental phenomena, anthropology, architectural design, travel, mountaineering and exploration. Offers a professional and comprehensive service for both commercial and academic use.

The Royal Photographic Society Picture Library

The Octagon, Milsom Street, Bath BA1 1DN
☎01225 462841 Fax 01225 469880
Email sam@collection.rps.org
Website www.rps.org/piclib.html

Contact *Samantha Johnson*

History of photography, with an emphasis on pictorial photography as an art rather than a documentary record. Photographic processes and cameras, landscape, portraiture, architecture, India, Victorian and Edwardian life.

RSPB Images

St Mark's House, Shepherdess Walk, London N1 7LH
☎020 7490 1710 Fax 020 7490 1511
Email rspb@sevenww.co.uk
Website www.rspb-images.com

Contact *Kristin Davidson*

Colour and b&w images of birds, butterflies, moths, mammals, reptiles and their habitats. Also colour images of all RSPB reserves. Growing selection of various habitats. Over 52,000 slides available digitally or in any desired format.

RSPCA Photolibrary

RSPCA Trading Limited, Causeway, Horsham, West Sussex RH12 1HG
☎01403 223150 Fax 01403 241048
Email photolibrary@rspca.org.uk

Photolibrary Manager *Andrew Forsyth*

Over 40,000 colour transparencies and over 5000 b&w/colour prints. A comprehensive collection of natural history images whose subjects include mammals, birds, domestic and farm animals, amphibians, insects and the environment, as well as a unique photographic record of the RSPCA's work. Also includes the Wild Images collections. Catalogue available. No search fees.

Russia and and Eastern Images

'Sonning', Cheapside Lane, Denham, Uxbridge, Middlesex UB9 5AE
☎01895 833508 Fax 01895 831957
Email easteuropix@btinternet.com

Architecture, cities, landscapes, people and travel images of Russia and the former Soviet Union. Considerable background knowledge available and Russian language spoken.

Peter Sanders Photography

24 Meades Lane, Chesham, Buckinghamshire HP5 1ND
☎01494 773674/771372 Fax 01494 773674
Email petersanders.photography@btinternet.com

Contacts *Peter Sanders, Hafsa Garwatuk*

The world of Islam in all its aspects from religion and industry to culture and arts. Areas included are Saudi Arabia, Africa, Asia, Europe and USA. Now expanding to all religions.

Science & Society Picture Library

Science Museum, Exhibition Road, London SW7 2DD
☎020 7942 4400 Fax 020 7942 4401
Email piclib@nmsi.ac.uk
Website www.nmsi.ac.uk/piclib/

Contacts *Angela Murphy, Venita Paul*

25,000 reference prints and 100,000 colour transparencies, incorporating many from collections at the Science Museum, the National Railway Museum and the National Museum of Photography Film and Television. Collections illustrate the history of science, industry, technology, medicine, transport and the media. Plus three archives documenting British society in the twentieth century.

Science Photo Library

327–329 Harrow Road, London W9 3RB
☎020 7432 1100 Fax 020 7286 8668
Email info@sciencephoto.co.uk
Website www.sciencephoto.com

Specialises in pictures of science, medicine, technology, earth, space and nature, with other 120,000 images in the collection..

The Scottish Highland Photo Library

Croft Roy, Crammond Brae, Tain, Ross-shire IV19 1JG
☎01862 892298 Fax 01862 892298
Email shpl@cali.co.uk
Website www.cali.co.uk/freespace/shpl

Contact *Hugh Webster*

150,000 colour transparencies of the Scottish Highlands and Islands. Not just a travel library; images cover industry, agriculture, fisheries and other subjects of the Highlands and Islands. Submissions from photographers welcome. Commissions undertaken. Call for CD catalogue.

Scottish Media Newspapers

195 Albion Street, Glasgow G1 1QP
☎0141 552 6255 Fax 0141 553 2642

Over six million images: b&w and colour photographs from *c.*1900 from the *Herald* (Glasgow) and *Evening Times*. Current affairs, Scotland, Glasgow, Clydeside shipbuilding and engineering, personalities, World Wars I and II, sport.

Kenneth Scowen Collection

See **Photos Horticultural**

Seaco Picture Library

Sea Containers House, 20 Upper Ground, London SE1 9PF
☎020 7805 5831 Fax 020 7805 5807
Email seaco.pictures@seacontainers.com

Contact *Maureen Elliott*

Approx. 250,000 images of containerisation, shipping, fast ferries, manufacturing, fruit farming, ports, hotels and leisure.

Mick Sharp Photography

Eithinog, Waun, Penisarwaun, Caernarfon, Gwynedd LL55 3PW
☎01286 872425 Fax 01286 872425

Contacts *Mick Sharp, Jean Williamson*

Colour transparencies (60 × 45mm and 35mm) and black & white prints (5 × 4″ and 60 × 45mm negatives) of subjects connected with archaeology, ancient monuments, buildings, churches, countryside, environment, history, landscape, past cultures and topography from Britain and abroad. Photographs by Mick Sharp and Jean Williamson, plus access to other specialist collections on related subjects. Commissions undertaken.

Phil Sheldon Golf Picture Library

40 Manor Road, Barnet, Hertfordshire EN5 2JQ
☎020 8440 1986 Fax 020 8440 9348
Email GolfSnap@aol.com

An expanding collection of over 400,000 quality images of the 'world of golf'. In-depth worldwide tournament coverage including every Major championship & Ryder Cup since 1976. Instruction, portraits, trophies and over 300 golf courses from around the world. Also the Dale Concannon collection covering the period 1870 to 1940 and the classic 1960s collection by photographer Sidney Harris.

Skishoot–Offshoot

Hall Place, Upper Woodcott, Whitchurch, Hampshire RG28 7PY
☎01635 255527 Fax 01635 255528
Email skishoot@surfersparadise.net
Website www.skishoot.net

Contacts *Jane Blount, Fiona Foote*

Skishoot ski and snowboarding picture library has 300,000 images. Offshoot travel library specialises in France.

The Skyscan Photolibrary

Oak House, Toddington, Cheltenham, Gloucestershire GL54 5BY
☎01242 621357 Fax 01242 621343
Email info@skyscan.co.uk
Website www.skyscan.co.uk

As well as the Skyscan Photolibrary collection of unique balloon's-eye views of Britain, the library now includes the work of photographers from across the aviation spectrum; air to ground, aviation, aerial sports – 'in fact, anything aerial!'. Links have been built with photographers across the world; photographs can be handled on an agency basis and held in house, or as a brokerage where the collection stays with the photographer; terms 50/50 for both. Commissioned photography undertaken. Enquiries welcome.

Snookerimages (Eric Whitehead Photography)

PO Box 33, Kendal, Cumbria LA9 4SU
☎015394 48894 Fax 015394 48294
Email eric@snookerimages.co.uk

Website www.snookerimages.co.uk

Over 20,000 images of snooker from 1982 to the present day. The agency covers local news events, PR and commercial material.

SOA Photo Library

87 York Street, London W1H 1DU
☎020 7258 0202 Fax 020 7258 0188
Email info@soaphotoagency.com
Website www.soaphotoagency.com

Contact *Brigitte Bott*

85,000 colour slides, 15,000 b&w photos covering *Stern* productions, sports, travel & geographic, advertising, social subjects. Representatives of Voller Ernst, Interfoto, Picture Press, Look and many freelance photographers. Free catalogues available.

Solo Syndication Ltd

49–53 Kensington High Street, London W8 5ED
☎020 7376 2166 Fax 020 7938 3165
Syndication Director *Trevor York*
Sales *Danny Howell, Nick York*
Online transmissions *Geoff Malyon*
(☎020 7937 3866)

Three million images from the archives of the *Daily Mail, Mail on Sunday, Evening Standard* and *Evening News*. Hard prints or Mac-to-mac delivery. 24-hour service.

Sotheby's Picture Library

34-35 New Bond Street, London W1A 2AA
☎020 7293 5383 Fax 020 7293 5062

Contacts *Joanna Ling, Sue Daly*

The library mainly consists of over 30,000 selected transparencies of pictures sold at Sotheby's. Images from the 15th to the 20th century. Oils, drawings, watercolours and prints. 'Happy to do searches or, alternatively, visitors are welcome by appointment.'

South American Pictures

48 Station Road, Woodbridge, Suffolk IP12 4AT
☎01394 383963/380423 Fax 01394 380176
Email morrison@south-american-pic.com
Website www.south-american-pic.com

Contact *Marion Morrison*

Colour and b&w images of South/Central America, Cuba, Mexico and New Mexico (USA), including archaeology and the Amazon. Frequently updated. There is an archival section, with pictures and documents from most countries.

The Special Photographers Library

21 Kensington Park Road, London W11 2EU
☎020 7221 3489 Fax 020 7792 9112
Email info@specialphotographers.com
Website www.specialphotographers.com

Contacts *Chris Kewbank*

Represents over 100 contemporary fine art photographers who are unusual in style, technique or subject matter. Also has exclusive access to the Bill Hopkins Collection – an archive of thousands of vintage pictures dating back to the early 20th century.

Frank Spooner Pictures Ltd

Unit B7, Hatton Square, 16–16A Baldwin's Gardens, London EC1N 7US
☎020 7632 5800 Fax 020 7632 5828
Email fsp/pix@compuserve.com

Subjects include current affairs, show business, fashion, politics, travel, adventure, sport, personalities, films, animals and the Middle East. Represented in more than 30 countries and handles UK distribution of Gamma Presse Images and Roger-Viollet of Paris. Commissions undertaken.

The Still Moving Picture Co.

67A Logie Green Road, Edinburgh EH7 4HF
☎0131 557 9697 Fax 0131 557 9699
Email stillmovingpictures@compuserve.com
Website www.stillmovingpictures.com

Contacts *John Hutchinson, Sue Hall*

250,000 colour, b&w and 16mm film coverage of Scotland and sport. The largest photo and film library in Scotland, holding the Scottish Tourist Board library among its files. Scottish agents for **Allsport (UK) Ltd**.

Still Pictures' Whole Earth Photolibrary

199 Shooters Hill Road, Blackheath, London SE3 8UL
☎020 8858 8307 Fax 020 8858 2049
Email info@stillpictures.com
Website www.stillpictures.com

Contacts *Theresa de Salis, Mark Edwards*

FOUNDED 1970, the library is a leading source of pictures illustrating the human impact on the environment, Third World development issues, industrial ecology, nature and wildlife, endangered species and habitats. 400,000 colour medium-format transparencies, 100,000 b&w prints. Over 400 leading photographers from around the world supply the library with stock pictures. Write, phone or fax for Still

Pictures' Environment and Third World catalogue and Still Pictures' Nature and Wildlife catalogue.

Stockfile
5 High Street, Sunningdale, Berkshire
SL5 0LX
☎01344 872249 Fax 01344 872263
Email info@stockfile.co.uk

Contacts *Jill Behr, Steven Behr*

Specialist cycling- and skiing-based collection covering most aspects of these activities, with emphasis on mountain biking. Expanding adventure sports section.

Sir John Benjamin Stone
See **Birmingham Library Services** under **Library Services**

Tony Stone Images
See **Getty Images**

Jessica Strang Photo Library
504 Brody House, Strype Street, Spitalfields, London E1 7LQ
☎020 7247 8982 Fax 020 7247 8982
Email Jessica.Strang@virgin.net

Contact *Jessica Strang*

Approximately 60,000 transparencies covering architecture, interiors (contemporary), gardens ('obsessive and not just small but tiny, or from almost no space at all'), couples and animals in architecture, recycling in the home, London (festivals, carnivals, etc.).

Joe Tasker Collection
See **Chris Bonnington Picture Library**

Tate Gallery Picture Library
Tate Gallery Publishing Ltd, Millbank, London SW1P 4RG
☎020 7887 8867 Fax 020 7887 8900
Email picture.library@tate.org.uk
Website www.tate.org.uk

Contacts *Carlotta Gelmetti, Chris Webster*

Approximately 8000 images of British art from the 16th century; international 20th century painting and sculpture. Artists include William Blake, William Hogarth, J. M. W. Turner, Dante Gabriel Rossetti, Barbara Hepworth, Henry Moore, Stanley Spencer, Pablo Picasso, Mark Rothko, Salvador Dali, Lucien Freud and David Hockney. Colour transparencies of more than half the works in the main collection are available for hire. For a fee, new photography is available depending on the location and condition of the art work. B&w prints of nearly all the works in the collection can be purchased. Colour slides and prints can be made on request providing a colour transparency exists. Picture researchers must make an appointment to visit the library. All applications must be made by fax or letter.

Telegraph Colour Library
The Innovation Centre, 225 Marsh Wall, London E14 9FX
☎020 7293 2939 Fax 020 7293 2930
Website www.tcl-images.co.uk

Contact *Zoë Fury*

Leading stock photography agency covering a wide subject range: business, sport, people, industry, animals, medical, nature, space, travel and graphics. Free catalogue available. Same-day service to UK clients.

3rd Millennium Music Ltd
22 Avon, Hockley, Tamworth, Staffordshire B77 5QA
☎01827 286086 Fax 01827 286086
Email Neil3MMLtd@aol.com
Website members.aol.com/Neil3MMLtd/
   NWCC.htm

Managing Director *Neil Williams*

Archive specialising in classical music ephemera, particularly portraits of composers, musicians, conductors and opera singers comprising of old and sometimes very rare photographs, postcards, antique prints, cigarette cards, stamps, First Day Covers, concert programmes, Victorian newspapers, etc. Also modern photos of composer references such as museums, statues, busts, paintings, monuments, memorials and graves. Other subjects covered include ballet, musical instruments, concert halls, opera houses, 'music in art', manuscripts, opera scenes, music-caricatures, bands, orchestras and other music groups.

Bob Thomas Sports Photography
See **Popperfoto**

Patrick Thurston Photolibrary
The Gallery, 12 High Street, Chesterton, Cambridge CB4 1NG
☎01223 352547/368109 Fax 01223 366274

Colour photography of Britain: scenery, people, museums, churches, coastline. Also various countries abroad. Commissions undertaken.

Rick Tomlinson Marine Photo Library

18 Hamble Yacht Services, Port Hamble, Hamble, Southampton, Hampshire SO31 4NN
☎023 8045 8450 Fax 023 8045 8350

Contacts *Rick Tomlinson, Julie Birchall*

ESTABLISHED 1985. *Specialises* in marine subjects. 60,000 35mm transparencies of yachting, racing, cruising, Whitbread Round the World Race, Tall Ships, RNLI Lifeboats, Antarctica, wildlife and locations.

Topham Picturepoint

PO Box 33, Edenbridge, Kent TN8 5PB
☎01342 850313 Fax 01342 850244
Email admin@topfoto.co.uk
Website www.topfoto.co.uk

Contact *Alan Smith*

Eight million contemporary and historical images, ideal for advertisers, publishers and the travel trade. Delivery online.

B. M. Totterdell Photography

Constable Cottage, Burlings Lane, Knockholt, Kent TN14 7PE
☎01959 532001 Fax 01959 532001

Contact *Barbara Totterdell*

Specialist volleyball library covering all aspects of the sport.

Tessa Traeger Library

7 Rossetti Studios, 72 Flood Street, London SW3 5TF
☎020 7352 3641 Fax 020 7352 4846

Food, gardens, travel and artists.

Travel Ink Photo & Feature Library

The Old Coach House, 14 High Street, Goring on Thames, Nr Reading, Berkshire RG8 9AR
☎01491 873011 Fax 01491 875558
Email info@travel-ink.co.uk
Website www.travel-ink.co.uk

Contact *Abbie Enock*

Around 100,000 colour images covering about 130 countries (including the UK). Close links with other specialist libraries mean most topics can be accessed. Subjects include travel, tourism, lifestyles, business, industry, transport, children, religion, history, activities. Specialist collections on Hong Kong (including construction of the Tsing Ma bridge), the Cotswolds, North Wales, Germany, Greece, France and many others.

Peter Trenchard's Image Store Ltd

The Studio, West Hill, St Helier, Jersey, Channel Islands JE2 3HB
☎01534 769933 Fax 01534 89191

Contact *Peter Trenchard, FBIPP, AMPA, PPA*

Slide library of the Channel Islands – mainly tourist and financial-related. Commissions undertaken.

Tropical Birds Photo Library

PO Box 100, Mansfield, Nottinghamshire NG20 9NZ
☎01623 846430 Fax 01623 846430

Contact *Rosemary Low*

Transparencies (35mm) of parrots and other tropical birds, and tropical butterflies. Also colour and b&w prints and large format transparencies of parrots. Specialises in parrots: more than 250 species.

Tropix Photo Library

156 Meols Parade, Meols, Wirral CH47 6AN
☎0151 632 1698 Fax 0151 632 1698
Email tropixphoto@talk21.com
Website www.merseyworld.com/tropix/

Contact *Veronica Birley*

Specialists on the developing world in all its aspects. Environmental topics worldwide. Assignment photography UK and overseas. 'New collections welcome. Must be 35mm or larger colour transparencies, top professional quality only, taken 1999 or later. See website for detailed submission guidelines. We advise you to email in the first instance.'

True North Picture Source

5 Brunswick Street, Hebden Bridge, West Yorkshire HX7 6AJ
☎01422 845532 Fax 01422 845532
Email john@trunorth.demon.co.uk
Website www.trunorth.demon.co.uk

Contact *John Morrison*

30,000 transparencies on 35mm and 6x4.5cm format on the life and landscape of the north of England, photographed by John Morrison.

Turnley Collection

See **Corbis Images**

Ulster Museum (National Museums and Galleries of Northern Ireland)

Botanic Gardens, Belfast BT9 5AB
☎028 9038 3000 ext 3113 Fax 028 9038 3103
Email patricia.mclean.um@nics.gov.uk

Contact *Mrs Pat McLean*

Specialist subjects: art – fine and decorative, late 17th–20th century, particularly Irish art, archaeology, ethnography, treasures from the Armada shipwrecks, geology, botany, zoology, local history and industrial archaeology. Commissions welcome for objects not already photographed.

Universal Pictorial Press & Agency Ltd

29–31 Saffron Hill, London EC1N 8SW
☎020 7421 6000 Fax 020 7421 6006
News Editor *Peter Dare*

Photo archive dates back to 1944 and contains approximately four million pictures. Colour and b&w coverage of news, royalty, politics, sport, arts, and many other subjects. Commissions undertaken for press and public relations. Fully interactive digital photo archive in addition to bulletin board accessible via ISDN or modem. Full digital scanning, retouching and transmission facilities.

UPI

See **Popperfoto**

V & A Picture Library

Victoria and Albert Museum, South Kensington, London SW7 2RL
☎020 7942 2487/2483 Fax 020 7942 2482
Email picture.library@vam.ac.uk

65,000 colour and half a million b&w photos of decorative and applied arts, including ceramics, ivories, furniture, costumes, textiles, stage, musical instruments, toys, Indian, Far Eastern, Islamic objects, sculpture, painting and prints, from medieval to present day.

Valley Green

Barn Ley, Valley Lane, Buxhall, Stowmarket, Suffolk IP14 3EB
☎01449 736090 Fax 01449 736090
Contacts *Joseph Barrere, Colette Barrere*

Masses of perennials – 'all correctly labelled'. Over 10,000 hardy plant transparencies in stock, plus watercolours and line drawings available. Commissions undertaken as well as commercial copywriting.

Venice Picture Library

2a Milner Street, London SW3 2PU
☎020 7589 3127 Fax 020 7584 1944

25,000 35mm images of Venice, its buildings, people, animals and atmosphere. Member of **BAPLA**.

Victory Archive

See **Popperfoto**

Vin Mag Archives Ltd

203–213 Mare Street, London E8 3QE
☎020 8533 7588 Fax 020 8533 7283
Email piclib.vintage@ndirect.co.uk
Website www.vinmag.com

Formerly the Vintage Magazine Company. Large collection of movie stills and posters, photographs, illustrations and advertisements covering music, glamour, social history, theatre posters, ephemera, postcards.

The Charles Walker Collection

Ramillies House, 1–2 Ramillies Street, London W1V 1DF
☎020 7734 7344 Fax 020 7287 3933

One of the foremost collections in the world on subjects popularly listed as 'Mystery, myth and magic'. The collection includes astrology, occultism, witchcraft and many other related areas. Catalogue available.

John Walmsley Photo Library

April Cottage, Warners Lane, Albury Heath, Guildford, Surrey GU5 9DE
☎01483 203846 Fax 01483 203846
Email john@johnwalmsleyphotos.co.uk
Website www.johnwalmsleyphotos.co.uk

Specialist library of learning/training/working subjects. Comprehensive coverage of learning environments such as playgroups, schools, colleges and universities. Images reflect a multi-racial Britain. Also a section on complementary medicine, with over 30 therapies from acupuncture and yoga to more unusual ones like moxibustion and metamorphic technique. Commissions undertaken. Subject list available on request.

Christopher Ware Pictures

65 Trinity Street, Barry, Glamorgan CF62 7EX
☎01446 732816/0802 865999 (mobile)
Fax 01446 732816
Contact *Christopher Ware*

Large collection of images (b&w and colour) of S. E. Wales, including Barry docks and the Steam Graveyard, railways, Vale of Glamorgan landscapes, civil and military aircraft over the last 40 years. Images available on CD-ROM or via email. Digital post-production. Commissions. Other photographers' work not accepted.

Warwickshire Photographic Survey
See **Birmingham Library Services** under **Library Services**

Waterways Photo Library
39 Manor Court Road, Hanwell, London W7 3EJ
☎020 8840 1659 Fax 020 8567 0605
Email watphot39@aol.com
Contact *Derek Pratt*

A specialist photo library on all aspects of Britain's inland waterways. Top-quality 35mm- and medium-format colour transparencies, plus a large collection of b&w. Rivers and canals, bridges, locks, aqueducts, tunnels and waterside buildings. Town and countryside scenes, canal art, waterway holidays, boating, fishing, windmills, watermills, watersports and wildlife.

Philip Way Photography
2 Green Moor Link, Winchmore Hill, London N21 2ND
☎020 8360 3034
Contact *Philip Way*

Over 5000 images of St Paul's Cathedral, historical exteriors, interiors and events (1982–2000).

Wellcome Trust Medical Photographic Library
210 Euston Road, London NW1 2BE
☎020 7611 8348 Fax 020 7611 8577
Email photolib@wellcome.ac.uk
Website www.wellcome.ac.uk
Contacts *Michele Minto, Julie Dorrington*

Approximately 160,000 images on the history of medicine and human culture worldwide, including modern clinical medicine. Incorporates the National Medical Slide Bank.

Eric Whitehead Photography
PO Box 33, Kendal, Cumbria LA9 4SU
☎015394 48894 Fax 015394 48284

Incorporates the Cumbria Picture Library. The agency covers local news events, PR and commercial material, also leading library of snooker images (see **Snookerimages**).

Wild Images
See **RSPCA Photolibrary**

Wilderness Photographic Library
Mill Barn, Broad Raine, Sedbergh, Cumbria LA10 5ED
☎015396 20196 Fax 015396 21293

Contact *John Noble*

Striking colour images from around the world, from polar wastes to the Himalayas and Amazon jungle. Subjects: mountains, Arctic, deserts, icebergs, wildlife, rainforests, glaciers, geysers, exploration, caves, rivers, eco-tourism, people and cultures, canyons, seascapes, marine life, weather, volcanoes, mountaineering, skiing, geology, conservation, adventure sports, national parks.

David Williams Picture Library
50 Burlington Avenue, Glasgow G12 0LH
☎0141 339 7823 Fax 0141 337 3031

Colour coverage of Scotland and Iceland. Smaller collections of the Faroes, France, Spain, Portugal, Czech Republic, Hungary and various other European countries; also Western USA. Landscapes, historical sites, buildings, geology and physical geography. Medium format and 35mm. Catalogue available. Commissions undertaken.

Vaughan Williams Memorial Library
English Folk Dance and Song Society, Cecil Sharp House, 2 Regent's Park Road, London NW1 7AY
☎020 7485 2206 ext. 207/208 Fax 020 7284 0523
Email library@efdss.org
Website www.efdss.org

Mainly b&w coverage of traditional/folk music, dance and customs worldwide, focusing on Britain and other English-speaking nations. Photographs date from the late 19th century to the 1990s.

The Wilson Photographic Collection
See **Dundee Central Library** under **Library Services**

Windrush Photos, Wildlife and Countryside Picture Agency
99 Noah's Ark, Kemsing, Sevenoaks, Kent TN15 6PD
☎01732 763486 Fax 01732 763285
Contact *David Tipling*

Specialists in birds (worldwide) and British wildlife. Photographic and features commissions are regularly undertaken for publications in the UK and overseas. The agency acts as ornithological consultants for all aspects of the media. Offers expert captioning service. **BAPLA** member.

Woodfall Wild Images

17 Bull Lane, Denbigh, Denbighshire
LL16 3SN
☎01745 815903 Fax 01745 814581
Email WWImages@btinternet.com
Website www.woodfall.com

Contact *David Hill*

Specialist environmental, conservation, landscape and wildlife photographic library including new material from the rainforest of Venezuela, covering various topics. A constantly expanding collection of images reflecting the natural world and man's effect upon it, both positively and negatively. Please call for a brochure, stock cards or prospective photographer notes. New specialist panoramic coverage available.

World Pictures

85a Great Portland Street, London
W1N 5RA
☎020 7437 2121/7436 0440
Fax 020 7439 1307
Email Worldpictures@btinternet.com

Contacts *David Brenes, Carlo Irek*

600,000 colour transparencies of travel and emotive material.

WWF UK Photolibrary

Panda House, Weyside Park, Catteshall Lane, Godalming, Surrey GU7 1XR
☎01483 426444 Fax 01483 861006

Contact *Rosie Lynch*

Specialist library covering natural history, endangered species, conservation, environment, forests, habitats, habitat destruction, and pollution in the UK and abroad. 15,000 colour slides (35mm).

Yemen Pictures

28 Sheen Common Drive, Richmond
TW10 5BN
☎020 8898 0150/8876 3637
Fax 020 8898 0150

Large collection (4000 transparencies) covering all aspects of Yemen – culture, people, architecture, dance, qat, music. Also Africa, Australia, Middle East, and Asia.

York Archaeological Trust Picture Library

Cromwell House, 13 Ogleforth, York
YO1 7FG
☎01904 663000 Fax 01904 663024
Email postmaster@yorkarch.demon.co.uk
Website www.yorkarch.demon.co.uk

Specialist library of rediscovered artifacts, historic buildings and excavations, presented by the creators of the highly acclaimed Jorvik Viking Centre. The main emphasis is on the Roman, Anglo-Saxon and Viking periods.

The John Robert Young Collection

61 De Montfort Road, Lewes, East Sussex
BN7 1SS
☎01273 475216 Fax 01273 475216

Contact *Jennifer Barrett*

50,000 transparencies and monochrome prints on religion, travel and military subjects. Major portfolios: religious communities; the French Foreign Legion; the Spanish Legion; the Royal Marines; the People's Liberation Army (China).

Balancing the Books – Tax and the Writer

'No man in the country is under the smallest obligation, moral or other, to arrange his affairs as to enable the Inland Revenue to put the largest possible shovel in his stores.

The Inland Revenue is not slow, and quite rightly, to take every advantage which is open to it ... for the purpose of depleting the taxpayer's pockets. And the taxpayer is, in like manner, entitled to be astute to prevent as far as he honestly can the depletion of his means by the Inland Revenue.'

Lord Clyde, *Ayrshire Pullman v Inland Revenue Commissioners, 1929*

Income Tax

What is a professional writer for tax purposes?

Writers are professionals while they are writing regularly with the intention of making a profit; or while they are gathering material, researching or otherwise preparing a publication.

A professional freelance writer is taxed under Case II of Schedule D of the *Income and Corporation Taxes Act 1988*. The taxable income is the amount receivable, either directly or by an agent, on his behalf, less expenses wholly and exclusively laid out for the purpose of the profession. If expenses exceed income, the loss can either be set against other income of the same or preceding years or carried forward and set against future income from writing. If tax has been paid on that other income, a repayment can be obtained, or the sum can be offset against other tax liabilities. Special loss relief can apply in the opening years of the profession. Losses made in the first four years can be set against income of up to three earlier years.

Where a writer receives very occasional payments for isolated articles, it may not be possible to establish that these are profits arising from carrying on a continuing profession. In such circumstances these 'isolated transactions' may be assessed under Case VI of Schedule D of the *Income and Corporation Taxes Act 1988*. Again, expenses may be deducted in arriving at the taxable income but, if expenses exceed income, the loss can only be set against the profits from future isolated transactions, or other income assessable under Case VI.

In the tax year 1996/97 a new tax system came into effect called Self Assessment. Under Self Assessment the onus is on the individual to declare income and expenses correctly. Each writer therefore has to decide whether profits arise from a professional or occasional activity. The consequences of getting it wrong can be expensive by way of interest, penalties and surcharges on additional tax subsequently found to be due. If in any doubt the writer should seek professional advice.

Income

A writer's income includes fees, advances, royalties, commissions, sale of copyrights, reimbursed expenses, etc., from any source anywhere in the world whether or not brought to the UK (non UK resident or domiciled writers should seek professional advice).

Agents

It should be borne in mind that the agent stands in the shoes of the principal. It is not always realised that when the agent receives royalties, fees, advances, etc. on behalf of the author those receipts became the property of the author on the date of their receipt by the agent. This applies for Income Tax and Value Added Tax purposes.

Expenses

A writer can normally claim the following expenses:

(a) Secretarial, typing, proofreading, research. Where payment for these is made to the author's wife or husband they should be recorded and entered in the spouse's tax return as earned income which is subject to the usual personal allowances. If payments reach relevant levels, PAYE should be operated.

(b) Telephone, faxes, Internet costs, computer software, postage, stationery, printing, equipment maintenance, insurance, dictation tapes, batteries, any equipment or office requisites used for the profession.

(c) Periodicals, books (including presentation copies and reference books) and other publications necessary for the profession, but amounts received from the sale of books should be deducted.

(d) Hotels, fares, car running expenses (including repairs, petrol, oil, garaging, parking, cleaning, insurance, road fund tax, depreciation), hire of cars or taxis in connection with:

   (i)   business discussions with agents, publishers, co-authors, collaborators, researchers, illustrators, etc.

   (ii) travel at home and abroad to collect background material.

   As an alternative to keeping details of full car running costs, a mileage rate can be claimed for business use. This rate depends on the engine size and varies from year to year. This is known as the Fixed Profit Car Scheme and is available to writers whose turnover does not exceed the VAT registration limit, currently £52,000.

(e) Publishing and advertising expenses, including costs of proof corrections, indexing, photographs, etc.

(f) Subscriptions to societies and associations, press cutting agencies, libraries, etc., incurred wholly for the purpose of the profession.

(g) Rent, council tax and water rates, etc., the proportion being determined by the ratio of the number of rooms used exclusively for the profession, to the total number of rooms in the residence. But see note on *Capital Gains Tax* below.

(h) Lighting, heating and cleaning. A carefully calculated figure of the business use of these costs can be claimed as a proportion of the total.

(i) Agent's commission, accountancy charges and legal charges incurred wholly in the course of the profession including cost of defending libel actions, damages in so far as they are not covered by insurance, and libel insurance premiums. However, where in a libel case damages are awarded to punish the author for having acted maliciously the action becomes quasi-criminal and costs and damages may not be allowed.

(j) TV and video rental (which may be apportioned for private use), and cinema or theatre tickets, if wholly for the purpose of the profession.

(k) Capital allowances for business equipment. These are now divided into three categories:

  (i) Computer equipment including printers, scanners, cabling, etc. For any such equipment purchased subsequent to 1 April 2000 there is a First Year Allowance of 100%. Prior to that the First Year Allowance was 40% of the cost of the equipment purchased after 1 July 1998 and 50% on equipment purchased after 1 July 1997. For equipment purchased prior to 1 April 2000, after the first year there is an annual Writing Down Allowance of 25% of the reducing balance.

  (ii) On motor cars the allowance is 25% in the first year and 25% of the reducing balance in each successive year limited to £3000 each year.

  (iii) For all over business equipment, e.g. TV, radio, hi-fi sets, tape and video recorders, Dictaphones, office furniture, photographic equipment, etc. there is a First Year Allowance of 40%. After the first year there is an annual Writing Down Allowance of 25% of the reducing balance. The allowances for all the three categories mentioned above will be reduced to exclude personal (non-professional) use where necessary.

(l) Lease rent. The cost of lease rent of equipment is allowable; also on cars, subject to restrictions for private use, and for expensive cars.

(m) Other expenses incurred wholly and exclusively for professional purposes. (Entertaining expenses are not allowable in any circumstances.)

NB It essential to keep detailed records. Diary entries of appointments, notes of fares and receipted bills are much more convincing to the Inland Revenue who are very reluctant to accept estimates. **The Self Assessment regime makes it a legal requirement for proper accounting records to be kept. These**

records must be sufficient to support the figures declared in the tax return.

In addition to the above, tax relief is available on:

(a) Premiums to pension schemes such as the *Society of Authors Retirement Benefits Scheme*. Depending on age, up to 40% of net earned income can be paid into a personal pension plan.

(b) Covenants to charities. (Deeds executed prior to 6 April 2000.)

(c) Gift Aid payments to charities. Any amount. (Prior to 6 April 2000, single payments of £250 or more.)

(d) Millennium Relief: Gifts for relief in poor countries ends on 31 December 2000.

Capital Gains Tax

The exemption from Capital Gains Tax which applies to an individual's main residence does not apply to any part of that residence which is used exclusively for business purposes. The effect of this is that the appropriate proportion of any increase in value of the residence since 31 March 1982 can be taxed when the residence is sold, subject to adjustment for inflation to March 1998 and subsequent length of ownership, at the individual's highest rate of tax.

Writers who own their houses should bear this in mind before claiming expenses for the use of a room for writing purposes. Arguments in favour of making such claims are that they afford some relief now, while Capital Gains Tax in its present form may not stay for ever. Also, where a new house is bought in place of an old one, the gain made on the sale of the first study may be set off against the cost of the study in the new house, thus postponing the tax payment until the final sale. For this relief to apply, each house must have a study and the author must continue his profession throughout. On death there is an exemption of the total Capital Gains of the estate.

Alternatively, writers can claim that their use is non-exclusive and restrict their claim to the cost of extra lighting, heating and cleaning to avoid any Capital Gains Tax liability.

Can a writer average out his income over a number of years for tax purposes?

Under Section 534 of the Income and Corporation Taxes Act 1988, a writer may in certain circumstances spread over two or three fiscal years lump sum payments whenever received and royalties received during two years from the date of first publication or performance of work. Points to note are:

(a) If the period of preparing and writing the work exceeds twelve months but does not exceed twenty-four months, one-half of the advances and/or royalties will be regarded as income from the year preceding that of receipt. If the period of preparing and writing exceeds twenty-four months, one-third of the amount received would be regarded as income from each of the two years preceding that of receipt.

(b) For a writer on a very large income, who otherwise fulfils the conditions required, a claim under these sections could result in a tax saving. If his income is not large he should consider the implication, in the various fiscal years concerned, of possible loss of benefit from personal and other allowances and changes in the rates of income tax.

It is also possible to average out income within the terms of publishers' contracts, but professional advice should be taken before signature. Where a husband and wife collaborate as writers, advice should be taken as to whether a formal partnership agreement should be made or whether the publishing agreement should be in joint names.

Is a lump sum paid for an outright sale of the copyright or is part of the copyright exempt from tax?

No. All the money received from the marketing of literary work, by whatever means, is taxable. Some writers, in spite of clear judicial decisions to the contrary, still seem to think that an outright sale of, for instance, the film rights in a book is not subject to tax.

Remaindering

To avoid remaindering authors can usually purchase copies of their own books from the publishers. Monies received from sales are subject to income tax but the cost of books sold should be deducted because tax is only payable on the profit made.

Is there any relief where old copyrights are sold?

Section 535 of the *Income and Corporation Taxes Act 1988* gives relief where not less than ten years after the first publication of the work the author of a literary, dramatic, musical or artistic work assigns the copyright therein wholly or partially, or grants any interest in the copyright by licence, and:

(a) the consideration for the assignment or grant consists wholly or partially of a lump sum payment, the whole amount of which would, but for this section, be included in computing the amount of his/her profits or gains for a single year of assessment, and

(b) the copyright or interest is not assigned or granted for a period of less than two years.

In such cases, the amount received may be spread forward in equal yearly instalments for a maximum of six years, or, where the copyright or interest is assigned or granted for a period of less than six years, for the number of whole years in that period. A 'lump sum payment' is defined to include a non-returnable advance on account of royalties.

It should be noted that a claim may not be made under this section in respect of a payment if a prior claim has been made under Section 534 of the *Income and Corporation Taxes Act 1988* (see section on spreading lump sum payments over two or three years) or vice versa. Relief under Sections 534 and 535 has now been withdrawn from partnerships.

Are royalties payable on publication of a book abroad subject to both foreign tax as well as UK tax?

Where there is a Double Taxation Agreement between the country concerned and the UK, then on the completion of certain formalities no tax is deductible at source by the foreign payer, but such income is taxable in the UK in the ordinary way. When there is no Double Taxation Agreement, credit will be given against UK tax for overseas tax paid. A complete list of countries with which the UK has conventions for the avoidance of double taxation may be obtained from FICO, Inland Revenue, St John's House, Merton Road, Bootle, Merseyside L69 9BB, or a local tax office.

Residence abroad

Writers residing abroad will, of course, be subject to the tax laws ruling in their country of residence, and as a general rule royalty income paid from the United Kingdom can be exempted from deduction of UK tax at source, providing the author is carrying on his profession abroad. A writer who is intending to go and live abroad should make early application for future royalties to be paid without deduction of tax to FICO, address as above. In certain circumstances writers resident in the Irish Republic are exempt from Irish Income Tax on their authorship earnings.

Are grants or prizes taxable?

The law is uncertain. Some Arts Council grants are now deemed to be taxable, whereas most prizes and awards are not, though it depends on the conditions in each case. When submitting the Self Assessment annual returns, such items should be excluded, but reference made to them in the 'Additional Information' box on the self-employment (or partnership) pages.

What is the item 'Class 4 N.I.C.' which appears on my Self Assessment return?

All taxpayers who are self-employed pay an additional national insurance contribution if their earned income exceeds a figure which varies each year. This contribution is described as Class 4 and is calculated when preparing the return. It is additional to the self-employed Class 2 contribution but confers no additional benefits and is a form of levy. It applies to men aged under 65 and women under 60.

Value Added Tax

Value Added Tax (VAT) is a tax currently levied at 17.5% on:

(a)   the total value of taxable goods and services supplied to consumers,
(b)   the importation of goods into the UK,
(c)   certain services or goods from abroad if a taxable person receives them in the UK for the purpose of their business.

Who is taxable?

A writer resident in the UK whose turnover from writing and any other business, craft or art on a self-employed basis is greater than £52,000 annually, before deducting agent's commission, must register with HM Customs & Excise as a taxable person. Turnover includes fees, royalties, advances, commissions, sale of copyright, reimbursed expenses, etc. A business is required to register:

- at the end of any month if the value of taxable supplies in the past twelve months has exceeded the annual threshold; or
- if there are reasonable grounds for believing that the value of taxable supplies in the next twelve months will exceed the annual threshold.

Penalties will be claimed in the case of late registration. A writer whose turnover is below these limits is exempt from the requirements to register for VAT but may apply for voluntary registration and this will be allowed at the discretion of HM Customs & Excise.

A taxable person collects VAT on outputs (turnover) and deducts VAT paid on inputs (taxable expenses) and where VAT collected exceeds VAT paid, must remit the difference to HM Customs & Excise. In the event that input exceeds output, the difference will be refunded by HM Customs & Excise.

Outputs (Turnover)

A writer's outputs are taxable services supplied to publishers, broadcasting organisations, theatre managements, film companies, educational institutions, etc. A taxable writer must invoice, i.e. collect from, all the persons (either individuals or organisations) in the UK for whom supplies have been made, for fees, royalties or other considerations plus VAT. An unregistered writer cannot and must not invoice for VAT. A taxable writer is not obliged to collect VAT on royalties or other fees paid by publishers or others overseas. In practice, agents usually collect VAT for the registered author.

Remit to Customs

The taxable writer adds up the VAT which has been paid on taxable inputs, deducts it from the VAT received and remits the balance to Customs. Business with HM Customs is conducted through the local VAT offices of HM Customs which are listed in local telephone directories, except for VAT returns which are sent direct to the Customs & Excise VAT Central Unit, Alexander House, 21 Victoria Avenue, Southend on Sea, Essex SS99 1AA.

Inputs

Taxable at the standard rate if supplier is registered	Taxable at the zero or special rate	Not liable to VAT
Rent of certain commercial premises	Books (zero)	Rent of non-commercial premises
Advertisements in newspapers, magazines, journals and periodicals	Coach, rail and air travel (zero)	Postage
Agent's commission (unless it relates to monies from overseas)	Agent's commission (on monies from overseas)	Services supplied by unregistered persons
Accountant's and solicitor's fees for business matters	Domestic gas and electricity (5%)	Subscriptions to the Society of Authors, PEN, NUJ, etc.
Agency services (typing, copying, etc.)		Insurance
Word processors, typewriters and stationery		
Artists' materials		
Photographic equipment		
Tape recorders and tapes		
Hotel accommodation		*Outside the scope of VAT*
Taxi fares		
Motorcar expenses		PLR (Public Lending Right)
Telephone		Profit shares
Theatres and concerts		Investment income
	NB This list is not exhaustive	

Accounting

A taxable writer is obliged to account to HM Customs & Excise at quarterly intervals. Returns must be completed and sent to VAT Central Unit by the dates shown on the return. Penalties can be charged if the returns are late.

It is possible to account for the VAT liability under the Cash Accounting Scheme (leaflet 731), whereby the author accounts for the output tax when the invoice is paid or royalties, etc., are received. The same applies to the input tax, but as most purchases are probably on a 'cash basis', this will not make a considerable difference to the author's input tax. This scheme is only applicable to those with a taxable turnover of less than £350,000 and, therefore, is available to the majority of authors. The advantage of this scheme is that the author does not have to account for VAT before receiving payments, thereby relieving the author of a cash flow problem.

It is also possible to pay VAT by nine estimated direct debits, with a final balance at the end of the year (see leaflet 732). This annual accounting method also means that only one VAT return is submitted.

Registration

A writer will be given a VAT registration number which must be quoted on all VAT correspondence. It is the responsibility of those registered to inform those to whom they make supplies of their registration number. The taxable turnover limit which determines whether a person who is registered for VAT may apply for cancellation of registration is £50,000.

Voluntary registration

A writer whose turnover is below the limits may apply to register. If the writer is paying a relatively large amount of VAT on taxable inputs – agent's commission, accountant's fees, equipment, materials, or agency services, etc. – it may make a significant improvement in the net income to be able to offset the VAT on these inputs. A writer who pays relatively little VAT may find it easier, and no more expensive, to remain unregistered.

Fees and royalties

A taxable writer must notify those to whom he makes supplies of the Tax Registration Number at the first opportunity. One method of accounting for and paying VAT on fees and royalties is the use of multiple stationery for 'self-billing', one copy of the royalty statement being used by the author as the VAT invoice. A second method is for the recipient of taxable outputs to pay fees, including authors' royalties, without VAT. The taxable writer then renders a tax invoice for the VAT element and a second payment, of the VAT element, will be made. This scheme is cumbersome but will involve only taxable authors. Fees and royalties from abroad will count as payments of the exported services and will accordingly be zero-rated.

Agents and accountants

A writer is responsible to HM Customs for making VAT returns and payments. Neither an agent nor an accountant nor a solicitor can remove the responsibility, although they can be helpful in preparing and keeping VAT returns and accounts. Their professional fees or commission will, except in rare cases where the adviser or agent is himself unregistered, be taxable at the standard rate and will represent some of a writer's taxable inputs.

Income Tax – Schedule D

An unregistered writer can claim some of the VAT paid on taxable inputs as a business expense allowable against income tax. However, certain taxable inputs fall into categories which cannot be claimed under the income tax regulations. A taxable writer, who has already claimed VAT on inputs, cannot charge it as a business expense for the purposes of income tax.

Certain services from abroad

A taxable author who resides in the United Kingdom and who receives certain services from abroad must account for VAT on those services at the appropriate tax rate on the sum paid for them. Examples of the type of services concerned include: services of lawyers, accountants, consultants, provision of information and copyright permissions.

Inheritance Tax

Inheritance Tax was introduced in 1984 to replace Capital Transfer Tax, which had in turn replaced Estate Duty, the first of the death taxes of recent times. Paradoxically, Inheritance Tax has reintroduced a number of principles present under the old Estate Duty.

The general principle now is that all assets owned at death are chargeable to tax (currently 40%) except the first £234,000 of the estate and any assets passed to a surviving spouse or a charity. Gifts made more than seven years before death are exempt, but those made within this period are taxed on a sliding scale. No tax is payable at the time of making the gift.

In addition, each individual may currently make gifts of up to £3000 in any year and these will be considered to be exempt. A further exemption covers any number of annual gifts not exceeding £250 to any one person.

If the £3000 is not fully utilised in one year, any unused balance can be carried forward to the following year (but no later). Gifts out of income, which do not reduce one's living standards, are also exempt if they are part of normal expenditure.

At death all assets are valued; they will include any property, investments, life policies, furniture and personal possessions, bank balances and, in the case of authors, the value of copyrights. All, with the sole exception of copyrights, are capable (as assets) of accurate valuation and, if necessary, can be turned into cash. The valuation of copyright is, of course, complicated and frequently gives rise to difficulty. Except where they are bequeathed to the owner's husband or wife, very real problems can be left behind by the author.

Experience has shown that a figure based on two to three years' past royalties may be proposed by the Inland Revenue in their valuation of copyright. However, this may not be reasonable and may require negotiation. If a book is running out of print or if, as in the case of educational books, it may need revision at the next reprint, these factors must be taken into account. In many cases the fact that the author is no longer alive and able to make personal appearances, or provide publicity, or write further works, will result in lower or slower sales. Obviously, this is an area in which help can be given by the publishers, and in particular one needs to know what their future intentions are, what stocks of the books remain, and what likelihood there will be of reprinting.

There is a further relief available to authors who have established that they have been carrying on a business, normally assessable under Case II of Schedule D, for at least two years prior to death. It has been possible to establish that copyrights are treated as business property and in these circumstances, Inheritance Tax 'business property relief' is available. This relief at present is 100% so that the tax saving can be quite substantial. The Inland Revenue may wish to be assured that the business is continuing and consideration should therefore be given to the appointment, in the author's will, of a literary executor who should be a qualified business person or, in certain circumstances, the formation of partnership between the author and spouse, or other relative, to ensure that it is established the business is continuing after the author's death.

If the author has sufficient income, consideration should be given to building up a fund to cover future Inheritance Tax liabilities. One of a number of ways would be to take out a whole life assurance policy which is assigned to the children, or other beneficiaries, the premiums on which are within the annual exemption of £3000. The capital sum payable on the death of the assured is exempt from inheritance tax.

Anyone wondering how best to order his affairs for tax purposes should consult an accountant with specialised knowledge in this field. Experience shows that a good accountant is well worth his fee which, incidentally, so far as it relates to professional matters, is an allowable expense.

The information contained in this section has been prepared by Ian Spring of Moore Stephens, Chartered Accountants, who will be pleased to answer questions on tax problems. Please write to Ian Spring, c/o The Writer's Handbook, *34 Ufton Road, London N1 5BX.*

Company Index

The following codes have been used to classify the index entries:

Subject Index